SUPERNATURAL FICTION WRITERS

SUPERNATURAL FICTION WRITERS

Fantasy and Horror

E. F. BLEILER, Editor

VOLUME 2

A. E. Coppard
to
Roger Zelazny

Charles Scribner's Sons · New York

Library of Congress Cataloging in Publication Data
Main entry under title:

Supernatural fiction writers.

Includes bibliographies and index.
1. Fantastic fiction — History and criticism.
2. Horror tales — History and criticism.   3. Supernatural
in literature.   4. Authors — Biography.   I. Bleiler,
Everett Franklin, 1920–
PN3435.S96   1985   809.3'876   84-27588
ISBN 0-684-17808-7

Acknowledgment is gratefully made to those publishers and individuals who have permitted the use of the following materials in copyright.

Ray Bradbury
Material from the introduction by Ray Bradbury, from *The Stories of Ray Bradbury*. Copyright © 1980 by Ray Bradbury Enterprises.   Reprinted   by   permission of Don Congdon Associates.

Avram Davidson
Material from "Eszterhazy and the Autogondola-Invention" by Avram Davidson. Copyright © 1983. First published in *Amaz-* ing, Nov. 1983. (*Amazing* is a registered trademark owned by TSR, Inc. for its science fiction stories magazine.) Reprinted by permission of the author and the John Silbersack Agency.

Lord Dunsany
Four lines from the poem "Waiting" by Lord Dunsany and about 95 words from one of Dunsany's letters reprinted in *Dunsany the Dramatist* by Edward Hale Bierstadt (Boston: Little, Brown, 1917). Reprinted by kind permission of Curtis Brown Ltd. on behalf of John Charles Villiers and Valentine Lamb as Literary executors of Lord Dunsany. Copyright Estate of Lord Dunsany.

VIII

*British Writers
of the Interbellum Period*

A. E. COPPARD

1878–1957

THE SON OF a radical, freethinking atheist tailor and a mother "widely given to romantic fiction" who believed that Satan walked the earth and who "suffered physical and mental prostration" from the pronouncements of "religious maniacs," Alfred Edgar Coppard grew up a skeptic and a thoroughgoing philosophical materialist with a lifelong fascination for religion and the supernatural. In his autobiography, *It's Me, O Lord!* (1957), he recounts a wager won by accepting a dare to walk through a cemetery when his mates expressed their fear of ghosts: "I scoffed, I laughed at them, I scorned them all. . . . That sort of squeamishness has never daunted me, and it seemed an easy way of winning a bet of anybody's shilling." He tells us in the foreword to the collection of his fantasy tales, *Fearful Pleasures* (1946), "I have not the slightest belief in the supernatural. If I should ever see a ghost I should know it was time for me to consult an oculist." Fantastic tales, he continues, are easy to write because "a writer can ignore problems of time and tide, probability, price, perspicuity, and sheer damn sense, and abandon himself to singular freedoms on the aery winds of the Never-was."

This might imply that Coppard, who during his life was often viewed as a simple, happy rustic with an accidental gift for writing, considered the writing of the short story as something less than an art. In fact, Coppard was an intensely self-conscious writer, aware of himself as author and aware of his fiction as the continuation of a line that he traced directly to Anton Chekhov, Guy de Maupassant, and

Thomas Hardy. Not an unlettered primitive, neither was he a British literary sophisticate.

As he liked to recall with amusement at his own audacity, Coppard began his life as a full-time writer on April Fools' Day, 1919, abandoning his secure job as a confidential clerk and cost accountant for an ironworks at Oxford to live in a small cottage in the woods at Shepherds Pit. He took with him fifty pounds, a love of literature, some success as a poet and short story writer, and a personal history that had long before begun to read like something out of a book. That story began on 4 January 1878, at Folkstone, Kent, where Coppard was born to George Coppard, a tailor, and Emily Southwell Coppard, a housemaid. Always poor, the Coppard family saw its fortunes plummet when George abandoned the family and then, after they had reassembled at Brighton, died of tuberculosis. At nine Coppard was taken out of school, supposedly because of poor health, and so ended his formal education. Almost immediately he was put to work — first as apprentice to a paraffin oil vendor; then as an errand boy for a tailor in London, where he lived with relatives; and finally as a messenger for Reuters. In 1892 he returned to Brighton and began the series of office jobs that he held until he became a full-time writer.

Coppard's surface life slowly moved from poverty to solid, middle-class respectability. But he was not simply a small-town petit bourgeois content with a merely respectable life. Something in his personality, some combination of curiosity, discontent, drive, self-awareness, romantic spirit, and sheer physical zest led him to an extraordinary, active engagement in the life of the mind and the body. At fifteen he became a professional sprinter, traveling to races to compete for cash prizes that he used to buy books, which he read with fierce, sometimes narrow, intensity. He became deeply informed in the works of the major British writers, loving especially Chaucer, Shakespeare, Milton, Keats, Wordsworth, and Robert Browning, and making it his particular ambition to read the long narrative poems that more conventionally educated readers might skim over. He trained dogs, learned to box, joined a rifle team, and took up the two activities that became lifelong pursuits—soccer and long-distance hiking.

The jaunts that he took through England and Ireland provided much of the material for his short fiction. As he walked, "Alf" stopped at inns and taverns, exchanging tales with the villagers. Early on, he began to write descriptive sketches of places and events, and this developed into a habit of carrying with him a notebook in which he logged the names of people and towns, always looking for the unusual. His continual talking and listening and writing down what he heard developed his remarkable skill at conveying an authentic-sounding country dialect.

Yet Coppard was never a cool, detached observer of "folk." At any gathering he was a strongly opinionated, argumentative fellow who followed his own fiercely held positions with a hearty laugh at himself. His first contact with educated, or even literary, persons came with a shock when he encountered the undergraduates at Oxford. Though they were a dozen years or more his juniors, they included him in their poetry and drama-reading circles, giving him for the first time a real sense of people living a life of the mind. Probably it was the emotional intensity of this experience that catapulted him away from his former life, motivating him by example and some self-confessed envy to attempt to write completely formed short stories and to submit them for publication, abandoning his common given name for the more literary sounding A. E.

Coppard drew on the scenes of "vulgar" life. Usually, his characters are common people with all the stereotypical weaknesses and virtues of peasants—guile, craft, simplicity. The fusion of the literary and the ordinary explains his insistence on calling his short stories "tales," a formal design that he carefully articulated. He declared in a 1931 interview in *Everyman* that "the writer should study the folk tale." And in Jacob Schwartz's *Bibliography* he says that he prefers to call his fictions "tales" because "a tale is told, a story is written. I have always aimed at creating for the reader an impression that he is being spoken to, rather than being written at." The voice that he intentionally worked at is designed for the reading pleasure of "the good average man who feels a response to art . . . but having no time to spare for study and instruction is content with what he likes." Coppard's love of the good tale well told can be seen in two examples: he describes the great joy with which on two occasions he unnerved an unlettered hiking companion with "terrible tales" from Edgar Allan Poe; he recounts his efforts to find origins for what he thought of as his folk tales, notably the source of his comic graveyard robbery story, "The Devil in the Churchyard" (*The Black Dog*, 1923). He got the story from a thatcher named Jim Massey in the Starr Inn, Stanton St. John, who swore it was true, but Coppard later traced it to a 1526 publication, *The Hundred Merry Tales*.

The success of Coppard's supernatural fiction can be traced directly to the technique of the tale. By relying on the effects of the oral tradition, Coppard can readily involve the reader in the voice of his narrator and draw him into the otherwise unbelievable or incredible. For example, "The Kisstruck Bogie" (*Dark-Eyed Lady*, 1947) is an amusing yarn told to the skeptical and impatient narrator by his friend Kisstruck, who had bought a haunted house. The ghost, only a voice, was amiable but ordinary, having grown lonely and despondent, fearing for his career and status as a haunt. Eventually, the ghost took up with a female spook, got her pregnant, and married her.

Described as poetic and Irish, Coppard's style became the focus of reviewers' attention from his first volume, *Adam & Eve & Pinch Me* (1921). Here, for example, are the opening lines of the first story, the religious-sexual allegory "Marching to Zion":

In the great days that are gone I was walking the Journey upon its easy smiling roads and came one morning of windy spring to the side of a wood. I had but just rested to eat my crusts and suck a drink from the pool when a fat woman appeared and sat down before me. I gave her the grace of the morning.

This invention of a kind of biblical Irish with its indefinite past tense sets a believable tone for the illusion that the reader is about to enter. The traveler-narrator, Michael Fionnguisa, tells of his adventures, first with Monk, a powerful, simple man who murders and robs three men whom they encounter in the act of committing crimes, then with Mary, a lovely, innocent, holy-minded young woman they take up with. Michael falls in love with Mary and coaxes her to tell him her strange dream. She dreamed that she was married to a carpenter named Joseph, and that while he was away a "dark handsome young man with black long hair and smiling eyes" came to her bed each night, stealing away each morning with one of the daffodils that she had carried to her wedding, until the flowers were gone. At Christmas time, she and her husband had a baby. Mary concludes her narrative, telling Michael that he is "like that lover of the darkness.'"

That night, says the narrator, "I lay with the bride of dreams in my arms." Waking the next morning, Michael finds himself holding a sprig of rowan. Mary is looking at the foot of the mountain, where she sees the empty crosses of Calvary. Neither Michael nor Monk sees anything but a field. Mary kisses Michael one last time and fades away, "growing vague like a ghost would be," leaving them "lonely in the world."

Any attempt to read this story strictly as a religious allegory creates more problems than solutions. Rather, it demands a more ambiguous interpretation. Perhaps each of the characters can be seen as a human type. Monk is the direct, physical, earthy man who acts to get what he wants. Michael is the poet, Mary his inspiration. Do we then read Mary as an actual character who appears and magically disappears? Or can we best see Mary as a projection of Michael's intense need for something beyond the material, something to fire his artist's imagination, that has taken on a life of its own? Zion, certainly, is not to be taken as a literal place on earth sought

by those on the "Journey," nor does it seem to be heaven. It suggests, metaphorically, the goal of a life's quest, a gathering spot for those faithful to some belief. Michael and Monk do not see the Calvary that Mary does. She alone recognizes the field of suffering to which life leads and by which it is redeemed. Michael has seen the beauty of life, but his poet's sensibilities are inadequate to offer him the insight to achieve transfiguration.

While speculating like this, the careful reader wants to know that Coppard based the setting and some of the incidents in the story on a walking trip he took to Ireland. And he wants to note that, while Coppard uses conventional religious or even biblical material, he gives more weight to amusement, diversion, and metaphor than to literal renderings of received belief.

At the end of his career, Coppard was still working with allegorical material derived from Christianity. "The Lion and Lord B." (*Lucy in Her Pink Jacket*, 1954) tells about a "Lord" who buys a lion to discourage thieves and keeps the beast in the desolate remains of his once thriving garden, which the robbers have denuded. Gradually, he tires of the novelty and tries to coax the animal to leave, making it resentful, furious, savage, until one afternoon it begins leaping into the air and vanishes. The story of the disappearance spreads and a cult of the "Assumption of the Beast" arises, gradually taking on its own energy, organization, and dogma.

As the only witness to the lion's life and death, Lord B. becomes the center of the controversies of the believers. He even begins to invent ghostly rematerializations that he starts to believe himself. Slowly he loses interest in life, resigns his office as Prime Chief Grand of the cult, takes to writing bad poetry, and dies. This obvious and heavy-handed treatment of Christianity as a sham might, if handled differently, have used fiction to achieve insight into the nature of belief; or it could have been simply, and honestly, angry. After all, Coppard saw religion as a fraud that fooled and betrayed the gullible. But he lost control of his artistry. Coppard used too many forced puns and an engineered cleverness. The steps of the lion pacing the garden actually form the sign of the cross.

But if Coppard's style eventually became forced,

stilted, and stylized, initially it imparted to his work a magic quite apart from the stories' contents. Often the tone is light, gently humorous. The reader has a sense that the narrator is as pleasantly surprised as he at the ongoing discovery of events. The stories move in unexpected ways, with sudden shifts of scene or mood, very much like tales told by a kindly, jolly, and slightly absentminded uncle who has remembered, once again, just one more detail. Seduced by the delights of language, defenses against disbelief already weakened, the reader falls effortlessly into complicity. So strong was this effect on the early readers of Coppard that he continued to have a reputation as a fantasy writer throughout his life, though, in fact, of over two hundred stories only about four dozen can be called "fantasy," and only about half of these deal directly with the supernatural.

Adam & Eve & Pinch Me established that reputation. Most of its tales have a distinct otherworldly quality; several deal directly with other worlds. "Piffingcap" (*Pearson's Magazine*, July 1918) is the name of a barber given a magic shaving mug that turns out to be both blessed and cursed. This story has the tone and meandering narrative line of a fairy tale. In "The King of the World" (*Voices*, October 1920) an Assyrian captain, lost in the desert, comes upon the ancient shrine of a god whose devotees became stone statues in exchange for brief but intense pleasure. The figure of a beautiful woman comes momentarily to life, to love the captain before they both become stone. Besides "Marching to Zion," the most important otherworldly work is the title story, a third-person account of an altered state of consciousness that, though it has an air of unreality, turns out to be true. The story opens:

> . . . and in the whole of his days, vividly at the end of the afternoon — he repeated it again and again to himself — the kind country spaces had *never* absorbed *quite* so rich a glamour of light, so miraculous a bloom of clarity. He could feel streaming in his own mind, in his bones, the same crystalline brightness that lay upon the land. Thoughts and images went flowing through him as easily and amiably as fish swim in their pools. . . .

Opening to ellipsis, the narrative suggests a continuation of an ongoing action. Images of fish and light and flashing fancy fill the mind of Jaffa Codling, wandering happily through his grand, preternaturally beautiful garden. Its Eden-like flavor is more than implied, for he watches the play of his three children, Adam, Eve, and Gabriel. Gabriel has a flaming golden sword, and he quizzes the gardener, Bond, about its true value: " Is this sword any *good?* " After much hesitation, the gardener responds, "No, Marse Gabriel!"

Throughout this scene, Codling, though emotionally involved, can only observe, because he has already discovered that he has become a kind of phantom who can see and hear but cannot interact with his family. He has already tried, with mounting aggravation and useless anger, to get into a room where his wife is making love to another man. He cannot open doors. He cannot get the servant's attention. Indeed, he finds himself passing right through people with whom he expects to collide. The only one who can see him, he discovers, is Gabriel, who performs for his benefit a series of miracles. He has found a box that Bond confirms is *good*. First Bond, then Gabriel, opens the box to release in succession a kingfisher, a golden carp "made wholly of fire," and a floating light that transforms into a sailing vessel, then bursts into three falling drops of colored fire. Codling has just come to realize what the reader has known for some time, that he is having an out-of-body experience, that the man with his wife is himself. But we discover with him, when he returns to himself, that his name is Gilbert Cannister and that, although he has only two children, his wife is pregnant: "We'll call him Gabriel."

The richness of imagery and the control of metaphor, even symbol, in the elaboration of this allegory of man's spiritual state, and the role of wonder and imagination, have made it a favorite of commentators on Coppard. The fish images (Codling), the Pandora's box (Cannister), the metaphors of illumination make possible a range of interpretations from the religious to the poetic. Once more, however, it is worth noting that Coppard did know a real gardener named Bond and had an actual garden in mind when he wrote the story.

One of the chief characteristics of Coppard's fiction is his almost effortless transition from the world of the everyday to the world of fantasy. Perhaps this is because his world is so often a pastoral one, and in that tradition one is in a kind of magical land to begin with. In "Crotty Shinkwin" (*Dunky Fitlow*, 1933), a butcher with a nagging wife sets out in a boat with a friend to fish. The anchor hooks onto the underside of an island that comes loose, turns over, and reveals a kind of alternate existence in which he sees signs of himself as a successful, happy man. In one of Coppard's best-known tales, the title story of *Clorinda Walks in Heaven* (1922), Miss Clorinda Smith dies and finds heaven to be very like the lovely English countryside. But this maiden discovers in heaven a long line of husbands, erotic entanglements from a history of passionate incarnations. Is heaven a dream, or is life? The narrative ends with a brief account of a woman of the same name who lay in a trance for a month, became known throughout the world, and ended as "one of those faded grey old maids who wear their virginity like antiquated armour."

Similarly, "Simple Simon" (*The Black Dog*) sets out one day for heaven, finally arriving in an elevator to find that heaven is an idealized version of his life on earth. His old, broken-down house in the forest has regained its youth. In this heaven the sins of the charitable are forgiven. Not so in the heaven of "Father Raven" (*Ugly Anna*, 1944). While out walking one day, his congregation finds itself on the way to final judgment. Unwisely generous where sin is concerned, the minister stakes his soul against the virtue of his charges and forfeits eternal joy.

Coppard's stories are more fanciful than fantastic, never ghoulish or terrifying; and when they turn to horror—and they do that rarely—it comes at the reader more like a sudden apparition on a dark night, soon to be nothing more than a slight night start, never the fang at the throat, the heart-skidding grab at the entrails, the descent into terror.

A tinge of horror touches us in "Ale Celestial?" (*You Never Know, Do You?*, 1939). Tavern keeper Barnaby Barnes—simple, sly, curmudgeonly—has never had good luck. He consumes himself in fantasies of easy wealth. One night, trying to force the

fortune at which his poor industry has failed, he intercepts a troll who has been stealing candles from the church, takes the candle from him, and, in return for the candle and a promise not to tell, receives in a dream a recipe for ale and a caution against greed. Reluctantly, Barnaby invests the heavy work and expense that the recipe demands. The ale

> lined the belly with rapture.... It was a moral ale as well as magical, it would make one drunk as a lord or leave him sober as a judge—according to the goodness of the person. A few sips of it would plant a lordly villain on his back or, in a manner of speaking, tilt a worthy man up to the level of magistrates.

The ale's fame spreads and Barnaby's wealth grows, but his greedy, grudging habits win out.

He brews an imitation of the troll's recipe. Although it tastes the same to him, his customers find it disgusting and leave. Day after day he consumes the counterfeit until, having become a "walking shade," he returns to the original recipe. Quaffing the true ale, he tastes it as "rank, fell and foul." Deceived and despairing, he dies among the barrels. At the foot of his corpse the villagers find a tall, fat candle, the flame dancing like a leaping, merry troll.

Coppard wrote his most direct tale of the supernatural near the end of his career. Very different in mood and style from his earlier work, it contains no narrative dialect, no clever punning, no idealized bucolic setting. Rather, it uses a very intense language that relies on un–Coppard-like images of the metaphysical. Published under two titles, "The Homeless One" (*Fearful Pleasures*) and "The Nameless One" (*Dark-Eyed Lady*), it is set in an insane asylum. The soul of Judas, freed to roam after he hanged himself, has drifted into the body of a modern suicide cut down at the moment of death. Now he learns about God from a crazed old cobbler who was a wayside preacher. Although he does not recall with certainty his former life and treachery, he feels the accumulated guilt of Christ's death and prays for forgiveness.

When we assess Coppard's work, we must remember that he became a full-time writer at forty-one without a long apprenticeship. In the prime of his life, he moved quickly to the height of his powers, wrote his best fiction in the 1920's, and began to decline in the early 1930's. Ironically, he was considered one of the most important "young" writers of that period. Ironically, too, although his finest writing is not ordinarily in the field of the supernatural, he is often remembered as a writer of fantasy. Since his death in London on 13 January 1957, no major published work has fully evaluated his achievement. He wrote about a dozen of the finest short stories in English but has had little direct influence on the writers of the modern short story, less on supernatural fiction. He was not part of any literary group; his time at the top of his form was too brief; he published far too much of what he wrote, so the reader is forced to sift for the gems. For the patient and careful reader, that sorting will lead to moments of quiet delight.

Selected Bibliography

WORKS OF A. E. COPPARD

Adam & Eve & Pinch Me. Waltham Saint Lawrence, England: Golden Cockerel Press, 1921. New York: Knopf, 1922. (The Knopf edition also contains the stories from *Clorinda Walks in Heaven.*)

Clorinda Walks in Heaven. Waltham Saint Lawrence, England: Golden Cockerel Press, 1922.

The Black Dog. London: Cape, 1923. New York: Knopf, 1923.

The Gollan. Printed, Not Published, for the Friends of Earl and Florence Fisk. [Green Bay, Wis.?], Christmas, 1929.

Crotty Shinkwin, a Tale of the Strange Adventure That Befell a Butcher of County Clare. The Beauty Spot, a Tale Concerning the Chilterns. Waltham Saint Lawrence, England: Golden Cockerel Press, 1932.

Fearful Pleasures. Sauk City, Wis.: Arkham House, 1946. London: Peter Nevill, 1951. (Collects twenty-two of Coppard's supernatural and fantasy tales.)

Selected Tales. From His Twelve Volumes Published Between the Wars. London: Cape, 1946. (Collects twenty-three tales. A good introduction to Coppard's work, but it contains only a few supernatural stories.)

The Collected Tales of A. E. Coppard. New York: Knopf, 1948, 1951. (Collects thirty-eight of Coppard's best tales, including a few described in this article. The best introduction to Coppard's canon.)

Lucy in Her Pink Jacket. London: Peter Nevill, 1954.

CRITICAL AND BIOGRAPHICAL STUDIES

Bates, H. E. *The Modern Short Story: A Critical Survey.* London: Nelson, 1941.

Beachcroft, Thomas O. *The English Short Story.* 2 vols. (*Writers and Their Work,* nos. 168 and 169.) London: Published for the British Council and National Book League by Longmans, Green, 1964.

————. *The Modest Art: A Survey of the Short Story in English.* London: Oxford University Press, 1968.

Coppard, A. E. "On First Getting into Print." *The Colophon,* 6 (May 1931).

————. *It's Me, O Lord!* London: Methuen, 1957.

Fabes, Gilbert H. *The First Editions of A. E. Coppard, A. P. Herbert, and Charles Morgan. With Values and Bibliographical Points.* London: Myers and Company, 1933.

Ford, Ford Madox. *Critical Writings,* edited by Frank MacShane. Lincoln: University of Nebraska Press, 1964.

Jehin, A. *Remarks on the Style of A. E. Coppard.* (English Pamphlet Series, no. 8.) Buenos Aires: Argentine Association of English Culture, 1944.

Morgan, Louise. "A. E. Coppard on How to Write Short Stories." *Everyman,* 4 (22 January 1931): 793–795.

————. *Writers at Work.* London: Chatto and Windus, 1931.

O'Connor, Frank. *The Lonely Voice: A Study of the Short Story.* Cleveland: World, 1963.

Schwartz, Jacob. *The Writing of Alfred Edgar Coppard: A Bibliography.* With foreword and notes by A. E. Coppard. London: The Ulysses Bookshop, 1931.

—FRANK EDMUND SMITH

E. R. EDDISON

1882-1945

NO ONE COULD predict the nature of Eric Rucker Eddison's fiction from an account of his life. Though no detailed biography of Eddison has been done, the basic facts may be found in *Who's Who* or, in slightly more detail, in L. Sprague de Camp's *Literary Swordsmen and Sorcerers* (1976). Eddison was born on 24 November 1882 in the Yorkshire village of Adel, near Leeds. He attended Eton and then Trinity College, Oxford, graduating in 1905. He married Winifred Grace Henderson in 1909, and they had one daughter, Jean. From 1906 to 1937 Eddison was a civil servant with the British Board of Trade, ultimately serving as deputy comptroller general of overseas trade. For his public service he was granted the titles of companion of St. Michael and St. George (1924) and companion of the Order of the Bath (1929). From 1934 to 1937 he was a member of the Council for Art and Industry. He retired to Wiltshire in 1938 and died on 18 August 1945.

In the course of this ostensibly prosaic life, Eddison wrote *The Worm Ouroboros* (1922) and the three novels of Zimiamvia, which are among the most passionate, violent, and luxurious of modern fantasy novels. Why does it seem less likely that a British bureaucrat should produce such tales than that an Oxford professor like J. R. R. Tolkien should write of elves, wizards, and apocalyptic battles? Perhaps because professors are known to read Malory and *Beowulf*. But Eddison read too. The sources of his fantastic vision lie mainly in three bodies of lit-erature: Norse saga, which he probably discovered through William Morris' translations but eventually learned to read in the original Icelandic; Greek epic and lyric poetry; and Elizabethan drama, especially John Webster's revenge tragedies. From these sources Eddison concocted sweeping plots, larger-than-life heroes and heroines, and a prose style that is sometimes florid but always—like his charac-ters—handsome, inventive, and commanding.

In England in the early twentieth century, the world of affairs was apparently not far removed from the world of letters. Eddison was not the only fan-tasist hidden, as de Camp says, "in a bowler." Kenneth Grahame, Walter de la Mare, and Charles Williams led similar double lives, as banker, book-keeper, and editor, respectively. By the 1940's, after Eddison was well established as a fantasist, he be-came acquainted with Williams, C. S. Lewis, Tol-kien, and the rest of the informal literary circle known as the Inklings. In a letter to his son dated 10 June 1944, Tolkien mentions having heard "Edison" read to the group a chapter from his current work (*The Mezentian Gate*) and praises its "undimin-ished power and felicity of expression" (Tolkien, *Letters*). Both Tolkien and Lewis admired Eddison's imaginative power and rich style but disliked the pagan philosophy implied in the stories (ibid.). It is doubtful on internal evidence that Eddison strongly influenced either writer, and his own themes and techniques had been set before he read anything of theirs.

Indeed, Eddison was part of a generation of writers whose most striking characteristic as a group is its fierce literary independence. Among the writers of fantasy and science fiction born between 1870 and 1886 are Saki, Lord Dunsany, de la Mare, G. K. Chesterton, Edgar Rice Burroughs, Jack London, David Lindsay, James Branch Cabell, E. M. Forster, James Stephens, Eddison, Williams, and Olaf Stapledon. These writers came of age after the Victorian era and before World War I. They grew up reading George MacDonald, Morris, H. Rider Haggard, and Edward George Bulwer-Lytton. The creation of fantastic worlds must have seemed to them to be a normal and desirable activity, granted the stolid, materialistic, and apparently stable world of the turn of the century. They had models but no formulas; of the group only Burroughs found a market in the specialty pulp magazines that were to both shelter and inhibit science fiction and fantasy in the twentieth century. Each writer found his own route to the marvelous.

When Eddison published *The Worm Ouroboros*, readers hardly knew what to make of it. The American edition (1926) was widely reviewed, and the epithets applied to it include "extraordinary," "strange," "bewildering," "amazing," and "sui generis." In judging the degree to which the work was out of step with its time, it helps to remember that it appeared in the United States the same year as Ernest Hemingway's *The Sun Also Rises*; nothing could be further from that book's lean style and Lost Generation anomie. Set on a version of the planet Mercury that no astronomer would recognize; peopled with witches, demons, imps, and goblins; alternating between lavish, leisurely description and strenuous action; introduced as a dream vision but with no corresponding awakening at the story's end; pitting noble but arrogant heroes against cruel but courageous villains, with a sympathetic turncoat shuttling in between; turning around at its conclusion to begin the plot all over again in an endless circle: the book is in all ways splendidly eccentric. And yet, as most reviewers recognized, Eddison is so sure of what he is doing—he sees his improbable world so clearly and chronicles it so convincingly— that we are willing to follow him down his strange byways.

A quotation may best illustrate this sense of conviction. A central episode in the novel is the ascent of the world's highest mountain, Koshtra Pivrarcha, by Lord Juss, ruler of Demonland, and his friend Brandoch Daha. Eddison spends a chapter on their climb, minutely detailing the difficulties and solutions, until at last the climbers stand at the summit:

> Presently a wind arose in the unseen spaces of the sky, and tore the mist like a rotten garment. Spears of sunlight blazed through the rifts. Distant sunny lands shimmered in the unimaginable depths to the southward, seen over the crest of a tremendous wall that stood beyond the abyss: a screen of black rock buttresses seamed with a thousand gullies of glistening snow, and crowned as with battlements with a row of mountain peaks, savage and fierce of form, that made the eye blink for their brightness: the lean spires of the summit-ridge of Koshtra Pivrarcha. These, that the Demons had so long looked up to as in distant heaven, now lay beneath their feet. Only the peak they climbed still reared itself above them, clear now and near to view, showing a bare beetling cliff on the north-east, overhung by a cornice of snow. Juss marked the cornice, turned him again to his step-cutting, and in half an hour from the breaking of the clouds stood on that unascended pinnacle, with all earth beneath him.
>
> (chapter 12)

This is Eddison's prose at its most straightforward. The images are precise; the language, dominated by verbs of action, is vigorous. Eddison, a mountain climber, takes a scene from some earthly peak, a scene that he knew and loved well, and heightens the scale to make it serve the purposes of his tale. However, even in this relatively plain bit of narrative, a few oddities of phrasing mark the language as not quite conventional, not quite modern. "Crowned as with battlements," "turned him again"—we do not speak or write like this in the twentieth century, and yet Eddison uses these constructions so fluently that it is difficult to label them archaisms. Like William Morris before him, he invents a language, drawing on older versions of English, and uses it to distinguish his invented worlds from our own.

In Eddison's first novel, this invented language sometimes gets out of control. His characters speak in a tongue that approaches the language of the seventeenth century more closely than does the narrative: "What in the stablished world is mine, that am thus in a moment reived of him that was mine own heartstring, my brother, the might of mine arm, the chiefest citadel of my dominion?" (chapter 5). Yet such speech is still vigorous, though not as direct as the prose in which it is embedded. It is in descriptions of sumptuous places, thrones, and costumes that Eddison overwhelms the reader. As in works by H. P. Lovecraft and Lord Dunsany, everything is carved of alexandrite or tourmaline, inlaid with gold, and encrusted with chrysoberyl and lapis lazuli. Every woman is a Helen, every man an Alexander. In contemplating such magnificence, Eddison lets the action flag. In the later Zimiamvian trilogy, the magnificence is less static and the characters not as interchangeably noble of countenance.

Other questionable features of *The Worm Ouroboros* include a plot rather thin for the length of the work, a reversal at the end for which the reader is not prepared (the victorious demons, having vanquished the evil Witch King Gorice, ask the gods to restore him so that they may have the fun of fighting him over and over, presumably to eternity), and a beginning section unrelated to the story proper. Scenes shift with an audible clunk, and proper names range from the silly (Zigg) to the tongue-twisting (Zora Rach nam Psarrion), with no system such as makes Tolkien's names convey character and paint scenery through sound alone. Nonetheless, *The Worm* remains a striking and original work of fantasy, and many readers prefer it to the more polished later novels.

Eddison's next work is a historical novel, *Styrbiorn the Strong* (1926), based on incidents from Norse sagas. Eddison recounts the short life of Styrbiorn, a hot-tempered tenth-century Swedish nobleman, in a manner reminiscent of Morris' *The House of the Wolfings*. As in the sagas themselves, deeds of high honor and rank treachery are presented impartially, and the characters reveal their inner conflicts only through terse speeches and impulsive acts. *Styrbiorn the Strong* is not fantasy except for a final chapter set in Valhalla, in which the character

of Odin suggests that of King Mezentius in the Zimiamvian books.

After *Styrbiorn*, Eddison again followed Morris' lead and translated an authentic saga, *Egil's Saga* (1930). In the introduction and notes, Eddison reveals how much he learned about characterization and style from Norse literature. His comments on the culture and art of Iceland could also stand as a defense of his own literary practice. He explains that "Iceland means three things: first, on the political field—aristocratic individualism of an uncompromising kind; secondly, in its broad outlook on human life and destiny—paganism; and thirdly, in art—a peculiar and in itself highly perfected form of prose narrative." Eddison's fantasies are based on the same three elements. His characters are nobly anarchic; their outlook is pagan, in that they profess and live by a "spirit of fatalism and fellowship with, not subservience to, the ultimate Power"; and he utilizes a mode of expression that "becomes more tense and curbed as the situation heightens, until words and phrases have effect individually and apocalyptically like lightning flashes, each trailing behind it . . . a turmoil of associations like rolling thunders."

Many of Eddison's readers (including C. S. Lewis) were bothered by the amorality (at least by Christian standards) of his characters. This too derives from the sagas; it is a part of their paganism. Eddison quotes E. V. Gordon, who points out that the standard of behavior of saga heroes and heroines is not moral but aesthetic. Likewise, in Eddison's fantasies the only sin is to be small-spirited. In sagas, says Eddison, temperance and moderation are "drab virtues of little men negatively withholding them from this and that"; the characters he admires "ride whirlwinds" of passion. Eddison's fantasies uphold a code that is unabashedly Nietzschean; had he written after World War II, his enthusiasm for supermen and heroic conflict might perhaps have been tempered.

Eddison sheds light on his stylistic preferences in his comments on translation:

The heroic age itself is old-fashioned to us to-day: it will seem not old-fashioned only but unreal and ridiculous if we attempt to galvanize it into a semblance of modernity by putting into its mouth the sophisticated parlance of our own very different times.

(pages 239–240)

According to Eddison, modern literary English is formal, abstract, and pompous because it is primarily a written language, whereas the language of the sagas was shaped by oral tradition. Contemporary terms "carry associations foreign to the background of daily life under the old, simple, unmechanized civilizations." Thus, in translating *Egil's Saga* or in creating imaginary worlds, the natural and appropriate language is "an archaic simplicity of speech," rather than a plodding modernity.

Eddison's last works are set primarily in his imaginary world of Zimiamvia. These three novels are loosely tied to *The Worm Ouroboros*: first, in that Zimiamvia is mentioned in the earlier book as a sort of Valhalla where the blessed dead are revived, "even they that were great upon earth and did great deeds when they were living, that scorned not earth and the delights and the glories thereof, and yet did justly and were not dastards nor yet oppressors"; and second, in that Lessingham, one of the heroes of the Zimiamvian books, first appears in the introduction to *The Worm*. There he is an Englishman who travels to Mercury in a dream and observes the drama of demons and witches. In the first strictly Zimiamvian novel, *Mistress of Mistresses* (1935), Lessingham is shown lying in state on the arctic island that he has attempted to establish as a latter-day Icelandic fiefdom. He has lived over eighty years as an adventurer, artist, and statesman. His oldest friend and his latest mistress, watching by his body, discuss his life, and the woman reveals herself as no mortal but as the Goddess. Lessingham's deeds and love of life have won from her a promised reward. He is reborn in Zimiamvia, and his adventures there make up a major part of the novel's plot.

Zimiamvia is less alien than the Mercury of *The Worm Ouroboros*. It is primarily a world of men and women, not demons and goblins, though among the secondary characters we find a naiad, a dryad, and an oread. Zimiamvia consists of city-states and small kingdoms: Meszria, Rerek, and rugged Fingiswold, with a barbaric land called Akkama beyond Fingis-

wold to the north. The three kingdoms have lately been unified by King Mezentius, who has just died. Likely claimants to his throne include the late king's son Styllis, Styllis' younger sister Antiope, their illegitimate half-brother Barganax, and the unscrupulous Horius Parry, the king's vicar (viceroy) in Rerek. Lessingham appears in this world as a cousin of the vicar's, lately returned from abroad. He supports the vicar, whose wolfish temperament he finds amusing.

When people in Zimiamvia are not engaged in battle and intrigue, they practice the arts of love. Lessingham falls in love with the Princess Antiope. His adversary, Duke Barganax, spends much of his time in dalliance with his mistress Fiorinda, a sort of Lucrezia Borgia whose politician brother has already arranged for her to be twice married and twice widowed. These two couples—Lessingham and Antiope, Barganax and Fiorinda—are mirror images of one another. Each pair includes one fair-haired member and one dark; the dark lovers, Lessingham and Fiorinda, are ambitious, in love with power, while the fair-haired lovers are amiable pleasure seekers.

As the novel develops, these four characters emerge as something more than human. They are incarnations of the two ruling principles of the universe, the God and Goddess, whom Eddison usually calls by their Greek names of Zeus and Aphrodite. Fiorinda knows that she is a goddess; the rest have occasional inklings. These four also share memories of a life on earth. Both Lessingham and Barganax remember being the earthly Edward Lessingham; and Antiope and Fiorinda recall existence as Lady Mary Lessingham, Edward's young wife, who was killed in a train wreck along with their daughter. These earthly memories surface only under the influence of a philosopher and magician named Doctor Vandermast and in the confines of his elusive House of Peace, which is remarkably like Lessingham's earthly house at Nether Wastdale (a real place in England's Lake District, usually spelled Wasdale), as described in the opening of *The Worm Ouroboros*.

Thus we see that the relationship between earth and Zimiamvia is a complex one, not explained clearly either in *The Worm* or in *Mistress of Mistresses*. The second Zimiamvian novel, *A Fish Din-*

ner in Memison (1941), provides a rationale for the interweaving of the two worlds. This novel takes place alternately in Zimiamvia and England. It describes the initial meetings and courtship between Barganax and Fiorinda and between Edward and Mary Lessingham. The Zimiamvian sections take place before the death of King Mezentius, who proves to be another incarnation of Zeus. At the fish dinner of the title, held by Barganax's mother, Amalie, the afterdinner conversation turns to philosophy. Fiorinda challenges the king to imagine a world like their own but inferior in that it is bound by mechanical laws and a rigid passage of time. He does so, and his imagining takes shape, spinning like a bubble in the air before them. It is our earth. On further challenge, Mezentius and Barganax enter into the created world, merging to become Edward Lessingham; Fiorinda and Amalie become Mary. They live out their lives in a moment of Zimiamvian time and return to their watching selves, whereupon Fiorinda pops the bubble-world with a hairpin. Earth, then, is a shadow Zimiamvia. What we know of beauty is an echo of that world. Thus Eddison ingeniously explains his use of earthly allusions, languages, and poems, such as the old French lyric sung by Fiorinda's maid Campaspe.

A Fish Dinner is in many ways the most satisfying of Eddison's books. The earthly lives of Edward and Mary make an effective counterpoint to the more perilous but less encumbered lives of the Zimiamvians. The Edwardian setting of their courting days is charmingly portrayed, with daylong cricket games, flirting chases on horseback, and formal dinners with witty conversations. Transitions between the worlds are dazzling, as when Fiorinda, at the book's opening, meets a young Lessingham in Italy, inspires him to return to England to win Mary, and then steps lightly from April in Verona to June in Meszria. Clicking castanets in England dissolve into Zimiamvian hoofbeats. Lights go out suddenly as Edward is painting Mary: the afterimage of her red hair and green dress becomes the painting of black-haired, red-robed Fiorinda that Barganax is executing. Mary's devastating death leaves Duke Barganax, at the fish dinner, shaken and silent until Fiorinda breaks the spell.

The third Zimiamvian novel was left incomplete at Eddison's death, but its completed beginning and ending were linked by a narrative outline, and so the whole was felt to be worth publishing as The Mezentian Gate (1958). In it, Eddison relates events from before the birth of Mezentius to his death soon after the fish dinner. This book further explores issues raised in the other two novels: the nature of love and beauty; the intricacies of politics; and the difference between being masters of time, as are Zimiamvians, and slaves to it. A major theme is King Mezentius' attempt to come to terms with his own newly discovered divinity. He seeks to test his powers by unmaking what he has made, including Zimiamvia itself, but love for his goddess, Amalie, restrains him. Instead, he chooses death and forgetfulness. When he is reborn as Lessingham, he is not as burdened with knowledge.

The Zimiamvian novels surpass The Worm Ouroboros in their philosophical content. Though some readers may tire of Doctor Vandermast's commentaries on Spinoza, Eddison effectively dramatizes his metaphysics. The adventure, intrigue, and lovemaking that keep the books in motion also help convey Eddison's views on life. Like all effective fantasies, the Zimiamvian books reveal their author's deepest convictions. Unlike most modern fantasy, they have at their center the relationships between persons, especially the passionate love between men and women. Perhaps for this reason they are entirely free of the elegiac longing of Tolkien's Middle Earth. Their central moment is not an elvish twilight but the glorious dawn that Fiorinda, in Mistress of Mistresses, recognizes as but another expression of her divine nature.

Selected Bibliography

WORKS OF E. R. EDDISON

The Worm Ouroboros. London: Cape, 1922. New York: Boni, 1926.

Styrbiorn the Strong. London: Cape, 1926. New York: Boni, 1926.

Egil's Saga, Done into English Out of the Icelandic. Cambridge: Cambridge University Press, 1930. New York: Greenwood Press, 1968.

Mistress of Mistresses. London: Faber and Faber, 1935. New York: Dutton, 1935.

A Fish Dinner in Memison. New York: Dutton, 1941.

The Mezentian Gate. Plaistow, England: Curwen Press, 1958. New York: Ballantine, 1969.

CRITICAL AND BIOGRAPHICAL STUDIES

de Camp, L. Sprague. *Literary Swordsmen and Sorcerers: The Makers of Heroic Fantasy.* Sauk City, Wis.: Arkham House, 1976.

Hamilton, G. Rostrevor. "The Prose of E. R. Eddison." *English Studies*, New Series, 2 (1949): 43–53.

Tolkien, J. R. R. *Letters of J. R. R. Tolkien*, edited by Humphrey Carpenter with the assistance of Christopher Tolkien. Boston: Houghton Mifflin, 1981.

Wilson, Sharon. "The Doctrine of Organic Unity: E. R. Eddison and the Romance Tradition." *Extrapolation*, 25 (Spring 1984): 12–19.

Zahorski, Kenneth, and Boyer, Robert M. "The Secondary Worlds of High Fantasy." In *The Aesthetics of Fantasy Literature and Art*, edited by Roger C. Schlobin. Notre Dame, Ind.: University of Notre Dame Press, 1982, 56–81.

—BRIAN ATTEBERY

DAVID GARNETT

1892-1981

BY THE TIME of his death in 1981 at the age of eighty-nine, David Garnett had, over the course of an active and varied life, published almost thirty-five books. Of these, only one is now widely remembered by the reader of fiction. Several should be. *Lady into Fox* (1922) may indeed be the most perfect book Garnett ever wrote, and perhaps his most memorable. All the same, his creative life was of a piece, even though it extended over many decades; and as late as *The Master Cat* (1974) Garnett was continuing intermittently to compose his allegories of metamorphosis, in which beasts and human beings exchange shapes and souls, so that we can gaze through mirrors upon our condition. Garnett's talent may at times seem slender and somewhat precious, and the deadpan amorality of his style may seem ultimately evasive; but he never sank into the dandy's world-weary silence, nor did he ever become (it has much the same effect as silence) loquacious.

Garnett's personal life, being extraordinary and lived in terms hardly describable in early-twentieth-century Britain, may have been an ideal one for a writer of allegories whose morals are never drawn. It was not, on the other hand, a particularly private life. David Garnett was born, a child of intellectual privilege, in Brighton on 9 March 1892 and was brought up in a physically remote part of rural Surrey. He was not isolated there, however. His mother was Constance Garnett, the famous translator from

the Russian. His father was Edward Garnett, an extremely eminent publisher's reader for most of his life and the literary discoverer of Joseph Conrad, D. H. Lawrence, and many others. His grandfather, Richard Garnett, the author of *The Twilight of the Gods* (1888; revised 1903), ended his influential career as a man of letters only with his death in 1906, when young Garnett was fourteen. The entire family was gregarious and maintained personal connections throughout the British literary establishment; indeed, they comprised a central part of that establishment. Among the visitors to the Surrey household were Conrad, Ford Madox Ford (then Hueffer), George Bernard Shaw, W. H. Hudson, Hilaire Belloc, Peter Kropotkin, and many others. It may not be surprising that a sense of companionable self-worth, of an unthreatenable eccentricity, permeates Garnett's life, as he has described it in the three volumes of *The Golden Echo* (1953, 1955, 1962), and affects his work as well.

Most of Garnett's formal education was in London, where from 1910 he studied botany for five years at the Royal College of Science. During this period he went on a walking trip with D. H. and Frieda Lawrence and first entered the circle of writers, artists, and intellectuals known as the Bloomsbury group. It included the Keynes brothers, Leonard and Virginia Woolf, Clive and Vanessa Bell, Duncan Grant, Roger Fry, and Lytton Strachey. For the rest of his life Garnett would live with, breed with, and memorialize these central figures. If there was a specific audience to which he spoke in his books, that audience was Bloomsbury.

Life soon became remarkably unusual for Garnett. He refused active combat in World War I, joining instead the Friends' War Victims Relief Mission, a Quaker organization. But he was soon back in England, involved in a ménage à trois with Duncan Grant and Vanessa Bell. He was for some years Duncan Grant's lover but intimate with both; one of Grant's most famous paintings, *Interior*, gives a life-enhancing view of the complexities involved in the ménage. All three worked intensely at painting or writing. Duncan Grant was the father of Vanessa's child Angelica, born on Christmas day, 1918. After the ménage dissolved, Garnett married the artist Ray (Rachell Alice) Marshall, who illustrated several of his novels. They had two children. She died in 1940. Two years later, Garnett married Angelica Bell, both of them seemingly aware of the other's relationship to Duncan Grant. They had four daughters, one of whom illustrated some of her father's last work. In a sense — it is a sense his novels reflect — the implications of the life Garnett led were too complex to handle in aesthetic terms. Though it is certainly the case that his best books are about sexual relations, those metamorphic dances that his characters discover themselves performing never receive an explanation, either worldly or supernatural.

Typically enough, Garnett's first novel was written under a female pseudonym, Leda Burke. But *Dope-Darling: A Story of Cocaine* (1919) is a work of only passing interest to the readers of his acknowledged fiction. Garnett always dated the beginning of his career with the startlingly successful *Lady into Fox*, which won both the Hawthornden and the James Tait Black prizes, and which, unfairly, has put all his subsequent work into the shade. It cannot be denied, however, that *Lady into Fox* is a finely executed tour de force, trim, polished, deadpan but deeply sly.

It has frequently been noted of this novel that it is told after the manner of Daniel Defoe, and there can be no doubt that Garnett made deliberate use of Defoe's characteristic techniques in telling his own tall tale. At the heart of Defoe's method is the pretense that he is reporting a preexistent (though fab-

ulous) story, that he is innocent of any implications the story may bear, and that he is a reporter rather than a creator. Therefore, he is not responsible for what the reader makes of his narratives. (There is an analogy here to some of the techniques of oral storytelling; the American tall tales describing the lives and exploits of figures like Pecos Bill are not so dissimilar to *Lady into Fox*, and help explain some of the novel's "mythic" resonances.) So, writing like Defoe, Garnett is able to disclaim any subversive intent in telling us of the tragic fate of Richard Tebrick's young wife.

In 1879 Mr. Tebrick marries Silvia Fox, whose only peculiarity, beyond having been raised in virtual isolation in a remote vicinity, lies in her hatred of fox hunting. He takes his new wife to his own remote dwelling in Oxfordshire and settles in with her. But, to his cost, he ignores her distaste for the formalized killing of wild animals and uses physical force to ensure that she witness hounds tearing after a fox. It is at this precise point that, suddenly, without explanation and forever, Silvia turns into a vixen:

> *Where his wife had been the moment before was a small fox, of a very bright red.* It looked at him very beseechingly, advanced towards him a pace or two, and he saw at once that his wife was looking at him from the animal's eyes. You may well think if he were aghast; and so maybe was his lady at finding herself in that shape, so they did nothing for nearly half-an-hour but stare at each other, he bewildered, she asking him with her eyes as if indeed she spoke to him: "What am I now become? Have pity on me, husband, have pity on me for I am your wife."
>
> (page 5)

Tebrick's shock is of course enormous but attaches more to the social consequences of what has happened than to the actual transformation. His wife is now naked, and he must clothe her. He must get her out of sight. He must keep her clean. She must not forget her table manners. Profoundly alienated though she may be from human demeanor, she must nevertheless continue to behave as his wife.

Despite Mr. Tebrick's best efforts, though, Silvia becomes more and more foxlike and eventually escapes from his home and becomes a wild animal. Deeply distraught, Mr. Tebrick looks for her constantly but finds her again only after she has borne a litter of pups. Even this does not divert him from attempting to maintain some semblance of propriety — though by now in his isolation and distress he has become deeply eccentric — and he tries to become a kind of father to the litter. This state of affairs cannot last, for we are in the latter years of the reign of Queen Victoria, and the realities of the world eventually impinge, fatally, upon the small family unit. The hunting season comes round again, and Silvia is viciously destroyed by hounds. The semblance is over. Mr. Tebrick goes insane, though he does eventually recover and, as the last sentence of the novel has it, "is still alive" when Garnett, in his implied role of disinterested reporter, puts the story into writing.

The touch is light throughout, but beneath the surface lie genuine metamorphic horrors, bearing (as they do) their message of the birth or death of an intolerable wrongness. Garnett's technique frees us to speculate endlessly on the nature of that wrongness, for assuredly he does not supply any reason for the cataclysm of change that so deeply violates (or perhaps expresses) Silvia's true being. Some contemporary reviewers treated her transformation as a misogynistic rewriting of the old plaint that when a man makes a woman into his wife, she is likely to turn into a vixen. This reading is possible, but also trivial.

More interestingly, *Lady into Fox* may be read as an allegory of the costs extracted of women in a patriarchal society when, on becoming adult, they must submerge their being in the hierarchical structure of a socially sanctioned marriage. If to be a woman in 1880 in Victorian England is in some way to be imprisoned, then Silvia's metamorphosis can be read as a refusal, however inarticulate on her part, to live in bad faith. In this light, Mr. Tebrick's unremitting constancy to his wife after the event can be seen as a refusal on his own part, for he refuses to admit her true nature.

It is also significant that the sport that Silvia abhorred is emblematic of the most established rituals of the life of the rural gentry. A pattern emerges: as fox hunting is death to foxes, so patriar-chal society is death to women. Speculation along this particular line of thought can become interminable, but one fact clearly expressed in the text itself does remain constantly relevant. At the heart of the tragedy of Silvia's metamorphosis lies the fact that it — that she — is fundamentally ignored.

With the exception of a few borderline tales, and of two novels whose implications are fabulous rather than realistic, Garnett published no further supernatural fiction for more than forty years. Of the short stories, "Purl and Plain" is of the greatest interest. It was originally published in the London edition of *Vogue* in 1927, and much later in *Purl and Plain, and Other Stories* (1973). Set in Poland in springtime, it is a seemingly absurdist fable whose implications, as usual in Garnett, ramify indefinitely. Two houses face each other across a river. An articulate and amorous oriole spies a silken thread in the garden of one house, entangles himself in it, flutters across to the other house, and escapes, leaving the thread to join the two families fatefully together. A woman from each house fastens upon the thread and begins to knit. The two draw together until, quarreling, they each tumble into the river that separates them, still bound by their silken thread to the perhaps flimsy but still sustaining rituals of normal life. Unfortunately, just as they begin to exchange confidences — one is a bride-to-be, the other about to become a grandmother — and just as they finish their knitting, the thread breaks, and they both drown in the springtime spate of waters. Seemingly offhand in its effects, "Purl and Plain" gains in retrospect a mysterious poignancy, a sense of meanings unraveled, implications unsounded.

Garnett's third and sixth novels, *A Man in the Zoo* (1924) and *The Grasshoppers Come* (1931), are both fables of metamorphosis in which the actual transformation is either encompassed only metaphorically, as in the first, or adumbrated, as in the second. In *A Man in the Zoo*, an engaged couple quarrel stiffly while visiting the London Zoo; and when she calls him "a survival—atavism at its worst," suggesting that he should be caged and put on show, he takes her at her word, escalating the cold war between them, and offers himself to the authorities. Only too glad to be able to exhibit a man, they give him an indefinite contract. But in this novel, just as relations between man and woman are frozen into a postured "engagement," so metamorphosis is stalled this side of realization. The young man does not change his shape. After a sojourn in the zoo as a man, he becomes reconciled with his young woman, his contract is canceled, and the two lovers depart, prepared to melt into one another's arms, to disappear in the crowd "chiefly composed of couples like themselves."

Far more impressively, *The Grasshoppers Come* presents the reader with an unassembled metamorphic equation that—if the proper connections are made—has explosive implications. Framed by descriptions of the growth and devastating progress of a horde of locusts in central Asia, the main story recounts the attempts of an ill-assorted trio to break a long-distance flying record. From England they aim their airplane deep into central Asia, where their miniature ship of fools duly crashes into the desert. The two passengers trek off into the wastes, while the injured pilot awaits certain death. The arrival of the locusts saves the pilot's life, though. With an ecstatic voracity equal to their own blind greed, he gorges himself on insects, becoming one with them. He is then rescued by a Chinese aviator, who has been tracking the horde. The thrust of the novel seems to lie in the juxtaposition of locusts and a humanity whose nature has become submerged in an onrushing, unstoppable technology. The airplane that surrounds its human passengers is singularly like an exoskeleton, and in its potent metamorphic latency the novel clearly allows a reading to the effect that—in the world we have created—human beings are nothing more than the soft stuff within the massed exoskeletons of a metal horde.

With reviewing and critical work, military service in World War II, and a subsequent publishing career (not his first), Garnett was fully occupied for many years; he also farmed semiprofessionally. He returned to fiction only in 1955, and to fiction of a supernatural character only in 1963, with the publication of *Two by Two: A Story of Survival*, which is the story of Noah seen through the eyes of twin sisters, stowaways on the ark and eventual mates to two of Noah's grandsons. While the story is in itself compactly and deftly told, and clearly worth attention for its measured deflation of the Old Testament

deity who drowns a world out of pique, readers may well be most intrigued by the close resemblance that *Two by Two* bears to much of the work of Garnett's old friend T. H. White:

> And Noah would pick up his speaking trumpet and bellow:
> "Beavers wanted. Beavers forward." And after a long wait the unfortunate beavers would come paddling forward side by side and modestly make their way up the gangway, horrified at having so much attention given to them....
>
> (Part One)

Indeed, in the person of Noah, Garnett has arguably composed a rather sharply etched portrait of White himself. Noah is drunken, self-pitying, monomaniacal, and melancholic; so was White, as Garnett knew well. *The White/Garnett Letters* (1968), which he edited, both makes this awareness evident and offers much clement insight into the creative anguishes that gave eventual birth to *The Once and Future King* (1958), White's masterpiece.

After *Ulterior Motives* (1966), in which matter transmission receives a treatment that shifts uneasily back and forth from science fiction to fantasy, Garnett returned one final time, in *The Master Cat: The True and Unexpurgated Story of Puss in Boots* (1974), to the tale of metamorphosis, implied or actual. It is preluded by a short story, "From 'Puss in Boots,'" which was published in *A Chatto & Windus Almanack* (1926) and republished in *Purl and Plain*. Here, to unfortunately coy effect, Garnett's cat prepares itself to tell him the true story of Puss in Boots, including the tragic sequel.

The novel itself avoids this sort of preciousness. It is divided into two parts, the first of which retells the famous Charles Perrault fable of 1697 from the viewpoint of the dexterous cat, and the second of which tells of the consequences of Puss's success in gaining wealth and position for his master, the miller's son. Once properly established, his master finds Puss in Boots an intolerable reminder of his humble origins, and (like any human) begins to lie to others and to himself about the nature of their relationship. Finally, with the aid of some visiting primitive Christians, whose minds are (as usual) boggled with superstitions and who (as always) are eager to extirpate any evidence of an earlier world not encompassed by their faith, the miller's son traps, imprisons, and tries to murder Puss. But the cat escapes and conveys to the natural world his message of betrayal. In the future no cat, no natural creature, should give final allegiance to man, for man is not to be trusted: "You must never serve one of the human race. Look at the rusty iron collar about my neck, look at the scars upon my body."

Taken as human whenever he wears his boots, hovering at the edge of metamorphosis, Puss is a tricksterlike figure; a passionate survivor with a cool, disinterested mind; an observer and manipulator both. He is perhaps Garnett's ideal protagonist, grave and gleeful, a rider of the waves of transformation. We do not know what he thinks. We do not know what Garnett thought of his own richly symbolic life. We do not know if his novels deliberately allegorize the unknowable. But we do know that both author and books clearly share one thing—a catlike equipoise, a catlike sangfroid. Garnett died on 17 February 1981, quite immensely old.

Selected Bibliography

FICTION BY DAVID GARNETT

Lady into Fox. London: Chatto and Windus, 1922. New York: Knopf, 1923.
A Man in the Zoo. London: Chatto and Windus, 1924. New York: Knopf, 1924.

The Grasshoppers Come. London: Chatto and Windus, 1931. New York: Brewer, Warren and Putnam, 1931.
Two by Two: A Story of Survival. London: Longmans, 1963. New York: Atheneum, 1964 (published in 1963).
Ulterior Motives. London: Longmans, 1966. New York: Harcourt Brace, 1967.
Purl and Plain, and Other Stories. London: Macmillan, 1973.
The Master Cat: The True and Unexpurgated Story of Puss in Boots. London: Macmillan, 1974.

CRITICAL AND BIOGRAPHICAL STUDIES

There is no substantial critical work on David Garnett's writing, although details of his life feature in publications on the Bloomsbury group. *David Garnett: A Writer's Library* (1983), published in the form of a catalog by The Golden Hind Bookshop (Deal, England), gives an intimate sense of his literary surroundings. His life is best told by himself:

The Golden Echo. London: Chatto and Windus, 1953. New York: Harcourt Brace, 1954.
The Flowers of the Forest. Being Volume Two of "The Golden Echo." London: Chatto and Windus, 1955. New York: Harcourt Brace, 1956.
The Familiar Faces. Being Volume Three of "The Golden Echo." London: Chatto and Windus, 1962. New York: Harcourt Brace and World, 1963.

Two further books are of interest:
The White/Garnett Letters. Edited by David Garnett. London: Cape, 1968. New York: Viking, 1968.
Great Friends: Portraits of Seventeen Writers. London: Macmillan, 1979. New York: Atheneum, 1980.

—JOHN CLUTE

DAVID LINDSAY

1878-1945

IF ONE CONCEIVES of fantasy and supernatural fiction as ranging along a continuum from the benign visionary fictions of a C. S. Lewis on the one hand to the unpleasant and often violent horrors of an H. P. Lovecraft on the other, David Lindsay presents a considerable problem. That his work is visionary in the truest sense there can be little doubt, but it is equally evident that few authors in the realm of the fantastic have achieved such unsettling visions of horror and violence as this strange and obscure "Scotsman." Harold Bloom claims of *A Voyage to Arcturus* that "no other fictional work inflicts such spiritual violence upon its audience," and indeed many readers find the book challenging in the most fundamental ways—many, in fact, find it almost unreadable, and not only because of its stilted style or its thoroughly unpredictable wealth of bizarre imagery. The novel is a deadly serious work of fantasy that forces readers to question and reevaluate constantly not only their own beliefs about reality, but also their reactions to the book as they are reading it. For many readers that makes it a potentially dangerous book.

Few of the readers of *A Voyage to Arcturus* know anything of the man who wrote it, and many assume that Lindsay was a one-book author whose novel is a fluke in an otherwise thoroughly anonymous career. This is true to the extent that none of his other works has ever found, or is ever likely to

find, a wide audience. But to regard *A Voyage to Arcturus* as anything other than a fundamental exploration of a philosophy that dominated Lindsay's entire life would be unfair both to the book and to the author. Lindsay did write other books—most of them fantasies—and to a large extent his career is a tragic tale of his constantly renewed attempts to bring his philosophical vision before the public in the wake of the commercial failure of his first and best novel.

Lindsay was born on 2 March 1878 in a London suburb named Blackheath, into a family soon to be devastated by the disappearance of Lindsay's father (who was later found to have deserted the family and gone to Canada). An isolated child and a brilliant student who reacted at an early age against his strict religious upbringing, Lindsay was forced by family circumstances to forgo a university education and take a position in a London insurance brokerage, where he worked from 1894 until 1916, taking time out to serve in the British grenadiers during the war (but never seeing action or leaving the British Isles). During this time Lindsay watched his older brother Alexander enjoy some modest success as an author of adventure novels (under the name Alexander Crawford), only to die prematurely at the age of forty. Lindsay, too, had literary ambitions, and his brother's death, together with his own marriage to an energetic younger woman named Jacqueline in

1916, may have influenced his rather dramatic decision that year to leave his job of twenty years and attempt a career as a writer.

Lindsay spent both his savings and his pension on a house in Cornwall—being, as it turned out, unrealistically optimistic about his future as a novelist—and immediately set to work on a novel then titled "Nightspore in Tormance." Submitted to Methuen in 1920, the novel was accepted, but it was cut by some 15,000 words and its title changed to *A Voyage to Arcturus.* The novel was published in September 1920, and that edition sold a total of only 596 copies. Turning to a more realistic—and thus perhaps more accessible—setting for his second novel, Lindsay finished *The Haunted Woman* in April 1921. This time the book was initially declined by Methuen but finally published in 1922 after it, too, had been cut, and it was serialized in the London *Daily News.* Again, sales were slow. A third novel, *Sphinx,* was declined by three publishers before it appeared in 1923. Lindsay's career, which had really never gotten under way, was already measurably in decline.

Perhaps out of desperation, Lindsay began in 1922 his only frankly commercial novel, *The Adventures of M. de Mailly.* Even this ingeniously complex historical romance did not find a publisher until 1926, although it did enjoy enough success to become the first work of Lindsay's to appear in the United States, under the title *A Blade for Sale* (1927). But Lindsay's real creative effort during these years was devoted to a long and heavily philosophical novel called "The Ancient Tragedy," which would be rejected repeatedly by publishers until Lindsay rewrote it as *Devil's Tor.* Accepted by Putnam in January 1932, a decade after Lindsay first began work on it, *Devil's Tor* was the last work of Lindsay's to see print during his lifetime. Some measure of the success of his career may be evidenced by the fact that this novel sold 650 copies, compared to 596 for *A Voyage to Arcturus* in 1920. Two other novels, *The Violet Apple,* written in 1924, and *The Witch,* which Lindsay worked on throughout much of the thirties but never finished, would not see print until 1976, in the wake of a modest revival of interest in Lindsay's work.

Needless to say, this spectacularly unsuccessful writing career had its effects on Lindsay's life, and

over the years he became increasingly bitter and reclusive. In 1929 he moved his family to a smaller house in Sussex, but financial difficulties did not abate, as evidenced by Lindsay's sad attempts to persuade Putnam to reissue *A Voyage to Arcturus* in 1932 directly on the heels of the failure of *Devil's Tor.* In 1938 the family moved again, this time to a suburb near Brighton, where Jacqueline Lindsay began to take in boarders to meet the family's financial obligations. Here the family remained through the war years, and here, on 16 July 1945, Lindsay died, following a bizarre series of mishaps that began with a bomb exploding near his house and causing a severe loss of blood when Lindsay was struck in his bath by broken glass, and ending with an abscessed tooth that went untreated and led to blood poisoning and gangrene. He also had carcinoma of the mouth.

Ironically, it was just about the time of Lindsay's death that the beginnings of his reputation as a unique fantasist began to spread. Already in the twenties he had begun to form a few literary friendships with such authors as L. H. Myers and E. H. Visiak, but those authors are if anything less well known today than Lindsay himself. But on 14 November 1940, C. S. Lewis praised *A Voyage to Arcturus* highly in a lecture delivered to the undergraduate literary society of Merton College, Oxford, and in 1944 he cited the novel as "the real father of my planet books," referring to his Perelandra trilogy. The lecture was reprinted in 1947 as part of a volume of essays dedicated to Charles Williams. In 1946 Gollancz finally reissued *A Voyage to Arcturus,* followed by another reprint in 1963, the year that also saw the first American edition of the book. *The Haunted Woman,* Lindsay's second novel, was reprinted in 1964. The year 1968 saw the first paperback edition of *Arcturus,* and in 1970 Lindsay's friend Visiak worked with the English novelists Colin Wilson and J. B. Pick on *The Strange Genius of David Lindsay,* the first critical volume devoted to Lindsay. *The Violet Apple* and *The Witch* appeared in 1976, and in 1981 came Bernard Sellin's *The Life and Works of David Lindsay.* By now Lindsay's work was a staple of college courses in fantastic literature, and was widely read by other authors. *A Voyage to Arcturus* was even listed as one of "ten representative novels" in Robert Scholes's and Eric Rabkin's 1977 text *Science Fiction: History, Science, Vision.*

A Voyage to Arcturus is hardly representative of anything, however, and certainly not of science fiction. Conceived manifestly as a dramatization of the author's philosophy, it is a work that in fact has more in common with the style and substance of earlier romantic philosophers. Critics have traced its ideas to Friedrich Nietzsche, Arthur Schopenhauer, Thomas Carlyle, and others in an effort to unravel the system that underlies the visionary surface of the novel. Whatever the sources of Lindsay's ideas, his form seems largely to have been borrowed from George MacDonald, whose *Phantastes* (1858) and *Lilith* (1895) inaugurated the form of English symbolic fantasy to which Lindsay's novel belongs, and to whom Lindsay once referred, in conversation with Visiak, as the greatest single influence on his fiction.

A Voyage to Arcturus opens unpromisingly, with a séance attended by two mysterious characters named Maskull and Nightspore. After witnessing the materialization promised by the medium Backhouse, Nightspore invites Maskull to accompany him to a remote observatory called Starkness, where they will join someone named Krag for a journey "to see the land where this sort of fruit grows wild." Mysteries quickly begin to multiply: at the observatory Maskull begins to hear a strange drumbeat that will stay with him for the rest of his journey (he is told it is his own heart). The observatory itself is in a tower that seems almost impossible for Maskull to climb, until he receives some of Krag's blood through a wound in his arm. And when the journey does take place, in a crystal vessel powered by "Arcturan back rays," it ends with Maskull alone on a scarlet desert, in pain and with his body growing new organs, which seem to be associated with love and sharing. Once Maskull awakes on Tormance, the planet of Arcturus, the narrative begins to reach its full power.

On Tormance, Maskull begins a series of adventures that give credence to C. S. Lewis' observation that the novel is "a lived dialectic." He encounters a succession of beings whose outer form reflects their inner nature, and in each episode Maskull

seems to arrive at the truth about this strange environment only to have this "truth" annihilated at the next turn. First he meets a couple named Joiwind and Panawe, who identify him with Prometheus, practice the virtues of "lovingkindness" and sacrifice, and warn him about the god Surtur, who they say is also known as Crystalman and sometimes as Shaping. Maskull is in search of Surtur, whom he had been told about by Krag.

Lindsay's odd nomenclature has been the subject of much speculation by students of *A Voyage to Arcturus*, and Surtur is one of the few names that seems to have a direct source: in the *Elder Edda*, the famous thirteenth-century compilation of Norse mythology, he is the guardian of the Muspel fire that will destroy the gods, and indeed in Lindsay's novel it is the light of Muspel that draws Maskull on toward whatever Surtur represents. After leaving Panawe and Joiwind, Maskull crosses the Lusion Plain into the violent region of Ifdawn Marest, where the landscape heaves and changes in treacherous ways. Here he meets a strong woman named Oceaxe and undergoes another change of organs, this time growing organs of control and will, and he quickly adapts by using his new powers to kill Oceaxe's lover Crimtyphon. But Crimtyphon's other lover, Tydomin, kills Oceaxe, and tries to occupy Maskull's body, during which experience Maskull finds himself back on earth, as the apparition at the séance he had witnessed earlier. No explanation is given for this apparent violation of chronology in the narrative, and it remains one of the more puzzling episodes in the novel.

Arcturus, it turns out, is actually a double star, and each of the twin suns that dominate Tormance represents a different moral realm. Oppressed by the heat of the sun named Branchspell, Maskull seeks to follow the light of the other, Alppain, and this is one beacon that remains consistent on his northward journey across Tormance. Maskull is "rescued" by Krag, who wrings the neck of the apparition Maskull has become, and he returns to Tormance ready to murder Tydomin. But first she leads him to Sant, a womanless plateau, where he meets Spadevil, a stern, iron-colored character who preaches the law of duty and changes Maskull's organs again to reflect this new moral realm. Sant is governed by a complex religion based on hatred of pleasure, led by the high priest Catice, and here Maskull learns that Surtur and Shaping are in fact not the same.

He continues through the Wombflash Forest with growing self-realization and an awareness that none of the realms he has visited have represented true reality. There follows a curious idyll with a simple fisherman named Polecrab and his visionary wife, Gleameil, who leaves her family to accompany Maskull to visit Earthrid the musician on Swaylone's Island. Earthrid's instrument is an entire lake, and his "music" violently alters the world, killing Gleameil. When Maskull insists on trying to play the instrument, he manages to destroy both it and Earthrid.

By now Maskull has learned that Crystalman is a god of illusion, and those who die in his power die with a hideous grin called "Crystalman's grin"; nearly everyone Maskull has killed so far has borne this grin. He enters a region of great fertility called Matterplay and sees in the water a vision of green sparks trying to achieve existence despite the clouds that repeatedly overpower them; this vision prefigures the final vision of the novel's end. He meets Leehallfae, a being of a third sex, who worships the god Faceny, a god that faces "nothingness" in all directions and lives in an underground realm named Threal. They find this realm, but there Leehailfae dies, also with the Crystalman grin. A new character, Corpang, explains that the true god of Threal is Thire, who exists as a trinity of existence, relation, and passion—but when they come upon an icon of this trinity, the light of Muspel changes each of the gods' faces to the Crystalman grin.

Corpang becomes the first character on Tormance to join Maskull as a follower, and the two of them are taken by a boatman named Haunte to a region of sexuality called Lichstorm, where they are joined by a powerfully sexual woman named Sullenbode. Her kiss destroys Haunte, but Maskull survives it, and she joins him as a disapproving Corpang departs. Crossing the Mornstab Pass into full Muspel-light, Sullenbode realizes that this light means more to Maskull than she does, and she dies. Alone again, Maskull enters Barey (the only place besides Muspel named from the *Elder Edda*, where it is called "the

frondiferous isle"). He meets Krag, who warns him that his apparent disillusionment may prove to be the last and strongest illusion of all, and Gangnet, who convinces him that his true goal is a kind of nothingness beyond nothingness—a renunciation even of the desire to achieve nonbeing. This seems to be as far as Maskull, the mask, the conscious man, can go in a world dominated by Crystalman. He dies and is replaced by Nightspore, revealing for the first time that they are aspects of the same man.

Nightspore is led by Krag to the tower of Muspel itself, which, like the tower at the observatory earlier, proves almost impossible to climb. But as he struggles upward, Nightspore catches ever more detailed visions of reality from the tower windows, realizing that Crystalman is a pleasure principle that separates life from will, that in fact feeds on the green sparks of life. The final vision, reached at the top of the tower, is that "Muspel consisted of himself and the stone tower on which he was sitting." Muspel is far from the powerful counterforce he had thought: Crystalman in fact controls the world, and he alone can hope to fight him. When he returns to the base of the tower Krag claims that he is himself more powerful than Crystalman, and that his name on earth is pain. The two of them set off in the darkness to continue the struggle.

Lindsay once claimed that his Muspel was identical with Schopenhauer's concept of "Nothing," or the reality that underlies all the snares of illusion. In *A Voyage to Arcturus* the quest for this reality is presented in heroic terms, and in the context of an elaborately worked out hierarchy of symbols involving colors, forms, sounds, and passions. While few of these symbols are allusive in the sense of requiring an understanding of referents outside the text, the considerable demands they make on the reader almost certainly contributed to the commercial failure of the novel. For his second novel Lindsay chose a more conventional setting—an ancestral home in Sussex—and a more conventional plot. If *A Voyage to Arcturus* is in the manner of a heroic epic, *The Haunted Woman* is more of a lyrical romance.

The "romance" is between a young woman, Isbel Loment, and an embittered older man, Henry Judge, in whose house her aunt is interested. But the house is haunted in a strange way: an ancient tower room, long since disappeared, reappears periodically to those few sensitive enough to perceive it. It is in this tower — reputedly built by the sixth-century Saxon named Ulf after whom it is named — that the romance unfolds. Those who enter the tower, however, later have no memory of what transpired there, with the result that Isbel and Judge, while in the "real" world, are never quite consciously aware of their romantic involvement with each other.

Ingenious as this device is as a barrier to romance, with its suggestions of the artificial inhibitions and social graces that prevent honest communication, Lindsay uses it mainly to suggest a more powerful reality. When a medium named Mrs. Richborough stumbles into the room, the experience so devastates her notions of what is important and what is real that she dies shortly afterward. Judge, coming to suspect that Mrs. Richborough's death may be connected with Isbel and the phantom room, decides to end his relationship with her and disappears. But when Isbel sees the apparition of Mrs. Richborough on its way back to the house, she follows and there realizes that Judge has entered the other world — called Ulf's world by now — and not returned.

Judge tries to bring her with him with exhortations to use her will, and with hypnotic music, but she is unable to overcome her sense of the world he inhabits and only catches a glimpse of him. He is on a hillside in the other world, looking upon the face of a musician whose music has been associated with the other world throughout the novel (it can be heard from the phantom room) and who may be Ulf himself. But the musician's back is to her and all she sees is Judge looking "as though he were beholding some appalling vision."

A sudden violent turn in the music causes Isbel to feel that this strange musician is the center of the landscape and that she is no more than his dream. Judge collapses just as the mist closes in, and Isbel is again in the real world. The next morning Judge is found dead in the house near where the phantom staircase leading to the tower room had materialized.

Lindsay is never quite able to generate enough sympathy for his characters for this novel to work as a romance, and his vision of the reality that underlies illusion — presumably the contrast between Ulf's world and our own — is so obscurely presented as to puzzle the reader more than persuade him. There are enough similarities with *A Voyage to Arcturus* to suggest the same concerns as in that novel. Music, for example, is an important image of the striving toward reality here also, but there are new strategies as well. Among the most important of them is Lindsay's decision to locate a portal to the other world in a recognizable landscape on earth. (To that extent, the influence of George MacDonald is more evident in this novel.) In general, however, Lindsay's rude style and stern outlook are not well suited to the domestic romance, and although he would return to such realistic settings in all his later books, he would never quite learn to invest his earthly characters with the kind of symbolic force that characterizes his best creations on the planet Tormance.

Romantic relationships are also at the center of Lindsay's next three fantasy novels, *Sphinx, Devil's Tor,* and *The Violet Apple. Sphinx,* which Lindsay revised often, goes even further than *The Haunted Woman* in attempting to create a web of character relationships against which to contrast the deeper reality represented by the supernatural world — in this case, the world of dreams. Nicholas Cabot, an amateur scientist who has come into an inheritance that frees him to continue his research on a machine that records dreams, arrives at an isolated village to pursue his work. Staying with a local family, he is soon ensnared in a complex of petty jealousies and domestic intrigues involving the family and their neighbors. The novel begins to take on the aspect of a light social satire in the tradition of Jane Austen, with the lady of the house trying to interest Cabot in one of her three daughters. Cabot instead develops a relationship with a woman who is a neighbor, and everyone gets involved in the potentially explosive relationship between a local composer named Lore Jensen and a rather foppish engineer who is assisting Cabot on his project.

For most of the novel, the sequences describing the dreams recorded by Cabot's machine seem arbitrary and unconnected to the main action, although they comprise by far the most compelling writing in the book. Gradually it becomes apparent that the dreams Cabot records are to serve a similar function to that of Tormance in *A Voyage to Arcturus* and the disappearing room in *The Haunted Woman*. This "deeper world" is also suggested by a musical composition of Lore Jensen's that gives the book its title. The riddle of the Sphinx, suggests Lindsay, is the perceptual world itself, which through nature and art presents clues to a deeper life that few can understand. Cabot and Lore are the destined lovers in this deeper world, but as in *The Haunted Woman* they are kept apart by pride and social convention, only to be united in another world after Lore has drowned (in a death foretold in Cabot's three recorded dreams—suggesting the three questions of the Sphinx) and Cabot has died from an overdose of a sleeping draught.

This final union is presented in a dream vision recorded by one of the daughters of the house, using Cabot's machine as her father sleeps. (Her father dreams of Lore, it is revealed, because he is secretly Lore's father as well.) This powerfully described vision almost succeeds in unifying the disparate threads of the plot and in lending the novel, momentarily, some of the richness of *A Voyage to Arcturus*.

Devil's Tor represents the last major statement of Lindsay's philosophy to appear during his lifetime. Unfortunately, the novel plods along for nearly five hundred pages to describe the action of only a few days, and much of the book is taken up with elaborate exposition and philosophizing concerning the myth of the Great Mother, which is the basis for the book. For the first time Lindsay attempts to cast his ideas in the context of a great public myth, and his detailed observations on the history and evolution of this myth are fascinating and often remarkably insightful in their own right.

The Great Mother, or Eternal Feminine, according to Lindsay's characters, once existed as a kind of primal unity in nature, before it was lost sight of through the fall into sexuality and the systematic rape of nature by man. Its presence is still evident, however, not only in aspects of the natural world, but also through art and through the careers of certain exceptional women who have entered into the myths of the world. In the Christian myth, for example, the most evident avatars are Eve and Mary. Someday, according to an ancient prophecy, the re-

turn of the Great Mother will herald the beginning of a new race on earth.

The plot of the novel, given this elaborately worked out backdrop, is remarkably simple: it concerns an ancient magical stone, broken in half in primeval times, and how the two halves of the stone are finally brought back together to herald the new age. (The stone, of course, is associated with the legends of the Great Mother.) This takes nearly four hundred pages and features an adventurer named Hugh Drapier, who returns from Tibet with one part of the stone and finds the other in an underground shrine opened by a bolt of lightning during a thunderstorm on Dartmoor. Two other explorers, Saltfleet and Arsinal, are pursuing Drapier. They are after the stone from Tibet, for they know its importance and feel he has stolen it from them. Ingrid Fleming, Drapier's cousin, with whom he is staying on Dartmoor, provides some initial romantic interest, but eventually emerges as the central character of the book as she realizes that she and Saltfleet are to be the parents of the new race when the stones are joined. And finally they are joined, in a thunderous visionary climax suggesting the return to the world of "the Ancient," a primal force of which even the Great Mother is only the demiurge. Saltfleet and Ingrid, joined by no human love but aware that they will found a race that will violently displace our own, set off to live in the north as the novel ends.

In many ways *Devil's Tor* seems to contradict *A Voyage to Arcturus*. The terrifying image of Crystalman is replaced by the equally powerful but more positive life force represented by the Great Mother, and the final vision of solitude is replaced by a final vision of union and creation. Lindsay himself acknowledged these disparities, and apparently hoped to resolve them in his unfinished last novel, *The Witch*. *The Witch* indeed recapitulates both the theme of the Great Mother and the theme of passing through worlds of illusion to achieve reality, but its style is if anything wordier than that of *Devil's Tor*, and in its unfinished state it is impossible to tell exactly what the nature of this resolution was to be.

The nature of reality—of an absolute reality that underlies the perceptual world—is the overarching theme of all of Lindsay's work, and it is perhaps ironic that he chose such fantastic tales as a means of containing this vision. (The choice may also suggest something about the potential of fantasy as a serious vehicle for philosophical art.) While he succeeded dramatically in *A Voyage to Arcturus*, he was never able to repeat that clarity of vision, and was acutely aware of his failures. His later novels often feature apparently autobiographical figures of failed artists, and in *The Witch* he says of one such artist that "some devil was in it that he should write his books, read by few, comprehended by fewer, wanted by none!" Lindsay's career was among the most tragic in the history of fantastic literature, and although he may never achieve the kind of wide readership he had hoped for, he may also have been accurate when he once told the publisher Victor Gollancz that "somewhere in the world, someone will be reading a book of mine every year."

Selected Bibliography

WORKS OF DAVID LINDSAY

A Voyage to Arcturus. London: Methuen, 1920. New York: Macmillan, 1963.

The Haunted Woman. London: Methuen, 1922. Hollywood, Calif.: Newcastle, 1975.

Sphinx. London: John Long, 1923.

The Adventures of M. de Mailly. London: Melrose, 1926. As *A Blade for Sale*. New York: McBride, 1927.

Devil's Tor. London: Putnam, 1932. New York: Arno, 1978.

The Violet Apple and The Witch. Edited by J. B. Pick. Chicago: Chicago Review Press, 1976.

The Violet Apple. London: Sidgwick and Jackson, 1978.

CRITICAL AND BIOGRAPHICAL STUDIES

Bloom, Harold. "*Clinamen:* Towards a Theory of Fantasy." In *Bridges to Fantasy*, edited by George E. Slusser, Eric S. Rabkin, and Robert Scholes. Carbondale: Southern Illinois University Press, 1982, 1–20.

Sellin, Bernard. *The Life and Works of David Lindsay*. Translated by Kenneth Gunnell. Cambridge: Cambridge University Press, 1981.

Wilson, Colin; Visiak, E. H.; and Pick, J. B. *The Strange Genius of David Lindsay*. London: John Baker, 1970.

Wolfe, Gary K. *David Lindsay*. Starmont Reader's Guide 9. Roger C. Schlobin, series editor. Mercer Island, Wash.: Starmont House, 1982.

—GARY K. WOLFE

EDEN PHILLPOTTS

1862–1960

EDEN PHILLPOTTS WAS born in India on 4 November 1862. He returned to England as a boy with his widowed mother and was brought up in Devon. In his late teens he went to London and worked as an insurance clerk while nursing the ambition to be an actor. When it became clear that there was no future for him in the theater he began writing, many of his earlier efforts appearing in *The Idler*. He went on to become a prolific novelist, short story writer, and playwright, also publishing several volumes of poetry. In all he published about 250 books, winning praise for his many novels and short stories set on Dartmoor, which began with *Children of the Mist* (1898). These novels are often reminiscent of the work of R. D. Blackmore, who encouraged Phillpotts in the early stages of his career, and have frequently been compared with the Wessex tales of Thomas Hardy. Phillpotts was active for more than fifty years as a writer, and was ninety-eight when he died on 29 December 1960.

As a writer of imaginative fiction Phillpotts is important primarily for the mythological fantasies that he produced in a twelve-year period between 1916 and 1927 and for a small group of science fiction novels, although there are other fantasies dating from every phase of his career.

Phillpotts' first stories in *The Idler* were both fantasies. "The Spectre's Dilemma" (1892) is an autobiographical statement by an ineffectual ghost. "Friar Lawrence" (1892) is a lighthearted account of a deal with the devil made by a friar required to write out the whole of *Lives of the Saints* in twenty-four hours as a penance for drunkenness. Phillpotts then changed tack, and for the next few years contributed anecdotes derived from his experiences while working temporarily in the West Indies. His first collection of stories, *Loup-Garou* (1899), consists mainly of stories based on his West Indian experiences; one, "The Obi Man," has some fantasy content.

"The Spectre's Dilemma," retitled "Alas, Poor Ghost!," was reprinted in a collection called *Fancy Free* (1901), along with many other pieces of a similar spirit. Some of these comic stories, including the fantasy "The Transmigrations of Tarver," are reminiscent of F. Anstey. The other stories include "Inoculation Day," a satirical vision of the future when men receive their character traits by injection, and "The Archdeacon and the Deinosaurs" (sic), the first of several idiosyncratic evolutionary fantasies. Phillpotts wrote one fantasy novel in this early period, *A Deal with the Devil* (1895), which is a lively comedy about a man nearing his hundredth year who bargains for a second lifetime with the devil and has to live it backward, getting younger all the time.

The only novel of fantasy that Phillpotts wrote in the next twenty years was the first of several juveniles, *The Flint Heart* (1910), although one of the thrillers that he wrote in collaboration with Arnold Bennett, *The Statue* (1908), is marginally science fictional in its use of an international radio broadcast. But a departure was signaled by the publication in

1916 of a sentimental novella set in the world of the Greek myths, *The Girl and the Faun*. The faun Coix falls in love with a human girl named Iole, and is pained when she prefers a human boy. Coix, though, remains unchanged through the years while Iole is withered by age. He meets her again when she is old but cannot recognize her because he has just seen "his" Iole looking as she was when he first saw her. This Iole is, of course, the granddaughter of the original, but the immortal Coix has his own special perspective on things, and it really is his Iole.

Three years later Phillpotts published *Evander*, a philosophically inclined story in a similar setting. Two gods, Bacchus and Apollo, contend for the worship of a woman whose husband worships the former. Evander, the disciple of Apollo, wins the woman away from her husband for a brief space, luring her with his beauty, intelligence, and grandeur. At heart, though, she is not cut out to be an Apollonian and accepts her Dionysian destiny. The author implies that there may be a message here for us all.

Phillpotts went on to write a series of such fantasies, using the Greco-Roman pantheon as a set of incarnated aspects of human nature and aspiration. As well as sympathizing with Bacchus despite the glamour of Apollo, Phillpotts spoke well of Pan (though well aware of the threat of Pan-ic possession). In *Pan and the Twins* (1922) he tells the story of two brothers separated at birth, one of whom preserves the faith of Pan while the other adheres to Christianity. In the meantime the emperors of the fading Roman Empire come and go, changing the "official" religion of the state as they please. The ideals of Christianity, like those of Apollo, are respected but gently criticized for their unreasonable asceticism; the brother who follows Pan is well served by his god, who chats with him god-to-man and gives him the gift of speaking to the animals. That brother lives a happier life without being, in the author's eyes, one whit less worthy than his eremitic sibling.

The Treasures of Typhon (1924) is an allegory in which an arrogant youth — a distinctly half-hearted follower of Epicurus — is sent into the world on a quest for a magical plant, armed with the power of communicating with the trees. His adventures serve to mend his character and to teach him to be a true Epicurean.

Circé's Island (1925) is a superb novella in which the boy Amphion, accompanied by his magical serpent Simo, voyages to Aea — the island home of the sorceress Circé — in search of Amphion's father, Dolius. Like all castaways on the island, Dolius has not amused Circé for long and has been turned, after her usual practice, into an animal. Circé likes Amphion, and is persuaded to release his father if he can figure out which particular creature Dolius has become. While he searches among the sad beast-men, Amphion is instructed in the business of living not only by Circé but by Odysseus, who is shipwrecked there in the meantime.

Another novella, *The Miniature* (1926), concentrates very heavily on the thread that runs through all these Greco-Roman fantasies almost to the exclusion of any semblance of plot. It presents a commentary from the viewpoint of the gods of Greece and Rome on the philosophical evolution of mankind, and dwells on the psychological utility of religion. The story ends with rather uncharacteristic black irony when mankind annihilates itself in a nuclear holocaust.

Arachne (1927), the last novel in the sequence, is perhaps the best insofar as it manages to integrate plot and philosophical allegory most comprehensively. It tells the story of Arachne, the legendary weaver and victim of hubris who challenges her mentor, Pallas Athene, to a contest. Athene is portrayed as an Apollonian character, magnificent in her way but prone to be overdemanding in her lectures on the cultivation of human wisdom. One of Arachne's suitors, Polydorus, falls completely under Athene's spell, but Arachne is interested only in her art. In this version of the story Arachne wins the verdict of the three divine judges and does not hang herself after suffering Athene's wrath (though Athene is persuaded to believe so). Instead, she runs away with her second suitor, Mopsus, while Polydorus founds an academy.

Arachne undoubtedly owes something to Richard Garnett's famous collection *The Twilight of the Gods* (1888), but Phillpotts' irony is much gentler and his didactic purpose is sweetened considerably by the leisurely affability of the tale. The tone is always light, the main aim is entertainment, and when the characters pontificate we are always allowed to take them less than seriously. For those who take notice of the messages, though, there is a neat and eloquent argument in favor of a patient and tolerant humanism. Thus, for instance, we find this argumentative core in Circé's parting advice to Amphion:

"Seek your account in humanity; be human; for within the scope and compass of man's nature lie waiting, as seed in Earth's warm bosom, greater virtue and wisdom, higher honour and dignity, than your race has yet achieved, or even imagined. Strive to win these treasures by the sole way in which they shall be won: seek them not from the unprofitable and empty skies, but within your own fertile heart."

(page 160)

Contemporary with this group of novels are several other pieces of interest to readers of fantasy. *The Lavender Dragon* (1923) is similar in all but setting, telling the story of a benevolent dragon who steals lonely humans to populate his utopian community, where tolerance and justice reign. This is in stark contrast to the medieval world outside (grim despite the presence of bold knights errant). *Number 87* (1922) is one of several thrillers written under the name Harrington Hext, and belongs to that prolific subspecies of early science fiction in which lone scientists use their inventions to blackmail the world in the cause of common sense and social justice. The collection *Peacock House* (1926) contains four fantasy stories, including two psychological horror stories, "Crazywell" and "The Iron Pineapple." Several other thrillers written during this period begin with apparently supernatural events that are later rationalized; these stories often feature the conflict between superstitious and scientific world views, which was a favorite topic of Phillpotts'. He was, of course, on the side of rationalism but remained generous in his respect for the opposition. His best work in this vein is *The Grey Room* (1921).

Phillpotts added two more fantasies to the tail end of this main sequence in his work. *The Apes* (1929)

is an interesting allegory of evolution, in which the wisest of the simians gather to offer up their greatest discoveries (for example, patriotism, house building, the joy of eating oysters). The wisest simian of all is about to be put to death for suggesting heretically that apekind might one day be displaced as the crowning glory of creation, but is saved by an apparition of man. The eventual fate of apekind is laconically described in an epilogue, and the moral offered to prideful man is made elegantly enough. *Alcyone* (1930) recalls some of the themes from the mythological fantasies, but is essentially a sentimental fantasy for children.

After a gap of some years Phillpotts returned to fantasy with *The Owl of Athene* (1936). This tale begins in the same spirit as the mythological fantasies, with a dialogue between Pallas Athene and her owl and a divine council that decides to test the mettle of mankind. The test, which takes place in the twentieth century, is an invasion of the land by giant crabs (they are finally destroyed by a new poison). The climax of the story is science fictional in character and pointed the new direction that Phillpotts' imaginative fiction was to take.

The Owl of Athene was followed in 1938 by *Saurus*, one of the classic scientific romances. The eponymous hero of the story is an intelligent lizard, hatched from an egg that has been carried by spaceship to earth from the asteroid Hermes. Saurus grows up in the home of a zoologist as a curious kind of feral child, and becomes an objective observer commenting on human affairs. The theme of the novel is similar to those of J. D. Beresford's *The Hampdenshire Wonder* (1911) and Olaf Stapledon's *Odd John* (1935), but Saurus is a gentler critic than either of those superhuman characters, with the magic and sympathy of Circé, although there is more than a touch of the cold-blooded Pallas Athene about him too.

In between *The Owl of Athene* and *Saurus* Phillpotts published *Lycanthrope* (1937; also known as *The Mystery of Sir William Wolf*), another of his thrillers in which rational and supernatural explanations compete until the final settlement. And soon after *Saurus* he published another juvenile adventure fantasy, *Tabletop* (1939).

Nearly a full decade was to elapse before Phillpotts returned to imaginative fiction with two more science fiction novels. *The Fall of the House of Heron* (1948) is an early novel about atomic power, notable for its uncharitable characterization of the scientist whose dedication to his work is so strong as to make him morally reckless. As did many other imaginative men, Phillpotts reacted with alarm and revulsion to the unveiling of the atom bomb and the destruction of Hiroshima and Nagasaki.

Phillpotts' preoccupation with the sins of science extended into *Address Unknown* (1949), which recapitulates the theme of *Saurus* but attaches a very different moral. Two young scientists contact a superior intelligence outside the galaxy who begins instructing them on how to secure the advancement of the human race toward the kind of passionless rationalism conventionally associated with science fictional superhumans. The protagonist of the novel, a stodgy and rather pompous conservative, has strong reservations about the propriety of such a destiny, and is ultimately relieved to witness the tragic end of the project. In the end, Phillpotts speaks directly to the reader, through a human character rather than a goddess or an amiable lizard:

"But this we know: that righteousness travels an upward way despite the chasms, tempests and high tides of evil that confound its progress among us. Our sense of rectitude persists and the venom poured against it must grow weaker and weaker as reason strengthens to cast out the old idols from our hearts and heads. Within ourselves lie the secrets of salvation: they are not the products of passing ideologies, egocentric philosophies, or the formulae of mutable faiths; nor does need exist to seek awakening by alien beings from any extra-galactic nebula."

(page 218)

For most of his long career as a writer Phillpotts lived a somewhat reclusive life, though he was married almost throughout. (His first wife died in 1928, which event coincided with the end of his sequence of mythological fantasies. He married again the following year.) Although he had friends in the literary world — Arnold Bennett and Agatha Christie both expressed gratitude to him for the encouragement he gave them in the early part of their ca-

reers — he was isolated enough for *Everyman's Dictionary of Literary Biography* (1958) to describe him with unusual bluntness as "unsociable by nature."

Despite this alleged unsociability Phillpotts was a convinced humanitarian, intensely sympathetic to the plights and pains of his fellow men. In his Dartmoor novels, in such reminiscences of childhood as *The Human Boy* (1899), and in such gentle comedies as his play *The Farmer's Wife* (1917), this humanitarianism is expressed directly. In his fantasies the sympathy is expressed by his affectionate and slightly ironic view of the essential human condition, mischievously transformed by the play of the imagination. He was well aware of the darker side of life — witness the bleaker aspect of the Dartmoor novels, which provokes the comparisons with Hardy — and Circé comments at one point to Amphion that "consciousness itself is a great suffering — so great that there have been philosophers who doubted whether the game was worth the candle." But he never allowed this darker perception to take over, and he remained an optimist.

Phillpotts was a committed champion of reason against superstition, though he rejected the adamantine amorality of scientism. Although the supernatural is featured occasionally in his nonallegorical fiction, he usually prefers a psychological (or, on rare occasions, a parapsychological) explanation to one that owes anything to religious metaphysics. Superstition is a prominent feature of his accounts of everyday life in rural Devon, but he never panders to it; his local witches, like Charity Crymes in *The Hidden Hand* (1952), always work by cunning and deception, not by magic. It is probable that he adopted the idiosyncratic form of his major fantasies partly to conceal or excuse the fact that they contain a frontal attack on religion in general and Christianity in particular. "Religion," says Pan in *Pan and the Twins*, "is with us that we shall not perish of too much truth." He adds that although people feel themselves safer in "cages" of faith they will one day find it possible to emerge from such cages to face the truth without fainting from exposure.

There is, of course, a certain irony in the fact that Phillpotts, like so many other modern Sadducees, found it convenient — and perhaps necessary — to use fantasy as a vehicle for his humanistic and rationalistic ideas. But no one can argue that those ideas are not decently and appropriately clad in the finest of his stories. His mythological fantasies do not seem to have been very widely read or liked, although Lin Carter was sufficiently impressed to feature *The Miniature* in his *Discoveries in Fantasy* (1972) and *The Lavender Dragon* in *Great Short Novels of Adult Fantasy Volume II* (1973) while he was in charge of Ballantine's excellent Adult Fantasy series. *The Miniature* and *The Lavender Dragon* are works that deserve more serious attention, both for their entertaining qualities and for the fact that they tell us what it is to be authentic Epicureans.

Selected Bibliography

WORKS OF EDEN PHILLPOTTS

A Deal with the Devil. London: Bliss, Sands and Foster, 1895. New York: Warne, ca. 1900.

Fancy Free. London: Methuen, 1901. (Collection.)

The Girl and the Faun. London: Palmer and Hayward, 1916. Philadelphia: Lippincott, 1917.

Evander. London: Grant Richards, 1919. New York: Macmillan, 1920.

Pan and the Twins. London: Grant Richards, 1922. New York: Macmillan, 1922.

The Lavender Dragon. London: Grant Richards, 1923. New York: Macmillan, 1923.

The Treasures of Typhon. London: Grant Richards, 1924. New York: Macmillan, 1924.

Circé's Island. London: Grant Richards, 1925 (also contains "The Girl and the Faun"). New York: Macmillan, 1926.

The Miniature. London: Watts, 1926. New York: Macmillan, 1927.

Arachne. London: Faber and Gwyer, 1927. New York: Macmillan, 1928.

The Apes. London: Faber and Faber, 1929.

The Owl of Athene. London: Hutchinson, 1936.

Saurus. London: John Murray, 1938. Westport, Conn.: Hyperion, 1976.

The Fall of the House of Heron. London: Hutchinson, 1948.

Address Unknown. London: Hutchinson, 1949.

—BRIAN M. STABLEFORD

SAX ROHMER

1883-1959

SAX ROHMER IS best known as the creator of the great Oriental villain Dr. Fu Manchu. Unfortunately, the "devil doctor" has overshadowed his other fiction, much of which is clearly superior. Indeed, the best of Rohmer's work is still very effective and readable. The action is gripping and carefully paced, the characters are well chosen and effectively presented, places and situations are clearly and vividly described, and the themes are interesting and deftly woven into the texture of the novel.

Sax Rohmer, who was christened Arthur Henry Ward, was born in Birmingham, England, on 15 February 1883. He completed his formal schooling in 1901 and adopted the name Arthur Sarsfield Ward. Ward read for the civil service but failed the examination. His first job, in a bank, ended because his figures were inaccurate; he lost a job with a gas company when he embellished letters to customers. He tried writing but received only rejections. Finally, he became a reporter for the *Commercial Intelligence*, where, under the direction of Swinborne Sheldrake, he received his only basic training in writing, but his tendency to embroider the facts resurfaced—and he lost another job.

After an unsuccessful attempt at illustration (his artistic skills were good), he returned to writing. Blending the fantasy and adventure of his imagination, fueled by tales of ancient Rome and Egypt, with the style of a news story, the next two stories he wrote resulted in his first sales: "The Mysterious Mummy" probably appeared in *Pearson's*, and "The Leopard-Couch" was published in *Chambers's Journal* (30 January 1904). Writing under the byline A. Sarsfield Ward, he continued selling stories and articles and was quite successful as a writer of lyrics and comedy sketches for the stage.

A trip to Holland (between the summer of 1904 and early summer 1905) led to the name Sax Rohmer. He claimed the name came from ancient Saxon, *sax* meaning blade and *rohmer* being a variation on "roamer." In 1905, Rohmer met Rose Elizabeth Knox. Though he cared little for most conventions, including marriage, they were married on 14 January 1909.

In 1911, Rohmer was assigned to do an article on a "Mr. King," reputed to be the guiding hand behind criminal activity in Limehouse. As a result, Rohmer learned a great deal about Limehouse and its activities, which he later used in many stories and novels. He also saw the man—perhaps the mysterious Mr. King—who inspired Fu Manchu.

Rohmer's career was boosted when Newman Flower, editor of *Story-Teller*, accepted an unfinished story that led to the series of stories later published as *The Sins of Séverac Bablon* (1914). Flower also took the first series of Fu Manchu stories, which were an immediate success. *The Mystery of Dr. Fu-Manchu*, the first book to bear the name Sax Rohmer, was published by Methuen in June 1913. Rohmer had mixed feelings about the Fu Manchu stories, especially later in his career, when he wrote them primarily to meet the demands of publishers and the public. He was aware that they were extremely popular but felt he could write better stories, even for the commercial market. Nevertheless, he wrote and revised them as carefully as he did all his work.

Rohmer believed firmly, based in part on his own experiences, in the existence of unseen forces and of secret or hidden knowledge. He was, however, content to speculate, rather than to take a set position, on such matters. Thus, he accepted neither the claims of Egyptologists that the pyramids were merely tombs nor other, less mundane explanations of their purpose and nature. Similarly, he did not believe in the concept of the supernatural, for he was convinced that nothing could exist outside the laws of nature, although many of these laws were not yet known. Rohmer's serious interest in the occult was reflected in *The Romance of Sorcery* (1914), a nonfiction study of occultism and its practitioners. The popularity of Fu Manchu and *The Yellow Claw* (1915) enabled Rohmer to branch out in a number of directions. He visited New York in 1919, and although he did not care for the hectic pace and materialism of America, he returned many times over the next forty years. His interest in the theater led to his involvement in two successful London ventures: *Round in Fifty* (1922), which exploited the comic possibilities of Jules Verne's *Around the World in Eighty Days* and introduced such innovative devices as film sequences, and *The Eye of Siva* (1923), a melodrama in which fantastic devices, including a death ray, abound.

A number of Rohmer's books were also filmed. *The Yellow Claw* was followed by a series of "two-reelers" based on the Fu Manchu stories. In 1929, Paramount Pictures filmed *The Mysterious Dr. Fu Manchu*, with Warner Oland in the title role, followed by *The Return of Dr. Fu Manchu* (1930) and *The Daughter of the Dragon* (1931), with Anna May Wong. Later, MGM filmed *The Mask of Fu Manchu* (1932), with Boris Karloff as Fu Manchu; this film brought a protest from the Chinese embassy about the rather stereotyped and generally unflattering portrayal of the Chinese in the film.

World War II affected Rohmer greatly: publishing activity was reduced because of wartime shortages, and Rohmer was busy with many war-related projects. Thus, after the war, he had to reestablish his position in a drastically changed market. His best hope, he thought, was in the United States, to which he emigrated in 1947. Stricken with Asiatic flu, he recovered enough to return to England on holiday but spent his last three weeks in the hospital with a combination of arteriosclerosis, pneumonia, and persistent hemorrhaging. He died on 1 June 1959.

It is difficult to categorize Rohmer's work. Although a mystic element or an element of the unusual appealed most strongly to him, he provided liberal amounts of adventure in his novels and generally approached them as tales of mystery and suspense. In addition, much of his fiction contains elements of horror, fantasy, science fiction, and the supernatural.

Rohmer's novels and stories are usually based on a strong threat to normal life or to our expectations of what should exist in a moral and ethical society. Time is always of the essence: the protagonist must rush to meet the thrusts of the antagonist and thwart him before preparations for the final attack are completed. On a simple level, the struggle pits good against evil, but it often has other levels as well.

Thus, these are usually carefully structured adventure plots. The opening scenes commonly attract attention, either by some unusual situation or by a description that endows an apparently normal situation with the promise of being unusual. The reader is then swept into the inciting incident and the development of the ensuing complications. Little time is spent on exposition; indeed, the plot often involves an investigation of some sort through which the background, and thus the nature of the opening situation, becomes clear to the central characters and to the reader. The pace, however, is skillfully varied. After the peak of each major action, there is a respite for reader and characters alike. A new element is then introduced, and the action gradually gains momentum until another peak is reached and another cycle begins.

Rohmer is also skilled in the use of the well-chosen, telling detail for his descriptions of scene, action, and character. His characters, although rarely rounded, serve their roles effectively. Rohmer's villains—always his most vivid characters—

have the most distinctive physical characteristics and the most exotic personalities. Frequently they are masters of great scientific, magical, or political power. In contrast, the central characters are often solid, stolid people who have been somehow drawn into a web of intrigue. They may, however, have become knowledgeable in the exotic lore that they need to combat their foes.

The Fu Manchu stories are fast-paced and packed with adventure, with the danger often exotic. Fu Manchu is vividly portrayed as a scientific genius who has great knowledge of many of nature's secrets. He uses this knowledge in the service of a covert society based in the East whose ultimate aim is world domination. He thinks nothing of eliminating anyone who might stand in his way, although he respects a worthy foe. Nayland Smith opposes Fu Manchu, never really winning a battle but often gaining a standoff as he struggles to uphold Western civilization. His knowledge of exotic lore has been gathered from his experiences in the East, and his manner and quick intelligence set him apart. The Fu Manchu stories pit these two adversaries against one another, with the fate of Western civilization hanging in the balance.

Although Rohmer did not accept the concept of the supernatural, the forces deployed in a group of his novels are removed from common experience and are beyond the understanding of current science. These are the novels that most interested him.

Brood of the Witch-Queen (1918) is an effective novel in which the secrets of ancient Egyptian sorcery are resurrected in twentieth-century England, threatening not only the protagonist but also the entire fabric of British society. Robert Cairn's account of the death of a king swan hooks the reader and establishes a sense of foreboding. Similar deaths follow, drawing Cairn into conflict with Anthony Ferrara. Later we learn that Ferrara is the child of an ancient Egyptian witch-queen somehow returned to life by Sir Michael Ferrara and Dr. Cairn, Robert Cairn's father. Furthermore, he has *The Book of Thoth*, a compendium of ancient knowledge and magic, which he uses to develop his control over the forces of nature. Ferrara progresses from the use of wax figures, to the projection of "glamours," to summoning the spirit of a vampire, to summoning elementals. Cairn's father has just enough knowledge to fend off these assaults, but he admits that he is at his limit. Thus, the destruction of *The Book of Thoth* is a last-ditch effort to halt and destroy Ferrara.

Thematically, *Brood of the Witch-Queen* suggests that there is an entire body of knowledge about controlling the forces of nature that most people are unaware of. A skeptical attitude toward such knowledge is clearly dangerous, for British society would be helpless against Anthony Ferrara if Dr. Cairn had not explored the occult lore of ancient Egypt. The novel also suggests the limited outlook of conventional Egyptology and its refusal to see beyond the obvious. Finally, Rohmer emphasizes the power inherent in the human mind, for that power enables Ferrara to control powerful forces and allows the Cairns to combat him.

The Quest of the Sacred Slipper (1919), although a good adventure, is less effective than *Brood of the Witch-Queen*. At the heart of this tale is the theft of one of Mohammed's slippers by Professor Deeping, a British scholar who visited Mecca posing as a Muslim. This theft arouses the ancient order of the Hashishin, led by Hassan of Aleppo, to violent efforts to recover the holy relic. The situation is complicated by the efforts of Earl Dexter, an American "cracksman" who wishes to steal the slipper and ransom it.

The weapons are the major elements of the unusual in this novel. Some of the methods seem to be supernormal, such as the glittering scimitar that warns Professor Deeping of his impending death and that apparently cuts off the hand of any non-Muslim who touches even the case containing the slipper. Other weapons, such as the mysterious tube that Hassan carries, seem to be the product of an advanced—or perhaps only different—science. Still others involve natural elements adapted to the needs of the Hashishin. For example, Professor Deeping is apparently killed by a person whose growth has been deliberately stunted so that he can fit inside a small box. In many cases, it is the setting, rather than the weapons themselves, that makes them seem so horrible.

The conflict in *The Quest of the Sacred Slipper* is complex, largely because of the three-way struggle for possession of the slipper. At one corner of the triangle are the Hashishin and their leader, the primary antagonists. Their goal is to rescue the slipper from the infidel and return it to its resting place in Mecca. At a second corner are Earl Dexter and his beautiful accomplice, Carneta, who wish to ransom the slipper to whoever will pay their price. At the third corner is Cavanaugh, the protagonist and narrator, who is supported by Inspector Bristol and New Scotland Yard. Cavanaugh's primary goal is to make sure that Professor Deeping's last wishes are honored, but his internal conflict is complex. Although he feels honor-bound to carry out Deeping's wishes, he feels that the slipper should be returned to Mecca. To that extent he agrees with Hassan of Aleppo, but he abhors the methods of the Hashishin and opposes them on that basis.

Grey Face (1924) has been called an outstanding example of the fashions in popular literature during the mid-1920's, especially because of its complex plot. It is, however, a less effective adventure and exploration of the occult than *Brood of the Witch-Queen:* the villain is not clearly delineated, the threats seem very mild, the larger threat is not clearly indicated until the end, the pace is slow, descriptions are less sharply focused, and the means for combating and defeating the villain come not from the actions of the protagonist and his associates but from an outside agency. In addition, the exploration of the occult, like the main thematic thread, is realized primarily through discussion.

Rohmer's novels frequently suggest that the universe contains many more secrets than science is willing to admit or investigate and that there is a scientific basis for much of what now seems occult or supernatural. In *Grey Face*, several of these ideas are advanced directly by Sir Provost Hope. He suggests that human society follows a rising and falling cycle, that there is an appropriate point in each cycle for certain discoveries or inventions to be made, and that if they are made before their proper time—and are therefore improperly controlled—the result is disaster or suffering for much of mankind.

These thematic statements have the effect of reducing the villainy of M. de Trepniak. Many of the evils that he caused resulted from his imperfect control over the unusual processes that he rediscovered,

rather than from a wanton desire to inflict harm. Unfortunately, all of these points are explained rather than shown in action.

The Bat Flies Low (1935) is one of Rohmer's best novels. Similar in theme to *Grey Face*, it explores those ideas in a much more thorough and satisfactory manner, and as a result all the elements in it work together more effectively.

Here, too, three groups work against one another. One is headed by Lincoln Hayes, owner of the Western States Electric Company and, like his father, an explorer of Egypt's past. A second group is headed by Simon Lobb, a business rival of Hayes. The third is an Egyptian group led by Mohammed Ahmes Bey and his beautiful niece Hatasu.

Lincoln Hayes's father had found the remains of an ancient Egyptian lamp that promised to revolutionize the electrical industry and, Hayes believes, to benefit many people. One of Hayes's men has discovered a manuscript that may reveal the lamp's secrets. Simon Lobb tries to steal this manuscript so that his company can gain an edge over Western States Electric; his purpose is strictly commercial. However, Mohammed Ahmes Bey takes the manuscript and disappears. Unable to understand Bey's motivation, Hayes follows him into the heart of Egypt, where he discovers a hidden community dedicated to the preservation of ancient knowledge.

He becomes convinced that its members are working to protect mankind and that the world is not yet ready for the revelation of the secrets of the lamp. He also becomes certain that his best route to self-fulfillment lies in this ancient order. Thus, when Bey discovers that Lobb's agent has stolen a working model of the lamp, Hayes uses his resources to try to prevent Lobb's scientists from completing a large-scale working model.

Clearly, when Lobb's scientists harness the force that produces light in the lamp, they have figured out many things about the lamp and its underlying principles. Just as clearly, the disaster and destruction that follow—explosions, earthquakes, tidal waves, great storms, and so on—show that they have not learned everything they need to know. Thus, *The Bat Flies Low* shows the destructive potential of discoveries based on evidence from past cycles of history but prematurely applied in the present cycle.

The sights and sounds of New York City and its people are skillfully integrated into the novel and confirm Rohmer's powers of observation and his ability to translate his observations to the written word. Lincoln Hayes is individualized by his monotonous voice and clipped speech, which nevertheless capture one of the many patterns of speech used by Americans. Although he appears only briefly, Simon Lobb is deftly portrayed as an up-and-coming entrepreneur who, in imitating his established rivals, overdoes everything. The characterizations of District Attorney Maguire and Detective Sergeant Hawley capture the skeptical, no-nonsense approach associated with American policemen. Maguire is individualized by his loud clothing and brusque voice, which seem more characteristic of American public figures than of those of other countries.

Wulfheim (1950), the kind of novel that Rohmer most wanted to write, contains deeper and more detailed explorations of character and relationships than do many of Rohmer's other novels—and even an element of humor. In addition, the style and language fit the needs of the story and situation; they are significantly different from those of Rohmer's more popular novels. Nevertheless, *Wulfheim* was submitted and published as by Michael Furey because Rohmer was convinced that such a book would not be accepted from Sax Rohmer.

Central to *Wulfheim* are the complicated interactions among love, lust, and loneliness; acceptance and rejection of life; and the social and religious forces that influence our relationships. Furthermore, these ideas are explored against a background in which psychic forces play an active, important role.

Count Wulfheim had been devoted to his first wife and was devastated when she died in childbirth. Though he had married again, he had kept his son, Otto, far from his home for many years. Thus, when his second wife died, Count Wulfheim was truly a lonely man, save for Fragia, the daughter of his second marriage.

Otto Wulfheim, after his only stay at Castle Wulfheim, had fled to a monastery. Believing he must explain his actions to his father, he returns as Brother Hilarius to Castle Wulfheim on Walpurgis Night. He surprises two grave robbers and thereby saves the heart of Abbot Caesar Wulfheim, an ancestor who had been cursed by Rome and whose heart had been buried with a knife through it because, in the depths of his loneliness, he had turned to satanism. Disinterment of this heart on Walpurgis Night and the similarity of the two monks, though separated by some three hundred years, unleash strong, long-suppressed psychic forces that test and teach the young monk.

The situation into which he returns is fraught with sexual tension. The servants and guests of Castle Wulfheim are all involved in the most complicated sexual relationships, actual and desired. This background is appropriate, for Otto Wulfheim had become a monk because he had fallen deeply and passionately in love with his half-sister. The desire to avoid incest is worthy but seems to have been only a part of his motivation in becoming a monk. Indeed, there is a strong suggestion that he wishes to suppress his desires totally, to avoid any thought or feeling of sexuality. In short, he fled to the monastery because he essentially rejects life. Nevertheless, he finds that he must deal with this aspect of it.

Otto's return leads Fragia to examine her feelings toward him. She had been naïve and open in her actions but had not considered the nature of her feelings. She finally recognizes that her love for Otto is other than sisterly; indeed, it includes a carnal element. However, she is more accepting of her feelings than Otto is of his.

Disturbing the heart of Caesar Wulfheim causes great turmoil in nature and in the castle; the sexual maneuverings seem to have become intensified by its presence. When Fragia unwittingly touches the heart, the long-pent force within it is released, and all the relationships in the novel are forced to a resolution. Fragia takes the full force of this psychic explosion and is unconscious and barely alive for several days. When she awakens, the spiritual side of her nature has been forced from her, with only her carnal nature surviving.

She suggests to the others that acceptance of sexuality is acceptance of life; the novel makes it clear that much more is involved. It is this side of her nature that causes her to deliberately and skillfully seduce Otto.

Although the sexual act drives Otto to the brink of madness, in that state he is able to communicate with Fragia in the garden of sleep, a psychic Eden reached only in a dreamlike state, and to learn what is true and enduring between human beings. Though he still mistrusts sexuality and abhors his incest, he realizes that both body and spirit are aspects of a single whole and that he and Fragia could have formed a complete, united personality had they been fully joined. It is only then that Otto Wulfheim is ready and able to learn that, had he only been willing to confide in Dr. Oberon rather than rushing blindly away to the monastery, the entire web of intrigue, death, and destruction that he brought to Castle Wulfheim could have been avoided: Fragia is not his half-sister.

There are recurrent suggestions, often voiced by Dr. Oberon, who seems to be a spokesman for Rohmer, that the teachings of the church are woefully narrow. Dr. Oberon, for example, insists that he is a Christian and has faith, though he rejects all formal religion. This commentary peaks at the end of the novel, when Dr. Oberon tries to make Otto/Brother Hilarius see the dichotomy between Christ's true teachings and their distortions by the church. Indeed, Dr. Oberon suggests, the Vatican and many church leaders know the truth though they do not make it widely known. In the end, Brother Hilarius seems called to spread a higher, revitalized vision of Christ and his teachings.

Of Rohmer's novels, the Fu Manchu works have been the most widely available, and Rohmer's name and reputation have been linked almost totally to them. That, however, gives only a very limited view of Rohmer's interests and literary ability. Only when all his works are seen together as a body does his true contribution as a writer of popular fiction become apparent.

Selected Bibliography

WORKS OF SAX ROHMER

The Romance of Sorcery. London: Methuen, 1914. New York: Dutton, 1914. (Historical work.)

Brood of the Witch-Queen. London: Pearson, 1918. Garden City, N.Y.: Doubleday, Page, 1924. (Novel.)

Tales of Secret Egypt. London: Methuen, 1918. New York: McBride, 1919. (Collection.)

The Orchard of Tears. London: Methuen, 1918. New York: Bookfinger, 1970. (Novel.)

The Quest of the Sacred Slipper. London: Pearson, 1919. Garden City, N.Y.: Doubleday, Page, 1919. (Novel.)

The Green Eyes of Bast. London: Cassell, 1920. New York: McBride, 1920. (Novel.)

The Haunting of Low Fennel. London: Pearson, 1920. (Collection.)

Grey Face. London: Cassell, 1924. Garden City, N.Y.: Doubleday, Page, 1924. (Novel.)

She Who Sleeps. London: Cassell, 1928. Garden City, N.Y.: Doubleday, Doran, 1928. (Novel.)

Tales of East and West. London: Cassell, 1932. Garden City, N.Y.: Doubleday, Doran, for the Crime Club, 1933. (The British and American editions differ considerably in content. The American edition picks up the supernatural stories from *The Haunting of Low Fennel.*)

The Bat Flies Low. Garden City, N.Y.: Doubleday, Doran, for the Crime Club, 1935. London: Cassell, 1936. (Novel.)

White Velvet. Garden City, N.Y.: Doubleday, Doran, 1936. London: Cassell, 1937. (Novel.)

Wulfheim, as by Michael Furey. London: Jarrolds, 1950. New York: Bookfinger, 1972. (Novel.)

BIOGRAPHICAL STUDY

Van Ash, Cay, and Rohmer, Elizabeth Sax. *Master of Villainy: A Biography of Sax Rohmer.* Bowling Green, Ohio: Bowling Green University Popular Press, 1972.

—L. DAVID ALLEN

FRANK BAKER

1908-1982

I

WRITING A SUCCESSFUL mainstream light-fantasy novel must be difficult, for very few authors have succeeded in doing it. Stella Benson wrote *Living Alone* (1919), Gerald Bullett wrote *Mr. Godly Beside Himself* (1924), Algernon Blackwood wrote *The Fruit Stoners* (1934)—although here other genres impinge—and Frank Baker, whose best work appeared in the circumbellum years of the 1930's and 1940's, wrote at least four such novels. Although Baker has received little serious attention, he was a gifted writer who, at his best, wrote about original ideas in a very individual way.

Frank Baker was born in London on 22 May 1908, the son of a broker in marine insurance. Since the family had a musical tradition and young Frank had a good voice, he was enrolled as a student chorister at Winchester Cathedral Choir School, where he remained until his voice broke when he was sixteen. In later life Baker was critical of the quality of education he received at Winchester, but he emerged as a trained musician steeped in church lore, and Winchester, suitably disguised, offered a setting for several stories.

When Baker left school there was no provision for taking the examinations for the university, and he became a clerk at an insurance office, where he served for about five years, until he was twenty-one. At this time the strong independence that marked his later life asserted itself, and he resigned. He

wanted to be a musician and a writer. He took a small job at the English School of Church Music, St. Nicholas College, Chislehurst, where he also continued his organ studies. During his spare time he tried to master the craft of letters. He remained at Chislehurst for about a year, when he was innocently caught up in a scandal at the school and fired. For a time he considered a lawsuit, but, instead, almost on the spur of the moment, he packed his few possessions and set out, with twenty pounds in his pocket, for Cornwall.

Cornwall in 1930 was still unspoiled. Baker, as he wrote in *I Follow But Myself* (1968), rented a small, isolated cottage, found a position as a church organist, and became Cornish by adoption. After several years of hard work, in 1935 he placed his first novel *(The Twisted Tree)*, under the sponsorship of the critic Edward Garnett, and was from then on a writer.

Up until the war years, Baker's life followed a pattern. He loved Cornwall and lived there when possible, although he occasionally found it necessary to move elsewhere. He earned his living as a musician, usually as a church organist, although he also gave music lessons. And, of course, he continued to write. Despite strong feelings of privacy and a fierce independence, he was a friendly and amiable man who delighted in pubs and congenial companions.

The splendid isolation of Cornwall, professional music, literary drive, and companionship were not everything for Baker. He may not have been aware of it in his early years when he reacted against the shabby treatment he had received at Chislehurst, but he was a profoundly religious man. Certain points arise over and over in his fiction: the relation of man to a higher principle, the permanence of identity through time, and sin and evil. For various reasons he gradually moved back to religion, and in 1938 he became a convert to Roman Catholicism, which he believed maintained certain truths he did not want to lose. This conversion was not limited to externals, for it permeates all his later work, sometimes as a point of view expressed by a lightly disguised character representing the author.

With World War II Baker found himself in difficulties, for he was a pacifist. For a time he worked in the East End of London, assisting victims of the Blitz, but this resulted in a near breakdown and he was forced to leave. Since he had trouble writing and had funds in hand from the sale of the motion picture rights to his novel *Miss Hargreaves*, he decided to try something new. He had long been interested in the stage and playwriting, and when he heard that actors were in demand, he decided that practical stage experience would be useful. He joined the Old Vic company and together with Sybil Thorndike, Lewis Casson, Paul Schofield, and others toured Great Britain. At a later date he worked with the Players' Theatre, and still later traveled about Britain under the auspices of the Council for Education, Music and the Arts producing his own play, *The Tragical Comedy of Punch and Judy*. During this stage career, which lasted about three years, he met his future wife, the actress Kathleen Lloyd, whom he married in January 1943.

As the war drew to an end, Baker returned to writing, and in 1944 decided to become a full-time writer. The decision proved to be justified. His novel *Lease of Life* was turned into a film starring Robert Donat, and his earlier works were translated into other languages. *Miss Hargreaves* was performed on the stage in 1953. At various times Baker worked for the BBC as a scriptwriter and editor, and for the British Arts Council as a reader. He delivered lectures on creative writing and worked on his novels.

In 1969 Baker was appointed artist in residence at Central State University, Oklahoma, where he conducted a course in creative writing. He wrote a book about his experiences there, but since it also dealt with the Kent State University incident, it was rejected by publishers. On his return to England, he continued his literary work, lectured, and organized poetry readings for the Shakespeare Institute, Stratford-upon-Avon, where he had many friends in the Royal Shakespeare Company.

Baker's last years were spent in Cornwall, where he was something of a celebrity, visited by notables of literature and the stage. He died of cancer on 6 November 1982. It is sad to see that his work is now nearly forgotten.

II

Baker's first novel, *The Twisted Tree* (1935), was not supernatural, but a novel of high passion in Cornwall, treating the Cornish much as Erskine Caldwell and William Faulkner treated their southern Americans. Although florid and flamboyant, it received favorable reviews as a first novel by a promising writer.

Baker's second novel, *The Birds* (1936), which preceded Daphne du Maurier's short story of the same title, is a symbolic fantasy with a considerable amount of social comment. It is told by an aged man of the future who looks back at the collapse of our civilization. The narrative: One day, a flock of birds appears near the Bank of England. An old woman starts to feed them, whereupon a bird attacks her and causes her death. Similar incidents take place elsewhere, and in a short time, birds, bringing death and foulness, attack mankind all over the world. Guns, traps, and chemicals are ineffective. The birds become larger and more aggressive, and it is gradually understood that they are in some way supernatural. The narrator, who lives in a small flat with a selfish and exploiting mother, is one of the few to understand the birds. He discovers that everyone has a personal bird, and if he or she can face it and accept it as part of himself or herself, the bird loses its power. But few can do this, and civilization falls. The birds thus symbolize sin or one's evil potential.

The Birds was not so successful commercially as *The Twisted Tree*. Only about 350 copies were sold, and some of the reviews that appeared were unfavorable. In retrospect it was handled too harshly, for if it is a young man's book, and too long, it is imaginative, suspenseful, and peopled with excellently drawn characters. Perhaps the highly personal mixture of social realism and fantasy that shades into allegory—which we today consider piquant—was simply untimely.

Miss Hargreaves (1940) is Baker's best-known work. Based on the theme of the sorcerer's apprentice—the thoughtless young man who evokes forces beyond his control and must suffer—it also exemplifies the catchphrase "Creative thought creates."

While on vacation in Northern Ireland, Norman Huntley and a friend visit an impossibly ugly modern church and, being young, exuberant, and cruel, proceed to pull the leg of the rather stupid, snobbish sexton. When the sexton talks about one of the late church notables, the young men invent a friend for the notable and pretend close acquaintance with her. This imaginary person, Miss Constance Hargreaves, is in her eighties, is wealthy, and is a niece of the duke of Grosvenor. She plays the harp, has a pet parrot named Dr. Pepusch, travels with a large portable bath, and writes (very good) bad poetry.

Trouble begins when Norman returns home and discovers that Miss Hargreaves is planning to visit him. She has come into existence. She arrives, as described—eccentric, demanding, high-handed—and proceeds to turn the Huntley family and the town topsy-turvy. At first she is likable, even lovable, if a nuisance, but as she assumes autonomy, she becomes less pleasant and falls out with Norman. This could be disastrous, for her wealth and social position command respect. It is soon a question of whether the creature will swallow the creator, a situation rendered perilous by Norman's ambivalence toward her.

Miss Hargreaves is a very agreeable romp, told with great vivacity. The characterizations are beautifully handled, with Miss Hargreaves, Norman, and Norman's highly eccentric father all vividly drawn. We can only regret not having seen Margaret Rutherford in the stage production of *Miss Hargreaves*, which opened in London in 1953.

With *Miss Hargreaves* and the nonsupernatural novel *Allanayr* (1941) Baker had hit a high level, but his next fantastic novel, *Sweet Chariot* (1942), is generally considered somewhat disappointing. It was written during Baker's troubled war years. Overlong, somewhat clichéd in subject matter, it seems undecided whether to be sentimental romance, humor, or an individuation story. It is probably best interpreted psychologically, as a story of emotional failure resulting in the appearance of a dissociated, unconscious personality fragment.

An inhibited middle-aged schoolmaster changes places with his guardian angel, and both fail. Spillett, the schoolmaster, tries to fly to heaven, and is beaten down as brutally as ever was Satan in *Paradise Lost*. Melchior, the angel, cannot understand social situations and is jailed when he sets the school buildings on fire as a protest. The merger of personalities that one expects in stories of this sort does not take place, and both return to their spheres. Neither has escaped responsibility by flight into fantasy.

Sweet Chariot is clear enough, but *Mr. Allenby Loses the Way* (1945) is perplexing. Baker seems to have tried a rather daring technical experiment: setting up mysterious situations, but explaining nothing, thereby letting the reader construct his or her own interpretation. The plot is simple enough—a man, abandoned as a baby, succeeds in identifying his parents—but the mechanisms that propel the search are elusive and far from simple.

In the subplot indicated by the title—other subplots being less relevant—Allenby, a small newsagent in London, is obsessed by the question of his identity. As a baby, he was found abandoned in a stone fairy ring in the Orkneys, and nothing is known of his parentage. One day an old man enters the shop and, after verifying that Allenby believes in the old Celtic fairies, offers him five wishes. Allenby makes his wishes and they come true. For his third wish he asks to meet his father, and finds himself talking to the old man—who really is his father.

But as is revealed early in the story, the five wishes are all wrong. It is all a hoax. The purported emissary of the fairies is an eccentric psychologist who plays elaborate tricks on others, partly as therapy, partly as cruel humor. The wishes are such a joke, devised on the basis of pub gossip, and small events that Allenby took to be supernatural were stage-managed. The situation thus anticipates John Fowles's *The Magus*.

Yet the wishes have come true, and some factor

other than fraud, cruelty, and irresponsibility must be at work, for the psychologist is caught in the same entanglement as Allenby. It is left to the reader to decide what this factor is and thereby determine what the book is really about. It may be a statement about the power of faith, expounding a universe of justice. The forces vaguely termed "fairies" may exist and may work with unwitting human tools. Perhaps a man who plays God may find himself to be a toy. The reader must decide.

Nor does Baker tell us what "way" Allenby lost. I am not sure how far one should push a religious allegory based on Christian dogma—probably not too far—but it seems safe to say that Allenby was alienated from life by his obsession. His end, off to war under an assumed identity, may have relevance to Baker's pacifism during the war.

Despite, or perhaps because of, this fluidity of idea, *Mr. Allenby Loses the Way* is very clever and entertaining, with good characters, exuberant imagination, and flashes of bizarre humor. A purist could find some of the subplots extraneous, but they are still amusing.

Baker's next novel, *Before I Go Hence* (1946), is more ambitious and more carefully written than his previous two novels. It is also superior technically. However, the comic element is lacking. Perhaps Baker realized that his forte was not thin situation comedy, but more serious metaphysical fiction. Or, since there are obvious autobiographical elements in *Before I Go Hence*, the subject matter may reflect Baker's own development.

There are two perceiving centers in the book—Maurice Hilliar and the Reverend Fenner Doble. Hilliar, who is openly equated with Baker, is a young musician and would-be novelist living in London in 1943 during the Blitz, tormented by the story he must write. Doble is a retired clergyman who in 1930 is living in an isolated house somewhere south of London. The house, named Allways, is much like the house in John Balderston's play *Berkeley Square*, a focus for time bridging, a place where kindred minds can meet across time. While wandering with friends, Hilliar comes upon the deserted Allways, which fascinates him, and as the story begins, he and his friends swing back and forth

between past and present while the weak, aged Doble watches.

Doble, who is seventy-six and is awaiting death, speculates much on eternity and the nature of time. He sets up his will to reach into the future, and as he lies dying, he sees that his life and his tragedy will be understood only by someone in another era who can enter his mind. In anguish he asks for that understanding. His problem is the death of his imbecile son. Until his last moments Doble is not sure whether he killed the son, by wish or deed, in order to free his daughter, who had already sacrificed too much of her life for the two men.

Hilliar becomes obsessed with his novel, and his time linkages with Doble enable him to reconstruct the tragic life at Allways. But this has its price, for it leads to Hilliar's estrangement from his wife and to poltergeistic activity.

Two themes dominate *Before I Go Hence:* isolation and the nature of time. Each of the major characters suffers from aloneness or psychological alienation, while time empowers Hilliar and Doble, linking them rather than separating them. For the phenomena of time bridging Baker drew upon J. W. Dunne's influential *An Experiment with Time*, but instead of accepting Dunne's cosmological explanation, he fell back upon religion. For Baker eternity exists in the mind of God, and therefore the moments that make up eternity are always in existence, even if they are not perceptible to man's limited psyche. In this, Baker was not completely orthodox, since it does not fit the Augustinian notion of straight-line developmental time and does not distinguish between time and eternity.

Before I Go Hence is the most powerful and most satisfying of Baker's fantasies, with a rich array of characters, excellent ideas, and virtuoso technique. It reveals enormous development since *The Twisted Tree*, with which it has thematic links.

Religious elements now begin to appear more openly in Baker's work, and *The Downs So Free* (1948) is structured on the concept of faith, presented in terms of Bishop George Berkeley's thesis about perception and existence. Set in Cornwall, with a good array of types (to some extent à clef) ranging from Jukes-like natives to sophisticates, it considers two persons who embody ideal positions. Mrs. Bardsley, a Catholic convert, represents externals in being charitable without having charity. Venables, a fussy rationalist, represents internals; when confronted by the supernatural, he has faith in it.

Venables, who is cultured and intelligent but shallow and crotchety, has entered into a Platonic marriage, partly to gain his wife's beautiful house. His wife accepts the situation, since she does not expect to live long, but she is hurt by his selfishness. As she lies dying, she misinterprets his actions, thinking that he is anticipating her death, and writes him a brutal letter, threatening him with punishment.

After her death Venables is violently assaulted by poltergeistic phenomena. He sees his dead wife and converses with her, and in a moment of exaltation and despair invites her into his body. The result is a message: the world will come to an end at a certain date. Venables thereupon invites the strange inhabitants of the Downs to a grand farewell dinner, at which he announces his prophecy. The world does come to an end for Mrs. Bardsley and Venables, but in an unexpected way. It is death for her and madness for him. His private Berkeleyan world has been destroyed, and he is now raving mad.

At one point in the novel, Venables, who is a skilled amateur magician, questions his supernatural experiences, deciding that he has duped himself by legerdemain and therefore must be mad. Baker cleverly shifts the reader's interpretation of Venables' mind back and forth, until the final solution: reality equals perception.

Talk of the Devil (1956), Baker's last supernatural novel, is a mystery story of a sort based in large part on historical events. The mystery, however, seems to have been of less interest to the author than the various psychological responses to supernatural evil. Behind the scenes of the story religious and rational philosophies clash. The paradoxical solution has the religious narrator (partly Baker himself) taking a rational view of evil, while the rationalist evildoer is self-forced into diablerie. As a thriller with a metaphysical background *Talk of the Devil* is thus comparable to the early work of Graham Greene.

As the story goes, the novelist Philip Hayes becomes attracted to a local event of a few years back. A woman had died in a purportedly haunted house, which she had intended to "dehaunt." The official explanation was heart failure, but Hayes thinks she was murdered, perhaps supernaturally. Connected with this death and an earlier murder is a black magic cult that Baker has obviously modeled on that of the historical Aleister Crowley. Hayes reaches a solution, but there is a twist.

Talk of the Devil has good Cornish local color, a well-sustained atmosphere, and believable characters. The haunted cottage, which is probably based on a local haunt described in Baker's *The Call of Cornwall* (1976), is a spooky place in a cold, nasty way. The ending of the novel, however, slips into melodrama, and the entry of politics is likely to break the spell for many readers.

Stories of the Strange and Sinister (1983), published posthumously, contains ten short stories, some of which had previously appeared in anthologies. It would be an overstatement to say that the book has a central theme, but time and its variations play an important part.

Five of these stories are outstanding. "Coombe Morwen" describes a restored old Devon farmhouse that in the eighteenth century was the scene of brother-sister incest and attempted murder. The house has been waiting for the right person to come along, so that the pattern can be repeated. A time tie causes "possession" and another attempted murder. Perhaps there will be a third. The theme of the story is threadbare, of course, but Baker has reworked it, what with a novel psychological interpretation, a triple frame-situation, and an open ending, into a very thought-provoking story. "In the Steam Room" is minimally supernatural, with a vision of a murder, but is extraordinarily vivid. "Art Thou Languid?" describes a haunting as two men who operate a music shop in a small town are faced with death. Baker handles the linked love and hatred between the two men very well. "Tyme Tryeth Troth" is a symbolic statement of the identity of the individual person through different stages of time. Told on almost a fabular level, it posits a familial scene, a profound human experience, as the central focus for past, present, and future. It is probably Baker's best short story, and is a very fine piece of work.

Somewhat atypical of the author's work, which is usually realistic within the established limits of a fantasy, is "Quintin Claribel," a fable based on figures of speech. When Quintin insults his governess, she utters two platitudes: she wonders that his words do not freeze in the air as a permanent reproach, and prophesies that he will eat his words. Both statements come literally true and dominate Quintin's life. It is a very amusing story.

In addition to his supernatural fiction Baker wrote six nonsupernatural novels: *The Twisted Tree* and *Allanayr*, which have been mentioned; *Embers* (1947); *My Friend the Enemy* (1948); *Lease of Life* (1948); and *Teresa* (1960), a novel with shifted time sequences, based on the life of his grandmother. Baker also wrote a collection of religious short stories, *Blessed Are They* (1951), several plays, journalism, and music.

Of these works, *Allanayr* (American title, *Full Score*) is the most attractive. Probably suggested, with suitable liberties, by Eric Fenby's experiences as music secretary and assistant to the paralyzed composer Frederick Delius, it is a personality study of a remarkable man. As was generally recognized when *Allanayr* appeared, Baker was entirely successful in creating the image of a rugged, sometimes unpleasant, egotistical, titanic, driven genius. It has many other virtues, although a conventional romance weakens the ending somewhat. All in all, *Allanayr* is an undeservedly forgotten novel.

Just as interesting as Baker's best fiction is his autobiographical volume *I Follow But Myself* (1968), which, as the title hints, is the story of a very independent young man who, in a pleasant, unassuming way, followed the life path he considered best, regardless of economics or the opinions of others. It is told in terms of friends and acquaintances who helped form his life. It is worth reading not only for its own sake, but for excellent personality sketches of Edward Garnett, Mary Butts, and Arthur Machen as an old man. A second autobiographical volume, *The Call of Cornwall*, describes the irresistible lure that Cornwall had for a Londoner. In both books, however, one has the feeling that Baker has left out much that would explain aspects of his work.

This is regrettable, for Baker really should have commented more on the ideas behind his work. He claimed not to be a satirist, yet some of his work has all the poking and prodding of good satire. He did not consider himself an allegorist or symbolist, yet his stories are rife with patterns and details that seem to mean more than, or point in different directions from, their literalness. And so we speculate.

There is the further question of the supernatural. Baker was one of the very few major authors of supernatural fiction who accepted traditional folkloristic phenomena. He claimed to have seen a ghost and relates that when he was a child, the house next door was haunted by a poltergeist. It would indeed be valuable to know how much of the other material he put into his fiction—notably the feeling of time dislocation—was personal with him.

III

"You throw idea after idea into your books, you've got a rich, perhaps slightly melodramatic mind, but you never seem to gather up the threads fully." This is an estimation that a literary critic offers to Philip Hayes, Baker's mask in *Talk of the Devil*. It is incomplete, but it is a fair statement about Baker as far as it goes. Baker is an imaginative writer who delights in occasional colorful events, but he sometimes has difficulty with form, particularly in "wrapping up" his story. Not that there are loose ends, but that Baker seems to see time and its embedded events so much as a continuum that he finds it difficult to break things off and twist characters and subplots into the smooth knot that classical form demands. When Baker does tie such a knot, it is sometimes loose or weak.

After the exuberance of his earlier work had waned, Baker became a very good stylist in the classical manner. He also had an exceptional imagination for original, convincing detail. His greatest strength, though, is in the area in which most writers of supernatural fiction are weak—the creation of characters. Some of his characters are delicately handled small middle-class British men and women. Others are gorgeously mad eccentrics or grotesques. They all live.

As this article is written, none of Baker's earlier

work is in print. A new generation of readers is missing a good range of supernatural experience.

Selected Bibliography

WORKS OF FRANK BAKER

The Birds. London: Peter Davies, 1936. Revised edition. London: Panther, 1964. (Novel.)

Miss Hargreaves. London: Eyre and Spottiswoode, 1940. New York: Coward McCann, 1941. (Novel.)

Allanayr. London: Eyre and Spottiswoode, 1941. As *Full Score.* New York: Coward McCann, 1942. (Nonsupernatural novel.)

Sweet Chariot. London: Eyre and Spottiswoode, 1942. New York: Coward McCann, 1943. (Novel.)

Mr. Allenby Loses the Way. New York: Coward McCann, 1945. London: Boardman, 1946. (Novel.)

Before I Go Hence. London: Andrew Dakers, 1946. New York: Coward McCann, 1947. (Novel.)

The Downs So Free. London: Andrew Dakers, 1948. (Novel.)

Talk of the Devil. London: Angus and Robertson, 1956. (Novel.)

I Follow But Myself. London: Peter Davies, 1968. (Autobiography.)

The Call of Cornwall. London: Robert Hale, 1976. (About Cornwall, with autobiographical elements.)

Stories of the Strange and Sinister. London: William Kimber, 1983. (Short stories.)

— E. F. BLEILER

ELIZABETH BOWEN

1899–1973

ELIZABETH BOWEN IS not widely known as a writer of supernatural fiction. Indeed her works that are clearly related to the supernatural amount to less than a dozen short stories. She is, however, a popular and critically respected writer of fiction and nonfiction. Her novels include *The House in Paris* (1933), *The Death of the Heart* (1938), and *The Heat of the Day* (1949); her nonfiction includes *Bowen's Court* (1942), *A Time in Rome* (1960), and *Afterthoughts* (1962). Born in Dublin, Ireland, on 7 June 1899 and educated in England, she was created a Commander of the British Empire in 1948. Bowen received honorary degrees from Trinity College, Dublin (1949), and Oxford University (1956); she was named Companion of Literature, Royal Society of Literature (1965); and she was awarded the James Tate Black Memorial Prize in 1970 for her last novel, *Eva Trout* (1969). At the time of her death, on 22 February 1973, Bowen was regarded as one of the best English novelists of the century.

Bowen is interesting as a mainstream writer who sometimes dabbled in the fantastic and, in particular, as one who turned to the fantastic with a demonstrated ability to observe humans in nonfantastic situations. Her most impressive fantastic work is to be found in a collection of stories that waft gently through different degrees of reality and that suggest some rather striking and disturbing things about the nature of "fantasy."

Bowen's early writing contains two stories of the fantastic, neither of which would demand much attention as an example of fantastic literature. The more successful as a whole story is "The Cat Jumps" (in Cynthia Asquith's anthology *Shudders*, 1929), describing how a weekend party of silly, one-dimensional "intellectuals" collapses into total funk in a house where a gruesome murder was committed. The result is a neat mixture of nervous dread and burlesque of the characters' pretensions. There may be a supernatural influence at work, but the characters' neuroses are quite sufficient to explain what takes place, and the effect is not unlike Saki's "The Open Window." The second story, "The Apple-Tree" (in Asquith's *When Churchyards Yawn*, 1931), has some striking moments depicting a young woman haunted by the apparition of an apple tree in which an unhappy schoolgirl companion she had forsaken had hanged herself. The story simply evaporates at the end, in a final paragraph that states that the apple tree somehow was exorcised and the young woman happily restored to her husband.

Much more impressive are the twelve stories collected in *The Demon Lover, and Other Stories* (1945; in the United States, with a different arrangement of contents and a new preface, as *Ivy Gripped the Steps*, 1946). Although only five can be labeled fantasy, all the stories must be considered to explain the subtle uneasiness that Bowen achieves in works balanced between mainstream and supernatural fiction.

Approaching the stories in the context of the book is a bit startling for one who first read them in a fantastic context. When "The Cheery Soul" was reprinted in the *Magazine of Fantasy and Science Fiction* (*MFSF*) in April 1952, for example, a reader knew what to expect. Not only the editors' introduction but the nature of the magazine settled the matter: there had to be a ghost. In the context of Bowen's collection, though, the reader does not know; he is in the position of the characters themselves, who do not know whether bizarre actions and statements represent actual supernatural intrusions or not. Puzzling over this ambiguity helps the reader understand how fantasy is created, since the stories illustrate the paradox at the heart of fantasy: supernatural elements are willed to exist, having their true origin in the human mind; yet their appearance frequently produces not satisfaction but horror.

In her preface to the American edition of the collection, Bowen explains that the stories are unified first by having been written during World War II; they are "studies of climate, war-climate, and of the strange growths it raised." Though the war is never shown directly and only one character is even described as a soldier, Bowen believes that the stories show how the war shook the consciousness of everyone who lived through it:

> The violent destruction of solid things, the explosion of the illusion that prestige, power and permanence attach to bulk and weight, left all of us, equally, heady and disembodied. Walls went down; and we felt, if not knew, each other. We all lived in a state of lucid abnormality.

She goes on to describe the order of the stories in the American edition of the book as showing "a rising tide of hallucination." This does not mean that the stories in the first part of the book are mainstream while later stories are increasingly fantastic; it does mean that they all take place in a disoriented, uncertain atmosphere in which the mind is apt to find itself pursuing strange notions to a disturbing length.

Bowen also suggests that her wartime stories show the resistance to depersonalization that filled everyone: "Outwardly, we accepted that at this time individual destiny had to count for nothing; inwardly, individual destiny became an obsession in every heart." Anticipating the objection that this escape from depersonalization actually means rushing into a new kind of tension, Bowen remarks that "one counteracts fear by fear, stress by stress." She insists that through the stressful episodes in several of these stories her characters discover themselves, painful though that discovery is. She further observes that the ghosts in several stories, whether actual or imagined, give a sense of certainty, of temporal continuity, needed by bewildered contemporary characters. Such is Bowen's intent. It is realized in the stories in a richer, more complex fashion than any discursive summary can suggest, and she goes some distance further.

The reader first observes in *Ivy Gripped the Steps* how fantastic the setting feels, even in a nonfantastic story. Never mentioning the war, the first story, "In the Square," begins by depicting a city square that looks "mysterious" because the area is deserted and the light is doing strange things to familiar objects. Furthermore, on each side of a breach evidently created by the destruction of several houses by a bomb, "exposed wallpapers were exaggerated into viridians, yellows and corals that they had probably never been." A man arriving at what had been a familiar house is struck by the change in appearance and then disconcerted by the behavior of the people in the house. Everything has become strange and insecure, even human relationships. As the woman of the house, someone the man once imagined he knew, remarks, "Who would think that this was the same world?" People are uncertain how to respond to that change. In a sense they are free from the constraints of the past, but all are confused by the freedom, some revolted or frightened, some actually annihilated. As a character in the next story, "Sunday Afternoon," remarks, one's sense of self depends on context, the stable system of values and facts that defines a person: "Those looks, those things that are said to you—they make you.... You may think action is better—but who will care for you when you only act? You will have an identity number, but no identity."

The fantasy story "The Cheery Soul" does appear to offer a comforting release from the tension of such a changing world. A reader certainly would prefer the company of its jolly, tradition-loving ghost to that of the obtuse, insecure narrator who must misinterpret events desperately to make them seem rational and nonthreatening as he stumbles about the deserted house to which he was invited by mock-hearty spies, searching for a smidgen of hospitality. By contrast, a policeman informs the narrator, the deceased cook was last observed "singing 'God rest you merry, gentlemen, let nothing you dismay.' She also shouted: 'Me for an English Christmas!' Accosting several pedestrians, she informed them that in her opinion times were not what they were." As a ghost, she devotes her time to bothering the (un-English) spies and giving the narrator the only truly welcoming gestures he receives.

In the editors' introduction to the reprint of the story in *MFSF*, it is described as an example of a rare subclass of fantastic fiction: the humorous ghost story. Certainly it is an extremely good-natured tale, especially in the way it presents the narrator's inability to respond to the ghost's heartiness.

In any case, a reader will feel that accepting the presence of a ghost in "The Cheery Soul" is preferable to accepting the point of the nonfantasy that precedes it, "The Inherited Clock." This story first appears to be fantasy because of the heavy symbolism of the clock's being associated with the survival of a family and because of the main character's inability to remember the incident that gave the clock such emotional significance in her life. In fact, she discovers that the clock has no supernatural power. Her cold-blooded cousin restores her memory of the time he hurt her with the clock and reminds her that the clock merely symbolizes the ways in which humans can injure each other. As a result, she realizes that she has been attaching significance to the clock only out of her own pain, her own human smallness. The discovery leaves her empty, without supernatural comfort or menace, trapped inside a mechanical system that she can see only too clearly. Nothing means anything.

The "supernatural" suggested in the collection's opening stories seems fairly straightforward, a survival of the past that works to preserve values that in turn work to preserve one's sense of self. Later stories look at this comforting support from another angle and qualify it strongly.

Like the people in "The Inherited Clock" and

"The Cheery Soul," the central character in "Songs My Father Sang Me" is "haunted" by the past, in her case an obsession with the father she loved but who fled while she was a child. Before he left, after one last argument with his wife, he had taken the little girl away for a drive that for her was a liberating holiday. He had talked while she ate chocolate, describing his past feelings. Then he had looked at her. As she recalls it later, "Something about me—my age?—was a proposition. Then he shut his eyes, like—I saw later, not at the time—somebody finally banishing an idea. 'No; it wouldn't work,' he said. 'It simply couldn't be done. You can wait for me if you want. I can't wait for you.'" His remarks obviously apply first to the idea of keeping her with him while deserting her mother. They also have a more than latently sexual meaning. In fact, the girl is still figuratively waiting for her father at the story's end, as her male companion suggests that for all she knows, her father might be in the same nightclub where they are sitting; when she looks for him in "an addled trio of men round the fifty-five mark," the companion twits her brutally with how she has fantasized the stoppage of time: "I thought we were looking for someone of twenty-six?" The woman ends where she began, caught inside a loop of time. This is not a comforting fantasy—or, if it is, the woman has bought comfort at the expense of the possibility of reaching out to anyone who is not the image of her father.

Following that story is one of the three best fantasies in the book, "The Demon Lover," in which someone does manage to defeat time by "waiting" for the woman he desires. The story is told from the viewpoint of a prosaic middle-aged woman who has forgotten that she pledged herself for all eternity to a ruthless young soldier later killed in World War I—until a letter mysteriously appears while she is visiting her closed-up London home during World War II and informs her that her lover intends to keep his promise by claiming her. She is a rather feeble creature of habit who had never truly loved the young man but had only been overwhelmed by his certainty; and over the years she has settled into a pleasant routine. Nevertheless, her dead lover's insistence that "nothing has changed" shatters that routine; all the safety of her normal life is at once voided. The story concludes, unlike "The Inherited Clock" or "Songs My Father Sang Me," with the character not returned to normality with stunned self-understanding or with resignation. Instead, she rushes from her house and climbs into the first taxi she sees, relieved until she realizes that the driver is her dead lover: "After that she continued to scream freely and to beat with her gloved hands on the glass all round as the taxi, accelerating without mercy, made off with her into the hinterland of deserted streets."

Surveying the stories in the book thus far, a reader realizes that Bowen actually offers no comfort in life. Fantasy evidently is produced by an impulse to impose personal will on time, against time. This is futile, for change must happen. Denying it is most unhealthy. Yet change seems to be unhealthy too. Progress leads to disappointment, for it has culminated in the superficial, brutal modern world. To account for this failure to grow in a healthy way, one must suppose that the impulse to deny real feeling in order to protect the tender self is a fundamental part of human nature, able to control perception and action even though it actually means smothering a vital part of the self. This being the case, life leads to disillusionment, and disillusionment to a frozen limbo worse than mere extinction.

"The Happy Autumn Fields," second of the three major fantasy stories in the collection, presents this realization in all its complexity. The story's two main female characters demonstrate how urgent and how doomed is the desire to preserve any moment unchanged forever. In the first part of the story, Sara, a young woman living in the country during Victorian times, is torn between her desire to preserve her closeness to her sister, Henrietta (and the happy stability associated with her family's closeness), and her attraction to Eugene, a neighbor's son who obviously is on the verge of declaring his love for her. Then the scene abruptly shifts, revealing that Sara's story was the dream-vision of Mary, a modern young woman who has just discovered a packet of family relics in her bomb-damaged London dwelling.

Mary yearns for the life that Sara seems to represent, as an escape from modern instability, and she manages to send her lover away so that she can slip back into Sara's consciousness. Sara is torn by a desire to hang on to the familiar, satisfying life that she has, as opposed to recognizing that she must give it up in order to respond to Eugene. Seeing that she is disturbed and desiring to comfort her, Eugene asks Henrietta to promise her that things will never change, whereupon Henrietta, who earlier had seemed to accept the idea that change must come, now flares out at him, "Whatever tries to come between me and Sara becomes nothing. Yes, come tomorrow, come sooner, come—when you like, but no one will ever be quite alone with Sara. You do not even know what you are trying to do. It is you who are making something terrible happen."

At that moment, Mary is jarred back to herself by the explosion of a bomb nearby. She is at first upset that she was not killed so that her consciousness could have stayed with Sara's. Her lover tells her that he has looked through the papers that she found and has discovered that both Sara and Henrietta died young and unmarried, for Eugene had been "thrown from his horse and killed, riding back after a visit to their home. The young man . . . was alone; and the evening, which was in autumn, was fine though late. Fitzgeorge [writer of the letter describing the event] wonders, and says he will always wonder, what made the horse shy in those empty fields."

The reader wonders too. What was Eugene "trying to do"—to pretend to preserve the past through an impossible promise or to shatter the link between the sisters in the name of natural change? And from whose perspective was his action "terrible"? It is clear that something terrible did happen to Eugene because of the conflict demonstrated in this story. It is impossible to be sure exactly what happened, and Bowen sets up the conclusion quoted above to leave the reader mulling this question. It could be the psychic energy of the adolescent Henrietta, acting as a poltergeist. It could be the bomb's explosion, somehow transmitted through the link to the present caused by Mary. But no matter how it happened, the obvious reason why it happened was Sara-Mary's irrational, antinatural desire to hold on to a past that must change.

The unhealthiness of fixing oneself to the past is further demonstrated in the next, nonfantasy story,

"Ivy Gripped the Steps," which shows a young widow who is so concerned with progress and niceness that she blithely ignores the approach of World War I, meanwhile heartlessly flirting with the son of her best friend, who visits her at a seaside resort. Fixated on her, in turn, the boy grows up to be a superficial sensualist who startles the young woman when she gets a look at him for the first time at the story's conclusion:

> She had seen the face of somebody dead who was still there—"old" because of the presence, under an icy screen, of a whole stopped mechanism for feeling. Those features had been framed, long ago, for hope. The dints above the nostrils, the lines extending the eyes, the lips' grimacing grip on the cigarette—all completed the picture of someone wolfish. A preyer. But who had said, preyers are preyed upon?

As in the passage just quoted, the stories in *Ivy Gripped the Steps* are full of supernatural images used figuratively. The last three stories in the collection show both the roots of fantasy and the presence of fantasy in everyday life.

"Pink May" is proclaimed a ghost story in the narrator's first sentence. Nevertheless, its tone is disconcertingly prosaic, because of the narrator's self-ish, superficial outlook. She is concerned about the ghost only because it bothers her as she is preparing to sneak out to meet her lover, while her husband works late at his war duties. The woman speculates that the ghost must be that of a puritan or of a woman who "must have taken a knock [been disappointed]"; she settles on the latter because "I know how a knock feels." Because she is haunted and distracted, she eventually loses her lover and then her husband when she breaks down and confesses to him. In conclusion, she admits that she never saw the ghost directly but protests that it did exist: "Not a ghost—when it ruined my whole life! Don't you see, can't you see there must have been *something*? Left to oneself, one doesn't ruin one's life!" But that is exactly what the reader has seen the characters in other stories doing, the supernatural only making possible the literal expression of their desires and fears.

"Green Holly" is the third of the collection's major fantasies as well as the last distinctly supernatural story in the book, showing again how one ruins one's life. The carol sung by two men and a woman at an isolated government installation is ironically appropriate: "Heigh-ho! sing Heigh-ho! unto the green holly: / Most friendship is feigning, most living mere folly." Proximity has created love affairs between the people shut in the place; time has broken and recombined the relationships until now the people peck at each other in irritated boredom. But one of the men, Mr. Winterslow, is haunted by the ghost of a beautiful woman. Seeing the action from inside the character of a ghost for the only time in the book, a reader realizes how much she resembles the living-dead man in "Ivy Gripped the Steps":

> Her own person haunted her—above her forehead, the crisped, springy weight of her pompadour; round her feet the frou-frou of her skirts on a thick carpet; in her nostrils the scent from her corsage; up and down her forearm the glittery slipping of bracelets warmed by her own blood. It is the haunted who haunt. . . . She was left with—nay, had become—her obsession. Thus is it to be a ghost.

She does not understand—let alone love—Winterslow; he is only an object of her obsession with being a lover. Winterslow is disconcerted by her, aware of his personal inadequacy as an object of love. But after the ghost fades, trapped again inside her timeless, meaningless self, Winterslow's vision is confirmed by Miss Bates, the spinster who at one time was intimate with him. She also has seen the apparition of the man who killed himself because of the ghost woman:

> "Stone dead, I saw the man of my dreams. . . . the hand that had dropped the pistol had dropped a white rose; it lay beside him brown and crushed from having been often kissed. The ideality of those kisses, for the last of which I arrived too late . . . will haunt, and by haunting satisfy me. . . . But who was *she* . . . to deceive him? Who could have deceived him more superbly than I?—*I* could be fatal," moaned Miss Bates,

pacing the drawing-room. "*I could be fatal—only give me a break!*"

The characters get no such break; they are only their grubby, nonideal selves, conscious of how much they lack and of what more they are losing all the time.

Finally, "Mysterious Kôr" shows once more the struggle between unsatisfying reality and appealing fantasy. In a silent, moon-drenched London, a soldier and his girl walk toward her apartment, she pretending that they are walking through the magical, timeless city of Kôr. Later, before the moonlight fades and the day returns, her soldier lover and her roommate, a repressed virgin who nevertheless has been thrilled to look out her window at the moonlit city, discuss their experience. The lover comments how his girl had committed herself to the fantasy of Kôr until "I could have sworn she saw it, and from the way she saw it I saw it too. . . . I tell you, I woke up just now not knowing where I'd been." He goes on to justify this desire: "Why not want Kôr, as a start? There are no restrictions on wanting, at any rate?" When the girl reproaches him with the question "Can't wanting want what's human?" he replies, "To be human's to be at a dead loss." They both return to their beds then, to try to sleep. The roommate is rather relieved that the moonlight is gone, thinking it safer not to be troubled; meanwhile, the other girl lies unmoving "in an avid dream, of which Arthur [the soldier] had been the source, of which Arthur was not the end. . . . He was the password, but not the answer: it was to Kôr's finality that she turned."

The word *finality* is typical of the skewed but precise choice of words that helps make Bowen's fiction memorable. It suggests the deadly glamour of fantasy. A reader certainly can understand how the characters are attracted to fantasy, but a reader also sees how fantasy (like the nonsupernatural lies that comfort as they deceive) leads them away from the real person and into the deserted avenues of the eternal city of Kôr. Such fantasizing seems a natural part of life, and the characters may have no real alternative, given their personal limitations and the chaos that surrounds them. Still, the results are coldly dismaying.

Following these wartime stories, Bowen continued her intermittent interest in supernatural fiction. Two more stories appeared in Asquith's anthologies: "Hand in Glove" in *The Second Ghost Book* (1952) and "The Claimant" in *The Third Ghost Book* (1955). They are better than average stories but lack the complexity of the stories in *Ivy Gripped the Steps*. They very skillfully but rather traditionally show representatives of modernity defeated by the supernatural representatives of tradition. Bowen also wrote the introduction to *The Second Ghost Book*, and her introduction to a 1947 edition of J. S. Le Fanu's *Uncle Silas* is a very intelligent commentary on that Gothic romance. Thus the bulk of the writing concerned with the supernatural that Bowen composed is slight. However, it is for the stories in *Ivy Gripped the Steps*—all the stories, both the overtly fantastic and the nonfantasies, which support the others by their atmosphere of hallucination and their fantastic images—that Bowen deserves the attention of readers of supernatural fiction. In that book she speculates convincingly on how fantasy emerges from the experience of ordinary people, and she depicts vividly one outcome of such fantasy: the ultimate, absolute horror of fulfilled desires.

Selected Bibliography

WORKS OF ELIZABETH BOWEN

Most of Bowen's fantastic short stories were first published in two volumes.

The Cat Jumps, and Other Stories. London: Gollancz, 1934. (Contains the title story and "The Apple Tree.")

The Demon Lover, and Other Stories. London: Cape, 1945. As *Ivy Gripped the Steps.* New York: Knopf, 1946. (With a new preface.)

The Collected Stories of Elizabeth Bowen. London: Cape, 1980. New York: Knopf, 1981. (Contains all of Bowen's fantastic stories, with the exception of "The Claimant." The contents of *Ivy Gripped the Steps*, minus the valuable preface, are found with a few additional stories in the section "The War Years.")

ELIZABETH BOWEN

CRITICAL AND BIOGRAPHICAL MATERIAL

Bowen has received considerable critical attention. However, most of it has been paid her novels, and very little of the criticism of her short fiction comments on the stories of the supernatural. The following items are worth noting.

Briggs, Julia. *Night Visitors: The Rise and Fall of the English Ghost Story*. London: Faber and Faber, 1977.

Heath, William. *Elizabeth Bowen: An Introduction to Her Novels*. Madison: University of Wisconsin Press, 1961.

Lee, Hermione. *Elizabeth Bowen: An Estimation*. London: Vision Press, 1981.

—JOE SANDERS

JOHN COLLIER

1901–1980

TO READERS OF supernatural fiction John Collier is known primarily as the author of the sardonic short stories collected in *Fancies and Goodnights* (1951), which won the first International Fantasy Award. In these tales Collier perfected a kind of fantasy fiction that has been widely imitated but never better realized. The narrative tone is detached, acerbic, and bright with wit; the characters are observed from a distance; their failings are sketched with brevity; and the tidy plot is concluded with an ironic twist. The effect is of light entertainment with a dash of bitters. The Collier of *Fancies and Goodnights* is always diverting and never ponderous. He is also seldom serious.

This was not always the case. On 16 May 1935, sixteen years before the publication of *Fancies and Goodnights*, Collier arrived in the United States for his first sojourn as a screenwriter for RKO Radio Pictures. His career up to that time had been one of a serious and diligent man of letters, a master of several modes. In the previous five years he had published a volume of poetry, a collection of stories, a modern edition of the seventeenth-century biographer John Aubrey's *Brief Lives*, and three novels—all before the age of thirty-five. His novels had been favorably received and reviewed; evidence of his growing stature at that time is given by the fact that John Gawsworth included a bibliography of Collier's works in the second volume of his book *Ten Contemporaries* (1933). But Collier would not publish another novel during his lifetime. Such an aban-donment is guaranteed to make a critic's eyes light up, and some indication of the several choices that Collier made is given by the preface that he wrote to the bibliography Gawsworth published:

There are two sorts of prose: the impressionistic, in which you give yourself up to the subject, the human heart or the light on the tree, and the other sort, Burton's sort, Fielding's sort, in which you hold your puppet-subject at arm's length, give it a jerk or two, then laying it down, you lean across the table, and with smile or leer address your ideal auditor direct, as one good fellow to another. Impressionistic prose has been most worked on lately: too much worked on. It is a fine medium, it has led up to *Ulysses*, but it seems it must lead on to *Haveth Childers Everywhere* [a fragment, published in England in 1931, of James Joyce's *Work in Progress*, later incorporated into *Finnegans Wake*]. The other sort is capable of quite a lot of development, and anyway I like it best. I wonder if, supposing I work hard for ten years, I shall find myself at forty in a position to write it well. That would be worth doing. Meanwhile I'll put some plots and things into my experiments, and by that means get some money.

(pages 110–111)

These lines foreshadow Collier's two forsakings: of "impressionistic" prose (which he used to good effect in the science fiction novel *Tom's a-Cold*), and of fiction that lacks immediate commercial possibility. It is more for the "plots and things" in *Fancies and Goodnights* than for his experiments in non-impressionistic narrative that Collier is remembered today. An examination of his early fiction shows him to have been a writer of considerable range, much of it unexplored in the latter years of his life.

John Collier was born in London on 3 May 1901. His family was affluent; his great-grandfather was physician to William IV, and his uncle Vincent Collier was a novelist. Collier was educated privately. He did not attend university but was writing poetry at nineteen and publishing it at twenty. During the 1920's he lived on a stipend provided by his father; he associated with London artists and writers and served as poetry editor of *Time and Tide*. His first novel, *His Monkey Wife; or, Married to a Chimp*, appeared in 1930, followed by *Tom's a-Cold* in 1933 (published in the United States as *Full Circle*) and *Defy the Foul Fiend* in 1934.

His Monkey Wife, as a first example of pre-1935 Collier, may be classified as fantasy although it contains no overtly supernatural elements. It is not easily classified at all, and this uniqueness is one of its chief virtues. The book concerns Mr. Fatigay, a British schoolteacher at a remote outpost in the Upper Congo. Mr. Fatigay is a believer in proper behavior and in the British Empire; he corresponds dutifully with his cold fiancée, Amy, back in London; and his domestic in the jungle is faithful Emily, a chimpanzee. The outré element of this tale is that much of the story is told from the point of view of Emily, a very intelligent and beautiful chimp, capable of reading, writing, and making the finest of social and moral distinctions. Unknown to Mr. Fatigay, she has fallen madly in love with him. Like the heroine of a Victorian novel (after the plot of which *His Monkey Wife* is most carefully modeled), Emily slavishly follows Mr. Fatigay as he returns to England and places her in service to Amy, who has no true love for him and who abuses the uncomplaining Emily severely. What Collier gives us is a novel in the manner of Charlotte Brontë, with an ape in the role of Jane Eyre. And Collier avoids none of the tropes or clichés of such a novel: Emily is perhaps the most self-sacrificing heroine in twentieth-century fiction, Amy the most cruel of mistresses, and Mr. Fatigay the densest of heroes.

Not only does Collier reproduce the plot of the Victorian novel; he also gives us the intensely rhetorical style and the intrusive narrator he tells us he "likes best" in *Ten Contemporaries:*

> As with a drowning man whom mermaid hands draw down to what is probably, after all, far better than the life he has hitherto led, yet who kicks and struggles regardless of this consideration, until he sees his whole past unfold before him in a series of vivid pictures, when he folds his hands and fills his lungs and sinks without further protest, so did Mr. Fatigay rebel bitterly against Emily's invitation into reason, an element as unfamiliar and as fatal to lovers as the sea is to any land creature. . . .
>
> (chapter 17)

The juxtaposition of these elements—the style and plot of the Victorian novel, the milieu of 1920's London, and the chimpanzee heroine—produces a wicked satire. While Emily supposes that her deferential manner and simple dress will commend her to the other passengers on the steamship as a creature who will not give herself airs though she has risen above her station, the other passengers take her to be a dumpy woman anthropologist. This cuts more than one way: against the class system (Emily is a parody of the good servant whose efforts to please are unappreciated by her social superiors), against racism (Emily's rude treatment is in part the result of her dusky complexion), and against the subjugation of women (only a dumpy woman, unable to compete in her proper sphere, would even consider a career as an anthropologist, and this one confirms the stereotype by looking like an ape). Though Collier would recoil at any suggestion that *His Monkey Wife* is a feminist novel (it mercilessly ridicules Amy, a "new woman"), the book abounds in examples of how the treatment of an ape in London is not much worse than the treatment of a woman.

Time and again the simple fantasy of placing the chimpanzee in the woman's role undercuts the manners and morals of Mr. Fatigay, Amy, and civilized London; and the insistence of the prose style that this is a conventional romantic novel is continually twisted to satiric effect by the absurd object at the center of its focus. As Anthony Burgess has pointed out in his introduction to *The John Collier Reader* (1972), though the conclusion of the book presents us with a romantic consummation of the marriage of Mr. Fatigay and Emily, described in the most decorous of terms, the mind cannot escape the knowledge that what is being described is a man copulating with a monkey. This disjuncture of manner and matter is the chief source of delight in *His Monkey Wife*. It is a method that Collier uses less often, and less lethally, in his short stories.

The elements of *His Monkey Wife* to which Collier was to hold fast in his short fiction are the intrusion of a fantastic event into a mundane world, a detached and often satirical narrator, and a cynicism about the human race. In the *Ten Contemporaries* essay, Collier says: "I cannot see much good in the world or much likelihood of good. There seems to me a definite bias in human nature towards ill, towards the immediate convenience, the vulgar, the cheap." This pessimistic view of humanity remains a constant in Collier's fiction.

Those elements of *His Monkey Wife* that Collier abandons are the extravagant style, gradually traded in for a more economical idiom, and the broad literary allusiveness that fills *His Monkey Wife* with references to John Donne, Alfred, Lord Tennyson, Shakespeare, Homer, and John Milton. The malice underlying this novel is muted in most of the stories, or perhaps it is simply that in them it has less space to express itself. Nevertheless, in comparison to *His Monkey Wife, Fancies and Goodnights* seems a less ambitious undertaking.

The change in Collier's style in his short fiction was not a sudden one. The stories that he published in the early 1930's are similar in manner to *His Monkey Wife*. In the version of "Green Thoughts" published in a special signed edition in 1932, for instance, Collier continually comments on the action with little sardonic asides. However, as he collected these stories into volumes during the next twenty years, reprinting some of them two and three times before the omnibus *Fancies and Goodnights*, Collier could not keep from tinkering with his prose in successive collections, pruning it of parenthetical statements. The version of "Green Thoughts" published in the collections *Presenting Moonshine* (1941) and

The Touch of Nutmeg, and Other Unlikely Stories (1943) is therefore subtly different from the original. By and large these changes consist of small deletions, but the overall effect is to clarify the narrative at some expense of wit and allusiveness.

This is not to say that Collier's short stories are trivial. But in general they are more skillful than disturbing. Partaking of some of the tone of the works of Saki, Ronald Firbank, and the early Aldous Huxley, the stories in *Fancies and Goodnights* and in Collier's other collections use the detached, omniscient narrator to comment, in language that ranges from the effete to the colloquial, on stories of moral choice. The people who inhabit these stories are not often described in depth; they are types, frequently not even named, whose moral flaws rebound against them in "surprise" endings that, at their weakest, are cloyingly pat. A good number of these stories contain no supernatural elements. The tone of both the fantasy and the nonfantasy is consistently sardonic. The tales insinuate a sly sexuality into screwball comedy sharpened by hints of malevolence.

A typical Collier fantasy such as "Fallen Star" presents the intrusion of some fantastic event or creature — in this case a fallen angel (female) — into the commonplace world — in this case the office of a New York psychiatrist. The angel has been lured away from heaven by Tom Truncheon, a comic demon who talks like a gangster from a 1930's Warner Brothers film and who hopes to ensnare both the psychiatrist and the angel in a carnal trap. The situation is treated with the lightest of satirical touches. Here, during their first analytical session, the psychiatrist begins to lose his professional detachment:

Delighted by his approbation, the angel asked one or two more questions, such as at last caused this worthy young analyst to rise from his chair and pace the room in a state of considerable agitation. "Unquestionably," he murmured, "I am experiencing the counter-transference in its purest form, or at least in its most intense one. Such a pronounced example of this phenomenon should surely be the subject of experiment. . . . In my paper I will call it 'The Demonstrative Somatic Method as Applied to Cases of Complete

579

Amnesia.' It will be frowned upon by the orthodox, but, after all, Freud himself was frowned upon in his time."

We will draw a veil over the scene that followed, for the secrets of the psychoanalytic couch are as those of the confessional, only more interesting.

The authorial comment that ends this passage is characteristic, Collier leaning across the table to leer at the reader. In the course of the story the demon's plans are thwarted, he is induced to undergo psychoanalysis (after which he does very well on Wall Street), and the analyst and the angel live happily ever after.

Demons, witches, genies, and magic appear frequently in Collier's short fiction. Stories like "Fallen Star," "Bottle Party," "Pictures in the Fire," "The Devil George and Rosie," and "Halfway to Hell" are frankly presented as divertissements, but some of the snap of *His Monkey Wife* surfaces in others that use these materials to more serious effect. "Thus I Refute Beelzy" presents the persecution of a boy, Small Simon, by his father, Big Simon, in the name of "learning from experience." One day the father returns home early from his office and discovers Small Simon playing with his imaginary friend, Mr. Beelzy. Big Simon insists, in proper psychoanalytical terms, that the boy give up this fantasy before he turns to a real lie. Collier, in a few pages, deftly sketches in the tyranny of the father, the mother's ineffectuality, their neighbor's embarrassment, and the boy's desperate defense, culminating in Big Simon taking his son upstairs to beat the fantasy out of him. For once there are no authorial intrusions: the story consists almost entirely of dialogue and ends on the horrific note of Beelzy's refutation of the father: "It was on the second-floor landing that they found the shoe, with the man's foot still in it, much like that last morsel of a mouse which sometimes falls unnoticed from the side of the jaws of the cat."

The plot of this story, complete to the supernatural reversal at the end, is similar to those of Collier's more whimsical tales, but the domestic drama that leads up to this conclusion raises it beyond the merely clever. This story is more powerful than "Fallen Star" because it starts from a situation closer to reality. Any aware reader is going to expect the departure into fantasy in the end, where father gets his comeuppance, but what is unexpected is its disproportionate savagery and the matter-of-fact way in which Collier leads us from the comic psychological brutality of dad (whose attacks are veiled, as are most attacks in the civilized family) to the grim supernatural brutality of Small Simon's protector (whose attack is graphically physical, unveiled to us in the gruesome final line of the story). We begin the story reading light comedy and conclude in grand guignol. No authorial comment is necessary or offered, as the tale moves from the whimsical to the minatory.

At its sharpest and most economical, as in "The Chaser," Collier's short fiction approaches parable. "The Chaser," not more than 1,500 words long, almost all of it dialogue, makes a point about love that is rapier sharp. Alan Austen, hopelessly in love with Diana, who does not care for him, visits an old man who sells potions. The man offers Alan a colorless, tasteless poison at five thousand dollars a teaspoonful, but Alan is desperately excited about the love potion that will make Diana his adoring slave, unable to bear being without him, intensely jealous, self-sacrificing, and devoted—for one dollar. The old man hints that those who buy the latter often return for the former, but Alan, in his joy, is oblivious. "Good-bye," he says. "*Au revoir*," says the old man.

Stories like "The Chaser" and "Thus I Refute Beelzy" demonstrate that Collier maintained the ability to write powerfully when he gave up the novel, that the loss in breadth did not necessarily demand a loss in acuity. They also exemplify a kind of short story not as dependent on depth of characterization as on acute observation of human nature in its broader aspects, a kind of fantasy where the fantastic element is used not to help the reader to escape from reality, but as a wedge to be driven into commonplace life in order to expose its inner workings. The love potion reveals what a pitifully distorted conception Alan—and, by extension, much of the populace—has of love. By providing such lessons, in such "crafty" packages, Collier's short stories are an effective antidote to the kind of fantasy that falsifies reality only to pander to its readers' escapism. Collier's stories may lack those qualities of characterization and verisimilitude that have traditionally been used to categorize a work as "serious," but they demonstrate that nonrealistic fiction is not by definition trivial.

To apply such a weighty analysis to most of Collier's short fiction is, however, to distort that fiction. Most of these stories consist of cleverness and polish, with the author's profound skepticism about humanity's goodness well submerged.

One might ask why Collier, after a fairly serious setting-out, chose to couch his criticism of life in the form of fantastic miniatures, to the point where he became known primarily for funny stories. Perhaps his desire to "get some money" may have influenced the course of his career; it would also be easy to blame Hollywood for the change in Collier's writing after he came to the United States. But the screenplays on which he worked, including *Sylvia Scarlett*, *Deception*, *The African Queen*, *I Am a Camera*, and *The War Lord*, are not without some access to bitter truths.

It is nevertheless true that the delight one takes in reading a collection of Collier's stories is often tinged with annoyance at the writer's reluctance to let down his jester's mask even for a moment to reveal plainly, without irony, his anger. This diffidence may be read, however, not as preciousness but as a defense against despair. Born into comfortable circumstances in Edwardian England, Collier lived through the major disasters of the twentieth century and had no illusions about progress or the perfectibility of man. Rather than grapple directly with these horrors in his fiction, he chose (with the possible exception of *Tom's a-Cold*) to spare himself, and perhaps his readers, by holding his indignation in check rather than letting it burst free. Certainly comedy has played better with the popular audience than savage indignation; and although Collier had something of the sensibility and brilliance to make a Swift or Voltaire, he was content in the end to retreat to the safer ground of a James Thurber. And it may be that he pursued exactly that path best suited to his talents, so that to pine for the novels he might have written is ill-considered as well as futile. Writ-

ing for the screen sharpened his dramatic sense, increased his economy, and gave him the ability to move an action through dialogue—all virtues that we find in Collier's short fiction. And Collier's experience as a screenwriter led directly to his final significant work of fantasy, *Milton's Paradise Lost*, a "Screenplay for Cinema of the Mind" (1973).

When *Milton's Paradise Lost* was published, John Updike in a *New Yorker* review asked "what possessed" this "excellent British fantasist" to convert Milton's epic into a screenplay. There is in this question some implication that it is all very well for an excellent fantasist to entertain us with comic tales of deals with the devil, but for him to write of Satan, hell, God, and Eden is presumptuous. Having touched on Collier's darker side, however, we can see that his effort to grapple with the large themes of *Paradise Lost*, whether successful or not, is a culmination of trends evident in his earliest fiction.

Collier's screenplay leaves out significant portions of Milton's story, notably the scenes set in heaven and the passages where the Archangel Michael tells Adam of the future and of the Son of God who is to redeem humanity. As he explains in his "Apology," Collier left out heaven because it would be hard to picture convincingly, and God because representing him in person would be impossible. The screenplay therefore concentrates on the actions of Satan and the fallen angels, and on the temptation and fall of Adam and Eve. The strength of Collier's version comes in his visualization of certain dramatic actions not clearly pictured in Milton, as in the breathtaking opening sequence depicting the fall of Satan's defeated army through space:

Nearer and louder explosions draw our eyes to the golden torrent ahead of us. It now has a finely rippled aspect, as if it might be made up of millions of newly hatched fish. . . . These are gigantic and glorious beings with beautiful, stricken faces and flying hair. . . . A brief but violent stepping up of the explosions finally disintegrates the cataract of doomed angels. . . . All space seems to be filled, as with big flakes of snow, with myriads of these falling creatures. Some mutilated, some in flames, they spread far and wide in a thick downpour, with now and then a single agonized face or a broken body sweeping past so close as almost to touch us.

(pages 4–6)

Collier makes good use of the advances in astronomy during the last three hundred years to simplify the often clumsy imagery of Milton's original. Collier's Satan glides through space more convincingly than Milton's; his sun and earth are seen more clearly, "as . . . from a modern satellite." His Garden is botanically precise and its geography detailed. The action of those parts of the story that Collier chooses to give us moves forward surely and swiftly.

In editing and rewriting Milton's language for the screen, considerable magnificence is lost, particularly when we are with Adam and Eve. Satan's speeches still retain some of the eloquence of Milton's original, and where Collier substitutes his own language the changes may be justified by the dramatic demands of the screenplay form; in many scenes the aural thunder of Milton has been transferred to the visual pyrotechnics of the film that Collier has in his mind.

The most significant difference between Collier's *Paradise Lost* and Milton's, however, is in theme. Milton explains that he writes in order to justify the ways of God to man; Collier, in his "Apology," openly mocks the notion of God's "infinite goodness, grace and mercy."

Collier's screenplay embodies criticisms that have been made of Milton's God since William Blake praised Satan's vitality and decried God's allowing the corruption of man, which he might have prevented. Thus, those portions of Milton's epic that show Satan at his most vital and heroic — notably the first two books — occupy a disproportionate part of Collier's screenplay. Those portions of *Paradise Lost* that show Satan at his weakest and most evil are left out or transformed. For example, in Milton's story, after Satan returns to hell and announces his victory in corrupting Adam and Eve, the assembled rebel angels and Satan himself are transformed into serpents. In Collier's version of this scene, the fallen angels are changed into the forms of all the heathen gods of human history, while Satan remains unchanged and triumphant.

Having given up the theological justification that is the heart of Milton's epic, Collier substitutes a different system of values. Instead of a struggle between good and evil over the soul of humanity, he gives us a struggle between the principles of change and stasis. Collier's God represents the perfection of a motionless, immortal crystal, while Satan represents the imperfection that comes through change: life, which implies death. This altered cosmology and its implications are carried consistently throughout the screenplay: sin and death, the two demons born of Satan's disobedience, are seen as by Eve to be love and birth.

These are not new ideas: the notion of a *felix culpa*, a happy fault, is present in Milton's original; Collier differs in that he presents this positive side to the Fall as a result of the actions of Satan and Eve more than as evidence of God's Providence. Like Mark Twain, Collier has a quarrel with God. His is a more modern theology, put forth with some diffidence.

This diffidence in the end causes Collier's screenplay to fall short of the achievement that it might have been. Updike's review points out that Milton was passionately involved in the theology that he explicated. Either Collier is not as involved in his own; or else his habit of self-concealment, developed over the forty years of his writing career, prevented him from approaching his story with Milton's high seriousness. In the final scenes of Collier's version there is a flagging of interest, more a playing out of the consequences of the action than an intense interest in the fate of fallen man. Collier's final dialogue, a quotation of the traditional marriage service, sounds paltry compared with Milton's description of Adam and Eve leaving Paradise: "The world was all before them, where to choose/Their place of rest, and Providence their guide:/They hand in hand with wand'ring steps and slow,/Through Eden took their solitary way."

Milton's Paradise Lost was the last book that Collier was to publish before his death, on 6 April 1980. In a sense, this screenplay is the culmination of his career: it exhibits the care for craft, the literary allusiveness, the delight in cleverness and invention, and the interest in fantasy as a means of exploring human nature evident in his best fiction. Most interestingly, despite its flaws it attempts to provide a justification for, and a reconciliation with, that recognition of the corruption of humanity that underlies all of Collier's work.

And it rounds off appropriately the career of a major fantasist of the twentieth century, whose writing has too long been deprived of serious consideration.

Selected Bibliography

WORKS OF JOHN COLLIER

Successive Collier story collections frequently reprint the same stories found in earlier collections. *The Touch of Nutmeg*, for instance, contains twenty-six stories, only nine of which did not appear previously in *Presenting Moonshine*, which in turn included *Green Thoughts* and the stories of *The Devil and All*.

His Monkey Wife; or, Married to a Chimp. London: Peter Davies, 1930. New York: Appleton, 1931. (Novel.)

Green Thoughts. London: William Jackson (actually Joiner and Steele), 1932. (Limited signed edition of the original short story.)

Tom's a-Cold. London: Macmillan, 1933. As *Full Circle*. New York: Appleton-Century, 1933. (Novel.)

The Devil and All. London: Nonesuch Press, 1934. (Short stories.)

Presenting Moonshine. London: Macmillan, 1941. New York: Viking, 1941. (Short stories.)

The Touch of Nutmeg, and Other Unlikely Stories. New York: Press of the Readers Club, 1943. (Short stories.)

Fancies and Goodnights. Garden City, N.Y.: Doubleday, 1951. Abridged version, as *Of Demons and Darkness*. London: Corgi, 1965. (Short stories.)

Pictures in the Fire. London: Hart-Davis, 1958. (Short stories.)

The John Collier Reader. New York: Knopf, 1972. (*His Monkey Wife* and short stories, with introduction by Anthony Burgess.)

Milton's Paradise Lost. New York: Knopf, 1973. (Screenplay.)

CRITICAL AND BIBLIOGRAPHICAL STUDIES

Collier, John. "Please Excuse Me, Comrade." In *Ten Contemporaries, Second Series*, edited by John Gawsworth. London: Joiner and Steele, 1933. (Sheds some light on Collier's view of his own work.)

Korn, Eric. "Monkey-Tricks and Minor Devils." *Times Literary Supplement* (26 December 1975): 1533.

Updike, John. "Milton Adapts Genesis; Collier Adapts Milton." *New Yorker* (20 August 1973): 85–86, 89.

—JOHN J. KESSEL

DION FORTUNE

1890-1946

I

MOST WRITERS OF supernatural fiction do not believe in their bogles or marvels. For some, supernaturalism is a literal way of shocking or entertaining readers; for others it is an allegorical or symbolic way of talking surreptitiously about something else. The only sizable exception to this rule of skepticism is occult fiction, whose practitioners are usually expounding what they believe is a valid field of knowledge.

Occult fiction, though not on the same level of excellence as other branches of supernatural fiction, has its own points of interest. It has a sometimes fascinating subject matter of its own, and in a strange way, it holds to a fairly mechanistic world view based on postulates different from those of science. Its followers consider it a science, albeit an esoteric science. This situation in turn creates a paradox: to form a story, the writer must reveal things, yet he or she must also conceal, for the heart of occultism is secrecy.

In the nineteenth century the subject matter of Theosophy was used notably by Mrs. Campbell Praed, Franz Hartmann, and Mabel Collins. In the twentieth century, the Hermetic Order of the Golden Dawn offered an occasional idea to Algernon Blackwood and inspired verse and stories by William Butler Yeats. Also connected with the Golden Dawn, though destructively, was the black-magi-

cian Aleister Crowley, whose *Moonchild* is a very amusing eccentric novel about magical feuds. But the occult novelist par excellence was Dion Fortune, a British mystic, expositor, and occult leader. Although Blackwood was a superior writer, Fortune made a larger mark on her world and was the clearest and most informative expositor of hitherto concealed ideas, the most devoted practitioner, and the most interesting personality.

II

Fortune's life is more mysterious than her fiction. Legends, some fostered by herself, have grown up around her, so that if one stays with verifiable fact, very little can be said about her. According to standard reference works, Violet Mary Firth was born in Llandudno, Wales, in 1890. When she was very young, she apparently settled on nursing as a profession and worked in a home specializing in the mentally ill. She then suffered a breakdown that incapacitated her for several years.

While still young, she entered the sequence of occult groups that other Britons have followed, moving from Christian Science to the Theosophical Society of Annie Besant; to the Hermetic Order of the Golden Dawn; to the Stella Matutina, a schismatic offshoot of the G.∴D.∴; and finally to an independent, eclectic position. While she was in the Golden Dawn, she received the hieratic motto-name "Deo non fortuna," which she adapted to the pen name Dion Fortune.

During the first quarter of the twentieth century, the occult societies that stressed ritual magic were being torn between two antagonistic forces: the exuberant, fantastic sexual Magick of Crowley and associates, and the milder mystically and religiously oriented approach of A. E. Waite and others. Fortune sided with the more religious group and in 1922 founded her own organization, the Society of the Inner Light, with as its organ the *Inner Light Magazine*. Her group has been characterized as Anglicanism gone sorcerous and polytheistic.

Fortune was greatly interested in the psychological ramifications of magic (and the magical basis for psychotherapy), an area that has since been greatly developed. She studied orthodox Freudian psychoanalysis, and it is said that she practiced as a lay analyst for a time. It has not been possible to discover exactly what she did, but she could not have been an authorized psychoanalyst. She had not been analyzed, had no formal training, and did not have a medical degree. Under the name Firth, she wrote three popular books expounding her points of view: *The Machinery of the Mind* (1922), *The Psychology of the Servant Problem* (1925), and *The Problem of Purity* (1928).

More important historically is a series of occult expositions published under the name Dion Fortune. The most significant of these are *The Mystical Qabalah* (1935) and *Psychic Self-Defence* (1930). The first explains an emanational cosmology ultimately based on Jewish mysticism, and the second is a rambling discussion of psychic experiences, her own and others'. Her writings, if not profound or scholarly, are clear and easily followed, hence have been popular.

In addition to leading her society, editing its magazine, lecturing, and writing journalism, Fortune turned to writing fiction, partly for financial reasons and partly (in her later books) to spread her ideas. In her early youth she had written two volumes of poetry, but these have not been available for examination.

Little more can be said about Fortune except that she seems to have been strong-minded and very sensitive to social problems. She was married to, and divorced from, T. Penry Evans, M.D. She died on 8 January 1946 in London.

On another level Fortune also lived a life of strange experiences—visions, horrors, ecstasies—some of which she recorded parenthetically in her books. While a rationalistic reader may refuse to take at face value her encounters with werewolves and vampires, experiences with projections, and psychic battles, they seem to have been real to her.

III

Fortune's first work of fiction, *The Secrets of Dr. Taverner* (1926), is a collection of eleven short stories that first appeared in the *Royal Magazine*. Taverner is a psychiatrist who specializes in cases that are best treated by occult means, but he is often in effect the equivalent of an occult detective. He maintains a sanitarium outside London, and his cases are recorded by a Watson-like figure. Taverner is said to have been modeled on a Dr. Moriarty, with whom Fortune worked and studied.

Taverner resembles Blackwood's John Silence in being both qualified as a medical man and endowed with supernatural knowledge and abilities. But whereas Silence, mirroring Blackwood, is a gentle person, Taverner has a certain ruthlessness and antinomian quality. He is a highly moral man, but his concept of morality is not that of Western culture. He does not hesitate to take the law into his own hands, and the implication is that right carries with it its own ethics.

As a personification of wisdom, Taverner is an embodiment of the traditional archimage. He is a very high initiate in the White Lodge (a benevolent occult group of great power) and, as a result of long training and many initiations, has acquired various supernatural abilities.

Taverner's exploits are thrillers and not didactic stories like Fortune's later work. "Scented Poppies" may be taken as typical. A solicitor consults Taverner. The heirs to a large fortune have successively acquired the curious habit of committing suicide by leaping out of windows. Under the circumstances, the suicides must be magically inspired. Suspicion falls on one of the surviving heirs, a dissolute young man who lives in Soho, eats un-British food, writes poetry, paints, and dabbles in occultism. Taverner discovers how the murders have been committed. The murderer gives his victims a beautiful dry bouquet that includes poppy capsules within which have been inserted seeds that open the pineal gland to psychic sensitivity, and a moonstone impregnated with thoughts of suicide. Taverner works the young man into a corner by offering to open his astral vision to the supersensual world. Taverner knows, but the culprit does not, that such vision will show the murderer his crimes and force him to madness or suicide.

Some of Taverner's cases involve reincarnation, with past crimes that must be atoned for or dead love that can now be fulfilled. Black magic, personality exchange, a vampire, a phantom dog, thought projections, and semihuman faunlike creatures all play parts. The final story, "The Power House," shows Taverner combating a black-magic lodge suggestive of Crowley's.

The Taverner stories are often considered Fortune's best work. The ideas are sometimes original, and individual stories have moments of Doyle-like sharpness. In "The Death Hound," for example, Taverner causes a magical sending in the form of a horrible hound to return to its originator. The evil magician races away in horror, with the monstrous hound after him. His body is found later. Taverner's wry comment is, "Six miles! He ran well!"

Fortune's *The Demon Lover* (1927) is a frankly sensational work that pulls out all stops in its succession of horrors. Modeled on the commercial fiction of the day, it is most closely paralleled by *A Brother of the Shadow*, by G. Colmore, which Fortune may have known. As an avid reader of supernatural fiction, she was also probably aware of similar work by Sax Rohmer, Mrs. Campbell Praed, and the authors of *Weird Tales*.

The Demon Lover is a story of action, but beneath the action exist ideas that often occur in Fortune's fiction. One such theme is that of the redemptive woman who saves the weak or errant man from either damnation or spiritual torpor. This salvation is usually done at a price to the man, either physical maiming, as in *The Demon Lover*, or submission and psychic emasculation elsewhere. This theme may have been personal for Fortune, or it may simply fit into the larger context of shopgirl romances that were rooted in the literary tradition of *Pamela* and *Jane Eyre*.

The central mechanism in *The Demon Lover* is black magic. Justin Lucas, an occultist of great ability and greater ambition, is executive secretary to a magical group that masquerades as a folklore society. The group wields enormous supernatural power, and Justin uses his position to steal secrets. To do this, he victimizes Veronica, a typist, and uses her as a medium. He is caught and sentenced to death, but before he dies, in a sharp twist from his usual selfishness, he protects Veronica by explaining that she was innocent. Justin dies and is buried, but his astral body is still undissolved and manifests itself as a vampire. The society decides to inflict on Justin the second death, which would be final. Justin, who has come to love Veronica, accepts, but a deus ex machina intervenes. A mahatmalike being appears and rules that Justin has been treated too harshly and should be restored to life. This is done. A supernatural flood exposes his coffin. But Justin returns to life blind as a result of the autopsy performed on his corpse. This is his punishment.

This brief summary does not indicate adequately Veronica's share in Justin's redemption. In past incarnations they had been lovers, and her love proved to be Justin's salvation.

The Demon Lover shows more imagination than the later novels, but even as supernatural fiction it lacks credibility. It is clumsy in presentation and amateurish in development. The supernaturalism involved, it should be noted, is that of contemporary fiction, not that of the secret occult lodges.

With her third book, *The Winged Bull* (1935), Fortune abandoned for the most part the thriller approach of the previous decade and began to write didactically, a tendency that increased with each succeeding novel. *The Winged Bull* deals with the supernaturalism that Fortune believed had a redemptive quality and is thus Fortune's first "serious" novel, as opposed to commercial work. It tries to create an authentic magical setting, skillfully compromising between attracting the reader and guarding secrets, and it presents a mild justification of ritual magic in terms of comparative religions. Like her other late novels it is ultimately about sexual intercourse, and it tries to align the physical aspects with great processes that rule the universe.

The surface text of *The Winged Bull* is about a demobbed, unemployed war veteran in desperate financial straits who encounters and finally accepts magic as a way of spiritual growth and salvation. The more interesting subtext, however, is a story of sexual bondage in which a disturbed young woman is prey to hostile forces. It is not until Fortune's last work, *Moon Magic,* that the woman, who is the thematic center, also becomes the narrative center.

As *The Winged Bull* begins, Ted Murchison, wandering through the British Museum after an unsuccessful job interview, is overpowered by a feeling of empathy for the great winged Assyrian bull that the archaeologist Austen Henry Layard stole from Nineveh. (The winged bull symbolized for Fortune the integration of body, mind, and sexuality.) In a moment of despair at his hopeless out-of-jointness with the times, he cries out aloud to the great god Pan and is heard—by an old friend, Brangwyn, his former commanding officer in the army. Brangwyn offers him a job as secretary and general factotum.

It soon becomes obvious that although Brangwyn means well, he has not been frank. Murchison's real function is to help Ursula, Brangwyn's half-sister, who has been entangled with a sex cult of black-magicians and is still emotionally enslaved and shattered. Both Brangwyn and the black-magicians plan to use Ursula in their sex magic, but their purposes are different. Brangwyn wants to heal her and bring her into harmony with the forces of growth in the universe; the black-magicians want to use her to control the hidden forces.

Murchison is humiliated when he learns that his real job is to be a stud, and would resign, except that he is penniless and feels an obligation to Brangwyn. He remains faithful and protects Ursula, even voluntarily undergoing a mock crucifixion at the hands of the evil magicians. Good eventually triumphs, and Murchison and Ursula celebrate the rite of the winged bull together.

In bald summary, *The Winged Bull,* like Fortune's other novels, may sound like mild pornography, but such is not the case. Sexuality is always Fortune's topic, but the sexuality is usually etherealized and rendered abstract in presentation. The emphasis is not so much on male and female as on man and woman.

As Fortune's first attempt at a psychological novel of a sort, *The Winged Bull* is a halting affair. The pacing is uneven, the plot creaks, and the characterizations are weak. The problem here and in Fortune's other novels is not that she could not create characters but that she could not sustain them. They change perpetually. This is a question not of growth or development but simply bad craftsmanship. For example, when Murchison enters the novel he is an average middle-class Englishman, reasonably well educated, sensitive, and cultured; by the end of the book he is a boorish lout whose virtue is a bullish power and endurance. Brangwyn, as the story opens, is a competent soldier; by the end he is a dithering, ineffectual fool.

Fortune apparently did not see this general weakness in her technique, although it is possible that editors who rejected her later work did. The heart of the problem seems to be that she adapted characters to suit the individual events.

Fortune's next novel, *The Goat-Foot God* (1936), is a story of rebirth, an individuation novel in which the powerful suppressed Dionysiac forces transform and heal a stifled, moribund personality. As such, it is related to the similar *The Blessing of Pan,* by Lord Dunsany; *Mr. Godly Beside Himself,* by Gerald Bullett; and the work of Thorne Smith.

The Goat-Foot God ties in with Fortune's concept of magic as a healing power and of psychology as a branch of magic. It is also concerned with sex, and the ultimate theme is freeing the libido by magical techniques. This relationship between magic and psychotherapy is, of course, not new in psychology or anthropology, but Fortune accepts literally what social scientists take figuratively: that magic works.

As the novel opens, Hugh Paston is broken emotionally. His wife has died in an accident while running away with a lover. Hugh now knows that she was never anything more than an adulterous gold digger and that he was imperceptive in not having seen it before. He understands that part of the fault is his, for he is a colorless, downtrodden man.

Hugh becomes acquainted with an old second-hand bookdealer who is sympathetic and is strongly associated with the occult. The bookseller has a remarkable library of occult books and is a defrocked or failed priest; hence, he has the power to perform ceremonies. Through the bookdealer Hugh regains some of his zest for life. He concludes that he can reinvigorate himself by evoking the deity called Pan.

Hugh buys a half-ruined monastery and plans to rebuild it as a chapel for pagan rites. A young woman artist, also oppressed and exploited, although in a different way, agrees to help him. But now the ancient powers manifest themselves. The monastery has a scandalous history. In the Middle Ages the authorities discovered that Abbot Ambrosius was running a pagan sex cult there. They walled up Ambrosius and then left him to die of starvation. And Ambrosius is Hugh.

The personality of the dynamic, powerful abbot emerges in Hugh, at first submerging him. The problem now is blending the power and vitality of Ambrosius with the steadiness and responsibility of Hugh, without losing the personality of Hugh. This is accomplished by an act of ritual magic; and Hugh, a new man, will continue the worship of Pan with his lover and wife, the artist.

Fortune is deliberately vague about Ambrosius, and the reader is offered a choice of explanations for the appearance of Ambrosius in Hugh. Is it reincarnation? Possession by the ghost of Ambrosius? Awakening of a configuration in Hugh's unconscious mind? All explanations are possible. In any case, *The Goat-Foot God* is Fortune's most pleasant work, even though it shows the author's usual weakness in characterization.

Fortune's last two novels, *The Sea Priestess* (1938) and the posthumous *Moon Magic* (1956), are best considered together, since they are concerned with the same central character and comprehend the same situation: the spiritual advancement of a woman, as Morgan le Fay (sometimes called Le Fay Morgan) advances from the Lesser Mysteries to the Higher Mysteries. In both novels she needs male help to accomplish her rituals and ruthlessly exploits the men she captivates with her sexual aura.

Morgan le Fay is the most satisfactory character that Fortune created, perhaps because there is a good deal of self-image embodied in her. If so, the image is not entirely complimentary. Relentlessly single-minded in her purpose, Morgan le Fay will let nothing stand in the way of her serving the goddess Isis and thus accelerating her own development. She smothers her consorts emotionally with glamour, drains their energy vampirically to add substance to her astral projections, tantalizes them sexually, and abandons them. Yet she is honest in declaring that her goddess comes first, and she salves her conscience after "sacrificing" a consort with the belief that she has re-created the old Atlantean magic that the world now needs and has awakened her male partner.

The Sea Priestess is told through Maxwell, a British real estate agent and auctioneer who helps Morgan set up her temple on the Bristol Channel and reestablish the worship of Isis. In the present world he is a family-pecked bachelor who needs arousing, but in the Atlantean past he was a lover to Morgan, who sacrificed him. Memories of Atlantis and Britain well up in his dreams as he works with Morgan.

Morgan is trying to reestablish the magic of Atlantis, where she had been a priestess. To do this she must create an astral projection of the goddess, receive power from it, and reestablish—although only on a spiritual level—human sacrifices. The auctioneer is her willing victim, and when the sacrifice is over, Morgan leaves. Maxwell had been in love with her, but he can now handle his own problems and establish a happy marriage with another woman.

Moon Magic is a sequel, set an indeterminate time later. For the most part, it is narrated by Morgan herself. She explains the reasons for her actions and the principles of the magic she employs. Again she sets up a shrine and, with a reincarnated sacrificial priest from Atlantis, attains the higher spiritual level to which she aspires.

In describing Morgan's magic Fortune is said to follow fairly closely the beliefs and rituals of her Society of the Inner Light. Behind her magic stands a complex cosmology; our world is paralleled by astral regions inhabited by superior entities that may be helpful to mankind. Some correspond to Madame

Blavatsky's mahatmas. Fortune is interested mostly in the lunar figure Isis, who symbolizes women's mysteries, either in the favorable aspect of Isis proper or in Black Isis, the destructive force of the universe. Morgan's magico-religious ceremonies consist of rituals (which have supernatural force) and psychic processes, in which thought-forms or projections are built up. This somewhat mechanical operation, which amounts to coercion of the godhead, is connected with a graduated scale of psychic development along which the successful worshiper moves.

Moon Magic is interesting in being one of the very few accounts of magic told from the point of view of the believing adept. It also offers a clear picture of what was being done in some circles in Great Britain in the 1930's and 1940's. As literature, however, the two Morgan le Fay novels are uneven. *The Sea Priestess*, which was rejected by commercial publishers, leaves much to be desired as a novel.

Although these six books, together with an account of Morgan le Fay's death as told by herself (published in the *Inner Light Magazine*), constitute Fortune's published fiction, there have been rumors of other, unpublished work that survives in manuscript. Nothing, of course, can be said about this.

Dion Fortune was not one of the great writers of supernatural fiction, but she is interesting typologically as perhaps the best author to emerge from the strange corner of the literary world where the supernatural and the occult overlap. It is also strongly suspected that if more information were available about her personal life, she would offer a remarkable example of the transformation of transcendental experience into fiction.

Selected Bibliography

WORKS OF DION FORTUNE

The Secrets of Dr. Taverner. London: Noel Douglas, 1926. St. Paul, Minn.: Llewellyn Publications, 1962. Revised, enlarged edition, 1979. (The Llewellyn 1979 edition contains an additional story, "A Son of the Night," that was not included in earlier editions.)

The Demon Lover. London: Noel Douglas, 1927. New York: Samuel Weiser, 1972.

The Winged Bull: A Romance of Modern Magic. London: Williams and Norgate, 1935. New York: Samuel Weiser, 1971. (Donald Tuck, *The Encyclopedia of Science Fiction and Fantasy*, lists a 1935 New York publication by Kyle. No other record of this edition has been found, and it is reasonable to assume that Kyle only sold imported copies of the London edition.)

The Goat-Foot God. London: Williams and Norgate, 1936. New York: Samuel Weiser, 1971.

The Sea Priestess. London: The Author, 1938. New York: Samuel Weiser, 1972.

Moon Magic: Being the Memoirs of a Mistress of That Art. London: Aquarian Press, 1956.

BACKGROUND MATERIAL

Howe, Ellic. *The Magicians of the Golden Dawn: A Documentary History of a Magical Order, 1887–1923*. London: Routledge and Kegan Paul, 1972. (Does not cover Fortune but provides historical background.)

King, Francis. *Ritual Magic in England*. London: Neville Spearman, 1970.

Knight, Gareth. "The Work of a Modern Occult Fraternity." In the postscript in *The Secrets of Dr. Taverner*. Llewellyn Publications editions, 1962, 1979.

————."The Books of Dion Fortune." *Gnostica* 3 (whole number 38, 1976): 51–54.

—E. F. BLEILER

WILLIAM FRYER HARVEY

1885-1937

I

WILLIAM FRYER HARVEY is remembered today for a handful of superlative uncanny tales, all regular anthology favorites: "August Heat," "The Ankardyne Pew," "The Beast with Five Fingers," and "Miss Cornelius." However, of the sixty-three short stories that came from his pen over three decades, only a comparatively small fraction fall into the category of the supernatural. It is strongly hinted throughout his work that witnesses to uncanny phenomena were suffering from varying degrees of imagination, panic, hysteria, psychosis, or complete insanity. He drew heavily on the new psychiatric lore of the irrational subconscious, and specialized in creating a lingering uncertainty in the reader's mind. Harvey is a master of the inconclusive or psychological ghost story, and his sardonic fantasies often come near to the genius of Saki and John Collier. Only very rarely did he attempt a traditional ghost story, the best example being "Across the Moors."

Harvey was born on 14 April 1885 at West View, Headingley, near Leeds in Yorkshire, the son of William Harvey, a retired merchant and prominent Quaker. His childhood, lovingly recalled in *We Were Seven* (1936), was extremely happy and made comfortable by a governess (a cousin), a nurse, an undernurse, a gardener, an undergardener, and a coachman. His mother, Anna Maria Harvey, was a

kind woman, and she and her husband were continuously busy with philanthropic work. The death of a bachelor uncle had made William Harvey wealthy, able to retire early and devote himself to his family of seven children. If there were ever any female dragons on the scene, like the fearful Miss Cornelius, Mrs. Ormerod, or Miss Avenal of his later stories, Harvey never referred to them in his memoirs, and he had hard words for no one. He grew up to be deeply religious, infinitely kind, and heroic.

The one book that Harvey remembered best from his childhood was a cheap reprint of Edgar Allan Poe's *Tales of Mystery and Horror*, and this was the main foundation stone of his own literary career. Harvey recalled:

I read it under the dining-room table, screened from casual observation by the long blue folds of the table-cloth. The light and the print were so poor, the tales themselves so frightening, that I took my stimulant in doses that were comparatively small. I read of the "Pendulum," of the "Descent into the Maelstrom," and finally, taking my courage in both hands, of the "Mesmerised Corpse" ["The Facts in the Case of M. Valdemar"]. The idea of a mesmerised corpse may be harmless when entertained an hour before a dinner of boiled beef, dumplings and carrots, with a rice pudding to follow that left nothing to the imagination. Twelve noon is a comfortable hour of the day, but what about twelve midnight, the witching hour when ghosts are abroad? There was the cistern room at the top of the house with its door which would not keep shut. Horrible things might have happened in the cistern room, a horrible thing might issue from it when all were sleeping, in the hope of finding someone who was still awake.

(*We Were Seven*, pages 200–201)

Harvey's childhood fantasies were allowed a free rein in regularly produced handwritten family papers, such as the *Pickle Jar* and, later, the *Missing Link*. Unfortunately, these have not survived.

He was educated at the Quaker schools at Bootham, York, and Leighton Park, Reading, and later at Balliol College, Oxford, and Leeds University, where he took his medical degree. His training was interrupted by ill health, and he then embarked on a voyage around the world, spending several months in Australia to recuperate. It was during this period that he passed the time writing "August Heat," "Sambo," and other early stories. On his return to England, the stories were published by Dent under the title *Midnight House, and Other Tales*, in 1910, when Harvey was twenty-five.

He became keenly interested in the adult education movement and went to Selly Oak, Birmingham, to assist Tom Bryan with the Working Men's College at Fircroft. At the outbreak of World War I he was one of the first to join the Quaker training camp at Jordans, and went with the first detachment of the Friends' Ambulance Unit to Flanders. Later he undertook much vital work as surgeon-lieutenant in the navy. Shortly before the end of the war, Harvey was awarded the Albert Medal for Gallantry by King George V. The official account of his heroism is as follows:

On 28 June 1918, two of His Majesty's torpedo-boat destroyers were in collision, and Surgeon-Lieutenant Harvey was sent to board the more seriously damaged destroyer in order to render assistance to the injured. On hearing that a stoker petty officer was pinned by the arm in a damaged compartment, Surgeon-Lieutenant Harvey immediately went down and amputated the arm,

this being the only means of freeing the petty officer. The boiler room at the time was flooded, and full of fumes from the escaping oil. This alone constituted a great danger to anyone in the compartment, and Surgeon-Lieutenant Harvey collapsed from this cause after performing the operation, and had to be hauled out of the compartment. . . . Surgeon-Lieutenant Harvey displayed the greatest gallantry and disregard of his personal safety in descending into the damaged compartment, and continuing to work there amidst the oil fumes at a time when the ship was liable to sink.

(*The Times*, 30 October 1918, page 3)

Only when Harvey was awarded the Albert Medal did his family and friends learn how he had risked his life to save the engineer. His lungs were badly damaged by the poisonous oil fumes, and he never fully recovered from the experience.

After the war Harvey married Margaret Henderson, daughter of John Henderson, who for many years was secretary of the National Liberal Club and the Omar Khayyam Society. Two of his brothers were now achieving some fame as writers: Thomas Edmund Harvey, member of Parliament for West Leeds, and later of the Combined English Universities; and John Wilfred Harvey, professor of philosophy at Leeds University.

Harvey returned to Fircroft as warden, but again ill health supervened, and he had to retire at the age of forty. During a subsequent long stay in Switzerland and later in a frequent sickbed at home in Weybridge, he wrote most of the short stories that appeared in *The Beast with Five Fingers* (1928) and *Moods and Tenses* (1933). His other books of this period include *The Mysterious Mr. Badman* (1934), which has a nice antiquarian flavor (it concerns the quest for a rare book by John Bunyan), with good atmosphere, but no supernatural content; and his two final works, both full of whimsicality and happiness, though written during a time of increasing pain and weakness: *Caprimulgus* (1936), a book for children "from 12 to 80," and *We Were Seven*. In the latter Harvey uses fictitious names for people and places (and calls himself "Richard" throughout), but otherwise this book is a true and entirely happy picture of his early years; through every page glow the goodness and affection of an ideal Quaker family.

At the age of fifty, Harvey moved from Weybridge to Letchworth in Hertfordshire, where he died two years later on 4 June 1937.

II

Harvey proved himself to be a master of the psychological short story in his rare first collection, *Midnight House, and Other Tales*, though only a minority are supernatural, with a few borderline cases. The title story features a traveler who spends a night at a lonely inn on the moors (a favorite situation in these tales), and endures two nightmares, which parallel the birth and death of a child during the same night.

"Unwinding" is a sequence game with an amazing coincidence implied in the climax; he uses the identical plot in a later story, "The Vicar's Web." In "Sarah Bennet's Possession," a Quaker widow of saintly character is contacted in different ways by the spirit of her wastrel husband, late of the Indian army. "Across the Moors" is Harvey's most traditional ghost story, in which a clergyman accompanies a woman across the moorland and relates how he was murdered by an ash stake eleven years before. "The Tortoise" is a memorable horror tale, certainly the best of those that have not been reprinted in later collections. A servant records in his diary that the spirit of his late master, Sir James, continues to live on in a strange and malevolent tortoise that has an uncanny resemblance to the dead man.

"Sambo" describes the behavior of a little girl who, under a mysterious compulsion, sacrifices her old dolls to her newest doll, believed to be a small puppet or idol from Africa. The reader is left to decide if this is a case of subconscious infantile sadism, or if there may still be some innate uncanny power left in Sambo. Eventually the doll is stolen and ends up displayed in an exhibition with a notice stating: "This idol affords an interesting example of the gods that were worshipped in the childhood of our race."

The most celebrated short tale in this early collection is "August Heat." The artist James Clarence Withencroft describes one blisteringly hot August day in his diary. He idly sketches the picture of a criminal in the dock accused of murder. While out

for a walk, the artist discovers a monumental mason, who has just carved a tombstone with the name James Clarence Withencroft engraved on it, complete with birth and death dates. The mason is the exact double of the man in the drawing; he proves to be extremely friendly, and invites the artist in to his house for supper. The stifling heat "is enough to send a man mad."

Alexander Laing, an enthusiastic admirer of Harvey's tales, described "August Heat" as "one of the most ingenious stories I have ever read.... We are concerned here... with a double coincidence, which, ghosts or no ghosts, *could* happen. Whether or not it did happen is a question we are inclined to forget in the fascination of a suspended climax of the first order."

The other story most linked with Harvey's name, "The Beast with Five Fingers," originally appeared in the *New Decameron* and is the title story of his second collection. It is certainly the most famous of all supernatural tales in the subgenre of the animated severed hand, but by no means the first. (Earlier examples include J. S. Le Fanu's "Narrative of the Ghost of a Hand," Guy de Maupassant's "The Hand," and Richard Marsh's "The Adventure of Lady Wishaw's Hand.")

Eccentric bachelor Adrian Borlsover goes blind at fifty but is favored with a peculiarly delicate sense of touch. He maintains a keen interest in botany, and "the mere passing of his long supple fingers over a flower was sufficient means for its identification." Not long before his death, his right hand appears to develop an independent personality and forges a message requesting that it be severed after the old man's death and sent to Eustace Borlsover (Adrian's nephew). The rest of the tale is excellently told, with Eustace chasing and fighting the malevolent hand until it finally causes his death in what appears to be an accidental fire. The hand's mode of progress resembles that of "a geometer caterpillar, the fingers humped up one moment, flattened out the next; the thumb appeared to give a crablike motion to the whole." It is suggested that the fingered beast may be animated by the spirit of a sinister, pagan-worshiping eighteenth-century ancestor.

This story differs from the majority of Harvey's plots in that several other people besides Eustace, including his best friend and various servants, witness the beast in motion. Eustace's pet parrot is one of its unfortunate victims when the thumb and forefinger squeeze it to death.

Many psychoanalytical critics have not been slow in pointing out that animated limbs and hands "spring from their association with the castration complex" (Freud's words). And Maurice Richardson, a leading writer on these topics, has conjectured that Borlsover is surely a significant name for a castrated, displaced father figure. However, it is just as unlikely that Harvey was totally unaware of this, as M. R. James was in "'Oh, Whistle, and I'll Come to You, My Lad.'"

Another well-known tale in this collection that has strong echoes of Le Fanu is "The Ankardyne Pew." A gloomy old house is haunted by strange sounds, including bird noises. These manifestations are described in passages from an 1890 diary, but the full explanation is discovered only later, in an entry from the *Gentleman's Magazine* for 1789. In the family chapel pew Squire Ankardyne once staged a cockfight and later tortured his defeated bird to death. A hundred years later, all birds show a rare antipathy to his descendant, Miss Ankardyne, and "seem to sense her coming and *run from the scattered corn.*"

"The Clock" is a typically inconclusive story in the same vein as Walter de la Mare's "A Recluse." A strange woman acquaintance asks the narrator to collect her travel clock, which she left behind in the narrator's house two weeks previously. The clock, which in theory should have stopped, is found to be completely wound up inside the locked bedroom, and there is a strange impression on the bed. Then an uncanny sound is heard "of something hopping up the stairs, like a very big bird would hop," followed by a curious scratching noise against the bedroom doors. Panic sets in, and the narrator beats a hasty retreat through the window. Looking back a few moments later, she sees that the window (which had been left wide open) is shut.

In "The Devil's Bridge," a stranger (probably the devil) builds a bridge across a river in a French village and claims the soul of the first person to cross to the other side. In "Two and a Third," a successful séance reveals a hidden connection between a wom-

an's dead son and her companion. "Ghosts and Jossers," the title of a story set during World War I, also signifies the losers and winners of a word game in which the losers "die." Three schoolboys "die" when they play the game with a stranger, their words being Coronel, Gallipoli, and Mesopotamia.

The same collection features some nearly supernatural stories ("The Tool," "Peter Levisham," "Six to Six-Thirty") and is especially noteworthy for the inclusion of two of Harvey's intensely sinister old women. "Miss Avenal" is a spiritual vampire, an old lady who seems to drain away her young nurse's energy and beauty, and replaces them with her own memories. The nurse becomes an inmate of a special wing in a euphemistically termed "rest home."

A similar fate befalls Andrew Saxon, the adversary of "Miss Cornelius," which many consider Harvey's finest story. The enigmatic Miss Cornelius, after being accused of faking a poltergeist, apparently bewitches Saxon's wife, though it is suggested that this may be a paranoid delusion of Saxon's. Eventually he takes his wife to a mental home, only to discover that he himself is about to be certified. (The narrator of "The Tool" also writes from inside an asylum.)

The Beast with Five Fingers was dedicated by Harvey to his wife; and his third collection, *Moods and Tenses*, was dedicated to his father-in-law, John Henderson. The introduction states that the eighteen stories in *Moods and Tenses* were written by his friend Dan Hartigan, an artist from New Zealand, who had a distinctly weird left eye. The stories can be divided into "left-eye" and "right-eye" stories, and it is up to the reader to decide which is which. One of the uncanny ("left-eye") tales is "Mrs. Ormerod," which concerns the third of Harvey's triumvirate of sinister women. She is a dominating housekeeper who seems to exploit the altruistic couple employing her. Again the reader is left to guess whether the character is a spiritual vampire, or whether the narrator is misinterpreting the actual situation. Her supernatural power is debatable and (like Miss Avenal's) has recognizable equivalents in the everyday world.

In "The Follower," an author invents a plot concerning a scholar who acquires some unusual palimpsests (connected with diabolism?) in Asia Minor and returns to England with a mysterious monk who is his "constant companion and follower." These two characters actually live half a mile away, across the valley, and the author is warned by them (supernaturally) to abandon his book. This tale has slight overtones of M. R. James, as does "The Dabblers." A secret tradition or game, descended from a form of the black mass, survives the generations at a public school: successive groups of five schoolboys sing at midnight on the same date every year, sacrifice a chicken, but are never caught. Like the majority of the stories in *Moods and Tenses*, the tale is extremely well-handled, but lacking in actual supernatural content.

Almost ten years after Harvey's death, his fame increased with the almost simultaneous release of Robert Florey's movie *The Beast with Five Fingers* (1946), starring Peter Lorre and Victor Francen, and the definitive collection of his short stories, edited by Maurice Richardson (1946).

The success of this book (*Midnight Tales* in Britain; *The Beast with Five Fingers* in the United States, not to be confused with the earlier edition with this title) led to the publication in 1951 of a new collection of unpublished tales written by Harvey in the early and middle 1930's, *The Arm of Mrs. Egan, and Other Stories*. The first twelve stories are interrelated, being told by Nurse Margaret Wilkie, who has witnessed or taken part in some peculiar happenings in the course of her professional life. Only three or four of these tales are up to the standard of Harvey's earlier work.

"The Arm of Mrs. Egan" suggests the writer's favorite device, the long arm of coincidence. When Mrs. Egan's young son dies, she blames (curses?) the bungling Dr. Gilbert Lennox, who is dogged by bad luck from that moment wherever he goes. He continually gives wrong diagnoses, and the victims are always linked in some way with the name Egan. He hides in a remote cottage in Lincolnshire, but a car crash in the vicinity involving Mrs. Egan results in his own death. Another of Harvey's eccentric women, in "The Flying Out of Mrs. Barnard Hollis," is an elderly widow who seems to have the power of liberating her astral body, plus an evil component. She takes a drug to induce the special psychic state and is evidently a white witch.

"Account Rendered" is a genuinely supernatural tale involving a mysterious figure engaged in psychological research into the relation of space-time and the unconscious. He needs to be anesthetized by a doctor on the same date every year. A strange old man fleetingly appears every time this is done: a ghost looking for his murderer. Failure to anesthetize can result in the central figure's death.

One of the four stories in *The Arm of Mrs. Egan* not related by Nurse Wilkie, "The Habeas Corpus Club," is a humorous fantasy. Peregrine Pollock is a prolific writer of crime stories and an insomniac. The spirits of all the corpses summarily dismissed in the early chapters of his books are all members of the Habeas Corpus Club. They leave the premises of the club only at night. "We go to haunt the authors who murdered us," say the members. "Do you wonder that Peregrine Pollock hardly ever sleeps?" Harvey's sardonic wit is well in evidence here, and the publishing firm in the tale glories in the name of Rape and Carnage!

It is usually difficult to distinguish the real situations from the disintegrating minds of Harvey's characters. Feverish moods and the unclear nature of personal relationships are the essential elements of his world. From the obsessive to the whimsical, William Fryer Harvey remains an excellent craftsman throughout the corpus of his engaging, sardonic fantasies.

Selected Bibliography

WORKS OF WILLIAM FRYER HARVEY

Since the full contents of Harvey's short story collections do not seem to be recorded elsewhere, they are listed here.

Midnight House, and Other Tales. London: Dent, 1910. (Contains "Midnight House," "The Star," "Across the Moors," "Last of the Race," "Deaf and Dumb," "August Heat," "Sambo," "Unwinding," "A Middle-Class Tragedy," "The Fern," "The Angel of Stone," "Sarah Bennet's Possession," "The Tortoise," "After the Flower Show," "The Desecrator," and "The Educationalist.")

The Beast with Five Fingers, and Other Tales. London: Dent, 1928. New York: Dutton, 1928. (Contains "The Beast with Five Fingers," "Six to Six-Thirty," "Blinds," "Miss Cornelius," "The Heart of the Fire," "Peter Levisham," "The Clock," "Ghosts and Jossers," "The Sleeping Major," "The Ankardyne Pew," "The Tool," "The Devil's Bridge," "Two and a Third," and "Miss Avenal." This edition is not to be confused with the Dutton 1947 edition, which is described below.)

Moods and Tenses. Oxford: Basil and Blackwell, 1933. (Contains "The Double Eye," "The Dabblers," "Full Circle," "Mrs. Ormerod," "Pelly's Gambit," "The Follower," "The King Who Could Not Grow a Beard," "Dung, Worm-Casts, Snow and Ice," "The Man Who Hated Aspidistras," "The Ivory House," "The Two Llewellyns," "Death of a God," "London Calling," "Double Demon," "Autumn Love," "Hypocrites," "Jimmy's Aunt," and "Shepherds and Kings.")

Midnight Tales, edited by Maurice Richardson. London: Dent, 1946. (Contains "Midnight House," "The Dabblers," "Unwinding," "Mrs. Ormerod," "Double Demon," "The Tool," "The Heart of the Fire," "The Clock," "Peter Levisham," "Miss Cornelius," "The Man Who Hated Aspidistras," "Sambo," "The Star," "Across the Moors," "The Follower," "August Heat," "Sarah Bennet's Possession," "The Ankardyne Pew," "Miss Avenal," and "The Beast with Five Fingers."

This collection was reprinted as *The Beast with Five Fingers, and Other Tales.* New York: Dutton, 1947. London: Dent, 1962. It should not be confused with the 1928 collection titled *The Beast with Five Fingers.*)

The Arm of Mrs. Egan, and Other Stories. London: Dent, 1951. New York: Dutton, 1952. (Contains "The Lake," "Chemist and Druggist," "Euphemia Witchmaid," "Ripe for Development," "Atmospherics," "The Vicar's Web," "Dark Horses," "The Arm of Mrs. Egan," "Old Masters," "No Body," "Account Rendered," "The Flying Out of Mrs. Barnard Hollis," "Dead of Night," "Mishandled," "The Habeas Corpus Club," and "The Long Road.")

RELEVANT WORKS

Harvey, William Fryer. *We Were Seven.* London: Constable, 1936. (Reminiscences.)

Laing, Alexander, ed. *The Haunted Omnibus.* London: Cassell, 1937. (Collection of ghost stories. Foreword by Laing.)

Richardson, Maurice. "The Psychoanalysis of Ghost Stories." *The Twentieth Century* (December 1959): 419–431.

"William Fryer Harvey." *The Times* (London) (7 June 1937). (Obituary.)

— RICHARD DALBY

JOHN METCALFE

1891-1965

JOHN METCALFE HAS a secure niche in the supernatural genre because of his memorable and powerful capacity for creating a strange atmosphere of indefinable fear. While only a small percentage of his oeuvre is genuinely supernatural, a strong sense of the macabre is present throughout his work. "The Bad Lands" (*The Smoking Leg, and Other Stories*, 1925), "Mortmain" (*Judas, and Other Stories*, 1931), and *Brenner's Boy* (1932) are some of the finest stories in supernatural literature. Although largely forgotten today, his work was greatly admired by many of his contemporaries, including Dorothy L. Sayers, Thomas Burke, Sir Hugh Walpole, and L. P. Hartley. A brief study of his life can unveil a few clues to the background of his weird tales.

William John Metcalfe was born on 6 October 1891 in Heacham, Norfolk, a small English town that closely resembles the area described in "The Bad Lands." His father, William Charles Metcalfe, had spent many years at sea in the merchant marine, and when he retired in middle age, he began a new career as a best-selling writer of sea stories for boys. His first success was *Frank Weatherall; or, Life in the Merchant Marine* (1886), based on his own experiences. It was followed by over two dozen more, all with a strong nautical flavor and very much in the G. A. Henty mold, with titles such as *Grit and Pluck*, *The Boy Skipper*, and *The Mystery of the Albatross*. He imbued his son with a love of the sea and small boats, and this love is evident in

several of John's best stories, including "Mortmain," "The Smoking Leg," and "The Double Admiral" (*The Smoking Leg, and Other Stories*).

When John was five, his parents were appointed superintendents of Dr. Barnardo's Girls' Home in Hazel Brae, near Peterborough, in Canada. Returning to England in 1901, they continued to perform similar work in the East End of London and later in Scotland, where they were in charge of an orphanage. His father's literary income enabled young John to have a good education of St. Felix College in Suffolk and Nelson's School in Norfolk. He graduated in philosophy at the University of London and in 1913 began a teaching job in Paris.

Following in the tradition of his family, Metcalfe joined the Royal Naval Division at the outbreak of World War I and later transferred to the Royal Flying Corps (coincidentally in the same team as Leslie Lewis, another future master of macabre fiction). After the war, he became a schoolmaster at Highgate School in north London. An active "scribbler" since early childhood, he now began to spend four or five hours a day writing short stories. The best of these appeared during the early 1920's in various literary periodicals, including *Land and Water*, the *Queen*, the *Adelphi*, and the *London Mercury*.

Metcalfe's first collection, *The Smoking Leg, and Other Stories*, proved very successful, quickly passing through three editions. Two of Metcalfe's best-known stories in this collection concern rubies with occult qualities from Burma. "Nightmare Jack" recalls Lord Dunsany's "A Night at an Inn" and at the same time is almost a tribute to the best horror stories of W. W. Jacobs; the dockland settings of that writer are incorporated here, complete with transcribed cockney dialect. "The Smoking Leg" is caused by a lethal ruby, once the eye of an idol, that, together with a restraining jade-green amulet, is inserted into a lascar's thigh by a deranged doctor. The lascar murders the doctor and escapes on a ship, where his leg continually emits smoke and flame. Now a veritable Jonah, the lascar and his smoking leg cause numerous ships to sink, until he is eventually washed onto the Cornish coast. The jewel exacts a horrific denouement on another doctor who removes it from the lascar's leg before he takes out the amulet.

"The Grey House" involves the mysteries of time and space. A man takes a mysterious taxi ride through south London and enters the past down a kind of drain or trapdoor, which circumstance, by an awful oversight, has left unclosed. Another strange and forbidding house is the focal point of "The Bad Lands." On a remote part of the Norfolk coast (probably very near Metcalfe's birthplace), two men are convinced that a tract of land past the dunes is an unutterably sad and abominable place, a *terre mauvaise* with definite geographical limits upon the earth, yet beyond and apart from them. The deserted house, diagnosed as evil only by the two men, is known to everyone else as a harmless farm dwelling. A spinning wheel in the house is the source of the evil, and possible madness caused by nightmare of the spiritual bad lands is suggested.

"The Double Admiral" is one of Metcalfe's most celebrated puzzle tales. Admiral Hood and a visiting psychic on the Hampshire coast see a brown, evil stain — an "island" — on the distant horizon. Together with a bishop, the two men sail out from the shore to take a closer look and endure a "vertigo of direction" involving a ghostly barque and their doppelgängers. The unearthly island has a mad, fantastic, and haunting beauty. Later the three men describe their "dream" to each other, and find they all had the identical dream simultaneously. The admiral appears to die on his boat and is then replaced by

his doppelgänger — the second admiral — from the ghostly barque.

In attempting to solve the intricate puzzles of "The Double Admiral," Dorothy L. Sayers wrote:

> Try to tidy it up and tuck in the ends if you can. Observe the deliberate delicacy with which the sinister island is introduced; the general dimness and queerness of the atmosphere; the complete absence of all the conventional apparatus of "ghaisties and ghoulies"; and ask yourself, at the end, what exactly did happen to the Admiral and at what precise point. The story has a trick in it somewhere; you follow it quite firmly and steadily until, somewhere in the green depths of spiritual mirror, the path "gives itself a little shake" and, like Alice, you find yourself walking in at the front door again. There is something indefinably but quite definitely wrong here — something that takes you on the blind side. If the thing could have a natural explanation, it would be as twisted and lop-sided as the supernatural explanation. But there is no explanation and no attempts to explain.

The nearest solution offered is the hourglass principle, with the sand or higher mass in the upper bulb leaking away to construct the growing mass in the lower bulb.

After the success of his first collection, Metcalfe worked on two novels. The first of these, *Spring Darkness*, was published in 1928. The plots of this novel and the next, *Arm's-Length* (1930), are rather similar, involving the passion of a young man of the lower-middle class for a young woman who is definably, but not absolutely, his social inferior.

A frequent visitor to the United States, Metcalfe decided to settle there permanently in 1928, when he became a barge captain on New York's East River. Hoping this would mean a more leisurely way of life, he worked hard on his second novel. Both he and his manuscript had a lucky escape when his barge sank after being struck by a tug. His next job was at sea, but his chief ambition — to buy a topsail schooner — was never realized.

Following the success of *Spring Darkness*, Metcalfe was a regular contributor to *Scribner's Maga-*

zine and other periodicals. He became acquainted with several literary figures in the Greenwich Village social scene, among them novelist Evelyn Scott (born Elsie Dunn in Tennessee), who was then working on her immense trilogy *Migrations*, *The Wave*, and *A Calendar of Sin*. She and Metcalfe married in 1930, a marriage that survived more than thirty years of various hardships and the simultaneous waning of their literary careers.

Metcalfe's second novel, *Arm's-Length*, is the story of an oversensitive young Englishman who is unable to deal with his own life or anyone else's, except at arm's length. His gradual involvement with the Pound family (a mother and three daughters), their secret terrors, and the ultimate catastrophe are well described. "The way in which this [atmosphere] is made to darken and to deepen into definite disaster and tragedy is wholly admirable. . . . He has written a remarkable and powerful book," wrote Gerald Gould in *The Observer*.

The following year saw the publication of *Judas, and Other Stories*, Metcalfe's second collection of short stories. Again these were very well received, although the book did not achieve an American edition. "Mr. Meldrum's Mania" is a strong and memorable tale of a man's gradual metamorphosis into the Egyptian god Thoth. In "Time-Fuse," an elderly lady who dabbles in spiritualism believes she can perform miracles and handle red-hot coals, through the power of faith and the assistance of a medium. But when the medium is shown to be fraudulent, she loses her faith and is horribly incinerated.

"Mortmain" is set in the same haunted area ("the land of the dead") of "The Double Admiral" and the later *Brenner's Boy*. This story may be based on Metcalfe's experience with barges and houseboats in the late 1920's (when this tale was almost certainly written) and on his father's nautical stories. John Temple marries Salome (Sally), whose late husband, Humphrey Child, about whom many strange tales are told, has been dead for only one month. John and Salome spend their honeymoon on a houseboat, sailing along Southampton Water and the Solent. At many different points along the route, both of them see the phantom of a prestidigitating, pestilential hulk — the ghostly shape of Humphrey Child's boat.

Also present are hideous carrion moths, both material and supernatural, emblematic of the dead man. Within a short distance of their destination, as "swollen, faeculent masses discharged tardily into a crimson vortex," the phantom vessel claims the life of Salome.

Of all atmospheric creepy stories, wrote Sir Hugh Walpole,

one of the most horrible is Mr. Metcalfe's "Mortmain." This is the art of suspense created by the deliberate contrasting of matter-of-fact and charnel horror. Nothing could be more tranquil and familiar than the easy rhythm of the river, its sights and sounds. Against this we have the horrible cloud of moths rising from their feast of corruption. There is little or no surprise here because we know that catastrophe must follow and we are aware from the very first page of the story that we are in the land of the dead.

The other stories in the book are macabre but not supernatural. "Funeral March of a Marionette" describes the antics of two boys who substitute a real body in place of the ritual effigy of Guy Fawkes. (The title was taken from Charles Gounod's orchestral piece, later used to introduce Alfred Hitchcock's television series.)

A mischievous child is also featured in one of Metcalfe's most unusual and puzzling tales, *Brenner's Boy*. Once again an apparently straightforward narrative gives rise to haunting overtones and culminates in a startling climax. Does the ill-mannered and unruly son of Admiral Brenner really stay for over two days uninvited at Warrant Officer Winter's house? And what links the incident so mysteriously with the meeting of Brenner and Winter back in 1898? The child's image fails to appear on photographs, and his father insists that the boy has never left home, where he is on the point of death. There are dark hints of the state of Winter's mind near the end of the story, but the phantom child is seen by his wife and two friends, Harry and Lydia — the latter mistaking him for a girl. This is the definitive cryptic Metcalfe tale, handled with remarkable skill.

599

Metcalfe published only one more book during the next decade, his magnum opus *Foster-Girl* (*Sally* in the American edition), which appeared in 1936. It was inspired by the part of his childhood spent in the Limestone and Stepney districts of the East End of London. This is a tragic tale of adolescent girlhood in the London underworld, with a gallery of eccentric and sinister types—the whole set against a lowering, uneasy panorama of the city's mean streets.

Metcalfe and Evelyn Scott traveled widely during the 1930's, especially to Santa Fe (New Mexico), and also to France, Spain, North Africa, and Colombia, where he contracted amoebic dysentery, for which extensive medical treatment was necessary for many years. In 1939 he rejoined the Royal Air Force in Canada, and the couple went to England in time to endure the London blitz.

After World War II, Metcalfe completed two strange, quirky novels. *All Friends and Strangers* (1948) concentrates on the theories of space and time touched on in "The Grey House" and his other tales. His final novel, *My Cousin Geoffrey* (1956), set in England between the two world wars, is a compelling study of obsession and psychic vampirism. Geoffrey Wheldrick, idolized by his young cousin Martin, has inherited strange psychic gifts from his grandfather. Martin's hero worship of his cousin gradually turns into an instinctive fear. Geoffrey's desire to subjugate Martin's personality is further stimulated when both men fall in love with the same woman, and the issue is resolved only in a protracted battle of opposing wills that stretches even beyond the grave.

In the late 1940's, Metcalfe befriended the eccentric poet John Gawsworth, who had just succeeded M. P. Shiel as "King of Redonda." In 1951, Gawsworth created the Dukedom of Bottillo for Metcalfe and, acknowledging his maritime experience, dubbed him Lord High Admiral of Redonda. Metcalfe and his wife endured poverty and neglect in London for a decade, and they were released from their destitution only when a fund subscribed to by many major English literary figures was set up to allow them to return to the United States in 1952. They landed lacking the money to pay their excess baggage allowance and, after a period at a charitable foundation during which Evelyn Scott recovered from a massive heart attack, they moved into a cheap hotel in New York that was to be their final home together. Although neither of them was in good mental or physical health, Metcalfe was able to hold a teaching position for some years.

During the two decades following the publication of *Judas* and *Brenner's Boy*, Metcalfe wrote nearly twenty more short stories, of which he considered nine suitable for publication. He assembled these into a collection to be called "The Feasting Dead, and Other Stories," comprising "The Childish Thing," "Not There," "Peter's Party," "Beyondaril," "Time and Again," "The Firing Chamber," "The Feasting Dead," "Corroboration," and "The Renegade." No British publisher could be found for these stories, which were possibly considered too strong in horror content. (Several other fine writers of the supernatural, including H. Russell Wakefield, were also unable to place their work in the British market during this period.) Metcalfe submitted the collection to August Derleth, who decided to publish "The Feasting Dead," the longest story in the collection, on its own. It appeared under the Arkham House imprint in 1954 and later had a wider circulation in Derleth's frequently reprinted anthology *When Evil Wakes*.

The Feasting Dead is an exceptional novella with multifaceted layers of horror and supernaturalism combined with veiled sexuality and insanity. It is an alternative version of the psychic vampirism suggested in *My Cousin Geoffrey*, with both moral and physical corruption. The narrator, Colonel Hapgood, and his young son, Denis, are acquainted with a French landowner, M. Vaignon (a distant cousin by marriage), who suggests regular exchange holidays, with his children staying in England and Denis spending more time at Vaignon's château in the Auvergne. During his holiday, Denis becomes oddly attached to a strange creature, supposedly a gardener or servant, named Raoul Privache, who eventually follows the boy back to Hapgood's house in England. Privache is one of Metcalfe's most unforgettable creations, an "ambiguous knot-in-a-board," a sinisterly unresponsive and ageless man whose face cannot be committed to memory. Hapgood reluctantly hires the obstinate Frenchman for menial duties and observes the man often squatting on the floor "with the bland corpulence and mindless sedentary persistence of some gigantic blow-fly." Denis is getting thinner all the time, and there are poltergeist activities in his bedroom at night. Privache is visible to many people, though a few others, including a local farmer, are unable to see him.

Colonel Hapgood endures a horrific nightmare in which the only words visible in a book are "shall feast upon thee," and soon after he discovers Privache attacking the boy. Hapgood fights off the Frenchman, who then mysteriously disappears. Later Denis escapes his father and makes his way back to the Auvergne in a desperate bid to find Privache. The colonel follows, and it becomes fairly obvious from the increasingly hysterical Vaignon that the family is plagued by a curse and that he attempted to rid the château of the ghoul by introducing it to Denis. Hapgood discovers the grave of Privache (dated 1873), who is evidently a vampiric parasite of the worst kind and cannot be destroyed. This memorable and involved tale includes several of Metcalfe's tantalizing puzzle elements.

Four of Metcalfe's eight other stories were retained by Derleth for use in later anthologies of new unpublished material. In "Not There," Miss Angela Snell admires, and identifies with, a statue on a London viaduct. When the statue is destroyed by a bomb in the 1944 blitz and not replaced, she takes its place by transmutation. There is a humorous final punchline. "Beyondaril" returns to the form of Metcalfe's early stories, with a lead character—who, like the characters in "The Bad Lands" and several other of his tales, suffers from a mental breakdown—haunted by the vision of a mysterious and forbidding house.

In "The Firing-Chamber," a third story, the Reverend Noah Scallard is grief-stricken when a local parishioner is accidentally incinerated at the local potteries while checking recently glazed china. A few days later he suffers the same fate supernaturally. In "The Renegade," a "normal" young woman with several werewolves and vampires in her family tree is disconcerted to find that her late uncle Theo-

dore, a fellow of the Zoological Society, was a were-rhino.

Metcalfe's evident mental instability in his later years was not helped by mild epilepsy and alcoholism. His wife died of complications following a cancer operation in 1963, and after a difficult year Metcalfe was bailed out of a New York hospital in the fall of 1964 and sent back to England by friends. He spent the last nine months of his life in Paddington, London, and became reacquainted with some of his old friends, such as John Gawsworth. The following April he was knocked down by a car, and three months later he suffered a fractured skull after an accidental fall down a staircase. Metcalfe died in a Wimbledon hospital on 31 July 1965.

Metcalfe wrote virtually nothing during his final ten years, but two short vignettes penned in London during his last year were published posthumously: "The Nuisance," written 30 June 1965, and "Why I Write the 'Macabre,'" written 26 March 1965. In the latter, he states:

> To many, apart from the consolations that religion may afford, the prospect of extinction, whether at 80, 90 or 100, is depressing, and we are drawn, maybe, for balm, towards such fields of exploration as planchette, telepathy, the leaping table. A major break-through on this psychic front—the eruption of something which might lend support to [Hamlet's] words that "There are more things in heaven and earth than" Science yet has countenanced or dreamed of—should hearten most of us and be immeasurably more important than any landing on the moon. Perhaps this is why, in my own case, I have been early given to the writing of novels and short stories which impinge upon the topic and are styled "Macabre."

John Metcalfe's work is unique among that of his British contemporaries. His expertise in creating an atmosphere of growing apprehension and unease, out of which some supernatural fear or horror takes definite shape, is unforgettable. All who appreciate the puzzling and enigmatic strangeness of his evocative prose will delight in rereading his work.

Selected Bibliography

WORKS OF JOHN METCALFE

The Smoking Leg, and Other Stories. London: Jarrolds, 1925. Garden City, N.Y.: Doubleday, Page, 1926.

Judas, and Other Stories. London: Constable, 1931.

Brenner's Boy. London: White Owl Press, 1932. (A limited signed edition of 125 copies containing a portion of the original manuscript, and a trade edition.)

The Feasting Dead. Sauk City, Wis.: Arkham House, 1954.

"The Firing-Chamber." In *Dark Mind, Dark Heart*, edited by August Derleth. Sauk City, Wis.: Arkham House, 1962.

"The Renegade." In *Over the Edge*, edited by August Derleth. Sauk City, Wis.: Arkham House, 1964.

"Not There." In *Travelers by Night*, edited by August Derleth. Sauk City, Wis.: Arkham House, 1967.

"'Beyondaril.'" In *Dark Things*, edited by August Derleth. Sauk City, Wis.: Arkham House, 1971.

CRITICAL AND BIOGRAPHICAL STUDIES

Callard, D. A. "Pretty Good for a Woman—A Quest for Evelyn Scott." *London Magazine*, 21, no. 7 (October 1981): 52–61.

Gawsworth, John. "In Memoriam: John Metcalfe." *Antigonish Review*, 1, no. 2 (Summer 1970): 73–75. (Followed by John Metcalfe's "Why I Write the 'Macabre'" and "The Nuisance": 76–78.)

O'Brien, Edward J. "John Metcalfe: An Intimate Study of the Author and His Work." *Argosy* (London), 16, no. 101 (October 1934): 19–20.

Sayers, Dorothy L. Introduction to *Great Short Stories of Detection, Mystery and Horror*, edited by Sayers. 2d ser. London: Gollancz, 1931.

Walpole, Sir Hugh, ed. *A Second Century of Creepy Stories*. London: Hutchinson, 1937.

—RICHARD DALBY

HOPE MIRRLEES

1887-1978

HOPE MIRRLEES IS one of those authors, like Margaret Mitchell or Austin Tappan Wright, whose reputation is based on one classic book. She lived to see *Lud-in-the-Mist* (1925) not just revived but revived to mass distribution and acclaim through Lin Carter's reprint of it in his popular Adult Fantasy series (Ballantine Books). *Lud-in-the-Mist* is a peak achievement of English fantasy, comparable with William Mayne's *Earthfasts* in emotional power and sense of the past, with J. R. R. Tolkien's *The Lord of the Rings* in nomenclature and sense of place, and with T. H. White's *The Once and Future King* in the charm of its language. Yet, for all its fantasy, it is grounded in the most British of qualities, common sense and respect for law. Jane Austen would never have written about Duke Aubrey and his cohorts of Fairyland, but if she had, the result might have been something very like this book.

Helen Hope Mirrlees was born in 1887, the daughter of a wealthy sugar merchant. The family name, common in East Anglia and Cambridgeshire, where the Mirrlees family lived, may be of Breton origin. Part of Mirrlees' childhood was spent in South Africa. Her elder sister Margot married into the landed Coker family in Oxfordshire, while her younger brother, William, was a professional soldier who ended his life a major general. Hope was educated partly at home by French governesses and partly at St. Leonard's School in St. Andrews, a boarding school. Then, like only a tiny minority of young women of her generation, she went to college—to Newnham College, Cambridge. There she studied under the great classical scholar Jane Ellen Harrison, thirty-seven years her senior, who was lecturer in classical archaeology at Newnham and a world-famous authority on ancient Greek religion. The middle-aged colleague of Gilbert Murray, Émile Durkheim, and Henri Bergson established a relationship with the young student that lasted twenty years, until Harrison's death in 1928. The Latinist F. M. Cornford wrote that Mirrlees, whom he called "a young novelist," gave Harrison "the devotion of an adopted daughter" (*Dictionary of National Biography*).

After the university Mirrlees began to write seriously. *Madeleine: One of Love's Jansenists* (1919) took several years to write and was accepted by Collins only after several other publishers had turned it down. It is a historical novel about a girl who wishes for the friendship of the famous bluestocking Madame de Scudéry, but whose adolescent egotism and clumsiness prevent her from being taken seriously. Virginia Woolf disliked the book but accepted Mirrlees' twenty-two-page *Paris, a Poem* (1919), which became the fifth book published by the Woolfs at the Hogarth Press. One hundred seventy-five copies were handprinted by Leonard and Virginia Woolf themselves, as were such influential works as T. S. Eliot's *Poems 1919. Paris* received a bad review from the *Times Literary Supplement* but was praised in the *Athenaeum*, which later published several of Mirrlees' literary essays.

Through letters and entries in Virginia Woolf's diaries one can get a dim glimpse of Mirrlees in the 1920's, "over-dressed, scented, extravagant," and, in Mrs. Woolf's opinion, "a spoilt prodigy" whose father gave her motor cars for her birthday. "I like her very much and think her very clever; but [she is] vain and lacking in self-confidence · · · and [has] greed, like the greed for almond paste, for fame." Mrs. Woolf came home from dinner with the Mirrlees family quite out of patience with the "vulgar," rich bourgeoisie. This opinion of the family was not shared by T. S. Eliot, who considered Mirrlees' mother and sister to be "really remarkable women" and Mirrlees herself his bosom friend. In fact, Eliot was given a temporary home by Mrs. Mirrlees during World War II, when he was driven from London by the blitz.

In the 1920's Mirrlees worked as well as lived with Jane Harrison; together they published two translations from Russian. *The Life of the Archpriest Avvakum by Himself* (1924) was their version of the first autobiography written in the Russian language, and *The Book of the Bear* (1926) was a collection of folk and literary tales about bears. Later scholars have criticized their version of the *Life* for inaccuracies and for not reflecting the colloquial vigor of Avvakum's language; nevertheless, it was the first English translation of this important work.

Mirrlees' last novel before *Lud-in-the-Mist, The Counterplot* (1924), was received favorably by several important critics. Raymond Mortimer said in the *New Statesman* (23 February 1924): "With *The Counterplot*, though [Mirrlees'] achievement is not yet comparable with that of Mr. E. M. Forster and Mrs. Woolf, she puts herself in their company." Gerald Gould, in the *Saturday Review* (1 March 1924), said that "a comparison with Aldous Huxley is inevitable," although he also criticized it for "that stupid vulgarity without which a book can nowadays scarcely hope to be accounted clever." He was evidently referring to the heroine's ruminations on sex.

A modern reader finds nothing vulgar in *The Counterplot*, which is a psychological study of a young woman torn between her Roman Catholic religion and her love for a young priest. Mirrlees was a Catholic convert, and *The Counterplot* may have been partly autobiographical. She seems to have converted to Catholicism after Harrison's death, for she spoke in a 1929 essay of "those of us who have had a Scottish nurse" as being brought up to detest popery, and in a poem, "The Rendez-Vous," of accepting Christ at an exhibition of Berthe Morisot's paintings.

Mirrlees' last novel was *Lud-in-the-Mist*, which Collins published in 1925. It received mostly favorable reviews. Mary Ross in the *New York Herald Tribune* (20 March 1927) wrote:

> Out of these themes [fairy tales, the Pied Piper, the despised Redeemer] Miss Mirrlees has woven a fugue so lovely that there is no need to ask its meaning. Yet its beauty, after all, is no surface decoration of pictures and cadences but the distillation of a rich knowledge of human beings.

L. P. Hartley, author of *The Go-Between*, wrote in a less friendly manner in the *Saturday Review* (18 December 1926): ". . . a fantasy which contains much that is poetic and significant, but more that seems confused, labored, and facetious."

The story of the book is quite simple, even though it puts on the mask of the detective story at one point. Lud-in-the-Mist is the capital of tiny Dorimare, a green land of villages watered by two rivers, the Dapple and the Dawl. The gift of the Dawl, agricultural wealth, is eagerly accepted by the folk of Dorimare; but the gift of the Dapple is fairy fruit, grown in Fairyland, across the Elfin Marches of the west. This fruit (with colors and tastes found in no other objects) is known to drive its eaters to melancholy, poetry, and similar madnesses, so that they run away to Fairyland and are never seen again. Since the revolution against the last ruler of Dorimare, the vanished hunchback Duke Aubrey, the great merchants have had everything their own way, and the Dapple's gift is forbidden by law. But the descendants of the revolutionaries are no longer the grim men of purpose who destroyed the decadent aristocrats, but complacent worthies, fond of jokes and of making speeches in their senate, whose most wearisome business is deciding who shall cater state banquets.

But their well-ordered world is not without its scandals, and one of the greatest occurs when Ranulph, the young son of the Mayor, Master Nathaniel Chanticleer, is found to have eaten fairy fruit. This event sets the plot in motion: for Master Nathaniel consults the foreign doctor, Endymion Leer, who prescribes a rest in the country for young Ranulph—at Swan-on-the-Dapple near the Elfin Marches, the farm of Leer's co-conspirator, the evil Widow Gibberty. In fact, it is Leer and the widow who are the chief importers of fairy fruit; Leer has been Duke Aubrey's missionary to Dorimare for thirty years and now engineers Ranulph's passage to Fairyland in order to disgrace the Mayor. But Master Nathaniel uses his sudden freedom from public office to solve the mystery of Farmer Gibberty's death thirty years ago, thus delivering his enemies into the hands of the law. Then Nathaniel, too, breaks the law: he goes alone to Fairyland to rescue his son. The former Mayor is the only Dorimarite who has ever loved his child enough to go there in search of him. And there he finds the unexpected: Duke Aubrey has already made him his initiate and his new deputy; for "there are many trees in my orchard, and many and various are the fruit they bear—music and dance and grief and, sometimes, joy. All your life, Chanticleer, you have eaten fairy fruit. . . ."

In *Lud-in-the-Mist* Mirrlees tells us that life is composed of both prose and poetry, and that death and life are merely aspects of the same thing. The past and the dead are present among the living, although they are often unseen and unfelt. The identity of the living fairies and the dead Dorimarites is emphasized at every turn; indeed, the country people of Dorimare are said to believe that people do not really die but are kidnapped by the fairies to labor in their fields of gillyflowers. The gallows (on which Endymion Leer and Widow Gibberty are hanged) is called "Duke Aubrey's wooden horse," and the cemetery is "the Fields of Grammary" (an old word for magic). A dead man's voice (Farmer Gibberty's) speaks to accuse Leer; a dead man's voice (Duke Aubrey's) converts Nathaniel from his opposition to all things fairy.

Mirrlees' treatment of the supernatural shows the influence of Jane Harrison, that great authority on myth. The fairies are the dead; the dead are not destroyed but transformed into supernatural creatures; the dead are the ancestors of the living. The living fear the fairies, except for the fey, who flee to live among the fairies as their slaves. And the prosy mercantile burghers who pride themselves on their solid common sense, who despise and loathe the very thought of Fairyland? They use the most astonishing oaths, like "By the Sun, Moon and Stars and the Golden Apples of the West!," little realizing that this (which they imagine is as meaningless as "Toasted Cheese!" or "By My Great-Aunt's Rump!") is the greatest oath of the fairies and Duke Aubrey's password. Dr. Leer asks them in his trial if they know how magical Dorimare is, for are not the hawthorn blooming, the sunset on the hayricks, as great miracles as any from Duke Aubrey's land?

Parallel to the equivalence of the past and the present, the quick and the dead, Mirrlees also equates poetry with law, showing them as fictions by which people live, and fantasies in which fruit may be defined as silk and men alive are considered dead. It is the law that Nathaniel uses to destroy Endymion Leer; it is the law that Nathaniel changes to ensure Duke Aubrey's triumph. When Ranulph Chanticleer grows up he becomes, not a man of law like his father, but the greatest of all Dorimarite poets, writing "songs that crossed the sea and were sung by lonely fishermen in the far North, and by indigo mothers crooning to their babies by the doors of their huts in the Cinnamon Isles."

Mirrlees' achievement in *Lud-in-the-Mist* was to create an entire world, costumed in the charming Jacobean fashion of seventeenth-century England but universal and timeless, showing life as the great dance of all aspects of being. The needs of the soul (religion, poetry, beauty) and the needs of the mind (law, logic, reason) are given equal reward and reconciled; neither triumphs alone, but both triumph together. Is it not, Mirrlees says, exactly in the most ordinary circumstances (for example, a party of laughing boys and girls dressing up in old-fashioned clothes) that one hears the blood-freezing "Note" of the music of Eternity? How poetic and noble, terrifying and incomprehensible is daily life; how mysteriously calm and ordinary are the fields of gilly-flowers. The book (like Tolkien's *Smith of Wootton Major*) owes to fairy lore its sense of lands "Beyond the Fields We Know," but unique to Mirrlees is the sense of the identity of those lands with our own.

After *Lud-in-the-Mist*, Mirrlees published three short literary essays in the *Nation and Athenaeum* but nothing else until 1962, when her lifework was published, *A Fly in Amber: being an extravagant biography of the romantic antiquary Sir Robert Bruce Cotton.* (This was the first volume; she intended, but never wrote, a second.) Four years after World War II she moved to South Africa and evidently stayed there for some time after 1962, but eventually returned to England and lived in Oxford.

In a biographical note on the jacket of *A Fly in Amber* Mirrlees said that Jane Harrison's friends had wished her to write Harrison's biography, but the research for that work had led her to write Cotton's instead. Harrison was an archaeologist in a day when archaeology was closer to philology, history, and the classics than it is now, and antiquaries like Cotton were the first archaeologists. So Mirrlees' research into the academic history of Harrison's lifework supplied the connection, which seems tenuous at first glance, between the life of a feminist, atheist, Victorian authority on Greek mythology, and the life of a Jacobean collector, legal scholar, and Parliamentarian. Mirrlees loved the seventeenth century; of her published works three are set in that era (the life of Avvakum, *Madeleine*, and *A Fly*), and *Lud-in-the-Mist* has a seventeenth-century atmosphere. She must have felt more confident tackling a life of that era than of her own.

Calling *A Fly in Amber* a biography is not strictly accurate; the first half of Cotton's life is merely the jumping-off point for a survey of the Elizabethan-Jacobean universe from every angle: literary, historical, political, economic, scientific, biographical, legal, and social. C. V. Wedgwood, writing in *History* (1962), found it unconventional but stimulating to the "relaxed reader." The book is, despite so many digressions that it begins to seem like nothing but a collection of digressions, a serious and scholarly treatment of the vanished Renaissance world that appears as Dorimare in *Lud-in-the-Mist*. The reader of fantasy will find new depth in the events and milieu of *Lud-in-the-Mist* when reading *A Fly in Amber*; each book reflects the other.

Mirrlees' last book, *Moods and Tensions: Poems*, was published by a small Oxford press in 1976. It contains about twenty poems, primarily on the themes of memory and religion, and is introduced by her lifelong friend the art critic Raymond Mortimer. It is interesting that the great themes of *Lud-in-the-Mist* and *A Fly in Amber*, namely, the intrusion of the past into the present and the identity of the past with the supernatural, are still present in these late poems. Consider this line, with its religious allusion, in the poem "Et in Arcadia Ego": "Spying on ghosts is my forbidden fruit." Master Nathaniel Chanticleer finds himself altering the present by spying on the past; while Sir Robert Cotton made his reputation as a politician through the exegesis of ancient law. At the end of her life Hope Mirrlees could truly say, as did her favorite historical character, Mary Queen of Scots, "In my end is my beginning." She died in 1978.

Selected Bibliography

WORKS OF HOPE MIRRLEES

Madeleine: One of Love's Jansenists. London: Collins, 1919.

Paris, a Poem. Richmond, England: Leonard and Virginia Woolf at the Hogarth Press, 1919. (175 copies printed by hand.)

The Counterplot. London: Collins, 1924.

The Life of the Archpriest Avvakum by Himself. Translated from the 17th-Century Russian by Jane Harrison and Hope Mirrlees. Richmond, England: Hogarth Press, 1924. Hamden, Conn.: Archon Books, 1963.

Lud-in-the-Mist. London: Collins, 1925. New York: Knopf, 1927.

The Book of the Bear, Being Twenty-one Tales Newly Translated from the Russian. Translated by Jane Harrison and Hope Mirrlees. Pictures by Ray Garnett. London: Nonesuch Press, 1926.

"Listening in to the Past." *Nation and Athenaeum*, 39 (11 September 1926): 670–671.

"The Religion of Women." *Nation and Athenaeum*, 41 (28 May 1927): 259–260.

"Gothic Dreams." *Nation and Athenaeum*, 42 (3 March 1928): 810–811.

A Fly in Amber: being an extravagant biography of the romantic antiquary Sir Robert Bruce Cotton. London: Faber and Faber, 1962.

Moods and Tensions: Poems. Introduction by Raymond Mortimer. Oxford: Amate Press, 1976.

CRITICAL AND BIOGRAPHICAL STUDIES

DuBos, Charles. "Introduction à *Le choc en retour* de Hope Mirrlees." *Approximations*, 4e série (1930). (An appreciative essay on *The Counterplot).*

Johnson, Reginald Brimley. *Some Contemporary Authors:* *Women.* London: Leonard Parsons, 1920. (Includes essay on Mirrlees.)

Matthews, T. S. *Great Tom: Notes Towards the Definition of T. S. Eliot.* New York: Harper and Row, 1973.

Sencourt, Robert. *T. S. Eliot, a Memoir.* Edited by Donald Adamson. New York: Dodd, Mead, 1971.

Travel and Leisure. "The Small Hotels of London" (February/March 1973).

Woolf, Virginia. *The Diary of Virginia Woolf.* Volume 2: *1920–1924.* Edited by Anne Olivier Bell, assisted by Andrew McNeillie. London: Hogarth Press, 1978.

————. *The Letters of Virginia Woolf.* Volume 3: *1923–1928.* Edited by Nigel Nicolson and Joanne Trautmann. New York: Harcourt Brace Jovanovich, 1977.

—DIANA WAGGONER

JOHN COWPER POWYS

1872-1963

T. F. POWYS

1875-1953

THE REVEREND CHARLES F. POWYS, vicar of Montacute in Somerset, had eleven children, six of whom were sons. Three of these sons became writers of note, and two of them are of some significance as writers of supernatural fiction. John Cowper Powys was the eldest child, born on 8 October 1872; Theodore Francis Powys was the third child, born on 20 December 1875. The Powys brothers numbered among their ancestors the poet William Cowper, and their family was remotely connected to that of John Donne, but none of the sons decided immediately upon a literary career. John became a teacher after taking his degree at Cambridge, and then went to the United States as a lecturer. Theodore did not bother with the university but tried instead to become a farmer in Dorset, with a conspicuous lack of success.

Both brothers obtained from their father a strong interest in matters of theology, but were drawn away from his orthodox piety (as were so many authors of imaginative fiction who were the sons of clergymen). Both were eventually to use fiction as a medium for constructing and displaying unorthodox theologies of their own.

Theodore's first venture into print was a privately published dialogue, *An Interpretation of Genesis* (1907). He apparently wrote similar interpretations of other biblical books for his own private purposes, but no others were published. By this time John had written his blank-verse narrative "Lucifer," a much more highly colored and consciously heretical work than his brother's, but it remained unpublished until 1956. In the poem Lucifer holds discourse with deities from several other religious traditions and then proceeeds to build his Cosmopolis.

The contrast between the content and style of these two works was to be retained throughout the careers of the two writers. Theodore remained a recluse, setting all his tales in an area of Dorset only a few miles across, presenting pictures of simple and unsentimental rural life where God wanders on and off stage in the enigmatic person of Tinker Jar, whose interventions in the bleak and quietly desperate human world are generally limited to bringing the blesssing of death. John cut a more colorful and extravagant path through life, and ranged in his fictions from hell to ancient Wales and outer space. His prose is decorated with stylistic embroideries and mythical presences, while the Manichaean and pantheistic substance of "Lucifer" was elaborated into a bizarre existential framework for novels in several different genres. (It is worth noting that the third writer brother, Llewelyn, was a rationalist and a dogmatic atheist; he wrote no supernatural fiction.)

John and Theodore both began to write novels during World War I. John published *Wood and Stone* in 1915 and *Rodmoor* in 1916, but there was then a long gap in his career until *Ducdame* in 1925. (His third novel, *After My Fashion*, languished unpublished for sixty years.) Theodore was even less successful initially. He wrote *Mr. Tasker's Gods* in 1916 and *Black Bryony* in 1917 but could not place them at the time, though he did manage to publish a book outlining his personal philosophy, *The Soliloquy of a Hermit*, in 1916. While John's career was languishing, however, Theodore's took off, and by the time John published his first really notable novel, *Wolf Solent*, in 1929, Theodore had become famous.

The unique world view of Theodore's fiction, which makes it so remarkable, is laid out with startling clarity (if not complete consistency) in *The Soliloquy of a Hermit*. It is a very detached point of view, which makes him careful to reserve judgment on people. He sees people's feelings as forces from without that take possession of them — "the moods of God," he calls them. He speaks frankly of his own uncontrollable moods of hopeless despair, all too rarely balanced by moments of preternatural contentment. He believes that every man harbors "something ugly in the dark of oneself," and looks to Christ with a truly fierce desire to be saved from that inner darkness; it is the role of Jesus to "stand in the way of the eternal moods," if only people will let him. Here, immortality is the ultimate horror, because it would be the perpetuation of this uneasy self-loathing; the greatest reward that God can offer men for lives lived well is the gift of cool oblivion. It is the bringing of this gift, to relieve appalling spiritual suffering, that climaxes a great many of his stories.

Theodore's first published book of fiction was a collection of three novellas, *The Left Leg* (1923). The title story is the first of his allegorical fantasies,

introducing the character of Mr. Jar. (The name is presumably derived from Jehovah, but Jar is as often Christ as he is God the Father.) As with the vast majority of Theodore's stories, "The Left Leg" is set in a small village close to Madder Hill. Jar has left the village, though rumors circulate that "something will happen" if he returns. In the meantime, the village is under the domination of the cruel and greedy Farmer Mew, whose crimes against his fellow men are clinically described. He contrives a murder and carries out a rape, each in the service of his mania for possession: he is equally unable to leave land and virgin girls outside his domain. He is on the point of possessing the village and its people totally when Jar — the one person he is afraid of, though he does not know why — returns to Madder. Mew tries to destroy Jar with gunpowder, but only succeeds in blowing himself up. The apocalyptic ending is, however, deliberately undercut by the striking last scene, in which Mad Tom Button finds Mew's left leg descending from the sky: a gift from Jar, for which he is properly grateful, but which he does not need as he continues to make his innocent and crazy way through life.

The stories in *The Left Leg* had been written between 1918 and 1921, and their success permitted the quick release of all the other works Theodore had stockpiled, which mingled with his newer works. The mood of the novels ranged from the dreadful bleakness of *Mr. Tasker's Gods* (1925) to the much gentler and more generous temper of his second major allegory, *Mockery Gap*, published the same year. In both novels the characters and their predicaments are similar: they are mostly innocents trapped in poverty and ignorance, victimized by the cruel and greedy men who contrive to get on in the world. In *Mr. Tasker's Gods*, though, there can be no release from suffering, while in *Mockery Gap* the good people can be relieved of their frustrations and anxieties through the agency of "the fisherman." The fisherman is a kindlier and more orthodox Christ figure than Jar in his Christly role; he never speaks but smiles a great deal and brings a gift of love that guides at least some of the characters away from danger and tragedy for a while. Theodore found it very hard, however, to maintain any real faith in the power of love; in his next novel, *Inno-*

610

cent Birds (1926), there is no cheerful redeemer and the plot focuses in harrowing fashion on the inability of the innocent and loving to withstand the cruel malice of those who would hurt and "possess" them.

The only one of Theodore's novels that remains constantly in print—it is regarded as his masterpiece—is Mr. Weston's Good Wine (1927). Here he gathers together the various threads in his work to solve the puzzle of the simultaneous existence in the world of dreadful cruelty and tender love, by inventing a God whose nature is such as to explain it. God here is not the furtive Tinker Jar but the amiable Mr. Weston, a wine salesman who comes to the village of Folly Down in his old car, accompanied by his assistant, Michael. While he is in the village, time stops so that existential accounts may be audited and settled.

Mr. Weston is not entirely suited to his godly role, which he seems to regard with less than total enthusiasm. He is certainly neither omnipotent nor omniscient; Michael has to remind him of the identities of the people of Folly Down and their standing as customers. He reveals that he rarely goes into churches, which are full of bad customers who expect to receive his wines free of charge. If Mr. Weston will seem to many a peculiar God, the villagers will seem an equally improbable array of human archetypes. The rector Nicholas Grobe refuses to believe in God, though he accepts Christ as an exemplary model for human conduct. His daughter Tamar is obsessed by the idea of making love to an angel. Thomas Bunce, landlord of the inn, asserts that all the world's sorrows and misfortunes are God's fault, while his daughter Jenny is in love with a hapless fool who preaches the Christian gospel to the birds and beasts because only they, in their innocence, can possibly have souls, as far as he can see. Bunce wants to sell his daughter more profitably than this, and in the meantime she is the target of a plot by the village's crabbed spinster, Jane Vosper, whose one delight is to procure the spoliation of the local maidens. Her agents in this scheme are the sons of the local squire, although she cunningly lays the blame on the church clerk, who is not displeased by these rumors of his exceptional virility.

Mr. Weston brings two wines to Folly Down. One is a light wine whose effect is exhilarating. The other is a dark vintage that brings the gift of oblivion. This dark wine is not death as such, but a special kind of death: a merciful granting of eternal peace. The plot shows us that there are other kinds of death: Jane Vosper's soul is dragged out of her, but Tamar Grobe dies of ecstasy when her strange dream comes true. What will happen to Jane Vosper is never made clear—and it remains permanently unclear in Theodore's work how the fate of those killed for their wickedness differs from that of those allowed release from their suffering. The devil is in the story—Mr. Weston carries him around in the back of his car, in the guise of a lion, and lets him out occasionally to throw a scare into people—but he seems to have no kingdom of his own and is even permitted to dissolve into his own oblivion in the end.

Like Mockery Gap, Mr. Weston's Good Wine is a reasonably gentle and generous allegory, where evil may be wiped out and love can triumph by means of small miracles like the one that lets Luke Bird pay Thomas Bunce's price for Jenny. There is no one in the novel like Farmer Mew—the squire is not a nice man, but he is no archetype of human evil. The ending is so very quiet that it can hardly be called apocalyptic, and it is undercut in much the same way that the conclusion of "The Left Leg" is undercut, reminding us that the day of judgment is now and forever and that life will nevertheless go on. It is not surprising that Mr. Weston's Good Wine proved to be the culmination of the first phase of Theodore's work, and for the next three years he concentrated on producing relatively unambitious short stories. Most of these stories are mundane, though some—like the early "The House with the Echo" (1922) and "I Came as a Bride" (1927)—are trivial stories of supernatural apparitions. It was not long, however, before he returned to the business of allegory.

Fables (1929; also known as No Painted Plumage) is a volume of eccentric surreal stories, each of which features a dialogue either between a man and some agent of nature ("John Pardy and the Waves" and "The Stone and Mr. Thomas," for example) or between nonhuman creatures and inanimate objects ("The Seaweed and the Cuckoo Clock" and "The Corpse and the Flea"). The dialogues are quirky and ironic, but combine to present the same sad and bleak commentary on the world as Theodore's other works. "Darkness and Nathaniel" is perhaps the best of his many stories singing the praises of merciful death. Only in connection with this volume does the possibility arise of an influence between Theodore and his elder brother. There is much in common between these stories and a small volume published in a limited edition by John in 1930, *The Owl, the Duck, and—Miss Rowe! Miss Rowe!*, which features an apartment in New York shared by various persons, human, divine, ghostly, and inanimate.

The stories in *The White Paternoster* (1930) show that Theodore's interest in the supernatural was again becoming prominent in his work, although here Christian mythology is utilized more straightforwardly. The best of these stories, which was also published separately as a booklet in the same year, is "Christ in the Cupboard," in which Jesus appears as a guest in a virtuous household, but is put away in the cupboard when his charity begins to threaten the growth of their wealth. When they finally let him out, having need of his saving grace, they find that he has changed into the devil.

Another small book published in 1930 is *The Key of the Field*, a novelette in which Jar features, uncharacteristically, as a squire whose beautiful garden can be glimpsed from an adjoining field. This field is initially let to a good man, but he is dispossessed by the machinations of his greedy neighbors. Their wickedness holds sway until Jar finds the good man reduced to desperation and welcomes him into his garden—via death, of course. Jar is a wandering tinker again in another novelette, *The Only Penitent* (1931), in which the vicar of Maids Madder opens a confessional that no one will visit, until Jar himself comes to confess the most terrible of sins:

> "I crucified my son. . . . 'Twas I who created every terror in the earth, the rack, the plague, all despair, all torment. I am the one who rips up the woman with child, every foul rape is mine act, all pain and all evil are created by me. Can you love me now?"

The vicar does not know quite how to react to this challenge, parrying the cry of pain with muttering of love and joy, but when Jar says that he casts men into a pit where "they become nothing" the confessor is glad to offer his forgiveness; it is the gift of death, not love, that is advanced here to reconcile man to God.

This same message is amplified in *Unclay* (1931), the longest of the allegorical novels, whose central character is Death. Death has been forced to take a holiday in the village of Dodder because he has mislaid the warrant instructing him to gather a few souls there. Jar is in the story, but he plays a minor role (as does the vicar to whom he confessed in *The Only Penitent*), intervening occasionally in a very small way to ameliorate some of the smaller sufferings of the characters. No one here can bring the kind of wholesale redemption that the fisherman brought to Mockery Gap. The axis of the plot is the determination of the miser James Dawe to sell his daughter Susie to the sadistic Farmer Mere.

Mere is foul enough to make his prototype, Mew, seem almost gentle by comparison. Theodore's preoccupation with the monstrousness of rape (which seems unhealthy to some of his critics) achieves its most powerful expression in the scene in which Mere "takes possession" of Susie, with her father's connivance, before the planned wedding. At this point the reader must begin to yearn for the moment when the innocent youth who loves Susie in a proper fashion will release the parchment he has found, entitling Death to gather in their two souls. In the abrupt climax Death is indeed released, to send Susie and her lover to a common grave, and to scythe down Mere and Dawe as well.

Unclay was Theodore's last novel, but his prolific period ended as it had begun with a collection of three novellas. As *The Left Leg* began with a tale of Tinker Jar returning after a long absence, so *The Two Thieves* (1932) concludes with one. The title story of this volume is the story of George Douse, who sees a man step out of a cloud on Madder Hill and steals from him four bottles labeled Greed, Pride, Anger, and Cruelty. He drinks down their contents swiftly, pleasing their erstwhile owner—the devil—who regrets that men in the modern age rarely drink as heartily as of old, and tend to water his spirits down. He warns Douse, though, about another thief who might yet steal back from him what he has stolen: Tinker Jar.

Douse becomes a paradigm of evil, more expansive even than Mere. He uses treachery to marry an innocent young woman so that he can dispossess her father and win a perfect victim for his sadism. He becomes a rich and powerful man, using and abusing his fellow men as he will, and subjecting his wife to the most appalling mental and physical torture, until the day when Jar returns and steals from him all four of his motive forces, leaving him nothing. As with *Unclay*, the ending is not exactly comforting: Douse hangs himself from the same tree that his wife's innocent onetime lover had used; there seems no difference in their destinies to justify the different ways that fate has treated them. The author observes at one point that "success always belongs to the Devil, failure to God," and is reiterating in the story the harsh moral of *The Only Penitent*, that God can be forgiven in spite of this simply because he sets a term to the extension of suffering by ordaining inevitable extinction. There are few Christians who would be ready to accept such a hard lesson, and it is not surprising that these later stories have been allowed to fall into their own oblivion, in spite of all their power and artistry.

After *The Two Thieves* Theodore continued to publish short stories for a few years. Four more collections of his stories were issued, but three reprinted or recombined earlier work. Only a handful of new stories appeared after the publication of *Captain Patch* in 1935 as Theodore put an end to his literary career and left it behind him. He lived quietly until his death on 27 November 1953, and his son records that these last years were the happiest of his life. Apparently, the moods of God no longer troubled him as they flowed through him.

In 1932, the same year that Theodore published *The Two Thieves*, John produced *A Glastonbury Romance*, the first of his novels in which the supernatural plays an important part. It is difficult to imagine a greater contrast than there is between the clinical allegory of rural life and the sprawling, vast, and ornate novel of ideas, but like all contrasts this conceals some significant common points. John, like Theodore, brings the supernatural into the everyday world as if it were a constant and unsurprising part of it. Apparitions of the dead and visions of the Holy Grail may be of great personal significance for those who experience them, but they are not anomalous irruptions into the world so much as focal points of meaning within it. There is something shared, too, in the ideas about human nature that the two brothers held. John, no less than Theodore, was preoccupied with his own dark moods and perverse impulses, unable conscientiously to disown them but equally at a loss to explain them. These dark moods and perverse desires are caricatured in John's characters as they are in Theodore's, but while Theodore remained scrupulously detached, never inserting himself into his creations, John tended to people his books with avatars of himself. In *A Glastonbury Romance* John Crow's uncertain and perverse love for his wife, Mary, is his; Sam Dekker's crisis of faith, which carries him away from his father the vicar, is also his; John Geard's sensations of supernatural power and mission are his too; and so is the unholy fascination with sadistic pornography that the Welsh antiquary Owen Evans cannot exorcise from his soul.

What places the two brothers poles apart, in literary terms, is a matter of method rather than concern. Whereas Theodore always wrote with simple directness, often with a deadpan mock-naïveté, John cultivated a striking, often coruscating style:

At the striking of noon on a certain fifth of March, there occurred within a causal radius of Brandon railway-station and yet beyond the deepest pools of emptiness between the uttermost stellar systems one of those infinitesimal ripples in the creative silence of the First Cause which always occur when an exceptional stir of heightened consciousness agitates any living organism in this astronomical universe. Something passed at that moment, a wave, a motion, a vibration, too tenuous to be called spiritual, between the soul of a particular human being who was emerging from a third-class carriage of the twelve-nineteen train from London and the divine-diabolic soul of the First Cause of all life.

This is the opening paragraph of *A Glastonbury Romance*, and similar references back to the cosmic context recur throughout the story. If a character prays we are told which of many deities intercepts the prayer, and whether it is the good or evil part of creation that makes fateful response. Here the First Cause is a combination of primal good and primal evil, in vaguely Manichaean fashion, but there are many other godlings, including the sun and (most importantly in human terms) the earth mother Cybele. It is with a strange hymn to her that the book ends, and the grail mythology that provides a frame for the story relates the Christian grail to a supposed pagan grail of the Druids, linked to her worship.

A Glastonbury Romance was the first of three long contemporary novels that constitute a distinct phase in John's career. The other two are *Weymouth Sands* (1934; also known as *Jobber Skald*), which is probably his best novel, and *Maiden Castle* (1936). The supernatural plays no role in the second, and only a subdued role in the third, though aspects of the same world view are clearly evident in all three. Between the first and last of these novels he also produced three nonfiction books: *A Philosophy of Solitude* (1933), *Autobiography* (1934), and *The Art of Happiness* (1935), all of which are essentially works of self-analysis. The middle volume has an almost painful intimacy and frankness concerning the darker side of the author's feelings and impulses.

Maiden Castle was quickly followed by *Morwyn* (1937), a novel of a very different kind that is isolated between two phases of John's career, although it foreshadows the out-and-out fantasies of his last years. It is called by its author a "novel against vivisection," but it is concerned not so much with the plight of experimental animals as with the evil of human addiction to inflicting pain. The narrator, together with the girl Morwyn (Welsh for "maiden") and his dog Black Peter, is thrust into the Underworld by a meteor strike that kills Morwyn's father, a "vivisector." They enter a hell that is the creation of its inhabitants—sadists all—who have transformed a sector of Elysium with their vile passions.

The Marquis de Sade becomes the visitors' guide, helping them to flee from Torquemada and the vivisector, who have designs on Morwyn and Black Peter. In the hope of escape they seek out Taliesin, the only man to venture into hell of his own free will; with him they discover Merlin, who sleeps with Cronos and other forgotten deities in the navel of the universe. There they witness the retrial of the titan Tityos, condemned long ago to be perpetually devoured by vultures as a punishment for attempted rape. He is now liberated on appeal, on the grounds that his was a "natural" crime far less heinous than those committed in the names of religion and science by the likes of the makers of hell. Sexual passion is thus granted a seal of approval, although the narrator's lust for Morwyn comes to nothing when she decides to pursue a separate destiny. (It appears that he is being punished for the tendency to cruelty that lurks within him.)

The metaphysical claim embedded in *Morwyn* is that the System-of-Things (a new version of the First Cause) has ordained that there shall be in human affairs a gradual evolution of pity and sympathy, which will eventually save mankind from torment but which is being blocked by science as it was once blocked by perverted religion. The moral is blurred, however, by the more enigmatic digressions into arcane mythological mystery, which attempt to bind together Welsh, Greek, and other varieties of myth into a syncretic system.

Morwyn was followed by a new phase in John's career, when he published very much less but devoted his main effort to the production of two massive historical novels set in ancient Wales. *Owen Glendower* (1940) has little supernatural content, though there is a prophetess and a certain amount of magic-working in the plot. There is also, of course, the customary undercurrent of mysticism and the usual veneration of nature, but here the author is much more restrained in offering his own commentary on events than in most of his works. The second of the historical novels, *Porius* (1951), is much more ambitious and enigmatic. It is probable that John never put as much work into any other of his novels, and he still had to cut and rewrite his own final version to the instructions of a publisher. Although almost as long as its predecessor, it has not the same strong story line, and is hardly concerned with events at all.

The book is named for a soldier-hero, but the real central character of *Porius* is Myrddin Wyllt—the Merlin of legend—who is both symbol of and spokesman for the primitive in man, attuned to nature and worshiping the earth mother. Only near the end of the novel does this Merlin perform an overt act of magic, but he is throughout the very embodiment of magic and "true" religion, around whom the pattern of history is gathered as a hard-bitten Arthur tries to hold back the invading Saxons to delay the downfall of Wales. The legacy of the Roman occupation has already faded away, and fading with it is another "legacy" — that of the "forest people" who were peaceful worshipers of the earth mother before any of the militaristic devastators came to take their land.

Porius was, in a sense, the climax of John's career: the last of his earnestly serious novels. It was followed, typically enough, by a new productive phase in which John elected to amuse himself. By this time, he was in his eightieth year. He produced one more historical fantasy, *The Brazen Head* (1956), based on the frequently quoted legend that Roger Bacon (or, sometimes, Albertus Magnus) built a magical head of brass to speak oracles, but missed his chance to learn what secrets it possessed because a novice set to watch over it failed to wake him at the propitious moment. In John's version Bacon and the great Albert are working together, on the same side as Saint Bonaventura, while opposed to them is the self-styled anti-Christ and soldier of fortune Peter Peregrinus. There is also a giant in the plot — John was fascinated by the symbolism of giants throughout his last years.

Between *Porius* and *The Brazen Head* John published two other novels. *The Inmates* (1952) is a curious story in which the inhabitants of a lunatic asylum rebel against their captors and eventually escape, with the aid of an Eastern mystic, in a giant helicopter. Although much that is in the book is not to be taken seriously, there is a sensitive treatment of the love affair between the hero, John Hush, and the lovely Tenna Sheer, and the author seems earnest enough in applauding the courage of those who have forsaken dreary sanity. It was followed by *Atlantis* (1954), which is also half-frivolous and half-serious, and deserves consideration as the last of John's philosophical novels.

Atlantis is a slow-moving but imaginatively adventurous account of the last voyage of the aging Odysseus, which takes the hero beyond the Pillars of Herakles to visit sunken Atlantis and America. Greek mythology is here represented in its own right rather than as a minor item in a syncretic the-ology (though the customary assumptions are still here); this seems to induce a change of tone, making the novel lighter and brighter than the other philosophical extravaganzas. A kind of riotous animism gives personalities even to inanimate objects, which take part in the constant debates that are interrupted periodically by episodes of stirring action. This venture into the Homeric world was followed up by an eccentric version of the *Iliad*, *Homer and the Aether* (1959), which is notable primarily for its peculiar introduction, "The Aether Speaks," in which the author attempts to superimpose his own world view upon Homer's.

John's last works of fiction were the two novellas in the volume *Up and Out* (1957) and the novel *All or Nothing* (1960). All three tales are exotic fantasies. In "Up and Out" the world explodes and four survivors — including a monster called Org and his inamorata, Asm — float through the cosmos, encountering personifications of time and eternity, debating with a few philosophers, and receiving dubious enlightenment from various deities. "The Mountains of the Moon: A Lunar Love Story" is a more focused and orderly work in which the moon is inhabited by the astral bodies of earthly dreamers, which have intuitive knowledge of metaphysical truths.

All or Nothing is a rambling story in which the young John o'Dreams and his sister Jilly Tewky embark upon a series of space adventures with various odd companions. They enjoy some remarkably strange encounters, and meet several giants. Philosophical notions jostle one another in a wild compendium of symbolic representations, but it is difficult to see in the novel anything other than an exercise in senile prolixity. On the other hand, it might be argued that the retreat into ideative chaos is merely an extension of a trend that can be seen in slow development throughout the author's career.

John Cowper Powys outlived his younger brother by ten years, dying on 17 June 1963. Although Theodore established a considerable reputation during the 1920's, being hailed by the influential literary magazine *Scrutiny* as one of the leading writers of the day (along with D. H. Lawrence and James Joyce), it is John's work that is better known now and that receives more critical attention. It is dubious whether this turnaround is warranted, and it may well represent a transient whim of fashion. Various biographies of the brothers show John to have had the more colorful and extraordinary character, and his fascinating *Autobiography* constantly tempts critics to the complicated task of unraveling the psychological threads tangled in his work. Theodore is often seen nowadays as a writer overly narrow in his concerns; time has blotted out the rural landscape in which he tried to see and display the whole human condition. In a way, he was too successful in retreating from civilization, and too honest in saying "no more" once he realized that he had said all he needed to. *Mr. Weston's Good Wine*, though, remains the finest allegorical novel written in this century, and John wrote nothing that can compare with it.

As eccentric theologians the Powys brothers invite comparison with David Lindsay, C. S. Lewis, and Charles Williams, but in fact all these writers produced very different work. This kind of fantasy provides so much scope that there is no real need for any one writer of it to resemble another very closely, even if the other is the writer's sibling. Now that God no longer exists, there are an infinite number of ways to invent him.

Selected Bibliography

WORKS OF JOHN COWPER POWYS

The Owl, the Duck, and—Miss Rowe! Miss Rowe! Chicago: Black Archer Press, 1930. London: Village Press, 1975.

A Glastonbury Romance. New York: Simon and Schuster, 1932. London: John Lane, 1933.

Maiden Castle. New York: Simon and Schuster, 1936. London: Cassell, 1937.

Morwyn; or, The Vengeance of God. London: Cassell, 1937. New York: Arno, 1976.

Porius: A Romance of the Dark Ages. London: Macdonald, 1951. New York: Philosophical Library, 1952.

Atlantis. London: Macdonald, 1954.

The Brazen Head. London: Macdonald, 1956.

Up and Out. London: Macdonald, 1957.

All or Nothing. London: Macdonald, 1960.

WORKS OF T. F. POWYS

The Left Leg. London: Chatto and Windus, 1923. New York: Knopf, 1923.

Mockery Gap. London: Chatto and Windus, 1925. New York: Knopf, 1925.

Mr. Weston's Good Wine. London: Chatto and Windus, 1927. New York: Viking, 1928.

Fables. London: Chatto and Windus, 1929. New York: Viking, 1929.

The Key of the Field. London: William Jackson, 1930.

The White Paternoster and Other Stories. London: Chatto and Windus, 1930. New York: Viking, 1931.

The Only Penitent. London: Chatto and Windus, 1931.

Unclay. London: Chatto and Windus, 1931. New York: Viking, 1932.

The Two Thieves. London: Chatto and Windus, 1932. New York: Viking, 1933.

Bottle's Path and Other Stories. London: Chatto and Windus, 1946.

God's Eyes A-Twinkle. London: Chatto and Windus, 1947.

CRITICAL AND BIOGRAPHICAL STUDIES

Brebner, John A. *The Demon Within: A Study of John Cowper Powys's Novels.* London: Macdonald, 1973.

Cavaliero, Glen. *John Cowper Powys: Novelist.* Oxford: Clarendon Press, 1973.

Coombes, Henry. *T. F. Powys.* London: Barrie and Rockliff, 1960.

Graves, Richard Perceval. *The Brothers Powys.* London: Routledge and Kegan Paul, 1983.

Hopkins, Kenneth. *The Powys Brothers: A Biographical Appreciation.* London: Phoenix House, 1967.

Humfrey, Belinda, ed. *Essays on John Cowper Powys.* Cardiff: University of Wales Press, 1972.

Hunter, William. *The Novels and Stories of T. F. Powys.* Cambridge: Gordon Fraser, 1930.

Knight, G. Wilson. *The Saturnian Quest: A Chart of the Prose Works of John Cowper Powys.* London: Methuen, 1964.

Powys, John Cowper. *Autobiography.* London: John Lane, 1934. New York: Simon and Schuster, 1934. Revised edition, London: Macdonald, 1967.

Ward, Richard Heron. *The Powys Brothers.* London: John Lane, 1935.

— BRIAN M. STABLEFORD

H. RUSSELL WAKEFIELD

1888-1964

LIKE HIS MORE talented and more famous predecessor M. R. James, Wakefield was English and produced several volumes of ghost stories without ever attempting a novel in the subgenre of supernatural fiction. The supernatural ghost story has always been recognized as a very English form of writing: by Englishmen, for Englishmen, and set in England. It has always been more restrained, subtler, more limited in scope, and less nasty than the horror story. Wakefield was a fairly typical exponent of the ghost story, although his contribution to the field tends to have been underrated.

Herbert Russell Wakefield was born in Kent on 9 May 1888, the son of the one-time bishop of Birmingham. He was educated at Marlborough College and at Oxford University, achieving a second-class honors degree in modern history. For a short while at the end of World War I he was secretary to Viscount Northcliffe. Between 1920 and 1930 he worked as a publisher (it was toward the end of the 1920's that he began to write ghost stories), and later he was a civil servant. His writing was mainly a part-time occupation. He produced about seventy-five supernatural stories, four nonsupernatural mystery novels, two nonfiction criminology studies, and some television plays. He lived in London for most of his life and died there in August 1964.

In its simplest and purest form the ghost story has only two basic plots. One is that a person carries out a premeditated murder and is afterward haunted — often to death — by the victim's ghost. The other is that, because a person or persons have been murdered there in the past, a particular place becomes haunted by the ghosts of those victims and is therefore unpleasant, or even dangerous, for any later occupants or passersby, even though they may have no connection whatsoever with the murderer. In other words, ghosts may be specific as to the person or the place they haunt. Wakefield employed one or the other of these themes in almost all his stories. Despite limiting himself in that way, and despite the comparative brevity of his stories (mostly they range between 3,000 and 5,000 words each, allowing little enough room for any complexities of plot), he succeeded in producing many original and gripping variations.

The recently dead returning to take revenge on their murderers was a clichéd theme even before Wakefield came to use it. By skillful handling he was able to base quite a lot of stories on it. The best of these, and one of his most memorable pieces of writing, is "Damp Sheets" *(Ghost Stories)*. Having squandered most of his money, Robert Stacey needs a loan from his rich old Uncle Samuel (whose money will come to Robert eventually, anyway). Robert and his wife, Agatha, invite Uncle Samuel to stay with them for the weekend.

Without Robert's knowledge, Agatha makes sure that the sheets on Uncle Samuel's bed are damp. The uncle catches a chill and dies, realizing Agatha's guilt in his dying moments. Robert and Agatha are quickly installed in Uncle Samuel's mansion, and all their financial worries are solved. But Agatha sees Uncle Samuel's ghost, and one day when she goes into the linen cupboard some piles of sheets fall on top of her, become tangled, and stifle her.

In one of Wakefield's deft changes of scene the last details of the story are given briefly in the coroner's court. The maid who found Agatha's body says that all the sheets in that linen cupboard were damp. The coroner asks what difference that makes, and the reader is able to nod wisely, acknowledging both the ironic humor of Uncle Samuel's ghost and the justice of the situation. In addition, the characters of Robert (weak and dissolute), Agatha (hard and cunning), and Uncle Samuel (crotchety but still perceptive) are well developed. It is a notably succinct story, only 3,000 words long, with every word made to count.

It is often the characters that make Wakefield's stories so memorable. In an interesting variation on the same theme, "Unrehearsed" *(Old Man's Beard)*, he deals with a vile actor-manager, Duncan Littlemore, who takes what he wants from people before casting them aside. Littlemore's final act of nastiness is to steal a good idea from a playwright who had sent him a play to read. The playwright, Arthur Wells, cannot prove plagiarism in court and, despairing of justice, shoots himself in Littlemore's dressing room. (This is a weak but necessary part of the plot.) Then the ghost of Wells kills Littlemore on the first night of the "stolen" play.

In both "Damp Sheets" and "Unrehearsed" the reader's sympathies are most definitely with the ghost. By contrast, in "That Dieth Not" *(They Return at Evening)*, the murderer, Sir Arthur Paradown, is the sympathetic character. His wife, Ethel, whom he murders, is an unpleasant social climber who married only for money and a title and who richly deserves her fate. (Perhaps the fact that Sir Arthur narrates the tale means that he appears better and his wife worse than would otherwise be the case.) Nevertheless, Wakefield keeps to the traditions of the ghost story, so Sir Arthur has to be driven to suicide by his wife's ghost. Moreover, Sir Arthur had been living in sin with another woman in Paris before he killed his wife, and the moral standards of the 1920's, when the story was written, would not have allowed such behavior to go unpun-

ished. This is one of Wakefield's longer stories—more than 10,000 words long—and is particularly well told.

Another example of an unusual variation on this theme is "And He Shall Sing . . ." *(They Return at Evening)*. Like several others of the author's stories, it is set in a publisher's office, and it concerns a book of poems submitted by a Japanese gentleman, Mr. Kato. By means of subtle hints the publisher (Mr. Cheltenham) and the reader discover that the book has been written by another Japanese, whom Mr. Kato has murdered. Not surprisingly, the ghost of the murdered man rises up to kill Mr. Kato on the day of publication.

The second major theme to be found in Wakefield's work is of the place haunted by ghosts of people murdered there, sometimes centuries before. Such a place is most often a house, though it may be just one room or an exterior location—a wood, a hill, a stretch of road. The essence of this theme is that anybody who enters that haunted place may suffer, or even die, particularly on the anniversary of the murder, so that later generations are at risk, even though neither they nor their ancestors have any connection with the murderer. Wakefield does not advance any means of satisfying or banishing such ghosts—all his stories of this type advocate leaving alone such haunted places.

Most memorable of this category is "The Frontier Guards" *(Imagine a Man in a Box)*, little more than 2,000 words in length. The place here is Pailton, "a charming little house" from the outside but haunted by a vicious ghost who has caused a string of deaths among tenants and, in one case, a burglar. Willy Lander, a writer, lives close by and knows something of Pailton's recent victims but not who the ghost might be or why it kills. His friend and guest, Jim Brinton, expresses an interest in seeing the inside of the house and, rather suprisingly, Lander readily agrees. They go after dark, and it is obvious to the reader that something very unpleasant is going to happen to them. What makes the story a classic is the subtle way in which the ending is handled, presenting a feeling of great menace without actually describing anything.

The subject of the author's first story, "The Red Lodge" *(They Return at Evening)*, is a less deadly haunted house. Based on his personal experience, it is less polished yet more enthusiastically written. The narrator and his wife and six-year-old son (and the servants) find unaccountable slimy footprints appearing from time to time in the big house that the family has rented for three months, and they see strange things, including a "green monkey." Although there are cases of deaths or suicides among previous tenants, this family escapes safely. From the local squire the narrator hears that an early-eighteenth-century owner of the Red Lodge forced his wife to drown herself and later committed suicide.

In the excellent "Mr. Ash's Studio" (*Ghost Stories*) the haunted house is an artist's studio. In "Ingredient X" (*The Clock Strikes Twelve*), it is just a room in a lodging house. In "Lucky's Grove" (*The Clock Strikes Twelve*), it is a grove of trees, haunted by pagan gods. In "Jay Walkers" (*The Clock Strikes Twelve*), it is a stretch of country road in Herefordshire, where people tend to be killed at a particular time on a particular day each year. Although a few stories cover the same ground (for example, "Into Outer Darkness" [*The Clock Strikes Twelve*] is very reminiscent of "The Frontier Guards" [*Imagine a Man in a Box*] but less polished), Wakefield's imagination enabled him to find exciting variations on this theme.

All of Wakefield's stories are intended as separate pieces, with no connection between them. Even so, the perceptive reader will notice a series of four stories in which a ghost hunter, Sir Anstruther Sawbridge, appears, and a fifth story in which he is mentioned. Yet there is no cult of personality here as there is, for example, in Algernon Blackwood's stories of Dr. John Silence, psychic detective. Only internal references to other stories in the series make it clear that Sir Anstruther Sawbridge is the unnamed narrator of two of them.

"The Third Coach" (*They Return at Evening*), "The Central Figure" (*Imagine a Man in a Box*), and "In Collaboration" (*The Clock Strikes Twelve*) all consist of strange documents written by mental patients that are shown to Sir Anstruther Sawbridge by Dr. Landon ("a distinguished alienist, and passionately absorbed in the study of insanity"). All three stories are unusual and gripping, involving psychic experiences, yet none of them is in accord with the patients' histories as known to Dr. Landon. "The Third Coach" is a wonderfully cynical tale of a rascally confidence trickster who, having had a vision of a train crash in which the third coach of the train is totally smashed, manages to persuade his wife (who is blackmailing him) to ride in that coach. However, the writer of the document is a mild-mannered curate. "The Central Figure," one of Wakefield's most intense stories, is narrated by a schizophrenic young playwright who has written a play on the eternal triangle theme. He himself takes the part of the man hopelessly in love with a woman who has no affection for him, and the play gradually becomes reality for the three actors rehearsing it. "In Collaboration" is a plagiarism fantasy. Two struggling young authors are sharing an apartment; one has a very good idea, which the other steals, writes into a book, and makes a fortune out of. The successful author is forced to receive mentally and write down the pitiful autobiography of his former friend, who is now on the point of starvation.

In "Jay Walkers" (*The Clock Strikes Twelve*) Sir Anstruther Sawbridge is an active participant. He notices a small newspaper filler about a haunted stretch of road in Herefordshire on which fatal accidents occur almost every year at the same time on the same date, and he cannot resist going there to investigate. At length he discovers that a murder was planned and put into motion there in 1888, when a young man, walking his fiancée home and feeding her berries picked from the hedgerow, deliberately gave her a few berries of deadly nightshade. The girl died that night, and it is obviously her ghost that haunts that section of road, causing cars to crash on each anniversary of her death. Sir Anstruther Sawbridge is also mentioned in the story "Happy Ending?" (*The Clock Strikes Twelve*), though he does not appear in it.

In describing Wakefield's more typical stories there is the danger of omitting some of his very best and most original tales, simply because they do not fit into any pattern of classification. A fine story of a peculiar psychic experience is "An Echo" (*They Return at Evening*), in which a famous clairvoyant, out bird watching, "sees" a murder of fifteen years before. In fact, it was a very mysterious killing, with the prime suspect, a beautiful young woman, being acquitted in court, mainly because the murder weapon, a pistol, was never found. Part of the psychic vision, though, suggests that the woman was guilty and hid the pistol in a hole in a nearby tree. The clairvoyant and a criminologist friend recover the pistol.

Much different from the author's normal ghost stories are a couple of excellent horror tales. "He Cometh and He Passeth By!" *(They Return at Evening)* is, at 15,000 words, exceptionally long for Wakefield; and it demonstrates that he was often a better writer at greater lengths, when there was room to present a fully convincing background, to build up characters, and to provide a plot with some complexities to it. "He Cometh and He Passeth By!" may be thought of as Wakefield's Aleister Crowley story, since the character of Oscar Clinton is obviously based on that of the real-life satanist. Its plot is largely a restatement of M. R. James's famous story "Casting the Runes."

Briefly, a barrister named Edward Bellamy tries to save a friend, Philip Franton, from the black magic curse of Clinton. He fails, then is determined to avenge Franton's death by killing Clinton. To do this he takes a short course in Oriental magic and mysticism from a convenient friend, and he deliberately makes Clinton's acquaintance. Clinton is presented as an intensely evil character—dissolute, sadistic, and a habitual user of illegal drugs. It is obvious that Bellamy will gain Clinton's confidence and use his own black magic to kill him, though the slow buildup is well handled.

Less predictable and equally unusual is "The First Sheaf" *(The Clock Strikes Twelve)*, the story of pagan harvest rituals, including human sacrifice, surviving in Essex as late as perhaps the 1870's and 1880's. The narrator is a middle-aged man looking back to the time when he was thirteen and his father had just become vicar of a small rural parish. There is local opposition to their presence, not just because they are outsiders but also because they are Christians. It is a first-rate, slightly gruesome horror story that is entirely out of character for Wakefield but that might have been written by August Derleth a decade or so later.

Over his writing career of about thirty-five years Wakefield's style and subject matter changed, though not dramatically; it is not possible to divide his output into neat, chronological compartments. His early stories, such as "The Red Lodge" and "The Third Coach," show him to have been competent from the start. Later stories, especially those written after 1946, display a greater vividness of characterization and a better eye for detail, on the whole. Also, these later stories are, in general, more overtly horrific and more sexually permissive; perhaps this is only a reflection of the age in which they were written. Their plots tend to become a little more complex, involving more characters, though this varied considerably and depended very much upon story length (his post-1946 stories are not, on average, any longer or shorter than earlier ones).

Typical of the later stories is "The Triumph of Death" *(Strayers from Sheol)*, written in 1949. In theme it is yet another haunted house situation, but by intention it is a horror story rather than a ghost story. Amelia is the middle-aged companion of the elderly and psychologically sadistic Miss Pendleham. Three of Amelia's predecessors have died, quite possibly of fright, and two others have "escaped quickly, declaring Miss Pendleham was a devil and the house hell." The house is full of dreadful things that Miss Pendleham professes not to hear or see but that give her a secret delight because they represent the ghoulish misdeeds of her ancestors. The local rector and his wife try to help Amelia but are too ineffectual and too late. It is not the sort of story that the author would have written twenty years earlier.

One of Wakefield's last stories (1964) is "The Last Meeting of Two Old Friends" *(Over the Edge)*, an amplification of "The Sepulchre of Jasper Sarasen" *(Strayers from Sheol)* from ten years earlier. Both deal with men who become too curious about tombs in local graveyards and die as a result. The tone in each case is more horrific than is to be found in any of Wakefield's pre-1946 stories.

Perhaps the strangest of Wakefield's later stories is "The Gorge of the Churels" *(Strayers from Sheol)*, from 1951. Set in India, presumably in the last days of British rule, it is full of ironic humor. Humor of any sort is virtually absent from Wakefield's stories, and so this very sharp form of it, which almost approaches black comedy, is unexpected. An English clergyman recently arrived in India, the Reverend Prinkle, delights in poking fun at the superstitious beliefs of the Indians, causing great (but concealed) anger to his Indian clerk, Mr. Sen. In his know-it-all fashion Prinkle completely disregards the clerk's advice and takes his wife and ten-year-old son to the Gorge of the Churels for a picnic. The Churels are women who have died in childbirth and whose spirits lie in wait near that gorge to steal any children who go there. The boy is almost captured, but Mr. Sen manages to swallow both his anger and his Christian beliefs long enough to save him — helped by a Bengali amulet that he carries secretly. The boy is unhurt and his parents never realize the danger.

As the stories described show, Wakefield almost always wrote from an upper-middle-class point of view. His characters are frequently lawyers, publishers, stockbrokers, or those living on large private incomes or investments. Some are baronets or peers; many live in mansions surrounded by large estates; all have servants. Although the servants appear in Wakefield's stories, it is noticeable that they do not play major roles. He adopts a condescending attitude toward them; he recognizes their presence and even their usefulness but feels it would lower the tone of his stories were they to voice anything more than the occasional "Yes, sir." Of course, during the late 1920's, when Wakefield began writing his ghost stories, many English households did have a servant or two, but they gradually become fewer and since 1945 have been almost nonexistent except in the richest families.

If Wakefield's stories are condescending toward servants they are downright rude toward the nouveaux riches. This attitude is displayed most overtly in "Look Up There!" and "The Dune" (both stories are in *Old Man's Beard*). (In the latter work the author spends half a page criticizing everything that his nouveau riche protagonist represents.)

It is not necessary for all of Wakefield's upper-middle-class characters to be rich. Some, indeed, are financially embarrassed; others are writers who have never had much money. This does not seem to matter so long as they have good family connections or have been to the right university.

One of the pastimes of the upper middle class that is mentioned frequently in Wakefield's stories is golf. He himself played regularly from his days at Oxford University onward, and many of his protagonists are regular players. "The 17th Hole at Duncaster" *(They Return at Evening)* is set on a golf course, where unpleasant things happen to people who are close to the new seventeenth green or in the wood behind it, especially after dark. Two other stories that revolve around golf are "A Peg on Which to Hang" *(They Return at Evening)* and "The Alley" *(The Clock Strikes Twelve)*, though in both cases it is the golfers' overnight accommodation that is haunted, rather than the courses on which they play.

A key to understanding Wakefield is provided by the fact that he believed in the supernatural. He never wrote a story that he did not feel could happen, and several of his tales were sparked off by supernatural experiences of his own or related to him by friends. Fortunately, his belief did not involve facile explanations or theories. Nor was he trying to convert readers to his views; his stories are equally enjoyable whether or not one believes in ghosts. A statement of Wakefield's beliefs on the subject is included in "Why I Write Ghost Stories," his introduction to the collection *The Clock Strikes Twelve* (1946 edition).

Wakefield was not the best or most important writer of English ghost stories — nor has he been imitated to any extent by more recent writers. Yet the best of his stories are very good indeed. If he had been more adventurous in his supernatural fiction — either covering a greater range of themes or producing a supernatural novel — he might be much more widely known today.

Selected Bibliography

WORKS OF H. RUSSELL WAKEFIELD

They Return at Evening. London: Philip Allan, 1928. New York: Appleton, 1928.
Old Man's Beard. London: Geoffrey Bles, 1929. As *Others Who Returned.* New York: Appleton, 1929.
Imagine a Man in a Box. London: Philip Allan, 1931. New York: Appleton, 1931.

Ghost Stories. London: Cape, 1932. (Reprints from the first three volumes, with four new stories.)

A Ghostly Company. London: Cape, 1935. (Reprints from the first three volumes, with two new stories.)

The Clock Strikes Twelve. London: Jenkins, 1940. Sauk City, Wis.: Arkham House, 1946. (The Arkham House edition contains four more stories than the Jenkins edition. These are taken from *Ghost Stories* and *A Ghostly Company*.)

Strayers from Sheol. Sauk City, Wis.: Arkham House, 1961.

"The Last Meeting of Two Old Friends." In *Over the Edge*, edited by August Derleth. Sauk City, Wis.: Arkham House, 1964.

—CHRIS MORGAN

DENNIS WHEATLEY

1897-1977

DENNIS WHEATLEY'S REPUTATION today rests largely on his occult novels, while most of his other works, primarily espionage thrillers and historical adventures, are ignored. Yet, by his own count, Wheatley wrote only nine occult novels or, as he labeled them, "Black Magic stories," less than a fifth of his total fictional output and about half of the books that can be fitted into the category of the supernatural.

There are several reasons for this critical imbalance. The extreme topicality of the espionage novels has dated them badly and, lacking the psychological and political sophistication of a John Le Carré or the comic-strip color and vitality of an Ian Fleming, Wheatley's spy thrillers have simply been supplanted by better books. The best of the occult novels, however, despite strong doses of political rhetoric, are not so dependent upon their historical and social contexts. Moreover, Wheatley was a writer of very uneven gifts. Although none of his books is without flaws, the Black Magic novels utilize the best of his talents and minimize his characteristic defects. Thus, despite the flood of horror stories in recent years, Wheatley's special brand of occult novel remains distinctive, original, and provocative.

At the same time, it would be a mistake to treat the occult novels as completely separate from Wheatley's other works. Although he referred to his Black Magic stories as belonging to a special category, he did not separate them from his other writings. He saw no problem in shifting his characters back and forth between a completely realistic world of political violence and machination or historical adventure and a supernatural one filled with diabolical forces, magic, and otherworldly confrontations. Thus, his series protagonists—Duke de Richleau, Gregory Sallust, Roger Brook—all face supernatural menaces in a few of their books, while directing their energies against purely human evil in the others. This easy movement between genres makes Wheatley a more difficult writer for the critic to pin down, but it is the primary factor in understanding his most important contribution to supernatural fiction, his synthesis of the intrigue novel and the horror story.

Despite Wheatley's large output, he did not begin writing fiction until his mid-thirties, and although always a well-read, cultured individual, he gave little indication in his prewriting days that he would someday be one of England's most versatile and prolific popular writers.

Born in London on 8 January 1897, Dennis Yeats Wheatley was the son and grandson of Mayfair wine merchants. He was a cadet on the HMS *Worcester* from 1909 to 1912, then spent a year in Germany studying winemaking. In September 1914, at the age of seventeen, he was commissioned in the army, then served in combat until gassed at the French front and invalided out of the service. From 1919 until 1931 he worked in the family wine business, which he inherited upon his father's death in 1926. Although Wheatley and Son would boast having had three kings, twenty-one princes, and many millionaires among its customers, it encountered severe difficulties during the Depression and had to be sold. Thus, in his mid-thirties, Wheatley found himself unemployed, except for a modest consulting position, untrained for anything but the wine business, and, although hardly reduced to penury, in relatively strained circumstances. It was at this point that he turned to writing. "Why don't you write a book?" his wife, Joan, suggested. "I'm sure you could." And then, if the account in his autobiography *Drink and Ink* (1979) is to be believed, he achieved instant commercial success with almost ridiculous ease. His first published novel, *The Forbidden Territory*, appeared in 1933 and launched Wheatley as a best-selling author.

The Forbidden Territory is a political thriller vaguely suggested by *The Three Musketeers*. Three friends, the French Royalist exile and epicurean Duke de Richleau, the Jewish financier Simon Aron, and the aristocratic Englishman Richard Eaton, journey to Stalinist Russia to rescue a fourth friend, the rich American Rex Van Ryn. Wheatley went on to write eleven novels featuring this foursome, three of which fit into the Black Magic category. The most important of these, and by general consent the best of Wheatley's novels, is *The Devil Rides Out* (1935).

Although the three novels between *The Forbidden Territory* and *The Devil Rides Out* all contain elements of the supernatural, it was probably not Wheatley's taste for the fantastic that led him into occult fiction so much as his calculation of its market possibilities. As he said in *Drink and Ink*:

> . . . I tried very hard to think of a subject for a book that would hit another high spot. It then occurred to me that, although in Victorian times there had been a great vogue for stories of the occult, in the present century there had been very few; so I decided to use the theme of Black Magic.
>
> (page 131)

Yet, at least in part, that may be a rationalization. Wheatley had a lifetime flirtation with the occult. Flirtation is the correct word, because, although he studied it assiduously and wrote about it at length

(most notably in his nonfiction treatise, *The Devil: And All His Works*, 1971), he never embraced it.

All the Black Magic novels contain short warnings to the reader, such as the one that prefaces *The Devil Rides Out:*

> Should any of my readers incline to a serious study of the subject, and thus come into contact with a man or woman of Power, I feel that it is only right to urge them, most strongly, to refrain from being drawn into the practice of the Secret Art in any way. My own observations have led me to an absolute conviction that to do so would bring them into dangers of a very real and concrete nature.

These prefatory admonitions are not commercial ploys; they are sincere warnings. To the day of his death Wheatley believed quite honestly and intensely that the devil does ride out, although his conception of the devil was complicated, ambiguous, and changeable.

To provide himself with the requisite background for occult books, Wheatley sought out knowledgeable individuals, notably Aleister Crowley, the most notorious "Black Magician" of the twentieth century; the Reverend Montague Summers, an eccentric cleric and historian of occult practices and literatures; and Rollo Ahmed, an Egyptian mystic and personal friend who could — safely — provide him with insights into the Secret Art. More important, Wheatley read most receptively everything he could find on the subject. He was an efficient, thorough, and perceptive researcher, with a knack for finding the most relevant, vivid details, whether the subject was the fine points of a black mass or the details of court life under Charles II. And nowhere is this capacity for detail more evident than in *The Devil Rides Out.*

The story line of the novel is simple and direct. The Duke de Richleau and Rex Van Ryn become concerned over the odd behavior of their friend Simon Aron, who has apparently fallen under the influence of the mysterious, sinister Damien Mocata. Once the duke determines that Satanism is involved, he and Rex kidnap Simon from Mocata's clutches, only to see him quickly retaken by the wizardry of the black magician. They subsequently learn that Simon is the key to Mocata's securing the "Talisman of Set," the mummified phallus of the god Osiris, who had been treacherously murdered and subsequently dismembered by his brother, Set. With this awesomely powerful charm in his possession, Mocata would be able to control the "Four Horsemen of the Apocalypse — War, Plague, Famine, and Death."

Striving now to save humanity as well as their friend, the two men make a second, more spectacular assault on the satanists in the midst of a sabbat and, with luck, daring, and surprise, succeed in getting Simon back into their hands. This successful attack unleashes the full fury of Mocata and his group, of course. The three retreat to the estate of their fourth friend, Richard Eaton, where they fend off the dark forces from within a protective pentacle. Their victory is short-lived, however, when Mocata kidnaps the Eatons' young daughter, Fleur, demanding Simon's return for the child's life. A wild chase to Paris follows, culminating in a confrontation with Mocata only moments before he is to sacrifice Fleur to Satan.

The climax has a Lord of Light intervening through Marie Lou, Fleur's mother, to stop Mocata and turn his own demonic forces against him. This last sequence, we subsequently learn, took place on the astral plane, but the results are real: Fleur is safe, Simon is cured, Mocata is dead, and the Talisman of Set is in the duke's hands, where he can destroy it at once.

In *The Devil Rides Out* Wheatley established the formula for the occult novel that he used in all the de Richleau books and, in varying degrees, in most of the Black Magic stories. De Richleau and his crew become aware of a serious satanic threat to a friend and/or humanity. They act against the threat and achieve a modest victory but, in doing so, alert the forces of darkness to retaliation. These aroused forces of evil then pursue and assault them in a seemingly uneven battle until, ultimately, good rallies and triumphs — usually quite suddenly — because of courage, resourcefulness, luck, and, frequently, divine intervention.

The Devil Rides Out is the best of Wheatley's novels for a number of reasons. The plotting is clear, direct, and logical. The heroes are capable and heroic, the villain is colorful and grotesque. The pacing is fast and well modulated. Given the novel's premises, the situations are believable and the climax, although it involves a deus ex machina, is foreshadowed and satisfying. And the occult material, which makes up so much of the fabric of the novel, is central to the plot and smoothly integrated into the action.

The novel is a veritable catalog of supernatural lore: satanism, black masses, demonic possession, magical incantations, the conjuring up of demons, necromancy, hypnotism, clairvoyance, numerology, palmistry, astrology, ghostly apparitions, enchanted pentacles, astral travel, curses, crystal-ball gazing, sex orgies, child sacrifice, time manipulation, and more — yet it all fits into the story without being unduly intrusive. Wheatley integrates his supernatural elements carefully into a solid, realistic milieu at those moments in the story when they fit most easily into the narrative flow. By doing so he creates a world in which the laws of black and white magic operate naturally and inevitably; the unseen becomes a palpable presence. From the point when de Richleau first postulates a supernatural explanation for his friend's errant behavior, there is a tension created in the atmosphere, a constant feeling of otherworldly menaces that steadily intensifies as the book progresses, reinforced by the continuing introduction of significant details.

This feeling of supernatural power and menace culminates in the book's major dramatic confrontations. Wheatley's most impressive ability, in both his realistic and his fantastic writing, is his capacity to create dramatic scenes that are exciting visually and viscerally. It is here that his skillful use of sharp, relevant details is most impressive. This can be seen even in such a minor scene as the one in which Marie Lou bars Mocata from the Eaton household by adroitly avoiding traps that would put her under his control. The scene generates considerable mounting tension in spite of its casual surface because of the verbal precision and suggestiveness of the dialogue, the characters' appropriate physical gestures, and the significance of the crucial details— a box of candy, a glass of water—as they become weapons in a very deadly duel of wills.

On a larger scale, this fusion of character, action, and detail gives the novel's two major confrontations—the assault by the duke and Rex on the sabbat, which results in Simon's release, and the comrades' defense of mind and soul against Mocata's demonic siege from within their precarious, magical pentacle—a sustained power that Wheatley was never quite able to match again. In no other book does he prove so emphatically that realistic detail is the key to making the fantastic believable—an artistic truth that, unfortunately, he did not always remember.

At the conclusion of *The Devil Rides Out*, Duke de Richleau expresses the hope that by destroying the Talisman of Set, he is barring the door against the Four Horsemen of the Apocalypse and averting World War II. Alas, as Wheatley and the rest of the world were soon to learn, the door had already been irrevocably opened. The forces that led to World War II, the war itself, and its repercussions, especially the cold war, were to dominate Wheatley's fiction for the remainder of his career.

This can be seen in *Strange Conflict* (1941), the occult sequel to *The Devil Rides Out*. And if the latter illustrates the black magic novel at its best, *Strange Conflict* demonstrates the worst. This novel is an uneasy, frequently chaotic mixture of adventure, espionage, occultism, patriotic zeal, and social moralizing.

In the early months of the war the Nazis have been able to damage British supply lines severely because of their unaccountably accurate knowledge of the shipping routes. Since the government's defenses have been completely unsuccessful, Duke de Richleau suggests that black magic is involved. Given unofficial permission to pursue his ideas, de Richleau investigates via the astral plane and learns that the Nazis have secured the services of a Haitian adept to do their spying.

The duke and his comrades—Simon Aron, Rex Van Ryn, and Richard and Marie Lou Eaton—journey to Haiti to confront their adversary. When their boat is stranded some miles from the coast, they are rescued by Dr. Saturday, a handsome, sophisticated

black doctor who turns out to be the villain. They fall under his power and are almost turned into zombies. However, de Richleau does battle with Saturday on the astral plane and defeats him. Like Mocata, Saturday is finally destroyed by a force—in this case the god Pan—that he has released but cannot control. Maddened by the sight of Pan, Saturday rushes off a cliff and is smashed on the rocks below:

> De Richleau hovered there until the spirit came forth from the mangled body. It was now quiet and submissive, with no more fight left in it. Since it had already been defeated on the astral, there was no need to take advantage of the momentary black-out which succeeds death to seize and chain it. Humbly it opened its arms wide and bowed its head in token of surrender. At the Duke's call two Guardians of the Light appeared and as they led the captive away a triumphant fanfare of trumpets filled the air.
>
> (chapter 22)

This quotation, a prime example of Wheatley's prose at its worst, pinpoints the most serious flaw in the book: a vague, sentimental mysticism that largely replaces the realistic occultism of *The Devil Rides Out*. The power of the earlier novel was produced largely by Wheatley's meticulous detailing of occult rituals and paraphernalia to create a frighteningly solid milieu. On the other hand, his abstract, generalized vision of life on the astral plane, where much of the later novel's action takes place, seems contrived and self-indulgent. Without the anchor of a realistic setting, Wheatley's flights into the fantastic lose most of their power and urgency.

Moreover, the book's loose structure lends itself to Wheatley's most damaging tendency, his heavy-handed introduction of "ideas"—political, historical, social, racial, moral, metaphysical, and theological—into the text, wherever they may or may not be appropriate. The social, political, and racial convictions, which were reactionary even in his own time, are positively offensive today, while the metaphysical and philosophical ones might be interesting if presented with some subtlety and indirection. But the quality of the ideas is not so annoying as their humorless intensity and their continual, pompous repetition.

And, as noted above, *Strange Conflict* also brings out the worst in Wheatley's prose. When telling his stories directly, dramatizing his characters in action, or describing relevant, vivid details, Wheatley handles the language adequately; but set free to describe life on the astral plane, or to deliver moralistic diatribes, or to indulge in generalized metaphysical speculation, it can be awful, a kind of late-blooming pseudo-Victorian prose, heavy on abstraction, ornate in diction and syntax, and glutted with sentimental clichés.

Shortly after the publication of *Strange Conflict*, Wheatley became directly involved in the strategic planning of the war, an experience that undoubtedly colored his writings even as it diverted most of his energies away from fiction. Initially rejected from all the services because of his age (he was forty-two), he began writing and submitting papers on home defense to the government. This eventually led to a commission on the Joint Planning Staff as a wing commander. (Wheatley's career as a strategic planner is chronicled in the last volume of his autobiography, *The Deception Planners*, 1980.)

His experiences are reflected in the best fusion of the occult and espionage genres in a story dealing with World War II, *They Used Dark Forces* (1964). This novel was the sixth and last in Wheatley's fictionalized history of the war via the exploits of Gregory Sallust, a dashing if suspiciously amoral hero based on Gordon Eric Gordon-Tombe, Wheatley's dashing, amoral boyhood chum. The series traces the career of Sallust from September 1939 through May 1945, using real events and historical figures as a background for the hero's adventures. *They Used Dark Forces*, the only one of the series that includes any occult material, is probably the best of the set and second only to *The Devil Rides Out* among the Black Magic stories, although the supernaturalism is considerably muted. *They Used Dark Forces* is also unique in that the black magic is used on the side of good, rather than evil.

This novel turns on the strange alliance formed between Sallust and Ibrahim Malacou, a Jewish black magician, who agrees to use his talents against Hitler in the interests of his own personal safety and of his persecuted brethren. Although both skeptical and wary of black magic, Sallust accepts Malacou's

help. Together they destroy the Nazi V-2 factory at Peenemünde, steal the German rocket plans, survive and secure release from a concentration camp, and gain access to the German high command. Finally, with the help of Malacou's clairvoyant talents, Sallust becomes occult adviser to Hitler himself and is, perhaps, instrumental in the führer's decision to commit suicide.

They Used Dark Forces is a fast-paced, absorbing book in which real events, such as the V-2 attacks on London, the Allied invasion, and the attempt on Hitler's life, are blended with fictional escapades and crises to create an adventure story. Wheatley's portrait of the Nazi high command in the midst of final collapse is memorable; and some of the individual portraits are quite vivid, especially that of the shattered, psychotic, drug-wracked, but still charismatic and obsessed Adolf Hitler. (Readers may bridle a bit, however, at the portrayal of Hermann Göring as a fine, courageous fellow, with excellent taste in food and art, whose only fault was to choose bad company.)

After the end of World War II Wheatley quickly seized upon the most important development in its aftermath, the cold war, in his fiction, and his blend of the spy thriller and occult novel was well suited to the topic. That the cold war was such an inviting subject for Wheatley is not surprising. From his first novel, *Forbidden Territory*, to his last, *Desperate Measures* (1974), Wheatley nurtured an almost obsessive hatred of communism and all such "revolutionary" movements. Even the Nazis at their worst never stimulated quite the vituperation that Wheatley heaped on communists and radicals. All the post–World War II Black Magic novels postulate an unholy alliance between the devil and communism or some like movement. This is demonstrated in two related spy thriller–Black Magic novels—*To the Devil—a Daughter* (1953) and *The Satanist* (1960). In the former, a black magician attempts to use a human sacrifice to create an army of homunculi for the communists; in the latter a satanist–mad scientist attempts to provoke World War III with a stolen atomic bomb.

The Satanist, the more interesting of the two, is one of the best examples of the thriller–Black Magic novel synthesis. The book breaks neatly in two: the first part is an occult mystery, as the hero and heroine infiltrate a satanic cult to investigate the murder of a government agent; the second part develops quickly into a pure spy thriller, almost a comic-strip "mad scientist in his mountain retreat trying to blow up the world" scenario.

What separates *The Satanist* from similar books is the character of its heroine, Mary Morden. She is a tough, honest, courageous, street-wise woman who even worked for a short time as a prostitute before marrying the murdered agent and who, late in the book, positively enjoys the sexual attentions of one of the book's villains. Mary may be the most sexually active "good girl" in the popular fiction of Wheatley's day and, as such, demonstrates an interesting quirk in his thinking. Despite his reactionary attitudes toward social class, politics, culture, and race, Wheatley had a surprisingly contemporary, "liberal"—if inconsistent—view of women and sexuality. He would place all sorts of restrictions on all sorts of "inferior" people, but a double standard in sexual conduct was not one of them.

In addition to the Black Magic novel, Wheatley explored one other fantasy category with some success, the "lost world" narrative. His first venture into this area was *The Fabulous Valley* (1934), followed by *They Found Atlantis* (1936), *Uncharted Seas* (1938), and *The Man Who Missed the War* (1945). The last three volumes were later collected in a single triple volume, *Worlds Far from Here* (1952). *The Fabulous Valley* is simply a bad mix of adventure novel and travelogue; but the other three are interesting, and the best of them, *They Found Atlantis*, is a well-structured novel of considerable charm and interest.

All three books have the same loose narrative structure. In each novel the main characters, either by choice or by necessity, embark on a journey to an unknown destination and discover a lost world. The trip takes up roughly the first half of each novel; their adventures in the strange new world and their escape from it make up the second half. (The characters' "escape," though, in *The Man Who Missed the War* is spiritual rather than physical. Actually they die heroically in an act that wins the war for the Allies and then immediately soar into space to view triumphantly the Allied victory.)

Uncharted Seas is most memorable for the scenes in which a group of shipwreck survivors do battle with horrifying creatures—giant squid, huge crabs—that emerge from the weed-gutted sea. It is reminiscent of William Hope Hodgson's maritime horror stories. *The Man Who Missed the War* is a disorganized, implausible, but generally entertaining book that is interesting as the fictional celebration of one of Wheatley's pet strategic ideas, the use of huge raft convoys to transport supplies to and from Great Britain as a way of neutralizing German submarines and airplanes. There is no indication that the government ever took Wheatley's notion seriously, but he was sufficiently dedicated to it to make it the subject of the novel.

The first half of *They Found Atlantis* is a suspense mystery in which an expedition in search of Atlantis is part of an elaborate ruse to steal the fortune of a beautiful duchess. The plot is foiled, but the duchess and her entourage are sent to the ocean bottom in a diving bell, where, after a harrowing encounter with semihuman creatures resembling H. G. Wells's Morlocks, they do indeed find Atlantis. It is an idyllic world made up of six men and six women, all physically and mentally perfect, who are able to absorb all human knowledge and survey all human activity via astral travel. The outsiders are provisionally admitted into the Atlantean society, but, less perfect than their hosts and hostesses, they allow evil into Atlantis, an offense punishable by exile. Although apparently doomed, they are guided to the surface by an Atlantean women, who has fallen in love with one of the party.

They Found Atlantis is a clever, well-developed narrative in which the suspense mystery of the first half is skillfully balanced with the fantastic Atlantis episodes, the characters are nicely set off against each other, and the imaginative world of Atlantis is rendered with detail, color, and imagination. *They Found Atlantis* does not deserve the obscurity into which it has fallen.

Wheatley's production declined gradually during his last years, although he was active until the end. His last Black Magic novel, *Gateway to Hell*, was published in 1970; his nonfiction history of the occult, *The Devil: And All His Works*, came out in 1971; and his last work of fiction, *Desperate Mea-*

sures, appeared in 1974. His final years were spent writing his memoirs, which were posthumously published. Wheatley died on 10 November 1977.

Dennis Wheatley was a master storyteller, with a solid grasp of narrative structure and pacing, an ability to create scenes of considerable power and immediacy, and a mastery of significant detail. As long as he confined himself to storytelling, the results were at the least entertaining and, at the most, memorable. But when the story became a vehicle for his ideas — social ideology, metaphysical speculation, sentimental mysticism, personal gripe — the novels collapsed. Unfortunately, these defects probably damage or ruin the bulk of his writing. There are, however, enough examples of Wheatley at his best to ensure him a permanent place among writers of dark fantasy.

Selected Bibliography

SUPERNATURAL FICTION BY DENNIS WHEATLEY

Such Power Is Dangerous. London: Hutchinson, 1933.

Black August. London: Hutchinson, 1934. New York: Dutton, 1934.

The Fabulous Valley. London: Hutchinson, 1934.

The Devil Rides Out. London: Hutchinson, 1935. New York: Bantam, 1967.

They Found Atlantis. London: Hutchinson, 1936. Philadelphia: Lippincott, 1936.

The Secret War. London: Hutchinson, 1937.

Uncharted Seas. London: Hutchinson, 1938.

Sixty Days to Live. London: Hutchinson, 1939.

Strange Conflict. London: Hutchinson, 1941. New York: Ballantine, 1972.

Gunmen, Gallants and Ghosts. London: Hutchinson, 1943. (Short stories, six of which deal with the supernatural.)

The Man Who Missed the War. London: Hutchinson, 1945.

The Haunting of Toby Jugg. London: Hutchinson, 1948. New York: Ballantine, 1972.

Star of Ill-Omen. London: Hutchinson, 1952.

Worlds Far from Here. London: Hutchinson, 1952. (A triple volume that includes *They Found Atlantis, Uncharted Seas,* and *The Man Who Missed the War.*)

To the Devil—a Daughter. London: Hutchinson, 1953. New York: Bantam, 1968.

The Ka of Gifford Hillary. London: Hutchinson, 1956. New York: Bantam, 1969.

The Satanist. London: Hutchinson, 1960. New York: Bantam, 1967.

They Used Dark Forces. London: Hutchinson, 1964.

The White Witch of the South Seas. London: Hutchinson, 1968.

Gateway to Hell. London: Hutchinson, 1970. New York: Ballantine, 1973.

NONFICTION

The Devil: And All His Works. London: Hutchinson, 1971. New York: American Heritage Press, 1971.

AUTOBIOGRAPHY

The Time Has Come . . . : The Memoirs of Dennis Wheatley. London: Hutchinson. Vol. 1. *The Young Man Said, 1897-1914* (1977). Vol. 2. *Officer and Temporary Gentleman, 1914-1919* (1978). Vol. 3. *Drink and Ink, 1919-1977* (1979). Vol. 4. *The Deception Planners: My Secret War* (1980). (All volumes are lively and interesting, but only Vol. 3, *Drink and Ink,* deals with Wheatley's writing career.)

CRITICAL AND BIOGRAPHICAL STUDIES

Barclay, Glen St. John. "The Devil and Dennis Wheatley." In *Anatomy of Horror: The Masters of Occult Fiction.* New York: St. Martin, 1978, 111–125.

Eckley, Grace. "The Devil Rides Out." In *The Survey of Modern Fantasy Literature,* edited by Frank N. Magill. Englewood Cliffs, N.J.: Salem Press, 1983, 383–386.

Heffelfinger, Charles. "To the Devil—A Daughter." In *The Survey of Modern Fantasy Literature,* 1954-1957.

Neilson, Keith. "The Haunting of Toby Jugg." In *The Survey of Modern Fantasy Literature,* 715–717.

———. "The Satanist." In *The Survey of Modern Fantasy Literature,* 1358–1362.

BIBLIOGRAPHY

Hedman, Iwan, and Alexandersson, Jan. *Fyra Decennier med Dennis Wheatley. En biografi & bibliografi.* Strängnäs, Sweden: DAST Forlag, 1973. (Thorough bibliography, with additional material. British first editions are collated in English.)

—KEITH NEILSON

CHARLES WILLIAMS

1886-1945

CHARLES WALTER STANSBY WILLIAMS, born on 20 September 1886 to Walter and Mary Williams, lived in London most of his life. As a youth he attended St. Albans School and University College until the money, always tight, ran out. He started work at Oxford University Press in 1908 as a proofreader, and remained there the rest of his life, taking his love of books and accuracy up the ladder to become an editor. Noted for his stimulating conversation and saintly air, he was also a prolific and challenging writer of unquestioned devoutness. When World War II took the press to Oxford, he was welcomed to C. S. Lewis' literary salon, the "Inklings," and the university gave him an honorary M.A. and a place on the English faculty. He died in Oxford on 15 May 1945.

Williams did not regard his "occult fantasy" novels as his most important works, but their unique combination of theology and sensationalism keeps them in print and read. While he has never had the large audience of fellow "Inklings" Lewis and J. R. R. Tolkien, devoted readers in his lifetime included such Anglican literati as Dorothy Sayers, T. S. Eliot, and W. H. Auden. The subject of several American doctoral dissertations, usually Christian-oriented, his writings cause critics either to fawn over him or to froth at the mouth. More objective criticism is harder to find, but Alice Mary Hadfield's recent biography and Glen Cavaliero's study of the

works ably supplement Mary McDermott Shideler's examination of his theology; Thomas T. Howard's recent book on the novels, however, seems to be a step backward from Robert Wilson Peckham's dissertation.

Always comfortable in the Church of England, Williams seems never to have experienced even a youthful revolt against religion. In an outwardly uneventful life, though, his faith was apparently tested by love relationships. In 1908, he met Florence Conway, whose laughter at his declamations of poetry earned her the biblical nickname Michal, after King David's wife, who laughed at the dancing before the Ark of the Covenant. Extended because of finances, their nine-year courtship was his first major test, as evinced by the emphasis on renunciation in *The Silver Stair*, his 1912 sonnet sequence for her. Despite his devotion, marriage and family (their son Michael was born in 1922) were not as expected and competed for time with his work. Another test, even less anticipated, was his unthinkable (and unconsummated) infatuation with fellow employee Phyllis Jones ("Celia," "Phillida," and "Chloe" in his writings).

Oppressed by the poverty of his parents and his own meager if secure income, Williams supplemented his earnings with adult evening-class lectures on poetry, enthusing about its relevance to life and quoting long passages from memory. He also offered his sacramental vision in writing in a dozen genres.

A longtime lover of medieval things, Williams saw the quest for the Grail as fundamental to Christianity as well as to the Arthurian legends. It suffuses his later poetry and his unfinished last book, *The Figure of Arthur* (1948). Explicit in one novel, the Grail is present symbolically in other objects of talismanic power subject to misuse. An equally important source was Dante, although Williams' own allegorical vision preceded his Dantean studies. *The Figure of Beatrice* (1943) praises romantic love as an intimation and embodiment of the love of God.

As these titles suggest, images of human love unite life, literature, and religion in Williams' "theology of romantic love." In it he recognized two traditional approaches to "Omnipotence" (his preferred nonsexist term for the Divine). Rejecting the mystical Way of the Rejection of Images (that is, seeking direct communication without intermediaries), he took as a writer the sensuous Way of the Affirmation of Images. Images that he especially affirmed include the Grail, Beatricean women, and "the City."

Unlike those who see God in country landscapes and Satan in the City, Williams envisioned London as the ideal human community, with elements of the Logres of King Arthur and the City of God of St. Augustine. With its masses of people whose cooperation—intentional or not—is needed in order for it to exist, "the City" (seldom more specifically named) is for him the proper locale in which to embody Christian doctrines of exchange, substitution, and "co-inherence." While everyone in a society "exchanges" goods and services, by sharing others' burdens we imitate the supreme "substitution" of Christ's death for every man. Belonging to each other, we create real civilization in the form of an idealized City. This city, then, is a model of "co-inherence," a mystical state of total interrelationship, overriding divisions of mind and body, intellect and plastic imagination, past and present, living and dead, which are ultimately artificial in the divine order of things.

Those who will not recognize the co-inherence selfishly refuse others or strive for power over them. Such was the goal of W. B. Yeats and other members of A. E. Waite's Order of the Golden Dawn, which Williams joined for a time (1917–1922). He seems to have had no interest in active participation in magic, a practice that he thoroughly condemned in *Witchcraft* (1941). Its attraction to others, however, permeates his novels, like the occult symbols and talismans that he may owe to the order.

The concerns that animated Williams' conversations permeate his writings, from early masques performed at Oxford University Press to lay theology and church history tests, from potboiling biographies and book reviews to morality plays and difficult modernist poetry on Arthurian themes. In every genre, he tried, not always successfully, to embody his positions in appropriate literary forms, rather than simply to argue his case. This was also true for the novels, which were not just a commercial diversion. As Lawrence R. Dawson, Jr., has shown, Williams read and reviewed mysteries and thrillers with enjoyment. In his own fiction, he sought, like Eliot in his plays, to reach the souls of a popular audience; only the surface was sensational.

The stories are complicated, but the plot details are relatively unimportant. All seven books deal with the invasion of contemporary society by occult forces, with characters lining up in the war between good and evil based on their attitudes toward the occult power. Poetic justice operates as in Dante: each person acts out in life the reward or punishment that he determines for himself after death. With the outcome foreordained in the eyes of God, the suspense is in how—not whether—good wins out. This makes for an accepting, even joyful, attitude toward pain and death and for a comic rather than tragic vision, well served by such literary forms as romance and masque. The formal spectacle of the masque is especially relevant to Williams' often static portrayal of the human, as well as divine, comedy of modern life.

As usual in romance (even more so in masque), his characters are types, with a few distinguishing features. Villains, always selfish, may be self-contained, refusing to acknowledge the co-inherence, or they may attempt to manipulate others and occult objects for their own ends. Largely stereotypes, they include scientists, publishers, historians, and a high proportion of foreigners. Jews, who as a group refuse the light of Christ, twice fill the role of villain; but so do Gypsies, Persians, and Greeks. Williams' virtuous characters are better realized. Not all of a kind, they may be found at various stages along the path of righteousness, from recent awakening (there seems always to be a chance of this even after death) to close communion with God. Included are noble pagans (an Iranian Muslim, a Zulu Christian, and two more Jews are among them), helpful but detached agnostics, Beatricean saintly women, and self-actualizing Christians.

The anonymous, omniscient narrators are usually urbane and ironic (especially toward those who have not seen the light), describing and commenting on the action; but they share the ecstasy of characters' epiphanies. Employing multiple points of view, Williams avoids the tighter unity of a limited narrator, preferring counterpoint and rapid changes of pace, from reckless speed to detailed exposition or intense meditation.

Usually economical, his language gets out of hand when he tries to persuade the reader of an abstraction that his story fails to establish concretely. Yet he insisted on accurate description, especially of spiritual states, seeing inaccuracy as part of the downfall of those condemned to infernal regions. In the cause of spiritual accuracy, Williams gives a privileged status to books, especially of poetry—not only what has been sanctified by the past, but also what his characters write now. In quest of literal accuracy, a common verbal device in the novels is to focus on literal meanings of clichés and dead metaphors, of which one of his favorites is "being in love." Characters may mistake for this state their desire to use others, or a vague discomfort (almost like spiritual indigestion); if "God is Love," however, we are all "in love," regardless of whether we know or acknowledge it in our behavior.

Occult, romantic, and Christian fantasies blend in a way not always easily distinguished. As Patricia Meyer Spacks notes, in *Shadows of Imagination*, Williams tries in his fiction to fuse the analogical levels of theological, supernatural, and psychological experience. In the context of the destination of one's immortal soul, however, which for Williams is absolute reality, both occult fantasy and realistic human psychology become trivial. Yet while veering toward allegory, another medievalism that

might have solved some of his artistic problems, he seldom goes that far. Natural and supernatural interpenetrate, as Eliot pointed out; and the commonplace, in which Williams delights, contains the miraculous, as it did for Hans Christian Andersen. In the first five novels, after the miraculous breaks through, the natural order is restored; but the last two establish an equilibrium in which the supernatural is itself commonplace.

On the occult level, witchcraft and black magic, though always overcome, have a palpable effect, at least on the user. On the romantic level, objects of power may be used for good or bad, or simply adored. Adoration is preferred if the phenomena are good in themselves, as are the Graal and the Stone of Suleiman; but undisciplined actions of Platonic forms and tarot cards need correction. On the theological level (not always explicitly Christian and never acknowledged as fantasy), the divine order is always present. Like Williams' inventions, contemporary disbelief in it produces only temporary aberrations. In each novel, at least one major character rediscovers the truth of the divine order by giving himself or herself over to some embodiment of it.

Shadows of Ecstasy (published in 1933, written in 1925) centers on the fascination of the Williams-like Roger Ingram, "professor of applied literature," with the 200-year-young Nigel Considine, who frees and arms the whole of Africa and challenges Western culture with a secret discipline of inward-turning power. According to Considine, the day of intellect is gone; even art and love—which attract Ingram—are only shadows of the ecstasy that ultimately can conquer death.

Confusing, ludicrously melodramatic, this apprentice novel features comic-opera disciples of Considine and a hoax that London has been invaded by Africans. The supernatural is curiously absent—even Considine's discipline has questionable results for others—and the villain arouses a curious ambivalence. The cast of characters includes Inkamasi, a noble Zulu king (a Christian whose life is sacrificed); Roger's saintly wife, Isabel; an agnostic surgeon, Sir Bernard Travers, and his son, Philip, in love with Isabel's spoiled sister, Rosamond; an Anglican priest, Ian Caithness, whose unsympathetic portrayal does not deprive the divine agency he serves of its potency; and two old, helpless Orthodox Jewish heirs to a vast fortune.

War in Heaven (published in 1930, written in 1926), Williams' first published novel, shows considerably more polish and a firmer sense of direction. It modulates from mystery to Mystery, from the discovery of a corpse in a publisher's office, through witchcraft and demonic possession, to an ethereal mass presided over by Prester John, using the Holy Graal (Williams' spelling).

Of the villains, three are strictly abstractions: Sir Giles Tumulty, a parody of the "disinterested scientist"; Menasseh, a Jew intent on destroying the Graal; and an unnamed Greek, who would destroy everything. The road to perdition starts with the error that belief is irrelevant to the quest for knowledge; each of the three is progressively more skeptical and more in thrall to Satan. The active villain, Gregory Persimmons, is still a "man of faith," who gives himself up to the forces for good when he realizes how far he was willing to go. Trafficking with Satan, he has sought young Adrian Rackstraw as a potential anti-Christ child; subjected the boy's Beatricean mother, Barbara, to demonic possession; committed or helped arrange two murders; and finally tried to bring back the spirit of one of his victims into the body of an Anglican clergyman.

The heroes include the saintly Archdeacon Julian Davenant, whose absentmindedness comes from listening for God's word; the Duke of the North Ridings, a sympathetic Roman Catholic; and Kenneth Mornington, a publisher's clerk whose passion for accuracy gradually turns into a defense of the Graal that costs him his life. Their invulnerability (death is not a defeat) is ensured by the presence on their side of a deus ex machina in the person of Prester John, legendary medieval guardian (and Incarnation) of the Graal.

Except for Prester John, a police investigator, and the unrepentant villains, everyone is connected with writing and the publishing firm, including Persimmons, who, though retired, still controls it when he wants to. Mornington and the duke are poets; Tumulty is on the publisher's list, and the Archdeacon would like to be. Another clerk, Lionel Rackstraw, has a gloomy outlook that events seem to justify,

until his wife and child are restored and the final curtain affirms the Archdeacon's fey blessedness.

Williams' comic vision is not limited to the happy ending, however. Chase scenes, sectarian squabbles over taking the Graal to Rome or Canterbury, the fatuousness of the Archdeacon's aide, and Prester John's gray-suited urbanity, which infuriates the villains even as it comforts everyone else, are all good for chuckles. Misused to show Adrian "pretty pictures," to "imprison" Barbara during her erotic seizure, and to invade the Archdeacon's soul, the Graal evokes smiles of triumph when its keeper rescues them and conducts the concluding ritual.

Many Dimensions (1931) is also dominated by a single Grail-object, the Stone of Suleiman (Solomon), sold by a Persian renegade to Giles Tumulty (the only character repeated in Williams' novels). Bearing the Tetragrammaton (Hebrew letters for Jahweh or Jehovah) and called by its spokesman, the noble Hajji, both the primal matter and "the End of Desire," it is subjected to blasphemous Western greed and curiosity. Infinitely divisible with no loss of substance, the Stone can conquer space and time, read and control minds, heal the sick, and destroy the ungodly. Activated by a young woman placing herself in its power, it pulses and radiates with an unearthly light that can kill as well as spiritually illumine.

Except for Tumulty, whom the Stone eventually destroys, there are no real villains, but almost everyone who hears about the Stone wants to use it for his own purposes. Williams creates comic effects with debates on the merits and demerits of instantaneous transport, time travel, and healing, in a complex, interdependent society. He broadly satirizes people who see the Stone as no more than a tool, such as an American airline owner, the General Secretary of the Transport Union, the Mayor of the town of Rich, the Home Secretary, and the Minister in charge of science.

Only two Britons are not satirized in this manner. Writing a book on "Organic Law" (a concept Williams treats with tolerant humor), Chief Justice Lord Arglay would apparently like to be justice incarnate. A wise and constructive agnostic, he decides to believe in God, given the apparition of the Stone, but does not become an adherent to any one faith. Even more under its spell, his secretary, Chloe (acknowledged by Williams as a Phyllis-figure), sacrifices herself to the Stone to restore it to Unity, calling back to itself all the copies (or "Types") made by Tumulty and others. Lying in a kind of coma at her employer's house for nine months before she dies, she is obviously intended as a symbol of (re)birth, but of what the narrator does not say.

Instead of a single Grail-object, *The Place of the Lion* (1931) subjects the world to invasion by supernatural animals representing the Platonic forms and the Middle Ages' nine ranks of angels. The mechanism by which they enter this world seems to be the deep thought of one Berringer, a philosopher of magic who lectures on the forms to a rural group of dabblers. As he lies stricken in a mysterious coma, his house becomes engulfed in a fire that does not consume; while around the house in steadily widening (Dantean?) circles, qualities ruled by the forms—strength (lion), subtlety (serpent), beauty (butterfly)—drain out of the world.

The saintly Anthony Durrant, subeditor of a literary journal, is the sole champion of resistance, supported by the eagle (wisdom), to which he surrenders himself. Rescued by it from a ledge in the symbolic chasm within Berringer's house, he becomes a new Adam, who by naming the animals returns them—the lion and the lamb among them—to where they belong. This triumphant scene, in a country field transformed into Eden, shows the Phoenix-like house as a tree of fire complementing the tree of life.

Anthony contrasts starkly with his London roommate, the fearful Quentin Sabot, and his village intended, the obtuse Damaris Tighe. Whereas Anthony is aware from the start that ideas are more powerful than things, Damaris, in selfish pursuit of her doctorate, dismisses and alienates other people and all but kills her subject, philosophy. In archetypal form, it almost kills her, until she extends herself for others (Anthony, then Quentin). In a wasteland terrain, sought by a zombielike version of the medieval thinker Peter Abelard, she is rescued by Anthony from a pterodactyl (her vision of the eagle).

A rare Williams portrait of someone who chooses the Way of the Rejection of Images, the bookstore clerk Richardson is a former follower of Berringer. Vouchsafed a vision of the sacred unicorn in a Methodist chapel, Richardson chooses to enter the mystic fire just when Anthony is putting it out. Other Berringer followers, who feel they must further the conquest by the forms, are physically transformed into pale human imitations of the lion and the crowned serpent.

The Greater Trumps (1932) expands the Grail-motif in the form of tarot cards and mysterious dancing figures that correspond to the tarot's twenty "Greater Trumps." As in a masque, these archetypes, like the animals in the previous book, are active in the world. Like the Platonic forms, they ensure natural and supernatural order when undisturbed. The original pack of cards, of which all others are copies, falls into the hands of Lothair Coningsby, a peevish minor government official (a "Warden of Lunacy"). The gypsy, Henry Lee, courting Lothair's daughter Nancy, sees them as a source of power. Brought into conjunction with mysterious golden figures in the house of his uncle Aaron, the cards control the four elements. Their misuse unleashes a supernatural snowstorm, which Nancy brings under control.

Representing basic types and relationships of people, the figures (and presumably the cards) are involved in the perpetual dance of life. The Fool in this pattern is both at the center and everywhere at once, which only Lothair's sister Sibyl can see. A saintly "fool" herself, Sibyl recognizes the Fool again in the snowstorm, when she comes upon him protecting Lothair. If her rescue of her brother is superfluous, the nobility of her intent is underlined by her gratuitous act of saving a kitten as well. Having contributed to the calamity by misadventure, Nancy, in saving the day, is also a Messiah-figure, recognized by Sibyl and by the Lees's crazy aunt Joanna, who is searching for a reborn child to play Osiris to her Isis.

In the longest scene of the book, Nancy's intervention unleashes a mystical golden cloud of human hands. This literal deus ex machina reeducates both the Lees and Lothair before the natural order is restored. Lacking any real villains or damage, the story is structurally comic, with a happy ending; but there is little humor (except some satire of Lothair and his family circle) in a work unusually dependent on spectacle.

Even more masquelike, *Descent into Hell* (published in 1937, written in 1933) is a departure in several ways. Its contrapuntal story lines introduce a purgatorial world of the dead interacting with the world of the living, and the suggestion of a change in the natural world precipitated by the Christian Apocalypse, and not restored to the natural order as in the previous novels. Ostensibly concerned with an amateur play production, the book expands that metaphor into the Last Judgment, toward which the roles of all concerned—amateurs at living—direct them. The play itself echoes Williams' own masques; the Christ-like playwright, Peter Stanhope, reflects the author himself. The claim that Battle Hill, the locale of the performance, has seen so much death that it is open to the world of the departed enables the place to stand for any human settlement.

The villains this time are guilty only of disregard for others, the heroes credited with acts of charity and literal substitution. The title points to historian Lawrence Wentworth, who progressively cuts himself off from human intercourse, refusing several chances to reinstate himself. In his unrequited infatuation with Adela Hunt, he accepts a succubus in her place, compounded from his own imaginings. In the guise of Lily Samile, who offers everyone whatever he desires, the Hebrew demon Lilith takes him even further into a symbolic reenactment of Adam and Eve in a wasteland Eden. A continuing dream of descending a long white rope to its bottom emblemizes his fall. For similar reasons, Adela succumbs to a mysterious sickness, less graphically depicted.

Their descent is counterpointed by the ascent of two other characters, Pauline Anstruther and the ghost of an unknown workman, who hanged himself with a rope when Wentworth's apartments were being built. Afraid of a doppelgänger that is approaching her more and more closely, Pauline is persuaded by Stanhope to let him bear her fear. Accepting this substitution enables her to see the double as a glorified vision of herself that centuries ago comforted an ancestor who was martyred for his faith. The confrontation takes place when her dying grandmother, Margaret, sensitive to the spirit world, takes pity on the workman, who has been moving up a mysterious mountain toward an equally mysterious radiance. Hearing his groan echoed by one that shakes the world (Christ's), she sends Pauline out to direct the ghost to London (the city, and a step toward paradise).

Consolidating some of the gains of its predecessor, *All Hallow's Eve* (1945) is weakened by a return to the black magic and melodrama of the earlier books. Opening on a purgatorial vision of the City, the novel introduces us to the ghost of Lester Furnivall, a self-centered young woman who finds salvation in substitution, and her foil, Evelyn Mercer, an acquaintance who chooses the path to damnation. A major role in this book is played by their actions in this gray London of the first states of the afterlife.

Links between their London and the city of the living are provided by several people. Lester and her widower, Richard, in fleeting contacts, discover and cement the love between them. The self-styled "Father" Simon Le Clerc, who enslaves his followers with false comfort and healing, communicates with the dead by occult means, even imprisoning the ghosts in a golemlike body. Having sent his daughter, Betty Wallingford, on sporadic visits to the future via the London of the dead, he tries to establish a permanent beachhead in it through her death.

Although Richard and his painter friend Jonathan Drayton, Betty's fiancé, are also brought to a sacramental view of the world, Lester and Betty are the major forces for good. Lester's salvation progresses with exchanges of sympathy for Richard, then Evelyn, and finally Betty. Substituting herself for Betty, when Simon tries to kill the girl, Lester accepts the agony of crucifixion. Lester's contribution to the girl's Beatricean beatitude is only possible, however, because Betty's nurse had secretly had her baptized as a baby. Betty's memory of being raised from that "lake" has echoes in the rain that she brings into Simon's church to purge it of his infamies, and in her ability to truly heal his followers, whose ailments his magic had only masked.

Five centuries old and trained in the black arts, this archetypal villain recalls Simon Magus, imitates—by inversion—all persons of the Trinity, and seeks worldwide dominion with the aid of two simulacra of himself. Ultimately foiled by Betty and Lester, Simon (like both Evelyn and Betty's mother) progressively deteriorates through his own acts. Although the story demands it, the narrator's insistent declarations of Simon's Jewishness are particularly unfortunate in a book appearing at the end of World War II.

On the angelic side Jonathan has the kind of insight into reality that only a symbolic artist could have. One of his canvases presciently shows an imbecilic Simon preaching to beetlelike followers, while another is animated by the light of glory. Betty recognizes the light in his painting as reality. Its counterpart in the afterlife is the radiance of the City, a blend of human and divine revealed through Lester's eyes. In the novel's metaphysic, this blend is particularly potent on Halloween, when the final chapter, "The Acts of the City," takes place. Echoing the biblical "Acts of the Apostles," Williams envisions the City or its spirit dispensing divine justice in these climactic scenes.

Williams' complex construction, the depth of his backgrounds, and his serious message all demand careful attention. But issues and spectacle take precedence over character and verisimilitude, as is proper in a masque but suspect in a novel. Read as novels, his books are studied like those of major writers, a dubious compliment that does not work to his advantage. He fares better in comparison with popular fantasy writers, in whose company his conventional ethnocentrism and anti-Semitism are, if not forgivable, at least more understandable.

Selected Bibliography

WORKS OF CHARLES WILLIAMS

The Silver Stair. London: Herbert and Daniel, 1912. (Poetry.)

War in Heaven. London: Gollancz, 1930. New York: Pellegrini and Cudahy, 1949. (Novel, written 1926.)

Many Dimensions. London: Gollancz, 1931. New York: Pellegrini and Cudahy, 1949. (Novel.)

The Place of the Lion. London: Mundanus (Gollancz), 1931. New York: Pellegrini and Cudahy, 1951. (Novel.)

The Greater Trumps. London: Gollancz, 1932. New York: Pellegrini and Cudahy, 1950. (Novel.)

Shadows of Ecstasy. London: Gollancz, 1933. New York: Pellegrini and Cudahy, 1950. (Novel, written 1925.)

Descent into Hell. London: Faber and Faber, 1937. (Novel.)

He Came Down from Heaven. London: Heinemann, 1938. (Theology.)

Taliessen Through Logres. London: Oxford University Press, 1938. (Poetry.)

Religion and Love in Dante: The Theology of Romantic Love. London: Dacre Press, 1941. (Theology and literary criticism.)

Witchcraft. London: Faber and Faber, 1941. (Theology and magic.)

The Figure of Beatrice: A Study in Dante. London: Faber and Faber, 1943. (Theology and literary criticism.)

The Region of the Summer Stars. London: Editions Poetry, 1944. (Poetry.)

All Hallow's Eve. London: Faber and Faber, 1945. New York: Pellegrini and Cudahy, 1948. (Novel.)

Arthurian Torso, Containing the Posthumous Fragment of "The Figure of Arthur" by Charles Williams and a Commentary on the Arthurian Poems of Charles Williams by C. S. Lewis. London and New York: Oxford University Press, 1948.

The Image of the City and Other Essays. Edited by Anne Ridler. Oxford and New York: Oxford University Press, 1958.

Collected Plays. Edited by John Heath-Stubbs. London and New York: Oxford University Press, 1963.

CRITICAL, BIOGRAPHICAL, AND BIBLIOGRAPHICAL STUDIES

Cavaliero, Glen. Charles Williams: Poet of Theology. Grand Rapids, Mich.: William B. Eerdmans, 1983.

Conquest, Robert. "The Art of the Enemy." Essays in Criticism, 7 (1957): 42–55.

Davies, R. T. "Charles Williams and Romantic Experience." Études Anglaises, 8, no. 4 (October–December 1955): 289–298.

Dawson, Lawrence R., Jr. "Reflections of Charles Williams on Fiction." Forum [Ball State University], 5 (Winter 1964): 23–29.

Eliot, T. S. Introduction to All Hallow's Eve by Charles Williams. London: Faber and Faber, 1945. New York: Pellegrini and Cudahy, 1948.

Glenn, Lois. Charles W. S. Williams: A Checklist. Kent, Ohio: Kent State University Press, 1975.

Hadfield, Alice Mary. *Charles Williams: An Exploration of His Life and Work.* New York and Oxford: Oxford University Press, 1983.

Hanshell, H. D. "Charles Williams: A Heresy Hunt." *The Month,* n.s. 9, no. 1 (January 1953): 14–25.

Hillegas, Mark R., ed. *Shadows of Imagination: The Fantasies of C. S. Lewis, J. R. R. Tolkien, and Charles Williams.* Carbondale: Southern Illinois University Press, 1969.

Howard, Thomas T. *The Novels of Charles Williams.* New York and Oxford: Oxford University Press, 1983.

Manlove, C. N. "Fantasy as Praise: Charles Williams." In *The Impulse of Fantasy Literature.* London: Macmillan, 1983.

Peckham, Robert Wilson. "The Novels of Charles Williams." Ph.D. diss., University of Notre Dame, 1965.

Reilly, Robert J. *Romantic Religion: A Study of Barfield, Lewis, Williams and Tolkien.* Athens: University of Georgia Press, 1971.

Sale, Roger. "England's Parnassus: C. S. Lewis, Charles Williams and J. R. R. Tolkien." *Hudson Review,* 17, no. 2 (Summer 1964): 203–225.

Shideler, Mary McDermott. *The Theology of Romantic Love: A Study in the Writings of Charles Williams.* New York: Harper, 1962.

Sibley, Agnes Marie. *Charles Williams.* Boston: Twayne, 1982.

Trowbridge, Clinton W. "The Beatricean Character in the Novels of Charles Williams." *Sewanee Review,* 79 (Summer 1971): 335–343.

Walsh, Chad. "Charles Williams' Novels and the Contemporary Mutation of Consciousness." In *Myth, Allegory and Gospel: An Interpretation of J. R. R. Tolkein, C. S. Lewis, G. K. Chesterton, Charles Williams,* by Edmund Fuller et al. Minneapolis: Bethany Fellowship, 1974.

Wright, Elizabeth. "Theology in the Novels of Charles Williams." *Stanford Honors Essays in Humanities,* 6 (1962).

—DAVID N. SAMUELSON

L. P. HARTLEY

1895-1972

EVEN THE MOST impassioned devotee of the "ghost story," L. P. Hartley once wrote, "would admit that the taste for it is slightly abnormal, a survival, perhaps, from adolescence, a disease of deficiency suffered by those whose lives and images do not react satisfactorily to normal experience and require an extra thrill." This wry little indictment appears in the introduction to Cynthia Asquith's *Third Ghost Book* (1955), a celebrated anthology series to which Hartley himself contributed extensively. In fact, Hartley indulged in this "slightly abnormal" genre throughout his long career, producing some of the most stylish and sophisticated ghost stories in the English language.

Hartley's reputation rests not on his supernatural fiction but on his skill at depicting the subtleties of class conflict. Novels such as *The Go-Between* (1953) and *The Hireling* (1957) and stories such as "A Condition of Release" are about people who try, usually with ugly or disastrous results, to bridge class barriers. Yet Hartley's work is seamless: both his realistic social sketches and his ghost stories fit into a single unified vision. The manner in which he manages to fuse the supernatural with an essentially secular world view is not only a technical tour de force but also a basic key to understanding his fiction.

Born in the Cambridgeshire town of Whittlesea on 30 December 1895 and educated at Oxford, Leslie Poles Hartley lived the demure, quiet life to which his more cultivated characters aspire. He served as a

gunner in World War I but otherwise led such an apparently undramatic existence that he was capable of admitting, "I have been more actively frightened by a book than by anything that has happened to me in my own life" (*Sketch*, 4 October 1939). This resolutely bookish attitude is cleverly projected into the ghost story "W. S.," the story of a novelist attacked by a murderous composite of his more unpleasant fictional characters, a tale that suggests that books are more threatening — indeed, more lifelike — than anything in life itself.

Certainly books were the center of Hartley's life. A full-time man of letters, he wrote book reviews and articles for *The Observer*, *Sketch*, *The Spectator*, the *London Magazine*, the *Times Literary Supplement*, and other publications. In the judgment of J. B. Priestley, he was the finest book critic in England. When he wasn't writing reviews, he was writing his own books — seventeen novels and five collections of short stories — which earned him high praise as a superior craftsman and an astute observer of social behavior and mores.

Hartley's critical writing on supernatural fiction, some of the most elegant in the field, is usually a reliable key to his own ghostly tales, in terms of both whom he admires and how he evaluates the genre itself. To Hartley, writing the supernatural tale was a delicate, risky undertaking: "If not the highest, it is certainly the most exacting form of literary art, and perhaps the only one in which there is almost no intermediate step between success and failure. Either it comes off or it is a flop" *(The Third Ghost Book)*. This is a rather severe, rigid argument—the antithesis, for example, of H. P. Lovecraft's more generous judgment that if a flawed work has "moments" of convincing supernatural dread it should be counted a success—but one utterly in keeping with Hartley's meticulous stylistic standards.

One writer who meets those standards for Hartley is Henry James, whose contribution to the genre was to show that "once a writer disclosed his meaning in plain language, something valuable was irretrievably lost. The veils were rent asunder; mystery ceased to exist" *(Sketch,* 15 February 1933). Actually, Hartley does not always follow this precept; some stories, such as "Feet Foremost" (1948) and "The Cotillion" (1948), are surprisingly "plain" and explicit, and his language is always more direct and economical than James's. Nevertheless, Hartley's ghost stories, which rely heavily on suggestion and ambiguity, are clearly in the James tradition.

Another writer Hartley singles out for praise (rather too generously, perhaps) is Cynthia Asquith, to whom he contributed his finest work in the genre. Asquith gives her ghosts "a natural as well as supernatural interest. Her living characters are not just fodder for her ghosts, nor are her ghosts just meant to terrify. Whether of flesh and blood or not of flesh and blood, humanity pervades them" *(The Third Ghost Book)*. In other words, in order for a supernatural tale to terrify, it must first do more than terrify; like any other fiction, it must present credible characters and settings.

In fact, the striking thing about Hartley's essays is the extent to which they refuse to segregate supernatural from mainstream fiction. When he praises Elizabeth Bowen for her ability to "heighten the mystery of existence by suggesting its unlimited ability to hurt and terrify" *(Sketch,* 28 August 1935), he is talking about all her work, both realistic and supernatural. When he praises Nathaniel Hawthorne's black depiction of supernatural evil, he makes the point that these excursions into the fantastic illuminate common reality.

Hartley's own macabre excursions began with the handful of horror stories in *Night Fears* (1924).

The title story is about an insomniac night watchman. As the story opens, he is optimistic, convinced that his insomnia will pass and that his endless circling in the dark demonstrates a "competent familiarity with a man's occupation" that will impress his wife.

Suddenly, out of nowhere, a mysterious figure appears who Socratically manages to call into question the stability of the watchman's health and job, the affection of his children, whom he rarely sees, and the fidelity of his wife, whom he rarely sees either. The faceless stranger speaks "in tones so cold and clear that they seemed to fill the universe; to admit of no contradiction." Under this pitiless inquisition, the watchman's basic life-supports crumble, his repressed despair leaps out, and he cuts his throat.

Since the story is told from the point of view of the watchman, the reader strongly suspects the stranger to be a destructive alter ego. But in the final paragraph, the apparition is shown to be very real, a solemn, almost medieval figure who looks down at the body, warms his hands on the brazier, then disappears into "a blind alley opposite, leaving a track of dark, irregular footprints." In the hands of a lesser artist this ending would be a disappointment, an unraveling of psychological subtlety. But with Hartley's steely prose—as "cold and clear" as the voice of the apparition—it becomes a final chill, a leap into the unknown.

"The Island," the sumptuous opening story in *Night Fears*, moves in the opposite direction. Its shadows and moonlit portents in a deserted house on a misty island virtually guarantee the appearance of something supernatural, yet what appears in the jolting climax is a corpse that is quite dead, a consequence of ordinary hatred and infidelity rather than anything unearthly. Another story in the collection that manages to be ghostly without any ghosts is "A Summons," a charming, creepy little mood piece depicting the "night fears" of a young man who hears a "deadly exaltation" and a "monotonous *memento mori*" in the buzz of a fly.

Five years after *Night Fears*, Hartley contributed a story for another Asquith anthology called *Shudders* (1929), a superb collection that includes Walter de la Mare's "Crewe," Arthur Machen's "The Cosy

Room," and Elizabeth Bowen's "The Cat Jumps." Entitled "The Travelling Grave," it is perhaps Hartley's most brilliant tale of terror, the one for which he is principally known to enthusiasts of the genre. The plot involves a basic situation that Hartley continued to use, with variations, throughout his career: the anxieties of a shy protagonist who reluctantly accepts an invitation to visit the house of a wealthy eccentric.

The oddball host is a collector named Dick Munt, a man who is "one of the exceptions—he's much older than he seems, whereas most people are more ordinary than they seem"; the reluctant visitor is Hugh Curtis, "a vague man with an unretentive mind." Hugh cannot remember what Munt collects, but "the mere thought of a collection, with its many separate challenges to the memory, fatigued him." Hugh assuages his fears of social awkwardness by planning to arrive late for dinner: "'Even if dinner is as late as half-past eight,' he thought to himself, 'they won't be able to do me much harm in an hour and a quarter.'"

As is usually the case in Hartley's horror fiction, what happens far exceeds even the neurotic hero's worst fears. Munt, as it turns out, collects coffins, and his newest, an exotic "charming toy," is a mobile grave with teeth, a mechanical monster that the jaded Munt plans to loose on Hugh during a game of hide-and-seek. In the end, Munt is accidentally devoured by his own monster, but not before Hartley has put Hugh through a harrowing example of what he calls "fear-fulfillment," the notion that projecting one's worst fears into a story "is a kind of insurance against the future. When we have imagined the worst that can happen, and embodied it in a story, we feel we have stolen a march on fate, inoculated ourselves, as it were, against disaster" (*Sketch*, 8 January 1936).

By the 1930's and 1940's, Hartley was turning out stories that range from curious mixtures like "The Travelling Grave" (which has elements of the psychological horror tale, the crime story, and the antiquarian monster story) to more traditional ghost stories such as "Feet Foremost" and "Three or Four, for Dinner?" (These stories can be found in *The Travelling Grave* [1948], one of the most distin-

guished of August Derleth's Arkham House books, and in an earlier book called *The Killing Bottle* [1932], although the easiest strategy is to go to *The Complete Short Stories* [1973].)

The most delightful aspect of all these stories is Hartley's suave, sardonic sense of humor. Like M. R. James, Ambrose Bierce, and E. F. Benson, Hartley uses humor not as a relief from horror so much as a biting intensification of it. In "The Travelling Grave," there is a long stretch of loony dialogue in which a character who thinks that Munt collects perambulators instead of coffins makes a series of accidental analogies between babies and corpses, at one point exclaming, "I do not care to contemplate lumps of flesh lacking the spirit that makes flesh tolerable." In "Feet Foremost," the heroine, upon hearing about the ghost of a woman who was tortured and murdered by her husband, surmises: "so now she haunts the place. I suppose it's the nature of ghosts to linger where they've suffered, but it seems illogical to me. I should want to go somewhere else." This urbane, dismissive talk makes the final appearance of the ghost much more striking and believable than the turgid theorizing that serves as a prelude in more occult spook tales.

The most memorable of Hartley's overtly supernatural stories is "A Visitor from Down Under" (from the first *Ghost Book*, 1926), the story of a man pursued by an icy avenging ghost, one who drops icicles from his trousers. The invocation of the ghost is connected to a children's party at Broadcasting House that the victim, Mr. Rumbold, hears on the wireless. Mesmerized by the droning chant of the children, Mr. Rumbold is taken ecstatically back to his own childhood. Gradually, however, the chant becomes sinister and ugly, finally intoning Mr. Rumbold's death knell and announcing the sending of the avenging ghost to "fetch him away."

Hartley's ghost scenes are frequently connected to this kind of regression to childhood, the time of magic and miracles. He once complained that many ghost story writers "cannot remember when a dressing gown hung over the end of the bed looked like a witch crouching or a man with a broken neck" and consequently wrote unconvincing supernatural scenes (*Sketch*, 3 May 1933). This statement is echoed in the doppelgänger story "A Change of Ownership" (in *The Travelling Grave*), when the doomed protagonist relives his childhood, a time when "the most familiar objects, a linen-press or a waste-paper basket, had been full of menace for him." Hartley objected to the determinism of Freud, yet his ghost stories are graceful embodiments of Freud's "Uncanny," the "dread and creeping horror" that arises when repressed childhood sensations suddenly erupt.

Eustace Cherrington, the hero of the *Eustace and Hilda* trilogy, continually relives these sensations, experiencing the

> contraction of the heart that the strangeness in the outward forms of things once gave him; the tingling sense of fear, the nimbus of danger surrounding the unknown which had harassed his imagination but enriched its life, which was the medium, the condition, of his seeing, bereft of which his vision was empty—far emptier, indeed, than that of people who had never known the stimulus of fear.
>
> (*Eustace and Hilda*, chapter 17)

In this rapt passage it is clear that the "stimulus of fear" is a life-enhancing force, but that is not the whole story; Eustace's weak heart, fear of relationships, and lifelong submission to the domination of his sister Hilda make it equally clear that fear can be neurotic, even fatal. Eustace is nourished by fear, but he is finally killed by it.

Eustace and Hilda (1947) is the most richly textured example of Hartley's major theme in his ghostly fiction—the idea that an encounter with childhood and an encounter with the supernatural are virtually the same thing, a momentary connection with the timeless and the transcendental. The potentially supernatural scenes in the childhood sections—including a beautifully realized encounter with a witchlike old lady and her haunted house—seem bereft of real ghosts; but in a scene in Venice near the end, Eustace, now an adult, sees a woman in black, "raising her arms in a wide gesture that might have been calling down a blessing or a curse." Eustace follows the woman up the stairs, in a sequence as labyrinthine and intricate as anything in

James or Walter de la Mare, but she vanishes. When he describes the woman to the maid, she screams *"Ha visto la larva!"* and flees the house. At first, Eustace is confused:

> *Larva, larva*, it was a Latin word. Groping among his classical studies, his memory brought out something pale with the milky glow of phosphorescence, something in an incomplete, provisional state of being. Now it came to him. Larva was a ghost. He had seen a ghost.
>
> (chapter 12)

One might expect Eustace to tell someone of this apparition or at least to muse upon it at length, but the aftermath is confined to a single remarkable sentence: "When the snarl of the word '*larva*' ceased to tear at his mind, the silence bit into the sore place like an acid." Eustace experiences so many preternatural moments that the appearance of a ghost in one of them is merely an overlay, a supernatural extension of feelings so intense—in this case, his childhood dread of his sister projected into a doomed future—that they burst the boundaries of normalcy. As "The Thought," "Night Fears," "A Change of Ownership," and other stories demonstrate, this escalation of intense feeling into the realm of the supernatural is a Hartley trademark; his ghosts grow organically out of the fears, relationships, and moral dilemmas of his characters.

The Go-Between (1953) is another novel that is rife with the fantastic—with "sensuous premonitions," curses that come true, and life-and-death struggles with a "hungry" deadly nightshade. This story of a little boy who acts as an unknowing go-between in an illicit affair between a lady of the aristocracy and a small farmer opens with an irresistible Hartleyan sentence: "The past is a foreign country: they do things differently there." This past is the year 1900, the "intoxicating" opening of a new century; it is also the narrator's childhood, which he relives after discovering a fifty-year-old diary, a talismanic document that virtually breathes malevolence: "I looked away and it seemed to me that every object in the room exhaled the diary's enervating power."

The diary tells the horrific story of the narrator's

loss of innocence—and, by extension, the new century's as well—in what is surely Hartley's most concentrated, sustained work of art. *Eustace and Hilda* attains its most magisterial supernatural heights during the moments when Eustace relives his childhood; here, the entire novel is such a moment, imparting a sinister magic that takes the reader's breath away.

The magic of *The Go-Between* is counterbalanced by its harshness—the remorseless exploitation of the little boy by the lovers and the traumatic impact of the terrifying discovery scene on the rest of his life. This tension exists in all of Hartley. Childlike rapture is set against a brutal, Hobbesian world of power and manipulation. In stories like "The Travelling Grave" and "St. George and the Dragon" the desire to hurt and dominate comes out in sadistic, pathological characters; but in most of Hartley's fiction, it is presented as depressingly normal, the human equivalent of the devouring of the shrimp by the anemone in *Eustace and Hilda* and the animal brutality depicted in "Podolo" (in *The Travelling Grave*).

After *The Go-Between*, Hartley continued to produce excellent supernatural fiction. Indeed, the ghost stories he wrote from his late fifties until his death are some of his finest. In addition to the brilliant "W.S." (from *The Second Ghost Book*, reprinted in *The White Wand* [1954]), there are several lesser-known tales. "The Waits" and "Someone in the Lift" (from *Two for the River* [1961]) are both Christmas tales, one a Dickensian story of a greedy businessman done in by the ghosts of two starving carolers, the other about a little boy who sees an elevator apparition that resembles his father. "Someone in the Lift" is one of Hartley's shortest, most gruesome, and most disturbing offerings. An economical compression of lifelong techniques and themes, it tells of a little boy's Oedipal role in the violent death of his father—all from the child's point of view, in a manner that seamlessly fuses the natural and the supernatural.

Hartley's wry humor persisted to the end as well. In "Fall in at the Double" (from *Mrs. Carteret Receives* [1971], his final collection), the new occupant of a house that was once an army barracks is hauled away in the night by a ghostly gang of soldiers reenacting the murder of their commanding officer. The protagonist is saved by his resourceful servant, who ends the story with: "'A hot bath, a hot bottle, a whiskey perhaps, and then bed for you, sir. And don't pay any attention to that lot, they're up to no good.'" It is as if Hartley is trying to make up for his rough treatment of servants in such stories as "The Travelling Grave" and "A Visitor from Down Under," making this one a hero instead of a baffled, terrified discoverer of horror.

The final story in *Mrs. Carteret Receives* (as well as in Lord David Cecil's 1973 edition of Hartley's *Complete Short Stories*) is "The Shadow on the Wall," a superb vampire tale and a fitting finale. It has all the tested Hartley ingredients—the neurotic middle-class character (in this case a woman) reluctantly visiting the home of a wealthy eccentric, the thickening of subjective fear into supernatural horror, the "fear-fulfillment" scenario in which things turn out even more grimly than the nervous character expects. Every time the heroine peers fearfully into her adjoining room (the bedroom of a decidedly suspicious character named Count Olmütz), she sees something more ghastly—monstrous shadows, severed heads, bloody bodies. "'Will the police find anything that I have found or haven't found?'" she wonders at the end. We'll never know, but as usual in Hartley, it hardly matters. The supernatural and the natural, the everyday and the marvelous, are two sides of the same mystery.

Selected Bibliography

WORKS OF L. P. HARTLEY

Night Fears and Other Stories. London: Putnam, 1924. (Short stories.)

The Killing Bottle. London: Putnam, 1932. (Short stories.)

The Shrimp and the Anemone. London: Putnam, 1944. As *The West Window*. Garden City, N.Y.: Doubleday, Doran, 1945. (The first novel in the *Eustace and Hilda* trilogy.)

The Sixth Heaven. London: Putnam, 1946. Garden City, N.Y.: Doubleday, 1947. (The second novel in the *Eustace and Hilda* trilogy.)

Eustace and Hilda. London: Putnam, 1947. (The third novel in the *Eustace and Hilda* trilogy.)

The Travelling Grave and Other Stories. Sauk City, Wis.: Arkham House, 1948. London: Barrie, 1951.

The Go-Between. London: Hamish Hamilton, 1953. New York: Knopf, 1954. (Novel.)

The White Wand and Other Stories. London: Hamish Hamilton, 1954. New York: British Book Service, 1954.

Eustace and Hilda: A Trilogy. London: Putnam, 1958. New York: British Book Centre, 1958. (Contains *The Shrimp and the Anemone*, *The Sixth Heaven*, and *Eustace and Hilda*.)

Two for the River. London: Hamish Hamilton, 1961. (Short stories.)

The Collected Short Stories of L. P. Hartley. London: Hamish Hamilton, 1968.

Mrs. Carteret Receives and Other Stories. London: Hamish Hamilton, 1971.

The Complete Short Stories of L. P. Hartley. London: Hamish Hamilton, 1973. (The title is misleading, as the book omits some stories from *Night Fears*.)

CRITICAL AND BIOGRAPHICAL STUDIES

Bien, Peter. *L. P. Hartley*. University Park: Pennsylvania State University Press, 1963.

Bloomfield, Paul. *L. P. Hartley*. London: Longmans, Green, 1962. Enlarged edition, 1970.

Jones, Edward T. *L. P. Hartley*. Boston: G. K. Hall, 1978. (With annotated bibliography.)

Mulkeen, Anne. *Wild Thyme, Winter Lightning: The Symbolic Novels of L. P. Hartley*. Detroit: Wayne State University Press, 1974.

—JACK SULLIVAN

MERVYN WALL

1908–

I

THE CHARMING FANTASIES of Mervyn Wall are not much known outside of Ireland, but they certainly should and undoubtedly will be. His main character, the inept and gentle medieval monk called Fursey, is as memorable and appealing as J. R. R. Tolkien's Bilbo Baggins; and poor Fursey in his two novels is plunged into a series of adventures as exciting and inventive as any that were inflicted upon Tolkien's superb and equally reluctant hobbit.

The best-known modern Irish writers have been men of strong and eccentric character, such as William Butler Yeats and James Joyce, or John Millington Synge and Sean O'Casey, or Patrick Kavanagh and Brendan Behan—men who were embroiled in literary wars, or riots in theaters, or brawls in pubs; men whose work is dramatically stamped with the mark of their own extraordinary individuality. Mervyn Wall is not overtly such a man or such a writer, yet he has quietly amassed a body of work that is coming to be recognized as among the very finest produced by any Irishman of the last fifty years. It is work that is unmarked (or unmarred) by the most distinctive quality of Irish writing, that gaudy rhetorical excess that has been the hallmark of Synge and Lady Augusta Gregory, and of Joyce and O'Casey.

Instead, Wall's voice has been quiet and reserved and unobtrusively fluent. And in that disarming fashion, he has created worlds as individual as Samuel Beckett's, and as horrible; worlds as richly invented as Flann O'Brien's, and as funny; and worlds as truly observed as Frank O'Connor's or Seán O'Fao-

láin's, and more devastatingly condemned. Beneath his politeness and mildness there lurk the most explosive booby traps for the mind. But despite a world view as bleak as Beckett's, Wall has also a sense of fun, of bemusement, and of tolerant concern for both his characters and his readers. His angers and his depressions may sometimes be almost Swiftian, but Jonathan Swift, as his readers and friends well knew, was the best of good companions. A writer like Wall, whose savagery can be conveyed by whimsy and whose despair is never embodied in a shriek, also is such a good companion. And when one's journey is beset by the most dismal perils, it is good to have an unperturbed and even cheerful companion whose useful store of information includes knowing how to defeat a basilisk and how to escape being burned at the stake.

Wall was born on 23 August 1908 on Palmerston Road, Dublin. Palmerston Road is a low row of large red brick Victorian houses. In 1908 it was distinctly a home for the upper middle class, and even now the Irish prime minister lives on it. These large, cold, high-ceilinged formal houses were largely inhabited by Irish professional men—doctors, lawyers, and businessmen who were solidly successful. Wall's own father was a barrister who had inherited money and so abandoned the law and devoted himself to music.

Wall himself was first educated at Belvedere College, the Jesuit school on Dublin's North Side, whose previous most eminent literary graduate had been James Joyce. Wall's family, however, was not so quickly or completely impoverished as Joyce's, and so in the years from 1922 to 1924 he was sent to

645

Germany, where he studied music and painting in Bonn. He learned German and read avidly, and it was for him a time of freedom and romantic adventure. Being brought back to Belvedere for a final year as a schoolboy was a considerable disappointment.

After Belvedere, Wall followed Joyce into University College, Dublin. There, after a year's uncongenial pursuit of medicine, Wall studied for an arts degree, which he received in 1928. In his generation, the National University had perhaps as talented a group of undergraduates as it had had in Joyce's day; and his best friends were the subsequently notable poets Denis Devlin and Brian Coffey, who introduced him to such exciting new writers as Ezra Pound and T. S. Eliot. There also he became entranced by the modern drama and was head of the university's dramatic society. He also became the secretary of the briefly revived Dublin Drama League, whose productions had so much influenced O'Casey, and he became a devotee of the Abbey Theatre and saw almost its entire repertoire.

These years of discovery, companionship, and vivid conversation ended abruptly upon his graduation. The world was on the brink of a great economic depression, and a degree in arts and a love for literature did not open many doors. His father, however, had become very religious and through a secret organization of Catholic laymen called the Knights of Columbanus was able to secure for his son a clerkship in the Agricultural Credit Corporation. There the young Wall worked from 1930 to 1932. In 1934 he entered the Irish civil service, where he labored unhappily for fourteen years. Life in the civil service he found to be poorly paid, profoundly boring, and full of repetitive details and petty tyrannies. Still, for his first years he was stationed in Dublin, with its convivial pub life and its flourishing Abbey Theatre, and he began to write.

James Joyce called Dublin "the centre of paralysis," and for Wall the most comatose aspect of that center was the civil service. Its influence upon his attitudes and upon his writing, from the very beginning up to his most recent work, can hardly be minimized. It pervades his stories, his novels, and his plays, and even in his fantasies there is some glancing satire about the medieval equivalent of the civil service.

Even his first notable work was a condemnation of life in an office. A play called *Alarm Among the Clerks*, it was produced by the Abbey's experimental Peacock Theatre in April 1937. Like Elmer Rice's *The Adding Machine* (1923), it is an ultrarealistic depiction of stultifying routine; but unlike Rice's Mr. Zero, Wall's Selskar kills his boss only in a drunken fantasy. Both in subject matter and in vehemence this was a play greatly different from the Abbey kitchen comedies of the 1930's.

Some people thought that Wall's denunciation of office life caused him to be transferred from Dublin to the provinces. However that may be, exile from Dublin was a depressing blow. Nevertheless, there was more time to write; and Wall's short stories began to appear in Irish magazines, in *Argosy* in England, and in *Harper's* and *Collier's* in the United States. Finally collected in 1974, these stories are wry, humorous studies of characters like Mr. Duffy of Joyce's "A Painful Case." However, in a few stories like "The Demon Angler" and "Leo the Terror," Wall verged on the supernatural or the fantastic.

In his next notable work, a play called *The Lady in the Twilight*, produced by the Abbey in 1941, only the overtones are ghostly. The body of the play is a Chekhovian study in comic realism; indeed, it is a play as subtly wrought and Chekhovian as anything in Irish drama save Denis Johnston's *The Moon in the Yellow River* and Brian Friel's recent *Aristocrats*. Perhaps it was too subtle, for it ran only a week, it was never revived, and Denis Johnston was about the only commentator to perceive its considerable accomplishment.

The major manners of Wall's mature work were now established, and they were the realistic, the humorous, the satiric, and the fantastic. So many manners are a bit unusual, for a writer will ordinarily discover what literary manner most aptly embodies his attitudes and utilizes his talents, and then ever after remain basically wedded to it. Thus Daniel Defoe is always a realist, Edgar Allan Poe always a romantic, and Mark Twain and George Bernard Shaw nearly always comedians. A great genius like

Shakespeare can shift easily from tragedy to comedy to fantasy; but often a lesser genius like Ben Jonson can hardly make the shift from comedy to tragedy without his audience feeling that he has shifted from success to failure. If we broaden our sights to include such overwhelming names as Shakespeare, Jonson, Twain, and Shaw, we can see that the public impact of a quieter writer from a small island on the outer edge of Europe might be lessened considerably by his writing in more than one manner.

Wall's major fantasies, *The Unfortunate Fursey* and *The Return of Fursey*, appeared, respectively, in 1946 and 1948; but we will postpone their discussion until we have briefly recapitulated the rest of his career.

In 1948 Wall escaped from the civil service to Radio Éireann, where he served as program officer until 1957. This work of planning and recording programs was quite congenial, and his colleagues included literary men like the novelist Francis MacManus and the poet Robert Farren. Indeed, his nine years at Radio Éireann threw him into contact with most of the well-known writers in the country. In 1950 he married Fanny Feehan, a young violinist and later a notable music critic, and they had four children.

In 1952 he published *Leaves for the Burning*, which the novelist John Broderick has described as "the best Irish novel ever written." It is at least one of the most realistic depictions of Eamon de Valera's depressing Ireland ever written; and that exact picture was, as Wall has stated, precisely his intention. In the book's sodden milieu of hypocrisy, jobbery, and philistinism, a Yeatsian idealism takes quite a beating. The small, absurd triumph of Wall's gentle, ineffectual hero (in foiling a robbery that might have netted a dollar) is such an inefficient and pointless gesture that initially we may merely smile—until we perceive that such a small celebration of duty and honesty may be all that we ourselves may ever be able to achieve.

No Trophies Raise (1956) was a heightened, satiric view of this same world. Many critics considered it a failure, for, lacking the warmth of the Fursey books and the solemnness of *Leaves for the Burning*, its satiric exaggerations seemed simply out-landish. But in retrospect many of the exaggerations appear both inventive and close to the bone; and, if there is not warmth, there is both sadness and mordancy in the death of the old philosopher.

In 1957 Seán O'Faoláin secured Wall's appointment as chief executive of the Irish Arts Council, and Wall remained in that post until his retirement in 1974. After those busy and pleasant years, he published his collection of stories, *A Flutter of Wings*, also in 1974. In 1978 a work of much greater substance, his longest novel, *Hermitage*, began to be serialized in the *Journal of Irish Literature* and in 1982 it was published separately. Like *Leaves for the Burning*, this is a meticulously observed realistic portrait of Ireland. But instead of a few weeks, this novel covers about fifty years of the life of a man and his country. Although its vision is glum and its pace ambling, the book is written with a lucid fluency that makes its 120,000 words a compulsive and even a quick read.

In 1982 the *Journal of Irish Literature* published a double issue devoted to Wall. It included an interview, a speech, a reprinting of *Alarm Among the Clerks*, and the first publication of the fantastic novella "The Garden of Echoes." At this writing Wall is working on a new novella to be called "The Odious Generation," and its central sequence is a drug-induced hallucination.

II

Wall began *The Unfortunate Fursey* while recovering from an attack of pleurisy. What sparked him off was a library book with

a strange title, something like *Of Ghosts, Demons, Witches and Other Such Matters*. I've forgotten the exact title, but it was a translation of the work of a French Abbé first published in the year 1600. The title page was missing, so I never learnt who the translator was. It fascinated me because of the elaborate language in which it seriously set out the absurd medieval beliefs and superstitions which attached to witchcraft. Incredible demons hopped in and out of every page. I don't think that ever in my life have I laughed so continuously.

(unpublished letter)

The wizards, witches, demons, familiars, vampires, and assorted other monsters that crowd the Fursey books are more of continental origin than indigenously Irish spirits such as pookas, banshees, and fairies. However, the religiously repressive society of Fursey's comic-strip medieval world had a direct relevance to Wall's modern Ireland. As he wrote:

I was subsequently told that the book had four times been submitted to the Literary Censorship Board, but that they could not find anything in it to justify banning. Of course, in the repressive atmosphere of the time, the Forties and the Fifties, when our Literary Censorship Board was banning an average of 840 books a year, many humorless people looked on Fursey with disapproval. Even in recent years when our parish priest was paying us his first pastoral visit, he asked sternly: "Are you the man who wrote *The Unfortunate Fursey*?" I was able to answer: "Yes, but before you say anything, I should tell you that two cardinals have congratulated me on it."

(unpublished typescript)

That some Irish clerics objected to the Fursey books was inevitable, for the greatest follies, bigotries, and barbarisms of Wall's medieval world are laid directly at the door of the church. Its chief representatives—such as that intractable bigot the bishop, the hyperzealot preacher Father Furiosus, and even the well-meaning abbot—are much more pernicious and uncivilized than the affable and urbane devil. Indeed, the ecclesiastical satire is at the center of the book, and the relevance of the satire to the modern Irish state is inescapable. Wall's crowning touch is almost Swiftian, as he has his clerics strike a bargain in which the devil offers Ireland immunity from that most heinous of all temptations, sex. And the church, for its part, promises not to "lay undue stress on the wickedness of simony, nepotism, drunkenness, perjury and murder." "The ferocious chastity of Ireland," as O'Casey called it, has seldom been better flayed. O'Casey, who struck at the same target in his later plays, was so much more perfervid that his fantasies had to wait years longer for acceptance. But the geniality and imaginative fancy of Wall's exaggerations quite disarmed most of his potential critics.

Wall's Fursey is a lay brother at the monastery of Clonmacnoise, and quite the most humble and inept member of the holy community. Indeed, the only task within his abilities is paring edible roots in the kitchen, and even in doing that he often cuts himself. When the devil and all his minions lay siege to Clonmacnoise, they are thoroughly repulsed, and so decide to concentrate on the one weak link of embattled holiness, Fursey. As the griffins, incubi, serpents, and undraped females invade his cell, poor Fursey is totally petrified with fear:

Brother Fursey's brain simmered in his head as he tried to remember the form of adjuration, but the only words that he could bring to mind were those of the abbot's injunction: "Be not over-confident in yourself and presumptuously daring."

(chapter 1)

The upshot is that Fursey is not only cast out into the world by his abbot, but also reluctantly married to an aged crone called The Old Grey Mare. This unpalatable female turns out to be a witch who is engaged in a battle to the death with the local wizard and church sexton. When she is defeated and dying, she tricks Fursey into a final (and, indeed, first) kiss, and breathes her powers into him.

Fursey, however, is a most untutored wizard who knows only how to ride a broomstick and how to produce food and drink by tossing a rope over a tree branch or convenient beam. His most unwelcome and occasionally palpable gift from The Old Grey Mare is her familiar, Albert, a shaggy, unkempt, doglike beast with bear paws who requires to be fed blood from a supernumerary nipple Fursey has now acquired somewhere on his anatomy:

Albert shambled over to the edge of the bed. Fursey put out his hand and patted him on the head. Albert wagged his hindquarters delightedly, and his smoky red eyes lit up with expectancy.

"Breakfast?" he repeated hopefully.

"No," reiterated Fursey.

Albert looked aggrieved. "If you expect nimble and courteous service from me," he asserted plaintively, "you'll have to keep me fed. I'm that

648

thirsty, the tongue is fair hanging out of my mouth for a drop of blood.''

"That's enough of that,'' rejoined Fursey.

(chapter 5)

Fursey's subsequent adventures include captures by and escapes from the civil and religious powers, both of which have great hopes of torturing him and burning him at the stake; an encounter with a holy hermit called the Gentle Anchorite, who shares his fleas, offers him moldy nuts to eat, and has an odor of sanctity that is almost overpowering, particularly in an enclosed space; and even an idyllic interlude in which he falls in love with the girl on whose father's farm he is working.

Idyllic interludes, however, are seldom Fursey's lot; and after many fruitless attempts at accommodation with church and state and many close escapes from the inevitably ensuing perils, Fursey finally becomes fed up with Ireland. He ignites the thatch on the bishop's palace, swoops down on his broomstick to rescue the beautiful Maeve just as she is about to be married to the soldierly lout Magnus, and:

Then he flew eastwards, over the grey-green fields, the crooked roads and the sluggishly rolling mountains of Ireland, the first of many exiles for whom a decent way of living was not to be had in their own country.

(chapter 10)

Such a skeletal summary may make plain the deft, satiric criticism of Ireland at its most insular, but it does no justice to the fey, fantastic, and whimsically imaginative details that are the story's chief delight. *The Unfortunate Fursey* is a book whose savage indictments are conveyed by a sweet sunniness. It will probably always be everybody's favorite Wall novel.

But *The Return of Fursey* shows no lessening at all in Wall's quality of imagination. The story is still full of crystallomancers, scryers, witches, fiends, and this time a roistering crew of Vikings led by one with the alarming name of Sigurd the Skull Splitter. If the adventures are as crammed with quaint and enchanting details as was the original book, the theme is more somber and sadder. The story tells how Fursey loses Maeve and returns to Ireland to recover her from Magnus, how he sells his soul to his friend the devil, and how he finally loses everything except his soul and his stoicism. The book might have been called *The Education of Fursey* or *The Coming of Age of Fursey*. After Fursey has again been battered by the funny, intractable, and sardonic realities of the world, he goes off by himself, having this time won nothing but perhaps a bit of wisdom. This is how Wall eloquently describes his final exit:

He was indeed a negligible figure, a small, bowed man holding his torn coat tightly about him, not only for warmth, but as if to keep from the vulgar gaze his terrors and the remnants of his dreams. And so, as he goes down the road, he is lost to view in the gathering shadows, glimpsed only for a moment at the turn of the track or against the vast night sky, just as we have managed to catch a glimpse of him through the twilight of the succeeding centuries.

Last spring I walked the road from Clonmacnoise to Cashel, and from Cashel to the Gap. Fursey and the others are still there, trampled into the earth of road and field these thousand years.

(chapter 10)

Yet such a sad view of the death of hope is related with the sprightliest invention and the drollest imagination. But as with the best of Charlie Chaplin, or of Anton Chekhov or O'Casey, the laughter is very akin to tears, and that quality is very akin to high art.

To date, Wall's most recent fantasy is "The Garden of Echoes,'' which was refused by several publishers as possibly a too glum children's story. Wall, however, describes it as "a humorous account of the adventures of two small girls in the World of Men. It is a sort of up-to-date Alice in Wonderland." By such a high standard this novella rather pales. Still, the travels of the two little girls through a whimsical and arbitrary world compel attention, and the inventiveness is not unworthy of the creator of Fursey. However, a Wall fantasy, no matter how much fun its details are, has always more to it than merely fun. So although the story is an adventure, the reader soon comes to see that its details, fetching as they are, really symbolize the difficulties the little girls will someday have to face in the adult world. Despite the book's charm and feyness, this dark meaning may have prejudiced some readers against it as a sunny children's book. But, as Wall wrote:

> I thought of it as a satire on adults from the child's point of view, but realized when I had finished it, that it was the author's protest against the inevitable passing of childhood. . . . None realized that the book was not aimed at children at all, but at those who have had children, like children or remember their own childhood.
>
> (unpublished typescript)

Behind all of Wall's work is such a sadness, a dark pessimism that moves him as an artist to melancholy rather than to outright misanthropy. However, the contrast between his basic feelings and both his artistic and public manner is striking. As an artist and as a public man, his manner is one of quiet and low-keyed benevolence, of reticent and even prudish courtliness. The manner, though, is something of a comic cloak, a donnish personality as useful as was Mark Twain's poker face when he told a joke. Wall's polite and stately tone camouflages a most surprising, ebullient, and inventive sense of fun; and through that shimmering play of invention emerge the author's most profound feelings of disillusionment and sadness.

In the work that Wall considers most important, probably the novels *Leaves for the Burning* and *Hermitage,* the fun, the fancy, and the fantasy are almost entirely absent; and the bleak, exact details accumulate like small, dark clouds on any Irish day. But in the Fursey novels and "The Garden of Echoes" the fun and fancy strangely and brilliantly become the manner of conveying his pervasive pessimism. In the Fursey books particularly, Wall so delightfully sugarcoats his eminently sour pill that one realizes only in retropect what tours de force these

two novels are. One might regret that this remarkable writer did not realize years ago how his comic manner could, even more successfully than his realism or his satire, truly embody his attitude. What a succession of droll yet moving achievements we would have had then.

But Fursey is probably achievement enough for any man.

Selected Bibliography

WORKS OF MERVYN WALL

Alarm Among the Clerks: A Play in Three Acts. Dublin: Richview Press, 1940.

The Unfortunate Fursey. London: Pilot Press, 1946. New York: Crown, 1947.

The Return of Fursey. London: Pilot Press, 1948.

Leaves for the Burning. London: Methuen, 1952. New York: Devin Adair, 1952.

No Trophies Raise. London: Methuen, 1956.

Forty Foot Gentlemen Only. Dublin: Allen Figgis, 1962. (Short local history of the Forty Foot bathing place that Joyce uses in the opening of *Ulysses.*)

The Lady in the Twilight. Newark, Del.: Proscenium Press, 1971.

A Flutter of Wings: Short Stories. Dublin: Talbot Press, 1974.

Hermitage. Dublin: Wolfhound Press, 1982.

"A Mervyn Wall Double Number." *Journal of Irish Literature,* 11 (January–May 1982). (Contains a speech, an interview, "The Garden of Echoes," and a reprinting of *Alarm Among the Clerks.)*

CRITICAL AND BIOGRAPHICAL STUDIES

Hogan, Robert. *Mervyn Wall.* Lewisburg, Pa.: Bucknell University Press, 1972.

Kilroy, Thomas. "Mervyn Wall: The Demands of Satire." *Studies,* 47 (Spring 1958): 83–89.

—ROBERT HOGAN

T. H. WHITE

1906-1964

IN NEW YORK, on 3 December 1960, the musical *Camelot* opened at the Majestic Theatre, to mixed notices. T. H. White was there. Critics then and since have felt that, in reducing White's *The Once and Future King* (1958) to the musical stage, the show's author, Alan Jay Lerner, fatally scanted the narrative and thematic complexities of the original book, and certainly even a cursory reading of *Camelot* (1961) will uncover the vulgarity of his treatment. White seems to have treated the transmogrification of his magnum opus with some aplomb.

"I have pretended to everybody that I am perfectly satisfied with this new version of my book," he wrote to his old friend and correspondent Sydney Cockerell (as quoted in Warner, *T. H. White*). His disapprobation can be read between the lines, but there is evidence, all the same, that performances of the musical triggered in the aging writer a deeply emotional response. According to an oral communication from the author Thomas M. Disch, who served as an usher at the Majestic Theatre during the weeks White was in New York, White was an extraordinary figure: he attended most performances, broke into tears at the first-act curtain, and remained emotionally distressed throughout the second act. He was dressed as an exaggeratedly tweedy rural English gentleman, but on his feet he wore cheap cowboy boots, brightly polished.

By 1960, White had become a ruined man, though at last a wealthy one; and in the urban fever of New York it may be he saw a ruined world. As *The Once and Future King* is a tragedy that closes in a state of etiolated solitude, it may be thought unsurprising that its author, in the unfertile twilight of his own days, amid the desiccating professionalism of a Broadway production of the most ardently ambitious work of his young maturity, become ungovernably vulnerable to weeping. He had little to look forward to. His alcoholism had worsened, his creative powers had greatly diminished, his health was declining, and he had for several years been trapped in an obsessive passion for a young boy, identified only as Zed in the sources; it was a passion that he could not express directly and one that, if requited in any fashion, he would have rejected, for he had never come to terms with his homosexuality. In addition, he was (as he had himself several times confessed in correspondence) a sadist, seemingly incapable of expressing love for other human beings without a concomitant inflicting of emotional pain; perhaps in compensation, he was physically a man of great gentleness. By the beginning of 1961, he was back on the English Channel island of Alderney, where he had lived in spiritual solitude since 1946, in his "desolate, well-appointed house" (Warner), brooding, with the aid of a daily bottle of brandy, over Zed.

From letters to David Garnett (7 and 12 February 1960) it is clear that White thought of his relationship with Zed as being similar to Merlyn's loving guardianship over the Wart in *The Sword in the*

Stone (1938), eventually to become the first volume of *The Once and Future King.* As with so many of his male characters—like Lancelot in *The Ill-Made Knight* (1940), the Professor in *Mistress Masham's Repose* (1946), Mr. White in *The Elephant and the Kangaroo* (1947), and the Master in *The Master* (1957)—both Merlyn and the Wart (who will become King Arthur) represent clear projections of aspects of White's own personality. The complex amalgam of melancholia, sense of aging, thwarted love, and narcissism that White must have experienced in New York in 1960 conveys an inescapable pathos but also points to an emotional vulnerability as central to his work as it is to any understanding of his life. Perhaps more poignantly than any other writer of fantasy, White constructs his novels so as to convey, and to elicit from his readers, emotions of remarkable intensity about the bright evanescence and woundedness of the world.

Terence Hanbury White was born on 29 May 1906 in Bombay, India. His father, of Irish descent, was a district superintendent of police; his mother, of Scottish and French blood, was the daughter of an Indian judge. Their marriage was disastrous. After eighteen months they stopped sleeping together, on her insistence. Her husband shot the pet dogs on which she flamboyantly doted. White was told that on one occasion his parents were discovered quarreling over his cot as to who would shoot the baby and then commit suicide. His mother insisted on possessing her only child but gave no love in return, and his father became a drunkard. In 1911 they took the boy to England and farmed him out to his grandparents, with whom he was relatively happy for six years. But then, in 1920, he was sent to one of those appalling English public schools whose claustrophobic mores—with enforced homosexuality and sadism bulking large—have haunted so many English gentlemen. White certainly considered that his experiences at Cheltenham College only deepened the emotional crippling begun in his early childhood.

He became a large, dashing, histrionic, lovable young man. He entered Cambridge University in 1925; in his third year, being diagnosed as tubercular, he was sent to recover in Italy, with the aid of a fund subscribed to by several of his teachers. In 1929, as well as graduating with distinction, he pub-

lished his first book, *Loved Helen and Other Poems;* the contents are promising, though the melancholy of his poetic style is somewhat declamatory. He had not yet learned how to trick the reader unawares into a shared vulnerability. He then became a schoolteacher, at St. David's preparatory school in Reigate, which suburban locale, it may be speculated, he found too close to London for comfort. In any case, he left St. David's under a cloud in 1932, having completed and published his first novels.

In 1932, White become head of the English Department at Stowe, in Buckinghamshire. His energy was seemingly unbounded: he taught a full schedule; he learned to fly; he became intensely involved in hunting and fishing, and rode to hounds; and he continued to produce books. Of these, the most interesting is the novel *Farewell Victoria* (1933). In the depth of its research into nineteenth-century England, in the glowing specificity of its treatment of humans and animals, in the power of its presentation of the past as something far more attractive than the present, and in the loving, meticulous, elegiac handling of its protagonist, the horse groom Mundy, *Farewell Victoria* has a polish and balance that seem deeply worked-through, the product of a man of mature years. (At the time, White was twenty-eight.)

His next two novels (his sixth and seventh), though much inferior to *Farewell Victoria,* are of interest to the reader of supernatural fiction. With *Earth Stopped; or, Mr. Marx's Sporting Tour* (1934), that interest must be minimal. Its satire on hunting resembles Anthony Powell's in *From a View to a Death* (1933), and its apocalyptic ending, when the world is apparently bombed into a wasteland, resembles the closing pages of Evelyn Waugh's *Vile Bodies* (1930); but it has none of the knowing savagery of either of those books. *Gone to Ground* (1935) is a direct sequel, and its narrative frame carries over the adolescent brittleness of the earlier book. (Whenever White attempted to satirize contemporary society, a bumbling Colonel Blimp–like fatuous indignation seemed to overwhelm him.) As *Gone to Ground* opens, it is clear to a group of survivors that the bombs have indeed fallen; luckily, they come across a dugout in possession of the centenarian fathers of two of them, and take it over. Trapped underground—the title refers to the behavior of an animal at bay, in this case humankind—they decide to tell one another tales of the world they have lost.

Their stories make up the bulk of the book; at least some of them had been written by White with no thought of their significance in this contrived context. Most are hunting stories and have supernatural content. Without acknowledgment, six of the best of them have been republished in a posthumous compilation, *The Maharajah and Other Stories* (1981); all the supernatural tales from that peculiarly edited volume are from *Gone to Ground*. "The Spaniel Earl" recounts, in a tone of hovering melancholic solicitude characteristic of White's later work, the efforts of his loyal family to protect, to cherish, and finally to mate the young earl, who, traumatized in early childhood, lives in the conviction that he is a spaniel; the conclusion is horrific, hopeful, and moving; he is mated to a Scottish girl who thinks she is a bitch. "The Troll" is a well-told conventional horror story set in Lapland. "The Point of Thirty Miles" carries a young hunter after his dogs for that distance, until they trap and rip to pieces a great wolf, which turns human as it dies. In "The Black Rabbit," a child poacher is caught by a keeper who turns out to be Pan and who responds to the child's compunctions about causing pain to animals with monotone paeans to the warp and woof of the natural world; it closes *Gone to Ground* on a note that is prophetic by implication, as though saying to the representative twentieth-century humans at bay, If your time has come, so be it.

Not included in *The Maharajah* are some lesser tales. Those constituting chapters two, four, five, seven, and twelve have supernatural content; in the last of these, a young man out fishing in a small river catches a mermaid swimming doggedly upstream, hopelessly lost; she speaks to him in (it is possible to surmise) highly colorful Greek. (Not many of White's readers, even in 1935, would have been able to decipher her remarks; there was always a bullying side to his need to make others learn what he had learned.) The story is amusing though anecdotal, a criticism that applies to much of *Gone to Ground*; despite some felicities, it is a bad book—the last bad book White would publish.

Something of his bullying side shows in the jour-

nal White kept of his sporting activities at Stowe, later published as *England Have My Bones* (1936). The book is about fishing, hunting, shooting, flying an airplane, driving a large car too fast, and so forth; White sees these activities as natural for a man, like himself, gifted with "a passion for learning" (preface) and, at the same time, practical behavior for a man trying to place himself, in the world, as an Englishman (entry for 3 March 1934). It is also possible to discern, in the strange way that his passion for learning conflates with his constant urge to terrify himself, something of the haunted muscularity of his wrestling with the devil of sadomasochism; this sense of a combative, precarious tenderness and abrupt brutality also informs his fiction, especially his treatment of characters, like Lancelot, who are self-projections.

At the end of 1933, White acquired an Irish setter bitch named Brownie, with whom he eventually fell in love. It was the only unhampered relationship he seems ever to have had, and when in 1936 he gave up his teaching post and the psychoanalysis he had undertaken in an attempt to "cure" his homosexuality, he moved into an isolated cottage on the Stowe estate with Brownie and entered into his happiest and most significantly productive years. From 1936 through 1944, first at the cottage and then in much greater isolation in Ireland, he wrote *The Goshawk* (1951); *The Sword in the Stone; The Witch in the Wood; The Ill-Made Knight;* "The Candle in the Wind," published as book four of *The Once and Future King; The Book of Merlyn* (1977), conceived as the fifth book of the Arthurian sequence but published only posthumously; *The Elephant and the Kangaroo;* and *Mistress Masham's Repose.* By 1944 he had also done much of the work on *The Bestiary: A Book of Beasts* (1954), *The Age of Scandal* (1950), and *The Scandalmonger* (1952), and had done preliminary work on *The Master.* Although Collins' refusal to publish *The Once and Future King* in 1941 must have been a serious blow and although his reclusive existence may have had a cumulatively disabling effect, it seems probable that Brownie's death on 25 November 1944 was the definitive tragedy from which he never recovered, as man and writer.

After leaving Ireland in 1945, White spent a year

at Duke Mary's, an isolated cottage owned by David Garnett, where much of his correspondence was destroyed by damp, further desolating him. In 1946 he moved to Alderney. In 1957 he fell into the destructive Merlyn-Wart obsession with Zed. The long-delayed publication of *The Once and Future King* in 1958 made him famous, and *Camelot* made him rich. It was all much too late. For many years, one of White's favorite personas had been that of a beery, bonhomous, elderly scamp-magus, a facade that overlaid abysms of obsession, loneliness, and loss. In his last years, this presentation of self coarsened into an unattractive caricature, and much of the time White appeared to friends and those he met in his travels as a lachrymose, touchy, repetitious, drunken bore. Behind this mask, of course, lurked a shadowy Wart for whom the world had become empty. When his creative life ended, White was thirty-eight years old; when, on 17 January 1964, he died of a heart attack alone in his cabin aboard the ship that had taken him from America to Greece, he was fifty-seven.

The original volumes of his Arthurian cycle as published before World War II and the definitive version presented as *The Once and Future King* constitute his memorial and are among the finest works of fantasy ever written. There are considerable differences between the original and revised versions of *The Sword in the Stone*; both *The Witch in the Wood*, which never satisfied White, and *The Ill-Made Knight* were revised for style throughout but lack substantive changes, and are best read in their final form. There is no textual history of the evolution of that final form; some data are available, all the same. The version of *The Once and Future King* that White presented to Collins in 1941 contained revised texts of the first three books, plus "The Candle in the Wind" and *The Book of Merlyn*. The 1941 version of "The Candle in the Wind," not then shaped so as to end the cycle, has not been seen; unaltered, *The Book of Merlyn* was published posthumously. Between 1941 and 1958, White returned to the cycle on more than one occasion. It may be surmised that agreement to its eventual publication came when he finally abandoned *The Book of Merlyn*, transferring two extended episodes from that text—the Wart's adventures as an ant and as a wild goose—to the final revised form of *The Sword in the Stone*. That *The Once and Future King*, as finally published, can be read as a single novel, despite some loss of balance toward its close, may be seen as a remarkable accomplishment.

The full text is a novel of fantasy in that it is derived from Sir Thomas Malory's *Le Morte Darthur* (1485), a compilation of Arthurian material permeated by elements of the supernatural; that these elements necessarily project far more prominently in any work of the twentieth century points to germane issues in the study and theory of the romance genre but need not directly concern the reader of White. It is significant, however, that the dominant supernatural element in the latter part of Malory, the search for the Holy Grail, is deliberately scanted in *The Once and Future King*; in order to maintain his focus on the central tragedy of King Arthur, and because he was in any case uncomfortable with some implications of the intrusive Grail legend, White has the tale recounted at second hand by a series of dejected knights on their return to the Round Table. This sidestepping of the Grail further intensifies the drastic austerity of the closing sections of White's novel.

It is perhaps generally the case that the childhood and adolescence of the heroes of legend subsist in a wash of the fabulous and that a dryness reflective of their world-weariness and experience supervenes in narrative of their subsequent long reigns. As with legends, so with the lives of men and women, for the ideal childhood might be described as a time of ontological plenty, with miracles abounding. If this is so, then most writers of high fantasy—and this is one of the deep appeals of the genre—reverse that exigent pattern. Almost without exception, modern tales of fantasy take their heroes from the world into a secondary universe, from scarcity into plenty. (Many never mention the world at all.) It is a sign of White's brave seriousness in *The Once and Future King* that he takes the opposite course.

As Malory deals with King Arthur's childhood in one short chapter, the sunny amplitude of *The Sword in the Stone* is almost entirely of White's own devising. Though riven with deliberate anachronisms—generally introduced by Merlyn, who, living backward in time, can recollect Victorian

England—it is set in a fantasized Dark Ages, an England covered with forests where magic works, supernatural creatures abound, and a sword embedded in a stone can be drawn only by the rightful future king of all the land, a Dark Ages imagined as though by a writer of the fifteenth century. It is the story of the Wart, brought up as an orphan by the kindly Sir Ector, and of his education at the hands of Merlyn, the magician who becomes his tutor and who transforms him into various beasts (a fish, a hawk, a badger, an ant, and a gray goose) in order to further his knowledge of the true world. The Wart, who is destined to become King Arthur, enjoys a childhood of unparalleled felicity, and Merlyn is an ideal teacher-companion—testy, lovable, protective, comical, fierce. He is White's happiest self-projection, and in his passionate engagement with the taste and feel of the working of the world, he embodies White's own extraordinary love of practical learning. In *The Sword in the Stone*—more especially in the unfettered exuberance of the original version—a magically potentiated vision of childhood and the plenitude of a secondary universe are married, seen as one thing.

But the Wart becomes King Arthur, and the stigmata of the real world begin to show through the fabric of that plenitude, which can only lessen. In "The Queen of Air and Darkness"—White's final title for *The Witch in the Wood*—the young King Arthur finds himself in a world of truculent, feuding warlords, whom he subdues at some cost to his innocence. Merlyn, along with all his salving magical potency, slips into enchanted sleep and does not awaken. And Arthur sleeps with his half-sister Morgause, who gives birth nine months later to Mordred. Arthur has seeded his own death:

It is the tragedy, the Aristotelian and comprehensive tragedy, of sin coming home to roost. That is why we have to take note of the parentage of Arthur's son Mordred, and to remember, when the time comes, that the king had slept with his own sister. He did not know he was doing so, and perhaps it may have been due to her, but it seems, in tragedy, that innocence is not enough.

(chapter 14)

This passage, which comes almost precisely halfway through *The Once and Future King,* marks the terminus of Arthur's childhood and a somewhat uneasy transition into the working-out of the tragedy that White conceives of Malory as having written. One of the most remarkable aspects of White's book—it may well be unique in fantasy literature—is that it begins as a tale written for children and moves, through several transitions of which the quoted passage is one of the more obvious, into a novel written for adults. *The Sword in the Stone* is a juvenile; "The Candle in the Wind" is anything but. The effect is curiously shocking. It offends our illusions.

In *The Ill-Made Knight* and "The Candle in the Wind" (possibly because in White's view they are not books written for children) there is relatively little fantasy of a free-floating sort, though the underlying structural premises of the Matter of Britain continue to shape the narrative. Benign, idealistic King Arthur retreats to the sidelines of the action, as befits a monarch who attempts to rule by law rather than force, and the center of the stage is taken by the story of Lancelot and his long adultery with Guenever as the Dark Ages turn—with an effect of superlatively ironic melancholy—into the late Middle Ages. Fully mature and sexually active, Guenever stands alone in the White canon; guilt-ridden, volatile, a sadist given to intensely gentle knightly courtesy to control himself, a solitary and berserker, Lancelot is White's most complex protagonist and represents his most difficult adult self-projection. The affair between Lancelot and Guenever lasts for decades. When Mordred finally forces Arthur to notice it in public, the quest for the Grail has already bled the Round Table of its youthful energy. Open warfare begins among the aged protagonists, and the Round Table ends in tragedy.

World War II had a complex effect on White. With his acute sense of the intricacies of giving and receiving pain, he was terrified of combat but attempted, all the same, through David Garnett, to acquire some sort of military role. Nothing happened—he was in any case overage and in dubious health—and he was soon trapped in neutral Ireland for the duration. It is in a sense as a substitute for active service that he wrote *The Book of Merlyn* in

1940—1941, and much of its didactic stridency can be accounted for by White's frustrated isolation from events he tended to think of as terminal for the human race.

It is the night before the last battle. The old king in his tent, caught on the wheel of fire of the tragedy of incest that has destroyed his hopes for a just comity, becomes suddenly aware that Merlyn is with him, for the first time in very many years. Merlyn invites him out for one last ramble, to meet his old friends, and to contemplate the lessons he has learned. There are touching scenes, until Merlyn, a mouthpiece at this point for White's polemical ire, begins to lecture: "War, in Nature herself outside of man, is so much a rarity that it scarcely exists. . . . If Nature ever troubled to look at man, the little atrocity, she would be shocked out of her wits" (chapter 3). Arthur's dreamed-of stateless comity must founder on man's nature as *homo ferox*, even though nothing else will save Man the Savage in the end but a world without borders. Man's fealty to the natural order—to the complex hierarchical plenitude experienced by the Wart while he was being educated—has become profoundly corrupted. All night, with some magical interludes later shifted into the 1958 version of *The Sword in the Stone*, the debate rages. In the morning, Arthur returns to the world to die and perhaps to sleep in Avilion.

As a return to the Wart's childhood felicity, *The Book of Merlyn* is a peculiarly disingenuous failure, for the logic of White's overall structure denies the possibility of any magical redemption of the sort routinely indulged in by writers of high fantasy, except in the form of a dream. In his Irish exile, White may have come to realize this. His next novel breaks radically from the Matter of Britain and the imparting of lessons about *homo ferox*. Despite the amused hyperbole of its attacks upon the character of the Irish, *The Elephant and the Kangaroo* is a formidably hilarious jeu d'esprit. Its fantasy elements are limited. A Mr. White, for some time resident in Ireland, and the farming couple he lives with are convinced that the archangel Michael has appeared to warn them of the Second Flood. With their somewhat bewildered assistance, the manic Merlyn-like White constructs a ramshackle ark and, when rain comes, sails down the Liffey to a comic apotheosis in

the Irish Sea near Dublin. A dog named Brownie plays a role. In the end, all are saved by a steamer.

Published before *The Elephant and the Kangaroo* though written after, *Mistress Masham's Repose* stands as the last fiction White was to compose at anything like full stretch. It is set in a vast estate called Malplaquet, which White describes with a plangent, sentimentalized nostalgia that closely recalls Evelyn Waugh's evocations of Brideshead in *Brideshead Revisited* (1945) but without the religious sanction. Heir to the estate but persecuted by evil guardians, vigorous ten-year-old Maria discovers a colony of Lilliputians living in Mistress Masham's Repose, an eighteenth-century "temple" set on a deserted island in a lake within the immense grounds. In a speech that hilariously parodies eighteenth-century conventions, their schoolmaster tells Maria how, two hundred years before, they had been abducted from Lilliput by Captain Biddel (a minor character in Jonathan Swift's *Gulliver's Travels*) and brought to England as a carnival attraction. Escaping Biddel at Malplaquet, they have been in hiding ever since. Being only human, Maria soon tries to make toys and vassals of them, until the professor (another version of White) who lives on the grounds forces her to realize that her behavior to the Lilliputians mirrors that of her guardians to her. She reforms; like the Wart, she is educable. Some contrived plot shenanigans follow the guardians' discovery of the creatures from Lilliput, whom they define as nonhuman and therefore exploitable; and the novel closes, after the wicked adults have been arrested, on a mechanically happy note. (Brownie died during the composition of the book.) What stays in the memory are the closely realized Lilliputians, Maria's admirable capacity to learn, the professor's comic vacuity, and the great circumambient grounds of Malplaquet.

The Master: An Adventure Story is a science fiction tale for older children. Although it has been unfairly dismissed by critics, it cannot be dealt with here at length. Of deepest interest to any reader of White is the character of the eponymous Master, a 157-year-old savant who has constructed on the Atlantic islet of Rockall a base from which he intends to rule the world. Last in the long line of White's self-projections, he is in one significant aspect different from all his predecessors: in attempting to evolve himself beyond the execrable human condition, he has so remotely immured himself within the upper labyrinths of the mind that he has almost lost the power of speech. He can only descend to faltering utterance, he can activate the necessary lower segments of his brain—only when drunk. And when he does speak, he utters only dense gnomic statements. He cannot bring the world eloquently to bear; he cannot teach. This silence, this despair at the human condition, this frozen removal from joyful contact with the young twins whose capture on the island provides the plot, and the grotesque hubris of his desire to rule the world for its own good, all mount to a self-portrait of the utmost desolation. At one point a boy finds him listening to music:

> He was wearing a quilted smoking-jacket and a round cap like a pill-box with a tassel—eerie, like a skeleton in rouge and lipstick. Three bottles of whisky stood beside him on the radiogram, the glass beside them chiming at the deep notes. His crackled face was infinitely distant in time and knowledge, blindly presiding over tumult in a world of stillness and silence, like a glimpse of Everest.
>
> (chapter 15)

In this fashion, White wrote his own epitaph. But the icy quietude of his close should not erase the memory of his prime. "The best thing for being sad . . . is to learn something," Merlyn tells the Wart in chapter 21 of Book I of *The Once and Future King*. With an almost sexual apprehension of the given world, the White who conceived Merlyn conceived domains of plenitude, whose workings he told with all his love. Merlyn's Isle of Gramarye seems more real than aging and the cold, though it is a dream.

Selected Bibliography

WORKS OF T. H. WHITE

Fiction

Earth Stopped; or, Mr. Marx's Sporting Tour. London: Collins, 1934.

Gone to Ground. London: Collins, 1935.

The Sword in the Stone. London: Collins, 1938. New York: Putnam, 1939. Texts differ. In revised form, makes up Book I of *The Once and Future King.* In a "special edition" form of the Collins printing, limited to six copies, White colored his own illustrations; copies are inscribed, as part of the inking of the edition, to John Masefield, Siegfried Sassoon, David Garnett, L. J. Potts, and Martin Trubshawe.

The Witch in the Wood. New York: Putnam, 1939. London: Collins, 1940. In revised form, and entitled "The Queen of Air and Darkness," makes up Book II of *The Once and Future King.*

The Ill-Made Knight. New York: Putnam, 1940. London: Collins, 1941. In revised form, makes up Book III of *The Once and Future King.*

Mistress Masham's Repose. New York: Putnam, 1946. London: Cape, 1947.

The Elephant and the Kangaroo. New York: Putnam, 1947. London: Cape, 1948.

The Master: An Adventure Story. London: Cape, 1957. New York: Putnam, 1957.

The Once and Future King. London: Collins, 1958. New York: Putnam, 1958. Comprises *The Sword in the Stone, The Witch in the Wood,* and *The Ill-Made Knight,* all revised, plus new material, "The Candle in The Wind."

The Book of Merlyn: The Unpublished Conclusion to "The Once and Future King." Austin: University of Texas Press, 1977. London: Collins, 1978.

The Maharajah and Other Stories. Edited with an introduction by Kurth Sprague. London: Macdonald Futura, 1981. New York: Putnam, 1981.

Correspondence

The White/Garnett Letters. Edited with a preface by David Garnett. London: Cape, 1968. New York: Viking, 1968.

Letters to a Friend: The Correspondence Between T. H. White and I. J. Potts. Edited by François Gallix. New York: Putnam, 1982.

CRITICAL AND BIOGRAPHICAL STUDIES

Crane, John K. *T. H. White.* Boston: Twayne, 1974.

Manlove, C. N. *The Impulse of Fantasy Literature.* London: Macmillan, 1983.

Warner, Sylvia Townsend. *T. H. White: A Biography.* London: Cape/Chatto and Windus, 1967. New York: Viking, 1968.

—JOHN CLUTE

IX

British Postwar Writers

C. S. LEWIS

1898-1963

WHEN C. S. LEWIS began to write science fiction and fantasy in the late 1930's, he came to these genres as an academic whose skill as a commercial novelist was untested. It is indeed unlikely that he ever conceived of his genre fictions as being commercial in any ordinary sense. He never pretended to have much concern about whether he was capable of writing "good" science fiction, and he persistently defined fantasy in terms that removed any of his products very far from the marketplace. After his mid-twenties, when he began his lifelong professional association with Oxford and Cambridge universities, he never needed to produce fiction that would earn a living, and he did not do so. It is in fact one of the more attractive aspects of his peculiarly complex and often abrasive personality, as man and writer, that for many years he anonymously allocated something like two-thirds of his writing income to various good causes and needy individuals. Charity being a Christian virtue conspicuously absent from most of his work, this quiet generosity should be kept in mind.

Being free to write or not to write popular literature, however eccentric, and quite possibly doing some damage to his academic career by indulging in the habit, Lewis was clearly motivated by suprageneric goals when he did choose to publish novels. Despite his disclaimers that he never began a story with a theological point in mind, everything he published deeply reflects adamantly held Christian convictions about the nature of the world and about the

appropriate rendering of Christian truths in words, image, and plot. That *Out of the Silent Planet* (1938) is a kind of science fiction and that *Perelandra* (1943) is a kind of fantasy is clearly and deliberately subordinate to the fact that they are at heart exercises in Christian apologetics. As such, they are of a piece with the rest of his voluminous output — which comprises poetry, literary criticism and history, popular theology and lay sermons, adult and children's fiction, and autobiographical works. All share common doctrinal, literary, social, and sexual prejudices.

In order to begin to understand his fantasy writings, which more uninhibitedly reflect the man than is usually the case in this generally commercial genre, one should look first at the shape of his life. Lewis abhorred depth psychology. Indeed, he abhorred much of twentieth-century thought and unreservedly despised the "soft" sciences for their presumptuous deciphering of the human condition, secular analysis of which he regarded as being close to obscene. Throughout his career he attempted to protect himself from what he conceived to be the destructive insights of non-Christian introspection. His early biographers often observed a similar decorum. All the same, significant patterns are difficult to muffle, as has been shown in such recent studies as Humphrey Carpenter's *The Inklings* (1978), a generally sympathetic, though revealing, analysis of Lewis and his friends.

The first fact may be the most important: born in Belfast on 29 November 1898, Clive Staples Lewis was an Ulster Protestant by upbringing, and he never quite lost, either in his work or in his manner, that flavor of uneasy bullying conservatism characteristic of the siege mentality of this surrounded but proselytizing faith. It should be remembered that Ireland's Roman Catholic majority has always treated the Protestants of Ulster as representatives of a foreign tyranny, religious and ethnic interlopers. Lewis was therefore a sort of stranger in the land of his birth, an internal exile tragically intensified by the death of his mother from cancer when he was nine.

Almost immediately afterward, his father banished him to school in England, where his experiences were more than usually miserable. Perhaps no child can fail to experience a sense of exile as adulthood looms with all its estrangements; but there can be little doubt that Lewis responded with unusual violence to his own eviction from Paradise. For the rest of his life he would use any weapon available to defend the sources of security he had managed precariously to attain: his Christian faith, to which he adhered with all the impenetrable assiduity of the true convert; his don's privileges; his sense of the proper scope and aims of scholarship and art, a sense that caused him to repudiate all forms of modernism because modernism (like depth psychology) does not shore up and celebrate its material but lays it bare and corrodes it; and, finally, the male friends who gathered about him to form the Inklings, a group of academics of conservative and religious inclination, including J. R. R. Tolkien and Charles Williams, who met regularly to drink and to read aloud from their works in progress. He became, in all his work, a strikingly adept manipulator of rhetorical argument and emotional imagery, sometimes to meretricious and sometimes to deeply moving effect, as can be seen in his fiction more clearly perhaps than anywhere else.

After 1914, when he was rescued from the last of his purgatorial stays at various boarding schools, Lewis' life became an outwardly undramatic record of success, though his private life was singular enough. His tutor very early noted his remarkable capacity to immerse himself in the world of imaginative literature and scholarship, and there was never much doubt that he would have an academic career. It was a distinguished one. After serving briefly in World War I, he took a Triple First (highest honors) at Oxford in classical moderations, ancient history and philosophy, and English language and literature; and from 1925 to the year of his death he taught, studied, and wrote book after book, first at Magdalen College, Oxford, and finally, from 1954 on, as professor of medieval and Renaissance English at Cambridge.

His private life was also fixed early. In 1918 he set up house with a Mrs. Moore, the mother of a friend who had died in World War I. He was twenty; she was forty-five. He lived with her for thirty-three years—celibately, it seems—until she died in 1951. As though to complete this parodic reconstruction of the prelapsarian family, his older brother moved in with them in 1932. A domineering, irascible, erratic, violently temperamental person, Mrs. Moore does not seem to have provided Lewis with anything like a far-ranging experience of the nature of women, and his views on their natural subordination to men—though rationalized in religious terms—do come at times very close to brute misogyny. His fiction, never so smugly punitive as when it is dealing with "modern" women, reflects this narrowness of vision, as it was almost all written before his late, transforming marriage to Joy Davidman Gresham. (*Till We Have Faces*, 1956, hints at this transformation.) The years until Joy's death in 1960 were, by his own account, his happiest. Her death, the effects of which he recounts in *A Grief Observed* (1961; published as by N. W. Clerk), shattered him. His health declined swiftly, and he died on 22 November 1963.

Curled up porcupinelike against the century in which he lived, Lewis focused his active emotional life inward and on the past. It is perhaps an unusual perspective for a writer of science fiction, however eccentric and even fantastic that science fiction may seem when compared to the normal product; but it is by no means an unprecedented angle of vision for a writer of fantasy. Lewis' bibliography is extensive, with at least fifty works published before his death and a considerable number—most of them collections of lay theology assembled for a Christian readership—posthumously released. Works that could be considered fantasy begin early, with *Dymer*

(1926; published as by Clive Hamilton), the second book he published; they extend to a posthumous volume, *The Dark Tower and Other Stories* (1977). All but the first come from the fully formed Lewis; that is, they are Christian, polemical, didactic, and adroitly palatable.

The eponymous hero of *Dymer*, a book-length narrative poem, escapes from the dystopian city of his birth, where "the State / Chose for eugenic reasons who should mate / With whom, and when," and finds himself translated to a myth-ridden world whose Nordic textures are the first mature declaration of Lewis' abiding love for northern landscapes, legends, imagery, and gods. In this new country—which in an inchoate fashion prefigures Narnia in seeming more real than the land he has left—Dymer fights a number of top-heavy allegorical battles, faces ambiguous challenges, and settles his mind.

The Pilgrim's Regress (1933; revised 1943) is based on John Bunyan's *Pilgrim's Progress* and is an explicit allegory. After Pilgrim has demonstrated a hearty contempt for the art, literature, thought, and social innovations of the first thirty years of the twentieth century, he "regresses" into childhood, where he ascends into the true comforting Christian faith and settles his mind. It may be remarked that Lewis' characters, saved or damned, generally pass through conflict into the firm repose of a settled mind and stop there.

During the period of his composition of the Ransom Trilogy, Lewis published two smaller works. In *The Screwtape Letters* (1942), a senior devil gives epistolary advice to a junior devil on how to tempt a young man into sin. The book is acutely witty and is probably the most winning expression of Lewis' powerful capacity to transmute convictions into dramatized argument. *The Great Divorce* (1945) demonstrates with a rather sourer humor the unyielding incapacity of the damned to comprehend the nature of Heaven, while they are on a bus trip to that locale.

It is with the Ransom Trilogy, which comprises *Out of the Silent Planet*, *Perelandra*, and *That Hideous Strength* (1945), that Lewis enters his full stride as an author of didactic fiction. The science fiction element in *Out of the Silent Planet* serves as a kind

of Venus'-fly trap for the unwary, inducing the reader to believe he is being told a tale of interplanetary adventure, perhaps in the tradition of H. G. Wells. On a walking tour of England, Dr. Elwin Ransom, who will be the guiding human spirit through all three volumes, is abducted by two scientists who, having visited Mars, have returned to Earth with imperialistic notions and the mistaken idea that the Martians, whom they think of as "natives," have demanded a human sacrifice from them. Ransom, whose name acquires theological significance as the trilogy proceeds, is their choice for the sacrifice: they have, of course, misinterpreted the request of the Martians. After Ransom has traveled through scenes of heavenly splendor, escaped his captors, and begun to understand the true nature of the Martian world, Lewis' underlying strategy starts to take shape.

As it turns out, the reader has been enticed into a world radically opposed to the secular universe of twentieth-century science fiction. The very essence of the universe that Ransom begins to comprehend can be read only as an intense, intricate testimony to the abiding and fully active existence of God. Long ago, after having lost his battle in Heaven (which to the trapped secular mind is only interplanetary space) against God, Satan, or the "Bent One," as he is called in the trilogy, had taken as his domain Thulcandra, or the Silent Planet, which has been in quarantine ever since. The Silent Planet is of course Earth. The scientists' impudent voyage to Mars—called Malacandra here, just as Venus is called Perelandra—breaks the long-held quarantine. This act has deep theological significance, for the Malacandrans are unfallen creatures, and Weston, the chief physicist and villain, speaks the language of the Bent One. The ancient conflict enters a new phase.

Out of the Silent Planet reaches its climax in an extended debate between Weston and Oyarsa, the chief of the "eldila," or angels, who occupies the same role on Malacandra as Satan does on Earth. Uttering constant technophilic imbecilities that demonstrate his obscene incapacity to understand the nature of an unfallen world, Weston attempts without success to suborn the angels of Heaven with his devil-worshiping scientific materialism. In this novel his failure is preordained and comic, and he is ignominiously sent back to Earth along with Ransom, who decides that he must try to live among fallen mankind despite the anguish this will cause him. (This identification of Ransom with Christ does not extend to the blasphemy of a Passion.) The novel ends with the quarantine apparently reinstated and with disingenuous hints of a science-fictional premise parodically inverted.

Lewis did not initially intend to write a trilogy; his first attempt at continuing Ransom's story, a fragment from 1940 entitled "The Dark Tower" and published in the volume of that name along with other minor efforts, is relatively slight and does not deal with large theological issues. Without any real doubt, and despite its overall thematic consistency, as an aesthetic whole the trilogy is misshapen. *That Hideous Strength* was written after *Perelandra* and is its chronological sequel. But it makes a sorry showing when treated in sequence—John Milton retold as Harriet Beecher Stowe. Despite its very considerable length, *That Hideous Strength* is a comparatively lightweight satire with melodramatic overtones. It is set on Earth, mainly at Bracton College in England, where the vile National Institute for Coordinated Experiments (NICE) is housed. Ostensibly an organization of scientists espousing rationalist values of the sort Weston represented, NICE is in truth a consort of superstitious devil-worshipers, among whom strides an official torturer. Lewis' early attempt at depicting an active woman, this torturer is an enormous, overmuscular, sadistic lesbian.

In the foreground of the action, and providing its mundane frame, are a young couple, Mark and Jane Stoddard, whose marriage is in trouble. Temporarily seduced by NICE, Mark soon finds himself at moral risk in his home life as well, for Jane has been expressing "modern" notions about the proper relationship between husband and wife, and about childbearing. In *That Hideous Strength*, the forces arrayed against the Bent One are led by a charismatic though etherealized Dr. Ransom; Lewis' characteristic punishment of the modern Jane Stoddard is (almost) meted out by Merlin, who is a kind of pre-Christian spirit of Old England unconvincingly resurrected to help save his beloved country. When he discovers that the woman has been practicing

birth control, he wrathfully suggests that "her head be cut from her shoulders." But Jane is saved and soon repents. As the forces of evil are defeated—in scenes rather reminiscent of the scouring of Toad Hall in Kenneth Grahame's *The Wind in the Willows*—a humbled Jane returns to Mark, who has himself been punished for his opportunistic liaison with NICE. Perhaps because the theological kudos bestowed on Ransom by Lewis have made it impossible for actions to be ascribed to him without blasphemy, Ransom performs more as a catalyst than as an agent; he calls down the angels from Heaven when they are needed for the assault on NICE, though to an oddly tepid effect, as they do little more than harrow Toad Hall.

It seems reasonable to assume that Lewis felt some discomfort in attempting to bring this book to an appropriate climax, probably because the real theological-apologetic issues had been dealt with earlier, in *Perelandra*. Perhaps he could see no way to transform the Silent Planet into a world of the unfallen (a sacrilegious effort if made), and therefore could not redeem *That Hideous Strength* from the smug farcicality that vitiates its climax. So the novel ends on a less-than-transcendent note, in the resumption of a Christian marriage properly endowed with children.

The imaginative heart of the trilogy and the natural resolution of its argument are to be found in *Perelandra*. In this superb resolution of his lifelong *Sehnsucht*, Lewis reaches his peak as a writer of fiction. (*Sehnsucht* [German, "longing"] here means a longing for unattainable beauty or a desiderium; it is a term frequently used in Lewis studies to point the inherent drive within much of his work.) The events of *Perelandra* take place after Ransom has returned from Malacandra. Having turned the premises of science fiction in upon themselves, Lewis no longer feels any need for mechanical appurtenances, and he transports Ransom to Perelandra through the agency of that planet's chief eldil. Because Weston, operating as the Bent One's tool, has broken quarantine, something new has happened in Deep Heaven. Awakening on Venus, which is almost completely covered by moving waters across which unceasingly float organic islands inhabited by pacific creatures, Ransom finds himself in a world unmistakably akin to Eden. The Miltonic parallel is deliberate.

Perelandra is governed by Tor and Tinidril—Adam and Eve—who have not fallen. But Weston soon arrives. He is horrible, whining, petty, sadistic, cursed. He begins to tempt Tinidril. (In repeating the biblical pattern, Lewis manifests his conservative reading of the Christian message; seemingly above temptation, the Adamic Tor is rarely encountered in the novel.) Ransom has been given the task of countering the Bent One's arguments. In the long debates that follow, the grotesque, insinuating "Weston" gets rather the better of the argument until, in a dark night of the soul, Ransom comes to realize that he must physically dislodge the Bent One from Perelandra and that he must actually destroy "Weston." He therefore terminates the debate and, in a series of actions of mounting brutality and considerable narrative force, he beats the "Un-Man" to death.

And the novel explodes into delight, with translucent innocence that is very convincing indeed. Perelandra has been saved from the Fall; there will be no history of exile and loss; Tor and Tinidril appear together and prepare to mount their throne:

> Paradise itself in its two Persons, Paradise walking hand in hand, its two bodies shining in the light like emeralds yet not themselves too bright to look at, came in sight. . . . And the gods kneeled and bowed their huge bodies before the small forms of that young King and Queen.
>
> (chapter 16)

In heightened language evocative of Tolkien and Williams, the novel closes with a dance of the gods and creatures of the unfallen heavens; it becomes apparent to the transfigured Ransom that he is beholding in this ceremony the warp and woof of reality, *Sehnsucht* transcended as the world dances in its true shape. This vision—not specifically Christian—of the Great Dance arguably translates Lewis' sectarian afflatus into the deep, hard, usable grandeur of myth.

Most of Lewis' remaining fiction comprises his series of children's stories about Narnia, a secondary universe inhabited by talking animals and ruled by Aslan, a Christ figure in the shape of a lion. (It is unfortunate that *Aslan* is now a word more evocative of computer languages than of a messiah.) In order of publication, though not of internal chronology, the series includes *The Lion, the Witch, and the Wardrobe* (1950), *Prince Caspian* (1951), *The Voyage of the "Dawn Treader"* (1952), *The Silver Chair* (1953), *The Horse and His Boy* (1954), *The Magician's Nephew* (1955), and *The Last Battle* (1956). The first two volumes show the haste with which they were composed; perhaps mainly for that reason, they displeased Tolkien, who up to that point had been a longtime intimate of Lewis and who was central, with him, to the success of the Inklings. Generally thought to be more successful, the middle volumes are written with a confident serenity that is appealing to many adults as well as to children; they depict a world transparent to God's immanence. The final volume, though more than competent, displays an almost sadistic pleasure in meting out punishment to the adversaries of Lewis' intensely literalist Christianity. A children's book is perhaps no longer a proper forum for the pious separation of those who are saved from those who are eternally damned.

Only the novel of Lewis' Indian summer remains. *Till We Have Faces: A Myth Retold* recasts as a complex Christian romance the myth of Cupid and Psyche, originally told by Apuleius in *The Golden Ass*. By virtue of doctrine, Lewis was convinced that to Christianize a "pagan" myth was to improve it, to make it tell the truth; and certainly in this book he has radically and successfully restructured the Apuleian tale. *Till We Have Faces* is a confession, a romance, an allegory, an adventure, a political tract, and a didactic rendering of the eternal Christ made manifest as the god of love. But if it is a fantasy, then the works of Dante and Bunyan also are fantasies. The supernatural elements in the book—Psyche being rescued by the West Wind from a place of sacrifice, living in a magic palace afterward with the god of love, and so on—are clearly subsumed under the Christ allegory. It is unnecessary to attempt to unravel the intricate metaphysical conundrums of *Till We Have Faces* in the present context.

All the same, it is of striking interest that in Psyche's sister Orual, who narrates the book, Lewis at last treats a woman without condescension. In her passions, both sexual and political, in the complex ambivalence of her feelings for the inhumanly beautiful Psyche, Orual is a fully fledged individual, and her grief at the loss of her sister strangely prefigures Lewis' own grief when Joy—his new wife and clear model for Orual—died of cancer a few years later.

At this point, for the reader of supernatural fiction, Lewis' career ends. Eloquent, learned, crystalline, his works are a solace to his fellow Christians and a temptation to the secular. The temptation is to try to read him for the pleasures and not the lessons that he imparts, the truths of which he is never in doubt. The solace for Christians is that he widens their house.

Selected Bibliography

WORKS OF C. S. LEWIS

Dymer. London: Dent, 1926. New York: Dutton, 1926. (Originally published as by Clive Hamilton.) Reprinted in *Narrative Poems*. New York: Harcourt Brace Jovanovich, 1969.

The Pilgrim's Regress. London: Dent, 1933. Revised edition. London: Geoffrey Bles, 1943. New York: Sheed and Ward, 1944.

Out of the Silent Planet. London: John Lane/ The Bodley Head, 1938. New York: Macmillan, 1943.

The Screwtape Letters. London: Geoffrey Bles, 1942. New York: Macmillan, 1943. (Reprinted with a new letter added in 1961; United States edition, 1964.)

Perelandra. London: John Lane/ The Bodley Head, 1943. New York: Macmillan, 1944. Retitled *Voyage to Venus*. London: Pan Books, 1953.

The Great Divorce. London: Geoffrey Bles, 1945. New York: Macmillan, 1946.

That Hideous Strength. London: John Lane/ The Bodley Head, 1945. New York: Macmillan, 1946. Abridged by author. London: Pan Books, 1955. Retitled *The Tortured Planet*. New York: Avon, 1958.

The Lion, the Witch, and the Wardrobe. London: Geoffrey Bles, 1950. New York: Macmillan, 1950.

Prince Caspian. London: Geoffrey Bles, 1951. New York: Macmillan, 1951.

The Voyage of the "Dawn Treader." London: Geoffrey Bles, 1952. New York: Macmillan, 1952.

The Silver Chair. London: Geoffrey Bles, 1953. New York: Macmillan, 1953.

The Horse and His Boy. London: Geoffrey Bles, 1954. New York: Macmillan, 1954.

The Magician's Nephew. London: The Bodley Head, 1955. New York: Macmillan, 1955.

The Last Battle. London: The Bodley Head, 1956. New York: Macmillan, 1956.

Till We Have Faces: A Myth Retold. London: Geoffrey Bles, 1956. New York: Harcourt Brace and World, 1957.

Of Other Worlds: Essays and Stories. London: Geoffrey Bles, 1966. New York: Harcourt Brace and World, 1966.

The Dark Tower and Other Stories. London: Collins, 1977. New York: Harcourt Brace Jovanovich, 1977.

CRITICAL AND BIOGRAPHICAL STUDIES

Carpenter, Humphrey. *The Inklings: C. S. Lewis, J. R. R. Tolkien, Charles Williams, and Their Friends*. London: Allen and Unwin, 1978.

Hillegas, Mark R., ed. *Shadows of Imagination: The Fantasies of C. S. Lewis, J. R. R. Tolkien and Charles Williams*. Carbondale: Southern Illinois University Press, 1969.

Lewis, C. S. *A Grief Observed*. London: Faber and Faber, 1961. (Published as by N. W. Clerk.)

Schakel, Peter J., ed. *The Longing for a Form: Essays on the Fiction of C. S. Lewis*. Kent, Ohio: Kent State University Press, 1977.

Walsh, Chad. *The Literary Legacy of C. S. Lewis*. New York: Harcourt Brace Jovanovich, 1979.

—JOHN CLUTE

SARBAN

1910-

FOR MANY YEARS the identity of "Sarban" was a mystery. Sarban wrote three books, published in quick succession in 1951, 1952, and 1953, and was not heard from again. Between them, the books contain three novellas and six short stories, all of them uncanny and disquieting, and each written with a confident air that has suggested to more than one reader that the person masquerading under that name was already a well-known professional. "Sarban . . . I should guess to be an established British writer preferring on occasion to become pseudonymous," wrote Kingsley Amis in *New Maps of Hell* (1961); he went on to suppose that it might have been the fetishistic content of *The Sound of His Horn* (1952) that had led to the necessary anonymity in that case.

Two of Sarban's books are collections. The first, *Ringstones, and Other Curious Tales* (1951), contains the novella "Ringstones" and four short stories. The other, *The Doll Maker, and Other Tales of the Uncanny* (1953), contains the novella "The Doll Maker" and two short stories. *The Sound of His Horn*, whose content unsettled Amis, is really a novella rather than a novel so far as length is concerned—a mere 154 pages of big print. It was published without any accompanying stories.

All of this is rather a slender body of work on which to sustain a reputation, more especially as the paperback reprints (the only editions of Sarban's work to achieve any real currency) did not include the short stories, so that most people know Sarban only for the three novellas. Indeed, *The Doll Maker, and Other Tales of the Uncanny* is now a very rare volume, and people who wish to read the two additional short stories in the book, "The Trespassers" and "A House of Call," may well have to visit a library of record.

Yet a sufficient number of readers found Sarban's stories haunting for his name to have been well remembered for over thirty years, especially by other writers. He has today a cult reputation as one of the most evocative "tellers of curious tales"—which, incidentally, is the meaning of the word *sarban* in Persian. A *sarban* is "one of those who, in former times, travelled the country with caravans of pack-animals. Story-telling was their diversion in the caravanserais where they made their halts" (so described in a letter written by John William Wall, a retired Britsh diplomat).

John W. Wall, in fact, is Sarban. He was tracked down via his publishers in the early 1980's by two British researchers operating independently, Michael Ashley and the present author. Career diplomats are not encouraged to publish while active in their profession, so Wall used a pseudonym. Sarban was a very appropriate name for one who was sent by his government to so many of the caravanserais of the Middle East. After graduating from Jesus College, Cambridge, he entered the Levant consular service in 1933 as a probationer. Subsequent posts included vice-consul at Cairo (1936); second secretary at Jedda (1939); and various quite senior positions at Tabriz (1944), Isfahan (1946), Casablanca (1947), Bahrain (1952), and Salonika (1955). From 1957 to 1959, Wall was British ambassador to Paraguay, and, from 1963 until his retirement in 1966, consul general in Alexandria. All this, of course, explains the eerie precision of some of his best stories' exotic settings: Cairo in "Capra," Tabriz in "The Khan," and Jedda in "A Christmas Story" (all three stories published in *Ringstones*). Except for *The Sound of His Horn*, which is set in Germany, Sarban's remaining stories are set in England.

In his fiction several strong themes recur over and over. They are clearly announced in the five stories of the *Ringstones* collection and developed in the two later books. The title novella, "Ringstones," was written in 1947; according to Sarban, it is the first story he wrote, apart from "some scrappy fiction writing . . . in the mid '30s . . . none survives."

"Ringstones," like most of Sarban's stories, has a "frame," a literary device that the author consciously borrowed from Joseph Conrad. In this case the framing story tells of two male university students, one of whom is very worried about a long handwritten manuscript he has received through the post from Daphne, a young woman friend. Unfinished, it tells — or purports to tell — of the strange experiences she has been having at a manor house in a remote corner of the Northumbrian moorlands, Ringstones, named after a nearby stone circle. A physical education student of lithe beauty and considerable athleticism, she has taken a vacation job looking after three children.

At first the work is idyllic, all picnicking and playing games. The children are charming and exotic, with a Middle Eastern appearance. The oldest is Nuaman, a handsome, eager, playful child of fifteen. The younger girls (twins?) are gazellelike "creatures of summer and some country of the sun." But a sinister note is struck quite soon. Nuaman is charmingly but aggressively domineering and mysterious. Daphne, the letter writer, sometimes thinks she sees him at a distance with other people, small and brown, on the hillside near the old stone circle; but there are no other people in this deserted spot. The games Nuaman laughingly organizes have a

mythic resonance; he dresses the Polish maid up as a pantomime bull but with horns that are really sharp, and he and his sisters practice bull-dancing. Daphne attempts to walk across the moors to the nearest village, though Nuaman had told her he did not want her to leave, even for a day. Very soon she becomes lost, as the landscape seems to develop a tortuous, labyrinthine topography that is foreign to its apparently open nature; the moorlands are now cloudy with an atmosphere of hostility. Daphne feels "panic" in the original sense of that word; it is as if the god Pan were not far away. After helplessly circling for many hours, she finds herself, bedraggled and unhappy, back at Ringstones, where she began, greeted by the child Nuaman, who knowingly tells her she should not have left.

Nuaman's games take on a strange, fetishistic air and involve his young, lithe dominance and the submissiveness of his playmates, including Daphne. He talks of harnessing her to a chariot, along with the Polish girl, who fears Nuaman. "He *do* weep," the maid tells Daphne, who does not realize that "weep" is a clumsy, foreign pronunciation of "whip."

Daphne's dreams (which may not be dreams) are bad. The manuscript ends abruptly at the point where she dreams she is harnessed with the bovine Polish maid to a chariot, with Nuaman lashing her with a whip. The reader now recognizes him as an avatar of some Syrian sun god, in league with the fairy people — ancient ironworkers — who built the sun-worshipers' stone circles.

The students who receive this manuscript (with no accompanying explanation) are disturbed and go off in search of Daphne. They find her a day later, quite unharmed, in a peaceful country village. She tells them the manuscript was merely an account of a vivid dream. Ringstones does exist, but it is a derelict, old, empty house. Daphne has been working as a child-minder for the perfectly respectable family of a village doctor. But beneath her laughing assurances that everything is all right lies a deep, frightening uneasiness, and the story ends with her looking miserably at a half-healed scar on her wrist.

On the surface "Ringstones" is a clever but conventional enough tale of mythic survivals in a remote British landscape, rather in the manner of Algernon Blackwood or Walter de la Mare (the latter, Wall told the author in a letter, being one of the strongest influences on his own writing). But the name of Arthur Machen springs to mind, too. Many of Machen's stories, notably "The Great God Pan" (1890), also deal on the surface with the continuing existence of ancient beings but have a subtext that tells of sexual terror. This terror is associated not only with the old gods but also, perhaps, with the most fundamental human emotions, which is to say, in terms of evolution, the most ancient emotions. The coming of the old gods is equated with the survival of the beast in man. A similar equation forms the subtext of many of Sarban's stories, but here the sexual terror is of a more complex kind, for it is preeminently something to be desired as well as loathed.

In "Ringstones" the prose is sensuous throughout; the reader is aware of Daphne's deep consciousness of her own body—not surprisingly, since she is a very physical woman and not long out of puberty. Her relationship with the children, particularly Nuaman, is described in especially sensuous terms: the running, the naked swimming, and so on. *Sensuous* is more apt than *sensual*, because Sarban is of that generation of writers who seldom wrote overtly of sexuality, but the implications—the prose is very evocative—are unmistakable. To submit to Nuaman would be, on the one hand, to bask in the rays of an ancient sun and, on the other, to accept shamefully a whimsical sadism. Nuaman represents a summer of the body and a winter of the spirit, though a winter not without joy. There is, that is to say, a strong element of masochism in Daphne, as there is in many of Sarban's protagonists. Typically a Sarban story pits a slightly masochistic protagonist against a supernatural sadist whose cruel potency, it is suggested, stands for something that has been lost to modern civilized society—or, at least, suppressed by it.

The repressions of modern life, particularly English middle-class life with its rather strangled emotions, are amusingly rendered in several of the stories. Children are the least liable to succumb to the death of the spirit that middle-class life, for Sarban, seems to represent, and it is children who are the protagonists of another story in the *Ringstones*

collection, "Calmahain," which tells of two children in the north of England during wartime. Their family is repressive and cruel, and as soon as it is learned that the children have found a game that they enjoy, then that game is banned, for pleasure is wicked. The children are thus forced to exist on their inner resources, and they begin to build up a vast, imaginary world into which they escape. The world is peopled by many dangers and by tiny fairy people. Eventually the family's home is bombed, and the neighbors assume that the children are dead along with their horrible elders, but the implication is very strong that they have escaped into the life of freedom represented by the world they have invented.

The old question that fantastic literature is so peculiarly well suited to pose is here asked again: What is real and what is imaginary? Solipsism is a fundamental theme in fantasy, the basic premise of which is nearly always to treat an imaginary world as if it were real and then to ask what happens next. This is the kind of "thought experiment" that is very useful in testing the limits of "reality" and, specifically, in asking whether things might be accepted as "real" only because we choose to perceive them as real. Thus, the solipsist spirit of Bishop Berkeley lives on, usefully, in the literature of the fantastic.

Sarban's stories are notable for the casual ease with which they build up nests and patterns of metaphor. Thus, the symbolic structure is at once rich and modest; that is to say, it does not loudly draw attention to itself as meaningful.

For example, the theme of repression, modernity, and the city (especially sexual repression) versus freedom, antiquity, and the wilderness (especially sexual freedom) is beautifully established in what is perhaps the best story in the *Ringstones* collection, "The Khan." The unhappy wife of a railroad engineer accompanies him on a difficult project in the Persian desert. The laborers are local tribesmen, rather wild and unpredictable, one of whom brings her a bear cub from "the Forest." She is amazed. Where would a desert conceal a forest? Her thick-skinned, ill-tempered husband wants to shoot the cub, and after a fierce fight, she rides out into the desert on a horse and high into a range of stony mountains. Here she finds a forest, a secret, honeyed homestead, with a strange group of women awaiting the return of their master, the Khan. She is bathed, oiled, scented, and at the end meets the Khan in a moment that movingly achieves a combination of exaltation and fear. The suggestion that she will make love to this mysterious giant of the wilderness is not overt, but the thrust of the story is unmistakably toward that consummation. What makes this so remarkable is that the Khan is not a man at all, but a great, powerful bear.

It is quite extraordinary how, without abandoning the language of polite society and while remaining the most English of writers, Sarban is able both here and elsewhere to evoke a positively tropical atmosphere of heated sexuality tinged with the slightest flavor of sadomasochistic perversity. This is not at all meant to suggest that he writes a kind of old-fashioned, soft-core pornography—far from it. For one thing, the dominance-submission theme in the work of any given pornographer is almost invariably of one kind, either of women to men or of men to women. In Sarban's stories sexual domination may be of either kind, and the focus of interest is on moral domination rather than erotic chastisement. In the longest of his works, *The Sound of His Horn*, Sarban has a male protagonist who undergoes experiences comparable to those of Daphne in "Ringstones" or the wife in "The Khan."

The theme is by no means exclusively sexual, for intimately involved with the idea of a sometimes gentle but always dangerous dominance is the idea of antiquity. The Khan comes from a time when the world was younger, as did Nuaman. Sarban's theme (often symbolized by supernatural powers) is in part that the potency of the past will always pose a threat and a challenge to the placidity of the middle-class present. Reason and good manners are confronted by feeling and unpredictability. The past is usually embodied in a single figure, usually a supernatural figure; but more subtly, it is also shown to survive even in the modern human psyche, for Sarban's supernatural figures seem to correspond to some part of the mind, as if something in humans is capable of calling them forth.

The framing story of "The Khan" is very elaborate—almost as long as the tale it frames. It involves the conversation between two European men (one of whom tells the story of the Khan to illustrate a point) in a dusty northern Persian town that has been taken over by a Russian-supported revolutionary party. Thus, in the framing story, too, ancient opposes modern, but this time in political terms, and the dualism occurs again, of course, in the story proper, with the theme of modern technology (the railroad) coming to a landscape previously untouched by modernity. Indeed, the symbolic structure of "The Khan" is extremely sophisticated, and the story deserves to be regularly anthologized (it seems never to have been republished), for not only is it a wonderful story in its own right, but also it has a notable relevance to the situation in present-day Iran.

The strangest thing of all about "The Khan" is that the story is told (crudely, as between hearty men) in the frame before it is told properly in the main story: "The wife . . . had been abducted by a bear and, as I gathered, either not objecting too strongly to the change of company, or perhaps not noticing it, had lived in conjugal relations with the creature for quite some time until found and restored to her rightful owner." Few writers would have the nerve to produce so rough an anecdote and then retell this bawdy, implausible, sexist piece of gossip as a tale of tragedy and regeneration. This achievement requires finesse.

The loneliness of the very old, the supernaturally surviving, is evoked in the least successful story of the *Ringstones* collection, "Capra." This time the mythic survival is a satyr, the setting a rather debauched weekend house party in modern Greece, and the frame a noisy conversation in the rush hour of wartime Cairo. The ingredients are perhaps too complex to jell, but the ending, as always, is good. The narrator is following the prints of cloven hooves and splashes of blood (the beast had been shot): "They stopped at the cliff. The mountain falls sheer away there, down into the Gulf of Corinth." This time around, the sexual potency of an ancient being is inadequate to cope with the sexual corruption of the modern world, which thus destroys him. (As with much of Sarban's imagery, the symbols seem often to have a Freudian or Jungian connotation; for a mythic being to perish by a plunge into the sea—

a sea of myth, so to speak—is almost for him to become reabsorbed by the "anima" of which Carl Jung wrote.)

Because Sarban's three books were published in such quick succession, it is not possible to detect any real development in his work, either thematic or artistic, although perhaps his narrative technique, which was remarkably polished from the outset, became even more finely wrought. The *Ringstones* collection is perhaps the best as well as the least known of the three books, but there is very little to choose between them in terms of outstanding quality. The other two books, especially *The Sound of His Horn*, have been discussed (though not widely) elsewhere, but *Ringstones* has been almost totally neglected.

The themes already discussed continue, in new contexts, in the second and third books. Curiously, *The Sound of His Horn* has usually been taken as science fiction rather than fantasy, perhaps because it can be readily pigeonholed as a "parallel universe" story. It tells what happens to an English soldier who escapes from a POW camp during World War II. The framing situation, however, is a country house party several years after the war. Alan Querdilion, who comes from a fox-hunting county family, is obviously deeply disturbed when the conversation turns to fox-hunting, and amazes his audience by saying, "It is the terror that is unspeakable." Later he confides the curious tale of his experiences to his oldest friend.

Querdilion, tired and frightened, stumbles into a woodland glade in the dark, through a strange glow. He awakens, badly burned, in a small infirmary. It gradually transpires that he has somehow crossed into a Germany more than a hundred years in the future, an alternate future in which the Germans had won the war.

The feeling of the story is that of pure fantasy, not science fiction (even though stories in which the Nazis win the war are not infrequent in science fiction; there are over a dozen, the best known being Philip K. Dick's *The Man in the High Castle*, 1962). The atmosphere of the story is terrifying—made more so by the timeless beauty of the forest and the almost attractively charismatic character of the Master Forester, Count von Hackelberg, the owner of the heavily wooded private preserve in which Querdilion finds himself.

One of Hackelberg's duties, which he carries out with humorous contempt, is to throw hunting parties for senior members of the Reich. Hunting takes place at night in this world. The title of the book reminds the reader of the old folk song "John Peel," whose line "O the sound of his horn woke me from my bed," should one stop to analyze it, suggests a very strange hunt—perhaps a wild hunt. Indeed, the clue to the ancestry of the story (nothing to do with science fiction, which Sarban had probably never read) is the Forester's name. A German name for the Wild Huntsman (Herne the Hunter in English versions of the legend) is von Hackelberg. He is the *wilde Jäger*. In one form of the legend his frightening, exultant task is to hunt human souls right down to the Last Judgment. Originally, of course, he was pre-Christian. The Norsemen called him Odin.

In this short novel his dominion extends not only over the forest but over humans as well. In scenes of extraordinarily perverse power, he uses naked women accoutred as birds of prey, fitted with iron-tipped gloves, and biologically altered (so that they are almost more cat than woman) as hunters. Naked women carrying flambeaux cast an eerie light over his banquets.

The members of the Reich are merely gross, cowardly, revolting; this is only incidentally a story about Nazism. The Master Forester, on the other hand, is a figure of dark, cruel attraction. Again, the figure is one out of myth exercising a dominion at once sexual and spiritual. *The Sound of His Horn*, in fact, displays a direct development of the themes of the previous book, *Ringstones*.

The development of the story itself—given its premises—is inevitable. Querdilion himself is hunted and reduced to a cringing beast in the woodlands. He meets an English girl who is also being hunted. This time they are not mock prey; this is the Forester's private hunt, and it is to the death. The girl sacrifices herself for Querdilion, who then is able to escape only because of a whim of the Forester, who perhaps prefers to meet him again, in another country and an alternate universe.

Querdilion, the very picture of the well-bred

Englishman, has thus been confronted with the archaic powers of death and sexuality, and it is hardly surprising that his present-day (1948) relationship with his fiancée, Elizabeth, is strained. Elizabeth has a "catlike gaze," and as Querdilion suggestively observes in the very last line, "Cats are a damn nuisance, whether you let them out or try to keep them in." The sentence is a splendid example of Sarban's sophistication and savage wit. It is very clear that he is awesomely conscious of the implications of his stories. In this case, of course, he is pointing to the central, concealed theme: that to a slightly repressed Englishman, intimations of the beast inside the human, and of the savage, sexual cat inside the woman, are the most frightening thing of all. Querdilion's experience with the Master Forester has taught him, it seems, that it is dangerous to let the cat out of its human disguise, but perhaps impossible to keep it in.

The title novella of *The Doll Maker, and Other Tales of the Uncanny* elaborates on a similar theme: the responsiveness with which a shy, unworldly, middle-class girl rewards the easy, cruel dominance of a sophisticated, worldly man. Put like this, it sounds like a romantic novel by Barbara Cartland, but although the story does use the conventions of this kind of romance (conventions that go back to the cruel, witty heroes—such as Darcy in *Pride and Prejudice*—of Jane Austen's novels), "The Doll Maker" is not fundamentally that kind of story at all. The irony is that its heroine thinks that what is happening to her is that kind of story.

She is a senior schoolgirl, almost alone in the world, spending a grim Christmas vacation at a tawdry, second-rate girls' boarding school in a rural area in the north of England. (Her family is not in the country, and she has nowhere to go.) He is the handsome young man who lives in the secret, tree-surrounded estate next door. She meets him—believing the meeting to be accidental—when she slips out of school one night, overwhelmed with claustrophobia. Strongly sensual feelings overtake her as their relationship grows, but she does not know that his desire is not to possess her in the normal sense of sexual passion (which is all too clearly what she feels for him); he wants to possess her forever as his toy. He has learned from an alchemist ancestor how to carve dolls and imbue them with human souls so that they strut and play and move about at his command.

The theme, oddly enough, is that of John Keats's poem "Ode on a Grecian Urn": Is it better to possess a superb work of art in the likeness of nature or to witness the free-flowing activities of nature itself? "The Doll Maker" is a frightening study of the immorality of the artist who sometimes sacrifices knowing and experiencing to controlling and shaping. It is more than that, of course; it always is with Sarban. "The Doll Maker" is also a study of the instinct to pervert sexual union away from mutuality and toward absolute possession. In earlier stories it sometimes seemed as if Sarban accepts the sadomasochistic elements of sexual attraction as an essential ingredient in the nature of human sensuality—an ancient ingredient that the modern world ignores at its peril. Now it is clear that he sees the danger in the old dominance-submission dualism. And yet, as ever in his work, the most disturbing element of all is not the presence of sadism (there is a nasty scene with a pin used to take a drop of the heroine's blood, needed for the animation of her puppet doppelgänger), but its attraction. The heroine escapes from, and destroys, her demon lover (who has been responsible for the seduction and effectively the murder of several of her schoolfellows, she learns) only by the most difficult exercise of courage and will. But she feels no triumph, only the most terrible sense of loss.

Readers may feel that there is something a little "nasty" about the persistence of this perversely sexual element in Sarban's work, but it ought to be said that the stories themselves, though they look clearsightedly at the darker side of human feelings, do not appear to be written gloatingly. They are not "bondage fantasies," though at times they come perilously close to this, for Sarban has an undoubted interest in the fetishistic, symbolic side of human relationships—the garments and the landscapes that form a frame for acts of love and death.

Sarban, in his quiet, almost unnoticed literary career, extended the metaphoric boundaries of fantastic literature considerably by contemplating areas of human feeling that are not very often dealt with in mainstream fiction, let alone in fantasy, even though fantasy is especially well equipped to deal with them. (Note the use of the word *fantasy* by psychologists, a use that may not be as far from its meaning in the literary-generic sense as is often supposed.)

The other two stories in *The Doll Maker* collection, as intimated above, are now almost impossible to locate. This is a great pity. "A House of Call" tells a good story about a man home from "flamboyant" India and looking forward to the calm of the English countryside, only to find himself thrown back in time, in a simple country inn run by a couple of viragoes, to the days of the Roman occupation (more dominance, this time political). The story is set outside Warminster, a place that even today has a reputation for the supernatural, being the center of a flying saucer cult. Much is made of England's Roman roads, "the rod of dominion laid across the high places of an enemy of the Roman people."

"The Trespassers" has two schoolboys breaking into a country estate to find a slightly older girl, mocking and confident, who promises them a "reward" if they help her find three golden hairs as long as her forearm. Here the mythic survival is a unicorn, which she entraps, just as she has enchanted the unfortunate boys, who are trembling on the brink of puberty. But to follow her, to get the reward, would be to be "torn from all that was living

and warm and real." Or maybe not; this time around they will not find out, though no doubt they will grow up eventually. Perhaps the whole thing was imagination (solipsism again)? When they return, the unicorn is shrunken in size and significance; it is merely a white pony. The story is a moving and subtle account of the difficulty of coping with the unaccustomed feelings of adolescence, as well as an excellent anecdote about unicorns.

Sarban is not among the major fantasy writers. There is, however, a strong case for arguing that he is the most memorable of all the minor fantasists. He has told the author that at least one unpublished (but unrevised) manuscript still exists.

Selected Bibliography

WORKS OF SARBAN

Ringstones, and Other Curious Tales. London: Peter Davies, 1951. Title story only, New York: Ballantine, 1961.

The Sound of His Horn. London: Peter Davies, 1952.

The Doll Maker, and Other Tales of the Uncanny. London: Peter Davies, 1953. Title story only, New York: Ballantine, 1960.

— PETER NICHOLLS

J. R. R. TOLKIEN

1892-1973

WHEN, ON THE back of an examination paper, J. R. R. Tolkien wrote the now famous sentence "In a hole in the ground there lived a hobbit," he could not have foreseen the vastness of the project he had begun or imagined its eventual effects on popular literature and culture. *The Hobbit* (1937) and *The Lord of the Rings* (1954–1955) proved that a public existed for a kind of writing that had long been out of critical fashion; in the years since *The Lord of the Rings* became a runaway best-seller, many similar but inferior fantasies have appeared, to feed a seemingly insatiable desire to escape into other worlds, like the faerie that Tolkien spoke of but lacking the historical and mythological depth he gave to Middle-earth. Only Ursula K. Le Guin's Earthsea Trilogy and Patricia McKillip's *Quest of the Riddlemaster* are better than threadbare copies of his originals.

Born on 3 January 1892 at Bloemfontein, South Africa, to Mabel and Arthur Tolkien, John Ronald Reuel Tolkien was brought back to England at the age of three. His father died when he was four; his mother became a Catholic when he was eight and died when he was only twelve, at which time he and his younger brother went to live with their aunt. In 1908, Tolkien met the slightly older Edith Bratt; in 1910, he was forbidden to see her by his guardian, Father Francis Morgan. At that time, he also formed a close brotherhood with a group of fellow students at King Edward's School. In 1911, he entered Oxford, where he graduated with first-class

honors in 1915, at which time he was commissioned in the Lancashire Fusiliers. In March 1916, he and Edith were married; by June he was in France, where he served in the trenches until November, when he was sent home with trench fever. He lost most of his closest friends in the school brotherhood to the war, and when he began to write "The Book of Lost Tales" (which eventually became *The Silmarillion*, 1977), it was both as an escape from the nightmares of World War I and as a homage to the lost hopes and possibilities of his dead companions.

After the Armistice, Tolkien returned to Oxford and joined the staff of the *New English Dictionary*. In 1920 he was appointed reader in English language at Leeds University. By 1925, he and Edith had three children, he was professor of English language at Leeds, and he and E. V. Gordon had published their influential edition of *Sir Gawain and the Green Knight*. In the summer of that year, the Tolkiens moved to Oxford, where he was elected Rawlinson and Bosworth professor of Anglo-Saxon and where they lived for most of the rest of his life. In 1926, he became friends with C. S. Lewis, which led to the eventual formation of the Inklings, a group that included Lewis' brother, Major Warren Lewis, R. E. Havard, Owen Barfield, Hugo Dyson, and Charles Williams. After the early 1930's, when he began to write *The Hobbit*, Tolkien's life moved on two parallel but separate tracks: he remained an important professor at Oxford (in 1945 he was elected Merton professor of English language and literature) whose work in Anglo-Saxon was increasingly influential; and he continued building his immense "sub-creation" of Middle-earth.

Tolkien retired from Oxford in 1959, and during the 1960's he began to reap the fruits of his labors on *The Lord of the Rings* while trying to complete *The Silmarillion*. Edith died in 1971 at the age of eighty-two; two years later, on 2 September 1973, Tolkien died at the age of eighty-one, better known for his tales of Middle-earth than for his lectures and writings on Old English, although his work in the latter had both changed the field completely and made possible his particular creative art.

Even Tolkien's children's book, *The Hobbit*, contains a larger world than the story of Bilbo and his quest for treasure reveals. When *The Lord of the Rings* appeared, it offered an epic quest in reverse and therefore a spiritual overturning of an ancient convention of such stories, as well as a tale of many peoples fighting to prevent the end of their world and to bring about the birth of a new age. Moreover, it also offered a complex portrait of Middle-earth at the end of the Third Age as a world with a long and extraordinarily rich history. We know now just how long that history had been building in Tolkien's mind and writings, for Humphrey Carpenter's *J. R. R. Tolkien: A Biography* has given us the background to its growth, while *The Silmarillion* and *Unfinished Tales of Númenor and Middle-earth* (1980) have provided much of Tolkien's invented documentation. They demonstrate Tolkien's great love for the Elves, bound eternally to Middle-earth, undying though they can be killed (while men, in contrast, have been granted "the gift" of death). The Elves are the living history of Middle-earth as well as its guardians; austere, proud, mythic figures inhabiting the landscape in which they are forever grounded on both sides of the ocean, they are the mythic ground of Tolkien's imagination.

When *The Lord of the Rings* first appeared, however, readers could only infer the earlier history of Tolkien's mythos from the carefully planted hints and allusions and the annotations of the appendices. Tolkien's ideal reader would read the appendices with pleasure and reread the trilogy in order to feel his or her way into the profoundly historical world of Middle-earth through its languages, for its history is bound up in its languages, especially the names. Recent criticism has begun to demonstrate how fully Tolkien's great work was, in Tolkien's words, "primarily linguistic in inspiration and was begun in order to provide the necessary background of 'history' for Elvish tongues."

As a writer of what has come to be called "high" or "heroic" fantasy, Tolkien is best known for his big books. But he also published a number of short fantasy fictions, "Leaf by Niggle" (*Dublin Review*, January 1945), *Farmer Giles of Ham* (1949), and *Smith of Wootten Major* (1967), as well as a collection of verses mostly based on Middle-earth material: *The Adventures of Tom Bombadil and Other Verses from The Red Book* (1962). All are enjoyable, and "Leaf by Niggle" is a highly personal spiritual fantasy, but they fade in importance when compared to the work rooted in his major mythology, which is itself centered in his love of languages and his desire to create, as Carpenter has pointed out, "a mythology *for England*."

It is T. A. Shippey's well-documented argument that for Tolkien such a mythology is rooted in Old English and in other languages that derived from a postulated common source. Tolkien knew a number of ancient languages, and their epics, but he especially knew Old English and loved the great stories told in it. His essay "Beowulf: The Monsters and the Critics" (1936) is not only a defense of the poem against the kinds of misreadings he felt it had received for too long, but also a defense of his own work against similar misreadings to come; and they did come. The negative critics not only disliked *The Lord of the Rings* (taste is, after all, personal), but they insisted that the work had no right to an audience because it was a "failure," and therefore must soon prove as unpopular as they wished it to be. Thus far they have been proved wrong. Tolkien's great work has touched a sympathetic chord in many readers, and that seems reason enough to treat it seriously. And there are other reasons as well: however eccentric his major writings may appear in this age of low mimeticism, they are works of literature; and they speak to their audience because they are carefully constructed and linguistically complex, expressing a moral vision.

Tolkien had written some of the major tales of *The Silmarillion* in various forms before he discovered a new race in Middle-earth, though he did not realize at the time that this was what he had done. Hobbits do not appear in any of the stories of the first two ages, and Tolkien had, by the early 1930's, written versions in both prose and verse of some of the major events in his mythic history. But he wrote these tales in a deliberately high mode, while composing light tales about characters with names like Tom Bombadil for his children's entertainment. As he discovered the whole narrative of *The Hobbit*, however, Tolkien began to fuse the two sides of his imagination, creating a work that would have great popular appeal and also touch on the deeper concerns of his slowly growing mythology. Although he did not realize it until later, the hobbits were the image of the ordinary that he needed to ground his grand vision in the popular imagination. As he

> once told an interviewer: "The Hobbits are just rustic English people, made small in size because it reflects the generally small reach of their imagination — not the small reach of their courage or latent power." To put it another way, the hobbits represent the combination of small imagination with great courage which (as Tolkien had seen in the trenches during the First World War) often led to survival against all chances. "I've always been impressed," he once said, "that we are here, surviving, because of the indomitable courage of quite small people against impossible odds."
>
> (Carpenter, page 176)

At the beginning of *The Hobbit*, Bilbo Baggins appears anything but indomitable. He is cute, and the dwarves and "Gandalf, the wandering wizard" seem like a lot of fun, too. But the tone of the story is pitched at children, and the humor is more important than anything else. The humor will remain important; indeed Bilbo's sense of humor is one sign of his slowly growing courage and intelligence, as we will see. However, before the story is over, his adventure will have touched on darker possibilities, which Tolkien himself would not fully discover until many years later. And, as readers of *The Lord of the Rings* know, Bilbo's original narrative of his finding of a magic ring, as he wrote it in *The Red Book* of Westmarch, is a somewhat whitewashed version of what really happened when he first met Gollum. When writing *The Hobbit*, Tolkien did not yet realize how important to his developing mythos that ring was to be.

For the time being, however, he was exploring the possibilities of an adventure story with a serious quest at its center that moved with comic energy to a well-earned happy ending. Children's literature is very difficult, as Tolkien probably found out in writing *The Hobbit*. Good children's writers do not talk down to their readers, and there are some failures of tone in the opening pages of his book. Soon, however, his basic interest in languages comes to the fore, as does his genuine delight in telling an exciting series of adventures. As a result, *The Hobbit* slowly takes on a thicker texture of implications without ever becoming too difficult for a child to enjoy.

One way Tolkien thickens the texture of his tale is by having the dwarves and Gandalf, and later Beorn, tell stories of their pasts and their homes. In comparison to the legends of ancient times that fill the landscapes of *The Lord of the Rings* with history, these tales are slight, but toward the end something begins to happen to the background — opening up vistas suggestive of a far larger and darker world than this particular work is privy to. Tolkien would spend some years finding out precisely how large and dark that world was, but the seeds of its growth were already planted — in the ring and in its former owner, Gollum.

The fun of *The Hobbit* has mostly to do with the changes undergone by Bilbo Baggins, that most ordinary of ordinary souls, as he gives in to the Took side of his character and agrees to go adventuring. As Gandalf remarks, "There is a lot more in him than you guess, and a deal more than he has any idea of himself." The book is dedicated to discovering how much more, by subjecting Bilbo to a series of tests that require him to show courage and concern for his companions and, finally, a moral concern for the good of all. Sometimes Bilbo has a hard time of it, for he has to overcome more than just fear; he has to overcome a bourgeois sensibility that is out of place in such adventures when they have a moral dimension. But Bilbo does come through, often by using his wits rather than his (small) strength. By the end he is a much better person for his adventures, one who can sacrifice his own gains for the common good. His moral stature has increased thereby; this too points the way to the later, greater work.

Language is important in two ways in *The Hobbit*. Although he has not yet named his world with the complexity and fullness that will come in *The Lord of the Rings*, Tolkien nevertheless tends to find his story in its names. Gandalf, the names of the dwarves, Beorn, and Smaug, to take just the main examples, all carry a kind of history, part of which will be inherent in Middle-earth, part of which has to do with the various linguistic traditions in which Tolkien discovered them. As Shippey points out, there is another way in which language plays an important part in *The Hobbit*. Much of its comedy resides in the clash of different forms of discourse. Thus, when one contrasts Bilbo's speech with that of Gandalf or the dwarves, one sees that an ancient and a modern tongue are at odds here. Bilbo is a modern materialistic type; the dwarves are heroic figures out of the old sagas (although Gandalf, as befits a wizard, can speak any tongue). The contrast between the two kinds of speech makes for some fine, occasionally near-satiric, comedy.

Bilbo remains something of an anachronism in the world of his adventure; although he does trick Smaug, he also disappears during the battle, which is no place for a Bilbo Baggins, however courageous he may have become. Before the battle, however, he exercises his courage and moral sensibility in his own tongue when he settles the conflict between Bard and Thorin by offering up his portion of the proceeds from the dragon's hoard (which just happens to be the Arkenstone). Here Bilbo's business English takes on a dignity previously lacking, but the major point, as Shippey notes, is that "Neither side is better than the other, or has any right to criticise. The contrast is one of styles, not of good and bad." By juxtaposing the two styles, Tolkien brings the world of ancient heroism into contact with the world of his readers, through linguistic entanglement. At the end, in Rivendell, Bilbo overhears Gandalf and Elrond discussing Gandalf's dangerous doings in Mirkwood; the language of the discussion is in the old high style, and it portends something much greater than one little hobbit's adventures. Tolkien spent the next seventeen years working out just how much greater it was and discovering that Bilbo's people had a very important role to play in the unfolding history of the One Ring.

At the very time he began work on what became *The Lord of the Rings*, Tolkien wrote two important essays on the kind of literature that he loved and had striven to create in the unpublished fragments of *The Silmarillion*. Both "Beowulf: The Monsters and the Critics" and "On Fairy Stories" (1938) explore tales in which "distance and a great abyss of time" are present. For Tolkien, such stories "open a door on Other Time, and if we pass through, though only for a moment, we stand outside our own time, outside Time itself, maybe." Such a "passing through" carries a particular emotional force, one that helps to explain *The Lord of the Rings*'s popularity. But the problem is to create the proper "door on Other Time."

Tolkien did it in two major ways. The most important and the most difficult to analyze has to do with his "invention" of languages for Middle-earth that themselves carry a great history — or rather two great histories. For, as recent students of Tolkien's linguistic explorations have shown, his names not only work self-referentially within his massive mythos, they also work in our world, weaving extraordinary connections back through Old English and other ancient tongues, often echoing three or four names from the past in one careful portmanteau. For Tolkien, history existed in words, and he worked with great care to see that the many names in *The Lord of the Rings* also contained history, thus enriching his story in ways that most fantasy writers cannot begin to guess at. Part of this enhancement comes from the way the words — for example, the names of the people and places of Rohan — connect to actual historical realities. We do not have to recognize consciously what Tolkien has done in the creation of his names to feel the effect of his complex constructions.

As well as inventing names and languages filled with their own history, Tolkien again brought a variety of discourses into juxtaposition, thus creating a world of great cultural depth. As Shippey shows,

"The Council of Elrond" chapter of *The Lord of the Rings* is packed with information, much of which is carried by the linguistic modes of the individual speakers, both those who are there and those, like Saruman, who are quoted within other characters' speeches. That Tolkien delighted in such speeches for their rhetoric alone is clear, but it is equally clear that he made them serve many simultaneous purposes. Their interest lies in the fact that they do not simply move the story forward but pull the reader further into the story world.

Speeches full of recent and ancient history are but one example of Tolkien's other major way of creating a sense of vast temporal panoramas: he inundates his landscapes with history and legend. Wherever they go, the hobbits and their companions run into legends, tales, historical sites that continually affect the way they feel, think, and act. Tolkien knew what he was doing when he studied the *Beowulf* scop's methods of interweaving history and legend into his narrative, for he does the same thing throughout *The Lord of the Rings*. Theoden knows that his ride to Gondor will be sung in afterages (if somehow Sauron is destroyed), just as Beowulf knew that his deeds would be sung. And both take comfort in the songs of earlier feats, which remind them that men have always had to choose which side they would battle on and have always had the freedom to choose.

What such presentiments of earlier days do is to keep reminding the protagonists of *The Lord of the Rings* (along with its readers) that they are connected to a great story. This is brought home most clearly in a conversation between Frodo and Samwise as they rest on the stairs of Cirith Ungol, on the Borders of Mordor. Sam speaks:

"Beren now, he never thought he was going to get that Silmaril from the Iron Crown in Thangorodrim, and yet he did, and that was a worse place and a blacker danger than ours. But that's a long tale, of course, and goes on past the happiness and into grief and beyond it — and the Silmaril went on and came to Eärendil. And why, sir, I never thought of that before! We've got — you've got some of the light of it in that star-glass that the Lady gave you! Why, to think of it, we're

in the same tale still! It's going on. Don't the great tales never end?"

"No, they never end as tales," said Frodo. "But the people in them come, and go when their part's ended. Our part will end later — or sooner."
(Book II, chapter 13)

By the time the hobbits make this discovery, they have long been part of the very warp and woof of the contemporary section of this tale, a tale known within *The Lord of the Rings* only in fragments, though we now have the posthumuous collections of works from the history of Middle-earth to fill in much that we (and the characters) can only infer during its passage.

I am not absolutely sure that it might not have been better to leave that history as a veiled context; still, now that *The Silmarillion* and *Unfinished Tales* exist there is no way to ignore them. But within *The Lord of the Rings*, Tolkien has created a marvelously complex mood containing the heroic-elegiac — the sense of loss for a world now gone — and a real consolation — for the world has been saved from the Darkness for men; and at least in the beginning of the Fourth Age elves and dwarves and others will still be there, working together to make it a bright place. Yet for the reader, even that world is so far in the past that it has long been utterly lost, except for snatches of legend and history, often hidden in words, now brought to light in Tolkien's massive invention.

Of course, Tolkien did have a great quest story to tell, one of the greatest, for unlike most others, including most of the near-copies of his masterpiece, it is a quest of renunciation. Nevertheless, some readers and critics are put off because the story "dawdles." But for Tolkien the dawdling, so to speak, is much of the story. He is not merely telling an adventure, he is creating a world, naming it in full and giving it a history. Still, the tale itself is important; and in its doubled, sometimes tripled and quadrupled, movements toward completion, it reveals a complex plot. Structurally, it is very much like *The Hobbit*, and many critics have pointed this out, though Pippin beat them to it at the end of book 5. Like, but unlike; for where *The Hobbit* had but one narrative line, *The Lord of the Rings* has many, and a kind of internal repetition of motifs and events thickens the narrative just as the history and legend foreground what would otherwise be conventional "empty" background landscape.

But Tolkien did not just borrow plot twists from his own work. Robert Giddings and Elizabeth Holland make a strong case for his having reworked into the narrative of *The Lord of the Rings* aspects of H. Rider Haggard's *King Solomon's Mines*, John Buchan's *The Thirty-nine Steps*, and Richard Blackmore's *Lorna Doone*, as well as some other popular fictions and legends, and traditional epic material. Their major point, however, and one supported by many other critics, is that Tolkien always improved upon his originals, giving his heroes qualities of leadership, self-sacrifice, moral vision, and nobility that their lesser originals lack. Some of his allusions are to acknowledged great works as well. There are a number of references to Shakespeare's plays: Aragorn rallying his men before dawn in Helm's Deep stands in contrast to Henry V with his soldiers in France, for example. In every case where an earlier version of an event or a character can be found, Tolkien will have given his version an archetypal significance different from, and usually more profound than, the original. Moreover, he usually takes various strands from other places and weaves them into a singular whole of his own.

Some readers complain that *The Lord of the Rings* is morally too simple, or that its characters are unrealistic, or that the background of the world has interfered with the proper realization of the foreground of adventure. These complaints miss the point. If the demarcation between good and evil is clearer than in "reality," the choices that each individual has to make are the same as they have always been. Tolkien's concept of characterization, consciously chosen, is at odds with realism, but is consistent and belongs to a long tradition; it demands a different kind of reading than does realistic fiction, but that kind is neither better nor worse, it is simply different. Tolkien sought to create a world that would enthrall his readers; part of the reading experience that *The Lord of the Rings* offers is the enchantment of entering such a world. Those who do not or cannot like it are free to leave, but they

surely err when they complain that it is a failure. For those readers who enter into its spirit, *The Lord of the Rings* offers rich rewards.

The rewards of *The Silmarillion* and *Unfinished Tales* are not the same as those of *The Lord of the Rings*. Most of the stories contained within these volumes had been written before *The Lord of the Rings* was begun, yet readers usually come to them after reading it. Tolkien was unable to complete the earlier books in his lifetime, and perhaps there were some complex literary reasons as well as the personal ones that Carpenter adduced in his biography. As his comments on *Beowulf* show, Tolkien especially valued the "impression of depth," the "effect of antiquity," and the "illusion of historical truth and perspective" that he found there, and that he created in *The Lord of the Rings*. But in it, Middle-earth is already ancient and contains a vast weight of history. The earlier tales lack precisely the depth he so valued. As it stands, *The Silmarillion* attempts to deal with the problem by erecting an implied scaffolding of divergent texts linked by commentary. The texts were supposedly written by men at different times as they tried to make sense of the ancient history of men and elves. Some of the *Unfinished Tales* are variant texts. To a certain extent Tolkien's strategy works, but what is indeed missing from these texts is the mediation performed by the hobbits. They represent ordinary us in the grand action of *The Lord of the Rings*; we have no such representatives in the earlier tales. Although these works have an austere beauty of their own, they will never entrance their readers as *The Lord of the Rings* does.

Still, they are impressive. "Ainulindalë" and "Valaquenta" form a wondrous myth of creation and fall. "Quenta Silmarillion" is a huge, many-stranded tale of the elves in revolt and in revengeful war against the Enemy. It is a truly northern myth of pride and courage, of heroism in the face of apparently hopeless odds. The story contains many heroic elvish figures, but some of the most important characters are men, especially Túrin and Tuor, both of whom are involved in great victories and great defeats. Yet Tuor is the father of Eärendel, the half-elf whose efforts bring about the final battle against

Morgoth and his eventual defeat, while Túrin moves in blind pride to bring disaster upon his family in fulfillment of the curse of Morgoth.

In its grand design the history of the Silmarils is as vast and complex as could be wished. Moreover, as Shippey says, in these tales Tolkien aims "at a tone, or perhaps better a 'taste' which he knew well but which had fallen outside the range of modern literature: a tone of stoicism, regret, inquiry, above all of awe moderated by complete refusal to be intimidated." In the best of these tales, he achieves that tone, and it is no small accomplishment. In the almost pure tragedy of Túrin Turambar, he is perhaps most successful, especially in the longer version of *Unfinished Tales*. The tale of Túrin is another example of recovering an earlier story and rewriting it so it becomes completely his own. The original for Túrin's tale, the "Story of Kullervo" in the Finnish epic the *Kalevala*, is crude and lacking in moral vision; Tolkien's story is tragic in itself, with a hero both truly great and deeply flawed, and it is also an integral part of the long work of loss that is *The Silmarillion*.

Perhaps his beloved tale of the love between the man Beren and the elf princess Luthien does not quite become his own; for though it is obvious that this story stood symbolically for his own love for his wife, it shows too clearly the traces of its progenitors and sometimes slips into sentimentality.

The "Akallabêth" reads more like straight history, though tales from Númenor will appear in *Unfinished Tales*. It too provides background for *The Lord of the Rings*, but it really only fills in gaps that had their own power as gaps in the actual text of the major epic. What is best about these two books is what Shippey calls their "inspiration" and "invention." The former is responsible for the many extraordinary images throughout Tolkien's creation; the latter for his lifelong struggle, often crowned with resonant success, to fit those images into a coherent pattern of history in Middle-earth.

As the creator of one of the greatest, if not the greatest, subcreated Other World in contemporary literature, Tolkien has achieved a prominence as a fantasy writer that few could hope to attain. In *The Hobbit* and *The Lord of the Rings*, especially, he has

crafted stories of the marvelous that should long continue to delight readers. They will do so partly because they are more than just adventure stories; they are richly textured, linguistically complex palimpsests expressing a profound moral vision of the cosmos.

Selected Bibliography

WORKS OF J. R. R. TOLKIEN

The following list includes only Tolkien's major fantasy works; his other publications can be found in West's bibliography, below.

The Hobbit; or, There and Back Again. London: Allen and Unwin, 1937. Boston: Houghton Mifflin, 1938. (Revised editions appeared in 1951 and 1966, the last being the final adjustment to *The Lord of the Rings*.)

Farmer Giles of Ham. London: Allen and Unwin, 1949. Boston: Houghton Mifflin, 1950.

The Fellowship of the Ring: Being the First Part of The Lord of the Rings. London: Allen and Unwin, 1954. Boston: Houghton Mifflin, 1954. (Revised edition. New York: Ballantine, 1965. London: Allen and Unwin, 1966.)

The Two Towers: Being the Second Part of The Lord of the Rings. London: Allen and Unwin, 1954. Boston: Houghton Mifflin, 1955. (Revised edition. New York: Ballantine, 1965. London: Allen and Unwin, 1966.)

The Return of the King: Being the Third Part of The Lord of the Rings. London: Allen and Unwin, 1955. Boston: Houghton Mifflin, 1956. (Revised edition. New York: Ballantine, 1966. London: Allen and Unwin, 1966.)

The Adventures of Tom Bombadil, and Other Verses from The Red Book. London: Allen and Unwin, 1962. Boston: Houghton Mifflin, 1962.

Tree and Leaf. London: Allen and Unwin, 1964. Boston: Houghton Mifflin, 1965.

Smith of Wootton Major. London: Allen and Unwin, 1967. Boston: Houghton Mifflin, 1967.

The Road Goes Ever On: A Song Cycle. With music by Donald Swann. Boston: Houghton Mifflin, 1967. London: Allen and Unwin, 1968.

The Father Christmas Letters. Edited by Baillie Tolkien. London: Allen and Unwin, 1976. Boston: Houghton Mifflin, 1976.

The Silmarillion. Edited by Christopher Tolkien. London: Allen and Unwin, 1977. Boston: Houghton Mifflin, 1977.

Unfinished Tales of Númenor and Middle-earth. Edited by Christopher Tolkien. London: Allen and Unwin, 1980. Boston: Houghton Mifflin, 1980.

Letters of J. R. R. Tolkien. Edited by Humphrey Carpenter with the assistance of Christopher Tolkien. London: Allen and Unwin, 1981. Boston: Houghton Mifflin, 1981.

The Book of Lost Tales, Part I. Edited by Christopher Tolkien. London: Allen and Unwin, 1983.

CRITICAL AND BIOGRAPHICAL STUDIES

Brooke-Rose, Christine. "The Evil Ring: Realism and the Marvelous." In *A Rhetoric of the Unreal.* Cambridge: Cambridge University Press, 1981, 233–255. (A fascinating structural reading of *The Lord of the Rings* from a position of distaste, so that the author always puts a negative valence on her insights.)

Carpenter, Humphrey. *J. R. R. Tolkien: A Biography.* London: Allen and Unwin, 1977. Boston: Houghton Mifflin, 1977.

Giddings, Robert, and Holland, Elizabeth. *J. R. R. Tolkien: The Shores of Middle-earth.* London: Junction Books, 1981. (Fascinating on possible sources for the narrative structures of *The Lord of the Rings;* Tolkien as a mythical/visionary artist.)

Helms, Randel. *Tolkien and the Silmarils.* Boston: Houghton Mifflin, 1981. (Sees *The Silmarillion* as Tolkien's "most complex and challenging work.")

Isaacs, Neil D., and Zimbardo, Rose A., eds. *Tolkien: New Critical Perspectives.* Lexington: University Press of Kentucky, 1981.

Shippey, T. A. *The Road to Middle-earth.* London: Allen and Unwin, 1982. Boston: Houghton Mifflin, 1983. (Perhaps the best single study of Tolkien's artistry and its roots, one that fully understands the need to approach his work via a linguistic path; not to be missed by students of Tolkien's oeuvre.)

BIBLIOGRAPHY

West, Richard C. *Tolkien Criticism: An Annotated Checklist.* Revised edition. Kent, Ohio: Kent State University Press, 1981. (755 entries; comprehensive to 1980.)

—DOUGLAS BARBOUR

X

American Early-Nineteenth-Century and Victorian Writers

WASHINGTON IRVING

1783-1859

NAMED FOR GEORGE Washington, first president of the United States, Washington Irving fittingly stands as the nation's first significant man of letters and true literary artist. Best known for two supernatural short stories, "Rip Van Winkle" and "The Legend of Sleepy Hollow," he would doubtless enjoy the current reviving interest in his fiction.

Irving's writing career, which he began as a journalist at nineteen, extended over more than fifty years. This was the era of America's coming of age as well, and Irving enjoyed the reputation of a literary lion in Europe and America. The long-running and condescending dismissal of Irving for producing what some readers perceived as little more than lachrymose, sentimental vaporizings in fiction — for being a febrile descendant of the Graveyard and Gothic schools in poetry and prose — has had to yield to reinterpretations in recent years that have raised his status as a literary artist.

Irving has emerged as a writer keenly aware of the supernatural and its artistic possibilities; but he was just as attuned to its excesses and sought to avoid them. Thus, he often experimented with what is termed "sportive," or humorous, Gothic; that is, he blended comedy with terror, as if to indicate his, and any other balanced person's, detachment from a wholehearted subscription to a belief in ghosts and goblins. Irving is also placed as a forerunner — and no mean pioneer at that — of the subtle psychological storytelling found in "ghostly" tales by later

nineteenth-century writers like Henry James, William Dean Howells, and Ambrose Bierce. In fact, Gothicism contributes far greater strength to the mainstream of American fiction than was for many years admitted by early historians of America's national literature.

Irving adds dimension to supernatural literature by creating ambivalence toward, and lack of interest in, his horrors. When *Tales of a Traveller* appeared (1824), he wrote to his American friend Henry Brevoort about several of his own attitudes toward fiction: "I consider a story merely as a frame on which to stretch my materials." He noted particularly the "half-concealed vein of humor that is often playing through the whole." Advocating the short story as a literary form, he added that an "author must be continually piquant." Such views apply to Irving's ghost stories. A devotee of folklore and legend, he constantly adapted from American and European sources such elements as would add piquancy to his own fiction. Consequently he becomes a transition figure between those who depended heavily upon foreign literary models and those who consciously strove to break new literary ground by using American materials.

After coauthoring *Salmagundi* (1807–1808) — a mélange of comic thrusts at persons, events, and publications of the time — with his brother William and James Kirke Paulding, Irving tried his hand alone at a comic work, *Knickerbocker's History of New York* (1809), a mixture of varied humorous forays upon persons, places, and things, old and new. The pretense of creating a history of New York is often put by as digressions gain forcible sway, although the persona of Diedrich Knickerbocker gives a measure of unity to the entire work.

Thwarted in love, Irving sailed in May 1815 for England, where he quickly entered the family hardware business. He moved thence into diplomatic posts, serving as a member of the American legation to Spain from 1826 to 1829; traveled to the Continent, where he spent much time in Spain; and finally returned to the United States in 1832. The years abroad were valuable for Irving's literary endeavors in that they provided him with materials for biographical works on Columbus and Muhammad and, more significantly, with backgrounds for supernatural tales. Irving also traveled through the American territories, turning out such accounts as *A Tour on the Prairies* (1835), *Astoria* (1836), and *The Adventures of Captain Bonneville, U.S.A., in the Rocky Mountains and the Far West* (1837). Subsequently appointed minister to Spain, Irving again journeyed to Europe, returning after this stint of diplomatic service to quiet leisure at his home, Sunnyside, near Tarrytown, New York.

Irving's first major work of fiction, *The Sketch Book of Geoffrey Crayon, Gent.* (the "editor" persona often used by Irving to place distance between himself and his readers; 1819–1820), contains his two renowned stories "Rip Van Winkle" and "The Legend of Sleepy Hollow," which have become classics because of their author's deft balancing of reality with unreality amid an unshakable skepticism accompanying the incredible events. Irving's opening remarks tell of his fondness for "observing strange characters and manners." Such inclinations expand: "I knew every spot where a murder or a robbery had been committed, or a ghost seen"—decidedly the attitude that Gothic tradition would nurture. Such predilections were to inform many of his stories.

"The figure of Rip Van Winkle presides over the birth of the American imagination," writes Leslie Fiedler, and Rip's story, the first spooky piece in *The Sketch Book*, merits close attention. Tormented by a shrewish wife, Rip neglects his farm and family for the pleasures of the bottle, the forest, and the streams, accompanied by his loyal dog, Wolf. One fall day they journey high into the Catskills, rightly dubbed "fairy mountains" early in the tale. Evening approaches, and Rip beholds a little old man, in old-fashioned Dutch garb, who asks his help in carrying a heavy keg of liquor to a group of oldsters as strange as the little man himself. They play at ninepins, and Rip quaffs repeatedly from the keg of apparently fine gin. He falls into a deep sleep. He awakens, old and changed, from his journey out of time. Returning to the inhabited world, he discovers that the American Revolution has occurred, that the country and its people are vastly changed, that his termagant wife is dead, and that his story is received with mixed responses. Did Rip really sleep in the mountains for years, or has he invented this weird account merely as a subterfuge for remaining away, free from responsibility and sexual obligation, for so long?

As far as distancing readers from the supernatural is concerned, the framing method of narration in "Rip Van Winkle" turns the screw of technique and intent through several revolutions. The story comes to the reader as a paper from Diedrich Knickerbocker, long a favorite with Irving's audiences, who in his turn had heard the story from Rip himself, as well as learning about it through general familiarity with its place in regional lore. Knickerbocker solemnly avers that he knows the Dutch settlements to have been "very subject to marvellous events and appearances." Given this kind of removal from the material and the mood of doubt established in the frame narrative (and that despite Knickerbocker's apparent attempts to contribute soundness to the story), the reader is left to wonder. Irving's story reminds one of Nathaniel Hawthorne's "Wakefield" (1835), wherein the titular hero decides on a whim to leave his wife for twenty years, returning to none of the excitement that greeted the homecoming of old Rip. No supernatural tinge enlivens Hawthorne's story; he prefers to unfold psychology from a realistic angle.

"Rip Van Winkle" heads a list of stories in which Irving keeps characters within the fiction and readers dangling between deciding on supernatural influences and the use of seeming supernaturalism to insinuate other implications. Whether Rip stayed for years among the mountains or whether his absence symbolizes the desire of all who wish to abrogate mundane responsibilities, he provides in his adventures a prototype for numerous American literary descendants. Herman Melville's Ishmael, in *Moby Dick* (1851), Mark Twain's Huck, in *The Adventures of Huckleberry Finn* (1884), plus a host of twentieth-century American fictional heroes, are in this family. Most notably, but without supernatural trappings, Ernest Hemingway's protagonists reveal kinship with precursors like Rip.

Like Rip, but depicted in more sensational terms, is Ichabod Crane, schoolmaster at Sleepy Hollow and would-be captor of the hand of blooming Katrina Van Tassel, heiress to a vast, wealthy farm. Crane's quest is foiled by an apparently demonic oppressor, the headless horseman of Sleepy Hollow, who may well be Abraham Van Brunt, or "Brom Bones"—so called because of his sturdy physique—in disguise. Bones is another, eventually successful, suitor for Katrina's hand.

Irving's rhetoric positions background characters (who function like the chorus in classical drama) and readers to react with ambivalence to the "ghostly" substance in this story. Sleepy Hollow, the reader immediately learns, is the narrator's first choice of a locale suited to escape from life: "A drowsy, dreamy influence seems to hang over the land, and to pervade the very atmosphere." To intensify this ambiguity, Irving says that "certain it is, the place still continues under the sway of some witching power, that holds a spell over the minds of the good people, causing them to walk in continual reverie." Therefore Sleepy Hollow undeniably promotes a suspension of disbelief in regard to what occurs there.

The region also sets up ideal conditions for that other kind of dream, the nightmare; and to this species of terror the hapless Ichabod is subjected by Brom Bones, masquerading as the headless specter of local fame, to quell Crane's passion for Katrina. Ichabod is ripe for such persecution; storehouse of supernatural lore that he is, he cannot detach himself from the hauntings that plague victims of fabled re-

nown. Prey as he is to night fears, the schoolmaster provides ready game for ignominious (but, to his opponent's and the reader's views, nonetheless comic) defeat by the more realistic and "heroic" Bones. The victor's name may reveal another meaning: Ichabod is brought low by his own "bones," or angular and unprepossessing physique, which finds no lasting favor with Katrina. She would rather be the beloved of daredevil Brom, whose masculine vitality courses unmistakably throughout this story.

Legend though the story may be, no genuinely supernatural "visitant" dogs Ichabod's tracks as he leaves Van Tassel's farm. His own expectations of confronting the galloping and headless spirit prime him for hallucinatory experience, although Irving cleverly manages what seems a meeting with a ghost, at just the spot where the legendary figure is reputedly most active. Details of this meeting are supplied with mounting suspense to impart realism to the fantastic chase, although alternate possibilities are hinted at. The most obvious is that Bones deliberately horrifies the susceptible Ichabod by means of a ghastly prank. Second, shamefully "used up" as he was in love, Crane's own Yankee ingenuity at saving face may have planted seeds for the story of otherworldly forces tormenting him. Knickerbocker's conclusion, or "postscript," which draws us back to everyday reality, combines with mentions of speculations concerning actual ghostly machinations to create indecisiveness. The very term *legend* in the title of Irving's story should alert attentive readers to the fact that definiteness may have no role in what ensues. Altogether, mystery envelops "The Legend of Sleepy Hollow."

A third tale in *The Sketch Book*, "The Spectre Bridegroom," smacks of the German legend of Lenore, wherein a dead groom rides away to the grave with a beautiful bride. In Irving's tale, Sir Herman Von Starkenfaust, son of the enemy of the Baron Von Landshort, knows that his friend, the young Count Von Altenburg, has died, sees Von Landshort's captivating daughter (the betrothed of Von Starkenfaust), and plays spook to win her hand. Ultimately the truth comes out, in a jolly context, such that ghosts and their doings are gently lampooned. This kind of explained supernaturalism recalls the similar tactic of the "mighty magician of Udolpho," Ann Radcliffe, mother to all writers of Gothic fiction, who ultimately supplied rational bases for what had appeared during several long volumes to be influences from the spirit world.

Irving's next book, *Bracebridge Hall* (1822), contains eerie touches, although they are not as well known as those in the stories from *The Sketch Book*. Only hints of supernaturalism crop up in the alchemical theme in "The Student of Salamanca." Later in the book the reader is prepared for weird happenings by the narrator's account of Squire Bracebridge's delight in superstitions and fairy tales, which leanings had earlier prompted his circulation of rumors that Bracebridge Hall was haunted and that spirits inhabited the surrounding countryside. A sketch of Diedrich Knickerbocker is given, with attention to his posthumous papers (this device became a favorite with Irving). These items, to be sure, illustrate the narrator's opinion, expressed earlier, that "twilight views of nature are often more captivating than any which are revealed by the rays of enlightened philosophy."

Whether these views mildly gibe at eighteenth-century rationalism, as they may, they epitomize the tenor of Irving's supernatural stories and his aims for infusing piquancy into them. "The Haunted House," which follows, demonstrates a deft transformation of the customary haunted castle of European settings to American locale and architecture. Thence Knickerbocker is led to recall his meeting with a storyteller whose narrative of Dolph Heyliger is set at a remove proper to allow for skepticism toward the house's eerie visitants.

Dolph Heyliger resembles Rip Van Winkle in his indolence, although his adventures take him into medical studies, which in their turn lead him into observing mysterious portraits—a stock gambit in Gothic tradition—that finally lure him to concealed treasure. Embedded within the tale of Dolph's rags-to-riches ascent is another, "The Storm-Ship," a reworking of the old legend of the Flying Dutchman, or ghost ship manned by a crew of spirits. Such materials were popular in Irving's day, with interesting assays of the legend by William Austin, in "Peter Rugg, the Missing Man" (1824), and Edgar Allan Poe, in "MS. Found in a Bottle" (1833).

Dolph continually meets persons who resemble the portrait in the haunted house, and he eventually learns that his own maternal ancestor was the subject. The strange Heer Antony, whom Dolph accompanies through some sensational travels, is also descended from the haunting figure. All in all, Dolph's is a sophisticated rendering of a trip into subliminal realms, and the reappearance of the old portrait's features suggests Jungian travels into the depths of the subconscious. Perhaps Irving so readily disclaimed firm belief in the supernatural because, employing it as symbolically for such psychic travels as Dolph's, he may have feared what deep probings might bring to the surface.

Tales of a Traveller (1824), much neglected and often maligned by critics, contains some of Irving's best art in the supernatural mode. Another of Irving's admired characters, Geoffrey Crayon, gives an opening frame, enters again after "Buckthorne and His Friends," and subsequently informs us that the contents of part 4 come from posthumous papers of Diedrich Knickerbocker. Ill at an inn in Mentz on the Rhine, Crayon decides to write a book. This background is a natural backdrop for ghostly legends and horrifying incidents, because in many minds of the early nineteenth century, *German* was synonymous with the lurid and the supernatural. Rifling his portfolio, Crayon warns readers to expect no overt "morals" in stories located there. Such implications will be found below the surfaces; the stories derive from varied sources (vague, too); and readers are asked to approach the pieces more with good humor than with other feelings. These qualifications again reinforce the separation of Irving the author from the beliefs in ghosts, goblins, and like phenomena evinced by his characters.

Tales of a Traveller divides into four sections, with supernatural elements predominating in parts 1 and 4. Part 1 is entitled "Strange Stories by a Nervous Gentleman," with an epigraph concluding, "Do you think I'd tell you truths?"—indicating that the horrors to come may not be entirely serious. These tales are the concluding entertainment at a great hunting dinner, when a call for ghost stories sounds.

"The Adventure of My Uncle" immediately plunges the reader into unresolvable circumstances.

Lodged in a strange bedchamber at the home of his friend the marquis, the uncle sees a lady walking about his room. Next day the host shows the lady's portrait, begins her history, and breaks off when the uncle recounts events of the preceding night. Other guests surmise that the befuddled uncle had actually seen the old housekeeper prowling, and the story ends inconclusively.

Another guest responds with "The Adventure of My Aunt," a vignette of commonsense reaction to mysterious portraits. The widowed aunt, dwelling in a wild, isolated country house, beholds a moving eye in a portrait, arms herself, and locates a robber hiding behind the picture—all couched in comedy and the belittlement of "straight" supernaturalism. Here Irving mocks the heritage of haunted portraits, devolving from Horace Walpole's famous first Gothic novel, *The Castle of Otranto* (1764). Debate over the ghostliness in this tale spurs an Irish captain of dragoons to spin yet a third family yarn, "The Bold Dragoon; or the Adventure of My Grandfather," rollicking with a drunkard's fantasy that a goblin piper accompanied a dance by the furniture in his room. Pressed for details, this narrator tells the hunting company how his relative often made "blunders in his travels about inns at night."

From this ridiculous comedy, attention turns to "The Adventure of the German Student," which introduces grisliness to hitherto comic offerings. The narrator heard the story from the hero, in a Parisian madhouse. There young Gottfried Wolfgang, former student at Göttingen, exists as a "visionary and enthusiast"—attributes that marked him for misfortune, as they did many others in fiction of the period. The stranger-hero in Poe's "The Assignation" (1834) is comparable in that both he and Wolfgang suffer great and fated passions. Irving's protagonist suspects that evil is hounding him to damnation. No man of the world, he envisions a female of "transcendent beauty" as his mate; meets such a young woman at the foot of the guillotine one dark, wild night; and bears her home. Black-garbed, she wears an arresting diamond-studded band of black velvet around her neck. After a night of passion, during which he pledges himself eternally to her, Wolfgang learns with horror that she is a corpse, sacrificed on the guillotine the previous day, and he goes

mad, certain that she is the agent of his destruction. Once more we wonder: Was this young woman actual flesh and blood, and, therefore, was Wolfgang necrophiliac, or did she spring only from his overwrought sensibility? Such considerations align Irving's tale with Poe's famous, less obtrusively funny "Ligeia" (1838). In both, the matter of "Germanism" infuses ambiguity into the fiction.

The greatest ambiguity of all follows, however, in a trio of linked tales, "The Adventure of the Mysterious Picture," "The Adventure of the Mysterious Stranger," and "The Story of the Young Italian." The framing narrator's words in these tales suggest the impact of too much food and drink as emphatically as they do a supernatural old portrait. Themes and character types from preceding pieces are reworked. The progress from possible ghostliness through the vicissitudes in love and fortune of a young artist (in other words, from the weird to the too-comprehensible) is subtle. Ultimately, the baronet, whose painting stimulates the narratives in this section, confidentially informs the frame-narrator, the Nervous Gentleman, that he tired of the group's banter and so directed them to a portrait different from the mysterious one. Overall, these interlocked stories cast doubts as to where the supernatural and the natural divide.

Part 4, "The Money-Diggers," offers in varied perspectives the legends of Captain Kidd's treasure and its seekers. "The Devil and Tom Walker," one of Irving's best weird tales, takes its rightful place among devil stories popular in the nineteenth century. "Wolfert Webber; or Golden Dreams," also in this section, features a compelling mariner from the netherworld whose frightening countenance and savage disposition create uneasiness and foreboding among those in his company at an old inn. Webber eventually returns from excursions into nightmare geography to gain his hoped-for riches from sales of land to the growing city of New York. *Tales of a Traveller* thus closes on a note of mild admonition to those who too earnestly subscribe to spooky happenings and beings.

The best of Irving's supernatural fiction has been surveyed above, although much more may be found in his complete writings. *The Alhambra* (1832), often designated his "Spanish Sketch Book," presents the "Oriental," or Near Eastern, variety of Gothicism, replete with magic, genies, and exotic, mysterious settings. The "Legend of the Arabian Astrologer" offers an indictment of greed just as much as it details mysterious events. Eroticism vies with magical happenstance to provide entertainment here. Love of money as the root of evil also supplies the theme in the "Legend of the Moor's Legacy." Both stories contain sufficient violence of realistic types — a concomitant of Oriental tales during these years — to make spectral interference in human lives rather pallid by comparison. In the "Legend of the Rose of the Alhambra" defeat of an elderly spinster's sheltering of her adorable niece is achieved through mysterious, amusing means. The blooming Jacinta and her mysterious lute, the gift of a spirit whose love was disappointed, cure the ills of the Spanish monarch, whose goodwill ultimately unites Jacinta with her own lover. Many of the mysteries in this tale are left delightfully ambiguous, attributes perhaps of the general confusion thought to underlie young love. Although the whole of *The Alhambra* has for preface a reminder of time's ravages of the old royal Spanish palace, the reader is told time and again about "tales of enchanted halls current in the Alhambra" during its era of magnificence. To this haunted castle of Gothic tales, Irving adds a dash of gentle comedy.

Elsewhere, too, Irving's veering toward the supernatural is evident. For example, a tour of Dryburgh Abbey acquaints the visitor with its mysterious legends, as recounted by an old retainer. Visits to Sir Walter Scott at Abbottsford brought forth an abundance of legendary lore, of which both men were fond, and even everyday visiting was turned in some measure into material for potential terrors. A kindred possibility for eeriness and ghostliness invested Lord Byron's ancestral hall, Newstead Abbey, in Irving's imagination. Not an obscure corridor or lonely glen is mentioned in his recollections of these spots, but each has its tragic legend or visitant from the far side of the grave to make a beholder's hair rise. Even the late work *Wolfert's Roost* (1855) abounds in hauntedness.

Washington Irving's signal contribution to supernatural fiction is his infusion of good-natured skepticism into tales of ghosts, goblins, and hauntings, which view does not obliterate possibilities for the existence of genuine diablerie. Diabolic visitations in Irving's stories generally tie firmly to human psychology rather than to inexplicable phenomena. Such skepticism has for a near neighbor, though, an inescapable uncertainty. It is as if Irving the literary artist, who was also a child of neoclassic rationalism, felt obliged to square with vestiges of the Enlightenment, while simultaneously wishing to avoid parodying Gothicism for the sake of parody alone. Bringing European literary tradition within the bounds of the American commonsense outlook — which often functioned in terms of humor that ran to tall tales or to roughness — Irving's multiple perspectives produced some far more sophisticated renderings of supernaturalism than he is customarily credited with. Such an outlook and method align him with contemporaries like William Austin and anticipate the handling of otherworldly phenomena by Hawthorne, Poe, and numerous other successors in American literature.

Selected Bibliography

WORKS OF WASHINGTON IRVING

There are, of course, almost countless reprints of Irving's individual stories.

Collected works
The Works of Washington Irving. New York: Putnam, 1860–1861, 21 vols. (This edition, the last supervised by Irving himself, will be superseded by the Twayne edition of *The Complete Works of Washington Irving*.)

Books with supernatural fiction
The Sketch Book of Geoffrey Crayon, Gent. New York: C. S. Van Winkle, 1819–1820, in 7 parts. London: John Miller, 1820, 2 vols. (Published as by Geoffrey Crayon.)
Bracebridge Hall, or The Humourists. A Medley. New York: C. S. Van Winkle, 1822. London: John Murray, 1822, 2 vols. (Published as by Geoffrey Crayon.)
Tales of a Traveller. London: John Murray, 1824, 2 vols. Philadelphia: Carey and Lea, 1824, in 4 parts. (Published as by Geoffrey Crayon.)

The Alhambra. A Series of Tales and Sketches of the Moors and Spaniards. Philadelphia: Carey and Lea, 1832, 2 vols. (Published as by the author of *The Sketch Book.*) London: H. Colburn and R. Bentley, 1832, 2 vols. (Published as by Geoffrey Crayon.)

Wolfert's Roost and Other Papers, Now First Collected. New York: Putnam, 1855. London: Bohn, 1855.

CRITICAL AND BIOGRAPHICAL STUDIES

Bowden, Mary Weatherspoon. *Washington Irving.* Boston: Twayne, 1981.

Clendenning, John. "Irving and the Gothic Tradition." *Bucknell Review,* 12, no. 2 (1964): 90–98.

Clyne, Patricia Edwards. "The Other Bicentennial: 200 Years of Washington Irving (1783–1983)." *Hudson Valley Magazine* (April 1983): 38–42.

Current-Garcia, Eugene. "Professionalism and the Art of the Short Story." *Studies in Short Fiction,* 10 (Fall 1973): 327–341.

Fiedler, Leslie A. *Love and Death in the American Novel.* New York: Criterion, 1960.

Fisher, Benjamin Franklin IV. "The Residual Gothic Impulse, 1824–1873." In *Horror Literature: A Core Collection and Reference Guide,* edited by Marshall B. Tymn. New York: Bowker, 1982.

Griffith, Kelley, Jr. "Ambiguity and Gloom in Irving's 'Adventure of the German Student.'" *CEA Critic,* 38 (1975): 10–13.

Hedges, William L. *Washington Irving: An American Study, 1802–1832.* Baltimore: Johns Hopkins Press, 1965.

Hoffman, Daniel G. "Irving's Use of American Folklore in 'The Legend of Sleepy Hollow.'" *Publications of the Modern Language Association of America,* 68 (1953): 425–435.

Irving, Pierre M. *The Life and Letters of Washington Irving, by His Nephew.* New York: Putnam, 1863–1864, 4 vols.

Myers, Andrew B., ed. *A Century of Commentary on the Works of Washington Irving, 1864–1974.* Tarrytown, N.Y.: Sleepy Hollow Restorations, 1974.

Pochmann, Henry A. "Irving's German Sources in *The Sketch Book.*" *Studies in Philology,* 27 (1930): 477–507.

Roth, Martin. *Comedy and America: The Lost World of Washington Irving.* Port Washington, N.Y.: Kennikat Press, 1976.

Wagenknecht, Edward. *Washington Irving: Moderation Displayed.* New York: Oxford University Press, 1962.

———, ed. *Washington Irving's Tales of the Supernatural.* Owings Mills, Md.: Stammer House, 1982. (The introduction offers interesting comment on Irving's methods.)

Wegelin, Christof. "Dickens and Irving: The Problem of Influence." *Modern Language Quarterly,* 7 (1946): 83–91.

Williams, Stanley T. *The Life of Washington Irving.* New York: Oxford University Press, 1935.

Young, Philip. "Fallen from Time: The Mythic Rip Van Winkle." *Kenyon Review,* 22 (1960): 547–573.

—BENJAMIN FRANKLIN FISHER IV

WILLIAM AUSTIN

1778-1841

LITERARY ANNALS SELDOM ascribe renown to an author on the basis of one story, yet such acclaim is William Austin's, for "Peter Rugg, the Missing Man." Published first in the *New England Galaxy* (10 September 1824; additions 1 September 1826 and 19 January 1827), this tale has secured a niche in America's literary history. In this chronicle of human solitariness touched by a supernaturalism that leads to a sad fate, Austin domesticates legends of the Wandering Jew and Flying Dutchman, tincturing them with New England homeliness. "Peter Rugg" aligns Austin with Washington Irving and Nathaniel Hawthorne, whose fiction delicately balances the natural and supernatural. The story also adumbrates Edward Everett Hale's *The Man Without a Country* (1863) and that song about Charlie's travels beneath the streets of Boston, "The Man Who Never Returned," popularized during the 1950's and 1960's by the Kingston Trio.

William Austin's more general fame is linked with the legal history of his native state, Massachusetts, to which he remained intensely loyal. Born on 2 March 1778 in Lunenburg, he was educated at Harvard and, for law, at Lincoln's Inn, London. Austin eventually won respect as an attorney and a wider reputation as a public figure throughout Massachusetts. His legal career touched but lightly his literary pursuits. The most direct result is *Letters from London* (1804), recording his meetings with famous persons in London and his opinions of the British national character. His outspoken political prin-

ciples drew censure from a few Federalist critics, but *Letters* gained overall commendation. Austin's later years were devoted to his law practice, and to serving several terms as representative for Charlestown to the Massachusetts General Court and as representative to the state senate. He died in Charlestown on 27 June 1841.

The other signal influence that Austin's legal career exerted on his literature was that it allowed him leisure to write. His imaginative productions totaled just six short stories and a fragment of drama involving Hesiod and Homer, and only the stories are noteworthy. They appeared during the 1820's and 1830's in newspapers and literary magazines.

Austin's tendencies as a writer reveal interesting parallels with the "Big Bear" humorists of the old Southwest: his profession, gentlemanly as were most of theirs, permitted time for creative endeavor. (This school included writers like Thomas Bangs Thorpe, whose yarn "The Big Bear of Arkansas" [1841] gave this brand of comedy its name, George Washington Harris, Johnson Jones Hooper, and William Tappan Thompson.) In their tall tales, horselaughs frequently shift toward irrational or horrific phenomena and incidents. So it is with Austin's tales: they persuade us initially of their verisimilitude and then take a turn toward the otherworldly. Like other humorists', too, Austin's tone is frequently condescending toward the supernatural, as if he himself rises above unsophisticated attitudes held by subscribers to the otherworldly. Although his stories feature wild extravagance, Austin, like these other writers, gives the impression — as evidenced by his small output — that he regarded literary work as the frivolity of spare hours. Finally, like the Southwestern school's work, Austin's bears the stamp of everyday reality — a reality, however, ever tending to slip into the irrational or the horrific. That he contributed to the *American Monthly Magazine* strengthens his ties to near-contemporary literary humorists. Not only does his fiction resemble theirs, but he keeps company with them in the magazine's pages. Francis A. Durivage, Albert Pike, and — if not wholly within the camp of Southwestern humor — Edgar Allan Poe circulate comic items here. Durivage and Poe, especially, incline toward comic renditions of supernatural phenomena.

Outwardly, Austin's fiction differs little from the ordinary run of stories published in periodicals in his day. "Peter Rugg," his first story, remains his best. A close second, "The Man with the Cloaks: A Vermont Legend" (1836), also probes the wellsprings of human psychical isolation and loneliness — again using the supernatural. Equally fantastic, but not so ambiguous as these, "The Sufferings of a Country Schoolmaster" (1825) recounts the anguish of a teacher who lodges and boards with an extremely parsimonious New England family and who well-nigh starves before he is paid. "The Late Joseph Natterstrom" (1831) embodies the popular Orientalism of the times in a moralistic tale about honesty and wealth. Supernaturalism is ever so lightly brushed into the character of the Turk, Eben Beg, who never actively partakes of the central incidents. He remains altogether a vague, shadowy personage, much as the mysterious stranger in "The Man with the Cloaks" never takes center stage but functions instead as some mysterious agency would in earlier Gothic fiction — although more realistically because of his mundane desire to borrow a cloak for warmth. Similar in solemn moralizing, "Martha Gardner" (1837), Austin's last story, is not fantastic. An earlier, lesser piece, "The Origin of Chemistry" (1834), moves from sociopolitical theorizing to a vision of the world's potential ending in poison warfare. Although the predictions for the future are vividly sketched, they feature no otherworldly horrors.

Like other such captivating supernatural fictions,

"The Man with the Cloaks" opens with firm grounding in mundane realism: "On the border of Lake Champlain you will find a beautiful declivity in the present town of Ferrisburg. . . ." Here lives old John Grindall, whose miserly ways have endowed him with great wealth. Another homely touch is the definite time: November 1780. A traveler, beset by the onset of cold weather, lodges at a neighboring inn. The landlord suggests that the traveler ask Grindall if he can borrow his old cloak, as the old man had recently purchased a new one. He concludes: "and, moreover, say to him, he will never be less warm for parting with it, as a deed of charity sometimes warms the body more than a blanket." This plausibility is causally undercut, however, in the narrator's observing that "time has probably added not a little to the real facts."

Naturally, as could be expected, Grindall turns the importuner away with no cloak, and the latter's departing words foreshadow the remainder of the story: "You may want more than two cloaks to keep you warm if I perish with the cold." Shortly afterward the community reports that a traveler had died along the lake, and Grindall "felt a sudden chilliness shoot through his frame." As if to maintain good New England common sense, the narrator quickly comments: "There was nothing supernatural in this; the body is often the plaything of the mind."

Supernatural or not, Grindall adds one cloak on each passing day, until at the end of a year, during which time he laments his long-standing parsimony and solitude, the stranger reappears. He prescribes a cure for Grindall — to shed a cloak each day for a year, and give it to somebody needy — and remarks that the cure for his cold heart will restore warmth. During this time, one day in August, Grindall cries out with such force that all the wild beasts depart the region for several years. And it seems as if each cloak he sheds is animated by spirits — whether good or evil none could decide — ultimately suspected to emanate from the "bounding heart" of Grindall as he approaches humanness. Finally, the stranger returns, compliments Grindall on his improvement (with the moral that charity surpasses mendacious solitude), and departs.

Mild though its horrors are, they permeate "The Man with the Cloaks." That this is a legend, descended to the narrator through oral tradition; that Grindall's opponent is simply "a stranger," or everyman; that he exists to serve as the mouthpiece for Grindall's conscience as much as he does to call up a character; and that the separation of the realistic and the frighteningly fantastic is exceedingly tenuous—these ambiguities create a deft psychological tale of supernatural proportions.

"Peter Rugg" contains stronger stuff, although its weird underpinnings also have foundations in everyday reality. The Yankee character type, generally very reserved, is noted for occasional irrationality and emotional outbursts. Peter Rugg's momentary irrationality produces a dire penalty—the loss of all that is dear to him; overall he loses the facility for human communion, and that loss creates eerie distortions in ordinary time and space, as regards his involuntary journeying.

Austin manages a subtle balance of reality with fantasy in this tale. Jonathan Dunwell relates his adventures by means of a letter to a friend. He opens with mention of his journey to Boston, riding atop the stage with the driver; he could thus see Peter Rugg and his child Jenny approach in their old-fashioned carriage and learned of Rugg's plight from the loquacious driver. Dunwell gleans more concerning Rugg from talks with a tin peddler and then with a lodger at an inn, designated a "bystander" or "the stranger." Further plausibility is gained as Dunwell hears more from Betsy Croft, an aged lady who lives near the spot of Rugg's former home, and from James Felt, possibly a dotard, whom she enlists to corroborate her words. Finally, lodging again at a hotel, Dunwell receives from "one of the company, smiling" the most numerous relevant particulars.

Peter Rugg, urged by his friend Mr. Cutter to remain sheltered from a storm, retorts: *"I will see home to-night, in spite of the last tempest, or may I never see home!"* Rugg's rejection of friendship and his defiance of the natural elements loose upon him a curse of perpetual travel toward home. Rugg and his daughter are apparently doomed to wander eternally. They and their carriage seem to age, while their horse grows younger and more vigorous. Thus Rugg ranks with Samuel Taylor Coleridge's Ancient Mariner, Irving's Rip Van Winkle, and a host of Wandering Jew and Cain figures. Not accidentally,

Rugg inquires, " . . . has John Foy come from sea? He went a long voyage; he is my kinsman," in what may well be a covert allusion to the Flying Dutchman legend.

The epistolary frame for the tale; the use of time past (Dunwell mentions 1820, although events of Rugg's journey occurred a half-century before); and the compounding of stories within the story in the form of reportage—all distance the narrator and us from the sensational circumstances enveloping Peter Rugg. Uneasiness is aroused by the oncoming storm; its clouds appeared "like a sort of irregular net-work, and displayed a thousand fantastic images." This sense of foreboding courses through the remainder of the tale, until Dunwell abruptly concludes. As if to reinforce his ambivalence toward supernaturalism, he states, as he watches the approaching storm, that he remains detached: "It is a very common thing for the imagination to paint for the senses, both in the visible and invisible world." The invisible world, nonetheless, lurks as a viable phenomenon throughout the story of Peter Rugg, whether in terms of lurid imagery or in the freewheeling shifts in space and time as Rugg and his carriage emerge from odd corners and eras.

Altogether, what with the many qualifiers about Rugg's sad fate—"Some of them treated it all as a delusion. . . . Others . . . shook their heads and said nothing"—Austin's tale aligns with those of Irving and, more important, is a potentially rich symbolic fiction. The very disjointedness of the narration, sometimes deemed a defect by critics, contributes to the story's legendary aura as well as its tall-tale quality. Human emotion—determined, even when awed or fearful—is reinforced as something unpredictable, as something that may create unintentional havoc, by means of the seemingly ragged edges in the chronicle of Peter Rugg.

Selected Bibliography

WORKS OF WILLIAM AUSTIN

"Peter Rugg, the Missing Man." *New England Galaxy* (10 September 1824, 1 September 1826, 19 January 1827).
"The Man with the Cloaks: A Vermont Legend." *American Monthly Magazine* (January 1836).

Literary Papers of William Austin, with a Biographical Sketch by His Son, James Walker Austin, edited by James Walker Austin. Boston: Little, Brown, 1890. (Collected works.)

CRITICAL AND BIOGRAPHICAL STUDIES

Anderson, George K. *The Legend of the Wandering Jew*. Providence, R.I.: Brown University Press, 1965.

Baldwin, Charles Sears. *Essays Out of Hours*. New York: Longmans, Green, 1907.

Buckingham, Joseph T. *Personal Memoirs and Recollections of Editorial Life*. 2 vols. Boston: Ticknor, Reed, and Fields, 1852.

Canby, Henry S. *The Short Story in English*. New York: Holt, 1909.

Duyckinck, Evert A., and George L., eds. *Cyclopedia of American Literature*. 2 vols. New York: Scribner, 1855.

Fisher, Benjamin Franklin IV. "The Residual Gothic Impulse." In *Horror Literature: A Core Collection and a Reference Guide*, edited by Marshall B. Tymn. New York: Bowker, 1981.

Higginson, Thomas Wentworth. "A Precursor of Hawthorne." *The Independent* (29 March 1888). (Reprinted as the introduction to William Austin, *Peter Rugg, the Missing Man*. Boston: Luce, 1910.)

Howe, Will D. "The Early Humorists." In *The Cambridge History of American Literature*. 3 vols. New York: Macmillan, 1931.

Mott, Frank Luther. *A History of American Magazines 1741–1850*. New York: Appleton, 1930.

Pattee, Fred Lewis. *The Development of the American Short Story*. New York: Harper, 1923.

Trent, William Peterfield. *A History of American Literature: 1607–1865*. New York: Appleton, 1903.

—BENJAMIN FRANKLIN FISHER IV

EDGAR ALLAN POE

1809–1849

I

THE MOST INFLUENTIAL nineteenth-century author of supernatural fiction, Edgar Allan Poe, was born in Boston, Massachusetts, on 19 January 1809. The child of actor parents, he was orphaned at the age of almost three and reared in the family of John Allan, a merchant of Richmond, Virginia, a hard, uncongenial man. Poe received the beginnings of a good education—five years of elementary school in England and, later, a year at the new University of Virginia—but he was removed from college for gambling debts.

From adolescence on, Poe's early life was conditioned by his quarrels with Allan, and instead of being heir to one of the wealthiest men in America, he eventually found himself a penniless, half-trained intellectual with no means of livelihood. Two years in the army under an assumed name were followed by a brief period at the U.S. Military Academy, from which he was court-martialed. This was in 1831, and from 1831 to 1849, the year of his death, he made a scanty living as a free-lance writer, journalist, and editor. His high achievement was recognized, but it was nearly impossible for a man to make a living from letters, and Poe had severe personality problems. He suffered from fits of depression, from which alcohol relieved him, and gradually became an alcoholic. When under the influence of liquor, the normally amiable, hardworking, conscientious Mr. Poe became an impossible person; as a result, he lost job after job and opportunity after opportunity. In 1835 he married his young cousin Virginia Clemm. Her prolonged illness and early death in 1847 were crushing for him. He died in mysterious circumstances in Baltimore on 7 October 1849. It is usually assumed that he was kidnapped by a band of political toughs, force-fed alcohol and drugs, and dragged around the election booths until he collapsed.

Despite his difficulties of personality and his wretchedly unhappy life, Poe was a man of enormous accomplishment. In addition to being an important poet, short story writer, and critic, he established the aesthetic basis of the modern short story and created the detective story. He also wrote theoretical essays on poetic technique. He was an excellent scholar, with a working knowledge of modern and ancient languages and their literatures, and he was widely read in contemporary American and British literature. His private reading reached into the sciences and philosophy, and his factual apparatus was enormous. As a writer he possessed a remarkable technical facility, and even critics who disparage his work usually do not deny his great analytical ability.

Poe applied this power of analysis to the supernatural fiction of his day and was perhaps the first to set up a working aesthetic. In an early review of a contemporary bad novel, Robert Montgomery Bird's *Sheppard Lee* (1836), he denounced the habit of dream endings and insisted that supernaturalism should be genuine and central to a work. He also suggested that, to create verisimilitude, an author should build up circumstantial detail in the background of the story, but leave the supernatural portions less developed. The narrative point of view should be that of awed, surprised acceptance. Elsewhere, notably in his famous review of Nathaniel Hawthorne's *Twice-Told Tales*, Poe set up criteria for story unity, which he compared to visual art. Further elements in his critical position were based on his lifelong struggle to define imagination and on the related question of what we would call symbolic structures and he called undercurrents.

Poe's fiction was written in a tradition based on English periodical fiction (notably in *Blackwood's Magazine*) and the German romantic short story. From *Blackwood's* he derived the first-person sensation and sensational narrative of exotic horror, and from the Germans his supernatural apparatus (doppelgängers, revenants, otherworlds, occultism) and much (ultimately, through Samuel Taylor Coleridge) of the theoretical position mentioned above. In later years he drew more heavily on French prototypes.

The question often arises why Poe concentrated on the less pleasurable emotions, for roughly half his fiction contains strong elements of horror, whether supernatural, sadistic, adventure-associated, or other. Poe stated in effect that he could write such material easily and that it sold well. In a letter (30 April 1835) to Thomas W. White, the proprietor of the *Southern Literary Messenger*, Poe, in discussing horror, stated that "these things are invariably sought after with avidity . . . and [their popularity] will be esteemed . . . by the circulation of the Magazine" (Quinn).

Like Poe's other rational explanations of his work this is at least partly true, but it should be remembered that other types of fiction also sold well and that on the American market horror fiction of Poe's sort accounted for only a small fraction of what was published.

In the same letter Poe offered to write for White stories in which "the ludicrous [is] heightened into the grotesque: the fearful coloured into the horrible: the witty exaggerated into the burlesque: [and] the singular wrought out into the strange and mystical." These are, of course, Poe's stories, and it is curious to note that Poe considered them to result from emotional magnification and distortion of the normal.

II

Poe's first published story, "Metzengerstein" (*Saturday Courier*, 14 January 1832), was one of a group of five stories submitted to a Philadelphia newspaper. The other four stories are humorous, even parodic, and "Metzengerstein," despite the effectiveness of its horror imagery, is undoubtedly a parody of Gothic and early-nineteenth-century extravagances, notably Horace Walpole's *The Castle of Otranto*. That it is sometimes taken to be only a horror story is perhaps due to the fact that Poe had not yet learned how to balance the thematic components of his fiction.

The story is based on a long feud between two noble German-Hungarian families, the Metzengersteins and the Berlifitzings, who are close neighbors. A fire destroys the Berlifitzing stables, and the old baron dies trying to save his horses. At this time a strange horse is captured by the Metzengerstein lackeys and brought to the profligate young Baron Metzengerstein. His immediate fascination with the horse turns eventually into an obsession, and the servants speculate that the horse is now controlling the man, instead of vice versa. The horse is also in some way connected with a tapestry showing an ancestral Metzengerstein killing a Berlifitzing. The suggestion, not stated directly, is that the horse, an embodiment of the dead baron, has emerged from the tapestry and that an ancient prophecy is to be fulfilled. A second fire breaks out, this time in Castle Metzengerstein, and the demonic horse carries its rider into the flames, to his death.

How seriously is the story to be taken? The ludicrous names alone are a giveaway. (They are probably derived from geography: Metz, Gerolstein or Geierstein [note Sir Walter Scott's *Anne of Geierstein*], and Berlin.) The incidents of the story do not always make sense. The prophecy does not fit its fulfillment, and the development is tongue in cheek. Much of what is assumed to happen—arson, emergence of the horse, metempsychosis—is supplied by the reader, not Poe. The rational story is simply that horses, as a nineteenth-century man would have known, usually do not try to run away from a fire, but try to dash through it. "Metzengerstein" is a nightmare, and a contemporary reader might have observed the resemblance between Poe's description of the tapestried horse and the artist Henry Fuseli's popular engraving *Nightmare.*

Two of the stories associated in early publication with "Metzengerstein" involve superficial supernaturalism to make a mundane point. In both cases the gentlemanly Devil of the many Faust stories is involved. "The Bargain Lost" (*Saturday Courier*, 1 December 1832; revised, retitled "Bon-Bon," 1835) uses diabolic temptation in reverse to provide a humorous critique of contemporary cultural patterns. In the revised version a French restaurateur is visited by the Devil, who discusses souls as gustatorial delights, piquancy depending on theological or philosophical position. Instead of trying to ensnare the restaurateur's soul, the Devil scorns it. More interesting is "The Duc de l'Omelette" (*Saturday Courier*, 3 March 1832; later revised), in which a French epicure dies, finds himself in Hell, and tricks his way out. The duke, scheduled for various torments, stakes his fate on a card game with the Devil and wins by palming a card. The story is written in the effervescent style of sensational French fiction. Because of certain details it is usually taken to be a parody of and mild attack on Nathaniel Parker Willis, with whom Poe had an off-and-on friendship. The same claim has been made for "Bon-Bon," but it is not strong. "Bon-Bon" is best left to specialists, but "The Duc de l'Omelette" is amusing even to a reader who does not know its point of reference.

The three early stories that have been described are among Poe's lesser work, but "Ligeia" (*American Museum*, September 1838) is generally considered one of his masterpieces. Poe thought it his best story. It is also important for integrating motifs that are associated with Poe's tales of horror or supernaturalism: the emphasis on isolation, amounting almost to an otherworld or pocket universe cut off from the world of life; the emasculated yet forcefully speaking male narrator, who tells of his subservience to and dislike of women; the pathological narrator, what with bad heredity, alcoholism, or drug addiction; the unusual, sometimes incestuous, sexual bonds between the characters; the elfin or gnomish outside environment; the interior decoration of morbid antiquarian clutter, like a bad stage set; the occult studies and obscure, strange-sounding book titles; the heightened, almost hysterical narrative tone; the emphasis on physical horror, yet sometimes with the lingering doubt whether it is meant seriously.

Despite a mostly clear narrative line, "Ligeia" is considered one of Poe's more problematic stories. Modern critics have differed greatly on interpreting it. It has been called a statement of incest and the Oedipus complex; a waking dream; a detailed parody of either the New England transcendentalists or the Gothic novelists; a nonsupernatural murder story told by a madman; a fictional exegesis of literary criticism, focusing on national varieties of romanticism; and even a literal supernatural story in which Ligeia resurrects herself.

In such cases one wonders whether the author might have indicated his intention. Surprisingly enough, Poe did. In a letter to Philip Pendleton Cooke (16 September 1839) he stated clearly that the story was meant as literal supernaturalism. But this letter has not dissuaded holders of other opinions, some of whom simply say that Poe lied.

To summarize the narrative: Ligeia is a learned, strong-minded German student of the occult who believes that the human will can be potent enough to stave off death. The narrator, her husband and subservient pupil, reflects her belief and, as she lies dying, is not surprised to hear her declaration of faith in her will. He mourns her death deeply and passionately, mostly because of her intellectual qualities. After a time he remarries, not another German magician, but an English county woman, the Lady Rowena, who is as insipid as Sir Walter Scott's Rowena. He soon tires of her and comes to hate her, dwelling on the memory of the wonderful Ligeia. He takes to opium, while Rowena falls ill. As he sits with her in the bridal chamber—which is decorated like a chamber of horrors with fixtures symbolic of death—he hears strange movements and sees an inexplicable shadow. A red liquor precipitates out of the air into Rowena's wine glass, and she dies not long after this. As the narrator sits by her corpse, he is horrified to see that it is showing signs of life. The dead body attempts several times to regain life, the narrator helping it, but with increasing emotional turmoil. At the last, when the corpse stands and faces him, he sees that it is black-tressed and too tall for the blonde Rowena; and when the wrappings drop away from its face, he recognizes Ligeia, who has occupied and transformed the body of the dead Rowena. As Poe indicated in his letter to Cooke, Rowena/Ligeia then collapses into final death—although this is not written into the story.

One of the cruxes in this simple recital of events is the origin of the red potion. Did Ligeia's ghost poison Rowena, or is the narrator indirectly confessing what he himself did in an opium fog? Poe left this for the reader to decide.

Even if we ignore the various speculative, metaphoric readings, there are strange elements in "Ligeia." The concept of emotional paradox that underlies the story is striking. As the narrator describes his situation, he is a subservient figure, yet his style is bold, dramatic, and ultramasculine. Nor does the narrator's description of his feelings coincide with his subject matter. He states that he hates Rowena (and he may have poisoned her), yet he tries to save her life. He dwells on his intense devotion to the intellectually gigantic Ligeia, but if his description of her is summarized, it does not reveal love. As described, Ligeia was subject to heavy rages; she was a know-it-all who put her husband down; she forced him to submerge his individuality and follow her pursuits; she lectured to him for hours; she was stern; in her last days she was scrawny and unattractive; and, finally, she revealed that she did not love him but thought of him only as a link to life. Is this a wife to cherish? On this basis it might be more apt to say that "Ligeia" is a hate story rather than a love story, a double episode in the battle of the sexes, one hate of which is stated frankly, the other concealed.

Before accepting an analysis of "Ligeia," a reader should take into account Poe's other Ligeia and the general fictional background to the story. Poe's other Ligeia is a being who is apostrophized in the poem "Al Aaraaf," a notoriously obscure early work. Here Nesace, the spirit of beauty sent out by God, invokes Ligeia, who is not identified but has the task of putting to sleep and awaking incarnate angels (men and women). She is associated with music. It is possible, in context, that Ligeia may symbolize a nightingale or similar nocturnal songbird, or, since Poe frequently used astral identifications, that she might stand for the planet Venus, as morning and evening stars. Associated with this Ligeia are many of the same tropes that the narrator uses to characterize his feeling toward the woman Ligeia: the sea, plants, the stars, and music. All this raises the question whether the Ligeia of fiction may not have been some sort of avatar, perhaps a star spirit that assumed human form, whence her great wisdom and supernatural abilities.

Vampirism may also be a factor—not that Ligeia was an animated bloodsucking corpse like Count Dracula, but that Poe might have written the story "Ligeia" with vampire lore in the back of his mind. What Ligeia does to the narrator and Rowena is spiritual vampirism of a sort. There is also the question of literary context. Two German stories are fairly similar to "Ligeia," and one of them would certainly have been accessible to Poe. In Ludwig Tieck's "Die Klausenburg," Elizabeth, a student of recondite philosophies, vows to her husband that by strength of will she will surmount death. (In her case she cites Fichte instead of Joseph Glanvill.) She returns from the dead as a monstrosity. Whether Poe could have known this story, though, is problematic, for it was not printed in German until 1836 (two years before "Ligeia") and not translated, so far as is known, until 1844, in John Oxenford's *Tales from the German*.

The second German story, called in English "Wake Not the Dead," appeared in the anonymously edited *Popular Tales and Romances of the Northern Nations* (1823). In it the husband's black-tressed first wife dies, and he marries a blonde, with whom he becomes unhappy. He languishes after his first wife and employs a magician to raise her from the dead. She returns, but as a vampire. Other details suggest "Ligeia." The story is attributed in this translation to Tieck, but a German original has not been found, and it may be supposititious.

The safest general conclusion about "Ligeia" is that it is a literal supernatural story, although murder may also be involved. As secondary elements or undercurrents it contains comparisons between German and English romanticism, as well as suggestions that Ligeia is more than human and that Poe was aware of vampirism in similar situations.

"Ligeia" is connected with two other stories, "Morella" (*Southern Literary Messenger*, April 1835) and "Eleonora" (*The Gift* of 1841). Both are concerned with the conscious return of the dead, though not as conventional ghosts. In "Morella," which Poe stated was in effect a forestudy for "Ligeia," a hated, dying wife vows to return. Her spirit passes into the body of her child, as it is born, but is not fully conscious of its identity until adolescence. "Eleonora" is a softened version of the same situation. When the narrator makes a second marriage despite his oath to the dead Eleonora not to marry again, he expects supernatural punishment. Instead, he hears her spirit voice blessing him and his new wife. Whether "Eleonora" is meant literally is disputable. Some critics regard the ghostly voice as simply self-justification in the narrator's mind.

If these three stories—"Ligeia," "Morella," "Eleonora"—are read backward, from the point of view of the woman involved, instead of from that of the overprotesting male narrator, a different emotional nexus arises. We see a woman who is loved not for herself but for an accidental. ("Berenice," in which the narrator is a mad tooth fetishist, could be added to this list.) She may even be hated for her superiority. The marriage collapses, and the woman may make an attempt to revive it but fails. Ligeia cannot assume a new identity; Morella cannot create herself permanently in her daughter; Eleonora simply gives up. Marriage is death.

Echoes of the "Ligeia" complex are to be heard beyond the quaternion of stories mentioned, in "The Fall of the House of Usher," where, witnessed by an outsider and epitomized, rather than told, by a victim/aggressor, we see the familiar sequence: love-hate, death, reawakening, love-hate, and final death for Roderick and Madeline Usher.

"The Fall of the House of Usher" (*Burton's Gentleman's Magazine*, September 1839) is often considered Poe's masterpiece. A story of utter depression told in supernatural terms, without the notes of irony or parody that sometimes emerge in the other supernatural stories, it is a remarkable example of sustained mood writing.

The wonderful first paragraph sets the tone of the story. Rhythmic prose, almost scansible as blank verse, using a vocabulary filled with negation words, it presents the main theme: the inevitability of catastrophe in a pocket universe that encompasses the characters, a humanoid house, and landscape—all of which are connected or identical. Poe's aesthetics required that the first part of a short story, like the overture to an opera (my comparison, not Poe's), should be built out of themes that will emerge later; here he accomplished this feat.

"The Fall of the House of Usher" is a failed mission. The narrator receives an urgent request to help his old schoolfriend Roderick Usher, who is in great trouble. He finds that the landscape around Usher's house is inexpressibly gloomy, dank, and dark, covered with a pall-like atmosphere that is almost tangible—a sort of Pittsburgh of the soul. The house at first glance seems sound but is really fissured and rotten. The narrator finds Usher a dying man, depressed beyond cure, helpless with fear, physically eroded by neural disorders, and emotionally broken by the anticipation of his twin sister Madeline's death. Madeline seems to die and is placed in the family vault, but awakens from catalepsy and emerges, torn and bloody. She falls upon Usher (whether in loving embrace or in attack is carefully clouded), and both collapse into death. The narrator rushes out and on looking back sees that the house, too, dies, crumbling into the dark tarn that stands beside it. The House of Usher is dead.

This is the surface narrative, but it is not accepted as the ultimate by many critics, for "The Fall of the House of Usher" may well be the most "interpreted" story in supernatural fiction. Usher, understandably, has been equated with Poe, and the story has been read as a figurative statement of Poe's own plight. (Actually, the story was written during one of Poe's more successful periods, when he was employed and abstaining from alcohol.) D. H. Lawrence considered the tale a love story, in which Roderick and Madeline drag each other down in incestuous love, thus betraying their inner essences. Others have called the story variously a psychological analysis of introversion; a poetic realization of a mechanistic theory of society; a murder story, in which Roderick, by burying his sister alive, eventually brings about his own destruction; a fate narrative; an allegory of the tripartite division of the human mind; a surreptitious vampire story; a failed alchemical experiment; a symbolic statement of psychosis, ego swallowed by the tarn of the unconscious; and an unsuccessful rebirth experience. In still other interpretations the narrator is taken as the central figure, a man who by his own folly pushes the Ushers to their doom.

"The Fall of the House of Usher" has also been read as a parody describing the destruction of the Gothic hero and the persecuted maiden; and, in contradiction, Roderick Usher has been identified as the first modern hero, the prototype of a succession of tormented, estranged, alienated, doomed men. Since this last judgment embodies literary history rather than subjective interpretation, it can be accepted.

Taken in the terms of the narrative, "The Fall of the House of Usher" is a story of fated collapse, not just of individuals, but of a family, as in Scott's *The Bride of Lammermoor*. The Ushers have decayed, and their decay, stated in supernatural terms, includes individuals and estates, which are linked. The present Ushers have been trapped in an error-world not of their own making; but since, in their decadence, they have yielded to it, they must die. There was once some hope when Roderick asked for outside help, summoning a champion to rescue him from his Slough of Despond. But the champion, the narrator, is no Help or Evangelist, and no counterpart to Ethelred of the chivalric tale read by Usher and the narrator. (It is worth noting that Poe here broke the usual pattern of using such märchen. Ethelred's adventures, instead of being symbolic of problems and solutions, are opposite to Usher's.) Fear and fate are too strong, and Hell is unsuccessfully harrowed.

Related in idea to "The Fall of the House of Usher" is "The Devil in the Belfry" (*Saturday Chronicle and Mirror of the Times*, 18 May 1839), which is superficially a humorous tale poking fun at Dutch (really German) lethargy and stick-in-the-mud conservatism. This aspect of the story is reminiscent of Washington Irving's portrayal of the Hudson River Dutch-Americans. The village of Vonder-

votteimittiss, inhabitants and milieu, is a glorified clock. Sixty houses corresponding to minutes are set around a central plain, or clock face, and surrounded by low hills, or a clock case. The humans are obsessed with clocks, and even the animals carry watches. Almost every detail of the people and their world is based upon time symbols. The leitmotiv of this otherworld is absolute conformity to what is established, and the symbol for this is the giant clock in the village belfry, tended by the belfryman. This culture is undisturbed until a demonic being invades it. A strange-looking creature, he darts about, performing outrageous actions, finally assaulting and overpowering the belfryman — at which the clock strikes not twelve, but thirteen. (Following the horological analogy, the demon would seem to be a malfunctioning second or minute hand.) The story ends with a plea for outside help to restore the primal harmony.

Beneath the narrative, the undercurrent seems to be a criticism of a clockwork universe, as postulated by perhaps Descartes or La Mettrie. The demon is the entry of an erratic, unpredicted event into a mechanistic world, causing the disruption of order until order is restored by outside aid. The theme is thus individuality against an established pattern. In "The Fall of the House of Usher" the preestablished pattern prevailed, perhaps in part because the outside irritant was not irritating enough; the opposite happens in "The Devil in the Belfry." There are, of course, the typical linkages of the land, buildings, and the human body.

Somewhat similar in thought is the much later story "The Angel of the Odd" (*Columbian Lady's and Gentleman's Magazine*, October 1844), in which the narrator is confronted by an imp who symbolizes the unpredictability of individual events, despite the overall reliability of statistics.

In the same year as "The Fall of the House of Usher" and "The Devil in the Belfry" Poe also published "William Wilson" (*Burton's Gentleman's Magazine*, October 1839, and *The Gift* for 1840). It can be taken as typical of a group of stories that also includes "Berenice" (1835), "The Tell-Tale Heart" (1843), "The Black Cat" (1843), and perhaps, in part, "Ligeia." These are mental picaresques in which an utter scoundrel or psychopath tells, with the utmost sangfroid, the horrible things that he has done, distancing himself at times from his deeds by a supernatural excuse. The narrators are abnormal: alcoholic ("William Wilson," "The Black Cat"), mad ("William Wilson," "Berenice"), or drug addicts ("Ligeia"). Their crimes are sadistic and horrible.

In "William Wilson" the narrator explains his lifelong difficulties with another William Wilson, who looks exactly like him and is his doppelgänger. They attend the same school, and while their lives separate, they meet occasionally, on which occasions the doppelgänger Wilson points out the iniquity of the narrator Wilson. On one occasion he reveals to a university group that the narrator has been cheating at cards, so Wilson is expelled. Finally, the narrator duels with his double, wounds him mortally, and then is told that he has killed the better part of himself. From here on his wickedness is untrammeled.

The motto at the beginning of the story and the doppelgänger's speech at the end both indicate that the doppelgänger is a dissociated personality fragment of Wilson's; it is his conscience, which has been so rejected that it leads a separate life. Yet "William Wilson" is not a simple allegory, for the relations of Wilson with Wilson are complex and elaborate, in the tradition of the works of Jean Paul and E. T. A. Hoffmann. (See Ralph Tymms, *Doubles in Literary Psychology*, 1949.)

One of the undercurrents of "William Wilson" takes a peculiar turn, bringing Poe into the story. The narrator, for reasons not known, is described as having been born on Poe's birthday, having gone to Poe's elementary school in England, and knowing Poe's friends. The other undercurrent links "William Wilson" with Poe's later story "The Masque of the Red Death." Although Wilson's school fits Poe's in name, location, and personnel, it is vastly different in plan and bears a close resemblance to Duke Prospero's fantastic abbey. It even has a sinister clock. Both stories describe psychic suicides, Wilson putting aside the better portion of himself, and Prospero succumbing to fear.

Poe published nothing similar in 1840, and in 1841, only the minor story "Never Bet the Devil Your Head" (*Graham's Lady's and Gentleman's Magazine*, September 1841). This is a difficult story to understand. Purportedly a denunciation of cursing written to contradict the accusation that Poe did not write moral fiction, it tells of Toby Dammit, who went through a life cycle in a year and literally lost his head to the Devil as the result of a bet that grew out of a careless oath. It is possible that the story is topical, but if so a convincing topicality has not been brought forward. (The Devil does wear an apron, symbolic of a freemason.) Some of the obscurity is removed if one assumes that Poe has mixed three story tracks, one of a human, one of a dog, and one of a horse — Toby perpetually changing form. A reader may nevertheless wonder why Poe bothered.

In 1842 appeared "The Masque of the Red Death" (*Graham's Lady's and Gentleman's Magazine*, May 1842), which vies with "The Fall of the House of Usher" for the reputation of being Poe's best story. It is popular probably because at first glance it lacks the difficulties present in other stories, although this simplicity of appearance is deceptive.

The story is a tableau imaging a single incident but reinforced with very strong painterly description. A virulent disease is sweeping through an Italianate land, and the ruling prince, Duke Prospero, to escape the plague seals himself and a thousand followers into an enormous fantastic building complex. The situation is thus reminiscent of Boccaccio's *Decameron*. Life in the abbey consists of a round of festivities and celebrations, while the plague rages outside. At the last costume ball, a figure garbed like a victim of the plague appears, horrifying and enraging the spectators. After some hesitation Prospero confronts and attacks the figure. He falls dead, and the figure is revealed to be empty cerements. Everyone thereupon dies of the Red Death.

The surface theme is obvious: one cannot escape fate, and hiding is of no avail. In this respect "The Masque of the Red Death" resembles early-nineteenth-century time-fate stories like the anonymous "The Fatal Hour." There is the further ironic note that the duke's precautions enhance his danger, so that unwittingly he commits suicide.

It soon becomes clear, though, that there is more to the story than a *Decameron*-like setting of palace revels or a narrative of terror. Poe took pains to establish the milieu, and two familiar undercurrents emerge: the identity of the building with the universe and with a human body. Prospero is a demiurge of a sort; he created in his abbey a Ptolemaic solar system, with rooms corresponding to the seven planets and their colors. His dancers, as Poe states, represent dreams. Present is a remarkable clock that obviously represents death; when it strikes, everything stops. When the clock strikes twelve, the end of time, Prospero's world dies along with its creator: "And Darkness and Decay and the Red Death held illimitable dominion over all." Time has entered eternity. The picture situation—the demiurge or earth spirit in battle with death—is thus reminiscent of Jean de Grainville's *The Last Man* (1805), although there seems to be no evidence that Poe had read the work.

There are, of course, other problems in "The Masque of the Red Death." Is it "masque," as Poe later spelled it, or "mask," as he first spelled it? What is the Red Death? Taken literally, it is imaginary, although undoubtedly related to the epidemics of the day, particularly pulmonary bubonic plague. Taken symbolically, it might be fear (as with Roderick Usher); for fear permeates the story, from the first withdrawal, to the cessation of dancing when the clock strikes, to the encounter with the masked figure. There is also the question of the relationship between William Wilson (who is partly identified with Edgar Allan Poe) and Prospero (a demiurge or author).

In an earlier, much simpler story, the prose poem "Shadow—A Parable" (*Southern Literary Messenger*, September 1835), Poe anticipated some aspects of "The Masque of the Red Death." The plague is present in Hellenistic Egypt, and a group of friends have secluded themselves as they drink and sing in a weird wake to a dead friend. A Shadow falls over them, a Shadow with the voice of multitudes, or the recognition of their mortality.

Similarly parabolic, although more obscure, is the later prose poem "Silence—A Fable," first published as "Siope" (*The Baltimore Book*, 1838). A demon takes the narrator to a remote, savage part of Africa, where a solitary, almost godlike man sits on a rock contemplating the turmoil of nature. The malicious demon steps up the elements, but this does not es-

pecially faze the man. But when the demon strikes everything silent, the man is distressed and leaves. The piece is sometimes taken to represent Poe's dislike of the New England transcendentalists, but it is more probably an allegory of the life of letters. The demon is the press; the man is an author who, although not happy with hostile displays, prefers them to silence or to being ignored.

Both these stories, themselves minor, were historically important in the later development of weird fiction in the United States, particularly with the Lovecraft circle, who lifted Poe's surface supernaturalism without considering a possible deeper meaning.

As the 1840's progressed, Poe stepped away from supernatural fiction, perhaps because his aesthetic theories were undergoing change. One late story, even though it is primitive science fiction of a sort, is important. This is "The Facts in the Case of M. Valdemar" (*American Review*, December 1845). Valdemar, a very ill man, dies as he is entering a mesmeric trance, but the mesmeric influence keeps him in a state of quasi-life, preventing dissolution. When the trance is broken, Valdemar immediately dissolves into a mass of corruption. The story is powerful, even if certainly parodic, and its crash ending is one of the most powerful in literature—on first reading. It was taken as a serious horror story by later writers, and it ultimately became the model for countless sensational stories with trick endings. Many writers, including H. P. Lovecraft, might have been better served if they had not read it.

III

The achievement of Edgar Allan Poe is still controversial, for it must be admitted that many major critics have damned his work. In some cases, this condemnation has been based on a lack of understanding of what Poe was doing; in others, it has been due simply to repugnance at a personality and work that are sometimes unpleasant; in still others, to a different zeitgeist or set of standards. Poe's position has thus changed cyclically, with a low point in the recent past and a considerable rise at present. It is safe to say that as his work is better understood in its complexity, it is more highly esteemed.

Where historical importance is concerned,

though, there can be no argument. In Europe his fantastic fiction set off whole literary movements, from the symbolism of nineteenth-century France to the expressionism of early-twentieth-century Germany. In Europe he has long been considered an author of world significance, indeed, perhaps the first modern author in that he was first to work (and that superbly) in the shadow areas of human personality. In genre work in the English language, he has been read and imitated by almost every major writer of supernatural fiction since his time. He stands behind the modern rise of pulp supernatural fiction, and today a large part of the new fiction is still only Poe updated and rewritten.

Selected Bibliography

WORKS OF EDGAR ALLAN POE

There are scores of editions of Poe's fiction containing some or all of the stories described in this article. In most cases the texts they follow are those of the Griswold edition (see below), which, while accurate for the versions it prints, does not always reprint Poe's best or final texts. Poe continually revised his work, but the changes are usually not important for the general reader.

Tales of the Grotesque and Arabesque. 2 vols. Philadelphia: Lea and Blanchard, 1840.

Tales by Edgar A. Poe. New York and London: Wiley and Putnam, 1845.

The Works of the Late Edgar Allan Poe. Edited by Rufus W. Griswold. 4 vols. New York: J. S. Redfield, 1850–1856.

The Complete Works of Edgar Allan Poe. Virginia Edition. Edited by James A. Harrison. 17 vols. New York: Crowell, 1902. (The closest to a variorum edition yet prepared and at the moment still the best edition.)

Tales and Sketches. Edited by Thomas Ollive Mabbott with the assistance of Eleanor D. Kewer and Maureen C. Mabbott. 2 vols. Cambridge, Mass.: Harvard University Press, 1978. (Volumes 2 and 3 of the Collected Works of Edgar Allan Poe. The set is still in the process of publication and will probably become the definitive edition of Poe.)

CRITICAL AND BIOGRAPHICAL STUDIES

The scholarly literature on Poe is vast, and even a listing of the more important studies would be beyond the scope of this article. The following items have been useful for the preparation of this article, or, as general works, can be recommended to the reader.

Bleiler, E. F. "Edgar Allan Poe." In Science Fiction Writers, edited by E. F. Bleiler. New York: Scribner, 1982. (Covers the stories more closely related to science fiction, including "Pym," "Pfaal," and the mesmeric stories.)

Campbell, Killis. The Mind of Poe and Other Studies. Cambridge, Mass.: Harvard University Press, 1933.

Howarth, William L., ed. Twentieth Century Interpretations of Poe's Tales: A Collection of Critical Essays. Englewood Cliffs, N.J.: Prentice-Hall, 1971. (Fifteen papers.)

Jacobs, Robert D. Poe: Journalist and Critic. Baton Rouge: Louisiana State University Press, 1969.

Pollin, Burton R. Discoveries in Poe. Notre Dame, Ind.: University of Notre Dame Press, 1970.

Quinn, Arthur Hobson. Edgar Allan Poe: A Critical Biography. New York: Appleton-Century-Crofts, 1941.

Regan, Robert, ed. Poe: A Collection of Critical Essays. Englewood Cliffs, N.J.: Prentice-Hall, 1967. (Thirteen excerpts and papers.)

Tymms, Ralph. Doubles in Literary Psychology. Cambridge: Bowes and Bowes, 1949.

Wagenknecht, Edward. Edgar Allan Poe: The Man Behind the Legend. New York: Oxford University Press, 1963.

Wilt, Napier. "Poe's Attitude Toward His Tales: A New Document." Modern Philology, 25 (August 1927): 101–105.

Woodson, Thomas, ed. Twentieth Century Interpretations of "The Fall of the House of Usher": A Collection of Critical Essays. Englewood Cliffs, N.J.: Prentice-Hall, 1969. (Fifteen excerpts and papers.)

—E. F. BLEILER

NATHANIEL HAWTHORNE

1804-1864

IN 1863, JUST a year before his death and after he had published all the fiction he was destined to complete, Nathaniel Hawthorne wrote his publisher, "I wish God had given me the faculty of writing a sunshiny book." This may seem to be a strange lament coming from a writer whose greatness is so much more closely allied with darkness than with light and with gloom than with sunshine, but it points to Hawthorne's crucial and deep-rooted ambivalence toward his characteristic qualities as a writer. Again and again in his notebooks and letters, Hawthorne reveals a tendency to be troubled by the dark and gloomy stirrings of his imagination. He was often concerned that his somber outlook and strange, haunting tales of guilt, isolation, and death might put on display an aspect of his mind that he would rather have kept from public view. Thus, he preferred *The House of the Seven Gables* (1851) to his much superior masterpiece, *The Scarlet Letter* (1850), because he considered *The House* "a much more natural and healthy product of my mind."

Indeed, one of the recurring themes in Hawthorne's commentary on his writings is a sense of struggle and conflict with the workings of his own imagination. His stories and novels seem to be continually attempting to wrestle out of his control, often with aims quite different from their author's. Hawthorne was to say of *The Scarlet Letter*, for instance, that it "is a positively hell-fired story, into which I found it impossible to throw any cheering light." Even the more overtly optimistic quality of

The House of the Seven Gables seems to have been purchased with some struggle. Hawthorne had intended all along to bring the book to a "prosperous close," but apparently he almost wrote an ending quite different from the happy one he had planned: "It darkens damnably towards the close," he told his publisher, "but I shall try hard to pour some setting sunshine over it." And, years after he had stopped writing short stories—some of which are among the greatest in the English language—Hawthorne would habitually belittle them, in some sense disowning these gloomy offspring of his "haunted" mind: "Upon my honor, I am not quite sure that I entirely comprehend my own meaning, in some of those blasted allegories."

This lifelong conflict stems to a large extent from a central division in Hawthorne's conception of himself as a man and his very different aims as an artist. Hawthorne's internal directives as an artist were clear. As he said in the preface to *The House of the Seven Gables*, he was allowed much leeway in his methods and techniques as long as he did not "swerve aside from the truth of the human heart." This, of course, was to be Hawthorne's constant subject. His most powerful and enduring work occurs when he peers unflinchingly into the depths of human psychology and moral responsibility. And, unlike his transcendentalist contemporaries, such as Ralph Waldo Emerson and Henry David Thoreau, Hawthorne refused to accept the prevailing optimism of his age; when he looked into man's soul what he saw was usually much darker and less agreeable than what others claimed to see.

One of Hawthorne's favorite metaphors for the human heart is the dungeon: "In the depths of every heart, there is a tomb and a dungeon, though the lights, the music, and revelry may cause us to forget their existence, and the buried ones, or prisoners whom they hide" ("The Haunted Mind," published in a gift book, *The Token*, 1835). It is little wonder that Hawthorne found it so difficult to pour "sunshine" into his works: his integrity as an artist led him again and again to descend into the dungeon.

Hawthorne the man, however, had another side. One important aspect of his personality that is sometimes underestimated by modern readers — who are occasionally too eager to believe the attractive but largely exaggerated myth of Hawthorne as neurotic, gloomy recluse — is the extent to which he saw himself as a conventional Victorian gentleman: cultivated, refined, even proper. Although he was never remarkably outgoing or gregarious, Hawthorne was certainly capable of functioning normally in his social world. Indeed, throughout his life he was to hold a number of positions — including United States consul at Liverpool — that would have required some degree of social ease and even urbanity.

An important consequence of this conventional side of Hawthorne was a lifelong reticence, a reluctance to disclose too much of his inner self in public. He was to say in the preface to his collection of stories *Mosses from an Old Manse* (1846), for instance:

> Has the reader gone wandering, hand in hand with me, through the inner passages of my being, and have we groped together into all its chambers, and examined their treasures or their rubbish? Not so. . . . So far as I am a man of really individual attributes, I veil my face; nor am I, nor have ever been, one of those supremely hospitable people, who serve up their own hearts, delicately fried, with brain-sauce, as a tid-bit for their beloved public.

Although this attitude would have been perfectly reasonable for a typical nineteenth-century gentleman, it clearly seems at odds with Hawthorne's dark and profound tendencies as a writer. And it is easy to see, given this ingrained reticence, why Hawthorne felt such ambivalence toward his literary productions — which so often reveal a mind deeply troubled by the negative capabilities of human nature and which went so utterly against the grain of the prevailing optimism of their times.

Hawthorne's recurrent use of the supernatural and the historical in his fiction is to some extent a reaction to this deeply felt ambivalence. His dark vision is so powerful and disturbing that he seems to have been temperamentally incapable of giving it expression without first achieving some emotional and aesthetic distance from it. By locating his fictions in contexts that are remote from his everyday life — by placing them either in the past or in the sphere of the supernatural — Hawthorne is able to comment more fully and truthfully than if he had attempted to write more directly from his own experience. Indeed, one can think of few writers who so rarely used the particulars of their day-to-day existence as material for their art. As Hyatt H. Waggoner says, Hawthorne was, paradoxically, "truest to himself when he wrote of others and truest to his own age when he ignored it and wrote of the past or the legendary and mythical."

Hawthorne's inclination toward the supernatural and the legendary was not motivated solely by the vagaries of his personality. There were also strong aesthetic reasons for employing these distancing devices. Perhaps most important was that by dealing with the remote and fantastic, Hawthorne could examine the underlying, elemental truths of human nature more closely. Together with his great contemporaries — Emerson, Thoreau, and above all Herman Melville — Hawthorne was engaged in a lifelong attempt to explore the more fundamental reality that lay just behind the world of the individual and the particular. (Indeed, all four writers would have agreed with Emerson's assertion that "every natural fact is a symbol of some spiritual fact.") And in this kind of endeavor, as Melville was to say of Hawthorne, "you must have plenty of searoom to tell the truth in."

Thus, Hawthorne was attracted to the supernatural and historical because they allowed him a wider fictive world through which to tell the truth as he saw it. In his preface to *The House of the*

708

Seven Gables he articulates the distinction he often made between two types of fiction: the romance and the novel. The romance is clearly the form that possessed for Hawthorne the greater range of aesthetic possibilities:

> When a writer calls his work a Romance, it need hardly be observed that he wishes to claim a certain latitude, both as to its fashion and material, which he would not have felt himself entitled to assume had he professed to be writing a Novel. The latter form of composition is presumed to aim at a very minute fidelity, not merely to the possible, but to the probable and ordinary course of man's experience. The former—while, as a work of art, it must rigidly subject itself to laws, and while it sins unpardonably so far as it may swerve aside from the truth of the human heart—has fairly a right to present that truth under circumstances, to a great extent, of the writer's own choosing or creation.

In "The Custom House," his introductory essay to *The Scarlet Letter*, Hawthorne locates this fictional ground even more precisely. It occupies a "neutral territory," he writes, "somewhere between the real world and fairy-land, where the Actual and the Imaginary may meet." Despite the domesticating language of this description ("fairy-land" sounds like a pleasant enough place), Hawthorne's exploration of this fictional terrain led him into some of the darkest and most somber regions any writer has ever visited.

Hawthorne's lifelong fascination with this "neutral territory"—especially as it manifested itself in the supernatural and historical—was to a large extent a direct result of the circumstances of his ancestry and early life. Born on 4 July 1804 in Salem, Massachusetts, young Hawthorne was part of a family whose roots could be traced back to the very beginnings of New England and that had been important and influential in the early history of Salem. The earliest of his American ancestors was a William Hathorne (Nathaniel added the *w* to the family name when he began to fancy himself a writer) who had come over from England in 1630 and won considerable reknown as a soldier and magistrate. He also won dubious fame by ordering the public whip-ping of a Quaker woman during the Quaker persecutions. His son John was a successful and prominent judge who presided over the infamous witchcraft trials of 1692. According to an apocryphal family legend, Judge Hathorne and his descendants were cursed by a woman he had sentenced to death: "God will give you blood to drink."

Young Hawthorne undoubtedly grew up listening to these and other stories of his family's past. In later years his attitude toward his ancestors would be highly ambivalent: respect for and pride in their many accomplishments would be inextricably mingled with disgust and guilt over their severity and intolerance. As he says in his essay "Main Street" (*Aesthetic Papers*, 1849), "Let us thank God for having given us such ancestors; and let each successive generation thank Him, not less fervently, for being one step further from them in the march of ages." Hawthorne was to incorporate much of what he had heard about his family's past into his fiction, including such elements as the persecution of the Quakers, an inherited family curse, witchcraft and devil worship, and the general historical context of Puritanism in early New England.

By the time Hawthorne was born, the family's fortunes had declined considerably from their former prosperity and prominence. When Hawthorne's father, a ship's captain, died during a voyage, his widow and three children, including four-year-old Nathaniel, were left almost totally without resources and were forced to move in with her affluent relatives. Thus, despite the early importance of the family, Nathaniel was destined not to grow up in a Hathorne home.

In 1825, upon graduation from Bowdoin College, where he had been a moderately successful and mildly popular student, Hawthorne returned home to Salem determined to become a writer. He completed a novel, *Fanshawe* (1828), about his college life but soon decided the book was unworthy of him and set about trying to destroy all copies. Meanwhile, Hawthorne was to spend the twelve years immediately after graduation living in the now-famous third-floor room (his "chamber under the eaves") in the Manning house, learning to write, refining and polishing his craft. He clearly learned his lessons quickly and well, for within seven years of his graduation — by the time he was only twenty-eight years of age — Hawthorne had already found his distinctive voice and had published some of his greatest tales, including "My Kinsman, Major Molineux" and "Roger Malvin's Burial" (both published in *The Token*, 1832). Hawthorne matured so rapidly as a writer that there is virtually nothing in either subject matter or quality that distinguishes most of his earlier works from his later ones.

Although Hawthorne had been fairly successful in getting his stories published in the magazines, annuals, and gift books that published short fiction in his day, he found it increasingly difficult to support himself from the income derived from his writing. Even after the publication of *Twice-Told Tales* (1837), his first volume of short stories, Hawthorne found it necessary to secure a position in the Boston customhouse as a measurer. Until the publication and success of *The Scarlet Letter* in 1850, he was forced to supplement his income as a writer periodically with outside work: first in the Bostom customhouse and later as a surveyor in the Salem customhouse. Indeed, his brief involvement with the Brook Farm community, an experiment in communal living, was in part an effort to provide a home for himself and his wife-to-be, Sophia Peabody, while also reserving some time for his writing. Hawthorne was disappointed and left the community just before his marriage in 1842, although his experiences there did provide the raw material for his novel *The Blithedale Romance* (1852).

Hawthorne's marriage to Sophia was to be an extremely happy one, and the next few years were to be the most satisfying of his life. In 1846 he published a second collection of tales and sketches, *Mosses from an Old Manse*, which was later reviewed enthusiastically and extravagantly by Melville, who would eventually become his neighbor. Hawthorne worked in the Salem customhouse from 1846 to 1849, when he was fired because of a change in political administrations. Being fired turned out to be a blessing in disguise, for Hawthorne, who had done virtually no serious writing during the previous three years, suddenly had the time to devote to his craft. In an intense outpouring of creative effort, he wrote *The Scarlet Letter* in just four months. The book was an immediate success, and Haw-

thorne soon followed with a number of others, including two important novels, *The House of the Seven Gables* and *The Blithedale Romance*, as well as a volume of short pieces, *The Snow-Image, and Other Tales* (1851).

The years 1850–1852 were to be Hawthorne's most intensely productive period. After this time, he was to have great difficulty writing any more fiction. His position as United States consul at Liverpool from 1853 to 1857 left him with enough free time to write, but during that period he could only fill up his notebooks with jottings from his travels in Europe. In 1860 he did manage to finish one last novel, *The Marble Faun*, which was drawn from his tour of Italy, but the remaining years of his life were marked by a frustrating series of false starts. His unfinished manuscripts were periodically interrupted by marginal notes asking, "What meaning?" Nathaniel Hawthorne died on 19 May 1864 in Plymouth, New Hampshire, at the age of fifty-nine.

In his earlier years Hawthorne rarely had to struggle with questions such as "What meaning?" Indeed, in the years between his graduation from college and *The Blithedale Romance* — from 1825 to 1852 — his mind fairly bristled with moral questions, insights into human nature, images and symbols, and ideas for stories. His work during these years falls into two distinct groupings: the tales, written for the most part before 1850, and the novels (or romances, as he called them), the three most important of which were written between 1850 and 1852. Hawthorne was to publish three major collections of stories in his lifetime: *Twice-Told Tales*, *Mosses from an Old Manse*, and *The Snow-Image, and Other Tales*. Although his novels all employ supernatural elements, it is in the tales that Hawthorne most consciously and consistently explores the fictional possibilities inherent in the supernatural genre.

Several stories written probably not too long after his graduation from college — "The Hollow of the Three Hills" (*Salem Gazette*, 12 November 1830), "An Old Woman's Tale" (*Salem Gazette*, 21 December 1830), and "Alice Doane's Appeal" (*The Token*, 1835) — indicate that right from the start of his career Hawthorne's fascination with the supernatural and otherworldly formed an integral part of his vision. If anything, these tales seem to be a kind of finger exercise in creating Gothic moods and in striking appropriately poetical atmospheric notes. One senses that Hawthorne, like Washington Irving, is experimenting with ways in which he can employ local materials—American legends, American landscapes, and American history—to help create the "neutral territory" that was to represent his favorite fictional terrain.

His early tales often attempt to locate themselves immediately in this fictional territory. Thus the opening sentence of his first published story, "The Hollow of the Three Hills," places his tale in an unusual, mythical location: "In those strange old times, when fantastic dreams and madmen's reveries were realized among the actual circumstances of life, two persons met together at an appointed hour and place." And the narrator of "Alice Doane's Appeal" tells his gloomy tale while seated atop "Gallows Hill," the burial ground of the unfortunate victims of the witchcraft hysteria of 1692. One can think of few settings in the New World more conducive to the kind of Gothic atmosphere Hawthorne was trying to create.

And yet Hawthorne was not interested merely in demonstrating the romantic possibilities inherent in American settings and history—Irving had already done that quite successfully. Instead, what distinguishes these early tales and marks them as valuable additions to the Hawthorne canon is the degree to which they employ Gothic formulas for purposes beyond simple sensationalism or atmosphere. Even this early Hawthorne is beginning to explore the themes and subjects that will concern him throughout his career as a writer: guilt, isolation, the complicated chain of consequences arising from human actions, and the impingement of the past upon the present. And so slight a sketch as "The Hollow of the Three Hills"—which is only a few pages long—manages to introduce a number of these themes in its minimal plot, in which a witch shows a young woman the many terrible consequences of her past sins.

Within only a few years of these early apprenticeship stories, Hawthorne was to reach his full stature as a writer of short fiction, discovering very early that his genius resided in the regions of the super-

natural and the mythical. Between 1832 and 1836 he was to publish, mainly in *The Token*, such masterpieces as "My Kinsman, Major Molineux," "Roger Malvin's Burial," "Young Goodman Brown" (*New England Magazine*, April 1835), "The Minister's Black Veil" (1836), and "The May-Pole of Merry Mount" (1836). The depth and range of his output are extraordinary for a writer so young. What appears to have happened in these years of such rapid growth is that Hawthorne suddenly mastered the technique of the symbolic tale. He found a way to fuse his deeply felt moral and psychological concerns with a fictional form that expressed these concerns in a highly evocative, symbolic manner. His greatest tales are perfect fusions of form and meaning: they operate forcefully and believably both on a literal, narrative level and on a profoundly symbolic level.

Hawthorne's weaker tales may be most instructive in helping to demonstrate the dynamics and potential shortcomings of this fictional technique. In many of the lesser tales, such as "Egotism; or, The Bosom Serpent" (*Democratic Review*, March 1843) or "The Man of Adamant" (*The Token*, 1837), the symbolic burden of the story clearly overwhelms the literal level. The reader tends to lose interest in the narrative aspect of the tale as it is presented and becomes almost exclusively concerned with its meaning. One of the dangers in Hawthorne's technique—especially in his supernatural fiction—is that the otherworldly and fantastic can easily become the merely figurative.

"Egotism," to take one example, is the story of Roderick Elliston, who, since his estrangement from his wife, has become so self-involved and isolated from all companionship that a serpent (the reader is left to decide for himself whether it is real or imaginary) has entered and feeds off his breast. "It gnaws me," he cries throughout the tale. At the end he is saved from the clutches of the serpent because he accepts the love of another human being, his wife. The serpent, which has pointedly been hissing throughout the story, shrinks away, and a minor character presents the moral of the tale: "A tremendous Egotism . . . is as fearful a fiend as ever stole into the human heart."

The tale is representative of a kind of symbolic

story Hawthorne attempted periodically but without much success. It never manages to achieve much power or emotional resonance. Elliston, for one thing, never comes alive as a character, and the serpent in his bosom—which so obviously represents egotism—never fully engages one's interest or belief. This story, as do many of Hawthorne's slighter efforts, comes very close to being outright allegory, with the result that to modern readers it is likely to seem altogether too obvious and labored. One reason for this is that the supernatural element in the story is never allowed to expand beyond its limited and rather heavy-handed role as an expedient literary device.

Although his interest is always primarily moral and psychological, Hawthorne's most successful fantastic fiction occurs when his energy is fully engaged by the supernatural mechanics of his stories. Indeed, in his weaker tales the supernatural and Gothic effects occasionally work more successfully than his sometimes ponderous moral musings. The single most memorable moment in "Egotism," for instance, is a brief but chilling description of Elliston's predicament: "At his bosom, he felt the sickening motion of a thing alive, and the gnawing of that relentless fang."

Likewise, the moral satire in another of his supernatural tales, "Feathertop: A Moralized Legend" (*International Magazine*, February–March 1852), is rather pedestrian: a witch turns a scarecrow into a human being who goes out into the world and, because his outward appearance and manners are so attractive, becomes popular and succcessful. The tale is interrupted by frequent moralizing: "Why should these imps rejoice so madly that a silly maiden's heart was about to be given to a shadow! Is it so unusual a misfortune?—so rare a triumph?" The real energy in the tale, though, occurs in a long and wonderfully eerie description of the scarecrow's transformation into a man. Although he is always the moralist, Hawthorne has many of the instincts and impulses of the supernaturalist: "And, half revealed among the smoke, a yellow visage bent its lustreless eyes on Mother Rigby."

In his great supernatural tales, Hawthorne manages to keep the reader's interest fully engaged on both the literal and symbolic levels, refusing to sac-rifice one level of meaning for the other. Also, and perhaps more important, is the fact that at his best Hawthorne avoids the rather sterile intellectuality of stories such as "Egotism" or "The Man of Adamant." Hawthorne himself occasionally complained that his work lacked passion; in the preface to the 1851 edition of *Twice-Told Tales* he said that his stories had the "pale tint of flowers that blossomed in too retired a shade." But at his absolute best, when all his faculties and resources are fully engaged, Hawthorne is quite capable of striking the deepest chords of human experience. Hawthorne wrote works such as *The Scarlet Letter* and "Young Goodman Brown" in a white heat. There is very little that is tame or retiring about them.

"Young Goodman Brown" represents Hawthorne at the very height of his powers as a writer of supernatural fiction: Melville called the tale as "deep as Dante." Of all Hawthorne's short fiction it expresses the darkest and most universal truths about human nature with the most simplicity and intensity. It works powerfully—even on a merely literal level—as a chilling supernatural tale about witches and devil worship.

The story is simple and well known: Young Brown goes into the forest one night for an admittedly evil, though unspecified, purpose. He leaves behind his young wife, Faith, telling himself, "She's a blessed angel on earth; and after this one night, I'll cling to her skirts and follow her to heaven." In the forest Brown meets the devil and, in a gradual series of revelations, learns that everyone in his world—including his minister, the pious old woman who taught him his catechism, all the elders of his church, even his father and mother—has gone into the forest before him, has met with the devil.

The climax of the story comes in a midnight meeting of the devil's congregation in which Brown and Faith are joined in a "communion with their race." The devil, surrounded by blazing pine trees that illuminate the unholy congregation in a lurid red light, promises to show them their nature and their destiny by revealing the darkest and rankest sins of each member of the congregation:

> "Lo! there ye stand, my children," said the figure, in a deep and solemn tone, almost sad, with

its despairing awfulness, as if his once angelic nature could yet mourn for our miserable race. "Depending upon one another's hearts, ye had still hoped, that virtue were not all a dream. Now are ye undeceived! Evil is the nature of mankind. Evil must be your only happiness. Welcome, again, my children, to the communion of your race!"

"Welcome!" repeated the fiend-worshippers, in one cry of despair and triumph.

Young Goodman Brown resists this inverted baptism and suddenly finds himself alone in the silent forest. He returns to the village a changed man: he now knows the truth — or at least part of the truth — about his fellow human beings, and from that point on he becomes "a stern, a sad, a darkly meditative, a distrustful, if not a desperate man." Having lost all faith in the human race, shirking all human contact, he spends a gloomy life cut off from what Hawthorne calls in another tale "the magnetic chain of humanity." And when he dies, they carve "no hopeful verse upon his tomb-stone; for his dying hour was gloom."

While the story works powerfully as a supernatural tale, it also operates on a profound moral level. In the story of the young Puritan, Hawthorne has constructed a compelling metaphor for what he saw as a universal human experience: the inevitable discovery that man is a flawed, imperfect creature. In his journey away from the certainties and fixed realities of youth and toward the dark forest of adulthood, with its hidden fears and desires, isolation, and ambiguity, Brown repeats a journey that all human beings eventually must make.

In a sense, Hawthorne is reminding his readers of something with which his Puritan ancestors would have agreed: the Fall is a continuing phenomenon and is not the result of the committing of sin but, rather, the knowledge of sin. Thus, once he discovers that all men are tainted, that everyone is to some extent in league with the devil, Brown has already fallen. And his refusal to join in the "communion of his race" — while in some ways admirable — paradoxically leads Brown not to salvation but to despair and further misery. He isolates himself from his fellow mortals and denies an integral part of his own

nature. For Hawthorne, this is always man's key temptation: to see reality in uncomplicated ways, to deny the essential ambiguity of being human. Brown is ultimately a pathetic figure, for in wholeheartedly accepting the devil's view of human nature, he denies the potential for goodness and even majesty that is also part of this nature. By adopting this limited view and cutting himself off from the rest of humanity, Brown commits what is in Hawthorne always a cardinal error.

The need to accept mankind's inherent duality is a central theme throughout Hawthorne's work. Indeed, it is curious that Hawthorne is so often regarded as an allegorical writer, when in fact he almost invariably condemns those who attempt to see reality in the black-and-white terms of pure allegory. "The Birth-Mark" (Pioneer, March 1843), for example, is about a brilliant scientist, Aylmer, who marries a beautiful young woman. The only imperfection apparent in Georgiana, in either body or soul, is a small birthmark on her cheek. Aylmer, however, becomes increasingly obsessed with the birthmark, seeing it as "the visible mark of earthly imperfection." By eradicating this symbol of mankind's flawed nature, Aylmer believes that he will be able to accomplish what nature has been unable to do: create a perfect human being. Using his science, Aylmer devises a series of potions that will gradually remove the mark. The drugs prove to be too strong, and so Georgiana dies even as the symbol of her earthly imperfection fades away. As with many of Hawthorne's self-involved characters, Aylmer's selfish and coldhearted quest for ultimate answers and absolute truths ends in the destruction of what he should have loved most.

Hawthorne's fiction is populated with a number of characters like Aylmer who love their theories and abstractions more than they love their fellow human beings. The ultimate sin for Hawthorne always involves a lack of respect for people; his most negatively drawn characters are those guilty of tampering with the hearts and lives of others for coldhearted or selfish purposes. In his supernatural fiction Hawthorne often employed the scientist-figure to explore the self-centered, emotionally frigid rationalism that he abhorred.

Dr. Rappaccini, in one of Hawthorne's most powerful tales, "Rappaccini's Daughter" (*Democratic Review*, December 1844), is perhaps the best known of Hawthorne's obsessed scientists. As one character in the story puts it, "he cares infinitely more for science than for mankind. . . . He would sacrifice human life, his own among the rest, or whatever else was dearest to him, for the sake of adding so much as a grain of mustard-seed to the great heap of his accumulated knowledge." Rappaccini has used his daughter as an unwitting subject in his experiments with poisonous plants. Through his experiments he has poisoned Beatrice's physical system, and although she is beautiful and utterly blameless, she kills whatever she touches or breathes upon. Thus, not only is Rappaccini guilty of callously using his daughter for his own selfish purposes, but the result of his experiments is Beatrice's isolation and estrangement from all other human beings.

The story ends tragically when Beatrice falls in love with a callow young boarder, Giovanni, who meets her in her garden. Although Giovanni initially falls in love with Beatrice, he cruelly rejects her after learning of her poisoned nature. Beatrice takes an antidote that she hopes will purify her of the evil in her nature and make her acceptable to Giovanni. The antidote, though, proves to be too strong and Beatrice dies. She is the victim of her father's obsessive scientific zeal and Giovanni's inability to accept her dual nature and love her in spite of the evil that is part — but only part — of her nature.

In Hawthorne's fiction the attempt to transcend the limitations of human nature almost invariably leads to tragedy. His supernatural tales again and again treat this theme. Indeed, several of the manuscripts that he left unfinished at his death — *Septimius Felton* (1872) and *The Dolliver Romance* (1876) — are late explorations of this theme. Both fragments deal with the search for an elixir of life that will bestow immortality. *Septimius Felton*, the more successful of the two fragments, is about a young student who has become fascinated with the idea of prolonging human life. After he has killed a British soldier — the story takes place during the revolutionary war — Septimius discovers in the soldier's pocket a manuscript that contains a recipe for an elixir. In his efforts to decipher the manuscript and learn the secret of immortality, Septimius alienates all his friends and relatives except for an aunt who is part Indian, and a strange character, Sybil Dacy, who appears after the soldier's death. Septimius manages to make the elixir and persuades Sybil to join him in drinking it. She drinks it first and dies because the recipe contains one wrong ingredient and is thus actually a poison. Septimius disappears at the end of the tale. Once again, the attempt to transcend nature ends tragically: the inability to accept one's place in the "magnetic change of humanity" always results in death, isolation, or ruin.

Hawthorne, finally, stands as a crucial figure in the history of supernatural fiction, for his best work demonstrates the ability of supernatural fiction to satisfy the narrative requirements associated with the genre, while at the same time revealing the universal and enduring truths demanded of great art. A tale such as "Young Goodman Brown" showed that a scary story about witches and the devil could explore the very depths of human experience. He found in his solitary explorations of the dark and somber regions of his imagination all the truth about human nature that he cared, or could stand, to learn.

Selected Bibliography

WORKS OF NATHANIEL HAWTHORNE

The standard scholarly edition of Hawthorne's work is *The Centenary Edition of the Works of Nathaniel Hawthorne*, edited by William Charvat et al., 16 volumes to date. Columbus: Ohio State University Press, 1962– . The editions listed below are first editions.

Twice-Told Tales. Boston: American Stationers, John B. Russell, 1837. London: Kent and Richards, 1849, with somewhat different contents. (Collection.)

Mosses from an Old Manse. 2 vols. New York and London: Wiley and Putnam, 1846. (Collection. "Feathertop" was added to the 1854 second edition by the same publisher.)

The Scarlet Letter. Boston: Ticknor, Reed and Fields, 1850. London: David Bogue, 1851. (Novel.)

The House of the Seven Gables. Boston: Ticknor, Reed and Fields, 1851. London: Henry G. Bohn, 1851. (Novel.)

The Snow-Image, and Other Tales. London: Henry G. Bohn, 1851. As *The Snow-Image, and Other Twice-Told Tales.* Boston: Ticknor, Reed and Fields, 1852. (Collection.)

The Blithedale Romance. London: Chapman and Hall, 1852. Boston: Ticknor, Reed and Fields, 1852. (Novel.)

Transformation; or, The Romance of Monte Beni. 3 vols. London: Smith, Elder, 1862. As *The Marble Faun; or, the Romance of Monte Beni.* Boston: Ticknor and Fields, 1862. (Novel.)

Septimius. London: Henry S. King, 1872. As *Septimius Felton.* Boston: Osgood, 1872. (Unfinished novel.)

CRITICAL AND BIOGRAPHICAL STUDIES

Fogle, Richard Harter. *Hawthorne's Fiction: The Light and the Dark.* Norman: University of Oklahoma Press, 1952.

James, Henry. *Hawthorne.* London: Macmillan, 1879. New York: Harper, 1880.

Kaul, A. N., ed. *Hawthorne: A Collection of Critical Essays.* Englewood Cliffs, N.J.: Prentice-Hall, 1966.

Male, Roy R. *Hawthorne's Tragic Vision.* Austin: University of Texas Press, 1957.

Matthiessen, F. O. *American Renaissance: Art and Expression in the Age of Emerson and Whitman.* New York: Oxford University Press, 1941.

Pearce, Roy Harvey, ed. *Hawthorne Centenary Essays.* Columbus: Ohio State University Press, 1964.

Stewart, Randall. *Nathaniel Hawthorne: A Biography.* New Haven, Conn.: Yale University Press, 1948.

Turner, Arlin. *Nathaniel Hawthorne: An Introduction and Interpretation.* New York: Barnes and Noble, 1961.

———. *Nathaniel Hawthorne: A Biography.* New York: Oxford University Press, 1980.

Waggoner, Hyatt H. *Hawthorne: A Critical Study.* Cambridge, Mass.: Harvard University Press, 1955.

BIBLIOGRAPHIES

Clark, C. E. Frazer, Jr. *Nathaniel Hawthorne: A Descriptive Bibliography.* Pittsburgh: University of Pittsburgh Press, 1978.

Ricks, Beatrice, et al. *Nathaniel Hawthorne: A Reference Bibliography, 1900–1971, with Selected Nineteenth-Century Materials.* Boston: G. K. Hall, 1972.

—ERICH S. RUPPRECHT

FITZ-JAMES O'BRIEN

1828-1862

FOR NEARLY FORTY years American literary historians and critics have neglected the work of Fitz-James O'Brien. Robert E. Spiller's *Literary History of the United States* ignores him; Arthur Hobson Quinn's *Literature of the American People* includes scattered remarks, essentially repeating what Quinn had written in *American Fiction* (1936). Brian Attebery excludes him from *The Fantasy Tradition in American Literature from Irving to Le Guin* (1980), while in *The Literature of Fantasy: A Comprehensive, Annotated Bibliography of Modern Fantasy Fiction* (1979), Roger C. Schlobin merely lists the titles published in *The Diamond Lens and Other Stories*, edited by William Winter in 1885. Giving no evaluation of the stories, Schlobin's brief notation reports that this volume excluded the poetry and personal reminiscences in Winter's *The Poems and Stories of Fitz-James O'Brien* (1881), the first and most complete collection of his works.

Fitz-James O'Brien has had his advocates, most of them from earlier generations. In *Supernatural Horror in Literature*, H. P. Lovecraft twice insists that the prototype for Maupassant's "Le Horla" occurs in "What Was It? A Mystery," which he calls "the first well-shaped short story of a tangible but invisible being." He gives a single line to "The Diamond Lens" before concluding that O'Brien's genius was not of the "same titan quality which characterized Poe and Hawthorne." In *Pilgrims Through Space and Time* (1947), J. O. Bailey praises the same tales,

declaring that "The Diamond Lens" foreshadowed "a great deal in later fiction." Perhaps the most enthusiastic response has come from Sam Moskowitz in *Explorers of the Infinite* (1963), who writes in superlatives of O'Brien's innovations, the poetic quality of some of his prose passages, and the breadth of his influence on subsequent writers, including A. Merritt, who, he infers, found his satanic dolls in the manikins of "The Wondersmith." Also, although Frederick Lewis Pattee refers to "How I Overcame My Gravity," published posthumously in *Harper's* in 1864, only Moskowitz gives it extended attention. Winter does not mention it in his 1881 collection.

The major problems in the critical appraisal of O'Brien's work occur either because even his editors compare him to writers like Poe or Bierce or because they speak of him in terms of his life-style instead of evaluating his fiction in terms of its own literary merit. Edward J. O'Brien considers him the finest writer of short fiction between Poe and Bret Harte. Pattee praises Fitz-James O'Brien for adding "a sense of actuality to Poe's unlocalized romance" by setting his stories in a familiar New York City.

During the 1850's in New York he moved among bohemian circles, especially the group that met at Pfaff's at 647 Broadway, a gathering place—however briefly—for such persons as Walt Whitman and Adah Isaacs Menken. He was also associated by Winter, his editor in 1881, with the actress Matilda Heron. So vague and contradictory were the accounts of O'Brien's life, especially of his youth in Ireland, that Francis Wolle undertook research leading first to an article in *American Literature* and then to a biography. Fitz-James O'Brien was born sometime in 1828 in Cork. His father, a county coroner, died when the boy was twelve, and Fitz-James spent his adolescence in Limerick. He began to write poetry early and, perhaps in 1849, went to London. For whatever reasons, he went to New York in 1852, possibly as early as January.

A *New York Times* article, "Funeral of Lieut. Fitz-James O'Brien" (10 April 1862), suggests that he went to London "with the intention of entering the university." Instead, he became a writer for the journals. Once he came to the United States, he became an immediate success. On this point no one disagrees. He was "for many years a valued contributor" to the *Times*, although he also published in such journals as *Putnam's*, *Atlantic Monthly*, and *Harper's*. Everyone has called him prolific, as he must have been to support himself solely by his writing. (Winter and others spoke of periods of poverty during which he showed bad temper even toward friends.) In addition to poetry, fiction, and at least one play, *A Cumulative Author Index for Poole's Index to Periodical Literature: 1802–1906* (1971) credits him with two unsigned notices of Herman Melville. He was most lionized, however, after the appearance of "The Diamond Lens" in the third issue of the new *Atlantic Monthly* (January 1858). The esteem of his contemporaries may be best measured by the *Times* article, which calls him "completely successful" as a literary man, saying that his work showed "a delicacy of fancy, a charm of style, a felicity of imagery, and a gentleness of feeling" that ranked him second only to Charles Dickens.

In 1861 he joined the Seventh Regiment of the National Guard of New York. He was appointed to the staff of General F. W. Lander. (Story has it that he gained the post when a notification to Thomas Bailey Aldrich went astray.) Despite the *Times* headline, apparently his lieutenancy was never finalized. He was cited for bravery after the fight at Bloomery Gap. He was wounded in a cavalry skirmish in February and died on 6 April 1862.

Perhaps the most astute judgment of O'Brien was Pattee's when he applied the word *journalistic* to his work, for Fitz-James O'Brien had to appeal to the audience of the popular magazines of the period in order to survive. Pattee also called him imitative, a characteristic one may expect of a writer of popular fiction, just as one may anticipate an unevenness in his work. Moreover, many of the tales are no more than two or three pages long. Yet evidence that he read widely, at least in the field of fantasy, reveals itself in his story "The Bohemian" (1855), in which he refers to Alexandre Dumas *père*, Edward Bulwer-Lytton, and Poe; in "What Was It?" he names Charles Brockden Brown's *Wieland* and Bulwer-Lytton's *Zanoni*, as well as speaking familiarly of E. T. A. Hoffmann.

At one pole of his fiction stands such a story as "My Wife's Tempter" (1858), a diatribe against Mormons. "The Dragon Fang Possessed by the Conjuror Piou-Lu" (1856) deals with a protagonist who wishes to expel the ruling Tartars from the Central Kingdom as well as gaining the hand of the lovely daughter of the Mandarin Wei-chang-tze. "Tommatoo" (1862) concentrates upon the efforts of the villain to kill the kindly old protagonist in order to gain his fortune and the hand of his niece. (As one might expect of popular magazine fiction, a love story figures in the plots of many of O'Brien's tales.) Such works as these, together with those dealing with the mundane social world, can be dismissed.

If one concentrates only upon those stories in which O'Brien deals with the supernatural, one still finds a similarity of plot and a basic reliance upon certain conventions. The protagonist of "The Bohemian" (1855) permits his fiancée to be hypnotized in order to find a treasure. The mesmerist steals the treasure, once found, and the shock of the experience kills the girl. In "The Pot of Tulips" (1855), an orthodox ghost story, the first-person narrator recalls the wealthy Van Koeren, whose "monomania" was jealousy. When his son is born prematurely, he cannot believe that he is the father. His cruelty causes the deaths of his wife and son, and he hides the evidence that would permit his beautiful granddaughter, Alice, to inherit. On his deathbed old Van Koeren cries out that he has been wrong, but he dies before he can rectify his errors. The protagonist and his close friend Jasper Joye take up residence in the Van Koeren home. The ghost of the old man appears, and the two young men deduce where he has hidden the deeds and legal papers. Of course, the protagonist loves the beautiful Alice.

The protagonist of "Seeing the World" (1857) is given the gift of all knowledge, but it isolates him from mankind. Not only can he read minds, but his senses attain a "frightful awareness," so that he cannot see his beloved as an attractive woman but only as an "anatomical preparation." He watches her heart beating. The wife of the protagonist of "Mother of Pearl" (1860) kills her child and attempts to kill her husband while under the influence of hashish. In "The Crystal Bell" (1856), General Dribbley gives the protagonist a bell that, the young man believes, rings whenever his fiancée lies to him. Distressed by this idea, he is reassured of her faithfulness when General Dribbley awakens him from his dream. "The Golden Ingot" (1858) focuses upon an alchemist who believes that he has transformed base metal into gold and that his daughter has stolen all his gold. The narrator, a medical man, shares that belief until the girl explains that "to save father from dying from disappointment" she purchased a bit of gold and inserted the same ingot into the crucible innumerable times during the past two years when her father conducted his experiments. The doctor allows the alchemist to demonstrate his ability at transmutation. The shock of failure kills the old man.

One of O'Brien's more effective shorter pieces is "A Terrible Night" (1856), apparently never anthologized. Despite its excesses, especially perhaps in its rhetoric, it reminds one of Ambrose Bierce's work. The narrator is the best friend of Dick Linton, to whose sister Bertha he is engaged. The dialogue emphasizes the depth of their friendship, as well as their love of Bertha. O'Brien uses this relationship in an attempt to increase the horror of what takes place. The two young men spend the night in a cabin in the forest; their host, a half-breed, terrifies them, and they take turns staying awake. The narrator, believing their host is about to knife him, shoots him. Only then does he awaken to find that he has shot Linton. Doctors tell the narrator that he suffered from "somnolentia" — sleep drunkenness. Bertha, of course, never sees him again, and he is overwhelmed by his grief, though not mad.

In most of these stories O'Brien, unlike Poe, does not effectively create the impression that he is portraying an abnormal state of mind. As noted, his rhetoric may be his worst enemy. Consequently, the actions are less convincing that they might be because they are so obviously external events instead of the ambiguities of madness.

O'Brien reveals the direction in which his imagination could or should have developed in the last line of "The Pot of Tulips." There he suggests that "if it suited me to do so I could overwhelm you with a scientific theory of my own on [apparitions], reconciling ghosts and natural phenomena." From Thomas Bailey Aldrich in *The Queen of Sheba* to Bierce and Henry James, subsequent writers were to do just this, explicitly or implicitly, as they transformed the traditional specter into psychological case studies of what has been termed an anxious state of mind. Francis Wolle, in *Fitz-James O'Brien*, underscored the strength of O'Brien's achievement when he said of "The Diamond Lens," that it "takes advantage of the interest in scientific description and scientific speculation which characterized the mid-nineteenth century."

Given O'Brien's seemingly obvious desire in even his lesser pieces to base his terror upon the rational and scientific instead of the supernatural in a traditional sense, one cannot easily understand why so many critics have praised "The Wondersmith" (1859). It is a hodgepodge of melodramatic, sentimental devices. Amid a number of ethnic slurs the first-person narrator (obviously in this instance O'Brien rather than a character) establishes Golosh Street, New York City, as a place of filth and corruption. Then he withdraws only to intrude later with several brief comments. The narrative then focuses upon Herr Hippe, the Wondersmith, a gypsy, several times called Lord Balthazar. With the aid of Madame Filomel, a fortune-teller who has collected the souls of "demon" children in a black bottle, he infuses life into wooden manikins that he has made with these souls of "ethereal demons." Violently anti-Christian, Herr Hippe and his gypsy cohorts plan to sell the manikins to Christian families as presents for the children. On New Year's Eve the manikins will come alive and kill the children with knives and swords that Hippe has equipped them with. When he throws a gold coin on a table, the manikins — now alive — fight greedily, stabbing each other. Satisfied that the creatures are fully evil, the plotters adjourn to the establishment of Pippel, a bird fancier, where the manikins kill all of the birds with swords anointed with a poison obtained from the Macoushu Indians of Guiana. Between these episodes, however, O'Brien inserts a scene depicting the love of the hunchback Solon for Zonéla, the beautiful young girl whom Herr Hippe forces to beg on the streets an organ-grinder with a monkey. Hippe discovers Solon and Zonéla together and ties up Solon. Zonéla is really the daughter of a Hungarian nobleman; Hippe kidnapped her as an act of vengeance because the nobleman caused Hippe's son to become an alcoholic. His son died from drinking too much brandy, the "curse" of the gypsies. On New Year's Eve the manikins get loose prematurely, killing Hippe and his colleagues as the gypsies, dying, throw handfuls of the satanic toys into the fire. The house burns, but the poetic Solon and beautiful Zonéla survive. There is no suspense or surprise; there is no adequate characterization. Because of the animated wooden manikins, Sam Moskowitz considers "The Wondersmith" important "as one of the earliest robot stories."

In sharp contrast, "The Lost Room" (1858) has an economy and a unity as the narrator describes his dark and gloomy room. He returns to find it brightly lighted and filled with revelers who first invite him to join them and then, when he refuses, challenge him to dice for the room. He loses and is evicted but briefly glimpses the room before it vanishes. He beats against the blank wall. Since there is no implication that he is mad, "The Lost Room" introduces the concept of multiple levels of space, though one may interpret the revelers and the bright room as some distortion of the narrator's past.

Although he may have been attracted to scientific material, "How I Overcame My Gravity" (1864) illustrates O'Brien's difficulty in handling such material. In a jargon that cannot be paraphrased, he explains how a whirling copper sphere overcomes gravity. The narrator constructs a globe in which to fly, but when it is catapulted into free flight, it begins to disintegrate. Fortunately, his wife awakens him from his dream.

O'Brien's two most successful stories work because of his control of point of view, his realistic detail, and his restraint. After locating the setting of "What Was It? A Mystery" (1859) on Twenty-sixth Street between Seventh and Eighth Avenues, the narrator explains that his landlady and her boarders are moving into the house because they expect it to be haunted. A "month of psychological excitement" passes without event. The narrator and his fellow boarder Dr. Hammond, who smoke opium together, speculate as to what "the greatest element of terror" is. That night, 10 July, in the darkness of his room "a something" falls onto the narrator and attempts to strangle him. He overcomes it, but when he turns on the light, it is invisible. The failure of his sense of sight is the greatest terror, and he is angry that his companions laugh at him — until they sense the creature's physical being. He and Hammond have it chloroformed in order to make a plaster cast of it. It is a dwarf with a grotesque face. Only after a fortnight does it starve to death. The exhibition of the plaster cast in a museum on Tenth Street provides a significant detail establishing the reality of the event. (To emphasize this, the editors of *Atlantic Monthly* added a note suggesting that an exhibition would be held.)

"The Diamond Lens" is a transitional piece. It looks backward to Poe and the Gothic, but it also anticipates the direction that much later fantasy would take. Obsessed with the science of microscopy, its first-person narrator dreams of a perfect lens. In a séance the spirit of Anton van Leeuwenhoek, inventor of the microscope, tells him to obtain a diamond of 140 carats and subject it to electromagnetic currents to realign its atoms. The narrator kills to get the diamond. In the world within a drop of water he sees a beautiful woman — Animula. To escape his enchantment with her grace, he goes to see the most famous dancer, Signoria Caradolce, but finds her gross in comparison. Rushing back to his room, he finds Animula dying because the drop of water has evaporated. The final ambiguity, which does not allow the reader to be certain that this is not a figment of a crazed imagination, helps make "The Diamond Lens" O'Brien's finest story as well as one of the classics of the nineteenth century.

The significance of the lengthy "From Hand to

Mouth," serialized in the *New York Picayune* (March–May 1858), remains more difficult to determine because it differs sharply from his other work. The problem, in part at least, may be that his first-person narrator never emerges as a distinct character but seems instead to be O'Brien himself. Sam Moskowitz, the latest to anthologize the story (*Horrors Unknown*, 1971), describes it as "extraordinary. . . [perhaps] the most striking example of surrealistic fiction to precede *Alice in Wonderland*." According to Wolle, O'Brien could not finish the story; it was completed by Frank M. Bellew, co-publisher of the *Picayune*.

Unlike O'Brien's other tales, "From Hand to Mouth" has no discernible plot line. In New York, the narrator attends a production of Meyerbeer's opera *The Huguenots*. The satirical intent of the narrative first reveals itself in his companion Cobra, music critic of the *Daily Cockchafer*, who "languidly surveyed the house" and "fortified himself" with a drink during the intermission.

Returning to his rooming house in a snowstorm after the performance, the narrator finds that his key will not unlock the door. Locked out in a foot of snow, he is accosted by Count Goloptious, who invites him to spend the night at the Hotel de Coup d'Œil, whose facade is a mosaic of stones representing the ear, the eye, the mouth, and the hand. Finding himself in a "den of enchantment," the narrator believes that the Count "intended to cook [his] head." Although he claims to awaken from a dream, he meets the Blond Head — he calls her Fair Rosamond — who asks him to rescue her. O'Brien's theme becomes apparent when Goloptious reveals himself to be a publisher. The story is O'Brien's satire of the relationship between the writer/artist and editors/publishers.

Resolved to rescue the captive damsel, the narrator refuses to leave the hotel. Told that he must write three columns a day to earn his room and board, he begins writing. A sculptor and a singer, Fair Rosamond modeled and painted the human organs and now makes a green bird out of terra-cotta. When the bird has breakfast with the narrator, it explains that to prevent Rosamond's escape, Goloptious has put her legs in the storeroom. Again she implores the narrator to help her escape but presents

him with a list of her luggage (including a portable bath) that must accompany them. The narrator searches for Rosamond's legs and instead finds the Count; when the narrator insists that he will rescue Rosamond, the Count and a companion (who carries his own head under his arm) pitch him into a flaming lake containing innumerable "poor wretches" — authors. Abruptly awakened in the snow-filled street by Dick Bunkler, the narrator blames his imaginings on brandy and goes into the house to prepare a nightcap.

One must make several inferences about this atypical work. First, in "From Hand to Mouth" — a phrase that might well describe his life in New York — O'Brien tried to adapt his talent to a comic weekly paper. A few incidents remain humorous. For example, after bringing him a light, a disembodied hand extends itself for a quarter tip. When Goloptious is asked why he is a "duellist," he replies that he is a member of Congress for South Carolina. But one suspects that many topical allusions that must have amused O'Brien's readers have by now been lost.

More obviously and effectively, O'Brien uses the narrative to satirize popular journalism and literature. Goloptious explains that his own work ranges from "gory essays on Kansas" to "sensational dramas for the Phantom Theatre." The narrator protests that for years he has resisted the process by which journalism sucks "the vitals out of a literary man." Before throwing him into the lake, Goloptious reminds him that he has "dared . . . theatrical managers . . . a fickle public."

In addition to numerous references to *The Arabian Nights* relating to Rosamond, the narrator tells the reader that "all the extensive descriptions of female loveliness you have ever read in two-shilling novels" must be combined and then "as much more added" to describe her. At the lake Goloptious points out an author who wrote "flash novels." The narrator replies, "Jack Sheppard. *The Bhoys*."

The narrative remains unique in that at no time does O'Brien attempt to evoke horror. He seeks to maintain a comic tone that will carry his extravagant satire. But he strikes out in too many directions. Some passages remain hilarious, however. "From Hand to Mouth" is his most interesting failure. It shows a different side of his talent that never achieved full development.

One must agree that O'Brien worked hastily and that he employed popular materials and techniques. Yet certainly his death cut short a promising career. As it is, he must be held in high regard because he introduced at least four elements of plot that shaped subsequent fantasy — the animated manikin, the lost room, the invisible creature, and the microscopic world. Such an imagination provides a brilliant transition between the traditions of Poe and the Gothic and the fantasy of the late nineteenth century.

Selected Bibliography

WORKS OF FITZ-JAMES O'BRIEN

Collections

The Poems and Stories of Fitz-James O'Brien, Collected and Edited with a Sketch of the Author by William Winter. Boston: J. R. Osgood, 1881. (The basic collection, with thirteen stories.)

The Diamond Lens and Other Stories. Edited by William Winter. New York: Scribner, 1885. (Contains thirteen stories, as in Winter, and Winter's biographical sketch.)

What Was It? and Other Stories. London: Ward and Downey, 1889. (Eight stories from the Winter edition.)

Collected Stories by Fitz-James O'Brien. Edited with an introduction by Edward J. O'Brien. New York: Boni, 1925. (Eight stories from the Winter edition.)

The Diamond Lens and Other Stories. With an introduction by Gilbert Seldes. New York: William E. Rudge, 1932. (Seven stories from the Winter edition.)

"What Was It?" "The Diamond Lens," and "The Lost Room" are often reprinted and can be found in many anthologies.

Stories not present in the above collections

"A Terrible Night." *Harper's Magazine*, 13 (October 1856). Reprinted in *Library of the World's Best Mystery and Detective Stories*, edited by Julian Hawthorne. New York: Review of Reviews, 1906.

"The Crystal Bell." *Harper's Magazine*, 14 (December 1856).

"Seeing the World." *Harper's Magazine*, 15 (September 1857).

"From Hand to Mouth," with Frank H. Bellew. *New York Picayune* (27 March–15 May 1858). Reprinted in *Horrors Unknown*, edited by Sam Moskowitz. New York: Walker, 1971.

"How I Overcame My Gravity." *Harper's Magazine*, 28 (May 1864).

CRITICAL AND BIOGRAPHICAL STUDIES

"Funeral of Lieut. Fitz-James O'Brien." *New York Times* (10 April 1862): 5.

Moskowitz, Sam. "The Fabulous Fantasist — Fitz-James O'Brien." In *Explorers of the Infinite*. Cleveland and New York: World, 1963.

Pattee, Frederick Lewis. *The Development of the American Short Story*. New York: Harper, 1923.

————. *The Feminine Fifties*. New York: Appleton-Century, 1940.

Wolle, Francis. "Fitz-James O'Brien in Ireland and England, 1828–1851." *American Literature*, 14 (1942–1943): 234–249.

————. *Fitz-James O'Brien: A Literary Bohemian of the Eighteen-Fifties*. Boulder: University of Colorado Press, 1944.

—THOMAS D. CLARESON

XI

American Fin-de-Siècle Writers

J. K. BANGS

1862–1922

I

AS A TOPICAL humorist John Kendrick Bangs, sometimes called "the humorist of the nineties," was unquestionably a historically important figure. He was the clearest representative of the genteel academic school of humor that flourished in the United States for the two decades straddling the century mark, and his works were more widely published than those of his greater contemporaries Mark Twain and Ambrose Bierce. He was good at catching ideas that were in the air, and he could spoof them in a gentle, appealing way.

Bangs was not a great writer of supernatural fiction, although some of his ghost stories are very amusing. But he was a form innovator. He was among the first to see that a traditional ghost need not be a horror figure but, instead, could be comic, and he was the first, for all practical purposes, to show that humorous—even comic—ghost stories could be written without dialect material or fake kindergarten fairylands. Bangs was not the only humorous supernaturalist of his time. Frank Stockton wrote a socially oriented light fantasy; and F. Anstey, the greatest of the three writers, used the raw material of supernaturalism for satirical purposes, poking fun at social classes and customs. But Bangs was rooted more deeply in the conventional ghost story and offered a broader, more comic note than either of the other two.

John Kendrick Bangs was born in or near Yonkers, New York, in 1862. There is a mystery about his birth, for no record has ever been found, and in later life he once had difficulty in proving his identity to the passport service for lack of birth records. He grew up in a bookish family, and his early taste for Mother Goose, *Gulliver's Travels*, Edward George Bulwer-Lytton, Edgar Allan Poe, and Nathaniel Hawthorne carried over into his adult life. He graduated in 1883 from Columbia University, where he had edited the student magazine, and shortly after leaving college he became an editor-contributor to the humor magazine *Life*. He later served on the *New York Evening Sun*, and then in 1889 joined the Harper publishing enterprises, where he rose to the position of humor editor for books and the four Harper periodicals. He wrote several best-sellers and was one of the most popular, most highly regarded writers of his day.

He married, prospered financially, and narrowly lost the race for mayor of Yonkers. He was an important member of exclusive social clubs, where he often served as a host for visiting dignitaries. A very affable man, he made friends easily, and a roster of his associates would look like a *Who's Who* of his day. This was a time when American club life was in its heyday, and the members of a small social group could direct the destinies of whole communities or even of the nation.

But around the turn of the century, everything began to go wrong for Bangs. His wife died. He had been fairly wealthy, what with family money and his own earnings, but in some way not disclosed he lost his money and was forced to dispose of his real estate, rare books, and other properties. His job collapsed when Harper's went under. In the reorganization he was assigned the editorship of *Harper's Weekly* but was forced to resign soon afterward. The management (J. P. Morgan's men) objected to his friendship with Theodore Roosevelt and did not approve of Bangs's coverage of the Cuban situation. Bangs had been assigned to do an exposé of the American occupation of Cuba after the Spanish-American War—but instead praised it.

Other journalistic jobs dissolved, and Bangs tried his hand at writing for the stage. He was reasonably competent as a librettist but, after some small initial success, was forced to recognize that the stage was not his métier. He moved to Maine and tried to conduct free-lance writing by mail, but his humor was now out of style.

By 1907, when he was forty-five years old, Bangs had only one ability left on which he had not tried to capitalize: his skill as an afterdinner speaker and lecturer. He had always been an enthusiastic clubman, and by all accounts he was the finest humorous speaker in the country. Only Mark Twain was in the same class, and if Bangs had less to say than Twain, he did not have Twain's fault of occasionally putting his foot in his mouth.

For the remainder of his life Bangs made a good living as a lecturer and speaker. A handsome, personable man of great charm and obvious intelligence, he was said to have been unbelievably rapid on the uptake and skilled at repartee.

During World War I Bangs worked at fund raising and toured army installations entertaining the soldiers. After the war he worked as a publicist and was useful to Warren G. Harding in his presidential campaign. By the end of 1921 it was obvious that Bangs was ill, and on 21 January 1922 he died at Atlantic City, New Jersey, following an operation for cancer.

This was the public life of J. K. Bangs. Surprisingly little is known about his private life, but there are hints that Bangs the humorist was not the only J. K. Bangs. Since the documentation is very shallow, a reader can only speculate on what went wrong with a gifted, once successful writer. In retrospect, though, it seems clear that he was a victim of over-

shadowing that he never outgrew. As a very young man he was thought of as the grandson of Nathan Bangs, an important Methodist Episcopal scholar, and he was often asked, about his writing, "What would your grandfather have thought of this?" And more important, Bangs never emerged from the shadow of his alcoholic father, Francis N. Bangs, a great trial lawyer of the day and one of the most violent personalities to terrorize a courtroom. In an age when lawyers came on strong, Bangs was unrivaled for his reckless trial behavior and his command of abuse and vituperation. He too was a humorist, but his humor consisted of trying to make his opponents look ridiculous, and his wit was furious, sadistic, and destructive. Bangs reacted against his father's ferocity, perhaps too much.

As a humorist J. K. Bangs was clever and facile. His work was smooth, pleasant, urbane, and, at its best, witty. It was usually concerned with ideas, in an academic sense. On the debit side it was so topical that it dated rapidly and was timid, superficial, and overly facile. Bangs once defined humor as "a delicate fancy intermingled with pointed wit." This is fine—if one can bring it across.

II

Bangs's first significant adult fantasy, *Roger Camerden* (1887), deals with psychopathology. Published anonymously, it is a problem story told in good Hegelian style as thesis, antithesis, and synthesis. At a rationalist club a college man reminisces about Camerden's sad history. Roger's father, he says, had been driven to suicide by a false friend, one Marville, who then disappeared. Roger tracked Marville down, hoping for revenge, but instead fell in love with his daughter. But then Roger died mysteriously. Perhaps he was murdered by Marville? One of the listeners objects. Marville, he says, was an honorable man and had no daughter. How can the contradictions be explained? Was the woman an adventuress and an impostor? A third party provides the resolution: both Camerdens were mad, Camerden, Sr., with psychotic guilt; Camerden, Jr., with rage and sexual excitement. In Roger's case the dementia was so strong that it amounted to a dissociated personality element.

Roger Camerden is stiffly written and so cerebral

as to be unconvincing, but it is one of the earliest stories to treat madness in terms of fantasy and mystery. Around the turn of the century this theme became more important with F. Anstey's *The Statement of Stella Maberly* and W. L. Alden's *A Lost Soul.*

Bangs's second novel, *Toppleton's Client* (1893), is curiously ambivalent in its mixture of humor and horror. Toppleton is the prototypical Bangs character that appears elsewhere—young, good-hearted, foppish, foolish, self-deprecatory, ineffectual. Sent to England to keep him from wrecking the family business with his incompetence, he meets the worst fate that can happen short of death or mutilation but is brave enough to see a good side to his predicament.

While in England Toppleton becomes entangled with two lawyer ghosts, one of whom stole the other's body and is currently residing in it, while the dispossessed true owner of the body drifts about helplessly. The bodiless ghost asks Toppleton to help expel the usurper. Toppleton agrees but is outwitted and finds himself displaced and shifted to an old, partly worn-out body, while the usurper makes off with Toppleton's strong, young body. But Toppleton accepts his new role gracefully.

More interesting than the supernatural part of the story are legal elements mentioned in passing that undoubtedly come from Bangs's family background. A dying man told one of his heirs to take cash from a certain drawer and keep it. But before the heir could open the stuck drawer, the other man died. The question is, which takes precedence, the living man's gift or the dead man's will, which would have disposed of the cash otherwise? The ghost lawyer won the case handily by bullying and terrorizing all the participants, so that his opponent had a breakdown and his own client tried to murder him. Surely this is a memory of Francis N. Bangs.

Neither *Roger Camerden* nor *Toppleton's Client* achieved commercial or critical success, but in other areas Bangs was beginning to be recognized. His greatest success began in August 1895, when "A House-Boat on the Styx" began serialization in *Harper's Bazar.* A jeu d'esprit, a single humorous situation stretched over three books, the heart idea is of a club in Hades (a very pleasant, mild place), where great men (real and fictional) could converse and meet socially. Most of the first book, *A House-Boat on the Styx,* is devoted to chitchat about cultural topics. Francis Bacon and William Shakespeare joust verbally about the authorship of the plays; Sir Walter Raleigh and Queen Elizabeth mince about coyly and say that their relationship is only that of cousins; Socrates gripes about Xanthippe; Charles Darwin and Baron Münchhausen discuss the possibility of simian speech; Napoleon and the Duke of Wellington admit that they do not really understand what happened at Waterloo. In all this, there is no central thread, although Raleigh comes close to being a focal point.

The clubhouse, which floats in the Styx, is restricted to men, and naturally the women in Hades are curious about it and resentful. One day, when the men are off watching a prizefight, Queen Elizabeth, Ophelia, and Xanthippe board the boat, snoop around, invite their friends on board—and then notice that the vessel is in motion. Captain Kidd and his pirates have stolen the boat—women and all. When the men return and see what has happened, some have regrets, but Socrates voices the majority opinion: "Give the ladies a chance. They've been after our club for years; now let them have it. Order me up a hemlock sour!" *A House-Boat on the Styx* appeared in book form in 1895 and became a national best-seller, perhaps the first time that an American book knowingly written as fantasy held such a position.

The sequel, *The Pursuit of the House-Boat* (1897), tells how the shades regained their club. Sherlock Holmes, whom Bangs's friend Arthur Conan Doyle had just killed over Reichenbach Falls, deduces where Kidd must be going, and the spirits set out in pursuit. In the meanwhile, the women, guided by Cassandra, have turned the tables on the pirates and are trying to navigate the vessel, but without much success, since the domineering Eve is totally incompetent as a sailor. The end result, after the men have regained the boat, is that the ladies become eligible for membership and "begin to think less and less of the advantages of being men and to rejoice that, after all, they were women." Or, in other terms, *Kinder, Kirche, Küche, und Bierstube?*

Today we can only marvel that the *House-Boat* books were so popular. Bangs was best at very short, snippet material, and the *House-Boat* books are padded and repetitive. The humor is donnish, and the great men receive no characterizations. Yet despite its weakness, the *House-Boat* was the founding document of a small subgenre of fantastic fiction, a humorous conversazione among the great dead. Bangs did not invent the idea, which is to be found in Lucian's *Dialogues of the Dead* and had cropped up in F. Marion Crawford's *With the Immortals* (1888), but he made the idea popular and accessible to the general reading public.

Just as important historically and typologically as the *House-Boat* stories were the ghost stories assembled and reprinted in *The Water Ghost and Others*, *Ghosts I Have Met, and Some Others*, and *Over the Plum-Pudding*. With them Bangs really founded the comic ghost story.

Before Bangs the ghost story had usually been on the surface a story of sensation and horror, and beneath the surface a moral document dealing with guilt and punishment. There were occasional humorous "trick" ghost stories, but these were usually rationalized. R. H. Barham's "Spectre of Tappington" and Charles Dickens' "The Bagman's Story" and "The Story of the Bagman's Uncle" come to mind, along with Washington Irving's "The Legend of Sleepy Hollow" and "The Bold Dragoon." Grant Allen had written a couple of rather heavy-handed stories that spoofed psychic research, and Oscar Wilde, in "The Canterville Ghost," had mingled sentiment, anti-Americanism, and a parody of boys' fiction. But it remained for Bangs to type the comic ghost story.

The ghosts in Bangs's three collections are not objects of terror but, rather, nuisances that must be evaded, outwitted, or canceled. And the reasons that ghosts appear are no longer murder, blood revenge, or guilt but usually social problems. They are trespassers on life.

The Water Ghost in "The Water Ghost of Harrowby Hall" (*The Water Ghost and Others*, 1894) appears each Christmas Eve, sopping wet, and soaks everything in sight. The narrator unsuccessfully tries many ways of getting rid of her, until he entices her out into subzero weather and she freezes solid. She is then stored in an icehouse, like a statue.

"The Spectre Cook of Bantletop," which owes a debt to Wilde's "The Canterville Ghost," provides an American answer to British snobbery. The ghost, a seventeenth-century cook, was unfairly fired and has vowed to haunt the kitchen until her back wages are paid — with compound interest. The total now comes to about £63 million. The American plays on her snobbery to be rid of her.

In "The Exorcism That Failed" (*Ghosts I Have Met, and Some Others*, 1898), the narrator accidentally jostles a Cockney ghost at a British street parade and is maliciously haunted ever since. The ghost has even taken to ghostwriting, using the narrator's name. In "The Amalgamated Brotherhood of Spooks" (*Over the Plum-Pudding*, 1901), which pokes fun at strikes and labor, a writer of ghost stories (perhaps Bangs) insults a ghost-walking delegate and is blacklisted by the ghost union. He can write no more stories.

The other supernatural fiction in these volumes follows similar patterns. The Devil, in "A Midnight Visitor" (*The Water Ghost and Others*), after annoying the narrator, goes to the narrator's club and performs remarkable magic tricks. The doings of Theosophy are reflected in "A Psychical Prank," in which the members of the Boston Theosophical Society travel invisibly in New York City streetcars in order to save carfare. "The Mystery of My Grandmother's Hair Sofa" and "The Dampmere Mystery" (both in *Ghosts I Have Met, and Some Others*) are based on figures of speech: in the first story the hair in a stuffed sofa turns white with shock and in the second the hair in a mattress stands on end when supernatural phenomena are occurring.

After the publication of *Over the Plum Pudding* Bangs does not seem to have written any more ghost stories in the strict sense, although, what with his writing under many pseudonyms, it is possible that isolated stories of his have not been identified.

But he did continue the celebrity humor that made the *House-Boat* books popular. *The Enchanted Type-Writer* (1899) is the third volume in the series. The narrator's typewriter begins to type out mysterious messages spontaneously. They come from James Boswell in Hades, where he runs the local newspaper. Boswell records another adventure of

Sherlock Holmes. In this case it is discovering the identity of Lohengrin, who, it will be remembered, worked hard to conceal his name and origin.

Olympian Nights (1902) takes the narrator on a visit to Mount Olympus, where things have been greatly modernized, with an elevator and restaurants. The gods even play golf—which was a fad sport of the time.

In addition to fiction that was supernatural in one way or another, Bangs wrote prolifically in many other fields. He wrote poetry, column humor, articles, plays, musical comedies, children's books, and much else, most of which has been forgotten. He even wrote a humorous account of his political defeat when he ran for mayor of Yonkers—one of his better works. At the moment his parodies of detective stories have a collector's market, since they involve Sherlock Holmes, Raffles, Raffles Holmes (the son of Sherlock), and others, but I do not think that many collectors read them for pleasure.

To be a developmental influence, but a somewhat inferior writer, is not uncommon in the history of literature. Horace Walpole originated the plot of the Gothic novel, but others have written better stories. Émile Gaboriau developed the modern detective novel, but others have written better novels. So let it be with John Kendrick Bangs.

Selected Bibliography

WORKS OF J. K. BANGS

Roger Camerden. A Strange Story. New York: G. J. Coombes, 1887. (Published anonymously.)

Toppleton's Client; or, A Spirit in Exile. New York: C. L. Webster, 1893.

The Water Ghost and Others. New York: Harper, 1894.

A House-Boat on the Styx, Being Some Account of the Divers Doings of the Associated Shades. New York: Harper, 1895. London: Osgood, McIlvaine and Company, 1896.

The Pursuit of the House-Boat, Being Some Further Account of the Divers Doings of the Associated Shades, under the Leadership of Sherlock Holmes, Esq. New York: Harper, 1897. London: Osgood, McIlvaine and Company, 1897.

Ghosts I Have Met, and Some Others. New York and London: Harper, 1898.

The Enchanted Type-Writer. New York and London: Harper, 1899.

Over the Plum-Pudding. New York: Harper, 1901.

Olympian Nights. New York: Harper, 1902.

CRITICAL AND BIOGRAPHICAL STUDIES

Bangs, Francis Hyde. *John Kendrick Bangs, Humorist of the Nineties. The Story of an American Editor–Author–Lecturer and His Associations.* New York: Knopf, 1941. (Very nicely written by Bangs's son, this is selective and more a hagiography than a biography, but it is necessary.)

Bangs, John Kendrick. "The Confession of John Kendrick Bangs." In Thomas L. Masson, *Our American Humorists.* New York: Moffat, Yard, 1922.

Blair, Walter, and Hill, Hamlin. *America's Humor from Poor Richard to Doonesbury.* New York: Oxford University Press, 1978.

Yates, Morris. *The American Humorist: Conscience of the Twentieth Century.* Ames: Iowa State University Press, 1964.

—E. F. BLEILER

AMBROSE BIERCE

1842–1914(?)

AMBROSE BIERCE IS a writer generally known only for a few stories, most notably the often anthologized "An Occurrence at Owl Creek Bridge" (1890), and for his masterpiece of jaundiced epigrams, *The Devil's Dictionary* (1906). But his relative obscurity is less the result of his skill as a writer, which was considerable, than of his deliberate opposition to many of the sacred cows of late nineteenth-century letters, most notably the novel form and the realistic mode. He disparaged the novel, citing it in *The Devil's Dictionary* as "a short story padded," and he despised realism, which he defined as "the art of depicting nature as it is seen by toads." *Romance* is one of the few entries in his dictionary against which irony is not turned: "Fiction that owes no allegiance to the God of Things as They Are. In the novel the writer's thought is tethered to probability, as a domestic horse to the hitching-post, but in romance it ranges at will over the entire region of the imagination — free, lawless, immune to bit and rein." It is this freedom of the imagination, along with the dedicated short-story writer's acute sense of craftsmanship, that makes Bierce important not merely as a writer of fantasy but as a writer of fiction.

Born on 24 June 1842 on a small farm in southeastern Ohio, Ambrose Bierce did most of his growing-up on a farm in northern Indiana. His journalistic career began with two years as a printer's devil for an antislavery paper but was interrupted first by a year in a Kentucky military school and then by the outbreak of the Civil War. Bierce enlisted a number of times. He was involved in what some historians call the first battle of the war, a skirmish at Philippi, West Virginia, and he served actively until the war ended in 1865, rising from raw recruit to first lieutenant.

The war experience left him with a complex set of impressions, the effects of which permeate his fiction: an intimate awareness of the horror and brutality of war and an ironic understanding of the frequent and outrageous stupidity of its conduct, together with an admiration for true military competence and courage and an intense pride in his own distinguished record. In his first campaign, under heavy fire he carried a wounded comrade more than one hundred yards to cover, and he fought in the very thick of battles such as Shiloh and Stones River. As a topographical engineer, he often approached perilously close to enemy lines while serving in major battles: Chickamauga, Lookout Mountain, and Missionary Ridge; he suffered a serious head wound at Kenesaw Mountain, Georgia; and he marched to the sea with Sherman's army. Though disillusioned, he seemed to hold on to his idealism with a proud and bitter tenacity. Indeed, one could call him an idealist without innocence.

In the summer of 1866 he joined the army again, serving on a mapping and surveying expedition of the West that took him through many gold-rush, mining-boom, and ghost towns, which were to provide settings for several of his stories. The expedition ended in San Francisco, where he resigned his commission in the spring of 1867. There he began seriously to train himself to be a writer, reading heavily and writing in the spare time afforded by undemanding jobs at the United States Subtreasury. His first published works, two poems in a local periodical in the fall of 1867, were followed by essays and sketches competent enough to earn him a job as editor of the *San Francisco Newsletter and California Advertiser* in December 1868. His satirical column, "The Town Crier," earned him admirers not only locally but also in New York and London. His first published story, "The Haunted Valley," appeared in the *Overland Monthly* in 1871, but he wrote primarily as an essayist for the next decade and a half.

From 1872 to 1875 he lived in England, writing for various humorous magazines and publishing his first three books, all collections of his journalistic writings: *The Fiend's Delight* (1873), *Nuggets and Dust* (1873), and *Cobwebs from an Empty Skull* (1874). His successful stay in England probably would have been more than a sojourn but for his wife, Mollie, née Mary Ellen Day, whom he had married on 25 December 1871; she returned to California for a visit, already two or three months pregnant with Bierce's third child, and when he learned of her condition, he followed and never saw England again.

In the United States, Bierce's reputation soon was reestablished, culminating in 1887 when his column "Prattle" began appearing in William Randolph Hearst's *San Francisco Examiner*; from 1896 to 1899, Bierce appeared regularly in both the *Examiner* and the *New York Journal*. In the meantime, he began publishing some of his best stories, most of which appeared in the *Examiner* between 1888 and 1891. His first story collection, *Tales of Soldiers and Civilians* (English edition, *In the Midst of Life*), was published simultaneously in America and England in January 1892, soon followed by his second, *Can Such Things Be?* (1893). The first was well received, especially in England, but his American publishers failed soon after Bierce's collections were printed, and their distribution was seriously limited until Putnam's brought out a revised and enlarged edition of *In the Midst of Life* in 1898.

Bierce published a number of other works: two volumes of poetry, *Black Beetles in Amber* (1892) and *Shapes of Clay* (1903); a collection of short tales, *Fantastic Fables* (1899); a novella in collaboration with Gustav Adolf Danziger, *The Monk and the Hangman's Daughter* (1891 in the *Examiner*; 1892 separately), which is in fact only an editing job by Bierce of Danziger's translation of the German story by Richard Voss; and the famous *Devil's Dictionary*, which appeared originally as *The Cynic's Word Book* (1906). He moved east in 1899, living in Washington, D.C., while continuing to work for the *New York Journal* and writing occasionally for the *New York American* and the *San Francisco Examiner*. In 1906 he left the *Journal* but continued to write for Hearst's *Cosmopolitan* from 1905 until 1909. From 1908 until its publication was completed in 1912, he worked on his twelve-volume *Collected Works*. During this period Bierce was lionized, especially during two trips to California in 1910 and 1912.

He left Washington on 2 October 1913 for what would be a fatal trip to Mexico. He traveled with the forces of Pancho Villa from Juarez to Chihuahua, where he was last heard from in a letter dated 26 December 1913. Though much has been made of his supposedly strange disappearance, Bierce clearly was aware of the dangers of the journey that he planned through Mexico to South America and beyond, especially for a seventy-one-year-old man; indeed, references in earlier correspondence to his aversion to dying in a comfortable bed suggest that he expected to die along the way. He was last reported seen by one of Villa's officers walking into the battle of Ojinaga on 11 January 1914, and there is little reason to suppose he was not among the heaps of corpses hastily burned to prevent typhus after the bloody battle.

As a fiction writer, especially as a writer of supernatural and horror fiction, Bierce's reputation rests primarily on the stories first collected in the two volumes of the early 1890's, *In The Midst of Life* and *Can Such Things Be?*, together with a few later stories added to *The Collected Works* under those two titles. His works remain bibliographically and textually a nightmare: dates of composition are rarely known, and original periodical printings are often unavailable and sometimes unknown, since Bierce gave no indication of original publication or composition either in his original collections or in the *Works* and often silently revised stories in both. Therefore, a reliable study of his development as a fiction writer has not yet appeared, but it is certainly possible to describe his achievement.

Bierce is notable for expanding and further Americanizing the settings of Gothic fiction, placing his stories in the semifrontier areas of the Western Reserve; in gold-rush, mining-boom, and ghost towns farther west; and in more civilized areas like San Francisco. He developed the potentialities of psychological terror in both supernatural and natural contexts; indeed, the psychological basis for his sense of horror is implicit in the definition of *ghost* in *The Devil's Dictionary:* "The outward and visible sign of an inward fear." Nevertheless, he was too much the skeptic to dismiss totally the possibilities of supernatural realities, a two-sided vision that leads to effective use of ambiguity in some of his best stories. Finally, this ambiguity is consistent with a pervasive irony that, combined with unsentimental urbanity and wit, gives his work an uncommon freshness and vitality.

Bierce's wit and the unconventionality of his approach are evident in "One Summer Night" (*Works*, vol. 3), a short piece on the old horror theme of premature burial. In this case, a buried man, very ill and suffering from "the invalid's apathy," falls asleep without fear in his coffin. Meanwhile, two medical students and a black named Jess dig up the body in the dead of night. As the casket is opened, thunder claps, and the "dead" man sits up, sending the students fleeing in panic. Jess is "of another breed," and so, later at the medical college, he confronts the students, asking for his pay; he has delivered the body, now surely dead of a blow from Jess's spade. The macabre joke is both on the students and on the stereotype of the frightened black.

Bierce typically handles the conventions of horror with unusual freshness. "The Secret of Macarger's Gulch" (*Can Such Things Be?*), for example, has a conventional structure, the presentation of a strange and perhaps hallucinatory event, followed by a later incident that confirms a supernatural agency. The first event is common horror fare. The narrator, Mr. Elderson, out hunting too late, camps for the night in an old shack in Macarger's Gulch. There he dreams of Edinburgh and of the Mac-Gregors, a scar-faced man and his plaid-shawl-draped wife. He wakes and in almost total darkness witnesses the sounds of a violent struggle culminating in "the sharp shrieking of a woman in mortal agony." But when he relights the fire, he finds no sign of any disturbance.

The confirming incident, which takes place several years later, is the most entertaining part of the story. At dinner with a friend named Morgan and his wife, Elderson learns that his host has traveled through the gulch and recently found a skeleton there. Morgan adds, moreover, that Macarger is a corruption of the name MacGregor. At this point a comic pattern of Elderson's shock and Morgan's polite response is set up. "My dear," says Morgan to his wife, "Mr. Elderson has upset his wine." The narrator comments, "That was hardly accurate — I had simply dropped it, glass and all." Morgan goes on, explaining that the skeleton, wrapped in a plaid shawl, was that of Mrs. MacGregor, apparently murdered there by her husband, and that the couple had come from Edinburgh:

> "My dear, do you not observe that Mr. Elderson's boneplate has water in it?"
> I had deposited a chicken bone in my fingerbowl.

Moreover, Morgan has found a picture of Mac-Gregor, which he shows to his guest. The picture clearly displays the scarred face of Elderson's dream. Morgan then asks why Elderson is so interested in this gulch, and the story ends with this exchange:

> "I lost a mule there once," I replied, "and the mischance has — has quite — upset me."
> "My dear," said Mr. Morgan, with the mechanical intonation of an interpreter translating, "the loss of Mr. Elderson's mule has peppered his coffee."

Bierce's ghost stories are notable not only for their occasional humor but also for their creation of eerie atmosphere. "An Inhabitant of Carcosa" (*In the Midst of Life*), for instance, is remarkable for its evocation of a timeless sense of decayed civilization. The narrator, an inhabitant of "the ancient and famous city of Carcosa," finds himself inexplicably wandering across an unknown and desolate plain punctuated by broken, half-buried gravestones and by larger stones, apparently the fallen remnants of larger monuments. The sense of desolation is heightened by unusual lighting effects: it appears to be day, but "low, lead-colored clouds [hang] like a visible curse" over the land; an uncouth figure, "half naked, half clad in skins" and carrying a burning torch, passes by without acknowledging the speaker's presence; nocturnal beasts of prey—a lynx, a few owls—seem active; and finally a break in the clouds reveals familiar stars rather than the sun.

The bewildered narrator's first conjecture—that he has wandered off in delirium from his sickbed—gives way to confusion and then to stunned certainty when he recognizes his own name on a crumbling tombstone and when the rising sun reveals that he casts no shadow: he is a spirit long dead but newly awakened to his condition, and the ruins about him are those of his own "famous" city. The story's ironic point looks back to Shelley's "Ozymandias," while its atmospheric effects and the name Carcosa look forward to stories by R. W. Chambers, Clark Ashton Smith, Robert E. Howard, H. P. Lovecraft, August Derleth, and Robert Bloch.

Bierce's ghost stories are often resolved in some variation of the convention of poetic justice, but there is usually a uniquely wry edge to his notion of justice. In "The Moonlit Road" (*Works*, vol. 3) a jealous man sets out to test his wife's virtue by planning to be gone overnight and coming home unexpectedly. As he returns in the dead of night he sees a man coming out of his house. In a jealous rage he goes to his wife's room and, without confrontation or questioning, strangles her. He avoids prosecution by attributing the murder to the unknown visitor, but sometime later he sees an apparition of his wife on a moonlit road near his home and flees in terror, living a number of years in guilty wandering before he commits suicide. In the final section of the story, narrated by the wife through a medium, we learn that the innocent wife had been cowering in fear as she heard her first visitor climb the stairs toward her room; but suddenly those footsteps retreated, only to return a few moments later and make their way to her room, where she was savagely strangled by an assailant still unknown to her. Sometime later, as she sought from the spirit world "to make my continued existence and my great love and poignant pity understood by my husband," she came upon him on that moonlit road. Ironically, she still does not know why he was so terrified or what has become of him since.

The ultimate horror, as this story shows, is in the human mind, and it is typical that horror in Bierce stories is generated in ways other than the supernatural. In the war story "One of the Missing" (1888; *In the Midst of Life*) a forward observer trapped in a collapsed building by an exploding shell is immovably pinned directly facing the muzzle of his own hair-triggered rifle. Though he is both brave and intelligent, he gradually disintegrates under the strain, first developing an excruciating ache at the spot on his forehead where the rifle points and finally, rather than wait indefinitely for the inevitable shot, managing with a stick and one free hand to depress the trigger. He dies of a shot unfired, for the rifle had discharged when the shell first struck. Similar elements of psychological terror and irony are apparent in "The Man and the Snake" (1890; *In the Midst of Life*), in which stories of the hypnotic powers of serpents lead a young man to hysterical death from what turns out to be a stuffed snake.

Although these are fine stories, at Bierce's very best the ironies of psychological terror touch deeper than the frailty of the human imagination. In "The Haunted Valley" (1871; *Works*, vol. 3) Jo. Dunifer is struck with terror and later dies from the sight of what he thinks is a ghostly eye peering through a knothole. It is the reasons for his terror that are of greatest importance: the apparition occurs as he explains to the narrator his "deep-seated antipathy to the Chinese" and his own experience with one of that "flight of devouring locusts." Bierce's satiric purpose becomes apparent as Jo. explains that he had hired one on his ranch five years before, at a time when he "didn't seem to care for [his] duty as a patriotic American citizen" and when he was "new to the trade" of Christianity and "full to the neck with the brotherhood of Man." He had fallen out with Ah Wee, he says, over the way the Asian cut trees, and he brags that he "had the sand" to fix things "so that he didn't last forever." The mystery deepens when the narrator discovers Ah Wee's tombstone, carved by Jo. with the line "She was a good egg," revealing that Ah Wee was in fact a woman.

It is not until four years later that the narrator learns the truth. According to his former hired hand, Gopher, Jo. had killed Ah Wee when he found her apparently in Gopher's arms; in fact, Gopher had only been trying to brush a spider out of her sleeve. The jealous Jo. was in love with her but "ashamed to acknowledge 'er and treat 'er white." The final irony is that Gopher does not even know that he himself precipitated Jo.'s death when he looked through that knothole four years before and brought to the surface the terrible guilt that brooded in his bigoted master.

Also among Bierce's best stories are those that poise ambiguously between natural and supernatural horror. Among the best known of these are two science fiction horror stories, "Moxon's Master" (*Works*, vol. 3) and "The Damned Thing" (*In the Midst of Life*). The former is a variation on the Frankenstein story; in this case the monster is an automaton that murders its creator after the man beats it in a game of chess. Through Moxon, the obsessed scientist, Bierce offers some interesting speculations based on Herbert Spencer's notion that man himself is a machine and that all matter may in some sense be sentient.

"The Damned Thing" is more finely wrought, one indication of which is the humor set up in wry contrast to the story's growing sense of horror. Part 1, for instance, titled "One Does Not Always Eat What Is on the Table," opens at a coroner's inquest into the death of Hugh Morgan, whose body lies on a table in the middle of his own one-room cabin. Part 2, "What May Happen in a Field of Wild Oats," is the narrative of William Harker, witness to Morgan's death. While out hunting with Morgan, he had seen a path being made toward them through a field of wild oats as if by an invisible creature. Morgan seemed to recognize the phenomenon, called it "that Damned Thing," fired on it, and then fled,

only to be caught and terribly mauled amid "an enveloping uproar of such sounds of rage and fury as I had never heard from the throat of man or brute." The state of the body is described in the title of part 3, "A Man Though Naked May Be in Rags," in which the jury decides that Morgan came to his death "at the hands of a mountain lion." The fourth and final part, "An Explanation from the Tomb," is an excerpt from Morgan's diary, suppressed by the coroner, who "thought it not worth while to confuse the jury." The diary reveals that Morgan had had a series of encounters with the creature, culminating in a flash of insight that concludes the story:

> There are sounds that we cannot hear. At either end of the scale are notes that stir no chord of that imperfect instrument, the human ear.... As with sounds, so with colors. At each end of the solar spectrum the chemist can detect the presence of what are known as "actinic" rays. They represent colors ... which we are unable to discern.... I am not mad; there are colors that we cannot see.
>
> And, God help me! the Damned Thing is of such a color!

Morgan's "solution" is in fact based on recent scientific discoveries that began to reveal the breadth of the electromagnetic spectrum. More important is that this story served as a model for the science fiction horror stories of such writers as Jack London, A. Merritt, and H. P. Lovecraft.

Like the best of Bierce's stories of natural and supernatural horror, the best of the supernaturally ambiguous stories have a greater satiric edge, like "The Famous Gilson Bequest," or expose more of the darker recesses of the mind, like "The Death of Halpin Frayser." "The Famous Gilson Bequest" (1878; *Can Such Things Be?*) is comparable to, though written some twenty years earlier than, Mark Twain's "The Man That Corrupted Hadleyburg." In a mining-boom town appropriately named Mammon Hill, Milton Gilson is a disreputable gambler suspected of thieving from other men's sluices. The whole town warmly approves when the respectable Henry Brentshaw, the most vocal in accusations against

Gilson, brings about his hanging, having caught him stealing horses, captured him, and testified against him. Nevertheless Gilson bequeathes everything he owns to Brentshaw, whom he names as executor. But a codicil turns up after the hanging: within five years anyone proving that Gilson stole gold from any sluice will receive the estate instead; otherwise it all reverts to Brentshaw.

Serious consequences follow when it is discovered that Gilson was a wealthy man, with sizable properties and bank accounts back east: the local newspaper, which had earlier attacked Gilson, prints "a most complimentary obituary notice," and every miner in the area brings suit against the estate. Brentshaw, now in the position of defending the man whom he had had hanged, first erects a costly monument over Gilson's grave with an inscription "eulogizing the honesty, public spirit and cognate virtues of [this] . . . 'victim to the unjust aspersions of Slander's viper brood'" and then employs "the best legal talent in the Territory to defend the memory of his departed friend," spending freely also in the suborning of witnesses and the bribery of judges. And the corruption spreads wider, invading "the press, the pulpit, the drawing-room," raging "in the mart, the exchange, the school; in the gulches, and on the street corners." At the end of the five-year period, "the sun went down upon a region in which the moral sense was dead, the social conscience callous, the intellectual capacity dwarfed, enfeebled, and confused."

The final scene occurs at night in the cemetery where Gilson's "now honorable ashes" lie. Brentshaw, visiting the scene, is a changed man. Though victorious in court, he is now gray and gaunt, his walk "a doddering shuffle," his former good humor replaced by melancholy, his understanding "narrowed to the accommodation of a single idea," having convinced even himself that Gilson was an honest man. He has also developed "a haunting faith in the supernatural . . . ominous of insanity," and in this state he sees the ghost of Gilson rise and flit back and forth between his own grave and those of his neighbors, panning dust from theirs and depositing it in his. We never know for sure whether this is Gilson's final comic revenge or a hallucination engendered by Brentshaw's repressed knowledge that his life has become a lie, but the next morning finds Brentshaw "dead among the dead."

"The Death of Halpin Frayser" (1891; *Can Such Things Be?*) is probably Bierce's most profoundly disturbing story. The first of its four parts begins with the conventional situation of a hunter, lost and out too late, spending the night in a forest, but there the conventional stops. Halpin Frayser awakens, inexplicably speaks the name "Catherine Larue," which he has never heard, and then falls into a strange dream. He wanders through a blood-drenched forest, seeking expiation for a terrible crime that he cannot remember, and finally being confronted by the soulless and malevolent body of his mother.

The second part takes us back to Frayser's youth. Twenty-six years old and the youngest in his well-to-do Tennessee family, he has been neglected by his father and spoiled by his mother, with whom he enjoys "the most perfect sympathy" and the "common guilt" of a love for poetry. Against his mother's wishes he is called away to California for a few weeks, which turns into six years' absence when he is shanghaied and then shipwrecked. He had only just returned as the story opened. Part 3 takes us back to the dream, where the monstrous mother attacks Frayser, and he "dreamed that he was dead." Part 4 occurs the following morning, when two lawmen, searching for Branscom, a man who had murdered his wife and is reported to be regularly visiting her grave, find the strangled body of Frayser lying in the cemetery. As they ponder the scene, we learn that the woman, recently widowed, had come to California in search of a missing relative before she married Branscom. Near Frayser's head the lawmen stumble over a gravestone marked "Catherine Larue," and remember that Branscom's real name is Larue and that his wife's former name was Frayser.

What "really" happened remains ambiguous. Possibly Branscom murdered the strange man he found sleeping on his wife's grave, but more important is what happened psychologically. Halpin Frayser's relationship with his mother is described in part 2 in considerable detail, the most suggestive of which is this passage:

... the attachment between him and his beautiful mother—whom from early childhood he had called Katy—became yearly stronger and more tender. In these two romantic natures was manifest in a signal way that neglected phenomenon, the dominance of the sexual element in all the relations of life, strengthening, softening, and beautifying even those of consanguinity. The two were nearly inseparable, and by strangers observing their manner were not infrequently mistaken for lovers.

It is hard to imagine a more ingenuous description of an Oedipus complex, all the more effective because it is never made explicit and because it explains the unconscious awareness implicit in Frayser's bloody dream and in the terrible guilt he feels but cannot identify. However Frayser was really killed, he was strangled by his mother's love.

No brief summary can do justice either to the story's numerous suggestive details or to the profound horror generated by the subliminal suggestion that man may be victimized by the most complex of monsters present in his own psyche. Bierce is often described as misanthropic, but a close reading of this story can change this view of him. The horror context emphasizes Frayser's position as victim, for he is by no means presented as evil. He serves to remind us that many of Bierce's stories deal with essentially decent men destroyed by circumstances, both internal and external, beyond their control. Though he often lost patience with mankind, Bierce possessed a deep though ironically understated compassion for a creature who little understands his own capacity for self-destruction.

Selected Bibliography

WORKS OF AMBROSE BIERCE

Tales of Soldiers and Civilians. San Francisco: E. L. G. Steele, 1891 (really published 1892). As *In the Midst of Life: Tales of Soldiers and Civilians.* London: Chatto and Windus, 1892.
Can Such Things Be? New York: Cassell, 1893.
Fantastic Fables. New York: Putnam, 1899.
The Collected Works of Ambrose Bierce. 12 vols. New York and Washington: Neale, 1909–1912.

Modern collections
The Collected Writings of Ambrose Bierce. New York: Citadel Press, 1946. (Introduction by Clifton Fadiman.)
Ghost and Horror Stories of Ambrose Bierce. Edited by E. F. Bleiler. New York: Dover, 1964.
The Stories and Fables of Ambrose Bierce. Edited by Edward Wagenknecht. Owings Mills, Md.: Stemmer House, 1977.

CRITICAL AND BIOGRAPHICAL STUDIES

Davidson, Cathy N. *Critical Essays on Ambrose Bierce.* Boston: G. K. Hall, 1982.
Fatout, Paul. *Ambrose Bierce: The Devil's Lexicographer.* Norman: University of Oklahoma Press, 1951.
————. *Ambrose Bierce and the Black Hills.* Norman: University of Oklahoma Press, 1956.
Grenander, M. E. *Ambrose Bierce.* New York: Twayne, 1971.
McWilliams, Carey. *Ambrose Bierce.* New York: Boni, 1929.
O'Connor, Richard. *Ambrose Bierce: A Biography.* Boston: Little, Brown, 1967.

—THOMAS L. WYMER

ROBERT W. CHAMBERS

1865-1933

ROBERT W. CHAMBERS was a popular and prolific writer, primarily of historical and society novels, who wrote some seventy-two volumes in all. Critics tended to dismiss him, not without justification, as a commercial writer. Yet, if the majority of his work is now forgotten, there remain some early pieces that contain a rare imaginative spark. As the critic Blanche C. Williams put it: "His best stories, of rare beauty and spirituality, are those of the supernatural. They should live so long as theories of metempsychosis last . . . and so long as revenants return."

The King in Yellow (1895), the book for which he is primarily remembered, is one of the most important works of supernatural horror between Edgar Allan Poe and modern horror fiction. *The Maker of Moons* (1896) is notable for its title story and a few others; and *The Mystery of Choice* (1897), which has fallen into undeserved obscurity, contains some very fine treatments of imaginative themes. Chambers continued to dabble in the supernatural in such later works as *The Tree of Heaven* (1907), *Athalie* (1915), *The Slayer of Souls* (1920), and *The Talkers* (1923), but by and large these lack the power and imagination of the earlier tales.

The horror in his fiction tends to be spiritual rather than physical, and the supernatural elements are generally mystical, although they sometimes approach conventional occultism. Many of the stories are about the human soul, and many offer tantalizing glimpses of strange mythologies. A good number include science fiction elements mixed with fantasy.

Robert William Chambers, the son of a successful lawyer, was born in Brooklyn, New York, on 26 May 1865. While a student at Brooklyn Polytechnic he became interested in painting. In 1886 he went with Charles Dana Gibson to Paris, where he studied at Julian's Academy for seven years. He exhibited at the Paris Salon in 1889. After returning to New York in 1893, he illustrated for such magazines as *Life*, *Truth*, and *Vogue*. During this period he wrote *In the Quarter* (1894), based on his life as a student in Paris. Though he had no formal training in writing, it came easily to him, and the book was a modest success. He was encouraged to write a second, *The King in Yellow*, and the resulting critical acclaim and notoriety induced him to turn from painting to writing as a career. One book followed another in rapid succession, and before long the supernatural tales were superseded by romances about the Franco-Prussian War and revolutionary New York State, and eventually by society novels about love and obstacles to marriage.

He married Elsa Vaughn Moller in 1898 and lived in a remodeled ancestral estate at Broadalbin in the foothills of the Adirondacks. He also maintained near Central Park an office, the location of which was a secret even to his own family.

His hobbies, accounts of which pervade much of his fiction, included collecting armor, Chinese and

Japanese antiques, and butterflies. He was extremely knowledgeable in these areas. He was also something of an outdoorsman and did quite a bit of hunting and fishing. He died on 16 December 1933.

The King in Yellow contains several Parisian sketches, a series of prose poems grouped under the title "The Prophets' Paradise," and five tales of the supernatural. Four of these are about the noxious effects of a play called "The King in Yellow" on those unfortunate enough to read it; the fifth is a haunting tale of dislocation in time.

The stories are introduced by the poem "Cassilda's Song." It is supposed to be taken from the play and introduces the reader to the mysterious city of Carcosa, with its black stars, twin suns, and towers rising behind the moon. Allusions to these and other strange names and images from the play are scattered through the four stories, creating a vague mythological backdrop.

The first story, "The Repairer of Reputations," is set twenty-five years in the future—that is, in 1920. It opens on an America that has just emerged unscathed from a war with Germany. Foreign-born Jews have been banned, a Negro state called Suanee has been created, and suicide has been legalized, the government providing government lethal chambers for those so inclined. The story is about a madman named Calvados de Castaigne. He is in league with a deformed and equally mad dwarf named Wilde and believes he is destined to be king of America. The dwarf has a manuscript, which names Castaigne's cousin the next in line and contains many allusions to "The King in Yellow." Castaigne plots to murder his cousin. The plans are foiled when Wilde is mangled to death by his cat in a rare instance of physical horror.

The power of the story is in its ambiguity. Is Castaigne mad because of his head injury or because he read the play during his convalescence? Are he and Wilde really mad, or do they actually have knowledge of things beyond normal human understanding? Wilde correctly predicts the location of a greave from a suit of armor, which has been missing for years. One wonders if the country would have risen up in revolt at the receipt of the Yellow Sign (a symbol or letter from no human language, further explained in the story of that title), as Wilde boasted.

"The Mask" is about a love triangle involving Boris Yvain, the sculptor whose statuary decorates the lethal chamber in the first story. It is also about falsity, self-deceit, and a chemical solution that turns living things to marble.

The woman, Genevieve, has professed her love for Boris; but Alec, who tells the story, discovers that she really loves him. There is a growing spiritual horror as he becomes aware of his own love for her and of the mask of self-deception he has been wearing. This is paralleled by the horror of Boris' solution, which petrifies first a lily, then a goldfish, a rabbit, and finally, by accident, Genevieve herself.

When Genevieve falls ill, Alec chances upon "The King in Yellow," reads it, and falls ill himself, becoming feverish and delirious. Is his illness due to a physical cause, or is it a result of reading the play? In his delirium he sees the play's Pallid Mask, which he seems able to relate to his own inner conflicts. Unlike Castaigne, he recovers and resolves to leave Genevieve with Boris. When he discovers that Boris has killed himself and Genevieve is petrified, he travels for two years. He returns and learns that the effects of Boris' solution were temporary. The story concludes as Genevieve awakens.

The protagonist of "In the Court of the Dragon" is not so fortunate. He goes to church for healing after "three nights of physical suffering and mental trouble" as a result of reading the play. He leaves the service after being upset by a strange, pale-faced organist, who then pursues him through the streets of Paris. He awakens to find himself still in the church and realizes that the organist had been hunting his soul through the streets. He now recognizes the organist from some dim primal memory. The church dissolves away to reveal black stars in the heavens, and he hears the King in Yellow whispering to his soul, "It is a fearful thing to fall into the hands of the living God!" The story is powerful, with strong imagery. Who or what the organist is, and the fate of the protagonist, are both left to the reader's imagination.

"The Yellow Sign" is about Scott, a young artist who breaks a taboo by falling in love with Tessie, who until then had been modeling for him in the nude. They are drawn together by morbid dreams that they share as a result of their possession of a talisman engraved with the Yellow Sign, and their pursuit by a dead graveyard watchman. As in "The Mask," the play provides revelation and understanding to the characters. It appears in Scott's library, although he purposely never purchased or even looked at a copy, because he had known Castaigne. They read it despite themselves, finding "words . . . more soothing than heavenly music, more awful than death itself." They sit dazed, talking of the play, until the watchman comes for his talisman, leaves Tessie dead and Scott dying, and disintegrates to a "horrible, decomposed heap on the floor" in an ending probably inspired by Poe's "The Facts in the Case of M. Valdemar."

The content of the play is always kept tantalizingly out of the reader's grasp and, on close inspection, does not seem to be consistent from one tale to the next. Characters read it and fall into reveries, babbling about the Pallid Mask, Hastur, Carcosa, or Aldebaran and the Mystery of the Hyades, but what these mean is deliberately unclear. Collectively, they seem to represent some forgotten truth or forbidden knowledge that the play awakens. Thus, the character in "In the Court of the Dragon" recognizes the organist as something returned from "Death and the awful abode of lost souls," to which the protagonist had long ago banished the organist; and Scott as he is dying says, "They of the outside world may send their creatures into wrecked homes . . . and their newspapers will batten on blood and tears, but with me their spies must halt before the confessional." He has glimpsed something beyond ordinary reality, and it will die with him. H. P. Lovecraft refers to it as "primordial Carcosa . . . some nightmare memory of which seeks to lurk latent and ominous at the back of all men's minds."

Several of the strange names from the play can be traced to two stories by Ambrose Bierce. "An Inhabitant of Carcosa," opening with a quotation ascribed to a sage called Hali, is told by a spirit whose middle name is Alar; the story contains a reference to the stars Aldebaran and the Hyades and is set in a city called Carcosa. "Haïta the Shepherd" has its title character praying to Hastur, the god of the shepherds. Chambers borrowed the names but imbued them with entirely different meanings. Therefore,

Hali is transformed from a man's name to that of a lake with waves of cloud, and Carcosa from an ancient city on earth to a mystical one that can be seen rising behind the moon.

Chambers' main inspiration was probably a scandalous current periodical called *The Yellow Book*. The word *yellow* had connotations of wickedness, decadence, and spiritual danger at the time. A contemporary review titled "More Yellowness" compared *The King in Yellow* to *The Yellow Book* and called Chambers "a martyr to degeneracy."

The King in Yellow has remained popular, and the entire work and the individual stories have often been reprinted. It has been influential, although there is a common misconception that the play was the inspiration for Lovecraft's Necronomicon. The contemporaneous play bears little resemblance to Lovecraft's ancient book of forbidden rites, and Lovecraft did not discover Chambers' fiction until 1927, five years after the Necronomicon made its first appearance in "The Hound." Lovecraft does include references to Hastur, the Yellow Sign, and the Lake of Hali in "The Whisperer in Darkness" (1930) but does not give them any significance, merely mentioning them in passing, along with strange names taken from other sources, much as Chambers did.

August Derleth incorporates these names into the Cthulhu mythos in his stories "Lair of the Star Spawn" (1932) and "The Return of Hastur" (1939), making Hastur the half-brother of Cthulhu. Marion Zimmer Bradley uses the name *Hastur* in a different way, making the Hasturs a caste of telepathic families in her Darkover books. Even more recently, a quotation from "The Mask" appears at the beginning of Robert Silverberg's *Thorns* (1967).

The fifth fantasy in Chambers' volume, "The Demoiselle D'Ys," is unconnected to the others, although it does have a character named Hastur. It is a haunting love story set in the Breton countryside. Philip, an American, is lost on the moors when he meets Jeanne D'Ys, a mysterious young lady who was raised by falconers and has never been off the moors. The falconing terms that she uses and the clothing she lends to Philip are distinctly medieval. Philip and Jeanne immediately fall in love. Before long, though, the bite of a poisonous snake lands Philip back in the present, where a shrine to

Jeanne's memory tells how she died in her youth "for the love of Philip, a stranger. A.D. 1573." Atop the shrine is one of her gloves, still warm.

It is a moving piece, despite the unlikely speed with which the two fall deeply in love. There is no attempt at an explanation of the dislocation in time, no hint of forbidden knowledge, as in the previous stories. With its rich description of the countryside and its eerie tone, the story is akin to a number of Chambers' later pieces set in Brittany.

The Maker of Moons is a collection of eight stories, four of which deal with the supernatural. The most notable is the title story, still read today, a novelette about Chinese sorcery near the Canadian border. It is based on the idea that gold is not an element but a compound. When it is found that moonshine gold is being manufactured and passed by a criminal ring, Roy Cardenhe, the narrator; Barris, a federal agent; and their entourage travel to Cardinal Lake to hunt, fish, and round up the moonshiners. In the woods, they find repellent creatures that look like a cross between crabs and reptiles, and discover an amulet engraved with images of the creatures that change color and move.

Roy has several encounters with a mysterious girl called Ysonde, who inhabits a glade that only he seems to be able to find. She tells him of her childhood in "Yian . . . where the river flows under the thousand bridges." She has had contact with no people except her stepfather, with whom she lives. She knows that the crab-reptile creatures are satellites of the Xin, a creature made from the bodies of the good genies of China by an evil sorcerer.

Barris realizes that they are up against the Kuen-Yuin, Chinese sorcerers who have "absolute control over hundreds of millions of people, mind and body, body and soul." Their leader is Yue-Laou, the maker of Moons.

Events move rapidly to a climax as the moonshiners are rounded up. Roy and Ysonde spy Yue-Laou by the lake, creating images of the moon that leave his fingers and float to the heavens. She recognizes the sorcerer as her stepfather. The crab-reptiles begin to move through the woods en masse, driving the wildlife before them, and the howling of Yeth hounds is heard. Barris shoots the sorcerer by the lake and is swallowed up by the Xin.

The story is colorful and effective but suffers from many flaws. The tone is too flippant, and How-lett, an English butler brought along by Barris, provides unnecessary comic relief. The storyline is overly dependent on coincidence, and the revelation at the end that Ysonde is probably Barris' daughter seems incredibly contrived. The idea of gold being a compound was absurd even then, and one cannot help but wonder why a Chinese sorcerer would be manufacturing it in the forests of New York State.

The sorcery in the story, while interesting, has nothing whatever to do with actual Chinese beliefs. Many of the names and terms in the story seem to be distorted versions of Chinese words. Sometimes these are used without regard for their real meaning, much as Chambers used Bierce's invented names in *The King in Yellow*. Thus, *Kuen-Yuin* may be from *Kuan-Yin*, the Buddhist goddess of mercy, and *Yian* may be a variant of *Yüan*, the name of an ancient Chinese dynasty, among other things. The word *Xin* may be a corruption of *hsien*, the Chinese term for "genius" or "spirit," or of *hsun*, "a hairy sea crab." Yeth hounds, the spirits of children in the form of headless dogs, are actually a part of Welsh folklore, but even if the reader is unaware of this, they seem to fit.

The real strength of the story comes from its wonderful images: the magical glade; Yian, with its thousand bridges; the Maker of Moons at work; and the Xin, with its repulsive satellites.

"The Silent Land" borrows some of the motifs of the previous story. It involves a pair of recreational fishermen who like to argue about the merits of their lures. They have the same comical butler, Howlett. One of them, Louis, meets a mysterious young woman, Diane. She has had a little more contact with civilization than Jeanne D'Ys or Ysonde, but she appears under similar circumstances in an unnaturally quiet wood called "the silent land." Louis is led there day after day by a spirit-bird until his partner finds out what is going on. In a revelation similar to Barris', the partner tells Louis that his father had been shot and killed by the girl's father.

The spirit-bird, which brings the couple together, is supposed to be a French legend but may well be an invention of Chambers. There are brief references to other legends: the Man in Purple Tatters, the werewolf, and "a King in Carcosa," a typical Chambers touch.

Like "The Maker of Moons," "The Silent Land" contains some nice descriptions, but it is flippant in tone and contrived. The two other supernatural stories are "A Pleasant Evening," and "The Man at the Next Table." The first is a rather long and tortuous story about an exiled French soldier falsely accused of treason, and the attempt made by the ghost of his girlfriend to clear his name after her death at sea. It is not particularly inventive, suffers from flippancy, and has an unsatisfying ending in which the reader discovers that it was all a dream . . . maybe.

The second is a comical piece about a man in search of a lost gemstone who is followed about by an eccentric old man with a beautiful daughter. Father and daughter both have powers of telepathy and teleportation, and reveal that they have been sent by the Mahatmas of the Trust Company to protect the man's great-aunt. It seems she became a cat when she died, and swallowed the gemstone.

The Mystery of Choice opens with a trilogy of tales sharing the same characters and set in the Breton countryside. They are reminiscent of "The Demoiselle D'Ys" in mood and setting.

"The Purple Emperor" is about the rivalry of two fanatical butterfly collectors and the death of one at the hands of the other. The narrator, Dick Darrel, an American, marries Lys, niece of the Purple Emperor, the murderer. The story is not supernatural, but it contains passing references to white shadows, which permeate the volume, and the Black Priest.

"The Messenger" is about the Black Priest, branded on the forehead and executed for treason during the Third Crusade and again in 1760. When his branded skull is disinterred in a gravel pit, he returns yet again, to the horror of the local Bretons and the disbelief of Darrel, who later discovers that an ancestor of Lys's was cursed by the priest. A type of sphinx moth called death's messenger flutters into the house, and the masked face of the priest is seen outside a window. Matters come to a grisly conclusion as the black-garbed figure, shot by Darrel, is chased into the woods, where he dissolves into a torrent of blood. It is an effective treatment of a conventional theme.

As in "The Demoiselle D'Ys" and "The Silent Land," there are passing references to Jeanne la Flamme and the Man in Purple Tatters. These may conceivably refer to actual Breton legends, but they have the feel of Chambers being playful.

The two stories are bridged by a short, moody piece called "Pompe Funèbre." It contains lush descriptions of a Breton forest as Dick Darrel follows a sexton beetle through the underbrush, searching for something to bury. He finds Lys crying because her uncle, the Purple Emperor, is dead. A bird flies overhead, casting a white shadow. The first line of the story is nearly the same as the first line of "The Yellow Sign," perhaps more playfulness on Chambers' part.

"The White Shadow" is an overlong story, tedious in places but innovative in others. A young man falls and is knocked unconscious. In this state, which seems to him to be a "magic second" that stretches to encompass years, he steps outside his body. He and his cousin Sweetheart transport themselves to Europe, where they marry and spend several happy years together, during which time the shadows they cast are white. Eventually, as the shadows turn darker, he sees a hospital room superimposed on his surroundings. The narrative breaks into poetry and then into an American Indian chant. He sees the figures of armor-clad gods and Indian chieftains. Finally, he awakens to find that a year has elapsed. Sweetheart, who was with him when he fell, is at his bedside. The story has a mystical aura, and the use of long poetical descriptions in the narrative seems to be a foreshadowing of the stream-of-consciousness technique.

"The Key to Grief" uses some of the same techniques and imagery. A man in a lumber camp escapes a lynching by taking a small boat to an almost inaccessible island called Grief. He meets an Indian woman there and leads a dreamlike existence with her. The same Indian words and chants as in "The White Shadow" permeate the narrative (they are a mixture of Ojibway and Sioux). When the woman bears the man a child, it casts a white shadow. His dreamlike existence comes to a vague end, and he dies in a way not made clear.

White shadows seem to function in a manner similar to the allusions to the play in *The King in Yellow*. They are obscurely symbolic and tie the sto-

743

ries together, but they are not used with any consistent symbolic intent. Thus, in "The White Shadow" they are said to be shadows of the soul, yet in "The Purple Emperor" they are cast by a shrine, and, in "Pompe Funèbre," by a bird.

"Passeur," another short, moody horror piece, separates "The White Shadow" and "The Key to Grief" and is reminiscent of "Pompe Funèbre" and "Street of the Four Winds," one of the Parisian sketches in *The King in Yellow*. A man waits for a ferry, once piloted by the woman he loves. It comes, but she is gone. It is piloted by Death. The story is quite effective.

The final story in the book, "A Matter of Interest," is rather out of place. It is a humorous science fiction story about a search for an unlikely creature called a thermosaurus. It was later included in *In Search of the Unknown* (1904), a collection of similar stories.

Chambers' last important work of supernatural fiction was *The Slayer of Souls*, an adventure novel of Oriental menace whose roots are clearly in "The Maker of Moons." The evil sorcerers are now called Yezidees instead of Kuen-Yuin, and they have graduated from counterfeiting gold to fomenting worldwide political discontent, being behind everything from anarchists to Bolsheviks. The action moves quickly as Tressa Norne, who has escaped from the Yezidee temple in Yian, destroys the eight Yezidee assassins one by one with her magic and psychic powers. Regarding the fate of the last, the Slayer of Souls, she says, "It is a fearful thing to fall into the hands of the living God!"—a sly reference to *The King in Yellow*.

Chambers' conception of the Yezidees reflects ideas that were prevalent during the period following World War I. Actually the Yezidees are a small religious group in Iraq who shun contact with the outside world. The fictional sorcerers are more closely modeled on the Assassins, a Muslim sect, which is based in Iran, not China. The novel also features a couple of temple maidens from Yian, who project their souls to America. The souls are indistinguishable from flesh and blood, as in "In the Court of the Dragon" and some other stories.

Chambers wrote several other books of minor interest. *In Search of the Unknown* is a collection of

humorous stories about a zoologist sent by the Bronx Zoo on quests for strange creatures. One tale concerns a pair of surviving great auks and a creature called the "harbour-master," which seems to be a prototype of the Creature from the Black Lagoon. A second is about a creature called the "dingue," which has one toe on each foot and a bell-like call. There is also a supernatural element as the Spirit of the North makes a physical appearance at the end. The stories are amusing and inventive. The collection, which is disguised as a novel, also includes "A Matter of Interest" and "The Man at the Next Table."

The Tree of Heaven (1909) is a collection of slight stories. They are presented in a framework in which the events of the stories are predicted by a mystic in a men's club. Each story is about a member of the club. "The Sign of Venus" is about a young man who meets a girl having an out-of-body experience. What he thinks is flesh and blood is a projected soul. "The Case of Mr. Helmer" is about an obsessed painter who meets the source of his obsession at a party—a woman who is Death.

The Talkers (1923) is a tedious novel about a love triangle between a young man named Sutton, a woman named Gilda Greenway, and an unpleasant hypnotist named Sadoul. Gilda is brought back to life after her mysterious death at a party by transplantation of her "nymphalic gland," another Chambers invention. It is part of a plan by Sadoul to win her affection by allowing a more cooperative soul to enter her body. Following her revival, she is plagued by a second soul, which gains occasional access to her body but is not friendly to Sadoul. Sadoul conveniently dies from snake venom (he had been treating himself with it for tuberculosis), releasing Gilda from the second soul. She is free to marry Sutton, but Sadoul's spirit becomes visible to the lovers before it departs and promises them that it will return. It is an unsatisfying book and not one of Chambers' better efforts. It does contain an oblique reference to *The King in Yellow*, for Gilda appears at a costume party as the "Queen in Green."

Chambers was a versatile but undisciplined writer. He discovered that he was a natural storyteller and that he could write what he chose and the public would devour it. But if his works are lacking in craft, if the characters are types rather than people, the best of them survive. The painterly eye from his days at art school, a love of nature and the outdoors, and a fine imagination still shine through in this handful of tales.

Selected Bibliography

WORKS OF ROBERT W. CHAMBERS

The King in Yellow. New York and Chicago: F. Tennyson Neely, 1895. London: Chatto and Windus, 1895. (Short stories.)

The Maker of Moons. New York: Putnam, 1896. (Short stories.)

The Mystery of Choice. New York: Appleton, 1897. London: Harper, 1897. (Short stories.)

In Search of the Unknown. New York: Harper, 1904. London: Constable, 1905. (Short stories.)

The Slayer of Souls. New York: Doran, 1920. London: Hodder and Stoughton, 1920. (Novel.)

The Talkers. New York: Doran, 1923. (Novel.)

The King in Yellow and Other Horror Stories. Edited by E. F. Bleiler. New York: Dover, 1970. (Selection from previous collections.)

CRITICAL AND BIOGRAPHICAL STUDIES

Baldwin, Charles C. *The Men Who Make Our Novels.* New York: Moffat, Yard, 1919.

Bleiler, E. F. Introduction to *The King in Yellow and Other Horror Stories.*

Bradley, Marion Zimmer. "The (Bastard) Children of Hastur." *Nyctalops,* 6 (1972): 3–6. Reprinted in *Essays Lovecraftian,* edited by Darrell Schweitzer. Baltimore: T-K Graphics, 1976.

Lovecraft, H. P. "Supernatural Horror in Literature." In *Dagon and Other Macabre Tales.* Sauk City, Wis.: Arkham House, 1965.

Weinstein, Lee. "Chambers and *The King in Yellow.*" *Starwind,* 2, no. 1 (1976): 24–30. Reprinted in *The Romantist,* no. 3. Nashville: F. Marion Crawford Memorial Society, 1979.

Williams, Blanche C. *Our Short Story Writers.* New York: Moffat, Yard, 1922.

BIBLIOGRAPHY

Clark, Kenneth. "Robert W. Chambers Re-Classified." *Journal of the Long Island Book Collectors,* 3 (1975): 18–20.

—LEE WEINSTEIN

F. MARION CRAWFORD

1854–1909

AN AMERICAN POPULAR novelist who chose to live abroad for almost his entire life, Francis Marion Crawford was born at Bagni di Lucca, in northern Italy, on 2 August 1854, the son of the sculptor Thomas Crawford. His was a thoroughly artistic family: his sister was Mrs. Hugh Fraser, well known during the last two decades of the nineteenth century and the early years of the twentieth for her novels and travel books. Brought up in Rome, Crawford was educated at St. Paul's School in New Hampshire; at Trinity College in Cambridge, England; and at Karlsruhe and Heidelberg in Germany. As a young man he was attracted by the languages and cultures of the East. He studied Sanskrit (initially in Rome) and traveled widely in Asia.

In 1879 and 1880 Crawford was the editor of the *Indian Herald* at Allahabad, an experience upon which he based his first novel, *Mr. Isaacs* (1882). It is even narrated by a brash and fairly young newspaper reporter. Its fantasy content is small, confined mainly to a few examples of supernatural powers (such as astral projection and the calling up of a mist) practiced by two elderly Indian mystics. These elements are not essential to the plot of what is basically a love story. *Mr. Isaacs* was extremely well received by readers (though less so by critics), establishing him as a popular novelist.

Crawford was essentially a romanticist. He concentrated on painting a glamorous (though not always accurate) picture of the lives of the rich and powerful of different centuries and diverse countries. He never attempted to be true to life or instructive in his novels; as he stresses in *The Novel, What It Is* (1893), he saw fiction as solely an entertainment. His plots are usually complex, though obviously contrived; his characters, while vivid, are most often painted either very black or very white; his settings are always richly detailed. His books sold well enough to be very remunerative, yet Crawford's high standard of living could be funded only if he wrote two books a year. Thus he wrote prolifically, normally producing 5,000 words a day. Such a high output prevented him from making the most of his talents.

For more than twenty-five years Crawford's books appeared regularly and were in great demand. Some of the most praised of his novels are *A Roman Singer* (1884), *Zoroaster* (1885), *Saracinesca* (1887), *A Cigarette Maker's Romance* (1890), and *A Rose of Yesterday* (1897). Crawford also wrote plays, short stories, nonfiction, and criticism. Although he maintained a home at Sorrento, Italy, for much of his life (from 1883) he continued to travel frequently. He died at Sorrento on 9 April 1909. His nonfantastic fiction is almost entirely forgotten today.

Crawford's fantastic works consist of four novels and seven stories, displaying the best and worst of his talents. The novels are *With the Immortals* (1888), *Khaled. A Tale of Arabia* (1891), *The Witch of Prague* (1891), and *Cecilia. A Story of Modern*

Rome (1902). The stories were collected as *Uncanny Tales*, published posthumously in 1911. In general the novels do not represent Crawford's best work and are inferior to the stories.

With the Immortals is a wish-fulfillment fantasy, blatantly self-indulgent and almost plotless. In 1887 a group of rich and idle English people (Augustus Chard; his sister, Diana; his wife, Gwendoline; and her mother, Lady Brenda) buy and refurbish an old castle on a rocky hillside near Sorrento. Augustus tries to tap the earth's "gigantic reservoir of electricity" by joining land and sea with masses of copper wiring. He succeeds (this is pseudoscience at its worst) and lights up the area as bright as day. The purpose of his experiment is to attract the ghosts of famous people to the castle. This, too, is a success, and all the ghosts who appear are those that Augustus and his family had earlier expressed an interest in meeting.

In ones and twos the ghosts make themselves visible: Heinrich Heine, Frédéric Chopin, Julius Caesar, Leonardo da Vinci, Francis I, Samuel Johnson, Chevalier Pierre de Bayard, and Blaise Pascal. The remainder of the novel (250 pages) is taken up with conversations between members of the family and the ghosts. They discuss, at inordinate length, such universal subjects as romance, love, religion, wit, and art, without coming to any firm conclusions. The entire situation is one of comic absurdity, a fact well appreciated by J. K. Bangs in his rather similar *A House-Boat on the Styx* (1895), but not by Crawford.

There is no development of plot or character. After several long sessions of conversation by night (initially) and by day, and after a brief appearance by the Sirens of mythology, the ghosts fade away, leaving Augustus and family unchanged.

The most successful of Crawford's fantasy novels is *Khaled. A Tale of Arabia.* It is a simple, lightweight story, very much in the mold of *The Thousand and One Nights*, and unlike anything else Crawford wrote. Khaled is one of the genies, an immortal servant of Allah. For an error of judgment he is punished by being made a mortal man. He is told that it is the will of Allah that he should marry Zehowah, the exceptionally beautiful daughter of the sultan of Riad, one of whose suitors he had arbitrarily killed. If he is able to make Zehowah love him he will receive an immortal soul and live in paradise when he dies; otherwise he will be condemned to hell. Khaled receives many advantages to help him on earth, including youth, good looks, great strength, a fine sword, and a magnificent horse. Khaled finds it easy enough to marry Zehowah but much more difficult to awaken her love. Military adventures, a rebellion, and erotic entanglements all take place before Zehowah finally succumbs to love and Khaled wins a soul.

It is difficult to find a moral in this outcome. Most probably Crawford did not intend any such thing; this is an entertaining rather than a deep novel. Although rather wordy and overlong by present-day standards, it is typical of Crawford's time. Its best aspects are the solidly believable Arabian setting (but suffused with the timeless romanticism of *The Thousand and One Nights*) and the rather Machiavellian logic. An example of the latter occurs in chapter 2, when Zedowah explains to her father why she believes Khaled to be a good choice of husband and future sultan. It is, she says, an advantage for him not to be a prince of another country, for he will not be torn between kingdoms. Having no other possessions, Khaled will never be distracted from Riad. Yet he is from outside Riad, another good thing, since for Zehowah to marry a young man of Riad would lead to jealousy and perhaps to civil war.

In a limited fashion *Khaled* is a successful novel. Its plot is very simple, however, hinging on Khaled's obtaining Zehowah's declaration of love. All other considerations are brushed aside, and Almasta (the only interesting character) just fades away at the end.

The Witch of Prague is a complex, yet flawed and unconvincing, tale of unrequited love that includes many supernatural elements. Its plot contains so many holes and inconsistencies that the novel must have been a potboiler — a first draft rushed into print to satisfy Crawford's fans. Its characters are all unnecessarily mysterious, as if the author could not be bothered to invent their backgrounds or motives. The information that is given is repeated frequently, making the novel longer by a third than it should be. As in *With the Immortals*, there are examples of poor science.

Despite these shortcomings, *The Witch of Prague* contains some impressive scenes and some memorable characters. Crawford had a knack for imbuing his physical descriptions with atmosphere, and he does this to good effect with wintry Prague of about 1890. Presumably he visited the city; certainly his descriptions of cold streets, a graveyard, and the interior of the great Tyn Church are convincing.

Unorna, known as the witch of Prague, is nasty but impressive. A beautiful young woman of twenty-five, she has one gray and one brown eye. She is a hypnotist of great power and spends most of her time in the heated conservatory of her house, surrounded by luxuriant tropical plants even in the depth of Prague's winter. Always she seems to love men who care little for her and to despise men who love her. The Wanderer (no other name is ever given him) visits Unorna by accident, and she falls in love with him and tries to make him love her through hypnotic power, though he is searching for his long-lost love, Beatrice.

Keyork Arabian, a powerful dwarf, is a friend of Unorna's and a fellow dabbler in the occult; he may even be an incarnation of the devil. He has a most impressively macabre collection of skulls and embalmed human remains. Although Dennis Wheatley, in an introduction to a 1971 edition of the novel, refers to Arabian as "certainly the most evil character" in the book, he is surely outdone in this respect by Unorna. Israel Kafka is a young man whose love for Unorna is repulsed and turns to hate, though Crawford prefers to forget about him during the closing stages of the novel. Beatrice, whose great love for the Wanderer has been maintained over several years despite her father's unexplained opposition to their marriage, just happens to be in Prague at the same time as the Wanderer, though Unorna finds her first and tries to thwart her by use of hypnosis. The interactions of all these characters are too involved to be described here, except to say that Unorna plots against them all, sometimes aided by Arabian.

Apart from a couple of brief ghostly visitations (a vision of Beatrice by the river and a groan from an embalmed head in Arabian's collection), the supernatural is confined to displays of hypnotism. Crawford tries very hard to convince the reader that the hypnotism shown here is scientifically accepted and accurate, although he is really ascribing much more power to the phenomenon than exists. At her house Unorna keeps a very old man under constant hypnosis as part of an experiment into the aging process and how to defeat it. Also, Unorna is shown hypnotizing the Wanderer, Israel Kafka, and Beatrice into performing actions that are very much against their will. (In Beatrice's case hypnotism even gives her the power to see in the dark!) Yet, at the crucial moment, Unorna's power always fails with melodramatic suddenness. The work as a whole is an obvious attempt by Crawford to write a Marie Corelli novel.

The last of Crawford's fantasy novels, *Cecilia. A Story of Modern Rome*, is a delightful tale of love, honor, and friendship set in the Rome of Crawford's time. Its main supernatural element (a small but important part of the plot) stems from the identical recurring dreams of two of the major characters. In general outline the plot concerns a love triangle and an arranged marriage that is finally called off. All the participants are members of the upper classes and of Rome's high society. Guido d'Este is untitled but closely related to kings and princesses; he is relatively poor but a handsome and very eligible young bachelor. Cecilia Fortiguerra, aged eighteen and just coming out into society, is exceedingly rich though only slightly titled. Their relatives introduce them expectantly.

Guido is at first cool toward Cecilia because of the family pressure; then he falls in love with her. Cecilia is pleased to have Guido as a friend, though she plans never to marry but to devote her life to study. After Guido falls in love with her she feels she would do better to marry him than anybody else, and she agrees.

A complicating factor is the presence of Guido's best friend, Lamberto Lamberti. He is introduced to Cecilia at about the same time as Guido, and he falls in love with her immediately. Both Lamberto and Cecilia realize that they have often dreamt of each other against a setting in ancient Rome, where she is a vestal virgin and he is her would-be lover. However, Cecilia is not attracted at first to the real Lamberto, while the latter (acting as a true friend should) conceals his love and endeavors to obtain a post (he is in the navy) away from Rome.

Once Guido and Cecilia are engaged, Cecilia begins to have doubts. She realizes that she does not love Guido and will never love him, but that she does love the man of her dreams—Lamberto. She breaks off the engagement, but only after Guido has survived a long and dangerous illness does he accept this rejection. And only after that acceptance does Lamberto dare to declare his love for Cecilia. She reciprocates and, at length, Guido accepts the situation with good grace.

The novel is slow-moving, though quite enjoyable, being largely taken up with plot complexities. The dreams of ancient Rome are striking yet brief— a plot contrivance to bring Cecilia and Lamberto together.

Much better crafted and much more satisfactory in general are Crawford's horror stories. Although all seven collected as *Uncanny Tales* (retitled *Wandering Ghosts* for United States publication and including the two stories from *The Upper Berth*, 1894) have been reprinted, some frequently, Crawford seems to have written no other, uncollected, fantasy stories at all. Most of the seven are ghost stories, though more horrific than usual for their kind. Three are firmly in the Gothic tradition, but the others are more original.

Best known, because most frequently reprinted, is "The Upper Berth." On a transatlantic passenger liner the upper berth in a certain cabin houses a lunatic who commits suicide. For three succeeding voyages that berth is haunted, forcing each new occupant to commit suicide too. The ghost's power is such that it is able to open the cabin's porthole, however firmly closed. The story's narrator is a big, strong man who happens to be sleeping in the lower berth. He tangles with the ghost and has his arm broken. It is this unexpected physical threat that makes the story so original and frightening. Additionally, the threatening atmosphere is skillfully built up, involving several senses (a damp smell, the feel of a man's arm in that vacated upper berth,

"smooth, and wet, and icy cold," as well as faint groaning). It is regarded as a classic of the genre.

Another ghost story set mainly at sea, but very different, is "Man Overboard!" Crawford was a very experienced seaman, especially in sailing vessels, and he held a master's certificate in navigation. Hence he was able to be totally convincing in depicting life aboard a four-masted schooner. During a storm one of a pair of identical twins goes overboard. His ghost returns to keep watch on the other twin, who was not responsible for the accident but makes use of it to marry his dead brother's sweetheart. The scenes of shipboard haunting are written with great subtlety and restraint. The story's gruesome final act is played out ashore and is narrated by the schooner's mate.

Set onshore but narrated by a retired sea captain is "The Screaming Skull." The theme, when it is eventually revealed, proves to be the traditional one of revenge by a murdered person. Yet there is much more to it than that. The narrator is so unsure of facts that he can only hint at the truth. He has inherited a small cottage from a doctor. The doctor's wife died a few years earlier, perhaps killed by her husband. Perhaps, even, she was killed by having molten lead poured into her ear while asleep, a method of murder mentioned lightheartedly by the sea captain on a visit to the doctor and his wife. It is possible that the skull the doctor kept in his cottage was that of his dead wife. If so, the thing that rattles inside the skull might be a small piece of lead. But surely the nighttime screams heard in the cottage cannot come from the skull. Surely, too, it was a coincidence that when the doctor was found dead on a nearby beach with his throat crushed, the skull happened to be there as well. Thus Crawford builds up the situation, detail by detail, in a chatty, nonlinear reminiscence just as one old sea captain might talk to another. From internal evidence the story was written around 1906 or 1907, near the end of Crawford's life.

Very different again is "The Dead Smile," a wonderfully atmospheric piece of Gothic melodrama set in a great old house in Ireland. A baronet, Sir Hugh Ockram, dies with a twisted smile on his face and a terrible secret in his head. He is buried in the traditional Ockram fashion, in the vault below the house in a shroud but no coffin. Later something drives his son and heir, Gabriel, to go down there at dead of night. In his father's decomposing hands he finds a document explaining the secret—that Gabriel and Evelyn, his wife-to-be, are in fact half-siblings rather than cousins. This is predictable. The twist is that Evelyn, reading the document over his shoulder, gives every indication of still wanting to marry him.

"For the Blood Is the Life" is an overly complex vampire tale, beautifully told and set against the scenic grandeur of the Italian west coast, not too far from Sorrento. Once again, the obvious drawing from life of so many aspects of background, character, and incident helps to lend conviction to the supernatural events.

"By the Waters of Paradise," concerned with the banishing from an old house and its gardens of a spirit of depression (which is never quite crystallized into a ghost), is a little weak and not helped by its artificially happy ending. "The Doll's Ghost" is the excessively sentimental story of how the ghost of a doll leads a doll repairer to the hospital bedside of his young daughter.

If Crawford's only contribution to fantastic literature had been his novels, that contribution might just as well have been forgotten. Of the four novels, only *Khaled. A Tale of Arabia* is worth reading today, and that is too lightweight to have any importance. It is Crawford's few horror tales that keep his name alive within the fantasy and horror genre. They predate H. P. Lovecraft, E. F. Benson, William Hope Hodgson, and most of the work of M. R. James. At their best they are important early examples of extremely horrific ghost stories told subtly

and with nicely calculated atmosphere. This subtlety, in particular, was a seminal feature, later copied by many other authors. It is exemplified by realistic settings, the building-up of believable characters, and the slow and careful provision of information. Whereas the novels concentrate on rich and powerful characters, tending to despise the working classes, the stories have much more of the common touch. Whenever anthologies of the greatest ghost and horror stories are compiled in the future they are likely to include something by Crawford.

Selected Bibliography

WORKS OF F. MARION CRAWFORD

Mr. Isaacs. A Tale of Modern India. London and New York: Macmillan, 1882.

With the Immortals. London and New York: Macmillan, 1888.

Khaled. A Tale of Arabia. London: Macmillan, 1891.

The Witch of Prague. London and New York: Macmillan, 1891.

The Upper Berth. London: Unwin, 1894. (Also contains "By the Waters of Paradise.") New York: Macmillan, 1894. (Contains only the title story.)

Cecilia. A Story of Modern Rome. London and New York: Macmillan, 1902.

Uncanny Tales. London: Unwin, 1911. As *Wandering Ghosts.* New York: Macmillan, 1911.

CRITICAL AND BIBLIOGRAPHIC STUDY

Moran, John C. *An F. Marion Crawford Companion.* Westport, Conn.: Greenwood Press, 1981.

—CHRIS MORGAN

FRANK R. STOCKTON

1834-1902

FRANK R. STOCKTON'S contemporaries would have been surprised to learn that he would be remembered mostly as a minor fantasist. A century ago, his popularity was comparable with James A. Michener's today. An 1899 *Literature* magazine poll put Stockton in fifth place among American authors, behind Mark Twain (in third place) but ahead of Henry James and Bret Harte. He was also famous as the subeditor, under Mary Mapes Dodge, of the great children's periodical *St. Nicholas*. Yet, by 1928, William Chislett, Jr., offered his essay on Stockton as a rehabilitation; and today most readers know him for only one story, "The Lady, or the Tiger?" The rest of his work is rarely read today, although he anticipated the twentieth-century ironic style by combining the extravagance of romance with the matter-of-factness of apparent objectivity.

Of his fifty-odd works, four novels and a number of short stories (his "fanciful tales") have science fictional or supernatural content. As a fantasist, Stockton was neither a supernaturalist nor a creator of worlds; indeed, he has been praised by some critics for sticking close to ordinary life. The shorter forms of fantasy, the ghost story and the fairy tale, simply appeared to him as suitable vehicles for charming entertainments. In his day he was best known as a humorist, but he was essentially a Victorian moralist, using fantasy to poke fun at solemnity and hypocrisy. He used elements of the supernatural, but his real interest was in their benignly humorous effects on the domestic surroundings.

The facts of Stockton's life are readily available in the standard biography by Martin I. J. Griffin (1939). Briefly, he was born Francis Richard Stockton in Philadelphia in 1834, the eldest son of a Methodist minister and his second wife. Frank's father had helped found the schismatic Methodist Protestant church, and his eldest half-brother, Thomas, was a famous preacher who preceded Lincoln as speaker at Gettysburg. Their father's interests were strictly theological and his beliefs puritanical; his influence was such that, barring attendance at weddings and funerals, Frank never entered a church during his adult life. Griffin thought that Stockton's devastating portrait of the hypocritical, selfish Reverend Mr. Enderton (in *The Casting Away of Mrs. Lecks and Mrs. Aleshine*, 1886) was actually of his father. Frank's mother, Emily Drean Stockton, is generally credited with encouraging his artistic and literary ambitions. He was lame from birth and delicate, and like many imaginative children in similar circumstances, he began making up stories to compensate for his lack of physical vitality.

On graduating from high school, Stockton apprenticed as a wood engraver, earning his living by this trade for fifteen years. In 1860 he married a South Carolina schoolteacher, Mary Ann (Marian) Edwards Tuttle. Marrying a Southerner in that year interested him, for the only time in his life, in politics; shortly afterward, in 1861, he published the pamphlet *A Northern Voice for the Dissolution of the Union*. This outlined a plan to eliminate slavery by compensating owners, while allowing the South to secede. However, although he did not participate in the Civil War, he withdrew the pamphlet when Fort Sumter was fired on.

After the war, Stockton became Mary Mapes Dodge's assistant first on *Hearth and Home* and then on *St. Nicholas*. As subeditor of both publications, Stockton wrote many different articles and stories, some under pseudonyms (Paul Fort and John Lewees) to disguise the number of his contributions. His reputation and income advanced until the Stocktons could afford to leave Philadelphia, in 1874, to buy a farm in New Jersey. This move inspired his first best-seller, *Rudder Grange* (1879), a collection of short pieces about the humorous domestic tribulations of a young married couple. Around 1876, Stockton's health and eyesight began to decline, and he was forced to leave *St. Nicholas*. Since he could neither read nor write for several years, his wife became his amanuensis until he could afford a secretary.

Stockton's earnings suffered in the early 1880's because of, ironically, his greatest success, the short story with the trick ending originally called "In the King's Arena" but retitled by the editor "The Lady, or the Tiger?" He returned from a trip to Europe to find himself famous, deluged with letters and manuscripts providing endless solutions and sequels. Fan clubs were even started expressly to debate the topic. But editors begin to reject his other stories, saying they were not up to the standard set by "The Lady, or the Tiger?" The nearest Stockton came to bitterness of soul, he said, was during this period; he even wrote a story about it, "His Wife's Deceased Sister" (*Century*, January 1884), reflecting his fears about ever achieving financial security.

However, his career soon recovered, and in 1886 he published one of the most popular of his longer stories, *The Casting Away of Mrs. Lecks and Mrs. Aleshine*. Most of his longer work, in fact, was written between 1886 and his death in 1902, including nearly all his science fiction. The Stocktons moved twice, first to Morristown, New Jersey, and then in 1899 to Claymont, near Charles Town, West Virginia. In both places Stockton lived, like many of his heroes, as a "gentleman farmer." He died of a cere-

bral hemorrhage on a visit to Washington, D.C. Marian survived him by four years. They had no children.

The majority of Stockton's work can be classified in one of three categories: fantasy, science fiction, and mainstream fiction. However, the differences among the types are largely those of incident and character; Stockton had no interest in the formal boundaries of genre or, indeed, in any literary theory, though he did occasionally experiment with narrative devices. Richard Gid Powers notes, "Had Jules Verne not written science fiction, Stockton would not have known how; had Verne's science fiction not sold well, Stockton would not have written science fiction at all." The general principle applies to all of Stockton's work: although Stockton was no hack, he wrote what would sell.

In fantasy, his place is beside such contemporaries and near-contemporaries as Hans Christian Andersen, whose stories he loved in childhood; the Americans Mark Twain and L. Frank Baum; and the Britons F. Anstey, Lewis Carroll, and E. Nesbit. However, he did not share the wild, motley vitality of Baum or the nonsensical exhilaration of Anstey, and he recognized both Twain and Andersen as far more serious and courageous artists than himself. Carroll's intellectual nonsense and Nesbit's unblinking reportage of childhood logic were more akin to Stockton's manner, centered on the absurdity of normal logic pushed to extremes. Instead of vitality, he displayed a vague and demure drollery; he was a master of the deadpan and the tongue-in-cheek. Pretension, deftly deflated, disappeared with a fizzle, not a bang. Charm was his hallmark, and his work is notable for its sweet temper and gentle dignity.

The first fanciful tales Stockton wrote were the various "Ting-a-Ling Tales," published in *Riverside* (1867–1869) as children's stories. The main characters are two friends, the tiny fairy Ting-a-Ling and the enormous giant Tur-il-i-ra. The plotting can only be described as minimal; a sense of plot was never one of Stockton's virtues, and these early stories are even more rambling than most. But Stockton's characteristic style is already well established in these tales. For example, consider this remark from "The Magical Music" (1870): "Standing on their heads . . . were many of those dreadful green lizards . . . whose bite causes their victim, together with all his blood relations, to gangrene in an instant." Apparently blood relations were no different a century ago than they are now. A small obsession with food, which is Stockton's only resemblance to the greatest of modern fantasists, J. R. R. Tolkien, is also evident in these early stories. But where Tolkien uses domestic items like food to give the reader a homely reference point in a fantastic universe, Stockton does exactly the reverse: the extravagance of his food is far greater than that of his secondary world.

A favorite theme of all Stockton's fantasies is the reversal of expectations and the relative absurdity of individual viewpoints. In "The Clocks of Rondaine" (St. Nicholas, 1887), a child learns the lesson that one's own point of view is just as silly as anyone else's; whose clock has the "best" time when all are different? The queen who punished her subjects for disliking "The Queen's Museum" (St. Nicholas, 1884) learns the same lesson through the efforts of a passing traveler and a band of rule-ridden thieves; and "Prince Hassak's March" (St. Nicholas, 1883) teaches the prince that even princes must take reality into account. "The Reformed Pirate" (The Floating Prince, 1881) laughs first at people who mistake bluster for threat and then shows how relationships change when sizes are altered. "The Philosophy of Relative Existences" (Century, 1892) shows a man meeting a ghost girl—or is it a girl meeting a ghost man?

Stockton often wrote about the absurdity of meddling in other people's lives. In a comic cautionary tale for busybodies, the sturdy "Bee-Man of Orn" is peacefully minding his own business when the ridiculous interference of the Young Magician sets him to discover the original form from which he was transformed. After an exciting adventure with a Languid Youth and a Very Imp, the Bee-Man discovers the astonishing truth: he was once a baby. The Young Magician's arcane knowledge, acquired through years of study, is shown to be somewhat less valuable than plain common sense.

In a more nostalgic mood are two of Stockton's better-known fairy tales. "Old Pipes and the Dryad"

receive youth and freedom through helping one another, despite the wicked machinations of the Echo-Dwarf and the stubborn prejudices of Old Pipes's mother. Similarly, in "The Bishop's Ghost and the Printer's Baby," the title characters achieve their desires through mutual aid. Both stories dwell on aging and death without much humor but also, unusually for a Victorian writer, without morbidity; Stockton dealt lightly with the solemn. "The Lady, or the Tiger?" and its equally frustrating sequel, "The Discourager of Hesitancy," bring O. Henry to mind because of their gimmick endings. In both tales the hero opens the fateful door not by trusting his luck but at a woman's direction; this is the main point of each story and the reason why the former, at any rate, has endured. Stockton had intended to show what happened when the door was opened. But he could not decide how the tempestuous, passionate barbarian Princess would have acted, so he left the decision up to the readers. It is the conflict in the Princess' heart, not the hero's fate, that occupies our minds and torments our curiosity. However, careful rereading shows that Stockton (who rewrote the ending five times!) loads the deck in favor of one choice.

"The Griffin and the Minor Canon" is Stockton's finest, most serious, and most deeply felt story. A griffin, hearing that his likeness adorns a great church, comes from the "dreadful wilds" to see it. The cowardly townspeople are terrified, and only the humble Minor Canon befriends the griffin. When the townspeople banish the Canon to the dreadful wilds, hoping the griffin will follow, the griffin takes over all the Canon's duties, teaching the naughtiest children and visiting the sick and the poor. Stockton amusingly describes the griffin's effect on these persons, most of whom discover reserves of energy and health they never knew they had.

This story is the only one in which Stockton takes a critical view of humanity. Fear, he says, not love, inspires people, except those few whose innate goodness makes them superior to the common run. Even love is not disinterested, for the griffin's love for the Canon is based on his attractiveness as a potential meal. This is a harsh judgment. Yet the story is deeply moving precisely because, for once, Stockton does not hide emotion but, instead, uses his whimsicality and charm to redeem the evil that he relates and to transmute contempt into compassion. Neither harshness nor sentimentality mars this classic tale of the power of goodness.

A burlesque of the Wandering Jew theme, *The Vizier of the Two-Horned Alexander* (1899), is a fantasy of many different eras similar to Edwin Lester Arnold's *Phra the Phoenician* (1891). In both books a man achieves immortality and meets adventure with all the most famous people of history. But Arnold's story is serious, while Stockton, true to form, treats the story as farce. Mr. Crowder, Stockton's hero, skips over exciting and dreadful events to recount how he wrote Herodotus' *History*, anticipating Robert Lawson's comic *Ben and Me* (1939), in which a mouse is really responsible for Ben Franklin's fame.

Three ghost stories show the influence of Spiritualism, the nineteenth-century philosophical and religious movement based on the belief that the spirits of the dead can communicate to the living through the power of a "medium," an extrasensitive living individual. The typical manifestations of these spirits included loud rapping noises, teleportation, levitation, ghostly voices, and materialized "ectoplasmic" hands and figures, some of which were "photographed." Spiritualism itself was never entirely respectable, but many of its believers were; the favorable testimony of one legitimate physicist who reported in 1874 that he had touched and spoken to the materialized spirit of a young woman was widely believed in spite of an immediately subsequent relevation of fraud.

Though any story including ghosts is today considered fantastic, in Stockton's day Spiritualism was thought by many to be the next stage in the evolution of science. All three of these stories deal with materialized ghosts rather than any of the lesser manifestations; in fact, the longest story, "Amos Kilbright: His Adscititious Experiences" (1883), is specifically about materialization. Amos, a farmer who drowned in 1783, is called up by Spiritualists who leave him in the "materialization process" too long and thus cannot return him to "the other side." A

local lawyer employs and befriends him but then is informed by the heartless Spiritualists that they intend to dematerialize Amos as a sideshow attraction for profit.

Stockton repeatedly refers to the Spiritualists' outward respectability and inward wickedness in their manipulation of the helpless Amos; at the same time, the materialization of a departed spirit is specifically compared to the newfangled telephone as a scientific marvel. It is consistent with Stockton's anticlericalism that he criticized Spiritualism as a scientific endeavor rather than joining with the large numbers of clergymen of all sects who opposed it on grounds of irreligion and devil worship.

"The Transferred Ghost" and its sequel, "The Spectral Mortgage," resemble the humorous ghost stories of Thorne Smith, in which the ghosts inspire exasperation, not awe, scientific curiosity, or *timor mortis*. Stockton amused his audience by pointing out the problems that supernatural creatures would have in trying to live like natural ones. Neither story deals with Spiritualism per se; Stockton simply uses the materialized spirits as eccentrics who ruffle the sensitivities of the stuffily respectable young hero, who, when confronted by the ghosts, fears that his fiancée will think it not quite nice to converse with them.

Three stories, "The Water-Devil," "What I Found in the Sea," and "The Knife That Killed Po Hancy," fall into a debatable land between fantasy and science fiction. The "science" in the first story (again, like Spiritualism) is laughable by today's standards, but Stockton included what were then the very latest developments out of the *Encyclopaedia Britannica*. In "The Water-Devil" the passengers on a ship think that a monster, which turns out to be a magnet, has the vessel in its grip. This tale displays another common theme of Stockton's, the misleading circumstance that makes fools of people; only one man, relying on common sense and courage, dares to hope that there is no monster, while everyone else precipitately flees.

"The Knife That Killed Po Hancy" still has on it the blood of a fierce jungle outlaw; when a sissified gent cuts himself with it, Po Hancy's savagery flows into his blood, getting him into some awkward social situations. The same device is used in "What I Found in the Sea": a diver breathes "sixteenth-century air" in the casks of a sunken English privateer. On returning to the surface, he swaggers about like Captain Kidd until the effects wear off. Both stories were inspired by the work of Louis Pasteur and others on the transmission of disease and blood transfusions. The literary inspiration was *Dr. Jekyll and Mr. Hyde*, but where Robert Louis Stevenson emphasizes the horror of the doppelgänger theme, Stockton's real interest in these stories is not in science, the supernatural, or abnormal psychology but in the amusing effects that these scientific oddities have on the characters' social relations.

Of Stockton's other work, a few books will interest fantasy readers. His most significant and popular science fiction novel, *The Great War Syndicate* (1889), describes the "war to end wars" run by a syndicate of American capitalists who convince the government that they can wage war better than it can. The book has been compared by Richard Powers to Mark Twain's fantasy *A Connecticut Yankee in King Arthur's Court*, which appeared in the same year. But where Twain's book uses many supernatural elements, including enchanters and travels through time, Stockton's is straight-faced utopian fiction.

Kate Bonnet, the Romance of a Pirate's Daughter (1902) is a story so ridiculous, in an eighteenth-century setting so far divorced from real history, that it best bears comparison with Joan Aiken's alternate-universe stories of Dido Twite. Kate's father, a Barbadian planter, becomes a pirate out of greed and boredom. Kate tries to bring him to his senses; after plot twists too numerous to mention, including Captain Bonnet's humiliation by a real pirate, the roistering Blackbeard, she is united with her true love, while Captain Bonnet, unrepentant to the last, is hanged, and good riddance. In spite of the nonsensical plot, the story retains its charm and readability.

The Casting Away of Mrs. Lecks and Mrs. Aleshine and its sequel, *The Dusantes* (1888), display one of Stockton's fortes: portraying sensible middle-aged ladies, who, he felt, were far more interesting than any youthful heroine. Mrs. Lecks and Mrs. Aleshine spout motherly aphorisms and eat a nour-

ishing luncheon even when swimming in the ocean after their lifeboat has sunk; they are the true heroines, and a rather insipid love story takes second place to their story. Another adventure novel, *The Adventures of Captain Horn* (1895), and its sequel, *Mrs. Cliff's Yacht* (1896), include elements of both *The Casting Away* and *Kate Bonnet*. Captain Horn and his passengers, including Mrs. Cliff, another of Stockton's sensible widows, discover a fabulous treasure of the Incas, which the corrupt Peruvian government is about to steal from its poverty-stricken rightful owners. Again, as in *Kate Bonnet*, the plot gallops along without much organization.

As a fantasist, Frank Stockton never created an all-encompassing secondary universe like those that Tolkien made the prerequisite of modern heroic fantasy; neither do his fantasies often achieve that sense of numinous wonder derived from the supernatural itself. For him, all wonders led inexorably back, via his skillful pairing of the grotesque with the commonplace, the amazing with the ludicrous, to the civilized domesticity that he cherished most.

Much of his work has failed to survive because he was so thoroughly a product of his time, place, and class. He was popular because he shared his audience's yearning for gentility and respectability and its reverence for "common sense" and financial success. Even so great an artist as Mark Twain allowed his genteel wife to sabotage his best work (*Huckleberry Finn* in particular) because she was shocked by its realistic crudity; Stockton was a craftsman, not a great artist, and his work was genteel by nature. Yet although Stockton and his audience bowed to the mammons of financial and social success, they also acknowledged a higher morality that held love and righteousness superior to money and position. For example, in "The Griffin and the Minor Canon" material success accompanies goodness: the gentle, humble Minor Canon, who "thought only of helping" the ungrateful townspeople, eventually becomes a bishop.

These contrary, complementary strains of the Victorian Protestant ethic dominate the impression that Stockton gives modern readers. *Kate Bonnet*, for example, contains the sentiment "No greater blessing can come to really good people than the absolute disappearance of the wicked,'' which brightens Kate's heart after she struggles to forget her father's evil deeds. Today that line seems laughably, even culpably, naïve. Yet one wonders what Stockton really meant by it, for he then says that the hearts of the other characters "brightened without any trouble at all, the disappearance of the wicked having such a direct and forcible effect upon them.'' Past years of suffering and evil that Stockton could not even have conceived of, we laugh out loud, just as he meant us to. Here is the authentic note of an individual, original artist. Perhaps Stockton's memory has faded because he was more civilized than we are, so that, in discovering the tranquil humor unique to this nearly forgotten spinner of tales, we can rediscover our better selves.

Selected Bibliography

WORKS OF FRANK STOCKTON

Henry L. Golemba points out that Stockton's works "amount to over fifty volumes, including twenty-nine novels, about fourteen volumes of short stories, eight books of travel, history, and natural philosophy, and five or more volumes of essays, letters, and various manuscripts.''

Collected works

The Novels and Stories of Frank R. Stockton (Shenandoah Edition). New York: Scribner, 1899–1904. 23 volumes. (Contains 21 novels, 66 short stories, a memorial sketch by Marian Stockton, and a partial bibliography.)

Fantastic fiction

The Floating Prince and Other Fairy Tales. New York: Scribner, 1881. (Includes "The Reformed Pirate," "The Magician's Daughter and the High Born Boy," and "The Castle of Bim.")

The Lady, or the Tiger? and Other Stories. New York: Scribner, 1884. Edinburgh: David Douglas, 1887.

Stockton's Stories. Second Series. The Christmas Wreck and Other Stories. New York: Scribner, 1886. Reprinted as *The Christmas Wreck.* (Includes "A Tale of Negative Gravity," "The Remarkable Wreck of the 'Thomas Hyke,'" and "The Discourager of Hesitancy.")

Stockton's Stories. First and Second Series. New York: Scribner, 1886.

The Bee-Man of Orn, and Other Fanciful Tales. New York, Scribner, 1887. London: Sampson Low, 1888. (Includes "The Griffin and the Minor Canon," "Old Pipes and the Dryad," "The Queen's Museum," "Christmas Before Last," "Prince Hassak's March," "The Battle of the Third Cousins," and "The Banished King.")

Amos Kilbright: His Adscititious Experiences, with Other Stories. New York: Scribner, 1888. London: Unwin, 1888. (Includes "Amos Kilbright" and "The Reversible Landscape.")

The Great War Syndicate. New York: P. F. Collier, 1889. London: Longmans, Green, 1889. (Novel.)

The Clocks of Rondains and Other Stories. New York: Scribner, 1892. London: Sampson Low, 1892. (Includes "The Tricycle of the Future.")

The Watchmaker's Wife and Other Stories. New York: Scribner, 1893. (Includes "My Terminal Moraine," "The Philosophy of Relative Existences," and "The Knife That Killed Po Hancy.")

Fanciful Tales. New York: Scribner, 1894.

A Chosen Few. New York: Scribner, 1895. (Includes "The Transferred Ghost.")

A Story-Teller's Pack. New York: Scribner, 1897. London: Cassell, 1897. (Includes "The Magic Egg," "Love Before Breakfast," "The Bishop's Ghost and the Printer's Baby," and "My Well and What Came Out of It.")

The Great Stone of Sardis. New York and London: Harper, 1898. (Novel.)

Afield and Afloat. New York: Scribner, 1900. London: Cassell, 1901. (Includes "The Governor-General," "Old Applejoy's Ghost," "Struck by a Boomerang," "The Skipper and El Capitan," "The Great Staircase at Landover Hall," "The Ghosts in My Tower," and "A Landsman's Tale.")

John Gayther's Garden, and the Stories Told Therein. New York: Scribner, 1902. London: Cassell, 1903. (A series of connected stories told by John Gayther—including "What I Found in the Sea"—and by the visitors to the garden.)

The Qveen's Mvsevm and Other Fancifvl Tales [sic]. New York: Scribner, 1906. (Includes "The Accommodating Circumstance" and "The Clocks of Rondaine.")

The Magic Egg and Other Stories. New York: Scribner, 1907. (Includes "His Wife's Deceased Sister," "Mr. Tolman," and "Our Archery Club.")

FRANK R. STOCKTON

BIOGRAPHICAL AND CRITICAL STUDIES

Chislett, William, Jr. *Moderns and Near-Moderns: Essays on Henry James, Stockton, Shaw, and Others*. New York: Grafton Press, 1928.

Golemba, Henry L. *Frank R. Stockton*. Boston: G. K. Hall, 1981. (Twayne's United States Authors no. 374. Bibliography included.)

Griffin, Martin I. J. *Frank R. Stockton: A Critical Biography*. Philadelphia: University of Pennsylvania Press, 1939. (Bibliography included.)

Powers, Richard Gid. Introduction to *The Science Fiction of Frank R. Stockton: An Anthology*. Boston: Gregg Press, 1976.

—DIANA WAGGONER

759

MARK TWAIN

1835–1910

I

BEST REMEMBERED FOR his creation of the world of Tom Sawyer and Huck Finn, Mark Twain (Samuel Langhorne Clemens) made use of the fantastic throughout his career. *The Mysterious Stranger* (1916), published posthumously, remains his most famous fantasy. Critics have long suggested that it voices the nihilistic views of Twain's embittered old age. In Austria in 1590 three teen-age boys, including Theodor Fischer (the narrator), befriend a youth, Philip Traum, who exhibits miraculous powers. He can, for example, turn clay figures into living people, and he can arbitrarily kill them. From the first he identifies himself and is accepted as the nephew of the Devil. The plot concerns itself chiefly with the persecution of a priest, Father Peter, and his niece, Marget, whom Traum has helped. The narrative serves as a vehicle for attacks upon humanity's "moral sense" and concludes with the speech in which Traum dismisses mankind, the universe, heaven, and hell as "a grotesque and foolish dream."

In *Mark Twain and Little Satan* (1963), John S. Tuckey introduces evidence that the text of *The Mysterious Stranger, A Romance*, as issued in 1916, is a "literary fraud" (*Mark Twain's "Mysterious Stranger" Manuscripts*, edited by William M. Gibson, 1969). Among the Mark Twain papers at the University of California at Berkeley, Tuckey found three unfinished manuscript versions of the story. Twain had given them the following titles: "The Chronicle of Young Satan," "Schoolhouse Hill," and "No. 44, The Mysterious Stranger." In each of them Twain unsuccessfully attempted to find an effective way to deal with the visit to earth of a youthful Satan, the unfallen nephew of *the* Satan.

Twain incorporated the earliest fragment—nineteen manuscript pages written in September 1897 while he was visiting Vienna—into "Schoolhouse Hill" (1898). In that version Satan, who gives his name as "Quarante-quatre . . . Forty-four," joins Tom and Huck in "Petersburg village" (Hannibal). Since this is the shortest version, one infers that Twain became dissatisfied with the intrusion of the stranger into the idealized world of his boyhood.

"The Chronicle of Young Satan" (it was begun in 1897 and the last half was written in 1900) shifts the scene to the village of Eseldorf in Austria, in 1702. It remains the most important fragment because it provides much of the action of the published text. After Satan plants a cherry seed from which grows a tree bearing varied fruit, he and Theodor go to the court of an Indian rajah, where Satan outwits a magician, placing a diamond within an ivory ball. The narrative ends abruptly. By far the longest version, "No. 44, The Mysterious Stranger," becomes a diffuse tale having little importance except that it concludes with Satan's famous speech.

In 1916, Albert Bigelow Paine, Twain's official biographer and literary executor, and Frederick A. Duneka, an editor at Harper and Brothers, bowdlerized "The Chronicle of Young Satan" and yoked to it the final chapter of "No. 44, The Mysterious Stranger," the speech in which Satan dismisses all life as "a Dream, a grotesque and foolish dream . . . a vagrant Thought . . . wandering forlorn among the empty eternities!"

If one compares "The Chronicle of Young Satan" as printed in Gibson's *"Mysterious Stranger" Manuscripts* with the 1916 text of *The Mysterious Stranger*, one finds the most blatant change to be the substitution of an unnamed astrologer for Father Adolph, taking from him his villainous actions as well as Twain's comments attacking Catholicism. Paine and Duneka removed a lengthy passage dealing, primarily, with the infatuation of several young women with Satan; they excised a sequence involving Satan's kindness to animals and his turning a gamekeeper to stone, and transformed the scene in which a woman is stoned to death for being a papist by a mob led by a Scottish minister. More specifically, from the discussion of the advance of civilization they deleted a paragraph denouncing the Inquisition and much of a passage condemning European imperialism. Ironically, they carefully preserved Satan's most nihilistic actions and speeches.

At the level of word choice, sentence structure, and division of the manuscript into chapters, one finds proof that Paine and Duneka edited the story heavily and arbitrarily. As a result, one cannot accept the text as Twain's work. Indeed, even the widely cited passage praising laughter as man's most "effective weapon" is altered. Nonetheless one should give some attention to what critics have said about it, for their insights throw light on the later fantasies of Twain, gathered primarily in Bernard De Voto's *Letters from the Earth* (1962) and Tuckey's *Mark Twain's "Which Was the Dream?"* (1967).

In 1952, Dixon Wecter referred to the "high celestial irony" in the story, calling its characters "Tom and Huck in medieval dress." He showed an awareness of the unpublished manuscript but accepted the 1916 text. Robert E. Spiller's *Literary His-tory of the United States* suggests that "it achieves a wintry serenity beyond grief," somehow solving "Twain's riddle of grief and self-reproach."

Such a judgment is indebted to De Voto's "The Symbols of Despair," first given as a lecture in 1940 and then included in *Mark Twain at Work* (1942). He outlined the biographical events forcing Twain to walk "the narrow edge between sanity and madness" and gave some description of the Twain papers. (One should recall that he had prepared *Letters from the Earth*, which appeared in 1962, for publication by 1939.) He believed that *The Mysterious Stranger*, as it appeared in 1916, showed that Twain had come "back from the edge of insanity . . . and brought his talent to fruition and made it whole again." Although he was then executor of the papers, he made no mention of Paine's and Duneka's tampering with the texts.

In *Mark Twain: The Development of a Writer* (1962), Henry Nash Smith did make note of the liberties taken by the editors but did not regard the "question [as] critical." In *Mr. Clemens and Mark Twain* (1966), Justin Kaplan acknowledged only that Twain had "survived" his ordeal.

What was his ordeal?

II

The life of Mark Twain is so readily accessible that a brief outline should be sufficient here. Samuel Langhorne Clemens, the son of a small merchant, was born in Florida, Missouri, on 30 November 1835. He grew up in Hannibal, Missouri, along the Mississippi River; he took the pen name Mark Twain from the cry of the rivermen as they took soundings.

After miscellaneous jobs, Clemens became a Mississippi River pilot, served briefly and mysteriously in the Confederate army, and at age twenty-six set out for the West, where he prospected for a short time. He became a journalist and in 1862 was a full reporter on a Virginia City newspaper. In 1864 he moved to San Francisco, where he worked under Bret Harte. He first achieved national renown with "The Celebrated Jumping Frog of Calaveras County" (*New York Saturday Press*, 18 November 1865), which was included in his first book. His fame continued to grow, and his second book, *The Innocents Abroad* (1869), was a best-seller.

This was followed by a succession of major works that included *The Adventures of Tom Sawyer* (1876), *Life on the Mississippi* (1883), *The Adventures of Huckleberry Finn* (1885), and others. He traveled extensively and was widely lionized in Europe and the United States. In his last years he settled in the East; he died in Redding, Connecticut, on 21 April 1910. Although he had achieved renown as a humorist, the work of his last years, fragmentary and mostly unpublished during his lifetime, reveals depths of pessimism and despair.

Scholars have found the genesis of Twain's late fiction in his personal catastrophes, which arose primarily from his business ventures. In 1880 he invested an initial $5,000 in the automatic typesetting machine invented by James W. Paige and developed at the Colt arms factory in Hartford. By February 1886 he had organized a company to perfect the typesetter, manufacture it, and market it throughout the world. In 1884 he had set up his nephew as Charles L. Webster and Company to act as his publisher. The two-volume *Personal Memoirs of U. S. Grant*—which he had undertaken, at least in part, to rescue Grant from bankruptcy—became a bonanza. So certain was Twain of his business success that he thought *A Connecticut Yankee in King Arthur's Court* (1889) would mark his permanent retirement from literature.

In August 1890 he signed a contract drawn up by Paige allowing him to buy out the inventor for $250,000. At that time he gained the backing of John Percival Jones, the millionaire senator from Nevada, who took a six-month option on the typesetter. In February 1891 the consortium that Jones represented refused to pick up the option. Twain was disconcerted. Neither had the publishing firm flourished. Webster had sold his interest to Frederick J. Hall. In 1890, Twain's wife, Livy, lent $10,000 of her money to the firm, while Hall borrowed from friends. The financial pressures grew so heavy that, in June 1891, Twain and his family sailed to Europe, giving up their Hartford home and Nook Farm. Twain's rheumatism had grown worse; Livy entered a long period of invalidism because of her hyperthyroid heart disease.

On 18 April 1894, Twain entered voluntary bankruptcy proceedings, with $100,000 in debts. Henry Huttleston Rogers, a power in the Standard Oil trust, became his financial adviser. Together with Livy, he counseled Twain to pledge himself publicly to repay every cent of his debt. To help do so, Twain undertook a yearlong round-the-world lecture tour beginning in July 1895. A year later he sailed from South Africa to England. Alone in Guildford, Surrey, on 18 August 1896, he learned that his beloved daughter Susy had died of meningitis in Hartford. Her death crystallized a nightmare anguish in him that never dissipated.

Yet, however traumatic such experiences, the qualities of mind and heart that caused Twain to react so intensely had gained expression as early as *Roughing It* (1872). Gazing at the volcano Haleakala on Maui, he "felt like the last Man, neglected of the judgment, and left pinnacled in mid-heaven, a forgotten relic of a vanished world."

One has only to turn to his *Notebooks* (1935) or the *Mark Twain–Howells Letters* (1960) to discover the despair that the concept of determinism caused him. It contributed, at least in part, to *What Is Man?*, published anonymously in 1906. Undoubtedly the impact of determinism could only intensify and, perhaps, distort the "incurably Calvinist mind" that he had inherited from his mother.

As early as "The Facts Concerning the Recent Carnival of Crime in Connecticut" (1876)—the tone of which borders on the burlesque—he dramatized a basic conflict within him that led to the young Satan and medieval Austria. The first-person narrator (a thin mask for Twain) anticipates a visit from his Aunt Mary: "my boyhood's idol; maturity, which is fatal to so many enchantments, had not been able to dislodge her from her pedestal." Only her nagging about his smoking could "stir my torpid conscience," but "a happy day came at last" when even her exhortations no longer affected him. As he admits this, he meets at his door "a shriveled, shabby dwarf"; he sees in "this vile bit of human rubbish" a grotesque caricature of himself, one who begins to berate him by enumerating his past thoughtless deeds. Interrupting the pygmy, the narrator accuses him of being Satan. The visitor identifies himself as the narrator's "Conscience," whose "business . . . and joy [are] to make you repent of *every*thing you do." Significantly, he reveals that human consciences are "merely disinterested agents."

Cursing and vowing vengeance, the narrator tries to seize the shrunken figure, but so lightweight is his conscience that the manikin "darts aloft" to avoid him. He throws anything within reach at the dwarf. Only when Aunt Mary arrives and begins "to abuse [him] a little" for recent misdeeds does his conscience grow heavy and tumble to the floor, where, because of the nature of the narrator's reaction to Mary, it falls asleep. As Mary stands "petrified with fear," the narrator seizes his "lifelong enemy" and strangles it. Announcing that he is now "a man WITHOUT A CONSCIENCE," he drives Mary from the house. In his "joy," he allows her to flee, although he could "throttle" her without remorse. "Since that day my life is all bliss," explains the narrator; during the first two weeks he killed thirty-eight persons "on account of ancient grudges," burned a house that "interrupted" his view, swindled a widow and some orphans, and now offers to medical colleges seeking cadavers the "assorted tramps" in his cellar. In *The Art of Mark Twain* (1976), Gibson describes the story as a struggle between ego and superego, while Kaplan notes that the tale explores "the roots of his black depressions."

That dark imagination led to "The Five Boons of Life" (1902)—the greatest of which is death—and to "Was It Heaven? Or Hell?" (1902), a kind of moralistic "The Lady, or the Tiger?" In the latter an angel of the Lord appears to the righteous, elderly sisters who have deliberately lied to their dying sister so that she will not suffer the knowledge that her daughter has already died of typhoid fever. They readily acknowledge their guilt and wait for the divine judgment of their lies. Returning, the angel whispers the verdict so that the reader can only guess.

Whatever else may be said of this group of works, it represents Twain's continuing distress regarding orthodox religion and includes such titles as *Eve's Diary* (1906), *Letters from the Earth*, and *Extract from Captain Stormfield's Visit to Heaven* (1909). Neither should one forget that in the 1890's, Twain

called *Huckleberry Finn* the "collision" between a "sound heart" and a "deformed conscience" in which conscience lost.

Tom Sawyer Abroad (1894), published in the midst of his financial collapse, adapted familiar materials into a balloon voyage echoing Jules Verne. *Tom Sawyer, Detective* (1896) attempted to cash in on the popularity of Arthur Conan Doyle's Sherlock Holmes. The earlier fragment *Huck Finn and Tom Sawyer Among the Indians* (1968; book form, 1969) faltered through reworked incidents and ended abruptly amid the sexual implications of Peggy's capture. In short, after 1885, with the exception of *Pudd'nhead Wilson* (1894)—so different from the earlier works—Twain did not achieve thematically or aesthetically a successful statement in fiction through the use of the world of Hannibal.

As early as "A Curious Dream" (1870), he had dealt with the supernatural. In this instance his tone recalls the broad humor of the tall tale, for the first-person narrator encounters a procession of skeletons carrying their coffins down a village street. One of them pauses and in a gossipy manner explains that such emigrations occur when descendants neglect old graveyards. But Twain has spoiled the fun with a giveaway title and opens with the assertion that this was, indeed, a dream; the narrator awakens at its end.

In "A Ghost Story" (1888), the first-person narrator is awakened by the ghost of the Cardiff Giant, who learns that he has been duped ("sold") into haunting a New York City museum that exhibits not his body but a plaster cast of it. He leaves, highly embarrassed. The most significant detail is incidental; early in the narrative the narrator tries to dismiss the incident as "a dream—a hideous dream."

Such a dream becomes a crucial element in *A Connecticut Yankee in King Arthur's Court*, in which Hank Morgan, master mechanic and superintendent of the Colt arms factory in Hartford, brings nineteenth-century enlightenment to sixth-century Britain. Its thematic complexities need not be dealt with here. In the prefatory "A Word of Explanation," Twain himself encounters in Warwick Castle a "curious stranger" who asks, "You know about transmigration of souls; do you know about transpositions of epochs—and bodies?" The stranger,

Hank Morgan, begins his story by saying that after he was knocked unconscious, he awoke near Camelot. Then he gives Twain a manuscript—perhaps the most often used narrative convention to establish the credibility of fantasy in the nineteenth century—outlining his adventures. Morgan, "the Boss," slaughters 25,000 knights with his gatling guns at the Battle of the Sand Belt, but he is wounded. His "boys" carry him to a cave where Merlin, his archrival, employs magic to keep Morgan asleep for thirteen centuries.

In a final note by Twain, Morgan dies, mumbling confusedly about "strange and awful dreams.... Dreams that were as real as reality." Thinking himself in the presence of Sandy, his wife in Camelot, he begs her not to leave him; delirious, he speaks ambivalently of reality. His life in Camelot seems a dream, yet it is more real to him than the "remote unborn" nineteenth century. He pleads, "Don't let me go out of my mind again; death is nothing, let it come, but not . . . the torture of those hideous dreams."

Such hideous dreams become the narrative frame for several stories included in *Which Was the Dream?* The plot centers upon the misfortunes of a man who has known great success. Although Twain planned *Which Was the Dream?* in 1895, he did not begin writing it until the spring of 1897, a few days after completing *Following the Equator* (1897). Alison, the rich wife of Major General Thomas X, explains that he has finally undertaken a biographical sketch "for the children to have when we are gone." It is a gala night: she and her daughters entertain Washington society at the first dress rehearsal of a play written by the precocious Bessie that will be given at her eighth birthday party on 19 March (the date of Susy's birthday). Alison notices the general doze momentarily over his cigar and then resume writing.

Thomas now becomes the narrator. His career has fallen short of the presidency only because of his youth (he is thirty-four, Twain's age when *The Innocents Abroad* succeeded and he married Livy). Using materials reminiscent of *Tom Sawyer*, the narrator dwells upon his first idyllic childhood meeting with Alison. Then, as he praises Bessie, screams interrupt him. The house is on fire. Lieu-

tenant Grant, who had served under the general briefly during the Mexican War, averts tragedy by directing the exit of the women and children.

The destruction of the house (Kaplan calls the fire Twain's "metaphor for Susy's death") uncovers disaster. To escape the onerous details of business life, the general has trusted his secretary, Jeff Sedgwick, giving him power of attorney. In a sense Sedgwick is his double (Twain's theme of disguise and confused identity); for example, he writes and signs letters in a hand that duplicates the general's. From his bankers Thomas learns that Sedgwick has systematically robbed him: lapsed insurance policies, overdrawn accounts, and the investment of Alison's money in a nonexistent California mine (the Golden Fleece). When the bankers accuse Thomas of forgery, he collapses. He regains consciousness in a log cabin near the town of Hell's Delight in California. For eighteen months he has lain in a coma. Alison has worked to support him; his friends have remained true.

Twain broke off the narrative in August 1897, the first anniversary of Susy's death. One infers that Twain drew upon autobiographical detail and the career of Grant until he became so emotionally involved that he could not continue the story as he had planned in his original notes.

In his second "dream-of-disaster story," to use Tuckey's phrase, Twain sought to gain a necessary distancing by shifting to the Mississippi Valley seventy years earlier for his setting. A brief manuscript, "Indiantown" (1899), establishes the characters who figure in the unfinished and unpublished novel "Which Was It?," begun in 1899 but written chiefly between 1900 and 1902. The wife's introduction duplicates the earlier effort, except that she plans to bring her manuscript to her husband, George Harrison, after the children's party is over. He begins his narrative abruptly fifteen years later, announcing that the fire destroyed the house and killed his wife and children on the night of the party. To protect his aged father and to save the family name and estate, Harrison commits murder and remains silent when Squire Fairfax is accused of the crime. The convoluted plot does not make a brief summary feasible.

Several points do merit attention. Harrison is

guilt-ridden because disasters result from his false pride. Squire Fairfax realizes that Harrison's father is senile and thus cancels the note payable on twenty-four-hours' demand, sending it to Harrison. Because he does not receive the note, Harrison accidentally commits murder. One might speak of the early chapters in terms of a conflict between the intentions of a good heart and the brutality of chance. Twain broke off the diffuse narrative before revealing that Harrison dreams everything within minutes, that his wife and daughters come to him, and that the dream experience ages him fifteen years in a brief interval.

Although Twain employed the same framing device in "The Great Dark," his most complete exposition of his concept of the dream life occurs in "My Platonic Sweetheart," rejected by *Harper's* in 1898 but published by the magazine in December 1912. Always concerned with the concept of multiple personalities, he became fascinated with the work in hypnosis then being done by the French. He wrote of the conscious self and the dream self, which at times became blurred in his imagination.

More a personal essay than a story, "My Platonic Sweetheart" opens in a Missouri town where the seventeen-year-old Twain meets a girl of fifteen. They know one another; he kisses her. Abruptly he awakens in Philadelphia. Ten years later, they meet in a magnolia garden near Natchez, and he carries her in his arms to a plantation house. Later his dream that his first public lecture in San Francisco failed dissolves into a scene in which he is with the girl near Haleakala on Maui. She says that she lived there when Hawaii was a continent and the volcano active; she speaks of traveling "in the stars a good deal." They meet an old Kanaka who has invented a gun that uses powder and has a percussion lock but shoots arrows. He fires one high into the air; it kills the girl. She dies in Twain's arms. He awakens while crossing Bond Street in New York during a seemingly uninterrupted conversation. That night, after making notes of his dream, as he always does, he dreams of being with her in Athens.

Awakening again in New York, Twain insists that "in our dreams—I know it!—we do make the journeys . . . we do see the things . . . ; they are the living spirits, not shadows; and they are immortal and indestructible." Just a week before he had seen her in India—Bombay was in sight, as were Windsor Castle and the Thames. Earlier he had mentioned "the two or three persons inhabiting us" and the "dream-artist who resides in us." After denouncing "the unreal life which is ours when we go about awake and clothed with our artificial selves in this vague and dull-tinted world," he concludes that "when we die we shall slough off this cheap intellect, perhaps, and go abroad into Dreamland clothed in our true selves." Anguish has given way to uncertain longing.

Before turning to "The Great Dark," one must examine the second group of fantasies contributing to it. The earliest of the nightmare voyages, discarded from *Following the Equator*, is "The Enchanted Sea-Wilderness," written late in 1896. Not only does it echo his impressions of his Pacific journey, but it also illustrates his use of two of the most popular elements of nineteenth-century fantasy: the barren wastes of the Antarctic Ocean and an adaptation of a becalmed area like the Sargasso Sea. It incorporates a brief, still-earlier fragment, "A Passenger's Story," in which a St. Bernard dog awakens the crew during a fire at sea just before flames reach powder kegs. Against the wishes of his men, the captain chains the dog aboard the burning ship before he and the crew abandon it. As a kind of divine retribution, in "The Enchanted Sea-Wilderness" the captain's boat is seized by the storm-shrouded "Devil's Race-Track," somewhere between the Cape of Good Hope and the South Pole. It is swept by concentric currents into the becalmed center, which is called the "Everlasting Sunday," where the crew finds derelict ships dating back to 1740. These are manned by shriveled mummies, in whom the crew foresees its own fate. The narrative breaks off in the midst of a description of a British man-of-war.

Another manuscript, "An Adventure in Remote Seas," dating from the spring of 1898, takes the crew of a sealing expedition through terrible snowstorms into the empty ocean somewhere southwest of Cape Horn. On an island no larger than a "little patch of rock," the crew finds a hut abandoned for at least a generation. A discussion of the intrinsic value of gold intrudes into the narrative, before the first-person narrator and a companion discover gold coins in a cave. They fight for possession of them but are separated. Within four days the crew accumulates $60 million in gold coins. Momentarily the narrator imagines that he has only dreamed that the gold exists. In the interim a storm has driven their ship from the island. They realize that they are marooned, for there is little or no chance that the mate can find the island again. The fragment ends with the image of the captain counting the gold.

Twain had not given a title to the manuscript that De Voto named "The Great Dark" when he included it in *Letters from the Earth*. Written in the autumn of 1898, it combines the dream motif and the voyage. Mrs. Edwards, the protagonist's wife, repeats the framing device that Twain had used earlier. But there is no fire. Instead, Edwards takes his daughters to the master bedroom to show them the grandest present of all, a microscope. He instructs his wife to strengthen the drop of water beneath the lens "with the merest touch of Scotch whisky [to] stir up the animals."

Perturbed by his thoughts, especially the idea of a microscopic world "unknown, uncharted, unexplored by man," Edwards throws himself onto his sofa. Immediately the Superintendent of Dreams appears to arrange for a ship and crew. Edwards finds himself and his family aboard a whaler. Such familiar landmarks as Sable Island, the Gulf Stream, and Greenland vanish; no one knows where the ship is or whither it is bound. In short, although the materials are familiar, Twain has found a way to give a distancing to his nightmare.

From his notes, one knows that he intended to maintain a humorous tone throughout much of the tale. He burlesques the work of the popular writer W. Clark Russell through the use of comic sea language, a device he had employed as early as the 1860's. He brings the Superintendent of Dreams aboard—invisible to all but Edwards—for a comic scene in which the Superintendent empties the coffee cups of the mate Turner. But the Superintendent's task is chiefly expository. When Edwards wants the dream ended, the Superintendent asks whether or not Edwards is certain that the voyage is the dream.

Mrs. Edwards reinforces this dilemma when she cannot recall such details from their former lives as a voyage to Europe. She suggests that they have been aboard the ship "always, for all I know"—at least since her father's death from heatstroke and her mother's suicide the same day.

Early in the second part of the story, Edwards asserts that the crew has mutinied several times during the past four years. By now his wife and children do recall details from their former lives, so that for "amusement" they draw upon memories of both lives. A "colossal squid," blinded by gatling guns, follows and attacks the ship. For a time the Edwardses fear that it has taken the children. When the ship is becalmed, the crew threatens to mutiny. Consciously or unconsciously, Twain undercut the captain's speech to the crew. Edwards praises the captain's strength of character, but he also announces that although they have private theatricals, concerts, and "the other usual time-passers," he does not want to miss the captain's speech.

After the captain asks the crew if they are "rational men, manly men . . . men made in the Image of God," he admits that he does not know where the ship is. He concludes: "If it is God's will that we pull through, we pull through—otherwise not. We haven't had an observation for four months, but we are going ahead, and do our best to fetch up somewhere."

The manuscript breaks off. One need not elaborately summarize the notes indicating that Twain intended a tragic ending. In the light beneath the lens, the sea was to dry up; the children were to die. Most important, Edwards would wake at home with his wife and children. But he would believe that they are the dreams and that the voyage was the reality.

Tuckey believes the captain made an "Odyssean speech"; he judges that the end, "as written, expresses strength and hope, rather than futility and despair." Certainly Twain scholars and readers would wish that he had reached some reconciliation in order to escape the anguish of the 1890's. The evidence of "My Platonic Sweetheart," for example, denies such a reconciliation. Instead, "The Great Dark" becomes a metaphor of stoic endurance, a classic fantasy of the period that grew out of the anguished reaction to the concept of determinism that marked Twain and many of his contemporaries.

Selected Bibliography

WORKS OF MARK TWAIN

"My Platonic Sweetheart." *Harper's Magazine*, 126 (December 1912): 14–20.

The Mysterious Stranger, A Romance. New York: Harper, 1916.

Mark Twain-Howells Letters. Edited by Henry Nash Smith and William M. Gibson. 2 vols. Cambridge, Mass.: Harvard University Press, 1960.

Letters from the Earth. Edited by Bernard De Voto. New York: Harper and Row, 1962.

Mark Twain's "Which Was the Dream?" Edited by John S. Tuckey. Berkeley and Los Angeles: University of California Press, 1967.

Mark Twain's "Mysterious Stranger" Manuscripts. Edited by William M. Gibson. Berkeley and Los Angeles: University of California Press, 1969.

The Devil's Race-Track. Edited by John S. Tuckey. Berkeley and Los Angeles: University of California Press, 1980.

CRITICAL AND BIOGRAPHICAL STUDIES

De Voto, Bernard. *Mark Twain at Work.* Cambridge, Mass.: Harvard University Press, 1942.

Gibson, William M. *The Art of Mark Twain.* New York: Oxford University Press, 1976.

Hill, Hamlin. *Mark Twain: God's Fool.* New York: Harper and Row, 1973.

Kaplan, Justin. *Mr. Clemens and Mark Twain: A Biography.* New York: Simon and Schuster, 1966.

Smith, Henry Nash. *Mark Twain: The Development of a Writer.* Cambridge, Mass.: Harvard University Press, 1962.

Tuckey, John S. *Mark Twain and Little Satan.* West Lafayette, Ind.: Purdue University Studies, 1963.

—THOMAS D. CLARESON

MARY WILKINS FREEMAN

1852-1930

MARY ELEANOR WILKINS was born on 31 October 1852 in Randolph, Massachusetts, a few miles south of Boston. Her father, a carpenter, was unable to make a decent living there, so he moved his family to Brattleboro, Vermont, when the girl was fifteen. She graduated from Brattleboro High School in 1870 and attended Mount Holyoke Female Seminary for a year. A bookish girl, she lived at home as a spinster daughter, teaching a bit, indulging a passion for art, and writing children's literature with some success. Her first books, published in 1883 and 1884, were collections of verse and short stories for children.

Her first short story for adults, "Two Old Lovers," was rejected by several magazines before being published by *Harper's Bazar* in 1883. In a literary career that spanned more than forty years, she published more than two hundred short stories in the leading magazines of the time and brought many of them together in eighteen story collections. She also wrote fifteen novels, a play, and a variety of nonfictional works. Respectful reviews and criticisms appeared, and she was regarded as one of the leading writers of the period.

In 1902, when she was fifty, Miss Wilkins married Dr. Charles Freeman; and they lived thereafter in Metuchen, New Jersey. The marriage was unhappy; her husband, an alcoholic, spent time in sanitariums and, in 1920, was committed to a state hospital for the insane. In 1926, Mrs. Freeman's long and distinguished literary career was given recogni-

tion by the award of the William Dean Howells Gold Medal for fiction and by election to membership in the National Institute of Arts and Letters. A well-chosen selection of her short fiction appeared in 1927. After several years of declining health and heart trouble, she died in Metuchen on 13 March 1930.

Almost from the first, Freeman's writings were recognized as an important part of the American literary scene. A review of *A New England Nun and Other Stories*, appearing in the *Atlantic Monthly* in June 1891, pointed out clearly the qualities that readers and critics prized in her fiction:

> . . . Miss Wilkins depends for her effects upon the simple pathos or humor which resides in the persons and situations that are made known through a few strong, direct disclosures. The style is here the writer. The short, economical sentences, with no waste and no niggardliness, make up stories which are singularly pointed, because the writer spends her entire strength upon the production of a single impression. . . . Now and then she touches a very deep nature, and opens to view a secret of the human heart. . . .

Behind such a critique is the recognition that the surface simplicity of the work, in its linear plotting, its clear prose style, and its straightforward delineation of character, leaves the critic little to say. As a result, critical opinion during the rest of her career, and even up to the present, offers little more than was said in 1891. Although books and articles about her contemporaries appeared regularly, her own work was not carefully scrutinized. Edward Foster's dissertation (Harvard, 1935), published in 1956, is brief and lacks important information, but it remains the indispensable biography. No collection of her letters has been published. Her books, long out of print, are hard to find. Some stories lie, unreprinted, in the magazines in which they first appeared. Perry Westbrook's critical study (1967) offers only a brief listing of secondary critical materials. In the years since Westbrook, however, it is heartening to observe that there have been articles that carefully examine some of Freeman's stories and various aspects of her career—and a number of promising dissertations have been completed.

Most of Freeman's work is realistic local-color fiction. Realism, the literary movement that took as its credo the portrayal of ordinary lives and commonplace events, had flourished in Europe since the 1830's but did not become a dominant literary mode in America until after the Civil War. The enormous expansion of the United States after 1865 made it inevitable that readers would be curious about their land and its inhabitants.

Local color was an important expression of the realist aesthetic, an attempt to depict the distinctive natural and social features of small, self-enclosed regions with their farms, villages, and towns. Loving care was taken in the description of each setting, in expressing the language of each place in its dialectal richness, and in portraying the individualism and stubborn identity of character formed by locale.

Each region had its chronicler: Sarah Orne Jewett wrote of Maine, Alice Brown of New Hampshire, Rose Terry Cook of Connecticut, Philander Deming of the Adirondack region of New York, Charles Egbert Craddock of the Tennessee mountains, George Washington Cable of Creole Louisiana, and Mark Twain of the village life of eastern Missouri in *The Adventures of Huckleberry Finn.*

Freeman's stories concern themselves with the lives of poor rural people of the parts of Vermont and Massachusetts that she knew best. A typical and famous example of her quiet art is the much reprinted story "The Revolt of 'Mother.'" An aging couple is in conflict over the building of another barn on its farm; the husband has gone back on his promise to replace the inadequate house he and his wife have lived in for years, bringing up a family, uncomfortably making do, and sacrificing to better the farm. The wife protests in vain, for the husband is obsessed with further costly improvements on his beloved farm. The new barn completed, the husband goes away for a few days to buy livestock, and "Mother" demonstrates the strength of her revolt by moving furniture and family into the new barn. Expecting anger and resistance from the father, the family is surprised at his reaction of acceptance and remorse.

The story is an exemplary model of Freeman's best work. Feelings run strong, but they are noticed below an apparently unruffled surface and are depicted in an understated way. Action is decisive but never violent; character is manifested in a few words and deeds. Here, the author is writing within the developing tradition of the American short story. The unity of effect, achieved without wasted motion, that Edgar Allan Poe urged in his criticism and practice, deeply affected the writers who followed him. Everything aims toward the strong, clearly etched situation and conclusion; anything that does not contribute to the inevitable movement of the tale toward that conclusion is rigorously excised. Each story that is successful has a perfection of form and makes its point with concision and clarity.

An extraordinary number of Freeman's many short stories achieve this economy of effect; among these may be cited "A New England Nun," "A Humble Romance," "The Apple-Tree," "A Village Singer," "Two Old Lovers," and "Gentian." All bear the marks of a careful and orderly art, practiced vigorously, aimed toward a clearly discernible goal. Sometimes they express a biting irony in gentle and unobtrusive language. With room in her subjects for satire, Freeman does not often use it but consciously restricts herself to comedy and sympathetic portrayal.

Although her best work is to be found in the short stories, at least two of Freeman's novels are outstanding. In *Pembroke* (1894) she portrays, as she says, "a study of the human will in several New England characters, in different phases of disease and abnormal development." A planned marriage is broken up because of an argument over politics; stubbornly, neither party attempts to marry someone else. Taking an episode from her own family's history, Freeman elaborates the story into a carefully planned depiction of willfulness and perversity. In *The Portion of Labor* (1901), she offers a study of poverty and revolt in a New England mill town, painting a large gallery of character types, from mill owners to workers and strikers. The cumulative power of the novel comes from its accurate description of the depressing setting.

Against the imposing bulk of her realistic fiction, Freeman's supernatural stories make a slender showing. There are only eleven stories assembled in *Collected Ghost Stories* (1974), and they have received a mixed reception. Foster gives them only a brief paragraph in his book, concluding that Freeman "does nothing fresh or interesting with this sub-literary genre." Westbrook is even more impatient, disposing of the stories in a short paragraph as "deficient in suspense and atmosphere" and "without merit." On the other hand, the brief but shrewd comments of H. P. Lovecraft in *Supernatural Horror in Literature* offer a sensible tribute to Freeman's art and make one wish that he had done more analysis of her work. Plainly, Freeman thought well of her ghost stories, for she collected six of them in one volume, *The Wind in the Rose-Bush and Other Stories of the Supernatural* (1903). Her other ghostly tales were scattered about in several short story collections.

In some of the tales, the influence of past evils manifests itself in the actions of her supernatural figures. The story of "The Vacant Lot" illustrates this theme. The descendants of the Townsend family, noted for its ancestral brutishness, move to Boston, where they are lucky to find an excellent house for a fraction of its actual value. The empty lot next door becomes the scene of disturbing events. The family can see the shadow of a woman hanging up wash but cannot see the figure casting the shadow. At night, lights appear in the lot, marking the windows of a house that must have long since been destroyed. In the Townsend house, loud crashes break all the mirrors and a crepe veil moves of its own volition. The family is unhurt but is shaken enough to move from its uncanny residence. It is innocent of wrongdoing, but a clue to events is offered by the quotation of a line from Psalm 51: "Behold, I was shapen in iniquity, and in sin did my mother conceive me." It must suffer for the sins of its cruel and murderous ancestors.

In "The Southwest Chamber," a room is possessed by the spirit of a dead occupant. Amanda and Sophia Gill have inherited the home of their Aunt Harriet by default, for the aunt hated their mother and did not make a will. This hatred is manifested only within the bedroom in which the old woman died. The spirit attempts to strangle a stubborn roomer who wants to take possession of the room for herself. A well-meaning minister who would exorcise the spirit is prevented from entering the room. The ghost is finally able to impose her own feelings on Sophia and, in a burst of power, to show her face in the bedroom mirror.

These tales deal with fairly familiar subjects, as do a number of other stories. In "The Shadows on the Wall," the elements of supernatural revenge are anticipated and rather too easily detected by the reader. In "The Wind in the Rose-Bush," a supernatural attempt at communication is made, as the ghost of a girl who was abused and allowed to die tries to make contact with the good-hearted aunt who, unaware of her death, has come to fetch her to a comfortable home. It can be argued that Freeman has not sufficiently worked out her subjects here, although the stories are sturdy and capable of offering supernatural fears. At times the language is a bit strained, and the reader is told that the characters are horrified. These criticisms acknowledged, however, the tales still establish their limited but legitimate area in supernatural horror.

At least two of Freeman's stories are unusual. A striking and subtle example of the vampire story that transcends the type is "Luella Miller," for Luella's vampirism consists, in part, of influencing people to look after her and make up for her practical incompetence by working themselves to death for her benefit. When Luella is engaged to teach at the district school, a girl does most of the work until she wastes away and dies. Erastus Miller marries Luella, but he dies within a year, consumptive and feeble from all he does for her. Lily Miller, his sister, then takes on the job of caring for Luella and changes quickly from a robust woman to a wan and feeble helpmate; as she is dying, she expresses anxiety about leaving Luella without help.

There are successive deaths: a friend, a servant girl, the doctor who wants to marry Luella and care for her, and another kindly woman who wants to help. When Luella herself dies, Lydia Anderson, the narrator of the tale, sees a strange sight—Luella's spirit leaving her house surrounded by the ghosts of all the friends and relatives who aided her in life, still helping her after death. Luella is a somewhat new figure in horror fiction; unlike the demonic bloodsucker of vampire stories, she is a mild-mannered, complaining, clinging-vine sort of personality. But she is hardly less fearsome for this bland guise.

Another story, "The Hall Bedroom," upsets the usual expectations of the supernatural. When the reader encounters the frame narrative, with its tale of people living in a certain room of a boardinghouse and then disappearing, anticipations of a tale of horror are aroused. Foul play is hinted, and it seems possible that murders have been committed. At the end of the story, as the frame narrative is completed, a hidden room is found behind the hall bedroom; a paper discovered there hints vaguely at connections with the "fifth dimension," and the uneasy landlady who tells the frame story decides to sell the boardinghouse and move away.

But this frame narrative is only a small portion of the entire tale, and it is contradicted by the long middle section of the story, given in the form of a journal kept by George Wheatcroft, the most recent occupant of the room to disappear. Wheatcroft is observant, and the story he tells is strange but not entirely fearsome. An oil painting of a landscape, mounted in the room, draws him by degrees into the scene it portrays. Moving about the room in darkness, he senses that he is in open country; but a light flashed by a neighbor returns him to the comfortable world of his room. In subsequent experiences in the dark room, he smells roses and tastes something strange but not unpleasant. The expansive response of his senses brings him more and more into the other dimension. He hears sounds, his fingers encounter strange carvings, he feels the wind on his face, and other hands touch his. The final interrupted entry reveals that he has seen this other world, which is beautiful and not horrible; and so he disappears into it.

For Freeman, the story is experimental and different; it offers a hint of directions that she might have explored had she chosen to continue her work with the supernatural tale. It is clear that she had a talent for the exposition of the ghostly, and one regrets that she chose to exercise that talent so infrequently.

Selected Bibliography

WORKS OF MARY WILKINS FREEMAN

A Humble Romance and Other Stories. New York: Harper, 1887. Edinburgh: David Douglas, 1891.

A New England Nun and Other Stories. New York: Harper, 1891. London: Osgood, 1891.

Pembroke, a Novel. New York: Harper, 1894. London: Osgood, McIlvaine, 1894.

Silence and Other Stories. London and New York: Harper, 1898.

The Portion of Labor. London and New York: Harper, 1901. (Novel.)

The Wind in the Rose-Bush and Other Stories of the Supernatural. New York: Doubleday, Page, 1903. London: John Murray, 1903.

The Best Stories of Mary E. Wilkins. Introduction by Henry W. Lanier. New York: Harper, 1927.

Collected Ghost Stories. Introduction by Edward Wagenknecht. Sauk City, Wis.: Arkham House, 1974.

CRITICAL AND BIOGRAPHICAL STUDIES

Foster, Edward. *Mary E. Wilkins Freeman*. New York: Hendricks House, 1956. (Contains bibliographical material.)

Hamblen, Abigail Ann. *The New England Art of Mary E. Wilkins Freeman*. Amherst, Mass.: Green Knight Press, 1966.

Hirsch, David H. "Subdued Meaning in 'A New England Nun.'" *Studies in Short Fiction*, 2 (1965): 124–136.

Knipp, Thomas R. "The Quest for Form: The Fiction of Mary E. Wilkins Freeman." Ph.D. diss., Michigan State University, 1967.

McElrath, Joseph R., Jr. "The Artistry of Mary Wilkins Freeman's 'The Revolt.'" *Studies in Short Fiction*, 17 (1980): 255–261.

More, Paul Elmer. "Hawthorne: Looking Before and After." In *The Shelburne Essays.* 2nd ser. Boston: Houghton, Mifflin, 1905.

Pattee, Fred Lewis. *Sidelights on American Literature.* New York: Century, 1922.

Thompson, Charles M. "Miss Wilkins: An Idealist in Masquerade." *Atlantic Monthly*, 83 (May 1899): 665–675.

Westbrook, Perry D. *Acres of Flint: Writers of Rural New England 1870–1900.* Washington, D.C.: Scarecrow Press, 1951.

———. *Mary Wilkins Freeman.* New York: Twayne, 1967.

BIBLIOGRAPHY

Westbrook, Perry D. "Mary E. Wilkins Freeman (1852–1930)." *American Literary Realism*, 2 (1969): 139–142.

—DOUGLAS ROBILLARD

XII

American Mainstream Writers
of the Early to Middle
Twentieth Century

GERTRUDE ATHERTON

1857-1948

I

GERTRUDE ATHERTON ENJOYED popularity from her first contributions to the *Argonaut* in 1883. From then until 1946 she published thirty-seven novels, five volumes of short stories, three separate collections of essays, a fictionalized biography of Alexander Hamilton and a selection of his letters, magazine fiction, an autobiography, a history of California, and two books about San Francisco. At the height of her popularity her novel *Black Oxen* (1923) succeeded Sinclair Lewis' *Babbitt* (1922) in first position on the best-seller list.

Gertrude Franklin Horn was born in San Francisco on 30 October 1857 to wealthy parents. She was privately educated, and traveled and lived abroad a great deal. She was married to George H. Atherton and used her married name in her writing. Although she was a reasonably popular author, she suffered from critical neglect, and it was not until near the end of her long life that she was honored with a doctorate of literature from Mills College in 1935 and with a doctorate of law from the University of California at Berkeley in 1937. She was awarded membership in the National Institute of Arts and Letters in 1938. In 1943 she became the first author to contribute manuscripts and memorabilia to the Library of Congress.

As a contemporary of both Henry James and Sinclair Lewis, she shared many of their themes and considerations, even though her work is often classified as regional Californian. She wrote about a mobile life-style that became common in the United States, particularly in her native California, after World War II. She was greatly interested in the interaction and conflict of people from more removed or less sophisticated areas (like California) with people of more cosmopolitan areas (like New York or Europe).

Atherton wrote largely about the "modern" woman, who wanted to be treated as the intellectual and political equal of men. She did not present the social differences between men and women didactically but, rather, rendered the inequities and their results (which were at times lamentable, as in "A Monarch of a Small Survey") as individual tragedies arising from accepted social prejudice. Her women tend to have more worldly experience than most heroines of her time. She sometimes used the mechanisms of marriage and divorce to move her women characters through society, a technique for which she was sometimes criticized. Her supernatural fiction does not stress these aspects of her mainstream fiction, although her attitudes and concerns are evident.

II

Atherton's standing as a writer of supernatural fiction is based on five stories. Four of them were collected in *The Bell in the Fog* (1905); the fifth appeared in *The Foghorn* (1934). They derive in part from a belief in the harmony between the individual and the spiritual and natural worlds, a point of view well set forth by Ralph Waldo Emerson in his essay "Nature":

Man carries the world in his head, the whole astronomy and chemistry suspended in a thought. Because the history of nature is charactered in his brain, therefore is he the prophet and discoverer of her secrets. . . . But it also appears that our actions are seconded and disposed to great conclutions than we designed. We are escorted on every hand through life by spiritual agents. . . . And the knowledge that we traverse the whole world of being, from the centre to the poles of nature, and have some stake in every possibility, lends that sublime lustre to death.

Atherton's supernatural stories often are concerned with the results of disrupting this harmony. Technically, she heightens the tension and impact of her work by "reporting" incidents that combine several elements of the supernatural without explaining the events. This ambiguity leaves the reader with a sense of the world out of natural order.

Five tales in *The Bell in the Fog* are mainstream stories based on psychological conflict. They are similar in manner, suggesting that the author viewed them as members of a single type: the clash between social morals and spiritual morals. The four supernatural stories, some reprinted from earlier sources, are "The Bell in the Fog," "The Striding Place," "The Dead and the Countess," and "Death and the Woman."

"The Bell in the Fog" tells the story of an American writer, Ralph Orth, who purchases a country seat in England. Atherton invokes ambiguity by never allowing the reader to know more than Orth knows. She introduces three related possibilities for the events that befall him: spiritualism, psychical phenomena, and reincarnation. Orth's psychical-spiritual tendency is established with the second sentence:

It was not so much the good American's reverence for ancestors that inspired the longing to consort with the ghosts of an ancient line, as artistic appreciation of the mellowness, the dignity, the aristocratic aloofness of walls that have sheltered, and furniture that has embraced, generations and generations of the dead.

Orth soon falls under the spell of a two-century-old portrait of a young girl, Blanche. Obsessed by her portrait, which is displayed with the portrait of her brother, he inquires about the children and is told (falsely) that they died in childhood. He writes a novel based on the morally pure, idealized child that he fantasizes from the portrait.

After the publication of the highly successful novel, Orth meets a little girl who is the living replica of his Blanche. She is Blanche Root, who is visiting her father's relations from New York State. Orth is even more taken with the living Blanche than he was with the portrait. Later he learns the true fate of the child in the portrait: she had lived to her twenties, when she had an affair with a tenant (one of Blanche Root's ancestors), and committed suicide.

The possible readings of the story intertwine spiritualism, communication with the dead, psychical phenomena, the physical manifestation of the spiritual in the temporal world, and reincarnation. One interpretation suggests that the first Blanche still haunts the area, though without manifestation. Orth, so spiritually caught up in the picture, writes from subconscious or supraconscious psychical knowledge the life that the reincarnated Blanche will live because of her purity. In writing his passionate book, he is directed by agents beyond his design, for purposes beyond his imagination.

Another reading suggests that Orth himself created Blanche Root when he wrote the story of the morally pure Blanche. The child whom Orth finds in the woods is the physical manifestation of his imagination. His story of the first Blanche is transferred into reality through this unusual, late-life child. This interpretation suggests a two-way flow between the spiritual and physical worlds. This old plot twist evokes the image of the author as god and suggests that the act of imagination can make something reality. There is no suggestion that the Blanche Root episode is a figment of Orth's imagination or a product of psychopathy. Atherton "reports" the progression of Blanche Root's life and death. The ambiguity reinforces the notion that the human condition transcends the physical element.

Atherton's sexual politics are evident in "The

Bell in the Fog." The Blanche of the painting, the reader learns, wanted to experience more than her society would permit her. In her affair with the young tenant, she broke with her society. Torn by the mores within which she was raised, she committed suicide.

"The Striding Place" uses the Celtic folktale motif of a treacherous and mystical locale that claims those who wander into it. Atherton adds to the Celtic folktale a gruesome twist based on the saying "You can't cheat death"—a saying so common and obvious it seems trite, yet it gives recognition of the futility of the desire for immortality. The story also draws a correlation between death and insanity.

The narrative follows Weigall's search for his friend Wyatt Gifford, who has been missing for two nights. Weigall is disposed to believe that Gifford is playing a practical joke, but, unable to sleep, he goes for a walk down to the river. Weigall's memories of Gifford add to the atmosphere of foreboding while planting the working hypothesis of the story:

> "I cherish the theory," Gifford had said, "that the soul sometimes lingers in the body after death. During madness, of course, it is an impotent prisoner, albeit a conscious one. . . . If I had my way, I should stay inside my bones until the coffin had gone into its niche. . . ."
>
> [Weigall says,] "You believe in the soul as an independent entity, then—that it and the vital principle are not one and the same?"
>
> "Absolutely. The body and soul are twins, life comrades—sometimes friends, sometimes enemies, but always loyal in the last instance."

Weigall's recollection of a poem by Wordsworth identifies the Strid as a mystical place:

> Weigall was not a coward, but he recalled uncomfortably the tales of those that had been done to death in the Strid. Wordsworth's Boy of Egremond had been disposed of by the practical Whitaker; but countless others, more venturesome than wise, had gone down into that narrow boiling course, never to appear in the still pool a few yards beyond.

As he walks, Weigall then sees in the foamy river a hand that he inexplicably knows to be Gifford's. The hand, "shaking savagely in the face of that force which leaves its creatures to immutable law," is raised as if in defiance of death. Atherton tells of Weigall's struggle to pull his friend from the river, at the same time describing his feelings of horror. Then, in the last sentence, Atherton introduces horror based on nightmares: Weigall cannot save his friend because Gifford has no face. His helplessness and loss of control provide the elements of horror, for the reader must consider the horror from Gifford's point of view.

Other elements of horror are suggested early in the story. Gifford is fighting for his life against all odds and cannot win, because the supernatural forces that control the Strid, while unable to make him yield, are able to take away his face and thus his ability to breathe, making him impotent to save his own life. The story, like a dream fugue, draws upon subconscious fears, and superimposes the fear of death on the fear of insanity. With this reading the story can be considered a metaphor for insanity.

"The Dead and the Countess" is a straightforward supernatural tale of the dead speaking from the grave to the living as a consequence of the desecration of a graveyard. It is set in Brittany during the early nineteenth century, when railroad trains were first being introduced. Concerned that the noise of the train passing the old cemetery will awaken the dead, the priest sprinkles holy water on the graves just before each passing of the train. Thus, the dead continue their sleep. The countess's fatal illness causes the priest to arrive late, after the train has awakened the dead. He hears their plaintive words from the graves.

The countess is buried in the old graveyard, at her request, so that she may hear the night train to Paris. For months the priest believes that she alone rests quietly in the graveyard, but actually the sturdiness of her coffin has muffled her cries. When the priest hears her, he tells the count, who is on the railroad board. While the count ponders what to do, the priest dies. The graveyard is later moved to a quiet, consecrated hill.

In "Death and the Woman," Atherton explores a

woman's psychological preparation and adjustment while waiting for her beloved husband to die; the prospect of life without him is as ominous for her as the wait is painful. The story resembles Atherton's mainstream psychological stories more than her other supernatural stories. The interior scenario carries it through the limited action, observing this woman living through what she knows are her husband's last minutes. The supernatural is not introduced until the end of the story, when death comes as a physical being to take her husband and she throws herself upon death. At this point, Atherton pulls the story back from the reader, in much the same manner as Hawthorne did in "Ethan Brand," revealing only the result of the wife's action: their bodies were found in their home. The psychological progression to a critical decision — in this case, suicide — fascinated Atherton. The lack of action may present a problem for readers who desire action or horror in supernatural fiction, and the supernatural elements may present a similar problem for readers seeking psychological fiction. Yet, by introducing death as a being, Atherton can allow the wife an immediate course of action that is the culmination of her personality.

"The Eternal Now," included in *The Foghorn*, relies on psychical phenomena. An American named Simon de Brienne is the host of a costume ball at his home, Briennelouvre, a replica, built from an old drawing, of the fourteenth-century Louvre. The house makes Simon vaguely uncomfortable when he recalls a story that a de Brienne of that period died an "atrocious death" in one of the Louvre's dungeons.

As Simon greets his costumed guests, he becomes increasingly preoccupied with the fourteenth-century historical personages whom they represent, and begins to transcend time and distance. A "mist" clouds his mind, and he finds himself amid the activities of the fourteenth-century Simon de Brienne, acting out the other man's life, while conscious that he has the historical knowledge that could allow him to change what had happened in the past. But he discovers that he cannot alter history and soon faces the fate of his nearly forgotten ancestor.

"The Eternal Now" is reminiscent of alleged supernatural experiences, notably the so-called Versailles adventure of Charlotte Anne Moberly and Eleanor Jordain. In this account, two Englishwomen claimed that while visiting Versailles in 1901, they had been transported back to the time of Marie Antoinette shortly before her execution. It is also obviously related to Henry James's *The Sense of the Past* and to John Balderston's play *Berkeley Square*, derived from it, in which excessive empathy with the past can literally absorb one. Atherton's approach, though, is not psychological, like that of her other supernatural stories, but historical.

III

Gertrude Atherton's position and importance as a mainstream novelist have yet to be established, since her work was discounted before any body of criticism concerning it had developed. Her fall into an obscurity bordering on disrepute involves a combination of factors including a lack of academic critical consideration. Until the early 1970's, the only academic assessment of Atherton's work was by Arthur Hobson Quinn. Critics relegated her to the classification of regionalist, ignoring the settings of her fiction and her life. They also missed the point of what she was doing, confusing her spare, unadorned prose style and vernacular dialogue with a paucity of content. She was also unjustly reproached on the basis of weak characterization, a criticism that contradicts the reviews of her work. In addition, her advocacy of eugenics hurt her even though many of her male counterparts held the same ideas without being ostracized. Then the well-known critic Arthur Hobson Quinn established the typical response to Atherton's work when, in a discussion of eight contemporary writers, he held that Edith Wharton, Ellen Glasgow, Anne Sedgwick, and Gertrude Atherton were without merit but praised the work of Floyd Dell, Ben Hecht, and Carl Van Vechten.

In the area of supernatural fiction, which constitutes only a small fraction of Atherton's production, her reputation is secure. During her lifetime her stories were compared with those of Henry James in their interest in psychological matters, but they are more direct and accessible. Though few in number, her stories are worth reading.

Selected Bibliography

WORKS OF GERTRUDE ATHERTON

The Bell in the Fog and Other Stories. New York: Harper, 1905. London: Macmillan, 1905.

The Foghorn. Boston: Houghton Mifflin, 1934. London: Jarrolds, 1935.

CRITICAL AND BIOGRAPHICAL STUDIES

Forrey, Carolyn D. "Gertrude Atherton and the New Woman." *California Historical Society Quarterly*, 55 (1975): 194–209.

McClure, Charlotte S. *Gertrude Atherton*. Boise State University Western Writers Series no. 23. Boise, Idaho: Boise State University, 1976.

————. *Gertrude Atherton*. Boston: Twayne, 1979.

————. "Gertrude Atherton (1857–1948)." *American Literary Realism, 1870–1910*, 9, no. 2 (1976): 95–101.

————. "A Checklist of Writings of and about Gertrude Atherton." *American Literary Realism, 1870–1910*, 9, no. 2 (1976): 103–162.

Van Domelen, John E. "Gertrude Atherton Inscriptions." *American Notes and Queries*, 10, no. 1 (1971): 7.

—MARILYN J. HOLT

EDITH WHARTON

1862-1937

THE CAREER AND writings of Edith Wharton have been linked, perhaps inevitably, with those of her friend and acknowledged mentor, Henry James. She admired James's writings, knew him well during the years in which she was most productive as an author, and was influenced by his choices of literary themes, settings, characters, and style. Like him, she sought to extend herself into the international scene, and she spent most of her mature life in Europe. Like him, she treated European themes and settings with ease and familiarity. This cosmopolitan and sophisticated range of her work gave it a distinctive air that set it somewhat apart from the writings of many of her American contemporaries, who restricted their fiction to a type of national or regional realism.

Like James, too, Wharton was concerned with the presentation of character within a restricted social fabric, and this kind of psychological realism allowed her to probe the complexities of personal motivations and values. Behind her portraits of upperclass men and women moving in a fairly narrow circle of winter pleasures and summer vacations, aesthetic and refined in their perceptions, bored sometimes by their world but at ease in it and, for the most part, satisfied with its rewards, unable at any rate to move into another orbit of life, there is often the bite of satire and irony. Wharton knew these people well, was one of their number, and had stud-

ied them with a detached and analytical eye. Better, she had transcended this futile idleness to become a hardworking teller of tales, and she was unlikely to be very kind in her depiction of this world. The fact is, another world was available to her pen, a rural, old-style New England scene of farms and small towns where tragedies were played out in a wild and grim wintry environment. This scene was familiar to her through observation rather than habitation; but she knew its quirks and fancies very well.

Edith Newbold Jones was born on 24 January 1862 in New York City, to parents who were wealthy and prominent members of the city's society. The early years of her childhood were spent in Europe; upon her return to the United States, she was accustomed to spending winters in New York and summers in Newport, Rhode Island. Her debut into this society took place in 1879. She began writing very early, and a volume of juvenile verses appeared privately in 1878. After her marriage to Edward Wharton in 1885, she traveled widely and continued writing poems; some were published in *Scribner's Magazine* in 1889. She began at about the same time to write short stories, and her first published effort was "Mrs. Manstey's View" (*Scribner's Magazine*, July 1891). By 1899 she was able to issue a collection of short stories, *The Greater Inclination*. Her first novel, *The Valley of Decision*, a long tale of Italy in the eighteenth century, appeared in 1902.

Her marriage to Wharton was unsuccessful. From the outset there had been sexual difficulties. He began, in the 1890's, to suffer from mental problems, and their lives were further complicated by his adulteries. By 1903 his illness had become a serious matter; in 1911 they were separated, and she divorced him in 1913. She had a long and intimate friendship with Walter Berry, an intelligent and cultured man who criticized her writings and gave her the encouragement she needed. From 1907 to 1910 she had a love affair with Morton Fullerton, an American journalist. She lived in Europe from about 1907 and rarely returned to the United States, except for brief visits.

Wharton's second novel, *The House of Mirth* (1905), is an excellent and successful example of her art, dealing with the leisured society she knew so well and detailing the decline of its heroine from wealth to poverty and tragedy. By contrast, the important short novel *Ethan Frome* (1911), set in rural western Massachusetts, arouses sympathy for farm people, characters of a class that Wharton did not usually describe. Frome, unhappily married to Zenobia, falls in love with her cousin, Mattie Silver, who returns his feelings. The situation is hopeless and the two attempt suicide. Ethan is crippled and Mattie becomes an invalid who must be cared for by the bitterly unhappy couple.

In 1920 Wharton published her best-known novel, *The Age of Innocence*, which looks back to the wealthy society of New York in the 1870's. The book, immensely popular, was awarded the Pulitzer Prize in 1921. It is a tale of a man in love with one woman and tied in marriage to another. His sense of duty is inflexible, life itself has a way of interposing difficulties, chances to act are lost, and he goes on to live a life that seems full but is somehow unsatisfactory. The detailed and careful delineation of setting, the well-managed and fully characterized persons in the tale, and the excellent, terse prose style make this a pleasurable book to read.

Wharton published short fiction prolifically throughout her career and assembled twelve collections that included most of her published work. Fourteen novels, a few novellas, and a number of works of nonfiction add to her achievement. An interesting study, *The Writing of Fiction* (1925), gives her thoughts on her art, and *A Backward Glance* (1934) is an autobiographical account. In 1923 Yale University awarded her the honorary degree of Doctor of Letters, and in 1930 she was elected to the American Academy of Arts and Letters. She died in France on 11 August 1937.

For most of her career Wharton's work was recognized for its high literary qualities; she was, moreover, a popular author as well. The dramatization of some of her works added considerably to her reputation and wealth. In 1935 Zoe Akins composed a play based upon the novella "The Old Maid," which had been published in *Old New York* in 1924. This extremely well-received work had a long run and received the 1935 Pulitzer Prize for drama. In 1936 a dramatization of *Ethan Frome* by Owen and Donald Davis, starring Raymond Massey, Pauline Lord, and Ruth Gordon, struck a popular note and had a good run in New York and on the road.

The best of Wharton's realistic fiction is notable for its carefully organized plots and its presentation of well-developed characters. Among other novels that stand out are *The Reef* (1912), *The Custom of the Country* (1913), and *Summer* (1917). Her best work as a novelist was done in the first two decades of the century and, although she continued to produce novels in the 1920's and 1930's, they fell off in quality. On the other hand her skills as a writer of novellas and short stories continued undiminished, and the four novellas that make up *Old New York* — "False Dawn," "The Old Maid," "The Spark," and "New Year's Day" — are excellent.

Of the many realistic short stories there are some very fine ones, including "The Pelican," "The Other Two," "Autres Temps," "Xingu," "After Holbein," "Atrophy," and "Roman Fever." Publication of these spans her whole career, from 1898 to 1936. Her keen sense of dramatic situation and significant detail is supported by her aesthetic theory. Commenting on short fiction in *The Writing of Fiction*, she remarked:

The shorter the story, the more stripped of detail and "cleared for action," the more it depends for its effect not only on the choice of what is kept when the superfluous has been jettisoned, but on the order in which these essentials are set forth.

She tried in all her fiction to meet these stringent requirements of selection and arrangement.

Wharton's supernatural fiction forms a part of her very large production that is quite small, about a dozen stories. She held them in special regard and published them in her various collections. At the end of her life she published *Ghosts* (1937), which brought together eleven of them, and she contributed a thoughtful preface on the reading and writing of ghostly tales. Recognizing the preeminence of Walter de la Mare and his influence, she dedicated the volume to him. In the preface she cites as important precursors Robert Louis Stevenson, J. S. Le Fanu, Fitz-James O'Brien, and F. Marion Crawford. She makes a point of speaking especially of Henry James's *The Turn of the Screw*, for its "imaginative handling of the supernatural."

Part of the preface is a lamentation that "the faculty required for their enjoyment has become almost atrophied in modern man," and she cites readers who have written letters to ask the wrong sorts of questions—how ghosts can write letters or carry them to letter boxes. Accepting the thesis that the ghost story ought to be read for enjoyment, she goes on to say:

It must depend for its effect solely on what one might call its thermometrical quality; if it sends a cold shiver down one's spine, it has done its job and done it well. But there is no fixed rule as to the means of producing this shiver, and many a tale that makes others turn cold leaves me at my normal temperature. The doctor who said there were no diseases but only patients would probably agree that there are no ghosts, but only tellers of ghost-stories, since what provides a shudder for one leaves another peacefully tepid. . . . The only suggestion I can make is that the teller of supernatural tales should be well frightened in the telling. . . .

This assertion repeats the view expressed in *The Writing of Fiction* that the ghost story gives rise to "simple shivering animal fear," and breaks boldly with the usual apologies for ghost stories that try to justify them on the grounds of their cathartic powers or their value in illuminating a social or moral question. The tale of the supernatural seeks to do just what she claims it does best: arouse in its reader a sense of fear and awe.

However, her first attempt at a story of the supernatural was not a horror story but an allegorical fantasy. It was, in fact, her second published story, "The Fulness of Life" (*Scribner's Magazine*, December 1893). Wharton evidently did not consider it an important work, for she failed to include it in any of her collections of short stories; but it does display some of her qualities as a storyteller. A woman has just died, and her soul finds itself on the threshold of eternal life surprised to discover that death is not oblivion. She is quizzed by the Spirit of Life and reveals that her earthly existence was disappointing, for its complexities were never fully engaged by her husband, he of the creaky boots, railway novels, and sporting advertisements in the newspapers. All of her pleasures were enjoyed alone, and they were always aesthetic and artistic. The Spirit locates an ideal soulmate for her who can share till eternity the joys of Botticelli, Leonardo, and the *Paradiso*. But she has a change of heart and decides, after all, to wait for her husband's death so that she can share the afterlife with him, creaky boots and all. He is going to need someone to choose his popular novels and keep his inkstand filled. He will expect to find her waiting, and she does not intend to betray his expectations. She will be the patient and cheerful wife and mate in eternity as she was on earth.

The story combines a tentative effort at fantasy with some of the hardheaded realism of the author. It is certainly satirical, somewhat whimsical, and, in relation to her own life, sharply ironic. Wharton had discovered, slowly, that marriage with the easygoing and empty Edward Wharton was going to be disappointing, sexually and intellectually; but she had at the outset an affection for this inferior man and had been prepared for cheerful resignation to the social amenities of a life without love. He was always admiring of her brains and creative talents, and, even if his boots, physical or intellectual, did creak, he seemed to fill some need in her life. In his treatment of her fiction, R. W. B. Lewis categorizes many of the fantasies as part of a group concerned with stories of marriage, and asserts that Wharton used the particular advantage of fantasy to act out, as it were, the frustrations of her life.

There are stories of protective ghosts, of malignant ghosts, of revenants from long-gone episodes of brutality, of ghostly women who still exert a hold on husbands. In "The Lady's Maid's Bell" (*Scribner's Magazine*, November 1902), one of the last situations emerges. Hartley, the narrator, is a servant who takes a position in a secluded country house as the personal maid of an invalid woman. The former maid has died after many years of faithful service. The newcomer sees a stranger, another maid, lingering about the servants' quarters but hardly marks it as important. She learns that the wife is unhappy; the husband is a coarse, brutish, and threatening individual with an eye for the female servants in the house. Fortunately he is more often away than not. Hartley is summoned to her mistress by the ringing of her bell, but she is puzzled to learn that her mistress did not call, in fact never uses the bell at all. Later, from a photograph, Hartley is able to identify the stranger in her quarters as Emma Saxon, the dead maid. We learn that the apparition is anxiously moving about the house, concerned for her mistress but unable to ward off danger. The ghost can ring the bell in Hartley's quarters, she can make a mute appeal by appearing plainly to the narrator and leading her through the snow to a neighbor's house for help, but she is unable to communicate her own sense of disaster to the new lady's maid. The story ends with the death of the mistress and the ghost manifesting herself to the husband.

A subtle and distinctive piece of fiction is "The Eyes" (*Scribner's Magazine*, June 1910). The frame narrative concerns a gathering of friends at the house of Andrew Culwin sitting about and swapping ghost stories. After the party the host, a detached, rather cold, elderly man, tells two remaining friends of his own supernatural experiences. Years ago Culwin impulsively proposed marriage to Alice Nowell, a plain cousin who loved him deeply. He felt ambivalent about his action: he had performed an act of goodness, but he was heavyhearted about his hasty proposal. Waking that night in his darkened bedroom, he became aware that a pair of eyes, old and repulsive, were glaring at him: "the thick red-lined lids hung over the eyeballs like blinds of which the cords are broken." The appalling vision of evil deeply disturbed Culwin. It recurred nightly, and he fled from it, abandoning his fiancée and going to Europe. Once away from the compromising situation, he found that the eyes ceased to appear.

Another incident with the eyes occurred some years later. He had been acting as friend and guardian to a young writer who depended on him for a good opinion of his work. The writer was almost ludicrously inept, and Culwin wanted to tell him so to spare him more difficulties, but he was unable, and in fact lied and spoke well of the young man's writing. Again the eyes began their nightly haunting. Culwin was spared the necessity of telling the harsh but salutary truth about his friend's work as a writer; it was finally borne upon the young man that he had no talent. When this crisis was past, the eyes again ceased their nightly vigil.

Culwin has thought about his experience but confesses that he can make little of it. He recognizes that the second appearance of the eyes was worse for him, for they had grown more hideous, as if there had been more to corrupt the body presumably attached to them; he recognizes that "what made them so bad was that they'd grown bad so slowly." As the story concludes, he learns what his listeners have already divined, that the eyes are his own. Looking in a mirror, he sees the eyes that he had remembered. His younger self has been haunted by the older, more experienced, more selfish man who has glared across the years at the bumbling would-be do-gooder of the past.

In the same year as "The Eyes," Wharton published "Afterward" (*Century Magazine*, January 1910), a more conventional tale of supernatural revenge. In "Afterward" the supernatural visitant is an outsider. The story echoes with the insistent remark that a house is haunted, that one will indeed see a ghost, but will not know it till long afterward. Ned and Mary Boyne have taken an old house in Dorsetshire after Ned has suddenly made a fortune in the United States under mysterious circumstances. They are to retire into the country and he is to write a book, long contemplated. All is peaceful in their house and they are enjoying their withdrawal from society. One day, from a vantage point upstairs, they see a stranger in the yard. Ned dashes downstairs to intercept him. When Mary follows and asks about the encounter, Ned denies that he has been out to see a stranger and makes up a lame story about noticing the gardener and wanting to speak to him. He is, however, disturbed by the old remark that one might see a ghost but know only later that such a meeting has occurred; and he wants to know just how much later.

Bits of a story then come to light about Ned's being sued for his part in a financial deal connected with his newly acquired fortune. A man named Elwell is suing. Confronted with this information, Ned says there will be no trouble, for Elwell has withdrawn the suit. A visitor looking for Ned shows up at the house and Mary, thinking little about it, courteously directs him to the library, where her husband is working. Some hours later, she learns that her husband has disappeared with the stranger. Ned never does return. Mary slowly puts the story together. There was a considerable amount of cheating in money matters. Elwell, a partner, attempted suicide after being bilked by Ned of his share in the fortune. Elwell initially survived his suicide attempt but died after a couple of months. When Mary sees a photograph of Elwell, she is able to identify him as the visitor to the house. His first attempt to visit had occurred just at the time of the suicide attempt, but he wasn't "dead enough." Only with his death was he able to carry out his vengeful and supernatural visit. And, of course, only afterward is someone able to know that there has been a ghost.

The remarkable substantiality of the story comes from the careful and full characterization of Mary Boyne, the perfectly ordinary surroundings in which the ghostly events take place, the fact that they happen during the daytime, and the decidedly commonplace appearance of the ghost as a quiet, polite visitor who has business with the husband. Every element of the story is underplayed so that it denies the horror of the events. Nowhere is language used to emphasize fearfulness.

This air of the plain and usual is a feature in a number of Wharton's best ghost stories. In "Miss Mary Pask" (*Pictorial Review*, April 1925), a narrator who must pay a duty visit to a dowdy old maid remembers, a bit late, having heard that she is dead. But the visit goes on, and he is disturbed by her conversation. In "Pomegranate Seed" (*Saturday Evening Post*, 25 April 1931), a second wife is losing her husband to the ghost of his first. The ghost acts in a peremptory fashion and writes letters to the husband that are delivered by hand to the home. The handwriting is familiar and thin. When the wife opens one of the letters she discovers that the writing is too faint for her eyes. The husband is terribly disturbed and aware of the identity of his ghostly visitor but cannot tell his second wife what is happening. The ghost finally draws him away from her, and he disappears; the wife is left to notify the police just as if "we thought it could do any good to do anything."

Two minor ghost stories did not appear in magazine form but were published in short story collections. In "Mr. Jones" (*Certain People*, 1930), the ghost of a caretaker to an English country house continues to control matters there and strangles the housekeeper when she is no longer able to prevent the new owner from interfering and learning the house's secrects. "All Souls," which first appeared in *Ghosts*, recounts some odd incidents that occur at an isolated house in Connecticut. Servants are called away from the house by a mysterious visitor, and for several days, beginning on All Souls' Eve, they abandon their mistress, who has injured her leg in a fall. It is possible that they have been summoned to a witch's coven. But this is not dramatized; it is offered by the narrator only as a conjecture, and the story suffers by not being resolved.

A more serious piece, "The Triumph of Night" (*Scribner's Magazine*, August 1914), presents the case of a young man who is granted the privilege of seeing the evil behind hospitality. But he fails to understand the apparition he has encountered and fails to save the life of his friend through his own fear and inaction.

In "Kerfol" (*Scribner's Magazine*, March 1916), the ghosts are dogs. When the story's narrator visits a country house in Brittany with the motive of possibly buying it, his way is barred by several dogs that form a circle about him in a quiet manner. He is impressed by their air of gravity and melancholy and believes, fleetingly, that they must have seen a ghost. But his fanciful idea is wrong. They are ghosts and they appear at an appointed day in recollection of an old episode of brutality.

In the seventeenth century a master of the château of Kerfol married a young woman. After giving her a dog as a present, he came to suspect her of infidelity and killed the animal. Afterward he killed all the dogs she befriended and put the corpses on her bed. Anne de Cornault did have a male admirer but was no adulteress. She met the man on several occasions and there was obviously an attraction between them. One night, having received a message from the man, she set out to meet him. The husband moved to intervene and was killed in a mysterious way. His wounds pointed to an encounter with animals, and Anne, forced to tell her story to the court, asserted that the ghosts of the dogs had killed her husband. Her unlikely story led the court to adjudge her insane.

Among Wharton's other stories, "A Bottle of Perrier" (published as "A Bottle of Evian" in the *Saturday Evening Post*, 25 March 1926) is a particularly good example of the Poesque tale of terror. "Bewitched" (*Pictorial Review*, March 1925) is a story of possession in which a man is ravaged by a dead girl. She is a succubus, draining him of his life and vitality.

Edith Wharton is one of the distinguished American authors of the first half of the twentieth century, and her eminent position lends authority to both her practice of the supernatural genre and her theorizing about it. She has a keen sense of how the world of the spirit can impinge upon the mundane, and one of her effective contributions to the field is the reality of that world. There is virtually no attempt to play upon the emotions by any heightened use of language. Instead all is presented with the dead-level, convincing reality of objects that one can touch.

Selected Bibliography

WORKS OF EDITH WHARTON

Ghosts. New York: Appleton-Century, 1937. Reprinted as *The Ghost Stories of Edith Wharton*. New York: Scribner, 1973.

The Collected Short Stories of Edith Wharton. Edited by R. W. B. Lewis. 2 vols. New York: Scribner, 1968.

CRITICAL AND BIOGRAPHICAL STUDIES

Bell, Millicent. *Edith Wharton and Henry James: The Story of Their Friendship*. New York: George Braziller, 1965.

Howe, Irving, ed. *Edith Wharton: A Collection of Critical Essays*. Englewood Cliffs, N.J.: Prentice-Hall, 1962.

Lewis, R. W. B. *Edith Wharton: A Biography*. New York: Harper and Row, 1975.

McDowell, Margaret B. "Edith Wharton's Ghost Tales." *Criticism*, 12 (Spring 1970): 133–151.

————. *Edith Wharton*. Boston: Twayne, 1976.

Wolff, Cynthia. *A Feast of Words: The Triumph of Edith Wharton*. New York: Oxford University Press, 1977.

BIBLIOGRAPHIES

Brenni, Vito J. *Edith Wharton: A Bibliography*. Morgantown: West Virginia University Library, 1966.

Springer, Marlene. *Edith Wharton and Kate Chopin: A Reference Guide*. Boston: G. K. Hall, 1976.

—DOUGLAS ROBILLARD

JAMES BRANCH CABELL

1879–1958

I

FOR SOME SIXTY-FIVE years critics have attempted, with less than satisfactory results, to classify James Branch Cabell as a writer, and he continues to elude neat classifications. Hailed as a consummate stylist, as an allegorist commenting wryly on the mores of his day, he is currently enjoying a vogue as one of the purer fantasists, as a creator of other worlds more satisfying to the questing ego than the shadowy posturing known as the real world. In commenting on Cabell's otherness, Louis D. Rubin, Jr. (in Inge and MacDonald), observes:

> His way of dealing with life in literature was and is sufficiently at variance with the literary practices of his day and ours as to create certain difficulties in dealing with him. These difficulties include form, language, audience, reputation, historical significance, and several other elements that affect his stature within both the literary community and the social community of his residence and ironic affiliation.

Cabell's environment and early life bore strongly on his desire to reshape a nebulous reality into the enduring structures of art. Late in his career he wrote, "All of every writer's youthfulness must enter into his books" (*Ladies and Gentlemen*, 1934).

Cabell was born on 14 April 1879 in what he liked to refer to as an upstairs room in the Richmond, Virginia, public library. In reality he was born on the third floor of his maternal grandmother's house, later razed to make way for the library at 101 East Franklin Street. His parents, Dr. Robert Gamble Cabell and Anne Harris Branch, were at that time following the local custom of newlyweds in living on the third floor of a parent's home until the children started arriving. James was the first of three children, all boys. When he was two, his parents moved to a house whose garden ran back to the garden of his grandmother.

For his fifth birthday party, James's fairy godmother and his real grandmother, Martha Louise Patteson Branch, summoned the small creatures of Richmond society to come dressed as characters in the Mother Goose rhymes. Young Master Cabell was dressed as Jack, Mother Goose's very own son, "in a lovely costume of pink and green satin, perfectly gotten up, even to the golden egg in his hand. By his side walked Mother Goose herself—viz., Miss Ella Moncure. The quaint figure performed her part to the life, watching over her son Jack and his precious egg with a vigilant eye" (*Richmond State*, 16 April 1884). Mother Goose would continue to peer into Cabell's dreaming for the rest of his life.

Cabell's family possessed a large library, and he read the works of Edgar Allan Poe at an early age. His grandfather Cabell had been a schoolmate of Poe's and was later an admirer of the poet's literary achievement. Feeling, however, that Poe was unsuitable for the impressionable mind of a young boy, he advised his grandson not to read Poe until he was older. James, age eight, forthwith read the complete works.

Cabell attended local private schools, starting at five under the tutelage of the later celebrated Miss Jennie Ellett. Later he studied under the equally noted John Peyton McGuire. He grew up in a Richmond that was industriously mythologizing the late Civil War. King Arthur had returned from Avalon in the form of General Robert E. Lee, with the knights of the Round Table becomingly dressed as Confederate generals. Jefferson Davis was wise Merlin, and Mordred's host that opposed King Arthur were called "Yankees." "It was confusing the way in which your elders talked about things which no great while before you were born had happened in Richmond. — Because you lived in Richmond: and Richmond was not like Camelot. Richmond was a modern city, with sidewalks and plumbing and gas light and horse cars" (*Let Me Lie*, 1947).

In 1894, Cabell was prepared to enter college at the relatively early age of fiteen. Just why he matriculated at William and Mary in Williamsburg is a point for speculation; it was a struggling private institution dedicated to preparing middle-class males for public school positions. He knew few if any members of the student body when he arrived there in the fall with yellow gloves and cane. Younger, more scholarly, less athletically inclined, essentially shy, he doubtlessly applied himself to his studies as much from a sense of alienation as from his natural aptitude for intellectual pursuits. The rurally oriented students found Cabell's city manners a cause for raillery and dubbed him "sister." In a sense barred from close relationships with most of his peers, he turned to two older persons whom he found sympathetic and who encouraged his scholarly, particularly poetic, endeavors. Charles Washington Coleman, college librarian and son of Cabell's landlady, took an increasing interest in the awakening adolescent. Then there was a dark-haired, brown-eyed young lady of nineteen, Gabriella Moncure. She lived only a street away, and Cabell read his poems to her in the evening. Established as a scholar, adjusted to an environment he found increasingly congenial, he returned to Williamsburg in the fall of 1895 a confident young man of sixteen.

The next three years were to prove critical to his development.

In his French studies Cabell read in the courtly romances of the medieval pages who served as youthful courtiers to noble ladies who tempered ardor into chivalrous expressions of love, so that the lover learned to extract from the transitory moment an enduring poem to immortalize his lady. Gabriella Moncure had been bred in the tradition; she was nobly born, and the boy had been entrusted to her care as a child, one bearing a golden egg. Cabell proved adept as a troubadour. In the background was the older poet, the whimsical, suggestive, decadent (poetically) Charles Coleman. In the garden was the lady, alternately defensive and receptive, increasingly aware of the ironies in the relationship. Cabell's poetic outpouring assumed the form of a verse diary capturing every nuance of his awakening passion. His fantasy women bear various names, but his inspiration is clearly Gabriella Moncure. His favorite cognomen for her is Heart o' My Heart, a play on the purported French origin of the name Moncure — *mon coeur* ("my heart").

Many of these poems were published in 1916 under the title *From the Hidden Way*. When queried as to his favorite of his works, he apologetically named this volume of youthful verse. He also included the poems in the Storisende Edition. If these poems do not succeed as poetry, they record a psychological progression and mark a growth in artistic ambition. A youth divided by love of the ideal and physical passion conveys with sensitivity the direction his feelings had taken from 1895 to 1898, from chivalry to gallantry, from the desire to worship to the desire to possess. Other seminal ideas are apparent, all developed and orchestrated in his later major works.

First, lust as the procreator of life is thereby also the creator of art, leading to his third attitude toward life (after the chivalrous and gallant), the artistic: life or experience is merely the raw material of art. Second, any act of creation can be construed as sin, as it invades the domain of God, who claims universal copyrights. Third, if man is imperfect and his nature divided, the cause may lie with God, who gives and withholds at the same time; at best, such seeming irrationality appears unjust, and at worst, inartistic. These ideas reach their fruition in *The High Place* (1923). The hero of that work observes: "Gods and devils are poor creatures when compared to man. They live with knowledge. But man finds heart to live without any knowledge or surety anywhere, and yet not go mad. And I wonder now could any god endure the testing which all men endure?" (chapter 23).

Cabell's last months at William and Mary, in contrast to the first three and a half years, were a time of intense emotional stress owing to rumors that linked his name homosexually with that of Charles Coleman. Two events gave rise to these rumors. On 18 January 1898, Cabell was host at a fraternity party at which the guests became so intoxicated that no one could recall what, if anything, had happened. At about the same time Charles Coleman fell from a ladder in the library, breaking a leg; shortly thereafter he accepted a position at the Library of Congress. Coleman's departure from Williamsburg appeared flight. The rumors grew, and Cabell's withdrawal from college in April appeared to the gossip-prone an admission of guilt. Williamsburg thought it had its very own Oscar Wilde in Coleman and its Lord Alfred Douglas in Cabell. Cabell's family had him immediately reinstated, but this bitter time saw him alienated from his former easy relationships and meditating on the essential falseness of appearances. In particular, his shame and his fear of linking Gabriella's name with his own discredited standing effectively ended their relationship. Her life, too, was soon to be drastically altered by her father's death, and what might have been a brief separation with a happy reconciliation was denied by other complications in both their lives. Gabriella Moncure remained Cabell's Heart o' My Heart for the rest of his life, becoming the witch-woman in his work, the inspirer of divine discontent. Always in an April twilight of his heart lived "Suskind," anagram for *unkiss'd.*

When Cabell left college, he worked the next three years for the *Richmond Times* (1898), the *New York Herald* (1899–1901), and the *Richmond News* (1901). While in New York, he frequently called on a cousin then living in Brooklyn, Miss Norvell Harrison. They played at the game of love, but their game resulted only in short-story material for both of them. In 1901, Cabell sent out five short stories to various magazines and had three of them accepted by *Harper's Monthly, Smart Set*, and *Argosy*. His output in the short-story form from this time on was prodigious; and, always an economical author, he later reworked many of these stories into his longer works. Indeed, his early stories grew out of his poems to Gabriella, and many of them incorporated poems, perhaps as secret messages to the one who had inspired them.

Also in 1901, Cabell underwent another period of stress that would contribute to the dark, satirical undertones that surfaced later in his work. When he had returned home from college three years earlier, he had found his parents separated. His mother, twelve years younger than her Presbyterian husband, dared to smoke and drink cocktails before other Richmond ladies confessed to these pleasures, and for these ladies Mrs. Cabell was entirely too friendly with an amusing cousin. On the evening of 13 November 1901, the amusing cousin was murdered in front of the house where Cabell and his mother lived. Through the years the gossips repeated the story that he had murdered his mother's lover. More than thirty years later he would write, "I was not really the philanthropist who committed it." His parents' divorce in 1907 added fuel to the gossip.

As a Cabell, he was "old family"; as a Branch, he was a pretentious plebeian. In *The Cords of Vanity* (1909) and *The Rivet in Grandfather's Neck* (1915) Cabell attempted to deal satirically with the mores of his society in "contemporary" novels, but sentiment intruded on his irony. Allegory would later allow him to maintain his ironic pose. Cabell's first novel, *The Eagle's Shadow*, appeared in 1904, as a result of his mother's taking the manuscript to a family friend, Walter Hines Page of Doubleday and Page, later ambassador to Britain.

In 1913, Cabell married Priscilla Bradley Shepherd. A widow four years older than he, she had five children as well as a comfortable inheritance from her first husband. They had one son when she was forty, Ballard Hartwell Cabell, a victim of Down's syndrome. Priscilla Cabell made her husband into her seventh child, giving him the privacy and means to weave his fantasies. While Gabriella Moncure was the model for all his dream women, Priscilla Cabell was the prototype of all the real, domestic women who enter as the voice of common sense, such as Dame Lisa in *Jurgen* (1919) and Niafer in *Figures of Earth* (1921).

In 1915, Cabell met Guy Holt, the editor who would help him define his literary philosophy and goals, giving his work the form that led to recognition of Cabell as a new voice in American letters. Cabell at that time was the author of six published books—*The Eagle's Shadow, The Line of Love* (1905), *Gallantry* (1907), *The Cords of Vanity* (1909), *Chivalry* (1909), and *The Soul of Melicent* (1913)—none of which had received popular or critical recognition. The Cabell-Holt relationship resulted in a lengthy correspondence extending from 1915 to 1933. While their initial collaboration was in the revision of Cabell's college poetry for publication in 1916, "it was in the making of *Beyond Life* (1919) that Holt and Cabell developed their most intimate connection" (Dorothy McInnis Scura, in Inge and MacDonald). *Beyond Life* is a collection of essays outlining Cabell's literary credo, a defense of romance, "the world as it ought to be," in a literary period of rampant realism. "'Realism,'" wrote Cabell, "is the art of being superficial seriously."

The Cream of the Jest (1917), Cabell's first serious essay into fantasy rather than historical romance or romanticized autobiography, became, in his words, "the most potent of all my books in its influence upon my career as a writer" ("Author's Note," Storisende Edition). It attracted the attention of Burton Rascoe, Sinclair Lewis, Joseph Hergesheimer, and H. L. Mencken, all of whom would help nourish his blossoming career. Underlying this work is the conviction that a psychological need for fantasy lies buried in everyone; obviously Cabell is his own hero. The writer Kennaston leads a dual life: during the day he lives in a real world with his pedestrian wife, but nightly he escapes into a dreamworld, lured there by Ettarre, the eternal witch-woman. But when Kennaston touches Ettarre, the dream vanishes, and he awakens again in his mundane surroundings. If Cabell does not come to terms with man's dual nature, he does hint at a compromise in the dubious satisfactions of (or perhaps, escape into) art.

With the publication of *Jurgen* in 1919, Cabell's days of obscurity were over. It was termed "lewd and lascivious" by the New York Society for the Suppression of Vice, and a court order banned its sale for two and a half years. Jurgen, an intrepid pawnbroker, does not hesitate to deal with the power brokers, whether gods or demons, or to "deal fairly" with the women he encounters in his quest through the shibboleths of man's mind. Given the opportunity to escape his wife, who has disappeared, he also has the chance to alter his fate by reliving a significant moment in the past, a moment he cleverly stretches to a year. Guenevere represents the springtime of chivalry, Anaitis (Venus) the summer of gallantry, and Helen the autumn of artistic creation; but in the end Jurgen elects to return to his wife, the winter of comfortable content.

The notoriety that accompanied the appearance of *Jurgen* colored all Cabell's subsequent work and made objective critical assessment difficult for his contemporaries. Jurgen-Cabell's skepticism was viewed as a rejection of American middle-class values, which he saw largely as a matter of pseudopious mouthings; World War I had been a "war to make the world safe for hypocrisy." The work also mockingly rejected the dictates of the naturalistic school, then in its ascendancy. Cabell burlesqued the realists as "mathematicians," and he evolved into an apologist for the "sophisticates," along with Mencken. Cabell, with Hergesheimer, Carl Van Vechten, Elinor Wylie, and others, would eschew moral earnestness as the death of art and would embrace style as the touchstone of literary immortality.

In the realist-romantic debate, Cabell saw an inherent flaw in the realist position; the realists, essentially enumerators, accepted their "facts" and were therefore passive. The romantics with their dynamic visions were the truly active, defying the transitory facts to achieve a "life beyond life." "Reality" was another form of "fantasy." Thus, Cabell anticipated such later writers as Joseph Heller and Kurt Vonnegut. And *Jurgen* contained a large amount of self-mockery. The failed poet would wear other guises in Cabell's later fiction. On a more universal psychological plane, the work embodied the post–World War I disillusionment usually credited to the Ernest Hemingway hero, who, though castrated, may be, in reality, a more sentimentally romantic creation than Cabell's philandering, cashiered poet, his honor (penis) held high even though accompanied by the shadow of Mother Sereda — common sense. *Jurgen* has rarely been out of print and has appeared in numerous editions. As a comic epic in the realm of fantasy, it remains unique in American letters.

While *Jurgen* was still banned, Cabell published *Figures of Earth* in 1921. The perceptive saw in it a vindication of Cabell's powers as an artist; it disappointed others who expected a "popular" novel from the controversial author. Eschewing the comic élan of *Jurgen*, Cabell probed more deeply into the demonic nature of creation. Set in the favored mock-medieval world, this work has a hero who is hell-bent on following the dictates of his ego rather than any external code of behavior. "I am Manuel," he declares; "I follow after my own thinking." In his blundering drive to give life to the figures of clay that he has shaped into human likenesses (a would-be realist?), he ironically gives birth to a chivalrous myth out of which grows a religious cult. Cabell realized that in Jurgen he had created a universal hero, one who appealed to the American's instinct to fantasize, especially about his sexual exploits. In addition, Jurgen's inate distrust of the "facts" of "economics" struck a responsive chord in the rebellious American heart. And so this hero had combined the classic traits of Don Juan's search for the ultimate orgasm and Faust's quest for ultimate knowledge.

Cabell envisioned another hero for *Figures of Earth*, one who would burlesque the realists' concept of the man of action. Not given to self-analysis in the style of Jurgen, Manuel blunders from exploit to exploit, using and betraying others in a ruthless "capitalistic" rise to power. Ironically, this "ape bereft of a tail" is eulogized as a "savior" of his people. Manuel may be considered another manifestation of Cabell's persona, the creative ego driving him to overcome all obstacles to win his literary realm. And in his defiance of the realists, Cabell sowed the seeds of his fall from critical grace, which was soon to be hastened by the New Deal critics of social reform.

The reviewers — "They that wore blankets" — soon took their revenge for Cabell's satire. But one doubts that Cabell would have altered his course if he had foreseen his critical fate, for in the writing of *Figures of Earth* he had made another profound discovery: all his work was biographical. It was really a biography with a capital B, his own as well as that of everyman, whose dreaming made him aspire to worlds that can exist only in the imagination.

The year after the publication of *Figures of Earth*, Cabell started writing *The High Place* (1923), in many respects his best work. He at last understood fully the psychological and artistic implications of the dreams that Gabriella Moncure had inspired in his impressionable youth; his firmness of purpose shines through this autobiographical allegory. Domestic women play no role in this comedy of disenchantment, but Gabriella enters the drama in two guises. She is the fairy Melusine, who guides all the dreaming of the young hero and determines all the conditions for the operation of the machinery. She is also the clairvoyant half-sister Marie-Claire, an adept at necromancy: "In their shared youth these two had not been strangers." Young Florian's desire is to incorporate beauty and holiness into his daily living, a desire so reasonable in his thinking that he violates every law of God and man in his quest. His inevitable disillusionment, a cosmic joke, is handled tenderly by Cabell.

Cabell was more pleased with *The High Place* than with any of his previous works. It had a well-defined plot, it had symmetry, it was really the type of work that he had intended to write all along. Ever ready to tell his readers what they should see in his work, he decided it was time to tell them that he was an epic romancer of no small accomplishment. He made the announcement in *Straws and Prayer-Books* (1924), another collection of essays, assuring his readers that the "Biography" was really begun in 1901 with his first story. Unfortunately, he would realize too late that he had to rewrite all his earlier work to make it conform to the notion of a projected perfection. Before setting out to accomplish this, he completed *The Silver Stallion* (1926), a sequel to *Figures of Earth* recounting the exploits of ten of Manuel's followers. It continued the high level of Cabell's best writing, but *Something About Eve* (1927) displays a lack of control about which Cabell temporizes in the preface. Its failure ironically exemplifies its theme: the failure of the poet to attain the perfection that he envisions in Antan.

Cabell then devoted three years to the crushing task of trying to make all his literary output—poems, fiction, essays—conform to the outline of a truly unified epic. The Storisende Edition (1927–1930) proved the reverse. Despite Cabell's reiteration that all goes by tens in his epic, his "twenty-volume" work ended up in eighteen covers; and despite his insistence that all his diverse writings fall neatly into three categories—the chivalric, the gallant, and the artistic attitudes toward life—the Storisende Edition of *The Works of James Branch Cabell* is a hodgepodge that generally moves from strong to weak. His prefaces speak bravely of its planned order, but Cabell knew better. He had been bound to a dream impossible to attain. He symbolically dropped the James from his name and wrote under the shortened Branch Cabell for the next decade and a half.

Smirt (1934), *Smith* (1935), and *Smire* (1937), a trilogy subtitled *The Nightmare Has Triplets*, constitutes Cabell's major effort in the supernatural idiom after the "Biography." As Cabell explained, this trio grew out of two of his dissatisfactions with his earlier work—its scrupulous avoidance of the method of naturalistic fiction and its use of the dream merely as a narrative device. Here he would apply the documentary veracity of Émile Zola to the matter of Lewis Carroll. He realized that the new gods, the critics of the 1930's, had replaced those of the 1920's, who had smiled on him, and that a new order of dreamer was being deified. In this trilogy, the subject is again a projection of the author, but his identity is constantly dissolving. In *Smirt* he is an ersatz Jehovah, in *Smith* a minor forest deity, and in *Smire* a decadent Holy Ghost. As Joe Lee Davis observes of these works:

Time is so scrambled and telescoped that anything not anachronistic seems improbable, and causality becomes wholly casual. . . . Although hearing and touch are not noticeably impaired, sight is at once sharper and hazier than in waking hours, while taste and smell are virtually nullified. Mythology, history, literature, statistics, and

journalism coalescently contribute to the continuing kaleidoscope of irreality.

This work has yet to be studied in depth. Edmund Wilson called for its reissue as an omnibus so that a wider audience could enjoy or judge "this amusing and original book—of dream comedies the most opalescent."

As Cabell moved into the autumn of his career, authorial intrusion became less evident in his fiction. Such major works as *The King Was in His Counting House* (1938), *Hamlet Had an Uncle* (1940), *The First Gentleman of America* (1942), and the lesser *There Were Two Pirates* (1946) and *The Devil's Own Dear Son* (1949) are more or less philosophical and historical disquisitions. The author moved directly into biography with *Let Me Lie* (1947), *Quiet, Please* (1952), and *As I Remember It* (1955).

Priscilla Bradley Cabell, his wife of thirty-six years, died in 1949, and a thoroughly domesticated and dependent Cabell married Margaret Waller Freeman the following year. He had known her in the early 1920's as one of the editors of the *Reviewer*, a little magazine published in Richmond, now credited with helping to create the corpus of literature known as southern. An efficient, strong-willed personality, Margaret Cabell nursed her husband in his final illness as well as his son, Ballard. Cabell died on 5 May 1958 in Richmond.

Cabell's literary fortunes have risen and fallen with the changes in the critical guard. The first eighteen years of his career were passed in relative obscurity. Then, just as he began to receive critical attention—notably from Rascoe in the *Chicago Tribune*, Mencken in the *Baltimore Sun*, and Wilson Follett in the *Dial*—the suppression of *Jurgen* in 1919 brought Cabell to the notice of a powerful and eloquent group of admirers, including Hugh Walpole, Carl Van Doren, Vernon L. Parrington, Louis Untermeyer, Carl Bechhofer in England, and Regis Michaud in France, who led a host of reviewers in hailing Cabell as the major new voice in American letters. Ironically, this James Branch Cabell period of the early 1920's is now known to the current critical establishment as the Fitzgerald period or the Jazz Age. As Ritchie D. Watson, Jr. (in Inge and Mac-

Donald), observes: "Certainly the most extraordinary aspect of Cabell criticism is the precipitous plunge his reputation sustained between the middle twenties, when he was the darling of the American intelligentsia, and the late forties and early fifties, when he was almost uniformly dismissed and forgotten by critics." The socialist arbiters of the 1930's and 1940's castigated Cabell as escapist, effete, and a "sleek, smug egoist." Among those who damned were Ludwig Lewisohn, Granville Hicks, Clifton Fadiman, Peter Munro Jack, Oscar Cargill, and Alfred Kazin. Cabell's literary fortunes took a turn for the better with Edmund Wilson's "The James Branch Cabell Case Reopened," which appeared in the *New Yorker* (21 April 1956). For Wilson, Cabell's elaborate web of fusions and confusions in the "Biography" grew out of the writer's rejection of the legends of the Old South and his disdain for the poverty of the New. The reader, confronted with "continual metamorphoses," is led to an understanding of life's radical uncertainty. This seminal reappraisal was followed by Wilson's obituary tribute in the *Nation* (7 June 1958), in which he extended his analysis of Cabell's oeuvre to the *Nightmare* trilogy. Here he detected a "misanthropic sadism," one growing out of a South that had to live on dead dreams, a thesis that allies Cabell to the Gothic element inherent in southern fiction. Since this time, much serious work has been done on Cabell (see bibliography).

II

With the overstatement that Cabell himself indulged in, he is credited with being the author of fity-two published books (titles would be more accurate). Of his major works, *Jurgen, Figures of Earth, The High Place,* and *The Silver Stallion* deserve to be included in any serious consideration of supernatural fiction. These four, along with his entry into the genre, *Cream of the Jest,* a few lesser excursions, and his "farewell" to other worlds, *Something About Eve,* constitute the corpus of Cabell's traffic with the supernatural in his major phase. At his technical best, his "distancing from the ordinary," to use Ursula Le Guin's term, is achieved through language, geography, "conductor" characters, and the ability to maintain the "anti-expected," to use

Eric Rabkin's term. As Mark Allen (in Inge and MacDonald) points out:

> Nearly all imaginable types of portals are found in the Biography. We have simple journeys across boundaries, magical ventures thorugh windows and doorways, sudden transformations of dream and vision, death and rebirth. We find conjuring spells like Manuel's invocation of Freydis, objects of power like Miramon's Bees of Toupan, sending spells by which Dolores projects Jurgen into hell. In each case, the device offers us a means to glimpse new sets of laws with the characters, unfamiliar geographies, and purely imaginative experiences.

The Cream of the Jest, Cabell's first critical success as well as his first excursus on the power of the dream world over the real, utilizes a distancing device that he had used only incidentally before—attribution of the story to another author. In this work he employs no less than three concentric narrators. In his study of point of view, *The Rhetoric of Fiction,* Wayne Booth uses this as an example in discussing the advantages of not providing a clear authorial voice, of deliberately confusing the reader through an observer who is himself confused. Cabell's trio of narrators "break down the reader's conventional notions of what is real" by undermining "the reader's normal trust in what the narrator says." Kennaston's talisman of power, the Sigil of Scoteia, which transports him through time and space, is revealed to be only half of a broken cover to a jar of cold cream. The jest is that all mundane objects have been imbued with their powers of magic by the enchanted themselves. Jurgen's "portal" is a centaur on which he rides in a race with the sun back in time to an enchanted garden between dawn and sunrise. In *Figures of Earth,* Manuel ascends Vraidex, the mountain of the sorcerer Miramon Lluagor, "lord of the nine kinds of sleep and prince of the seven madnesses." Later Manuel passes through the Window of Ageus (anagram for *usage*) to retrieve a lock of hair from Suskind (anagram for *unkiss'd*). In *The High Place,* Florian ascends Vraidex, where Holiness and Beauty lie sleeping; ironically, when he awakens the sleeping princess, he awakens to disenchantment. In *The Silver Stallion,*

Coth's "maps served faithfully to guide him, until Coth perforce went over the edge of the last one, into a country which was not upon any map." Another portal in this work is Kerin's fall down the Well of Ogde. Gerald Musgrave (Mustwrite) in *Something About Eve* exchanges bodies with a Sylvan, the latter desiring the use of Gerald's human body; Gerald, freed from the shackles of humanity, voyages to the worlds he could only imagine previously.

Cabell wrote essentially of voyages, quests into wonder, and of the inevitable return to less than satisfactory compromises in a dubiously "real" world. In the 1920's his quests were welcomed as sophisticated allegory; today they are read primarily as beguiling fantasy. Judging from the sustained if limited recent interest in his work, one may safely predict that Cabell will continue to be discovered by a respectable number of readers who are willing to accept his portals for their journeys into the worlds of the imagination, worlds that irradiate mundane reality.

Selected Bibliography

WORKS OF JAMES BRANCH CABELL

The Cream of the Jest. New York: McBride, 1917.

Jurgen. New York: McBride, 1919.

Figures of Earth. New York: McBride, 1921.

The High Place. New York: McBride, 1923.

The Music from Behind the Moon. New York: John Day, 1926.

The Silver Stallion. New York: McBride, 1926.

Something About Eve. New York: McBride, 1927.

The White Robe. New York: McBride, 1928.

The Way of Ecben. New York: McBride, 1929.

Smirt: An Urbane Nightmare. New York: McBride, 1934.

Smith: A Sylvan Interlude. New York: McBride, 1935.

Smire: An Acceptance in the Third Person. Garden City, N.Y.: Doubleday, 1937.

CRITICAL AND BIOGRAPHICAL STUDIES

Davis, Joe Lee. *James Branch Cabell.* New York: Twayne, 1962. (An erudite and sympathetic reading that denies that Cabell wrote novels; claims that Cabell's works are blends of romance, anatomy, and confession.)

Inge, M. Thomas, and MacDonald, Edgar E., eds. *James Branch Cabell: Centennial Essays.* Baton Rouge: Louisiana State University Press, 1983. (Based on the 1979 Cabell symposium sponsored by the Friends of the James Branch Cabell Library, Virginia Commonwealth University, Richmond. Papers by Mark Allen, Leslie Fiedler, Joseph M. Flora, William Leigh Godshalk, Edgar E. MacDonald, Louis D. Rubin, Dorothy McInnis Scura, Ritchie D. Watson.)

Tarrant, Desmond. *James Branch Cabell: The Dream and the Reality.* Norman: University of Oklahoma Press, 1967. (Treats Cabell as a Jungian mythmaker probing the unconscious for universals.)

Wells, Arvin. *Jesting Moses: A Study in Cabellian Comedy.* Gainesville: University of Florida Press, 1962. (Places Cabell in the tradition of Rabelais; sees the pattern of Cabell's work as based on the contrast between illusion and perception of reality, resulting in rebellion followed by reluctant acceptance.)

BIBLIOGRAPHICAL STUDIES

Brewer, Joan Frances. *James Branch Cabell: A Bibliography of His Writings, Biography and Criticism.* Charlottesville: University Press of Virginia, 1957. (Definitive with regard to published writings, but arranges entries according to Cabell's later concept of his work as a "planned whole.")

Bruccoli, Matthew J. *James Branch Cabell: A Bibliography, Part II. Notes on the Cabell Collection at the University of Virginia.* Charlottesville: University Press of Virginia, 1957. (Planned as a second volume to Brewer's bibliography listed above. Includes all editions of Cabell at the University of Virginia, annotates 414 letters, catalogs manuscripts.)

Duke, Maurice. *James Branch Cabell: A Reference Guide.* Boston: G. K. Hall, 1979. (Flawed by "selectivity" or oversights and general unevenness of annotation.)

Watson, Ritchie D. "James Branch Cabell: A Bibliographic Essay." In *James Branch Cabell: Centennial Essays,* edited by Thomas M. Inge and Edgar E. MacDonald. (An overview of Cabellian criticism in major scholarly journals, with coverage of specialist Cabellian periodicals.)

PERIODICALS

The Cabellian. Eight issues published, fall 1968 through 1972. No longer published.

Kalki. First number issued in 1965. Still sporadically published.

—EDGAR MacDONALD

STEPHEN VINCENT BENÉT

1898-1943

I

THE DEMISE OF Stephen Vincent Benét's literary reputation is a stark reminder of how fleeting fame can be. Heralded after the publication of *John Brown's Body* in 1928 as "the national poet" and certainly one of the most popular short story writers of his day, Benét now is largely forgotten, having been relegated to the nether ring of minor poets by such influential critics as F. O. Matthiessen and remembered by others only as the author of "The Devil and Daniel Webster." With his relentless concern for the glories of the American past and with his often folksy diction, Benét is deemed old-fashioned, an upholder of overblown patriotism and outgrown values. This is unfortunate, for by writing ordinary people into his historical poems, he brought a new immediacy to the Civil War and the Western frontier and discovered a medley of regional dialects. Furthermore, although certainly not in the mainstream of supernatural writers, Benét worked some wonderful experiments with the fantastic folktale, infusing the genre with a peculiarly modern spirit by suggesting that while the supernatural is more pervasive than we generally acknowledge, it is also much more banal.

II

Stephen Vincent Benét was born in Bethlehem, Pennsylvania, on 22 July 1898 into an old army family that prided itself as much on intellectual incli-

nation as on military achievement. Among his relatives were the co-inventor of the Benét-Mercier machine gun and a famous brigadier general. His father, also a career officer, ran his home as a kind of literary salon, according to Benét's biographer Charles Fenton. As a result, the three Benét children (all of whom grew up to be writers) were raised in a rather heady atmosphere, listening to their father recite poetry, being encouraged by their poet-mother to try their hands at verse. The family idyll was disrupted for Benét by nine unhappy months at a military academy (later described in thoroughly Dickensian terms in his first novel, *The Beginning of Wisdom*, 1921). He was also left severely weakened by a childhood case of scarlet fever. Nevertheless, he managed at age seventeen to publish his first collection of verse and sell a poem to the *New Republic*.

This and subsequent publications induced Malcolm Cowley, then editor of the *Harvard Advocate*, to dub him "the bright star not only of Yale but of all eastern colleges"—an impressive epithet at a time when Archibald MacLeish, F. Scott Fitzgerald, and T. S. Eliot were on the class lists. And yet, although Benét trod many of the same paths as his contemporaries (working as a cryptographer with Thornton Wilder at the beginning of World War I and, like F. Scott Fitzgerald and Sherwood Anderson, doing a stint in a New York advertising firm after receiving his B.A. from Yale in 1919 and before going on to earn his M.A. there in 1920), he never thoroughly aligned himself with the Lost Generation. He chose a more domestic, if not quieter, existence.

After marrying the writer Rosemary Carr in 1921, Benét spurned the New York literary scene (which he termed "fraternity politics all over again") and began churning out short stories and serials for the popular magazines. Poetry he allowed himself only on vacations or when, as in 1926, he won a Guggenheim to study in Paris. He used this reprieve remarkably well, writing the Pulitzer Prize–winning *John Brown's Body* in less than a year. But his hopes of subsidizing a few more years of poetry with its earnings were soon dashed by the Great Depression. Shortly after returning to the United States, he was forced to resume the grind of commercial writing that lasted the rest of his life.

A diary entry from the mid-1930's suggests how difficult this must have been for Benét: "This degrading, humiliating, and constant need of money stupefies the mind and saps the vitality. Will I ever get free of it and be able to do my work in peace?" (Fenton, *Stephen Vincent Benét*). And yet, what is striking about Benét is the rigor with which he pursued even the kind of writing that he detested. Twelve weeks of working nonstop on the script of D. W. Griffith's *Abraham Lincoln* were followed by the press of writing more stories for "the chewing gum trade" and, despite an attack of arthritis, a brisk tour on the lecture circuit. At the same time he was working on a novel, collaborating with his wife on a collection of children's verse, and writing an increasingly dark series of poems for the *New Yorker*. Only near the end of the decade did he begin to take his short fiction more seriously, daring, for instance, to address the financial desperation of the decade in "The Devil and Daniel Webster" and developing his own brand of fantastic folktale in "Doc Mellhorn and the Pearly Gates."

Despite a second and almost crippling attack of arthritis and a brief period of mental collapse, Benét's output between 1937 and 1942 was greater than ever. According to Fenton, Benét was writing six to eight stories a year and, for the first time in his life, working simultaneously on his poetry and prose. In addition, in 1940 he began writing a number of poems, pamphlets, and radio scripts for the war effort. One of these, a poetic radio script called "Listen to the People," read as a preface to President Roosevelt's Fourth of July broadcast in 1941 and published the same week in *Life*, made Benét, by Fenton's calculation, "heard by more Americans than any other serious writer in the history of the United States." It also stepped up the demand for his political writing. Even when he seemed to know that the end was near ("Get dummy for collected edition," says an entry in his diary. "A very handsome tombstone" [Fenton]) he continued to write for the Office of War Information while trying to complete *Western Star*, a companion to *John Brown's Body*. He never finished it. Recuperating from a heart attack, Stephen Vincent Benét died in his New York City apartment on 13 March 1943. Two weeks later the *Saturday Review of Literature* paid tribute to him with a memorial issue, and in 1944 *Western Star* was awarded a Pulitzer Prize.

III

The titles of Stephen Vincent Benét's first two collections of short stories, *Thirteen O'Clock* (1937) and *Tales Before Midnight* (1939), can be misleading. Only seven of these twenty-five stories (published posthumously in 1943 in a volume called *Twenty-five Short Stories*) employ the supernatural, and then primarily as a vehicle for Benét's chief concern—defining a distinctly American culture that has grown out of a uniquely American past.

The most famous of these, "The Devil and Daniel Webster" (*Saturday Evening Post*, 24 October 1936), is a case in point. Benét was quite direct about what he considered the thrust of this story:

> It's always seemed to me that legends and yarns and folk-tales are as much a part of the real history of a country as proclamations and provisos and constitutional amendments. . . . "The Devil and Daniel Webster" is an attempt at telling such a legend. . . . I couldn't help wondering what would happen if a man like that ever came to grips with the Devil—and not an imported Devil, either, but a genuine, homegrown product, Mr. Scratch.

> (Fenton, page 295)

Interestingly enough, Benét makes his "homegrown Mr. Scratch" a dapper American businessman, quick to leap on the oath that Jabez Stone utters when he runs into financial trouble on his farm, and equally eager to get the soul of Daniel Webster when the orator comes to the farmer's aid. More mincing than menacing, Benét's Satan is too stylized to be truly frightening. But he is a droll symbol of the greed that threatens our country's values and a welcome foil for the somewhat overblown Webster, who is convinced that "if two New Hampshire men aren't a match for the devil, we might as well give the country back to the Indians."

The collection of butchers, witch burners, and pirates called from the dead to sit on the trial for Stone's soul, on the other hand, is genuinely ghastly. And, in addition to raising the awful possibility that the final arbiters of life are consummately evil, they neatly undercut the sentimentality of the tale. When they are finally moved by Webster's speech, it is out of respect for what Webster calls "the failures and the endless journey of mankind," and not only because of Webster's power. This seems to suggest that the story is as much about the obdurate pioneering spirit as it is about an American Faust or a New World Job, as some critics claim. In any case, it has proved to be a popular story, having been produced as an opera in 1939 (with libretto by Benét), a film (*All That Money Can Buy*, 1941), and several stage and television plays, as well as having been reprinted in many anthologies.

After the success of "The Devil and Daniel Webster," Benét wrote two more Webster tales for the *Saturday Evening Post*: "Daniel Webster and the Sea Serpent" (22 May 1937) and "Daniel Webster and the Ides of March" (28 October 1939). Only "Daniel Webster and the Sea Serpent" has been reprinted (*Thirteen O'Clock*).

A comic folktale in the tradition of the Paul Bunyan stories, the "Sea Serpent" purports to explain how Daniel Webster, secretary of state, got himself out of an awkward social predicament at the same time he got the United States out of a war. This time "Dan'l" is up against Samanthy, a leviathan of no ordinary intelligence who falls madly in love with him. Following him to Washington, she stirs up a ruckus, threatening his negotiations with England and demanding the return of her affections. It is not long, however, before Dan'l, with his mythological wit, comes up with a solution: he makes Samanthy part of the American navy, which has the double effect of scaring off the British ambassador and of consigning the enamored fish to the South Seas.

The implication seems to be that more went into the making of this country than we usually imagine. But this is a theme Benét handles better in a later story such as "O'Halloran's Luck." In "Daniel Webster and the Sea Serpent" the heavy-handed paean to Webster's ingenuity is only barely buoyed up by the narrator's winking good humor and by amusing details like Samanthy's predilection for Italian sardines.

Set in contemporary New York and somewhat critical of the people it finds there, "The King of the Cats" (*Harper's Bazaar*, February 1929) is a completely different kind of story. It is based on a European folktale that reflects a very primitive way of regarding animals as the possessors of hidden supernatural powers and institutions. In Benét's hands, the story gets not only an American setting but also a comic touch.

Here the supernatural feline comes in the shape of Monsieur Tibault, a European conductor human in every respect except for his extraordinary tail—an appendage he uses to conduct the orchestra and to captivate New York society. Only Tommy Brooks, a thoroughly shallow Princetonian, remains immune. It seems his almond-eyed girlfriend—a descendant of Siamese royalty—has also fallen for Tibault. Jealousy, of course, whets suspicion, and it is not long before Tommy finds out exactly why Tibault likes to curl up on the couch. But even after he learns the magic of the famous legend and sends Tibault up in a cloud of smoke, Tommy hardly triumphs. He loses his princess and winds up with a pedestrian wife from Chicago.

While this tale lacks the liquid elegance of, say, Algernon Blackwood's otherworldly cat story "Ancient Sorceries," it has plenty of comic bite. One can only surmise that the supernatural cats are far too elegant for the superficial Tommy, who is incapable of appreciating any world but his own.

For the stories collected in *Tales Before Midnight*, Benét turns from legendary to commonplace characters and sends them on great American journeys, the goal of which is usually work.

In "Johnny Pye and the Fool-killer" (*Saturday Evening Post*, 18 September 1937), the journey begins when Johnny's harsh foster parents, a miller and his wife, threaten him once too often with their image of death — the demon who destroys all fools. A smart boy, Johnny suspects that "the Fool-killer got you wherever you went." Nevertheless, he decides to "give him a run for his money," and, leaving home, the boy begins his search for work that might help him escape the folly of ordinary mortals.

The story then catalogs the men Johnny meets along the way, everyone from a quack selling "Old Doctor Waldo's Unparalleled Universal Remedy" to the president of the United States. Although one is clever and another rich or brave, they all make some mistake that sets Johnny to hearing the approach of the Fool-killer, so eventually Johnny acknowledges the futility of his quest and decides to return home. This is a decision the Fool-killer seems to respect; when the scissors-grinder finally comes for Johnny, he offers to let Johnny live if he can solve this riddle: "How can a man be a human being and not be a fool?" In an amusing twist, Johnny's answer, "When he's dead and gone and buried," and his subsequent refusal to accept immortality without immortal youth, make a fool of the Fool-killer; he has to take Johnny even though the man is not a fool.

Benét reappraises the stature of death again in "Doc Mellhorn and the Pearly Gates," a matter-of-fact fantasy about the afterlife of a crusty old country doctor (*Saturday Evening Post*, 24 December 1938). What gives the story its crispness is the narrator's droll omnipotence and indulgent patience with skeptics like the good doctor and us. It also offers one of Benét's best opening lines: "Doc Mellhorn had never expected to go anywhere at all when he died. So, when he found himself on the road again, it surprised him."

Once past the Pearly Gates, Mellhorn, of course, has to accept the existence of heaven. But, he reasons, he does not have to stay there; he elects to go to hell instead, where people need him. The problem is that his clinic there is such a success it plays

"merry Hades with the whole system," and Mellhorn is kicked upstairs once again. En route, he falls into a deep depression, until he finds that he is not necessarily doomed in heaven to eternal rest.

"O'Halloran's Luck" (*Country Gentleman*, May 1938) is another tale told to correct popular misconceptions, especially those which maintain that leprechauns are confined to Ireland or that the supernatural life of America is not as rich as that of the old country. In this story, such spirits are fundamental to the strength of this nation. O'Halloran's luck is only one example.

The title refers to the leprechaun that Tim O'Halloran rescues from wolves on the Western prairie. After exchanging stories about old times in County Clonmelly and about how hard it is for Irishmen, no matter what size, to make their way in this country, Tim and the leprechaun decide to throw in their lot together on the railroad. Posing as a nephew of Tim's named Rory, the leprechaun proves more than a little mischievous around camp. But with his second sight, he also proves extremely useful. Giving Tim prescient tips on how to build the railroad, he helps the Irishman first to a promotion and then to a girl. In return, Tim's kindness helps Rory to leprechaun liberty. At times, swelling lessons about hard work, happenstance, and freedom threaten to engulf this story, but in the end, irascible characters and rolling dialect lend it a salutary charm.

A fantastic truth about the birth of the nation is also the subject of "A Tooth for Paul Revere," the only fantastic folktale in Benét's *Selected Works* (1942) that did not appear in earlier collections. First published in the *Atlantic Monthly* (December 1937), the story posits that the American Revolution began not with Paul Revere or the Founding Fathers, but with an apolitical Lexington farmer in search of a cure for his aching tooth. Having been told that Paul Revere is as good at forging artificial teeth as he is at silver, Lige Butterwick travels to Boston, where he cannot help noticing the tension between Redcoats and colonists. Meeting Paul Revere raises his patriotic consciousness still further, so when he accidentally takes the magic box that Revere has filled with "gunpowder and war and the makings of a new nation," he knows that he must take his own ride to join Revere on the road between Lexington and Concord.

In his critical study of Stephen Vincent Benét, Parry Stroud says that with this story Benét makes "in fresh fashion the point that the American Revolution began when the common man, through whatever homely circumstances, joined the leaders in becoming involved in political issues." But contemporary readers may find that freshness marred by the quaintness of the characters and the cuteness of the supernatural machinery, which seem to work against each other and the theme.

As a rule, Benét is much more successful when he reverses the formula and exposes the homeliness of the not-necessarily-supernatural. This is what he does with such wit in "Doc Mellhorn" and "Johnny Pye" and what he does again, with equal drollery, in "The Angel Was a Yankee" (*McCall's*, October 1940).

A wry little story about "the biggest attraction" P. T. Barnum "never got," "The Angel Was a Yankee" recalls how, after winning the angel from a recalcitrant farmer, the circus owner suffers a pang of conscience and lets the little fellow go. It seems that he cannot quite bring himself to hold a fellow Yankee. He does, however, manage to ask the angel if death will afford him "the opportunities to meet celebrities—er—such as George Washington, for instance." But the New England angel, a captain in his lifetime and a captain now, only gives this unsatisfying reply, "Ain't seen 'em. I'm telling you—Coast Guard duty. Far as the Grand Banks. Can't tell you I've seen 'em when I ain't."

Crackling dialogue and salty characters form the comic soul of this story. Especially good are the sketches of Barnum, the wily Yankee who is ultimately outwitted, and the laconic little angel who confesses that he just cannot believe the circus midget is real.

Benét took a darker view of beings from the otherworld and their earthly counterparts in the stories he wrote after 1940. Although it occasionally strains against his optimism, most of the stories published in *The Last Circle* (1946) reflect a growing sense that human life might not amount to much and that the afterlife cannot comfortably be mocked. "The Danger of Shadows" (*Harper's Bazaar*, May 1941), for instance, questions the value of both work and family and gives harrowing form to the spirit that would have life another way.

Tired of the dull routine of Harbison's job and marriage, Harbison's shadow grows defiant, tugging him toward his young secretary and resisting him on the walk home. At first, Harbison puts up a struggle. But as the winter wears on, he grows weary, while his shadow seems "to grow more corporeal everyday." Once the shadow convinces him to leave his wife and children, however, Harbison realizes that he has to get rid of his shadow; suicide seems the only way.

An unfortunate domestic denouement flattens the ending of the story. But before that, the threatening figure on the wall and the suggestion that our shadows may lead very active lives of their own are as unsettling as the image of Harbison's drab existence.

Work also fails to bring salvation in "The Minister's Books" (*Atlantic Monthly*, August 1942); in fact, ambition to succeed contributes to the main character's demise.

Set in the late nineteenth century, the story traces a young minister's seduction into a coven of ghostly witches. Alone in a new town and struggling with his ministry, Hugh McRidden finds himself strangely drawn to the books in his library. Each marked with a bookplate picturing a stern-looking group of Puritans gathered "for what appears to be prayer" in an open glade, the tomes seem at first to be religious histories. But *An Examen into the Invisible* soon opens his eyes, and it is not long before he succumbs to the magic. Although ridden with guilt, the minister relishes the "fearsome joy in crossing to the other side" and his miraculous ability to save the town from a deadly epidemic. When the time comes to pay for these favors with a human sacrifice, however, McRidden's original ministry wins out, and he choses to kill himself instead.

Although once again the suicide is aborted, this time the character's salvation is far from secure. The warlock from the eighteenth-century bookplate catches up with McRidden, and Benét provides no clue as to whether the meeting is the product of madness or not. Full of dark hints about the evil done in the guise of Christianity and about the villagers' chilling indifference, this is one of Benét's bleakest and deepest tales.

"William Riley and the Fates" (*Atlantic Monthly*, November 1941) is also about the intrusion of the extraordinary in ordinary American life, but this time the story is weighed down by heavy-handed homilies and the implausible prospect of the Fates picnicking in a public park.

Benét's portrait of William Riley — a young man eager for the achievements he is sure he is going to attain — is wonderful. But the Fates — three women who seem "to be knitting all the time" and a wizened old man spinning a wheel of fortune — are an obvious crew, sent in to warn him against taking the future for granted. The trouble is that the story, published barely two months before the attack on Pearl Harbor, dissolves into propaganda, and Benét's best devices, like the Fates's futuristic newsreel of a war-torn Europe, are undermined by William's facile conversion from isolationism and his glib pronouncement that "fate's Fate, but a country's what you make it."

"The Gold Dress" (*Cosmopolitan*, July 1942) works much better. Eschewing broad statements about the national character, Benét explores the yearnings of a repressed old maid and brings a touch of comic poignancy to the ghost tale.

The mechanism is standard: never having gotten what she wanted in life, Louella Weedon comes back to demand her due — love, merriment, and the young banker she had hoped to marry. The sad twist is that even as a ghost Louella is bound by propriety. All she can do is sit primly in her parlor and ask her young man to help with the sewing. Only under the hilariously understated threat of exorcism can Louella blurt out what she really wants — one of the fine dresses that have lain hidden in her closet for twenty years. Clearly, it is difficult to fulfill even the simplest desires.

Even the most optimistic story in this group, "The Land Where There Is No Death" (*Redbook*, October 1942), contains a strain of uncertainty. On the surface a comforting allegory about the inseparability of life and death, the tale also suggests that the best of stories can lead us astray.

The title refers to the land that young John invents to console his childhood companion Hilda, distraught over her first experience with death. As the two children grow older, they elaborate upon the myth and then forget it until, under the pressure of taking his clerical exams, John resurrects and begins to believe in the fantasy. Reasoning that death cannot exist if God is truly good, he leaves school to travel "into strange lands, among strange folk" only to end, not surprisingly, where he began. An old man, with nothing but the stories he has told along the way to show for his life, John tries to frame one last tale to warn others against such delusions. But his story of death turns into a story of life as he realizes that without death there could be no life, that people would not know "what it was to be safe if they knew not danger." The implication is that death is not an end but a beginning. Still, it does not squelch the possibility that, near death himself, Benét was seriously questioning the worth of a lifetime spent telling stories.

IV

One might question the significance of Benét's fantastic fiction with the same misgiving, and first because it was not his primary medium. Benét was a poet who turned to short stories only under financial duress and then with some contempt. Fenton reports that Benét went into the business with some reluctance, confessing, "The short story is not my forte," and Benét himself was in the habit of deriding his "bright, gay stories about gay, bright, young dumb people." Of one he said, "It is a dear little candy laxative of a tale. . . . I do not see how it can fail to sell — it is so cheap." Second, even when, in the mid-1930's, he began to take the form seriously, he was more interested in writing folktales that would enrich our literary heritage than he was in the possibilities and implications of the fantastic itself. But as he worked with the form — fitting otherworldly beings with contemporary concerns and re-imagining the spiritual life of the past — he did add a new dimension to the genre that might still be exploited. One wonders what a Doc Mellhorn would find en route to heaven today, or how a contemporary writer would handle Daniel Webster's confrontation with the devil.

Selected Bibliography

WORKS OF STEPHEN VINCENT BENÉT

The Devil and Daniel Webster. New York: Farrar and Rinehart, 1937. (Separate publication of the short story that was first printed in the *Saturday Evening Post*, 24 October 1936.)

Thirteen O'Clock. Stories of Several Worlds. New York: Farrar and Rinehart, 1937. London: Heinemann, 1938.

Johnny Pye and the Fool-killer. Weston, Vt.: Countryman Press, 1938. (Separate publication of the short story that was first printed in the *Saturday Evening Post*, 18 September 1937.)

The Devil and Daniel Webster. New York: Dramatists Play Service, 1939. (One-act play.)

The Devil and Daniel Webster: An Opera in One Act. New York: Farrar and Rinehart, 1939. (Libretto, the music to which was written by Douglas Moore.)

Tales Before Midnight. New York: Farrar and Rinehart, 1939. London: Heinemann, 1940.

Selected Works of Stephen Vincent Benét. 2 vols. New York: Rinehart, 1942. (Reprints.)

"All That Money Can Buy." In *Twenty Best Film Plays,* edited by John Gassner and Dudley Nichols. New York: Crown, 1943. (The screenplay version of *The Devil and Daniel Webster,* issued in 1941.)

Twenty-Five Short Stories. New York: Sun Dial, 1943. (Reprints *Thirteen O'Clock* and *Tales Before Midnight.*)

The Last Circle. New York: Farrar and Straus, 1946. London: Heinemann, 1948. (Previously uncollected material.)

Stephen Vincent Benét: Selected Poetry and Prose. Edited by Basil Davenport. New York: Holt, 1960. (Paperback edition.)

CRITICAL AND BIOGRAPHICAL STUDIES

"As We Remember Him." *Saturday Review of Literature,* 27 March 1943. (Memorial issue with tributes from Philip Barry, William Rose Benét, John Farrar, Archibald MacLeish, and Thornton Wilder, among others.)

Fenton, Charles A. *Stephen Vincent Benét: The Life and Times of an American Man of Letters.* New Haven, Conn.: Yale University Press, 1958.

————, ed. *Selected Letters of Stephen Vincent Benét.* New Haven, Conn.: Yale University Press, 1960.

Matthiessen, F. O. "The New Poetry." In *The Literary History of the United States,* edited by R. E. Spiller and others. Vol. 2. New York: Macmillan, 1946.

Stroud, Parry. *Stephen Vincent Benét.* Boston: Twayne, 1962.

BIBLIOGRAPHY

Maddocks, Gladys Louise. "Stephen Vincent Benét: A Bibliography." *Bulletin of Bibliography and Dramatic Index.* Part I (September 1951): 142–146; Part II (April 1952): 158–160.

— ROBIN BROMLEY

THORNE SMITH

1891–1934

THORNE SMITH WAS—with the possible exception of James Branch Cabell—the naughtiest of important American fantasists. But while time has transformed this quality in Cabell's work from the shocking to the quaintly nostalgic, leaving the substance of his complex, ironic vision for contemporary readers to appreciate, Smith's work must still be approached primarily in terms of its social and moral context. The word *naughty* still applies, with all of its connotations. Smith's novels, like that archaic word that describes them, are dated beyond redemption.

This is not to say that they cannot be enjoyed today, nearly a half-century after their publication, but only that these works were the product of sensibilities and attitudes characteristic of a particular moment in American history, a time when Victorian innocence and prudery had collapsed in serious writing, and the cracks were showing—but only barely—in the popular media. It was the age of the tease and the double entendre. In this atmosphere the sly, boisterous, frivolous wit of Thorne Smith, coupled with his extravagant imagination and doctrine of playful, hilarious irresponsibility, could thrive.

James Thorne Smith, Jr., was born on 27 March 1891 at the U.S. Naval Academy at Annapolis. His father, Commodore James Thorne Smith, U.S.N., supervised the Port of New York during World War I. The younger Smith was educated at the Locust Dale Academy (Virginia), St. Luke's School (Wayne,

Pennsylvania), and Dartmouth. His career in advertising was interrupted by the war when, following the family tradition, he enlisted in the navy. It was during his naval service that he began to write fiction. While editing the service newspaper *Broadside*, he published his first effort, *Biltmore Oswald* (1918), and its sequel, *Out of Luck*, in its back pages.

Although realistic in approach, these protracted sketches of the bewildered naval recruit's shipboard experiences exhibit Smith's whimsical humor and situational inventiveness, and were commercially successful when subsequently published in book form. However, it was not until Smith combined this humor with a fantastic premise in *Topper* (1926) that he found the personal formula that was to characterize his brief, prolific career as a best-selling fantasist of America's middle-class manners and morals in transition.

Cosmo Topper is the quintessential Smith hero: in his late thirties, safely ensconced in his job as a banker and in his marriage, his neighborhood, and his predictable life-style: "So completely and successfully had he inhibited himself that he veritably believed he was the freest person in the world." Yet as the novel opens Topper has nagging doubts, an impatience with his wife's routine and a stifled desire to protest her choice of lamb for dinner, a dream of escape to Calcutta, a preoccupation with eyes—the predictable eyes of his friends and associates, the mysterious eyes of his cat, and his own uncharacteristic eyes: "His face was unremarkable save for his eyes, which were extremely blue and youthful, as if the fire in them had been banked for the sake of conservation." In short, all Topper needs to set his rebellion going is the right sort of spark.

That spark comes when Topper impulsively buys a notorious automobile formerly owned by George and Marion Kerby, a fun-loving couple killed when they drove the vehicle into a tree. What Topper does not realize is that with the purchase of the automobile he has also acquired its former owners in the form of "low-planed" spirits—temporarily earthbound ghosts, a condition that allows the newly dead to get used to their situation before moving on.

Considering his stuffiness, Topper adjusts with remarkable alacrity to his ghostly traveling companions. Indeed, one of the characteristics of Smith's fantasies is that the fantastic event or condition enters his mundane characters' lives with very little fanfare and almost immediate, matter-of-fact acceptance, at least by the novels' protagonists. There is as much humor generated by Topper's casual acceptance of George and Marion as there is later by the chaos that these creatures generate. Thus, *Topper* illustrates two conditions that operate in Smith's novels: the relationship between the protagonist and the fantastic situations he is thrust into, and the humor provoked by the bizarre intrusions of spirits or other incredible phenomena into the real world of America in the 1920's and 1930's. Add to that Smith's dramatic sense and verbal dexterity, and the formula is complete. When these elements are in a proper balance, the novels are entertaining and at times enlightening; when they are not, contrivance and literary slapstick replace characterization and satiric perception.

Once the Kerbys have established themselves as Topper's companions, the book turns into a series of episodic confrontations between Topper and his ghostly companions and various would-be authority figures. Since Topper is the only corporeal member of the group, he is constantly thrust between the Kerbys' rambunctious, selectively amoral behavior and that of the most staid members of social institutions. The Kerbys continually get him into trouble, exacerbate the problem, then eventually rescue him or absent themselves long enough for him to extricate himself.

But *Topper* is more than a series of bizarre situations, ludicrous characters, and running gags. The real center of the novel lies in the education of Cosmo Topper from straitlaced philistine and secular puritan to generous, fun-loving, free spirit. Once he meets the Kerbys, they quickly introduce Topper to the first ingredient in his emancipation, hard liquor. Marion, rather indirectly and coyly, subsequently adds the second—sex. The rejuvenation of Topper is not simply behavioral but moral as well, and implies at least a semiserious message.

Published in the heyday of Prohibition, *Topper* offers alcohol as a psychological and moral panacea—an elixir capable of freeing the imagination from stultifying assumptions, the moral sense from bigotry and blind adherence to false values, the soul from greed and self-doubt, and the body from slothful passivity. Even the fact that strong drink propelled the Kerbys into their fatal tree is treated as a lark.

More subtle and interesting to the contemporary reader is Smith's handling of sexuality. In *Topper*, as in most of Smith's fantasies, women are the primary agents of both repression and emancipation. In the best of the novels the Topper-like figure is caught between the wife, who represents social stability, moral rigidity, and behavioral inhibition, and a femme fatale of a kind, a younger, prettier, livelier female who challenges the hero's staid way of life. Sex is at the center of the freedom offered, although Smith teases us with evasions and hints. While the antidrink fortress is immediately attacked and demolished in Smith's novels, the sexual citadel is approached much more indirectly and delicately, especially in *Topper*. Yet it is sex more than booze that finally converts Topper into a free soul.

After George and Marion initially jolt Topper loose from his moral moorings, quickly converting him to the joys of drink and general carousing, George vanishes and Marion remains to guide Topper through the more complicated and subtle stages in his reformation. "You're my first and only child," she tells him. "I'll make a man of you yet." And, after a fashion, she does.

Topper falls in love with Marion and becomes her willing accomplice in all areas of general misbehavior—drinking, partying, breaking and entering, petty theft—perhaps copulation ("perhaps" because Smith is so evasive about it; not until *Topper Takes a Trip* do Topper and Marion become unambiguous lovers). All the while, Topper protests his fidelity to Mrs. Topper. While never made explicit, the promise, via gesture, innuendo, and constant verbal tease, of idyllic, illicit sexual bliss fuels Topper's erratic rebellion. By the time George reappears, Marion has lured, shocked, coerced, and possibly seduced Topper into a new view of life. As he bids farewell (he thinks) to the Kerbys, he makes a farewell toast:

"I toast you all," he said, "as a revelation to me of a larger life and a lighter death. And I thank you all for the changes you have wrought in me. Once I was a law-abiding, home-loving and highly respected member of my community. Within a few short months you have changed all of that. Now I am a jailbird, a hard drinker, a wife deserter and an undesirable dissolute outcast. And I am glad of it. Only a few short miles now separate me from my home, but let me assure you that they will be the hardest miles I have ever travelled in my life."

(chapter 20)

Then, wistfully, Topper adds an aside to Marion:

"You've created happiness in me.... You've awakened dreams and left memories. You've made me humble and you've made me human. You've taught me to understand how a man with a hangover feels. You've lifted me forever out of the rut of my smug existence. I'll go back to it, I know, but I won't be the same man."

"You never were," she answered logically, "you never were intended to be. Nobody is, but life gets you, life and the economic urge—success, esteem, safety. How many of our triumphs in life spring from negative impulsives, the fear of losing rather than the wish to win. It's a lot of talk, Topper, the whole damn show. And no one alive today is to blame. We must thank the ages past and bow to their false gods. We dress them up in new garments, but in their essence they're just the same—power, property and pride. You can't get away from them, the subsidized steps to salvation."

(chapter 20)

Topper does return home to resume his old life, of course, a changed, sadder, and wiser man. And he is pleased to discover that as a side effect of his rebellion, Mrs. Topper has also loosened up. Thus, the book ends on a happy yet sadly wistful note.

Topper was published just four years after Sinclair Lewis' *Babbitt*, and the two novels have much in common: a middle-class businessman conformist meets a free-spirited woman who tempts him into a brief rebellion. The rebellion is transitory, and the rebel returns to the fold; but in the process he has learned much about himself, his society, and life. If Lewis' realistic comedy is more memorable than Smith's fantastic one, the difference lies not in any superiority of realism over fantasy but in the greater intensity of Lewis' uncompromising bitterness over Smith's rather wistful cynicism.

The commercial success of *Topper* launched Smith's career as a best-selling novelist and, a few years later, stimulated a sequel, *Topper Takes a Trip* (1932). But, despite the quality of its predecessor, *Topper Takes a Trip* is one of Smith's weakest novels—or, rather, *because* of the success of *Topper*, *Topper Takes a Trip* is poor. And the failure of the latter is most instructive in analyzing Smith's strengths and weaknesses.

Smith moves the setting of *Topper Takes a Trip* from Glendale, New Jersey, to the French Riviera, thus avoiding any uncomfortable references to the American depression economy. Cosmo Topper has settled comfortably into the role of middle-aged sophisticate that he had secured by the end of the previous novel. His experiences with the Kerbys have "not so much changed his character as ventilated it, giving it a chance to breathe good, honest vulgar air vitalized by the fumes of grog." He has retired from banking in favor of the life of a leisured expatriate, and although still married to Mrs. Topper, he has left her behind in the States. But he has become bored with his passive, idle-rich existence and yearns for the return of the Kerbys, who show up immediately to reanimate their protégé. But Smith's old joke has worn thin. With Topper now liberated, the humor provoked by his progressive emancipation is lost. Smith must fall back on the zany humor of invisible ghosts pranking the living, verbal wit, and plot contrivance. The novel becomes a series of humorous bits, with little real direction. And to squeeze more humor out of character conflict, Smith lets Topper regress periodically to his old state of moral and behavioral rigidity, thus adding laughs at the expense of character. The book is quite funny at times, but except for the account of the physical and emotional culmination of Topper's romance with Marion Kerby, the novel is little more than a sequence of amusing but strained comical vignettes.

Thus, Smith's satire requires a sympathetic, evolving character as a spine for the novel's development and as a foil for its fantastic intrusions. With the education of such a character at the center of the action, the best novels have a balance that keeps Smith's tendency to directionless slapstick and overextended verbal exchanges in check. But without such a character, the books become protracted fantastic jokes, enlivened by witty dialogue and individual scenes, but generally contrived and dated.

The Stray Lamb (1929) has a Topper-like figure in T. Lawrence Lamb, a well-to-do investment broker whose complacent life is upset when a "little russet man" gives him the unwished-for power to change into a variety of animals. Lamb had been made vulnerable to the russet man's wizardry by Sandra Rush, a pretty young model, who, encouraged by Lamb's teenage daughter Hebe, has set her sights on Lamb. Sandra is, of course, the Marion Kerby of this novel, and the conformity and hypocrisy that bind are again represented by his wife, Mary (who has been renamed Sapho by her daughter because of her penchant for amateur dramatics). The progressive metamorphoses give *The Stray Lamb* more comic variety than do the ghosts of *Topper*; and one chapter, "Less Than the Dust," in which Lamb surveys the world through the eyes of a mongrel stray, allows Smith a kind of bitter, poignant satire that is probably unmatched in his other works. Particularly striking is a brutal vignette in which one reveler dies of drink while his wife makes love to a friend in the next room—demonstrating with a vengeance the dark side of the Kerbyian party ethos. Lamb's education is more believable than Topper's because Sandra is more real, their relationship is more convincing, and the resolution is more satisfying, since Lamb finally breaks free of his social and marital restraints to begin a trium-

phant new life abroad with Sandra. (Sapho Lamb has taken a lover, so he is relieved of all moral responsibilities to her.)

After creating Topper and Lamb, Smith decided to experiment with a different sort of protagonist in his next fantasy novel, *The Night Life of the Gods* (1931), and that is the primary reason why the novel, for all its exuberant humor, fails. Crackpot inventor Hunter Hawk is already unorthodox, so he has little to learn from his bizarre experiences. In his persistent search for an "amusing" discovery, Hawk almost blows himself to pieces but, in the process, develops two quasi-magical rings, one with a white ray that turns living things into stone and the other with a green one that reverses the process. Immediately Hawk uses his new powers to turn all of his nagging relatives to stone, except Daphne Lambert, his high-spirited niece. Freed at last from his obnoxious family, Hawk takes to the woods with two bottles of burgundy; there he meets a small man in rags. This creature, who turns out to be one of the ancient "little people," leads Hawk to his daughter, a passionate, hot-tempered, nine-hundred-year-old female named Magaera (Meg) Turner. The couple instantly fall in love and set off for a grand party, armed with Hawk's rings and Meg's similar gifts (she can turn statues into living beings). After a number of farcical adventures, they end up at New York's Metropolitan Museum of Art, where they use their powers to bring the statues of figures from Greek mythology — Mercury, Hebe, Apollo, Perseus, Venus, Bacchus, Neptune, Diana, and Medusa's head — to life.

Thus, Smith creates two fantastic gimmicks in a single book, Hawk's romance with a passionate she-leprechaun and their animation of Greek deities in the middle of New York City. This all produces a considerable amount of comic activity but not much substance. The Hawk-Meg romance is amusing, especially when juxtaposed with Daphne's affair with her disreputable suitor, but the ribald antics of the living statues are more forced than funny. There is little in their behavior to suggest reawakened Greek gods except perhaps Bacchus' taste for liquor and Neptune's for fish. They are simply a gang of rowdies out on the town. Thus, the poignancy of their being turned back into stone is considerably blunted. And one is unprepared for Hawk's decision to turn himself and Meg into stone. The book ends on a sad and somewhat uncomfortable note; the shift from the farcical to the wistfully bittersweet is too sudden. Smith's apparent theme—that there is no place in the modern world for the truly unique and free-spirited—is provocative, but his fantasy characters are not real enough to sustain it.

Turnabout (1931) is arguably Smith's best book because its premise, while not completely original, is perfectly suited to his comedic and satirical talents. Tim and Sally Willows, having grown bored with their lives and marriage, constantly bicker over their respective roles in marriage and society. This finally provokes Mr. Ram, the Egyptian statue on their bedroom bookshelf, to some disciplinary magic: Tim's consciousness is transposed into Sally's body and vice versa. In the usual manner of Smith's heroes and heroines, Tim and Sally adjust quickly to the mutual metamorphosis, but the practical problems of functioning in each other's body and social-professional roles are another matter. Sally, with no training or experience, is thrust into the world of big-time advertising, where, acting with simplicity and honesty, she/he is a miraculous success. Tim, after finally mastering the intricacies of makeup and brassieres, finds himself/herself defending his/her "honor," enduring church suppers, and eventually becoming pregnant.

The turnabout premise in this novel is especially effective because it forces the characters to deal directly with the social institutions that Smith wants to satirize—suburbia, big business, the church, the courts, and medicine—while commenting on sexual role behavior in the America of his day. This is not to say that *Turnabout* is a major social document; the observations are clever, humorous, and perceptive, but they lack the bitterness and implications of true satiric invective.

The most significant development in the novel is the new and believable relationship between Tim and Sally that results from their strange experience. In the end, after Mr. Ram has transformed them back to normal, they have achieved a new respect and affection for each other, an enlightenment shared with pleasure by the reader.

Turnabout is Smith's only successful novel without a Topper-like inhibited male as its central char-

acter, and it is the only one in which the husband and wife grow together. *Turnabout* is a shade more serious than the bulk of Smith's work and whets an appetite for social perceptions and character complexities that was, alas, never to be satisfied.

The Bishop's Jaegers (1932) is not actually a fantasy; however improbable, there is nothing impossible about a group of lost ferryboat passengers ending up in a nudist colony. The structure of the novel, however, does come close to the alternate-world fantasy in which one or more characters are suddenly lifted from the real world and set down in a fantastic one. In his next novel, *Rain in the Doorway* (1933), Smith goes the rest of the way, combining the secondary-universe idea with his favorite motif, the education of the inhibited middle-aged man.

Trying to avoid the rain, Hector Owen steps into the doorway of a nondescript department store, only to be suddenly whisked inside the building and into a new world, where his hidden and not so hidden desires are miraculously satisfied, leaving him permanently changed. The novel is a legitimate alternate-world fantasy, although the secondary universe that Owen enters differs only psychologically and morally from his own. His guide—and mistress—through this hedonistically oriented world is a beautiful young woman named Satin. She is, of course, the primary embodiment of the new, free way of life, in contrast with Owen's wife, Lulu, who again represents middle-class respectability and hypocrisy (if not morality, since she, like Sapho Lamb, has a lover). The world that Owen finds himself in is a large, unconventional department store, where he is instantly made a partner and put in charge of the pornographic-book department. The humor is produced by Owen's fumbling attempts to simultaneously flee and embrace the possibilities offered by his new environment, ultimately finding himself in bed with the wife of each of his three partners. Although hardly explicit by contemporary standards, this scene is much more daring than anything in *Topper* and Smith's other early novels. By the end of his career, his handling of sex had become more honest and direct. Owen's magical department store ultimately burns down, destroying his playful alternate world. It then turns out that this new world was simply a dream-hallucination, as he is informed by Satin, the one element in his fantasy that turns out to be real: "You've been on a mental binge. . . . I picked you up in a department store. You were dazed among a lot of books. Since then you've been mine to take care of—and you still are." While thinner in plotting than some of the other books, *Rain in the Doorway* is a generally entertaining, believable work because the humor is less coy and more direct.

Skin and Bones (1933) is probably Smith's poorest novel—grotesque, strained, characterless, and unfunny. Unlike the earlier books, the fantastic element in this novel—Quintus Bland's sporadic transformations into a living skeleton—is never quite explained, and it does not have any special point, like Lamb's animal identities or the Willows' gender reversal. The fantastic just happens and becomes the stimulus for a series of ribald adventures involving alcohol, sex, disguises, and corpses. Perhaps Smith was attempting a serious venture into black humor, but his sensibility and techniques seem all wrong for it. *The Glorious Pool* (1934), the last novel that Smith completed, is somewhat more successful. A group of aged hedonists happen upon a fountain of youth and get somewhat carried away; their actions culminate in the protagonist's regression all the way to babyhood.

While vacationing in Sarasota, Florida, Thorne Smith died suddenly on 20 June 1934, at the age of forty-three, of a heart attack. A last novel, incomplete at the time of his death, was subsequently finished by Norman Matson and published under the title *The Passionate Witch* (1941). The situation, that of Topper-like T. Wallace Wooly, who inadvertently marries a witch, is typical Thorne Smith, but the mix of the two authors is imperfect and the result quite uneven.

Enormously popular in his own day, Thorne Smith is perhaps today best represented by showings on late-night television of the films or even old television series based on his works. The best known and most successful is the film adaptation of *Topper* (1937), starring Roland Young as the beleaguered hero and Cary Grant and Constance Bennett as the Kerbys. Young and Bennett returned in *Topper Takes a Trip* (1939), and Young in a third, original

film, *Topper Returns* (1941). In the mid-1950's a popular television series based on the novels was produced, with Leo G. Carroll in the title role. *The Passionate Witch* also had noteworthy reincarnations in René Clair's film *I Married a Witch* (1942), with Fredric March as Wooly, and in the television series *Bewitched* (1964–1972), starring Elizabeth Montgomery, a sitcom more loosely suggested by the novel.

These successful adaptations seem entirely appropriate. Smith's writing career occurred at the same time that sound was becoming a part of the movies and, particularly in the United States, when verbal wit was merging with visual farce to usher in the era of "screwball comedy." Thus, his fast, visual, imaginative blend of social observation, zany slapstick, and verbal dexterity is perfectly suited to the screen. This filmic quality is just another indication of how perfectly Smith fit into his era. Paradoxically, his final claim to lasting recognition lies in the fact that he was thoroughly a man of his own time, a most astute and entertaining chronicler of its tastes and mores.

Selected Bibliography

WORKS OF THORNE SMITH

Topper: An Improbable Adventure. New York: McBride, 1926. London: Holden, 1926.

The Stray Lamb. New York: Cosmopolitan, 1929. London: Heinemann, 1930.

The Night Life of the Gods. Garden City, N.Y.: Doubleday, Doran, 1931. London: Barker, 1934.

Turnabout. Garden City, N.Y.: Doubleday, Doran, 1931. London: Barker, 1935.

Topper Takes a Trip. Garden City, N.Y.: Doubleday, Doran, 1932. London: Barker, 1935.

Rain in the Doorway. Garden City, N.Y.: Doubleday, Doran, 1933. London: Barker, 1933.

Skin and Bones. Garden City, N.Y.: Doubleday, Doran, 1933. London: Barker, 1936.

The Thorne Smith 3-Decker. Garden City, N.Y.: Doubleday, Doran, 1933. (Contains *The Stray Lamb*, *Turnabout*, and *Rain in the Doorway*.)

The Glorious Pool. Garden City, N.Y.: Doubleday, Doran, 1934. London: Barker, 1935.

The Thorne Smith Triplets. Garden City, N.Y.: Double-day, Doran, 1938. (Contains *Topper Takes a Trip, The Night Life of the Gods,* and *The Bishop's Jaegers.*)

The Passionate Witch. Completed by Norman Matson. Garden City, N.Y.: Doubleday, Doran, 1941. London: Methuen, 1942. (Published posthumously.)

The Thorne Smith Three-Bagger. Garden City, N.Y.: Doubleday, Doran, 1943. (Contains *The Glorious Pool, Skin and Bones,* and *Topper.*)

CRITICAL STUDIES

Elchlepp, Elizabeth. "Turnabout." In *Survey of Modern Fantasy Literature,* edited by Frank N. Magill. Vol. 4.

Englewood Cliffs, N.J.: Salem Press, 1983, 1983–1985.

Goldin, Stephen. "The Stray Lamb." In *Survey of Modern Fantasy Literature.* Vol. 4, 1848–1850.

———. *"Topper* and *Topper Takes a Trip."* In *Survey of Modern Fantasy Literature.* Vol. 4, 1958–1962.

Van Doren, Carl. *The American Novel: 1789–1939.* Revised and enlarged edition. New York: Macmillan, 1940, 331–332.

Watson, Christine. *"The Night Life of the Gods."* In *Survey of Modern Fantasy Literature.* Vol. 3, 1111–1115.

—KEITH NEILSON

ROBERT NATHAN

1894-

ROBERT NATHAN WAS born in New York City on 2 January 1894, the son of Harold Nathan and Sarah Gruntal Nathan. Nathan's family included several notable Jewish educators, among them founders of both Barnard College and Columbia University.

At college Nathan edited the *Harvard Monthly*, but his college days came to an end when he left school in 1915 to marry Dorothy Michaels. Nathan and his wife returned to New York, where he worked in advertising. His experiences in the world of business and his reminiscences of college days are recollected in his first novel, *Peter Kindred* (1920).

Peter Kindred, like Nathan, leaves college to live in the city; unlike Nathan, he chooses an unconventional life of free love with a young woman from Radcliffe. The two struggle in the city but are tragically torn apart by its squalor and by the stillbirth of their child.

Peter Kindred is an uneven novel, reflecting Nathan's inexperience in dealing with the harsh world of reality, yet had it not appeared at almost the same time as F. Scott Fitzgerald's *This Side of Paradise* or had it been successful, it might have convinced Nathan to continue to write realistic novels. Instead, he felt that the Fitzgerald novel "completely stole the show." Perhaps he was fortunate that Fitzgerald's work was so successful, because Nathan started writing the sort of fantasy novels that have made him popular for fifty years.

After the early failure of his novel Nathan went to California. In 1921 he returned to New York, where he continued to write. Nathan taught at the New York University School of Journalism in 1924–1925. The next years were spent in the East, writing and building up a reputation. In 1943 he moved permanently to California, where he worked for Metro-Goldwyn-Mayer as a screenwriter. He still lives in California and had been married seven times as of 1970.

Nathan's fantasies fall into three major categories: rural and urban pastorals, religious fantasies, and (best known of all his works) fantasies of love and time.

Autumn (1921), the first of his pastorals, is the story of the village of Barly, nestled in the mountains of New England. The novel shows, for the first time, some of the techniques that Nathan was to use successfully in later works: a fantasy setting, magic, talking animals, and the lovely, poetic language that is characteristic.

The Fiddler in Barly (1926), which continues the story of the village, became so popular that it was collected with four other novels in *The Barly Fields* (1938). The introduction to this collection was written by Nathan's friend Stephen Vincent Benét, who therein outlines some of the traits that readers have enjoyed in Nathan's work. Benét compares Nathan's novels to William Blake's "Songs of Innocence," because they are so unlike the grimly realistic novels of the time. Of Nathan's works Benét says, "Here was a kind of writing of which there is never much in any one time — a style at once delicate, economical and unobtrusively firm, sharp enough to cut without rancor, and clear as water or air. . . . With it also went a sensitive love of life and a deep hatred of all those who would maim and distort it for any end."

It might be logical to expect that, after the success of the Barly novels, Nathan would continue in much the same vein, with tales of the country. But his novel *The Orchid* (1931) was set in his hometown, New York. In this work a marriage is saved by a magic carousel and the odd, Gepetto-like character who runs a merry-go-round. *The Orchid* is romantic but ordinary in character and structure. It was his first urban pastoral, a form Nathan used for a number of later works. The urban pastoral retains the simplicity, romance, and evocative language of the rural fantasy. The only difference is its setting, the city, the usual site of a realistic novel. As in the rural pastorals, however, unusual and magical events occur.

Although the early fantasies are charming, with touches of wit and a great deal of insight into the human need for love and understanding, they are not the only fantasies that Nathan wrote in the 1920's and 1930's. During those years he became interested in his Jewish heritage. He had been brought up in a liberal, reform Judaism. Although his mother would have liked him to be a rabbi, Nathan did not share her desire. He describes his early faith as universal in scope, and he saw many universals and parallels in man's view of the creator: "I found it almost impossible to distinguish between Judaism and Christianity. I never thought of myself as a Christian, but I experienced the same feelings of love and wonder from God's relation to Jesus as I did from his relation to Moses and Elijah" ("On Being a Jew," *Scribner's Magazine*, June 1933). Perhaps because of Nathan's ecumenism, his novels, while religious in tone, are universal, reflecting a love for the godlike qualities in mankind: love and generosity that transcend any particular religion. But occasionally Nathan did write novels reflecting his Jewish heritage.

In *Jonah* (1925), he depicts the rebellious prophet. Jonah does not want to be a prophet and indeed frequently rebels against God. Nathan's portrayal of

Jonah is traditional. He shows the prophet's cries to the Lord and does not attempt to make Jonah a modern man. As in earlier novels, Nathan uses animals to tell something about the human race. Here a fox thinks that God must be a jackal. When the fox's wife is eaten by a jackal, the fox concludes that God must be a raven. By having the fox change his mind about God, Nathan shows the human trait of shaping God in man's image instead of seeing human qualities as a reflection of God.

In his novel *There Is Another Heaven* (1929), the Jewish hero, Mr. Lewis, had become a Protestant, not out of conviction but because he thought that his conversion would make him more acceptable to the businessmen with whom he associated. So after death he finds himself in a heaven that is alien to him: an odd little village of white clapboard houses and a museum filled with mementoes of the Protestant Reformation. Lewis feels very much out of place. He wonders where his mother and father are, and where Jesus is. All of the people Lewis most wants to see are in another heaven. Finally he recrosses the Jordan and sets out to find his own heaven.

Another religious fantasy, *The Bishop's Wife* (1928), shows the effect of earthly life on an angel. The bishop of the title is a modern clergyman concerned primarily with business and only secondarily with God. At first, the bishop is collecting money to build a great cathedral. When he wishes for a deacon to help him, the bishop's prayers are answered and Michael appears to become his assistant. Michael is all the bishop could ask for: he preaches magnificently, he cares for the bishop's small daughter, and he spends time with the bishop's neglected wife, Julia. Julia's repressed sensuality responds to the angel's masculine beauty, but she is conscious of her duty as wife and mother. She refuses the love of the smitten angel and gently reminds him of his own duty. Michael begins to understand that the spiritual ecstasy once possible in paradise is no more, and that all that is left for human beings is physical love, its pale shadow. In addition, the body that Michael has assumed does not have the sexual organs to make physical love possible. By portraying the pain of an angel who loves a woman, by showing true humanity as a willingness to sacrifice ecstasy for duty, Nathan praises humanity. Julia is stronger than Michael because she has had to sacrifice all of her life.

The Devil with Love (1963) retells the Faust legend as it might occur today. Alfred Sneeden promises to sell his soul for the love of the much younger Gladys Milhouser. Unfortunately, Lucifer cannot take Alfred up on his offer in the traditional manner, for hell is packed with souls. So Lucifer decides instead to take only Alfred's heart. The devil, calling himself Dr. Hod, sets up a medical practice and begins the treatments supposed to make Alfred irresistible to the lovely Gladys. The town priest, Father Deener, feels uneasy about the new doctor and eventually recognizes him as the devil. Meanwhile, Gladys not only ignores Alfred but also falls in love with Dr. Hod. Alfred is saved by the love of a woman his own age, who volunteers to take his place in hell; Gladys and Dr. Hod have an affair in which the devil finds the human woman too much for him; and Father Deener finds that even though people are often selfish and cruel, human love, especially a woman's love, is stronger than the power of hell.

Two saints appear in *The Rancho of the Little Loves* (1956). Arriving in the Mojave Desert by mistake, they meet Conchita, the only employee of a very small whorehouse. Her only customer is Mr. Teargarden, the headwaiter of a casino in Las Vegas. Predictably, she has fallen in love with her customer, but Teargarden fears what his mother might say if he marries Conchita. The saints, who are throughly enjoying their unexpected vacation in Las Vegas, help Teargarden and Conchita to marry.

These fantasies contain much that is superficial. For example, in the Barly novels, though one sympathizes with young Metabel as she loses her love, one does not sense in her loss a great tragedy. True, she would like to marry her woodsman, but she recovers quickly from the affair. The other novels portray little of that tenderness and passion which mark great love stories. The bishop's wife is content to let her angel return to his traditional heaven, and Mr. Teargarden has to be tricked into marrying his Conchita. One senses a glibness in the portraits that make even the heros and heroines seem shallow. Perhaps some of the fault for this lack of depth may

be attributed to Nathan's inexperience as a writer. He was also writing in a genre that had few American or British counterparts. Instead, Nathan reveals that much of his inspiration in those works came from Anatole France, whose own writings portray a satiric view of human nature.

Though Nathan's pastorals, novels of the Jewish experience, and supernatural novels were popular, his most successful novels were those of love and time. Perhaps some experience that Nathan had in his middle years taught him the essential tragedy of love: love is not permanent but, like life itself, slips rapidly away. The first work to show Nathan's mature view of love and time was *Portrait of Jennie* (1940).

Set in the last years of the Great Depression, *Portrait of Jennie* tells the story of an artist who meets and falls in love with a girl from another time. Eben Adams is twenty-eight years old, poor, and hungry. But more worrisome to Adams than his physical discomfort are the artistic doldrums in which he finds himself. His landscapes are mediocre, and the only work that catches the eye of a gallery owner is a pencil sketch of a girl, Jennie, five or six years of age.

The owner is eager to see more sketches of Jennie, so Adams sketches her again a few weeks later. To his artist's eye she appears a little older, perhaps seven or eight. While Jennie chats about the war, Adams gradually begins to understand that she is talking about World War I and that something marvelous is happening to him. With each meeting Jennie ages: to ten, to her early teens, and finally to the last year of school, while for Adams only a few weeks pass. She keeps telling him, "I'm hurrying."

During their fifth meeting, Adams asks Jennie to let him paint her picture, and it turns out even better than he thought it would. By the sixth meeting, he tells Jennie that he is a success.

When the two meet for the seventh time, Jennie appears to be about twenty, and Adams realizes that he is in love with her. That afternoon they picnic in the park; they return to his studio and spend the night together. When Jennie leaves in the morning, she promises to return when they can be together forever.

At their final meeting they are caught in a hurricane in which they lose one another. Jennie is torn from the life she shares with Adams back to the separate life that she has been living. At the moment that she drowns in the hurricane Jennie is, in her parallel life, drowning as she falls from the deck of the ocean liner on which she is a passenger. *Portrait of Jennie* is by far Nathan's best work. It combines the charm of his early pastorals with a tragic love story. It is intensely emotional in its idea of a love so strong that time and space are no barriers.

Critics have suggested that Nathan may have intended to write more than a love story here, for there are hints of allegory in the novel: the mysterious appearance of the child, Jennie; her return time after time to serve as inspiration for Adams; and finally her sacrificial death as she is washed away in a hurricane. There remains the question of what exactly Jennie is. She is not a ghost, for she is living a "real" life somewhere at the same time that her relationship with Adams takes place in New York. Her death occurs at about the same time in real life as it does in the hurricane scene with Adams. Is there part of her personality, or her soul perhaps, that is destined to love Adams even though her conscious mind and body are somewhere else living a supposedly normal life? E. F. Bleiler, in his *Guide to Supernatural Fiction*, says that "Nathan apparently considered her an embodiment of Dunne's theory of serial time." J. W. Dunne, a British philosopher, wrote several books on the nature of time and the universe. *An Experiment with Time* (1927), *The Serial Universe* (1934), and *The New Immortality* (1938) contain, among other ideas, Dunne's conception of time as a series of events in which an observer participates. Thus an individual, ever in a state of flux himself, experiences a series of events that are also always changing. So each person's present moment is unique and differs from the present moment of any other human being, or of the universal present moment. In addition, while all this movement and change is occurring, all humans are also involved in interacting one with another. Dunne illustrates the difference between the individual's time and time in the absolute. The individual's personal time might move at a different rate from absolute time's rate. The movement of absolute time can be measured by clocks and calendars, but the individual's time rate cannot be measured, except by the individual himself.

Portrait of Jennie seems to illustrate Dunne's theories in at least one particular, in Jennie's ability to move forward in time at her own pace instead of at the rate that one expects relative to absolute time. At her first meeting with Adams she is a little girl, and by the time of her death she is a mature young woman. In her own personal time Jennie has matured from the age of four to about twenty. Yet in absolute time only a few weeks have passed.

Nathan says that he never read Dunne's books until after he wrote *Portrait of Jennie*, but this claim does not necessarily mean that the book could not have sprung from current theories. There were a number of books and articles investigating interaction between time and the individual. Among the works that Dunne cites are H. G. Wells's *The Time Machine* and the philosophical works of Henri Bergson. In addition there are hints that possibly Nathan was influenced by some of the literary theories of Marcel Proust, himself a follower of Bergson. Many instances in Nathan's novels of love and time serve to illustrate Proust's theories. For example, in *Portrait of Jennie* the child Jennie suddenly appears just at the time that Adams reaches the period of greatest despair about his career. At each appearance, the child and later the adolescent Jennie gives some indication that she knows that Adams wants or needs her to come. At first it is his despair, and later his growing passion, that calls the girl from another part of the world, where she is living a life quite removed from his.

Another example of the elasticity of time occurs in *Mia* (1970), in which the narrator, Baggot, an elderly widower, falls in love with the middle-aged Emmeline, while meeting and being enchanted by a charming twelve-year-old girl, Mia. He sees the child from time to time during the months that follow and, as in *Portrait of Jennie*, is struck by her quick maturation into a beautiful adolescent.

As Baggot's passion for Emmeline deepens, he tries to make love to her. When she refuses, he returns home to find Mia offering herself to him. Baggot refuses the child: "I saw myself . . . as I was, an old man—and I saw the young Thomas of so long ago, who would have loved her; and I wanted to weep." Eventually Baggot comes to realize that in some strange fashion Mia is Emmeline as she was as a child. When he realizes that he can have Mia in her older personality, he determines to marry Emmeline. As the novel nears its end, Emmeline sets out on a bus to join him. There is an accident, and the only passenger killed is Emmeline. The bus driver recalls seeing an angry young girl standing in the road pointing a rifle at the bus and grimacing as she dropped to the ground dead.

Mia is similar to *Portrait of Jennie* in several ways. First, Baggot, like Adams, is in a period of stress. He has been a successful writer and is writing his autobiography. But as he writes, he begins to remember, painfully, much of the past: he remembers his dead wife and her "quiet little sigh as she left me forever." He also mourns the past that overtakes the present almost before he lives it: "Where are they gone, the good years, the loving years? . . . It seems to me that it is always yesterday, even before today is over. And it is already too late."

As in *Portrait of Jennie*, there is symbolism. The most obvious symbol is the autobiography, standing for the empty years that are being written down because there is nothing more to be lived. When Baggot thinks of his marriage to Emmeline, he says, "I was not to be lonely anymore. I could stop writing my autobiography." Another hint that the autobiography symbolizes an empty, useless life is found early in the novel when Baggot says, after a particularly depressing episode, "Perhaps it had been a mistake to attempt an autobiography. I should have tried a novel again, with all things ending hopefully. Not happily, necessarily—but hopefully."

Like Baggot, Emmeline is unhappy with what she is now. She feels that she has never been a success and has never fulfilled the potential of the child she was. Mia, of course, is that unhappy child, offering herself to a man many years her senior, as she grasps for the love and life that she will never experience.

Although *Mia* is not as well done as *Portrait of Jennie*, it is very readable and very sensitive in its presentation of the role of the past in the life of an aging man. Baggot's sorrow as he sees his life slipping away and his delicacy in refusing to take advantage of the unhappy Mia humanize him and make him a very sympathetic character.

A love-and-time motif is also found in *The Wilderness-Stone* (1961), in which a novelist experiences his own remembrance of things past as he relives a friendship with a poet who died some twenty years before. As in Proust's works, physical sensations take Edward back to the times he spent with his friend, Bee. The fragrance of the spring flowers, for example, returns him to the time when his life was in its spring. The experiences are not dreams; instead Edward travels back across time to his youth, "fresh and sweet and eager, still shining with its own light in the darkness of time."

Edward shares his reminiscences of the past with a young neighbor, Miranda. From the first, he senses that Miranda is as in love with the past as he. As Edward shares his memories of Bee, Miranda comes to feel very strongly about the young poet. Edward's remembrances of Bee and of parties they both attended become more frequent, and as he remembers he catches glimpses of a young woman at the parties with Bee. The woman was not at the parties when he actually attended them in the past, but somehow she seems to be intruding in his memory. He cannot see her face, except one time; then he is astonished to see that she is his neighbor, Miranda. Somehow Miranda has become a part of Edward's past life. The climax comes when Bee asks Miranda to come to him: "'I've asked her to come live with me. . . . But it's very difficult.' . . . Difficult indeed, I thought; that must be the most difficult of all voyages." Although not previously noted by critics, Nathan's debt through Proust to Bergson is obvious.

Perhaps the success of these novels prompted Nathan to try once again to deal with the question of how love and time are related. The result, *The Elixir* (1971), introduces a college professor on holiday in England. He meets a young woman who reminds him of the sort of girl that Merlin's Nimue might have been. He falls in love with her, although he knows that he has only a few remaining days of vacation. Going home, the professor's plane is hijacked by Palestinian guerrillas, and as he waits in the desert, Nimue appears and leads him to the Old Man of the Mountain. Along the way they meet King Richard the Lionhearted on his way home from the Crusades. Finally, after journeying through time and space with his young lover, the professor returns home to find that his young graduate assistant reminds him of Nimue.

Nathan tries hard with this novel, perhaps too hard, for the effect is not beauty but a confusing mixture of times, periods, people, and legends. There seems to be no reason for the various personages to appear, and although the use of legend is interesting, the novel falls far short of his earlier triumphs.

These are the major novels dealing with a love relationship affected by time; Nathan used myth and symbolism in many other works. One example is *So Love Returns* (1958), a novel in which a widowed author, the father of two, falls in love with a girl whom he meets on the beach. Although he is not aware of the fact until later, the girl is a mermaid. The novel is beautifully written and contains some very poetic touches. Indeed, Nathan wrote several books of poetry and liked to play with language. In the foreword to the 1936 collection of his poetry he says, "When I was young, poems were loved for their beauty. Designed to stir the heart rather than to tease the mind, they were remembered with emotion and recited like music." When an author displays such an attitude toward language, it is no wonder that even his prose is poetic.

A different use of myth is found in *But Gently Day* (1943). Here the mind of a soldier remains alive for a while after his death in a plane crash. He returns to his home, not in the present but in the years following the Civil War, when his grandparents settled the area. He falls in love with a girl but is accidentally shot. When his body is found in the plane wreck, it has a bullet hole. This story is a version of the motif used by Ambrose Bierce in his short story "An Occurrence at Owl Creek Bridge." A young man is hanged, and at the moment that his own body dies, his mind makes a sort of leap and he finds himself experiencing an entire, separate life. Only at the moment of death in the new existence does he return to his old body to find himself falling, once again, at the end of the hangman's noose.

In *The River Journey* (1949), a dying wife wants to give her husband a trip on a houseboat as a final gift. During one stop, Death comes aboard in the person of a handsome young man. A young manicurist, presumably his next victim, comes with him.

Minerva, the wife, falls in love with the young man and asks him to take her at once instead of at the end of the journey. He hesitates, and Minerva accuses him of cowardice. She intends to give her husband one last gift, the love of the young woman, and she will not be denied.

Death agrees, but at a stop along the river, everyone attends a circus, at which both women are killed in an accident. The lesson here is only too obvious: no one can bargain with Death. When the husband, the only survivor of the trip, returns home, he remembers the years of love and, as he falls asleep, seems to hear the voice of his lost wife: "What . . . is love, but remembering?" she asks.

Nathan also wrote a number of topical novels during World War II; two novels about a Yorkshire terrier, Tapiola, and his friends; *Sir Henry* (1955), the adventures of a Don Quixote sort of knight; several books of poetry; juvenile novels; plays; screenplays; and one mock-archaeological treatise, *The Weans* (1960).

Not all of his novels are love stories. Two in particular, *The Innocent Eve* (1951) and *Heaven and Hell and the Megas Factor* (1975), reflect Nathan's concern about atomic weapons. He seems to suggest that as long as humans continue to manufacture and stockpile weapons, they are in danger of destroying themselves and their world.

Nathan has several very noticeable characteristics: first is his choice of the short novel or novella form. His works are generally quite short, sometimes set with large margins in a large typeface. Second, although some of the early novels use an omniscient point of view, the later novels often have an older man, usually an artist or writer, as the narrator. It is tempting to think that the narrator may be a persona of Nathan, especially when the narrator echoes a bit of philosophizing from an earlier work.

One characteristic of Nathan's language is his use of long sentences. These sentences are never too long or convoluted, but rather they take advantage of the rhythmic possibilities of certain words and combinations of words. Similarly, Nathan relies heavily on poetic descriptions of nature and on the use of sensory imagery.

Nathan is unashamedly sentimental, especially when describing children and animals, yet he is quite impatient with adult weakness and fallibility. He is a rarity, a writer whose works, although they span over fifty years, are as readable now as when first written.

Selected Bibliography

WORKS OF ROBERT NATHAN

Peter Kindred. New York: Duffield, 1919. (Published in January 1920.)

Autumn. New York: McBride, 1921.

Jonah. New York: McBride, 1925. As *Son of Amittai.* London: Heinemann, 1925.

The Fiddler in Barly. New York: McBride, 1926. London: Heinemann, 1927.

The Woodcutter's House. Indianapolis: Bobbs-Merrill, 1927. London: Mathews and Marrot, 1932.

The Bishop's Wife. Indianapolis: Bobbs-Merrill, 1928. London: Gollancz, 1928.

There Is Another Heaven. Indianapolis: Bobbs-Merrill, 1929.

The Orchid. Indianapolis: Bobbs-Merrill, 1931.

The Barly Fields: A Collection of Five Novels. New York: Knopf, 1938. London: Constable, 1939.

Portrait of Jennie. New York: Knopf, 1940. London and Toronto: Heinemann, 1940.

But Gently Day. New York: Knopf, 1943.

The River Journey. New York: Knopf, 1949.

The Innocent Eve. New York: Knopf, 1951.

Nathan 3: The Sea-Gull Cry, The Innocent Eve, The River Journey. London: Staples Press, 1952.

The Rancho of the Little Loves. New York: Knopf, 1956.

So Love Returns. New York: Knopf, 1958. London: W. Allen, 1959.

The Wilderness-Stone. New York: Knopf, 1961. London: W. Allen, 1961.

The Devil with Love. New York: Knopf, 1963. London: W. Allen, 1963.

Mia. New York: Knopf, 1970. London: W. Allen, 1970.

The Elixir. New York: Knopf, 1971.

Heaven and Hell and the Megas Factor. New York: Delacorte, 1975.

CRITICAL AND BIOGRAPHICAL STUDIES

Benét, Stephen Vincent. "The World of Robert Nathan." Introduction to *The Barly Fields.* New York: Knopf, 1938.

Dorian, Edith McEwen. "While a Little Dog Dances— Robert Nathan: Novelist of Simplicity." *Sewanee Review,* 41 (1933): 129–140.

Fay, Eliot G. "Borrowings from Anatole France by Willa Cather and Robert Nathan." *Modern Language Notes,* 56 (1941): 377.

Laurence, Dan H. "Robert Nathan: Master of Fantasy." *Yale University Library Gazette,* 37 (1962): 1–7.

Magarick, Pat. "The Sane and Gentle Novels of Robert Nathan." *American Book Collector,* 23, no. 4 (1973): 15–17.

Roberts, Francis. "Robert Nathan: Master of Fantasy and Fable." *Prairie Schooner,* 40 (1966): 348–361.

Sandelin, Clarence K. *Robert Nathan.* New York: Twayne, 1968.

Tapley, Roberts. "Robert Nathan: Poet and Ironist." *Bookman,* 75 (1932): 607–614.

Trachtenberg, Stanley "Robert Nathan's Fiction." Ph.D. diss., New York University, 1963.

BIBLIOGRAPHY

Laurence, Dan H. *Robert Nathan: A Bibliography.* New Haven, Conn.: Yale University Press, 1960.

—JULIA R. MEYERS

CHARLES FINNEY

1905–

THE SON OF a railroad superintendent, Charles Finney was born on 1 December 1905 in Sedalia, Missouri. He was named for his great-grandfather, who founded Oberlin College. Finney went to grade school and high school in Sedalia and to the University of Missouri in 1925. Finney says in an autobiographical sketch in *The Unholy City* (1937) that after a year and a half at Missouri he "ran out of money, quit, couldn't find a job, and ended everything by enlisting for China as a private in the 15th Infantry."

Finney's experiences with the army in Tientsin in 1927–1929 proved to be central to his writing career, providing the atmosphere and the direct or indirect background for much of his fiction; *The Old China Hands* (1961) records this experience. Finney says that he "wasn't a very good soldier" but that he "did finally make Private, 1st Class, and got Excellent Character on my discharge." Although told that he could make corporal if he reenlisted, "I didn't have that much faith in myself." He left the army.

Since his brother was living in Tucson, Arizona, Finney went there, "and in just eight months landed a job as proofreader on Arizona's second largest newspaper, the [*Arizona Daily*] *Star*." Proofreader from 1930 to 1945, Finney became night wire editor (1945–1953), copy reader (1953–1965), and financial editor (1965–1970), and retired in 1970. He married Marie Doyle in September 1939. Children were born to them in 1942 and 1947.

Although he had a full-time job with a newspaper, Finney launched a writing career in the 1930's, completing a novel that he began in Tientsin, *The Circus of Dr. Lao* (1935), which was well received and won the National Booksellers Award for most original novel of 1935. Finney's subsequent works were not so well received, but his story "Life and Death of a Western Gladiator" (1958) has been widely reprinted and adapted for television, and *The Circus of Dr. Lao* was filmed as *The Seven Faces of Dr. Lao* in 1963. After about 1968, Finney retired from writing, saying in R. Reginald's *Science Fiction and Fantasy Literature: A Checklist* that he "enjoyed writing, but ran out of ideas and gave it up." He suffered a stroke in 1972.

Even the most superficially naturalistic of Finney's stories are drenched in the supernatural. Most take place in his literary universes, the Arizona towns Manacle and Abalone, where normalcy is suspended. Tucson, Finney says in his foreword to *The Ghosts of Manacle* (1964), was not what he wanted as a background city, so he invented imaginary towns, and all his stories "are about nonexistent people and beings in a nonexistent town. Hence, in a way, all are ghosts."

Finney's work is, somewhat paradoxically, both influenced by literary modernism and an influence on subsequent science fiction and fantasy. Edward Hoagland discusses the influence of Gustave Flaubert, James Joyce, Joseph Conrad, and others, easily detected in Finney's fascination with language, his creation of a self-contained universe of discourse, and his sense of irony. At the same time, readers coming to Finney from science fiction and fantasy will think first of Ray Bradbury, who has anthologized *The Circus of Dr. Lao* and whose *Something Wicked This Way Comes* and other works were avowedly written under Finney's influence.

Both Finney and Bradbury depict American small towns invaded by traveling circuses; both writers dwell on the narrowness of these towns, as well as their paradoxical closeness to the threshold of wonder. The dark presences of Nathaniel Hawthorne and Edgar Allan Poe are behind each writer, along with the more recent influences of Sinclair Lewis, H. L. Mencken, and the Sherwood Anderson of *Winesburg, Ohio*. But Finney's writing is far less reducible than Bradbury's. It is all too possible to summarize Bradbury's Mars but not Finney's Abalone.

The Circus of Dr. Lao bears only a superficial resemblance to Bradbury's work. In both Finney and Bradbury, magic comes through the looking glass into the world of here and now; in both, magic infuses the prosaic with the romantic. But whereas Bradbury provides a total if sentimental confirmation of the infusion, Finney's response is much more complex. The effects of Finney's circus, for example, are gradual. The ad for the circus in the *Tribune* seems straightforward until the proofreader, Mr. Etaoin, notices that the circus is not named. Railroad workers soon conclude that it came by truck, although highway workers, likewise having failed to spot it, conclude that it came by rail.

Finney understates, rather than overstates, these growing supernatural hints. As the circus marches through town, onlookers are disappointed to find that it has only three wagons; later, these onlookers extensively discuss whether one of the cages contained a bear or a Russian. And as if to dull the edge between the natural and the artificial, Finney stresses that lawyer Frank Tull, one of the onlookers, has many artificial parts to his body. Even when the horrors commence, Finney uses understatement. When the medusa turns a woman to stone, for example, the tone of the writing is whimsical. Finney's works locate a threshold between the natural and

the supernatural, but it is perceived only with difficulty.

When Finney's supernatural circus enters Abalone, childlike, romantic values penetrate the metropolis. The Desk Sergeant in *The Circus of Dr. Lao* says, "I ain't paid no 'tention to circuses since I was a kid"—which means exactly what it would mean in Charles Dickens' *Hard Times*: that he is cut off from the source of life, the imagination. Looking at the unicorn, Larry Kemper says, "It ain't no unicorn; I know that, 'cause there ain't no unicorn nor ever was." His rationalism leads him to conclude that it is a horse, but when he is told it is not, he says, "I guess it's a freak of some kind then," as if putting labels on things rendered their essences. Kemper, the Desk Sergeant, and the citzens of Abalone are cut off from both the natural and the supernatural. Dr. Lao's circus affords them an opportunity to apprehend the natural world again, a Wordsworthian way to travel back, although they neither accept nor seem to understand this opportunity.

Finney again crosses the threshold between the natural and the supernatural in "The Door" (1962; collected in *The Ghosts of Manacle*, 1964). In the hospital for tests, the narrator meets Simon Bowles, huge and philosophical, who taps the fire exit every day with a cane and wonders if there is fire on the other side of the door of death. Bowles's philosophy is that there is only so much energy in the world, that things are always dying so that other things may live. Bowles punches himself every day so that he does something, if only something small. The reader gradually realizes that death is already touching Bowles, that Bowles realizes he will soon pass through the door. And death comes, in a pleasant way, taking Bowles soon after the Amerind Maribeth Yazzi gives him a back rub. Finney asks us to wonder, but not to fear, what is behind the door. The supernatural threshold is delineated subtly in "The Black Retriever" (1958; collected in the same volume), which proceeds from the premise that a dog has been incompletely transformed into a woman. This becomes certain when both a dog's footprints and nail scratches are found on top of a car.

The nature of this threshold between natural and

supernatural is further exemplified by Finney's view of the supernatural as nature intensified, nature seen properly. This view was born in the romantic movement: one thinks of Thomas Carlyle's "Natural Supernaturalism," a chapter in his *Sartor Resartus*. Dr. Lao's circus is most notable for its exuberant beasts—not all natural, true, but most containing natural elements in strange combinations. The chimera combines eagle, lizard, and lion; the hedge hound is part plant and part animal; mermaid and medusa, too, are nature intensified. In general, Finney seems to present the natural in extremis: in "The Gilashrikes" (1959; collected in *The Ghosts of Manacle*), for example, a man crosses gila monsters and shrikes.

The alignment of magic and the natural is equally clear in a neglected work, *Past the End of the Pavement* (1939), the very title of which suggests an antithesis of the works of man and the works of nature. Once again, a small rural town is on the threshold of the supernatural. Mrs. Helen Farrier's boys, Willie and Tom, have a special relationship with natural things; their dominating passion is for a series of pets that they capture. The Reverend Jackson suggests to a troubled Mrs. Farrier that they get chickens, domesticated pets that will calm the boys down. But they select instead a vicious white muscovy drake that escapes and kills three of neighbor Tar Smith's chickens. Smith tries unsuccessfully to kill the drake and concludes "that duck ain't nacheral." Finney's irony is that nature itself isn't natural to those who have shut themselves off from it.

The boys, by contrast, have two mothers. One is Mrs. Farrier, "and the other . . . was Nature herself, a vast, amorphous thing, unnamed and undefined, the midwife of the world; and she offered them ecstasy." But there are soon hints of the boys' eventual alienation from nature's magic. The boys steal baby screech owls and raise them in the woodshed. When the owls grow up, they fly away, out "for a time, they returned now and then in the early evening to drive Mrs. Farrier nearly crazy with their strange and beautiful night songs. But eventually they left the Farrier back yard for good, and the boys never see them again." Natural magic drives adults crazy,

and the young soon become adults, for the boys make their peace with the adult world when they sell a puff adder, Benji, to the Missouri State Game and Fish Exhibit, providing their family with enough money to pay the electric bill. Thus, the bishop can come to dinner, but "his smile and his appetite reminded them of Benji," the snake. While the bishop and other adults may think they live in a world apart, they are within the natural-supernatural system that includes Benji.

"The Life and Death of a Western Gladiator"(*The Ghosts of Manacle*) makes a similar point about nature's potency. It is the story of Crotalus, a twenty-year-old rattlesnake. When he kills a German shepherd, he precipitates man's attack on the cave of snakes; but by leading the reader to identify with Crotalus, Finney implies that to attack the snake is to attack what is valuable in oneself.

In Finney's literary universe, then, nature intensifies as magic moves to confront an often oblivious humanity. But humans, too, are usually engaged in quests; in fact, Finney often structures his works as quests or, more accurately, as ironic antiquests, laced with black humor. For example, two Americans in "The End of the Rainbow" (collected in *The Ghosts of Manacle*) visit a fortune-teller who advises them to go to Nogales, Sonora; buy a map from the first person offering one; and discover the Frémont treasure. The reader knows from the tone of the scene that their quest is hopeless, as it generally is for Finney's protagonists. After Dr. Lao's circus, "the people of Abalone went homewards or wherever else they were going." They are going nowhere.

The ironic quest is, likewise, at the center of *The Unholy City* (1937). When his plane crashes, Captain Butch Malahide goes beyond the threshold of magic. He finds Vic of Ruiz, who serves to parody the epic or utopian guide and whose first offer is to use the captain's money to pay off his debts. Soon the captain and Ruiz join in quest of a bacchanal in the city, a quest they never fulfill. The best they can do is to find two women, Mrs. Schmale and Mrs. Schwackhammar, whose names explain how far short of the bacchanalian these women fall. Malahide and Ruiz continue to wander without a goal through a ludicrously disorganized city.

But if motion is often futile in Finney, lack of motion is also a problem. In "The Captivity" (1961; collected in *The Ghosts of Manacle*), an "elderly oddball" narrates the story of one hundred men in a prison camp of no precise location. The men seem to be aware of unstated rules; though in close quarters, they never kill each other. There are deer within their enclosure, and they run these deer to their deaths or let them escape through a door in the fence. The men never seem to consider their own escape, however; neither do they question their pacific stance toward one another and their violence to the deer. After three years, the camp's doors open and all one hundred walk out together, but with fifty of them insane. They have been in a prison in more ways than one. Although not allegorical in a mechanical way, the story does suggest that violence toward nature combined with stasis toward human norms produces insanity.

This story highlights another aspect of Finney's supernatural stories—social commentary. The men in captivity might have escaped, but they are held within narrow codes according to which restraint toward one another prevents a breakout. The snake in *The Circus of Dr. Lao* says to Etaoin, the proofreader, "You have your cage, too." The cage of social codes receives complex treatment in "The Horsenapping of Hotspur" (1958; collected in *The Ghosts of Manacle*). Henry Percy, a rich rancher, gives orders that no snakes in the area are to be killed; the ready compliance with this absurd order establishes the atmosphere of fairy tale. Meanwhile, Poverty Booger and Injun Joe prepare to steal Percy's horse Hotspur. But the bird Molina tells the horse Julie, who tells the snakes. Grateful to their protector, the snakes save his horse by scaring off the would-be robbers. However, since it becomes fashionable for the rich of Manacle to dine at Injun Joe's, he is in effect rewarded for his indiscretion. Finney states his ironic support for social codes: "For the Code of the West says a man's past shall never be held against him, particularly when he starts making money." If class differences are absurd, the triumph of money is even more absurd.

Economics are in fact the final reality in a good number of Finney stories, for Finney is very much the 1930's writer. While Abalone and Manacle are realms of magic, they are also typical 1930's towns, in which economic demands are never too far away. The landlady's threats are ubiquitous in *Past the End of the Pavement*. The National Federation of the Unemployed threatens the quest in *The Unholy City*, and a young politician schemes to destroy the federation. In *The Unholy City* Finney also devotes considerable space to a black man on trial, as well as to mercenary soldiers. Abalone's interest in the circus of Dr. Lao is the interest a depression-era town has in escape, exactly as depression audiences must have identified with Fay Wray, rescued from poverty by a showman only to fall into the clutches of the infamous King Kong.

Less fortunately, Finney is also the 1930's writer in his use of stereotypes as a mainstay of his humor: thus, Injun Joe and Poverty Booger, among many others. Dr. Lao is the mysterious Oriental, and Miss Agnes Birdsong, who in *The Circus of Dr. Lao* looks for Pan only to find the satyr, is the stereotypical old maid. College students, carefree and troublesome, conform to another now-vanished stereotype. All of Finney's blacks shuffle their feet; not a single one of his female characters has any depth. True, Finney is using stereotypes to attack the narrowness of small towns, but today it is the stereotypes that seem narrow.

Far less conventional is the collision in Finney's works between the supernatural and organized religion, a collision most evident in *The Circus of Dr. Lao*. The circus's parade of supernatural and mythological creatures is inevitably pagan. The townspeople seem to lose their Christianity when they enter the circus, for when the seer Apollonius holds out the cross to disperse demons, "the applause was sparse and unconvincing." Apollonius asserts that he has "been alive since the Christian era began" and proves his power to rival Christianity by resurrecting a dead man. Further, Finney attacks the town's narrow dualism. When Apollonius presents a witch's sabbath, Satan appears, and Miss Agnes Birdsong complains that Dr. Lao mixes horrors into everything, instead of preserving unadulterated goodness apart from badness. Dr. Lao counters that "the world is my idea," referring presumably to the plastic creativity of his magic and its ability to transcend the simple categories of naïve Christianity.

The extensive final spectacle of *The Circus of Dr. Lao* is an apparent parody of all organized and anthropomorphic religion. The people of Woldercan, suffering from drought, pray through a priest to their god, Yottle. When the priest emphasizes their sins, the people of Woldercan complain that "we don't want forgiveness. We want rain and something to eat." So the priest demands food of Yottle, who in turn demands the sacrifice of a virgin. When the would-be lover of the chosen virgin resists, Yottle (in the form of a heavy statue) falls, killing executioner, priest, and virgin. Manna and rain at last fall, but only after the religious apparatus has been swept away.

A similar attack on simplistic world views is contained in "The Iowan's Curse" (1958; collected in *The Ghosts of Manacle*). The Iowan moved to Manacle for the climate but is convinced that he has put a curse on the town, because his every act of benevolence causes him reversal and disaster. For example, the Iowan is kind to a little boy, paying him to watch his car, but the car is stripped. In Finney's world, Christian ethics are inverted; his is truly an unholy city.

A long, late story, "The Magician Out of Manchuria" (1968; collected in *The Unholy City*, 1968 ed.), not only illustrates many of the themes of Finney's work but also points to what Finney may see as the political meaning in magic. The backdrop of the story is the change that communism has brought to China, from the transformation of villages into communes to the Great Leap Forward (1959–1961). The magician of the title comes south from Manchuria to escape the new politics. Soon he joins up with the Lustful Queen of La, who has been deposed from her kingdom by Khan Ali Bok, an opportunist who has made a deal with new leaders. Nominally the situation has changed, but in essence the power structure still oppresses the people. Although not legally a monarch, Ali Bok keeps all power after he ousts the queen, throwing her in the ocean to drown. After fishermen haul her in, the magician restores her to life and gives her a beauty that she never had. The magician plans to restore her to her rightful kingdom; he and his company, in typical Finney fashion, begin an inverted quest to find the kingdom. A hermit advises the magician that the political times are not fortuitous and that he should attempt not to restore the queen but merely to survive. Accordingly, the magician's company fades into the Moonbeam Mountains to join the "company of the compassionate," brigands who resist the Great Leap Forward.

Soon the quest continues in the boat *Flower of the Lotus*, which magically takes to the air, not in search of the queen's country—now an impossible dream—but to a river bank populated by elders who say that "magic is our life work. . . . But now we find ourselves fettered." In the modern world, magic is at odds with the prevailing social winds; the best it can find is a refuge. Finney has always located the source of magic in the mysterious East, and he now laments that political changes have cut off the source. The hermit presumably speaks for Finney: "A way of life is passing, and all that once was mysterious, poetic, and beautiful is being transformed—at the point of the bayonet—into crass materialism." Perhaps one should not be surprised that Finney stopped writing.

But while he was writing, Finney effectively used understatement to show the power of magic. Apollonius may speak best for Finney: "I don't do tricks. I do magic. I create; I transpose; I color; I transubstantiate; I break up; I recombine; but I never trick." Finney is as much the modernist as the romantic or the conveyor of horror. He is the ironist of form; he ends *The Circus of Dr. Lao* with a twenty-page catalog of ideas and characters. Dr. Lao's creatures are not primarily romantic but are by turns grotesque, marvelous, and banal, reminding us not so much of John Keats's nightingale but of Charles Baudelaire's pelican waddling into Paris. Readers of Finney can expect black humor as well as soaring skylarks.

Selected Bibliography

WORKS OF CHARLES FINNEY

The Circus of Dr. Lao. New York: Viking, 1935. London: Grey Walls Press, 1948. (Novel.)

The Unholy City. New York: Vanguard, 1937. (Novel. The 1968 Pyramid reprint edition also contains the story "The Magician Out of Manchuria.")
Past the End of the Pavement. New York: Holt, 1939. (Novel. Reissued as *This Is Past the End of the Pavement.)*
The Old China Hands. Garden City, N.Y.: Doubleday, 1961.

The Ghosts of Manacle. New York: Pyramid, 1964. (Short stories.)

CRITICAL AND BIOGRAPHICAL STUDY

Hoagland, Edward. Introduction to *The Circus of Dr. Lao*. New York: Vintage, 1983.

—CURTIS C. SMITH

JAMES THURBER

1894-1961

WHEN ONE THINKS of the great writers of fantasy and horror fiction, James Thurber does not leap to mind. This is hardly surprising. For one thing, Thurber's reputation is most firmly established as a humorist — many would say he is the greatest American humorist of the twentieth century. For another, although his contributions to fantastic fiction are both original and important, they are concentrated in areas generally outside the mainstream of the genre. While writers of fantasy traditionally gravitate toward the remote and exotic, Thurber delighted in the trivial and mundane. Throughout his career he insisted on keeping at least one foot firmly rooted in the world of the commonplace. Finally, in a genre dominated by the large canvas, Thurber resolutely remained a miniaturist, achieving his most memorable effects in stories and sketches of just a few thousand words.

This is not to say that Thurber eschewed the literary forms generally associated with fantasy. Indeed, he experimented — with much success — with such diverse vehicles as fables, parables, and fairy tales. His most brilliant work as a fantasist, however, is not to be found exclusively in these more familiar fantasy forms. Instead, Thurber is at his most exciting and innovative whenever he approaches the world of fantasy through the gateway of the everyday, when the world of dream and the world of the commonplace mysteriously intersect and collide. And these collisions take place everywhere in his work, not only in his fairy tales and fables but also in his short stories, essays, humorous sketches, and even in his autobiographical pieces. No matter what the literary form, Thurber refused to draw a very distinct line between the real and the fanciful.

Perhaps Thurber's drawings most clearly illustrate this brilliant interplay between reality and fantasy. Although Thurber himself tended to downplay his popular and critical success as an artist (he disliked being thought of as "Thurber, the bird who draws," preferring to see himself as "a painstaking writer who doodles for relaxation"), his drawings are important both in and of themselves, and for the light they shed on his literary productions. In the best of his drawings there is often the same curious admixture of the everyday and the bizarre that can be found throughout his written work. A well-known early cartoon, to take just one example, shows an annoyed woman in bed saying to her obviously henpecked husband, "All right, have it your way — you heard a seal bark" (*The Seal in the Bedroom and Other Predicaments*, 1932). Meanwhile, just out of sight of the arguing couple, a seal sits perched on the headboard looking off inscrutably into the distance. Pure Thurber.

Thurber's literary work is replete with such moments. Indeed, one of his most distinctive and appealing characteristics as a writer is how easily and naturally he allows the bizarre and fantastic to invade his rhetorical world. One such instance occurs in the preface to his funny and critically acclaimed collection of autobiographical pieces, *My Life and Hard Times* (1933). In this preface, Thurber says that humorists are often misunderstood: "This type of writing is not a joyous form of self-expression but the manifestation of a twitchiness at once cosmic and mundane." He goes on to describe the proclivity of writers such as himself for getting into "minor difficulties": walking into the wrong apartments, drinking furniture polish instead of stomach bitters, driving their cars into prize tulip beds. While cataloging the miseries of being a humorist, Thurber describes some of the things that "set in motion" the "little wheels" of the humorist's invention. The passage ends with a characteristic Thurber fantasy vision:

> He can sleep while the commonwealth crumbles but a strange sound in the pantry at three in the morning will strike terror into his stomach. He is not afraid, or much aware, of the menaces of empire but he keeps looking behind him as he walks along darkening streets out of the fear that he is being softly followed by little men padding along in single file, about a foot and a half high, large-eyed, and whiskered.

This use of fantasy to give life and texture to his private fears and apprehensions is one of Thurber's hallmarks as a writer. Although he occasionally indulges in a flight of fantasy for its own sake, Thurber usually employs the fantastic to express his inner demons more vividly. In "Recollections of the Gas Buggy" (*The Thurber Carnival*, 1945), for instance, Thurber is working with a very familiar theme for a modern-day humorist: the difficulties and tribulations of having to live with the automobile. What gives this sketch its uniquely Thurberian quality, however, is the way in which the author allows his private fears to assume a wonderfully dramatic reality: "I have felt the headlights of an automobile following me the way the eyes of a cat follow the ominous acitivies of a neighbor's dog. Some of the machines I have owned have seemed to bridle slightly when I got under the wheel." Thurber brilliantly taps a common source of anxiety and illuminates it with his own perspective. At times, Thurber suggests, cars seem to display an almost deliberate perversity, a kind of "antic intelligence." Thurber mentions a car he used to own that, resenting a remark he had made about its value, decided to "get even" with him: "Once, driving into a bleak little town in the Middle West, I said aloud, 'I'd hate to be stuck in this place.' The car promptly burned out a bearing, and I was stuck there for two days."

Thurber's special qualities as a writer can to some extent be explained by several biographical factors. For one thing, although Thurber achieved his greatest fame (and did his best work) writing for the *New Yorker*, an Eastern magazine known for its wit, urbanity, and sophistication, his own roots were actually quite different. Born in Columbus, Ohio, on 8 December 1894, James Grover Thurber had an upbringing that was thoroughly Midwestern and solidly middle-class. He was raised in a town of wide, tree-lined streets, large, comfortable homes, and stable, traditional values. He attended grade school, high school, and even college (at Ohio State University) all within the comfortable confines of his hometown. Thurber always displayed a great deal of affection for these Midwestern roots, and many of his pieces over the years—including *My Life and Hard Times*—would revisit this terrain. In later years Thurber was to say, "I am never very far from Ohio in my thoughts, and . . . the clocks that strike in my dreams are often the clocks of Columbus." Thus, although he traveled widely, lived in New York and Connecticut, and received a great deal of recognition from the Eastern literary establishment, a part of him always retained the point of view of the realistic, levelheaded Midwesterner.

If Thurber's upbringing led him to develop something of a Midwestern sensibility, his strong impulse toward fantasy was also decided early on. At the age of seven Thurber suffered a serious injury that would affect his entire life. While playing cowboys and Indians with his brothers he was struck by an arrow, leaving him totally blind in one eye. By his early fifties complications from the injury would cause blindness in the other eye as well. But the immediate effect of the handicap was to prevent young Thurber from engaging in strenuous activities with other boys his own age. In compensation, as Charles S. Holmes points out, he began to develop his "already rich inner life," and, indeed, Thurber's inclination toward fantasy was to stay with him throughout his career as a writer.

Although his handicap did not allow him to join the armed forces, Thurber spent the years from 1918 to 1920 in Washington, D.C., and then in Paris as a code clerk for the State Department. He returned to Columbus to work as a reporter for the *Dispatch*, but like so many members of his generation he felt the allure of Paris and moved back in the mid-1920's, working for the Paris bureau of the *Chicago Tribune* and trying unsuccessfully to write a novel. During this time he had begun to write short humorous sketches but was unable to get them published.

A turning point in Thurber's career occurred in 1927, for in that year he began to work for the *New Yorker*, a fledgling magazine founded two years earlier by the brilliant but eccentric Harold Ross. Thurber's relationship with the magazine would continue for the rest of his life; he began briefly as a managing editor, worked as a staff writer for a number of years, and was a leading contributor for many more. The *New Yorker* was a perfect forum for Thurber's special brand of short humor, and his sketches and stories found a wide and appreciative audience. And conversely he was a major factor in setting the tone of urbane wit that the magazine established in those early days. Thurber's highly entertaining reminiscences of his relationship with the *New Yorker* are recounted in *The Years with Ross* (1959).

The publication of *The Thurber Carnival* in 1945 represents a watershed in Thurber's popular and critical reputation. Although all but one of the pieces in the collection had already appeared in the *New Yorker*, and most had been collected in one of Thurber's dozen previously published books, *The Thurber Carnival* placed Thurber's best work side by side for the first time. Thurber had been a popular and critically respected writer before this, of course, but the publication of the book seemed to galvanize readers' responses to his work. Not only was *The Thurber Carnival* a best-seller, but, more important, it had the effect of solidifying and to some extent validating Thurber's growing reputation as a first-rate artist of substantial literary importance.

In one of the most perceptive and important reviews that Thurber ever received, "James Thurber's Dream Book" (*New Republic*, 12 March 1945), Malcolm Cowley presented a much more complicated view of Thurber than had been popular up to that time. Although Cowley agreed with the popular conception of Thurber as an extremely gifted humorist, he went further and suggested that Thurber was at the same time a "serious and skillful" artist who was often after much bigger game than merely making people laugh. What Cowley noticed, and what *The Thurber Carnival* helped make clear, was that Thurber's best work often has a serious, even dark, streak running through it. Much of it did not "bother to be funny," and even the overtly humorous pieces frequently "balance on the edge between farce and disaster." Cowley pointed out that many of the stories and sketches in *The Thurber Carnival* deal with such subjects as hallucinations, nightmares, murder, suicide, and madness. "Entering Thurber's middle-class world," Cowley wrote, "is like wandering into a psychiatric ward and not being quite sure whether you are a visitor or an inmate."

It is important to realize that Cowley, as many critics have since recognized, correctly attributed the source of much of Thurber's power as a writer to the fantasy element in his work. When one surveys Thurber's literary output, particularly his short fiction, it is clear that fantasy holds a central position: not only do his stories and sketches often incorporate fantasy, but, more fundamentally, many of them are about fantasy. Indeed the relationship between fantasy and reality, between the world of the extraordinary and the world of the mundane, is Thurber's great theme. And it is a tribute to Thurber's integrity as an artist that, although he spent a lifetime exploring this theme, it never becomes tired or predictable in his hands. Instead, his exploration of the relationship between the real and the fantastic always remains subtle, complex, and ultimately mysterious.

For Thurber the world of fantasy is seen as a locus of positive values, as a place of escape from the boredom and stifling mediocrity of everyday living. Thurber's work is full of characters who try to flee from the dulling grind of their lives by employing fantasy. Sometimes this attempted escape works; often it doesn't. But more important is the fact that despite the regular triumph of the mundane and trivial over the fanciful, Thurber—especially in his earlier work—usually champions fantasy.

There are numerous examples of this theme in Thurber's books, but perhaps the best is his familiar masterpiece, "The Secret Life of Walter Mitty" (*My World—And Welcome to It*, 1942). Almost everyone knows the story of Walter Mitty, one of Thurber's meek little men, who in the face of an unpleasant and continually intimidating reality seeks refuge by constructing for himself an elaborate fantasy life pieced together from the clichés and shopworn situations of dime novels and third-rate adventure movies. Thurber's attitude toward Mitty is wonderfully complicated. On the one hand, Mitty is a pathetic character who is totally ineffectual in dealing with the real world. His heroic fantasies are inevitably intruded upon by a reality seemingly bent on demeaning him. Thus, at the beginning of the story he daydreams of being a commander guiding a "huge, hurtling, eight-engined Navy hydroplane" through a terrible storm: "The crew . . . looked at each other and grinned. 'The Old Man'll get us through,' they said to one another. 'The Old Man ain't afraid of Hell!'" The fantasy is abruptly interrupted by his wife: "Not so fast! You're driving too fast! . . . What are you driving so fast for?" Mitty's daydreams are invariably terminated by similar kinds of intrusions.

On the other hand, despite the tawdry stuff of Mitty's dreams, Thurber obviously feels a great deal of affection for his hero. As Mitty is confronted by a world of surly parking-lot attendants, truculent traffic cops, and aggressive, overbearing wives, his retreat into fantasy is understandable and perhaps even admirable. We may laugh at him and his third-rate fantasies, but he is indulging in so common and elemental an activity that we also cannot help but feel a certain kinship with him. Indeed, it is signif-

icant that the story ends by generously allowing Mitty to keep his last fantasy intact:

> He put his shoulders back and his heels together. "To hell with the handkerchief," said Walter Mitty scornfully. He took one last drag on his cigarette and snapped it away. Then, with that faint, fleeting smile playing about his lips, he faced the firing squad; erect and motionless, proud and disdainful, Walter Mitty the Undefeated, inscrutable to the last.

Thurber's celebration, or at least endorsement, of fantasy is at the heart of his more traditional fantasy works. In "The Unicorn in the Garden" (*Fables for Our Time and Famous Poems Illustrated*, 1940), Thurber tells the story of a man who sees a unicorn in his garden one day. He feeds the unicorn a lily and excitedly tells his wife that the mythical beast has chosen to visit their garden. She refuses to believe that unicorns exist and arranges to have her husband committed. Luckily, there is a mix-up with the psychiatrist, and she is committed instead: "So they took her away, cursing and screaming, and shut her up in an institution. The husband lived happily ever after."

Rarely in Thurber is the triumph of the fanciful so complete and unequivocal. Only in the fairy tales—*Many Moons* (1943), *The Great Quillow* (1944), *The White Deer* (1945), *The 13 Clocks* (1950), and *The Wonderful O* (1957)—does Thurber consistently present situations in which the forces of creativity and imagination manage to overcome the negative forces of cold conformity and deadening unimaginativeness.

Thurber's exploration of the relationship between reality and fantasy also led him, however, to a group of stories that examine the dark, nightmarish side of fantasy. In these tales, the world of fantasy impinges upon the world of reality in strange, bizarre ways. In "A Friend to Alexander"(*My World—And Welcome to It*), Andrews, the main character, begins the story by declaring, "I have taken to dreaming about Aaron Burr every night." The story ends with a duel—fought in a dream— between Andrews and Burr. But the surprising result of the fantasy duel is Andrews' real death: "'Extraordinary,' said Dr. Fox the next morning, letting Andrews' dead left hand fall back upon the bed. 'His heart was as sound as a dollar when I examined him the other day. It has just stopped as if he had been shot.'" In another story, "The Whip-Poor-Will," also from *My World*, a character loses his mind—he ends up killing three people before committing suicide—because the call of a whippoorwill outside his window has given him continual nightmares: "Its dawn call pecked away at his dreams like a vulture at a heart." In both stories the world of dream and fantasy has a shocking and disastrous influence on the real world.

But Thurber does not insist on this negative and nightmarish view of fantasy. His more common attitude is to see fantasy as a means of moving beyond the confines of routine, everyday life toward some sort of liberation. He ends a superb sketch on his faulty eyesight, and the different and wonderful shapes that reality assumes when he removes his glasses, with this revealing and touching passage:

Some day, I suppose, when the clouds are heavy and the rain is coming down and the pressure of realities is too great, I shall deliberately take my glasses off and go wandering out into the streets. I daresay I may never be heard of again. . . . I imagine I'll have a remarkable time, wherever I end up.

("The Admiral on the Wheel,"
Let Your Mind Alone!)

After a career that spanned five decades, James Thurber died in New York City on 2 November 1961 of pneumonia and a pulmonary embolism.

Selected Bibliography

WORKS OF JAMES THURBER

For a representative selection of Thurber's best short work, two sources are particularly recommended: *The Thurber Carnival* and *Alarms and Diversions.*

My Life and Hard Times. New York and London: Harper, 1933. (Autobiography.)

The Middle-Aged Man on the Flying Trapeze. New York and London: Harper, 1935. (Collection.)

Let Your Mind Alone! And Other More or Less Inspirational Pieces. New York and London: Harper, 1937. (Collection.)

Fables for Our Time and Famous Poems Illustrated. New York and London: Harper, 1940. (Fables and drawings.)

My World—And Welcome to It. New York: Harcourt, Brace, 1942. London: Hamilton, 1942. (Collection.)

Many Moons. New York: Harcourt, Brace, 1943. London: Hamilton, 1945. (Fairy tale.)

The Great Quillow. New York: Harcourt, Brace, 1944. (Fairy tale.)

The Thurber Carnival. New York and London: Harper, 1945. (Collection.)

The White Deer. New York: Harcourt, Brace, 1945. London: Hamilton, 1946. (Fairy tale.)

The Beast in Me and Other Animals. New York: Harcourt, Brace, 1948. (Collection.)

The 13 Clocks. New York: Simon and Schuster, 1950. London: Hamilton, 1951. (Fairy tale.)

Further Fables for Our Time. New York: Simon and Schuster, 1956. London: Hamilton, 1956. (Fables.)

Alarms and Diversions. New York: Harper, 1957. London: Hamilton, 1957. (Collection.)

The Wonderful O. New York: Simon and Schuster, 1957. London: Hamilton, 1958. (Fairy tale.)

CRITICAL AND BIOGRAPHICAL STUDIES

Bernstein, Burton. *Thurber.* New York: Dodd, Mead, 1975.

Holmes, Charles S. *The Clocks of Columbus: The Literary Career of James Thurber.* New York: Atheneum, 1972.

———, ed. *Thurber: A Collection of Critical Essays.* Englewood Cliffs, N.J.: Prentice-Hall, 1974.

Morseberger, Robert E. *James Thurber.* New York: Twayne, 1974.

Tobias, Richard C. *The Art of James Thurber.* Athens: Ohio University Press, 1969.

BIBLIOGRAPHY

Bowden, Edwin T. *James Thurber: A Bibliography.* Columbus: Ohio State University Press, 1968.

—ERICH S. RUPPRECHT

XIII

Early American Pulp Writers

A. MERRITT

1884-1943

I

REPUTATIONS COME AND reputations go, but in the fields of science fiction and fantasy there is probably no other great reputation of the past that has suffered as much as that of A. Merritt. During the 1930's and 1940's he was widely considered the greatest fantasy writer of modern times. He even had the then unique distinction of having a magazine, *A. Merritt's Fantasy Magazine*, named in his honor. All this, of course, was in the precritical days, and today Merritt is seldom ranked among the more important authors of the pulp era. His merits seem to have crumbled along with the magazines in which his stories appeared, and his flaws now seem more perceptible than his strengths. This is particularly true of his earlier work, which, oddly enough, had been treasured more than his later novels.

For a man who held a high position in the newspaper world and was highly regarded during his lifetime, Merritt has always been astonishingly vague as a personality. Although he was accessible personally, very little has ever been known about him beyond bare biographical facts, and even some of these are very hazy.

Abraham Merritt was born in 1884 in Beverly, New Jersey, an across-the-river suburb of Philadelphia. He attended local elementary schools and Philadelphia High School, and was intended for the law. He matriculated at the Law School of the University of Pennsylvania, but dropped out because of financial difficulties. Merritt then took a job as a cub reporter with the *Philadelphia Inquirer* (1902); he later became a city reporter, assigned to such matters as crimes, suicides, strikes, and catastrophes. According to an interview that he gave in the 1930's, he was considered the best man to cover executions, even though he loathed the assignment. He would attend the execution "strongly fortified," write up the event suitably, "resign," and spend a few days recovering, before returning to work.

During this early period of newspaper work occurred one of the mysteries in Merritt's life. Details have never been released, although Merritt often made teasing comments about it. He seems to have been a witness to a criminal act or, as a reporter, to have uncovered dangerous material. His superiors, for one reason or another, did not want him to be summoned as a court witness, and packed him off out of the country on a paid vacation. According to one account, he spent a year traveling around the world; according to another, he spent most of his time in Central America, particularly in Yucatán, poking around Maya ruins, trying to interest someone in dredging the cenote at Chichén Itzá.

After a year, the crisis, whatever it was, was over. Merritt returned to Philadelphia, where he resumed work at the *Inquirer*, and by 1911 he had become night city editor. In 1912 he joined the Hearst papers in New York, as assistant to Morrill Goddard, editor of the *American Weekly*. This was a large, luridly colored Sunday supplement distributed with the

Hearst papers. It was filled with sensational articles on popular science, scandal, occult matters, exposés, current events, as well as some fiction—in short, anything that might be pleasing to the Hearst readership. Under Goddard and Merritt the circulation rose to 7,500,000 copies, an enormous figure for the day. In 1937, following Goddard's death, Merritt became editor in chief, a position he held until his own death.

In 1943, while in Florida examining his business interests, Merritt died of a heart attack. In addition to being a first-rate newspaperman, he was apparently also an excellent businessman, with many profitable holdings in Florida real estate. His personal interests seem to have paralleled his fiction to some degree, since he was greatly interested in archaeology, anthropology, magic, and history of religions, although he was by no means a scholar in any of these fields. One of his hobbies was raising curious and poisonous plants.

Merritt is said to have been a pleasant, affable man, with a hospitable bottle in his desk drawer, and with a good sense of humor. In person he was small and chubby. According to an anecdote that he liked to tell about himself, one of his many fans pestered him for an interview, which he finally granted. On seeing him, she recoiled in horror, exclaiming, "Oh, *you* never wrote *The Moon Pool!*"

II

Merritt's publications range in time from 1917 through 1935, but it is his work written before 1932 that has been most highly regarded by his fans. This earlier fiction, beginning with "Through the Dragon Glass" and ending with *Dwellers in the Mirage*, is adventure fiction with supernatural or science fiction trappings, and is modeled on the pulp adventure fiction of the day. Merritt's later work, the two novels *Burn, Witch, Burn!* and *Creep, Shadow!*, on the other hand, are thrillers emergent out of a supernatural basis, using the techniques of the contemporary mystery story.

Merritt's first story, "Through the Dragon Glass" (*All-Story*, 24 November 1917), uses the soldier-of-fortune theme common in the contemporary pulps. Herndon, an acquisitive millionaire, helps to loot the imperial palace in Peking during the Boxer Re-

bellion. He is impelled supernaturally to take a mirror that stands hidden in a secret room. As Herndon tells his story, it is revealed that the mirror is a gateway to another world, one from ancient Chinese mythology. Herndon enters this world, meets an amiable young woman, encounters the malevolent magical lord of the land, and barely escapes. He plans to return. There is an implication of reincarnation and previous encounters in the otherworld.

Although it is sketchy and underdeveloped, "Through the Dragon Glass" contains many elements typical of Merritt's early fiction, though not of his journalism. The style is essentially "fine writing," which later progressed to attempts at rhythmical patterns, often broken and interrupted rhetorically. Inversions of normal word order, omission of definite and indefinite articles, and listings without a final conjunction became more and more frequent mannerisms, which editors apparently were powerless to change.

Merritt was also greatly concerned with the imagery of sound and color, and he often tried to create a visually brilliant picture or a sensuous mood by selective tone color. The result is sometimes a shower of terms, at best conveying a sense of alienness, at worst almost constituting a parody of bad, late-nineteenth-century verse. Yet behind all these odd mannerisms, which came to be accepted as "trademarks" by his admirers, was a very skilled verbalist who was well aware of what he was doing. His was not a sin of ignorance.

Another curious feature of Merritt's writing appeared in this early period. His hobby was the study of mythology and religions, and he delighted in mythological syncretisms—raided, obviously, from popular works. Thus, characters, in otherwise ordinary conversation, are likely to make odd references to Chinese godlings, Islamic peris, and Irish sidhe. Herndon of "Through the Dragon Glass," while lying badly wounded, describing his experiences in the otherworld can say, "We drank of green water that sparkled with green fires, and tasted like the wine Osiris gives the hungry souls in Amenti to strengthen them."

Unfortunately, Merritt was not a scholar, nor was he usually able to integrate this material into his stories very well. For the most part it lies heavily and inappropriately (like the Egyptian references in the quote above, in what was a Chinese wonderworld) on the surface verbal texture. In a sense, one must admit, Merritt was paralleling the art forms of his formative period, around the turn of the century, when, as with the British art nouveau lapidaries, a flash of decoration might be thrown upon an otherwise bare surface.

It might seem odd that the pulp-reading public would stand for these idiosyncrasies, yet they were among the aspects of Merritt that were most treasured. They meant culture, exoticism, and learning to those who were delighted by something more than slash-bang sensation or the bread-and-butter work of most of the other pulp writers.

Merritt's next story, "The People of the Pit" (*All-Story*, 5 January 1918), is a science fiction horror tale. Unlike "Through the Dragon Glass," which is a story of sentimental longing beneath its hard exterior, this story is a recognition of arbitrary, incomprehensible horrors lurking beneath the surface. Set in Alaska, told in a story-frame, it is a narrative told by a dying man. He had descended an almost infinite number of steps into a bottle-shaped chasm, and had encountered an alien world dominated by hostile, alien beings that seemed to be animated light. They captured him, chained him to an altarlike structure, and subjected him to a conditioning that was seemingly intended to adjust him to their strange activities. He escaped, surviving only long enough to tell his story.

There is no explanation of "The People of the Pit," simply a fictional statement that man is powerless against evil higher beings. (One can reject the facetious suggestion that the story is really a semi-allegory of alcoholism and the d.t.'s.) It is also worth noting that two themes that were present in "Through the Dragon Glass" and are otherwise recurrent in Merritt's work are absent: a linkage between beauty and evil, and an intense interest in the resolution of dualism, usually that of good versus evil.

The stories that created Merritt's reputation were "The Moon Pool" (*All-Story*, 22 June 1918) and its sequel, "The Conquest of the Moon Pool" (*All-Story*, 14 February–29 March 1919). That the two do not fit together very well is usually overlooked because of the imaginative sweep of the second story.

"The Moon Pool," a short story told in an unnecessarily complex story-frame, is essentially a variant of the monster-from-the-crypt theme. It takes place (mostly) on and around the megalithic ruins at Metalinim in Micronesia, which Merritt claimed to have visited. A shining, seemingly insubstantial light-being, accompanied by a shower of tinkling sounds, emerges from a pool in an underground vault among the ruins, and absorbs those it encounters. A curious aspect of this monster is the feelings that it arouses in its victims:

> "It caught me above the heart, wrapped itself around me. There rushed through me a mingled ecstasy and horror. Every atom of me quivered with delight and shrank with despair. There was nothing loathsome in it. But it was as though the icy soul of evil and the fiery soul of good had stepped together within me."

In another passage Merritt refers to the effects of the so-called Dweller as "that unhuman mingling of opposites." The story ends with the narrator fleeing over the ocean, hoping to escape. But the Dweller follows along the moonlit path on the water and takes its prey. As with much of Merritt's other work, there are possible interpretations in terms of classical psychoanalysis that may or may not have been in Merritt's mind.

When Merritt wrote the short story "The Moon Pool," it was, as far as anyone knows, an independent story, and it is by no means clear how he would have explained the Dweller, scientifically or supernaturally. But when at the request of Bob Davis, the editor of *All-Story*, he wrote a long sequel, "The Conquest of the Moon Pool," he pinned the Dweller down in terms of science fiction. It had been created or manufactured in the remote past by a race of reptilian beings with intelligence and science far superior to those of mankind.

"The Conquest of the Moon Pool" is a lost-race story set in a huge, subterranean world beneath the Caroline Islands, inhabited by descendants of people from a lost continent. These Murians are divided into factions. With one faction, which is planning the conquest of the surface world, is associated the Dweller (now called the Shining One). With the other faction are three surviving members of the ancient reptilians, who are doomed to imprisonment of a sort until they find the will or courage to destroy the Shining One and the evil associated with it. Four men from the outer world (representing strength, courage, wisdom, and evil) become enmeshed in the resulting conflict.

Unlike "The Moon Pool," which is essentially a mood story, "The Conquest of the Moon Pool" is a fast-moving adventure story with extremely wicked villains, muscular heroes, a lustful vamp, a virginal "good girl," monsters, fantastic weaponry, and superscientific devices. Yet love, as in all Merritt's major work, is the motive power behind both stories, with both sacred and profane, familial and sexual varieties present.

Both stories were combined into a single narrative published in book form as *The Moon Pool* (1919). The original short story is unusual for its attempted splendor of description, as applied to an old theme; the sequel story, despite moments of imagination, is much weaker, and today seems very dated.

Merritt's next story was a short fantasy, "Three Lines of Old French" (*All-Story*, 9 August 1919), which seems to have been his most popular work. A highly sentimental tale reeking of the lowest levels of World War I propaganda—what with wicked Boches, saintly French, charming houris awaiting the dead soldier in a paradise, and refutation of cynical materialists—it is more interesting in showing an aspect of Merritt's writing process than for its content. It is based on a story by another author. Thus, "Three Lines of Old French" seems built on "The Demoiselle d'Ys" by Robert W. Chambers; *Burn, Witch, Burn!* on "The Wondersmith" by Fitz-James O'Brien. By this, I am not implying that Merritt was a plagiarist. What he wrote was his own, but he seems to have needed or liked external stimulation to start the writing process.

"The Metal Monster" (*Argosy All-Story*, 7 August–25 September 1920), Merritt's next work, is a science fiction novel that Merritt referred to as his "best and worst" novel. By this he probably meant that it contained good ideas, but was spoiled by bad development. Set in Central Asia, it is a lost-race novel (ancient Persians) with, as a sideshow, a metal being, larger than a city block, composed of living metal modules comparable to the molecules of a human body or the pieces of an erector set. This strange being, sentient and intelligent, is involved in an erotic empathy with a human female. But it carries within itself the potential of civil war and it short-circuits itself, its plans for geometrizing the world unrealized. Among other things, the story might be taken as a parable of human activity, but this does not seem to have been Merritt's intention. The story is an early exemplar of a powerful motif in later science fiction: alien life forms cannot resist the sexuality of human females.

"The Ship of Ishtar" (*Argosy All-Story*, 8 November–13 December 1924) reveals another aspect of Merritt's writing habits. It was first written as a long short story or nouvelle, which the editor of *Argosy All-Story* suggested should be expanded to a novel. Merritt simply added a long sequel, much as he had done previously with the coalesced book *The Moon Pool.*

In magazine form "The Ship of Ishtar" is a long novel set in a parallel world where the divinities of ancient Mesopotamia openly interfere in human life and themselves carry on a strongly felt feud. The cause of this feud was an incident in the past. The universal life principle and the death principle, as embodied in a human priestess and priest, had coalesced momentarily because of human sexual passion and almost shattered the universe. This incident forced a conflict between Nergal, god of death, and an aspect of Ishtar, goddess of life and love.

The gods then built a marvelous ship model in our world, a simulacrum of a real ship in an otherworld. The real ship was divided into two parts, black for Nergal and his priests, and white for Ishtar and her priestesses. Over the millennia the two forces have fought a drawn battle aboard the ship. (The model was apparently devised to transport persons to the otherworld.)

In the twentieth century, Kenton, a wealthy young dilettante archaeologist, receives a gift from a friend on a dig in the Near East. A block of stone, it suddenly "dissolves," revealing the model ship. Through the model Kenton is drawn into the otherworld to fight the evil priest of Nergal and win the love of Sharane, priestess of Ishtar. These are not easy tasks, since he is driven off as an impostor by Sharane, and chained as a slave to a galley bench by the priest of Nergal. Flashes back and forth to our world, the acquisition of loyal comrades, the winning of Sharane, victory aboard the Ship of Ishtar, interviews with the gods, adventures in a neo-Babylonian land all culminate in a final sea battle, figuring love against hatred. As the story ends, all the major characters, good or evil, are dead, although the souls of Kenton and Sharane have been taken to herself by Ishtar. Despite the sentimental sop at the end, this is a very unusual closing to a pulp tale of romantic adventure.

In the late 1930's *Argosy* conducted a survey to determine the most popular story ever to appear in *Argosy* and *All-Story*, and ''The Ship of Ishtar'' was apparently a wide winner. Today, though, it is not so readily judged. On its credit side are many fine strokes of the imagination and two good, original characterizations. On its debit side are many stagy, sensational sections that do not carry conviction, weak or stereotyped characterizations, and evidence of hasty writing. Despite the cosmic rationale—the quarrels of gods and goddesses—a reader is likely to finish the story wondering why it ever took place.

''The Face in the Abyss'' (*Argosy All-Story*, 8 September 1923) and its sequel, ''The Snake Mother'' (*Argosy All-Story*, 25 October–6 December 1930), abridged and combined as *The Face in the Abyss* (1931), are science fiction stories set in an isolated pocket of the Andes, where descendants of the ancient Atlanteans survive. The themes are a dualism of good and evil, and the power of love; the story vehicle is the struggle to keep a long-submerged evil from emerging and encompassing the land. Among the more original features of the stories are hypostatized abstractions, Greed and Folly, which were condensed into human form ages ago by a fantastic science, and the Snake Mother, a somewhat kittenish being who is the last survivor of superintelligent serpentine beings who first set man on the path to civilization.

The Face in the Abyss is an uneven work. While there are excellent flights of imagination in activities and equipment, the fictional mechanism has now become trite. The sequel novel is weaker than the original short story, which has some period charm in its quaint juxtaposition of love and greed, brutality and decency.

The second most popular work to appear in *Weird Tales* was Merritt's ''The Woman of the Wood'' (August 1926). (The first was C. L. Moore's ''Shambleau.'') Reminiscent of the work of Algernon Blackwood, although more sensational, it is on one level a story of madness and on another of supernatural empathy. McKay, staying in a small hamlet in the Vosges, suddenly perceives the local trees as beautiful, sensual women and handsome men. They beg his protection, for the woodcutter Polleau and his sons have a feud with them. While trying to protect the trees, McKay is responsible for the deaths of the Polleaus. Horrified by what he has done while as if possessed, yet equally torn by regret that he has not entered the world of the trees, he leaves. In many ways this is the best of Merritt's short stories.

The most significant of Merritt's early works is ''Dwellers in the Mirage'' (*Argosy*, 23 January–27 February 1932). It is built upon three motifs: the survival of an ancient Central Asiatic culture in a lost valley in Alaska, hidden beneath a miragelike atmospheric lens; the emergence of a horrible monstrosity that figures in the religion of the lost land; and the mental self-torture of a man cursed with ancestral memory (or psychosis) that takes over his personality and wreaks havoc on himself and his friends. With the exception of *Land Under England* (1935) by Joseph O'Neill, which is essentially political, it is the last significant lost-race novel written in English. It is also the culmination of the tradition established by H. Rider Haggard. Yet it is also something of a hybrid work, for the monstrosity, which is first put forth as the spirit of death and destruction, is ultimately explained as a being from another universe, beyond our space-time. This explanation establishes ''Dwellers in the Mirage'' as science fiction.

''Dwellers in the Mirage'' is a powerful story, if one can accept its conventions. The frequent mythological comparisons are, for the first time in Merritt's work, integrated with the story and not just obtrusive atmospheric devices. Leif, the tortured, buffeted hero, gnawed by conscience and driven by the emergence of unconscious personality (no matter what its origin), and the power-mad, erotic Lur, the only one of Merritt's femmes fatales to come to life, are memorable. One has the impression that in this book Merritt set out to do the best work he could.

"Dwellers in the Mirage" was the last of Merritt's "fairyland" romances. It is possible that with the detailed, mythic structure of the story (which would give a Jungian analyst a remarkable field for exegesis), he worked something out of his psyche, or the answer may simply be economics. Lost-race science fiction with an element of fantasy did not sell.

Merritt's first work in his later style was "Burn, Witch, Burn!" (*Argosy*, 22 October–26 November 1932). (His earlier thriller, "Seven Footprints to Satan," 1927, was an unsuccessful novel in the mode of Sax Rohmer.) "Burn, Witch, Burn!" was apparently an attempt to link up with the extraordinary popularity of the detective story in the early 1930's. It begins as a mystery, with a baffling death under exceedingly strange circumstances, followed by similar deaths. The story then proceeds as a repeated dialogue between the "ancient wisdom" (of witchcraft) and modern medical materialism. Materialism, in the person of Dr. Lowell, an elderly psychiatrist, is buffeted, belittled, and crushed as evidence mounts. It is, of course, now impossible to know how seriously Merritt's contemporaries took this dialectic of points of view, but to a modern reader the rational side is only a straw man used to fill pages.

The heart idea of "Burn, Witch, Burn!" is that an evil force, in some way linked to beauty, can gain control of a soul-fragment within man. But it must follow certain procedures, including partial consent of the victim. This assault, though, must eventually fail, for it overlooks a basic factor: humanity.

The two chief characters in "Burn, Witch, Burn!" are cast as basic typological responses to supernatural evil, yet are also clichéd. The incredulous narrator, Dr. Lowell, is a too-familiar figure in the supernatural fiction of the day, and his credulous counterpole, Ricori, a romanticized gang lord — suave, intelligent, handsome — might have stepped out of an early issue of *Black Mask*. These personal polarities also predetermine their reactions to evil: temporizing on Lowell's part, and direct action on

Ricori's. Neither approach, though, is efficacious. As is often the case in Merritt's fiction, a third factor is necessary — humanity, individuality, sacrifice of individuality, or love.

According to the plot of "Burn, Witch, Burn!" an ancient form of black magic suddenly appears in New York City. A modern witch, for delight or aesthetic satisfaction, is creating animated dolls by extracting personality fragments from the persons she magically kills. She then sends her dolls out on murder-errands, sometimes definite, sometimes random. One of her victims is a member of Ricori's gang; another happens to be Nurse Walters, in Lowell's hospital. This chance makes Lowell and Ricori allies in a search for the witch, which search is accomplished mostly by Ricori's men. When the witch, Madame Mandilip, is found, Ricori tries a direct confrontation with her, and is fortunate to survive. Lowell tries subtlety and is badly outwitted and fitted with a disastrous posthypnotic suggestion. After these debacles it is decided that the dollmaker should be "executed" in a gangland raid, but again Madame Mandilip is too strong, and Lowell, Ricori, and his henchmen would meet horrible deaths were it not for the doll of Nurse Walters. This doll retains an unconquerable spark and rebels at a crucial moment. It stabs Madame Mandilip as she holds it. The doll workshop is destroyed by fire.

It would seem fairly obvious that Merritt took the basic idea of this story from O'Brien's short story "The Wondersmith," adding a background of history of religions, parapsychology, and the trappings of a gangster tale.

"Burn, Witch, Burn!" was adapted into a motion picture, *The Devil Doll* (1936), starring Lionel Barrymore. It probably also served as the inspiration for Sarban's novel *The Doll Maker* (1953), where once again we find the strange link between evil and an aesthetic sense. Sarban's novel, which is less blatant and raucous than Merritt's, is on the whole superior, but Merritt can better convey sudden frantic thrills and a sense of immediate peril.

Merritt's next novel, "Creep, Shadow!" (*Argosy*, 8 September–6 October 1934), is a sequel of a sort to "Burn, Witch, Burn!" Its ultimate theme is the unchanging nature of fate. If historical occult circumstances are repeated, the resulting complications will be the same. In this case, there is a parallelism between lovers in the pre-Christian megalithic world of Brittany and the same lovers today. This concept of repeated patterns in fate is not uncommon in supernatural fiction, but in most cases, like Algernon Blackwood's *Julius Le Vallon* (1916) or H. Rider Haggard's novels about She-Who-Must-Be-Obeyed, it is built on the concept of reincarnation. In Merritt's novel, however, the reemergence of personalities from the past is explained mechanistically. Paralleling instinct in animals, humans possess buried in their brains certain cells upon which are graven the experiences of their ancestors. These records are not present in all persons, nor to the same degree, but when they are perfect, they can be awakened—in which case the individual is as if possessed by the ancestral personality. (This was an explanation advanced for Leif's situation in "Dwellers in the Mirage.")

In "Creep, Shadow!" two persons are governed by this psychological reversion: Alan Caranac, an anthropologist, and Dahut de Keradel, both of Breton descent. Alan is at times overpowered by the personality of Alain de Carnac, his distant ancestor who was lord of the great stonework at Carnac, and Dahut has merged with her wicked ancestress Princess Dahut of the lost city of Ys, the memory of which has been preserved in Breton folklore.

According to a common version of the legend of Ys, the city existed below sea level, and was protected from the sea by great walls, in which were set sea gates. A young man from a hostile people came to Ys, and won the heart of the princess. As a token of her love, she stole the keys of the sea gates from her father and gave them to her lover, who let in the sea, drowning Ys. In most versions, the princess, who was quite depraved, died, but the lover escaped, sometimes with their child. Norman Douglas, it will be remembered, made use of this same legend in *They Went* (1920), which probably inspired Merritt.

Merritt enlarged the legend by making Princess Dahut a most potent sorceress who worked evil magic by means of shadows—or "ghosts" equivalent to Homeric shades. Eventually, Princess Dahut was destroyed by her shadow slaves.

In the present circumstance, Dahut d'Ys de Ker-

adel, with her ancestress' personality awakened and merged with her own, also controls shadows and has some sort of affinity with or control of the sea. She is currently using her magic partly to get money for herself and her father and partly for the cruel pleasure it gives her.

As the story begins, Alan Caranac returns to New York after a long absence, to find that one of his closest friends has mysteriously died. It was suicide, but also murder, since the friend had been driven by a supernatural manifestation. As in Arthur Machen's "The Great God Pan," there have been several such suicides, and they are linked to the Keradels. Dahut, an incredibly beautiful woman, sees in Caranac the memory packets of her ancient lover and evokes them, seeking ambivalently both revenge and renewed love. To protect his friends—among whom is Dr. Lowell of "Burn, Witch, Burn!"—Caranac is forced to yield to her and to love her, at her establishment in Rhode Island. Surreptitiously, though, he is working with Ricori (of "Burn, Witch, Burn!") to destroy the menace of the shadows.

A further complication is Dahut's father, a very brilliant savant who is also a ruthless fanatic, a most powerful warlock, and a monomaniac. He is determined to evoke a pre-Celtic horror-god or monster, and is conducting human sacrifices, at which Alan, in his ancestral reawakening, assists.

With Ricori and his men in the background, Alan plays a dangerous game, which seems lost when Dahut catches him in treachery. She sends him out as a vampiric shadow. But here Merritt invokes his principle of sacred versus profane love, and a good woman's love breaks Dahut's magic. Alan's path is now that of the ancient Alain: to use Dahut's love for him, despite her anger, to destroy her father and his fearful magic, and then, himself, to kill Dahut. The plan almost works. Dahut invokes the sea to kill her father and dispel the god-monster (the Gatherer in the Cairn), but she herself is drowned by her rebellious shadows. As may emerge from this plot summary, Dahut de Keradel is the true cryptagonist of "Creep, Shadow!," not the insipid "anthropologist" Alan Caranac, to whom the story has been offset.

After "Dwellers in the Mirage," "Creep, Shadow!" is Merritt's most successful novel. The surface texture is not as obtrusive as in his earlier work, and is skillfully varied — hard-boiled, lyrical, humorous. The characterizations, allowing for pulp simplistics, are reasonably drawn, and the integration of mythological elements is firm. One may cavil at a single unnecessary episode (part of Alan's adventure when he was a shadow in a shadow world), but even here a strong pictorial aspect is worth noting.

With "Creep, Shadow!" Merritt, in effect, stopped writing, for the few short stories and fragments that may have been written later are trivial and not memorable. This is lamentable, for Merritt had at last gained full control of his material.

III

If one wanted to characterize Merritt in simple terms, one could call him the most romantic (in the late-nineteenth-century sense of the word) major science fiction and fantasy writer of his day. This romantic quality was highly regarded, and Merritt was one of the authors most frequently imitated by young writers.

Today, we are more apt to find things in Merritt's writing, particularly his early writing, that should not be imitated, but admitting weaknesses should not preclude seeing strengths. He had a fine imagination, and each of his stories was innovative in significant ways. He had the knack of treating each motif as a fulfillment, exhausting its potential. Thus, one can take sentimental treatment of survival after death no further than "Three Lines of Old French."

Merritt could be an exciting writer, and he could digress from the pulp milieu in unusual ways. He was an excellent craftsman when he wanted to be, and his skills evolved as he grew older. If he was always concerned with love and dualism (good versus evil) he constantly varied their embodiments.

Yet, despite these strengths, the ultimate feeling today is that Merritt was for the most part an unsatisfying writer. Perhaps the problem was lack of literary integrity, a too great cleaving to the attitudes and wish fulfillments of his fleeting audience, with the result that his stories are filled with now-dated material. If he was cleverer than most of his colleagues in doing this, he has paid a higher price in the end, for what appealed to readers of the Munsey pulp magazines of the 1920's may strike readers of the 1980's as itself a fantasy world.

In many instances Merritt carried out his emotional topicality to such an extent that when the Zeitgeist changed, the older position was difficult to accept, or even ludicrous or repellent. Such is the case with "Three Lines of Old French," which today seems obscene, a deliberate attempt by a very intelligent writer to play upon feelings of bereavement arisen out of World War I.

Perhaps there was an element of cynicism in Merritt's work that his contemporaries did not see. Could a professional newspaperman high in the Hearst empire be other than intellectually hard-boiled? Or was there perhaps a situation like that of William Sharp and Fiona Macleod, where Sharp, a professional journalist, wrote florid, mushy stories about the Hebrides under the pseudonym of Fiona Macleod, and threatened to stop writing if the secret was revealed? Was Merritt equally wrapped up in his work? We do not know.

Is any of Merritt's work worth reading today, other than as historical documents? The mythic quality of *Dwellers in the Mirage*, with its formal structuring and inner drama, is still vital. A sense of peril emerges from *Burn, Witch, Burn!*, and *Creep, Shadow!* is an excellent suspense story. There are also moments in the other major works. As for the rest of Merritt's fiction, it belongs back in the 1920's and 1930's, perhaps occasionally to be stroked for nostalgia, but maintainable only by taxidermy.

Selected Bibliography

WORKS OF A. MERRITT

The following are first book editions of Merritt's more important fiction. There have also been a few separate pamphlet editions of individual short stories and many reprint editions of the novels. For these, consult Currey and Tuck in the general bibliography at the end of this volume.

The Moon Pool. New York: Putnam, 1919. (A combined version of "The Moon Pool" and "The Conquest of the Moon Pool." Later editions sometimes change the villain from a German to a Russian Communist.)

The Ship of Ishtar. New York: Putnam, 1928. (Badly abridged from the magazine version. The 1956 Borden [Los Angeles] edition, with illustrations by Virgil Finlay, reprints the full magazine text.)

The Face in the Abyss. New York: Liveright, 1931. London: Futura, 1976. (A combined version, with some abridgment, of "The Face in the Abyss" and "The Snake Mother.")

Dwellers in the Mirage. New York: Liveright, 1932. London: Skeffington, 1933. (This follows the magazine text, in which Evalie, a girl from outside, survives and leaves the valley with Leif. The Avon reprint [New York, 1944] offers a different ending, picked up from Merritt's manuscript, in which Evalie is killed. Most later reprintings follow the tragic ending.)

Burn, Witch, Burn! New York: Liveright, 1933. London: Methuen, 1934.

Creep, Shadow! Garden City, N.Y.: Crime Club/Doubleday, Doran, 1934. As *Creep, Shadow, Creep!* London: Methuen, 1934.

The Metal Monster. New York: Murder Mystery Monthly, 1946. (Sometimes titled *The Metal Emperor*.)

The Fox Woman and Other Stories. New York: Avon, 1949. (All Merritt's published short stories, sometimes with textual variations from other versions. Also three fragments of unfinished work.)

CRITICAL AND BIOGRAPHICAL STUDIES

Bleiler, E. F. "A. Merritt." In *Science Fiction Writers*. New York: Scribner, 1982. (The same point of view as the present article, but fuller discussions of the science fiction works and descriptions of minor work not covered here.)

Spence, Lewis. *Legends and Romances of Brittany*. New York: Stokes, [1917]. (Discussion of the various Ys legends, with scholarly references, prepared while Spence was still a serious student of folklore. Probably Merritt's source for *Creep, Shadow!*)

—E. F. BLEILER

TALBOT MUNDY

1879–1940

I

TALBOT MUNDY MIGHT conceivably have objected to being included in this volume, since he claimed that the topics he wrote about were not supernatural. In his article "A Jungle Sage" (*Adventure*, 15 March 1932) he wrote, "I firmly disbelieve in the supernatural, being convinced that natural laws pervade and govern the whole universe; but it is perfectly obvious that some men know more of the laws than others do, and those men can work what look like miracles to the ignorant observer." And in *Full Moon* (1935), even more to the point, "Magic is the crumbled remains of an ancient science."

Yet to a mundane viewer this is supernaturalism based on an occult concept—the Ancient Wisdom, a body of knowledge said to have been widespread in the past, perhaps in prepyramid times, perhaps in Atlantis, perhaps in preglacial times, compared to which our science is kindergarten material. Further, the intelligent beings of those days, whether fully human or not, could accomplish by mental power what we do physically, with great difficulty. This concept Mundy derived from Theosophy, an occult movement started by Helena Petrovna Blavatsky in the 1870's. According to Blavatsky the Ancient Wisdom is not dead, but survives in the hands of mahatmas (or Masters) in the Himalayas, who sometimes interfere for good in the doings of modern man. The present age, without the Ancient Wisdom, is the Kali yuga, or a horrible time, but it will be succeeded by something better. Talbot Mundy, the foremost writer of Oriental adventure stories, also believed this.

II

Until very recently it was not possible to speak authoritatively about the life of Talbot Mundy, for he had effectively clouded his early life, and the data in reference works and in publicity articles were contradictory and self-inconsistent. According to Stanley Kunitz's and Howard Haycraft's *Twentieth Century Authors*, for example, Mundy acquired his expertise on Africa and India by serving as a colonial official; according to interviews in *Adventure* magazine, he had been a seeker of fortune who sometimes skirted the edge of a too strict law. But now, thanks to the researches of Peter Berresford Ellis, it is possible to see Mundy as a man whose life was divided symmetrically into two almost equal segments.

Talbot Mundy was born as William Lancaster Gribbon in London on 23 April 1879. His father was a wealthy owner of an accounting business and a pillar of society, and his mother came from a cadet branch of the great Lancaster family descended from John of Gaunt. At the appropriate age, young Gribbon was sent to Rugby School, where he remained until he was sixteen years old. At first he was a good student, but adolescence and his father's death seem to have caused a personality change, and he was expelled. The next five years of his life are little known, but he claimed to have gone to India as a newspaper reporter, to have served in the British army, and to have fought in the Boer War—but these claims range from unlikely for the first to untrue for the second and third.

In 1901, however, Gribbon's name is to be found in records, first in Bombay; then, later, in England, where he married; then in Africa. He was a handsome, charming, gracious, plausible, and enterprising young man—whom it was most unwise to trust with one's money or wife. The records show a series of aliases—Thomas Hartland, Lord Hartland, Sir Rupert Harvey, Talbot Chetwynd Miller Mundy (in which last identity he drew upon Debrett to declare himself the illegitimate son of the Earl of Shrewsbury). He was arrested for alienation of funds, swindling, and impersonation; received prison sentences for swindling; and was deported from Africa. He was an ivory poacher and a cattle rustler. And he had a reputation as a womanizer that gained him a special nickname among the blacks. With such a trail of misdeeds reaching from England to Cape Town, to Mombasa, to Lake Victoria, Mundy could fittingly be called an all-around bad egg.

By 1909 the British Empire apparently grew too hot for Mundy and the second of his five wives, a woman who had a reputation of her own, and they went to New York. His welcome was violent, for while gambling with gangsters not long after his arrival, he received a nearly fatal beating and was long in Bellevue Hospital recovering. It was in Bellevue that Talbot Mundy the writer was born.

What happened around 1910 or so to change an irresponsible rogue into a man of almost irreproachable behavior in later life may never be known. But at this middle point of his sixty-one years of life, Mundy transformed himself into an honest man, respected and esteemed, with no further sins than acquiring two or three more wives than the law would have allowed him. As is to be expected, he tried to conceal his unsavory past, and very few knew of William Lancaster Gribbon, the family black sheep.

From 1911 until his death in 1940, Mundy was a professional writer; and although his career had ups and downs, during the 1920's, when he was one of the most popular pulp authors, he received from *Adventure* magazine alone (not counting book royalties and monies from foreign printings) $30,000 per year—an enormous sum for the day. During the later depression years, though, what with changing reading tastes and shaky magazines, he was at times not far from being broke.

How Mundy learned to write, where he picked up the skill that enabled him to leap with immediate success into one of the most difficult, most competitive occupations, can be answered only with a cliché: native ability, perhaps developed by some fifteen or sixteen years of living by telling victims plausible stories. He sold his first piece, an article on pigsticking (boar hunting with lances) in India to *Adventure* in 1911, beginning an association that lasted most of his life. This was a coup, for the newly founded *Adventure* was the most literate and most respectable of the pulp magazines. Most of Mundy's later books were reprinted from its pages.

Mundy's fiction is mostly adventure fiction set in exotic locations—Africa, Palestine, India, and Tibet. One might have expected his work to have been picaresque of a sort, justifying roguery, but oddly enough, it stresses honor, decency, noblesse oblige, and a general pukka sahib (establishment) orientation. He was alive to the best traditions of the British military caste, the self-sacrificing attitude of the better colonial administrators, although he was by no means priggish and wrote hotly about persons who abused power. In World War I he was caught up in the jingoism of the day, as much against the Turks as against the Germans. In later years, however, he wrote more critically against officialdom, nationalism, and similar complexes, and gradually substituted for civil authority another range of control, an ethical one. Throughout his life, one concept stood foremost in the subtext of his fiction: loyalty.

If the reminiscences of "A Jungle Sage" (1932) can be believed, Mundy was interested in the supernatural as early as 1905 or so. He tells of a search in Kenya and German East Africa for witch doctors who could work magic. Naturally, he found something of what he sought, but most of what he found was native herbalism that was superior, for some ailments, to Western medicine.

This interest moved to Christian Science, which Mundy did not join formally, although he liked some of Mary Baker Eddy's ideas, and eventually to

Theosophy, which he accepted eclectically as the creed of his later life. In the early 1920's he moved to California, where he joined the Universal Brotherhood and Theosophical Society, more commonly known as the Point Loma Rosicrucians or the Tingley Theosophists, after its then head, Katherine Tingley. A small schismatic group, ultimately descended from Madame Blavatsky's original Theosophical Society, Tingley's group never had the economic power of the mail-order San Jose Rosicrucians (the AMORC) nor the cultural impact of the British Hermetic Order of the Golden Dawn. But so far as an outsider can judge, it was more reasonable than its immediate rival, Annie Besant's Theosophical Society, centered at Adyar, India. It was concerned not so much with pseudoscience attained by clairvoyance, like Besant's group, as with spiritual wisdom and character growth.

At about this time the central concept of the Ancient Wisdom began to filter unobtrusively and smoothly into Mundy's supernatural fiction as the ultimate story source. It was presented in a general way that offended no one. But this did not keep Mundy's early fiction from being essentially male-oriented action stories filled with swashbuckling rogues from the northern provinces of India, utterly evil magicians, muscular he-men, hard-boiled femmes fatales, murder-prone demoiselles in Indian whorehouses, and cosmopolitan, chic mahatmas of supernal wisdom and paranormal abilities. Almost fairy tales of a violent nature, these stories are set in beautifully suggested exotic locales—ancient ruins in the jungle, the slums of Delhi, the hidden caverns beneath Benares, the windblown passes over the Himalayas, the placid lamaseries of Tibet—all done with an extra little touch that lift the stories above ordinary action fiction.

As Mundy grew older, though, it became obvious that his concept of both action and mankind had changed. Action no longer was a tulwar that ripped open a man's guts, but tension-laden repartee; mankind was no longer essentially hairy-chested soldiers of fortune and lewd shaktic priestesses, but more nearly average men and more humane women—most of whom had quests and purposes of one sort or another and pondered about the reason for life.

By the time of his death in Florida on 5 August 1940, the Oriental adventure story had become in his hands a story of interlocking personalities, propelled by clashes that expressed *in parvo* both the cultural aims of a people and high ethical notions. It was essentially a mainstream novel of character (though of character with supernatural attributes), concerned ultimately with spiritual crises.

Along with this development, which was accomplished with admirable craftsmanship, grew a sense of message. Mundy now felt it more and more necessary to exhort or nag the reader to a sort of Vedantic Christianity that included the *Bhagavadgita* and the *Yoga Sutras* of Patanjali. In this, of course, he was not too far removed from Aldous Huxley, Gerald Heard, and Alan Watts. Mundy expounded this system in *I Say Sunrise* (1947) and in chapter heads to his novels. These were usually presented in bombastic, paradoxical form and read like collaborations between Nietzsche and G. K. Chesterton at their worst.

But by this time the old Talbot Mundy was gone, and if a reader felt the urge to read excellent adventure with supernatural trimmings or supernaturalism with adventure trimmings, he had to return to the older books and magazines.

III

Most of Mundy's fiction was written in story chains in which permanent characters peregrinate from story to story. There are notably an African chain, a Near Eastern chain, a Classical Roman chain, and an Indian chain.

The Indian chain is where most of Mundy's supernatural fiction is to be found. It is built around several personalities: Athelstan King, an officer in the Indian Army, exemplifying the best in British military tradition; Cotswold Ommony, a forest ranger of great expertise and probity; Jeff Ramsden, an American mining engineer and strong-arm man; Narayan Singh, a Sikh soldier of fortune; Chullunder Ghose, a very intelligent Bengali babu of great unscrupulousness, but intense personal loyalty; and, most important of all, Jimgrim.

Jimgrim, or James Schuyler Grim, an American, was modeled upon Lawrence of Arabia and first served as a troubleshooter and kingmaker in the postwar Near East. In some odd way Mundy came to identify with Grim, and Grim grew in stature from political manipulator to seeker after enlightenment and then to self-sacrificing Christ figure.

The first significant Indian fantasy is *Caves of Terror* (*Adventure*, 10 November 1922, published as "The Gray Mahatma"), with Athelstan King and Jeff Ramsden. In a previous adventure, *King—of the Khyber Rifles* (1916), King had encountered Yasmini, the most interesting of Mundy's femmes fatales, who usually combine aspects of Mata Hari and Eva Peron. Yasmini had been organizing an invasion of India with German aid, but King was able to control her by means of sex, since she fancied that they were reincarnated lovers. (She may have been right on reincarnation; the influence of H. Rider Haggard is obvious here.) But now Yasmini is back and a renewed peril. She has stumbled upon the Nine Unknown, the keepers of the Ancient Wisdom, and is blackmailing one of them. This is the Gray Mahatma, a most remarkable holy man possessed of great occult powers and learned in incredible sciences—but outwitted by a woman. If Yasmini gains his secrets, India is lost. King and Ramsden undertake to stop her, and after adventures in the underground caverns of the Nine Unknown, where they witness all sorts of marvels, they succeed. For his weakness, the Gray Mahatma is placed under a death sentence by his organization. Even though he was an enemy, King and Ramsden respect and pity him, but cannot save him. He voluntarily becomes the subject of vibratory experiments, and all that is left of him is a handful of dust, which a priest kicks contemptuously.

Caves of Terror is a fast-moving adventure story, with many thrilling passages as King and Ramsden court danger. The Gray Mahatma is well conceived, and Yasmini is always amusing. But there is a certain ambiguity of theme and creakiness of resolution.

In a semisequel, *The Nine Unknown* (*Adventure*, 20 March–30 April 1923), Mundy shifts the story center away from King to Jimgrim, who is now in charge. Just before this Grim had been peripherally concerned with the discovery of King Cheops' tomb in the Fayum ("Khufu's Real Tomb," *Adventure*, 10 October 1922, published in book form as

The Mystery of Khufu's Tomb). The tomb was found by analyzing the cosmic proportions embodied in the measurements of the Great Pyramid. While this is a notion from occultism, the story is not supernatural.

In *The Nine Unknown* Jimgrim has left the Near East. He has been charged with discovering what happens to the world's supply of gold and silver, which for centuries has disappeared into India. This leads to the Nine Unknown—and many perils natural and supernatural. Grim, Ramsden, Chullunder Ghose, Narayan Singh, and others are surprised to learn that the Nine Unknown is an altruistic organization that conceals its incredible knowledge in order to prevent the world from destroying itself. The real problem is a similar but evil organization of shaktists and Kali worshipers armed with supernatural power, including thuggee-death, who want to acquire the supersciences. Grim and his associates help to destroy the false Nine, and as a reward are permitted to witness some of the missing gold being turned into atomic energy. The Nine Unknown retreat back into obscurity, and the gold is still lost. The reader, however, has met very fine ethnic characters and outstanding Indian local color.

The Devil's Guard (*Adventure*, 8 June 1926, published as "Ramsden") is often considered the finest of the Jimgrim stories. By now the focus of the Indian fantasies has changed. *The Nine Unknown* consisted of thrills and action without a thematic idea, but *The Devil's Guard* is ultimately concerned with spiritual quests. Enlightenment has become more important than metallurgy or economics, and it is recognized that each man has his own grail, which he is entitled to seek.

Ramsden receives a letter from Rait, an old acquaintance, appealing for help. Rait had penetrated Tibet in search of Shamballah—here a hidden school for occult instruction of the highest order—but has been captured by Tibetan black magicians. He offers as inducement not only the way to Shamballah but also manuscripts written by Jesus when he was in Tibet. Jimgrim, Ramsden, Chullunder Ghose, and Narayan Singh set out but are completely overmatched by the evil sorcerers, among whom Rait is now to be counted. Grim and his associates survive only through the help of a protective lodge of benevolent "white magicians." Singh is dead. Ramsden and Ghose are almost shattered physically and emotionally. Only Grim fares a little better, because he attained to a higher stage of development than his friends and is able to respond to evil with a quietism much like the Chinese Taoist *wu wei*. Grim is to go on to Shamballah for instruction.

Jimgrim (*Adventure*, 15 November 1930–15 February 1931, published as "King of the World"), the sequel to *The Devil's Guard*, is a strange novel, so highly compressed and so elliptic that it sometimes seems like the skeleton of a much longer work. It is essentially a story of selfishness versus self-sacrifice. One Dorje, a highly intelligent Tibetan, has discovered the lost cities buried beneath the Gobi Desert (a Theosophical concept) and has deciphered from golden plates secret knowledge of the past: controlled telepathy, antigravity, longevity, and superbombs. Building onto the common Asiatic belief in a coming King of the World (the future Buddhist savior Maitreya), he plans world conquest. He has accomplished quite a bit but is now burning out from advanced age and exhaustion. Grim and his associates enter the fight against Dorje. In a confrontation between the two men, Mundy reveals that they are surprisingly similar, except that one has chosen good, the other evil. Grim voluntarily takes a drug to heighten his mental abilities, knowing that it means his death, and blows up Dorje and his organization. His death is conceived as a self-immolation for the sake of mankind.

Although the Near Eastern and Indian fiction involving Grim (with the exception of *Jimgrim*) is genre adventure fiction, certain of the Indian stories peripheral to Grim are more concerned with working out central moral ideas. Such a novel is *Om. The Secret of Ahbor Valley* (*Adventure*, 10 October–30 November 1924), which is an exegesis of trust and good faith as experienced under varying circumstances.

In *Om*, Cotswold Ommony, the superintendent of a huge reforestation project in a primitive area of India, undertakes several quests, all of which interlock in the Ahbor Valley. This is a semiautonomous area in northeast India to which primitive natives forbid entry, on pain of death. From the valley has come a curious fragment of crystal that has the power to arouse mental sensations. It is later revealed to be a chip from a gigantic sphere set up tens of thousands of years earlier by wielders of a science far superior to ours, as a device for spiritual development. Ommony is also trying to discover what happened to his sister and her husband, who disappeared into the Ahbor Valley about twenty years earlier. The most interesting part of the novel, however, is Ommony's experiences traveling about India in disguise, performing a miracle play with a native dramatic troupe headed by a Tibetan lama. The description of life on the Indian stage is as fascinating as the train ride in Kipling's *Kim*. Uniting these themes are trust and good faith: Ommony with the lama; the lama with the Ahbors; Ommony with his long-lost niece, who has been reared in the Ahbor Valley. She is spiritually perfect and is to be a new redeemer sent to correct the corrupt Western world. Here, of course, there are echoes of Mundy's involvement with the Tingley Theosophists and of the earlier missions of Vivekananda and Krishnamurti.

A much less significant work is *Black Light* (1930), an extended parable on justice. It is told in Mundy's later style of tense confrontations and grandiloquent yogis. Beddington, a wealthy young American, falls in love with Amrita, a Western girl who has been reared in a heterodox Hindu temple. Against the romance are Beddington's viciously possessive mother (Mundy had a thing against domineering women) and a maharaja who wants Amrita for his harem. The yogi Ram Chittra invokes the Black Light—the projection of the akashic record (a Theosophical concept: all actions are recorded on the *akasa*, or ether). The wicked are punished and the good rewarded.

Less moralistic is *Full Moon* (*American Weekly*, 28 October 1934–13 January 1935), which is an odd mixture of Mundy's typical story and science fiction. Set mostly in northwest India, it is based on disappearances. Various parties—a beautiful Eurasian madam, the C.I.D., Afghan cutthroats, the Army—are all frantically following a trail to the most remarkable archaeological find in history. Unfortunately, the discoverer, General Frensham, has disappeared—literally. In caves beneath a mountain in Rajputana lie the remains of a preglacial culture, the product of nine-foot-tall giants, superior to modern man in every way. Even more remarkable, these beings had discovered the way to enter the fourth dimension, at full moon. The Great Race then moved there en masse. So did General Frensham.

The giants and the nature of their civilization are based on Theosophical concepts; the dimensional ideas come in part from E. A. Abbott's *Flatland* (1884); and the notion of strange disappearances is derived from the books of Charles Fort, a very interesting crank.

As fiction, *Full Moon* is a lackluster performance that plods along mechanically, without the zest or conviction of the earlier novels. It is filled with clichéd ideas—Indian whorehouses, beautiful Eurasian spies, blustering Afghans, scoundrelly hypnotists, and stiff-upper-lip Englishmen in native disguise.

At this time, 1935, Mundy was fifty-six, tired, and ill from an undiagnosed diabetic condition, and his day was done as a premier writer of pulp fiction. He decided to gamble on a new mode of life and became a radio script writer, for the last five years of his life writing *Jack Armstrong, the All-American Boy*, one of the more popular serials. This proved successful. During this period he wrote his last two novels, *The Thunder Dragon Gate* (1937), which is not important, and a quasi-sequel, *Old Ugly Face* (*Maclean's Magazine*, 15 April–15 May 1938), which is vital and worth reading, if one skips long passages of inspirational material.

Old Ugly Face is a novel about loyalty and honesty, told in terms of local Tibetan politics, and of the eternal battle between good and evil. The old Dalai Lama has died, and his successor (or reincarnation) is a child, control of whom is a high card in the game of politics. Russians, Germans, Japanese, British are all eager to own him, and, in the hands of corrupt Tibetans, he is practically up for auction. The one loyal high official in his regime is the old lama Lobsang Pun, Old Ugly Face, who has been proscribed as an outlaw by the corrupt officials. The story is told through two Westerners, Andrew Gunning and Elsa Burbage Grayne, who become entangled in the plots and counterplots and are exploited supernaturally by Lobsang Pun. The remarkable lama, to gain his objective of an independent Tibet and to preserve the sanctity of the Dalai Lama, manipulates fate and uses a gamut of paranormal abilities. There is action in the book, but suspense is maintained mostly by dramatic confrontations. There is death, but even more, there is life, in a remarkable character, Lobsang Pun.

IV

Altogether Mundy wrote about 160 stories, roughly one third of which are nouvelles or novels. (It is not possible to be more precise, since he often combined shorter pieces into longer works.) By far the greater portion of these stories is nonsupernatural adventure fiction, although there is one sentimental novel, *Her Reputation* (1923), which was made into a silent motion picture.

Most of these stories are fitted into series. There is an early group of sports stories written under the pseudonym Walter Galt, and there are the Monty stories of pre–World War I Africa. Jimgrim had ten Near Eastern adventures before shifting his operations to India, and Ommony and Ghose appear in many other stories than those described above. Most important of all the nonsupernatural chains, though, is the series about Tros of Samothrace, set around the time of Julius Caesar. Tros is present, aiding the Trinobantes during Caesar's invasion of Britain, and it is Tros who takes Cleopatra back to Egypt after Caesar's assassination. Tros's ambition is to sail around the world, but before he could reach Mexico, as planned, Mundy died. The later, better Tros stories are really mainstream historical novels, at times in the modernizing manner of George Bernard Shaw's *Caesar and Cleopatra*.

Today, Mundy is remembered mostly for the Indian supernatural stories, in which he showed himself to be the finest writer in his day of Oriental adventure fiction. Like much genre fiction these stories are by necessity simplistic in certain ways, yet they are highly imaginative, and the author's art can make the reader believe, for a couple of hours, in colorful activities off the Chandni Gowk in Delhi, and in the manifestations of the Ancient Wisdom.

Selected Bibliography

WORKS OF TALBOT MUNDY

King—of the Khyber Rifles. Indianapolis: Bobbs-Merrill, 1916. As *King, of the Khyber Rifles.* London: Constable, 1917. (The Beacon [New York, 1954] edition has been altered textually by an unknown hand, with erotic material added.)

Caves of Terror. Garden City, N.Y.: Doubleday, 1924. London: Hutchinson, 1932.

The Nine Unknown. Indianapolis: Bobbs-Merrill, 1924. London: Hutchinson, 1924.

Om. The Secret of Ahbor Valley. Indianapolis: Bobbs-Merrill, 1924. London: Hutchinson, 1925.

The Devil's Guard. Indianapolis: Bobbs-Merrill, 1926. As *Ramsden.* London: Hutchinson, 1926.

Black Light. Indianapolis: Bobbs-Merrill, 1930. London: Hutchinson, 1930.

Jimgrim. New York: Century, 1931. London: Hutchinson, 1931.

"A Jungle Sage." *Adventure,* 82:1 (15 March 1932).

The Mystery of Khufu's Tomb. London: Hutchinson, 1933. New York: Appleton-Century, 1935.

Full Moon. New York: Appleton-Century, 1935. As *There Was a Door.* London: Hutchinson, 1935.

Old Ugly Face. London: Hutchinson, 1939. New York: Appleton-Century, 1940.

I Say Sunrise. London: Andrew Dakers, 1947. Philadelphia: Milton F. Wells, 1949. (Nonfiction.)

BIOGRAPHICAL AND BIBLIOGRAPHICAL MATERIAL

Day, Bradford. *Talbot Mundy Biblio.* New York: Science-Fiction and Fantasy Publications, 1955. (Bibliography of books and magazine publications, together with miscellaneous material.)

Grant, Donald M., ed. *Talbot Mundy: Messenger of Destiny.* West Kingston, R.I.: Donald M. Grant, Publisher, 1983. (A collection of material: "Autobiography," a semifictional piece by Mundy. "Talbot Mundy" by Dawn Mundy Provost, Mundy's fifth wife; reminiscences from about 1927 to Mundy's death. "Willie — Rogue and Rebel" by Peter Berresford Ellis; an authoritative biography of Mundy's early years. "Books" and "Magazines," full bibliographies, with annotations, by Donald M. Grant. An indispensable volume.)

[Hoffman, Arthur Sullivant]. "The Camp-Fire." *Adventure,* 1 January 1927. (Anonymous editorial material with a personality sketch of Mundy.)

BACKGROUND READING

Besant, Annie. *The Ancient Wisdom.* Adyar, India, and London: Theosophical Publishing Society, 1897. (Theosophical anthropology.)

Williams, Gertrude Mervin. *Priestess of the Occult (Madame Blavatsky).* New York: Knopf, 1946. (Biography of Blavatsky and history of the Theosophical Society.)

—E. F. BLEILER

H. P. LOVECRAFT

1890-1937

ALTHOUGH HE HAS secured a firm position in the field of horror-fantasy writing, Howard Phillips Lovecraft is decidedly one of that field's most unconventional figures. Surprises await the reader beginning to explore Lovecraft's work and expecting to encounter stock horror—settings in cobwebbed and thunder-shaken Old World ruins, episodic and earthbound plots full of human interest, shock value derived from the graphic and wholesale spilling of blood. Lovecraft in the full maturity of his narrative powers deals in none of these things, preferring rather to place most of his settings in his native New England, to deal in a cosmos that transcends human interests, to favor atmosphere and mood over characterization and plot, and to derive the real thrust of his horrific powers not from shock effect but from veiled implications that the reader is left to ponder when the tale is told.

Indeed, the central feature of Lovecraft's fictive world—of the Lovecraft Mythos and its pantheon of such invented "gods" as Yog-Sothoth, Azathoth, Nyarlathotep, Shub-Niggurath, and Cthulhu—is horror by implication, to the effect that typically a Lovecraft protagonist, rationalizing desperately to avoid facing some ominous truth threatening to break through, must finally face that truth and its implication that humankind has a really motelike insignificance in the scheme of things. While the thinking, feeling human protagonist is the conduit through which the decisive experiences and revelations flow, this very figure is reduced, with his hap-

less species, to a self-understood evanescence by the very experiences that he so sensitively undergoes. This "ironic impressionism"—this effect of the human protagonist's being an organism just sufficiently well developed to be made to realize his own insectoid meaninglessness in the face of ultimate cosmic indifference and chaos—is virtually unprecedented in literature.

Lovecraft began his serious literary career at a relatively late age, and his brief life then gave him only two decades to develop it. Born on 20 August 1890 in Providence, Rhode Island, he was given intellectual direction in childhood (in the absence of his father, who died in 1898 after years of institutionalization) by his maternal grandfather. From his grandfather's large and varied old library Lovecraft, a precocious reader, imbibed early fascination with colonial New England history, the stylistic proprieties of eighteenth-century English writers, the lore of Greco-Roman antiquity, and the world of *The Arabian Nights*, from which he derived so vivid a view of the provincial nature of the Christian tradition that he developed a lifelong aversion to religion in general. Discovering and reading Edgar Allan Poe at the age of eight, he saw his interests take a turn toward the realm of horror; but it would be almost twenty more years before he turned his efforts to the fiction for which he has come to be known.

After leaving high school (without a diploma, due to a nervous condition and sporadic attendance) in 1908, Lovecraft entered a five-year period of near hermitage, indulged by his mother and aunts, sitting home, reading voraciously, and writing reams of imitative eighteenth-century verse. These poetic efforts, though in themselves of little literary value, served to give him a grounding in metrical competence and, more important, a poetic cast of mind that would come to have a great deal to do with the sonorous, alliterative, balanced quality of his later prose style. His reading during this period amounted to a remarkable self-education, as is evident to anyone who thoughtfully peruses the thousands of his extant letters, which brim with a wide erudition and mark him as an epistolarian (by habit, all his life) whose equal in output is scarcely to be found.

However, Lovecraft needed an exit from this secluded way of life; it came in 1915 when he was drawn into amateur journalism, an activity that would provide him with a circle of like-minded friends and an impetus to develop as a writer — for it was the amateur journalist W. Paul Cook who persuaded Lovecraft, in 1917, to begin writing stories in earnest. From that point, his career in fiction developed gradually, from competent but relatively unimpressive beginnings to works of great power in his last years.

Although he traveled in the eastern and southeastern United States and in Canada, he would live in his beloved Providence all his life, except for a two-year (1924–1926) "period of exile," as he was fond of putting it, in New York, corresponding to a brief and finally unsatisfactory marriage; and he would weave New England into a fabric of increasingly cosmic narratives until his death on 15 March 1937, at the age of forty-six, from intestinal cancer and kidney inflammation.

Lovecraft enjoyed a certain modest acclaim among the readers of the pulp magazines that printed his stories, but he died convinced that his work would find no wider acceptance, that he would not be remembered as a writer of any importance; he had long since termed himself an "inconsequential scribbler." That his works would be translated into many languages, that he would one day be the subject of serious criticism and scholarship, that he would continue to be read and pondered, all would have astonished him utterly.

In some respects Lovecraft was a writer of the idée fixe. Even in some of his early and comparatively unsophisticated tales one finds the germinal stirrings of things to be developed with greater success later on; certain compelling notions seemed obsessively lodged in his mentality, and he was often able to use and reuse a given theme or motif with freshness and increasing appeal over a long span of time.

One important such theme is the notion that the earth has known immensely long cycles of early intelligent life before man, cycles so ancient that they are now reflected, in Lovecraft's fictive world, only in obscure myth as set forth in such (invented) moldy and inaccessibly rare grimoires as the *Necronomicon* and the Pnakotic Manuscripts.

This idea surfaced as early as 1917, when Lovecraft wrote "Dagon," the first of his stories to be published in *Weird Tales* (October 1923). Only hinted at in "Dagon," the idea finds somewhat more extensive articulation in "The Nameless City," which Lovecraft wrote in 1921 (*The Wolverine*, no. 11, November 1921). This story, inspired by Lovecraft's reading of Lord Dunsany and of Thomas Moore's *Alciphron*, first quotes the fictitious Abdul Alhazred's celebrated couplet from Lovecraft's invented grimoire the *Necronomicon* (without yet naming the volume, which Lovecraft first does in "The Hound," written in 1922; *Weird Tales*, February 1924) and describes its protagonist's discovery, in subterranean vaults beneath an abandoned desert city, of the remains of an ancient crocodile-like race of beings. Their history is set forth in pictorial narrative murals, a motif that Lovecraft would explore with much greater power in "At the Mountains of Madness" (written in 1931; *Astounding Stories*, February, March, April 1936) and "The Shadow out of Time" (written in 1934–1935; *Astounding Stories*, June 1936). In the latter tale, the narrator's final, awful moment of truth is perhaps the central moment in all the Lovecraft Mythos. Nowhere does Lovecraft bring home with more force the awesome implications, for his protagonist and for mankind, of the earth's newly understood prehistory. The reader feels, with Lovecraft's Peaslee, the soul-shaking poignancy with which that character finally opens an eons-old book in a forgotten vault to face ineluctably what he has refused to admit concerning the evanescence of mankind, to accept for truth what he has fervently hoped to be only myth-inspired dream. The novelette has pointed its tensions, its focus, toward this moment literally from the first line.

The notion of ancient life cycles predating man is central also to "The Call of Cthulhu" (written in 1926; *Weird Tales*, February 1928), a highly significant tale in that Lovecraft here begins to impart substantial form to his Mythos, describing the prehuman tenancy of the planet, suggesting the existence of the obscure cults devoted to the return to power of great Cthulhu (an ancient, octopoid horror trapped beneath Pacific waters), and eliciting requests for more "Cthulhu stories" from readers of *Weird Tales*. August Derleth would later hold this trailblazing work in such esteem as to coin the phrase "Cthulhu Mythos," one that has been widely used, but of which Lovecraft would scarcely have approved, since in the final analysis Cthulhu is a minor figure in the Lovecraft pantheon. The author himself later regarded the story as cumbrous, probably because of its multilevel "frame" mode of narration (the account of the cult of the Old Ones being technically a story within a story within a story within a story!), but the work stands nevertheless as a powerful tale presaging further development of the Mythos.

One finds further exploration of the life cycles motif in "The Whisperer in Darkness" (written in 1930; *Weird Tales*, August 1931) and *The Shadow over Innsmouth* (written in 1931; published privately in book form in 1936 and posthumously reprinted in *Weird Tales*, January 1942). In all these revisitings of the theme, Lovecraft's protagonists are devastated by the implications of their discovery that humankind, far from being the undisputed lords of earth, must accept a most transitory role in the planet's newly understood history; but the author manages to rework his cherished theme with such freshness each time that it seems new and intriguing.

Lovecraft also seems to have had certain character types in mind over considerable periods of time, developing them gradually from inchoate foreshadowings in early tales to stark and striking figures of horror in later works. In particular, the notion of a character with unnaturally prolonged life seems to have been much in his imagination. Expressing this notion (in the form of a character named Charles Le Sorcier) as early as 1908 in a piece of juvenilia called "The Alchemist" (*United Amateur*, November 1916), Lovecraft reformulates the character type in various subsequent stories.

In "The Terrible Old Man" (written in 1920; *The Tryout*, 7, no. 4, July 1921), the figure in question is an incredibly aged sea captain who converses with shipmates from days long past in a locally feared little house by the sea. Later the same year Lovecraft wrote "The Picture in the House" (*Weird Tales*, January 1924), in which an unnaturally long-lived man owes his longevity to cannibalism. Then, in 1925, during his New York period, Lovecraft wrote "The Horror at Red Hook" (*Weird Tales*, January 1927), in which Robert Suydam, allied with ancient cults and evidently unchanged by the passing of decades, seeks to regain social respectability by marrying into a well-regarded family.

This motif is brought to grand fruition finally in the haunting character of Joseph Curwen, in Lovecraft's Providence novel *The Case of Charles Dexter Ward* (written in 1927; *Weird Tales*, May, July 1941). Curwen, whose life is uncannily prolonged by sorcery, is ill regarded, like Suydam, for his seeming refusal to grow older even after more than a century, and marries into a respected family to mollify his neighbors. Finally he is killed. Brought back to life by his descendant Charles Ward after two centuries to visit horrors upon the modern Providence community, Curwen stands as a vivid culmination of several years' development of the character type that he represents.

Lovecraft, still unable to abandon the idea, revisited it in 1933 with "The Thing on the Doorstep" (*Weird Tales*, January 1937), in which the wizard Ephraim Waite possesses the body of his daughter and seeks to go living on and on by usurping body after body, with a suggestion that his consciousness has already long outlived its customary time. Yet despite the continuity of conception that runs through all these characters, Lovecraft manages to make each successive reappearance of the character type seem newly engaging.

Another notable facet of Lovecraft's art is his ability to make striking fictional use of travel impressions, particularly with respect to his treks to western Massachusetts and southeastern Vermont; it was an unusual talent that could transmute these locales the way he did. He was doing so as early as 1927, with his story "The Colour out of Space" (*Amazing Stories*, September 1927), which draws upon his knowledge of the then much-discussed plans to flood the Swift River Valley in western Massachusetts, inundating four evacuated towns to create a water supply for Boston. Lovecraft's narrator is thankful for the intended effacement of the region after he learns of a horror that has occurred there: a meteorite has poisoned the region with a creeping blight affecting the vegetation and livestock first, then the hapless farm family on whose land the stone fell. The story is in effect a tone poem, narrated with somber, mood-evoking poetic balance. It was Lovecraft's own favorite among his tales—and he was generally an extremely harsh self-critic.

Perhaps the most interesting use of travel impressions, however, is "The Dunwich Horror" (*Weird Tales*, April 1929), written in 1928 immediately after the author's return home from a trip to western Massachusetts to visit friends in the towns of Athol and Wilbraham. This widely read story transmutes a real ravine called Bear's Den in North New Salem, near Athol (mingled with scenic impressions from Wilbraham Mountain), into a hellish lair, called Cold Spring Glen, in which the monstrous Yog-Sothoth-spawned Wilbur Whateley's twin brother lurks. The brother is an invisible horror who rages through the remote countryside bringing death to the Dunwich farm families.

The curious thing about "The Dunwich Horror" is that on the face of it the tale seems to be a "good guys versus bad guys" confrontation running quite contrary to Lovecraft's usual philosophical indifference to such merely human concerns as good and evil. Protagonist Henry Armitage is given such moralizing and corny lines that one may wonder whether Lovecraft has lapsed here. Yet, there is abundant internal evidence that Armitage's "victory" over the teratological twins is a hollow one, bereft of significance in the cosmic scheme, in which the Old Ones who seek to prevail over the earth must ultimately do so.

Furthermore, there are suggestions that Wilbur and his gargantuan brother are really the heroes of the tale, in terms of the mythic hero archetype and the pattern of the hero "monomyth." The theme of death and rebirth is patently present in symbolic terms when Wilbur dies and the brother bursts forth from the decayed Dunwich farmhouse in which he (it) has been nurtured, a symbolic womb; the mythically usual descent to the underworld is given by the brother's slithering down into Cold Spring Glen; and the climactic scene atop Sentinel Hill (named after Sentinel Elm Farm in Athol), in which the twin is magically sent back to the god-father Yog-Sothoth, is a delectable parody of the Crucifixion. All in all, "The Dunwich Horror" contains so many in-jokes, so many levels of meaning, that one can scarcely take its superficial appearances seriously.

There are other notable adaptations of travel experience among Lovecraft's best-known tales. Just previous to his visits to Athol and Wilbraham, Lovecraft had stayed for two weeks with his friend Vrest Orton in Guilford, Vermont; and after letting the locale's remote rural impressions incubate for a couple of years he wrote, in 1930, his Vermont story "The Whisperer in Darkness," indulging in his penchant for character isolation by presenting Henry Wentworth Akeley (patterned on an artist-recluse whom Lovecraft met in Vermont) as a sort of hermit progressively encroached upon by nonhuman fungoid creatures inhabiting the nearby woods. Lovecraft derived the name Akeley from Samuel Akeley, the builder of the old house in which Orton hosted him.

Besides these locales, Lovecraft made much use of the historic Massachusetts towns of Marblehead (called Kingsport) and Salem (called Arkham). It was not long after his first visit to the charming little seacoast town of Marblehead that he wrote, in 1923, his Yuletide story "The Festival" (*Weird Tales*, January 1925), telling of a protagonist drawn back to the town by old family traditions and compelled to partake of ancient and repellent winter solstice rites in an underground chamber beneath an old church (based on the real St. Michael's in Marblehead).

Lovecraft's uses of Salem range over a number of tales, notably "The Thing on the Doorstep" and "The Dreams in the Witch House" (the latter written in 1932; *Weird Tales*, July 1933). In his Salem witch story, Lovecraft makes bold to subsume the traditional witchcraft lore into his own unique Mythos, suggesting that the conventional notions of witches' sabbats and devil worship are really only a facet of an immeasurably more ancient lore involving the (Lovecraftian) god Azathoth. The story is marred, however, by an uncharacteristic dependence upon such conventional trappings as crucifixes used against witches, and shows some signs of overexplanation and hasty writing. Nevertheless, Lovecraft evinces an altogether uncommon capacity for responding to New England place impressions, which were every bit as sentient and eloquent to his imagination as the South was to William Faulkner.

The literary influences on Lovecraft are many and varied, if one counts even minor ones, for he read insatiably; but only four writers can be identified as major influences: Edgar Allan Poe, Lord Dunsany, Nathaniel Hawthorne, and Arthur Machen.

Early in his career, Lovecraft emulated Poe at times to the extent of outright imitation, as can be seen in such tales as "The Outsider" (written in 1921; *Weird Tales*, April 1926), "The Hound," and, as late as 1926, "Cool Air" (*Tales of Magic and Mystery*, March 1928). "The Outsider," a tale enigmatic in its interpretative potential, may owe something thematically to Ambrose Bierce's "An Inhabitant of Carcosa" but is more strongly suggestive of the opening of Poe's story "Berenice." By 1927, when he was writing "The Colour out of Space," Lovecraft had certainly abandoned his stylistic dependence on Poe and had found his own style, but a certain Poe influence lingers throughout his career — the general narrative mind-set by which a horror tale thrives best in the soil of the well-understood psychology of fear, a psychology in which the protagonist must endure his horrors utterly alone, unsure of his sanity and deeply shaken by the implications of what happens to him.

Even near the end of his career, with the dream-haunted narrator of "The Shadow out of Time," Lovecraft reflects a lasting indebtedness to the general psychology of Poe. It pervades Lovecraft's literary effusions in the form of the highly effective character isolation that informs such works as *The Case of Charles Dexter Ward* and "The Shadow Over Innsmouth." This influence is more pervasive, more general, than the merely stylistic influence that Lovecraft soon enough outgrew.

One cannot, however, carve Lovecraft's writing career up into exclusive periods of influence in any facile way, for even at the time of his most pronounced imitativeness of Poe he was also strongly moved by the dreamy, ethereal fictive world of Lord Dunsany. He had such a mental predisposition to be receptive to Dunsany's style that he actually wrote one "Dunsanian" story, "Polaris" (*The Philosopher*, no. 1, December 1920), in 1918, before he had begun to read Dunsany. The lofty, quasi-biblical Dunsanian influence is thereafter overtly visible in such works as "Celephaïs" (written in 1920; *The Rainbow*, no. 2, May 1922), "The Quest of Iranon" (written in 1921; *The Galleon*, 1, no. 5, July–August 1935), the splendidly poetic tale "The Strange High House in the Mist" (written in 1926; *Weird Tales*, October 1931), and the novel *The Dream-Quest of Unknown Kadath* (written in 1926–1927; *The Arkham Sampler*, Fall–Winter 1948).

In the Kadath novel the protagonist, Randolph Carter, becomes a Lovecraftian version of the Homeric Ulysses, voyaging through Dreamland in quest of archaic gods who can tell him how to find a once-glimpsed marvelous city of his deep dreams. He learns in the end that he carries his goal within him, for his dream city is merely the sum total of all that he has loved and remembered from youth; this theme is adumbrated in the earlier "Celephaïs." The novel exemplifies the fact that even when Lovecraft is stylistically and thematically reflecting the manner of Dunsany, he does so with a dark suggestiveness that goes beyond the Irish master. What lingers of the Dunsany influence for Lovecraft is the notion of a pantheon of invented gods or primordial entities. Moved by Dunsany's creation of such ancient gods as Māna-Yood-Sushaī, Lovecraft pursued his own gods throughout his career, even when Dunsany had long abandoned the notion of creating them himself. Beginning with "The Call of Cthulhu" in 1926, Lovecraft breathed life into his own highly original theogony.

The influence of Nathaniel Hawthorne is diffuse and not confinable to a particular period. Although Lovecraft had no taste for Hawthorne's moralizing didacticism in fiction, he derived from Hawthorne a number of particular points of imagery and thematic usage. The gloomy meditations upon puritanical furtiveness found in Lovecraft's "The Picture in the House" have their clear source in Hawthorne. The influence of *The House of the Seven Gables* upon Lovecraft's "The Shunned House" (written in 1924; privately published in book form in 1928; *Weird Tales*, October 1937) is obvious, even to the extent of near-parallel passages of description. Lovecraft's use of the motif, in *The Case of Charles Dexter Ward*, of ancestral papers hidden behind a portrait owes a similar debt to the same Hawthorne novel.

In all likelihood, Lovecraft obtained the germinal idea for his fictive tome the *Necronomicon* from a description of such an ancient book in Hawthorne's *American Notebooks*, which he is known to have read sufficiently early to be thus influenced. He even derives certain motifs from Hawthorne's unfinished novels, taking, for instance, the idea of the witch Keziah Mason in "The Dreams in the Witch House" from *Septimius Felton*, in which Hawthorne's character is named Keziah and is engaged in a struggle with the Black Man of witchcraft lore. The pervasive and lasting Hawthorne influence, however, consists of the use of New England as an eminently suitable setting for ponderous and terrible happenings.

Lovecraft's debt to Arthur Machen is found in various thematic points, notably the notion of a pagan god's siring a horrific hybrid offspring, which Machen explored in "The Great God Pan." Lovecraft uses this idea in "The Dunwich Horror," in which he even mentions Machen and the Machen title, as if he wants the influence to be seen. Other such thematic derivations can be observed as well. Machen's most lasting influence on Lovecraft, however, is the notion of unthinkable survivals from the past, survivals of ancient, myth-presaged entities that, if they ever really lived, ought now to be still but are not. Lovecraft, already much given to literary speculations about the impact of the past upon the present, was well disposed to be receptive to this Machenian notion of unsuspected survival. It shows up most clearly in "The Whisperer in Darkness," where Lovecraft's fungoid denizens of the Vermont woods form a living linkage with an unsuspected

past not yet dead, and where again Lovecraft even mentions Machen (by way of Machen's "little people") as if to call attention to the influence.

Despite all these significant influences, Lovecraft is no mere "derivative" writer; he ventures well beyond those literary forces that helped to shape him. Lovecraft's survivals from the past are not Machen's "little people" of the wood; they imply in their immemorial alienness a cosmic sense unreached even by Dunsany's theogony. Lovecraft retains his Poesque fear responses and character isolation but employs them in tales of far-flung implications that in no way imitate Poe directly. He keeps his Hawthornian predilection for the somber side of old New England, but he weaves that setting into tales far outside the world view of Hawthorne.

In short, H. P. Lovecraft is more than the sum of his parts, for in his mature style he transcends his sources of influence, assimilating them and blending them with his own ideas to achieve high originality. Lovecraft's imaginative world, a vast and awesome realm in which human wanderers are reduced to ironically self-understood insignificance, is ultimately his alone. Philosophically, one may be attracted to or repelled by this bleak view of man's place in the universe, just as one may approve or disapprove of Lovecraft's avoidance of dialogue and his heavily atmospheric descriptive style. One may like or dislike Lovecraft—but one must ponder him in either case.

Selected Bibliography

FICTION BY H. P. LOVECRAFT

The following four items constitute the first editions of Lovecraft's more important fiction. Occasional juvenilia and minor items are to be found in *Marginalia* (Sauk City, Wis.: Arkham House, 1944) and *Something About Cats* (Sauk City, Wis.: Arkham House, 1949).

The Shunned House. Athol, Mass.: The Recluse Press, 1928. (Approximately 300 sets of sheets were printed by W. Paul Cook, a few of which were bound at a later date by various hands. Only a few copies are known to survive. Would-be purchasers are warned that there is a counterfeit edition and are advised to consult Lloyd

W. Currey's *Science Fiction and Fantasy Authors* for points.)

The Shadow Over Innsmouth. Everett, Pa.: Visionary Publishing Company, 1936. (Approximately 400 sets of sheets were printed, about half of which were bound. Exceedingly rare.)

The Outsider and Others. Sauk City, Wis.: Arkham House, 1939. (The first major Lovecraft collection, edited by August Derleth and Donald Wandrei. Now extremely rare. 1,268 copies printed.)

Beyond the Wall of Sleep. Sauk City, Wis.: Arkham House, 1943. (The second major Lovecraft collection, edited by August Derleth and Donald Wandrei. Now extremely rare. 1,217 copies printed.)

Since the above first editions are rare books and collectors' items of considerable value, the following books are suggested as reasonably accessible reprints. It should be noted that there have been many other reprintings of Lovecraft's fiction in the United States and Great Britain, and that the bibliographic situation is complex.

The Dunwich Horror and Others. Sauk City, Wis.: Arkham House, 1963. (Contains "The Rats in the Walls," "The Outsider," "The Colour out of Space," "The Music of Erich Zann," "The Call of Cthulhu," "The Dunwich Horror," "The Whisperer in Darkness," "The Shadow Over Innsmouth," "The Shadow out of Time," and others.)

At the Mountains of Madness and Other Novels. Sauk City, Wis.: Arkham House, 1964. (Contains the three novels, "The Shunned House," and others.)

Dagon and Other Macabre Tales. Sauk City, Wis.: Arkham House, 1965. (Contains "Dagon," "Polaris," "Celephaïs," "The Nameless City," "The Quest of Iranon," "The Festival," "The Horror at Red Hook," "The Strange High House in the Mist," "The Alchemist," and others. Also included is Lovecraft's important critical survey "Supernatural Horror in Literature.")

The Horror in the Museum and Other Revisions. Sauk City, Wis.: Arkham House, 1970. (Contains the major stories "revised" by Lovecraft for other authors, actually nearly pure ghostwriting in most cases. Includes "The Mound," an important facet of the Lovecraft Mythos.)

OTHER WORKS BY H. P. LOVECRAFT

Supernatural Horror in Literature. New York: Ben Abramson, 1945. (The first really scholarly study of horror fiction. Lovecraft here provides one of the earliest competent, critical treatments of Poe, among others, and the essay is also valuable for the insights that it provides into influences on Lovecraft.)

Selected Letters 1911-1924. Sauk City, Wis.: Arkham House, 1965. (Edited by August Derleth and Donald Wandrei.)

Selected Letters 1925-1929. Sauk City, Wis.: Arkham House, 1968. (Edited by August Derleth and Donald Wandrei.)

Selected Letters 1929-1931. Sauk City, Wis.: Arkham House, 1971. (Edited by August Derleth and Donald Wandrei.)

Selected Letters 1932-1934. Sauk City, Wis.: Arkham House, 1976. (Edited by August Derleth and James Turner.)

Selected Letters 1934-1937. Sauk City, Wis.: Arkham House, 1976. (Edited by August Derleth and James Turner.)

CRITICAL AND BIOGRAPHICAL STUDIES

Burleson, Donald R. *H. P. Lovecraft: A Critical Study.* Westport, Conn.: Greenwood Press, 1983. (A critical study of all Lovecraft's fiction and selected poetry.)

de Camp, L. Sprague. *Lovecraft: A Biography.* Garden City, N.Y.: Doubleday, 1975. (A factually thorough biography with photographs.)

Joshi, S. T. *H. P. Lovecraft.* Mercer Island, Wash.: Starmount House, 1982. Starmont Reader's Guide 13. (A brief but philosophically very insightful survey of Lovecraft's works.)

————, ed. *H. P. Lovecraft: Four Decades of Criticism.* Athens: Ohio University Press, 1980. (Essays by Fritz Leiber, Dirk Mosig, George Wetzel, J. Vernon Shea, and others.)

Long, Frank Belknap. *Howard Phillips Lovecraft: Dreamer on the Nightside.* Sauk City, Wis.: Arkham House, 1975. (A memoir by one of Lovecraft's closest friends.)

Lovecraft Studies, edited by S. T. Joshi. (Periodical published twice yearly, beginning Fall 1979. Devoted entirely to serious literary criticism on Lovecraft.)

BIBLIOGRAPHY

Joshi, S. T. *H. P. Lovecraft and Lovecraft Criticism: An Annotated Bibliography.* Kent, Ohio: Kent State University Press, 1981. (A highly valuable scholarly compilation.)

—DONALD R. BURLESON

ROBERT E. HOWARD

1906-1936

I

ON ABOUT 10 November 1932 an important story appeared on the newsstands of America. This was "The Phoenix on the Sword," which appeared in the December 1932 issue of *Weird Tales*, a shaky, low-budget pulp magazine that was highly regarded by a clique of semiprofessional writers and a band of vocal fans.

"The Phoenix on the Sword" was the first story about Conan the Cimmerian, the type specimen of the ultra-macho blood-and-guts, sword-and-sorcery hero, and it told of a muscle-clad hero who by strength, courage, and stubbornness defeated evil. It was not a very good story, but it held the reader's attention, and it established a subgenre—the heroic supernatural adventure story. It was followed by better stories about Conan, was imitated by other writers, and became the source of a not-so-minor industry in the 1970's and 1980's.

The author of the story was Robert Ervin Howard, a twenty-six-year-old Texan who was building himself a reputation as a more than routinely competent writer of pulp adventure stories. His work was narrow in range, often carelessly written, and occasionally self-projective in an unpleasant way, but it showed great imagination and enormous narrative vigor and drive.

Robert E. Howard was born in Peaster, Texas, on 22 January 1906, but spent most of his life in Cross Plains, Texas, a small town of about fifteen hundred people, roughly fifty miles southeast of Abilene, in the post-oak country of small ranches and shallow oil fields. His father was a country physician. His mother's family, the Ervins, were from the Deep South, and there were traditions that they had once enjoyed extensive holdings in slaves and land. This background undoubtedly had much to do with Howard's racial attitudes.

Howard spent his formative years in small Texas towns and had almost no experience of any other sort of life. He attended a local high school and spent two years at a nearby business college, but was otherwise self-educated. A desperate, omnivorous, moneyless reader, he found books difficult to get. He tells of raiding local schoolhouses and filling his saddlebags with books, which he then took home to read. He also devoured the omnipresent pulp magazines that formed the culture of small-town America. Among the authors who influenced him most were Jack London, Arthur Conan Doyle, Talbot Mundy, Rudyard Kipling, and H. Rider Haggard. Howard was highly intelligent, and he eventually picked up a wide, if haphazard, range of knowledge, particularly in history, but often showed a lack of intellectual balance and perspective.

At an early age Howard decided to become a writer, and taught himself by analyzing the stories in *Adventure* and perhaps other pulps. Since he sold fiction while still a teenager, we can watch a stubborn, persistent young man bulling himself forward in his chosen field, despite great cultural handicaps. He developed over his eleven-year writing career but, sadly, this development was not so much broadening of outlook or sophistication as technical improvement. At the time of his suicide in 1936 he defined fiction in much the same way as when he started to write: a highly colored description of a direct physical onslaught against or in anticipation of a threat.

At first Howard sold his stories and an occasional poem to *Weird Tales*, and this remained his favorite market. It paid poorly and belatedly, but Howard liked it, perhaps because of the sort of story it printed, perhaps because here alone did he have a following. But over the years he gradually expanded his writing to include sports stories, Westerns, and adventure stories, so that at the last he was writing for many different pulp markets. He apparently had no strong urge to go beyond the pulps. He was a reasonably competent businessman, and he made a good living for Cross Plains, but it was nothing compared to what the major pulp writers like Talbot Mundy and Max Brand were earning.

At the time of his death Howard was not a fully mature writer, although his work was showing signs of a new leap forward. But at his best he could convey a visual scene as sharp as a motion picture set. He could double-plot and multiple-plot with great skill, so that no matter what the faults of a Howard story might be, the parts usually slid neatly into place. Characterization was not a strong point, but he could pour emotion into his stories and drag the reader along at a headlong pace. His other great strength was imagination. He could always see new aspects in trite situations and say things that had not been said before.

Howard was an impatient man, and seldom reworked a rejected story, but would dash off a new one to take its place. It was easier, he said, to write twice as much material as he needed to sell. He worked feverishly when the mood struck him, and often wrote carelessly and sloppily. He never met the good editor he needed.

Texas was Howard's world, and it was not until 1930, at age twenty-four, that he reached the outside world and came into contact with intellectual equals of similar tastes. At that time he began to correspond with members of the Lovecraft circle—H. P. Lovecraft himself, Clark Ashton Smith, August Derleth, and E. Hoffmann Price. This correspondence gave him a few intellectual jolts, and it also offered him some badly needed self-esteem in being recognized by peers. (Locally, he was considered a lazy eccentric.) Yet this correspondence may also have reinforced his resolution not to leave his mother and Cross Plains.

There were reasons that Howard should have left Cross Plains, apart from its handicaps as a very small town. He lived in a family situation that was like a bear garden, with an irascible, domineering father and an invalid mother to whom Howard was much too close.

At age thirty Howard was a brawny, two-hundred-pound six-footer who talked and wrote as macho as could be. He made a fetish of rough and tough athleticism (despite tachycardia), and was an arms enthusiast. His correspondents compared him to Conan, and he seemed to enjoy life.

But this was all on the surface. Beneath the Hemingway facade was a timid, emotionally immature man who on many occasions swore that he would commit suicide when his mother died. He also seemed at times to move and talk in a private world away from reality. Enemies were after him, he said, and he would pack a gun, hone his oversized pocketknife, and slow down in his car to examine thickets that might hold an ambush.

When on 11 June 1936 Howard heard that his mother had entered terminal coma, he kept his oath. He took his pistol, went out to his car, and blew out his brains.

Apart from its needlessness, Howard's suicide was tragic, for he was a very gifted, gentle man (despite the foolish noises he made) who was trapped by genetics and geography, and deserved a better fate.

At this point it is necessary to speak about a dark aspect of Robert E. Howard. As will be seen from the story descriptions that follow, Howard was an extreme racist who hated and feared blacks. Yet this fear and hatred were theoretical only, and there is no suggestion that Howard ever applied it or focused it on individuals. From what is recorded, he was a kindly man, if moody, and not the vicious cracker that his stories sometimes suggest. In all this he paralleled his friend Lovecraft, who was also able to maintain a sharp dichotomy between the theory and practice of intolerance.

II

Howard's fiction that was written before 1932 is by and large either immature or undistinguished, and does not require much comment. There are, though, occasional stories that are interesting for reasons other than literary quality, and the early heroic story chains are so personally revelatory that they cannot be ignored.

His first published story was "Spear and Fang" (*Weird Tales*, July 1925), which anticipates a strong theme in his later work: racial conflict. A handsome young Cro-Magnon woman is almost raped twice, once by a fellow tribesman, and once by an apelike Neanderthal man. As in the work of Edgar Rice Burroughs, the operative word is "almost," for the hero comes along at exactly the right moment. Written when Howard was eighteen, "Spear and Fang" is clichéd and false, but it is cleanly written and holds the reader's attention.

The most ambitious of Howard's early tales is the serial novel "Skull-Face" (*Weird Tales*, October–December 1929). It is about a revived Atlantean mummy of great malice who causes trouble on the international scene. The mummy's name, Kathulos, may have been borrowed from Lovecraft's god Cthulhu (although this has been denied), but the story is a weak imitation of Sax Rohmer's Fu Manchu stories.

Before the Conan series Howard developed three other heroic story chains, although not all their story components were published in his lifetime. The earliest of these heroes is Solomon Kane, a sixteenth-century English Puritan whose most characteristic adventures take place in an Africa modeled on those of H. Rider Haggard and Paul du Chaillu. In the hands of an author more skilled at rendering character, Kane might have been interesting, since he is complex, but Howard could never make him convincing. A dour, tormented, rage-driven man, Kane believes that he has a divinely inspired mission to rid the world of evil. (Is there a memory here of the holiness preachers of Howard's post-oak country, with their crusades against sex, liquor, and playing cards?)

The only story about Kane that is worth reading is the last, "Wings in the Night" (*Weird Tales*, July 1932), which is noteworthy for a sustained atmosphere of savagery and brutality. Kane, wandering across Africa, comes upon a small tribe of friendly natives who trust him to defend them with his firearms against frightful semihuman winged beings. Kane fails and the tribe is exterminated in a surprise attack. Almost mad with guilt, Kane takes one of the most ferocious revenges in pulp fiction.

The inner situation of most of the stories about Kane is guilt and anger, but the emotion most common in Howard's next series, the tales about King Kull, is suspicion.

Kull, who lives around 100,000 B.C., is an Atlantean barbarian who has usurped the throne of Valusia, a more civilized but somewhat decadent land. Kull rules well and is a champion against evil, but he is hated as an outsider without social graces and legitimacy. Someone is always plotting against him.

Kull's first adventure, "The Shadow Kingdom" (*Weird Tales*, August 1929), tells of an attempt by prehuman serpent men to take over the land and ultimately displace mankind. The plot is aimed at Kull, and one of the enemy assumes his likeness by magic. "The Shadow Kingdom" is ingenuous cloak-and-dagger work, and a reader may ponder over a summary that can be extracted from it: "I'm surrounded by snakes and they're trying to steal my stuff!" This same idea is to be found in other stories about Kull. They are undistinguished, and Kull achieves as much life as a hitching post.

If Kull is dull fictional fare, he is interesting as a projection of Howard, who used him on occasion to expound a "philosophy of life." Howard was also in Kull's position: a Westerner, a barbarian who had to force recognition the hard way, who might be laughed at by members of the "effete" Eastern establishment but would win, anyway. All this, of course, is a pattern in American history—frontier versus seaboard—but for Howard it had great personal relevance.

A third heroic series centers on Bran Mak Morn, a Pictish chief who is trying to withstand the Romans in Britain. Howard was fascinated by the Picts, and brought them into his work whenever possible — with Kull, Conan, and elsewhere. Most of the stories about Bran and other Picts are trivial, but "Worms of the Earth" (*Weird Tales*, November 1932) is noteworthy for its emotional level — a prolonged shriek. Bran has vowed revenge on the governor of a Roman frontier post, and risks his life and sanity forcing the underground pre-Pictish serpent people to help him. Although Howard portrayed Bran's emotional turmoil simplistically, the story maintains a remarkable level of near-hysteria.

More interesting work is sometimes found in later independent stories than in the early series. Three of these stories are worth mentioning.

"The Valley of the Worm" (*Weird Tales*, February 1934) uses a favorite device of Howard's: a twentieth-century man remembers a life in the remote past, perhaps through reincarnation, perhaps through ancestral memory. This device permitted a modern commentary on events that a primitive man would not have understood.

In "The Valley of the Worm," which despite a need for editorial tightening is the best of these stories about memory, the narrator remembers the life of Niord, a warrior in a proto-Indo-European völkerwanderung, including the incident that gave rise to the general legend of the dragon slayer. Niord and his people, the Aesir, warlike blond giants, wander into the Pictish jungles. Warfare and massacre result, with the Aesir winning. In the Pictish territory is a valley with ancient ruins. Niord's people ignore a warning to stay out, and settlers are torn to shreds by a monstrosity that emerges from underground. Niord avenges his friends, killing the Lovecraftian horror with poisoned arrows, but dies in the conflict.

The story is told simply, but with a tone of muscle arrogance that makes Jack London's most exuberant work seem restrained. It projects two emotions — xenophobia and hatred — stating directly ideas that underlie much of Howard's fiction: the inevitability of war when peoples meet, and the superiority of Indo-Europeans. But once "The Valley of the Worm" starts to move, it is the most powerful fantasy ever written about primitive man. Unlike the Conan stories, which are in a way playful stories

and a little tongue-in-cheek at times, "The Valley of the Worm" is serious, and deadly.

In two Southern regionalist stories, "Black Canaan" (*Weird Tales*, June 1936) and "Pigeons from Hell" (*Weird Tales*, May 1938), Howard uses local folklore. "Black Canaan" is a projection of antiblack hatred and fear, and is based on a historical conjureman named Kelly. In the story, the whites — a sturdy, self-reliant group — anticipate a black uprising when Saul Stark, a powerful juju man, comes to the area. It is obvious that the white men will be massacred and the women raped, and that the blacks will set up a magical kingdom ruled by Stark. The whites band together to kill Stark and his evil, oversexed mulatto priestess, but succeed only by chance, and the narrator has a narrow escape from being transformed into an aquatic horror. But success is success, and the blacks are put back in their place. "Black Canaan" is a vicious story, but as a projection of fear raised to almost mythic levels it is an interesting document, and it is a powerful story.

"Pigeons from Hell" is based on folktales that Howard heard from his Ervin grandmother. There is some racist bile in the story, but the larger point is fear of the malignant dead or undead, as the narrator spends a night in a haunted, deserted house where voodoo had once been practiced. The situations anticipate the sadistic horror comic books of the 1940's and 1950's, but Howard conveys the emotions of the experiencer with great skill.

III

When one thinks of Howard, one thinks of Conan, the first great macho hero in popular literature. Conan started in a small way but today is a figure known around the world, as the following translations indicate: *Conan el Conquistador, Conan il Conquistatore, Conan La naissance du monde, Seifuku-Ō Conan, Conan von Cimmeria,* and *Schimmen en Zamboela.*

During Howard's lifetime eighteen stories about Conan were published. Written in haphazard order, though with a life history in mind, they took Conan from his youth as a savage gaping at the marvels of civilization to the kingship of Aquilonia. Along the way he was variously a thief, pirate, Cossack het-

ROBERT E. HOWARD

man, chief of desert raiders, leader of mountain cutthroats, mercenary, and all-around soldier of fortune. Howard never wrote a story telling exactly
how Conan became king.

The first Conan story, "The Phoenix on the
Sword," was adapted from an earlier story about
King Kull that Howard was not able to sell. It was
insipid, and to vitalize it, Howard added a new second subplot, an explosion of supernatural revenge
that by chance includes Conan.

In this story Conan is not individualized; the elemental gusto and rogue elements come later. But
the world of Conan is present in at least foreshadowings. Although Howard's history is somewhat
confused, Conan's world is the preglacial, precata-
clysmic world of about 10,000 B.C., when the Mediterranean is still a dry valley and much of western
Africa is under water. The Nile curves westward,
running through the Ur-Mediterranean lands to the
sea. The so-called Hyborian countries correspond
roughly to modern Europe. Conan's Aquilonia is an
Ur-France; Nemedia (Russian *nemetz*, "German") is
Ur-Germany; Vanaheim and Asgard are an enlarged
Scandinavia; Stygia, the home of magic, is an expanded ancient Egypt. Conan himself is a Cimmerian, or the rough equivalent of an Irishman. Howard
knew of Herodotus' Cimmerians, but he was probably thinking of the vaguer, more remote Cimmerians mentioned by Homer.

This world abounds in great kingdoms and petty
city-states, high barbaric cultures and savage tribes,
world religions and primitive shamans, magicians of
power and malice, and demons galore. Howard
treated history and geography loosely, and did not
hesitate, for example, to bring Nahuatl colonies to
Africa.

Conan embodies certain of Howard's ideals and
those of the post-oak country: strength, resilience,
courage, rough integrity, and "badness"—a sort of
preglacial John Wesley Hardin with muscle. In a letter to Clark Ashton Smith (23 July 1935) Howard
described Conan as

the most realistic character I ever evolved....
Some mechanism in my subconsciousness took
the dominant characteristics of various prize-

fighters, gunmen, bootleggers, oil field bullies,
gamblers, and honest workmen I had come into
contact with and combining them produced....
Conan.

The name itself is a not uncommon Celtic name
of great antiquity.

As Howard stated, Conan seized upon him, and
he found it difficult to write about anything else.
Since there is much personal projection in the stories, this is not surprising. Nor, considering Howard's writing habits, is it astonishing that the stories
vary greatly in quality.

Among the better stories are "The Tower of the
Elephant," "The Pool of the Black One," "Shadows
in Zamboula," and "Queen of the Black Coast."
They display less of Howard's weaknesses than
usual, and many of his strengths: plotting, color, and
imagination.

In "The Tower of the Elephant" (*Weird Tales*,
March 1933) Conan is a young man, fresh from the
backwoods of the distant north, but a man of daring.
He scales the dreaded Elephant Tower of the magician Yara looking for loot, finds there a strange being
from the stars, and witnesses great sorcery. In this
story, which is narrated economically, the influence
of the Lovecraft circle can be seen in the concept of
the extraterrestrial.

In "The Pool of the Black One" (*Weird Tales*, October 1933) Conan is on an unknown isle far out in
the Atlantic, where gigantic black hominids are associated with a supernatural well. Just as Saul Stark
in "Black Canaan" could turn white men into
aquatic monsters, the black giants in this story dip
white captives into the well, whereupon they
shrink to stone doll-like images. A dreamlike ending, in which the water from the well chases Conan
and his pirate comrades, is effective.

"Shadows in Zamboula" (*Weird Tales*, November 1935), set in a frontier town in the Ur–Near East,
postulates a slave population of black cannibals who
terrorize and "run" the town, but contains imaginative incidents and complex plotting that inter-
mesh as neatly as clock wheels. Within Howard's
form limits, this tale is close to perfection.

Perhaps the best of the Conan stories is "Queen

865

of the Black Coast" (*Weird Tales*, May 1934), in which Conan becomes the consort of a bloodthirsty female pirate. Together they spread murder and rapine along the coasts of Africa, but doom comes on them when they interfere with an ancient monstrosity in a black, ruined city. The story is told almost as simply as a saga, but with many imaginative touches and high emotion. Its ultimate point is the power of love. It is effective in being the only Conan story that is based on another emotion than greed, lust, or hatred.

In other Conan stories there are occasional good touches, even though the stories may be marred by hasty writing, pulp clichés, or unsuccessful tone. In "Shadows in the Moonlight" (*Weird Tales*, April 1934) there is a ruined hall lined with black iron statue-men waiting for the moonlight to release them temporarily; outside, parrots scream about the punishment for the bestial crime the black statue-men have committed. (The blacks had tortured and castrated a white demigod.) In "The Devil in Iron" (*Weird Tales*, August 1934) an evil humanoid being is the result of the evolution of metal "flesh" over millions of years. "A Witch Shall Be Born" (*Weird Tales*, December 1934) contains the most extravagant feat that ever pulp hero performed. As Conan, crucified by his enemies, hangs helpless on the cross, he is attacked by a vulture. Damned if he will die meekly, he seizes the vulture's neck with his teeth and bites it to death!

Howard wrote only one novel about Conan, "The Hour of the Dragon" (*Weird Tales*, December 1935–April 1936; book title, *Conan the Conqueror*). Written in 1934, it is hasty and crude (though with excellent moments), but is interesting psychologically. Conan is "dead" at least four times in the story, but always returns to life. Is this alternation of life and death a reflection of Howard's internal debate about suicide? On one occasion Conan is guarded and preserved by a maternal figure, the only such character in Howard's work, in which women are otherwise hellcats or clinging-vine bedmates.

The theme of "The Hour of the Dragon" is mythic, the return of the king. Conan has lost his kingdom through a combination of evil magic and worldly enemies, and before he can regain it, he must find the "heart" of his kingdom. This turns out to be the Heart of Ahriman, a fabulous gem from another world, which in some fashion is apart from the magic of earth and can protect one against earthly wizardry.

A comparison between "The Hour of the Dragon" and the Aragorn subplot of J. R. R. Tolkien's *The Fellowship of the Ring* is illuminating, especially since Tolkien apparently liked Howard's work. Both stories are based on the same idea, although Tolkien diversified it and wove side issues into it, while Howard used a straight-line plot. Tolkien strove for a uniform, smooth urbanity, but Howard strove for tension, high emotion, and dynamism. Whereas Tolkien expanded his material to the limit desirable (and sometimes beyond), Howard compressed his incidents to bare idea, sometimes excessively. Tolkien's imagination swathed fantastic ideas in realistic trappings; Howard's brought exotic novelty to realistic events. Both men had difficulties with their symbol-tokens. In *The Hobbit*, the Fouqué-Wagner-Tolkien ring suffered a misdirection that proved difficult to correct; whereas Howard treated his token with careless ambivalence. It came from beyond earth, yet bears the name of an evil earth god. It is said to be a force for good, yet it worked the utmost evil in awakening the great magician Xaltotun, Conan's most powerful enemy, from the dead.

All these Conan stories were written to an aesthetic that described violence precisely and luridly. Heads fly off at Conan's sword strokes; villains are cloven to the chine; backs are broken like rotten wood; and entrails flop on the ground and entangle one's feet. During his lifetime Howard was criticized for this charnel approach, but today it seems mild when compared with what others have written since.

With Conan, Howard had finally perfected the literary model that he had been working toward for most of his career—the supernatural adventure story. Conan was an interesting character who sometimes came to life, and he was easy to write about, for finesse was not needed to get him out of scrapes. As Howard stated, probably with a chuckle, all Conan had to do was bull and chop his way through obstacles.

The world of Conan was familiar enough to

evoke recognition, yet alien enough that almost anything might turn up—poisonous serpents the size of telephone posts; "dragons" reconstituted by magic from dinosaur bones; relics of prehuman civilizations; strange hallucinogens; magicians, demons, and even an occasional god.

But what came next?

Conan could not go on forever, and there was no reviving the dull earlier heroes. *Weird Tales* was feeling the depression, and Howard knew that the writing he liked best to do was coming to an end. Was this recognition a hidden factor in his suicide?

IV

The posthumous fate of Howard's work should be a lesson to authors.

Howard did not destroy rejected or abandoned manuscripts, but threw them into a box. As a result, well over two hundred stories in various stages of completion turned up after his death: sports stories, Westerns, supernatural stories, adventure stories—six about Conan, at least five about Kane, and ten about Kull.

Over a third of this *Nachlass* has been published. A few stories were printed as Howard wrote them, but more have been scraped, pounded, and stretched by other writers. Finishing another man's rejects is a thankless task, but Howard's "collaborators" deserve some reproach. They have seldom bothered to say what they have done, but have shifted stories from series to series, rewritten, abridged, added material, changed names to fit their own theories of nomenclature, and written weak sequels. It is to the credit of E. Hoffmann Price, Howard's friend, that he refused to join in this pastime, saying, in effect, "Are you crazy? Only Howard could write a Howard story!" He was right.

Also right were the early editors who rejected this *Nachlass*, and Robert E. Howard, who threw it aside, for very few of these stories deserved to be taken from the cardboard box.

This deutero-Howard, composed of remnants and the work of other men, did much to damage the already lopsided reputation of Howard, but worse was to come. In late 1970, Marvel Comics, Inc., issued the first number of *Conan the Barbarian*, a comic book series based very loosely on Howard's work.

Other series followed. These brought Howard to the "big time," made his work valuable literary property, and culminated in the motion picture *Conan the Barbarian* (1982), about which nothing need be said.

From this commercial high point Howard and Conan can go only downhill, but let us hope that during this necessary descent some of the accretions will drop away and leave only those dozen or so stories in which Howard projected his flawed and pitiable personality into compelling, compulsive work that has more than a spark of vitality and is still the best of its kind.

Selected Bibliography

WORKS OF ROBERT E. HOWARD

The following entries offer first book publication of almost all Howard's supernatural fiction that was published during his lifetime, together with occasional nonsupernatural fiction. The texts involved are those of magazine publications in almost all cases. Beyond these first editions, the publishing situation is chaotic, what with reprints, collections with altered texts, "collaborations," and pastiches. This later material is not included.

Stories about Conan
Conan the Conqueror. New York: Gnome Press, 1950. (Novel, originally titled "The Hour of the Dragon.")
The Sword of Conan. New York: Gnome Press, 1952. (Four stories, including "The Pool of the Black One.")
The Coming of Conan. New York: Gnome Press, 1953. (Five stories, including "The Tower of the Elephant" and "Queen of the Black Coast," with "The Shadow Kingdom" and another Kull story.)
King Conan. New York: Gnome Press, 1953. (Four stories, plus a collaboration.)
Conan the Barbarian. New York: Gnome Press, 1954. (Five stories, including "Shadows in the Moonlight," "A Witch Shall Be Born," "Shadows in Zamboula," and "The Devil in Iron.")

Other supernatural fiction
Skull-Face and Others. Edited by August Derleth. Sauk City, Wis.: Arkham House, 1946. (The Howard memorial volume, with nineteen stories, one article, and one poem; including "Black Canaan," "Worms of the Earth," "Skull-Face," "The Valley of the Worm,"

"Wings in the Night," and "The Tower of the Elephant." Also present are biographical appreciations by H. P. Lovecraft and E. Hoffmann Price.)

The Dark Man and Others. Sauk City, Wis.: Arkham House, 1963. (Contains fifteen stories, including "Pigeons from Hell.")

King Kull. New York: Lancer Books, 1967. (All the Kull stories and a ballad.)

Red Shadows. West Kingston, R.I.: Donald M. Grant, 1968. (All the Kane stories and ballads.)

Bran Mak Morn. New York: Dell, 1969. (All the Bran Mak Morn stories.)

Humorous Western fiction

A Gent from Bear Creek. London: Herbert Jenkins, 1937. Reissued, West Kingston, R.I., by Donald M. Grant, 1965.

The Pride of Bear Creek. West Kingston, R.I.: Donald M. Grant, 1966.

Nonfiction

Letter to Clark Ashton Smith, 25 July 1935. *Amra*, 2:39 (1966).

"Kelly the Conjure-Man." *The Howard Collector*, 1:5 (1964).

"On Reading—and Writing." In *The Last Celt*, by Glenn Lord; see below.

CRITICAL, BIOGRAPHICAL, AND BIBLIOGRAPHICAL STUDIES

de Camp, L. Sprague. "Memories of REH." *Amra*, 2:38 (1966a). (Description of a visit to Cross Plains, Texas, and memories of the Howards gathered from friends.)

————. "Bibliotechnical Bonanza." *Amra*, 2:42 (1966b). (Comments on posthumous manuscripts.)

————. "On the Trail of Tranicos." *Amra*, 2:45 (1967a). (Comments on textual alterations to Howard's story "The Black Stranger," retitled "The Treasure of Tranicos.")

————. "Superaddendum to the Exegesis." *Amra*, 2:45 (1967b). (Comments on posthumous manuscripts.)

————. *Literary Swordsmen and Sorcerers: The Makers of Heroic Fantasy.* Sauk City, Wis.: Arkham House, 1976. (Excellent chapter on Howard.)

————; de Camp, Catherine Crook; and Griffin, Jane Whittington. *Dark Valley Destiny: The Life of Robert E. Howard.* New York: Bluejay Books, 1983. (Received too late to be used in this article. An excellent, full biography with a wealth of new material. The authors' point of view and conclusions are much the same as those of this article, but the pathological side of Howard is stressed more.)

Lord, Glenn. *The Last Celt: A Bio-Bibliography of Robert Ervin Howard.* West Kingston, R.I.: Donald M. Grant, 1976. (Complete bibliography of prose and poetry, published and unpublished. Also contains autobiographical fragments by Howard; articles by Lovecraft, Price, and others.)

Lovecraft, H. P. "Robert Ervin Howard: A Memoriam." *Fantasy Magazine* (September 1936). Reprinted in *Skull-Face and Others*, by Robert E. Howard, and in *The Last Celt*. (A rather stiff literary appraisal.)

Preece, Harold. "The Last Celt." *The Howard Collector*, 2:4 (1968). Reprinted in *The Last Celt*. (Reminiscences of a friend.)

Price, E. Hoffmann. "A Memory of R. E. Howard." In *Skull-Face and Others*. Reprinted in *The Last Celt*. (The basic source of information about Howard's personality and writing circumstances.)

————. Letter to H. P. Lovecraft, 25 June 1936. *The Howard Collector*, 1:2 (1962). Reprinted in *The Last Celt*. (Comments on Howard's personality.)

Schweitzer, Darrell. *Conan's World and Robert E. Howard.* San Bernardino, Calif.: Borgo Press, 1978. (Mostly plot summaries of the Conan stories, with comments.)

Smith, Tevis Clyde. "Report on a Writing Man." *The Howard Collector*, 1:3 (1963). (Reminiscences of an occasional collaborator.)

Weinberg, Robert. *The Annotated Guide to Robert E. Howard's Swords and Sorcery.* Mercer's Island, Wash.: Starmont House, 1976. (Discussion, criticism, plot summaries of all Howard's fantastic adventure. Useful.)

—E. F. BLEILER

FRANK BELKNAP LONG

1903–

FRANK BELKNAP LONG, JR., whose career as an author of supernatural and science fiction stories has spanned over sixty years, is perhaps most widely recognized as a colleague and close friend of H. P. Lovecraft, whose more celebrated career has to some extent overshadowed Long's own. And indeed in many ways Long has encouraged this situation, since he frequently gives lectures and interviews on his association with his mentor; he has also written an informal biography, *Howard Phillips Lovecraft: Dreamer on the Nightside* (1975). For all this, Long's own work includes some significant contributions to the field of the supernatural horror story, even though in recent years he has more often chosen to write science fiction.

Long was born in New York City on 27 April 1903, the son of a dentist. One of his maternal ancestors was a passenger on the *Mayflower* and reportedly the first man to fight a duel on American soil, and another forebear was the only general to die in battle during the Civil War. His paternal grandfather erected the pedestal for the Statue of Liberty. Long has written that he enjoyed "a fairly typical 'all American' boyhood" (*The Early Long*, 1975), with few environmental influences that would explain his eventual interest in the fantastic.

As a boy Long considered becoming a naturalist, and although he had been exposed to the imaginative fiction of Edgar Allan Poe, Nathaniel Hawthorne, Jules Verne, and H. G. Wells, "it was probably meeting and talking with Howard Phillips

Lovecraft in my adolescent years that actually tipped the scales and made it inevitable that I would become a science fiction and fantasy writer" (*The Early Long*). Even before that meeting, the impulse was already evident, for what brought the two of them together was Long's pastiche of Poe called "The Eye Above the Mantel," which had appeared in the little magazine the *United Amateur*. Lovecraft, who was active in the United Amateur Press Association, wrote to Long to praise the story, and as a result, Long became the first of many disciples to follow Lovecraft into the field of supernatural fiction. The two first met when Lovecraft visited New York in 1922, and the relationship was cemented during the period of Lovecraft's marriage and residence there.

Long attended New York University, but an attack of appendicitis and his subsequent hospitalization precipitated his decision to leave school and embark on a career as a free-lance writer. Although he calls his plan "foolhardy," he nonetheless carried it out with some initial financial assistance from his parents. It was two years before he was able to make his first professional sale.

Long acknowledges that Lovecraft was instrumental in placing his early work in the then recently inaugurated pulp magazine *Weird Tales*. His first stories to appear in its pages were "The Desert Lich" (November 1924) and "Death Waters" (December 1924); Long was startled to find the second illustrated on the magazine's cover. The story itself is a fairly conventional narrative about a native curse of a plague of water snakes; a similar subject appears in Long's next effort, "The Ocean Leech" (*Weird Tales*, January 1925). This tale is considerably more unusual, however. While its plot of a sea monster attacking a ship is somewhat commonplace, its combination of fevered melodrama and understated dialogue, though not entirely successful, marked a step forward in the author's technique. Thematically, the story is distinguished by the idea that the creature exerts a seductive spell, so that the captain loses the respect of his mate when he is temporarily unable to resist its influence.

Long gradually expanded his market to include periodicals publishing fiction in other genres, but he also continued to write for *Weird Tales*, contributing "Men Who Walk Upon the Air" (May 1925), "The Were-Snake" (September 1925), "The Sea Thing" (December 1925), and "The Dog-Eared God" (November 1926). During the same period, his first book was published, a privately printed volume entitled *A Man from Genoa, and Other Poems* (1926).

"The Man with a Thousand Legs" (*Weird Tales*, August 1927) is a bizarre tale about a young scientist whose experiments transform him into the title character; it is chiefly distinguished by a complex structure in which nine separate narrators are employed to unfold the fragmented story. Far more important was "The Space Eaters" (*Weird Tales*, July 1928), in which Long became one of the first writers to draw on the synthetic mythology that Lovecraft was gradually shaping in his own fiction. Moreover, Lovecraft himself is a character in "The Space Eaters," an author of strange stories named Howard; the narrator is named Frank. Thus, the story has something of the quality of a private joke, one that was perhaps not apparent to many of its original readers.

Howard is described as frustrated in his desire to "suggest a horror that is utterly unearthly, that makes itself felt in terms that have no counterpart on this earth," but the sensation he seeks is near at hand. Half-seen entities have invaded a village, their icy tentacles piercing the brains of residents for some unknown purpose, but they are eventually driven off by the mystic powers of a cross. When Howard cannot resist the temptation to embody the incident in prose, the horrors from beyond return to destroy him. "The Space Eaters" is a bizarre, uneven story, with some of the same melodrama that marred "The Ocean Leech," but its very extravagance creates some powerful passages interspersed with wry humor. In retrospect, this odd effort looks like a dry run for the story that would become Long's most famous, "The Hounds of Tindalos" (*Weird Tales*, March 1929).

Long reports in his biography that both he and his mentor agreed that Long lacked a sense of the "cosmic," which was one of Lovecraft's principal contributions to the tale of terror: an awareness of the infinity of space and time and of humanity's insignificance in relation to the universe. "The Hounds of Tindalos" is the story in which Long comes closest to expressing this feeling, and it is not only an important variation on Lovecraftian themes but also a work with a unique flavor.

The use of exotic or imaginary drugs has been frequent in supernatural fiction, but they have most often been used to effect physical transformations. Long's protagonist, Halpin Chalmers, takes an oriental potion to alter his perceptions in the hope of discovering the fourth dimension. The idea that chemicals can provide transcendent experiences is more fashionable now than when this story was first published, which may help to explain its continued popularity. But what Chalmers discovers is hardly an inducement to experiment with drugs. The Hounds of Tindalos are alien entities, "lean and athirst," who sense Chalmers as he perceives them in his visionary state and travel across time and space to destroy him.

Along with "The Black Druid" (*Weird Tales*, July 1930), "A Visitor from Egypt" (*Weird Tales*, September 1930), and "Second Night Out" (*Weird Tales*, October 1933), "The Hounds of Tindalos" is one of the stories that Long and many of his readers regard as the most important of his *Weird Tales* period. All of these tales but "Hounds" lack the grandeur of conception for which Long had originally striven, yet the smaller scale of these later stories, combined with a more fully integrated irony, make them among the more effective examples of the genre.

"The Black Druid" seems to show some of the influence of the English author M. R. James, in both its sly humor and its antiquarian protagonist. Stephen Benefield, an eccentric pedant who haunts libraries for information concerning obscure cults, takes the wrong overcoat from a rack, and gradually realizes that it has transformed him into a ghastly revenant of the ancient past. Benefield discards the garment and returns to his old self, none the worse for wear except for a nocturnal visit from the garment's owner, who seems to want nothing more than his property. Long stresses the comic humiliation of becoming a monster as much as its terror, and the result is one of his most genuinely amusing tales.

Some of the same atmosphere comes through in the museum setting of "A Visitor from Egypt," but this is a much grimmer piece, climaxing in madness and death. Buzzby, the pompous curator of a New England museum, entertains a visitor who purports to be an Egyptologist but whose strange conversation about the powers of the old gods is more disturbing than enlightening. Before the tale is over, the museum is in flames, Buzzby is insane, and the awesome figure of Osiris has returned from the past to claim the relics that are his due. Long's depiction of the verbal dueling here is skillful, and the horrors, although only half seen, are fully realized and quite convincing.

"Second Night Out" (this is Long's preferred title, although the story was first published as "The Black Dead Thing") returns to the familiar theme of the haunted ship, this one a passenger liner bound for Cuba. The narrator is almost the victim of an eerie manifestation that recurs on every voyage, a supernatural creature whose origin is never explained, however strongly it makes its presence felt. Despite Long's vivid description of the thing's unpleasantness, the story is most impressive in its depiction of the narrator's subjective sense of unease as he lies seasick on the deck where horror has stalked before.

Long's most extended work of supernatural fiction during this period was the Lovecraftian novella *The Horror from the Hills* (*Weird Tales*, January, February–March 1931). Lovecraft not only influenced this tale but also might almost be said to have collaborated on it, since it grew out of one of his dreams that he described to the younger writer. Lovecraft originally planned to write the story himself but finally turned it over to Long, who employed it as one section of his episodic novella. The nightmare had concerned a Roman expedition to destroy a cult in the mountains of ancient Spain, which Long employed to demonstrate the extensive history of an imaginary and elephantine deity called Chaugnar Faugn.

The Horror from the Hills begins in a museum, where a young curator, Algernon Harris, receives a stone figure of Chaugnar Faugn from Clark Ulman, the mutilated archaeologist who discovered it in Asia. Much of the first chapter is a monologue in which the terrified Ulman describes his experiences; many of the nine subsequent chapters include extensive lectures from the various characters whom Harris encounters, especially a psychic named Roger Little, who recounts the episode from Lovecraft's dream. Some of these digressive discussions seem intended only to fill out Long's first lengthy work of fiction, and even when they are relevant to the business at hand, they often seem wordy. Commenting on the difficulty that a theorist experiences in converting others to a cause, Little says:

He doesn't perceive that new truths must be presented to the human mind vividly, uniquely, as though one were initiating a mystery or instituting a sacrament, and that every failure to so present them decreases the likelihood that they will gain proponents, and that an entire civilization may pass away before any one arises with sufficient imagination and sufficient eloquence to take truths which have been enunciated once or twice coldly and forgotten because of the repugnance with which the common man regards fact barely recited and to clothe them in garments of terror and splendor and awe and so link them with far stars and the wind that moves above the waters and the mystery and strangeness that will be in all things until the end of time.

(chapter 5)

This sort of speech and some other incidents suggest that Long did not take *The Horror from the Hills* completely seriously. When Harris cannot resist fiddling with Little's "time-space machine," which is intended to destroy the rampaging Chaugnar Faugn, he blasts a huge hole in Little's wall and simply says, "I fear I've ruined your apartment." "Not important, really," Little replies. "It's eerie, of course, having all one's secrets open to the sky, but my landlord will rectify that." In short, this novella is not comparable in quality to the short stories that Long was writing at the same time. When he later began to concentrate on science fiction, he did some of his best work in novels.

An odd combination of supernatural and science fiction marked Long's one true collaboration with Lovecraft, which also included contributions from A. Merritt, C. L. Moore, and Robert E. Howard, three of the era's most prominent fantasy writers. Julius Schwartz, who edited a "fan" periodical, convinced the five to write a chapter apiece of a story called "The Challenge from Beyond" (*The Fantasy Magazine*, September 1935). Although irritated when he was obliged to yield his assigned second section to the more renowned Merritt, Long was eventually persuaded by Lovecraft to write the ending instead. The two of them seem to have provided most of the plotting, with Lovecraft conceiving the idea of an exchange of bodies between a human and an extraterrestrial, and Long devising the denouement, in which the hero triumphs on his alien planet while his counterpart on earth goes mad.

By this time Long was beginning to show more interest in writing science fiction, due in no small measure to the magazine *Astounding Science-Fiction* and its editor, John W. Campbell, Jr. Long has written that he prefers his work for Campbell to all but a handful of his earlier supernatural stories, and he might have drifted away from fantasy almost entirely but for the magazine Campbell inaugurated in 1939, *Unknown* (later *Unknown Worlds*). This magazine, Long writes, "greatly surpassed *Weird Tales* in many ways, for it contained no cliché-ridden, pulp magazine stories at all" (*The Early Long*). It certainly provided Long with one of his best forums; the understated, often wryly humorous stories that he produced for the magazine are among his best.

"Dark Vision" (*Unknown*, March 1939) was originally submitted to *Astounding*, but Campbell held it for the first issue of his new magazine, where he believed it would be more appropriate. The story concerns an electrical accident that gives the protagonist a unique sort of extrasensory perception: he perceives not only other people's conscious thoughts but also their unconscious desires, and his mind becomes the agonized recipient of the basest impulses of everyone around him. The idea and its treatment are powerful and succeed in transcending the sentimental introduction of a sympathetic female character who is apparently the only person on the planet without an id.

In "The Elemental" (*Unknown*, July 1939), a gambler at a racetrack is possessed by a supernatural force that provides him with incredible powers but eventually leaves him stranded at an inopportune moment; like several of Long's stories from this period it shifts gradually from humor to horror. "Johnny on the Spot" (*Unknown*, December 1939), although not one of Long's most widely known stories, is one of his most ingenious. Written in the manner of the "hard-boiled" crime fiction of its time, it concerns a tough but troubled killer who is, in slow stages, revealed to be no ordinary thug but rather Death himself. This is a cleverly controlled tale in which what might have been no more than a gimmick is raised to the level of metaphor.

In "Fisherman's Luck" (*Unknown*, July 1940), an innocent angler finds that his rod is actually the staff of the god Mercury, and with it he catches everything from a nineteenth-century lover to a severed human head. The story mixes horror, humor, and pathos. However, "The Refugees" (*Unknown Worlds*, February 1942) is pure farce, the tale of a man plagued by the mischief of leprechauns who have fled to America from the misery of World War II.

"Grab Bags Are Dangerous" (*Unknown Worlds*, June 1942) is an impressively odd little story in which the protagonist acquires a sinister sack that is meant to hold toys for children but seems intent on drawing him into it instead; the author blends comedy and uneasiness with a light, undeniably deft touch. "Step Into My Garden" (*Unknown Worlds*, August 1942) is reminiscent of "Fisherman's Luck" in its use of Greco-Roman mythology, but this time the reference is to the garden of Proserpine, which appears in the hero's backyard when he hovers between life and death. The theme might have been treated with mysticism, and indeed there is a touch of it; but for the most part Long chooses grotesque comedy, with corpses bound for the underworld who balk at the strange fruit they are offered by a dwarf attendant who mutters about "shants," "digglies," and "gnores."

The casual and playful air of most of these tales from *Unknown* is consistently delightful, even though they do not attempt the cosmic themes of some of Long's famous stories for *Weird Tales*. It was for the latter magazine that Long produced "The Peeper" (March 1944), which combines something of his light approach with a more serious theme. Mike O'Hara, a cynical newspaper columnist who once had higher aspirations, is being haunted. The ghost is his former self, the youthful poet whom time betrayed.

Although he had published several volumes of poetry, it was not until 1946 that Long's first volume of stories appeared. This was *The Hounds of Tindalos*, which contains most of his significant work from *Weird Tales* and *Unknown*; it remains his most memorable book of supernatural fiction, if only because by the time of its publication he had vitually abandoned the genre. Instead he became active in science fiction, writing stories for a number of magazines and producing such books as *John Carstairs, Space Detective* (1949), *Space Station #1* (1957), *Mars Is My Destination* (1962), and *It Was the Day of the Robot* (1963).

Long also took on several editorial positions, serving as associate editor on such publications as *Satellite Science Fiction* and *Mike Shayne's Mystery Magazine*; these jobs, Long says, involved doing the work at home along with his own writing, "beginning in 1951 or 1952, for about ten years" (*Twilight Zone*, January 1982). Among the many books by Long to appear during this period was the 1931 serial *The Horror from the Hills*, published in hard cover in 1963. Most of his remaining books are science fiction; among them are *The Martian Visitors* (1964), *Mission to a Star* (1964), *This Strange Tomorrow* (1966), *Lest Earth Be Conquered* (1966), *The Three Faces of Time* (1969), and *Survival World* (1971).

Despite its title, *The Horror Expert* (1961) is not supernatural fiction; it concerns a woman whose morbid quest for sensation leads to criminal compli-

cations. Long did return to fantasy with *The Night of the Wolf* (1972), but this novel suggests again that his fantasies are most effective in shorter form. A fairly simple plot about a werewolf attacking a household is treated with considerable digression and circumlocution. Apparently the intention is to emphasize atmosphere and character, but having characters engage in long discussions of theories and opinions even when faced with the most desperate emergencies often reduces the pace of the novel to a crawl.

The Rim of the Unknown (1972) is a collection of several decades of Long's short stories; it contains some of his best work, but only a few of the selections, such as "The Man with a Thousand Legs," can be considered fantasy. Most of the book is devoted to science fiction.

The year 1975 again brought Long closer to supernatural fiction. Partially inspired by the growing reputation of Lovecraft, the first World Fantasy Convention was held in that writer's native city of Providence, Rhode Island. Long spoke on his association with his mentor, and the same year saw the publication of his memoir of Lovecraft. Although it is not a formal study, Long's sympathetic book was especially welcome to many readers in contrast to L. Sprague de Camp's highly critical *Lovecraft: A Biography* (1975). Long returned to Providence as the fifth convention's guest of honor in 1979; in Fort Worth in 1978, he had been given the World Fantasy Award for lifetime achievement.

Collections of Long's early stories continued to appear. *The Early Long* is virtually identical to *The Hounds of Tindalos* but is noteworthy because it contains the author's notes on the tales, along with a lengthy autobiographical introduction. *Night Fear* (1979) is a mixed bag: along with a number of science fiction stories are such rarely reprinted fantasies as "The Were-Snake" and "Johnny on the Spot," and the novella *The Horror from the Hills* is included in its entirety.

Long also began to write supernatural short stories again. His later tales are neither as wild as his work in *Weird Tales* nor as humorous as his work in *Unknown*; what the newer stories do possess is an emphasis on humanistic values, so that the plot elements seem less significant than the effects that they have on the characters. Thus, Long returned in two stories to his long-standing theme of sea monsters but with the new wrinkle that in both cases the horror is perceived through the eyes of a sensitive child with latent psychic powers. In "Cottage Tenant" (*Fantastic*, April 1975), a young boy fascinated by tales of mythical creatures actually succeeds in conjuring one out of the ocean with the power of his unconscious mind; yet less attention is paid to the horror itself than to the power of the imagination that created it. "Dark Awakening" was written as a tribute to Lovecraft for Ramsey Campbell's *New Tales of the Cthulhu Mythos* (1980). In this story the Lovecraftian demons in which Long once reveled are conspicuously absent; there is only a sinister amulet that exerts an irresistible attraction on an adventurous boy. While hardly devoid of chills, both stories seem more intent on exploring personal relationships than exploiting opportunities for terror.

A more conventional plot emerges in "Woodland Burial," written for Stuart David Schiff's anthology *Whispers III* (1981). This is a simple tale about a murder victim seeking revenge from the grave, but it is tautly told, with characters and dialogue more immediate and concrete than in most of Long's previous fiction. After six decades of work, Long is still growing as a writer and is still able to surprise his readers.

Selected Bibliography

WORKS OF FRANK BELKNAP LONG

The Hounds of Tindalos. Sauk City, Wis.: Arkham House, 1946. London: Museum Press, 1950 (abridged edition). (Short stories.)

The Horror from the Hills. Sauk City, Wis.: Arkham House, 1963. London: Digit, 1965. (Novel.)

The Night of the Wolf. New York: Popular Library, 1972. (Novel.)

The Rim of the Unknown. Sauk City, Wis.: Arkham House, 1972. (Short stories.)

Howard Phillips Lovecraft: Dreamer on the Nightside. Sauk City, Wis.: Arkham House, 1975. (Biography.)

The Early Long. Garden City, N.Y.: Doubleday, 1975. London: Hale, 1977. (Short stories.)

Night Fear. New York: Zebra Books, 1979. (Short stories.)

CRITICAL STUDIES

Collins, Tom. "Frank Belknap Long." *Twilight Zone*, 1:10 (January 1982): 13–19.

de Camp, L. Sprague. *Lovecraft: A Biography.* Garden City, N.Y.: Doubleday, 1975.

—LES DANIELS

CLARK ASHTON SMITH

1893-1961

URING THE 1930's, Clark Ashton Smith was one of the most important writers of fantasy fiction appearing in the pulp magazines. With Robert E. Howard and H. P. Lovecraft, he dominated the pages of *Weird Tales;* and a fair amount of his fiction was published in *Wonder Stories* and other science fiction magazines. The appeal of his work was its exotic otherworldliness. His selection of a title for his first Arkham House collection of tales, *Out of Space and Time* (1942), was a perceptive measure of his themes and settings; it was drawn from Poe's remarkable poem "Dream-land" (1844), which describes "a wild weird clime, that lieth, sublime,/Out of SPACE—out of TIME." This extramundane region—in some unknown part of earth, in another dimension, another planet, or another time—is central to Smith's conception of fantasy, which seeks to disorient the readers' senses by removing familiar landmarks. Some of the best supernatural stories of other authors make their point by the frightful events that occur in familiar surroundings, but Smith usually plunges his readers outside their normal world and lets them flounder toward some uneasy familiarity with strange circumstances.

Smith was born in Long Valley, California, on 13 January 1893 and spent his life there, in quite restricted surroundings, without much travel. His schooling was minimal, and he was largely self-educated. Beginning early as a writer, he published stories in the *Overland Monthly* in 1910 and in the *Black Cat* in 1911 and 1912. But his main effort was

given to poetry, and in 1912 he had published *The Star-Treader and Other Poems*, to favorable critical reception. For more than a decade, he seems to have restricted his writing to poetry, though recent research indicates that he may have written a short novel, *As It Is Written*, and submitted it to the magazine *Thrill Book* in 1919, where it was accepted but not published. He numbered other California writers among his acquaintances and was particularly friendly with George Sterling, who contributed brief introductions to two of his volumes of poetry. Upon Sterling's suicide in 1926, Smith memorialized him affectingly, in both poetry and prose.

Around 1926, Smith resumed the writing of fantasy fiction, and for more than a decade he was a prolific author of short stories. In 1933, he undertook the publication of a pamphlet, *The Double Shadow and Other Fantasies*, containing six stories, and sold it by mail from his address in Auburn, California. The establishment of Arkham House and its publication of his fiction and poetry helped his reputation to grow. Smith died on 14 August 1961, but there were several posthumous Arkham House publications. In the 1970's, many of the stories and some of the poems were published in paperback, in a careful thematic ordering by Lin Carter, and thus were made available to a wider audience. Although these volumes are out of print, republication of the stories in the 1980's is once again offering them to a potentially large reading public.

The recognition of Smith has been nothing like

the widespread recognition granted H. P. Lovecraft, with the publication of his letters, a biography, and critical and bibliographical studies. But Smith has had his devoted followers, who have produced an impressive body of material. *Emperor of Dreams* (1978) is an important bibliography with some reminiscences. A collection of letters would be welcome, and a well-researched biography would do much to place Smith properly among his contemporaries.

That place should include a fair estimate of Smith's poetry. Like a number of other excellent poets of his time, Smith was relatively unaffected by the revolution of modernism that took place around 1912. When poets like Ezra Pound, T. S. Eliot, and William Carlos Williams shifted the bases of poetry, their techniques left behind some of the practitioners of a more traditional brand of poetry. Unaffected by these changes, Smith and a number of other poets continued to write in the manner of their nineteenth-century literary ancestors. His work displays technical skills in blank and narrative verse, Alexandrines, odes, sonnets, and quatrains. His poetic diction often has an antique air, using such forms as "fain," "knowest," "foldeth," and "thee" and "thou" in place of a more contemporary diction. There are poems descriptive of his fictional worlds, Averoigne and Zothique. One finds the influence of Edgar Allan Poe very strong in the poems, as in "Luna Aeternalis." His prose poems show the powerful effect of the French romantic and symbolist poets, whose works he read and often translated. It is, perhaps, inevitable that the writings of many poets — perhaps most poets — will be neglected for the work of a few major talents in any century. With all its faults, Smith's poetry displays excellences of form and theme that continue to make it appealing.

One of Smith's most interesting posthumous publications is a notebook that he kept for many years, in which he wrote down "used and unused plot-germs, notes on occultism and magic, synopses of stories, fragments of verse, fantastic names for people and places" (*The Black Book*). In this regard, he greatly resembles Nathaniel Hawthorne, whose notebooks recorded many of the story ideas and themes used in his fantasy fiction. Smith's jottings offer useful clues to the workings of his mind. He makes lists of names and possible story titles, and recounts promising themes for unwritten stories. There are experimental lines of poetry, revisions of poems, and trial passages of prose tales.

The notebook displays Smith's attention to the problem of arranging his stories in orderly groups to indicate their themes and settings. He classifies the tales as belonging to "The Book of Hyperborea," for example, or lists the "Tales of Zothique," obviously considering their order for book publication. Smith's care in the ordering of his tales is also evident in the Arkham House editions of his first two story collections. In *Out of Space and Time*, the stories are grouped under such headings as "Judgments and Dooms," "Hyperborean Grotesques," "Interplanetaries," and the volume's title. In *Lost Worlds* (1944) the grouping has been fine-tuned, with stories placed under headings consisting of Smith's fantastic locales: "Hyperborea," "Atlantis," "Averoigne," "Zothique," and "Xiccarph." Entries in the notebook indicate that stories about each of these worlds were to be linked to form histories of his imaginary realm.

Donald Sidney-Fryer has offered a very useful description of the typical Smith story:

> Many of the more characteristic tales are actually poems in prose in which Smith has united the singleness of purpose and mood of the modern short story (as first established by one of Smith's literary idols, Edgar Allan Poe) together with the flexibility of the *conte* or tale; an entire short story being unified and, in part, given its powerful centralization of effect, mood, atmosphere, etc., by a more or less related system or systems of poetic imagery.
>
> (*In Memoriam*, page 11)

Sidney-Fryer's insistence on the poetic qualities of the stories is well taken. As a poet, Smith understood how he could hold a story together by a pattern of images; some of his best stories possess a chain of connected images. For example, *The White Sybil* (1935) depends on pervasive images of ice, coldness, and death; these are juxtaposed against the images of a shadowless, windless landscape full of blossoming flowers and trees in the paradisiacal world of the sybil.

Sidney-Fryer's association of Smith's fiction with Poe's is also much to the point. In a list of his favorite weird stories, Smith cited "The Fall of the House of Usher" and "The Masque of the Red Death." His list included stories by Robert W. Chambers, M. P. Shiel, Algernon Blackwood, Ambrose Bierce, Arthur Machen, and Lovecraft, all of whom can be said to have worked in the tradition of Poe, since they also used special diction to establish setting and mood. The criticism, sometimes made, that Smith unnecessarily burdened the diction of his stories with learned and obscure words has only enough truth in it to be misleading. While we can be brought up short by words like "terebinth," "machicolated," "malisons," and "thallophytic," among other curious forms, we soon learn that Smith uses the words with precision and that they add a dimension to the incantatory tone of his work that is obvious when it is read aloud. And, by way of balance, Smith can also affect another manner in his narration, one that is straightforward, plain, almost journalistic.

Many of the outstanding writers of fantasy made this genre only a part, often a small part, of their work in fiction. Unlike them, Smith published over a hundred stories, and all of them fall into the closely related categories of weird, horror, fantasy, supernatural, and science-fantasy stories. In the tales of Hyperborea he evokes a fantastic past for the earth, creating countries and cities of a geological period before the time of man. In "Ubbo Sathla" he writes that the land of Hyperborea flourished in the Miocene epoch, which is a world as far from reality as any off-world setting. As the name indicates, Hyperborea is located beyond the northern regions of the habitable world. Mhu Thulan, within its borders, can be associated with Lemuria and the Ultima Thule, perhaps Smith's version of Poe's "ultimate dim Thule." Lin Carter's effective ordering of the tales in his edited volume *Hyperborea* (1971), his map, and his geography help to impose a pattern and a cohesiveness upon the group.

Several of the stories are predominantly ironic and even satiric in tone. In "The Seven Geases" (*Weird Tales*, October 1934) the hunter Ralibar Vooz disturbs a sorcerer in the midst of his incantations and is punished by having a terrible "geas," or spell, placed upon him. He is sent on a subterranean

odyssey as a gift to a a horrible monster, which rejects him and sends him on his way in the grip of an even more potent geas. After being rejected in turn by increasingly awful creatures, he is freed to make his way back to the dreadful limbo of the outer world, but, after escaping terrible fates, he perishes by accident. Similarly, the miser in "The Weird of Avoosl Wuthoqquan" (*Weird Tales*, June 1932) is ungenerous to a prophesying beggar and is victimized as a result of his avarice.

A particularly noticeable characteristic of the Hyperborean tales is the multiplicity of monstrous creatures. Smith mentions, on one occasion, "the great sloths and vampire bats," the "small but noxious dinosauria," the subhuman Voormis, the batlike toad-god Tsathoggua, the spider-god Atlach-Nacha, and others. The narrator of "The Testament of Athammaus" (*Weird Tales*, October 1932) is an executioner who has the unsavory task of attempting to put to death an immortal semihuman figure who becomes more horrible and less human at every resurrection and finally causes the Hyperborean city of Commoriom to be deserted. The loathsome creature in "The Coming of the White Worm" (*Stirring Science Stories*, April 1941) bleeds from its wounds a black, foul liquid far in excess of what it could be expected to hold.

It is difficult for a fantasy writer who creates a succession of monsters to achieve a continuous suspension of disbelief, and sometimes the creatures slip from the horrible to the absurd. To Smith's credit, his descriptions are careful and realistic and hold the attention successfully; moreover, some of his monsters betray a sour, biting wit that has its own appeal.

Smith's Hyperborean tales are unlike the action-filled Hyborian stories of Robert E. Howard, and none of his characters is like Conan. A prose poem, "The Muse of Hyperborea" (*Hyporborea*), clearly defines Smith's vision: "And in some dawn of the desperate years, I shall go forth and follow where she calls, to seek the high and beatific doom of her snow-pale distances, to perish amid her indesecrate horizons." It is a poetic vision of ancestral memory and lamentation.

In Atlantis, says Smith in "The Muse of Atlantis," one of his prose peoms, "we will go down through streets of blue and yellow marble to the wharves of oricalch." For the poet, Atlantis offers a vision of color and richness, and he sets a number of stories in Poseidonis, the last remaining island of that lost continent. Atlantis has been a land of dark knowledge, and the magician Malygris is Smith's prototypical character for these stories. One of the two tales devoted to him has a touching and affectionate tinge. In "The Last Incantation" (*Weird Tales*, June 1930) the aged sorcerer recalls from the dead a girl he had once loved; but, once she is back, he learns with disappointment how different from his memories of her she now seems. He is disillusioned to learn that what he cannot call back is his own youth with all its idealism. A very different sort of tale is "The Death of Malygris" (*Weird Tales*, April 1934), a more conventional horror story of a magician exercising his power after death against plundering enemies.

When Smith published a small collection of his tales in 1933, he gave it the title *The Double Shadow and Other Fantasies*, signaling his favorable opinion of the title story. His confidence is well placed, for it is one of the most carefully wrought of his stories. Pharpetron, the narrator, tells of discovering, with his mentor, Avyctes, a strange, triangular metal tablet carved with ciphers in the language of a lost race of serpent-men more ancient than the inhabitants of Hyperborea. It is a difficult and tedious task to decipher the tablet, but Pharpetron and Avyctes eventually learn the substance, if not the import, of the spell it contains, which gives the formula to raise an extraordinary and unspecified entity but not the counterspell to exorcise it. Avyctes displays hubris by believing that he is powerful enough to control whatever being he can call up. The two men are disappointed when they carefully perform the incantation and nothing immediately appears, but they presently become aware that Avyctes is being haunted by a distorted shadow thrown from no visible source and that it is slowly closing with his own shadow. He is finally possessed by the demon he has raised, and Pharpetron is left to tell the story and meditate on his own approaching doom.

Smith sold the pamphlet by mail, advertising it as "a booklet containing a half-dozen imaginative and atmospheric tales—stories of exotic beauty, glamour, terror, strangeness, irony, and satire." With the booklet in the "Science Fiction Series" (Stellar Publishing Company, 1932) that printed "Immortals of Mercury," it probably represented all that he could hope for in the way of book publication for his stories, though his work was popular in the magazines and he was an executive director of the Science Fiction League.

One of Smith's strong themes is the horrible fate of "those who go too far," but he also displays a talent for turning a potentially horrible story into an attractive and moving one. An unusual interplanetary journey is the subject of "A Voyage to Sfanomoë" (*Weird Tales*, August 1931). Two scientists of Atlantis, foreseeing the destruction of their foundering world, build a spaceship driven by "explosion of atoms in sealed cylinders." The construction takes years, and the journey to Venus is long, so that when they arrive they are old men. They find their new home a torrid garden of Eden, where they are gently led to forget their past, painlessly die, and are metamorphosed into flowers. It is the mildness and pensiveness of the story that are most impressive. Death is usually the most shocking event in a horror story, but here it is a desirable and pleasing end or, perhaps, another beginning.

Among Smith's created lands, the most vivid is probably Zothique, "a latter coast/Where cities crumble in the black sea-sand/And dead gods drink the brine." In these lines, from a poem entitled "Zothique" (*The Dark Chateau*), Smith celebrates an earth of the far distant future. The sun has become dim, whatever is left of the world is old and decadent, the world we live in is as ancient to that future as Hyperborea is to us. The concept has within it an almost hypnotic power, and it yields often to Smith's most incantatory style: "I tell the tale as men shall tell it in Zothique, the last continent, beneath a dim sun and sad heavens where the stars come out in terrible brightness before eventide." The strong sense of age and decay, of spaces, infinitude, and flatness, are the archetypal images of the sublime as Edmund Burke defined the term and as it makes its way into literature and the visual arts. These lines are from "The Empire of the Necromancers" (*Weird Tales*, September 1932), the most successful of the stories of Zothique.

The necromancers, Mmatmuor and Sodosma, have been driven into exile for their desecration of the respected dead. They make their way across the deserts to Cincor, where a plague in the distant past destroyed a flourishing kingdom; here they revive the corpses of men, women, and animals and set up to rule in the capital city of Yethlyreom. The situation is spectacularly fantastic in this kingdom of the living dead. The corpses move about mutely, caring for the castle grounds or working in the fields and mines, tending to the needs of the old necromancers; some of the women "whom the plague and the worm had not ravaged overmuch" are taken as lovers by the old men. It is affecting to read of the dead, roused from oblivion by magic, dim of memory and yearning vaguely for a new dissolution, but hardly able to resent, protest, or rebel. At last the youngest of the dead emperors, feeling a rage stronger than the others', is able to ally himself with the oldest of the necromancers to discover the secret that will release them all from their enchained life-in-death, destroy their dictators, and earn for them the return to rest. They carry out the prophecy of destruction and lead their subjects back to a death by fire in the vaults below the palace:

All that night, and during the blood-dark day that followed, by wavering torches or the light of the failing sun, an endless army of plague-eaten liches, of tattered skeletons, poured in a ghastly torrent through the streets of Yethlyreom . . . to wend downward by a thousand thousand steps to the verge of that gulf in which boiled the ebbing fires of earth. There, from the verge, they flung themselves to a second death and the clean annihilation of the bottomless flames.

Here Smith is able to take the language of the horror story and transform it into an instrument of compassion by turning his poor, ravaged, living corpses into believable and sympathetic characters.

But there is a sharply ironic side to his literary character, and it is shown to its best advantage in the fable of "Morthylla" (*Weird Tales*, May 1953). After publishing many stories during the 1930's, Smith had become much less prolific and during the 1940's and 1950's had only an occasional story in the magazines. But he had not lost his skills. "Morthylla" would have made a fine prose poem or narrative poem. Its themes are eternal return, weariness and disillusionment with the constant and appalling repetitions of earthly life, and the desire for death. Although these themes are often the tiredest conventions for symbolist and decadent poets, Smith seems to take them personally. They call up his deepest feelings and recur often in his poetry and fiction.

He makes the protagonist of the tale a poet, world-weary, infected with "a curiosity toward the unseen, a longing for things beyond the material world." In a graveyard he meets a lamia and, for a time, is satisfied with life. But she turns out to be a sham, a mortal posing as a lamia, and, in his bitter disappointment, he commits suicide. His death is only another beginning: "After his death, he forgot that he had died; forgot the immediate past with all its happenings and circumstances." He is ready to repeat, unknowingly, the events of his past life. The fable is a devastating one, ornate in its insistence on demonstrating mankind's useless longing for something beyond mortality; what is beyond mortality is more mortality. The technique of the story depends upon an economy of means: the scene of the meeting of man and lamia early in the story is repeated at the end, almost word for word.

Although Smith apparently thought well of his Averoigne stories, set in his version of medieval France, the few that he wrote seem somewhat more conventional than his other tales, possibly because a more or less historical setting imposed limitations that he did not have with his invented epochs and continents. Certainly the more spectacular stories that he composed for the science fiction magazines offered a greater range of strong images. Among these works, the one most consistently reprinted and cited for excellence is "The City of the Singing Flame" (*Wonder Stories*, January 1931), a tale of a gateway from this world to other dimensions. Traveling to another world, the narrator finds himself drawn to a sirenlike flame that is attracting life forms to what appears to be self-destruction. In "The Master of the Asteroid" (*Wonder Stories*, October 1932), the narrator is a man trapped in a wrecked spaceship and doomed to slow death. The strange life forms of the asteroid, insectile and short-lived, visit him and regard him as a divinity until he is overcome by a mysterious, superior, godly being. Here, as in some of the other stories that Smith published in the science fiction magazines, there is a strong tinge of the horror story; the writer emphasizes the strangeness of the interplanetary experience and presents otherworldly monsters rather like the ones he has developed for our planet. There were, in fact, protests that Smith's stories were not science fiction at all.

In "The Immortals of Mercury" (1932), the reader encounters an unending stream of off-world wonders: savage natives of the planet, "heat lizards" similar to crocodiles, and the ruling race, the wise, immortal, and murderously detached Oumnis. Most of the story is given over to the protagonist's attempted escape from the dangers around him; but Smith typically offers the ironic horror-story conclusion in which, having gotten past all dangers, the poor man mistakenly emerges to the surface of the planet on its dark side and freezes to death. Likewise, "The Vaults of Yoh-Vombis" (*Weird Tales*, May 1932), which might well have appeared in *Wonder Stories*, presents an evil and alien Mars whose chief denizen is a parasitic creature that controls its human victim while feeding on him. And "Dweller in the Martian Depths" (*Wonder Stories*, March 1933), which could as easily have been featured in *Weird Tales*, puts in the way of its human explorers a being that blinds and enslaves them.

In his interesting study of Smith, L. Sprague de Camp calls attention to his "elaborately euphuistic style," neglecting to mention that in stories like "The Uncharted Isle" (*Weird Tales*, November 1930) Smith resorted to a plain narrative suitable for the sailor-narrator. De Camp also comments upon Smith's ironic sense of humor and his "uninhibited bent for the macabre." With no little humor of his own, de Camp allows that "nobody since Poe has so loved a well-rotted corpse." The fact is that with all his predilection for the macabre, Smith never seems to become morbid about it. There is an ironic, poetic vision always at play behind the looming horrors, somewhat detached, alert, and observant. A strong sense of beauty, even in strangeness, often gives the tales a fascination they might otherwise lack; and here the poetry that Smith composed for so many years adds an element of charm that is often lacking in the fantastic story.

Selected Bibliography

POETRY OF CLARK ASHTON SMITH

The Star-Treader and Other Poems. San Francisco: A. M. Robertson, 1912.
Odes and Sonnets. San Francisco: The Book Club of California, 1918.
Ebony and Crystal: Poems in Verse and Prose. [Auburn, Calif.: Author, 1922.]
Sandalwood. [Auburn, Calif.: Author, 1925.]
Nero and Other Poems. Lakeport, Calif.: Futile Press, 1937.
The Dark Chateau. Sauk City, Wis.: Arkham House, 1951.
Spells and Philtres. Sauk City, Wis.: Arkham House, 1958.
Selected Poems. Sauk City, Wis.: Arkham House, 1971.

STORIES OF CLARK ASHTON SMITH

The following listing offers first editions. There are many more recent collections under different titles.

The Double Shadow and Other Fantasies. [Auburn, Calif.: Author, 1933.]
Out of Space and Time. Sauk City, Wis.: Arkham House, 1942. London: Neville Spearman, 1971.
Lost Worlds. Sauk City, Wis.: Arkham House, 1944. London: Neville Spearman, 1971.
Genius Loci and Other Tales. Sauk City, Wis.: Arkham House, 1948. London: Neville Spearman, 1972.
The Abominations of Yondo. Sauk City, Wis.: Arkham House, 1960. London: Neville Spearman, 1972.
Tales of Science and Sorcery. Sauk City, Wis.: Arkham House, 1964. London: Panther, 1974.
Other Dimensions. Sauk City, Wis.: Arkham House, 1970. London: Panther, 1977, in 2 vols.
As It Is Written. West Kingston, R.I.: Donald M. Grant, 1982. (Attributed to Smith. Hitherto unpublished novel, the manuscript of which was discovered in the files of *Thrill Book*.)

ESSAYS OF CLARK ASHTON SMITH

Planets and Dimensions: Collected Essays of Clark Ashton Smith. Edited by Charles K. Wolfe. Baltimore: Mirage Press, 1973.

The Black Book of Clark Ashton Smith. Sauk City, Wis.: Arkham House, 1979. (Smith's notebook, and biographical essays.)

CRITICAL AND BIOGRAPHICAL STUDIES

Chalker, Jack L., ed. *In Memoriam: Clark Ashton Smith*. Baltimore: Anthem, 1963. (Memorial chapbook with biographical and critical articles. Some work by Smith is included.)

de Camp, L. Sprague. *Literary Swordsmen and Sorcerers*. Sauk City, Wis.: Arkham House, 1976. (Chapter 8, "Sierran Shaman," is a biographical study of Smith.)

BIBLIOGRAPHY

Sidney-Fryer, Donald, et al. *Emperor of Dreams: A Clark Ashton Smith Bibliography*. West Kingston, R.I.: Donald M. Grant, 1978.

—DOUGLAS ROBILLARD

AUGUST DERLETH

1909-1971

AT THE HIGH point of his career in 1942, August William Derleth remarked that he was "probably the most versatile and voluminous writer in quality writing fields." His record supports that claim. In addition to more than 400 short stories and numerous poems, essays, and sketches published in over 500 different magazines, Derleth's bibliography includes 137 of his own books and 41 anthologies of the works of others. The yearly output of this industrious and methodical writer, by his own estimate, came to between 750,000 and 1,000,000 words. In addition, as the founder and often sole employee of Arkham House Publishers, he published the fantasy works of many other writers.

The breadth of Derleth's work is as impressive as its volume. With the exception of drama, there is little he did not write. Short stories, novels, poems, journals, essays, biographies, mysteries, juveniles, history, science fiction, and fantasy poured regularly from his workroom in Sauk City, Wisconsin, for forty years.

Derleth's writing fell primarily into two categories: regional writing and horror fiction. The novels, essays, poems, and journals expressed his regional interests, while the bulk of his short story output was written for *Weird Tales* and other pulp markets. Today, Derleth has two separate, small, but loyal audiences: those for whom he is a regionalist, and those for whom he is an important, if minor, figure in the weird tale genre.

Even among readers of the macabre, however, he is considered more important as a publisher than as a writer. In 1939, two years after the death of H. P. Lovecraft, Derleth and Donald Wandrei established Arkham House to perpetuate Lovecraft's works in book form. The Lovecraft volumes issued by Arkham House since 1939, as L. Sprague de Camp notes, "have more or less kept Lovecraft's name alive and his books in print since his death." Many other fantasy writers owe a similar debt to Derleth. Fritz Leiber, Ray Bradbury, A. E. van Vogt, and other now well-known names owe their first book publication to Arkham House.

Derleth has received little recognition for either his own work or his encouragement of other writers. He was awarded a Guggenheim Fellowship in 1938, sponsored by Sinclair Lewis, Edgar Lee Masters, and Helen White, but for a lifetime of contributions to the field of fantasy, he has received but little mention in passing.

August Derleth was born on 24 February 1909 in Sauk City, Wisconsin, one of the fourth generation of Derleths, who had arrived in Sauk City in 1854. This site on the banks of the Wisconsin River had been an important Indian village. It lay on the edge of Wisconsin's "driftless area," that haunting circle of bluffs, wooded hills, and deep valleys somehow missed by all the glaciers. This was the location of Hamlin Garland's *Main Travel'd Roads* and Clifford Simak's strange loners in *Way Station*. Derleth, too, was fascinated by its mysteries—the "dark laws which geese and men obey."

Derleth attended parochial and then public school in Sauk City, where his early abilities to read and write were encouraged by sympathetic teachers. Although he began with pulp adventure stories—he was a reader of *Weird Tales* from its first issue in 1923—Derleth found Ralph Waldo Emerson, Nathaniel Hawthorne, Walt Whitman, Masters, H. L. Mencken, and, above all, Henry David Thoreau, whose *Walden* became "a sort of Bible." Among pulp writers, he quickly came to single out Lovecraft as superior. These early discoveries set Derleth on his career as a writer, and aspects of each of these authors are easy to identify in Derleth's work. "Nothing thereafter," he wrote, "was to alter the course upon which these mentors had so firmly set me."

For the rest of his life, little was to distract Derleth from this call to letters. He attended the University of Wisconsin from 1926 to 1930 and toyed briefly with teaching, but he had already sold his first story, "Bat's Belfry," to *Weird Tales* as a teenager and had seen it published in the May 1926 issue. As a college student he invented a Holmesian detective, Solar Pons, who became the hero of twelve novels and many short stories.

After graduating from college, Derleth made a brief foray into the commercial world in 1930–1931 as editor of *Mystic Magazine* for Fawcett Publications in Minneapolis, but left when the magazine folded. He spent a brief period in 1931 as editor of *The Midwestern* in Madison, Wisconsin, but he had already determined to return to spend his life in Sauk City and to write. Derleth took occasional writing jobs—he was contributing editor to *Outdoors Magazine* for a while, he was literary editor of the Madison *Capital-Times* from 1941 until his death, and he taught several regional literature and creative writing courses at the University of Wisconsin—but he was never emotionally far from Sauk City. He returned to Sauk City with a larger plan than these odd jobs.

That plan was the Sac Prairie saga, the history of Sauk Prairie and its people from the beginning to the present—the "most ambitious project ever undertaken in the history of literature," wrote Derleth. He claimed the projected fifty-volume series of novels, stories, poems, histories, and journals had only two literary competitors: Honoré de Balzac's *Human Comedy* and Marcel Proust's *Remembrance of Things Past*. The first story in this series, "Old Ladies," in the January–February 1932 issue of *Midland* magazine, was followed eventually by 152 short stories, ten novels, and seven collections of essays, journals, and autobiography.

Along with the Sac Prairie saga came other volumes loosely connected into a Wisconsin saga—novels and histories of Wisconsin and its people. By 1940 these works had earned Derleth a reputation as a major regional writer—a young writer on his way up. In 1939 he built an estate on the edge of Sauk City, with a house thatched with marsh grass. From this "Place of Hawks" he became a spokesman for regionalism to the many younger writers who made pilgrimages to Sauk City.

While attending to his "serious work" (his own name for it), Derleth had not neglected his early love, the macabre. "Bat's Belfry" was followed during the 1930's by more than 200 similar stories written for *Weird Tales* and for the many other horror magazines that had begun to appear. He wrote so many stories for these pulps that he was forced to use pseudonyms to avoid the too frequent use of his name. For *Weird Tales* he often used the name Stephen Grendon, and, for other publications, Simon West, Michael West, Kenyon Holmes, Will Garth, and Romily Devon.

Derleth's macabre fiction during this period revealed a craftsmanlike writer who knew the genre but possessed little innovation or originality. The stories for the most part followed formulas set down earlier by English ghost stories: haunted houses; ghosts returning for revenge; jewels; talismans; idols' eyes—all with curses; secret passages; and pictures that move. Many of the shortest pieces were intended, by Derleth's own admission, as fillers between the featured stories in each issue.

Had it not been for H. P. Lovecraft's early death in 1937, Derleth's reputation might have remained that of a regional writer. Derleth had written to Lovecraft, a fellow writer for *Weird Tales*, in 1926 to inquire about an Arthur Machen story. Lovecraft's response initiated a voluminous correspondence during the remaining twelve years of his life, a correspondence that Derleth ranked with reading *Walden* as a shaping experience. Derleth and Lovecraft never met, but Derleth claimed that he "seldom knew a man so well."

Following Lovecraft's death, Derleth and another *Weird Tales* associate, Donald Wandrei, obtained publication rights to Lovecraft's work, intending to collect his work and publish it as books, a form more permanent than pulp magazines. It was not a good time for such a venture. The horror genre had not yet caught on in the United States, in spite of a long tradition in England. Even *Weird Tales* had an estimated readership of no more than 50,000.

Nevertheless, Derleth and Wandrei put together an initial collection of Lovecraft stories as *The Outsider and Others*, and submitted it to Derleth's own publisher, Charles Scribner's Sons. When Scribner's and then Simon and Schuster both rejected it because of poor sales for short fiction and because of Lovecraft's relative obscurity, Derleth and Wandrei determined to publish the volume themselves. They hoped to pay for the volume with advance sales advertised in *Weird Tales*, but when advance orders amounted to only 150 by 1939, the two men went ahead with 1,268 copies, paid for with a loan Derleth had received from the bank to build his house, and a small loan from Wandrei.

The new venture was called Arkham House after Lovecraft's fictional name for Salem, Massachusetts, the location of his Cthulhu Mythos stories. In addition, Lovecraft's "hills behind Arkham" must have reminded Derleth of his own dark Wisconsin hills.

Sales of *The Oustider and Others* were slow — it took four years to sell out the edition — but they were enough to convince Derleth that there might be a market for small editions of similar fantasy books. He assumed sole financial responsibility for Arkham House, although Donald Wandrei continued to edit occasional volumes. Over the next thirty years a steady stream of nearly one hundred fantasy and science fiction novels, short story collections, and anthologies came from the small firm in Sauk City, seldom in runs of more than 5,000. Seventeen of these volumes, and two edited by Derleth for London publishers, were Lovecraft items: stories, novels,

essays, and letters. In addition, almost thirty nonfantasy books (detective stories and Wisconsin history) appeared under other Derleth imprints: Stanton and Lee, and Mycroft and Moran. Arkham House and the other two are still in business.

Derleth's dedication to Lovecraft did not end with book publication. Before his death, Lovecraft had encouraged his small circle of friends — most of them, like Derleth, contributors to *Weird Tales* — to add to the Cthulhu Mythos with stories of their own. The Cthulhu Mythos, invented by Lovecraft, suggested that unspeakably horrible and evil "Old Ones," who inhabited earth prior to human beings, lay hidden under the oceans and earth or beyond the sky waiting for deluded people to permit their return and takeover. Lovecraft had left many hints, suggestions, outlines, and notes for the Cthulhu Mythos before he died. Using these scattered fragments, Derleth completed a novel, *The Lurker at the Threshold* (1945), and sixteen short stories, collected in *The Watchers Out of Time* (1974). He published these as "collaborations," but they were actually written by Derleth based on ideas suggested by Lovecraft.

Derleth also published two volumes of his own Cthulhu Mythos stories, *The Mask of Cthulhu* (1958) and *The Trail of Cthulhu* (1962); and he edited a volume called *Tales of the Cthulhu Mythos* (1969), containing Cthulhu stories by others of the Lovecraft circle, including Clark Ashton Smith, Robert E. Howard, Frank Belknap Long, and Robert Bloch.

Many of these same writers, including Derleth himself, were given a measure of permanence by Arkham House publication. The second Arkham House book was *Someone in the Dark* (1941), a collection of Derleth stories from *Weird Tales*. Several collections of Derleth fantasy followed over the years. Other important Arkham House publications include Henry S. Whitehead's *Jumbee and Other Uncanny Tales* (1944), Frank Belknap Long's *The Hounds of Tindalos* (1946), Robert E. Howard's *Skull-Face and Others* (1946), A. E. van Vogt's *Slan* (1946), Ray Bradbury's *Dark Carnival* (1947), and Robert Bloch's collection *The Opener of the Way* (1945).

All of these Derleth acquaintances were American, but Derleth was especially fond of the much longer tradition of English macabre fiction and helped make that popular in the United States. Lord Dunsany, Cynthia Asquith, A. E. Coppard, J. S. Le Fanu, and others found new audiences through Arkham House. Derleth's publication of an omnibus volume of four novels by William Hope Hodgson, *The House on the Borderland and Other Novels* (1946), rescued that fantasy writer from the obscurity into which he had fallen since his death in World War I.

Two volumes of verse, *Dark of the Moon: Poems of Fantasy and the Macabre* (1947) and *Fire and Sleet and Candlelight* (1961), became important collections in an area of fantasy that had previously received scant attention. *Dark of the Moon*, covering sixty-four English and American poets from William Blake and John Keats to Lovecraft, has been called by Marshall B. Tymn the "single most vital volume in any collection of supernatural verse."

The modest success of Arkham House was a beacon to the small-press movement in the United States. Derleth showed that a small specialty publishing house could make a place for itself alongside the publishing giants. While Arkham House and the Sac Prairie saga occupied much of Derleth's attention after 1940, he continued to write his own macabre stories for the pulp magazines, occasionally collecting them in Arkham House editions. However, he never listed these stories among his serious works. Writing them was usually relaxation at the end of the day, and they have never achieved the importance in the fantasy field that his editing and publishing efforts have.

Almost all the stories are imitative of styles and formulas developed by others. The ease with which Derleth was able to imitate Lovecraft extended to other writers whom Derleth particularly admired. Nelson Algren once wrote that "it takes August Derleth . . . to write verse like Fearing, MacLeish, Anderson, Whitman, Sandburg, and Masters—with a faint dash of 'Dover Beach' tossed in—and still write something like himself."

Derleth's first collection of stories from *Weird Tales, Someone in the Dark,* is arranged in three sections, each of which shows Derleth's debt to a particular fantasy writer whom he admired. Section One, "Not Long for This World," contains stories in the manner of M. R. James, an English ghost story writer. Here are stories of amulets, vengeful ghosts, a glory hand (a severed and preserved human hand with supernatural powers that can be sent around by its owner to do evil deeds, such as choking enemies), and other stock English devices. Section Two, "A House with Somebody in It," contains stories such as "The Sheraton Mirror" and "The Paneled Room," which owe their simplicity, dry humor, and sense of place to the New England regionalist Mary E. Wilkins Freeman and her depiction of lonely, frustrated lives. Section Three, "Visitors from Down Under," contains two stories based on the Cthulhu Mythos.

Derleth's writing methods may have contributed something to his lack of originality. He claimed to have written the stories in his best collection, *Mr. George and Other Odd Persons* (1963), for *Weird Tales* at the rate of one a day for a month—all late at night after his serious work was over. They were all published in *Weird Tales* under Derleth's Stephen Grendon pseudonym. Derleth's friend Mark Schorer confirmed this hectic pace. In 1931 they collaborated on a series of stories for the pulps, ranging from 3,000 to 8,000 words. Together they wrote one a day for a month. After plotting out a week's worth of formulas (Monday, Canadian setting—werewolf gambit; Tuesday, New Orleans country—zombie gambit; Wednesday, Massachusetts—dead/alive theme; and so on), Derleth outlined the story and then Schorer wrote a first draft. As Schorer went on to the second story, Derleth polished the draft. A collection of these stories was published as *Colonel Markesan and Less Pleasant People* (1966).

In spite of the haste of these and other Derleth stories, they all seem competent and even craftsmanlike, if conventional. Derleth believed that in some strange way horror fiction was an escape from the horror of real life, and he treated the stories as escape fiction. He felt that characterization, plot, and meaning were unimportant in the genre, or less important than "mood and phenomena." He was opposed not only to a "heavy ladling out" of horror but also to a psychological explanation for what ought to be supernatural. The one requirement that Derleth considered essential is that the writer "believe in his horror, at least for the duration of his writing." A number of these light but well-crafted stories were adapted well for early television programs such as *Suspense* and *Thriller*.

Here and there in this mass of conventional macabre fiction, however, are a number of stories that return to Sac Prairie in mood, locale, and character and that stand out from the body of Derleth's pulp efforts. Although they retain many of the conventions of the traditional ghost story, they also reflect more of Derleth's own moods and observations about nature and people—especially his neighbors. Nearly every collection has one or two of these stories, but the main collection of local ghost stories is *Lonesome Places* (1962).

Walden West (1961) is the journal that best expresses Derleth's views of life—views that are both nostalgic and somber. Whereas Thoreau's retreat to Walden Pond produced solitude, Derleth's return to Sauk City uncovered loneliness in the lives of its inhabitants. Derleth intersperses sketches of his neighbors and their homes, whose peaceful facades hide terror and isolation, with scenes of a faintly malevolent nature, which surrounds and waits. These excursions into the wooded hills or down to the river are most often at night, the best time to sense "the facets of nature which quicken my pulse with that awareness that both life and death are inextricably associated with the loneliness of man's mote-like existence in the cosmos—and acceptance of man's essential solitude on earth."

This "village on its paw of land, the encircling hills, the undulating prairie between" frustrates the lives of its residents and twists them into what Sherwood Anderson called "grotesques": the woman who suffered a stroke in New York and came home to Sauk City to die—and did so for the next forty years; the spinster whose father once offered to sell her to a passing rich man when she was still a child, and who now spends her days telling whoever will listen how she wishes she had been sold.

To move from the real darkness of these neighbors to the supernatural darkness of ghost stories is but a slight extension. The idol's eye and the severed hand disappear, and in their places are lonely people, often children, whose psychological states are at one

with the ghosts who haunt them. Characterization becomes more important. Even in a short sketch such as "Birkett's Twelfth Corpse" (*Strange Stories*, August 1940), Derleth delineates with grim humor two grizzled Wisconsin rivermen who have established reputations for finding drowning victims.

In one of Derleth's most reprinted stories, "The Lonesome Place" (1948), two boys hate to run errands downtown in the evenings because they must pass an especially dark place near the grain elevator. Their imaginations have filled it with supernatural creatures. The narrator of the story recalls this lonesome place years later when he reads that a child has been murdered there and that the townspeople have cleared the entire area of trees and bushes. Whatever haunted the lonesome place will move to another town and another lonesome place—and wait.

Here and in other stories, Derleth is at his best when dealing with the relationship between ghosts and children. The relationship is usually sympathetic, in contrast to that between children and an adult world that does not understand and has no time for children. In "Mr. George" (*Weird Tales*, March 1947), a young girl's adult friend returns after his death to keep the girl company and to protect her from three scheming relatives who try to do away with her in order to inherit her house and money. Mr. George causes each of their plans to backfire, killing them off one by one.

In "Alannah" (*Weird Tales*, March 1945), a lonely boy whose mother has no time for him makes friends with the ghost of a woman who had drowned herself in a pond years before to end a childless existence. The ghost eventually invites the boy into the pond, where he drowns willingly. The narrator, a tutor who has witnessed the drowning and is horrified, changes her mind when she arrives at the pool and sees "the grass move in the moonlight as if two people walked there." "What I felt," she says, "was not cold, it was not ... that terrible loneliness—no, it was warm and fulfilling, ineffably beautiful, as if the heart and soul of love itself had become briefly, briefly tangible there."

Similarly, a terminally ill child's dying is eased in "Just a Song at Twilight" (*Weird Tales*, August 1930) by the ghost lullabies of his mother from a previous reincarnation who has come for him. Following his death, his parents see, down the hall, "a woman, and at her side, clasping her hands, a boy, and as they were walking along, through the wall and out into the sky, there came the sound of the song."

These tales of sympathetic ghosts not only are well done, they are handled with more originality and deftness than Derleth's more conventional stories. What haunts the readers of these stories is not the horror but the sadness. In "Mrs. Bentley's Daughter" (*Weird Tales*, October 1930), a child who has drowned in a well remains in the neighborhood to play and to comfort his mother, who accepts this as better than nothing. "Mara" (*Arkham Sampler*, Winter 1948) recounts a troubled love affair that becomes smoother and richer when the ghost of the woman returns after suicide to comfort her lonely lover, sexually and otherwise, in the house they had lived in together. As the man notes to a confidant, "we never lived more like man and wife before than we have lived since then."

Two of Derleth's best stories are "The Extra Child" (1950) and "The Dark Boy" (1957). The first story centers on a picture above a mantel in Jason Corscott's home. Jason is fond of this picture of six children playing because they are the children he might have had, had he settled down and married his youthful love, Evelyn Howe. After her death in Ceylon, however, Jason notices a change in the picture. Day by day a seventh child gradually appears from behind a tree, arms outstretched. Jason finally sees that it is Evelyn who is beckoning to him, and he walks through the picture and disappears. A niece discussing his disappearance with an inspector notices that there are now eight children in the picture and an old man sleeping in the shade in the background. Jason and Evelyn have their children.

"The Dark Boy" is the story of a lonely young widow who comes to a remote rural area to teach school. After being drawn to a quiet "dark boy" in her class, she learns that he is the ghost of Joel Robb, who had died two years before. Rather than suffering a breakdown, as the previous teacher had, she befriends the lonely ghost, reading stories to him after class and eventually reuniting him with his still grieving father (whose wife has also died). "If you could just get used to not being afraid of him," she tells the father, "you'd never notice him. . . . He's just lonesome. And so are you. And if it comes down to it, so am I. Most people are. After all, you're his father; he's got a right to look for some affection from you." As the father walks the teacher back to school, there is a hint that these three lonely people will be together for some time.

August Derleth died in Sauk City on 4 July 1971, with little of the recognition he deserved and wanted. He received no major awards other than the Guggenheim, and aside from accounts by friends, and features in Midwestern newspapers and magazines, there have been few serious treatments of his works and no attempts to publish any of his manuscript material and voluminous correspondence. Even before publication of *Walden West* in 1961, his reputation as a regionalist had begun to fade, and his most frequent mention in fantasy circles is in connection with Lovecraft.

In 1977 a Derleth fan, Richard Fawcett, founded the August Derleth Society to correct the neglect he had been shown. The society publishes a quarterly newsletter and has a current membership of about 250. Collections of Derleth and Arkham House material may be found in the libraries of Brown University, the University of Virginia, and the University of Southern California at Los Angeles. The Lilly Library at the University of Indiana has some 2,000 Derleth manuscripts, complete first editions of his works, and a comprehensive Arkham House collection. These rich, untapped resources await the researcher and the critic.

Selected Bibliography

FICTION OF AUGUST DERLETH

Country Growth. New York: Scribner, 1940. (Sac Prairie collection.)

Someone in the Dark. Sauk City, Wis.: Arkham House, 1941. (Collection.)

The Lurker at the Threshold, with H. P. Lovecraft. Sauk

City, Wis.: Arkham House, 1945. London: Museum Press, 1948. (Novel.)

Something Near. Sauk City, Wis.: Arkham House, 1945. (Collection.)

Not Long for This World. Sauk City, Wis.: Arkham House, 1948. (Collection.)

Wisconsin Earth: A Sac Prairie Sampler. Sauk City, Wis.: Stanton and Lee, 1948. (Collection.)

The Survivor and Others, with H. P. Lovecraft. Sauk City, Wis.: Arkham House, 1957. (Collection.)

The Mask of Cthulhu. Sauk City, Wis.: Arkham House, 1958. London: Consul, 1961. (Collection.)

Wisconsin in Their Bones. New York: Duell, Sloan and Pearce, 1961. (Sac Prairie collection.)

Lonesome Places. Sauk City, Wis.: Arkham House, 1962. (Collection.)

The Trail of Cthulhu. Sauk City, Wis.: Arkham House, 1962. Jersey, England: Neville Spearman, 1974. (Collection.)

Mr. George and Other Odd Persons. Sauk City, Wis.: Arkham House, 1963. Retitled *When Graveyards Yawn.* London: Tandem, 1965. (Collection.)

Colonel Markesan and Less Pleasant People, with Mark Schorer. Sauk City, Wis.: Arkham House, 1966. (Collection.)

The Shadow Out of Time and Other Tales of Horror, with H. P. Lovecraft. London: Gollancz, 1968. (Collection.)

The Watchers Out of Time and Others, with H. P. Lovecraft. Sauk City, Wis.: Arkham House, 1974. (Posthumous collection of all the Derleth-Lovecraft stories. As has been mentioned elsewhere, Lovecraft's contribution was minimal, sometimes a short passage or two, or only an idea.)

Harrigan's File. Sauk City, Wis.: Arkham House, 1975. (Collection of science fiction.)

Dwellers in Darkness. Sauk City, Wis.: Arkham House, 1976. (Posthumous collection.)

NONFICTION OF AUGUST DERLETH

Village Year: A Sac Prairie Journal. New York: Coward-McCann, 1941.

Writing Fiction. Boston: The Writer, 1946.

August Derleth: Thirty Years of Writing—1926-1956. Sauk City, Wis.: Arkham House, 1956.

Some Notes on H. P. Lovecraft. Sauk City, Wis.: Arkham House, 1959.

Walden West. New York: Duell, Sloan and Pearce, 1961.

Collected Poems, 1937-1967. New York: Candlelight Press, 1967.

Thirty Years of Arkham House 1939-1969: A History and Bibliography. Sauk City, Wis.: Arkham House, 1970.

WORKS EDITED BY AUGUST DERLETH

Derleth, August. *Who Knocks? Twenty Masterpieces of the Spectral for the Connoisseur.* New York: Rinehart, 1946. St. Albans, England: Panther, 1964. (Anthology. The Panther edition is abridged.)

——— . *Dark of the Moon: Poems of Fantasy and the Macabre.* Sauk City, Wis.: Arkham House, 1947. (Anthology of poems.)

——— . *Night's Yawning Peal: A Ghostly Company.* New York: Pellegrini and Cudahy for Arkham House, 1952. London: Consul, 1963. (Anthology.)

——— . *Fire and Sleet and Candlelight: New Poems of the Macabre.* Sauk City, Wis.: Arkham House, 1961. (Anthology of poems.)

——— . *When Evil Wakes: A New Anthology of the Macabre.* London: Souvenir Press, 1963. (Anthology.)

——— . *Tales of the Cthulhu Mythos.* By H. P. Lovecraft and others. Sauk City, Wis.: Arkham House, 1969. (Anthology.)

——— . *Dark Things.* Sauk City, Wis.: Arkham House, 1971. (Anthology.)

Lovecraft, H. P. *The Outsider and Others.* Edited by August Derleth and Donald Wandrei. Sauk City, Wis.: Arkham House, 1939.

——— . *Beyond the Wall of Sleep.* Edited by August Derleth and Donald Wandrei. Sauk City, Wis.: Arkham House, 1943.

——— . *Marginalia.* Edited by August Derleth and Donald Wandrei. Sauk City, Wis.: Arkham House, 1944.

——— . *The Dunwich Horror and Others: The Best Supernatural Stories of H. P. Lovecraft.* Sauk City, Wis.: Arkham House, 1963.

——— . *Selected Letters 1911-1924.* Edited by August Derleth and Donald Wandrei. Sauk City, Wis.: Arkham House, 1965.

——— . *Selected Letters 1925-1929.* Edited by August Derleth and Donald Wandrei. Sauk City, Wis.: Arkham House, 1968.

——— . *Selected Letters 1929-1931.* Edited by August Derleth and Donald Wandrei. Sauk City, Wis.: Arkham House, 1971.

CRITICAL AND BIOGRAPHICAL STUDIES

Bishop, Zelia B. "A Wisconsin Balzac: A Profile of August Derleth." In *The Curse of Yig.* Sauk City, Wis.: Arkham House, 1953.

Tierney, Richard L. "The Derleth Mythos." In *Essays Lovecraftian.* Baltimore: T-K Graphics, 1976.

Wandrei, Donald. *100 Books by August Derleth.* Sauk City, Wis.: Arkham House, 1962.

BIBLIOGRAPHY

Wilson, Alison M. *August Derleth: A Bibliography.* (The Scarecrow Author Bibliographies, No. 59.) Metuchen, N.J.: Scarecrow Press, 1983. (A thorough descriptive bibliography of all Derleth's works.)

—ROALD D. TWEET

C. L. MOORE

1911-

I

THE CONSIDERABLE REPUTATION of C. L. Moore rests on two bodies of work, the science fiction and supernatural fiction written alone or with her husband, Henry Kuttner, between 1940 and 1958, and two series of stories written by her alone and published between 1933 and 1939. This essay is primarily concerned with Moore's solo work in supernatural fiction, although, as will be seen, it is often difficult to disentangle Moore from Kuttner or the supernatural from the science fiction.

Born on 24 January 1911, Catherine Lucille Moore was raised in Indianapolis, where her childhood followed the pattern, not uncommon among writers, of illness-enforced inactivity accompanied by wide reading of mythology, fantasy, and eventually science fiction. The Great Depression interrupted her college education in 1930, and she found work as a secretary in a bank. It was while practicing her typing that she wrote the opening of what was to become her first published story, "Shambleau" (*Weird Tales*, November 1933). This was by no means the first story that she had written, however; Moore reports that she had been telling stories from the time she learned to talk and writing them down since she could write (see Sam Moskowitz). The immediate success of Moore's first publication is not, in retrospect, surprising; "Shambleau" and the tales that followed it over the next seven years sprang from a mind well stocked with the materials of Western myth and writing skills practiced for years.

It is not merely convenient to divide Moore's work into periods before and after her marriage to Henry Kuttner; it is unavoidable. From 1933 to 1940 she wrote alone (with two exceptions) and published in *Weird Tales* (with four exceptions), and the bulk of this work falls into two cycles. There are eleven stories of Northwest Smith (nine appear in the book of that title) and six of Jirel of Joiry, with one tale, "Quest of the Starstone" (the first Moore-Kuttner collaboration, published in *Weird Tales* in November 1937 and never reprinted), involving both characters. After 1940 the Moore-Kuttner partnership was literary as well as marital, and nearly all of the work produced by either from that time was to some degree collaborative, no matter what by-line it might carry.

Insofar as it is possible to separate the voices in the collaborative work (and until there is an autobiography this will remain a highly speculative matter for most stories), the Moore contribution is thought to be in characterization, mythological and literary awareness, and what may be called a dark romanticism (as distinct from Kuttner's dark cynicism). It would be an oversimplification to call Kuttner a "craftsmanlike" and Moore an "intuitive" writer, but it is a useful half-truth. A brief account of her writing practices (see her Afterword to *The Best of C. L. Moore*) and some correspondence published by Forrest J Ackerman (see *Gosh! Wow!*) suggest the extent to which Moore relied on intuition and the promptings of the unconscious mind to shape her fiction.

In any case, her early work does use mythological and supernatural motifs to explore the complex emotional lives of her characters and to portray the infinite, wonder- and terror-filled universe that stretches beyond what humanity can understand. If supernatural fiction can be either metaphysical—aimed at suggesting the nature and structure of reality—or psychological—aimed at depicting extraordinary psychic states or the hidden parts of the mind—then Moore's early work is primarily psychological, dedicated to exploring those realms of heightened experience that border on the abnormal. In an interesting development, the work produced after her marriage to Kuttner shows a use of Freudian psychological models, which suggests that Moore's career might be seen to recapitulate the history of the supernatural tale from the late nineteenth to the early twentieth century. That tradition also dealt extensively with the forbidden contents of the unconscious mind, but when scientific psychology began to provide another way of confronting these contents, the supernatural tale declined in favor of other forms, including science fiction.

In her early work Moore often uses the language of science or pseudoscience to describe supernatural events and beings, and in the Northwest Smith stories she mixes genres by setting supernatural motifs in a science-fictional world. The result does not feel much like science fiction. Her 1930's version of a solar system peopled by Martians, Venusians, and various lost races and strange creatures strongly recalls the exotic Far Eastern, African, or *Arabian Nights* backdrops of the pulp adventure tradition; and these tales, with their wonders, hidden byways, and ancient evils, have more in common thematically with the work of A. Merritt or H. P. Lovecraft than with the space operas of E. E. Smith or John Campbell. Even the Jirel stories, with their medieval setting, make it clear to the reader that the magical realms that Jirel visits should be understood as other worlds or other dimensions. "Jirel Meets Magic" (*Weird Tales*, July 1935) is especially interesting in this regard. Pursuing an enemy through an extra-dimensional doorway, Jirel confronts the sorceress Jarisme, who traps her in a corridor full of doorways to other worlds, some of which are clearly science fictional. The third doorway, in particular, looks out on interplanetary space and a flame-tailed rocket.

II

Moore's first four stories, appearing between November 1933 and August 1934, feature the spaceman Northwest Smith, a Byronic pulp hero with the requisite tragic past (see the brief, allusive "Song in a Minor Key," *Scientisnaps*, February 1940), acknowledging no law, willing to steal or kill but not to betray his own sense of right, both passionate and chivalrous as only a pulp hero can be. Into Smith's space-opera world Moore introduces elements of Lovecraftian supernatural horror. The series formula pits Smith against an inhuman, otherworldly threat of a psychic or spiritual nature, usually in the course of helping a woman in distress. One of Moore's most frequently used motifs, in this series and elsewhere, is the psychic vampire, and Smith faces variations of this theme in eight of the ten collected tales, starting with "Shambleau."

The horror motif in this story is a combination of the vampire and classical Medusa that serves to highlight the psychological symbolism of both figures. There is a strong erotic strain in vampire stories, at least since the Victorian period, and it is generally recognized that there is in the night side of the mind an attraction to this creature. The Medusa, according to Joseph Campbell (*The Masks of God: Occidental Mythology*, 1964), is the demonic manifestation of the Mother Goddess that results from the patriarchal subjugation of her cult. Given Moore's adaptation of other powerful mythic females—Circe, the lamia, Lilith—it is likely that something more than routine horror-mongering is her aim.

Whatever Shambleau's mythological roots, she provides a means of treating, through Smith's unwilling attraction to her, one of Moore's signature themes—the soul divided against itself. Smith's conscious mind is not seriously attracted to Shambleau—in fact, when he briefly embraces her, he is instinctively repelled by her touch and by the "dark knowledge" he sees in her eyes. But at night Shambleau calls to his dreaming mind, and Smith thinks her first feeding is a nightmare of horrible pleasure from which he cannot awaken. At the next feeding he is awake, but her power holds him helpless, and his conscious mind is revolted by what some deeper level cannot resist, a pleasure that he finds repellent and that he knows will eventually destroy him. As the language reaches for ways to describe the indescribable, there are images of snakes, slime, crawling things, and writhing worms—the physical correlatives of the sensation of Shambleau's embrace of Smith's soul.

The profundity of the division within Smith is indicated by his rescue by his Venusian partner, Yarol, who recalls an old story and looks into a mirror to aim his flame gun at Shambleau. While Smith often requires some assistance to throw off the influence of a Power, never again is his *will* so undermined; a sane part of him was sickened by sharing the alienness of Shambleau's thoughts, but there was also, Smith says, "some nucleus of utter evil in me—in everyone" that would not leave the creature's embrace. When Yarol asks his partner to promise to destroy any Shambleau he might meet in the future, all Smith can say is, "I'll—try."

Important elements of "Shambleau" are repeated in the *Weird Tales* stories "Scarlet Dream" (May 1934), "Julhi" (March 1935), and "Yvala" (February 1936); in each, Smith faces a mixture of eroticism and psychic vampirism (with echoes of classical myth) in which the feeding of the vampire gives back to the victim an unclean and deeply dangerous pleasure, one that leads to the death of the soul. In "Scarlet Dream" the myth is that of the lotus-eaters, but the "lotus" is the blood that runs from the spigots in a temple in a pocket universe that Smith has entered. It is the only food in this world, the basis of a vampiric food chain that includes bloodsucking grass and, at its top, the Thing that occasionally materializes to feed on the humans. The blood from the spigots gives not only nourishment but also an unwholesome euphoria that transfers itself to the erotic relationship between Smith and the woman who is his companion—the "faintly acrid bitterness of her kisses" is the taste of blood. Smith's fundamental personality finally reasserts itself, however, and he resolves to leave the "colored lotus-land." After a confrontation with the Thing, the woman takes

Smith to a room in the Temple where the fiery pattern of the magical Word that is the gateway to this world writhes on the walls. She places Smith at the safe center of the room, utters the Word, and is destroyed, while Smith is sent back to his own world.

"Julhi" and "Yvala" are both closer to "Shambleau" in that the vampirism is fundamentally psychic and the vampire herself is the focus of erotic interest. Julhi combines Cyclops and the lamia, and lives on "the sensations and emotions of the flesh" as well as blood. The danger to Smith is that the feelings she stimulates will kill him. Yvala is a Circe figure who lives on the worship offered to her transcendent beauty; the worshipers are emptied of humanity, reduced to beast-spirits haunting her magical wood on a moon of Jupiter. Both these creatures are ancient and inhuman. Yvala's human appearance is an illusion; her true shape is that of "a blaze of avid light." Julhi is one of a race whose true home may not be in our universe; and strange as her shape appears, her true form is even more alien.

These tales and the others show Smith able to tear loose from the influence of the vampire by a kind of spiritual brute force that is described explicitly in several stories (see "Lost Paradise," July 1936, or "Tree of Life," October 1936). In "Yvala" it is described as "a bedrock of savage strength which no power he had ever met could wholly overcome"—though in "Shambleau" he is clearly unable to help himself.

This concern with the lowest substratum of sentience runs through these early stories; one finds not only the "bedrock" strength of Smith and Jirel but also a vision of the inhuman forces at the roots of all life (recall Smith's "nucleus of utter evil"). In "Black Thirst" (April 1934), Smith confronts the Alendar, an ancient, immortal creature who has guided the evolution of humanity to "its limit of loveliness" in order to feed on that beauty. The woman Vaudir tells Smith, "Life rises out of dark and mystery and things too terrible to be looked upon"; the Alendar's true form, one presumably closer to the roots of life than humanity's, is a black slime, and his mind is full of "worm-thoughts." But one need not regress all the way to the primal ooze. Yvala's victims, stripped of their humanity, linger on as shame-filled animal spirits; and Smith, in an inversion of the Actaeon myth, becomes not the victim stag but "a wolf-memory."

In other tales Smith confronts gods that, like Lovecraft's Old Ones, are ancient, unimaginably alien beings from other dimensions. In "Dust of Gods" (August 1934), he and Yarol journey to Mars's north polar region to find the physical remains of Pharol, one of the Three, the deities of the vanished fifth planet between Mars and Jupiter. Their experiences are less horrific than disorienting as they cope with the leftover extradimensional physics of the gods; and Smith has little real difficulty in finding Pharol's dust, which he destroys, judging it too dangerous to allow back in the world. He has little more trouble with another Three in "Lost Paradise," in which his life-instinct successfully resists their efforts to devour him and incidentally causes the destruction of the prehuman lunar civilization of the Seles that the Three supported in return for their willing sacrifices.

Only in "The Cold Gray God" (October 1935) does Smith find more than he can handle by himself. The nameless god of ancient Mars, desiring to return to the place from which it withdrew long ago, sends a Thing that possesses Smith's body in order to open the doorway to the Beyond where the god waits. The language echoes both "Shambleau" and "Black Thirst" in its images of slimy, writhing tendrils of gray smoke that invade Smith's body; and as in "Shambleau," he needs outside help to defeat the god — though this time his will is not corrupted but only overwhelmed.

III

Jirel of Joiry is in some ways a female version of Northwest Smith — she may be lawful ruler of Joiry rather than an outlaw, but in Moore's medieval France that entails a high degree of violence and an anarchic individualism that echoes Smith's. Like him, Jirel encounters otherworldly threats to her psychic health and must find the strength to resist; like him, she lives in a world where one can be eaten up by forces beyond human comprehension or betrayed by the darker side of one's own nature.

The first of the Jirel series is "Black God's Kiss" (November 1934). Guillaume, a rival lord, conquers Castle Joiry, captures Jirel, and — as if to emphasize

the completeness of his victory — forces a kiss on her. The kiss makes Jirel's desire for revenge personal as well as feudal-political, and to find a suitable means of retribution she descends into a strange dark world under the castle. The otherworldly setting of this tale allows a symbolic as well as a literal interpretation: it can be seen as Jirel's own mind. The entry to the underworld is a trapdoor deep in Castle Joiry, which is identified with Jirel (in medieval fashion, she refers to herself as "Joiry"). The descent through the spiral tunnel to the dark cave that is the anteroom to the underworld is a transition from the waking to the dream state; it involves the leaving behind of waking inhibitions, as represented by the crucifix that must be abandoned before the underworld can be seen. The dreamscape through which Jirel moves is her own undermind, though it is not the deepest level possible; she moves through that world's night, not seeing all that it contains, and she knows that to see it during its own day would be more than she could stand — it would destroy her waking-world mind.

Forces from the id are present here. From even deeper in the underworld rises a tower of cold flame, within which dwells a being of light that directs Jirel to the black god, whose temple rises from the waters of a lake. The light-being mirrors Jirel's own features and must be an aspect of herself (despite the alienness of its voice), as the black god also must be, though both perhaps rise from that level of being where the individual connects with the inhuman or prehuman forces of nature. The alienness alluded to so frequently in the story would then represent the waking mind's rejection of its connection to those chthonic powers that feed all consciousness — the bestial mind with its reptilian drives and cold-blooded desire for retribution. In this interpretation, Jirel's revenge springs from the deepest and darkest levels of her psyche, whereas her attraction to Guillaume is the product of a merely human unconscious. The kiss must be carried up from the underworld and passed on to the victim before it damages the carrier. Released from the burden of the kiss and the rage that drove her to bring it up from the depths, Jirel too late realizes the complexity of her feelings toward Guillaume.

If "Black God's Kiss" shows revenge, then its sequel, "Black God's Shadow" (December 1934), shows if not redemption, at least some recognition on Jirel's part of the complex mixture of good and evil in the human personality. In this tale she realizes that she both loved and hated Guillaume; and, haunted by his voice, accusing and pleading for mercy, she returns to an underworld that now resembles a mixture of dreamscape and an objective, Dantean hell. The "undermind" reading is suggested by the reflections that she encounters—her distorted image in a brook, her shadow cast by the green moon, the Jirel-faced girls who dance about a black image of Guillaume—and by the half-heard voices in the water and wind. But whether the underworld is inside or outside Jirel, it is certainly a place in which she learns about herself. She must face not only her remorse and the ambiguity of her feelings for the man she killed, but also the duality of human nature in general. Guillaume's punishment is for the noble part of his spirit to be bound to the image of his bestial side, and Jirel must face her own double nature (thus the reflections) in order to save the good side of Guillaume.

Just as the nature of the underworld seems to change, so does the significance of the black god; here it is less a chthonic component of the human spirit than a universal force of death and despair. The motif of doubling or mirroring is repeated in the god's manifestation as a freezing "chill of inhumanity" that Jirel opposes with the warm spark of her life and the heat of her emotions, especially the "fire-hot memory" of Guillaume's kiss. Three times the god tries to freeze her into hopelessness, and twice her "stores of passion" enable her to throw off the spell. The third time, as she feels herself being drawn out of her body, Guillaume's spirit passes through hers, kindling a flame that thaws the black god's ice. She realizes that she has come full circle in her pursuit of Guillaume, who has found "clean death, perhaps," as she has found "a peace beyond all understanding."

It is quite possible that the intuitive writer of 1934 did not consciously construct the allegorical machinery of these tales, but a later Moore certainly would have recognized the possibility of such symbolism. In any case, the worlds that Jirel encounters in subsequent tales are objectively real, with more

melodramatic and conventional magical encounters; the "Black God" tales stand alone in the cycle as projections of the contents of the mind onto a dreamscape, a symbolic journey through the undermind. No other Jirel story is quite so psychologically powerful; though in the third, "Jirel Meets Magic," the sorceress Jarisme torments Jirel by forcing her mind back on its own past, to view "all the futility and pain of life, all the pain that thoughtless or intentional acts have caused others, all the spreading consequences of every act. . . ." Jirel's mental view inevitably focuses on her killing of Guillaume, and her response is grief and rage that break Jarisme's magic and allow her to destroy the sorceress. Unlike Northwest Smith, whose confrontation with his own dark nature leaves him shaken and uncertain whether he would be able to resist a second encounter with a Shambleau, Jirel comes away from her experiences strengthened and genuinely indomitable.

IV

Between 1934 and 1939, Moore published four nonseries stories in *Astounding*, stories similar in motif to, but different in emotional charge from, the horror pieces for *Weird Tales*. Despite its place of publication and some quasi-scientific rationalization, "The Bright Illusion" (October 1934) is romantic fantasy rather than science fiction. Dixon is transported by a golden light-being from the Sahara to a world far across space and dimensions to help it displace IL, the flame-god of a people so alien that Dixon can barely manage to look at them or their world. The motifs of the Jirel and especially the Smith tales are here: alienness that defeats attempts of the human mind to comprehend it (the golden being, so alien that it does not even possess individuality, comes from somewhere beyond space and time for purposes that Dixon can barely comprehend); vampirism of sorts (IL consumes the life-force of his worshipers as they voluntarily sacrifice themselves to maintain it—reminiscent of the sacrifices of the Seles in "Lost Paradise"); the illusion of beauty covering an unbearably alien reality (the priestess and her fellows); the idea of an essential being far beneath the surface of the individual (here something deeper than life itself, since there is a part of the sacrificed ones that escapes, and IL does not know what it is or where it goes); and the primal emotional lives of the characters, the instant, archetypal, romantic love that is paramount.

These motifs function not in their usual mode but to show love transcending the horror and alienness that the protagonists experience on the surface. Although constantly aware that the beauty he sees is an illusion, that the reality is something he can hardly comprehend or bear to see, Dixon finds that he loves the priestess, and even when she discovers his true nature and mission, she still loves him. Theirs is a romantic yearning for infinite fulfillment, too intense for the real world; the only resolution is death, which IL grants them.

The second *Astounding* story, "Greater Glories" (September 1939), has never been reprinted; the third, "Tryst in Time" (December 1936), again depicts the triumph of love. It begins with a conventional science fiction scientist using his time machine to send the Northwest Smith–like Eric Rosner to randomly sequenced points in time. In each period he encounters incarnations of the same woman, who gradually comes to recognize in him, as he gradually comes to discover in himself, an overpowering love and admiration. After many time-jumps, Rosner finds himself in a "living darkness, pulsing with anticipation"; she is there and tells him that their "forgotten sins" have been expiated and that they "can escape into [their] own place at last." This stock romance of reincarnation is made palatable by the vitality of Moore's writing and by recognizing in its straining toward an impossible fulfillment of desire the other side of the demonic "loves" of the Northwest Smith stories.

V

After 1940, Moore's name rarely appears in the magazines, and when it does it is likely to be attached to such science fiction stories as "Vintage Season" (*Astounding Science-Fiction*, September 1946), "No Woman Born" (*Astounding*, December 1944), or "Judgment Night" (*Astounding*, August 1943). The Moore-Kuttner marriage and writing partnership has been mentioned above, and James Gunn has shown how they developed a series of pseudonyms to fill the pages of the wartime *Astounding*. There are two C. L. Moore supernatural tales from

1940 and after, however, as well as an interesting body of collaborative science fantasy under the Moore-Kuttner by-line and the Lewis Padgett and Lawrence O'Donnell pseudonyms.

"Fruit of Knowledge" (October 1940) appeared in *Unknown*, John Campbell's fantasy analogue of *Astounding Science Fiction.* Its retelling of an apocryphal version of Genesis emphasizes Lilith's love for Adam (if that word can apply to the attraction of an elemental being to a newly created creature) and how it leads to the Fall. The mythographic treatment and the love motif are characteristic of Moore, but there are touches of humor—the cherubs who fly through Eden chattering like small boys, Lucifer's swaggering style—that are unlike anything in her earlier work, and which must show the influence of Kuttner.

"Daemon" (*Famous Fantastic Mysteries*, October 1946), the last supernatural fantasy to carry the Moore by-line, has none of the Kuttner humor or irony. As with "Fruit of Knowledge," the story portrays the spiritual outsider. In this unorthodox version of Christian theology, humans have, in addition to souls, *daemons* (perhaps inspired by the Platonic spirit of that name) that reflect the moral state of the soul by their colors: dark for bad men, pearly for good, and for the story's most evil man, Captain Stryker, an unbearable blood-red. The tale is the dying statement of Luiz, a Brazilian simpleton who, because he has no soul, can see the *daemons* and who, marooned on a Caribbean island, also comes to know the spirits of the pagan world. These pre-Christian deities and powers have been banished from the lands of believers since the Incarnation, and they are unable to touch the "men with souls" or to approach a cross.

While the plot tells how Luiz is shanghaied, terrorized by Stryker, and eventually abandoned on the island with one of the passengers, its emotional center is in its portrait of the isolation of the soulless among those who possess souls and the comfort that Luiz finds with those other exiles, the pagan spirits. During his time with the oread of the mountain, Luiz becomes less "*o Bobo*" (simple), better able to understand himself and the world. When Stryker returns to cover up the evidence of his crime, it means the end of this Edenic existence, but Luiz is not altogether sad. "It was," he tells the priest, "a chilly comfort we gave each other, at the best. . . . [The nymphs] will never guess how warm and wonderful it must be to own a soul."

The rest of the short supernatural fiction is written with Kuttner, whose ironic voice dominates. "The Devil We Know" (*Unknown*, August 1941) and "Compliments of the Author" (*ibid.*, October 1942), for example, present variations on deals with the devil and feature the sort of hero-as-heel that would seem to be Kuttner's specialty. (In reporting on the writing of *Fury*, Moore says that she "can't identify" with its unpleasant protagonist.) On the other hand, given Kuttner's long experience as a pulpsmith, one might expect the short adventure novels written for such secondary markets as *Startling Stories* and *Thrilling Wonder Stories* to carry his mark, but Moore's epic and romantic sensibility is clearly present. These Merrittesque tales feature motifs and atmosphere that look back to her solo work of the 1930's, especially what was published in *Astounding*—heroes are transported across gulfs of space, time, and dimension to face alien threats and find transcendent love. *The Dark World* (*Startling Stories*, Summer 1946) is especially Moorean, with its double hero, the evil Ganelon and the good Edward Bond, inhabiting the same body, and with its use of different mythic or legendary figures (Medea; Medusa; the British god of the sea, Llyr; the werewolf) in a single frame.

Even while Kuttner was still alive, the couple were moving away not only from science fiction and supernatural fiction but also from print altogether, toward television, a move that Moore completed after her husband's death in February 1958. After 1958, no new supernatural science fiction appeared under either by-line, although the best of their short fiction has been collected in hardback and paperback editions since the 1960's.

Selected Bibliography

WORKS OF C. L. MOORE

Shambleau and Others. New York: Gnome Press, 1953. London: Consul, 1961. (Short stories.)

Northwest of Earth. New York: Gnome Press, 1954. (Short stories.)

Jirel of Joiry. New York: Paperback Library, 1969. Reissued as *Black God's Shadow.* West Kingston, R.I.: Donald M. Grant, 1977. (Contains the Jirel stories from *Shambleau and Others* and *Northwest of Earth.*)

The Best of C. L. Moore. Edited by Lester Del Rey. Garden City, N.Y.: Doubleday, 1975.

Scarlet Dream. West Kingston, R.I.: Donald M. Grant, 1981. (Contains the Northwest Smith stories from *Shambleau and Others* and *Northwest of Earth*, together with "Song in a Minor Key.")

WORKS OF C. L. MOORE AND HENRY KUTTNER

No Boundaries. New York: Ballantine, 1955. London: Consul, 1961. (Short stories.)

Earth's Last Citadel. New York: Ace, 1964. (Novel.)

WORKS OF HENRY KUTTNER

The Dark World. New York: Ace, 1965. London: Mayflower, 1966. (Novel.)

The Mask of Circe. New York: Ace, 1971. (Novel.)

WORK AS BY LEWIS PADGETT

Line to Tomorrow. New York: Bantam, 1954. (Short stories.)

CRITICAL AND BIOGRAPHICAL STUDIES

Ackerman, Forrest J. "[Introduction and] After Notes on 'The Nymph.'" In *Gosh! Wow! (Sense of Wonder) Science Fiction*, edited by Forrest J Ackerman. New York: Bantam, 1982, 487–488, 503–508. (Includes part of the correspondence between Ackerman and Moore.)

Edwards, Suzanne. "The Best of C. L. Moore." In *Survey of Science Fiction Literature*, edited by Frank N. Magill. Vol. 1. Englewood Cliffs, N.J.: Salem Press, 1979.

Gunn, James. "Henry Kuttner, C. L. Moore, Lewis Padgett, *et al.*" In *Voices for the Future*, edited by Thomas D. Clareson. Vol. 1. Bowling Green, Ohio: Bowling Green University Popular Press, 1976. (Concentrates on Moore-Kuttner collaborations in *Astounding*.)

Mathews, Patricia. "C. L. Moore's Classic Science Fiction." In *The Feminine Eye: Science Fiction and the Women Who Write It*, edited by Tom Staicar. New York: Ungar, 1982. (Nearly half deals with the early supernatural fiction.)

Moore, C. L. Introduction to *Fury* by Henry Kuttner. New York: Lancer, 1972. (Brief account of Moore-Kuttner collaborative methods.)

————. "Afterword: Footnote to 'Shambleau' . . . and Others." In *The Best of C. L. Moore*, edited by Lester Del Rey. Garden City, N.Y.: Doubleday, 1975.

————. "C. L. Moore: Poet of Far-Distant Futures." In *Pulp Voices or Science Fiction Voices #6: Interviews with Pulp Magazine Writers and Editors*. San Bernardino, Calif.: Borgo Press, 1983, 45–51. (Interview conducted by Jeffrey M. Elliot.)

Moskowitz, Sam. "C. L. Moore." In *Seekers of Tomorrow*. Cleveland: World, 1966.

Shroyer, Frederick. "C. L. Moore and Henry Kuttner." In *Science Fiction Writers*, edited by E. F. Bleiler. New York: Scribner, 1982.

— RUSSELL LETSON

XIV

American Pulp Writers
of the Circumbellum Period

ROBERT BLOCH

1917–

ROBERT BLOCH, WHOSE long literary career began when he was still a teenager, is perhaps the twentieth century's most representative writer of horror fiction. Influential, prolific, and thoroughly professional, he has survived and prospered through both talent and adaptability. His style has ranged from Lovecraftian formality to humorous slang; his genres include mystery and science fiction as well as fantasy; and he has worked on scripts for films, television, and radio as well as written short stories and novels. His most famous book, *Psycho*, while not completely typical of his total output, has had a significant impact on the tale of terror through its emphasis on psychological rather than supernatural oddities.

Robert Albert Bloch was born in Chicago on 5 April 1917. An avid moviegoer as a child, he was frightened by Lon Chaney's performance in *The Phantom of the Opera* in 1925, but he was also fascinated, later describing his vocation as a response based on the maxim "If you can't lick 'em, join 'em" (*Fangoria*, October 1979). Two years later he acquired his first copy of the pulp magazine *Weird Tales*, and among the issues he subsequently read was one including the H. P. Lovecraft story "Pickman's Model" (*Weird Tales*, October 1927). A few years later a correspondence began between the two that eventually led to Bloch's first fiction sales. Although they never met, Bloch became one of Lovecraft's disciples, along with such others as Frank Belknap Long, August Derleth, and Fritz Leiber.

Bloch has consistently expressed his appreciation for Lovecraft's advice and encouragement; the older writer's influence on his early work is evident.

After a few minor appearances in semiprofessional and fan publications, Bloch broke into the professional magazines with the story "The Feast in the Abbey" (*Weird Tales*, January 1935). Written before he graduated from high school, this is a slight but hardly negligible tale about some demonic monks who, under the guise of hospitality, feed the protagonist his own brother. The first-person narration, the formal diction, and the lack of dialogue all reveal the influence of Lovecraft, who was to have an even greater effect when Bloch began to employ his mentor's subjects as well as his style.

In "The Shambler from the Stars" (*Weird Tales*, September 1935), Bloch uses Lovecraft's theme of a sinister volume of spells that summon a demon from another dimension, and he also employs a thinly disguised Lovecraft as one of the monster's victims. Although the tale is set forth in a straightforward manner, its origin indicates a tongue-in-cheek attitude that would become increasingly prominent in Bloch's later fiction, and the idea that a perpetrator of imaginary horrors might encounter real ones recurs frequently in Bloch's work.

For the time being, however, Bloch continued to follow the Lovecraft pattern, producing stories about nameless terrors and ancient, evil entities. One of the best of these is "The Faceless God" (*Weird Tales*, May 1936), in which an unscrupulous archaeologist uncovers the sinister statue of Lovecraft's dark messenger Nyarlathotep and lives just long enough to regret it. In "The Dark Demon" (*Weird Tales*, November 1936) Bloch describes another writer of supernatural fiction, this one possessed by a horror discovered in the dreams that inspire his work. Again this seems a disguised portrait of Lovecraft, who is even mentioned in the text, and who was more or less simultaneously slaughtering Bloch (called "Robert Blake") in his story "The Haunter of the Dark" (*Weird Tales*, December 1936).

A few months later, Lovecraft was dead after a short illness. Bloch was desolated, but he kept writing, and for a time his stories continued to emulate Lovecraft's style and structure, particularly through the use of a devastating (and often italicized) revelation contained in the last line. Yet Bloch was beginning to change. Lovecraftian themes gave way to other plot ideas, often in exotic settings. "Waxworks" (*Weird Tales*, January 1939) portrays a morbid Parisian poet, and "The Mother of Serpents" (*Weird Tales*, December 1936) is a tale of voodoo vengeance in Haiti. Bloch's favorite story of this period is "Slave of the Flames" (*Weird Tales*, June 1938), which depicts a pyromaniac responsible for the Chicago fire of 1871 who discovers that he is the reincarnation of the man who burned Rome for Nero, and learns that such atrocities can bring the reward of eternal life. That theme would become the basis for one of Bloch's most celebrated stories five years later, "Yours Truly, Jack the Ripper," while pyromania would later become the subject of his suspense novel *Firebug*, published in 1961.

After only a few years of work, Bloch started to vary his technique and expand his markets, selling several pieces to such science fiction magazines as *Amazing Stories*. Perhaps because he was working in a genre that Lovecraft had rarely touched upon, Bloch began to develop a style less formal than his mentor's. A major turning point in his development was "The Cloak" (*Unknown*, May 1939). The new magazine's editor, John W. Campbell, Jr., encouraged a different sort of supernatural fiction, in which ancient legends clashed with contemporary culture, creating a hybrid form containing substantial doses of screwball humor. Although *Unknown* was never an important outlet for Bloch, who placed

only three stories there, it gave him an opportunity to break out of his *Weird Tales* formula. The first few lines of "The Cloak" say it all:

> The sun was dying, and its blood spattered the sky as it crept into a sepulcher behind the hills. The keening wind sent the dry, fallen leaves scurrying toward the west, as though hastening them to the funeral of the sun.
> "Nuts!" said Henderson to himself, and stopped thinking.

With that vernacular epithet cutting through the florid imagery of the opening paragraph, Bloch began to come into his own. From this time on, more and more of his work would express the cynicism and humor that had always been part of his personality. In fact, it had been his childhood ambition to be a comedian, an ambition that was partly realized in some of his fiction as well as in his later public speaking. In time Bloch would become the greatest exponent of gallows humor in American supernatural fiction since Ambrose Bierce.

Although "The Cloak" also has its serious side in describing the fate of a man who rents authentic vampire garb for a costume party, Bloch's next effort for the magazine, "A Good Knight's Work" (*Unknown*, October 1941), is completely farcical. This tale, about a good-natured petty criminal involved with a knight sent into the future by the magic of Merlin, shows the influence of Damon Runyon in its use of stylized underworld slang. The comedy continued in "Nursemaid to Nightmares" (*Weird Tales*, November 1942), concerning an eccentric millionaire who collects mythological monsters, and the unemployed writer who is hired to be their keeper. Bloch has acknowledged that the inspiration for this story came from Thorne Smith, author of *Topper* (1926) and *Night Life of the Gods* (1931). At the same time he was producing these light fantasies, Bloch inaugurated a series of twenty-two humorous stories about one Lefty Feep, beginning with "Time Wounds All Heels" (*Fantastic Adventures*, April 1942).

Still, Bloch was primarily an author of terror tales, and soon produced one of his most important. Although he initially attached no particular significance to "Yours Truly, Jack the Ripper" (*Weird Tales*, July 1943), and still does not consider it one of his best efforts, it brought him more recognition than he had ever received before. The story was widely anthologized, and adapted for radio on four separate occasions. It introduced one of Bloch's most frequent subjects: the sadistic, psychotic mass murderer. However, this killer, like the protagonist of "Slave of the Flames," takes lives to prolong his own. The idea that the unsolved crimes of Jack the Ripper might be the work of an immortal fiend struck a responsive chord, and Bloch also provided an ingenious and unexpected twist ending for a tale told largely through pithy dialogue.

Bloch had married in 1940, and to ensure a steady income he took a job as an advertising copywriter in 1942. As it turned out, the job lasted for ten years and, along with work as a ghostwriter for political speeches, helped to solidify Bloch's sardonic attitude toward much of modern civilization, an attitude that would be expressed with increasing frequency in his later work.

In 1945 Bloch had his first major experience as a dramatist when he wrote thirty-nine scripts for the radio series "Stay Tuned for Terror." Most of the material was adapted from stories that Bloch had written for *Weird Tales*, and years later some of these would turn up as scripts for television or motion pictures. Bloch has stated that many of his stories "already were consciously or unconsciously shaped for adaptation," so that "they could easily be transformed or translated" (*Twilight Zone*, June 1981).

Also in 1945, Bloch's period of development was consolidated with the publication of his first book, *The Opener of the Way*, which contained the best of his early *Weird Tales* work, flanked by "The Cloak" and another piece of zany horror called "One Way to Mars" (*Weird Tales*, July 1945).

A number of Bloch's most vivid and chilling short stories appeared over the next decade, even though it marked the decline and eventual demise of pulp magazines specializing in tales of supernatural horror. "Enoch" (*Weird Tales*, September 1946) is narrated by a simpleminded backwoods youth who believes he possesses a sinister familiar who demands murders in exchange for his supernatural

gifts. When the protagonist is arrested, he is naturally assumed to be suffering from delusions, but a chilling denouement demonstrates that the elusive Enoch is all too real. The tale exemplifies Bloch's growing ability to put himself into the minds of the most unlikely characters, and shows an increasing interest in psychology that was nonetheless combined with a distrust of psychiatry as a profession. A counterpoint to "Enoch" was provided by "The Sorcerer's Apprentice" (*Weird Tales*, January 1949), in which a naive derelict assumes, with disastrous results, that the tricks of a stage magician are authentic miracles.

In the ambitious "The Cheaters" (*Weird Tales*, November 1947) Bloch combines several narratives to recount the history of a pair of spectacles that enables its owners to perceive the truth. Characteristically, the author sees to it that this heightened perception results in heightened horror. On a smaller scale, stories like "Catnip" (*Weird Tales*, March 1948) demonstrate the author's fondness for a joke; this entire tale of witchcraft, death, and retribution apparently exists only to provide the setup for an outrageous pun in the last line, almost a parody of Bloch's former Lovecraftian technique.

Bloch's last two stories for *Weird Tales* show a range that virtually encapsulates his career. "Notebook Found in a Deserted House" (May 1951) is a return to the artificial mythology created by Lovecraft, with the significant difference that the tale is told by a boy of twelve. "Lucy Comes to Stay" (January 1952), however, is a psychological study of a woman whose troubles all seem to stem from the misdeeds of her amoral companion; but Lucy is finally revealed to be the product of a madwoman's disturbed imagination. As Bloch himself has noted, "Lucy Comes to Stay" provided the germ of the idea that would later be expanded into his most notorious novel.

Bloch had become a novelist some years earlier, with the publication of *The Scarf* (1947). He had expanded his market to include mystery magazines, but his short stories were less likely to involve detection than straightforward depictions of hideous crimes. His horror stories had become naturalistic rather than supernatural. Bloch later wrote that death and madness had become his principal themes, and noted that his stories in this vein demanded a form different from that of conventional detective fiction because "psychopathology defied the deductive method" (*The King of Terrors*, 1977). Still, Bloch frequently managed to include a twist ending that was the equivalent of a detective's solution to a baffling crime. *The Scarf*, described by its author as "a first person account of the activities of a psychopathic strangler" (*The King of Terrors*), nevertheless contains a surprise ending in which the killer's apparent motive is revealed as a self-serving delusion that masks an even darker guilt.

His next novel, *The Kidnapper* (1954), is one of Bloch's favorites and also one of his least popular, apparently because of its brutal realism. Still, other crime novels followed it, including *Spiderweb* (1954), *The Will to Kill* (1954), and *Shooting Star* (1958). During the same period Bloch also created his most extended comic fantasy, "The Big Binge" (*Imaginative Tales*, July 1955), which was later expanded into the novel *It's All in Your Mind* (1971). Since the book's premise involves a machine that transforms ideas into realities, it might be said to have at least a flimsy connection to science fiction, but a story filled with pink elephants and squeamish vampires can hardly be considered a piece of serious scientific speculation. As Bloch noted, "The science fiction magazines would print fantasy and label it science fiction. But I know nothing about science at all" (*Castle of Frankenstein*, 1971). In any case, the comparatively unknown *It's All in Your Mind* is a wild and amusing combination of wordplay, slapstick, and satire.

An even less accurately labeled tale is "That Hell-Bound Train" (*Magazine of Fantasy and Science Fiction*, September 1958), which won the Hugo Award as the best science fiction story of the year even though it is pure fantasy. This unique piece, ironic and wryly philosophical, contains little of the horror or humor that are Bloch's stock in trade. Based on an old folk song about sinners on their way to perdition, "That Hell-Bound Train" concerns a young man who makes a deal with the devil, exchanging his soul for a watch that will stop time for him when he finds happiness. Years pass, and despite a full life Martin dies still hoping for more. Yet all is not lost, for he still has the watch

and the ability to make time stand still when he is forced to board that "Hell-Bound Train" and join its raucous passengers. Bloch's skillful evocation of the tragedy of passing time, combined with a happy but unsentimental ending, make this a very special story.

Nonetheless, this was a period in which Bloch began to become disillusioned, both with his writing career and with the world in general. The narrator of "The Hungry Eye" (*Fantastic Science Fiction*, May 1959), a comedian, gives this view of the modern scene:

There is no place in this modern world for ogres or bogeymen. We are well aware that we deal with nothing more alarming than sadists, psychopaths, paranoiacs, schizophrenics, manic-depressives, necrophiles, zooerasts, pyromaniacs, and other deviates and borderline neurotics whose combined total is probably less than one third of the entire population.

And as if that weren't enough, a horror from another world shows up as well. Even more negative is "The Funnel of God" (*Fantastic Science Fiction*, January 1960); the hero spends a lifetime searching desperately for a meaning in life, but ends up lost in a dark void as the universe itself is destroyed by his quest.

By this time, though, Bloch had already written *Psycho* (1959), the book that would change his life and open the way for him to become one of the most successful horror writers of his generation. The novel was well received on publication, but gained its greatest fame through its motion picture adaptation by the noted director Alfred Hitchcock. Although it would be ridiculous to deny the brilliance of Hitchcock's work, especially since *Psycho* has become one of his most celebrated and analyzed films, it is equally absurd to suggest, as some commentators have, that the director somehow succeeded in making a silk purse out of a sow's ear. Bloch's novel is an indisputable tour de force, the distillation of twenty-five years of experience and experimentation: it provided not only the plot for the movie, but many of the clever little touches most critics assume are Hitchcock's own. For instance, those who praise the director for the suspenseful scene in which a car carrying incriminating evidence sinks with agonizing slowness into a swamp should realize that the incident is also in the book, and in fact was prefigured fourteen years earlier in the story "Enoch."

Psycho is the story of Norman Bates, a lonely motel keeper apparently doomed to spend his life nursing his senile but tyrannical mother. When it seems that she has murdered a guest named Mary Crane, Bates feels obliged to cover up the crime, but the investigating detective is killed too, and further deaths are prevented only when Mary's sister and fiancé discover the secret of the Bates motel. The once startling revelation has by now become almost folklore: the mad murderer is actually Norman, who had poisoned his mother years before, preserved her body, convinced himself that she was still alive, and assumed her identity and her clothing in moments of stress or excitement.

Bloch got his inspiration from the factual case of a Wisconsin killer named Ed Gein, but the story and its treatment are largely original. What is most memorable is the cleverness of the trick (since Bates believes his mother is responsible, the reader does as well), but the story is so well told that it is gripping even when no surprise is expected. *Psycho* is a landmark, if only because after its appearance horror stories were more likely to deal with madmen than monsters. Yet more than a touch of the supernatural is implied; despite all the glib psychological explanations, the fact remains that Norman Bates has been, in one way or another, possessed by the spirit of his dead mother.

Hitchcock's *Psycho* (1960), from a script by Joseph Stefano, cleaves remarkably close to the original; the most significant variation in the film is that the adventures of Mary (renamed Marion) are expanded, so that she seems to be the movie's heroine; thus her sudden death comes as a special shock to the audience. And this murder, which Bloch dismisses in one sardonic line, becomes a savagely sexual stabbing in a shower that set a new standard for vivid horror. If the scene seems austere now compared with the lurid events in more recent thrillers like John Carpenter's *Halloween* (1978) and Sean Cunningham's *Friday the 13th* (1980), there can

still be no doubt that these films and countless more owe their inspiration to *Psycho*.

Although the success of this book and this movie gradually led Bloch away from the short story form toward more novels and screenplays, 1960 saw the publication of his second and perhaps finest collection of tales, *Pleasant Dreams—Nightmares*, which included much of his best work since *The Opener of the Way* in 1945. And Bloch's fame resulted in the publication of numerous further collections of old and new tales, including *Blood Runs Cold* (1961), *Bogey Men* (1963), *The Living Demons* (1967), *Dragons and Nightmares* (1969), *Fear Today, Gone Tomorrow* (1971), *Cold Chills* (1977), and *Such Stuff as Screams Are Made Of* (1979).

It is generally believed that the success of Hitchcock's *Psycho* brought Bloch to Hollywood, but in fact he was already there. He had been hired to write a script for the television crime program *Lock-Up* in 1959, and soon received assignments for more prestigious suspense shows like *Alfred Hitchcock Presents*, hosted by the director, and *Thriller*, hosted by actor Boris Karloff. Bloch wrote the screenplays for such stories as "Waxworks" and "The Sorcerer's Apprentice," while other writers adapted such Bloch tales as "The Cheaters" and "Yours Truly, Jack the Ripper."

Before long Bloch was working in film, a medium that had fascinated him since childhood and had been the subject of many stories, beginning as early as "Return to the Sabbath" (*Weird Tales*, July 1938). Bloch's first movie script, based on a story by Blake Edwards, was for the psychological thriller *The Couch* (1962); Bloch also wrote a novelization in the same year. *The Cabinet of Caligari* (1962), a remake of the silent German classic, proved to be a disappointment for Bloch since his script was extensively rewritten by producer-director Roger Kay. An association with producer-director William Castle brought better results, including a chance for Bloch to write original screenplays. *Strait-Jacket* (1963), which starred Joan Crawford, was a movie about an ax murderer containing a long suspense sequence that is one of the writer's favorites; *The Night Walker* (1964), with Robert Taylor and Barbara Stanwyck, contains an apparent haunting that turns out to be a hoax.

A longer and more fruitful association, with a British film company called Amicus, began in 1965. *The Skull* (1965), expanded from Bloch's short story "The Skull of the Marquis de Sade" (*Weird Tales*, September 1945), was written by Milton Subotsky and directed by the distinguished cinematographer Freddie Francis, who would also direct the next three Bloch films for Amicus. *The Skull*, which featured the popular British horror stars Peter Cushing and Christopher Lee, was the first of Bloch's supernatural stories to appear on the screen. The next movie, *The Psychopath* (1966), had an original script by Bloch in the suspense genre. *The Deadly Bees* (1967) was an adaptation of H. F. Heard's mystery novel *A Taste for Honey* (1941).

The most important of the films that Amicus produced from Bloch scripts were the last three, each of them a compendium of four of his previously published short stories. *Torture Garden* (1967) featured such stories as "Enoch," and performances by Burgess Meredith and Jack Palance. Despite a title that Bloch deplored, *The House That Dripped Blood* (1970) is widely regarded as the finest film from one of his scripts, with the dramatization of "The Cloak" proving especially successful. This movie was directed by Peter Duffell and starred Peter Cushing, Christopher Lee, and Ingrid Pitt. *Asylum* (1972), which included such tales as "Lucy Comes to Stay," was directed by Roy Ward Baker; the cast included Cushing and Herbert Lom. This proved to be Bloch's last motion picture to date, although he continued to provide scripts for such television films as *The Cat Creature* (1973) and *The Dead Don't Die* (1975).

During the period of his greatest activity in the realm of screenwriting, Bloch continued to produce novels, but virtually all of them were crime fiction, however horrific, rather than fantasy. In fact, Bloch was president of the Mystery Writers of America in 1970–1971. The novels of suspense that followed *Psycho* included *The Dead Beat* (1960), *Firebug* (1961), and *Terror* (1962), which contains slight supernatural overtones in its depiction of a murderer pledged to the cult of the sinister goddess Kali. This was followed by *The Star Stalker* (1968), *Night-World* (1972), and *American Gothic* (1974), a fictionalized account of the career of H. H. Holmes, who plied his trade during the 1893 Chicago World's Fair, and eventually confessed to killing twenty-seven people.

Although Bloch was writing less supernatural fiction, he was nonetheless guest of honor at the first World Fantasy Convention (1975), which was held in Providence, Rhode Island, to honor H. P. Lovecraft, Bloch's mentor and that city's native son. Bloch received the convention's first life achievement award for his contributions to the field.

Comparatively few of Bloch's recent short stories have employed supernatural themes, at least partly because, as Bloch explains, there is very little market for such work. Yet he continues to write fine supernatural tales from time to time. "The Movie People" (*Magazine of Fantasy and Science Fiction*, October 1969) is a nostalgic elegy for silent movies; its hero vanishes into an old film to be reunited with his lost love. More typical of Bloch is "A Case of the Stubborns" (*Magazine of Fantasy and Science Fiction*, October 1976), a gleefully revolting piece about the tribulations of a rural family saddled with a grandfather too cantankerous to admit that he has been dead for several hot summer days.

Much of Bloch's latest writing has been both playful and reflective, using his previous work as a springboard for meditations on the tale of terror. In a take-off on an earlier story, he made himself the protagonist of "The Closer of the Way" (in Stuart Schiff's 1977 anthology *Whispers*), and depicted himself as a murderer as mad as any in his fiction. One of his infrequent supernatural novels, *Strange Eons* (1978), is based on Lovecraft's fiction and takes as its premise the idea that the stories may have had a basis in reality. Even if some of the book seems a trifle self-conscious, its cataclysmic climax is impressive. *Psycho II* (1982) is a sequel that begins with Norman Bates escaping from an asylum and ends with a twist so outrageous that it almost seems a practical joke on readers who wanted more of *Psycho*. Perhaps because Bloch's trick was virtually unfilmable, the motion picture *Psycho II* (1983) was based not on Bloch's novel but on an original script by Tom Holland.

Honored as an author of fantasy, mystery, and science fiction, Robert Bloch is all of these, but regardless of genre he is primarily a creator of tales of terror, anticipating for his readers what he calls, in his introduction to *The King of Terrors*, the day when "we'll all learn the joke that makes skulls grin."

Selected Bibliography

WORKS OF ROBERT BLOCH

The Opener of the Way. Sauk City, Wis.: Arkham House, 1945. London: Neville Spearman, 1974. (Short stories.)

The Scarf. New York: Dial, 1947. London: New English Library, 1972. Also reprinted as *The Scarf of Passion*. (Novel.)

Psycho. New York: Simon and Schuster, 1959. London: Hale, 1960. (Novel.)

Pleasant Dreams—Nightmares. Sauk City, Wis.: Arkham House, 1960. London: Whiting and Wheaton, 1967. (Short stories.)

Bogey Men. New York: Pyramid, 1963. (Short stories.)

The Living Demons. New York: Belmont, 1967. London: Sphere, 1970. (Short stories.)

Dragons and Nightmares. Baltimore, Md.: Mirage Press, 1969. (Short stories.)

It's All in Your Mind. New York: Curtis Books, 1971. (Novel.)

Fear Today, Gone Tomorrow. New York: Award Books, 1971. London: Tandem Books, 1971. (Short stories.)

Cold Chills. Garden City, N.Y.: Doubleday, 1977. London: Hale, 1978. (Short stories.)

The King of Terrors. New York: Mysterious Press, 1977. London: Hale, 1978. (Short stories.)

Strange Eons. Chapel Hill, N.C.: Whispers Press, 1978. (Novel.)

Such Stuff as Screams Are Made Of. New York: Del Rey Books, 1979. London: Hale, 1980. (Short stories.)

CRITICAL STUDIES

Collins, Tom. "Robert Bloch: Society as Insane Asylum." *Twilight Zone* (June 1981): 13–17.

Elliot, Jeffrey. "Robert Bloch." *Fangoria* (October 1979): 43–47.

Moskowitz, Sam. "'Psycho'-Logical Bloch." In Robert Bloch, *Bogey Men*. New York: Pyramid, 1963.

Stanley, John. "An Interview with Robert Bloch." *Castle of Frankenstein*, no. 16 (1971): 4–11; and no. 17 (1971): 21–26.

BIBLIOGRAPHY

Flanagan, Graeme. *Robert Bloch: A Bio-Bibliography*. Canberra City, A.C.T., Australia: [Author], 1979.

—LES DANIELS

LEIGH BRACKETT

1915–1978

I

LEIGH DOUGLASS BRACKETT was born in Los Angeles on 7 December 1915 and grew up on the unspoiled California coast, living in her grandfather's house on the shores of Santa Monica Bay. She was an only child, an early reader, a dreamer, and something of a rebel. Her childhood was solitary but apparently happy, and left her impatient of the conventional restraints placed on girls. She once wrote (quoted in Walker):

On or about my eighth year, a milestone event occurred and changed my entire life. Someone gave me a copy of Burroughs' *The Gods of Mars.* I had always refused to read girls' books. I liked stories where things *happened,* the wilder and more exotic the better . . . but suddenly, at one blazing stroke, the veil was rent and I had a glimpse of the cosmos. I cannot tell you what a tremendous effect that idea of Mars, another planet, a strange world, had upon my imagination. It set me firmly on the path toward being a science-fiction writer. From then on, I could not get enough of fantasy.

In the early 1940's, Henry Kuttner introduced her to the Los Angeles Science Fiction Society, where she met the then little known Ray Bradbury. They "became close friends, and spent many a Sunday at the beach going over each other's manuscripts, talking writing and science fiction . . . a couple of thirsty castaways in a cultural desert"

(Walker). Brackett also met other, better-known science fiction writers, among them her future husband, Edmond Hamilton. They married in 1946. For most of their married life, she and Hamilton divided their time between Los Angeles, where Brackett often worked as a scriptwriter, and the small town of Kinsman, Ohio, where they lived in a restored farmhouse.

After the mid-1960's, she and Hamilton traveled a good deal, visiting Egypt, Iran, and other parts of the Middle East. The visit to Iran in 1966 enabled Brackett to do the research for her last mystery, *Silent Partner* (1969), which is set mostly in Iran. She died of cancer on 18 March 1978; her husband had died the previous year.

For a writer remembered today only for her science fiction and science fantasies, Brackett had a career full of surprises. She was remarkably versatile and had demanding standards for herself. One example of her versatility is the often praised *The Long Tomorrow* (1955). It stands with Walter Miller's *A Canticle for Leibowitz* as the best of that decade's many post-Holocaust stories. The original impetus for the book was Brackett's interest in her Amish neighbors in Ohio, and the finished work contains a sympathetic, finely drawn portrait of their way of life. The narrative is slow to unfold, is without fantastic elements, and is idea-oriented, traits not typical of her science fiction.

Brackett was a well-established professional writer who defined her job as "the ability to turn out a story to order and still make it *good.*" Among her other nonfantastic fiction are four mystery novels under her own name and one (*Stranger at Home*, 1946) ghost-written for the actor George Sanders. Her single western novel, *Follow the Free Wind* (1963), won the Silver Spur award as the year's best western story. She also wrote radio, television, and film scripts. Among her major film scripts are *The Big Sleep* (1946, in collaboration with William Faulkner), *The Long Goodbye* (1973), and the first draft of *The Empire Strikes Back* (1979), which she finished one month before her death.

Her favorite kind of writing was pulp science fantasy. She started there and returned to it whenever possible. In fifteen years of writing for the pulp magazines, she published over fifty science fantasies, most of them of novella length. Life with Hamilton refined her already considerable talent for the form. She credited him with helping her to plot more tightly. Consequently, her later pulp stories are better shaped and better paced than the earlier.

Brackett had several strengths that set her apart from the run of pulp authors. She was a highly visual writer, good at stylish descriptions, and she imagined things in convincing detail. Her prose was always serviceable, sometimes evocative and sensual. She could write crisp, tight prose or, when the need arose, heavily rhythmical, image-laden periods, as in this example from "Enchantress of Venus" (*Planet Stories*; Fall 1949; line division and capitalization mine):

> Beneath the surface Stark could see
> The drifts of flame where the lazy current ran,
> And the little coiling bursts of sparks
> That came upward and spread
> And melted into other bursts,
> So that the face of the sea was like
> A cosmos of crimson stars.

This is prose that flirts with a metrical beat. It would require only light editing, at least as far as the rhythm is concerned, to turn it into a heroic song similar to those about Roland and Beowulf. Many of Brackett's best stories have sections written in this chantlike manner. Above all, Brackett had an unusual gift for the apt metaphor, which was probably her most striking quality as a stylist.

These stylistic strengths made it inevitable that Brackett would become adept at creating a powerful sense of atmosphere within a story. This in turn made her interplanetary romances among the best in the field. The essence of this kind of tale has been defined by Terry Carr as "the writer's ability to evoke the beauty of scenes on other planets, the chill sense of evil in a half-seen creature." From the start Brackett's work was notably rich in color and poetic image.

Leigh Brackett's best pulp fantasies—including "The Last Days of Shandakor," "Enchantress of Venus," *People of the Talisman*, "The Lake of the Gone Forever," "The Veil of Asteller," and "Shannach—the Last"—are almost without exception moody, intense, and sad. The action is skillfully presented but always subordinate to the often symbolic, always emotionally charged images. Indeed, the action is mostly a way of getting from one image to another, since it is not what the protagonist does but what the reader feels and experiences through him that counts most.

II

The term *pulp fiction* is sometimes used in a derogatory sense to refer to mindless, emotionally superficial, badly written adventure stories. This, of course, is not correct, for *pulp fiction* is descriptive, not pejorative, and the best pulp fiction is not only good but also difficult to write. It has a kinetic quality, color, strong feeling, striking images, and a focused emotional appeal. While the stress is often on action, such action must point to a clear-cut and definite conclusion.

Within the range of pulp science fiction, Brackett's work tends toward the fantasy end of the spectrum and might properly be called science fantasy. She was good at exotic and symbolic landscapes, and for her, atmosphere and setting mattered as much as plot. These, not character, were her primary mechanisms for evoking emotion.

For such science fantasies Brackett adopted the pulp conventions about the solar system. For her, Mercury has a narrow twilight zone in which life is marginally possible; Venus is a watery, misty young world, rife with savagery; and Mars is an old, dying planet, bone-dry and cold, full of mystery and ancient menace.

Mars became the setting for most of her pulp fiction, and the mark of Edgar Rice Burroughs' Martian novels is clear. Brackett's heroes also set out on quests and encounter odd mixes of barbarism and superscience, sword fights and high-energy weapons. Lost races and forgotten cities older than time are plentiful. Brackett, though, improves on her model in every way, especially in terms of style, theme, and emotional depth.

Brackett's first published story, appropriately titled "Martian Quest," appeared, atypically, in *Astounding Stories* (February 1940). Elizabeth Lynn has described the story as a "rather ill-yoked pairing of brute courage and modern chemistry" (Introduction to *The Sword of Rhiannon*).

Later in 1940, Brackett sold her first story to *Planet Stories*, establishing a relationship that lasted as long as the magazine did, until 1955. *Planet Stories* was congenial to her, since the stories published in it stressed not so much intellect as sensation. She was the magazine's most popular writer.

The pulp Mars in particular became her personal planet. She formed the world from romance, so much so that often the invading Terran rocket ships seemed incongruous, much as they would in Oz. The Brackett Mars was a sometimes uneasy mix of fantasy and science fiction but remained fertile territory for the writer long after the physical realities of the actual planet became better known. Significantly, her Martian stories explore the conflicting claims of imagination and scientific logic, setting the power of a beautiful illusion over the bleakness of reality.

Brackett's best pulp stories are collected in three volumes: *The Coming of the Terrans* (1967), *The Halfling and Other Stories* (1973), and *The Best of Leigh Brackett* (1977). The best of these is *The Coming of the Terrans*, which is almost a progress report on her career, showing her growing mastery of the form and her increasing self-awareness. It also shows the wide variety of effects that can be achieved in writing interplanetary adventure fiction.

The Coming of the Terrans opens with the steamy, erotic, fast-moving "The Beast-Jewel of Mars" (*Planet Stories*, Winter 1948). Burt Winters,

a rocket ship captain, leaves his command and the safety of the Terran trade city (that is, the daylit world of reason and common sense) to venture by night into the Martian hinterland (the shadowy world of the unconscious, which is creative, chaotic, and teeming with lurking monsters of uncensored emotions). The captain comes in quest of a vanished love, but he stays to fight for his soul, a much more interesting predicament. A half-naked Martian princess acts as villain, though one admires and pities her more than one does the spoiled, useless Terran girl who is the nominal heroine.

The beast-jewel of the title is a device for allowing the body to revert pleasurably to the animal by throwing off the mind and its constraints. As a ruse, Winters embarks on "shanga" (Martian for "the going back"), but he is horrified to learn that he now wants the release offered by addiction to the beast-jewel. He is simultaneously fascinated and repelled. In the unholy wild garden of the queen, Winters sees earthmen who have become addicts collapsing into twitching heaps of polymorphous sexuality, while sadistic Martian spectators watch the human debasement below them. Predictably, Winters resists, rescues his lost love, and returns to his rocket ship, but he is not untouched by his experience.

As the plot summary shows, the story is melodramatic, sensational, even lurid, but beneath its shiny surface it is a Martian version of Robert Louis Stevenson's *The Strange Case of Dr. Jekyll and Mr. Hyde*. Brackett uses human anxieties about sexuality, doubts about human nature, and the fear of hidden desires as the emotional fuel that makes the plot run. Readers are given a long and powerful look into the heart of a man (after having been artistically deceived into thinking he will take them through quite a different tale) who from now on will live in fear of himself, unsure whether he is an ape or an angel.

The next story, "Mars Minus Bisha" (*Planet Stories*, January 1954), is very different. It is understated in style, slow-paced, muted in emotions, and rife with mounting psychological tensions. It tells of the relationship between a sensitive, humane scientist and the small abandoned Martian girl he comes to see as a daughter. Unfortunately, the scientist's hard-edged, rational world view causes him to misunderstand all that happens. His prejudice against Martian superstitions means that his heroism, though real, is misguided, making what is already a tragedy still worse.

The first story offers a sophisticated reworking of a Burroughs plot and situation, and the second shows the influence of Ray Bradbury. The best story in *The Coming of the Terrans* is "The Last Days of Shandakor" (*Startling Stories*, April 1952), which is Brackett's own, not derivative of any other writer of Martian stories. In a sense it is a personal statement, a writer's farewell to the pulp Mars. The protagonist is hard-bitten scholar and adventurer John Ross (half planetary anthropologist, half pirate; a pulp hero of the type that served as model for Indiana Jones of the film *Raiders of the Lost Ark*), one more Terran who encounters and is half-destroyed by a Martian mystery too big for human dreams of knowledge, avarice, and fame. The story is also a bitter metaphor for the poisoning of the soul that follows hard upon the failure of the imagination. Without the transforming quality of the imagination, it tells the reader, life is a desert, beauty has fled, and men are barbarians. The vision is austere to the point of bleakness, and no happy ending is pulled out of a hat.

The critic Anthony Boucher gave the next story, "Purple Priestess of the Mad Moon" (*Magazine of Fantasy and Science Fiction*, October 1964), its name. He made up the intentionally ridiculous title as an example of the kind of writing that he claimed Brackett did better than anyone else, a somewhat backhanded compliment. She in turn wrote a story around the title and sold it. The result is a fable of another sort on the potency of the imagination. Harvey Selden, a tidy-minded team player from the Bureau of Interworld Cultural Relations, is kidnapped on Mars and has an encounter with a demon, who is revealed to be evil and frightening. Selden is released unharmed but cannot forget or come to terms with the memory. The not-so-buried implication is that he has encountered a repressed fragment of his own nature, a theme that "The Beast-Jewel of Mars" also employs. After returning to earth (a statement that can serve as plot description and metaphor), Selden obsessively attempts to deny the validity of his

fantastic experience, evoking psychology to exorcise the terrors of the imagination.

"The Road to Sinharat" (*Amazing*, May 1963) is the weakest story in *The Coming of the Terrans* and, not coincidentally, is the closest of the five stories to the mainstream of science fiction and the furthest from fantasy. The story sounds an ecological warning, citing an example from the Martian past. A key character is Howard Wales, "Earth's best man in Interpol" and a firm believer in helicopters, high technology, and methodical police work. Wales is not badly drawn; he is, however, strikingly out of place set against a background of Martian romance, at times seeming to have wandered in by mistake from a police procedural. The story is in many ways a rewrite of a much earlier story, "Queen of the Martian Catacombs" (*Planet Stories*, Summer 1949; expanded as *The Secret of Sinharat*, 1964). Both have as the central plot conflict the prevention of an impending jihad by Martian desert tribesmen and hill barbarians against the Terrans, and both make use of the Ramas, a Martian elder race of near-immortal psychic vampires, to provide a touch of the fabulous. Both works, however, are straightforward adventure stories that could as well have been set in tribal Arabia or the Indian Northwest Frontier of Talbot Mundy.

The stories in *The Coming of the Terrans* have been discussed in detail because they are representative of the author's pulp science fantasy, showing the range of her techniques and some of her concerns and methods. But *The Coming of the Terrans* is not an exhaustive sampling of her work. There is more to Leigh Brackett.

III

Planet Stories ceased publication in 1955, and for roughly the next decade Brackett's work was published in paperback-book form as Ace Doubles. (This was a publishing format in which two stories were bound together back to back.) Seven of Brackett's novels were published in this manner, all based on earlier work.

Four of them were novels of science fiction adventure: *The Galactic Breed* (1955; abridged from *The Starmen of Llyridis*), *The Big Jump* (1955), *The*

Nemesis from Terra (1961), and *Alpha Centauri— or Die!* (1963). They are alike in having as their theme liberation and as their heroes hard-nosed, two-fisted nobodies who become somebodies on a great scale. The best is *The Nemesis from Terra*, set on Mars; it is the one closest to a fantasy.

Three science fantasies were also published in the Ace Doubles: *The Sword of Rhiannon* (1953), *The Secret of Sinharat*, and *People of the Talisman* (1964), the last two being bound together. *The Sword of Rhiannon*, an enlargement of "Sea Kings of Mars" (*Thrilling Wonder Stories*, June 1949), recreates the Mars of a million years ago, a planet sparkling with oceans, forests, and vitality but menaced by evil serpent beings and graced by the presence of a repentant god. Brian Aldiss has called it "the most magical sub-Burroughs of them all, the best evocation of that fantasy Mars we would all give our sword arm to visit" (*Billion Year Spree*, chapter 10).

The Secret of Sinharat and *People of the Talisman*, both expansions of much earlier work, are tales of Eric John Stark, Brackett's best-known pulp hero and her own favorite character. *The Secret of Sinharat* is the weakest of the Stark stories, while *People of the Talisman* is among the best of Brackett's work. The latter contains a splendid narrative set piece depicting the fall of a walled city to a barbarian horde, and it also contains the most atypical female character in Brackett's fiction: a charismatic warrior maid cut from the same fierce mold as C. L. Moore's Jirel of Joiry. The Lady Ciaran leads the conquering army and beats Stark in a hand-to-hand duel. The final reason for rating *People of the Talisman* high is that it is a perfectly constructed pulp story, exemplifying the requirement of concentrated unity of effect for maximum emotional impact. Every aspect of the work is connected: the fates of the twin cities; the fates of the major characters and most minor ones; the perfect placement of incident in the narrative; and the accomplished interweaving of plot and subplots so that all demonstrate a common theme—the necessity for individuals to be self-created and self-reliant, and the illusory nature of most things to which humans give their belief or their lives.

Stark is the only character that Brackett featured in a series and her best-drawn hero. Dark, blunt, grim, a man seen always standing apart, Stark is an orphaned Terran who was raised by the subhuman aborigines of Mercury. His lineage and actions serve to link him with both mythology and popular culture, a dual heritage that Brackett obviously intended. Terry Hansen (*Extrapolation*, Spring 1982) has pointed out that the structure of Brackett's "Enchantress of Venus" follows the archetypal pattern for the mythic hero's story: separation, initiation, return. Hansen also quotes from Joseph Campbell's *The Hero with a Thousand Faces* (1949) the standard path of the heroic quest; it might serve as a tight plot summary of the story: "A hero ventures forth from the world of common day into a region of supernatural wonder: fabulous forces are there encountered and a decisive victory is won: the hero comes back from this mysterious adventure with the power to bestow boons on his fellow men."

At the same time, Stark is an offspring of the worlds of popular culture. He can be seen as a scaled-down, moodier version of Superman, while his history shows obvious kinship with Tarzan's. Like Robert E. Howard's Conan, Stark is generally taciturn and unsmiling, and has an unconcealed contempt for civilized softness and corruption. His toughness is genuine and is presented with a gritty realism reminiscent of Raymond Chandler's Philip Marlowe, who is a cross-genre grandfather of Brackett's wild man. Stark is raw and ruthless, quite amoral— not a noble savage; yet he is nonetheless a decent man in many ways and a loyal friend.

In 1974–1976 the *Book of Skaith* trilogy appeared, three short novels published separately: *The Ginger Star*, *The Hounds of Skaith*, and *The Reavers of Skaith*. It is Eric John Stark's showcase, continuing the *Planet Stories* tradition while significantly enlarging it. It is a somber tale, one touched by the qualities of epic and myth.

The Book of Skaith contains the best integration of science fiction and fantasy elements that Brackett ever achieved. Much of her best writing is here. Skaith is a new world, a new canvas for Brackett. Lost in the distances of the galactic fringes, Skaith occupies a literary terrain halfway between fairyland and science fiction. On one level the trilogy offers a dying sun circled by a worn-out planet whose inhabitants are suffering the effects of severe depletion of resources, a receding technology, a stagnant social order, and an oncoming ice age. Artfully intermixed with this are hidden citadels; seal people, mole people, bird people; wizardlike immortal Lord Protectors and their agents, the robed Wandsmen; giant telepathic Hellhounds; queens, Wise Women, and Corn Kings; and everywhere true prophecy and the visible workings of fate. Magic, or something very like it, flourishes on Skaith, coexisting amicably with space ships and laser cannons.

Skaith is a fine setting for adventure. *The Book of Skaith* offers readers more, however. The action is viewed on a planetary scale, and events have an epic significance. Stark is a hurtling missile who collides with every element of Skaithian society. His person signifies the smashing impact that star ships and access to the universe outside its skies will have on all Skaithian institutions and beliefs. Stark is the future incarnate. Further, Stark is given a mythic dimension. He moves against a background of the supernatural and the inexorable working of fate, whose chosen instrument he unwillingly is. Stark is a savior, the Dark Man of ancient prophecy. His consort, Gerrith, is herself a Wise Woman and born to wear the robe and crown of her people's fate.

Skaith and its predicament are explicable in rational terms, but a strong element of the fantastic is associated with the dying planet. In the shadows of human clashes and combats are conflicting archetypes, the primal opposition between the energies of life and the death wish.

The Book of Skaith can bear comparison with any of the major fantasy or science fantasy trilogies of the last fifty years. Its scope is large. The reader is introduced to any number of social groups, which are presented in their entirety: customs, culture, history, legends, problems, gods, and devils. Brackett tells her story with an awareness of economic and political realities seldom found in pure fantasy. Her battles and sieges are realistically portrayed. She is unsentimental in her presentation of hardship and suffering, and possesses a refreshing awareness of the moral ambiguities that surround great events.

Leigh Brackett does a thoroughly persuasive job of creating the late-autumn bleakness of Skaith, a world that is fading and running down before the reader's eyes. *The Book of Skaith* remains at the moment an undeservedly obscure but major work by one of the important figures in the history of American science fiction and supernatural fiction.

Selected Bibliography

WORKS OF LEIGH BRACKETT

Books written by Brackett
Book bibliography is followed by original magazine title and date of publication. Ace Doubles were paperback volumes in which two novels, often by different authors, were bound together, back to back.

Shadow over Mars. Manchester, England: Sydney Pemberton, 1951. ("Shadow over Mars," 1944.) Reissued in expanded form as *The Nemesis from Terra.* New York: Ace, 1961, an Ace Double bound with *Collision Course* by Robert Silverberg.
The Starmen. New York: Gnome Press,1952. London: Science Fiction Club, 1954. ("The Starmen of Llyridis," 1951.) Reissued in abridged form as *The Galactic Breed.* New York: Ace, 1955, an Ace Double bound with *Conquest of the Space Sea* by Robert Moore Williams.
The Sword of Rhiannon. New York: Ace, 1953, an Ace Double bound with *Conan the Conqueror* by Robert E. Howard. London: Boardman, 1956 (*The Sword of Rhiannon* alone).
The Big Jump. New York: Ace, 1955, an Ace Double bound with *Solar Lottery* by Philip K. Dick. ("The Big Jump," 1953.)
The Long Tomorrow. Garden City, N.Y.: Doubleday, 1955.
Alpha Centauri—or Die! New York: Ace, 1963, an Ace Double bound with *Legend of Lost Earth* by G. McDonald Wallis. (Expanded from "Teleportress of Alpha C," 1954.)
The Secret of Sinharat and *People of the Talisman.* New York: Ace, 1964, an Ace Double. ("Queen of the Martian Catacombs," 1949, and "Black Amazon of Mars," 1951.) Both stories reissued together as *Eric John Stark: Outlaw of Mars.* New York: Del Rey Books, 1982.
The Coming of the Terrans. New York: Ace, 1967. (Short stories.)
The Halfling and Other Stories. New York: Ace, 1973. (Short stories.)

The Ginger Star. New York: Ballantine, 1974. London: Sphere, 1976. (Novel.)

The Hounds of Skaith. New York: Ballantine, 1974. (Novel.)

The Reavers of Skaith. New York: Ballantine, 1976. (Novel.)

The Book of Skaith. Garden City, N.Y.: Doubleday, 1976. (Reissue of the three preceding books.)

The Best of Leigh Brackett, edited by Edmond Hamilton. Garden City, N.Y.: Doubleday, 1977. (Short stories.)

"Stark and the Star Kings," with Edmond Hamilton. (The only formal collaboration between Brackett and Hamilton, this story was written in the early 1970's and will be included in Harlan Ellison's anthology *Last Dangerous Visions*.)

Books edited by Brackett

The Best of Planet Stories #1. New York: Ballantine, 1975. (Contains the Brackett–Ray Bradbury collaboration "Lorelei of the Red Mist," 1946, and an introduction by Brackett.)

The Best of Edmond Hamilton. Garden City, N.Y.: Doubleday, 1977. (Introduction and Afterword by Brackett.)

CRITICAL AND BIOGRAPHICAL STUDIES

Aldiss, Brian, ed. *Space Opera: An Anthology of Way-Back-When Futures*. Garden City, N.Y.: Doubleday, 1974.

————, and Harrison, Harry, eds. *SF Horizons*. 2 vols. New York: Arno, 1975.

Anderson, Poul. "Starflights and Fantasies: Sagas Still to Come." In *The Craft of Science Fiction*, edited by Reginald Bretnor. New York: Harper and Row, 1976.

Arbur, Rosemarie. "Leigh Brackett: No 'Long Goodbye' Is Good Enough." In *The Feminine Eye: Science Fiction and the Women Who Write It*, edited by Tom Staicar. New York: Frederick Ungar, 1982.

Budrys, Algis. "Pulp!" *Science Fiction Review*, 45 (November 1982): 16–20.

Carr, Terry, ed. *Planets of Wonder*. New York: Thomas Nelson, 1976.

Hamilton, Edmond, ed. Introduction to *The Best of Leigh Brackett*. Garden City, N.Y.: Doubleday, 1977. (Also contains an Afterword by Brackett.)

Hansen, Terry L. "Myth-Adventure in Leigh Brackett's 'Enchantress of Venus.'" *Extrapolation*, 23 (Spring 1982): 77–82.

Lynn, Elizabeth. Introduction to *The Sword of Rhiannon* by Leigh Brackett. Boston: Gregg Press, 1979.

Truesdale, David, and McGuire, Paul. "An Interview with Leigh Brackett and Edmond Hamilton." *Science Fiction Review*, 21 (May 1977): 6–15.

Walker, Paul, ed. *Speaking of Science Fiction*. Oradell, N.J.: Luna Publications, 1978.

BIBLIOGRAPHY

Arbur, Rosemarie. *Leigh Brackett, Marian Zimmer Bradley, Anne McCaffrey: A Primary and Secondary Bibliography*. Boston: G. K. Hall, 1982.

—JOHN L. CARR

RAY BRADBURY

1920-

IN THE WORDS of Ray Bradbury, "the ability to fantasize is the ability to survive." His writing has exhibited this exuberance for nearly four decades. Bradbury is nostalgic, optimistic, and apocalyptic by turns; his own ability to fantasize, to create monuments of the imagination, has long placed him in the forefront of current American writers specializing in speculative fiction. Whether the incarnations of that imagination find their outlet in plays, movie scripts, short stories, novels, public lectures, poetry, or almost sermonic essays, they have made an indelible impression on the conscious and unconscious spirit of his contemporaries. In fact, it could be maintained that Bradbury's depictions of both the light and dark sides of human nature have enabled many to face the unknown and thereby enabled them to survive.

Considering the collected works of Bradbury—his complete bibliography runs to many, many pages—the reader immediately faces a number of anomalies. Is this man writing science fiction? Fantasy? Supernatural horror stories? Nostalgia for the future? Evocative re-creations of a never-never land of the golden days of his midwestern youth? However Bradbury's work could finally be classified, it remains provocative, intense, personal, immediate, and, above all, magical.

Distinguishing between fantasy and science fiction has long been a difficult if not impossible task. In no other author is the problem so clearly shown as in Bradbury. This genial master of English prose has stationed himself squarely in the center of the issue, and indeed, it may well be that his writings have contributed to its definition. For example, is *The Martian Chronicles* (1950) fantasy or science fiction? How about *The October Country* (1955) or *Something Wicked This Way Comes* (1962)? Are Bradbury's excursions into the heart of humanity really explorations of our shadow side? For that matter, the questions could be reversed. Do not Bradbury's evocations of darkness and evil, in the end, celebrate the upward aspirations of the human race? Does Bradbury's eternal optimism find some negative correlation in his visions of the perverted, twisted machinations of his evil characters in stories too numerous to mention?

These stories, novellas, and novels overlap; science fantasies shade into symbolic dystopias; and Mars becomes Green Town becomes Mars becomes Waukegan. . . . It is virtually impossible to distinguish form, substance, medium, message, style, darkness and light, vision and dream, past and present, present and future, future and past, fantasy and science fiction. Yet with all of these difficulties, two things remain constant in his writing—magic and the ability to enchant.

Enchantment may well be the proper word for Bradbury, enchantment in the sense that he seems to have cast a magic spell on his audience. He delights them, bewitches them, charms them completely with his verbal evocations, with his vision of a timeless past, a provocative future, and a challenging present. His enthusiasm is contagious, his emotional response to his surroundings is profound, and his perceptions of his intuitive interior life seem to intensify the ordinary. Moreover, his ability to communicate those enthusiasms, perceptions, and emotions marks him as a genuine rara avis, a writer who is at once respected by his peers and beloved by his readers. But success did not come easily for Bradbury. Rather, he inched his way along, crafting story after story, destroying reams of what he considered garbage, and selling an occasional short piece of fiction for a half cent per word.

Born on 22 August 1920 in Waukegan, Illinois, Ray Douglas Bradbury as a boy soon discovered L. Frank Baum's magic land of Oz, the never-never Africa of Edgar Rice Burroughs' Tarzan of the Apes, and Barsoom, Burroughs' impossible, romantic Mars, where John Carter always saved and served the incomparable Dejah Thoris. Bradbury also never forgot the timeless summers of the American Midwest, a locale that he has revisited frequently in such works as *The Martian Chronicles* and *Dandelion Wine* (1957). Indeed, the past is always present for Bradbury: he shapes its materials and illumines them with his particular insights, and he places, almost full blown, an alter ego of himself, such as Douglas Spaulding in *Dandelion Wine*, in some era of his own past that he wishes to evoke.

So impressionable was Bradbury as a boy that it almost seems as if he has forgotten nothing; no incident from his past escapes his artistic vision and revision; the joys and terrors of youth become artistic materials to be molded, shaped, and given birth in a luminous, timeless prose. In fact, it could be maintained that this tendency to display or exhibit himself—his emotions, his feelings, his intuitions—in print has caused the very problem of critical artistic differentiation faced by his readers. If Bradbury himself is a person of complex, often differing reactions to people, events, and things, then his prose reflects that very complexity. It is almost as if Bradbury were echoing Walt Whitman (whom he curiously resembles in many usually unnoticed ways) by admitting that he contradicts himself. If he contains multitudes, his stories will also contain them. If he is at once a fantast, a preeminent creator

of highly imaginary fictions, he is also a celebrator of the dark in *Something Wicked This Way Comes*.

This novel may well have its roots in Bradbury's discovery of magic when he was barely eleven. The famous Blackstone the Magician included the boy in his act as a member of the audience—and young Ray was enchanted by the magic of magic. His meeting with another magician, Mr. Electrico, who performed with a circus, proved to be a crucial experience for him:

> Every night for three nights, Mr. Electrico sat in his electric chair, being fired with ten billion volts of pure blue sizzling power. Reaching out into the audience, his eyes flaming, his white hair standing on end, sparks leaping between his smiling teeth, he brushed an Excalibur sword over the heads of the children, knighting them with fire. When he came to me, he tapped me on both shoulders and then the tip of my nose. The lightning jumped into me. Mr. Electrico cried: *"Live forever!"* . . .
>
> A few weeks later I started writing my first short stories about the planet Mars. From that time to this, I have never stopped. God bless Mr. Electrico, the catalyst, wherever he is.
>
> (Introduction to *The Stories of Ray Bradbury*)

Shortly thereafter the Bradbury family moved to Arizona and then, in 1934, to Los Angeles, where he has lived ever since. He graduated from Los Angeles High School in 1938, sold newspapers, bought a typewriter, rented an office, and launched his career. Today, millions of words and thousands of sales later, he still remembers the thrill of his first sale: a short story, "Pendulum," on which he had collaborated with a friend, Henry Hasse, and published in *Super Science Stories* in November 1941. His share of the check was $13.75. Within a year he was a full-time writer; within a decade *The Martian Chronicles* was published, and Bradbury found himself famous.

It is impossible to mention here all the stories he has written since. His collection *The Stories of Ray Bradbury* (1980) skims the surface in presenting a mere one hundred stories, but a collection of the total contribution of this transplanted midwesterner, this eternally joyous boy, might require an entire bookshelf. To be sure, Bradbury is certainly aware of the darker side of things, and his writing often portrays the darker vision. Yet even in such an apparently pessimistic novel as *Fahrenheit 451* (1953), in which mankind ingests poisons of various kinds, both real and psychic, the final affirmation is quite clear.

Pessimism and optimism combine in *Fahrenheit 451*, "future-scene" fiction with some relatively obvious overtones of allegory and sermon. However, a later novel, *Something Wicked This Way Comes*, cannot, by any stretch of either the imagination or literary classifications, be termed science fiction. It is at once Gothic fantasy, supernatural or preternatural horror, and a rattling good story replete with mystery, wonder, awe, and terror. Yet the nostalgia it invokes, particularly in its descriptions of Green Town, Illinois, in another time, another place, is essentially the same nostalgia for the future depicted at the end of *Fahrenheit 451*. It is a reassuring vision; it is light after darkness, good after evil.

The two novels, then, apparently so unlike, have far more similarities of theme than might appear on the surface. This centrality of theme infuses almost all of Bradbury's writing, and it is this thematic unity that gives his writings such centricity of appeal. The works are varied, to be sure, sometimes unclassifiable as to genre, but they are distinctively—to coin an adjective—Bradburian.

What have Bradbury's themes been? What is the source of his particular genius, his unique ability to reach the fuzzy-cheeked adolescent and the sophisticated eastern-establishment book critic? Of course it is not the mere genres of science fiction and fantasy, which he has invested with his own distinctive stamp; neither is it the nature of the subjects—Mars, book burning, and so on—that he has chosen. Rather, it is his sense of what is best in America and the American people or, indeed, what is best in humanity as a whole. While he may well be caught up in Frederick Jackson Turner's thesis that the unique quality of American life was determined by the existence of the frontier and the response of Americans to it, nevertheless Bradbury has been almost as popular a writer in other countries as in the United States. His concerns are often expressed in terms of

the metaphor of the wilderness, and all peoples seem to respond to the challenge that the wilderness conveys. It is almost as though Bradbury were appealing to some Jungian collective unconscious, recalling the dim ancestral memories of how humans feared but faced the saber-toothed tiger and eventually conquered it, and looking ahead at how humans will fear but face the expanses of space and eventually conquer its vastnesses.

According to Bradbury, the final, inexhaustible wilderness, the final frontier, is the wilderness of space, and in that last challenge mankind will eventually both find and renew itself. That vision of ultimate rebirth is essentially religious, but Bradbury is rarely explicit about it. The theme infuses much of his writing as a sort of susurrus, quietly whispering in the background. He seems to be saying in his luminous manner that in space, as atoms of God, humans will live forever. Thus, the conquest of space becomes for him a religious quest, although a directly religious theme is sounded very seldom in his stories. One story, "The Fire Balloons" (1951), tells of the debate two priests have on Mars about whether or not some native blue fireballs have souls; in "The Man" (1949), Christ leaves a distant planet the day before an earth rocket lands. The poem "Christus Apollo" (1969) states his faith quite explicitly: "Christ wanders in the Universe / A flesh of stars."

The central tensions that permeate all of Bradbury's work are those of stasis, entropy, and change. He reveals these tensions frequently in short stories; but even the major works like *Something Wicked This Way Comes*, *Fahrenheit 451*, and *The Martian Chronicles* depend on complex interrelationships of time, setting, place, character, and dialogue. These matters are not simple ones in his books, despite the ostensible simplicity of the themes or subjects. *Something Wicked This Way Comes* will illustrate the many harmonic variations in the novels and in many of his short stories.

Something Wicked has its roots in an earlier collection of short stories, *The October Country* (1955). Bradbury's introductions to this collection remind the reader that many of the stories were written before he was twenty-six and that some date back to

1943. Nonetheless, they reflect his absorption in Edgar Allan Poe's short pieces of fiction, which served to introduce him to the Gothic mode. Gothic devices of all kinds suffuse these stories—catacombs, death, atmospheric effects, terror, awe, dread, superstitions, grotesqueries, haunted houses, and so on. To be sure, Bradbury often masks them with accustomed twentieth-century devices or patterns of behavior, but even these reappear in some very unfamiliar guises. To cite only two examples, catacombs that have become a local tourist attraction in Mexico and haunted houses are transformed in "The Man Upstairs" (1947) into a new boarder in Grandma's house who has a collection of triangles, chains, and pyramids instead of the usual heart, lungs, and stomach. The metaphors may well be those of contemporary society, but they are also those of geometrical figures or universal abstractions.

Something Wicked presents a major expansion on the theme of the horrible and horrifying residing in the pedestrian, the conventional, the ordinary. Even the names of the two major characters illustrate something of the ambivalence with which the author views this romantic re-creation of his own youth: William Halloway and James Nightshade. Halloway can equal Holy Way, and nightshade is, after all, a poisonous weed. Yet neither boy is a mere stereotype of good or evil. Rather, what Bradbury seems to suggest is that everyone, even adolescents in edenic Green Town, can harbor both the lightness and darkness of the human imagination. Yet, with almost typical thematic reversal, Bradbury has Jim Nightshade look ahead, wishing to grasp life, while Will Halloway remains enchanted by the past. Commentators have often noted that these two boys seem to typify the two major aspects of Bradbury's writing—nostalgia for the past and eagerness for the future.

Other themes in the novel present still other aspects of Bradbury's complex visions and enthusiasms. The virtual disruption of Green Town by Cooger and Dark's Pandemonium Shadow Show—what a significant name that is—can certainly be construed as the challenges that all of us must face. If evil has many aspects, many are presented in the kaleidoscopic vision of Cooger and Dark's minicircus. Bradbury celebrates the lure of the side-show—the Illustrated Man, the Dark, the Shadow. It is pandemonium loosed. All of the characters must react to these strangely seductive evils, including Charles Halloway, Jim's father, and the other townspeople—and, hence, the readers. The Halloween vision that Bradbury so carefully portrays and his loving attention to detail are trademarks, as uniquely his own as are his visions of Mars. Yet Bradbury never seems to forget that Halloween (or All Hallows' Eve) is the vigil of the Feast of All the Saints and is traditionally followed in the church calendar by All Souls' Day. Everything combines: the good and the sainted *are* among us; perhaps only by their sufferance are the creatures of Dark also among us. This is a complicated allegory, to be sure, but one that Bradbury continually seems to suggest.

During the 1950's Bradbury turned out dozens of stories of fantasy and science fiction, and not a few that were both. He was a busy writer, and gradually, perhaps because his style was inimitable, he began to be noticed by many writers and critics outside the field of speculative literature. Such diverse writers as Aldous Huxley, Christopher Isherwood, and Gilbert Highet hailed him as a stylist and a visionary.

Perhaps even more important, the film director John Huston asked him to write the script for his version of *Moby Dick* (released in 1956). While it may be true that Herman Melville's *Moby Dick* cannot be captured in any other medium, some film critics have said that Melville was better served by Bradbury than by Huston. In the end, Melville's white whale provided Bradbury with another parameter to a central metaphor or symbol that had entranced him for years: just as the cylindrical shape of Jules Verne's submarine of Captain Nemo and the Martian rocket ships of H. G. Wells had long fascinated Bradbury, so the shape of the whale itself provided still another metaphor. For Bradbury, metaphor is not merely a figure of speech; it is a vital concept, a method he uses to comprehend one reality and express it in terms of another, to permit the reader to perceive what he is saying. For example, *Fahrenheit 451* is structured around book burnings, and while the moving tattoo was superimposed on an otherwise loosely connected series of stories, it nonetheless provides the final form of *The Illustrated Man* (1951) with a coherent metaphoric unity. As has already been noted, all of Bradbury's writing might be described as a metaphor of generalized nostalgia, not merely for the past but also for the future. In his slow progression through Verne, Wells, and Melville, Bradbury was searching for his own authentic voice, and the concept of metaphor helped him find it.

The pattern of the whale, often disguised as a rocket ship or spaceship, is an image to which Bradbury returned again and again. It provided him with a convenient symbol that, for example, brought the colonists to Mars and ultimately led to the events described in *The Martian Chronicles*. Here for the first time Bradbury explored the implications of a metaphysical or social problem in depth. Many commentators have remarked that Bradbury is essentially a short-story writer, that his novels are merely expansions of short stories, as is the case with *Fahrenheit 451*, or are merely collections of loosely connected stories, such as *The Martian Chronicles*. He is a dash man, they say, not a long-distance runner; but they add that it may well be more difficult to turn out gem after gem of short fiction consistently than to hone, develop, and give birth to a new novel every five years or so.

Indeed, that reservation about his writing may have some validity. Yet it is also certain that the apparently loosely connected series of stories found in *The Martian Chronicles* and in *The Illustrated Man* have more coherence and unity than is generally claimed for them. In *The Martian Chronicles*, Bradbury does not hesitate to juxtapose the familiar tensions between fantasy and reality, time and eternity, or past and present. Moreover, he explores the implications of these tensions in greater detail than in any of the fiction that he had previously written, as if he had found his mature voice for the first time and was delighting in its possibilities.

What is most remarkable about this series of stories is that Bradbury himself is intensely involved with it while at the same time remaining dispassionately objective. He seems to be saying, "I feel this way; I'm enchanted by it and I hope you are too, but let's be careful lest we be swept away by the creation we are both involved in." This ambiguity of passionate involvement with an equal degree of objective distancing is a remarkable technique, not only for

itself but also for its appearance in the hitherto much maligned genre of science fiction. How, then, in *The Martian Chronicles*, does Bradbury achieve this goal of what might be called "perspective by ambiguity"?

To answer this question, one must direct attention not so much to the stories themselves and what they say directly but to the interchapters, the brief interstices between the longer stories. Dated by year and month, these sections seem to force the reader to fill in the gaps that they leave. What happened between the stories? we ask. And no sooner do we do so than Bradbury has achieved a major goal: profound involvement by his readers in the very act of creation. But because no two readers will create the same material in the same way, we are faced, in the end, with ambiguity coupled with both intensity and perspective. It is a remarkable accomplishment, and that Bradbury is able to bring it off so well is not the least of the book's many merits. Throughout the succession of stories, Bradbury poses many questions but answers very few of them. What is going on? we also ask. Is the re-creation of the old family home real or a hallucination? Is it amicable or dangerous? Do Martians really exist, or are they found only in our minds, and even if they are only in our minds, isn't mental reality just as real as extramental reality?

Throughout the book Bradbury is too good a storyteller to let questions, answers, or even suggestions, hints, or illusions get in the way of the tales themselves. Thus, he carries us through one apparently isolated story after another until we finish the book. Then we wish only to begin it again, in an attempt to recapture the charm and magic of the initial reading. The reader's curiosity is not merely tweaked by the stories or by what Bradbury has chosen to tell us or, sometimes, chosen not to tell us. Rather, we become fascinated by the ambiguities. The reader welcomes them and the inferences found in the pages or in his or her mind.

Such subtlety of vision and intensity are often found in imaginative literature. What is surprising is that they are habitually present in Bradbury's work, which, after all, had its wellsprings in the pulps. More than one critic has wondered if what Bradbury writes should be called "science fiction." It is more like fantasy, they say, and Bradbury is a fantast, a creator of entire worlds; or they may say that his writing, no matter in what category it is placed, has simply made the imagination live once more. By and large, such statements do not concern Bradbury in the slightest. He cares little either for critics or for what they say about his work. "Critics come from the head," he has remarked, "and I write for the heart!" In fact, one reviewer recently tried to disparage his writing by calling him the "Norman Rockwell of science fiction," and Bradbury quite naturally took it as a compliment.

To be sure, even when Bradbury's stories are set on Mars or a rocket ship, they are not what has been termed "hard-core" science fiction, or soft-core fantasy, for that matter. He has no particular fondness for the technological products of civilization. Although he owns a car, he does not drive. He has rarely, if ever, been on a plane, and his passion for old trains, old buses, and old streetcars and his habit of bicycling all over West Los Angeles have given him the perhaps undeserved reputation of a man who might have been happier living in the first two decades of this century or even in the last two decades of the nineteenth.

Yet his pleas for an expansion of the space program and his ability to share his dreams with everyone from America's astronauts to third-graders have placed him firmly as a man of the last third of this century. He would not give up, say, the automobile, no matter how he might deplore what pollution has done to the cities or the countryside.

One of the most intriguing aspects of Bradbury's writing is that it appeals to virtually everyone in his audience. He himself has analyzed that appeal: he recognizes that the sources for his stories are usually, if not always, found in the events of his ordinary day-to-day life, and as such, they are easily recognizable by his readers as something that they themselves have often perceived but not really recognized. Such is certainly the case, to cite only one example, in one of his most famous short stories, "The Fog Horn" (1951), first published (and soon thereafter filmed) under the title *The Beast from Twenty Thousand Fathoms* (1953). Bradbury describes its origin as follows:

One night when my wife and I were walking along the beach in Venice, California, where we lived in a thirty-dollar-a-month newlyweds' apartment, we came upon the bones of the Venice Pier and the struts, tracks, and ties of the ancient roller-coaster collapsed on the sand and being eaten by the sea.

"What's that dinosaur doing lying here on the beach?" I said.

My wife, very wisely, had no answer.

The answer came the next night when, summoned from sleep by a voice calling, I rose up, listened, and heard the lonely voice of the Santa Monica Bay fog horn blowing over and over and over again.

Of course! I thought. The dinosaur heard that lighthouse fog horn blowing, thought it was another dinosaur arisen from the deep past, came swimming in for a loving confrontation, discovered it was only a fog horn, and died of a broken heart there on the shore.

(Introduction to *The Stories of Ray Bradbury*)

Here is the apotheosis of Bradbury's vision, its pure essence — the leaping imagination, the lure of the past clashing with the reality of the present, all combined with something that the reader can readily perceive. Of course, one says while reading the story, how often one has been moved by that lonesome booming sound. As Bradbury puts it:

A sound like the birds flying south, crying, and a sound like November wind and the sea on the hard, cold shore. . . . Whoever hears it will weep in their souls, . . . whoever hears it will know the sadness of eternity and the briefness of life.

(ibid.)

Here is Bradbury at his most magical, transforming the most simple, most transitory phenomena into memorable beauty. His style is perhaps the feature that contributes most to his imaginative vision.

Today, after over forty years of writing, after hundreds of short stories, plays, film and television scripts, and dozens of poems, Bradbury remains one of the most popular American writers. He is a very charismatic figure on the lecture circuit, almost a happening, a loving and much loved man. It may be, in the end, that the future will recognize him as a bard in the grand, antique sense of the word. He has captured past, present, and future as has perhaps no other writer, and his bardic song will undoubtedly enchant the future as much as it has enchanted both the present and the past.

Selected Bibliography

WORKS OF RAY BRADBURY

The Martian Chronicles. Garden City, N.Y.: Doubleday, 1950. As *The Silver Locusts.* London: Rupert Hart-Davis, 1951.

The Illustrated Man. Garden City, N.Y.: Doubleday, 1951. London: Rupert Hart-Davis, 1952.

Fahrenheit 451. New York: Ballantine, 1953. London: Rupert Hart-Davis, 1954.

The October Country. New York: Ballantine, 1955.

Dandelion Wine. Garden City, N.Y.: Doubleday, 1957. London: Rupert Hart-Davis, 1957.

Something Wicked This Way Comes. New York: Simon and Schuster, 1962.

The Anthem Sprinters and Other Antics. New York: Dial, 1963.

The Vintage Bradbury. New York: Vintage Books, 1965.

When Elephants Last in the Dooryard Bloomed. New York: Knopf, 1973. London: Rupert Hart-Davis, 1975.

Where Robot Mice and Robot Men Run Round in Robot Town. New York: Knopf, 1977. London: Rupert Hart-Davis, 1979.

The Stories of Ray Bradbury. New York: Knopf, 1980.

CRITICAL AND BIOGRAPHICAL STUDIES

Anonymous. "Ray Bradbury and the Irish." *Catholic World,* 200 (January 1964): 224–230.

Ash, Lee. "WLB Biography: Ray Bradbury." *Wilson Library Bulletin* (November 1964).

Federman, Donald. "Truffaut and Dickens: *Fahrenheit 451.*" *Florida Quarterly* (Summer 1967).

Forrester, Kent. "The Dangers of Being Earnest: Ray Bradbury and *The Martian Chronicles.*" *Journal of General Education* (Spring 1976).

Gladish, Cristine. "*The October Country.*" In *Survey of Science Fiction Literature,* edited by Frank Magill. Englewood Cliffs, N.J.: Salem Press, 1979.

Grimsley, Juliet. "*The Martian Chronicles*: A Provocative Study." *English Journal* (December 1970).

Hamblen, Charles F. "Bradbury's *Fahrenheit 451* in the Classroom." *English Journal* (September 1968).

McNelly, Willis E. "Bradbury Revisited." *CEA Critic* (March 1969).

———. "Ray Bradbury, Past, Present, and Future." In *Voices of the Future,* edited by Thomas Clareson. Bowling Green, Ohio: Bowling Green University Popular Press, 1976.

———, and Neilson, Keith. "*Fahrenheit 451.*" In *Survey of Science Fiction Literature.*

McReynolds, Douglas J. "The Short Fiction of Ray Bradbury." In *Survey of Science Fiction Literature.*

———. "The Short Fiction of Bradbury." In *Survey of Modern Fantasy Literature,* edited by Frank Magill. Englewood Cliffs, N.J.: Salem Press, 1983.

Mengeling, Marvin E. "Ray Bradbury's *Dandelion Wine*: Themes, Sources and Styles." *English Journal* (October 1971).

Moskowitz, Sam. "Ray Bradbury." In *Seekers of Tomorrow: Masters of Modern Science Fiction.* Cleveland: World, 1966. Reprinted. Westport, Conn.: Hyperion Press, 1974.

Nolan, William F. "Bradbury: Prose Poet in the Age of Science." *Magazine of Fantasy and Science Fiction* (May 1963).

———, ed. *The Ray Bradbury Companion: A Life and Career History, Photolog, and Comprehensive Checklist of Writings and Facsimiles from Ray Bradbury's Unpublished and Uncollected Work in All Media.* Detroit: Gale Research, 1975.

Olander, Joseph, and Greenberg, Martin H., eds. *Ray Bradbury.* New York: Taplinger, 1980. (Includes a bibliography.)

Reilly, Robert. "The Artistry of Ray Bradbury." *Extrapolation* (December 1971).

Sisario, Peter. "A Study of Allusions in Bradbury's *Fahrenheit 451.*" *English Journal* (February 1970).

Slusser, George Edgar. *The Bradbury Chronicles.* San Bernardino, Calif.: Borgo Press, 1977.

Stupple, James A. "The Past, the Future, and Ray Bradbury." In *Voices of the Future,* edited by Thomas Clareson. Bowling Green, Ohio: Bowling Green University Popular Press, 1976.

Sullivan, A. T. "Ray Bradbury and Fantasy." *English Journal* (December 1972).

Wolfe, Gary K. "*Something Wicked This Way Comes.*" In *Survey of Modern Fantasy Literature.*

— WILLIS E. McNELLY

L. SPRAGUE DE CAMP

1907–

FLETCHER PRATT

1897–1956

LYON SPRAGUE DE CAMP was born on 27 November 1907 in New York City. He studied aeronautical engineering at the California Institute of Technology and worked for a while giving courses on patents. He began writing fiction in the mid-1930's but his first full-length book, written in collaboration with A. K. Berle in 1937, was *Inventions and Their Management*—a guidebook for would-be inventor-entrepreneurs. He was soon able to devote himself full time to writing.

Fletcher Pratt was born on 25 April 1897 in Buffalo, New York. After leaving school he became a librarian and also pursued a career as a flyweight prizefighter. He gave up the latter occupation because it was not considered appropriate to the dignity of the former. He began college but had to leave for financial reasons to work as a reporter. He held various jobs on the fringe of the literary world and began selling science fiction stories to the pulp magazines in 1928. Sometimes he worked in collaboration and often used collaborative by-lines even for his solo efforts. He also translated novels from French and German for Hugo Gernsback's magazines. In the late 1930's he began to produce serious nonfiction, mainly books on history.

De Camp and Pratt met in 1939, and Pratt quickly suggested that they write in collaboration for John W. Campbell, Jr.'s, new fantasy magazine *Unknown*. De Camp was already very much at home in the pages of *Unknown*, which offered far more scope for his sense of humor and his idiosyncratic imagination than its science fiction companion, *Astounding*. Both writers were used to writing in collaboration with others—de Camp's first novel, *Genus Homo* (1941), had been written with P. Schuyler Miller.

The work that de Camp had already done for *Unknown* was quite impressive. In the first year of the magazine's publication, 1939, he had published a short novel, a revision of a manuscript submitted by H. L. Gold, which appeared as a collaboration, and a full-length novel. "Divide and Rule," the short novel, is an eccentric story about man's rebellion against alien invaders of earth who look like kangaroos and have restored feudalism (complete with the chivalric code and the institution of knight-errantry) as part of their program of social control. "None But Lucifer," revised from Gold's original version, is the story of a man who figures out the devil's secret and bids to take over his job. *Lest Darkness Fall* (in book form, 1941) is a classic novel of alternate history, telling the story of a modern man who slips through time to sixth-century Rome and saves Europe from the Dark Ages.

One might have expected, given Pratt's interest in history and the seriousness of his own later excursions into fantasy writing, that the two writers might produce novels like *Lest Darkness Fall* together. (In fact, much later, Pratt was to write his own story of time slipping and changing history in "The Spiral of the Ages," 1954, but it was a relatively mediocre effort never reprinted in book form.) What they elected to produce was exuberant comic fantasy closer to the spirit of "Divide and Rule." This is not wholly surprising; as well as their common interest in history the two men shared a wholly skeptical fascination with the idea of magic, an interest in mythology, and a sense of humor that delighted in the farcical play of ideas.

They selected as their first hero a clever but conceited psychologist, Harold Shea, a man definitely not cut out to be a hero but with resources to draw upon in cases of emergency. Shea is the research assistant to Reed Chalmers, who holds the theory that a gateway to an infinite array of possible worlds might be opened by retuning the senses. He is right, but finds the job of tuning in to the correct target world a little more difficult than anticipated. However, by means of Chalmers' method Shea is able to undertake a series of exotic adventures in other worlds glimpsed and described (or even created) by poets and myth makers.

In the first novella of the series, "The Roaring Trumpet" (1940), Shea finds himself in the world of the Norse gods, with Ragnarök approaching too rapidly for comfort. Good old American know-how and a little extra cleverness of his own allow him to outwit the various hostile forces he encounters until he is thrown back to his own world just as Heimdall blows the trumpet to signal the battle that will end the world. This novella was quickly followed by "The Mathematics of Magic" (1940), in which Shea and Chalmers enter the world of Edmund Spenser's *Faerie Queene* in order to help Gloriana's knights "straighten things out." Shea is bursting with confidence after his success in the world of Norse mythology, but matters inevitably turn out to be more

complicated than he expected. When things are straightened out, Chalmers decides that he likes Gloriana's kingdom better than his own world and elects to stay, while Shea is able to bring his dream girl, Belphebe, out of the poem and into reality. These two novellas were published together in book form as *The Incomplete Enchanter* in 1941.

This settled situation was recomplicated in a novel-length sequel, *The Castle of Iron* (1941; in book form, 1950). Here Shea and several friends are snatched out of their own reality by Chalmers, who has been tempted by curiosity to inspect the world of which the *Faerie Queene* is partly a copy: Ludovico Ariosto's *Orlando Furioso*. While there he has gotten into trouble, and when his rescuers arrive, more quickly develops. Belphebe is absorbed back into her parallel character, Belphegor, facing Shea with a very awkward problem of recovery. The story is not as good as its two predecessors but retains the same heady combination of humor and high adventure.

Pratt and de Camp went on to write two more novels together, with *Unknown* in mind. The first, *The Land of Unreason*, appeared there in 1941 (in book form, 1942), but the second, *The Carnelian Cube*, remained unpublished for some years, finally appearing as a book in 1948.

In *The Land of Unreason* an American visiting England is carried off by the little people (who are drunk on whiskey he has inadvertently provided) to be a rather overaged changeling. Just as it was with the world of the Norse gods, King Oberon's fairyland is a realm in which common sense and logic are useful primarily because they are so new and unexpected. The hero's attempts to come to terms with magic are plagued by error and misfortune, but he muddles through the quest on which he is dispatched, to reach an altogether appropriate destiny. Even in the revised version published in book form the novel seems untidy and rather slapdash, but it makes amusing reading.

The Carnelian Cube is even less successful. It tells the story of an archaeologist who finds the philosopher's stone, by means of which a man can dream himself into a new world. Impatient with our own dull world he tries to take himself into a rationally ordered one, but finds that order has distinct disadvantages. He has to find the stone again in order to escape. Next he wishes for a world in which a man can be an individual and receives an absurd redneck utopia. Undaunted, he finds the stone yet again and asks for a world in which history is a genuine science afforded proper respect. Consequently, he finds himself involved in a nightmarish experiment in historical reconstruction that threatens to kill both himself and the woman he has been pursuing, unsuccessfully, through a series of avatars. At the end of the book we lose sight of him as he regains the stone and sets out yet again; we can easily imagine him lost forever in an endlessly frustrating search for elusive perfection. The novel is certainly not uninteresting, but the repetitive invocation of the deus ex machina to wipe out situations at the point of inextricable complexity is too easy an artifice, and the second and third worlds are ineptly drawn, as if the authors could not be bothered to pay enough attention to their task.

The method by which de Camp and Pratt worked was first to decide on a plot; then de Camp would do a first draft and Pratt a final one. All of their early writing must have been done very quickly (de Camp wrote one other novella and two novels for *Unknown* in the same period, plus numerous short pieces for *Unknown* and *Astounding*); it is not really surprising that the authors sometimes seem to be failing to make the most of their premises. Only in the first two novellas, where the whole business was so new and exciting, did they muster the verve and vitality to make everything flow smoothly and perfectly; the three novels became steadily more mechanical as they materialized.

The three long stories that de Camp wrote on his own for *Unknown* during the period of his collaborations with Pratt are much the same kind of work. "The Wheels of If" (1940) is a lively story of alternate possibilities. *The Undesired Princess* (1942; in book form, 1951) takes yet another not very heroic hero into a fairy-tale world painted in primary colors, where statements are taken altogether too literally. Though *Solomon's Stone* (1942; in book form, 1957) seems to have been written in the same frenetic rush, it is perhaps the best of the three. Prosper Nash, an accountant whose body is borrowed by a demon, finds himself on the astral plane, which is inhabited by the dream creations of men in the real world. He finds that his fantasy self is a dashing cavalier, and in that form he must steal the eponymous talisman from an enchanter if he is to stand a chance of recovering his own body.

All these stories demonstrate that de Camp—with or without Pratt's help—was rather limited in his plotting strategy. Either he thrusts a hero into an awkward situation where the story is kept rolling simply by recounting the hero's attempts to stay alive or, more often, he provides the hero with a motive for searching out and securing an object of some kind. Because of these limitations his longer stories—including the longer collaborations with Pratt—are nothing but a series of exotic encounters strung together like beads in a necklace. The strand usually has some gems but other beads seem to be there only to fill in the gaps. In general de Camp seemed to be careless in connecting up the episodes of his longer stories and ended up arbitrarily switching from one briefly sketched situation to another. (Such recent de Camp novels as the otherworldly adventure fantasy *The Great Fetish*, 1978, show that he has never overcome this difficulty.)

The de Camp–Pratt partnership was broken in 1942 by World War II, when de Camp went to work in the United States Naval Reserve. Pratt returned to journalism, serving for a while as a war correspondent in Latin America, and wrote several books about the war. *Unknown* was a casualty of the war, killed by the paper shortage in 1943, and when the two writers got back together again there was no such obvious market for their wares.

Despite this de Camp and Pratt did write two more Harold Shea novellas, "The Wall of Serpents" (1953) and "The Green Magician" (1954), later issued in book form as *Wall of Serpents* (1960). In the former story Shea and various associates visit the world of the Finnish *Kalevala* and in the latter they encounter the heroes of Irish mythology. Both pieces seem somewhat tired by comparison with the *Unknown* stories, and there is evidence of a certain carelessness in composition in the fact that one character is mislaid between episodes. Between 1950 and 1954 de Camp and Pratt also produced a series of short anecdotal fantasies—tall tales with a supernatural slant. The early ones were collected in *Tales from Gavagan's Bar* (1953). These easy, relaxed narratives are good examples of their kind and are more successful than de Camp's recent series of stories of a similar stripe, collected in *The Purple Pterodactyls* (1980). In the postwar decade, however, both writers did better work on their own than in collaboration.

Pratt wrote prolifically for *Startling Stories* and *Thrilling Wonder Stories* between 1951 and 1954, producing several notable science fiction novellas. These include two transfigurations of stories from Greek mythology: "The Wanderer's Return" (1951) is a version of the *Odyssey* and "The Conditioned Captain" (1953; reprinted that year in book form as *The Undying Fire*) is the story of Jason.

But his two most considerable works were published outside the magazines. *The Well of the Unicorn* (1948), originally issued under the pseudonym George U. Fletcher, was Pratt's first attempt to write a serious novel. It contrasts strongly in its technique with the slapdash carelessness of his science fiction potboilers, having the same painstaking quality as his best nonfiction. It is set in an imaginary realm partly derived from Lord Dunsany's play *King Argimenes and the Unknown Warrior* (1911), though very much elaborated. It is the story of Airar Alvarson, the son of a dispossessed landowner, who joins a revolt against the militaristic Vulkings who have occupied his homeland and are ambitious to rule the whole empire of which it is a part. He has some small skill in magic, but it is his intelligence as a leader of soldiers in battle that helps him to make a major contribution to his cause. At first everything goes badly and he spends much time running away or in hiding, in company with various ill-assorted allies. He loves and loses one woman, is loved by and rejected by a second, and finally loves and wins a princess of the empire. He is never quite convincing as a leader or as a lover, but the book is only part Bildungsroman; it is also a conscientious attempt to describe an imaginary world in detail and to bring an unaccustomed realism to the writing of heroic fantasy. There are excursions into political philosophy as Airar tries to identify what is wrong with Vulking rule and what kind of system ought to replace it, but they are tentative. The role played by magic is subdued, stifled by the hard-bitten realism.

The mythical Well of the Unicorn, whose waters are supposed to cleanse the soul of violent impulses, is an enigmatic and rather unconvincing element in the background.

The Well of the Unicorn is a failure, but only because it aspires to such a high standard. It tries to do so much and falters, but it does serve to demonstrate that there is more potential in the heroic fantasy genre than most writers look for or try to exploit. Pratt tried again in *The Blue Star*, originally published in a volume called *Witches Three* (1952), one of a series of three-story collections that Pratt was editing for Twayne Publishers.

The Blue Star is set on another world, similar to our own in all respects save that magic works there. Magic is primarily the prerogative of female witches, but their power can be transferred in part to their lovers, along with emblems called Blue Stars. Rodvard Bergelin, the hero of the novel, seduces a witch named Lalette in order to take possession of her Blue Star so he might use it in the service of a revolutionary movement to which he belongs. The star is a rare prize, because witchery has almost been hounded out of existence by a jealous church. The political order against which Rodvard conspires is a medieval empire, but the principles for which he is fighting are not clear even to him. He goes to court to use his Blue Star for the cause, but circumstances quickly lead him into danger and force him to flee. Lalette, left behind, has also been forced to escape from her native land. They make their separate ways to Mancherei, a country dominated by a heretical cult that has established a curious kind of Catharist communism. Both find the demands of the new state oppressively threatening, and after an uneasy reunion are forced to escape again. Their reunion is not without bitterness on account of past betrayals, but they love one another enough to try to make some kind of life together.

As in *The Well of the Unicorn*, magic plays a subdued role in *The Blue Star*, but with better reason. Political philosophy is much more to the fore, and the hero's painful sentimental education is described in loving detail. It is rather a dour novel, but it is more fluently written than its predecessor and more intricate in its plot. It is one of the best heroic fantasies of its period.

These two novels demonstrate the extent to which de Camp and Pratt had developed in different directions since their early days. De Camp always remained committed to the proposition that fiction should be pure entertainment and that even when it was not actually comic it should be lighthearted and fast-moving. His own heroic fantasy novel of the early 1950's is anything but dour: *The Tritonian Ring* (1951; in book form with three short stories, 1953) is a pure adventure story in which Prince Vakar of Lorsk has to venture forth in search of a magic talisman that even the gods fear, in the hope of saving his homeland from invasion. In the end, having survived many dangers, he finds the talisman — a fragment of an iron meteorite that holds the potential of ending the Bronze Age and banishing supernatural power from the world. It is an eminently readable story, but by comparison with Pratt's heroic fantasies it is simply playing with stereotypes. De Camp set several shorter stories in the same world as *The Tritonian Ring*, the best of which is "The Eye of Tandyla" (1951).

Neither Pratt nor de Camp had much success with their fantasy writing in the early 1950's. Their books were issued by specialty publishers and made little money. (Presumably Pratt could not persuade anyone to release *The Blue Star* as an individual novel. Apart from being serious it also contained a lot of sex, some of it perverse, which would have been considered a risky undertaking.) It is not altogether surprising that both writers virtually abandoned fantasy in 1954, devoting their efforts mainly to nonfiction. Pratt returned to popular history and was just achieving some notable success in this area when he was struck down by cancer of the liver. He died on 10 June 1956 and did not see the renaissance of heroic fantasy in the late 1960's that brought all his own books back into print, including the collaborations with de Camp.

De Camp was more fortunate than his friend, and was able to exploit the new boom to the fullest. He helped to begin it by editing a series of excellent paperback anthologies of heroic fantasy and figured prominently in the line of Ballantine Adult Fantasy paperbacks edited by Lin Carter. Together with Carter he became heavily involved in the spectacular posthumous career of Robert E. Howard, whose pi-oneering sword-and-sorcery hero Conan became the focal point of a cottage industry.

In 1955 de Camp had completed or adapted four unpublished Howard manuscripts for the collection *Tales of Conan*, and in 1957 he revised Björn Nyberg's Conan story "Conan the Victorious," later expanded as *The Return of Conan* (subsequently retitled *Conan the Avenger*). When the series was reedited for publication as a long series of paperbacks de Camp and Carter began completing other fragments or adapting non-Conan stories left behind by Howard at his death in 1936. After this material ran out they collaborated to produce new stories and novels. Later other writers got into the act too.

De Camp returned to writing heroic fantasy on his own account with *The Goblin Tower* (1968), the first of a series featuring Jorian of Xylar, who accepts magical aid in order to escape ritual beheading when his term as king comes to an end. Sequels to this novel are *The Clocks of Iraz* (1971) and *The Unbeheaded King* (1980); *The Fallible Fiend* (1973) is set in the same milieu. The world of these novels is analogous to the Mediterranean in the Hellenistic period. De Camp draws upon his interest in ancient technology, especially in the second volume. Jorian is a cross between the standardized sword-and-sorcery hero and the clever but flawed characters he and Pratt favored (Pratt always had a strong aversion to mighty-thewed barbarians).

As usual, the plots of these novels are simple fight-for-survival and quest stories, but they never flag and they are written with care and flair. Although they do not reach the standard set by Fritz Leiber's stories of Fafhrd and the Gray Mouser, they combine wit and adventure in an enterprising fashion. *The Fallible Fiend* is more offbeat than de Camp's other ventures in the genre; its protagonist is a demon named Zdim who is trapped into servitude to the wizard Dr. Maldivius. He is perhaps the only sword-and-sorcery hero who regularly devours people. Still, he remains likable as he provides a suitably ironic commentary on human affairs from the demonic standpoint.

As well as writing fantasy, de Camp began to write a good deal about it. He published articles in the amateur magazine *Amra*, some of which were collected in *The Conan Reader* (1968). Later he became Howard's biographer in *The Miscast Barbarian* (1975), which followed his long and scrupulously detailed biography of H. P. Lovecraft, *Lovecraft* (1975). Another small volume of essays was issued as *Blond Barbarians and Noble Savages* (1975), but of greater significance is a series of pieces written for *Fantastic* in the early 1970's that was published in book form as *Literary Swordsmen and Sorcerers* (1976). This is a light and informal survey of the whole field of heroic fantasy and is perhaps the best introduction for the interested reader.

It is probable that both de Camp and Pratt were capable of producing much stronger works of fantastic fiction than they ever did. They were both men of great intelligence, armed with useful stocks of knowledge about ancient history and mythology. They were both well read in fantasy fiction, and in their nonfiction they demonstrated themselves to be literary craftsmen of no mean ability. De Camp did use his talents to great advantage in writing historical fiction—*The Bronze God of Rhodes* (1960) and *The Dragon of the Ishtar Gate* (1961) are classics of their kind—but in his fantasy he usually seems to be pedaling in a lower gear or just coasting. Pratt certainly tried to write fantasy novels as good as any that had previously been done, but became discouraged before he had quite found the appropriate idiom. Their best work is their most relaxed, written when they were entertaining themselves in extravagant fashion. *The Incomplete Enchanter* is perhaps the archetypal *Unknown* product, embodying the elusive esprit of that excellent magazine.

Even had he survived, Pratt might have been too old to seize the opportunities offered by the fantasy boom of the last fifteen years, but he would surely have tried. It is possible that he might have persuaded his collaborator to do a little more with his own fiction. In the article on Pratt in *Literary Swordsmen and Sorcerers* de Camp disapproves of *The Blue Star* on the grounds that the leading characters are too unheroic and that they achieve too little, but this is perhaps a slight blind spot of de Camp's; he has always considered it unprofessional for writers of popular fiction to stray too far from stereotypes. It is possible that Pratt, if he had lived longer, might have been able to persuade his friend that commercial common sense is not the only vir-

tue to be applauded in popular fiction. But at his own chosen level de Camp is certainly to be respected as a writer, and in their earlier days together the two collaborators did find a certain synergistic magic of their own.

Selected Bibliography

WORKS OF L. SPRAGUE DE CAMP AND FLETCHER PRATT

The Incomplete Enchanter. New York: Holt, 1941. London: Remploy, 1974.

The Land of Unreason. New York: Holt, 1942. London: T. Stacey, 1972.

The Carnelian Cube. New York: Gnome Press, 1948.

The Castle of Iron. New York: Gnome Press, 1950. London: Remploy, 1974.

Tales from Gavagan's Bar. New York: Twayne, 1953. Augmented edition, Philadelphia: Owlswick Press, 1968.

Wall of Serpents. New York: Avalon, 1960.

FICTION OF L. SPRAGUE DE CAMP

Lest Darkness Fall. New York: Holt, 1941. London: Heinemann, 1955.

The Wheels of If and Other Science Fiction. Chicago: Shasta, 1948.

The Undesired Princess. Los Angeles: F.P.C.I., 1951.

The Tritonian Ring and Other Pusadian Tales. New York: Twayne, 1953. London: Sphere, 1978.

Solomon's Stone. New York: Avalon, 1957.

The Goblin Tower. New York: Pyramid, 1968. London: Sphere, 1979.

The Reluctant Shaman and Other Fantastic Tales. New York: Pyramid, 1970.

The Clocks of Iraz. New York: Pyramid, 1971.

The Fallible Fiend. New York: Pyramid, 1973. London: Remploy, 1974.

The Great Fetish. Garden City, N.Y.: Doubleday, 1978.

The Purple Pterodactyls. Huntington Wood, Mich.: Phantasia Press, 1979.

The Unbeheaded King. New York: Del Rey, 1980.

NONFICTION OF L. SPRAGUE DE CAMP

The Conan Reader. Baltimore: Mirage Press, 1968. (As editor and contributor.)

L. SPRAGUE DE CAMP AND FLETCHER PRATT

Blond Barbarians and Noble Savages. Baltimore: T-K Graphics, 1975.

The Miscast Barbarian: A Biography of Robert E. Howard. Saddle River, N.J.: Gerry de la Ree, 1975.

Literary Swordsmen and Sorcerers: The Makers of Heroic Fantasy. Sauk City, Wis.: Arkham House, 1976.

Dark Valley Destiny: The Life of Robert E. Howard. New York: Bluejay Books, 1983. (With Catherine Crook de Camp and Jane Whittington Griffin.)

WORKS OF FLETCHER PRATT

The Well of the Unicorn, as by George U. Fletcher. New York: William Sloane, 1948. London: Futura, 1977.

The Blue Star. In *Witches Three.* New York: Twayne, 1952.

—BRIAN M. STABLEFORD

FRITZ LEIBER

1910–

FRITZ REUTER LEIBER, JR., was born on 24 December 1910, the son of a Shakespearean actor who also appeared in a number of films. He graduated from the University of Chicago in 1932, having taken courses in biology, psychology, and philosophy. His long series of stories about Fafhrd and the Gray Mouser has established him as the leading American writer of sword-and-sorcery stories, but he has also written a good deal of first-rate supernatural fiction and some excellent science fiction. His stylish artistry and prolific imagination combine to make him one of the best modern writers of fantastic short stories, and though his ventures into novel-length fiction have been relatively infrequent, at least three of his novels may be counted classics of their respective genres. He has won six Hugo awards, three Nebulas, three World Fantasy Association awards, a Grand Master of Fantasy award, and a Mrs. Ann Radcliffe award. Although his career has been punctuated by several dry periods, he has shown no loss of ability over the years.

Leiber began to write in the mid-1930's. He shared with his wife, Jonquil Stevens, a strong interest in weird and supernatural fiction, and he was further motivated to try his hand at such fiction by his friendship with Harry Otto Fischer. He and Fischer provided an audience for one another, and it was out of their experiments with sword-and-sorcery fiction that the characters of Fafhrd and the Gray Mouser were born. Fischer invented the characters and both men used them for a while, though the

only substantial project to be completed at this stage was Leiber's novella "Adept's Gambit," which failed to sell in the thirties and eventually appeared in his first collection of stories, *Night's Black Agents* (1947).

The first story that Leiber did sell was the Fafhrd and Gray Mouser story "Two Sought Adventure," which appeared in *Unknown* in 1939. Leiber's fiction during these early years was mostly slanted toward *Weird Tales*, which published several of his short supernatural tales, but it was *Unknown*'s editor, John W. Campbell, Jr., who gave Leiber the encouragement that he needed. Despite Campbell's support, though, Leiber could not write quickly enough to make a good living as a pulp writer, and when *Unknown* closed in 1943 Leiber relegated his writing to his spare time. He went to work for Douglas Aircraft, and later became assistant editor of *Science Digest*, where he remained for twelve years.

Apart from the early sword-and-sorcery stories, *Unknown* published several important supernatural stories by Leiber during this early phase of his career. Leiber delighted in devising hauntings and supernatural creatures specifically adapted to contemporary urban environments. The settings of his stories are city landscapes—tenements, factories, lighted streets—and Leiber proved that such settings could contain supernatural phenomena just as aptly and convincingly as the ancient mansions and stagnant swamps that were still conventional in the weird fiction of the day. In his brilliant early story

"Smoke Ghost" (1941) he provided a prospectus for this kind of fiction:

> Have you ever thought what a ghost of our times would look like, Miss Millick? Just picture it. A smoky composite face with the hungry anxiety of the unemployed, the neurotic restlessness of the person without purpose, the jerky tension of the high-pressure metropolitan worker, the uneasy resentment of the striker, the callous opportunism of the scab, the aggressive whine of the panhandler, the inhibited terror of the bombed civilian, and a thousand other twisted emotional patterns. Each one overlying and yet blending with the other, like a pile of semi-transparent masks?

This method of populating characteristic twentieth-century environments with appropriate monsters and specters was to help Leiber produce some of his best fantasy stories throughout his career. It was most impressively displayed during this early period in his first novel, *Conjure Wife*, published in *Unknown* in 1943 and reprinted in book form in 1953. *Conjure Wife* describes the practice of modern-day witchcraft, not as a bizarre survival from some bygone era but as a matter of routine, used by faculty wives at a small American university to promote their husbands' careers. The implication of the story is that only men have become rationalists, abandoning magic for science; women have remained mystics, preserving their traditions in secret. The hero of the story, an anthropologist, discovers his wife's secret by accident, and insists on liberating her from the grip of superstition. Immediately he finds himself prey to nightmares as the jealous wives of his faculty rivals realize that he is unprotected and vulnerable to their malevolence. In the end, he himself is driven by desperation to practice magic in order to save his wife from a fate worse than conventional fates worse than death. The story is a masterpiece of suspense, written with a compelling authority that wavers only in the final chapters.

After the demise of *Unknown* Leiber invested more effort in science fiction, and in the early forties sold two novels and several shorter pieces to Campbell's *Astounding*. His output dwindled in the later forties, though, and apart from *Night's Black Agents*, an Arkham House collection with a good deal of original material, he published only a few relatively trivial horror stories. The best of these was "The Girl with the Hungry Eyes," a story about advertising imagery and supernatural glamour, which appeared in 1949.

This first lean spell ended in 1950, when Leiber suddenly began publishing on a prolific scale in various pulp magazines. Most of the stories were science fiction, but they included one very fine fantasy story published in abridged form in *Fantastic Adventures* as "You're All Alone." The full-length version, with some slightly pornographic sex scenes added to it by an editor, appeared in an obscure paperback edition as *The Sinful Ones* (1953). The volume also included a nonfantasy novel by David Williams, *Bulls, Blood, and Passion*. This full-length version was revised by Leiber for a new edition in 1980.

The story properly belongs to Leiber's early phase; the first chapters were written for *Unknown* before he learned that the magazine was to close. "You're All Alone" is based on the premise that most of the people in the world are robots caught in a deterministic web, acting out a script. The hero of the story is one of the few "real" people who can step outside his "role" and act freely, without being attended to by the robots. Other people have this freedom, too, but many have used their opportunities in a malevolent fashion, and they pose a deadly threat to the hero and to the real woman with whom he falls in love. The story is dramatically powerful, combining an appealing wish-fulfillment fantasy with a gripping story of menace. Although the abridged version has been reprinted several times, the full-length version is very much better.

During the early fifties Leiber was encouraged by H. L. Gold, the editor of *Galaxy*, much as he had earlier been taken up by Campbell. For this reason Leiber's main effort was directed toward science fiction, though he did produce a couple of sword-and-sorcery stories and some strange surreal fantasies for the *Magazine of Fantasy and Science Fiction*. Despite the interruption of a three-year dry spell in the middle years of the decade, he produced a good deal of excellent fiction, culminating in the production of his Hugo-winning novel *The Big Time* (1958). It is about the "Change War," a war fought across the ages by the Spiders and the Snakes, whose armies are human mercenaries and whose battles are attempts to alter events in history to their own advantage.

There was an important change of direction in Leiber's career in 1959, by which time Gold had become less enthusiastic about his work. He was taken up instead by Cele Goldsmith, the recently appointed editor of *Fantastic*, who was in the process of overhauling the image of that magazine and improving it greatly. She built a special issue of the magazine around Leiber's latest sword-and-sorcery story, "Lean Times in Lankhmar," filling it with stories that showed the versatility of the author. Leiber became a regular contributor to *Fantastic*, publishing stories of Fafhrd and the Gray Mouser and bizarre horror-fantasies like "Hatchery of Dreams" (1961) and "Dr. Adam's Garden of Evil" (1963).

Apart from the stories of Fafhrd and the Gray Mouser that he wrote for *Fantastic*, the best fantasy stories Leiber produced during the early 1960's were "The Black Gondolier" (1964), about the haunting of the Grand Canal in the oil town of Venice, California, and "Four Ghosts in Hamlet" (1965), one of several stories inspired by his love for the theater.

Another brief dry spell followed the virtual demise of *Fantastic*, which became a reprint magazine in 1965. He began publishing again, near the end of 1967, quickly producing "Gonna Roll the Bones," a phantasmagoric story of gambling with the devil that appeared in Harlan Ellison's anthology *Dangerous Visions* and won Leiber the first of several awards for shorter fiction. He won another in 1969 for his science fiction story "Ship of Shadows," and also collected both the Hugo and the Nebula for his 1970 story about the first meeting of Fafhrd and the Gray Mouser, "Ill Met in Lankhmar." As with many of the stories he wrote in the years following the death of his wife in September 1969 the last is a harrowing and tragic story. Leiber would probably have written much less in these years had it not been for the fact that Ace Books was issuing a series assembling all the stories of Fafhrd and the Gray Mouser into a coherent group, and extra material was needed to fill in gaps.

Since 1974, Leiber's productivity has been steady, but far from prolific. What it has lacked in quantity,

though, it has made up in quality. Among his fantasy short stories have been "Midnight by the Morphy Watch" (1974), one of several excellent stories about chess; the award-winning "Belsen Express" (1975), perhaps the most chilling of all his stories of contemporary hauntings; and "The Button Molder" (1979), an eerily intimate, quasi-autobiographical story. In the same period Leiber produced two fantasy novels—an adventure of Fafhrd and the Gray Mouser published initially in two parts as "The Frost Monstreme" (1976) and "Rime Isle" (1977); and *Our Lady of Darkness* (1977), which combines the method of "Smoke Ghost" with the curious intimacy of "The Button Molder" and adds a little flavoring of Lovecraftian influence.

Leiber's stories are highly various, and they reveal him to be one of the most versatile fantasists. He is one of the few modern writers to be intimately familiar with the whole tradition of fantasy writing, and although he has never been influenced by other writers in the trivial sense of wanting to imitate their work (a kind of influence that is the curse of contemporary American fantasy fiction), his familiarity with the motifs and methods of the best in supernatural fiction has helped to furnish his own imagination and has assisted him to enrich the tradition with his own contributions. His most considerable contribution to contemporary fantasy, however, is undoubtedly to be found in his sword-and-sorcery tales. The stories of Fafhrd and the Gray Mouser span the entirety of his career, from the time before his first sale to his most recent work; it is in these stories that his development as a writer can be tracked, and they display most of his virtues as a storyteller.

The bibliography of the series is complicated, but almost all the stories are now collected into a series of six volumes. In the order of the series' internal chronology, these are: *Swords and Deviltry* (1970), *Swords Against Death* (1970; this includes seven stories from an earlier collection, *Two Sought Adventure*, 1957), *Swords in the Mist* (1968), *Swords Against Wizardry* (1968), *The Swords of Lankhmar* (1968), and *Swords and Ice Magic* (1977).

Leiber's initial interest in this kind of fiction was partly inspired by the fact that in the early 1950's *Weird Tales* regularly featured Robert E. Howard's tales of Conan the Barbarian and derivative stories by several other writers—most notably C. L. Moore. Leiber and Fischer, however, adopted a very different tone and manner when they began to write of Fafhrd and the Gray Mouser. They knew more about ancient mythologies and cared more about matters of style.

The first completed story of the two heroes, "Adept's Gambit," is a deliberately baroque tale, spiced with ironic wit; it is an exercise in pure grotesquerie as well as a tale of high adventure. Fischer had already identified the characters with the imaginary city of Lankhmar, but had not specified its location; thus "Adept's Gambit" takes place not in the wholly imaginary world of Nehwon, where all the other stories are set, but in our world, beginning in ancient Tyre at the time of the Seleucid Empire. Fafhrd finds himself cursed, so that whenever he makes love to a woman she turns into a pig. He and his friend set off to search for the adept of the title, in order to make him remove the curse. But most of the story is an account of the careers of the adept and his enthralled sister, which tends to draw the narrative out of shape; this may have been the reason *Weird Tales* rejected it in 1935.

The five stories that Leiber sold to *Unknown* are rather more conventional than "Adept's Gambit," featuring a series of encounters between the heroes and various magical entrapments. There is more emphasis on action and suspense, but the stories are nevertheless distinctive. "The Bleak Shore" (1940), in which the heroes are summoned by a personification of death to meet their fate, has a quasi-symbolic character that foreshadows the later surreal fantasies Leiber incorporated into the series. Although Leiber kept a tight rein on his sense of irony and his love of the grotesque in these early pulp stories, they often have a somber atmosphere and a delicately nightmarish quality that are typical of the author. These show up particularly well in one of the two stories that Leiber added in the early 1950's: "Dark Vengeance" (1951; retitled "Claws from the Night" in the book versions).

"Lean Times in Lankhmar," the story that led off the all-Leiber issue of *Fantastic* in 1959, offered a dramatic change of pace. This is a magnificently exuberant tale, gaudy and humorous. Fafhrd becomes,

for a while, a follower of the minor god Issek the Jug, leading a revival of his cult and allowing its high priest to make rapid progress toward the better end of the Street of the Gods. Inevitably, he comes into conflict with the Gray Mouser, who has taken a job with a gang running a protection racket for the "benefit" of the more prosperous religions on the street. This is the most lighthearted story in the series, and perhaps the best—Leiber is clearly enjoying himself hugely in filling in all the local color pertaining to Nehwon's most decadent city.

Leiber's next series story for *Fantastic* was the relatively trivial "When the Sea King's Away" (1960), but this was soon followed by the impressive novella "Scylla's Daughter" (1961), developed from a fragment left over from the 1930's. Fafhrd and the Mouser are hired as guards to defend a fleet of grain ships against sabotage. Also aboard ship are Hisvet, the daughter of a grain merchant, and her bond servant Frix. The sailors become convinced that Hisvet and her troop of performing rats are the enemy, but Fafhrd and the Mouser (who entertain the ambition of seducing the two women) will not believe it—to their eventual cost. The situation is further complicated by the appearance of a two-headed sea serpent and an otherworldly visitor who is trying to collect it for his menagerie. More by luck than by judgment the heroes save the fleet.

Leiber took up the story again when he extended the novella into the full-length novel *The Swords of Lankhmar*. Here the rats of Lankhmar Below and their human allies wage war for control of the city. The Mouser makes himself tiny in order to follow Hisvet into the underworld, while Fafhrd tries to rouse other forces to come to the city's aid. In the end he has to recruit the awful Gods of Lankhmar (a very different and much more sinister crew than the Gods *in* Lankhmar, whose cults occupy the Street of the Gods) and the fearful War Cats. The story moves at a furious pace, but it is the fabulous decoration of the plot with bizarre ideas and the sparkling irony of the narration that make the novel a classic of its kind.

Another novella from *Fantastic* in this period is "The Lords of Quarmall" (1964), which is rather different in tone—presumably because a substantial part of it is a fragment by Fischer. The two heroes are separately hired as bravos by the two sons of Quarmal of Quarmall, who are waging a sorcerous war against one another. The heroes lose interest when they realize how sadistic their employers are, but have difficulty in escaping from the deteriorating situation with their own skins intact.

"The Lords of Quarmall" is starker and more horrific than most of Leiber's solo efforts in this period, but it matches up well with the "The Unholy Grail" (1962), originally a nonseries story that was rewritten to make it an early episode in the career of the Gray Mouser (here merely an apprentice wizard named Mouse). This is a fierce tale of supernatural vengeance with no leavening of humor. There is a certain propriety in the fact that when Leiber came to write two companion pieces, one about Fafhrd's early life and one about the first meeting of the two characters, the darker side of his imagination was very much in the ascendant because of the death of his wife.

"The Snow Women" (1970) is dominated by the icebound forest in which it is set and by the cold witchery of the matriarchs who rule Fafhrd's Snow Clan. Despite the presence of a group of traveling players who draw Fafhrd into a rejection of his heritage, the story is bleak and cynical. "Ill Met in Lankhmar" is even bleaker, explaining how the two heroes lose their loved ones because of a frightful spell unleashed by the resident sorcerer of the local Thieves' Guild. It is a powerful story, built on an undercurrent of pain and anguish. Other vignettes written in the following years, like "The Sadness of the Executioner" (1973) and "Trapped in the Shadowland" (1973), also feature brushes with death, but in a rather stylized and surreal manner.

The series regained its imaginative vigor as Leiber's sense of loss eased a little, and his ironic humor became evident again in the dream story "Under the Thumbs of the Gods" (1975) and the philosophical reverie "Trapped in the Sea of Stars" (1975). Leiber was back in his stride by the time he wrote the novel compounded out of "The Frost Monstreme" and "Rime Isle" (which takes up most of the book *Swords and Ice Magic*). Here the two heroes are commissioned by two enigmatic women to buy ships, recruit crews, and sail to the aid of Rime Isle, which is under threat from the Sea Mingols and

their sorcerer Khahkht. Khahkht fails to stop them from reaching the island, but the inhabitants will not admit that they are threatened and the only allies Fafhrd and the Mouser can find are two alien gods who have come to Nehwon in search of new worshipers. These gods, strangely like the two heroes in some ways, are Odin and Loki, and they eventually prove to be as much of a menace to Rime Isle and the heroes as the Sea Mingols. Fafhrd and the Mouser win, but their victory is purchased dearly; Fafhrd loses one of his hands, which testifies to the fact that Leiber had not altogether banished his feelings of pain. (Leiber always tended to identify himself with the tall barbarian Fafhrd rather than with the small and cunning Mouser, who was Fischer's alter ego.)

It is because Leiber has always tended to project himself into his work in this way that he is such an unusually effective writer. He is frequently a playful writer, juggling ideas for the sheer pleasure of it, but he possesses the ability to conjure up bizarre situations with a brilliant vividness and realism. Like a good Method actor he can put himself into the position of his characters, conjuring up the fantastic worlds they inhabit and feeling his way around them as though they were solid. This personal quality in his work has come more and more to the fore as his career has advanced — *Our Lady of Darkness* almost invites consideration as a roman à clef. (The hero of the novel, a pulp writer named Franz Westen, lives in an apartment building in San Francisco under circumstances very similar to those under which Leiber was living during 1976. The plot is, of course, imaginary, involving paramental entities — city-demons whose occult secrets are revealed in a modern grimoire and in a journal supposedly written by Clark Ashton Smith — that encroach upon the hero's life and threaten to destroy him, although it would not be too difficult to imagine them as symbolizations.)

Probably no ability can serve a writer of supernatural ficiton as well as the gift of becoming a haunted man — using the power of imagination to supernaturalize his own environments and to solidify the fragile tissue of fanciful dreamworlds. Leiber has capitalized on this talent as well as anyone, adding to it his own species of mordant wit. Although his keen intelligence makes him a good science fiction writer in any vein, he has benefited more than most writers nurtured in the Campbell school from the relaxation of convention that allowed surrealism to invade science fiction in the 1960's. He is at his best when dealing with an enchanted world in which the domestic and the fantastic are so close together that the one begins to permeate the other.

Leiber is also at his best when dealing with ordinary characters whose weaknesses are more obvious than their strengths. One of the great virtues of his heroic fantasy is that he succeeds where the vast majority of writers in the genre fail: he gives his heroes a true human dimension. In a brief introduction to *The Swords of Lankhmar* he observes that Fafhrd and the Mouser are "rogues through and through" and that "they drink, they feast, they wench, they brawl, they steal, they gamble, and surely they hire out their swords to powers that are only a shade better, if that, than the villains." Unlike the characters in much heroic fantasy, Fafhrd and the Mouser stand in no particular relationship to the ultimate powers of good and evil—and, indeed, in Nehwon as in our world there is no evidence of such a moral order. Fafhrd and the Mouser are not evil, but they are not particularly scrupulous, either, and their main priorities are survival and pleasure. These kinds of characters are the men Leiber seems to admire most: survivors who can endure the persecutions of ill fortune and hostile forces, sometimes exuberantly and sometimes with difficulty. He is unfailingly sympathetic to characters victimized by circumstance, allows them their black moods as well as their celebrations, and seduces the reader into the same concern for them that he has.

Leiber has not produced as much as most of the writers who came under Campbell's wing at about the same time, and he certainly struggled harder than many to establish himself as a writer. The sheer variety of his work and the fact that he was always testing the limits of what his various editors would permit has made it difficult for him to build up a following of loyal fans. On the other hand, though, his very isolation may have helped to maintain the power and intensity of his best works. He has certainly never allowed himself to lapse into the production of merely routine work. He has had his failures, but he has never written a pure potboiler. The cream of his supernatural stories will certainly endure: the best of them will stand as the classic stories of urban hauntings. His sword-and-sorcery stories will also stand as evidence of what really can be achieved within what has unfortunately become one of the most limited and convention-bound of all modern literary genres.

Selected Bibliography

WORKS OF FRITZ LEIBER

Night's Black Agents. Sauk City, Wis.: Arkham House, 1947. London: Neville Spearman, 1975.

Conjure Wife. New York: Twayne, 1953. Harmondsworth, England: Penguin, 1969.

The Sinful Ones. New York: Universal Giant, 1953. Revised edition, New York: Pocket Books, 1980.

Shadows with Eyes. New York: Ballantine, 1962.

Swords Against Wizardry. New York: Ace, 1968. London: Prior, 1977.

Swords in the Mist. New York: Ace, 1968. London: Prior, 1977.

The Swords of Lankhmar. New York: Ace, 1968. London: Hart-Davis, 1969.

Night Monsters. New York: Ace, 1969. Expanded version, London: Gollancz, 1974.

Swords Against Death. New York: Ace, 1970. London: New English Library, 1972.

Swords and Deviltry. New York: Ace, 1970. London: New English Library, 1971.

You're All Alone. New York: Ace, 1972.

The Best of Fritz Leiber. London: Sphere, 1974. Garden City, N.Y.: Doubleday, 1974. (The story contents of both volumes are the same, but the secondary material is different.)

The Book of Fritz Leiber. New York: DAW, 1974.

The Second Book of Fritz Leiber. New York: DAW, 1975.

Our Lady of Darkness. New York: Berkley/Putnam, 1977. London: Millington, 1978.

Swords and Ice Magic. New York: Ace, 1977. London: Prior, 1977.

Heroes and Horrors. Chapel Hill, N.C.: Whispers Press, 1978.

CRITICAL, BIOGRAPHICAL, AND BIBLIOGRAPHICAL STUDIES

Leiber, Fritz. "Fafhrd and Me." *Amra*, October 1963. Reprinted in *The Second Book of Fritz Leiber*, 92–114.
————. "The Profession of Science Fiction, XII: Mysterious Islands." *Foundation*, 11–12 (March 1977): 29–38.

Morgan, Chris. *Fritz Leiber: A Bibliography 1934–1979*. Birmingham, England: Morgenstern, 1979.
Stableford, Brian M. "Fritz Leiber." In *Science Fiction Writers*. New York: Scribner, 1982.

—BRIAN M. STABLEFORD

THEODORE STURGEON

1918-

THEODORE STURGEON WAS born Edward Hamilton Waldo in New York City on 26 February 1918. When his mother married for a second time he changed his surname to his stepfather's. He had hopes of becoming a gymnast but these were destroyed by a bad attack of rheumatic fever when he was fifteen. After graduating from high school he went to sea for three years; during this period he began selling short stories to newspapers, and eventually moved on to the pulp magazines edited by John W. Campbell, Jr., *Astounding Science-Fiction* and *Unknown.* His first story aimed at these markets, "Helix the Cat," failed to sell then but eventually appeared in the Campbell memorial anthology *Astounding* (1973), edited by Harry Harrison. When "A God in a Garden" did sell to *Unknown* in 1939 Sturgeon decided to forsake the sea in order to make a living writing. He was a regular contributor to Campbell's magazines until World War II broke out, but then abandoned his writing career for some years, working at various jobs outside the United States.

Sturgeon was encouraged to begin writing again by Campbell in 1946, and published prolifically for some fifteen years in all the leading science fiction and fantasy magazines. The great majority of the works on which his reputation now rests were published in this period. Although he enjoyed another short burst of creativity in the years 1969 to 1971, he never really got going again and published only a handful of works in the next decade.

The stories that Sturgeon produced in the early phase of his career are slick and clever by the relatively undemanding standard of the pulp magazines of the day, but most of them are trivial. Although his science fiction story "Microcosmic God" (1941) is fondly remembered, the one real strength in his work during this initial phase was a certain dexterity with touches of pure horror. This allowed him to enliven otherwise unremarkable stories like "Shottle Bop" (1941) and "The Hag Seleen" (1942; revised from an original version by James H. Beard), and helped him to produce the remarkable "It" (1940), the ultimate monster story, in which a little girl falls prey to a thing that is the very essence of noisomeness. Sturgeon was to retain throughout his career a very keen sense of the horrible, which he combined with a frank and intimate style of character presentation that makes the gruesome aspects of his stories perceptively vivid. At his best he is an affectively powerful writer who makes the reader feel with and for his characters, and thus care when the characters are exposed to frightful circumstances. As in "It," he frequently uses children as characters in his pure horror stories.

The most disturbing of all the horror stories Sturgeon wrote during this period was "Bianca's Hands," but it proved to be too strong to find a market. It is an intense story of an obsession that ultimately proves fatal, of a man who falls in love with the hands of an idiot girl. The consummation of this strange passion is his death by strangulation, after which the beautiful hands wither away (perhaps having never existed except in the protagonist's mind). The story eventually won a competition run by the British magazine *Argosy*, where it was published in 1947. "Bianca's Hands" shares the same strengths as "It," intimate characterization and affective writing, but the story has an extra dimension as an exercise in abnormal psychology.

The work of Sturgeon's second period includes a number of remarkable stories that feature similar studies of obsession. In all of them Sturgeon gives the impression that he understands perfectly what it is to be obsessed. He is not always sympathetic to the curious forces that drive his characters, but we feel that he appreciates the strength and demonic pressure of such forces. Like F. Scott Fitzgerald, Sturgeon is a connoisseur of "taking things hard," and much of his writing is a virtual celebration of the many ways in which people can be cruelly mistreated by fate. At his most extreme, he can be a very nasty-minded writer indeed.

The one story that Sturgeon wrote during the war was the science fiction suspense tale "Killdozer!" (1944), in which a giant bulldozer is infested by a malign and homicidal alien intelligence. The stories that he wrote for Campbell after his return to the United States were mostly gentler, even sentimental, although he produced some striking alarmist fantasies about the dangers of atomic power and atomic war. *Unknown* no longer existed, and he began to slant his fantasy stories toward *Weird Tales*. His earliest pieces for that magazine all include people who are savagely victimized by outside forces. One work—"Fluffy" (1947)—retains something of the flip irony of his *Unknown* stories, but the others are fearful tales of possession: "Cellmate" (1947), "The Professor's Teddy Bear" (1948), and "The Perfect Host" (1948) all feature human beings placed under awful compulsions by cruel and homicidal things whose nature usually is not made clear. The novella "One Foot and the Grave" (1949) is not dissimilar, although it is concerned with two warring agencies whose supernatural battle draws in various innocent bystanders, afflicting the hero and heroine with diabolical stigmata. Sturgeon refuses to characterize these two agencies as good and evil, although he promises that the outcome of the contest

will be beneficial for man. One of the entities, which has been imprisoned but is now set free, represents the power of human will; now it will complement rather than oppose the other force, which is the power of human reason.

A similar pattern of underlying ideas recurs in "Excalibur and the Atom" (1951), a novella published in *Fantastic Adventures*, which attempts to combine the hard-boiled detective story with Arthurian fantasy. Again, there are two contending agencies that are not to be reckoned as good and evil; one is a force encouraging construction, the other destruction. It is the destructive force that has been confined, and this has made people too ready to cling to their edifices of belief and too determined to resist change. Hostility to the crystallization and stultification of ideas and beliefs is a constant feature of Sturgeon's work; in more recent pieces he states it explicitly over and over again.

Fantastic Adventures replaced *Weird Tales* as the principal market for Sturgeon's fantasy after the publication there of his first novel, *The Dreaming Jewels*, in 1950. As with much of Sturgeon's work this is a story on the borderline between science fiction and fantasy. Sturgeon was never particularly interested in science or in the conventional hardware of science fiction, but he was equally uninterested in the stereotyped repertoire of *Weird Tales* horror stories: ghosts, premonitory dreams, ancient curses, and pallid vampires. Sometimes the agents engaged in fantastic actions in his stories are described as alien beings, sometimes as human beings with strange powers of the mind, and sometimes simply as "things" beyond our comprehension. However, the roles they play are similar no matter how they are characterized.

In *The Dreaming Jewels* a child brutalized by his adoptive father runs away to find shelter in the freak show that is part of a carnival run by the obsessive misanthrope Pierre Monêtre. Most of Monêtre's freaks are the creations of mysterious crystals whose power he is trying to understand and control. The child, too, is a creation of the jewels, but a very different one—complete where they are imperfect.

Monêtre is a truly demonic character, a paradigm of evil born of obsessive misanthropism. The fact that a science fictional jargon is used to justify the existence of the jewels is largely irrelevant to the story, since they simply provide a source of power that can be used either wrongly (as Monêtre would do, for his own selfish advantage) or rightly (generously and altruistically, as the boy hero must learn to do in order to grow to maturity).

Most of Sturgeon's stories of the 1950's share this theme: there are wellsprings of supernatural power that can be diverted into good or evil channels. The human characters are faced with stern challenges to their moral sensibilities as they try to figure out where the right channel leads, which is always toward tolerance, especially tolerance in sexual matters. This is the message of science fiction stories about ESP and other hypothetical mental powers like ". . . And My Fear Is Great" (1953) and of eccentrically delicate fantasies like "The Silken Swift" (1953), which explains what kind of young woman ought to be able to harness a unicorn.

In the majority of Sturgeon's stories the characters manage to discover the right way to use supernatural power. It is frequently difficult for them, because they are often social misfits or outcasts, but they generally learn moral discipline along with the mental discipline that allows them to make the most of the abilities that lie latent within them. The science fiction novel *More Than Human* (1953) is perhaps Sturgeon's best story of this kind, paying scrupulous attention to the responsibilities attached to superhumanity. A similar pattern of thought can be seen in the nonfantasy story "To Here and the Easel" (1954), where artistic creativity is substituted for literal superhuman powers.

At the same time, though, Sturgeon retained a keen awareness of the possibilities inherent in the abuse of power. "Talent" (1953) is a gruesome story about a spoiled little boy who has the power to make anything he wishes come true, but who comes to grief as a result of indulging in a reckless and ill-thought-out whim for the sake of a nasty impulse. Much more powerful is "A Way of Thinking" (1953), in which a man celebrated for his talent for finding unusual solutions to problems is driven into a terrible rage when his brother dies as a result of an amateur witch carelessly working magic by means of a voodoo doll. He takes his revenge not upon the would-be witch, who had no real idea that her magic

was working, but upon the doll, which permitted her thoughtlessness to be transmuted into evil. He achieves his revenge after reasoning that if a human being can be destroyed by torturing the doll, the doll might be destroyed by reversing the symbolism and the ritual. The story is all the more horrible because the reader is encouraged to regard the central character as a hero until the final revelation of what he has done.

During the latter years of Sturgeon's prolific period there were almost no markets for fantasy among the popular magazines. *Weird Tales* finally died in 1954. *Galaxy*'s fantasy companion *Beyond* lasted only ten issues. *Fantastic*, after briefly entertaining higher ambitions, was transformed into a stereotyped science fiction magazine. Sturgeon's main market during the late 1950's was *Galaxy*, and most of the magazine stories that he wrote were science fiction. None of his last three significant fantasy stories of this period was initially published in American magazines.

"The Graveyard Reader" (1958), which appeared in the British magazine *Science Fantasy*, is an unusual and delicate story that begins in a graveyard, where a man is contemplating the newly made grave in which his wife is buried. She was killed in a car crash, running away from him; his feelings are very mixed, his bitterness compounded by the fact that he never knew or understood her. In the graveyard he meets a stranger who claims to be able to read graves: to decode their strange symbolism and thereby to empathize with the dead. Intrigued by the notion that the secrets of his lost marriage are not beyond recall, the protagonist sets out to learn this peculiar natural language, intending eventually to find out all the things about his wife he never knew while she lived. It takes him a year to learn, but in that year the need to know disappears; in the end he puts a headstone on the grave inscribed with the words "Rest in Peace": a message intended not for the dead woman but for himself.

This story represents Sturgeon in his gentlest mood. It is one of the few in which the supernatural "solution" to the problem of human disconnection is discarded in favor of a polite acceptance of isolation.

"Need" (1960) is a novella originally published in

the collection *Beyond*. It is the story of a man gifted with an extraordinary empathy; he can feel the need of others as a pressure within his mind that always threatens to become unbearable. He is forced to help wherever he can, not because of innate altruism, but simply to relieve the agony inside himself. He cannot bear to be near the hospital in his hometown, and he forces drug addicts to stay away by violent threats. The protagonist of the story becomes involved with this strange character by accident, helping him in some of his desperate errands of mercy while hoping to be helped in turn. The protagonist is searching for his wife, who has left him. But he does not find things as simple as he imagines, and is told—much to his discomfort—that not only does his wife not need him, but his need for his wife is not enough to awaken more than the slightest ache in the head of the empathetic man.

"Need" is not as gentle a story as "The Graveyard Reader"—it has its raw moments—but it is similarly contemplative in focusing on what people look for and require in their relationships with one another. The supernatural element in the story is introduced to dramatize the points that are made, not to offer an artificial transcendental solution. Sturgeon has moved on from such solutions in his science fiction, too: *Venus Plus X* (1960) contrasts strongly with *More Than Human* and with a cavalier novel of salvation by acquired superhumanity, *The Cosmic Rape* (1958).

By the time "Need" was published, Sturgeon's prolific phase was dragging to a halt, but he had yet to produce his most famous fantasy novel. In the more than twenty years since it was published he has completed no others. The novel in question is *Some of Your Blood* (1961), and it is itself rather short.

Like the central section of *More Than Human*, which was originally published independently as "Baby Is Three" (1952), *Some of Your Blood* takes the form of a case study in psychoanalysis. A young soldier, having committed an assault against a superior officer, has been sent home for psychiatric treatment. Exactly why this has been done is not made clear at first. Certain vital documents are withheld so that the reader and the psychiatrist can approach the case afresh and solve the puzzle by degrees. Even

without the aid of the title it probably becomes obvious to readers at an early stage what the big secret is that the soldier is hiding. He is a vampire who has been used to slaking his strange thirst by drinking the menstrual blood of a girl and who has suffered awkward withdrawal symptoms because of his foreign posting.

Although the story is framed as though its appeal to the reader is based on the shock of this eventual revelation, there is in fact a great deal more of interest in the story. To some extent it is a strong plea for sexual tolerance, presenting an impassioned argument in favor of a brilliantly unorthodox perversion. (It hardly needs to be noted that the human imagination is faced with a difficult task in seeking to invent forms of eccentric erotic behavior that have not previously been recorded; Sturgeon's achievement in this area should not be underestimated.) More significantly, however, it is a story that aspires to make some very important points about human psychology and about the element of need in relationships. The tale has strong links with "Need," where great emphasis is placed on the sheer diversity of human needs and the manifold ways in which relationships can or must be created in order to accommodate needs.

The plight of the vampire in *Some of Your Blood* serves to emphasize the aspect of Sturgeon's work that is in one sense his main strength and in another his main weakness. He tends to see people as helpless victims of repressed cravings, driven by compulsions that circumstances forbid them to express clearly. For Sturgeon a happy ending is a meeting of individuals who can satisfy one another's cravings—with or without the aid of some kind of supernatural force. This attitude adds strength to his work because it allows him to create tension in his work as ill-shaped people struggle to find the eccentric complementary shapes into which they can lock and meld. It also adds weakness, though, because in the vast majority of cases the situations are artificial; too often the author is in the business of supplying bizarre solutions to bizarre problems. The implication that these tales can stand as metaphors for the problems of people everywhere is not altogether convincing. The rhetorical fervor of his stories makes them compelling reading, and one has to admire the sympathy and generosity of his more constructive fantasies, but when one compares these to such savage horror stories as "A Way of Thinking," one can hardly help suspect that Sturgeon is not convincing even himself.

This lack of conviction seems obvious in the stories that he wrote in the brief third phase of his career, where the artifice is blatant and no vestige of subtlety is left to cloak the moralizing. Virtually all the stories published after 1961 are either science fiction or nonfantasy, but it is worth noting that one of the most recent is a horror story as nasty-minded as anything Sturgeon ever wrote. This is "Vengeance Is" (1980), published in Kirby McCauley's anthology *Dark Forces*, in which a man is driven by anger to beg his wife to submit to two would-be rapists because he knows that they will catch a particularly dreadful venereal disease if they carry out their intention.

Sturgeon played an important role in the development of postwar American science fiction, helping to transform it into a more relevant and more interesting genre. His supernatural fiction has always seemed to be a sideline, although it is arguable that much of the "science" in his work is merely jargonized magic. He has been a remarkably effective author of horror stories, though never a particularly prolific one: "It," "Bianca's Hands," and "A Way of Thinking" are brilliant exercises in that genre and will always guarantee him some status as a fantasy writer. "The Graveyard Reader," too, will always command attention as a unique and sensitive

fantasy. He has time still to add to this list, if only he can find the imaginative energy.

Selected Bibliography

WORKS OF THEODORE STURGEON

Without Sorcery. Philadelphia: Prime Press, 1948. Abridged as *Not Without Sorcery*. New York: Ballantine, 1961. London: Futura, 1976.

The Dreaming Jewels. New York: Greenberg, 1950. London: Nova, 1955. Also titled *The Synthetic Man*. New York: Pyramid, 1957.

E Pluribus Unicorn. New York: Abelard, 1953. London: Abelard-Schuman, 1959.

Beyond. New York: Avon, 1960.

Some of Your Blood. New York: Ballantine, 1961. London: Sphere, 1967.

The Worlds of Theodore Sturgeon. New York: Ace, 1972.

Visions and Venturers. New York: Dell, 1978. London: Gollancz, 1979.

The Golden Helix. Garden City, N.Y.: Doubleday, 1979.

CRITICAL AND BIOGRAPHICAL STUDIES

Friend, Beverly. "The Sturgeon Connection." In *Voices for the Future*, edited by Thomas Clareson. Bowling Green, Ohio: Bowling Green University Popular Press, 1976.

Moskowitz, Sam. "Theodore Sturgeon." In *Seekers of Tomorrow*. Cleveland: World, 1966.

—BRIAN M. STABLEFORD

MANLY WADE WELLMAN

1903-

I

MANLY WADE WELLMAN may be the only American writer born (21 May 1903) in what is now called Angola, where his father headed a mission hospital. When Wellman was six, his family returned to the United States. He began writing fiction early and sold his first story while a junior at Wichita State University. Except for brief periods with the WPA Writers' Project and during World War II, he has always been a free-lance writer. During the Great Depression he moved to New York City, but in 1946 he relocated to Chapel Hill, where he later taught creative writing at the University of North Carolina.

A prolific author, Wellman has been able to move with facility from field to field for half a century: besides fantasy, he has written dozens of books, including more than thirty juvenile novels, science fiction, nonfiction (mostly Civil War and local histories), and mysteries. He successfully combined the last two interests in *Dead and Gone: Classic Crimes of North Carolina*, a work that won the Edgar Award of the Mystery Writers of America for best fact-crime book of 1955. He has written biographies and plays, and has even compiled a collection of Confederate songs from the Civil War, *The Rebel Songster* (1959).

So large has his output been that for discussion here his fantasy will be divided into three groups, with the first group admittedly a catchall: it includes everything from ghost stories to sword-and-sorcery tales. Its settings likewise vary widely: medieval France, Edgar Allan Poe's Philadelphia (with that author as the hero), and Civil War battlefields. The second group contains the stories labeled "occult detective"; and the third, and most recent, may be called the "Carolina fantasies," from their setting. The "miscellaneous" group includes some of his earliest as well as some of his most recent work. But the other categories have almost a chronological unity: the great majority of the occult detective stories were written between 1938 and 1951, while all of the Carolina fantasies appeared between 1946 and the present.

II

Within the group of Wellman's stories that neither feature an occult detective nor are set in North Carolina, there are several notable subgroupings, beginning with standard tales of horror. Most of these were written early in his career, and appeared under his own name, or that of "Levi Crow" or "Gans T. Field" (the pen name is an adaptation of the Wellman family motto, *Contra campa*, "against the field," into English). They were printed in several magazines—in *Strange Stories*, in John W. Campbell, Jr.'s, *Unknown*, and most often in *Weird Tales* (from whose editor, Farnsworth Wright, Wellman says he received "great and understanding help").

In 1975, Wellman won the award for best collection, at the World Fantasy Convention, for *Worse Things Waiting* (1973), a large selection of his early stories. It would have been hard to write horror fantasy in the 1930's and 1940's uninfluenced by H. P.

Lovecraft; it is therefore not surprising that among these early stories is "The Terrible Parchment" (*Weird Tales*, abbreviated *WT* hereafter, August 1937), concerned with Cthulhu, the *Necronomicon*, and other elements of the Lovecraftian mythos. The collection has werewolves ("Among Those Present," *WT*, March 1937); the dead rising from their graves ("The Undead Soldier," *WT*, May 1936); changelings ("The Changeling," *Strange Stories*, February 1939); vampires ("The Devil Is Not Mocked," *Unknown Worlds*, June 1943), in which a Nazi officer meets Count Dracula; and others in the same vein.

The miscellaneous stories have an impressive range of settings and characters: from medieval France, as in "These Doth the Lord Hate" (*WT*, January 1939, under the pseudonym Gans T. Field), in which a peasant turns in his wife and daughter as witches; through the seventeenth-century England of "The Liers in Wait" (*WT*, November 1941), in which Charles II refuses the help of witches against Cromwell; to nineteenth-century Philadelphia in "When It Was Moonlight" (*Unknown*, February 1940), in which Edgar Allan Poe appears as a character, rescuing a husband from his vampire wife and gaining the idea for the story "The Premature Burial" as well.

A second subcategory of the miscellaneous group has American Indians and their folklore as its subject, in stories written between 1939 and 1960. For at least three of them, Wellman used the pseudonym Levi Crow. Their settings may be the past, as in "Young-Man-with-Skull-at-His-Ear" (*Magazine of Fantasy and Science Fiction*, abbreviated *MFSF* hereafter, May 1953), in which "Ancient Ones" befriend a young brave, bring him victory in battle, and make him chief of the tribe; or as in "The Hairy Thunderer" (*MFSF*, April 1960), in which the spider-spirit helps a young Indian to defeat a white trader who has enslaved his tribe with whiskey. They may be set in the present, as in "For Fear of Little Men" (*Strange Stories*, June 1939), in which tiny malevolent creatures try to disrupt the sculpting of a statue of Hiawatha; or as in "Dhoh" (*WT*, July 1948), in which a folklorist is killed by the bear-spirit to prevent his reality from becoming known. Or the stories may even look to the future: in "War-

rior in Darkness" (*MFSF*, June 1954), a blind young man seeks death at the hands of the legendary Indian Strike Eye, who turns out to be a stranded visitor from another planet. Strike Eye gives the warrior a view of a future when white men destroy each other in wars and when the Indian tribes return to their old ways.

An even larger subgrouping consists of the fantasy tales set during the Civil War, a period in which Wellman has shown much interest (in works of nonfiction as well). These stories, with the exception of his novels, are Wellman's longest, a sign of their generally fuller development. An example of this class of story is "His Name on a Bullet" (*Strange Stories*, April 1940); here a witch gives a Virginia soldier the bullet that will kill him. Since he guards it well, he comes safely through the war, but since he can die no other way, in his old age he must ask a friend to use it on him. A theme that often appears in Wellman's work—the book of magic—also shows up here. A warlock in "The Valley Was Still" (*WT*, August 1939) uses a book of charms to enchant a Union detachment into immobility; he offers the devil's aid to a Confederate soldier, with the assurance of victory for the South. The soldier refuses, and history takes its course.

But the book of spells is an effective weapon for good in the hands of Wellman's Civil War Pennsylvanian, Sergeant Jaeger. Readers first met Jaeger in the serialized "Fearful Rock" (*WT*, February–April 1939). He is among the Union soldiers who defeat a detachment of Quantrill's raiders near the Arkansas-Missouri border. But the area has an eerie quality about it and, the soldiers discover later, a tradition of devil worship. Soon they find themselves attacked by the dead but risen Confederates. The sergeant uses the spells of J. G. Hohman's *Pow-wows: or Long-Lost Friend* to defeat the evil forces that have raised the cavalrymen, and at the end, Jaeger resolves to return to the area after the war, but this time as a minister of God.

An episode from Jaeger's earlier life is shown in "Coven" (*WT*, July 1942). A captured fourteen-year-old rebel soldier helps the sergeant to locate the grave of a vampire, whom they then destroy. Years later, in 1876, the now-grown boy finds himself in

948

MANLY WADE WELLMAN

the Ozarks. He meets Jaeger, who has kept his promise to return, and helps him to destroy a coven of witches.

Almost forty years were to pass before Wellman returned to the character of Jaeger, telling the story of his return to the Ozarks in "Toad's Foot" (*MFSF*, April 1979) and continuing the sergeant's adventures in "What of the Night" (*MFSF*, March 1980).

Far from considering his work done when he retired from teaching at the University of North Carolina in 1971, Wellman produced a spate of stories, most of them with Carolina settings but a few branching into fields of fantasy that he had never tried before. At the invitation of the science fiction writer Andrew J. Offutt, he started a series of sword-and-sorcery pieces—not all that different a form from space opera, but a new direction for Wellman. These stories appeared in *Swords Against Darkness* and *Heroic Fantasy* between 1977 and 1979. Not much sword-and-sorcery shows a sense of humor (the link between high fantasy and high seriousness has yet to be explored critically), but Wellman's does. His hero, Kardios, is the last survivor of Atlantis, which sank beneath the waves when, contrary to warnings of ancient legend, he kissed its queen. With a beginning like that, the reader is well prepared for burlesque, such as is encountered in "The Dweller in the Temple": here, at the behest of the high priest Athmar, Kardios becomes the sacrificial king of the ancient city Nyanyanya. The Kardios stories show that Wellman's imagination is as fresh now as it was at the beginning of his career, when he gained a reputation with his stories of psychic investigators.

III

Occult detective stories are those that feature a hero who combats supernatural forces with their own weapons. The form was popular in the 1930's and 1940's, as Seabury Quinn's Jules de Grandin stories testify. Wellman explored this genre near the beginning of his career in stories that, with one exception, were published between 1938 and 1951. They are more readily accessible than any of his works but the most recent. In 1981, there appeared *Lonely Vigils*, a collection of all but one of Wellman's occult detective stories.

The volume deals with the exploits of three investigators. One of these, Professor Nathan Enderby, appeared in only a single story, "Vigil" (*Strange Stories*, December 1939), for which Wellman used the pseudonym Hampton Wells. "Vigil" is Wellman's least successful venture in this form: the character of the reclusive, misogynist professor is more caricature than characterization, and his Chinese servant is a cliché. Wellman's handling of the supernatural menace is more sure-handed, though, and he was to achieve better effects with his other two detectives, Judge Pursuivant and John Thunstone.

Judge Keith Hilary Pursuivant was the earlier of these; "The Hairy Ones Shall Dance" (*WT*, January–March 1938) marked his debut, and in three more stories he continued his adventures until 1941. Apparently independently wealthy, he devotes himself to the extermination of malevolent supernatural forces, which are usually brought to his attention by someone in his wide circle of social acquaintances. In "The Hairy Ones Shall Dance," for example, it turns out that his adversary is a werewolf.

Since the judge is an authority on the works of Lord Byron, he is invited to examine the manuscript of a Byronic play in "The Black Drama" (*WT*, June–August 1938). He discovers that although the play was composed in the 1930's, Byron did indeed write it, having made a compact with the devil to live for 150 years. Pursuivant sends Byron to his overdue rest. "The Black Drama" is the longest Pursuivant adventure, the best developed in characterization, and the most original in its plot. The other two stories are much shorter and much more typical tales of psychic investigation. "The Dreadful Rabbits" (*WT*, July 1940) suffers principally from its title, and "The Half-Haunted" (*WT*, September 1941) is a competent but unexceptional story of the exorcism from a haunted house of not one but several ghosts.

All of the Pursuivant stories were published under the pseudonym Gans T. Field in *Weird Tales*. After "The Half-Haunted," perhaps out of a desire to do away with the pen name or perhaps simply because of the difficulties posed by Pursuivant's de-

949

pendence on chance encounters to find adventures, Wellman changed detectives.

In appearance, his new investigator looks like a younger Judge Pursuivant: both are tall, broad, dark-haired, and mustachioed (in these respects resembling their creator, also). But unlike the judge, John Thunstone goes looking for trouble. He actively seeks out the users of black magic, and not surprisingly (given his activities), many of those dark forces seek John Thunstone.

Especially in the Thunstone stories Wellman explored the darker sides of folk beliefs, a practice that he continued throughout his career, and he moved with ease from the legends of one culture to those of another. For example, in "The Third Cry to Legba" (*WT*, November 1943), the title names the voodoo god appearing in the story; and the next story, "The Golden Goblins" (*WT*, January 1944), switches to American Indian mythology for its supernatural machinery. Later stories deal with real or invented folk sources, from those of the Eskimo ("Sorcery from Thule," *WT*, September 1944) to the Gurkhas of Nepal ("The Dai Sword," *WT*, July 1945). Wellman created his own folk beliefs from time to time, one of which he was to use for forty more years—the Shonokins.

The Shonokins are a species unrelated to humans, a race of great antiquity who had established a civilization in the New World before the coming of the Indians. The Shonokins have intelligence, magical powers, and a likeness to human beings that allows them to pass among humans unnoticed. One characteristic physical difference is that on a Shonokin's hand, the ring finger is the longest digit. Their origin is a mystery—no one has ever seen a Shonokin female, for example—but there is no mystery about their ambition to reestablish their dominance over the earth. John Thunstone encounters and defeats the Shonokins in four stories: "The Dead Man's Hand" (*WT*, November 1944), "The Shonokins" (*WT*, March 1945), "Blood from a Stone" (*WT*, May 1945), and "Shonokin Town" (*WT*, July 1946).

Wellman provides an interesting sidelight on the Shonokins in the foreword to *Lonely Vigils*, where he says:

I had thought that they were my own invention. But various readers assured me that the Shonokins were fearfully known by name in various parts of the country, including New England, upstate New York, the Ozark Mountains and California. Letters like that are always a delight to read, what time they do not cause you furiously to ask yourself what you might be stirring up without intending to do so.

Whatever the provenance of the Shonokins, Wellman's hero Silver John was to meet and checkmate them forty years later (and to refer to John Thunstone while doing so).

These stories frequently create an air of authenticity through Wellman's penchant for citing (even quoting from) a book of magic. Yet, as has often been pointed out, the books mentioned in Wellman's works are not pseudobiblia like Lovecraft's *Necronomicon*. Wellman claims to own many of them. In the course of the occult detective stories, he mentions, or his characters encounter, a whole library of the occult.

The success of the Thunstone stories depends on Wellman's careful working to build plausibility into his horror, the most difficult genre in which to establish the suspension of disbelief. To this end, he employs such techniques as the use of folk motifs and quotations from real books (how much more effective are a few lines in authentic sixteenth-century English than in a modern imitation). And he uses still another practice, that of continuing a number of characters from story to story. One such is the villain Rowley Thorne, similar in some respects to the writer and diabolist Aleister Crowley. In the foreword to *Lonely Vigils*, Wellman mentions receiving a warning that Crowley might sue him for libel, but Wellman did not take the threat seriously, and in fact Crowley never did sue. A more attractive character encountered several times is the Countess Monteseco, the American widow of a nobleman; Sharon, the countess, provides a romantic interest for Thunstone and someone to protect against the machinations of Thorne. Continuing figures allow for deeper exploration of character than in a single story and therefore can reduce stereotypes.

All but one of the John Thunstone stories appeared in *Weird Tales* between 1943 and 1951; the exception is "Rouse Him Not," published in the fanzine *Kadath* in 1982, in a special occult detective issue dedicated to Wellman. In that story, Thunstone still wields a silver sword forged by St. Dunstan; and although he has "gray streaks" in his hair, his adventures continue in *What Dreams May Come*. The last of the earlier Thunstone adventures, though, was "The Last Grave of Lill Warran" (*WT*, May 1951), which looks both backward and forward in the course of Wellman's writing. Lill Warran, a werewolf, had been killed but not in the prescribed way, and so she returns as a vampire. In investigating her case, Thunstone writes a letter about the situation to Quinn's character, Jules de Grandin (who is mentioned in several of Wellman's stories). The setting and the characterization of the story point toward Wellman's fiction to come: the tale takes place in the Sandhills region of North Carolina, and the reader will later encounter the atmosphere of the story in the Silver John adventures. In addition, one of the main characters is a man who had loved Lill and buried her corpse when it was refused burial in hallowed ground. Both the story's setting and its emphasis on natural human emotions in the face of supernatural events give it a dimension that lifts it above the common tale of ghosts and goblins, a quality found throughout the stories of the third category — the Carolina tales.

IV

When Wellman moved to North Carolina, he found a region that enchanted him, one on which he could lavish his attention. His love for North Carolina's mountains, for its people, and for its flora and fauna is the foundation of his best work. Wellman's use of the area began almost immediately after his relocation. His story "Frogfather" (*WT*, November 1946), for example, not only takes place there but, as if to foreshadow the creation of Silver John, has as a character a young boy named Johnny. Like the carnivorous pitcher plant or the Venus flytrap — both indigenous to the region — the gardinel — a man-eating plant that looks like a house — appears in "Sin's Doorway"(*WT*, January 1946) and

in "Come into My Parlor" (in *The Girl with the Hungry Eyes and Other Stories*, 1949). The Shonokins adapted to the new region as easily as their creator, starting with "The Pineys" (*WT*, September 1950).

Before looking at the stories of Wellman's most successful character, one should note that other tales besides those of Silver John fall under the heading of Carolina fantasies. Through the 1970's and early 1980's, a number of more or less traditional horror stories appeared in *MFSF*; these include "Dead Man's Chair" (*MFSF*, October 1973), surely one of very few tales about haunted furniture and its owner's revenge; "Where the Woodbine Twineth" (*MFSF*, October 1976), in which feuding ghosts are put to rest by the Romeo-and-Juliet-like union of their offspring; and "Hundred Years Gone" (*MFSF*, March 1978), in which a traveler arrives at a mountain cabin just in time to prevent a vampire's rampage.

Wellman's best-known work, the Silver John stories, first appeared in *MFSF* in December 1951 with "O Ugly Bird!" and continued steadily through 1958, with a few very short pieces in March 1962 under the title "Wonder As I Wander: Some Footprints on John's Trail Through Magic Mountains." These eleven pieces, plus a few more vignettes, were reprinted as *Who Fears the Devil?* (1963); all quotations from the Silver John stories are from this edition. Then, in 1979, Silver John appeared in a novel, *The Old Gods Waken*. Since then, novels have followed regularly: *After Dark* (1980), *The Lost and the Lurking* (1981), and *The Hanging Stones* (1982).

The narrator of all these tales, whose last name is never revealed, takes his epithet from the metal of his guitar strings. Even his name shows how folklore is woven into the stories, in this case, "O Ugly Bird!": "'Silver?' said the storekeeper. 'Is them strings silver? Why, friends, silver finishes a hoodoo man.'" The presence of many such folk beliefs in the stories lends them an air of truthfulness and verisimilitude.

Fantasies so often present a wholly imaginary world that the concrete reality of the setting of these works almost startles the reader. They prove that a skillful writer can blend fantastic themes with realism of setting, but few do it with the mastery of Wellman, with his thorough understanding of a locale real enough to be visited. For instance, in "One Other" (*MFSF*, August 1953), John visits a place to see a local sight and is asked, "When you talk about bottomless pools, you mean the ones near Lake Lure on Highway 74?" John has seen them, and so can anyone who travels to Rutherford County. The fictional Flornoy College, where "country boys who mightn't get much past common school can come and work off the most part of their board and keep and learning" ("Old Devlins Was A-waiting," *MFSF*, February 1957), sounds much like Warren Wilson College, not far from Asheville, in Swannanoa. References like these—and there are many—root the stories in their setting.

Wellman has a keen ear for the poetry of the region, which finds expression in its speech and its song. The stories show the metaphoric luxuriance of the mountain speakers, a frequent exuberance of speech that can only be hinted at in examples like "Polly Wiltse's beauty would melt the heart of nature and make a dumb man cry out, 'Praise God who made her'!" ("The Desrick on Yandro," *MFSF*, June 1952).

And songs fill the Silver John stories with authentic samplings of the Appalachian store of folk music: the short story "The Little Black Train" (*MFSF*, August 1954) takes its title and one verse from a folk song recorded in Durham in 1922. John knows what his audience favors ("'I love the old songs better,' said Mr. Bristow") and plays them: "Staying off the wornout songs, I smote out what they'd never heard before—'Rebel Soldier' and 'Well I Know that Love Is Pretty' and 'When the Stars Begin to Fall'" ("The Desrick on Yandro"). Wellman is also quite able to add some lines or verses to a real ballad to fit it to his fictional context because like John, Wellman is a student of ballad literature, a guitarist, and a banjo player. His county history *The Kingdom of Madison* (1973) has a chapter entitled "What Shall I Sing?" showing his familiarity with ballad literature and its collectors.

Along with folk speech and folk song, folk belief and custom make up the third support of the Silver John stories. Wellman includes such statements as

"You'll never see a man exactly six feet tall, because that was the height of the Lord Jesus," or, "If you step down a mullein stalk toward your true love's house, ... if it grows up again she loves you" ("Dumb Supper," *MFSF*, March 1954).

All of this richness of setting forms the perfect background for as rounded a character as John. Born next to Drowning Creek and baptized in its waters, orphaned early but taught to read and write by "an old teacher lady," he grows into a man a little taller than most, a widely read roaming balladeer. In "Nine Yards of Other Cloth" (*MFSF*, November 1958), he meets and betroths a girl named Evadare; in the first two novels he plans to marry her and take up farming (although she is willing to wander along with him), and in the next two, his plans have come to fruition.

John illustrates well the centrality of religion to a culture; these stories are filled with the religion of the region. It is a sectarian (but not in any derogatory sense of the word), believing, Scripture-reading, fundamentalist Christianity. Although many Christians both worthy and unworthy of the name live in John's southern mountains, few match John's virtue, his determination to do right, or his modesty. For these characters, and especially for John, religion is an everyday, full-time matter, a guide to conduct and a comfort in distress. Even those who trade it for powers in the black arts know the worth of what they have given away. Their faith is the assumed background of their lives, and in that respect, it is like the religion in a medieval tale.

Perhaps the finest story in *Who Fears the Devil?* is "On the Hills and Everywhere," which appeared in the January 1956 issue of *MFSF*. Since January issues of the pulps are on the newsstands during December, the story was one of the editor Anthony Boucher's Christmas gifts to his readers. It is surely one of the quietest and simplest stories ever to appear in a pulp magazine, more like a medieval saint's legend than a space opera or a ghost story. Its beauty is a tribute to Wellman's skill and a confirmation that with the Silver John stories, especially, he has picked a setting and a genre that allow him to create art.

Less critical attention has been paid to Wellman

than his work is worth, but that neglect may soon be remedied. The collections *Worse Things Waiting* and *Lonely Vigils* rescued many of his early tales from the obscurity of moldering issues of pulp magazines. The Silver John novels will soon be available in paperback; a new John Thunstone novel has appeared to join Wellman's recent stories of Silver John. And the attention that will result from this increased availability will be deserved.

From Mark Twain to Flannery O'Connor, the tradition of southern realism has been strong in the United States; and more attention to Wellman, even if it served no other purpose, would show that a technique like realism of setting is adaptable to a wider variety of themes than has been realized. But more attention would serve another purpose: stories as honest and as colorful as his simply deserve a wider audience.

Selected Bibliography

WORKS OF MANLY WADE WELLMAN

Books

Who Fears the Devil? Sauk City, Wis.: Arkham House, 1963. (Contains all the Silver John short stories except as indicated below. Paperback reprint editions do not have the full text of "Wonder As I Wander.")

Worse Things Waiting. Chapel Hill, N.C.: Carcosa, 1973. (Short stories. Contains all Wellman's miscellaneous fantasies as described in the text, all the Indian stories, Civil War stories, and Sergeant Jaeger stories except as indicated below. In some instances texts have been reworked from magazine versions or restored to manuscript versions.)

The Old Gods Waken. Garden City, N.Y.: Doubleday, 1979. (Novel about Silver John.)

After Dark. Garden City, N.Y.: Doubleday, 1980. (Novel about Silver John.)

Lonely Vigils. Chapel Hill, N.C.: Carcosa, 1981. (Short stories. Contains all the stories about Professor Enderby, Judge Pursuivant, and John Thunstone except as indicated below.)

The Lost and the Lurking. Garden City, N.Y.: Doubleday, 1981. (Novel about Silver John.)

The Hanging Stones. Garden City, N.Y.: Doubleday, 1982. (Novel about Silver John.)

What Dreams May Come. Garden City, N.Y.: Doubleday, 1983. (Novel about John Thunstone.)

Uncollected stories

"Frogfather." *Weird Tales* (November 1946). (Carolina.)

"Dead Man's Chair." *Magazine of Fantasy and Science Fiction* (abbreviated *MFSF* hereafter) (October 1973). (Carolina.)

"The Ghastly Priest Doth Reign." *MFSF* (March 1975). (Carolina.)

"Caretakers." *MFSF* (October 1977). (Carolina.)

"The Dweller in the Temple." In *Swords Against Darkness II*, edited by Andrew J. Offutt. New York: Kensington, 1977. (Kardios.)

"Straggler from Atlantis." In *Swords Against Darkness*, edited by Andrew J. Offutt. New York: Kensington, 1977. (Kardios.)

The Guest of Dzinganji." In *Swords Against Darkness III*, edited by Andrew J. Offutt. New York: Kensington, 1978. (Kardios.)

"Hundred Years Gone." *MFSF* (March 1978). (Carolina.)

"Trill Coster's Burden." In *Whispers II*, edited by Stuart Schiff. Garden City, N.Y.: Doubleday, 1978. (Silver John.)

"Where the Woodbine Twineth." *MFSF* (October 1978). (Carolina.)

"The Edge of the World." In *Swords Against Darkness IV*, edited by Andrew J. Offutt. New York: Kensington, 1979. (Kardios.)

"The Seeker in the Fortress." In *Heroic Fantasy*, edited by Gerald W. Page and Hank Reinhardt. New York: DAW, 1979. (Kardios.)

"The Spring." In *Shadows II*, edited by Charles Grant. Garden City, N.Y.: Doubleday, 1979. (Silver John.)

"Toad's Foot." *MFSF* (April 1979). (Sergeant Jaeger.)

"Owls Hoot in the Daytime." In *Dark Forces*, edited by Kirby McCauley. New York: Viking, 1980. (Silver John.)

"What of the Night." *MFSF* (March 1980). (Sergeant Jaeger.)

"Can These Bones Live?" *Sorcerer's Apprentice* (Summer 1981). (Silver John.)

"Nobody Ever Goes There." In *Weird Tales III*, edited by Lin Carter. New York: Zebra, 1981. (Silver John.)

"Rouse Him Not." *Kadath*, 2, no. 1 (1982). (John Thunstone.)

CRITICAL AND BIOGRAPHICAL STUDIES

Meyers, Walter E. "The Silver John Stories." In *Survey of Modern Fantasy Literature*, edited by Frank N. Magill. Vol. IV, 1744–1748. Englewood Cliffs, N.J.: Salem Press, 1983.

Wagner, Karl Edward. "Manly Wade Wellman." In *Twentieth-Century Science-Fiction Writers*, edited by Curtis C. Smith. New York: St. Martin, 1981, 572–574. (Contains a partial bibliography and a brief statement by Wellman.)

—WALTER E. MEYERS

XV

British and American Modern Writers

ROBERT AICKMAN

1914-1981

I N 1955, QUITE obscurely, there was published in the United Kingdom a concise paperback guide to the English canal system, which then as now was severely threatened by the march of progress. The author of *Know Your Waterways*, Robert Aickman, who had cofounded the Inland Waterways Association in 1946 to lobby for the preservation of the canals, was, by the time he wrote his guide, over forty years old. He had already made some kind of mark in several fields, had already argued himself into a systematic disdain for most of the nineteenth and all of the twentieth century, and was just launching himself into his final career; for it was also in 1955 that he published "Ringing the Changes," his fifth tale of the supernatural, and began to attract widespread though bemused notice as a writer of fiction. Before his death in 1981, Aickman would publish forty more stories, a novel, and a superb autobiography, becoming the finest English writer of supernatural fiction of the last fifty years. From the very first he wrote as a mature man who had already experienced and, by his own testimony, suffered much.

The cover of *Know Your Waterways* features a small photograph of a barge being steered toward the camera along a tree-lined canal by a man with thick hair and glasses. Squatting or lying on this barge, and seemingly attentive to him, are two figures, possibly women, but one can see only the backs of their heads. Around them are the makings of an ornate meal, an open purse, a large canister with Romany

markings. In the background, at a point where the trees seem to have met above the sun-shot canal, a dark shape rather like a gondola seems to be following the barge, though there is no sign that the helmsman is aware of this. He is instead responding to the intrusion of the camera; his mien is assured, seemingly competent, but in the strong glare of the sun oddly exposed, as though something were about to crumble. Although he is not identified in any way, it is clear that the helmsman in the photograph is Aickman himself.

Two women together whose relationship may not be clear; a helmsman of their company, but at the same time isolated, perhaps by age; a stretch of seemingly navigable water encroached upon by undergrowth; Romany runes; a mysterious doppelgänger shape as deep in the background as it is possible to discern; exposing sunlight and intrusive shadow; Mammon and Styx—the effect may be accidental, but in this photograph, one is thrust directly into the complexly ominous universe of Aickman's fiction. Just as in that fiction Aickman's own life everywhere shows through, so in this photograph one can sense an urgent welling-up of personal significance from everything hinted at or merely visible, for in Aickman's world everything signifies, everything contributes to the quest for the terrible secret meaning of the world.

Aickman published his first stories as late as 1951, so that the composition of almost all of his work would seem to postdate what Carl Jung identified as the midlife crisis, that time of troubles which, in his view, afflicts for a time any normal adult who has lived long enough to pass through the period of youthful heroism. Understandably, most writers of popular fiction concentrate on the first period and are generally reluctant to extend their interest into the time or staleness or hidden retribution (as in the tragedy of Oedipus) that follows on from the moments of triumph. But in the real world, the hero must face his midlife crisis or die in nescience. His past now seems full of sound and fury, his present life seems intolerably void of novelty, and the future lacks any conceivable meaning. At this stage the hero may divorce his wife and take up a new career.

For Jung, though not perhaps in his words, the hero's psyche has now become a kind of wasteland or battlefield, in which the archetypes that figured and inspired the exploits of his youth jostle sourly for advantage. If he is to pass through his crisis, the hero must somehow integrate these discordant aspects of his personality into the full, harmonious "individuation" of the mature Jungian self; he must somehow transform these clamorous images of internecine warfare into a kind of chivalry. Only thus redeemed can he face the most important remaining challenge—which is death—with equanimity.

If a man fails in this endeavor, then he will be haunted, for when the archetypes appropriate to young manhood fail to integrate into a mature selfhood, they tend to manifest themselves in the form of ghosts. It is in this sense that so many of Aickman's finest efforts can be read as ghost stories, in which the world itself becomes the deranged battlefield of the self. If it is at the heart of fantasy to treat the objective world as a manifestation of the subjective, then it is a matter of dubious interpretation whether the ghosts in an Aickman story are objective or subjective in nature. And if these ghosts represent a failure on their victim's part to construct out of the jarring cohorts of his psyche a meaningful selfhood, then it can come as no shock to find that many of Aickman's stories are virtually indecipherable, that by their very nature they resist paraphrase. It is enough in an Aickman story that the victim recognize the nightmare world he inhabits;

by definition, understanding that world is beyond him.

Many come to the midlife crisis; few surmount it. Whether Aickman himself gained the repose of full adulthood would be impertinent to question, though he very clearly hints throughout *The Attempted Rescue* (1966), his significantly titled autobiography to the age of twenty-five or so, that he does not judge himself to have gained anything like equipoise in later life. What is surely clear is that his fiction is conceived from the other side of heroism. His stories come from a distant shore.

Despite occasional episodes of self-exposure, of which the autobiography is the most prominent, Robert Fordyce Aickman remains a figure of seemingly deliberate obscurity. Although *The Attempted Rescue*, for example, clearly ties his childhood to the period dominated by World War I and supplies sufficient internal evidence for one to establish his year of birth as 1914 (27 June, to be precise), nowhere in the book is that date given; neither did it appear in biographical summaries while Aickman was alive. Facts do emerge, however. He was born in London and was an only child. His parents were affluent, though not excessively so. His maternal grandfather was the popular novelist Richard Marsh, now best known as the author of *The Beetle*. Other relatives were more eminent than this, and Aickman spent long periods visiting large, imposing residences, the like of which haunt his fiction from beginning to end.

Aickman attended several private schools with outward success, though he was deeply unhappy. He discovered the theater and developed a lifelong obsession with opera. In 1934 he published "a toy pagoda of words" called "What Is a Flounce?" in the *New English Weekly*. But then he gave up writing. He was variously employed and became the theater critic for *The Nineteenth Century and After*. His childhood obsession with travel blossomed into the founding of the Inland Waterways Association, and he was either a founder of or moving force in several other associations, including the London Opera Society. At some point he married and divorced. He was heterosexual. His relationships with women were many and intense; he got along less well with men. With Elizabeth Jane Howard—each writing three stories independently—Aickman published *We Are for the Dark* (1951). In 1964 he edited with great success *The Fontana Book of Great Ghost Stories*, producing seven similar volumes by 1972. Before his death, on 26 February 1981, he published eight further volumes of fiction.

It all seems to have meant little or nothing, as *The Attempted Rescue* makes clear:

> For years I seem to have regarded myself as what F R Rolfe called a Nowt: a being without independent volition, directed wholly by circumstances and the will of others. If the circumstances were right (which was very infrequently), I could shine in a moment, and rise too, but I could do nothing to penetrate or to discover these circumstances. I was as the clown in a French mime; with wild hair in place of long sleeves. I turned almost all my suffering inwards, until it became unbearable, because nothing ever happened, neither break-out nor breakdown, so that I never ceased to bear it. Doubtless the suffering was unconsciously purposive, in the true neurotic fashion. The only possibility in my mind was that I might become an author.
>
> (chapter 18)

As his autobiography also makes clear, Aickman was convinced that much of his suffering lay in his failure to escape the influence of his extraordinary parents even after their deaths.

He was intensely devoted to his supple, delicate, frustrated mother and lived in terror of his monstrously domineering, eccentric, clockwork father; indeed, by quoting Samuel Butler in the "Proem" to his autobiography, Aickman makes it evident that he conceived of his life as bearing anxious witness to the parent-son catastrophe depicted in *The Way of All Flesh*. His father, who appears in various guises throughout the fiction, was by nature mechanical and impulsive, time-bound and insanely dilatory, a figure locked into lunatic obsessions like a robot into its program. Supremely deficient in human integration (or chivalry), Aickman's father, like a deranged archetype, clearly haunted his son's life and stalks through his work. Unmistakable portraits of him occur in "The Inner Room" (1966) and

in "The Fetch" (1980), the first of the two late novelettes that constitute in coded form an autobiographical summa; in "The Stains" (1980), the second of these stories, the ghosts are laid and death embraced.

In "The Fetch" no such reconciliation is possible. "In all that matters, I was an only child," the narrator of the tale begins, and draws a portrait of a personality irretrievably bound to his own childhood and to a family "curse" that, though alien to him, he cannot transcend. His father seems to be "a wraith with a will and power that no one available could resist." His mother is deeply adoring but dies while he is a child, under horrific circumstances, after a visitation from the family fetch, a doppelgänger-like witch who comes to one who must die and shows him, in its hooded visage, his own face.

From this point his father utterly abandons the child but owns him still. Like a vulnerable helmsman beginning his transit of something ominously like the Styx, the narrator spends the remainder of his life affirming and denying the terms that define him: "I had long recognized that many people would have said that I was obsessed. But the whole business seemed to me the explanation of my being." He goes through the motions of a career and falls desperately in love and marries, but the fetch comes for his wife. His second wife, by refusing any credence to that which binds him, isolates him all the more.

His life a shambles and an imprisonment, he retreats to the deserted family seat in rural Scotland, and the fetch comes for him at last. But the narrator barricades the doors and windows so as not to see his own face. As the story ends he is still alive, which is heroism of a sort, but is misplaced. Youthful heroism will not solve the crisis of a soul in extremis, for the narrator has failed to live, and his survival is an ironic jape, for neither can he face his death.

Aickman is quite explicit about his sense of the nature of supernatural manifestations. Introducing *The Fontana Book of Great Ghost Stories* (1964), he makes clear his lack of interest in random sensation:

> The ghosts are the returned dead whom once we knew, or our uncle knew. They are creatures

we once knew, but now know no more. . . . They are, occasionally, creatures we never knew (or think we didn't), like angels or devils or toys possessed by a spirit. They are things within us which we have, as psychologists say, projected outside us. They are little children beating on the glass. They are free; at least from us. They are real. We are glad to meet them when we are glad to meet ourselves, but that is to be one man (or woman) marked out of ten thousand.

There is much that is inexplicable in his forty-five stories but very little that is truly arbitrary. And the terrible secret meaning of the ghost-ridden world of Aickman's fiction lies precisely in its binding complicity, for the world *means* what you have become; it is therefore a fiction of consequences. If a man fails to become chivalrous to the knowledge of the approach of death, then he will end up as much a ghost as that which haunts him. If (as he must) he fails to understand the world that mirrors the wasteland of his fragmented psyche, the world will not for that reason cease to bind him.

Sometimes clearly, sometimes obscured by bizarre cacophonies of symbol and event, this sustaining moral import can be perceived throughout Aickman's work. At times, as in "The Insufficient Answer" (1951), "Choice of Weapons" (1964), "Bind Your Hair" (1964), and "Ravissante" (1968), the internecine warfare between self and world may be too jangled for the reader easily to parse.

The insistent striving for meaningfulness in his fiction is perhaps most poignantly effective in what might be called the tales of failed transcendence, those stories whose protagonists are compelled by their sense of inward crisis to attempt to change their lives, perhaps utterly. They set out on doomed journeys, as in "The Inner Room," which is a virtual maze of journeys into the mirror, with no exit. They come to islands, as in "The View" (1951), "Just a Song at Twilight" (1965), and "The Wine-Dark Sea" (1966), only to find their sense of exile supernaturally confirmed. In "No Time Is Passing" (1980), a river suddenly discovered at the foot of the protagonist's garden demands that he cross it; but the god or monstrous parody of a man who rules the other side sends him scurrying back across the exact same river, for nothing has changed; the man remains lost in the petty, cushioned shambles of his life.

In "The Hospice" (1976), which offers a horrific and hilarious vision of the aesthetic and human costs of living in modern, middle-class, industrial England, a lured traveler confronts another's death probably prophetic of his own, for which "he should not have to wait long." The grounds of the sanatarium for insomniacs in "Into the Wood" (1968) draw the sleepless protagonist into a forest advertised as transcendental, but it is no more than a labyrinth that returns one to the institution. A similar poverty awaits the woman in "The Next Glade" (1980), who is drawn into the woods by a phantom lover but finds only her failed marriage there.

The significance of these terminal landscapes is not exhausted by the force with which they manifest individual fates, for the typical Aickman protagonist inhabits a wasteland whose origin and contours also represent a complex failure of Western civilization to sustain, through its artifacts and imperial progress, an organic human dimension. It is worth noting that at about the time Aickman was beginning to write fiction, the social thought of John Ruskin was finally receiving due notice. As Sir Kenneth Clark, speaking of Ruskin's magisterial abhorrence of industrial "values," put it in *The Listener* for 1 April 1948,

We do not yet believe in the greatest of all his truths: that any ugly lamp-post is a wicked lamp-post. We are all inclined to take ugliness for granted, as something which has always existed and for which we are not responsible. . . . [But] every form we create will betray us; and to the sensitive eye our utility furnishings will tell their tales as surely as if they were covered with flowers and scrolls or embossed views of the Forth Bridge.

As Aickman himself says in *The Attempted Rescue*, "Possibly, as Wilde suggested, the awful truth is that appearances are true."

A conviction that appearances are indeed terrifyingly true is manifest throughout the fiction, clearly underpinning the sense that the world, for an Aickman character, means what it says. Not only, however, does the world mirror the lone protagonist's failure to pass through the crisis of his mortal life into a state of internal chivalry, but it also confesses to the moral-aesthetic collapse of an entire culture. Limned in a prose whose mandarin irony barely masks exorbitant disgust, this marriage of appearance and truth effectively puts into the terms of fiction the nub of Ruskin's thought; Aickman also shares his political inclinations: "I am," Ruskin says in *Praeterita*, "a violent Tory of the old school;—Walter Scott's school, that is to say, and Homer's."

From *We Are for the Dark* down to the last uncollected tales, the reader finds himself always in a world shaped by these convictions, recounted in the same tone. It is not a simple or a young man's world. Neither is Aickman finally able to direct his consuming rage at the loss of virtue into works of a scope ample enough to express it. Stories that are clear allegories of the West's current cultural straits—like "Growing Boys" and "Residents Only" (both 1977)—tend to disintegrate into sour skits; and the unremitting irony of their telling becomes carping, indeed sanctimonious.

In the extraordinary complexity of the intellectual and emotional repertory he brings to his fiction, Aickman may evoke comparison with a writer such as Thomas Mann rather than with any predecessor in the field of supernatural fiction proper, with the possible exception of Walter de la Mare. But any such comparison exposes the limits of Aickman's imaginative hold. In Mann's only major novel of supernatural import, *Doctor Faustus*, a repertory not dissimilar to Aickman's undergoes a scouring ironical metamorphosis into an aesthetic shape so encompassing that one can descry within it a full vision of the fate of Western man without cramping, piety, or shortcuts into sarcasm. Aickman's mind may well be as complex as Mann's, but its lack of a grasp equal to its reach can be seen in the failure of *The Late Breakfasters* (1964), his only novel. Its supernatural content (a lissome ghost) is flimsy and soon dissipates; in its coquettish figurations of stylish writing it registers as apprentice work (the date of composition is unknown), and it breaks down into two mismatched halves. After this, Aickman never wrote (as far as is known) a story longer than 25,000 words.

Of these stories, several highly polished professional tales stand rather to one side. That they are his most popular works only demonstrates Aickman's intelligence as a craftsman. "The Waiting Room" (1956) adroitly traps a lost traveler in a waiting room built over a burial ground for hanged felons; he awakens with a bad crick in his neck. "Ringing the Changes," the most reprinted of his stories, introduces a newly married couple to an isolated village in the East Anglian fens on the night when the dead awaken to the sound of all the church bells ringing at once; the ensuing imbroglio obscurely taints the new marriage. "Pages from a Young Girl's Journal" (1973), which won a World Fantasy Award, details a young girl's unfolding awareness that she has been changed into a vampire by a dark stranger at a ball. Set in Italy and featuring cameo roles for both Byron and Shelley, it is a vivid period masquerade. Aickman's impersonation of the young English girl is deftly marmoreal and chillingly virtuoso.

Ongoing references have been made to stories more typical of Aickman's career as a whole. Given his complex seriousness of intention as a writer, and what seems in his later years the freedom to write as he wished, it is not surprising that few of those stories yet unmentioned are much inferior to his best work. But although his canon is remarkably uniform in quality, some further tales do stand out.

With *Dark Entries* (1964), Aickman makes his debut as an independent author. Beyond "Ringing the Changes," "The Waiting Room," and "The View," it contains, in "Bind Your Hair," a fantasia on the theme of the rite of passage that is both funny and alarming. Sequences reminiscent of Ivy Compton-Burnett reveal that the engagement of Clarinda to Dudley is faltering because of his fatal lack of sexual affect, so that it is impossible for her to envisage any meaningful passage into a different order of human existence. The supernatural intervenes in the form of a bacchanalian fertility rite in a sacred grove that casts together old gods, middle-aged gypsies, young children, and the stalled, tremulous Clarinda. At story's end, still with the blank Dudley, she remains poised at the brink of a genuine passage, though the reader is left free to doubt—as with so many Aickman characters—that she will ever make a move to save her life.

Along with the political satire and soul-bondage of "My Poor Friend," the numbing social backdrop of "A Roman Question," and the metaphysical slapstick of "Larger than Oneself," *Powers of Darkness* (1966) contains, in "The Visiting Star" (all stories 1966), Aickman's most complex transformation of his vast knowledge of the theater. In a barren Midlands city, as a cold Christmas approaches, an assortment of provincial types awaits the arrival of Arabella Rokeby, a great star from a time impossibly remote. Preceded by her agent, whose name, Superbus, reflects his tyrannical nature, she soon enchants everyone, as though she were something magical, as though she literally incarnated the thaumaturgy of true theater. And indeed this is the case. Any actor wears masks, but Rokeby is nothing more (or less) than an intricately wedded procession of masks; a manikin of Superbus; a psychic vampire. All the same, and very movingly, she remains humble in the face of the art she serves so completely. After hints of ritual extravagances and depths and after a catastrophe that ushers in Christmas, the magical, breathtaking show in which she stars does go on.

As noted, many Aickman stories present the failure to achieve an integrated world in terms of attempted transcendental journeys, as though into a better future. In a second broad category, usually signaled by someone's arrival at a meticulously described house, the attempted rescue has already failed by the time the tale begins, and within the house will be discovered an inverse ghost, a mummy, perhaps still breathing. The finest of these stories is probably "The Unsettled Dust," first published in *Sub Rosa* (1968). The narrator, who represents a controlling bureaucracy, visits one of the stately homes under his aegis, where he finds everything covered with dust and the two resident sisters (the home's former owners) locked into an icy covert feud. He inadvertently uncovers the source of the quarrel when he, too, finds himself haunted by the ghost of the young man with whom one of the sisters had long ago attempted to elope. The young man's mysterious death has frozen all life in their persons. There is no passage for them, no resolution of their sibling warfare, no future. As the ghost runs through its fixed reiteration of the tragedy, dust is

briefly unsettled; but when the ghost has passed, there is once again dead silence:

And, interestingly enough, the dust had by then ceased to swirl, though I am sure it still lay thick on the room floor, the floors of all the other rooms, the passages, the stairs, the furniture, and all our hearts.

From the same volume comes a further example of this category of the tale of frozen belatedness, "The Houses of the Russians," though it is less frigid in its implications.

"Meeting Mr. Millar" (1972), "The Same Dog" (1974), and "The Clock Watcher" (1974), all from *Cold Hand in Mine* (1975), and "Compulsory Games" (1976), "Wood" (1976), and *Le Miroir*," all from *Tales of Love and Death* (1977), are also stories of psychic mummification. Near the end of Aickman's career, his figures of horrific immobility, whatever their ostensible age or sex, became more profoundly estranged from humankind, more desperately caught in that clockwork of obsessive reiteration that disqualifies them from genuine being; more and more they came to resemble his dreadful father. In both "Meeting Mr. Millar" and "Wood," characters who first seem no more than psychic mummies (but still human) are revealed horrifyingly as literal clockwork, as simulacra that savagely mock human nature in their fixed reiteration of human traumas, human longings for change, growth, redemption.

The most representative of these stories is probably the superb "Compulsory Games," in which failed transcendence and mummification conjoin in ghastly wedlock. Colin has lived too mildly, too cautiously, ignoring the world as it changes; he is a mummy (though not literally so) but is ignorant of his condition. His wife leaves him for someone real, and the charade of his trivial existence collapses into a succession of unendurable ghostings. The world becomes a deranged, gloating nightmare, in which he must recognize his own shattered being and from which he cannot escape: "He was being mashed up and transmogrified before his own inner eyes; and the new entity, deprived of all egoism, would live for ever." For Colin, there is no passage. For the reader, his fate has a wider significance in that the wasteland to which "the new smiling Colin" is abandoned wears the hectic lineaments of the modern world.

Apparently, Aickman was unwell for several years before his death from cancer. Though the stories in *Intrusions* (1980) are as fine as anything he wrote earlier, they speak in measures more deeply elegiac than before. Married in tone to "The Fetch," "No Time Is Passing," and "The Next Glade," though not collected in the same volume, "The Stains" can stand for all of them. Although cancer is not mentioned as such, in the inexorable suffusion of staining throughout the tale, stainings of body and world, one recognizes an irreversible and growing consanguinity with death. But "The Stains" is also a story of redemptive love, a *Liebestod*. His wife dead from an unspecified disease, Stephen visits his feckless brother in the bleak north of England, ostensibly to recuperate. Walking alone on the moors, he sees an oread, or mountain nymph, at the end of the visible path. Her name is Nell (knell). He is stricken with love for her, though a great stain on her body frightens him. To wrap up his affairs, they go to London, which seems fungoid; the world is indeed disintegrating. But they escape for the moment, making their way back to a secret dwelling in the heart of the moor, where Nell's dread father—who is like death and the past but also like the natural world beyond human psychoses—begins to shake the earth in his search for them. For he will not be gainsaid.

The stain on Nell's body has migrated to Stephen's, where it belongs. But he has been happy, and for a time he has "counted the good things only, as does a sundial." At the heart of their secret home is a stone slab and, under it, a small room—"more a coffer than a room, Stephen apprehended." Here, as the father breathes stertorously outside, they come indissolubly together, married. Stephen is, of course, dead.

Most remarkable in this tale is the sense it imparts of earned reconciliation between Stephen and a world engorged with stains but redeemed by the fact that he has been capable of greeting its terminal message in the shape of Nell. She is the very image of chivalry. It is Aickman's sole successful marriage. If he wrote further stories, they have not been published. It is not, in any case, easy to comprehend that a man may reach much closer to the other side of the Styx, and tell the tale.

Selected Bibliography

WORKS OF ROBERT AICKMAN

We Are for the Dark: Six Ghost Stories, with Elizabeth Jane Howard. London: Cape, 1951. (Aickman's stories are "The Trains," "The Insufficient Answer," and "The View.")

The Late Breakfasters. London: Gollancz, 1954.

Dark Entries. London: Collins, 1964. (Contains "The School Friend," "Ringing the Changes" [1955], "Choice of Weapons," "The Waiting Room" [1956], "Bind Your Hair," and "The View.")

Powers of Darkness. London: Collins, 1966. (Contains "My Poor Friend," "Your Tiny Hand Is Frozen" [1953], "The Visiting Star," "A Roman Question," "The Wine-Dark Sea," and "Larger than Oneself.")

Sub Rosa: Strange Tales. London: Gollancz, 1968. (Contains "Ravissante," "The Inner Room" [1966], "Never Visit Venice," "The Unsettled Dust," "The Houses of the Russians," "No Stronger than a Flower" [1966], "The Cicerones" [1967], and "Into the Wood.")

Cold Hand in Mine: Eight Strange Stories. London: Gollancz, 1975 (published 1976). New York: Scribner, 1977. (Contains "The Swords" [1969], "The Real Road to the Church" [1975], "Niemandswasser," "Pages from a Young Girl's Journal" [1973], "The Hospice," "The Same Dog" [1974], "Meeting Mr. Millar" [1972], and "The Clock Watcher" [1974].)

Tales of Love and Death. London: Gollancz, 1977. (Contains "Growing Boys," "Marriage," *Le Miroir*, "Compulsory Games" [1976], "Raising the Wind," "Residents Only," and "Wood" [1976].)

Intrusions: Strange Tales. London: Gollancz, 1980. (Contains "Hand in Glove" [1979], "No Time Is Passing," "The Fetch," "The Breakthrough," "The Next Glade," and "Letters to the Postman.")

Painted Devils: Strange Stories. New York: Scribner, 1979. (Contains. "Ravissante," "The House of the Russians," "The View," "Ringing the Changes," "The School Friend," "The Waiting Room," "Marriage," "Larger than Oneself," and "My Poor Friend.")

Uncollected Fiction

"Just a Song at Twilight." In *The Fourth Ghost Book*, edited by James Turner. London: Barrie and Rockliff, 1965.

"Laura." In *Cold Fear: New Tales of Terror*, edited by Hugh Lamb. London: W. H. Allen, 1977.

"Mark Ingestre — The Customer's Tale." In *Dark Forces*, edited by Kirby McCauley. New York: Viking, 1980.

"The Stains." In *New Terrors*, edited by Ramsey Campbell. London: Pan Books, 1980.

Autobiography

The Attempted Rescue. London: Gollancz, 1966.

There is no extended critical work on Aickman. The short essays and checklist in *Nyctalops 18* (1983) (Albuquerque: Harry O. Morris, Jr.) are useful.

—JOHN CLUTE

LLOYD ALEXANDER

1924-

OF ALL THE modern writers who have written fantasies based on the legends and myths of Wales, Lloyd Alexander is by far the best known, perhaps because his Prydain series is aimed at a younger (and therefore wider) audience than that which is likely to appreciate Evangeline Walton, Alan Garner, Kenneth Morris, or Susan Cooper. Yet his best work — his short stories and picture books, his novel *The First Two Lives of Lukas-Kasha* (1978), and the Westmark novels of the 1980's — has little to do with Wales and almost nothing to do with the supernatural, barring the appearance of a wizard or two. Alexander's real genius is not for the epic fantasy form, in which he made his first great success, but for the didactic fable, the moral lesson wrapped up in an amusing tale. His didacticism is consistent throughout his work and reflects his genuine moral seriousness, relieved by a facetious humor and enhanced by a narrative skill that he has greatly polished since he began writing fantasy in the early 1960's. Though the Prydain books remain a valuable introduction to fantasy for children, Alexander's shorter stories and later novels are more attractive to adult readers.

Lloyd Chudley Alexander was born on 30 January 1924 in Philadelphia but spent most of his life in nearby Drexel Hill, where he still lives. His father, who had a brokerage business, seems to have been a man of strict formality; in Lloyd's words, "For him, casual dress consisted of a black derby, pearl-gray spats, a black chesterfield and a cane; he was

the least droll person I knew" (*Janine Is French*, 1959). Like many writers, Lloyd had a sickly childhood enlivened by wide reading, a taste encouraged by an elderly aunt who left him her accumulation of classic novels when she died. School stifled rather than encouraged his intellectual development, and at sixteen he went to work as a bank messenger boy. After a time he attended West Chester State Teachers College for a year but found it as airless as high school had been.

World War II gave him entrée to the wider world: as well as various assignments to the artillery, to a military band, and as a medic, the army sent him to Lafayette College, the first school he ever liked. A short tour of duty in Wales during 1943 made a deep impression: the foreignness of the language, the beauty of the landscape, and the kindliness of the people sank into his consciousness, surfacing twenty years later in his first Prydain story, *The Book of Three* (1964). Eventually he went into combat intelligence and then, as the war wound down, into counterintelligence in Paris, where he attended the Sorbonne and married Janine Denni, whose young daughter he later adopted. After the war Alexander tried to become a writer through the simple expedient of writing family-saga novels set in social and cultural milieus that he knew very little about. None of the novels was published, but he managed to eke out a living in a series of jobs and to win a small reputation by translating French authors, including Jean-Paul Sartre.

After several years of unsuccessful struggle, it occurred to Alexander to try writing stories from his own experience rather than in imitation of best-sellers, and he began to achieve a moderate success. His time as a bank messenger was fictionalized in *And Let the Credit Go* (1955); his love of cats found expression in *My Five Tigers* (1956); his wife's amusing malapropisms and difficulties in adjusting to American life were memorialized in *Janine Is French*; and his admiration of, and attempts to imitate, professional musicians were humorously described in *My Love Affair with Music* (1960). The last book was praised by critics as a document of the genuine love of an amateur performer for the music to which he could not do justice. Two further books centered around animals were *Park Avenue Vet* (1962; written with Dr. Louis Camuti) and *Fifty Years in the Doghouse* (1964), a history of the Society for the Prevention of Cruelty to Animals.

His first children's books had nothing to do with his own background or experience: he was commissioned to write a biography for a children's series on Jewish-American patriots. To Alexander's surprise, the book, *Border Hawk: August Bondi* (1959), won the National Jewish Book Award. This success won him a second commission, this time for a book on the patriot and financier of the American Revolution Aaron Lopez, *The Flagship Hope* (1960). Well-received as these books were, they are outside the mainstream of Alexander's work, which has fallen into three major groups: the French translations, the semiautobiographical books of the 1950's, and the fantasies for which he is best known, the first of which was *Time Cat* (1963).

Time Cat is a fantasy of a type that was once more common than it is now, the historical travelogue. Gareth, a black cat belonging to a small boy named Jason, asks his young master to visit nine different times (his nine "lives") in which cats influenced the human lives around them. In each tale the combination of Gareth's intelligent feline nature and Jason's human sense proves a blessing to the people they meet. The strongly didactic and moral nature of Alexander's gift is displayed in this early fantasy, as various characters are guided into right paths or shown resisting tyranny with Gareth's help. A visit to ancient Japan provides an appealing and unusual side trip; although the rest of the episodes could have come straight out of the syllabus of any college course on Western civilization, Alexander was one of the first fantasy writers to show interest in non-Western traditions.

Time Cat was followed by the five books of the Prydain series. The series' hero is Taran, the ignorant, brash, and clumsy Assistant Pig-Keeper, who dreams of warlike glory. In *The Book of Three*, Taran leaves the house of his master, the wizard Dallben, for a chance at glory in the train of Gwydion, Prince of Don, but finds that being a hero is neither as easy nor as fulfilling as he had thought. Though Taran takes part in the rescue of Princess Eilonwy from Spiral Castle and the finding of the enchanted sword Dyrnwyn, which alone can defeat the evil Arawn, Death-Lord of the underworld realm of Annuvin, he realizes that he mostly got in the way and made mistakes. His friends, the would-be bard Fflewddur Fflam, the grouchy dwarf Doli of the Fair Folk, and the affectionate wild man Gurgi, behave more heroically than he does, precisely because of his thirst for glory.

In *The Black Cauldron* (1965), Taran acquits himself better: he sacrifices the magic brooch that has given him the gift of understanding nature so that a greater mission — the destruction of the Cauldron, which turns dead men into zombie warriors — can succeed. In *The Castle of Llyr* (1966), Taran learns patience when driven nearly mad by the stupidity of Prince Rhun and the selfishness of the giant Glew, and begins to exercise the authority that his assumption of responsibility for his friends has given him.

In *Taran Wanderer* (1967), Taran goes off to search for the secret of his parentage, hoping that he was born noble, so he may ask for Eilonwy's hand. After several adventures that bring him no closer to this objective, Taran tries to learn the humble crafts of smithing, weaving, and potting; but although he does well enough, he knows he does not have the talent that would allow him to be satisfied with his own work. At last he realizes that his quest has been not for his parents but for himself, so he returns to Caer Dallben determined to do whatever may be necessary in his life, even if it means staying Assistant Pig-keeper forever.

But in *The High King* (1968), which begins on Taran's journey home, Taran achieves his true destiny. Arawan Death-Lord has gathered all his forces for the final conquest of Prydain, while Dyrnwyn, which only one "of able worth" may wield, has been stolen and lies hidden in Annuvin with other treasures and lore of Prydain. Huge armies of the unkillable Cauldron-Born have joined with rebellious southern kings and are marching on Caer Dathyl, stronghold of good King Math. A great battle before Caer Dathyl fails to hold back the onslaught; Math is slain and the castle thrown down. But Taran, with his faithful friends, gathers together a troop of survivors who travel by difficult mountain passes to Annuvin and defeat Arawn when Taran finds that in great need he is able to use Dyrnwyn.

It is after the last battle that the true climax of the series comes. Gwydion, Son of Don, announces that all the Children of Don must now leave Prydain and return to their home in the Summer Country, where no one ever dies; and those who helped them in their struggle against Arawn are to be rewarded by going with them. But Taran has made promises to friends who died in the war, there is rebuilding to be done, and he gives up his right to passage to the Summer Country. At this, Dallben gladly reveals the truth at last: Taran was prophesied to be the High King of Prydain but could take power only when he gave up a kingdom of happiness for a kingdom of sorrow—that is, when the boy's dreams of glory gave way to the mature adult's acceptance of responsibility.

The widespread acclaim that Alexander now enjoys in the world of children's books began when *The Book of Three* was published. In the *New York Review of Books* (3 December 1964), Janet Adam Smith sounded the first note in what was to become a symphony of praise: "As in T. H. White, voices of today echo in a fabulous world of dwarfs and warriors and talking creatures. It is a book to suit all who delight in *The Sword in the Stone.*" Other well-known critics, including Virginia Kirkus and Ruth Hill Viguers, joined in agreement with Smith's assessment as the Prydain series developed and culminated in the Newbery Award winner *The High King.*

Yet this comparison with T. H. White now seems inapt. Alexander's casual American diction injects contemporaneity into the Welsh mythic material that he used to create Prydain, as does White's use of anachronisms in Camelot. In *The Sword in the Stone*, the anachronisms, like Sir Ector's school song and Morgan le Fay's movie-star appearance, illuminate the epic material, because they show how modern culture still contains the culture of that older world. But in the Prydain books the anachronisms clash with, and distract the reader from, the epic, for White blended twentieth-century humor with mythic power more convincingly than Alexander did. The Prydain books display neither White's narrative fluency nor his inventiveness, and the first two books are so clumsily written that their continuity is seriously affected. For example, characters who were nowhere nearby a moment ago are suddenly in the midst of the action, while the time scale of the action often seems to stretch out or speed up for no apparent reason. Alexander could hardly be expected to meld modernity with myth successfully when he had not solved basic problems of narrative, although this problem lessened with time.

This difficulty with tone is symptomatic of a more serious problem that the Prydain series presents to the reader: its attempt to substitute the moral seriousness of fable for the mythic seriousness of epic. The purpose of fable is to teach by satirizing; the purpose of myth, particularly in its grand epic form, is to reinforce whatever view of the meaning of reality is held in common by all whose culture partakes of that specific mythic tradition. But the reality behind Prydain is not creation but instruction, for every episode contains a lesson, usually restated in bald terms at its conclusion. Many fantasies are about a character's struggle toward maturity, but Alexander harps relentlessly on the theme; there is no subtext, no depth. Without side issues and seemingly unnecessary details, the Secondary World simply does not come to life. For example, Arawn Death-Lord, who in the Welsh mythic tradition represents the blessed necessity of death, which clears the ground for new growth, is simplified into a mere villain. This reduction of Arawn from a natural force and supernatural person to a black hat is paralleled by similar reductions throughout the series, which have the cumulative effect of distorting, and finally destroying, the units of the mythic material, too intractable in itself to be successfully shaped into the straightforward moral lesson that Alexander was trying to teach.

But when Alexander turned from his ambitious epic to the shorter forms of fairy tale and fable, his didacticism stopped being a liability. The successful fable does not need a whole new universe to support it; it thrives on the archetype. A character like Taran, so unsatisfactory as a full-fledged character in a novel, is perfectly credible when conceived as a swineherd who wins a princess and a kingdom. Alexander's breezy humor lends his tales and fables an individuality and a freshness that the Prydain books lack. For example, the title story of *The Town Cats and Other Tales* (1977) tells how a back-alley tomcat saved a town from the ruinous exactions of the king's corrupt envoy by convincing the towns-folk to sacrifice their dignity—and sacrifice it they do, to the cat's and the reader's amusement.

In *The Truthful Harp* (1967), the story of how Fflewddur Fflam got his magical instrument, the bard's kindness, generosity, and courage appear in a brighter light when contrasted with his laughable self-importance and bragging. *Coll and His White Pig* (1965) recasts, using a character from the Prydain series, the Grimm story of the youth who aided even the humblest of animals and was aided in his turn. Coll's baldness and his worry over his turnips are not sufficient to make him memorable in the context of a novel, but in this short tale they are just enough to add humor and perspective to the fairy-tale atmosphere. *The King's Fountain* (1971) lacks the drama of some of Alexander's other stories yet depicts with great tenderness the dilemma of the poor man who found that his own courage and honesty made him wiser than the elders, stronger than the blacksmith, and richer than the merchants of his land.

This turn to shorter and less epic works enabled Alexander gradually to refine his narrative facility. His next two or three novels, including *The Marvelous Misadventures of Sebastian* (1970), *The Cat Who Wished to Be a Man* (1973), and *The Wizard in the Tree* (1975), show progressive enhancement in style and polish, leaving behind the awkward and flat-footed prose of the Prydain books. *Sebastian*, in-

spired by the youth of Mozart, tells the adventures of a Baron's Fourth Fiddler, dismissed from his post by the evil Regent's lackey, who discovers his own musicianship, finds true friends in the traveling Gallimaufry-Theatricus, and meets and loves a princess. The story races breathlessly along, perhaps too precipitately at moments, as full of twists and turns as the back streets of Loringhold, where the Regent's paid assassin tries to kill Sebastian and Isabel. But although, once again, the tale centers on the hero's increasing maturity and willingness to accept responsibility, the moralizing is restrained; and charming details like the Gallimaufry's balloon, which thrills yokels by lifting them ten feet in the air, give the story a sense of ease and gusto.

The Cat Who Wished to Be a Man is Lionel, cat to the enchanter Stephanus, whose adventures as a human bring him into contact with more cruelty, greed, and outright villainy than any cat could imagine. The mere contrast between the innocence of the boy-animal and the all-too-human evil of the people of Brightford provides the moral lesson; the lack of specificity in the tale—its vaguely "long ago and far away" setting, its almost generic characters of grasping mayor, irritable enchanter, bombastic quack, and feisty heroine—provides a ready-made fairy-tale world; so Alexander can concentrate on the story, which displays a nice balance among elements of suspense, adventure, first love, and intrigue. A particularly amusing touch is Lionel's gradual loss of his feline abilities as he falls ever deeper in love with Gillian.

The Wizard in the Tree, set in the Victorian era, has a heroine whose dreams of noble wizardry are sadly dispelled when she meets a real enchanter. Mallory rescues Arbican, who does eventually aid her with his magic; but his unreliability finally teaches her what he has been telling her all along— that she never really needed his magic in the first place. This lesson, borrowed from *The Wizard of Oz*, is distinguished by a suspenseful and exciting plot and Dickensian villains, including the gloating murderer Squire Scrupnor and the unjust, nagging Mrs. Parsel.

The First Two Lives of Lukas-Kasha (1978) is more substantial than any of Alexander's previous work, although it does not represent any sort of drastic change. Indeed, the three main characters—impish Lukas; his friend the logorrheic bazaar-poet Kayim; and Nur-Jehan, the disdainful, malapert slave girl—have the same appearances and mutual relationships as Taran; Fflewddur, the amusing bard; and Eilonwy, the acerbic princess. Nevertheless, the characters are far more distinctively individual than their predecessors, and the action of the story arises organically out of Lukas' canny and roguish personality, not from any didactic scheme. Lukas' character grows more lively and believable with each episode, like the ones in which he cozens the horse thief Katir, makes the mayor of Zara-Petra an honest man, and convinces the arrogant Nur-Jehan that common sense is better than honor thirsting for blood. These vignettes of character display Alexander's talent for the clever twist and provide comic relief that does not clash with the more serious side of this story of an evil ruler's misuse of power and war against the innocent.

Westmark (1981) is a reprise, in plot at least, of *Sebastian*. It is set in a land with the same vague eighteenth-century Viennese aura: for instance, Princess Isabel's castle is called the Glorietta, while Princess Augusta's is the Juliana. The evil Regent of the earlier book becomes the evil minister Cabbarus; Quicksilver of the Gallimaufry becomes the Cagliostro-like Count Las Bombas; the Regent's nameless hired assassin is reborn as the professional killer Skeit. Yet the two stories are not about the same things: whereas Sebastian needs to know what he can do, Theo needs to know what sort of man he is—and fears the answer.

Alexander has never written a sequel to *Sebastian*, so its happy ending remains that of a fairy tale; but *The Kestrel* (1982), the sequel to *Westmark*, shows the difference between fairy tale and reality. The story of *Westmark* continues with almost no break, and it is a painful story, for Theo's forgiveness of the wicked Cabbarus leads to the even worse evils of treason and war. And Alexander pulls no punches for juvenile readers: this war is real. Again and again Theo is revolted by some new cruelty, only to become accustomed to, and then even outdo, the savagery he has seen. Friends die horribly, enemies are butchered, the innocent and guilty suffer alike.

Theo finally gets his answer—the same answer

that is all anyone gets. He is a human being like any other, and the redemption of his hopes and the forgiveness of his sins are the same: in remembering those who have died, both enemy and friend, and acting accordingly—that is to say, in learning from experience. But this time Alexander does not tell the reader his lesson; rather, he shows it. His own experience in World War II and his desire to point a moral are finally melded into a work that is wholly organic and deeply felt.

As well as continuing to publish novels and stories, Alexander became one of the founders, and an active member of the editorial board, of the children's literary magazine *Cricket*. He has also been author-in-residence at Temple University and has written several articles and essays on fantasy, including an introduction to a well-received annotated bibliography of modern fantasy literature, *Fantasy Literature: A Core Collection and Reference Guide* (1979). There he has stated syncretic beliefs about reading fantasy: "We read fantasy any way that pleases us at a given moment: as mythologists, historians, theologians, psychoanalysts, or social critics. In the end, I must agree with what Elizabeth Cook says about these perspectives in *The Ordinary and the Fabulous*: "None of them are right separately, and all of them are right collectively." This is a view that is perhaps too narrowly focused on the use, rather than the nature, of fantasy, but it is consistent with Alexander's work. His own fantasies have been presented to readers in terms which make it clear that he has perceived moral instruction as their greatest need, and who can say, in this era of barbarism, that he is wrong?

The moral instruction that Alexander has given is notable for its benevolence. Throughout his work he has praised good sense, humor, tolerance, humaneness, kindness, generosity, courage, and respect for intelligence, skill, and hard work. If he has sometimes praised them rather more baldly than subtly, they are still, after all, what fantasy is about: the moral life, reified in the fiction of myth. His lack of interest in the supernatural per se is summed up in the wizard Arbican's farewell to Mallory: "There's nothing of true value I could give you that you don't have already." The powers outside humans are already within them. Alexander's best works reify fable and fairy-tale traditions and, at the same time, express real experiences—the suffering of war, the pleasures of friendship and craftsmanship, and the contentment in helping others. If this is not "high" fantasy, the creation of worlds, it is at least good fantasy.

Selected Bibliography

FICTION OF LLOYD ALEXANDER

The Prydain books

The Book of Three. New York: Holt, Rinehart and Winston, 1964. London: Heinemann, 1966.

The Black Cauldron. New York: Holt, Rinehart and Winston, 1965. London: Heinemann, 1967.

Coll and His White Pig. New York: Holt, Rinehart and Winston, 1965. (A picture book illustrated by Evaline Ness.)

The Castle of Llyr. New York: Holt, Rinehart and Winston, 1966. London: Heinemann, 1968.

The Truthful Harp. New York: Holt, Rinehart and Winston, 1967. (A picture book illustrated by Evaline Ness.)

Taran Wanderer. New York: Holt, Rinehart and Winston, 1967. London: Fontana, 1979.

The High King. New York: Holt, Rinehart and Winston, 1968. London: Fontana, 1979. (Winner of the Newbery Medal, 1969.)

The Foundling and Other Tales of Prydain. New York: Holt, Rinehart and Winston, 1973. (Six short stories set in the time before the birth of Taran.)

Other novels and stories for children

Time Cat: The Remarkable Journeys of Jason and Gareth. New York: Holt, Rinehart and Winston, 1963. As *Nine Lives*. London: Cassell, 1963.

The Marvelous Misadventures of Sebastian: Grand Extravaganza, Including a Performance by the Entire Cast of the Gallimaufry-Theatricus. New York: Dutton, 1970. (Winner of the National Book Award, Children's Books, 1971.)

The King's Fountain. New York: Dutton, 1971. (A picture book illustrated by Ezra Jack Keats.)

The Four Donkeys. New York: Holt, Rinehart and Winston, 1972. London: World's Work, 1974.

The Cat Who Wished to Be a Man. New York: Dutton, 1973. London: World's Work, 1974.

The Wizard in the Tree. New York: Dutton, 1975.

The Town Cats and Other Tales. New York: Dutton, 1977.

NONFICTION OF LLOYD ALEXANDER

"Substance and Fantasy." *Library Journal*, 91 (15 February 1965): 6157–6159.

"The Flat-Heeled Muse." *Horn Book*, 41 (April 1965): 141–146.

"Wishful Thinking—or Hopeful Dreaming?" *Horn Book*, 44 (August 1968): 382–390.

"Newbery Award Acceptance." *Horn Book*, 45 (August 1969): 378–381. (Alexander's acceptance speech.)

"No Laughter in Heaven." *Horn Book*, 46 (February 1970):11–19.

"Identification and Identities." *Wilson Library Bulletin*, 45 (October 1970): 144–148.

"Literature, Creativity, and Imagination." *Childhood Education*, 47 (March 1971): 307–310.

"High Fantasy and Heroic Romance." *Horn Book*, 47 (December 1971): 557–584. (Reprinted in *Crosscurrents of Criticism*, edited by Paul Heins. Boston: Horn Book, 1977.)

"Fantasy as Images: A Literary View." *Language Arts*, 55 (April 1978): 440–446.

Foreword to *Fantasy Literature: A Core Collection and Reference Guide*, by Marshall B. Tymn, Kenneth J. Zahorski, and Robert H. Boyer. New York: Bowker, 1979.

"The Grammar of Story." In *Celebrating Children's Books*, edited by Betsy Hearne and Marilyn Kaye. New York: Lathrop, 1981.

CRITICAL AND BIOGRAPHICAL MATERIAL

Carr, Marion. "Classic Hero in a New Mythology." *Horn Book*, 47 (October 1971): 508–513.

Commire, Anne. *Something About the Author: Facts and Pictures About Contemporary Authors and Illustrators of Books for Young People*. Vol. 1. Detroit: Gale, 1971.

De Montreville, Doris, and Hill, Donna, eds. *Third Book of Junior Authors*. New York: Wilson, 1971.

Townsend, John Rowe. *Written for Children: An Outline of English Language Children's Literature*. Philadelphia: Lippincott, 1974.

Wintle, Justin. "Lloyd Alexander." In *The Pied Pipers*.

New York: Paddington Press, 1975. (An interview with Alexander.)

BIBLIOGRAPHY

Zahorski, Kenneth T., and Boyer, Robert H. *Lloyd Alexander, Evangeline Walton Ensley, Kenneth Morris: A Primary and Secondary Bibliography*. Boston: G. K. Hall, 1981. (An exhaustive bibliography with a lengthy essay on each writer's work.)

—DIANA WAGGONER

POUL ANDERSON

1926-

POUL ANDERSON RETAINS more than a touch of his Danish seafaring and storytelling ancestors. For more than three decades, as his best critic has noted, he has "roved time's fartherest reaches—backwards, forwards, and sideways" (Sandra Miesel, "Of Time and the Rover"). He has traveled in no single vessel. Since the publication of "Tomorrow's Children" (*Astounding,* March 1947) while Anderson was still an undergraduate at the University of Minnesota, he has experimented with and mastered nearly all of the forms in the spectrum from fantasy to science fiction, with mystery, juvenilia, poetry, and criticism tossed in. He is as comfortable with sword and sorcery and space opera as with hard science fiction.

Anderson has been as prolific as he is versatile, with more than fifty books and over two hundred stories to his credit. Almost all of these are well crafted, and most of them represent new uses for the older forms that Anderson inherited from the golden age of science fiction. The beliefs of that early era remain: a love of storytelling, a sense of epic adventure, and a belief that what humans do can make a difference in the universe.

These fruitful voyages out have made Anderson a difficult writer to categorize. He is usually treated as a science fiction writer who uses elements of fantasy, and it is true that his body of science fiction works—many of them part of his vast future history—outnumber the fantasy. Anderson attributes that to the greater market for science fiction and still claims fantasy as his first love. Heroic fantasies such as *The Broken Sword* (1954), *Three Hearts and Three Lions* (1961), and *Hrolf Kraki's Saga* (1973) hold their own with such hard science fiction as *Brain Wave* (1954), *Tau Zero* (1970), and *The Avatar* (1978) as works of imagination.

Anderson is at his best, in fact, when combining fantasy and science fiction. When the world of faerie and the world of technology meet, as in "The Queen of Air and Darkness" (*Magazine of Fantasy and Science Fiction* [hereafter abbreviated *MFSF*], April 1971) and "Goat Song" (*MFSF,* February 1972), the result is not only new twists of plot and character but also serious reflections on the place of humans in the cosmos. By far the bulk of Anderson's fantasy includes at least an element of science fiction, if only to transport the reader to alternate worlds, and even his hardest science fiction has increasingly introduced elements of fantasy.

Characteristic of both Anderson's fantasy and science fiction is the epic scope and feel of the Scandinavian saga. His future-history series, about an age called the Technic Civilization, chronicles the movement of humans out into the universe from A.D. 2100 to 7100. The two heroes of these novels and stories, Nicholas van Rijn, a merchant trader, and Dominic Flandry, a military officer, carry with them into the future the qualities of old Norse heroes. Lasers may replace swords, but the pattern of human endeavor remains the same. Planets light-years away still bear old epic names: Rustum, Roland, Beowulf.

Because Anderson has been adept at whatever form he tries, he has never cut out a niche that is exclusively his own. His admirers often offer this as an explanation of why, in spite of the quality of both his craft and his imagination, none of Anderson's novels has ever won either a Hugo or a Nebula. In short fiction, however, he has won his share, with seven Hugos and two Nebulas: Hugos for "The Longest Voyage" (*Analog*, December 1960), "No Truce with Kings" (*MFSF*, June 1963), "The Sharing of Flesh" (*Galaxy*, December 1968), "The Queen of Air and Darkness" (1971), "Goat Song" (1972), "Hunter's Moon" (*Analog*, November 1978), and "The Saturn Game" (*Analog*, February 1981); and Nebulas for "The Queen of Air and Darkness" and "Goat Song."

Poul Anderson was born on 25 November 1926 in Bristol, Pennsylvania, to parents of Danish ancestry. He lived briefly in Denmark prior to World War II. After returning to the United States, he attended the University of Minnesota along with Gordon R. Dickson, a science fiction writer with whom he later collaborated on several stories. He graduated in 1948 with a degree in physics and an interest in writing. His interest in science and his familiarity with Scandinavian languages and culture, especially saga, folklore, and mythology, influenced the shape of both his science fiction and his fantasy. He drifted into these genres, too, because he felt that, unlike mainstream fiction, these old forms still encouraged "storytelling."

Anderson's first efforts at science fiction were welcomed by John W. Campbell, Jr., editor of *Astounding*, but he moved slowly at first, with only ten stories published by 1951. His first novel, *Vault of the Ages*, a juvenile post–atomic holocaust story, was published in 1952. The following year, his imagination seemed to explode. In 1953 he published nineteen stories and the magazine versions of three novels, including the heroic fantasy "Three Hearts and Three Lions," which he expanded to book form in 1961, and the hard science fiction novel *Brain Wave*, which was published in book form in 1954. These two novels, which indicated

the directions in which Anderson's writing was to go, remain among his most enduring works.

Brain Wave established his reputation for hard science fiction. The story imagines what happens when earth moves out of a galactic cloud that had blanketed the solar system since the beginning and that had inhibited the intelligence of all organic life. As the cloud departs, intelligence levels skyrocket: animals develop memory, retarded humans become normal, and geniuses become superhuman. The novel delineates in detail how this could happen and what the effects would be on society, culture, and religion. Like later Anderson works, *Brian Wave* is remarkable for its careful world-building and for posing serious questions—in this case, how much intelligence is actually desirable for humans.

Three Hearts and Three Lions showed Anderson equally capable of heroic fantasy. He took a favorite pulp genre and not only crafted it better than earlier efforts but also made something more of it than sword and sorcery adventure. Holger Carlsen, a Danish commando during World War II, is knocked unconscious during a raid and wakes to find himself in an apparently ancient world, whose inhabitants know who he is and have been awaiting him. With the help of a dwarf, Hugi; a "swan-may," Alianora; and a Saracen turned Christian, Carahue, Holger sets out on a quest to discover who he is. He soon discovers that this is Middle Earth in a parallel universe and that a major battle is building between the worlds of faerie, on the side of Chaos, and human beings, on the side of Law—the same conflict between the forces of evil and good that he had been involved in in the twentieth century. At first Holger's inexperience and innocence make him weak. He barely survives a series of enticements from the faerie world, offering him love, pleasure, sex, and release from cares. He finds it especially hard to resist Morgan le Fay, who leads the forces of Chaos. But with the help of his companions, each new temptation strengthens him, and he proves victorious over Morgan le Fay and her giants, dragons, trolls, werewolves, and hell horses. He eventually learns that in the earlier world he is Holger Dansk, the Defender, the continental equivalent of King Arthur, and that Morgan has sent him into the twentieth century in order to weaken the forces opposing her. When his quest is done, he returns to a mundane middle-class existence, where he meets the narrator, who tells the story. Middle World is left with the promise of his return in the future, when he will again be needed in the eternally recurring war against the forces of evil and Chaos.

Three Hearts and Three Lions shows many of the techniques and themes that Anderson would develop in his heroic fantasy. Sword and sorcery fiction had always used a large canvas and other epic devices, but Anderson's incorporation of authentic Scandinavian folklore, names, styles, rhythms, dialects — enough to give the flavor of the sagas without distracting the modern reader — gives his work a solidity that the old space operas lacked.

Anderson's stylistic adaptation of the sagas is at its best in *Hrolf Kraki's Saga*, which is hardly even fantasy. It is, rather, an attempt like Thomas Malory's in *Le Morte d'Arthur* to draw scattered accounts of a legendary hero together. Hrolf Kraki is mentioned in *Beowulf* and other early texts. The heavy beat and alliteration of Anglo-Saxon translate well into a kind of poetry-prose. In this heavy style, full of understatement and grim humor, Anderson captures the brutal but joy-filled sensuous life of his hero.

Most prominent among the themes of Anderson's heroic fantasies is the war between Chaos and Law. So widespread and ancient is this battle, so much a pattern behind the rise and fall of whole civilizations, that Holger Carlsen finds it taking place at the same time in parallel worlds. It is a theme Anderson repeats in both science fiction and fantasy. In *Operation Chaos* (1971) a werewolf and witch team is sent by the military (in a world based on magic rather than gunpowder) to harrow hell itself and confront ultimate Chaos. Chaos, in Anderson's world, is always the aggressor seeking to bring down Law. Dominic Flandry and Nicholas van Rijn, the future-history heroes, fight the same battles on a technological rather than supernatural level.

Of greatest importance in this battle, from Anderson's perspective, is the individual man (and woman, in his more recent fiction). He would agree with Carlyle that "history is nothing but the biography of great men." As in the sagas (and as in the ideal of rugged individualism rampant in nine-teenth-century American culture), it is the individual who discovers a continent or settles a country, who carries the human spirit forward. Only a Hrolf Kraki can forge a kingdom and wield peace. Chaos awaits the death of the hero.

Further, the saga hero is not born heroic; he earns his greatness by direct experience. He needs the native gifts of brawn and brains, but until he survives an often brutal rite of passage, he cannot lead. Nearly the whole of *Three Hearts and Three Lions* deals with Holger Carlsen's preparation.

Even experience is not enough. The hero's success depends upon his fate — his *wyrd* — which hangs over him and will eventually bring him down. The gloomy overtones that critics have noticed in Anderson are not his alone. The old saga hero is filled with the joy of being alive in this world, loving and fighting, but is surrounded by a tragic vision more desperate than that of the Greeks. The great Scandinavian heroes celebrate with the gods in Valhalla — but only until Ragnarok, that twilight when the universe and even the gods themselves will perish to nothingness.

The contrast between human and faerie seen in *Three Hearts and Three Lions* is made clearer in Anderson's second heroic fantasy, *The Broken Sword*, loosely based on the *Hervarar Saga*, *The Second Lay of Helgi Hundingsbane*, and the medieval Danish ballad "Aage and Else." Vulgard is stolen away from his parents as an infant by Imric, the elf-earl, and raised as Imric's own child. As he grows up and learns elf ways, he is also forced to confront the poignant differences between human and elf: the brevity of human life and the nonhuman grace of the elves. Scafloc (his elf name) becomes a hero in a war between Trollheim and Alfheim (Elfland), because he can wield iron, but doubts his own worth until he finally confronts the evil elf-troll whom Imric had put in Scafloc's place, and who has been raised as the real Valgard. Only then does he discover his self.

For much of his career, this remained Anderson's portrait of the world of faerie. Elfland is a false Eden, a green world that would seduce humans away from their responsibilities, away from their quests and their tragedies, which alone can make them fully human. The world of faerie is attractive, but as Anderson once reported, "I myself am of skeptical temperament, and I cut my philosophical teeth on the most hard-boiled logical positivism." Anderson heroes, too, must learn to shake off the enthrallment of fancy; duty must overcome pleasure; the hero must learn to stand alone.

Anderson heroes have changed little during his career, aside from becoming a bit older and more reflective, but the world of faerie has grown more and more problematic in his works. However far in the future Anderson roved, however complex his machine civilizations, faerieland would not go away.

"The Queen of Air and Darkness" illustrates Anderson's growing dilemma. Written nearly twenty years after *Three Hearts and Three Lions*, the story is better crafted and more disturbing. As the story opens, two changelings, Mistherd and Shadow-of-a-Dream, are enjoying a magical twilight. A pook (child-stealing fairy), Ayoch, brings a human child into the clearing, seeking approval of the Queen of Air and Darkness, a beautiful but terrifying figure who, in guises such as Lilith and Morgan le Fay, has appeared in every culture and in the works of writers such as T. H. White and C. S. Lewis. Here she rules a kingdom of pooks, nicors (sea sprites), elves, giants, and changelings, those humans who have been stolen away and raised in the world of faerie.

The reader soon discovers that this is all taking place on the planet Roland, so distant from earth and other human civilizations that its million humans, who live mostly in the city of Christmas Landing, are visited by spaceships only two or three times a century. The kidnapped child is Jimmy Cullen, three-year-old son of Babro Cullen, a recent arrival on Roland. Babro hires a very Holmesian detective, Eric Sherringford, to find her son.

Like the other humans on Roland, Eric has never actually seen any natives, and no artifacts have been found. All Eric has to go on are the many rumors of the Queen and her kingdom that isolated settlers have reported for many years. Though children have disappeared, the rumors are generally discounted as leftover folklore that the Rolanders brought with them from earth. Yet Eric proposes that there is some truth to these myths and, with Babro, sets out for the northland, where the Queen supposedly reigns.

Shortly, Eric captures Mistherd, and almost at the same time, Babro is captured when she responds to a call from her son and leaves the vehicle they have come in. On the way to Carhedin, home of the Queen, Babro discovers that the horse carrying her is identical to one she owned as a child, and that her captor is her husband, who has been dead for four years. He urges her to remain with him and Jimmy at Carhedin, a reunited family. Her son also pleads with her to remain.

Meanwhile, Eric convinces a defiant Mistherd of the deceit practiced by the Queen by turning on a machine that filters out the telepathy that had maintained Mistherd's illusions. Mistherd sees that the Queen and the other natives are saurian humanoids, and is bitter at the deception. Together she and Eric break through the Queen's defenses and rescue Babro and Jimmy.

Seen from this perspective, the world of faerie has once again been a deceit from which humans need rescuing. However, disturbing questions haunt Eric and Babro. In the first place, although the natives have used the memories of human folklore brought to Roland as weapons to entice the humans, the fact that these myths and archetypes have lasted in those memories even on this distant planet suggests to Eric that they are more than mere inventions. They must satisfy some suprarational need that science and the machine do not. Why, Eric wonders,

across that gap of centuries, across a barrier of machine civilization and its utterly antagonistic world-view . . . why have hardheaded, technologically organized, reasonable, well-educated colonists here brought back from the grave a belief in the Old Folks?

Babro supplies an answer when, sitting with Eric in the blue twilight of Roland amid the glowing lanterns of firethorn bushes, she admits that she has trouble thinking of stars as "balls of gas, whose energies have been measured." Eric denies her suggestion that such feelings are nonsense and tells her that "emotionally, physics may be a worse nonsense . . . man is not at heart rational."

Later, when Babro stands before the Queen, attracted by the dream, she struggles only weakly to be rational and scientific, for "why should we believe ashen tales about . . . atoms and energies, nothing else to fill a gape of emptiness?" Anderson supports this position himself in a 1981 essay, "Fantasy in the Age of Science":

No matter how far we have wandered or how much artifice we have raised around ourselves, we are still creatures of sea and forest, open skies full of wings, sun, moon, stars, the night wind; we were meant to marvel at the world and to stand in awe before the unknown.

In the second place, the world of the Queen is only partly dream and illusion. The natives actually are faerielike in that they can live only in the twilight northern hemisphere, they are gentle, and they do communicate with telepathy and other nonrational means. Further, their world does have much that seems superior to the humans' machine culture. They are expert biological scientists but have decided against the machine to live in harmony with nature and with each other. Human lifestyle has its problems, too. When Babro begs the Queen to send her back to her human world, the Queen, with deceitful half-truth, responds, "back to prison days, angry nights, works that crumble in the fingers, loves that turn to rot or stone or driftweed, loss, grief, and the only sureness that of the final nothingness." Babro cannot gainsay the Queen's accusation that humans are "not wholly alive." Nor can Babro and Eric deny that it is the humans who are transgressors on this planet and that the human methods of fighting are far worse than the enticements of the Queen.

Nevertheless, the Queen and her faerieland are sham, and to fall for the dream that she offers would end in the gradual disappearance of human life from Roland. The position that Anderson arrives at in the end is an uncomfortable one, a paradox in which belief and doubt must exist side by side. The rationalist Eric comes to accept aspects of human experience — feelings and telepathy — that lie outside hard science. He knows that in order to study the folklore of the planet "he must get an understanding — not an anthropological study; a feeling from the inside out." He explains to Babro that myth and archetype

are powerful because such figures as Christ, Buddha, Hamlet, and the Earth Mother "crystallize basic aspects of the human psyche, and when we meet them . . . our reaction goes deeper than consciousness."

Humans need these myths. In *Orion Shall Rise* (1983), Talence Ferlay, one of a small group of leaders who are shepherding the earth back to civilization after a holocaust, permits the people to think of him as a "saint," though it makes him uncomfortable, because "every society must have a myth to live by, else it's a walking corpse."

At the same time, to fall under enchantment is stultifying. Anderson injects himself into the "Queen" narrative to suggest that Homo can truly be called sapiens when he practices his specialty of being unspecialized: "His repeated attempts to freeze himself into an all-answering pattern or culture or ideology . . . have repeatedly brought ruin." Eric and Babro have themselves let the archetypes of the rational detective and the grieving widow limit their lives. Only when they free themselves to experience a richer world can they begin to fall in love.

Eric suggests that the answer is to live "with" our archetypes but not "in" them. Rather than destroy the natives' culture, he hopes that humans will learn to share, because both cultures have much to teach each other. Machine and faerie need not be at odds.

A similar viewpoint is suggested in "Faun" (*Boy's Life*, September 1968). On the planet Arcadia, Edmund Wylie, a "product of city and machine," becomes lost in the wilds. Unable to cope by himself, he is saved from a saber-toothed dire lizard by a boy-faun, whose cynopard pet chases the lizard away. The boy could have killed the lizard with the gun he was carrying; but when confronted by Wylie for his refusal to shoot, he replies that he wouldn't use the gun when there was a chance of saving Wylie "in a better way," that is, naturally.

The faun turns out to be Wylie's own son, who is part of a carefully controlled scientific plan to terraform the planet for human use without upsetting the balance of nature, as was common human practice. The faun is therefore half human, carrying biological equipment on his back to collect and analyze specimens, and half sentient being, whose lowered threshold of perception allows an "ocean of visual detail, sounds, odors, tastes, vibrations, temperatures to roll over him." The Arcadian scientists realize that "an ecology is too vast and complex for blind changes." "Shall we make another mechanical desert," they ask, "or shall we make it bloom? To help nature help us, we must trace out the myriad relationships in the web of life, their interactions, significance, meaning."

If the faeries of Middle Earth have not followed humans out into space, the values of that world have, and they have tempered Anderson's perceptions and his rugged heroes. In *The Avatar* a typical Anderson hero, Dan Broderson, accompanied by Joelle Ky, a "holothete" who guides spaceships by connecting her mind to the on-board computers, and Caitlin Mulryan, a fun-loving earth mother, range through space to discover the secret of the Others, mysterious aliens who have placed T machines around many suns with inhabitable planets for unknown reasons. The T machines permit instantaneous transport to other T machines light-years away, making interstellar space-travel possible.

This time, however, it is neither Broderson's derring-do nor Joelle's keen intellect that leads them to the Others. Rather it is Caitlin who finally makes contact through her intense feelings and intuitions. The Others turn out to be advanced beings capable of experiencing the pains and joys of life in the universe from leaf to fish to bird to human through "avatars" of that life. They are content to experience life rather than interfere because they believe that "every kind of life is equally precious, with an equal right to go its own unique way." Caitlin herself turns out to be an avatar of the Others and must decide whether to merge with them or remain human.

The values of faerie are no longer deceitful, an evil Eden, but a total part of human experience, feeling and reason together. What one critic calls Anderson's dual and paradoxical vision of "bard and technocrat" has fused.

Anderson's most sympathetic view of Middle Earth's inhabitants can be found in *The Merman's Children* (1979). Based on an old Danish verse tale, "Agnete and the Merman," the novel chronicles the last days of a colony of mer-folk toward the end of

the Middle World when humans have begun to dominate all life. The point of view is primarily that of three halflings—children of Vanimen, leader of the mer-folk colony of Liri, and Agnete, a human who lived with Vanimen for eight years. The children are part of both worlds, and as human life encroaches on Liri, they must decide which world to be a part of. As mer-folk, they could live happily and at peace for centuries; as humans, their lives would be transitory and troubled, but they would have souls and attain heaven. Mer-life seems preferable. Humans are cruel slaveholders who "wrangle about such snailshell matters [as theology] when they might be savoring this world." But Vanimen also senses something tragically attractive in transitory humanity. "Amidst every misery," he wonders, "what do they glimpse, that we are forever blind to?"

Both human and mer-folk, then, have gifts that could be valuable to the other; the tragedy is that each culture and race wants only its own ways. For Anderson, the marvel of the universe is its diversity: "how marvelous and manifold this universe is which we have the joyous privilege of inhabiting." At the end of the novel a puzzled priest who should be cursing the soulless mer-folk, but cannot help loving them, sermonizes: " 'For God so loved the *world*. . . .' I take that to mean everything He ever made, and there's nothing He did not make. . . . I've a notion He creates nothing in vain."

But to dwell too long on the philosophical underpinnings that support Anderson's epics of the imagination is to miss out on the fun that he feels to be the basis of fantasy. It is, he says, the "purest form of fiction . . . it keeps imagination alive, playfulness, wonder . . . [and] helps maintain our basic humanity." Much of Anderson's fantasy, then, is just good clean fun.

In *The High Crusade* (1960), a spaceship full of Wersgorix who make the mistake of landing near a peaceful English village in A.D. 1345 intend to take over the earth as they had many other planets. They overlook English pluck and common sense, however, and are no match for Sir Roger de Tourneville and his small band of English knights, who quickly prove the superiority of arrow and sword over laser. With the one spaceman left alive as pilot, Sir Roger and the whole village use the ship as easy passage to Europe and the Crusades. The Wersgor spaceman heads instead for home, where he supposes Roger will get what he deserves. The Englishmen are not to be outdone, however, and soon the Wersgorix planet's defenses—including space craft, force-shields, and advanced weaponry—surrender to medieval tactics. From here, English feudalism spreads throughout the universe, planet after planet held by Roger against the day when the English king may happen to find them.

In another English fantasy, *A Midsummer Tempest* (1974), Anderson assumes that in a parallel universe Shakespeare was a historian rather than a playwright, and that his characters were real. Here Oberon, Titania, Puck, Prospero, and Caliban bemoan the coming of science and Puritanism. They ally themselves with Prince Rupert of the Rhine, nephew of Charles I and leader of his troops. Aided by Prospero's magic, talismans, and all the dead of Glastonbury Tor, royalist and faerie forces defeat Cromwell. *A Midsummer Tempest* also shows Anderson's stylistic skill at its best. Writing almost entirely in iambic pentameter, Anderson carries off the dangerous act of imitating Shakespeare.

Anderson's playful fantasy shows itself best, perhaps, in his many short fantasy pieces. Titles such as "Bullwinch's Mythology" (originally "Poulfinch's Mythology," *Galaxy*, October 1967) and "On Thud and Blunder" (1978), and characters such as Cronkite, in "The Barbarian" (*MFSF*, May 1956), indicate the playfulness. One of his best short pieces is "House Rule" (1976), which takes place at the Old Phoenix Tavern at a crossroads between universes. Here Albert Einstein and Leonardo da Vinci can meet and discuss relativity; Eric the Red, Sancho Panza, and Anderson's own Nicholas van Rijn can meet for a beer; and Héloïse can meet an Abélard from a parallel world in which he is still whole, and spend one passionate last night with him. All this is managed by Taverner, the innkeeper, who decides who comes and when, and from which of the many universes. He keeps life at the tavern interesting.

There is more than a little of Taverner in Anderson himself. Like the innkeeper, he can range the universe for a good story and for characters whose meetings will delight the reader. Anderson has run

his literary Old Phoenix Inn for many years and shows no sign of diminishing in quality or quantity—or in the broad sweep of his canvases—his work supported by a belief that "no matter what we learn in the future, what we confront will always be a mystery."

Selected Bibliography

FICTION BY POUL ANDERSON

Vault of the Ages. Philadelphia: Winston, 1952.

Brain Wave. New York: Ballantine, 1954. London: Heinemann, 1955.

The Broken Sword. New York: Abelard-Schuman, 1954. Revised edition. New York: Ballantine, 1971. London: Sphere, 1973.

War of the Wing-Men. New York: Ace, 1958. London: Sphere, 1976. As *The Man Who Counts* (magazine-version title). New York: Ace, 1978.

Guardians of Time. New York: Ballantine, 1960. London: Gollancz, 1961.

The High Crusade. Garden City, N.Y.: Doubleday, 1960. London: Corgi, 1981.

Three Hearts and Three Lions. Garden City, N.Y.: Doubleday, 1961. London: Sphere, 1974.

Trader to the Stars. Garden City, N.Y.: Doubleday, 1964. London: Gollancz, 1965. (Collection.)

Flandry of Terra. Philadelphia: Chilton, 1965. London: Coronet, 1976.

Tau Zero. Garden City, N.Y.: Doubleday, 1970. London: Gollancz, 1971.

Hrolf Kraki's Saga. New York: Ballantine, 1973. London: Futura, 1978.

The Queen of Air and Darkness and Other Stories. New York: New American Library, 1973. London: New English Library, 1977. (Collection.)

The Many Worlds of Poul Anderson. Radnor, Pa.: Chilton, 1974. As *The Book of Poul Anderson*. New York: DAW, 1975. (Collection.)

A Midsummer Tempest. Garden City, N.Y.: Doubleday, 1974. London: Severn House, 1976.

A Knight of Ghosts and Shadows. Garden City, N.Y. Doubleday, 1975. As *Knight Flandry*. London: Sphere, 1978.

The Best of Poul Anderson. New York: Pocket Books, 1976. (Collection.)

The Avatar. New York: Berkley/Putnam, 1978. London: Sidgwick and Jackson, 1980.

The Earth Book of Stormgate. New York: Berkley/Putman, 1978. (Collection.)

A Stone in Heaven. New York: Ace, 1979.

The Merman's Children. New York: Berkley/Putnam, 1979. London: Sidgwick and Jackson, 1981.

Fantasy. New York: Pinnacle, 1981. (Collection.)

Orion Shall Rise. New York: Simon and Schuster, 1983.

NONFICTION BY POUL ANDERSON

Is There Life on Other Worlds? New York: Crowell-Collier, 1963.

"The Creation of Imaginary Worlds: The World-Builder's Handbook and Pocket Companion." In *Science Fiction, Today and Tomorrow*, edited by Reginald Bretnor. New York: Harper and Row, 1974. (A detailed account of how Anderson determines the parameters of distant planets on as scientific a basis as possible.)

"The Profession of Science Fiction VI: Entertainment, Instruction, or Both?" *Foundation: The Review of Science Fiction*, 5 (1974): 44–50. (Discusses the role of the science fiction writer.)

"Star-Flights and Fantasies: Sagas Still to Come." In *The Craft of Science Fiction*, edited by Reginald Bretnor. New York: Harper and Row, 1976. (Anderson discusses his affirmative view of humans and the universe, and his preference for saga and epic forms.)

"Fantasy in the Age of Science." In *Fantasy*, a collection edited by Poul Anderson. New York: Pinnacle Books, 1981.

CRITICAL AND BIOGRAPHICAL STUDIES

Elliot, Jeffrey M. "Poul Anderson: Seer of Far-Distant Futures." In *Science Fiction Voices No. 2*. The Milford Series, Popular Writers of Today. San Bernardino, Calif.: Borgo Press, 1979. (In this interview Anderson discusses his craft and his preferences in science fiction.)

Elliott, Elton T. "An Interview with Poul Anderson." *Science Fiction Review*, 7 (May 1978): 32–37. (Anderson comments on his early career, ideas, characters, themes.)

McGuire, Patrick L. "Her Strong Enchantments Failing." In *The Many Worlds of Poul Anderson*, by Poul Anderson. Radnor, Pa.: Chilton, 1974, 85–113. (A discussion of "The Queen of Air and Darkness" that is applicable to the rest of Anderson.)

Miesel, Sandra. "Challenge and Response: Poul Anderson's View of Man." *Riverside Quarterly*, 4 (January 1970): 80–95. (Examines Anderson's themes with reference to specific works.)

————. *Against Time's Arrow: The High Crusade of Poul Anderson.* San Bernardino, Calif.: Borgo Press, 1978. (Covers Anderson's career from his first story to 1978.)

————. "Of Time and the Rover: An Afterword." In *The Guardians of Time*, by Poul Anderson. New York: Pinnacle Books, 1981.

BIBLIOGRAPHY

"Poul Anderson: Bibliography." *Magazine of Fantasy and Science Fiction* (April 1971): 56–63. (This whole issue is devoted to Anderson.)

—ROALD D. TWEET

PIERS ANTHONY

1934–

ODERN FANTASY ATTEMPTS to capture an uneasy union between logic, quite often drawn from the contemporary sciences, and something akin to mythology. Much as science fiction makes halting efforts to consolidate the ethos of twentieth-century society, so science fantasy and pure fantasy peer beyond the physical universe as limned by science and technology and try to provide links with another part of man's mortality, a parcel of human intellect universally represented by myth. In the *Iliad* and the *Odyssey* Homer encapsulated for early Greek society both tales of the powers of the gods and the quest tale. Twentieth-century writers of fantasy have created many mythic worlds just beyond the ken of men, yet just within reach.

The enormous popularity of J. R. R. Tolkien's trilogy *The Lord of the Rings* demonstrates the deep modern-day attraction of myth and universes inhabited by mythical beings; one of the great strengths of Tolkien's tales (in addition to his minute command of what might be called, paraphrasing Yeats, the Anglo-Saxon twilight) is the unity in his otherworldly characters, who are simply and clearly identified with "real" things. Without the matrix of myth and the gods and powers from which are derived purpose, fantasy has little cohesion other than as an adventure story, most commonly seen in the many quest novels that festoon the paperback sections of bookstores. The best of the modern craftsmen of fantasy know this, and they give some of their tales a gossamer beauty, even though these fic-

tional myths live only on the pages and in the minds of millions of readers.

Piers Anthony is certainly a typical example of a writer of fantasy and science fiction, and most of his work combines elements from both genres. One could separate his novels and short stories into fantasy or science fiction, but since there is a continual integration of fantasy and science in almost all of Anthony's works, his fiction is best viewed as a whole, shorn of artificial divisions or labels.

Piers Anthony is the pen name of Piers Anthony Dillingham Jacob, who was born in Oxford, England, on 6 August 1934. After childhood moves from England to Spain and then to the United States, he gained a B.A. degree from Goddard College in 1956. Having served in the United States Army from 1957 to 1959, he attended the University of South Florida in Tampa and obtained a teaching certificate in 1964. As is the case with many science fiction writers, Anthony practiced several professions before he became a full-time free-lance writer in 1966, including a stint as a technical writer for Electronic Communications, Inc., in St. Petersburg and as an English teacher at the Admiral Farragut Academy there.

Although Anthony's popularity as a fantasy and science fiction writer began with the publication of *Chthon* in 1967, he had already produced eight short stories between 1963 and 1967, which had been published in various main-line science fiction periodicals (*Fantastic, Amazing, Analog, If,* and *Gal-*

axy). In these early stories, Anthony demonstrates a fine skill in description coupled with a natural talent for fashioning detailed and convincing pictures of alien worlds, sometimes well within the usual definitions of science fiction but quite often encompassing baroque elements of fantasy. His writing is well paced and occasionally manifests exceptionally great artistry, but Anthony's greatest fault may be that he writes too easily. Many of his stories bear the marks of unrevised initial drafts, written quickly for a known market.

The majority of Anthony's almost three dozen novels are parts of a series, in which themes and characters reappear in altered worlds or dimensions as the novels succeed one another. Intriguing is the Magic of Xanth sequence, which includes *A Spell for Chameleon* (1977), *The Source of Magic* (1979), *Castle Roogna* (1979), and *Night Mare* (1982). In *A Spell for Chameleon*, Bink, the main character, is confronted with the questions of whether there is indeed magic in the universe and, in particular, whether he has magical powers. The answer to the first question is yes, but Bink also discovers that he has the ability to resist the harm or evil that magic can impose. This revelation then casts the themes that Anthony has disguised within a chain of intricate, consistent definitions of the nature of magic. A magician named Humfrey appears to instruct in the proper use of this peculiar power, which has its own rules and limits, and soon the reader understands that Anthony is employing magic as a metaphor for nature in all its forms and that conservation of magic is absolutely essential. The point is clear: conservation of the earth's natural resources is essential. Xanth cannot understand the lesson proffered by the magician, and *The Source of Magic* develops the thesis that only after a demon (literally) has been released will conservation become understood as a necessity; the techniques of understanding are wrapped in the bright ribbons of ecological balance. Science, the reader is told repeatedly, has its rules of logic and perception but can lead only to what Anthony sees as a rationality defined by formula, a soulless existence countered only by emotion.

In spite of the weighty, repeated admonitions, Anthony is able to sustain an interest in the story of Xanth by a facile ability to suggest a shift from one physical state into another, nicely illustrated in *Night Mare*. In this fifth novel of the Xanth series, one meets Night Mare, who provides dreams of fear and who has the uncanny and normal ability to slide through physical barriers as if they did not exist. As a horse, she stands as one of Anthony's more believable characters, and *Night Mare* draws tightly the tapestry woven in previous novels in the Xanth series: initially Mare Imbrium (puns abound in Anthony's work) finds that she has not performed her stated job well enough, but she is unable to improve the quality of bad dreams that she visits on sleeping mortals; that failing allows the Night Stallion to send her into exile, into the world of light, where she is charged to deliver a message for a king. "Beware the Horseman!" she is told to say. Does this message allude to the invasions of barbarians in the north of Xanth, or does it signify the demise of the king? The question seems explicit, but Anthony focuses attention on how a world can be saved by a king who abdicates his power; what he calls a "soul-horse" can easily succeed where a mere king cannot. Science and its rigid logic have failed, in contrast to a combined feeling of color and space and an internally consistent system of dream conservation and the touch of soils, which have succeeded.

If the Xanth series is a piquant exploration of how perceptions of magic and science may be placed side by side and overlapped, the ecological-physiological trilogy consisting of *Omnivore* (1968), *Orn* (1970), and *Ox* (1976) indicates the fine intellect and literary gifts that Anthony too seldom exploits. *Orn* may be one of the best novels that consider the problems of mammal and avian physiology, and one is struck by its account of how wasteful is the underlying pattern of metabolism characteristic of higher animal life, with the exception of birds. The plot, such as it is, is rather wobbly, consisting of the adventures of curiously (usually monosyllabically) named human protagonists (Cal, Veg, and Aquilon) on a planet that is Earth at the close of the Cretaceous, and the beginning phases of the Eocene. Cal, Veg, and Aquilon are also the leading characters in *Omnivore* and *Ox*, yet Anthony's strongest portrayals are not of these three human explorers but of the Mantas and Orn in *Orn* and the eponymous Ox. The Mantas are alien companions of the three humans (two men and a woman) and have qualities of both fungi and mammals, together with the ability to fly (in the manner of the manta ray in Earth's oceans) and a panoply of sense perceptions that function as multiple antennae for the humans.

Orn is a giant flightless bird clearly recognizable as a Diatryma, a creature found fossilized in the lower Eocene beds of Wyoming. Anthony imbues his Diatryma with a millennia-deep racial memory that enables Orn to "think" in terms of the countless variations of environmental experiences since the dawn of life itself. In *Orn*, Anthony reveals an unusual interweaving of the elements of fantasy and science fiction with sociobiology and structural anthropology. He skillfully stitches fragments of Edward O. Wilson's concept of biological variables to applications of similar limitations found in the structural anthropology of Claude Lévi-Strauss and then uses the techniques of fantasy to bind these disparate elements into a convincing image of a giant, flightless bird who knows without thinking, who understands without knowing. Especially memorable in *Orn* are the passages depicting Orn's pursuit of Ornette, the female of the species:

Ornette stopped, panting. Orn, hardly two wingspans behind, stopped also. The chase had to halt when the sun dropped, to resume in place when it rose again. The night was for feeding and resting and . . . courtship. Thousands of generations before them had determined this, and the pattern was not to be broken now.

The swamp spread out below from a comparatively thin tributary stream here, and there were fish in it and mams in burrows adjacent and arths available for the scratching. They hunted separately, and fed separately. Then, as full darkness overtook them, they began to dance.

Ornette crossed the plain, away from him, until she was a female silence in the distance. Orn stood, beak elevated, waiting. There was a period of stillness.

Then Orn stepped forward, spreading his wings and holding them there to catch the gentle evening breeze. He gave one piercing, lust-charged call. She answered demurely; then silence.

Orn moved toward her, and she toward him, each watching, listening, sniffing for the other.

Slowly they came together, until he saw the white of her spread wings. The remiges, the rowing feathers, were slightly phosphorescent when exposed in this fashion, slick with the oils of the courtship exercise; and so she was a winged outline, lovely. He, too, to her.

In the sight of each other, they strutted, he with the male gait, she the female. They approached, circled, retreated, their feet striking the ground in unison, wings always spread. Then Orn faced her and closed his wings, becoming invisible, and she performed her solo dance.

(chapter 11)

In *Ox*, Anthony continues with an occasionally skilled combination of fantasy and the stock settings of science fiction (a prehistoric planet populated by dinosaurs, as well as by quasi-robots), but with the Presence of Ox, who—or which—is a "Pattern." But the major concern in *Ox* is not the brittle trappings of pseudoworlds, robots, and dinosaurs, or even the presumed plights and narrow escapes from earthquake and giant reptiles by the three human explorers; rather, Anthony probes the question of why and what dreams are. "What happens to any dream artifact when the sleeper wakes?" asks one of the characters as they all contemplate the "vision of sexuality" that has been evoked. Anthony may not intend to turn H. G. Wells's famous novel *When the Sleeper Wakes* slightly askew, but the echoes are certainly strong.

Anthony has other objectives in mind than Wells's waking dreamer in tomorrow's world: Anthony, as in most of his novels, looks backward into the immeasurable depths of the human subconscious and repeatedly asks questions about the nature of fantasy and its connections (if any) with the so-called real world; he inquires into the nature of dreams as potential illustrations of the existence of man as man within himself, physically inchoate yet well defined in and on other planes than the waking ones. With Orn and Ox he seeks memory that is stored rather than learned—a problem raised by Plato, who inquired in the *Meno* about the knowledge of the soul prior to birth; Anthony asks if such "folk memories" were not typical of man's earliest life, as Jean Auel suggests in her richly detailed novels *The Clan of the Cave Bear* (1980) and *The Val-*

ley of Horses (1982), which depict the dawn of man in Europe 50,000 years ago. In *Macroscope* (1969), Anthony asks similar questions through the tarot and astrology; he proposes that space opera and astrology are both symbols of the basic pattern in human history: the "discovery" of rigid and carefully defined blueprints in the universe and the sense of wonder attending the "discovery" of something that is simply invariable.

These splendid questions demand solid writing and thoughtful solutions, which Anthony cannot seem to provide: his novels and their weak characters are not able to bear the weight of these very significant, often philosophical, problems. In *Chthon* and *Phthor* (1975) the reader meets an underside world, perhaps like many claustrophobic nightmares, but the action turns on an escape from garnet mines, some flimsy pseudosex, and the inevitability that man will discover the necessity of ecological balance through his shadowy visions in the half-waking state. The settings are suggestive, the premises are exciting, but Anthony cannot or will not exercise his intellect and his writing power to raise his novels above the level of adventure.

Even when Anthony turns to what a critic might call "pure" fantasy, these themes are repeated. In *Hasan* (1977), Anthony employs the venerable form of the bazaar stories of the Middle East (best known through *The Arabian Nights*) in an ornate and picaresque way to delineate sexual fantasies, and morality and immorality as defined by magic and ecology. *Hasan* is pleasant reading, but the weak portrayals of Hasan, a would-be magician; Bahram, an evil child-killer; and Dahnash, a true magician, cannot bear the weight of significance that Anthony places on them in terms of his theme of conservation: magic (again nature) is good, but good only when used carefully and subject to the laws of conservation. The reader recalls the far more involving tales in the original *Arabian Nights*, and concludes that *Hasan* is merely trite.

Devices in fantasy intrigue Anthony. *Macroscope* illustrates his conviction that astrology and the tarot just might hold some "truth"; *Chthon* shows his idea that nightmare worlds depict a piece of real existence; the Xanth series suggests an extension of dreams into magic; and the Cluster series—

Cluster (1976), *Chaining the Lady* (1978), *Kirlian Quest* (1978), and *Thousandstar* (1980)—projects the tarot into a literal system of solutions to the struggle between determinism and free will. By employing the fantasy device that what are presumed to be symbols for something else are, in reality, the things themselves, Anthony has delved into a fictional realm that bears much affinity to the world of very ancient religion. If the starships of *Chaining the Lady* have the literal structures of tarot symbols (cups, swords, and so on), then one perceives that Anthony is arguing that the deeper mythological and religious memories of humans demand a literal existence, as did old Roman religion when it spoke of the Temple of Mars containing war: inside the temple was a sword, which *was* war, and when a soldier took up his sword for a war, he grasped war (the god) literally and directly, not a symbol.

Anthony muffles much of his insight with the expected sexual derring-do that consumes many pages in his novels—for example, the "conquests" of females in *Chthon* and the surprisingly angry view of women in *Refugee* (1983), the first volume of *Bio of a Space Tyrant*. Moreover, Anthony's facile ability with words has led him into greater dependency on the "names" of the protagonists to speak of their essential qualities: in *Omnivore*, *Orn*, and *Ox*, Veg is, indeed, a vegetarian, with all the fussiness expected of a stereotypical abstainer from meat; in *Refugee*, one finds the tasteless Hope Hubris, who indulges in whims of savagery and sadomasochism (in response to a current market demand?) as he seeks his ideal woman—named Helse Hubris, no less. *Refugee* stands as a shallow polemic directed at a number of contemporary irritations (such as "poverty-stricken foreign freeloaders"), and the use of spirits as opposites of physical humans is almost smothered by Anthony's ire at the state of the world.

The publication of *All* in 1978 brought together the three novels of Anthony's Battle Circle trilogy, *Sos the Rope* (1968), *Var the Stick* (1972), and *Neq the Sword* (1975). Recognition by the science fiction and fantasy professionals had come to Anthony when he won the 1968 prize given by Pyramid Books, the *Magazine of Fantasy and Science Fiction*, and Kent Productions for *Sos the Rope*, the first of three books on what might happen on a post-atomic war Earth if mankind had indeed learned any lessons from the inevitability of destruction preceding the nuclear holocaust. By contrast with Anthony's later, complicated scenarios, which murkily fuse magic, the tarot, astrology, dreamlore, and various psychological viewpoints, the Battle Circle trilogy is written with a refreshingly spare use of pseudoscientific lore, and one can easily follow the linear development of civilization after the nuclear wars.

First, there is a stage of rejuvenation of bureaucracy in the large Tribe of Sol, accompanied by a seemingly monastic preservation of "odd knowledge" (technology inherited from the old days), suggesting an orderly and careful rediscovery of that technology. As a character, Sol is a little more convincing than many in Anthony's novels. Sol must wage wars of conquest to compensate for his own lack of power to produce children. Sos concocts strategies for struggles undergone in the name of vengeance, and the reader gains a warning against the reassertion of pride, jealousy, and sex. Finally, the political order realized by Neq and what are called "the crazies" makes certain that this bright new world will not be polluted by pride, jealousy, sex, and stupidity and its first cousin, instant rage.

By comparison with Anthony's later writing, the Battle Circle books are streamlined, albeit simple in an occasionally negative way, but when set beside the more recent Adept trilogy — *Split Infinity* (1981), *Blue Adept* (1981), and *Juxtaposition* (1982) — they can be approached with a sense of gratitude. *Blue Adept* may be the worst of Anthony's novels, even though one meets there a peculiar brand of unicorn who experiences the usual dimension-slippages expected in Anthony's works. The author cannot hide his boredom with his own prose, and any reader who recalls *Orn* will instantly recognize the "dances" of the unicorns as simply reworked from the courtship rituals of the prehistoric birds.

Piers Anthony is an excellent example of a great writing talent who has been seduced by the apparent freedom of fantasy but who has forgotten what all great modern psychologists have taught about fantasies, both private and public: they generally tend to become repetitive, following a carefully laid plan predetermined by one's own childlike recollections of "what it would be like to have power over the parent," or, later, in adolescence, "what it would be like to have power over women (or men)." The finest writers of modern fantasy have clearly understood that myths, rooted within a lengthy, historical folk tradition, are the most fertile grounds for fantasy worlds and that childhood daydreams soon become trite, boring, and ultimately uninteresting except to one's psychiatrist. A single fundamental idea drives almost all of Anthony's writing: conservation. One fundamental question haunts Anthony: What do the persistent assumptions of magic, astrology, and similar forms of human perception (or misperception) of the physical universe mean about human existence in that universe? In some respects, Anthony is a contemporary counterpart of John Wyndham, who pleaded for a return to a more "balanced time" when life was uncomplicated by human emotions, which are nicely and constantly represented by the surging emotions of sexual attraction. Memory will recall how splendid existence was before sex became a drive, an urge that brought jealousy, hate, politics, and power struggles.

Anthony's novels and short stories demonstrate why talented writers, with some notable exceptions, normally turn to science in their attempts to grapple with the basic question concerning reality. One need only mention "Things Are Not Always What They Seem" by Paul Davies in his *Other Worlds* (1980) to show the would-be writer of fantasy just how fruitful and instructive are the speculations of modern physics to an author who seeks "fantasy worlds" far beyond childhood repetition. Anthony may be correct in emphasizing the long history of magic and astrology; but in voicing anger at the new, uncertain world of science, he has forgotten that magic itself laid the foundations of science.

Selected Bibliography

WORKS OF PIERS ANTHONY

Chthon. New York: Ballantine, 1967. London: Macdonald, 1970.

Omnivore. New York: Ballantine, 1968. London: Faber and Faber, 1969.

Sos the Rope. New York: Pyramid, 1968.

Macroscope. New York: Avon, 1969. London: Sphere, 1972.

Orn. New York: Avon; Garden City, N.Y.: Doubleday, 1970. London: Corgi, 1977.

Var the Stick. London: Faber and Faber, 1972.

Neq the Sword. London: Corgi, 1975.

Phthor. New York: Berkley, 1975. London: Panther, 1978.

Cluster. New York: Avon, 1976. As *Vicinity Cluster.* London: Millington, 1979.

Hasan. San Bernardino, Calif.: Borgo Press, 1977.

Ox. New York: Avon, 1976. London: Corgi, 1977.

Piers Anthony's Hasan. San Bernardino, Calif.: R. Reginald/Borgo Press, 1977.

A Spell for Chameleon. New York: Ballantine, 1977. London: Futura, 1978.

Chaining the Lady. New York: Avon, 1978. London: Panther, 1979.

Kirlian Quest. New York: Avon, 1978. London: Panther, 1979.

Castle Roogna. New York: Ballantine, 1979. London: Futura, 1979.

The Source of Magic. New York: Ballantine, 1979. London: Futura, 1979.

Thousandstar. New York: Avon, 1980.

Split Infinity. New York: Ballantine, 1981. London: Granada, 1983.

Blue Adept. New York: Ballantine, 1981.

Night Mare. New York: Ballantine, 1982.

Juxtaposition. New York: Ballantine, 1982. London: Granada, 1983.

Bio of a Space Tyrant. Vol. 1: *Refugee.* New York: Avon, 1983.

CRITICAL AND BIOGRAPHICAL STUDY

Barrow, Craig Wallace. "Anthony, Piers." In *Twentieth Century Science Fiction Writers,* edited by Curtis C. Smith. New York: St. Martin, 1981. (Includes a listing of uncollected short stories.)

BACKGROUND WORKS

Davies, Paul. "Things Are Not Always What They Seem." In *Other Worlds: A Portrait of Nature in Rebellion, Space, Superspace and the Quantum Universe.* New York: Simon and Schuster, 1980.

Dawood, N. J., ed. *Tales from the Thousand and One Nights.* Baltimore: Penguin, 1973.

Matthew, W. D., and Granger, W. "The Skeleton of *Diatryma,* a Gigantic Bird from the Lower Eocene of Wyoming." *Bulletin of the American Museum of Natural History,* 37 (1917): 307–326.

Romer, Alfred Sherwood. *Vertebrate Paleontology.* 3rd ed. Chicago: University of Chicago Press, 1974.

Rose, H. J. *Religion in Greece and Rome.* New York: Harper and Row, 1959.

Scarborough, John. "Greeks and Myth." In *Facets of Hellenic Life.* Boston: Houghton Mifflin, 1976.

————. "John Wyndham." In *Science Fiction Writers,* edited by E. F. Bleiler. New York: Scribner, 1982.

Shalvey, Thomas. *Claude Lévi-Strauss: Social Psychotherapy and the Collective Unconscious.* Amherst: University of Massachusetts Press, 1979.

Thorndike, Lynn. *A History of Magic and Experimental Science.* 8 vols. New York: Columbia University Press, 1925–1958.

—JOHN SCARBOROUGH

PETER S. BEAGLE

1939-

PETER BEAGLE'S GIFT for fantasy is rare in contemporary literature. In seven books and numerous shorter works, he has shown himself equally capable of evoking glamour from the mundane and of deflating high-flown romanticism. Both enamored and suspicious of poetry and myth, his is a contemporary sensibility. A guitarist and folk singer, infatuated with song and its promise of immortality, he is also a naturalist, comfortable with animals and suspicious of humans' pretentious claims.

Born in New York City on 21 April 1939, to Simon and Rebecca Soyer Beagle, both teachers and inveterate readers, Beagle claims to have been a writer all his life. A fat, asthmatic, lonely child, he compensated with a rich fantasy life, working up his own imaginative creations to supplement those that he knew from books and films. If, as he says, he "slept" through his formal schooling and much of his childhood, he read voraciously, maybe more than was good for him. He learned enough to earn a B.A. degree from the University of Pittsburgh in 1959, and to write a well-received first novel, *A Fine and Private Place* (1960), published before he was twenty-one.

After a trip to Europe, Beagle accepted a writing fellowship to Stanford University, where he wrote the short story "Come, Lady Death" (*Atlantic Monthly*, September 1963). His trip to California with a painter friend is chronicled in his second book, *I See by My Outfit* (1965). As he tells it, they rode their motor scooters across the continent, singing songs and seeing myths wherever they went. An eastern city boy, allergic to many of the animals he loved, he took on a western menagerie outside Santa Cruz, California, along with a wife and three children from her previous marriages. Now divorced, he lives in nearby Watsonville.

As a free-lance writer, he has written only two other explicit fantasies: *The Last Unicorn* (1968), produced from his script as an animated feature film (1982), and "Lila, the Werewolf" (1969), a short story. Of his long-promised third novel only a fragment, "Sia" (1977), has appeared, but he has not stopped writing.

Besides reviews and articles (some autobiographical), he has written television and movie scripts (including Ralph Bakshi's animation of J. R. R. Tolkien's *The Lord of the Rings*, 1978). He has also collaborated on four illustrated nonfiction books. *The California Feeling* (1969) combines Beagle's prose with photographs by Michael Bry and others. Their attempt to record the real California responds to a fear that Beagle claims to share with all immigrants to the Golden State: that what attracted them to it will soon disappear. In the purely commercial *American Denim: A New Folk Art* (1975), his text identifies myths and UFO visions grafted onto homely materials. His own favorite of his books, *The Lady and Her Tiger* (1976, officially by Pat

Derby, an animal trainer originally from Tolkien country, England's Sussex), laments the loss of the wild and man's failure to live with it.

Beagle's latest book, *The Garden of Earthly Delights* (1982), is a commentary on the symbol-laden paintings of the fifteenth-century Dutch artist Hieronymus Bosch. The commentary, explicitly not that of a professional art critic, sympathizes with a moralistic view of the world that is largely out of favor in the world. Both medieval and modern, realistic and fantastic, Bosch's images, although impossible, center on this world, not that of the hereafter. Incongruous at first glance, the topic fascinates Beagle. His whole oeuvre testifies to the common ground of the Jewish writer and the Christian painter. Both are witty, distinctly conscious of death and social injustice, disdainful of a society committed to shortsighted materialism, and attuned to the marvelous in daily life. These qualities are abundant in Beagle's fantasy fiction. "Come, Lady Death" is set in eighteenth-century England, when class differences were marked and seemed likely to remain so. At the last formal ball of the aged and bored Lady Neville, the guest of honor, Death, attends as a beautiful young girl. Asked to remain by the terrified yet fascinated guests, then to choose her replacement, she picks logically enough: Lady Neville has lived a full but useless life and was heartless enough to send Death's invitation via a dying child.

Setting and characters—a romantic poet, a death-seeking soldier, newlyweds, an aging beauty clinging to her last days, the hairdresser whose child is dying—are lovingly detailed. As much fantasy goes into re-creating the period as into portraying the title figure. Yet reversals of expectations (both characters' and readers') undercut the fantasy's escapism. Even the glamour of the setting reminds us of the cruelty and inequities of society and of life. Lacking the self-consciousness and humor of Beagle's other fantasies, the story evokes memories of Edgar Allan Poe. Exorcising his gruesomeness, it plays with his poetic ideal of the death of a beautiful woman. In Beagle's fairy tale, nobody "lives happily ever after."

More explicitly mordant, "Lila, the Werewolf" tells of a discovery by Joe Farrell (also the protagonist of Beagle's unfinished third novel). Lila Braun, who lives with him, has a grisly secret life every full moon, which ravages the neighborhood's pet population. Fascinated—even aroused—by her "problem," Farrell does nothing about it except talk with his friend Ben. "It's only Lila," he points out reasonably, exercising his "gift for acceptance."

Having forgotten to take her special pills one month, Lila in heat attracts every male dog in the neighborhood. Assisted by her mother, Bernice (whom he calls the "real werewolf"), Farrell possessively tries to protect *his* werewolf. Becoming human again to survive the silver bullet of the apartment building's central European custodian, Lila escapes in haste. Farrell cannot escape Bernice, however, who keeps him apprised of Lila's status: a Stanford psychologist marries her and gets a perfect research topic.

This story exemplifies "modern" fantasy for many. Into an otherwise ordered, rational world a single impossibility intrudes. The solidity of the New York setting and of Farrell's acquaintances is a continual reminder that the premise is absurd. Yet their acceptance raises the question of whether modern man's unflappability might be simply amorality or apathy. Beagle claims to be embarrassed by the tale's misogyny and bizarre eroticism, which suggests a darker side to his liberal personality and a literal reading of his "love" for animals.

Mundane in both setting and action, Beagle's first novel, *A Fine and Private Place*, is a comedy in a city graveyard. Yorkchester Cemetery, in his hometown, the Bronx, shelters the living as well as the dead. Jonathan Rebeck, a former druggist who could not satisfy his customers' demands for medicinal magic, has hidden out there for nineteen years. His simple needs are taken care of plausibly, if the mechanics of housekeeping are not scrutinized too carefully. Housed in a mausoleum, served by public toilet facilities, Rebeck is fed by a loquacious raven, not because he is a prophet, but because it is the nature of ravens to bring things to people. That the first meal he brings is baloney should not go unnoticed.

Besides Rebeck, the cemetery houses both corpses and their ghosts, until the latter (in the nineteen-year-old author's metaphysics) become as separated from life mentally as the former are physically. Rebeck's first companion is Michael Morgan, a somewhat pompous history professor allegedly poisoned by his wife. They are soon joined by the plain and bookish Laura Durand, who died unloving and unloved. Rebeck also has living company in Doris Klapper, builder of a gaudy mausoleum to the memory (if not according to the wishes) of her husband, Morris. Intertwining these couples' relations, the novel ultimately bears out its epigram from Andrew Marvell's poem "To His Coy Mistress":

The grave's a fine and private place
But none, I think, do there embrace

Ostensibly hardheaded realists, Michael and Laura turn romantic in contemplation of what they no longer have: they can talk but not touch. Opposites at first—she is tired and wants to forget; he wants fiercely to keep his memories—they are drawn together by their postmortem education. Both learn their lessons, but Michael's are harder to take. Recognizing himself in life as precisely the kind of person he hated, he also comes to remember—thanks to the raven's headline-reporting service—the way he really died. As a suicide, he must be moved from sacred ground, parting him from the first "person" he has ever really loved.

Meanwhile, Mrs. Klapper's advances threaten Rebeck's security and revive her own interest in life. Klapper (as she calls herself) also lives in the past, trying to fend off the living death of older Jewish women she knows. Having done without for so long, Rebeck likes her company but rebuffs her gifts (Morris' old clothes). His epiphany comes from Morris' ghost, reminding him of their simple but profound difference: Rebeck is still alive.

Rebeck sometimes doubts that the ghosts are real, but Michael's disinterment tips the balance. Enlisting the help of Mrs. Klapper and the night watchman, Campos, who also is familiar with ghosts, he gets Laura's body moved to a public cemetery, where Michael's now lies. Passing through the gates, Rebeck leaves the graveyard for good.

Beagle plays off these facile romances against common sense, humor of situation, even a certain poetry of observation. Rebeck may think he is hallucinating, but the narrative point of view recognizes the consciousness of Michael and Laura, even of the raven. No Poe-like bringer of doom, he talks like Jimmy Durante, hitches a ride on Campos' truck, and even gets into an argument with a cheeky squirrel. Doing what a bird's got to do, the raven (like Morris Klapper) acts as a reference point against which to measure the irrational behavior of the others, living and dead.

On the other side of realism, the narrator is given to flights of poetry. Hardly a line of description lacks its own sprightly metaphor or simile, to comic or poignant effect. This surfeit of metaphor can be tedious, but it is hardly incongruous, since the main characters are trying to recall what things are like. Michael and Laura try to remember poetry, and Rebeck reads it to them, underlining the vivid sense of life that heightened language conveys. Characters are also aware that they are thinking of each other in "literary" terms, as "types" and "symbols" at "crossroads" of decision-making.

Clever and stylistically surefooted as it is, Beagle's first novel pales next to *The Last Unicorn*, a half-fledged Tolkienian "secondary universe." This is a world of mythic power, where spiritual sterility has produced a waste land, where magic works (sometimes controllably), and where unicorns are not just possible but inevitable. Yet the raven and the squirrel would find company in a blue jay and a butterfly. Indeed, this book has more humor (wit, comedy of incongruity, satire, even slapstick) than Beagle's other fictions combined.

A female unicorn, in quest of her fellows, is accompanied by a bumbling magician and an improbable virgin. On the edge of a waste land, they find the unicorns confined to the sea by King Haggard. Confronted by his defender (and the unicorns' keeper), the fearsome Red Bull, the last unicorn survives when the magician's unreliable powers make her a beautiful mortal. Castle-bound, she almost forgets her mission, courted by the king's adopted son. Her presence brings out the hero in him, the artist in the magician, and the worthy companion in the spinster. Reluctantly restored, the unicorn drives the Bull into the sea, after he kills the foolhardy prince. The unicorns are freed, the castle falls, the waste land blooms, the hero is resurrected, and the questers separate, their lives forever changed.

Explicitly identified as a fairy tale by the magician, the story has as its obvious themes the restoration of the waste land (Olderman) and the conquest of time (Norford), yet neither theme is quite what it seems. Blessed (and cursed) by a witch, the village of Hagsgate (like the king) fears what it must eventually lose. Refusing to breed or cultivate the soil, it is affluent but sterile. Failing when the castle falls, it must produce for itself. In contrast to them and to the carnival witch who earlier imprisoned the unicorn with her other prize creatures, the protagonists accept time's burden by denying its relevance to ideals. The unicorn is as reluctant to reassume immortality as she had been to lose it; the magician finds immortality a curse, gladly exchanged for control over his magic.

Despite the traditional ingredients, in other words, the story is far from conventional. Rich in symbols, it is not a strictly allegorical reading of the world. A singer as well as a storyteller, Beagle studs his narrative with songs, both haunting and mocking, and prose that is usually poetic, but switches to wisecracks at the drop of a pun. The characters, too, are variants from the fairy-tale or romance norm. Complex rather than sterotypical, half-serious and half-satirical, they have one foot in the fictional world, the other in the real one. Self-conscious about their roles, they stand in for a contemporary audience, itself unsure of how to relate to such obvious wish-fulfillment.

Unicorns are traditionally male; Beagle's is female. Immortal as a mythical ideal (that of immutable natural beauty), she sacrifices her conventional solitude in an effort to restore order. Yet if this age is remiss in not believing in unicorns, she is also incomplete, lacking the knowledge of companionship and of transience. Her regret at becoming Lady Amalthea is that mortality cannot be beautiful. Re-educated by the magician and the love of her prince, she returns reluctantly to her original form, having known love and feared death and experienced time.

Schmendrick the Magician (the name is Yiddish for "incompetent," with echoes of the comic strip's Mandrake) is an "artist" figure, gradually coming into his power. To open the unicorn's cage in Mommy Fortuna's Midnight Carnival, he must use keys; his spells won't work. When he and the unicorn are in the hands of Captain Cully and his men, Schmendrick's magic unexpectedly summons the spirits of Robin Hood and his men. Neither promising nor threatening, his very incompetence gains them entrance to King Haggard's castle. Yet his self-recognition and coming of strength prompt the unicorn and the hero to their climactic acts. It is Schmendrick, moreover, who names the roles and the story, and interprets their meanings.

Cully's middle-aged drab, Molly Grue, is only symbolically a virgin. "Where have you been?" she demands in a heartrending confession of lost time, when she first sees the unicorn. Unlike Cully, she can see the authenticity both of Robin Hood and of the unicorn's quest. Among her new companions, she blossoms, making the castle glow and winning the confidence of an oracular cat. As Schmendrick's adviser and Lady Amalthea's mentor, Molly improves with age, unlike Mommy Fortuna, whose illusions cannot overcome her melancholy fear of time.

A pathetic villain, King Haggard gains little from his power or conquest because he, too, is haunted by transience. Aptly situated on a "bluff," his castle overlooks not only a cursed land but also the sea full of unicorns, his dubious "possessions" and only solace. Identified in appearance with the castle, stabled in the cliff beneath it, the blind Red Bull is its support, Haggard's master as much as his servant. An emblem of rage, fear, and the underpinnings of social and political power, it never fights, only intimidates.

Despite his mysterious birth and upbringing, Prince Lír is an unpromising hero, first seen dallying with a princess and reading a magazine. Smitten by the Lady, he performs a panoply of heroic deeds, until Molly advises a more modern approach. Soft words may win Amalthea's affection, but self-sacrifice helps her achieve her mission, him his potential. Thus he recognizes that his role as hero is to make Haggard's moral decisions. Bringing about King Haggard's downfall as foretold, he becomes (in an almost unforgivable pun) "King Lír." He even gets his own princess to rescue, but the unicorn's love he can have only as an ideal.

Lesser roles are also filled with charming, unexpected characters. The scatterbrained butterfly first

990

alerts the unicorn to her quest and its danger with snatches of news, poetry, and commercial jingles. The blue jay (regrettably absent from the film) suffers his wife's censure for stopping to pay homage to the unicorn. A real harpy revenges herself on Mommy Fortuna (the goddess Fortune, or Lady Luck) when the carnival's cages are sprung, and the carnival's spider weeps at losing the illusion that she is Arachne. Captain Cully reverses Robin Hood's feats and writes interminable ballads, hoping the famed collector Samuel Childs will bring him immortality. Lír's natural father, Drinn, who abandoned him in infancy, when the signs that his life fitted the heroic pattern had become "too obvious," comes forward to share in the prince's accession. The cat speaks only once, to good effect; and a wine-bibbing skull, as the cat promised, shows the way to the Red Bull's lair, an exit through a clock that denies the reality of time.

Beagle's debts to other writers (among them Robert Nathan, James Thurber, Tolkien, C. S. Lewis) have been amply documented. Equally apparent is his obligation to the entire tradition of literary romance, including the metafictional reflexiveness of contemporary literature (Foust). His vision of the fanciful as real and the real as fanciful may be "anaemic" to some (Manlove), but the tradition is fresh again in his hands. He may still tend to overwrite a little and to sentimentalize, but his language makes much of his writing seem newly minted. Beagle's contribution to the fantasy shelf is slim, but even if it grows no more, it is potent word-magic.

Selected Bibliography

WORKS OF PETER S. BEAGLE

A Fine and Private Place. New York: Viking, 1960. (Novel.)

"Come, Lady Death." *Atlantic Monthly*, 212 (September 1963): 46–53. (Short story.)

"Tolkien's Magic Ring." *Holiday*, 39 (June 1966): 128, 130, 133–134. (Essay.)

The Last Unicorn. New York: Viking, 1968. (Novel.)

"Lila, the Werewolf." *guabi* (1969), as "Farrell and Lila the Werewolf." Separate publication, Santa Barbara, Calif.: Capra Press, 1974, Capra Chapbook #17. (Short story.)

The Zoo. CBS, 1973. (Filmscript.)

The Dove. E. M. I., 1974. (Filmscript.)

"Sia." In *Phantasmagoria: Tales of Fantasy and the Supernatural*, edited by Jane Mobley. Garden City, N.Y.: Doubleday, 1977, 214–221. (Fragment.)

"The Self-Made Werewolf." Introduction to *The Fantasy Worlds of Peter S. Beagle*. New York: Viking, 1978. (Omnibus edition.)

CRITICAL AND BIOGRAPHICAL STUDIES

Carter, Lin. *Imaginary Worlds: The Art of Fantasy*. New York: Ballantine, 1973.

Evory, Ann, ed. *Contemporary Authors, New Revision Series*. Vol 4. Detroit: Gale, 1981. (Includes interview with Beagle.)

Foust, R. E. "Fabulous Paradigm: Fantasy, Meta-Fantasy, and Peter S. Beagle's *The Last Unicorn.*" *Extrapolation*, 21 (Spring 1980): 5–20.

Hark, Ina Rae. "The Fantasy Worlds of Peter S. Beagle." In *Survey of Modern Fantasy Literature*, edited by Frank N. Magill. Vol. 2. Englewood Cliffs, N.J.: Salem Press, 1983.

Kiely, Benedict. "American Wandering Minstrel: Peter S. Beagle and *The Last Unicorn.*" *Hollins Critic*, 5:2 (April 1968):1–9, 12.

Manlove, C. N. *The Impulse of Fantasy Literature*. London: Macmillan, 1983.

Norford, Don Parry. "Reality and Illusion in Peter Beagle's *The Last Unicorn.*" *Critique: Studies in Modern Fiction*, 19:2 (1977): 93–104.

Olderman, Raymond M. *Beyond the Waste Land: A Study of the American Novel in the Nineteen-Sixties*. New Haven, Conn.: Yale University Press, 1972.

Stevens, David. "Incongruity in a World of Illusion: Patterns of Humor in Peter Beagle's *The Last Unicorn.*" *Extrapolation*, 20 (Fall 1979): 230–237.

Taylor, Henry. "*The Last Unicorn.*" In *Survey of Contemporary Literature*, edited by Frank N. Magill. Vol. 6, revised and enlarged edition. Englewood Cliffs, N.J.: Salem Press, 1977.

Tobin, Jean. Introduction to *The Last Unicorn*, by Peter S. Beagle. Boston: Gregg Press, 1978.

Van Becker, David. "Time, Space, and Consciousness in the Fantasy of Peter S. Beagle." *San Jose Studies*, 1 (1975): 52–61.

—DAVID N. SAMUELSON

RAMSEY CAMPBELL

1946-

IN RAMSEY CAMPBELL'S "Above the World" (*Whispers II*, edited by Stuart Schiff, 1979), a middle-aged Manchester man named Knox retraces his honeymoon trip in the mountains of England's Lake District, where his ex-wife and her new husband recently died of exposure when the evening mists converged on them. Morosely introspective, Knox literally reels from his panic-stricken moment of existential awareness when he peers into the heather as dusk and the fog overtake him:

All around him plants reproduced shapes endlessly: striving for perfection, or compelled to repeat themselves without end? If his gaze had been microscopic, he would have seen the repetitions of atomic particles, mindlessly clinging and building, possessed by the compulsion of matter to form patterns.

Suddenly it frightened him—he couldn't tell why. He felt unsafe.

As chronicled in over 200 short stories published since 1962 and in an increasingly more accomplished series of occult and suspense novels, most of Campbell's characters, after similar epiphanies, feel just as unsafe. Nearly every one of his protagonists must face up to the absurdist dread that accompanies Campbellian self-discovery. In "Potential" (*Demons by Daylight*, 1973), for example, a reticent young fellow who has never indulged in the excesses of the counterculture tempts himself into attending a ri-

tualistic "happening" that, perhaps supernaturally, transforms him into a knife-wielding murderer.

Not all of these usually fatal brushes with the dark side of existence are so ambiguous. In "Above the World," Knox may only seem to hear voices coaxing him on to his doom, but the mossy, human-looking slate figures bearing down on him at the end of the story are horribly real. In "Cold Print" (*Tales of the Cthulhu Mythos*, edited by August Derleth, 1969), a bookshop customer is promised the ultimate pornographic thrill if he just peruses a rare volume of perverse mysticism:

As the desk was thrust aside by the towering naked figure, on whose surface still hung rags of the tweed suit, Stratt's last thought was an unbelieving conviction that this was happening because he had read the *Revelations*; somewhere someone had *wanted* this to happen to him. It wasn't playing fair, he hadn't done anything to deserve this—but before he could scream out his protest his breath was cut off, as the hands descended on his face and the wet red mouths opened in their palms.

Such terrifying revelations are repeated in much of Campbell's fiction. The hideous fates that befall his banal and usually inoffensive victims are not only pointlessly extreme but are also, if not exactly deserved, somehow inevitable and even grotesquely logical. Campbell sets up these revelatory moments with meticulous care: he evokes an almost palpable

993

atmosphere of urban decay in descriptions of Liverpool and London and effectively uses fragments of surrealist imagery to reflect the distorted perceptions of his protagonists, creating confusion over what is real and what is imagined. Campbell creates this murky psychological ambience with such narrative skill, sustained stylistic precision, and visceral power that he has been hailed by critics on both sides of the Atlantic: "With the possible exception of Robert Aickman," Michael Ashley declared in 1980, "Ramsey Campbell now stands supreme amongst Britain's writers of horror and supernatural fiction"; Jack Sullivan asserted in a *Washington Post* review (25 April 1982) that "Campbell is surely the most sophisticated stylist in modern horror"; and in *Danse Macabre* (1981), Stephen King noted that "good horror writers are quite rare . . . and Campbell is better than just good."

Campbell has the ability to tap his own neurotic anxieties and dramatize them within revitalized pulp-fiction formulas. His love for the fantasy and horror genres began at a very early age, and his youthful plunges into active fandom compensated for what he found frightening in both his environment and temperament.

John Ramsey Campbell was born in Liverpool on 4 January 1946 to Alexander Ramsey and Nora Walker Campbell. Because of what he regarded as a "posh" accent and a glandular disorder lasting until mid-adolescence that made him extremely fat, Campbell was painfully shy and sensitive throughout his youth. It did not help his "extremely nervous" demeanor when his parents enrolled him at St. Edward's College in Liverpool, an expensive, rigorous all-boys grammar school operated by the Christian Brothers. There Campbell acquired both peculiarly Catholic guilt feelings and an unhealthy fear of women.

Campbell learned early on to retreat from these psychological handicaps creatively through reading and writing. With the encouragement of his mother and one of his English teachers, he started writing his own Cthulhu Mythos imitations, stolidly mimicking H. P. Lovecraft's florid style. He also began corresponding with August Derleth, co-founder of Arkham House, which publishes Lovecraftiana and similar material by newer writers. The Derleth connection encouraged both his talent and ego, as Campbell reminisced in the introduction to *Dark Companions* (1982): "Derleth liked [the Lovecraft pastiches] enough to tell me how to improve them—by describing fewer things as eldritch and unspeakable and cosmically alien, for a start, and by re-reading the ghost stories of M. R. James to learn suggestiveness—and eventually he published a book of them." With that collection, *The Inhabitant of the Lake and Other Less Welcome Tenants* (1964), "J. Ramsey Campbell" became, at eighteen, the youngest author ever published by Arkham House, although his professional literary career had actually begun earlier, when Derleth published "The Church in High Street" in his *Dark Mind, Dark Heart* (1962).

Campbell's Lovecraft imitations were serviceable at best; at worst, they carried the older writer's often stylistically tone-deaf allusiveness to an extreme. Yet even a very young Campbell knew that it would be pointless to unleash his monstrosities on Lovecraft's traditional Arkham, Massachusetts, locales. Campbell invented his own fictional domain, the Severn Valley of central England, with its cursed Roman ruins, seemingly bucolic countryside, dying industrial towns, and creepy villages. More positively, from Lovecraft, Campbell learned the absolute importance of careful organization. Indeed, Campbell's admiration for Lovecraft's structural design could also be a comment on the construction of his own work: "The story's movement has far less to do with plot than with a gradual accumulation of telling detail, presented with relentless logic; the story moves singlemindedly toward terror" (introduction to *New Tales of the Cthulhu Mythos*, edited by Campbell, 1980).

Campbell's increasing confidence in his ability to identify and express metaphorically the sources of his own fears gradually forced him to move beyond the Lovecraft orbit. This change in literary style corresponded with changes in his personal life. After leaving school, Campbell worked first for the Inland Revenue, beginning in 1962, and then, in 1966, for the Liverpool Public Library, getting new settings for his work. He continued to write, revise, and sell the occasional story as he slowly found his own stylistic voice.

The breakthrough for him came with "The Cellars" (*Travellers by Night*, edited by Derleth, 1967), which is about an office girl who discovers that the male co-worker she accompanied into Liverpool's catacombs is slowly being transformed into a dripping mound of white mold. Many of Campbell's central thematic concerns and favorite stylistic devices found their first mature expression in this horrific little gem: a visceral fear of the dark; the feeling that male-female relationships could somehow mutate into apocalyptic events; his knack for creating truly disturbing tactile imagery; and his already noted talent for investing his grimy Liverpudlian locations with eerie surrealistic beauty: "The rain still streamed down the toadstool-buff or sooty buildings to the kaleidoscopic shops which served as their foundations, their windows full of lifeless shoes and dresses; over all, detached, the streetlamps pored, and above the roofs the Liver Building clock stood with hands on hips."

While growing as a writer, Campbell also became more active as a fantasy and science fiction fan. It was through his fandom connections that Campbell met and, in 1971, married Jenny Chandler, the daughter of the Australian science fiction writer A. Bertram Chandler. (The couple have two children and currently live in Merseyside.) In 1973, Campbell quit his library post to become a full-time writer, at first living off his wife's earnings as a teacher. Campbell's activities as a fan did not diminish, however, when he settled into domesticity and began writing daily. He is president of the British Fantasy Society, a participant at many British and American science fiction and fantasy conventions, film reviewer for BBC Radio Merseyside, and editor of a number of important and well-received anthologies of original horror stories.

Campbell's shrewdness and intelligence about his field are evident in all of his work, whether as editor or author, even when he is discussing his own contributions to the genre. With characteristic perceptiveness and detachment, Campbell incisively delineated what he regarded as his major themes in a 1982 interview with Dr. Jeffrey M. Elliot for *Whispers* magazine:

Repressed fears, often from childhood, erupt in supernatural forms; hence, external terrors which relate to the psychology of the victim but which cannot be explained by it. A good example of this is "In the Bag," which appeared in Hugh Lamb's book *Cold Fear*. Another major theme is the instability of reality, especially at its most mundane. Stories such as "Litter" and "The Man in the Underpass" exemplify this, I think. Like much horror fiction, these stories have something in common with surrealism, of which I'm quite fond, not least the new perception of things we've taken for granted. . . . My writing also explores still another theme—namely, the effects of extreme situations and experiences on ordinary people. There are undoubtedly other themes, some carrying over from my childhood Catholicism. For example, the idea that evil thoughts are as dangerous as evil deeds, which occurs in "The Height of the Scream." But I don't believe it's necessarily beneficial to be too aware of one's themes, even the ones I've mentioned.

Within this precise and self-conscious listing, other recurring motifs suggest themselves to careful readers of Campbell's work. The "instability of reality" idea, which Campbell mentioned in conjunction with "Litter" (*Vampires, Werewolves and Other Monsters*, edited by Roger Elwood, 1974), a tale about a sentient pile of debris swirling around a drably impersonal Liverpool shopping complex, is also found in his many stories dealing with metamorphosis. These metamorphoses occur through the blurring and merging of individual personalities either into their ominous surroundings, as in "Napier Court" (*Dark Things*, edited by Derleth, 1971), or into their feared doppelgängers or hated rivals, as in, respectively, "The Scar" (*Magazine of Horror*, Summer 1969) and "Second Chance" (*The Height of the Scream*, 1976). Sometimes the point of view is that of the victim of the transformation; at other times it is the vantage of a helpless bystander, like the young woman who walks hand in hand with her lover into a pitch-dark cave on a Brighton guided tour, only to re-emerge moments later holding onto a blind old man, in "The End of a Summer's Day" (*Demons by Daylight*). It is a change that no one else in the tourist group notices. Loss of identity and the psychic dislocations resulting from schizophrenic trauma are twin fears that Campbell masterfully evokes.

Yet even more powerful perhaps are the terrors that Campbell conjures up from his dreaded "childhood Catholicism," most particularly "the idea that evil thoughts are as dangerous as evil deeds"—indeed, might even have an objective existence of their own, as the protagonists of "The Depths" (*Dark Companions*) and "The Height of the Scream" (title story of the 1976 collection) both discover. In Campbell's fiction, the concept of original sin and its horribly inevitable everyday effects has a special validity for children, who must face up to the harsh consequences of succumbing to momentary temptations, as do the little girls who fear and taunt the baleful neighborhood recluse in "Trick or Treat" (*Weird Tales 2*, edited by Lin Carter, 1981). The aimless viciousness of urban teenage hooliganism boomerangs on its perpetrator in "Mackintosh Willy" (*Shadows 2*, edited by Charles Grant, 1979). And a secretive little girl leads her reluctant chums to meet her mysterious newfound friend, in "The Man in the Underpass" (*The Year's Best Horror Stories III*, edited by Richard Davis, 1975), who turns out to be the incarnation of a bloodthirsty Aztec god.

When little Tonia emerges from the underpass at the conclusion of this last story and proudly announces to an inquisitive policeman, "Pop a cat a petal did it to me too," the murkily suggestive ending exemplifies one of Campbell's favorite narrative devices. When it works, as it does here, it may seem puzzling at first, but coupled with clues carefully planted throughout the story, its implications slowly sink in; and the revelation for the reader parallels the dawning, sickening realization that the characters experience. When this tendency toward narrative obliqueness does not work, Campbell can be accused of a kind of willful obscurantism, a problem that a number of his critics have noted and that Campbell himself has acknowledged. "More often than not," T. E. D. Klein observed with some exasperation in his 1977 study of Campbell's work, "I came to the end [of a Campbell story] without realizing it, turning the page only to find myself faced with a new story." Sometimes, as Klein went on to say, rereading the last couple of pages is essential to understanding the point of the whole thing; the risk that Campbell takes is that the reader might think that the extra effort is not worth it.

Other problems become noticeable in Campbell's longer works. His coldly distanced attitude toward his characters, although not so apparent in a short story, can be intrusive and alienating in a novel. In *Danse Macabre*, Stephen King observed about Campbell's first novel, *The Doll Who Ate His Mother* (1976), "Campbell is good, if rather unsympathetic, with character (his lack of emotion has the effect of chilling his prose even further, and some readers will be put off by the tone of this novel; they may feel that Campbell has not so much written a novel as grown one in a Petri dish)." Despite the brooding Liverpool atmosphere and the inspired lifting of certain plot elements from Bram Stoker's *Dracula*, the rushed quality of the ending of this first novel undercuts the book's overall impact. Like *Dracula*, the story concerns a disparate group of scared and outraged ordinary folks who find themselves reluctantly thrown together to combat an evil force that has radically disrupted their lives. Also as in the Stoker classic, the members of this group do not realize that their occult enemy is intimately present among them, and it is this obliviousness to their immediate danger that generates much of the book's suspense. The novel builds to what should have been an extremely frightening confrontation in the cellar of an abandoned house between the now totally unbalanced villain and the heroine, a lonely young woman attracted to what she views as his engaging vulnerability. But the scene does not quite come off because of Campbell's inexperience in pacing and structuring a novel-length horror story.

If the climax of *The Doll* is not as effective as it should have been because the buildup to it is perfunctory and undeveloped, the endings of Campbell's next three novels share similarly unsatisfactory payoffs, but for the opposite reason: the earlier sections that lead up to them promise far more than Campbell can deliver.

The Face That Must Die (1979) is a "straight" (that is, nonsupernatural) suspense thriller centering on the characterization of a textbook-case paranoid schizophrenic who is convinced that the dour, aging hippie he spots outside a shabby apartment building is a mass murderer deserving vigilante-style execution. From chapter to chapter, Campbell expertly alternates point of view between the psychotic middle-aged pensioner and the unfulfilled wife of his intended victim, providing a telling commentary on the desiccated underbelly of the contemporary urban body politic in a demoralized English welfare state. But the claustrophobic atmosphere sustained throughout the book is subverted at the end by moving the action to the countryside, thus dissipating the tension and disrupting the taut mood.

To Wake the Dead (1980) is another occult novel with a flawed ending. Its central character, Rose Tierney, was infested as a child with the spirit of a power-hungry Victorian magician, Peter Grace. As Grace's influence over her increases and as his followers gradually get close to her and her husband, Rose begins to manifest certain precognitive powers. The novel contains some of Campbell's best descriptive writing, especially in the extended passages dealing with Rose's out-of-body experiences, which Campbell makes seem both exhilarating and foreboding. But again the book's climax and denouement are conceptual letdowns, too predictable and pat to be aesthetically satisfying: during the climactic seance-ritual, the kidnapped Rose initiates a kind of psychic Mexican standoff by calling forth a godlike force to thwart Grace's imminent return to human form. Her triumph is short-lived, however, for she experiences a vision months later implying that Grace has returned anyway as an infant. This literal deus ex machina cosmic-cavalry rescue and its pessimistic last-page reversal must have seemed lame and derivative even to Campbell, for he dropped the original epilogue for the American edition of the novel, retitled *The Parasite*, and added a slightly more upbeat finale; unfortunately, the change is no improvement. In the revised version, Rose turns out to be the one pregnant with the reincarnated magician and must heroically sacrifice her own life to frustrate his earthly ambitions, an inside-out gloss on the final actions of the young mother in Ira Levin's *Rosemary's Baby* (1967), but without the earlier novel's cheeky deadpan irony and mordant black humor.

The Nameless (1981) also depends on last-minute reversals and surprise twists that dramatize the constant tug-of-war between the forces of absolute negation and pitifully finite human love. Another of

Campbell's put-upon yet resourceful heroines, this time a widowed literary agent guilt-ridden by the kidnapping and disappearance of her little daughter years before, learns that the girl may still be alive and a hostage to a Manson-like cult. The mother tracks down the cultists to their lair, only to discover that the daughter is their psychically gifted leader. Campbell was hard pressed to find a plausible way to conclude this book on a hopeful note: at the very moment that the daughter is about to summon some awesome demonic entity, the spirit of her dead father appears to convince her into a change of heart. The ending prompted Michele Slung to declare in her review of *The Nameless* for the *Washington Post* (20 November 1981), "I don't think it's unfair to say that, despite his technique, Campbell is better at opening the door on bad things than he is at closing it."

This Lovecraftian lurker-at-the-threshold motif receives its fullest and most assured expression, however, with *Incarnate* (1983), Campbell's most confident and best-sustained longer work so far. His central conceit in this book is that the products of the human subconscious are as physically real as the more mundane aspects of people's waking lives, as the half-dozen volunteers of an Oxford ESP/dream-research project and their families slowly learn years after the experiment was suddenly terminated. It becomes only gradually apparent to the group members that the dream they shared on the last day of the project has opened a door into another dimension, that its inhabitants want that door to stay open, and that only the subjects of the experiment can be used to fulfill the interlopers' nefarious designs. Campbell switches from character to character and from one suspense set piece to another, slowly building to the logical climactic confrontation between the scared, confused, and terribly vulnerable humans and their archetypal alter egos from the Jungian dreamworld. Campbell's knack for combining surrealistic and naturalistic imagery has never been utilized better or for a clearer and more incisively focused thematic purpose. And for once he evinces some natural sympathy for his terrified and hapless characters, dropping the usual chillingly detached pose of impersonality and indifference for a more sensitive and openly empathetic tone, thus making

Incarnate his most mature and accessible novel, structurally and emotionally.

In the introduction to his landmark horror-story anthology, *Dark Forces* (1980), editor Kirby Mc-Cauley declares that "the tale of horror is almost always about *a breaking down*. In one way or another such stories seemed concerned with things coming apart, or slipping out of control, or about sinister encroachments in our lives." Ramsey Campbell's stories, however, are almost always about things being pieced together, patterns being recognized, tantalizing clues obsessively being followed up and eventually strung into some newly understood overriding order, as the crime writer investigating a particularly loathsome homicide tries to do in "The Depths": "He remembered thinking that the patterns of life in the tower blocks had something to do with the West Derby murder. They had, of course. Everything had." Sometimes even the positioning of Campbell's words on the page yields its own secret pattern, its own hidden meaning, as happens in the anagrammatic (and enigmatic) "The Words That Count" (*The Height of the Scream*). "There were patterns and harmonies everywhere," muses Campbell's artist-protagonist in a story appropriately entitled "The Pattern" (*Superhorror*, 1976):

You only had to find them, find the angle from which they were clear to you. He had seen that one day, while painting the microcosm of patterns in a patch of verdure. Now he painted nothing but glimpses of harmony, those moments when distant echoes of color or movement made sense of a whole landscape; he painted only the harmonies, abstracted. Often he felt they were glimpses of a total pattern that included him, Di, his painting, her writing, life, the world: his being there and seeing was part of the pattern. Though it was impossible to perceive the total pattern, the sense was there. Perhaps that sense was the purpose of all real art.

These reflections could easily sum up Campbell's own approach to his craft and his unrelievedly fatalistic vision of the kind of world he writes about. To their horror, Campbell's characters discern their own integral place in the pattern when they eventually find out that the pattern exists in the first place in order to reflect their own most deeply buried fears and most carefully suppressed needs. The little boy in "Just Waiting" (*Twilight Zone Magazine*, November–December 1983) learns what it would be like to have his most secret wish come true—but first he has to consciously recognize what that wish really entails. The troubled teenager in "The Telephones" (*The Height of the Scream*) is sadistically stalked through the Liverpool outdoor telephone booths by his own latent homosexual yearnings. "He was approaching panic," Campbell relates, describing the last mortal moments of the mountain-climbing Mr. Knox in "Above the World," retracing the steps of his honeymoon trip alone and unloved: "As much as anything, the hollow at the centre of himself dismayed him."

"Dismayed" usually does not quite cover it: as Campbell time and again artfully reminds the reader, the void lies within, a truly terrifying thought. The pattern is all too clear, and one ignores it at one's peril, but each person will have to make that final connection for himself. For Campbell, pointing out the pattern and the reader's connection to it is a vital, compulsive, even ennobling activity, because for him it is indeed the words that count.

Selected Bibliography

WORKS OF RAMSEY CAMPBELL

The Inhabitant of the Lake and Other Less Welcome Tenants. Sauk City, Wis.: Arkham House, 1964. (Short stories. Signed as J. Ramsey Campbell.)
Demons by Daylight. Sauk City, Wis.: Arkham House, 1973. London: Star Books, 1975. The Jove edition (New York, 1979) deletes two stories and adds three others. (Short stories.)
The Doll Who Ate His Mother. Indianapolis: Bobbs-Merrill, 1976. London: Millington, 1978.
The Height of the Scream. Sauk City, Wis.: Arkham House, 1976. London: Millington, 1978. (Short stories.)
The Bride of Frankenstein. New York: Berkley, 1977. London: Tandem, 1978. (Novelization of the 1935 Universal Pictures motion picture. Signed as Carl Dreadstone, a house pseudonym.)
Dracula's Daughter. New York: Berkley, 1977. (Noveliza-

tion of the 1936 Universal Pictures motion picture. Signed as Carl Dreadstone.)

The Wolfman. New York: Berkley, 1977. (Novelization of the 1941 Universal Pictures motion picture. Signed as Carl Dreadstone.)

The Face That Must Die. London: Star Books, 1979. (Novel.)

To Wake the Dead. London: Millington, 1980. As *The Parasite.* New York: Macmillan, 1980. (The American edition is slightly revised; the original epilogue is dropped and a new ending is added. Novel.)

The Nameless. New York: Macmillan, 1981. London: Fontana, 1982. (Novel.)

Dark Companions. New York: Macmillan, 1982. London: Fontana, 1982. (Short stories. The Fontana edition drops four stories from the Macmillan edition and substitutes four others.)

Incarnate. New York: Macmillan, 1983. (Novel.)

Night of the Claw. New York: St. Martin, 1983. (Novel. Signed as Jay Ramsey.)

Campbell also edited and contributed to the following anthologies:

Superhorror. New York: St. Martin: 1976. As *The Far Reaches of Fear.* London: W. H. Allen, 1976.

New Tales of the Cthulhu Mythos. Sauk City, Wis.: Arkham House, 1980.

The Gruesome Book. London: Piccolo Books, 1982. (Written for young people.)

New Terrors. 2 vols. London: Pan Books, 1980.

CRITICAL AND BIOGRAPHICAL STUDIES

Ashley, Michael. "Unshackled from Shadow." *The Fantasy Reader's Guide. No. 2: The File on Ramsey Campbell,* edited by Michael Ashley. Wallsend, England: Cosmos Literary Agency, 1980.

Campbell, Ramsey. "As Far as I Can Recall." In Ashley, *The Fantasy Reader's Guide.*

Crawford, Gary William. "Campbell, Ramsey." In *Horror Literature: A Core Collection and Reference Guide,* edited by Marshall B. Tymn. New York: Bowker, 1981.

———. "The Parasite." In *Survey of Modern Fantasy Literature,* edited by Frank N. Magill. Vol. 3. Englewood Cliffs, N.J.: Salem Press, 1983.

———. "The Short Fiction of Campbell." In *Survey of Modern Fantasy Literature.*

Elliot, Dr. Jeffrey M. "Ramsey Campbell: Journey into the Unknown." *Whispers,* 4, nos. 3–4 (March 1982).

King, Stephen. *Danse Macabre.* New York: Everest House, 1981.

Klein, T. E. D. "Ramsey Campbell: An Appreciation." *Nyctalops,* no. 13 (May 1977). Reprinted in Ashley, *The Fantasy Reader's Guide.*

Sullivan, Jack. "Ramsey Campbell: Premier Stylist." In Ashley, *The Fantasy Reader's Guide.* Reprinted as "No Light Ahead," *Whispers,* 4, nos. 3–4 (March 1982).

BIBLIOGRAPHY

Ashley, Michael. "The File on Ramsey Campbell." In Ashley, *The Fantasy Reader's Guide.*

—KENNETH JURKIEWICZ

AVRAM DAVIDSON

1923-

AVRAM DAVIDSON HAS acquired a glamorous but somehow unfocused image as a writer. But though his work is difficult to classify — let alone analyze — it cannot be ignored. Its brilliance makes it necessary to examine the nature and limits of Davidson's achievement.

Davidson was born on 23 April 1923 in Yonkers, New York, and educated at New York University, Yeshiva University, and Pierce College. He served with the navy during World War II as a hospital corpsman in the South Pacific and China. His first professional sale was to *Orthodox Jewish Life Magazine* in 1946, and his first appearance in the genre of supernatural fiction was "My Boy Friend's Name is Jello" (*Magazine of Fantasy and Science Fiction* [*MFSF*], July 1954). He has published nineteen volumes of fantasy or science fiction — short story collections or novels — plus a collection of essays on crime and two detective novels under the pen name Ellery Queen. His fiction has won the Hugo Award and the World Fantasy Award, plus the Ellery Queen Award and the Edgar Allan Poe Award; he also won a Hugo as best editor while at *MFSF* (1962–1964).

Despite this impressive record, Davidson has been largely ignored by critics of science fiction or fantasy. Critics who do mention him seem unsure whether to consider Davidson a writer of science fiction or fantasy, and they are not certain whether specific stories are science fiction or fantasy. This, however, is part of a larger inability to place David-

son's work within either category. He cannot be considered the culmination of a trend in either genre, nor can he be said to have inspired others to emulate him. He remains a unique figure, to be approached respectfully but gingerly.

Davidson's uniqueness becomes apparent the moment one starts reading one of his stories. A Davidson story probably will be set in a locale that a reader has never dreamed of and will deal with a subject that he or she has never really stopped to think about, such as the carving of cigar store Indians or the odd way that safety pins and coat hangers seem to appear and disappear at frustrating moments. A Davidson story will be written in a distinctive style, and the skillful dialogue will fit the age, race, and personality of each character. Many stories include apparently purposeless bits of detail, pauses, interruptions, and fragments that gracefully create the setting and mood, as in the opening paragraph of "Dr. Bhumbo Singh" (*MFSF*, October 1982):

Trevelyan Street used to be four blocks long, but now it is only three, and its end is blocked by the abutment of an overpass. (Do you find the words *Dead End* to have an ominous ring?) The large building in the 300 block used to be consecrated to worship by the Mesopotamian Methodist Episcopal Church (South) but has since been deconsecrated and is presently a glue warehouse. The small building contains the only Bhutanese grocery and deli outside of Asia; its trade is small. And the little (and wooden) building lodges an extremely dirty little studio which sells spells, smells, and shrunken heads. Its trades are even smaller.

This chatty, casual tone is achieved by the loose relation of ideas, interrupted whenever the narrator has yet another (perhaps seemingly irrelevant) fact to add or feels like dropping in an offhand comment. But Davidson also can introduce details in series of parallel elements that draw the reader into a story's sensuous intensity, as in his novel *The Phoenix and the Mirror* (1969), where a languid city of Cyprus is presented:

> The city of Paphos might have been designed and built by a Grecian architect dreamy with the drugs called talaquin or mandragora: in marble yellow as unmixed cream, marble pink as sweetmeats, marble the green of pistuquim nuts, veined marble and grained marble, honey-colored and rose-red, the buildings climbed among the hills and frothed among the hollows. Tier after tier of overtall pillars, capitals of a profusion of carvings to make Corinthian seem ascetic, pediments lush with bas-reliefs, four-fold arches at every corner and crossing, statues so huge that they loomed over the housetops, statues so small that whole troops of them flocked and frolicked under every building's eaves, groves and gardens everywhere, fountains playing, water spouting . . . Paphos.
>
> (chapter 10)

Then again, Davidson can build a scene out of flashes of vision, fragments that demonstrate his sharp ear for dialect, as in "Bloody Man":

> Brown man, glass of brown rum in his brown hand. Sweat on his face. Voice rising. "Ahn so me di *know*, mon, Me di know *who* eet is, mon. Eat ees de blood-dee *Cop*-tain. Eet ees Cop-tain *Blood!*"
> Brown man spun around by another Brown man. Brown fist shaken in brown face. "Me say, 'Hush you mout', mon!' Ah else, me gweyn mahsh eet shut fah you—you hyeah?" And a shove which spins the other almost off his balance, careening against the bar. But not spilling the drink. First man saying nothing. Shaking. Sweating.
>
> (*Fantastic*, August 1976)

Despite Davidson's versatility, his work shows certain recurring concerns. However details are presented, each story contains a lot of them, encouraging absorption or immersion in that story's subject and world. Davidson especially loves unfamiliar landscapes, strange people, and arcane lore. His stories often call attention to some network of unnoticed detail or mass of forgotten facts—another reason why his fiction is difficult to classify. Davidson is fascinated by the kind of systematically arranged, self-consistent information that at one time looked like science but that now has been excluded from scientific "truth." "King's Evil" (*Or All the Seas with Oysters*, 1962), for example, might be classified as science fiction because it deals with mesmerism, ancestor of hypnotism; still, Dr. Mainauduc seems to be doing more with that primitive "science" than its refined form would attempt. He is a mesmerist, not a hypnotist, and imagines his powers to be much greater than they are. Yet he displays powers greater than our understanding of science can accept. He has something of the scientist about him, something of the fraud—and a great deal of the creative fantasist. Without endorsing Mainauduc's ignorant vanity, Davidson clearly is delighted by people like him, through whom he can show the imagination extending itself, registering perceptions and making connections unimagined by the staid, "correct" people in the mainstream of society.

Science fiction is a body of literature based on extrapolations from currently accepted knowledge and the assumption that the universe is (or will be) comprehensible and/or controllable by humanity. Fantasy is a body of literature based on extrapolations from concepts that are not "factual" and the assumption that the universe is not (and never will be) comprehensible and/or controllable by the human mind. Davidson's fiction resists classification not only because he explores the gathering of information in unacceptable fields but also because, in giving a dazzling account of what the human mind can do, he also shows how vast is the knowledge and power possessed by the mind.

Davidson's recurrent subject is the acquisition of knowledge. As to mastery, however—of comprehension, let alone control—many of his stories nod in the direction of fantasy. In his introduction to "What Strange Stars and Skies" in *The Best of Avram Davidson* (1979), for example, Davidson notes that Edward Ferman of *MFSF* (where the story was first published, in December 1963) observed: "'It's really not . . . exactly . . . a story. But it has a *style* . . . The Style is Everything.'" He also quotes another comment that the story received: "'You deserve some sort of congratulations for having devoted thirty perfect pages to setting a stage on which absolutely nothing ever happens.'" In fact, these comments neatly illustrate what Davidson accomplishes—a story in which style (or Style) prevents the narrator from appreciating what has happened.

The story, which Davidson describes as having begun as a spoof "of a certain type of Anglo-British literature," is an expertly mimicked rendition of late Victorian melodrama. As such, it is notable both for its insistence on extreme displays of emotion—as in the first sentence, beginning "The terrible affair of Dame Phillipa Garreck, which struck horror in all who knew of her noble life and mysterious disappearance, arose in large measure from her inordinate confidence in her fellow-creatures"—and for its reluctance to actually show what could justify such feeling. The facts that the narrator relates are easy enough for a modern reader of fantastic literature to piece together. But the story cannot come to grips with its subject. The lumbering rhythm, combined with abstract nouns and adjectives, seems utterly inappropriate to relate the story of a woman kidnapped by an alien monster in a spaceship that has stopped to pick up a cargo of humans for some unknown purpose. And inappropriate it is—as Davidson intends. If, as Ben Shahn maintains, style is the shape of content, it follows that some content may elude some styles. In Davidson's story, the narrator's efforts to untangle events only show his inability to stretch his mind wide enough to take in what happened. The style reflects his truncated, merely conventional powers of observation.

Brute force is no more successful when used to obtain knowledge or power. At the beginning of "Sacheverell" (*MFSF*, March 1964), one of David-son's best-known stories, a man is sleeping in a littered, wretched room, then becomes aware of a "thin and tiny" voice that carries one side of a formal tea party conversation with a "Princess," someone called "Madame," a "General," and a "Professor." As the incongruity becomes obvious between the present setting and the atmosphere that the speaker craves, the man awakens and drags in the chain tethering the speaker—an ape. From the beginning, Davidson sets up a sharp contrast between the brutal human, George, and the refined animal, Sacheverell. George has stolen Sacheverell from his owner, the circus showman Professor Whitman (George insists much too urgently that Whitman died of natural causes), and doesn't know what to do with him. He is sure that there must be some way to exploit the talking ape, but he can't figure it out and is reduced to tormenting Sacheverell for the answer: "He poked again. Sacheverell made a sick noise, struggled. 'Come on,' George said. 'Level with me. There's a million dollars inside of you, you dirty little ape. There's *gotta* be. Only I don't know *how*. So you tell me.'" But before he can be satisfied, George is killed by Sacheverell's friends from the circus sideshow: Princess Zaga, the bearded lady; General Pinkey, the midget; and Madame Opal, the fat lady. In a deft touch, George is now dismissed as not evil but merely ignorant: "'he didn't know any better.'" Safe with his friends, Sacheverell describes the horrors he has suffered: "'He treated me *very* mean. But worst of all, you know, Madame Opal, he *lied* to me—he lied to me all the time, and I almost believed him—that was the most horrible part of all: I almost believed that I was a monkey.'" George's efforts at gaining knowledge clearly are foolish and self-destructive. The kind of knowledge worth having is that shared by the characters onstage at the end of the story: that they are what they believe themselves to be, so that if Sacheverell does not want to be a monkey he doesn't have to be a monkey.

Suggested at least obliquely at the end of both stories is the idea that true understanding comes only with love, that any degree of true mastery can be exercised only out of sympathy. At the end of "What Strange Stars and Skies" the narrator in effect throws up his hands and admits that he cannot make sense of the clues that he has been given but finds some comfort in the "conviction that Dame Phillipa's noble and humanitarian labors still continue, no matter under what strange stars and skies." Though that statement must be qualified by awareness that the narrator's fondness for such rodomontade would prevent his supposing anything else, it is fair to note that "Sacheverell" does demonstrate how "noble and humanitarian" desires can operate through grotesque agents in bizarre circumstances. As a further demonstration of the point, in "The Golem" (*MFSF*, March 1955), sometimes considered an odd science fiction story, an elderly Jewish couple sitting on their front porch are approached by a menancing figure that they can interpret only as a golem, an animated statue from Hebrew folklore. Actually, the being tells them, he is an artificial human being who has read Mary Shelley's *Frankenstein* and other stories of hostile robots and has come to strike terror into the hearts of two likely human victims. They ignore him, rambling in the loving natter of two people who have spent most of their lives together. Only when the stranger calls the wife a "foolish old woman" does the old man pay real attention to the outsider and strike him. This happens immediately after the couple's ironic, kindly squabble, and the man still is deaf to any direct threat the stranger may pose; he just wants the golem to speak respectfully to his wife. When the artificial human is damaged by the blow, the old couple patch him by writing some Hebrew letters on his forehead and fiddling with the wires inside his head. When he regains consciousness, he accepts their version of reality and goes off to mow their front lawn. And thus the story neatly shows the defeat of science (and the horror associated with it) by slightly addled affection.

By contrast, consider what happens in "Dagon" (*MFSF*, October 1959). Set in China just after World War II, the story is narrated by an American who surveys the setting avidly until he finds what he desires: a native woman he can dominate utterly. He first manipulates her man into offering her as a concubine, then has the Chinese man shot when he interferes with the narrator's process of remaking her: "She was a world which I had created, and behold, it was very good." The narrator obviously sees himself in the role of God, and the story's style reflects

his isolation in Davidson's least richly textured, most unloving writing. The narrator is less and less conscious of the outside world except as it relates to him and his perfect power. He is aware of no danger when the murdered man's father, a magician, appears on the scene. At the story's end, the narrator still is utterly vain, satisfied with himself and his life. A reader, however, observing the narrator's final limited, fragmented description of his condition, realizes that he now exists as a goldfish in the Chinese magician's bowl. By imposing his pattern on experience to gratify his sense of mastery, the narrator has found madness and the doom he deserves. For the transition from vain human to vain fish is almost imperceptible as the narrator is relating the story; he certainly has not lost any humanity in the transition, because he already has made himself subhuman.

Thus, in Davidson's fiction those people who claim the most accomplish the least, while those who are too preoccupied with others to worry about getting things done for themselves are actually the most productive. Knowledge is acquired not so much by formal study as by love. It follows that one must be ready to drift with the currents of feeling, following whatever side channel is interesting rather than sticking to a set course. Perhaps this explains Davidson's striking inability to shape long projects successfully. Several times in his career, he has broken off impressive multivolume works, returning to one years later but leaving most achingly unfinished. None of Davidson's book-length fantasies represents a complete work, though their own qualities deserve some discussion and though Davidson regards one of them as his masterpiece.

To take these works in order of importance, *Ursus of Ultima Thule* (1973) is Davidson's sometimes vivid, sometimes hazy version of a sword-and-sorcery quest adventure. The story is unfinished at the book's end, and considering how labored the book feels there is little reason to imagine that it ever will be completed. On the other hand, *The Island Under the Earth* (1969) is a marvelous fragment, the first volume of a trilogy that was to include *The Sixlimbed Folk* and *The Cap of Grace*. The novel sets a fascinating scene in a land that is the reverse imprint of "the Island above the earth" (our world) and is told in a style that shimmers and shifts as does the landscape. Fanning hopes that this work someday will be completed is the fact that Davidson did return to one unfinished project: *Peregrine: Secundus* (1981) continued the story begun in *Peregrine: Primus* (1971). Peregrine's story is deliriously picaresque, a technique justified by the fragmented setting of the early Dark Ages, as tiny sects and kingdoms posture madly. And Davidson's writing, especially in the second book, exploits the humor of digression to the ultimate.

Of all Davidson's book-length works, the most striking is *The Phoenix and the Mirror*. Davidson himself speaks of it with the greatest affection and sees it as the beginning of a major artistic commitment. In his introduction to chapter 8 of the novel, reprinted in *The Best of Avram Davidson*, he explains that during the Dark Ages the Roman poet Vergil was thought of as a magician. By the same token, the ignorant people of that later time thought of ancient Rome in terms of their own culture. So Davidson has used the legends of Vergil as the basis for what is in effect an alternate world, one using names and facts from our history but showing strange distortions of this world's past and natural laws. *The Phoenix and the Mirror* is the only portion yet published of what Davidson intends to be "a trinity of trilogies." However, Davidson admits in his introduction that he has

> not kept on writing the rest of the novels. I have kept on gathering my materials for the background of the medieval Vergil Legend, and, as of the date I write this (July 19, 1977), I have at hand twenty-five large notebooks and over five thousand file cards bearing on the matter: the ensuing year of my life is to be mainly devoted to reworking it all, going backward over it *at an angle*, and so producing, both systematically and by inspiration, *The Encyclopedia of the World of Virgil Magus*—

Apparently, this encyclopedia was to be preparation for the actual writing of the additional novels; in any event, no further novels of Vergil have appeared.

The Phoenix and the Mirror is an impressive work even by itself. The novel is largely the story of Vergil's efforts to make a virgin mirror, one uncontaminated by human gaze, in order to locate a missing girl, her mother, Cornelia, having robbed him of part of his soul to force him to undertake this project. When the mirror is finished, the novel becomes Vergil's quest for the girl he has seen in the mirror and fallen in love with. All this is told in a style of tightly wrought opulence reflecting the many oddities Vergil observes during his travels and the multiple motives he suspects in most of the characters he meets. The novel is a richly sensuous experience. Perhaps the reason why legends and stories about Vergil have so fascinated Davidson is the way Vergil's world offers a chance to look at ours "at an angle" by its alterations of what we accept as fact. Even the legends of that world are different. When Ebbed-Saphir relates the story of the fall of Tyre, he gives a variant version of the story of the Trojan War; in the variant, however, the prince of the city is asked to judge not the beauty but the wisdom of supernatural beings. Proud in *his* wisdom, he accepts and is doomed along with his city. Thus Davidson is able to use legend-at-an-angle to echo his familiar theme that pride in understanding is folly.

It also is appealing to realize that the poet-artist Vergil is the person considered the center of real understanding. But though others respect Vergil for his wisdom, Davidson always describes him as an experimenter, a seeker, rather than one who claims to have achieved mastery. Vergil has discovered that at the deeper levels of being there is neither good nor evil but only differing degrees of potency; this gives him the opportunity to realize how any power he discovers can be used according to human choices. In fact, Vergil's power derives from his understanding that one must not prejudge experience; he discovers truth by observing directly what he is studying, rather than relying on commentaries. Visiting the camp of the Sea Huns, for example, he gets not an explanation so much as a demonstration of how a shaman became a bear, and he realizes that this is the proper way to acquire knowledge: "so had history been . . . before first drama and then writing had severed the unity." Awareness of that unity, a sense of the unsevered complexity of life, is what makes Vergil superior. Here, for instance, he is conversing with a character later revealed to be a supernatural being who has a longer-than-human existence but who has lost the sense of wholeness:

> A breeze touched their faces. "I smell the wild herbs of the countryside," Vergil said, his melancholy tinged with a shadow of pleasure.
> The Red Man sniffed. "And I smell the rotting garbage and the man-stale in the streets," he said.
> "This, too, is life," said Vergil, after a slight pause.
>
> (chapter 11)

As a character, Vergil is thus more impulsive than clinically analytical. Following impulses sometimes gets him in trouble, as it entraps him in Cornelia's plotting at the beginning of the book; overall, though, the novel justifies Vergil's willingness to respond to situations, pressures, or a glimpse of a girl's face.

Better than Davidson's other book-length fantasies, then, *The Phoenix and the Mirror* justifies its loosely developed plot, which appears to be a series of accidents. After all, planning ahead would do Vergil no good unless he were willing to alter his plans to fit momentary opportunities. A more serious drawback, however, is Vergil's lack of fixed character to display. True, this can be justified because he is driven throughout; also true, in the first part of the book he is less than a whole person because Cornelia has stolen a portion of his soul. But one still wonders what he might *be* as a person otherwise. For that matter, who (or what) is a whole person? What, after all, is the relation of the acquisition of knowledge to the conduct of life? These are questions that the depth of Davidson's skill raises and the width of his range of thinking reinforces — but that this novel or Davidson's other fiction never quite answers.

Perhaps Davidson will finish the tasks he has set himself; certainly he seems dedicated to continuing his efforts. "The Redward Edward Papers" (1978), a long prose work first published in the collection of the same title, is a nonlinear exploration of characters, incidents, interests, and styles, somewhat in the manner of *Tristram Shandy*. At the end, Davidson proclaims that all the characters are aspects of himself, in all their variety and turmoil. He also discusses his writing, wondering what his career has accomplished: "if what I have been writing is shit . . . , how come I cannot even go easily to stool but must be painfully costive and bloody, not once and again." He returns to the question at the end of his afterword to the entire book: "We must in any event suffer and die. The question is not, Are we to suffer and die? The question is, Having suffered and having died, what have we left behind us?" He finally finds a bearable answer in a quotation from a biography of Isak Dinesen, describing a writer as one of

> . . . *that small band of independent writers who dared to write as they please, and as they must, little, early, late; the grand and lonely ones who had the courage and genius to keep—at their cost—to their vision and eccentric disciplines . . . without regard to fashion, the mainstream and the time, not because they were dilettantes but because they were artists.*

Davidson is an artist. Even if he has not fully mastered his chosen subject, he will be remembered for his fiction, which shakes readers loose from their preconceptions. In many of his stories, Davidson involves readers in one aspect of a situation, then abruptly reveals that the story has been about something else altogether. "Faed-Out," (*MFSF*, October 1963), for example, seems to be a clever variant on the traditional ghost story, in which a dead actor appears to people he knew in Hollywood to beg that the movies in which he debased his art not be shown on television. The story is told from the viewpoint of a former actor who was typecast as a villain because he is so ugly but who is really kind and considerate; it is logical that he should be the one to piece together the ghost's messages. But the story's conclusion deepens its meaning quite a bit by revealing that this character, who thought of the dead actor as a friend, is hurt because he is the only one who has not been haunted; despite his concern for others, he himself is unseen and ignored.

In much the same way, "Dr. Bhumbo Singh" begins as a parody of the traditional disastrous-purchase-at-a-magical-shop story but ends with the revelation not only that the purchaser of a murderous piece of magic is foolishly deluded but also that all human aspiration is madness.

Finally, Davidson recently has added to the stories about Dr. Eszterhazy (native of an eastern European nation bordering on Graustark and Ruritania, in the days before World War I), whose later life was covered in the award-winning collection *The Enquiries of Dr. Eszterhazy* (1975). The most recent, "Eszterhazy and the Autogondola-Invention" (*Amazing*, November 1983), details at considerable length the martial squabbling of petty nations, then suggests that the dispute was settled not by human ingenuity but by the workings of magic, only to pull still further back from the temporal concerns of humanity to remind readers that "overhead shone the glittering stars." Just before that conclusion, readers (and Eszterhazy) overhear several young men discussing how old themes keep reappearing in the world:

"Look, here in today's evening paper, *Report from the Rural Districts*, listen to this, it's being said that a country girl near Poposhki-Georgiou saw a bull with a wreath of flowers round its neck and she climbed up to get on and then the bull ran off with her still clinging to its back. . . . "

"Silly girl!"

"What was her name; it wasn't Europa I suppose?"

"No it wasn't; what kind of a name is that; it certainly isn't good Scythian Gothic, what?"

The one with the newspaper gave it a second look. Said, "Olga."

"*Olga?*"

"See right here in the paper: Olga. *Here.*"

"Zeus and *Olga*? Doesn't have quite the same ring to it as —"

His friend shrugged. "Oh well. Other times, other mirrors."

Eszterhazy felt he liked this, came closer.

"What chap was it who said, nature always holds up the same mirror, but sometimes she changes the reflections?"

The other sipped from his glass of bullblood wine while he considered. "Don't know who said it. You're sure somebody said it? Well, it's either very profound or very silly."

Davidson's abiding concern has been with showing such strange, shifting combinations of tone and fact. He is willing to risk someone's questioning whether his own work is "very profound or very silly." What sometimes seems an obsession with oddity he would call a sensitivity to shades of fresh, undiscovered meaning. In that light, studying how people of the past delved into byways of thought may suggest how we can appreciate the multiple, co-existing half-truths that form the only certainty we can have.

In *Peregrine: Secundus* the hero is able to hear warnings from dryads because he has not yet received a Christian baptism, which the natural spirits describe as *"those waters which close the ears of man and child and woman against us forever."* Peregrine replies that he is "'a heathen still. . . . A child of the wild heath. And I hear you and I listen.'" Impossible as it may finally prove, Davidson intends no less than to combine the wide-ranging knowledge of an adult with the receptiveness of a child. He wants to open his readers' senses so that they can hear. And he wants to make them more receptive to unfamiliar ideas so that they can listen. As yet, he has not been able to bring together these extremes of consciousness, to show a purposeful, sympathetic, whole character. Nevertheless, his work remains constantly vital. There is no supernatural fiction like his in range of skills and depth of defiant commitment. Whether or not he ultimately is successful in his efforts, he deserves respect for his proud, lonely effort.

Selected Bibliography

WORKS OF AVRAM DAVIDSON

Or All the Seas with Oysters. New York: Berkley, 1962. London: White Lion, 1976. (Includes "The Golem," "King's Evil," and "Dagon.")

What Strange Stars and Skies. New York: Ace, 1965. (Includes "What Strange Stars and Skies" and "Faed-Out.)

The Island Under the Earth. New York: Ace, 1969. St. Albans, England: Mayflower, 1976.

The Phoenix and the Mirror. Garden City, N.Y.: Doubleday, 1969. St. Albans, England: Mayflower, 1975.

Peregrine: Primus. New York: Walker, 1971.

Strange Seas and Shores. Garden City, N.Y.: Doubleday, 1971. (Includes "Sacheverell.")

Ursus of Ultima Thule. New York: Avon, 1973.

The Enquiries of Doctor Eszterhazy. New York: Warner, 1975.

"Bloody Man." *Fantastic Stories*, August 1976.

The Redward Edward Papers. Garden City, N.Y.: Doubleday, 1978. (Includes "Sacheverell," "Dagon," and "The Redward Edward Papers.")

The Best of Avram Davidson, edited by Michael Kurland. Garden City, N.Y.: Doubleday, 1979. (Includes "The Golem," "King's Evil," and "What Strange Stars and Skies.")

Peregrine: Secundus. New York: Berkley, 1981.

Collected Fantasies, edited by John Silbersack. New York: Berkley, 1982. (Includes "Sacheverell," "The Golem," and "Faed-Out.")

"Eszterhazy and the Autogondola-Invention." *Amazing Science Fiction Stories*, November 1983.

Editor, *Magic for Sale*. New York: Ace, 1983. (Includes "Dr. Bhumbo Singh.")

CRITICAL AND BIOGRAPHICAL STUDIES

Feeley, Gregory. "The Davidson Apocrypha." *Foundation*, no. 27 (1983).

Lawler, Donald L. "Davidson, Avram." In *Twentieth Century Science Fiction Writers*, edited by Curtis Smith. New York: St. Martin, 1981.

Mulcahy, Kevin. "Avram Davidson." In *Twentieth Century American Science-Fiction Writers*. Detroit: Gale, 1981.

— JOE SANDERS

STEPHEN R. DONALDSON

1947-

BRITISH FANTASY WRITERS often turn to their art at a mature age: No one can say what J. R. R. Tolkien's early fantasies were like when they were first written, but his first published work, *The Hobbit*, appeared in 1937, when he was forty-five. C. S. Lewis' *Out of the Silent Planet* appeared in 1938, the author's fortieth year.

But American writers of fantasy sometimes start much younger: Peter Beagle began his publishing in 1960, at twenty-one, and it is to this tradition of early beginnings that Stephen R. Donaldson belongs. Born on 13 May 1947 in Cleveland, he started at age thirty and by 1983 had published seven books of one enormous story: two connected trilogies — The Chronicles of Thomas Covenant, the Unbeliever (*Lord Foul's Bane*, *The Illearth War*, *The Power That Preserves*); The Second Chronicles of Thomas Covenant, the Unbeliever (*The Wounded Land*, *The One Tree*, *White Gold Wielder*) — and a seventh work, *Gilden-Fire*, which consists of material cut from *The Illearth War*.

And he started with spectacular success. *Lord Foul's Bane*, his first book, won high praise from Clifford D. Simak, Marion Zimmer Bradley, Robert Bloch, and Terry Brooks. The books of the first trilogy were compared with Tolkien's saga by the *Los Angeles Times* and the *Montreal Star*. In 1978 *Lord Foul's Bane* was selected as best novel of the year by the British Fantasy Society. And at the World Science Fiction Convention in 1978, the attendees voted Donaldson the John W. Campbell Award

(sponsored by *Analog* magazine) for best new writer of the year.

The two trilogies must surely be unique in having a leper — Thomas Covenant — as their hero. The books, especially the first few, present a good deal of medical information about Hansen's disease — and the author knows what he is talking about: when he was three his father, James R. Donaldson, an orthopedic surgeon, moved the family to India, where he treated many lepers. (The First Chronicles is, in fact, dedicated to his father, and Donaldson credits one of his father's speeches on leprosy with giving him the idea of having a leper as his hero.) When Stephen was sixteen, he returned to the United States and later entered the College of Wooster, from which he graduated in 1968. American involvement in Vietnam was intensifying then; Donaldson registered as a conscientious objector and spent two years in alternative service at a hospital. He then began graduate work at Kent State University and received a Master of Arts degree in 1971.

His next few years are well accounted for: as he explains in the foreword to *Gilden-Fire*, he originally planned the First Chronicles as a work of four parts, not three, and when he delivered the manuscript to Lester Del Rey at Ballantine Books, the work ran to 261,000 words. Del Rey advised him to cut it by 250 pages, resulting in a trilogy and also, as Donaldson admits, in a better work.

The improvement came about in this way: In parts one, three, and four of the original version,

Thomas Covenant was the character from whose point of view the story was told; but in part two another character, one from the fantasy world, had been central. The removal of part two meant that all events would be seen through Covenant's eyes; that singularity of view is crucial to the work and is needed to explain the main conflict of the first trilogy.

Covenant is a man of our own times, similar to the reader in every respect but his leprosy. Near the beginning of the first book, he sees a car speeding toward him and knows he will be struck. But when the impact comes, he finds himself in the fantasy world, the Land. Like us all, he believes that he knows what is real and what isn't, and he gains his epithet, the Unbeliever, from his refusal to accept the reality of the situation in which he finds himself.

His refusal is understandable: the discovery that he had leprosy completely changed his earlier way of life, and he was able to endure his existence only by eliminating hope from his life. Not only did he become reconciled to the incurability of his disease—he depended on it. His doctors succeeded in impressing on him that only an unfailing vigilance could make up for the most potent effect of his disease, the absence of pain. They tell him:

"... from now until you die, leprosy is the biggest single fact of your existence. It will control how you live in every particular. From the moment you awaken until the moment you sleep, you will have to give your undivided attention to all the hard corners and sharp edges of life. You can't take vacations from it. You can't try to rest yourself by daydreaming, lapsing."

(chapter 2)

Because leprosy attacks the nerves, the leper lacks the pain that warns the healthy person of a bruise, a burn, a cut. Without that pain, the slightest injury can lead to infection and perhaps to gangrene.

When Covenant awakes in the Land, he soon notices that his palms and his soles, formerly numbed by leprosy, now have sensation. If the Land is real, then he has been healed; since he lives on the belief that leprosy is incurable, the Land can therefore not be real. As one might expect, his insistence that all

he experiences is a hallucination hampers his contacts with those he meets in the Land.

The Land challenges his sense of reality in other ways, too: in some respects the very earth is alive with a force—Earthpower—that the inhabitants take for granted, use, and control in ways that seem magical to Covenant. And he himself is a potent center of magical power, in part because of who he is and in part because of what he has.

Covenant's initial discovery of his disease cost him two fingers of his right hand, and their amputation left him resembling one of the legendary figures of the Land, a hero named Berek Half-hand, whose return had been prophesied. Moreover, the magical object that he possesses is one about which he has intense and ambivalent feelings—his wedding ring.

Covenant's wife, Joan, had not been able to conquer her revulsion at his disease. She took his young son and moved away, and Covenant loves and yearns for both of them. Too much in love to forget her, he is also too knowledgeable about people's reactions to leprosy to hate her. He knows that she is gripped by an unreasoning emotional response that society has burdened her with. He may think she is weak, but he cannot think she is wicked. His wedding ring is therefore more than a symbol of his nominal marriage: it is a constant reminder of the place of the leper—*his* place—in the world. Yet that same ring is made of white gold, an ordinary enough alloy in our world but one that does not exist in the Land. Through it volcanic, even world-destroying, energies may be channeled. The first trilogy is in large part the story of Covenant's learning to control himself and thereby control those energies.

What is perhaps most difficult for Covenant to believe is the hint that he is a pawn in a cosmological struggle. A Satanlike demigod has brought Covenant to the Land to gain control of his white gold; this figure has many names, but his most descriptive title is "the Despiser." Part (perhaps all) of the figure's strength comes from human hatred, and Covenant must continually struggle to keep from allowing himself to hate others, even those who have ostracized him out of fear of his disease. If he gives way to that hatred, he becomes like the Despiser and will become his tool. Of course, this is the way the people of the Land see the struggle; for Covenant the Despiser is one more vision in a vivid dream, an externalization of the frustration that life has loaded on him. But Covenant cannot deny the harsh lessons that the Land teaches. In union with the Lords, he undertakes a quest for the Staff of Law, a source of power that has been captured by one of the Despiser's minions. Through the hardships of the journey, Covenant learns to appreciate the truth that we become similar to what we hate. But when, after all their struggles, the questors recover the Staff, Covenant finds that his achievement is short-lived: he begins to fade and when he awakens he is back in our world, in a hospital, recovering from being hit by the car.

Still rejected by his community, he is twice again called to the Land, and each time returns in a way that confirms neither explanation of his experiences. They could have been real; they could have been a hallucination. But at the climax of the trilogy, just before his return at the end of the third volume, he denies those who wish him to kill the Despiser: he rejects scorn, rejects hatred, and by so doing either eliminates the Despiser's power to harm or masters himself—and perhaps both. He awakes again in a hospital bed; to keep intravenous tubes in place, his hands are tied to the sidebars "as if he had been crucified" (*The Power That Preserves*). The day is Easter.

Before discussing the plot of the second trilogy, we should consider some of Donaldson's literary techniques, especially those that aid materially in his creation of a "secondary world," in J. R. R. Tolkien's terms.

It is generally conceded that Tolkien's invented languages are one of the main devices he uses to add depth and texture to his world. Almost every writer of fantasy does something similar, uses language in some way to bring an atmosphere of strangeness to the story. One traditional way to achieve this sense of remoteness is the use of archaic language: Edmund Spenser uses archaic words in *The Faerie Queene*; or Tolkien creates Quenya and Sindarin Elvish, Orcish, and all the rest. Writers of fantasy commonly invent languages (although seldom with Tolkien's skill and thoroughness), and Donaldson is no exception. He coins words here and there for new

things, practices, offices, and the like, but this coinage is not the most striking literary device that he employs.

In the passages that describe Covenant's activities in our world, Donaldson's word choice, while apt, is contemporary. But after Covenant enters the fantasy world, the diction of the narration becomes unusual. For the most part, the words are familiar, but perhaps once or twice per page (especially in the more exotic passages), he uses a word that subconsciously reminds the reader that these are not humdrum events being described. The word may be of native origin but simply obsolete; or it may be Latinate, a modern inkhorn term. Either way, the effect is the same. For example, in *The Wounded Land*, the first book of the second trilogy, Donaldson describes a character as "in the brittle caducity of age" (page 247). On page 256, rather than call something a "nameless power," it is termed an "innominate power." Again, on page 262, "exhaustion etiolated her sobbing."

The effect is certainly not confusing or overpowering: *caducity*, then nine pages later *innominate*, followed, after six more pages, by *etiolated*. In a climactic scene, the night unfurls "like an oriflamme"; or a bizarre creature is called *roynish*. These are not the stock *plights* and *hights* and *wights* of run-of-the-mill archaizing fantasy.

If we look through fifty pages, we find a dozen or so of these words; say, *anadem, gangrel, gelid, gravid, indefeasible, infrangible, irrefragable, macerate, mephitic, reticular, stridulation*, and *telic*. All but two of these words are of Latin derivation, and some of them are less rare in medical use than in common use. Perhaps Donaldson first learned some of the words at home from his father. Whatever brought them to his attention, they certainly deviate from common use and mark off the narration in which they appear as unusual. It should be noted, though, that Covenant remains a man of our own time: characters in the fantasy world may say things like, "Avaunt, Marid! Ware us!" but Covenant himself always sounds like a twentieth-century American.

The metaphors of the work are often Christian. The symbolism of Covenant's posture in the hospital bed is noted above; in *The Wounded Land* Covenant is bitten by a poisonous snake and some of the venom remains within him. Later on, as the poison works on him, we read, "Fangs fixed like crucifixion," and again, "He saw fangs crucifying his forearm." And, of course, the hero's name is consistent with this kind of metaphor: he becomes the sign of a promise.

The language of the series does not change in the second trilogy, but Covenant's character does. By the opening of the second major section, Covenant accepts the Land as real, although he cannot explain its existence or the way he was transferred there. The focus in these three books is not exclusively fixed on Covenant, because Donaldson introduces a second major character, Linden Avery. She is a doctor who moves to Covenant's town and meets him professionally. Through a series of circumstances, they both find themselves translated to the Land, but the place has been almost devastated by inexplicable extremes of weather, repeated over and over for only a few days at a time.

Covenant has long known that time passes at a different rate in the Land: the lapse of a few days on earth may equal decades in the Land. When Covenant and Avery are transferred, thousands of years have passed since Covenant's last visit, and the Despiser has resurged, seeking again to escape his imprisonment in the Land. Now Covenant (with Avery's help) is called on again to restore the special balance of Earthpower that formerly invested the Land with an exquisite beauty. But his task is much more difficult this time: in the first trilogy, he had the aid of many. On his side were the Lords, special wardens of the Land, and their armies. He was helped by their elite corps, the Bloodguard, undying (but not invulnerable) protectors of the Lords. And he had the help of a giant, Foamfollower.

Now the Lords have changed, seduced by the Despiser: they have gone from being protectors to oppressors, demanding human sacrifice from the people. The Bloodguard is enslaved; three of the giants have been possessed by evil spirits obeying the Despiser, and their community has been slaughtered. The Staff of Law, which had tapped the Earthpower and allowed the Lords to balance the forces of nature, has been destroyed. Still another check to the will of the Despiser has been lost.

Moreover, Covenant finds himself changed: in the first trilogy, he had been able to sense evil, perhaps, he conjectured, because he was not of that world. In the second trilogy he lacks that sense. But Linden Avery has it, and the feeling of evil that she has at some times and in some places is so oppressive that it almost overwhelms her.

This time Covenant will have no help from the rulers of the Land, but he does have his experience to guide him. Consequently, Avery's transition to the Land is much less wrenching than his was. And her medical skills make her especially valuable: with her health sense, she can make certain diagnoses and effect cures by a power much like telekinesis.

Prophecy had played a part in the first trilogy, but not to such an extent as in this one. Covenant had long known that the "wild magic" focused through his ring had the power to threaten the existence of the Land, and on this trip more than one character foretells that he will in fact destroy it. Avery, too, is the subject of prophecy. Her arrival with Covenant was not the result of chance. In some mysterious way, she should have been the ring bearer; she is the hope of the Land. Covenant's heaviest burden is his scrupulous nature. Throughout the first trilogy his guilt rode him like a fury. Now it is made even heavier by the knowledge that many regard him as a bystander in the deliverance of the Land.

The second trilogy ends with Covenant defeating the Despiser and triumphing in a surprising but logically necessary way. Although Covenant's story is finished, he will surely remain one of the best-drawn characters in modern fantasy. In his introspection Thomas Covenant is more like Hamlet than like Conan. In his power he is like Tolkien's Gandalf, but in his lack of control of that power he is only a sorcerer's apprentice. In his vulnerability, he is like Frodo; yet Frodo does not torment himself, as Covenant does incessantly, with thoughts of his past sins and missed opportunities. Like Frodo, Covenant successfully endures, and that is his chief virtue; his will is trustworthy, even if his conscience is troubled. One last comparison: again like Frodo, Covenant finds that his experiences ultimately make him unfit to return to an ordinary life. All in all,

Thomas Covenant is a remarkable character, one able to bear the weight of six long volumes, and his creation is a remarkable accomplishment. Although his achievements are already considerable, Donaldson is a writer still in the morning of his career. If his works to come equal the Chronicles of Thomas Covenant, he will have helped measurably to make the twentieth century memorable for the quality and diversity of its literary fantasies.

Selected Bibliography

WORKS OF STEPHEN R. DONALDSON

Lord Foul's Bane. New York: Holt, Rinehart and Winston, 1977. London: Fontana, 1978. (First trilogy, book one.)

The Illearth War. New York: Holt, Rinehart and Winston, 1977. London: Fontana, 1978. (First trilogy, book two.)

The Power That Preserves. New York: Holt, Rinehart and Winston, 1977. London: Fontana, 1978. (First trilogy, book three.)

The Wounded Land. New York: Ballantine, 1980. London: Sidgwick and Jackson, 1980. (Second trilogy, book one.)

Gilden-Fire. San Francisco: Underwood-Miller, 1981. (Material cut from *The Illearth War.)*

The One Tree. New York: Ballantine, 1982. London: Fontana, 1982. (Second trilogy, book two.)

White Gold Wielder. New York: Ballantine, 1983. (Second trilogy, book three.)

—WALTER E. MEYERS

HARLAN ELLISON

1934-

I

HARLAN ELLISON WAS born in Cleveland, Ohio, on 27 May 1934, the son of Louis Laverne Ellison and Serita Rosenthal. Ellison's fiction, which is often autobiographical, points to the formative importance of his early life. Comic books and radio helped to mold his imagination.

Ellison was a part-time actor at the Cleveland Playhouse from 1944 to 1949 and was a founder of the Cleveland Science Fiction Society in 1950. In the early 1950's he briefly attended Ohio State University. Science fiction fandom was another formative experience, as were the ten weeks in 1955 during which he ran with a teenage gang; this experience inspired not only early writing attempts but also four books on juvenile delinquency.

Ellison served in the army in 1957–1959. He married Charlotte Stein in 1956; after what he describes as "four years of hell" (*Gentleman Junkie,* 1961), he was divorced in 1959. As an editor of *Rogue* in 1959–1960, Ellison lived in Chicago. But dissatisfied with his writing and with his materialistic life-style, Ellison left for New York. Dorothy Parker's favorable review of *Gentleman Junkie* in *Esquire* (January 1962) established Ellison as a serious writer.

In 1962 Ellison moved to Los Angeles, where he remains. In the early to mid-1960's he was married and divorced twice more; it is no wonder that his writings often depict tempestuous relationships. During the 1960's, too, Ellison became an infamous

enfant terrible at science fiction conventions. To go to the World Science Fiction Convention was to hear stories of his abrasive personality and angry responses to small provocations. During this time Ellison became a prolific television writer, producing scripts for such shows as *Route 66, The Man from U.N.C.L.E., The Alfred Hitchcock Hour, Cimarron Strip, Outer Limits, The Young Lawyers,* and *Ghost Story* from 1962 to 1973. Ellison wrote the script for one of the best *Star Trek* episodes, "The City on the Edge of Forever."

Ellison had the unfortunate experience of being the creator, under the pseudonym Cordwainer Bird, of the short-lived NBC-TV series "The Starlost" in 1973. He was also the screenwriter for such films as *The Oscar* and *The Dream Merchants.*

Perhaps Ellison's most important contributions to science fiction in the 1960's were his edited volumes *Dangerous Visions* (1967) and *Again, Dangerous Visions* (1972). In these collections Ellison fulfilled his promise to bring his readers stories not otherwise publishable within the conservative science fiction code, stories containing sex (at that time taboo in science fiction) and violence. More important, he presented stories that were stylistically experimental. Thus, Ellison can claim to be one of the creators of science fiction's new wave, which moved the genre in the direction of literary modernism.

Ellison was an instructor for the Clarion Writers' Workshop at Michigan State University from 1969 to 1977; from 1973 to 1977 he created for Pyramid Books the Harlan Ellison Discovery Series of first novels; and in 1976 he was married and divorced for the fourth time.

Ellison has collected numerous Hugo awards (given by science fiction fans at the annual world conventions) and Nebula awards (given by the Science Fiction Writers of America), as well as the Edgar Allan Poe Award of the Mystery Writers of America. Although his writing has its roots in science fiction, Ellison now loudly proclaims (with some justice) that he is not a science fiction writer. With his usual fanfare, he resigned from the Science Fiction Writers of America, claiming, among other things, that the organization was not adequately protecting the professional interests of its members.

II

Ellison's interest in the supernatural is that of the moralist. The supernatural allows him to present his characters with otherwise impossible moral challenges. Ellison's supernatural fiction, science fiction, and realistic fiction cannot be clearly demarcated, for his "science" is generally the fantastic or the fanciful, and many of his realistic stories have too many bizarre twists to warrant that designation. While concentrating on Ellison's overtly supernatural stories, this article will also mention other stories that are thematically similar.

If Ellison is ever the moralist, he is also an autobiographical and confessional writer. The introductions to his stories, in which he often describes a story's genesis, are often as long as the stories themselves. Ellison turns repeatedly to his childhood. In "One Life, Furnished in Early Poverty" (1970; collected in *Approaching Oblivion*, 1974), a man magically goes back in time to find himself. He finds Gus, as he is called, in an Ohio winter of long ago and hopes to save Gus from the bullying aggression of his parents and peers. The narrator enters Gus's world, which is dominated—as Ellison's early life evidently was—by the imaginative escape of radio shows, comics, and science fiction. One of Ellison's themes is the power of that culture of the 1930's and 1940's; having read comics, the narrator says, "My scripts sold so easily because I had never learned

how to rein-in my imagination." Although the narrator becomes fast friends with his younger self, his body begins to shrink, and he knows he must return; but Gus is so resentful at what he interprets as desertion that he resolves to "show" Mr. Rosenthal (the narrator). Not friendship but resentment spurs Gus on, as apparently it spurred Ellison on. Ever the follower of Freud and Jung, Ellison depicts overcompensation.

The lure of the past, especially of the old radio shows, is again the theme of "Jeffty Is Five" (1977; collected in *Shatterday*, 1980). Jeffty not only is five but remains five as the years go by. Moreover, his radio remains tuned to "The Green Hornet" and "The Lone Ranger" after these shows are no longer on the air for anyone else. The narrator begins a friendship with Jeffty, and as the years go by, he wonders, "Things may be better, but why do I keep thinking about the past?" Ellison again suggests the degeneration of American culture, which is no longer as fulfilling as "The Shadow" or "Dick Tracy."

However, Ellison is far from depicting childhood as uniformly romantic. He teaches us to look at particular situations rather than at generalities. In "Final Shtick" (1960; collected in *Love Ain't Nothing But Sex Misspelled*, 1968), a successful comedian approaches his hometown in triumph, only to remember the anti-Semitism he once experienced there. Ellison is ever the ironist of particular situations.

Nonetheless, a world view can be derived from Ellison's fiction. Ellison has been called an existentialist and has been compared to Thomas Hardy and D. H. Lawrence. Just as Hardy's universe often seems to suggest the hard justice of fate, so Ellison's does. In "Rain, Rain, Go Away" (1956; collected in *Ellison Wonderland*, 1962), Hardy's inexorable cosmic justice comes to Hobert Krouse, forty-six and paunchy, who all of his life asked the rain to come another day. One day all of the deferred rain does come, even as past indiscretions return to haunt Michael Henchard of Hardy's *The Mayor of Casterbridge*.

Ellison's fiction, moreover, shows him to be influenced by D. H. Lawrence. First and most evident is

Ellison's view of the importance of sexual relations; and both Lawrence and Ellison warn of the apocalypse. Lawrence's clearest end-of-the-world statement is *Women in Love*; he expresses a similar view in the title of one of his books, *Approaching Oblivion*. Lawrence counters oblivion with vitalism, and so does Ellison in "Ernest and the Machine God" (1968; collected in *Over the Edge*, 1970). The antagonism between human sensuousness and the machine in this story is as clear as that between the gamekeeper's life-force and the deathlike fixation of Lord Chatterley's motorized wheelchair. In "Ernest and the Machine God," Selena, who has psychic powers, kills a government man, escapes to a North Carolina town, and develops car trouble. She tunes in to the sexual-sensuous power of Ernest, who fixes her car with his apparently supernatural hands. After they have sex, he loses his powers, but her car runs; what Lawrence would call the blood power of human beings has yielded to the mechanism.

"Rock God" (1969; collected in *Over the Edge*) suggests, too, the phoenixlike vitalism of Lawrence, with every new age developing its appropriate religious forms to match the vital forces. Other Ellison stories suggest the universe's inexorable justice meted out to presumptuous characters in a Hardyian or Lawrentian fashion: in "All the Birds Come Home to Roost" (collected in *Shatterday*), a man experiences "some kind of terrible justice" when all the women he has ever known revisit him. In "Shoppe Keeper" (1977; collected in *Shatterday*), supernatural bureaucrats limit the dimension of wonder by making a supernatural shopkeeper take back the "stones of power" that he sold to a human.

Ellison resembles Lawrence, too, in his belief that socially conscious art can shock the world into change. Shock, the smashing of icons, is clearly an Ellison goal; he takes delight in depicting subjects taboo in American mass culture, from lesbianism to the joy of violence. But to Ellison shock is purposeful, for he is a modernist prophet who believes in the power of art to stave off the apocalypse. In "Paulie Charmed the Sleeping Woman" (1962; collected in *Approaching Oblivion*), Paulie, a horn player, performs in the cemetery at the crypt of his dead love, Ginnie, and raises her, Lazarus-like: "We heard the noise outta that crypt. We heard her coming." Art could bring the resurrection.

Ellison perhaps diverges from Hardy and Lawrence in his emphasis on individual identity. To have no identity or to be dependent on the identity of another is a most dire situation in Ellison's fiction. In "All the Sounds of Fear" (1962; collected in *Love Ain't Nothing But Sex Misspelled*), a method actor, asked in a sanatorium to discard all of his roles, emerges without any features on his face. Ellison believes humans are responsible for what they are or are not, for they have created it. "In Fear of K" (1975; collected in *Strange Wine*, 1978) concerns a couple in a maze whose fear of a monster they have created by their fear keeps them from escaping. Similarly, "In the Fourth Year of the War" (1979; collected in *Shatterday*) focuses on a man whose second self seemingly forces him to kill people who have wronged him in the past. Ellison's conclusion is that "the horrors are the ones we create for ourselves."

"Strange Wine" (1976; collected in *Strange Wine*) leads to a similar conclusion. A man becomes convinced that he is an alien and that the earth is a place of special punishment to which sinners from other planets are magically sent. But when he dies and his spirit returns to his home planet, he discovers that the earth is in fact the most comfortable place in the universe. He had made his own suffering on earth by imagining that cosmic forces were stacked against him; in reality, he was being tortured by his own failure to take responsibility.

Humans cannot take responsibility unless they face and feel what they are; many of Ellison's characters cannot. In "World of the Myth" (1964; collected in *I Have No Mouth and I Must Scream*, 1967), a man commits suicide because antlike creatures in a magical alien world form a mental mirror that forces him to confront himself; in "At the Mountains of Blindness" (1961; collected in *Gentleman Junkie*), musicians force a drug pusher to listen to the music of a horn player dependent on him; the pusher must hear in the horn player's music the effect that his drug sales have had. Similarly, a bearded man (probably the devil) in "Enter the Fanatic, Stage Center" (1961; collected in *Gentleman Junkie*) sets up an art studio with paintings of the townspeople designed to make them acknowledge the sordid truths of their lives.

To feel, in Ellison's world, often is to suffer. In "Grail" (1981; collected in *Stalking the Nightmare*, 1982), a demon gives Christopher Caperton the clues allowing him to determine what has been his loftiest moment of love; but he has been given an "awful gift," for his life must continue beyond that moment. Similarly, Clotho in the magical bookstore of "The Cheese Stands Alone" (1981; collected in *Stalking the Nightmare*) grants Dr. Cort his wish of telling him the happiest moment of his life, which Cort assumes is in the future. Instead, it was when he caught a baseball at ten. Cort is condemned to feel the sense of loss for the rest of his life.

If to feel is to suffer, not to feel is a moral failing. In "Night of Black Glass" (1981; collected in *Stalking the Nightmare*), a man who has survived both the war in Vietnam and his wife's death takes a bus to the "edge of the world," a beach in Maine. There the ocean, a black glass, yields ghosts of his wife and his dead war buddies. His crime lies not in surviving but in feeling no guilt at having survived.

Ellison's characters seem to face innumerable threats to their identities, from suicidal loneliness to psychological doubling to murderous antagonisms. But there are ways to answer these threats, for in Ellison's world, as in Lawrence's, the moral source of the threat is often so clear that revenge against wrongdoing is possible, although revenge also carries its own risks and temptations. Violence is the solution as well as the problem in "The Whimper of the Whipped Dogs" (1973; collected in *No Doors, No Windows*, 1975). Threatened by a burglar in her New York apartment, a previously naive Bennington graduate prevails by invoking the god of violence. Ellison quotes Rollo May on "violence . . . as a daimonic necessity for contact."

But violence and revenge are risky even for the morally strong and just. In "Status Quo at Troyden's" (1958; collected in *No Doors, No Windows*), a man murders the greedy landlord about to evict him and then steps into the same role. The title character of "The Man Who Was Heavily into Revenge" (1978; collected in *Shatterday*) is Fred Tolliver. When William Weisel, a contractor, refuses to

correct flaws in Tolliver's house, Tolliver does him in with a series of supernatural plagues. The reader sympathizes until he finds out that Tolliver has not fulfilled his agreement to repair Evelyn Hand's musical instrument. Tolliver has been to Hand what Weisel has been to Tolliver. Ellison quotes S. J. Lec: "No snowflake in an avalanche ever feels responsible."

A variation on the revenge theme is the perfect crime, in Ellison's fiction the occupation of those who wish the easy evasion of responsibility. Madge in "Do-It-Yourself" (1961, with Joe E. Hensley; collected in *Ellison Wonderland*) wants to kill her husband with the techniques suggested by a magical talking murder kit; but she is so geared to habitual proprieties that she cannot follow its precise instructions. Not only does she fail, but her husband kills her.

Another threat to identity is what Ellison calls lack of belief. In "O Ye of Little Faith" (1968; collected in *Love Ain't Nothing But Sex Misspelled*), Niven believes in nothing. Although he loves Bertha, he cannot say so, as he cannot express dependence on anything or anyone. The couple wander into a soothsayer's shop. Gloomy and aggressive, Niven hits the soothsayer, who sends him to a realm containing the minotaur, Jesus, and Odin, all gods floating in this limbo because they have no one to believe in them. Ellison concludes of Niven that "he had believed in no god. . . . No god believed in him."

So many are the threats to authentic identity that Ellison seems at times to be saying that human nature itself falls short. At such times Ellison shares the misanthropic gloom of Alexander Pope or Jonathan Swift. Gremlins, for example, in "Working with the Little People" (1977; collected in *Strange Wine*), have been helping human beings for years to find artistic inspiration. But the story shows that the gremlins have now become disillusioned with humans and in fact no longer believe that they exist.

Usually, though, Ellison presents the difficulty rather than the impossibility of moral redemption. His characters sometimes get a second chance, although they do not always take it. In "Delusion for a Dragon Slayer" (1966; collected in *Love Ain't Nothing But Sex Misspelled*), a wizard gives a man a chance at a happy afterlife if he can perform the heroic feats that he only dreamed of in life. But the man fails again.

Sometimes in Ellison's fiction moral redemption seems to come through being a savior or following one; but the theme is ambiguous, for it is also possible to have one's identity absorbed by another. In "Diagnosis of Dr. D'arque Angel" (1977; collected in *Strange Wine*), a man inoculates himself against death by absorbing bits of the threat of death. His idea is to kill his wife in a car crash and not be killed himself. But when he does kill her, he discovers that his very need to kill her shows his dependence on her and that she had a whole series of men similarly dependent. His identity is so dependent on hers that he cannot live without her.

For the most part, Ellison's redeemed people act contrary to social expectations. In "Djinn, No Chaser" (1982; collected in *Stalking the Nightmare*), a couple enter a magical store and buy a lamp containing a genie. But the genie is trapped inside and expresses his frustration by inflicting a series of plagues on his owners. Danny, a male chauvinist, cannot cope with this situation; but his wife, Connie—whom the reader had perhaps thought stupid—thinks of the simple expedient of freeing the genie with a can opener.

More serious is the character transformation in "Lonelyache" (collected in *I Have No Mouth and I Must Scream*). Ellison correctly assesses this as one of the best stories he has ever written. "Lonelyache" contains the theme that people create their own ghosts, but in this story the ghost is exorcised. A lost and lonely man creates a ghost that only he can see, which lives in a corner of his apartment. The man has a series of empty, dreary affairs. Finally he learns how to interpret a sequential dream he has been having: the dream means that he fears commiting suicide by shooting himself through the eye. He performs this action. Although his suicide is gruesomely violent, it represents to Ellison a triumph of self-knowledge.

III

Ellison has written an enormous amount—perhaps too much—and his themes and subjects are many. He is always interested in men and women, sex, and abortion. Not many stories written for American magazines in 1960 had lesbianism as a theme, as does "A Path Through the Darkness" (collected in *Love Ain't Nothing But Sex Misspelled*). Although from time to time Ellison affirms the equality of women and has worked for the Equal Rights Amendment, many of his stories are marred by an apparently unconscious sexism. An early example is "Nedra at f: 5.6" (1957; collected in *No Doors, No Windows*), about a woman with perfect proportions who does not show up on photographic plates, for she is apparently a demon. Other Ellison stories, though, are much more evenhanded. "Erotophobia" (1971; collected in *Approaching Oblivion*) is about a man who is weary of being pursued by women. A man in a bar points out to him that every person is both male and female. Apparently it is true, for when the protagonist looks into a mirror he sees himself turn into a beautiful woman. But "she" rebuffs him, and he withdraws into himself: the solution to promiscuity is isolation.

Other of his stories deal with a Blakean inversion of good and evil. "Hitler Painted Roses" (1977; collected in *Strange Wine*) portrays a woman in hell wrongly accused of mass murder. She escapes from hell and confronts the real killer, a man who has managed to make his way to heaven. But God is not impressed with this revelation; he escorts her back to hell, where, just inside the portal, there is a lovely fresco of roses painted by Hitler. Perhaps George Bernard Shaw's point that hell contains the interesting people is also Ellison's.

Although Ellison's stories characteristically deal with the morality of individual choice, several also present social criticism. At the height of the civil rights movement, Ellison wrote a number of stories sympathetic to black liberation. "The Night of Delicate Terrors" (1961; collected in *Love Ain't Nothing But Sex Misspelled*) shows how close to the supernatural Ellison's realistic stories can come, as blacks, turned away from a motel on a cold winter's night, think about the revenge that would come from black revolution; readers are to know, simply from this vignette, that the revolution will come. Another widely reprinted story is "Pennies, Off a

Dead Man's Eyes" (1969; collected in *Over the Edge*). The near-supernatural basis of this story is the folk belief that stealing pennies from the eyes of a dead man will send him to hell. Yet the narrator forgives Jed's daughter, who is passing for white, for stealing the pennies from her father's eyes, as she has "paid her dues."

A number of Ellison stories denounce television's perversions. "!!! The!!Teddy!Crazy!!Show!!!" (1968; collected in *Stalking the Nightmare*) presents Satan as the guest on a talk show who praises the good work of the host; similarly, demons in "Flop Sweat" (1971; collected in *Shatterday*) make a talk-show hostess into their priestess. As the themes of these stories suggest, several Ellison supernatural stories are rather thin jokes. "Mom" (1976; collected in *Strange Wine*) was written in response to a dare that no more ghost stories could be written. Ellison took up the dare and created a Jewish-mother ghost. But other Ellison stories are more ambitious. "Catman" (1974; collected in *Approaching Oblivion*) presents a situation so abstract that, in the fashion of Anthony Burgess' *A Clockwork Orange*, it requires some time for readers to absorb the extrapolated language, and one is never certain of one's orientation.

Ellison's best science fiction stories develop themes similar to those of his supernatural stories. "I Have No Mouth and I Must Scream" (1967; collected in the volume of the same title) concerns the struggles for identity of a group of people trapped inside a resentful computer of the far future that tortures them with archetypal beasts. Violence is again affirmation: it is a triumph when the protagonist kills everyone in the group except himself. "A Boy and His Dog" (1969; collected in *The Beast That Shouted Love at the Heart of the World*, 1969), another postdisaster vision, shows a man's assertion of identity in hip violence and in the rejection of small-town, "square" violence. Collected in the same volume is "The Pitll Pawob Division," a small gem about the lack of communication between alien species.

Ellison has struggled against the formulaic restraints of American publishing; his greatest fear, he repeatedly says, is that he will become too comfortable. His weapons are shock and iconoclasm. While some of his supposedly avant-garde stories turn out to be crude or trite, in his best works Ellison combines striking narration and prophecy.

Selected Bibliography

WORKS BY HARLAN ELLISON

The Deadly Streets. New York: Ace, 1958. London: Brown, Watson, 1959.

Gentleman Junkie and Other Stories of the Hung-Up Generation. Evanston, Ill.: Regency Books, 1961. Revised edition with different contents. New York: Pyramid, 1975.

Ellison Wonderland. New York: Paperback Library, 1962. As *Earthman, Go Home*. New York: Ace, 1964. As *Ellison Wonderland*. London: Signet, 1974 (with different contents).

From the Land of Fear. New York: Belmont Books, 1967.

I Have No Mouth and I Must Scream. New York: Pyramid, 1967.

Love Ain't Nothing But Sex Misspelled. New York: Trident Press, 1968. New York: Pyramid, 1976 (with different contents).

The Beast That Shouted Love at the Heart of the World. New York: Avon, 1969. Abridged. London: Millington, 1976.

The Glass Teat: Essays of Opinion on the Subject of Television. New York: Ace, 1970. London: Savoy, 1978.

Over the Edge: Stories from Somewhere Else. New York: Belmont Books, 1970.

Alone Against Tomorrow. New York: Macmillan, 1971. London: Panther, as two books, *All the Sounds of Fear*, 1973, and *The Time of the Eye*, 1974.

Partners in Wonder. New York: Walker, 1971. (Collaborations with other authors.)

Approaching Oblivion: Road Signs on the Treadmill Toward Tomorrow, with Edward Bryant. New York: Walker, 1974. London: Millington, 1976.

Deathbird Stories: A Pantheon of Modern Gods. New York: Harper and Row, 1975. London: Millington, 1978.

No Doors, No Windows. New York: Pyramid, 1975.

The City on the Edge of Forever. New York: Bantam, 1977. (Novelization of television play in "Star Trek" series.)

Strange Wine. New York: Harper and Row, 1978.

Shatterday. Boston: Houghton Mifflin, 1980. London: Hutchinson, 1982.

Stalking the Nightmare. Huntington Woods, Mich.: Phantasia Press, 1982.

WORKS EDITED BY HARLAN ELLISON

Dangerous Visions. Garden City, N.Y.: Doubleday, 1967. London: Bruce and Watson, 1971, in 2 vols.

Again, Dangerous Visions. Garden City, N.Y.: Doubleday, 1972. London: Millington, 1976.

CRITICAL AND BIOGRAPHICAL STUDIES

Porter, Andrew, ed. *The Book of Ellison*. New York: Algol Press, 1978.

Slusser, George Edgar. *Harlan Ellison: Unrepentant Harlequin*. San Bernardino, Calif.: Borgo Press, 1977.

BIBLIOGRAPHY

Swigart, Leslie Kay. *Harlan Ellison: A Bibliographical Checklist*. Dallas: Williams Publishing Company, 1973. (Updated in the *Magazine of Fantasy and Science Fiction*, July 1977.)

—CURTIS C. SMITH

ALAN GARNER

1934-

I

ALAN GARNER RANKS among the most highly regarded children's fantasy writers, although his work has moved steadily away from the realm of fantasy and is considered by many not to be directed toward children at all. His first two books, *The Weirdstone of Brisingamen* (1960) and *The Moon of Gomrath* (1963), are fast-paced narratives full of the traditional apparatus of fairy tale and legend: wizards, elves, dwarfs, and enchanted weapons. *Elidor* (1965), his next novel, is a threshold story: the emphasis is not on the realm of magic but on its effect upon the everyday world, where the characters must live between moments of enchantment.

Garner won the Carnegie Medal for his fourth book, *The Owl Service* (1967), in which a Welsh legend becomes embodied in the relationships of three contemporary teen-agers; this novel differs from the earlier ones in its stripped-down narrative style, extensive use of dialogue, striking characterizations, and reliance on implication rather than outright statement. In *Red Shift* (1973), Garner uses dialogue and between-the-lines implication so intensively that many reviewers rejected the book as a needlessly obscure puzzle. The Stone Book Quartet (1976–1978), a set of four elegantly wrought stories about several generations of English craftsmen, is not fantastic, though it carries on Garner's characteristic themes and occasionally suggests the mysticism more explicitly represented in the magic of the earlier volumes.

In addition to these stories, Garner has written plays and librettos and edited volumes of folktales. An interest in folklore runs throughout his career, as evidenced by the list of traditional sources appended to *The Moon of Gomrath*. Among his unpublished works are papers on the oral traditions and vernacular architecture of his native Cheshire.

Discussing his intended audience, Garner comes down solidly on both sides of the question: "I don't write for children, but entirely for myself. Yet I do write for children, and have done so from the very beginning" ("A Bit More Practice"). The best way to gauge Garner's range is his statement "I try to write onions"—stories that function on every level, from page-turning plot to symbolic drama, and yet are the same throughout, so that naïve and sophisticated readers confront variations of the same experience. Like George MacDonald, Garner writes for the childlike; that is, for those who are willing to follow him through whatever strange realms and events are necessary to pursue a theme.

Publishing for children has given him a core audience that reads, as he says, with an intensity unmatched by most adults. He uses the limitations imposed by such an audience as a way of disciplining himself, enforcing direct presentation and focus. Like many books originally published for children, his works have been reprinted in paperback for a general audience.

II

Alan Garner was born on 17 October 1934 and grew up in Alderley Edge, a village on the outskirts of Manchester, England. A series of illnesses kept him out of school during most of his childhood, but he did attend the prestigious Manchester Grammar School. After two years of service in the Royal Artillery, Garner studied classics at Magdalen College, Oxford, but did not complete his degree. He returned to the Cheshire countryside near Alderley Edge in 1956 and, with the aid of four years of welfare payments from the National Assistance Board, wrote his first book. Since then he has been a full-time writer. He has been married twice: to Ann Cook in 1956 and to Griselda Greaves in 1972. He has three children by his first marriage and two by his second.

The primary sources of Garner's fiction are his working-class background, the Cheshire countryside, his education at Manchester Grammar School and Oxford, and his knowledge of myth and folklore. These elements are intermingled to explore a set of recurring themes: family relationships, the nature of time, the fate of the intelligent misfit, the continuity of human interactions. In the early books Garner's themes are often veiled in the symbolism of magic or the conflicts of archetypal characters. In the later works magic disappears, symbolism becomes more elusive, and archetypal conflicts are internalized within the minds of the protagonists. To Garner, this change represents improvement. He is a conscientious writer who spends years researching and revising a single story. After each book is completed he is likely to proclaim it the first good thing he has done, and all the earlier efforts apprentice pieces.

Nonetheless, each of his works has its devotees. Even the first, *The Weirdstone of Brisingamen*, which Garner now finds condescending and empty of believable characters, continues to engage readers with its freewheeling plot and vivid setting. The book is really about its setting, the countryside around Alderley Edge. All the magical beings, including wizards, witches, trolls, dwarfs, "svarts," elves, "stromkarls," and a lady of the lake, are tied to the Edge, a forested bluff in the flat Cheshire landscape. These creatures and their actions express a sense of living among abandoned quarries, caverns, prehistoric monuments, sturdy small farms, swamp, forest, cliff, and plain, settings bearing such a weight of human associations that any feature not tied to some eerie legend can easily support one borrowed from Scandinavian or Celtic lore.

Garner begins with a local legend incorporating the sleeping king motif associated in England with King Arthur. The story describes the sale of a milk-white mare to a wizard who guards 140 sleeping knights in a cavern under Alderley Edge. When farmer Gowther Mossock tells the tale to two visiting children named Colin and Susan, they set out to find the Iron Gates that lead to the wizard. The children's game leads abruptly to an attack by a pack of grinning svarts and rescue by the wizard himself, who calls himself Cadellin. After that there is scarcely a moment's rest. A missing treasure, a witch, and Cadellin's evil counterpart, Grimnir, keep the story roiling with chase, capture, and escape. The best-sustained episode is an extended crawl through a series of tunnels and caves; this claustrophobic sequence takes five chapters in a book of twenty-one.

Each chase brings out new attackers; each escape calls forth a new ally. Ultimately, there are too many of both. In a single volume there are as many supernatural races as in the entire *The Lord of the Rings*. The book's primary strength — its relentless activity — is also its chief weakness. There is no overall shape to the story, and the implications of no single element are worked out to the reader's satisfaction.

A measure of Garner's development between his first book and *The Moon of Gomrath* is in his dialogue. Much of the speech in *The Weirdstone* rings false. The children speak flat, modern English, the local people speak broad dialect, and the magical characters speak like actors in a costume drama. The effect is rather like a puppet show in which the puppeteer rushes from one set of strings to another, providing all the voices and sometimes throwing in an "I dunner" or a "must needs" for variety. Colin and Susan are particularly blank. In *The Moon of Gomrath*, Colin and Susan still sound as if they had no family, no interests outside of magic, and no existence prior to their arrival at Alderley Edge, but they speak believably of the things they experience, and during the course of the novel they begin to react as individuals.

The Moon of Gomrath begins, as does *The*

Weirdstone, with the children playfully seeking the world of magic. Once again their entry into it is unexpected and violent, and again a large cast and a hectic pace make for a confusing, engrossing story. A major strand of this story concerns Susan's acquisition of magical power and Colin's mastery of his own strengths of courage and comradeship. The chief magic of this book is not the "high magic" of Cadellin and Grimnir, the manipulative, intellectual magic that divides neatly into black and white, but the "old magic" of emotion, natural cycles, and sexuality. Garner seems more comfortable with this unpredictable, passionate magic than with abstract wizardry. In the first book, Cadellin is described with the typical wizardly attributes: he is wise, stern, kindly. But when the action begins he seems less wise than clever, less stern than inflexible, and downright chilly toward the children when they interfere with his duty.

In *The Moon of Gomrath*, Garner seems not only to have grown aware of this unacknowledged side of the wizard archetype but to have exploited it. Cadellin watches grumpily as Susan and Colin unlock the old magic bound ages ago by the wizards because, as Susan says, "It just got in the way." The counter to Cadellin in this book is the Hunter. Wild, graceful, lawless, man-shaped but crowned with stag's antlers, the Hunter evades the categories of good and evil.

The plot of *The Moon of Gomrath* is unified by the theme of the freeing of the old magic, which is also the unlocking of Colin and Susan's emotional individuality. So long as Garner stays with this double theme, events follow one another inevitably. Susan's power is symbolized by a silver bracelet given her in the previous book. When she lends the bracelet, she is open to possession by the Brollachan, a traditional British evil spirit and a sexual symbol. In pony shape, it seduces Susan into riding, and then gallops away into the lake. She can neither control it nor get off. When she returns, her hair is wet and full of weeds and her hand feels like a hoof. The Brollachan is cast out by clasping the bracelet on her wrist, but her spirit is still out of her body and it is up to Colin to find the herb, a part of the old magic, to call her back. Colin succeeds, but his actions wake the Hunter and rouse the Wild Hunt. With every move they make, the characters are more deeply embroiled in supernatural affairs, until at the end Susan stands poised at the brink of another existence, no longer quite human or content to be. Colin has also been too deeply touched by magic to find peace in ordinary life.

Insofar as it concerns this change, the story moves surely from childlike beginning to bittersweet end; however, other elements in the story do not tie in neatly with this progression or match its emotional impact. Ailing elves, noble and treacherous dwarfs, and an Irish hero are not explored in the same depth as Susan's coming of age, and so they become merely distracting. Additionally, the forces of evil are less compelling than they were in *The Weirdstone*. Garner has lost his interest in personifying evil, in externalizing the sinister side of human behavior, but he has not yet evolved alternative strategies for portraying conflict.

The open-endedness of *The Moon of Gomrath* would seem to call for a sequel to bring the story of Susan and Colin to a conclusion. However, Garner felt that these characters did not warrant a third visit. Instead, in *Elidor* he explores the themes that emerged at the end of the second book through new actors and in a very different setting. Though still set in Cheshire, Elidor contains no comfortable old farmhouses or wooded hills. It takes place in the anonymous suburbs and decaying heart of Manchester.

Four children, playing a game with a street map, wander into the slums, where a ragged fiddler unlocks a gateway into another world. In that world Roland, the youngest child, finds himself alone in a forest as dead as the slum neighborhood; this new land, Elidor, is somehow analogous to our own. The fiddler reappears as a king named Malebron and sends Roland into a burial mound to rescue his siblings and to retrieve the lost treasures of Elidor. Those will help Malebron fight the blight on his land. Roland succeeds, and the children bring the treasures to Malebron, as foretold in an ancient Elidorian prophecy.

When the quest is accomplished, the story seems to be over, barely a quarter of the way into the book, but Garner has begun to question the fairy-tale structure of trial and happy ending that sufficed in his first two books. What happens next, he asks, when enchantment must be tested against daily life? Having seen the golden towers of Elidor, having held the glowing spear, sword, stone, and bowl, how can the four children resume their lives of school, play, and television?

Malebron and the children are attacked. He rushes them back through the barrier to the slums, sending the treasures with them. But back in the city, the treasures change form, becoming an iron railing, a piece of lath, a keystone, and a cracked cup. These the children are to guard, with no more guidance than a prophecy about the song of a being named Findhorn.

When the children return from Elidor, the narration combines the urgency of a magical quest with the reality of the Manchester setting. The children must slip home unnoticed and store the treasures where they will not be taken for trash. Further problems arise because the treasures are focuses of power in Elidor, and because the forces of evil there turn their energies toward locating the treasures in this world.

Power, force, energy: the words are appropriate to the magical context, but they also have significance in the everyday world. Both magical and electrical energy are invisible, potent, and dangerous. The power of the treasures manifests itself in a form adapted to their new surroundings: jammed radio and television, static electricity that cannot be "earthed" (since its proper earth is not our earth), a smell of ozone, an electric razor eerily buzzing with the cord unplugged. Burying the treasures stops these phenomena but does not hide the treasures from Malebron's enemies.

Throughout the novel, Roland remains passionately loyal to Malebron and to his vision of a restored Elidor. His eldest brother, Nicholas, grows increasingly skeptical of Malebron, of the worth of the treasures, and even of the experience in Elidor. The others, David and Helen, remain uncommitted, although Helen finds the first clue to Findhorn's identity, an ancient jug with a painted unicorn. It is also Helen, as a "makeless maid," who attracts the unicorn when it emerges from Elidor and thus inadvertently lures it to its death at the hands of the Elidorians. Findhorn, like the legendary swan, sings at its

death, thereby fulfilling prophecy and restoring the wasted lands and maimed king of Elidor. As in all of Garner's fantasies, the materials of Arthurian romance are used in such a way as to make the reader forget their overfamiliarity. This wasteland, this cup and lance do not merely echo Thomas Malory or T. S. Eliot; they operate as necessary elements of the plot and coherent symbols within the theme.

The ending of the story is presented as a series of intense, disjointed scenes, as if illuminated by lightning flashes. It is a difficult ending, partly because it counters our expectations even while fulfilling the pattern laid out by omen and prophecy. Chief among the reversals is Roland's reaction. Having confronted in Findhorn a pure, elemental truth, Roland regrets its sacrifice even to save a world. The unicorn, by coming through the barrier between worlds, has become more real than any of the splendors of Elidor, as Garner's descriptions make clear. Elidor is described in conventional phrases, while Findhorn is portrayed in words conveying movement, danger, and physical presence. It bleeds; its hoofs clatter on paving stones. No vague golden fairyland can match its sharply etched, terrifying beauty. The end of the book throws earlier assumptions into new perspective. Like Cadellin, Malebron becomes a questionable figure: does a wise and good wizard or king throw children in danger to save a weapon, or call upon others to make sacrifices he is unwilling to make? Has Roland abandoned his own world for a world to which he does not belong? If we read *Elidor*, as Justin Wintle suggests, as "metaphorical autobiography," we see Garner turning away from the innocent, lyrical side of fantasy and toward the darker, more mythical side, and that is indeed the direction of his next book.

The Owl Service differs from the earlier novels in concentrating on a single traditional narrative, the Welsh story of Lleu Llaw Gyffes and Blodeuwedd, his bride made of flowers. Like the story itself, the setting, in a remote valley in Wales, is stark and stylized. A few key sites — an attic, a large stone in a shallow river, a fish pond, a mountain road — are presented through imagery of sound, smell, and touch as well as sight, so that the reader feels not so much a spectator at a play as a silent participant in the midst of the action.

While writing *Elidor*, Garner did a series of radio and television interviews, and he credits that experience with a new awareness of language that shows in his subsequent works. In *Elidor*, his dialogue has lost its awkwardness, but only Roland really reveals himself through his speech. In *The Owl Service*, ascriptions for dialogue—"He said," "She replied"—become unnecessary because each character speaks from a unique perspective, personality, and experience. So much of the characterization is etched through shadings of dialogue that the reader must attend closely to nuances, especially at the beginning of the book, when the characters are still strangers to him.

There are no capsule descriptions to sort out relationships and attitudes, but one becomes not only acquainted but also deeply involved with the two sets of characters. One group includes the English family that owns an old house in the valley: Alison; her stepbrother, Roger; Roger's father, Clive; and, never seen, but felt throughout as an ominous presence, Alison's wealthy mother. The other group includes the housekeeper, Nancy; her bright, defensive, illegitimate son, Gwyn; and the seemingly balmy handyman, Huw Halfbacon, who is also lord of the valley and spokesman for the forces that haunt it.

These forces are keyed to the tale of Lleu, Blodeuwedd, and Gronw Pebyr, whose tragedy of love, betrayal, and murder repeats itself again and again as young lovers come of age in the valley. Garner exercises his new control over language to render an atmosphere of rising tension that belongs both to the unearthly drama and to the deepening loves and hates among the living characters. Natural and supernatural merge as Alison becomes possessed by Blodeuwedd and Gwyn and Roger are forced into the roles of lover and betrayer.

In the legend, Lleu Llaw Gyffes is doomed to marry neither mortal woman nor goddess, and so a woman is made for him from flowers: blossoms of oak, broom, and meadowsweet. Unfortunately, no spell ensures that Blodeuwedd loves him. She and Gronw conspire to kill Lleu, meeting the improbable conditions that constitute his Achilles' heel. Lleu does not die, though, but is transformed into an eagle. He seeks out his guardian, the wizard Gwy-dion, who returns him to human form. He kills Gronw, throwing a spear through the rock Gronw shelters behind, and Blodeuwedd is punished by being turned into an owl. From this story Garner takes not only the tragic pattern, but also a cluster of recurring images: the pierced stone in the river, the flash of a spear, the clatter of beaks and claws, the rank sweet smell of meadowsweet. All the elements are still present in the valley, and once the characters become aware of the legend it becomes a filter altering the look of everything they see.

Though little happens in the book, each event is charged with suppressed violence, which occasionally flashes through like a knife glinting under water, as when Alison's anger sends a book, poltergeist fashion, flying at Gwyn. Nothing is histrionic; at the most intense moments Garner is most likely to understate, but the careful choice of word and image can halt the reader's breath. In the case of the book, he uses the unexpected word "swarmed" to bring it to fearsome life.

Some readers have complained that all the violence, misdirected passion, and mythic beauty rest on the shoulders of three rather ordinary teen-agers. In earlier generations, the recurring drama has led to madness, murder, and the creation of art: the painted plates that are the "owl service" and a portrait of Blodeuwedd discovered under a plastered wall. In this generation the drama seems likely to spend itself on snide comments from Roger, Alison's withdrawal, and the despair of Gwyn, most susceptible of the three. Yet, it is this contrast between the physical and social reality limiting the protagonists' actions and the emotions burning through them that gives the work poignancy. When Alison, Gwyn, and Roger confront class snobbery, ethnic prejudice, emotional tangles inherited from parents, and the need to establish individual identities, the magic of owls and flowers sharpens the dilemmas, renders them more urgent, even deadly. However, it does not alter the nature of adolescence, which, Garner believes, holds within it the pain and beauty from which myth is born.

His next novel, *Red Shift*, retains a number of elements from *The Owl Service*: a disaffected, visionary hero; a relationship thwarted by parental misunderstanding and circumstance; a love triangle;

violence born of wounded pride; and the repetition of all these things over time. Garner splits his narrative among the parallel stories of Macey in Roman Britain, Thomas Rowley in Oliver Cromwell's time, and Tom in the present, all living in the same locale and all finders, in turn, of a prehistoric stone ax that represents stability in the face of turmoil.

The ax is not overtly magical, unlike the plates in *The Owl Service*. Its significance is portrayed strictly through the emotions of the characters who value it. Likewise, the similarities among Macey, Thomas, and Tom are not presented as the result of a brooding supernatural force. One may hypothesize reincarnation or a common genetic twist or merely coincidence: the narrative does not rule out a fantastic interpretation but neither does it particularly encourage it. A more strongly suggested link is the way each shift in the narrative, from Tom's story to Thomas' to Macey's, can be interpreted as indicating that one character is seeing, in a vision, a part of the life of another. All three see "bluesilver," the color that triggers berserk trances in Macey and shows up in Thomas' epileptic auras; the color of the star Delta Orionis, significant to all three, and of the train that takes Tom's lover, Jan, away from him.

"Bluesilver" is opposed to a "red shift." The latter's astronomical association suggests that the novel may be closer to the conventions of science fiction than to those of fantasy. Though there is little technology, there is a central concern with the nature of time. The narrative structure intimates that time may be cyclical or that all times are coexistent. Tom is interested in entropy, red shifts, and the time lag between an event, like a nova, and our knowledge of it. The novel is part science fiction, part mystery, part experiment with perception and point of view, and only glancingly a fantasy. Garner claims that, as usual, he had a model in folklore—the ballad of Tamlain and Burd Janet—but a comparison of the ballad with the novel reveals little direct borrowing. The ballad may have suggested a theme, the rescue of a troubled youth by a faithful lover, but none of its supernatural machinery appears in the story.

Beginning after or perhaps with *Red Shift*, Garner ceases to be a fantasy writer. His interest in crafting stories of love, family life, and growth continues, and so does his affection for traditional magical tales, but the two interests have become separated. The latter is expressed in the volumes of folktales edited and sometimes retold by Garner: *The Hamish Hamilton Book of Goblins* (1969), *The Guizer* (1975), *Alan Garner's Fairy Tales of Gold* (1980), and *The Lad of the Gad* (1980). The former is realized in the spare, deceptively simple volumes of the Stone Book Quartet. Though Garner is reluctant to discuss anything not yet in print, his comments on the Quartet as well as the direction his work has taken since *The Moon of Gomrath* make it seem unlikely that he will return to fantasy.

Lovers of fantasy may find themselves wondering what masterpiece could be concocted by combining Garner's early facility with magic with his later depth and skill. However, he has conclusively shown that his writing goes its own way, regardless of the wishes or expectations of its audience. When he began to write fantasy, he was unaware of the work of other British fantasists like J. R. R. Tolkien and C. S. Lewis (and has since expressed a lack of interest in the first and a positive dislike of the second); he was re-creating the form from its folkloric roots. He then chose to abandon the formula he established in the popular stories about Alderley Edge, and with each succeeding work has ventured into new techniques, some fantastic and some not, for exploring his primary concerns.

Garner stands in contrast to many contemporary fantasy writers who establish a magical world and a storytelling formula, usually modeled on Tolkien's, and then repeat them again and again. "Each book," he says, "is the first—or ought to be" ("A Bit More Practice"). Each of his works represents his attempt, to the best of his ability at the time of writing, to tell a moving and suggestive story. Though some of his innovations are controversial, his successes and his range have won him deserved popularity in the United States and near adulation in England.

Selected Bibliography

WORKS OF ALAN GARNER

The Weirdstone of Brisingamen: A Tale of Alderley. London: Collins, 1960. New York: Watts, 1961. Revised edition. London: Penguin, 1963. New York: Henry Z. Walck, 1970.

The Moon of Gomrath. London: Collins, 1963. New York: Henry Z. Walck, 1967.

Elidor. London: Collins, 1965. New York: Henry Z. Walck, 1967.

The Owl Service. London: Collins, 1967. New York: Henry Z. Walck, 1968.

Red Shift. London: Collins, 1973. New York: Macmillan, 1973.

The Stone Book Quartet

The Stone Book. London: Collins, 1976. New York: Collins/World, 1978.

Granny Reardun. London: Collins, 1977. New York: Collins/World, 1978.

Tom Fobble's Day. London: Collins, 1977. New York: Collins/World, 1979.

The Aimer Gate. London: Collins, 1978. New York: Collins/World, 1979.

Folktale collections

The Hamish Hamilton Book of Goblins. Edited by Alan Garner. London: Hamish Hamilton, 1969. As *A Cavalcade of Goblins.* New York: Henry Z. Walck, 1969.

The Guizer: A Book of Fools. Edited by Alan Garner. London: Hamish Hamilton, 1975. New York: William Morrow, 1976.

The Girl of the Golden Gate. London: Collins, 1979.

The Golden Brothers. London: Collins, 1979.

The Princess and the Golden Mane. London: Collins, 1979.

The Three Golden Heads of the Well. London: Collins, 1979.

Alan Garner's Fairy Tales of Gold. London: Collins, 1980. New York: Philomel Books, 1980. (The previous four books combined in one volume.)

The Lad of the Gad. London: Collins, 1980. New York: Philomel Books, 1981.

Essays and interviews

"A Bit More Practice." *Times Literary Supplement* (6 June 1968). Reprinted in *The Cool Web: The Pattern of Children's Reading,* edited by Margaret Meek, Aidan Warlow, and Griselda Barton. New York: Atheneum, 1978, 196–200.

"Real Mandrakes in Real Gardens." *New Statesman* (1 November 1968): 591–592.

"Alan Garner." Interview with Justin Wintle. In *The Pied Pipers: Interviews with the Influential Creators of Children's Books,* edited by Justin Wintle and Emma Fisher. New York and London: Paddington Press, 1974, 221–235.

"Inner Time." In *Science Fiction at Large,* edited by Peter Nicholls. New York: Harper and Row, 1976, 122–138.

"An Interview with Alan Garner." Interview with Aidan Chambers. In *The Signal Approach to Children's Books,* edited by Nancy Chambers. Metuchen, N.J., and London: Scarecrow Press, 1980, 276–328.

CRITICAL AND BIOGRAPHICAL STUDIES

Benton, Michael. "Detective Imagination." *Children's Literature in Education,* 13 (1974): 5–12.

Cameron, Eleanor. "*The Owl Service:* A Study." *Wilson Library Bulletin,* 44 (1969): 425–433.

Chambers, Aidan. *The Reluctant Reader.* Oxford and New York: Pergamon Press, 1969.

————. "Letter from England: Literary Crossword Puzzle . . . or Masterpiece?" *The Horn Book Magazine* (October 1973). Reprinted in *Crosscurrents of Criticism: Horn Book Essays 1968–1977,* edited by Paul Heins. Boston: Horn Book, 1977, 315–318.

Finlayson, Iain. "Myths and Passages." *Books and Bookmen* (November 1977): 74–79.

Gillies, Carolyn. "Possession and Structure in the Novels of Alan Garner." *Children's Literature in Education,* 18 (1975): 107–117.

Pearce, Philippa. "*The Owl Service.*" *Children's Book News* (July–August 1967). Reprinted in *The Cool Web: The Pattern of Children's Reading,* edited by Margaret Meek, Aidan Warlow, and Griselda Barton. New York: Atheneum, 1978, 291–293.

Philip, Neil. *A Fine Anger: A Critical Introduction to the Work of Alan Garner.* London: Collins, 1981. New York: Philomel Books, 1981.

Townsend, John Rose. "Alan Garner." In *A Sense of Story: Essays on Contemporary Writers for Children.* Philadelphia and New York: Lippincott, 1971, 108–119.

—BRIAN ATTEBERY

SHIRLEY JACKSON

1919–1965

IN A EULOGY to Leonard Brown, her college English teacher, Shirley Jackson wrote that his invaluable gift to her was the insight that "the aim of writing was to get down what you wanted to say, not to gesticulate or impress." Jackson followed this credo throughout her career. A master of the plain style, she was a supremely economical artist whose angular, clear diction gave the American Gothic tale a precision not to be found in Edgar Allan Poe, Nathaniel Hawthorne, or her other predecessors. What she "wanted to say"—that human cruelty and the precariousness of life are the only certainties in our otherwise enigmatic lives—was harsh, and she got it down honestly, without fuss. "The Lottery," one of the most widely anthologized stories in English, expresses the objective, social side of her vision; practically everything else in her serious fiction, from the bleak attenuations of the short stories to the strange rapture of *We Have Always Lived in the Castle*, expresses the inner side, the sense that the human psyche is as treacherous as human behavior.

Yet one of the most striking qualities of Shirley Jackson is her offbeat charm. Her content is severe, but her bright, quirky sense of humor and her sheer oddness soften the blow. Furthermore, no matter how bizarre her characters are—and she consistently creates some of the most bizarre people in fiction—she displays compassion and an almost frightening empathy. Her maddest, most dangerous character, Merricat Blackwood in *We Have Always Lived in the Castle*, is sketched with startling ten-

derness. Not since Poe has there been a more passionate poet of the freakish and abnormal, the "grotesque and arabesque," but Jackson goes further than Poe; rather than being tragically destroyed, Merricat is "happy" in her final lunacy—indeed, the only character to come out happy in all of Jackson's serious fiction.

In the evolution of the supernatural tale, Jackson's was a distinctly original voice, but her methods were too personal and idiosyncratic to attract disciples or imitators. Her version of the genre took ambiguity to its furthest extremity, beyond Henry James, Walter de la Mare, or her favorite ghost story writer, Elizabeth Bowen. She wrote what are simultaneously some of the most exasperatingly confusing and peculiarly satisfying tales in the genre.

Jackson slyly referred to herself as the only practicing witch in New England, a joke that had an undercurrent of truth. She did dabble in magic, with a Ouija board and tarot cards, and she had a library of some five hundred occult books. Yet most of her comments on the subject—such as her delightful description of how the supernatural, which had never previously harassed her life, suddenly turned up everywhere when she started work on *The Haunting of Hill House*—are laced with irony and gentle self-deprecation. Surprisingly, her fiction contains little sense of spirituality; the supernatural, both real and imagined, lurks as one of life's nasty little surprises rather than as a subject for mystical contemplation.

Jackson's life, far from being witchlike or mysterious, was one of cluttered domesticity and tireless devotion to her art. Born in San Francisco on 14 December 1919, she moved to Rochester, New York, with her family and enrolled at the University of Rochester, only to drop out after two years to devote a year to learning to be a writer. She trained herself to produce at least a thousand words a day, a habit she tried to maintain throughout her life and to which we owe the six novels, two autobiographies, three children's books, and numerous short stories that she managed to turn out despite that life's brevity. By 1937, ready for school again, Jackson enrolled at Syracuse University, where she launched her career with the publication of "Janice," a brilliantly compressed single-page story of a suicidal coed that forecast Jackson's lifelong obsession with mental anguish. She also wrote biting satirical editorials for the *Spectre*, a controversial student literary magazine; her nonfiction, which focused on bigotry and hypocrisy, was as prophetic as her fiction. During this period she met Stanley Edgar Hyman, the managing editor of the *Spectre* and future literary critic, whom she married in 1940.

Jackson's married life, engagingly documented in *Life Among the Savages* (1953) and *Raising Demons* (1957), revolved around four children, five cats, two dogs, a hamster, and a husband who divided his time between teaching at Bennington College and writing columns for the *New Yorker*. Jackson herself wrote fiction for the *New Yorker*, where she placed a dozen stories. One of these was "The Lottery," published in June 1948, which instantly made her famous—indeed, infamous. This horrifying parable of an annual human sacrifice in a cozy, normal American village inspired a torrent of hate mail and canceled *New Yorker* subscriptions. Readers either demanded to know "the locale and the year of the custom" or accused Jackson of being un-American and "perverted." "If I thought this was a valid cross section of the reading public," Jackson quipped, "I would give up writing."

Actually the situation was grimmer than that—this, after all, was a cross section of the *New Yorker* reading public—but Jackson continued writing anyway. Even during her most time-demanding periods of "raising demons," she turned out a steady stream

of work, stalling only during periods of depression and anxiety. As might be guessed from her fiction, these were rather severe and became steadily worse. By 1960 she was often afraid to go shopping alone or leave the house. For *Hangsaman* (1951) and *The Bird's Nest* (1954), both novels about mental disintegration, she did extensive research in abnormal psychology; but she also wrote from personal experience. Near the end of her life, Jackson's condition, with the help of a psychiatrist, began to improve significantly. Ironically, it was at this point that she died suddenly of a heart attack on 8 August 1965 at age forty-five.

Many of Jackson's finest supernatural short stories can be found in *Come Along with Me*, a collection of fiction and nonfiction assembled by Stanley Edgar Hyman three years after his wife's death. One of the most chilling and hauntingly typical pieces in the collection is "The Beautiful Stranger," the story of a woman who hates her husband so much that one day she envisions him, on his return from a Boston business trip, as a stranger, a man who *almost* looks like her husband but is really someone else.

At first she is terrified by this weird displacement, but then she feels a huge relief, fearing only that the "beautiful stranger" will come home one day as her husband again. Increasingly fragmented and disoriented from reality, she is literally lost at the end, unable to find her own doorstep in the endless row of suburban houses. Hers is surely a story of mental breakdown—yet there is a tiny possibility that her fantasy is real. In a chilling moment of conversation, the "stranger" casually remarks to his wife that someone at his office told him "'that he had heard I was back from Boston, and I distinctly thought he said that he heard I was dead in Boston.'"

Another chilling, potentially supernatural tale is "The Daemon Lover," from *The Lottery, or The Adventures of James Harris* (1949), a collection of stories featuring the same mysterious, continually transforming character. Again, the story involves a woman's collapsing mental state, this time under the stress of being jilted on her wedding day by an unseen suitor, James Harris, whom she gradually traces to the top floor of a shabby apartment building. Her frantic, repeated knocks are answered only by "low voices and sometimes laughter. She came back many times, every day for the first week. She came on her way to work, in the mornings; in the evenings, on her way to dinner alone, but no matter how often or how firmly she knocked, no one ever came to the door."

Three hypotheses seem possible with this strange, desolate story: that James Harris is truly a phantom lover, a modern version of the "daemon lover" suggested by the ballad to which the tale alludes; that he is simply a deranged, sick personality; or that he is a figment of the heroine's imagination. All three paths lead to the same loneliness. In Jackson's disturbed world, madness and the supernatural are practically interchangeable.

Ambiguity is the ruling principle in this fiction. In "Home," which appeared in the *Ladies' Home Journal* the month of Jackson's death, we never know whether the heroine's car is haunted by ghostly hitchhikers or the character's imagination. In "The Summer People" (collected in *Come Along with Me*), we never know whether the terrified old couple in their summer cottage are victims of their own paranoia or of a horrible plot by villagers — who may or may not have tampered with their car, cut their phone lines, and deprived them of food — resentful of outsiders. (If stories featuring sinister villagers, such as "The Lottery" and "Trial by Combat," are any guide, the prognosis is not good.) The old couple are huddled together in the last paragraph, waiting for the worst — and the story simply stops.

To the frustration and "confusion" of her critics, Jackson wraps everything in enigma — not only the implications of a story (as in James's *The Turn of the Screw*) but often the story itself. These nightmarish little pieces have a way of beginning as genre thrillers, only to turn into aggressively "modern" short stories, brief flashes of disturbing insight (or delusion?) that turn the story sharply inward as outer events vanish from the page.

Still, there are enough clues to construct tentative hypotheses. Furthermore, the language is so clean and finely honed that the reader experiences considerable pleasure as the puzzle unfolds. In "The

Rock," an atmospheric horror tale inexplicably discarded until Hyman resurrected it in *Come Along with Me*, the reader gradually surmises that the short, timid Mr. Johnson, who somehow looms large and threatening by the end, is Death and that he has fastened on the heroine after waiting impatiently for her sister-in-law: "It had to be one or the other," he tells her at the end, before moving "swiftly and silently away."

The most exquisitely open-ended of Jackson's supernatural stories is "The Visit" (in *Come Along with Me*), a haunted house story played out on two planes of reality, each of which presents many possibilities. The first puzzle involves an unusual couple, a dashing young man and an old lady who "died for love," and who are seen only by Margaret, the young heroine who is visiting the lovely old house of a friend from school. The tale is so deftly constructed that we don't realize Margaret is the only seer — or that the couple are ghosts — until the end.

Unless we assume Margaret to be hallucinating, we are faced with several tantalizing mysteries that compel us to reread the story. Why does the man stay young while the woman grows old? And is it significant that the old woman, like the heroine, is named Margaret? Could it be that they are really the same person, the old Margaret being a future projection of the young one, who is already enraptured with the young man?

Then there is the puzzle of the house itself, the most elaborate and magical house in Jackson's short fiction, an enchanted world of endless tapestries within tapestries and mirrors within mirrors, a place where "it was impossible to tell what was in it and what was not." Reality is always tenuous for Jackson's nervous, vulnerable characters, but this tale goes a step further, with the chilling suggestion that the heroine is forever trapped in the house by her friend's mother, who throughout the story embroiders the heroine into her bewitching tapestries.

"The Visit," which is dedicated to Dylan Thomas, is the most intricate and lyrical of Jackson's supernatural tales; it presents her world at its most lonely and brilliantly artificial, a succession of mirrors, doublings, and possibilities within possibilities, where lost connections between people continually multiply. Whenever the young Margaret encounters the strange couple, the words "lost, lost" echo through empty space.

Jackson's mastery of the inconclusive supernatural tale reaches its highest development in her spook novels *The Sundial* (1958) and *The Haunting of Hill House* (1959). *The Sundial* is the less attractive and entertaining, but it is also the more original, unpredictable, and savagely funny. The opening sets the somewhat crazed tone immediately:

> After the funeral they came back to the house, now indisputably Mrs. Halloran's. They stood uneasily, without any certainty, in the large lovely entrance hall, and watched Mrs. Halloran go into the right wing of the house to let Mr. Halloran know that Lionel's last rites had gone off without melodrama. Young Mrs. Halloran, looking after her mother-in-law, said without hope, "Maybe she will drop dead on the doorstep. Fancy, dear, would you like to see Granny drop dead on the doorstep?"
>
> (chapter 1)

The remaining members of the Halloran household are equally unpleasant and unhinged. The supernatural element in the plot gets under way when Aunt Fanny, seemingly the craziest of them all, is visited by the ghost of her father, who forecasts the imminent end of the world, with "'black fire and red water and the earth turning and screaming.'" At first everyone thinks she has finally gone mad, "but Aunt Fanny mad was so much more palatable than Aunt Fanny sane that Mrs. Halloran bit her tongue, averted her eyes, and winced only occasionally." Eventually the members of the household succumb to Aunt Fanny's hysteria, boarding themselves up in the house and planning to emerge after the apocalypse as rulers of a new world. All of Jackson's characters are isolated and hemmed in, but these go all the way. "'We are a tiny island in a raging sea,' says Mrs. Halloran, 'a point of safety in a world of ruin.'"

What they really are, the reader thinks, are lunatic crackpots—yet as the fateful prophesied day in August gets closer, the weather does turn freakishly ominous and people on the outside do begin behaving even more strangely than Jackson's people usually behave. By the last page, with everyone boarded up in the house during a raging storm that is supposed to be the end of the world, the reader has the eerie sensation that the cracked Aunt Fanny could be right—and then the novel ends.

Jackson goes too far this time: *The Sundial* is a frustrating novel, an excruciating exercise in unfulfilled expectations. Yet before its nonending, it does treat us to an astonishing array of superb Gothic scenes, including a moving statue, a demonic snake "full of light," a voodoo scene, a mysterious murder in the night, and a scene involving a sadistic villager (Jackson's most persistent personification of evil) that briefly turns this caustic, largely comic fantasy novel into a bloodcurdling tale of horror. If nothing else, Jackson's frequently declared love of eighteenth-century Gothic fiction is brilliantly apparent throughout. What mainly comes through, however, is her characteristically somber vision: if these people are microcosms of the world, as several reviewers have suggested, the world is clearly in trouble—whether it ends or not.

In *The Haunting of Hill House*, Jackson's ambiguity is brought under firmer control, as is her characterization. Although it takes a while to get under way, this tightly written modern Gothic manages to sustain mood, credibility, and narrative variety, and to come up with a powerful ending as well—a combination that is rare in the history of supernatural novels. The center of the book is Hill House itself, "a place of contained ill will" and one of the supreme haunted houses in literature:

> No human eye can isolate the unhappy coincidence of line and place which suggests evil in the face of a house, and yet somehow a maniac juxtaposition, a badly turned angle, some chance meeting of roof and sky, turned Hill House into a place of despair, more frightening because the face of Hill House seemed awake, with a watchfulness from the blank windows and a touch of glee in the eyebrow of a cornice.
>
> (chapter 2)

The marvelously threatening houses that Jackson created in "The Rock," "The Little House," "The

Visit," and *The Sundial* show that she had been building up to Hill House for some time, developing a style of stark lines and odd angles—much like Hill House itself—that turns Gothic clichés into art. But part of the key to the novel's success is Jackson's refusal to be solemn. Her irrepressible sense of humor is fully indulged, as when the obligatory psychic doctor tells the nervous characters involved in the haunted house investigation how to get to sleep in a house full of ghosts: "'I wisely brought *Pamela* with me. If any of you has trouble sleeping, I will read aloud to you. I never knew anyone who could not fall asleep with Richardson being read aloud to him.'" (Jackson was actually a passionate admirer of Richardson; her joke, as is often the case, was on herself.)

Eleanor Vance, who is one of the novel's four psychic investigators, is the archetypal Jackson heroine: apart from family oppressions, hatreds, and jealousies, her life has been empty—for her entire existence she has "been waiting for something like Hill House." Hill House is waiting for her too and claims her at the end in a suicide that is the hideously logical resolution to her life. Does her precarious mental state imply that the novel's memorable spectral occurrences—including a magisterial booming and hammering in the night that is one of the great scenes in supernatural literature—are all in her head, since they are detailed from her point of view? Not necessarily, because Theodora, the chic lesbian who comes closest to being Eleanor's friend, experiences some of them too, and because the house, as we have seen, is most shudderingly alive during moments of omniscient narration. A lifelong fan of eighteenth-century fiction, Jackson had no scruples about jumping from interior monologue to old-fashioned, omniscient commentary; the counterpoint of her own voice with the disturbed thoughts of Eleanor creates the most memorable ambiguity in Jackson's fiction.

Jackson's last completed novel was *We Have Always Lived in the Castle* (1962), which won a National Book Award. Like its two predecessors, it is a modern Gothic, complete with madness, mass murder, and a haunted house that is burned down at the end by the nastiest villagers since "The Lottery." Although the novel contains nothing supernatural, it is narrated by a young psychotic who views her inner world as "the moon" and the outer world as a magic place inhabited by demons and ghosts. No actual ghosts appear, but Merricat Blackwood's story has the most ghostly texture of any Jackson novel.

As a depiction of madness, this novel is peerless. With a hallucinatory, intensely musical style that locks us into the psyche of a murderous psychotic, *We Have Always Lived in the Castle* is not so much a study of psychosis as a participation in it. The limpid simplicity of the language is reminiscent of Arthur Machen's "The White People," another magic work that makes a young girl's seemingly mad world come to vivid life. Unlike Machen, however, Jackson refuses to provide a denouement: as usual, she leaves us in breathless suspension, with the narrator declaring, "We are so happy," as she peers out from her "great ruined structure overgrown with vines, barely recognizable as a house."

At the time of her death, Shirley Jackson was working on *Come Along with Me*, a seemingly autobiographical novel about a forty-four-year-old woman who dabbles in magic. What would have happened after the séance scene in this delightful work—and what would have happened in the rest of Jackson's potentially long writing career—was truncated by her sudden death. Her life ended like her fiction—by stopping abruptly, without climax or denouement.

Selected Bibliography

WORKS OF SHIRLEY JACKSON

The Lottery, or The Adventures of James Harris. New York: Farrar, Straus, 1949. London: Gollancz, 1950. (Stories.)

The Sundial. New York: Farrar, Straus, 1958. London: Michael Joseph, 1958.

The Haunting of Hill House. New York: Viking, 1959. London: Michael Joseph, 1960.

We Have Always Lived in the Castle. New York: Viking, 1962. London: Michael Joseph, 1963.

The Magic of Shirley Jackson. Edited by Stanley Edgar Hyman. New York: Farrar, Straus and Giroux, 1966.

(Stories plus *The Bird's Nest, Life Among the Savages,* and *Raising Demons.*)

Come Along with Me. Edited by Stanley Edgar Hyman. New York: Viking, 1968. (Unfinished novel plus stories and essays.)

CRITICAL AND BIOGRAPHICAL STUDY

Friedman, Lenemaja. *Shirley Jackson.* Boston: Twayne, 1975.

BIBLIOGRAPHY

Phillips, Robert S. "Shirley Jackson: A Checklist." *Bibliographical Society of America. Papers,* 56:1 (January 1962): 110–113.

————. "Shirley Jackson: A Chronology and Supplemental Checklist." *Bibliographical Society of America. Papers,* 60:1 (April 1966): 203–213. (Approved by Jackson.)

—JACK SULLIVAN

STEPHEN KING

1947–

I

IN HIS AUTOBIOGRAPHY and analysis of horror archetypes in modern culture, *Danse Macabre* (1981), Stephen King succinctly states his philosophy of writing: "I recognize terror as the finest emotion . . . and so I will try to terrify the reader. But if I cannot terrify him/her, I will try to horrify; and if I find I cannot horrify, I'll go for the gross-out. I'm not proud." King's definition of the "gross-out" involves the shambling, decaying, revenge-bent animated corpse of E. C. comics fame. The "gross-out," however, is most often seen in King's earlier novels, those written prior to 1979. King is maturing as a writer, and his recent works are predominantly combinations of terror and horror.

With very few exceptions, King's fiction aims to convince his readers that the universe is scarier, filled with more inexplicable evil, than they suppose. For example, the short story "The Monkey" (*Gallery*, November 1980) uses as an object of terror an innocuous, almost comical device, a windup toy monkey with cymbals fastened to its hands. Every time the monkey claps the cymbals together, someone or something close to Hal Shelburn dies violently. "The Monkey" begins when Hal Shelburn, as a mature, married man, rediscovers the grinning monkey, which was his childhood nemesis, in its original box. King overcomes the reader's disbelief by describing in flashbacks the deaths that took place when Hal was a child and his futile attempts to destroy the evil, lethal toy.

Shelburn succeeds in removing this malign thing from his life. Good triumphs. This is not an unusual ending for one of King's stories, for most of his fiction is moral and grimly optimistic. As King states in his *Playboy* interview (1983), he is "convinced that there exist absolute values of good and evil warring for supremacy in this universe [and that] people can master their own destiny and confront and overcome tremendous odds."

In King's fictional world choosing between good and evil is an assertion of individuality, and King seems to believe that the best of us are rugged individualists who defy group pressures to do what is right. We should also know right instinctively. It is not an oversimplification to say that good and common sense are closely connected for King.

Conversely, the human villains are persons who have surrendered to groups or symbols and have lost their goodness by doing so. The bad in King's books are high school cliques, politicians, scientists, the military, the rich, bureaucrats, those who wear designer clothes, religious groups that distribute poorly written tracts, and so forth. These "politics" of King's may be simplistic, but they undoubtedly offer one reason for the popularity of his fiction.

King's political views have rarely been questioned, but his prose style has often been severely criticized. King admits that he often writes clumsily but adds that even though he cannot write "elegant prose," he can respond to it in the work of others. Yet, despite his modesty, his "plain style" may be partly responsible for his commercial success. Unlike earlier fantasists like H. P. Lovecraft and Algernon Blackwood, King does not have a private mythology—nor does he flaunt his erudition. He frankly states that he is writing for general America, not just for the initiated few; this means that he writes to be understood. King also believes that the "story *must* be paramount, because it defines the entire work of fiction. All other considerations are secondary—theme, mood, even characterization and language itself" (*Playboy*).

One of King's stylistic tricks, for which he has been criticized, is the use of recognizable brand names from popular culture, but few critics seem to have recognized the purposes served by such references. Allusions to a popular beer, for example, add verisimilitude and make the story more immediately accessible. Even more important, King's constant references to the "real" enable him to blend the "unreal" with it until both are equally believable. Such a subtle amalgam occurs in *The Shining* (1977) when little Danny Torrance compares the dumbwaiter at the Overlook Hotel to the secret passage in *Abbott and Costello Meet the Monsters*. No such motion picture exists, although most readers undoubtedly accept its reality.

King is a witty writer; his recent works often contain subtle and humorous allusions to his earlier novels, as well as many quietly sly jokes that are never belabored. Even evil is not immune to King's humor. The first words of Randall Flagg, the evil force in *The Stand* (1978), after he yells to see if a starving Lloyd Henreid will respond, are from Maurice Sendak's children's book *Where the Wild Things Are*. They provide an amusing connection between Sendak's title and Flagg's location—a maximum-security prison.

Despite the judgments of some reviewers, King's writing reveals him to be well read in both mainstream and genre literature. Even an early work like *The Shining*, in addition to many references to Edgar Allan Poe's "The Masque of the Red Death," contains allusions to Frank Norris' *McTeague*, William Carlos Williams' philosophy of poetry, and Shirley Jackson's *The Haunting of Hill House*. The earlier *'Salem's Lot* (1975) combines dozens of references to vampires (drawn from motion pictures, plastic models, cartoons, books, and comic books) with Wallace Stevens' poem "The Emperor of Ice Cream"—odd though it seems, an effective combination.

II

Stephen Edwin King was born on 21 September 1947 in Portland, Maine. His father deserted the family when King was about two, leaving behind a few possessions, including an Avon collection of supernatural fiction and a volume of stories by H. P. Lovecraft about which King has said, "That book, courtesy of my departed father, was my first taste of a world that went deeper than the B-pictures which played at the movies on Saturday afternoon or the boys' fiction of Carl Carmer and Roy Rockwell" (*Danse Macabre*).

In 1970 King graduated from the University of Maine at Orono, with a B.S. in English teaching. He sold a few short stories, primarily to *Startling Mystery Stories*, and by 1972 he had written four non-horror novels, all of which remain unpublished to date.

Although King had written and sold horror short stories, before 1973 it had never occurred to him to write a horror novel. However, in 1972 King and his family were financially desperate. They had removed the telephone from their house trailer because they could no longer afford it, and King was drinking heavily and was discouraged about becoming an established writer. He had started a short story called "Carrie" but was dissatisfied with it, feeling that he was not capable of writing believably about teenage girls. He threw out what he had written, but his wife pulled the pages from the wastebasket and urged him to finish the story. As King later stated, though, he finished *Carrie* not to please his wife, not because he had any suspicion of its future success, but because he was suffering from writer's block and had nothing else to write about. He considered *Carrie* a dog.

King's misgivings were wrong. *Carrie* (1974) was accepted, and his first published novel became a paperback best-seller. Since then, almost all of King's novels have made the best-seller lists. The two exceptions to date, *The Dark Tower: The Gunslinger* (1982) and *Cycle of the Werewolf* (1983), were published in limited editions, as collectors' items.

The plot of *Carrie* centers on the coming of age of Carrie White, a tormented high school student. She menstruates in the school's shower, and when she believes that she is bleeding to death, her bestial classmates deride her. Carrie, however, is strongly telekinetic. After her classmates play an especially vicious joke on her by showering her with pig's blood at the prom, she destroys them and the town. She herself dies from wounds inflicted by her mother, a religious fanatic.

King had several subtexts (his word) in mind while writing *Carrie*. He wanted to show that

> high school is a place of almost bottomless conservatism and bigotry, a place where the adolescents who attend are no more allowed to rise "above their station" than a Hindu would be allowed to rise above his or her caste . . . , [and that Carrie is] Woman, feeling her powers for the first time and, like Samson, pulling down the temple on everyone in sight at the end of the book.
>
> (*Danse Macabre*)

Although the subtexts are noble, *Carrie* is often crudely written, with sometimes laughably leaden dialogue. King admits the faults of the story and generously praises the film version (1976), directed by Brian De Palma, as superior.

Carrie provides an excellent indication of King's interests, for although it is technically science fiction and Carrie White's powers are explained as "genetic recessive," King's explanation can be safely ignored since he concentrates on the results of Carrie's gift rather than its cause. In all of his work, in fact, King is less interested in causes than in results, and explanations are kept to a minimum. In his novella "The Mist" (1980) no explanation is offered for the deadly creatures that appear from an eerie mist and trap people in a supermarket. Everything may have been caused by a secret government organization, the Arrowhead Project, but the only persons who could possibly provide answers commit suicide in the supermarket.

King's next three novels, *'Salem's Lot, The Shining*, and *The Stand* (1978), are concerned with external evil. *'Salem's Lot*, in which vampires overrun the small Maine town of Jerusalem's Lot, shows many of King's strengths. The town itself is believable, and King manages to create more than a hundred (generally sexually neurotic) characters, although the novel is not so much about people or vampires as about the death of a small town. *'Salem's Lot* also contains a strong irony concerning faith. Father Callahan, a Catholic priest, loses his faith, and although he has an expensive crucifix, he is humbled by the chief vampire. Two men who have faith are able to repel a vampiric attack with impromptu crosses made of tongue depressors and adhesive tape. Also well handled is a sex-death linkage—death from the vampire's bite is erotically stimulating—that makes the vampires eerily attractive. All in all, the most serious fault in *'Salem's Lot* and its short sequel, "One for the Road" (*Maine*, March–April 1977), is conceptual: at the rate that men and women are bitten and become vampires, the United States should long since have become a nation of the undead.

A peripheral element of *'Salem's Lot* was a haunted house, but it did little except lend atmosphere. King's next novel, *The Shining*, is "set in the apotheosis of the Bad Place: not a haunted house but a haunted hotel, with a different 'real' horror movie playing in almost every one of its guest rooms and suites" (*Danse Macabre*).

The title of *The Shining* refers to psychic powers possessed by five-year-old Danny Torrance, for in the novel "to shine" means to possess paranormal abilities. But Danny is less interesting than his father, Jack Torrance, a former teacher and former alcoholic who also happens to be a talented writer. Jack Torrance is powerfully drawn and more "real" than the men in *Carrie* or *'Salem's Lot*, perhaps because, as King has admitted, Torrance is a semiautobiographical part of himself. King adds that, but for the success of *Carrie*, he could easily have turned into a sort of Torrance, a bitter, hostile teacher surrounded by his unsuccessful manuscripts. The other characters are less interesting.

The Shining is essentially the story of Torrance's

gradual collapse. While serving as a winter care-taker, Torrance is seduced by the evil Overlook Hotel and is led to try to murder his son and wife when they will not yield to the hotel. Only the timely arrival of Dick Hallorann, the Overlook's black chef, summoned from Florida because he, too, has the "shining," saves Wendy and Danny from meeting the fate of the previous caretaker's family. Jack and the Overlook perish when its boilers burst.

The Stand simultaneously demonstrates King's strengths and weaknesses and is a watershed in his career. The first part of the novel tells of the accidental escape of a "superflu" from a bacterial warfare installation. The flu, nicknamed "Captain Trips," is 99.4 percent fatal, mutating until the victim's body is no longer capable of producing antibodies. The world is soon almost depopulated when the American military, seeing that the United States has become vulnerable because of mortality from the flu, spreads the virus to other countries. Those who survive Captain Trips are offered a choice via dreams: join either the evil Randall Flagg in Las Vegas, or the good, 108-year-old, black Abagail Freemantle in (eventually) Boulder. Most of the survivors, with the general exception of scientists, conservatives, militarists, and criminals, move to Boulder and the "Free Zone."

Fantasy enters late in the first part of *The Stand* with the dreams, which are shared by all, and with Flagg, who is also called "The Walkin Dude" or "The Dark Man." Flagg is a creature born of modern anxieties and fears, and his powers are formidable. He can control crows, weasels, and wolves, and he can also change into these forms. He can open electrically sealed cells with magically created keys; hypnotize and madden with his eyes and voice; send his consciousness flying as an eye to observe potential enemies; levitate; and create ball lightning to destroy his foes. "Mother" Abagail has no comparable powers, but the people in Boulder, with two exceptions, are pure of heart.

The second part of *The Stand*, in which the government of the Free Zone is formed and its representatives confront Flagg, is anticlimactic and, worse, overlong. King has also been criticized for setting up Flagg as a straw man who topples when his plans go wrong, but this criticism seems to miss King's point.

At the beginning of the book Flagg is too powerful for the Free Zone ever to defeat him, but King skillfully undermines him and withdraws his powers as the story progresses. Flagg's eye develops blind spots, and he is weakened by bursts of emotion and temper tantrums. And, of course, Flagg's powers, being evil, cannot prevail against courageous, "decent" people.

King finds it difficult to make his women and minority members believable. He has candidly admitted that Mother Abagail and Hallorann, the cook in *The Shining*, are "cardboard caricatures of super-black heroes, viewed through rose-tinted glasses of white-liberal guilt" (*Playboy*). The self-criticism is justified. Nor are Frances Goldsmith and Nadine Cross, the two other women who figure prominently in *The Stand*, any more believable.

Before *The Stand*, King tended to end his novels by destroying everything. Something is saved in *The Stand*, but the novel has what amounts to two endings, neither of which is satisfying. In the first, the long-expected confrontation between good and evil never takes place. Instead, the captured representatives of the Free Zone, Flagg, and Flagg's cohorts in Las Vegas are all destroyed by an atomic bomb. In the second ending, Stu Redman, the only surviving Free Zone representative, is nursed back to health by Tom Cullen, a well-meaning retarded man; and their slow journey back to Boulder is very much a letdown.

The Stand, nevertheless, has much to commend it. It has King's usual convincing mass of detail. The male characters come to life, and King does not make everything *too* sweet at the end. When Redman returns to Boulder, he discovers that society (in a largely pejorative sense) has begun again. Boulder has gotten politics, and deputies are about to be issued guns. Will Captain Trips and atomic weapons inevitably follow?

King's next two novels are more closely allied to science fiction than to horror. In *The Dead Zone* (1979) the topics are paranormal abilities and the potential for an American Hitler. Johnny Smith, as a child, is hit on the head with a hockey puck and acquires a mild precognitive ability. As an adult, he is critically injured in a car accident, and when he awakens from a four-year coma, part of his brain (the "dead zone") is permanently damaged, but his psychic abilities are much greater. Smith need only touch someone or something belonging to a person to perceive his or her fate.

The Dead Zone is more ironic than King's previous works. Smith, after his coma and a number of operations, is hideous but gentle. Greg Stillson, a rising politician, seems bluffly friendly but conceals a tigerish personality, and his political rise is due to blackmail and intimidation. Eventually, after discovering the identity of a rapist, Smith attends a political rally, shakes Stillson's hand, and learns that Stillson will become president and cause a nuclear war—if not stopped.

Smith's problem is clear: his powers are taken seriously only in retrospect, and he cannot wait. King thereupon expertly rehashes the old science fiction clichés about preventing World War II by entering a time machine and assassinating Hitler before his rise to power. He also shows Smith becoming desperate as his health deteriorates and the "dead zone" of his brain becomes a malignant tumor.

Although King's next novel, *Firestarter* (1980), shares with *Carrie* the theme of a young girl (with powers) edging into maturity, there are few other similarities between the two works. Charlene ("Charlie") McGee, who can start fires by paranormal means, acquired her ability because her parents partook of Lot Six, an experimental drug that also gave her father the ability to "push" people into obeying his orders. The Shop, the government agency that administered the drug, has watched closely as the McGees "fire-trained" young Charlie. Thinking that the McGees are fleeing, the Shop captures Charlie, killing her mother. Although her father, Andy, frees Charlie for a short time, both are recaptured and imprisoned by the Shop. Andy's powers are temporarily exhausted, and Charlie, who does not wish to use her powers, is tricked into starting fires by John Rainbird, a monstrously disfigured Indian assassin. Eventually Andy McGee "pushes" himself into recovering his powers and tries to escape with Charlie. He does not succeed, and Charlie alone escapes, after destroying the Shop and its installations.

Firestarter has more depth than its simple story line indicates. The Shop itself is the villain. "Cap" Hollister, who heads its operations, is unpleasant,

but ultimately he is pathetic and less vicious than his bureaucracy and its enforcers. Rainbird is a larger-than-life figure, intelligent, amoral, and fascinated with death. He genuinely likes Charlie, even though he is aware that he is cynically manipulating her. His ultimate desire is to look into her eyes while killing her, as he did with Dr. Wanless, the developer of Lot Six. Finally, *Firestarter* is almost a paean to "common people," for they constantly aid the McGees with rides, rooms, food, and money.

Cujo (1981), whose title refers to a rabid St. Bernard dog, is a study of personalities, marriages, and our society, which emerges as the villain. False ideals of youth and beauty have led Donna Trenton to take a lover, so that she can pretend she is not getting old. Cheapness and mass production cause her car to stall and delay rescue attempts while she and her four-year-old son are trapped in the car and attacked by Cujo. Donna's husband, Vic, is an adman whose product, a cereal sold with the ironic slogan "Nope, nothing wrong here," causes its eaters to vomit. He has had to leave town in a desperate attempt to keep the advertising account. Cujo's owners, the Cambers, are fighting for possession of their son, for Charity Camber is afraid that the son will become limited and uncultured like her husband. Indeed, as King wishes us to observe, Cujo is merely an unfortunate dog doing what he must. Cujo has no free will, but human beings have brought their fates upon themselves.

King seems to have written himself into *Cujo* as Steven Kemp, Donna Trenton's erstwhile lover, a psychotic poet and playwright who has published one book. Kemp also works as a restorer of old furniture, an apt metaphor for King's writing, since King himself admits that he is not the most original of writers. This identification of Kemp with King does not mean that Kemp is King in every respect; it is merely that King seems to be making a sophisticated joke about himself, his craft, and his position in life.

In 1982 King published two works, *The Dark Tower: The Gunslinger* and *Different Seasons*. The first book is a strange, atypical short novel made up of five linked novellas. Best described as a surreal Western, a combination of fantasy and science fiction, it is the first in a planned series chronicling the quest of Roland, the last gunslinger, as he searches for answers in a strangely desolate world. Roland eventually finds the man in black, whom he has been seeking, but his quest is by no means over. He must find still more answers and the Dark Tower.

Different Seasons is a collection of four loosely connected novellas, only one of which, "The Breathing Method," transcends the literal. "The Breathing Method" is dedicated to King's friend and collaborator Peter Straub, and to some extent King has modeled his story on Straub's *Ghost Story*, imitating Straub's prose style as he tells of a club of old men who tell stories to each other. On the less literal level, "The Breathing Method" is symbolic: the men's club is a metaphor for the mind, and its numerous rooms are all the stories that King has told or plans to tell. King himself is in the story as Stevens, the caretaker of the club.

Nonetheless, "The Breathing Method" is less vital than the other three novellas, particularly "Apt Pupil," which is superb as it shows what happens when a young boy learns that an elderly neighbor is really a former concentration camp commandant. But "The Breathing Method" is a conscious attempt to do something different, and King should be commended for experimenting and taking chances, even if the experiments are not wildly successful.

Christine (1983) is also experimental, in narration. The first and third sections are told by Dennis Guilder, a high school senior; the middle is told by an omniscient observer. As Guilder's status as a student might indicate, *Christine* is about maturation and coming of age. Not only are Guilder and his friend Arnie Cunningham maturing, but Christine, a 1958 Plymouth Fury, has just reached twenty-one. She, too, is of age. Maturation involves the loss of innocence, and by the end of the novel few of the characters are innocent and fewer still remain alive, for Christine is possessed by the vindictive spirit of her late previous owner, a misanthrope. She runs over everyone who has offended her, threatened her, or hurt her in any way.

Christine is King's best novel to date. Not only is it impressive as contranatural horror, but it can also stand on its own as mainstream literature.

In late 1983, with *Christine* still on *Publishers Weekly*'s paperback best-seller list, King published two more books, *Cycle of the Werewolf* and *Pet Sematary*. As its title indicates, the former involves werewolves; it is an enjoyable story although routine in its treatment of the theme, but Bernie Wrightson's many illustrations are excellent.

Pet Sematary attracted considerable prepublication attention because King said it scared even himself. Modeled on W. W. Jacobs' famous horror story "The Monkey's Paw," *Pet Sematary* tells what happens when Louis Creed, a Maine doctor, learns that the land behind the children's pet cemetery (childishly misspelled "Pet Sematary") will restore the buried dead to life.

Although King keeps Jacobs' irony, demonstrating that changing fate merely makes life worse, *Pet Sematary* has few of the subtle terrors of Jacobs' story. King shows what is knocking at the door, and after the first shock the story becomes predictable, involving "gross-outs" rather than terrors. Nonetheless, the ending is terrifying; and *Pet Sematary* is by no means a bad book.

In addition to the aforementioned *Carrie*, movies have been made of *The Shining, The Dead Zone, Cujo, Christine,* and *Firestarter*, and King himself has written and starred in *Creepshow*. Unfortunately, King's supernatural novels do not adapt well as movies: Stanley Kubrick's *The Shining* (1980) bears little resemblance to the novel, except for its title, and is a disappointment as a horror film. *Creepshow* (1982) is routine and derivative in its episodic horrors, although King emerges as an amusingly bad actor. And John Carpenter's *Christine* (1983) lacks the careful development and sense of menace found in the novel: Christine seems perfectly justified in her homicidal activities.

On the other hand, King's more realistic novels have become fairly good motion pictures. David Cronenberg's adaptation of *The Dead Zone* (1983) keeps fairly closely to King's story and has a number of excellent, memorable scenes. Furthermore, Lewis Teague's *Cujo* (1983) is also an excellent adaptation, although Teague felt compelled to change King's downbeat ending.

III

King has also written an impressive number of short stories. The tales in *Night Shift* (1978), his only collection to date, range from inexplicable shock-horror, as in "The Boogeyman," to terror, as in "The Last Rung on the Ladder." At least two of the stories in *Night Shift* were cannibalized for later work: "Night Surf" became *The Stand*, and "Trucks" served as the basis for *Christine*. "The Lawnmower Man," perhaps King's best humorous effort, is a cheerfully gruesome tale in which Harold Parkette, a suburban Everyman, discovers that the man hired to trim his grass swears by Circe, has strangely cleft feet, and runs naked after his lawn mower, eating all that it spews out. Occasional embarrassing stories like "Jerusalem's Lot" (unrelated to '*Salem's Lot*), in which King attempts to be Lovecraftian and Victorian, may easily be forgiven.

In the large body of King's uncollected stories, one may find many fine tales, but only two need be mentioned. "Big Wheels: A Tale of the Laundry Game" (1982) is a conscious attempt at surrealism. Two lower-class laundry workers who need an inspection sticker for their car discover that an old friend runs an inspection station. They get him drunk enough to pass their car, but this is only part of the story, and its conclusion is ambiguous and dreamlike.

"The Wedding Gig" (1980) is also impressive. Set in 1927, "when jazz was jazz, not noise," it is a completely mainstream story of jazz musicians hired to play at the wedding of Maureen Scollay, the fat, ugly sister of a minor gangster. Maureen Scollay is perhaps the most realistic woman King has created. Furthermore, the story also touches upon the racist attitudes prevalent in the 1920's: the narrator is relieved when the one black member of his band quits, for "Lots of places wouldn't even audition us with a Negro in the group." The crowning irony is that the narrator sympathizes with Maureen, who is a cold-blooded murderess, but is indifferent to the fate of the black piano player, a decent young man named Billy-Boy Williams.

Any article about Stephen King must of necessity be open-ended, for King is still young. Nevertheless, it is a reasonable assumption that he will continue to dominate the terror-horror field. His forthcoming novels — *The Talisman* (with Peter Straub), *IT* (a sequel to '*Salem's Lot*), *The Cannibals*, and *The Plant* — are terror-horror combinations, and King will probably continue in this vein, since he genuinely enjoys what he is doing.

Writers often produce their best work later in life, and if King continues to experiment and improve, his critical reputation can only grow. It is likely that he will be recognized and remembered as a man who wrote his way out of clichés and sensationalism and brought new life into the terror-horror field. He is undoubtedly one of the most able writers working today.

Selected Bibliography

WORKS OF STEPHEN KING

The following lists first trade editions of King's books. King's recent works have also been published in limited editions issued simultaneously with the trade editions. No attempt has been made to list such deliberately created variants and collectors' items. For such material see Underwood and Miller, and Winter, below.

FICTION

Carrie. Garden City N.Y.: Doubleday, 1974. London: New English Library, 1974.

'*Salem's Lot*. Garden City, N.Y.: Doubleday, 1975. London: New English Library, 1976.

The Shining. Garden City, N.Y.: Doubleday, 1977. London: New English Library, 1977.

Night Shift. Garden City, N.Y.: Doubleday, 1978. London: New English Library, 1978. (Short stories.)

The Stand. Garden City, N.Y.: Doubleday, 1978. London: New English Library, 1978.

The Dead Zone. New York: Viking, 1979. London: Futura, 1980.

Firestarter. New York: Viking, 1980. London: Macdonald, 1980.

Cujo. New York: Viking, 1981. London: Macdonald, 1982.

The Dark Tower: The Gunslinger. West Kingston, R.I.: Donald M. Grant, 1982.

Different Seasons. New York: Viking, 1982. London: Macdonald, 1982.

Christine. New York: Viking, 1983.

Uncollected short stories mentioned in this article
"The Mist." In *Dark Forces*, edited by Kirby McCauley. New York: Viking, 1980.

"The Wedding Gig." *Ellery Queen's Mystery Magazine,* December 1980.

"The Man Who Would Not Shake Hands." In *Shadows Four,* edited by Charles L. Grant. Garden City, N.Y.: Doubleday, 1981.

"The Monkey." In *Fantasy Annual IV,* edited by Terry Carr. New York: Pocket Books, 1981.

"Big Wheels: A Tale of the Laundry Game." In *New Terrors,* edited by Ramsey Campbell. New York: Pocket Books, 1982.

AUTOBIOGRAPHICAL MATERIAL

"Introduction." In *Night Shift.* Garden City, N.Y.: Doubleday, 1978.

Danse Macabre. New York: Everest House, 1981. (An autobiography.)

"Afterword." In *Different Seasons.* New York: Viking, 1982.

"On Becoming a Brand Name." In *Fear Itself: The Horror Fiction of Stephen King,* edited by Tim Underwood and Chuck Miller. San Francisco and Columbia, Pa.: Underwood-Miller, 1982.

"On *The Shining* and Other Perpetrations." *Whispers* (August 1982).

CRITICAL, BIOGRAPHICAL, AND BIBLIOGRAPHICAL MATERIAL

"Interview: Stephen King." *Playboy* (June 1983). (Comprehensive and recent. Wide coverage, including King's childhood; his views on sex, marriage, ghosts, drugs, writing, etc.)

Underwood, Tim, and Miller, Chuck, eds. *Fear Itself: The Horror Fiction of Stephen King.* San Francisco and Columbia, Pa.: Underwood-Miller, 1982. (Essays, bibliography. Includes an abridged version of Douglas E. Winter's *Stephen King.*)

Winter, Douglas E. *Stephen King: Starmont Reader's Guide 16.* Mercer Island, Wash.: Starmont House, 1982. (Much original material, but overadulatory. Includes bibliography.)

— RICHARD BLEILER

R. A. LAFFERTY

1914-

OF ALL THE contemporary authors generally considered to be part of the fantasy and science fiction genres, Lafferty is without doubt the most original. His originality—and, indeed, his uniqueness, for nobody has been able to imitate him—stems from his themes, approach, and writing style. Lafferty's major themes, particularly in his novels, are inevitably religious, mythological, or both; while his minor themes most often involve the dissemination of peculiar, little-known pieces of knowledge. (He is a man of great erudition, particularly fond of word derivations, folklore, and the more abstruse aspects of mythology and theology, examples of all of which he delights in explaining to the reader.)

While some of Lafferty's fiction is easily recognizable as fantasy or as science fiction, more falls into neither category or, possessing an allegorical underlay, transcends genres; other portions of his work are strongly autobiographical, or moralistic, or historically based. Yet because of its uniqueness it is better to ignore definitions and categories and to consider all his fiction together.

Lafferty's uncommon approach is one of obliqueness. It is not that he tries to be unclear but that much of his subject matter is too effervescent or too incredible to survive full, detailed scrutiny—only an impression consisting of brief hints and half-truths, analogous to glances from the corner of the eye, can provide the proper setting. The result, however, is one of complexity and, on occasion, a certain degree of confusion for the reader.

Not really divisible from Lafferty's themes and approach is his pixilated, often outrageous, writing style. While quite a few fantasy authors have a readily identifiable style or a strong auctorial presence, Lafferty has both to an unequaled degree. Examples are necessary here:

When you have shot and killed a man you have in some measure clarified your attitude toward him.

("Golden Gate," 1982)

This had been one of the heroic labors required that one of the Argonauts should do. Had Hans failed, they would all have been destroyed by the furies.

This is hero stuff? This?

Yes, yes. Such were the high feats of the primordial heroes and of the early Irish heroes. Do not be fooled by later classical instances. They are derivative.

(*Archipelago*, chapter 1)

The word Surround isn't related to the word Round. It is a short doublet form for Superundate, to be completely covered as with waves. An Island isn't a body of land completely surrounded by water. A Lake is a body of land completely surrounded by water.

(ibid., chapter 6)

Apparitions are as stone-deaf. They speak their message but they do not hear. You may have noticed this yourself.

("Frog on the Mountain," 1970)

These quotations are typical, although Lafferty always seems to be trying to avoid the typical in his writing. Most of his work contains much wit, humorous asides, narrative hooks, and apparent overstatements.

Raphael Aloysius Lafferty was born in Neola, Iowa, on 7 November 1914. When he was four his family moved to Tulsa, Oklahoma, where he has lived ever since. His father was Irish Catholic and worked in the oil-lease business, and Lafferty attended a Roman Catholic school. He had an almost eidetic memory when young, and he always read greatly. His only extended absence from Tulsa was during World War II, when he served in the army for about four and a half years. This included a long posting to the islands of the South Pacific, which had a considerable influence on him and to which references recur throughout his writing. He was an electrical engineer until he retired from that profession in 1970. He did not write at all until he was forty-five (1959); since then he has been fairly prolific, with seventeen novels and about 175 stories published, and a lot of unpublished work. He had a nonspeculative story published in 1959 and his first speculative story, "Day of the Glacier," in *The Original SF Stories* magazine of January 1960. He is a bachelor and lives in his parents' former home in Tulsa.

Between 1960 and 1968 (when his first novels appeared in print) he had almost fifty stories published. Their originality was recognized very quickly, and they were very well received by critics and readers alike. Nearly all were published as science fiction, principally in the *Galaxy* stable of magazines—*Galaxy*, *If*, and *Worlds of Tomorrow*—which were all then under the editorship of Frederik Pohl, and during a period when they were regarded as the best of the science fiction magazines, with *If* winning three consecutive Hugo awards.

Even at the outset of his writing career, Lafferty's stories were strikingly different from everything else appearing in the science fiction magazines. They were refreshingly zany but often concerned with problems pertinent to the 1960's. Certainly they stretched the definition of science fiction, dealing in new ways with some of the older science fiction themes and conventions. They resulted in Lafferty's being regarded as part of a new wave of American fantastic fiction that appeared in the mid-to-late 1960's and included such writers as Samuel R. Delany, Thomas M. Disch, Harlan Ellison, Ursula K. Le Guin, and Roger Zelazny.

An example of Lafferty's high quality from the beginning is his third story to be published, "Through Other Eyes" (1960), in his Institute for Impure Science series. The main characters of the series, Gregory Smirnov, Valery Mok, and Charles Cogsworth, are all there (though not Epiktistes, the sentient computer), and the quality and tone of the story give no indication of its earliness. Typically, it concerns the testing of a new invention—one that enables people to see the world through the eyes of others. The effect is, naturally, shattering, but it is a thinly disguised plea by Lafferty for better human understanding. A well-known later story in the same series is "Thus We Frustrate Charlemagne" (1967). Its time paradox theme is the familiar one of trying to change history, though it contains first-rate historical research and a streak of wild humor, both of which single it out as different. The series includes that complex episodic novel *Arrive at Easterwine: The Autobiography of a Ktistec Machine* (1971), and it is continuing, with recent stories such as "Great Tom Fool or The Conundrum of the Calais Customhouse Coffers" (1982).

The stories from the 1960's are Lafferty's best work in the sense that they are simpler, more easily understood, and thus more entertaining than his later stories. Several of them have become minor classics, with many reprints to their credit.

"The Six Fingers of Time" (1960) is one such story. It describes how a young man, Charles Vincent, discovers that he possesses the special talent of being able to move faster than the eye can follow. He can enter and leave this speeded-up condition at will. There is the suggestion that this talent is an inherited one, connected with the possession of an extra digit on one's hand (and Vincent has an odd double thumb). Vincent misuses the talent in a puerile manner, playing cruel tricks upon members of the public. A man of similar talent whose face he never sees informs him that he must learn responsibility, and later invites him to join the brotherhood of those who have learned to conquer time—an invitation that Vincent refuses. Yet the moral position of this refusal is not clear, for the shadowy man has the "smell of the Pit" on him. Clearly this is not a God-given gift. Within a year Vincent has worn himself out by this speeded-up living, and he dies of senility.

Lafferty has a liking for writing about groups of prepubescent children. His general standpoint seems to be that they instinctively know things—especially about secret and magical subjects—that adults have forgotten. A delightfully humorous version of this is "Seven-Day Terror" (1962), which is Lafferty's most reprinted story. Clarence, a nine-year-old, makes a device that causes objects to disappear, and his eight-year-old sister manages to take the credit for their reappearance, because she knows they will all reappear after exactly seven days anyway.

A much more serious story is "Among the Hairy Earthmen" (1966), in which a group of alien super-children spend an afternoon playing on earth. But their afternoon is three centuries of our time, during which they appear repeatedly as various kings and queens of the Middle Ages and Renaissance, using ordinary human beings as cannon fodder in their games. It is an allegory of irresponsibility.

The idea of a group of children with special powers recurs in *The Reefs of Earth* (1968), and an analysis of an educational system that could produce very able children (if enough survived) is found in the bitterly satirical "Primary Education of the Camiroi" (1966).

The frequently reprinted "Slow Tuesday Night" (1965) points to the ephemeral nature of any achievement by postulating a world in which all processes of business and the arts move at a phenomenally rapid pace, so that a lifetime's experience can be had in just one night. An office can be rented and furnished within a minute; a new product can be manufactured and marketed in three minutes; a

work of philosophy is written in seven minutes, with a little help from machines ("This was truly one of the greatest works of philosophy to appear during the early and medium hours of the night"); a marriage may last only thirty-five minutes, including honeymoon; a panhandler can become the richest man in the world in just an hour and a half and then be reduced to penury again five minutes later; during the night the entire city is usually rebuilt "pretty completely at least three times."

Lafferty's high regard for American racial minorities, especially Amerindians, Mexicans, and Gypsies, stems from his childhood days when, as an Irish Catholic, he was himself persecuted to some extent and forced to join the racial-minority fringe. His best-known Indian story is "Narrow Valley" (1966), wherein an old Indian spell (aimed at tax avoidance) makes a 160-acre plot of land look like a five-foot ditch. A Gypsy story is "Land of the Great Horses" (1967).

In 1968 Lafferty had his first three novels published. The earliest to appear was *Past Master*, a final nominee for both the Hugo and Nebula awards and still regarded by some as his best novel. Religion and myth are interwoven in a battle between good and evil against a complex background. The human-settled planet of Astrobe is in turmoil despite the near perfection of its wonderful cities, where leisure is the norm and every luxury is available. Millions of people are leaving this society, preferring to live in the dangerous squalor of new slums where they must work hard and have very low life expectancies. To help the situation, Thomas More is brought from the earth of a thousand years earlier, chosen because he may be popular and because of his one honest moment (for which he was executed).

Once on Astrobe, More is manipulated by the governing group, which consists mainly of Programmed Persons—perfect mechanical men, virtually indistinguishable from humans, in whose hands most of the power has been placed. The one fault of the rule of these Programmed Persons, and of Astrobe's utopian ideal, is that it is purely materialistic, suppressing the spiritual side of life. Yet even the Programmed Persons have a spiritual ruler—Ouden, a nothingness, a vortex, which seems

1047

to personify evil. On More's side, trying to protect and guide him, are various human mythical archetypes. More runs for world president and wins an overwhelming victory. Very soon, though, he discovers that he is being used to help stamp out everything spiritual upon Astrobe, and he rebels against his lawmakers. He refuses to agree to a clause of this nature and, just as he was a thousand years before, is sentenced to death. A revolution precipitated by the death sentence fails to save More's life but might lead to a new world order.

The Reefs of Earth was the first novel finished by Lafferty (in 1966) but it was published a month or two after *Past Master*. Reminiscent of "Among the Hairy Earthmen," though somewhat less serious, *The Reefs of Earth* is deceptively simple. At one level it concerns a group of six alien children (plus a seventh who is a ghost) determined to kill off all earth's inhabitants and take over the planet. The children are Puca, a race very similar to humans, though sometimes very ugly, like goblins or Neanderthals, and possessing special talents. Generally they are rejected and persecuted by humans, though accepted by Amerindians and blacks. The children fail in their aim (they are, after all, under ten, and there is the suggestion that they may succeed later), and their four parents (they are two families of cousins) all die from a combination of persecution and earth allergy sickness.

At a second level the novel shows up most normal humans (specifically the WASP inhabitants of whichever southern state the novel is set in) as being spiritually deficient and unworthy to live in this world—let alone rule it—while the ethnic minorities are depicted as more intelligent and capable. At another level the whole novel is not to be taken at face value or as an allegory, but is an excuse for a succession of tall tales and doggerel verses. The children delight in telling each other brief ghost and horror stories. This is the *aorach*, a Puca art form. But other characters in the book tell such tales too, and Lafferty inserts many unbelievable snippets into the narration:

> Phoebe Jane piloted them down the river about a mile. She put them in an inlet so hidden that the stars didn't even shine. It was like the inside of a blind shed.
>
> "A family lived in this inlet for three generations once, and they never did see the sun," she said. "The parents never saw the faces of their own children. It's so dark in here that you strike a match here and it shines dark instead of light. It's so dark here that you didn't see me go, and I left my voice here to talk with you for two minutes after I'm gone."
>
> (chapter 6)

The other art form of the Puca is the *bagarthach* verse, which can make the person at whom it is aimed do anything, even die. It is doggerel, for which Lafferty has an obvious weakness. All the chapter titles in the novel fit together to make a sixteen-line example of it.

The same verse form, complete with forced rhymes of an outrageousness to rival those of Ogden Nash, is a feature of the author's third 1968 novel, *Space Chantey*. This is another excursion with the archetypes of myth, as a far-future space captain and his crew, returning from war, relive the adventures of Homer's *Odyssey*. The novel is short and patchily episodic. It reaches its greatest heights when the parallels with Odysseus are forgotten and new adventures included. Somehow Atlas is in here, holding the universe together by knowing everything about everything. From Norse myth come some giant trolls (including one who can repair and even improve spaceships with his stone hammer). Most original is a gamblers' world, where the captain, Roadstrum, wins 1,000 planets and then loses 1,024 to a lavatory attendant. As one might expect of mythological archetypes, Roadstrum and his men are occasionally killed, but they never stay dead for long. It is a lightweight work, though one of Lafferty's own favorites.

Myth and religion go hand in hand again in *Fourth Mansions* (1969), another Nebula nominee. The main question in this tremendously complex novel is whether mankind can manage to rise to a new superhuman level (the Fifth Mansion) or whether it must continue its cyclical progression through the previous levels. (The progression is spiritual and mental in nature rather than physical.) As usual in Lafferty's books, the final result is left unclear.

The novel's protagonist is Freddy Foley (there is frequently alliteration in Lafferty's character names), a young journalist who is naive but lucky, an obvious everyman hero type, who comes to fill a Parsifal role and has greatness (a metaphorical Holy Grail) thrust upon him. Circling about him are four power groups who could help or hinder, each characterized by an animal. Already superhuman are the brainweavers, a seven-person mental gestalt (pythons), who want humanity to progress. Opposed to them and trying to control Foley are the revenants, immortal and almost omniscient, changing bodies at will (toads). Then there is a secret Christian brotherhood, the patricks (characterized by the badger), who help Foley and make him their emperor. Last of the four is a young revolutionary, Miguel, who is the self-proclaimed champion of the people (unfledged falcon). Great stress is placed throughout on secret groups who wield enormous power and manipulate large sections of humanity. Despite the complexity there is considerable narrative drive and much violent action, blending to make a very satisfying novel.

The Devil Is Dead (1971) must be considered in tandem with *Archipelago* (1979), the latter being Lafferty's favorite among his novels. Both were finished in 1967, and they are, respectively, volumes 2 and 1 in the *Devil Is Dead* trilogy, or, as the author prefers to call it, the Argos Mythos. Each volume contains many references to the other, and there are characters in common. Neither is fantasy in the accepted sense except that the author hints that *Archipelago* may be viewed as a mythological allegory and *The Devil Is Dead* as both a religious and mythological one. *Archipelago* recounts some of the exploits of the Dirty Five, a group of men who meet while serving in the army in the South Pacific in 1943–1945. They are Finnegan, Hans, Casey, Vincent, and Henry, who are also reincarnations of five of the Argonauts (respectively Jason, Orpheus, Peleus, Meleager, and Euphemus). Sometimes their present-day adventures parallel those of the Argonauts, though they seem to spend most of their army service drink-

ing. Later, in civilian life, some of them (together with wives or girlfriends) set up a printing company in New Orleans. Although Lafferty provides details of the earlier lives of all five (sometimes at excessive length), it is the later wanderings of Finnegan upon which he concentrates:

> Was Finnegan a simple schizo in his living several lives? No. He was a complex schizo. His travels ended only with his life, though X. (who claimed to have later congress with him) said they did not end even then. The apocryphal, of the Finnegan adventures cannot be separated from the canonical. They raise the question: are there simultaneous worlds and simultaneous people?
>
> (chapter 7)

At the end Finnegan seems to be killed, though this is not clear, and it seems obvious that he will reappear. He does so in *The Devil Is Dead* (a final nominee for the Nebula award), which concentrates on his adventures. The first half of the book consists of a sea voyage from a southern American port to the Greek islands on a small ship owned by the eccentric millionaire Saxon X. Seaworthy. Most, if not all, of the crew and passengers seem to be mythological archetypes. One, named Papadiabolous, is said to be the devil, though Finnegan knows that he is not who he appears to be, because Finnegan has helped to bury a man with the same face on the eve of the voyage.

After a monumental battle between good and evil on the island of Naxos, in which several of the crew are killed, Finnegan becomes a fugitive, hunted around the world by Seaworthy and his associates. An explanation in the last two chapters of how both Papadiabolous and his double were sons of a Pole, Ifreann Chortovitch, who had, literally, been fathered by the devil, is too long and too late. This is a particularly confusing novel at the allegorical level, because personalities and alliances are never made clear. There is even a double of Finnegan, who is either murdered by or merges with him.

Lafferty had four other books published in 1971. *Arrive at Easterwine* has already been mentioned.

The Fall of Rome is a straightforward nonfiction account of the decades leading up to the entry into Rome by Alaric and his Goths in 410 A.D. (Although it is referred to in some reference works as a novel, it is an undramatized factual account.) *The Flame Is Green* consists of three years of the rollicking, slightly bawdy adventures of Dana Coscuin, a young Irishman from Bantry Bay, in Spain, France, and Poland just before and during the revolutions of 1848. Coscuin becomes involved with various revolutionary groups. Although Coscuin seems to make some miraculous recoveries from severe (or mortal) wounds, these may be attributed to Lafferty's love of the paradoxical overstatement; the novel would not be classifiable as speculative except for the reappearance as a minor character of Ifreann Chortovitch, the son of the devil. Nevertheless, the novel was nominated for a Nebula Award. It is the first in a planned series of four books about Dana Coscuin. Lafferty also published *Strange Doings*, a collection of science fiction stories. The following year, 1972, he had another historical novel published, *Okla Hannali*, the biography of a nineteenth-century Choctaw Indian.

Lafferty's four more recent novels, *Not to Mention Camels* (1976), *Apocalypses* (1977, two novels in one volume), and *Aurelia* (1982), are less satisfactory and have not had the same impact as his earlier works. *Not to Mention Camels* returns to the theme of recurring archetypes. ("'But there *are* no other people!' he cried then. 'There are a dozen or so people. That is all. And they are repeated billions and billions of times.'") They often die but at the instant of death manage to jump to another world, appearing fully adult, though under a different (yet similar) name. Thus Pilger Tisman becomes Pilgrim Dusmano and then Pelian Tuscamondo. He should not be able to recall any of his previous existences, yet he can. A complicating factor is that he is at least partly an artificial creature. He is, perhaps, analogous to the revenants in *Past Master*.

A feature of *Not to Mention Camels* is blood lust, expressed in various unpleasant deaths (such as having one's thoracic organs pulled out by hand and the cavity filled with molten gold) and cannibalism. There are references to *Archipelago*, even though none of the parallel worlds in *Not to Mention Camels* appears to be earth.

Of the two 180-page novels in *Apocalypses*, "Where Have You Been, Sandaliotis?" tells of the greatest confidence trick in the world—the creation of Sandaliotis, a peninsula in the Mediterranean larger than Italy. It is investigated by Constantine Quiche, "the best detective in the world," who discovers it to be an evanescent confection of sea foam and illusion, created to be sold as real estate. It is a memorable work but never convincing.

Also in *Apocalypses* is "The Three Armageddons of Enniscorthy Sweeny." Here Lafferty employs an even more elliptical and indirect approach than normal to suggest that on a parallel earth three stunningly powerful operas (*Armageddons I, II, and III*), performed in 1916, 1939, and 1984, have served to prevent world wars (though it is uncertain whether the final 1984 disaster can be averted, or even whether the world can survive the impact of the third opera).

Aurelia is an extension of "Primary Education of the Camiroi" with added religious symbolism. Aurelia, a fourteen-year-old, is trying to complete her world government project by flying in a spaceship she has built to a backward human-settled planet and governing it for a year. There is no mention here of Camiroi, her advanced planet being known only as "Shining World." Being a poor student, she crash-lands on the wrong planet. Its name is never divulged to the reader: probably it is earth; possibly it is counterearth. She never has a chance to govern the planet but is hailed as a kind of messiah; a cult quickly establishes itself around her. Her death is prophesied within three days. Another young off-worlder who has just arrived is Cousin Clootie, there to help Aurelia do a proper job. He is her "dark companion." They are light and dark (her name means golden, while his is a Scottish term for the devil), yin and yang, both with cult followings, and they die together by the agency of a spiked yo-yo with yin and yang symbols painted on it. The symbolism is confusing, and a succession of homilies from Aurelia slows down what action there is.

From 1968, when his first novels appeared, Lafferty's short stories began to change. Gradually they became heavier and more intense in their themes and more esoteric in their audience appeal. Rather than appearing in *Galaxy* and *If*, most were first published in original anthologies, notably Damon Knight's *Orbit* series, which favored experimental stories. For about four years Lafferty's stories were better received than ever, with several award nominations and one Hugo; but since 1973 the pendulum has swung the other way, with his stories being regarded as incomprehensible by increasing numbers of readers.

Examples of some of his most admired efforts include the Nebula nominee "Continued on Next Rock" (1970) and "All Pieces of a River Shore" (1970). Several stories from this period share themes with his novels. For instance, "About a Secret Crocodile" (1970) deals with some of the many secret groups that control aspects of society; it could be part of *Fourth Mansions*. Another highly regarded story, and a Nebula nominee, is "Sky" (1971), about a drug of that name that makes people think they can fly. In 1973 Lafferty won a Hugo Award for his 1972 story "Eurema's Dam," a poignant piece edging into black comedy about Albert, the last of the idiots, who is unable to write properly or to add figures but has to invent tiny machines to do these jobs for him. In adulthood he builds larger and more useful machines that will fill high government office, and they look down on him. His only friend is Charles, a machine that he builds to be as stupid and awkward and inept as himself.

Perhaps it is a testament to Lafferty's originality and unwillingness to compromise the erudite obscurity of much of his later work that he has a good deal of unpublished material of all lengths, including about fourteen novels. But two of his books, *Annals of Klepsis* (a fantasy novel) and *More Than Melchisedech* (the third Argos Mythos novel), were published in 1983 and three collections are scheduled for early publication.

Lafferty is a writer who often demands considerable effort from his readers. Undoubtedly his best work is of shorter lengths, and he is unable to sustain his highest standards for more than a few pages. All his novels are episodic; all contain some good passages and many clever lines along with overlong or confused patches. His great originality has taken fantasy and science fiction into new areas—a tribute that can be paid to only a handful of twentieth-century authors.

Selected Bibliography

WORKS OF R. A. LAFFERTY

Past Master. New York: Ace, 1968. London: Rapp and Whiting, 1968.

The Reefs of Earth. New York: Berkley, 1968. London: Dobson, 1970.

Space Chantey. New York: Ace, 1968. London: Dobson, 1976.

Fourth Mansions. New York: Ace, 1969. London: Dobson, 1972.

Nine Hundred Grandmothers. New York: Ace, 1970. London: Dobson, 1975. (Short stories.)

Arrive at Easterwine: The Autobiography of a Ktistec Machine. New York: Scribner, 1971. London: Dobson, 1977.

The Devil Is Dead. New York: Avon, 1971. London: Dobson, 1978.

The Flame Is Green. New York: Walker, 1971.

Strange Doings. New York: Scribner, 1971. (Short stories.)

Okla Hannali. Garden City, N.Y.: Doubleday, 1972.

Does Anyone Else Have Something Further to Add? New York: Scribner, 1974. London: Dobson, 1980. (Short stories.)

Funnyfingers & Cabrito. Portland, Oreg.: Pendragon Press, 1976. (Chapbook containing two stories.)

Horns on Their Heads. Portland, Oreg.: Pendragon Press, 1976. (Chapbook.)

Not to Mention Camels. Indianapolis: Bobbs-Merrill, 1976. London: Dobson, 1980.

Apocalypses. Los Angeles: Pinnacle Books, 1977.

Archipelago: The First Book of the Devil Is Dead Trilogy. Lafayette and New Orleans, La.: Manuscript Press, 1979.

Aurelia. Norfolk–Virginia Beach, Va.: Donning, 1982.

Golden Gate and Other Stories. Minneapolis: Corroboree Press, 1982. (Short stories.)

Four Stories. Polk City, Iowa: Chris Drumm, 1983. (Chapbook.)

Laughing Kelly and Other Verses. Polk City, Iowa: Chris Drumm, 1983. (Chapbook.)

Heart of Stone, Dear, and Other Stories. Polk City, Iowa: Chris Drumm, 1983. (Chapbook.)

Ringing Changes. New York: Ace, 1983. (Short stories.)

Snake in His Bosom, and Other Stories. Polk City, Iowa: Chris Drumm, 1983. (Chapbook.)

Through Elegant Eyes: Stories of Austro and the Men Who Know Everything. Minneapolis: Corroboree Press, 1983. (Short stories.)

CRITICAL AND BIBLIOGRAPHICAL STUDIES

Bain, Dena C. "R. A. Lafferty: The Function of Archetype in the Western Mystical Tradition." *Extrapolation,* 23 (Summer 1982): 159–174.

Drumm, Chris. *An R. A. Lafferty Checklist.* Polk City, Iowa: Chris Drumm, 1983.

—CHRIS MORGAN

TANITH LEE

1947-

TANITH LEE IS today one of the most versatile and original writers of fantasy, horror, and science fiction. She is a leader of the women who have brought new perspectives to speculative fiction during the last decade, particularly in treating sex, violence, and mythological themes; and her success has paralleled and strengthened that of such recent stars as Julian May, Elizabeth A. Lynn, Marion Zimmer Bradley, C. J. Cherryh, and Anne McCaffrey. Lee has humor, vision, and an understanding of human nature, especially adolescent nature, and she is an expert practitioner of that old and respectable type of fiction, the Bildungsroman, the coming-of-age novel.

Lee was born on 19 September 1947 in London. She attended Catford Grammar School and Croydon Art College. Art college is a way station for many talented English youths, like Lee's contemporary John Lennon, who do not aspire to attend a university. Lee's own expressed artistic interests include writing, painting, and music; she is also interested in psychic powers and past civilizations. She worked in a succession of dead-end or entry-level jobs until she had made enough money from writing to live on; now she resides in London and writes full time. In 1979 she won the August Derleth Fantasy Award for her novel *Death's Master* and in 1980 and 1981 was the guest of honor at several major American conventions of science fiction and fantasy fans.

In a 1979 interview, Lee said:

I began to write, and continue to write, out of sheer compulsion to fantasize. I can claim no noble motives, no aspirations that what comes galloping from my biro [ballpoint pen] will overthrow tyranny, unite nations or cause roses to bloom in the winter snow. I just want to write, can't stop, don't want to stop, and hope I never shall. . . .

(Contemporary Authors)

True to her word, Lee has produced over twenty full-length novels, four collections of short stories, and four radio plays, and continues to turn out at least two books per year; and there seems to be no limit to her ability to maintain a consistently high level of achievement. But it is not true, as she implies, that her books are mere storytelling, pleasant escapist recreations; her imaginative sympathy for her characters powerfully depicts their deepest emotions and demonstrates that modern fantasy is primarily concerned with the life of the soul. Moreover, she has frequently dealt with some of the most important themes of twentieth-century literature: genocide, alienation and anomie, and the conflicts between societies with advanced technology and those less developed.

Most of Lee's stories center on unusual characters, gifted (or cursed) with abilities far beyond the common, learning to know themselves and grappling with their destiny. For example, the *Birth-*

grave trilogy describes the education of a goddess and a god, her son; *The Storm Lord* is the story of a rightful king who rises from youthful obscurity to predestined power; *Volkhavaar* shows the development of a would-be witch into a powerful sorceress; in *Don't Bite the Sun* and its sequel, *Drinking Sapphire Wine*, the adolescent heroine learns that she can overcome the luxurious meaninglessness of her life; in *Day by Night* the relationship of the hero and heroine is the focus of their whole world's history; in *Sabella* and *Lycanthia*, vampires and werewolves, respectively, are the protagonists. Lee often uses supernatural motifs to treat questions of identity: doppelgängers in the *Birthgrave* trilogy, *East of Midnight*, and *Electric Forest*; possession in *Sabella* and *Volkhavaar*; shape-changing in *Don't Bite the Sun*, *Lycanthia*, and her children's book *The Dragon Hoard*. The survival of the spirit after death, shown in *Companions on the Road, Kill the Dead, Cyrion, Volkhavaar, The Silver Metal Lover, Sung in Shadow, Death's Master*, and *Night's Master*, is another expression of Lee's constant interest in the meaning of personality.

Another frequent theme is the nature of good and evil. Those powers that ordinary folk call evil are so in Lee's worlds by their created nature, not by a postulated fall from grace. For example, in *Night's Master*, Azhrarn is lord of beautiful demons, all wickeder than humans can dream; but he saves humanity from an absolute evil that tries to destroy it, for without humanity to love and torment, the Demon Prince has no reason for being. Lee as creator takes pride in the balance between good and evil in her worlds, and does not go in for great epics of the struggle of good versus evil. Her stories are more typically about the struggle of the soul to reach wisdom and maturity, and much of her ability to create credible characters derives from the fact that she does not label some "good" and some "bad." In *Volkhavaar* (1977), for instance, a woman's love transforms a man-devouring god into a spirit of peace rather than destroying him. Related to this is Lee's frequent celebration of the abilities of the underappreciated and downtrodden, and of the ability of the spirit to survive under the most appalling conditions.

Another major theme is love in all its manifold forms; there are love stories in all Lee's books. Her approach to sex is frank, and her descriptions of sexual relations are usually forthright and matter-of-fact. But she also has an understanding of the world of feeling in which passion is triumphant—indeed, can be simultaneously triumphant and ridiculous. Though her female characters are often stronger, more capable, and more interesting than her male characters, Lee is not a feminist in the manner of those writers who seem to believe that all depictions of relationships must be politically correct, and she often portrays love as a romantic dream of all-enveloping passion.

The worlds that Lee's stories take place in have some common characteristics. In technology, they are either primitive and magical, or so far advanced that the technology seems like magic. Descriptively, Lee can invent convincing geography, but few of her places are notable as places. In this she shows a strong resemblance to Robert E. Howard, who vividly described locations yet could not make them memorable; the lavish pageantry of her places soon begins to blur in the mind, so that one vast hall or blood-smeared temple or smoking battlefield or haunted ruin seems much like the next. The invented races and peoples who inhabit the worlds are more successful; particularly striking are the cruel demigods in *The Birthgrave*, the genocidal masters and their telepathic slaves in *The Storm Lord*, the gorgeous Sophisticated Formats (robots) in *The Silver Metal Lover*, and the conquered devotees of the God of Flies in *Vazkor, Son of Vazkor*.

The theme of coming-of-age is most powerfully expressed in Lee's first major works: the *Birthgrave* trilogy and *The Storm Lord. The Birthgrave* (1975) is the first half of a double work; its sequels, *Vazkor, Son of Vazkor* (1978) and *Quest for the White Witch* (1978), are the parallel second half, one long story in two volumes (probably because of its length and the fondness of readers for "trilogies"). Karrakaz, the last child of a race whose fabulous beauty, strength, and psychic powers accompanied behavior so evil as to be demonic, wakes under a smoldering volcano into a world where her lack of self-knowledge makes her the pawn of any man with the daring to dominate her. The sorcerer Vazkor is the strongest of those who try, but Karrakaz's own nature soon motivates her to fight back and destroy him. After bearing his child, whom she leaves with a young mother whose own child has died, she travels on in search of her own identity. Her son, Vazkor, grows up as a barbarian but, on reaching adulthood, learns what he thinks is the truth about his parentage: that his father, from whom his extraordinary powers came, was murdered by his mother. He sets out to find and destroy her while developing his abilities. But when through arrogance and pride he becomes responsible for the deaths of those he loves, he begins to realize that his powers cannot have come from his ambitious, cruel father and eventually learns his true nature and history. Both protagonists vow to use their powers to heal and help ordinary people, not to dominate them.

In *The Storm Lord* (1976) another lost child, Raldnor, grows to manhood unaware of the telepathic power he has inherited from his mother's people and the kingship he has inherited from his father. Like Vazkor, he is a half-breed conceived in rape; like Vazkor, he searches for his true parents, is aided by women who die through loving him, achieves secular power before he is ready for it, then loses it suddenly, searches further and learns wisdom, and finally adjures his worldly power insofar as he can. In both stories genocide and racial hatred color history and politics, but all three protagonists, though doing their utmost to fight against these evils, finally turn their backs on the worldly power that it was so easy for them to grasp. To these superior persons, other things are more important.

One may ask: what is the use of reading about characters who cannot die, whose powers reach beyond any human powers, and whose worlds are nothing like the real world? One answer is that there are more ways of dying than the physical: Lee reminds us that the soul can die when it succumbs to arrogance and hatred, whether the body is at risk or not. Another is that we ourselves use powers that people "only yesterday" never dreamed were within human reach. And our world is full of peoples who lack the advanced technology of the developed countries; Lee asks us if we can avoid treating them as Karrakaz's race treated its "inferiors." But even ignoring the social relevance of these stories, we can see that they provide a powerful insight into the kind of domination that Karrakaz, Vazkor, and Rald-

nor rebel against, the domination of the powerful over the powerless. It is easy to believe that Lee is sincere in saying that she has no political purpose in writing, but she is so good at creating real characters that their lives, however different in externals from "real" lives, can be understood and appreciated as humanly relevant.

Lee's effortless style materially contributes to her success; she not only is a brilliant descriptive writer but also has a pithy turn of phrase. Not a conscious "stylist" like Lord Dunsany, she rarely sinks into the pretentiousness that so often accompanies an effort to create heroic fantasy. She displays few mannerisms and seems as much American as British. For example, here is a passage from the novella *Companions on the Road* (1975), describing the final confrontation of the hero with pursuing sorcerer-ghosts:

> Two men and a woman stood at the horses' heads. The men were all black, hooded, gauntleted, and on the thin fingers of the gauntlets glittered topaz and diamonds, but in the eyeholes of their hoods glittered nothing, only shadow. The woman, too, wore black, and a black veil wound around her head, but her face and her shoulders and her hands were bare, and white as wax. She wore no jewels, no rings, but she had eyes—gold fringed eyes with irises as black as jet. . . . This is how they remember themselves beyond the grave, so this is how they are.
>
> (chapter 9)

Here all the images are straightforward, the sentences simple in structure and vocabulary, and the similes not quite clichés—"as white as wax," "as black as jet." Yet this understatement intensifies the terrifying presence of the ghosts, just because it is so simple. This persuasive simplicity is also evident in the proverbs that Lee, like J. R. R. Tolkien, invents, like this one from *Vazkor, Son of Vazkor*: "Don't weep on board a ship—the sea is salt enough."

Occasionally, as in *Sung in Shadow* (1983), Lee's adaptation of the Romeo and Juliet story, the beauty of her style takes over; the story, which introduces a supernatural element but otherwise is little different in plot from William Shakespeare's, cannot sustain the weight of words. But at her best, especially in action sequences, the beauty of her style comes not from its elaborate descriptions but from its functional ability to make things happen before the reader's eyes. A parallel power is her ability to transmute violence; often horrifying yet never casual, never without affect, her violent scenes make us exclaim in shock, yet we recognize the reality of violence in life that she portrays. Many of her characters commit acts of ghastly violence, but unless these characters are fully evil, they are never unchanged by doing so.

Shorter than the adventure fantasies and more like fairy tales are some of Lee's best books. The romantic *Volkhavaar* is the story of Shaina, a slave girl who falls in love with an actor from a strolling company, not knowing that his soul is in bondage to an evil magician. Like Hans Christian Andersen's Little Mermaid, Shaina sacrifices herself to save him, but this is the beginning, not the end, of her story. *The Winter Players* (1976) pits another young girl against another wicked magician, and again a willing sacrifice leads to unexpected joy and fulfillment. The *Companions on the Road* are three evil ghosts pursuing a soldier who has stolen their link to hell, a jeweled chalice, to compensate the bereaved family of a comrade. But only one daughter has survived plague and battle. However, the living force of her dead family's love for her proves stronger than the ill spells of the unholy three. *East of Midnight* (1977) is a variation on the common fantasy and science fiction theme of the world ruled by women. Opposed to this world is its reflection, a world (like ours) ruled by men, from which the hero emerges to destroy its outdated religion and remold the society of the former; unlike many recent women writers, Lee does not portray a feminist utopia but two worlds out of balance (like ours) because of their mistreatment of one sex. The triumph of the downtrodden slave, Dekteon, and the equally downtrodden king, Zaister, is shown in fairy-tale terms, even to the happy ending for both.

Actual fairy tales include those collected in *Red as Blood* (1983), a deliberate alteration of familiar children's tales. In these tales Snow White is the wicked witch, Cinderella is a hag bent on revenge, the Pied Piper is a god scorned, Rapunzel's prince is

the demon Ahriman, and Beauty is as alien as her Beast. *Cyrion* (1982) details the picaresque adventures of a mysterious wanderer in a thirteenth-century kingdom of Jerusalem a bit different from the historic one. Lee's "Romulan and Iuletta" story, *Sung in Shadow*, appears to be set in the same world as *Cyrion*, a world whose history is "Remusan" rather than Roman, in which (of course) magic really works and both good and evil spirits abound. *The Dragon Hoard* (1971), a children's story that was Lee's first published novel, is a humorous tale of a misbegotten quest, an unfortunate prince who becomes a raven at inopportune moments, and a sorceress (appropriately named Maligna) who treats the dragons pulling her chariot as nastily as she treats everyone else.

Lee's horror fantasies include *Night's Master* (1978) and its sequel, *Death's Master* (1979), *Sabella* (1980), *Kill the Dead* (1980), and *Lycanthia* (1981). The Masters of Night and Death dwell in an underworld that for the former is luxurious and ornate, for the latter dim, bare, and ghostly. When Azhrarn, the Master of Night, interferes with the life of a beautiful child, his meddling provides the impetus for a series of loosely connected stories that end when he becomes mankind's savior. Typically, he does this by trickery. When the gloomy Master of Death accepts the service of a witch, he inadvertently causes the birth of his worst enemy, a sorcerer who builds a city of immortals where Death can never enter. But immortality proves less delightful than those who become immortal had thought, and one of them in turn gives her service to Death.

Lycanthia is an intensely sexual tale, set in France in 1913, in which the hero proves no hero by defending his werewolf lover and her brother; for he defends them "wrongly, with the wrong weapons" and loses his chance at both love and power. The eponymous heroine of *Sabella*, the lonely vampire of faraway Novo Mars, kills once too often but, by so doing, finds her true lover and discovers that vampirism is not really her problem. *Kill the Dead* is the tale of an exorcist whose vocation of destroying ghosts is stronger than death and ghosthood. Here again love, however unworthy its object, struggles and then triumphs over whatever and whoever it is that obstructs it.

Lee's five science fiction books seem as magical as her fantasies because all are set in worlds of miraculous technology. In *Don't Bite the Sun* (1976) and its sequel, *Drinking Sapphire Wine* (1979), life span has been so greatly extended that adolescence lasts more than fifty years, and adolescents are expected—even required—to spend their time in vandalism and casual sex. But when decadence is mandatory, and the only restrictions are on things that are worthwhile, how can the young validate, or even endure, their existence? *The Silver Metal Lover* (1981) similarly depicts a decadent society but shows how love can survive even when no one believes in it or in lovers. *Day by Night* (1980) portrays (like *East of Midnight*) two mirror societies, this time on the dayside and nightside of a nonrevolving planet. Neither society knows that the other exists; but the best man and the best woman of each, driven by envy from their homes, finally meet and thus fulfill the destiny of the whole world. *Electric Forest* (1979) is another doppelgänger tale, in which a hideous monster becomes a beautiful woman. The book has the Byzantine complexity typical of Lee's peer C. J. Cherryh, but while it is readable and enjoyable, a plot full of double-blind stratagems is not really Lee's forte.

Though her work shows the influence of pulp adventure fantasists like Robert E. Howard and the early Leigh Brackett, Tanith Lee has long since transcended the limitations of pulp and has used its conventions to create work that is original and psychologically valid. Particularly attractive is her ability to convey the agonizing pain of growing up while convincing one that the pain is worth it. Lee understands and likes adolescents—she is a grown-up who has not "forgotten what it's like"—but she also understands that adolescence is a transition between states of being, not a state in itself. Her characters suffer to become more mature, more capable, and more sensitive than they have been—to become adults, not just stronger adolescents.

So far Lee has rarely dealt with the further development of the newly adult, and it is reasonable to ask whether she should attempt it. Her statement of her working methods implies that she writes directly from the subconscious and thus might find it difficult to create any other type of story. She has achieved financial and aesthetic success at a rate of production that would certainly burn out many writers. But Tanith Lee is too good a craftsman and too sensitive an artist to let her subconscious do her work for her. Her skills are so polished, her invention is so unflagging, and her gift of empathy is so pronounced that even a failure on the grander canvas of maturity might be worth the effort, while a success might take a central place in the fantasy tradition. Few fantasists have dealt as sympathetically with so many facets of human emotion as she has, and her readers can anticipate with eagerness tales that will widen the scope of her art.

Selected Bibliography

WORKS OF TANITH LEE

The Birthgrave. New York: DAW, 1975. London: Futura, 1977.

Companions on the Road. London: Macmillan, 1975. In *Companions on the Road and The Winter Players.* New York: St. Martin, 1977.

Don't Bite the Sun. New York: DAW, 1976.

The Storm Lord. New York: DAW, 1976. London: Futura, 1977.

The Winter Players. London: Macmillan, 1976. In *Companions on the Road and The Winter Players.* New York: St. Martin, 1977.

East of Midnight. London: Macmillan, 1977. New York: St. Martin, 1978.

Volkhavaar. New York: DAW, 1977. London: Hamlyn, 1981.

The Castle of Dark. London: Macmillan, 1978.

Night's Master. New York: DAW, 1978. London: Hamlyn, 1981.

Vazkor, Son of Vazkor. New York: DAW, 1978. As *Shadowfire.* London: Futura, 1979. (Sequel to *The Birthgrave.*)

Quest for the White Witch. New York: DAW, 1978. London: Futura, 1979. (Sequel to *Vazkor, Son of Vazkor.*)

Death's Master. New York: DAW, 1979. London: Hamlyn, 1982.

Drinking Sapphire Wine. New York: DAW, 1979. London: Hamlyn, 1979.

Electric Forest. New York: DAW, 1979.

Shon the Taken. London: Macmillan, 1979.

Day by Night. New York: DAW, 1980.

Kill the Dead. New York: DAW, 1980.

Sabella; or, The Blood Stone. New York: DAW, 1980.

Delusion's Master. New York: DAW, 1981.

Lycanthia. New York: DAW, 1981.

The Silver Metal Lover. New York: DAW, 1981.

Unsilent Night. Cambridge, Mass.: The NESFA Press, 1981. (Includes the short stories "Siriamnis" and "Cyrion in Wax" and several poems.)

Cyrion. New York: DAW, 1982. (Includes "Cyrion in Wax" and several other stories.)

Red as Blood. New York: DAW, 1983.

Sung in Shadow. New York: DAW, 1983.

CRITICAL AND BIOGRAPHICAL MATERIAL

DAW Books. "Tanith Lee Biography." (Unpublished publicity material.)

Evory, Ann, ed. *Contemporary Authors*. Volumes 37–40. First revision. Detroit: Gale, 1979.

Tymn, Marshall B.; Zahorski, Kenneth J.; and Boyer, Robert H. *Fantasy Literature: A Core Collection and Reference Guide*. New York: Bowker, 1979.

Weinkauf, Mary S. "Tanith Lee." In *Twentieth-Century Science Fiction Writers*, edited by Curtis Smith. New York: St. Martin, 1981.

—DIANA WAGGONER

URSULA K. LE GUIN

1929-

ALTHOUGH SHE WON fame in the 1960's and early 1970's for her science fiction, and more recently has gained acceptance from an audience that reads the *New Yorker* and *Kenyon Review*, Ursula Kroeber Le Guin has been basically a fantasy writer. In her writings about speculative literature, collected in *The Language of the Night* (1979), she stresses language over technology, children's literature as an antidote against the conventionally adult, and characterization of "the Other" in preference to the creation of other worlds in space. Her science fiction is far less concerned with the promise of new technology than with the continuing problems of human psychology and social dynamics, in locales that pose alternatives to the way we live now. Most of her work takes place somewhere that is not, from science fictional planets to the "high fantasy" world of Earthsea, with its wizards and dragons, and the country of Orsinia, which but for history could almost pass for a real central European nation.

The progress of her career, however, illustrates some of the pitfalls awaiting a writer of fantasy who continues to grow, as a person involved in the real world, rather than being content to repeat old formulas. Reflecting a growing feminism and more strenuous opposition to the technological imperative, her fiction after 1970 has become more circumscribed in its locales, in its characters' freedom of action, and even in its expression. Some of it has no recognizable impossibility (fantasy) at all. That

which does tends toward hallucination, parody, and propagandistic shrillness, making it progressively harder for a reader to suspend disbelief.

Both Le Guin's success and her problems may be traced in part to her origin as, in her words, "an intellectual born and bred." Her father was the famed anthropologist Alfred Louis Kroeber, her mother, Theodora Kroeber, the author of the ethnological classic *Ishi in Two Worlds* (1961) and subsequent children's books. Born on 21 October 1929, in Berkeley, California, their daughter was exposed from childhood to magic and folklore, to respect for cultural diversity and human unity, and to the vices and virtues of the academic community.

Her acknowledged influences in literature range from Lord Dunsany to the trashiest pulp magazines she could find in her youth. The list also includes eight "romantic" poets (three from the twentieth century), four English and four Russian novelists, and a handful of contemporary writers of speculative fiction. Educated at Radcliffe and Columbia, where she specialized in Romance literature of the Middle Ages and Renaissance, Ursula Kroeber won a Fulbright fellowship to study in Paris. There she met and married Charles Le Guin, a history professor, with whom she settled in Portland, Oregon, to nurture a family and a career.

First published in 1962, Le Guin soon became known as a competent storyteller, weaving images and allusions in increasingly complex ways through nine science fiction and fantasy novels published between 1966 and 1974. Critical attention was paid less to her style, however, than to the alternative she offered to the technocratic, capitalistic, male-dominated Western ideals then ruling American science fiction. Taoism, Jungian psychology, anarchism, ecology, and gender liberation resonate in her vision of humankind's potential for unity and balance, in the individual, the society, even the galaxy. Essentially the same themes dominate Earthsea, Orsinia, her Hainish Cycle of science fiction stories and novels, and her utopian, dystopian, and surrealistic works characteristic of the 1970's.

This background made Le Guin unusual in science fiction and her contributions significant. But her understanding of the constraints on behavior posed by nature, often known through science, gives an unusual relevance to her fantasy writing as well. This double viewpoint is illustrated indirectly in the stories published as *Orsinian Tales* (1976) and in *Malafrena* (1979). Dating from the 1950's, at least in original concept, they show a strong involvement in commonplace events and the very real heartaches of everyday life. Their nostalgia for a simpler existence is revealing, and their style is reminiscent of nineteenth-century Russian fiction, possibly filtered through Constance Garnett's translations. No romantic fairyland, Orsinia has a gritty physical existence and a sense of social oppression out of which its characters garner real but small victories.

During the 1960's, Le Guin generally published "high fantasy" and science fiction with a large quotient of fantasy. A charming story of black magic, "April in Paris" (1962), brings four lonely people from different eras into a brace of romantic alliances in the year 1482. Reflecting her stay in Paris and the beginning of her marriage, it has a character from the future and the science fictional motif of time travel, but is centered on magical means for fulfilling wishes. A divided soul is also suggested by "Darkness Box" (1963), in which the heroic prince of a magic kingdom is enabled to "unfreeze" time so that he can conclusively meet his fate in battle with his brother. More science fictionally, this division between wrongheaded opposites is projected onto a postcatastrophe Earth in "The Masters" (1963). There, a ritual-dominated antitechnological society

is resisted by the perseverance of essentially irresponsible scientific inquiry.

Two 1964 stories of "high fantasy" introduced the Earthsea Cycle and served as "cartoons" for the trilogy to follow. Central to both are the magic of words and wizards punished by their own shortsightedness. Comic in tone, "The Rule of Names" brings a greedy wizard to Sattin's Island in quest of a dragon's treasure. Mistaking the disguised dragon for another wizard, he tries to use against it its "true name," only to have its *true shape* emerge, devour him, and wreak havoc on the citizenry. More somber is "The Word of Unbinding," whose hero must choose death in order to defeat a villain capable of devouring magic itself.

Published during the same period as her major science fiction novels, the Earthsea trilogy occupies a position central to Le Guin's early career. Freed from the constraints of either realistic events or science fictional speculation, the characters of these books for children are limited solely by the author's moral imagination. Though wizards and dragons and magic spells are familiar properties of "high fantasy," their powers and limits are set by the author, who spells out the rules for her readers and does not depend on their familiarity with storytelling conventions.

The few hundred islands and surrounding waters of Earthsea approximate in global latitude and extent the contiguous United States. Their locus in history, based on technological sophistication and social organization, could be any time more than 500 years ago. In this imaginary world magic works, in the service of government and religion, trade and technology. A discipline there as much as science is here, magic is zealously guarded and maintained by people who take their responsibility seriously. They know that each action brings a reaction, that magic brought to one place or person is taken from another. The wisest of wizards avoids being corrupted by its power by using magic rarely, even in diluted forms.

Central to each book is the journey motif, the traditional romance quest for balance and understanding of both the microcosm and the macrocosm, achieved by magical means. Unlike the objective ideal of science, magic is openly participatory, its language not numbers but words. Theoretically each practitioner truly knows what he summons and addresses ("the rule of names"). Magic makes the natural medium for education the story or song, whose pattern both approximates and evokes its subject. Implicit, too, is the importance of the storyteller or writer, who makes from words something of lasting value.

The central figure of the trilogy bears several names. His childhood name is Duny, his "use" name Sparrowhawk, his "true" name Ged (with echoes of "get" and "god"). His story alone is *A Wizard of Earthsea* (1968), winner of the *Boston Globe* Award for children's literature. In it a young goatherd becomes a mage, through formal education at the wizards' academy and rigorous experience in the world. More dangerous to him than either dragons or evil sorcerers are his own pride and ambition. They cause him when still a child to summon from darkness a "shadow" that almost destroys him before he is strong enough to withstand it. Rescued, healed, fully trained, and tempted again, he finally faces it, names it, and merges with it in pure Jungian fashion.

Ged's adventures are continued less directly in *The Tombs of Atuan* (1971), winner of the Newbery Medal for children's literature. The central character this time is Tenar, renamed Arha, "the eaten one," at the age of five. She is believed to reincarnate generations of high priestesses of "The Nameless Ones," powers of death and darkness. Disabled by her humanity from killing Sparrowhawk when he invades the labyrinthine tombs of her domain, she helps him escape instead, causing her temple and its grounds to collapse. From him she regains her original name; with him she reunites the lost ring of Erreth-Akbe, marked by the "lost rune" of peace. Sexually awakened by his penetration of her unconscious, she is reborn into the fear and joy of freedom in the world of the living.

"Coming of age" has several meanings in *The Farthest Shore* (1972), winner of the National Book Award for children's fiction. Now the Archmage, Ged seeks and finds the hole in the world through which light and life and magic are leaking, and

closes it at the cost of nearly all his powers. The "girlish" Prince Arren, skilled in both song and swordplay, accompanies Ged on earth and sea, through misgivings, despair, and the land of the dead, lured on in part by the constellation of the lost rune of peace in the sky. Emerging as the True King, he promises the restoration of order and goodness to Earthsea. The world they save, however, by defeating the evil sorcerer Cob, with his false promises of immortality, is also one to which age has come. Ged and Arren, and by implication all of us, must accept death as part of the greater equilibrium, the balance of powers that ensures the quality of life, that is, its magic.

Instant "classics" of children's literature, the Earthsea books bear out the observations of C. S. Lewis and others that good children's literature can also be enjoyed by adults. There is little doubt of their verbal economy, their excellence of composition, the suitably varied style of each volume, and the power of their interwoven tales and images. Le Guin has also been praised (by Robert Scholes among others) for her moral vision of an "ecology" of magic and her dedication to the power of the Word, though some readers may object to her determined attack on secular or religious leaders who promise immortality.

Themes from the Hainish Cycle are clearly visible in the Earthsea trilogy in pure or isolated form, from quest and patterning motifs to the overall emphasis on "wholeness and balance" (Douglas Barbour's phrase). *A Wizard of Earthsea* was preceded by three quest novels set on alien worlds that focus on identity, communication, and community. The theme of the exploited female was explored in *The Tombs of Atuan* just after *The Left Hand of Darkness* (1969) introduced the reading public to the androgynous people of Gethen. The tension between hope and despair confronted in *The Farthest Shore* (and hinted at in her earliest work) echoes through *The Lathe of Heaven* (1971), *The Dispossessed* (1974), and beyond.

The Hainish Cycle consists of five novels, two novellas, and three short stories; it spans 2,500 years in the world of the fiction, ten years of publication. It was named by critics after the Hainish civilization alleged to have spread human/humanoid seed across the galaxy millions of years ago. The Hainishmen play no large role as characters in these works, but their influence is felt explicitly in the life forms they foster, implicitly in the challenge they pose to Earthmen who would surpass them.

The earliest works in the cycle are the most romantic, the most heavily tinged with high fantasy, none more so than "Semley's Necklace" (originally titled "The Dowry of Angyor," 1964), Le Guin's fifth published story, decked out in the trappings of Norse mythology. In quest of her dowry, which was lost to the "Star-folk," an imperious heroine, invincibly ignorant of science and technology, undertakes a near-light-speed journey to a distant world. Returning eighteen years later, she is driven to distraction by the discovery that her warrior husband is dead and the baby daughter she left behind is now her own (apparent) age.

Reprinted as the prologue to *Rocannon's World* (1966), this story introduces that world, two of its five sentient races, Rocannon himself, and the "League" (of All Worlds) that he serves as a "hilfer," a student of *high intelligence life forms* (that is, an interstellar anthropologist). His subsequent quest explains how the planet Fomalhaut II came to bear his name in League annals.

Heedlessly accelerating the technological development of hilfs in defense against a nameless enemy, the League has created a world intent on empire. To defend Fomalhaut II from the invaders, Rocannon must invade their headquarters, half a continent away, to call down destruction upon them. On his long journey, he learns what five races of hilfs can teach him, from brotherhood to "mind-speech," accepting the trade-offs involved in each lesson. Under the heavy weight of ideas, allegory is never far away, as with the stark division of one race into the light elves and dark dwarfs of fantasy.

Fearful of direct interference, League emissaries try not to intervene at all on Gamma Draconis III in *Planet of Exile* (1966). They recoil from the intimacy of mindspeech, until the City people and the neighboring village natives discover that they need each other. The positive results of their integration are not evident until the end of the third novel in the cycle.

Played out on a conquered Earth, *City of Illusions* (1967) is largely a battle of minds, with much of the abstract weakness that battle implies. The quest of the amnesiac Falk takes him across a ravaged America into the stronghold of the Shing (the "enemy" that scattered the League into disarray). Dealers in lies and illusion, they offer Falk his old identity at the cost of the new, so they may strike at his home world. A sacred book, however, helps Falk regain his old self (as the starship navigator Remarren), escaping with a captured Shing to Gamma Draconis. Rich in both mental and mechanical technology, his world will rout the Shing and restore democracy to the galaxy. Least satisfactory of the apprentice novels, this book at least completes the trilogy and prepares the way for its successors.

Although the rest of the Hainish Cycle is more prosaic, it is not devoid of fantasy. *The Left Hand of Darkness* and the short story that prefigured it, "Winter's King" (1969; revised 1975), concern a world of people essentially human but different from us in terms of their sexuality. The people of Gethen are sexually neuter except during "kemmer" (estrus), when either gender may emerge, with no perpetual pattern of gender domination. Both works involve controlled parapsychology: "mind-handling" (brainwashing) in the story, "foretelling" (oracular interweaving of the minds of adepts) in the novel. Folklore is also important in the novel, which approaches in form an anthropological field report, with myths, legends, and religious ceremonies incorporated into the body rather than in an appendix.

As the cycle continues, however, political questions occupy Le Guin's attention more and more, along with social satire directed largely at American behavior patterns. Although the totalitarian oligarchy of Orgoreyn is not spared, the "comic opera kingdom" (George Edgar Slusser's term) of Karhide is also flayed for indecision and paranoia. The entire planet of Gethen, moreover, serves as a reproach to the supposedly open and tolerant Earth-based "Ekumen of Known Worlds," successor to the earlier League. Its ambassador (or "Mobile"), Genley Ai (the name suggests both vision and selfhood), balks at taking seriously the "feminine" (to him) Gethenians. On his Le Guinian quest, however, he achieves not only political asylum and association but also a new sense of identification with "the Other." Like Gulliver after living among the Houhnhyms, however, Ai feels uncomfortable at the sight of his blatantly bisexual colleagues at the end.

Perhaps having reached the limits of her imagination, Le Guin began bringing her future history closer to home, with two versions of the timeless fantasy of the "green world" into which man brings discord. In "Vaster than Empires and More Slow" (1971), an Earth crew of ten "mad" scientists (that is, representatives of irresponsible Western civilization) visit a world of vegetable life. They are almost destroyed when their own paranoia induces fear into the vast alien mind, and one of their number deserts, a "bioempathic receptive" who prefers the company of the forest to that of his hated crewmates. An explicit condemnation of colonial exploitation, "The Word for World Is Forest" (1972; separate book publication, 1976) is Le Guin's self-proclaimed "Vietnam story." In it, traditional Western scorn for native populations is defeated by a people living symbiotically with their trees and practicing a kind of "thinking" that combines both waking and dreaming consciousness.

The Hainish Cycle apparently ended in 1974 with one more novel and a footnotelike story. *The Dispossessed: An Ambiguous Utopia*, like *The Left Hand of Darkness*, won both the Hugo and Nebula awards for best science fiction novel of the year. Linked to its predecessors by ambassadors from Hain and Earth among other things, it is primarily a novel of political analysis. Today's East and West and Third World are all represented on the world of Urras; while its arid "moon," Anarres, represents a flawed attempt at anarchist rule, theoretically devoid of personal property, aggrandizement by position, and gender inequality. Whatever its faults (pointed out by Samuel R. Delany and other sympathetic critics), *The Dispossessed* is outstanding as a novel of utopia, transcending the traditional guided tour of a perfect world. Even more committed to realism, the Nebula-winning story of the last day of Laia Odo, Anarres' founder, suggests that no one can live up to anarchist ideals and that every day, like the story's title, is "The Day Before the Revolution."

The fantasy elements in these works are largely restricted to the presence of alternatives to the actualities of our history. Le Guin's utopian preoccupation carries over into several other works of the 1970's. "The Ones Who Walk Away from Omelas" (1973) meditates on William James's question of the worth of happiness that rests upon cruelty. "The New Atlantis" (1975) counterpoints a dystopian future Oregon with a mysteriously rising midocean continent and its collectively sentient "inhabitants." "Diary of the Rose" (1976) and "SQ" (1978) sardonically comment on the health of a state obsessed with the "sanity" (political conformity) of its citizens. Only "The Eye of the Heron" (1978) is overtly utopian, with its diagrammatically simple victory of nonviolence over machismo on an alien world with plenty of frontier territory.

Differing perceptions are crucial in these tales, as they are in the parodies and parables that dominate the rest of her fiction. Even the ostensibly "hard" science fiction of "Nine Lives" (1969) reorients the reader, demonstrating the unexpected superiority of two imperfect, isolated people over a team of clones. "Field of Vision" (1973) shows explorers of Mars driven mad by the sight of God (or a reasonable facsimile). "The Eye Altering" (1976) uses the symbol of painting to show settlers acclimating to a new world. Most hackneyed of all, "Pathways of Desire" (1976) posits an entire alien world subjectively created by an introverted teen-ager.

Le Guin labeled some of her earlier works "psychomyths," a term that may encompass more recent fictions as well, both long and short. In "Things" (1970, as "The End"), a bricklayer builds a bridge into the sea, to get to more fortunate isles, during "the last days." A man with the initials L. S. D. mentally takes "The Good Trip" (1970) to Oregon's Mount Hood instead of dropping acid. "A Trip to the Head" (1970) uses another forest setting to explore surrealistically the problem of labels. Even more surrealistic, "Schrödinger's Cat" (1974) envisions a world in which people keep "coming apart," dramatizing a famous thought experiment in physics.

Le Guin's major psychomyth is *The Lathe of Heaven* (1971; adapted for television, 1980). Set in Portland, it concerns the "active dreams" of George

Orr, which actually change reality, usually for the worse, under the direction of a willful psychiatrist. Dr. Haber manipulates George's dreams for his own fame and fortune, and incidentally the improvement of the world, but almost everything goes sour. When we seek to "improve" the world, the novel argues, we do more harm than good. Echoing Le Guin's earlier pleas for social responsibility, this book also illustrates her growing pessimism.

Parody is one suitable response when a writer of fantasy no longer accepts fantasy's adequacy as a substitute for reality. At least six stories since 1974 fit that category, from the heavy-handed *Star Trek* burlesque "Intracom" (1974) to the clever pastiche "The Author of the Acacia Seeds and Other Extracts from the *Journal of Therolinguistics*" (1974), with its pseudoscholarly studies of the "art forms" of ants, penguins, and trees. Rather more trivial is another pastiche, "Some Approaches to the Problem of the Shortage of Time" (1979), objectifying by the clock a purely subjective impression; "Direction of the Road" (1973), a tree's-eye-view of man's progress in locomotion; "Mazes" (1975), in which an "alien" (a rat?) is tortured by a psychologist unwilling to communicate with his subject; and "The Wife's Story" (1982), a wolf's version of the horror of her mate's being a were-human.

Faced with a breakdown in belief, a writer can reorient herself to the known world, as Le Guin has also done with Orsinia and some stories in *The Compass Rose* (1982). "The First Report of the Shipwrecked Foreigner to the Kadanh of Derb" (1978) is a thinly disguised sketch of impressions of Venice. Equating sanity with death, "The Water Is Wide" (1976) is a passable hallucination. An East Indian girl's sale into marriage in "The White Donkey" (1980) is barely turned into fantasy by her brief, unknowing relationship with a unicorn. Either a hallucination or a ghost story, "Small Change" (1981) focuses on another young woman's sense of loss. And in "Sur" (1982), a South American woman recalls (or imagines) her expedition to the South Pole, kept secret so that men could later reap the glory of discovery.

Metafantasy is active in three other later works, which strongly attract personal readings. In the juvenile novella *Very Far Away from Anywhere Else* (1976), the imaginary country of "Thorn" is a refuge and an inspiration to its teen-age protagonists. The relationship between fantasy and reality is not always that simple.

In an illustrated children's book, *Leese Webster* (1979), Le Guin allegorized her own dilemma. An insignificant little spider who just wants to make pretty webs sees people turn her room into a gallery. Unable to eat because her webs are behind glass, Leese is unceremoniously dumped outside the house, where her webs catch the dew and the sunlight, take care of her survival needs, and attract no critical attention at all.

In the short novel *The Beginning Place* (1980), two young people, superfluous in suburbia, discover a secret gateway to a land vaguely like Orsinia. Hugh and Irene do not want each other in their unwillingly shared fantasy world. They need each other, however, and the town of Tembreabrezi needs them both. Undergoing pain and hardship, they slay a vague, hermaphroditic sort of dragon and become better able to cope with reality.

Neither traditional fantasy nor science fiction, much of Le Guin's later work is "modern" or "postmodern," poised between belief and disbelief. Such uncertainty is not rare today, but neither is it the stuff of enchantment. It is probably no accident that the last decade found her writing nonfiction, giving lectures, and participating in writers' workshops more than before. Even if, as seems likely, Le Guin detaches herself still more from the writing of fantasy, a considerable body of work will remain, including three additions to the small shelf of children's fantasy classics.

Selected Bibliography

WORKS OF URSULA K. LE GUIN

Planet of Exile. New York: Ace, 1966. With a new introduction by Le Guin, New York: Harper and Row, 1978; London: Tandem, 1978. (Novel.)

Rocannon's World. New York: Ace, 1966. With a new introduction by Le Guin, New York: Harper and Row, 1977; London: Gollancz, 1979. (Novel.)

City of Illusions. New York: Ace, 1967. London: Gollancz,

1971. With a new introduction by Le Guin, New York: Harper and Row, 1978. (Novel.)

A Wizard of Earthsea. Berkeley, Calif.: Parnassus Press, 1968. London: Heinemann, 1973. (Juvenile fantasy novel.)

The Left Hand of Darkness. New York: Ace, 1969. London: Macdonald, 1969. With a new introduction by Le Guin, New York: Ace, 1976. (Novel.)

The Lathe of Heaven. New York: Scribner, 1971. London: Gollancz, 1972. (Novel.)

The Tombs of Atuan. New York: Atheneum, 1971. London: Gollancz, 1972. (Juvenile fantasy novel.)

The Farthest Shore. New York: Atheneum, 1972. London: Gollancz, 1973. (Juvenile fantasy novel.)

"The Word for World Is Forest." In *Again, Dangerous Visions*, edited by Harlan Ellison. Garden City, N.Y.: Doubleday, 1972. Reprinted alone, New York: Berkley, 1976. With a new introduction by Le Guin, London: Gollancz, 1977. (Short novel.)

The Dispossessed: An Ambiguous Utopia. New York: Harper and Row, 1974. London: Gollancz, 1975. (Novel.)

The Wind's Twelve Quarters. New York: Harper and Row, 1975. London: Gollancz, 1976. (Contents: "Semley's Necklace," "April in Paris," "The Masters," "Darkness Box," "The Word of Unbinding," "The Rule of Names," "Winter's King," "The Good Trip," "Nine Lives," "Things," "A Trip to the Head," "Vaster than Empires and More Slow," "The Stars Below," "The Field of Vision," "Direction of the Road," "The Ones Who Walk Away from Omelas," and "The Day Before the Revolution.")

Orsinian Tales. New York: Harper and Row, 1976. London: Gollancz, 1977. (Nonfantasy stories.)

Very Far Away from Anywhere Else. New York: Atheneum, 1976. (Juvenile nonfantasy short novel.)

Earthsea (*A Wizard of Earthsea, The Tombs of Atuan, The Farthest Shore*). London: Gollancz, 1977.

"The Eye of the Heron." In *Millennial Women*, edited by Virginia Kidd. New York: Delacorte, 1978. (Short novel.)

Three Hainish Novels (*Rocannon's World, Planet of Exile, City of Illusions*). Garden City, N.Y.: Doubleday, 1978.

The Language of the Night: Essays on Fantasy and Science Fiction, edited by Susan Wood. New York: Putnam, 1979.

Leese Webster. New York: Atheneum, 1979. (Illustrated juvenile fantasy.)

Malafrena. New York: Putnam, 1979. London: Gollancz, 1980. (Nonfantasy novel.)

The Beginning Place. New York: Harper and Row, 1980. (Juvenile fantasy novel.)

The Compass Rose. New York: Harper and Row, 1982. (Contents: "The Author of the Acacia Seeds," "The New Atlantis," "Schrödinger's Cat," "Two Delays on the Northern Line," "SQ," "Small Change," "The First Report of the Shipwrecked Foreigner to the Kadanh of Derb," "The Diary of the Rose," "The White Donkey," "The Phoenix," "Intracom," "The Eye Altering," "Mazes," "The Pathways of Desire," "Gwilan's Harp," "Malheur County," "The Water Is Wide," "The Wife's Story," "Some Approaches to the Problem of the Shortage of Time," and "Sur.")

CRITICAL AND BIOGRAPHICAL STUDIES

Barbour, Douglas. "Patterns and Meaning in the Science Fiction Novels of Ursula K. Le Guin, Joanna Russ, and Samuel R. Delany." Ph.D. diss., Queen's College (Kingston, Ontario), 1976.

Bittner, James W. "The Fiction of Ursula K. Le Guin." Ph.D. diss., University of Wisconsin, 1979.

De Bolt, Joe, ed. *Ursula K. Le Guin: Voyager to Inner Lands and to Outer Space*. Port Washington, N.Y.: Kennikat Press, 1979. (Includes biographical essay by De Bolt and review of criticism by Bittner.)

Delany, Samuel R. "To Read *The Dispossessed*." In *The Jewel-Hinged Jaw: Notes on the Language of Science Fiction*. Elizabethtown, N.Y.: Dragon Press, 1977. New York: Berkley, 1978.

Ketterer, David. "The Left Hand of Darkness: Ursula K. Le Guin's Archetypal Winter Journey." *Riverside Quarterly*, 5 (April 1973): 288–297. Reprinted in chapter 4, *New Worlds for Old: The Apocalyptic Imagination, Science Fiction, and American Literature*. Bloomington: Indiana University Press, 1974. Garden City, N.Y.: Doubleday / Anchor, 1974.

Olander, Joseph D., and Greenberg, Martin Harry, eds. *Ursula K. Le Guin*. Writers of the 21st Century Series. New York: Taplinger, 1979.

Perry, Joan. "Visions of Reality: Values and Perspectives in the Prose of Carlos Castaneda, Robert M. Pirsig, Ursula K. Le Guin, James Purdy, Cyrus Colter and Sylvia Plath." Ph.D. diss., University of Wisconsin, 1976.

Siciliano, Sam J. "The Fictional Universe in Four Science Fiction Novels: Anthony Burgess' *A Clockwork Orange*, Ursula K. Le Guin's *The Word for World Is Forest*, Walter Miller's *A Canticle for Leibowitz*, and Roger Zelazny's *Creatures of Light and Darkness*." Ph.D. diss., University of Iowa, 1975.

Slusser, George Edgar. *The Farthest Shores of Ursula K. Le*

Guin. Milford Series: Popular Writers of Today. San Bernardino, Calif.: Borgo Press, 1976.

Wood, Susan. "Discovering Worlds: The Fiction of Ursula K. Le Guin." In *Voices for the Future,* edited by Thomas D. Clareson. Vol. 2. Bowling Green, Ohio: Bowling Green University Popular Press, 1978.

See also "The Science Fiction of Ursula K. Le Guin." *Science-Fiction Studies,* 2 (November 1975): 203–274. Includes articles referred to by Darko Suvin and Ian Watson and a postscript by Douglas Barbour to his article in *Sci-ence-Fiction Studies,* 1 (Spring 1974): 164–173. See also "Special Ursula K. Le Guin Issue," *Extrapolation,* 21 (Fall 1980): 197–297. In addition, articles can be found in other issues of *Extrapolation* and *Science-Fiction Studies,* as well as in *Foundation: The Review of Science Fiction* and *Science Fiction Commentary.*

BIBLIOGRAPHY

Bittner, James W. *Ursula K. Le Guin: A Primary and Secondary Bibliography.* Boston: G. K. Hall, 1981.

—DAVID N. SAMUELSON

PATRICIA McKILLIP

1948–

THE YOUNG ADOLESCENT protagonist of Patricia McKillip's autobiographical novel, *Stepping from the Shadows* (1982), laments:

> "I don't have their voices in my head. The women's voices. I have only the men's voices. . . . The sea, horses, swords, dragons, songs, churches, magic words, ships, and stars—I don't have any other way to think about them. All the storytelling words belong to men."
>
> (chapter 3)

She expresses something of the problems of a woman struggling to write in a tradition dominated by a male world view. This is a problem McKillip has attacked in most of her major work, attempting to restructure traditional narrative patterns and symbols, indeed, to reassess archetypal patterns, in ways compatible with a female—not necessarily a feminist—perspective.

Born on 29 February 1948 in Salem, Oregon, the daughter of Wayne T. McKillip and Helen Roth McKillip, Patricia grew up an Air Force child, living in Arizona, Germany, England, and California. She earned two degrees from San Jose State University, the B.A. in 1971 and the M.A. in English in 1973; in the latter year her first two books, both aimed at children, were published. *The House on Parchment Street* is a ghost story set in a three-hundred-year-old house in London, while *The Throme of the Erril of Sherill* is her first quest fantasy.

The ghosts in *The House on Parchment Street* are not creatures of horror but spirits trapped in a daily repetition of a violent act, the assassination of a priest during the time of Oliver Cromwell. Part of the plot concerns the detective story of how three adolescents discover these and other details that explain the appearance of the ghosts, but the center of the story is how these adolescents come to accept themselves as unique individuals in a world that imposes conformity. The ghosts thus supply a historical example of intolerance against which the youngsters' problems are measured. Intolerance is also related, though not obtrusively, to sexual stereotyping. Carol, the American visitor who is the central character, is fiercely independent and quick to anger. Her British cousin Bruce is terrified of the ghosts and frightened as well of revealing his real passion, one that is socially unacceptable among adolescents: he is a talented artist. Similarly, his friend Alexander is a closet poet. As the ghostly mystery is solved, the three youngsters discover in one another sources of strength and sensitivity that help them accept themselves, the boys becoming more open about what they really love doing, and Carol becoming less belligerent without becoming any less strong.

In *The Throme of the Erril of Sherill* the femininist theme is a bit clearer, although it is lightly handled. The "Throme," one of many whimsical neologisms in this fantasy, is itself a fantasy within the story: "a dark, haunting, lovely Throme . . .

made of the treasure of words in [the] deep heart" of the Erril of Sherill. The Erril is himself the stuff of fables in the kingdom ruled by Magnus Thrall, King of Everywhere. The king desires the Throme, believing, "If I had it, the most precious of all precious things, my heart would be at rest in its beauty, and I could stop wanting." His daughter, "the King's Damsen," who "sat with him and wept and embroidered pictures of the green world beyond the walls," is loved by Caerles, "a moon-haired Cnite" who asks for her hand. He is refused by the selfish king but accepts the seemingly hopeless quest for the mythical Throme, the one thing the king will take in exchange for his daughter.

The quest develops in a manner marked by McKillip's concern for reassessing archetypal patterns in terms of values appropriate to a nonsexist vision. The king's castle is a patriarchal prison, "a tall thing of great, thick stones and high towers and tiny slits of windows," set over against "the green world," the natural world of fertile balance between masculine and feminine. The moon-haired Cnite bears other signs of sympathy with the White Goddess and the feminine principle; his shield and his doublet bear a device of three moons. But although he is a good Cnite, he is not a perfect one, and his quest, like all proper quests, is a learning experience. In a series of encounters with precocious children and sometimes wise and sometimes deceiving women, he exchanges the symbols of masculine dominance that he bears for symbols suggesting a fuller awareness of and participation in life: his horse for a "dagon," a giant, fiery-breathed hound; his sword for a star-wand, "the guiding light to the Floral Wold, the candle that illumines dreams"; his shield for a golden harp; his coat of mail for a cloak of many-colored leaves; even his mouse-colored boots for a ferry ride across a bottomless river to a green wood.

But the green wood, to the Cnite's dismay, is the very one outside King Magnus' castle, and the quest seems to have failed. But on the advice of a "sweet-eyed mother," Caerles himself writes the Throme, "a dark, haunting, lovely Throme . . . made of the tales and dreams and happenings of his quest." When he returns to the castle, the usually weeping Damsen breaks out laughing—not, however, deri-

sively: "I never knew before how much I want a barefoot, leaf-cloaked Cnite." The king accepts the Throme in delight, but the Cnite confesses his authorship; and Magnus, in spite of its genuine loveliness, destroys the Throme, withdrawing his Damsen's hand. But having changed irrevocably, she declares: "I will not . . . wither here in these stones. . . . I want this moon-haired, barefoot Cnite, and I will have him, Throme or no Throme. I want to walk in the singing world. I want to laugh instead of weep. You can weep here alone. I will go with him."

The lady's transformation is perhaps the most important departure from the conventional quest pattern in the story. Once the Cnite abandons the masculine stereotypes, the Damsen is able to see that she has a real choice: choosing Caerles does not in fact mean, as her father suggests, "From my stone walls to his stone walls you will go." Instead, the Cnite will take her to "a place with quiet water and wind singing through the trees, where I will build a house for you with flowers at your doorstep and cows with cowbells in your field." Thus she is able to reject her former passive role and become her own person, integrated into the green world of fertile life.

The Forgotten Beasts of Eld (1974), which won the 1975 World Fantasy award, is McKillip's first novel-length work, her first adult fantasy, and her first work to focus fully on the development of a female hero. It is especially interesting to recognize in this story how effectively, often how subtly, McKillip has adapted the formulas of the hero's development to a female protagonist—not by merely plugging a female into the male formula but by reflecting many of the realities of a female maturing in a male-dominated culture. The novel opens, for instance, with the epic and romance convention of the hero's lineage, but this one is notable for its ironic partriarchal bias: "The wizard Heald coupled with a poor woman once . . . and she bore him a son." That son and his son Ogam conceive their children in equally impersonal terms and on similarly anonymous women. But Ogam's woman bears him a child who, "unaccountably, was a girl."

Growing up in the isolated setting of Eld Mountain, both of her parents having died by her sixteenth year, Sybel is uncommonly free, though ignorant of the uniqueness of her freedom. Herself a wizard, she is able to "call" to her and hold in her power a collection of fabulous beasts that brood like living archetypes within her stonewalled house. "Ancient, powerful as princes, wise and restless and dangerous," they include a lion, a falcon, a cat, a swan, a boar, and a dragon. Thus, like many heroes, she is identified with the natural, the animal-haunted green world of her mountain forests, and she grows up in a kind of exile from a usurped land. But in this case that land is the world of human society wrongly dominated by an imbalanced masculinity, the lowland plains of the lords of Sirle and the king of Eldwold.

The imbalance of that world is suggested by its preoccupations with possessions, heirs, and wars, problems that intrude on Sybel's world when Coren, one of the lords of Sirle, appears at her gate with the infant Tamlorne, orphaned child of Sybel's aunt, the former queen of Eldwold, by an adulterous relationship with one of Coren's brothers. The infant prince, hidden with Sybel, will be safe from vengeance from the king and handy for the lords of Sirle to use in power struggles to come. But all is not wrong in the masculine world. Coren, like Caerles in *The Throme of the Erril of Sherill*, is an unusual male. He is able to identify Sybel's wondrous animals because he has studied long-neglected tales; he is respectful of Sybel's strength and beauty and aware that what the child requires most is her love. Also like Caerles, however, he has weaknesses: he is consumed with vengeful hate for Drede, who killed his brother, and even he betrays minor sexist assumptions; when Sybel says she knows nothing of caring for babies, he is surprised: "You are a girl. You should know such things."

Nor is all balanced in Sybel's world, though her weaknesses are the result of her youth and isolated upbringing. Thus, as with many romance heroes, her maturation will be a socialization process, a learning to accept other human beings and to love. Her incompleteness is indicated also by her quest for the Liralen, the most beautiful of fabulous beasts, a great white bird that functions as the symbol of a fully developed and integrated self.

In addition to involvement with the magical beasts, symbols of her harmony with the natural world, Sybel's quest involves other variations on romance conventions. Coren, after an initial trial, turns into the faithful lover whom she must learn to trust. The old woman guide is not the usual crone but a loving and motherly witch woman, both independent of the world and wise in its ways. The obstacles for the hero to overcome are a series of trials, but, more appropriately for a female hero, they take the form of men who try to use Sybel, to reduce her to a tool or a prize in their power games.

The most serious trials come from Drede, who wants to appropriate Sybel's power by making her queen. She easily declines his initial offer, but then he employs Mithran, a wizard more powerful than she, to "call" her to his castle and strip her of her will. He hopes to create a mindless queen who will "give to Drede, without question, forever, what he asks." In desperation Sybel offers to marry him freely, but the insecure king must have certainty, absolute possession. Mithran, however, ready in his lust to betray the king, offers not to break her will if she will accept him instead of Drede. But Sybel finds little choice between the two: "Drede will have me helpless and smiling, or you will have me helpless and afraid." Overcome with lust, Mithran's hold on Sybel's mind slips long enough for her to summon the Blammor, the most dangerous of fabled beasts, which destroys by giving back an image of one's own dark self. The sight of the creature slays Mithran, and Sybel escapes, but she leaves nursing an all-consuming hate for Drede.

What Sybel has undergone, perhaps the most significant adaptation of the archetypal pattern to a female hero, is what Annis Pratt in *Archetypal Patterns in Women's Fiction* (1981) calls the rape-trauma. Central to woman's development, as Pratt describes it, is her confrontation with uncontrolled male lust, an experience often overwhelming in the helplessness and anger that it creates in the victim. Sybel's struggle to come to terms with this experience, her misdirected quest for vengeance, is the subject of the last half of the story. She marries Coren and uses him, his family, and everything possible to engineer Drede's destruction. The climax comes when Coren discovers how he has been used and when Sybel, having realized how much she has hurt Coren, learns, with the help of a vision of the

Blammor that she survives, how she has debased and perverted herself. On the eve of the great battle that she has arranged between Eldwold and Sirle, she renounces her hate, frees all her beasts, and returns alone to Eld Mountain.

But Coren loves her still, and Sybel, having finally learned to accept love, realizes as she again summons the Blammor that it is in fact the Liralen, the beautiful image of the integrated self available only to those who have been reconciled with their dark selves. Her realization is a fitting conclusion to a female version of the archetypal journey.

McKillip's longest work, the Riddle-Master trilogy, is not as successful as *Forgotten Beasts*, though it is certainly more ambitious, an attempt at a fantasy with dual heroes, a male and a female. *The Riddle-Master of Hed* (1976) concerns the male hero, Morgon, Prince of Hed, a small agricultural island isolated from a mainland of kingdoms being subverted by unknown forces and beginning to disintegrate into general warfare. It is the time of the ending of an age, with, it seems, only Morgon standing between chaos and the birth of a new age.

Like most of McKillip's male heroes, Morgon already approaches, and through the trilogy becomes, a nonsexist ideal. In the tradition of the reluctant hero, most of the first novel concerns his flight from a destiny fraught with overwhelming responsibility; but he is humble, not weak, stubbornly committed to peace and preferring weapons like a magic harp whose sound shatters metal. His development centers on a growing sympathy with nature, beginning with his "land-ruler's" sensitivity to his own land and later adding, under the schooling of wise and ancient guides, shape-changing, the ability to become and enter into the life first of animals, then of trees. Riddlery, another major passion of Morgon's, implies a historian's hunger for the tales of the past and a philosopher's and a literary scholar's concern for their meaning and application to life. His major decisions are made on the basis of virtues like curiosity, compassion, a sense of responsibility, and love for Raederle, the female hero. He finally learns, however, that five attempts on his life and the current general unrest are caused by a revival of an ancient war between the long-dead Earth-Masters and the shape-changing sea people, who are invading the

land. The volume ends with Morgon in despair, having been betrayed by his guide and companion Deth and by "the High One," a kind of supreme wizard who is spoken of almost as a god.

The second volume, *Heir of Sea and Fire* (1977), centers on Raederle, strong and independent in spite of being expected to perform only the limited role implied by those who characterize her as "the second most beautiful woman" in her father's kingdom. Whereas the reluctant Morgon has confronted a series of guides, all aiding and encouraging him in his quest, Raederle is surrounded by avid suitors and well-meaning male protectors urging her to remain safe, to let others—men—face dangers. Indeed, such would-be helpers are her major external sources of opposition as she pursues her own quest, a journey to the High One's mountain to investigate rumors of Morgon's death. Her major opposition, however, comes from within. She learns that she is descended from the sea people, who are Morgon's and her own people's enemies, that she shares their powers and passions, associated with control of sea and fire, energies within her that she does not understand and fears will betray Morgon. It is an allegory of woman bred in a tradition of passivity that leads her to fear and deny her own capacities, but gradually learning to accept and respect herself and all her potential.

In the third volume, *Harpist in the Wind* (1979), Raederle, having helped Morgon overcome a consuming hate for Deth, convinces him to accept her as a full partner in their mutual quest to keep their world free, sharing in all its dangers. Yet the quest is interestingly different for each. For Morgon it centers on his learning how to wield power. Deth, it turns out, is the real, long dispossessed High One who has been training Morgon to fight a last battle against the forces of lawless and loveless destructiveness and to become his heir. Morgon must be reconciled with this spiritual father before he can understand power and bring peace to the realm. Raederle must learn power too, but her spiritual fathers, such as they are, are the destructive, domineering male spirits of the past from whom she must declare her independence. She also has spiritual mothers, but there is no real problem of alienation from them. The powers she learns are not finally concerned either with ruling, as they are for Morgon, or with helping Morgon, although they have important external effects and often save Morgon at crucial moments. Rather their ultimate effect seems to be simply to free Raederle, to make it possible for her to be herself.

The end of the novel reflects this conclusion in that Morgon and Raederle, though they obviously love each other, do not wed; their relationship is far more complex than that. "I loved the sea," she says. "Maybe I'll live in it." "I'll live in the wastes," he replies. "Once every hundred years, you will shine out of the sea and I'll come to you, or I will draw you into the winds with my harping." Their relationship is not so much a union as a balance, her sea and fire with his earth and wind making up a cosmos.

Stepping from the Shadows, McKillip's most recent novel, is not, strictly speaking a fantasy; rather it is an autobiographical *Künstlerroman*, her portrait of the artist as a young woman. Yet the work is appropriate to examine here because, being a portrait of a fantasy writer, it is pervaded by the spirit and the symbols of fantasy. Though its settings are realistic, its form and techniques recall Nathaniel Hawthorne's concept of the romance, fiction admitting the marvelous and not strictly bound by the principle of "minute fidelity . . . to the probable and ordinary course of man's experience." Indeed, the story is as much about the female artist's imaginative life as about anything, and it comments significantly on much that McKillip has written before.

The central character, Frances Stuart, is a young girl whose confusion and internal division are portrayed in part by an unusual technique of point of view: the narrator is Frances' unnamed alter ego, usually the more rational side of the personality. Frances, the more imaginative side, "was always slow, always dreaming, and I had to nag her just to do things the way ordinary people did." A number of factors—fear and guilt about her own body; bewilderment at a world characterized in part by fear of World War III in the mid-1950's and by President John Kennedy's assassination and the antiwar movement in the 1960's; rootlessness occasioned by the nomadic life of her Air Force family—these and other factors combine to drive her into a life of imaginary worlds. Central to her problem is the lack of a

satisfactory myth to express and contain her dreams and her emptinesses. Awakening to the mystery of life as she looks through the door of her third-grade classroom, she asks:

> Where was I . . . before there were words and numbers and saints. When there was only the hot earth and the sky, and I had no name. . . . I wanted to know suddenly. I needed to know. . . . The desert outside was old, old; even heaven and hell were old. I was something new in an old world, and I did not know why.
>
> (chapter 1)

The traditional, ordered Catholic vision taught at her school does not seem to help, and Frances begins to tell stories, then to write them, as a way of coping with problems that she cannot otherwise resolve.

A central story she tells herself, the development of which parallels her personal growth, is about two sisters, one beautiful and clever, one ugly and mute, the two parts of her divided self. In Frances' sixth grade the sisters live in a house near a secret forest that one yearns to enter and the other fears. In the seventh grade her dream vision of a beautiful stag is merged into the story: the sisters see the stag and are drawn into the forest in pursuit of it, seeking its meaning. In the tenth grade the stag becomes a horned god, the Stagman: "She clothed him, armed him, sent him into the world to find his name." Not yet human, "he was searching for the path out of his godhead," and in a remarkable reversal of Apollo and Daphne, Frances dreams of him as a tree that under her touch turns "soft, muscular, warm with light [and] dangerous." Yet the Stagman remains nameless, and in her first year of college, with protest rising against the Vietnam War, the narrator complains that Frances is "escaping into the Stagman's tale, leaving me to fend for sanity in a world that was rapidly losing its lovely medieval geometry." The Stagman wanders across a wasteland that merges with the real world, his aimlessness an expression of her own sense of namelessness and alienation from a world defined in male terms: "I wondered wearily if life might make more sense to me, lose its cumbersome, historical burden of masculine despair, if I simply filled my head with a different pronoun."

Frances has a long way to go, including a brush with death that revives her will to live, success as a writer when her Stagman story is published, and several failed attempts to find the Stagman in relationships with men before she learns that "the Stagman was part of me, not part of the world around me . . . part of my own shadow, or my dreams, to be endlessly challenging, forcing the best of strength, creativity, passion from me." It is a resolution that Carl Jung would describe as Frances' reconciliation with her *animus*, but the experience is not so much an illustration of psychoanalytic patterns as a convincing portrayal of a deeply personal transformation, as the two sisters are merged into a single, whole person.

In many ways *Stepping from the Shadows* is as much McKillip's *Moby Dick* as it is her *Portrait of the Artist*, not only because of its powerful dominant symbol but also because it seems to represent a culmination, an end of a pattern of development suggesting that whatever comes next will represent new kinds and levels of achievement. We can only wait and wonder.

Selected Bibliography

WORKS OF PATRICIA McKILLIP

The House on Parchment Street. New York: Atheneum, 1973.

The Throme of the Erril of Sherill. New York: Atheneum, 1973.

The Forgotten Beasts of Eld. New York: Atheneum, 1974.

The Riddle-Master of Hed. New York: Atheneum, 1976.

Heir of Sea and Fire. New York: Atheneum, 1977.

Harpist in the Wind. New York: Atheneum, 1979.

Stepping from the Shadows. New York: Atheneum, 1982.

—THOMAS L. WYMER

RICHARD MATHESON

1926-

STEPHEN KING CREDITS Richard Matheson (along with Jack Finney) with having radically changed the shape and direction of American horror fiction:

> At about the same time Jack Finney was writing *The Body Snatchers*, Richard Matheson was writing his classic short story "Born of Man and Woman." ... Between the two of them, they made the break from the Lovecraftian fantasy that had held sway over serious American writers of horror for two decades or more.... They represent the birth of an almost entirely new breed of American fantasist. ...
>
> (*Danse Macabre*, 1981)

The importance to King of this "non-Lovecraftian" influence is that it moved the horrific from the ornate, bizarre, and self-consciously "mythic" worlds of H. P. Lovecraft and the *Weird Tales* tradition to the everyday world of ordinary people. To be sure, there are otherworldly menaces in Matheson's stories and novels, but they operate in the most mundane and "normal" environments and are most often made from the stuff of our own distorted realities.

"In a way," Matheson has said, "as a fantasy writer I'm a mainstream writer. Once I've established the twist, I proceed almost in a non-fantasy manner." Or, as he says at another point in the same interview, "George Clayton Johnson once said that the typical Richard Matheson story is where a hus-

band and wife are sitting down to have coffee and cake when something strange pops out of the sugar bowl. I just think that people identify with fantasy more if you can get the story closer to their daily lives" (*Twilight Zone*, 1981). This running tension between the normal and the bizarre gives the best of his writing its distinctive suspense, horror, and, frequently, humor.

There was, as Matheson himself admits, little in his background to foreshadow his development as a major American fantasist. He was born in Allendale, New Jersey, on 20 February 1926; graduated from Brooklyn Technical High School in 1943; served in the army (experiences later chronicled in his mainstream novel *The Beardless Warriors*, 1960); and after the war studied journalism at the University of Missouri, graduating in 1949 with a B.A. As King noted, Matheson attracted attention with his initial publication, "Born of Man and Woman," in the *Magazine of Fantasy and Science Fiction* (February 1950). The flood of stories and novels that followed culminated in two novels, *I Am Legend* (1954) and *The Shrinking Man* (1956). But impressive as these novels may be, it is probably in his short fiction that the full range of Matheson's themes, images, situations, characters, and virtuosity can best be seen.

In the usual Matheson short story, the "thing from the sugar bowl" may threaten the entire world, as does the irrational urge to mass self-destruction in "Lemmings" (1957). Not surprisingly, given their time of composition, Matheson's stories frequently present a threat of nuclear holocaust and focus on a threatened couple or family ("The Last Day," 1953; "Descent," 1954; and, with an unusual twist, "Third from the Sun," 1950). This couple or family unit is also threatened by a variety of menaces, including kidnapping ("Being," 1954; "Dying Room Only," 1953), alien impregnation ("Mother by Protest," also known as "Trespass," 1953), a voodoo curse ("From Shadowed Places," 1968), rampaging insects ("Crickets," 1960), a vanishing child ("Little Girl Lost," 1953), an unruly child ("The Doll That Does Everything," 1954), and a grotesque, radiation-mutated child ("Born of Man and Woman").

The focus in "Born of Man and Woman" is not, however, on the beleaguered family but on the chained creature; and this points to an even more common situation in Matheson's fiction: the man in a trap. Once the protagonist in these stories finds himself in his trap, he fights to get free, finally succeeding or, occasionally, failing. The traps vary greatly from straightforward physical ones—a chain on a wall, a closed car, an apartment, a casket; to elaborate, complex situations—a barricaded house in a world full of vampires, an unorthodox haunted house, a time loop; to personal afflictions—a "shrinking" sickness, a "wild talent," a terminal illness, death itself.

But if the traps differ considerably, the protagonists are usually similar. They are almost always male (even "Mother by Protest" is told from the husband's point of view), usually sensitive and intelligent. Often they are moderately successful writers, family-oriented but sometimes estranged, comfortable in bourgeois surroundings and modest in desires, but acutely aware—or made aware—of the precariousness of life and the ambiguity of reality. This perennial protagonist is, as Matheson acknowledges, a fictionalized version of himself.

In some stories the protagonist finds himself with no way out. For example, in "The Children of Noah" (1957), the vacationing Mr. Ketchum is stopped for a traffic violation and taken into the small town of Zachry, Maine, where, he discovers at the last moment, he ends up in a huge oven. A different, more complicated kind of trap, a sexual one, confronts David Lindell in "Lover When You're Near Me" (1952). Left to manage mining operations

for six months on Space Station Four, he is given a "Gnee" servant, a pink, hairless, one-nostriled female with telepathic powers. The creature's strong mind and grotesque lust gradually overwhelm Lindell until, by the end of his tour of duty, he is a mental and physical wreck. Even more frightening is the fate of John in "Wet Straw" (1953), who is pursued and finally destroyed by the ghost of his murdered wife. As her presence grows and erotic memory vies with fear, John's mind deteriorates rapidly. Yet the story's end leaves no doubt that the vengeful ghost is real and not hallucinatory.

This emphasis on the collapse of mental processes points to an even more harrowing situation, being trapped in a world that is going mad or disintegrating altogether. Paranoid visions, as Peter Nicholls has pointed out, are central to Matheson's vision. This paranoia can be simple and straightforward, as in "Legion of Plotters" (1953), but it usually is more complicated. In "Mad House" (1953), for example, not only do people plot against Neal, but even the objects in his house eventually become animated and kill him. But it is his own anger, as Matheson shows, that has been absorbed by Neal's "things" and used against him. "Brother to the Machine" (1952) and "Deus Ex Machina" (1963) are actually the same provocative story told from very different angles. In each of them a man discovers, in the last moments of his life, that he is really a robot/android (the stories are reminiscent of Philip K. Dick's "Imposter"). Just as disturbing is the experience of Robert Graham in "The Curious Child" (1954), who progressively forgets everything about the life he is living, although he is rescued by a happy ending; it was all a time-travel accident and he is reunited with his proper time. Less fortunate is Don Marshall in "The Edge" (1958), who goes out for lunch one day and inadvertently wanders into a parallel universe, where he is trapped. Still more unlucky is the protagonist of "Disappearing Act" (1953), whose world simply disappears around him; the story ends in midsentence.

Not all Matheson heroes accept their fates passively; some fight back, despite the odds. Unbeknown to his fellow passengers, Arthur Jeffrey Wilson in "Nightmare at 20,000 Feet" (1961) saves them all from a destructive gremlin on the wing, despite his almost hysterical fear of flying. When he pulls a gun, opens the plane's emergency exit, and shoots the creature, we applaud his heroism, although those around him see only a maniac.

"Duel" (1971) is probably Matheson's best-known short novel due to the popular television adaptation. Although not technically a fantasy, it is perhaps the purest and most intense of the trapped-man stories. Mann, a salesman en route to San Francisco, passes a massive truck-and-trailer rig on a hill, provoking a cat-and-mouse duel between motorist and truck driver. Matheson describes every movement of his near helpless hero's existence as Mann attempts to outrun, outmaneuver, and outthink his implacable opponent. The ardors of driving, the sights and sounds of the highway, the mechanical fragility of Mann's vehicle, and the truck's awesome presence combine in a story that has rarely been exceeded for sheer physical intensity. At the same time, the struggle is as much mental as physical, as fear, panic, rage, helplessness, and, finally, primal joy surge through Mann's mind. And while Matheson never suggests that the truck is other than a truck driven by a psychotic driver, "Duel" does become a kind of primal struggle of man versus beast. "He visualized the truck as some great entity pursuing him, insentient, brutish, chasing him with instinct only" — proof that the everyday world can produce "monsters" every bit as terrifying as those found in the cosmos of Cthulhu and company.

I Am Legend, the first of Matheson's science fiction/fantasy novels, extends and expands the man-in-a-trap motif. "I got the idea for it," he told *Twilight Zone* magazine, "when I was seventeen years old in Brooklyn and saw *Dracula*. I figured that if one vampire was scary, then a whole world full of vampires should really be scary." Nuclear war and a series of severe dust storms unleash a virulent disease, semilatent for centuries, that turns everyone into a vampire except the hero, Robert Neville, who lives barricaded in his home, venturing out only during the day to forage and to kill as many of the creatures as he can.

The central irony is that in a world of vampires the "normal" man is the real "vampire." Like his nemeses, Neville's life is regulated by the sun; he must return to his "casket" — his fortress home — be-fore the sun sets or be destroyed by hoards of rampaging vampires. It is he who ravages the countryside, indiscriminately killing sleeping victims. And, like the traditional vampire, he kills not only in the name of survival but also — defining the word broadly — for pleasure.

The novel is in four parts divided by time (January 1976; March 1976; June 1978; January 1979) and, more important, by stages in Neville's growth. Initially, he simply reacts to the situation with raw emotion. Memories of the cataclysm that destroyed the world, his life, and his family persist, along with intense erotic needs. The futility of his actions is self-evident; the music, films, and amenities with which he has surrounded himself become increasingly meaningless; and his behavior, especially his drinking, becomes increasingly self-destructive. He contemplates suicide or simply surrender. Thus, he kills not so much for physical survival — his barriers are more than enough to keep the moronic undead at bay — as for psychological survival: it gives him something to do and a kind of meaning and direction to his life.

By the second segment of the book, the killing of vampires has become less of an emotional outlet and more of a scientific ritual. Striving for more efficient ways to kill leads to a study of vampirism itself. The detachment of the scientist replaces the fanaticism of the revenger, although the latter is never far out of sight.

In part three, the "human" Neville clashes with the scientific one when he meets Ruth, another apparently "normal" person. Logic tells him to test and, if need be, kill her; reawakened feelings and memories induce him to postpone the test. The result is mixed. Ruth is a vampire after all, although of a new and different variety, and their meeting was not accidental: she had been sent as a spy. On the other hand, during their brief relationship she falls in love with him (although he had killed her husband); when she departs she leaves a note warning him about the "new vampires." He rejects the suggestion that he flee to the mountains and, in part four, waits passively to accept his fate.

Why does Neville ignore Ruth's warning? Because, apparently, he realizes that he is an anomaly in a world that has no place for him. In the end he identifies with the mindless vampires who must be destroyed so that the new society — however primitive and brutal it may be — can come into being. Neville has been not only trapped but also obsessed. Despite his extensive study of vampires, he has ignored the most important and obvious fact about them: that there are not only mindless, animated corpses but also infected, still-living human beings. His hatred is too intense and narrow to enable him to consider the nature and implications of the living vampires, so he is unprepared for their metamorphosis into the new society. Robert Neville is unable to escape from his trap because it is, in the end, one of his own making.

In *The Shrinking Man*, Scott Carey's trap is even more isolating and frightening because it is progressive. As the result of accidental exposure to radioactive mist coupled with ingestion of a pesticide — the evils of nuclear testing combining with environmental pollution — he shrinks an inch a week. Thus, he is constantly forced to adjust to new and even more threatening environments, as well as to the loss of his humanity and the prospect of imminent physical annihilation.

The Shrinking Man is probably Matheson's best and certainly his most exciting novel, because the concept maximizes his ability to trace the physical and psychological experiences of an isolated character and his knack for constructing vivid, economical, dramatic scenes. The first brief chapter describes Carey's encounter with the radioactive mist that activates the shrinking process; the second jumps ahead to the point where, having shrunk to four-sevenths of an inch, Carey fights for his life against a spider in the cellar of his own home. Matheson continues this rhythm throughout the novel; vignettes dramatizing the stages of Carey's decline alternate with scenes of his battle for survival, as he awaits his final dissolution. Thus, the poignancy of the hero's loss of humanity is juxtaposed against his courageous "last stand."

The power of the book comes not from Carey's hardships but from his reactions to them. We share his anguish and embarrassment when sex with his wife becomes "grotesque," when he transforms their ugly baby-sitter into an object of sexual adoration, when his daughter abuses him like an unruly pet,

and when the family cat chases him as a juicy morsel. At the same time, we share his tentative joy amid despair when he has a brief, idyllic love affair with a circus midget — the last act he can perform as a viable "human being." When Carey accepts annihilation with equanimity we sense a tragic reconciliation; when he awakens to find that he has not vanished after all but has been reborn into a new, submicroscopic world, we share his joy and sense of infinite possibility.

Matheson's next book, *A Stir of Echoes* (1958), reflects both his lifelong interest in psychic phenomena and his experiences in California suburbia. A more modest novel than its immediate predecessors, it is less extreme in its actions and situations, less grotesque in characterization, and confined to a single neighborhood. Yet within these limits, it is engaging and provocative, an interesting mix of psychic horror story, suburban melodrama, and whodunit.

When Tom Wallace, a southern California aerospace worker, is hypnotized by his brother-in-law at a party, his latent psychic powers are set free. He begins to foresee events, to more or less read the minds and feelings of his family and neighbors, and, most disturbing, to see a female ghost in his living room at night. Thus, like Scott Carey, he is the victim of an unexpected, disrupting condition that he can neither understand nor control. He is trapped within himself, and as his powers reveal his neighbors' dark secrets, he is drawn into their duplicitous, lustful, and ultimately homicidal intrigues.

But this suburban melodrama is less interesting than the protagonist's inner drama. Like John Smith, hero of Stephen King's *The Dead Zone* (1979), Tom Wallace needs to come to terms with his wild talent and to keep it from destroying his relationships with the world; this need provides the book's real tension. But while King treats John Smith's condition and fate as public tragedy, Matheson presents his hero's experience as a matter of private, intimate anguish. Tom Wallace's idyllic marriage, like Robert Neville's and Scott Carey's, is threatened by his bizarre situation. His pregnant wife, Anne, further upset by the sudden death of her mother (which Tom had predicted), cannot accept her husband's frightening abilities. And as the marriage deteriorates, Tom's emotional stability grows increasingly precarious, until his sanity becomes the novel's primary concern.

Finally a psychiatrist gives Tom a lucid explanation of his condition and another round of hypnosis; Tom immediately gains confidence and control over his talents, stabilizes his marriage, solves the "ghost" problem (it was a previous tenant murdered by a neighbor), and is then conveniently wounded in the head—thus eradicating his discomfiting abilities. Obviously, this resolution is too fast and easy, denying the novel the final impact of *I Am Legend* or *The Shrinking Man*, but it is well designed and adroitly executed. And the relationship between Tom and Anne is quite believable and sympathetic, a solid foreshadowing of the intense love relationships that are the focus of Matheson's two later novels, *Bid Time Return* and *What Dreams May Come*. But between *A Stir of Echoes* and these later books comes *Hell House* (1971), perhaps Matheson's oddest book, one that is both his most conventional horror story and his least characteristic novel.

In basic plot, *Hell House* is a traditional "haunted house" narrative, structurally resembling Shirley Jackson's classic *The Haunting of Hill House* (although Matheson denies any influence). Three experts in the paranormal are hired by an eccentric millionaire to definitively answer the question of life after death by investigating the mysterious phenomena that pervade the Emerick Belasco mansion, more commonly known as "Hell House."

Although aware that two previous investigations ended in disaster, the chosen trio eagerly accepts the challenge. Lionel Barrett, a scientific investigator of the supernormal, brings along his invention, a machine called an EMR, or "Reversor," which will neutralize the electromagnetic forces that (he thinks) cause all paranormal activities. He thus hopes to demonstrate that such phenomena are physical, not spiritual, in origin. Florence Tanner, a spiritualist, vows to understand and deal with the forces of Hell House through love. For the third investigator, Benjamin Franklin Fischer, who at fifteen was the sole survivor of an earlier debacle, a second chance at the Belasco mansion represents the opportunity to salvage his self-respect as well as to give his psychic abilities a definitive test.

Almost from the beginning of the novel, the group is attacked by every conceivable form of psychological and physical horror. These assaults are reinforced by the pervasive atmosphere of sexual perversion and moral chaos. The mansion itself projects an aura of evil comparable to that in Lovecraft's classic "Rats in the Walls" and, more recently, Basil Copper's "The Grey House." The atmosphere of Hell House is totally absorbing.

But the characters, unfortunately, are not. *Hell House* is the only novel in which Matheson abandons the trapped male protagonist in favor of a shifting focus. This technique might work with distinctive and interesting characters, but here they are thoroughly bland and unsympathetic. Lionel Barrett is petty and arrogant; his wife, Edith, who assists in his experiments, has almost no personality at all. Florence Tanner is too hysterical to be taken seriously. Benjamin Franklin Fischer, the typical Matheson hero, is largely wasted, remaining well in the background before emerging in the last chapters to explain the mysteries of the mansion. Fischer's stiff speeches simply add an implausible, contrived rationale to this occasionally powerful but ultimately bothersome book.

It would be difficult to find a greater contrast than that between *Hell House* and Matheson's two latest major novels, *Bid Time Return* and *What Dreams May Come*. Most simply stated, *Hell House* is about the power of hate, while the others are about the power of love. Matheson deserts the horror genre completely in favor of romantic fantasy—which is not to say that they are of equal merit. *Bid Time Return* is a powerful and sensual narrative of desperate love found and lost, while *What Dreams May Come* is an ambitious failure, a love story turned into a well-meaning but garrulous metaphysical tract.

Bid Time Return (1975), also known as *Somewhere in Time*, is Matheson's most poignant novel. Richard Collier, a thirty-six-year-old screenwriter, is the victim of a progressively destructive brain tumor. Given only a few months to live, Collier severs all ties and sets out from Los Angeles on a motor trip east. He gets no farther than the Coronado Hotel in San Diego, where he sees the picture of Elise McKenna, a turn-of-the-century actress, and falls in

1077

love with her. Obsessed by love, intrigued by accounts of the mystery in Elise's life, and stimulated by notions of the relativity of time as stated in J. B. Priestley's *Man and Time*, Collier determines to visit 1896 by sheer force of will—and he does. He meets and woos Elise, over the determined, ultimately violent opposition of her manager, W. F. Robinson, and wins her for a brief, intense affair, only to be whisked back to 1971 by a seemingly insignificant detail in his costuming.

Although there is a fairy-tale aura about the story, it is set in a world that is very real. As Collier drives through southern California, Matheson renders the landscape in detail, conveying a powerful sense of contemporary California, with its rush, superficiality, and odd mixture of frivolity and frenzy. This image is effectively juxtaposed against the world of 1896, with its slow pace, formality, seriousness, and relaxed, sympathetic view of human relationships. Matheson captures the mood, feeling, style, and texture of both eras, making each more real by the comparison, although he is not, like Jack Finney in *Time and Again*, comparing the two in order to emphasize the superiority of the earlier era. Despite obvious similarities, the two novels are quite different: *Time and Again* is a time-travel story with a love affair in it; *Bid Time Return* is a love story in a time-travel context.

The reader identifies with Collier because of his sensitivity, his intense emotions masked by frail, cynical defenses, and the courage with which he confronts his fate. Thus, we share his exhilaration at the prospect that passion can surmount terminal illness and time itself. But we also share the sense of pervading doom that underscores his every action. When he is suddenly and unexpectedly wrenched back to his own time to die, we are shocked but not surprised.

What Dreams May Come (1978) again presents a pair of separated lovers but estranged by the barrier between life and death. Killed in an automobile accident, Chris Nielsen is thrust into the afterlife. After initally resisting the transition, he gives in, to begin a new life. The middle third of the novel is a guided tour of the netherworld, with incidental satire of religious, moral, social, and psychological ideas. This semi-idyllic afterlife is interrrupted by the news that, despairing over Chris's death, his wife, Ann, has committed suicide. This violation of the natural order threatens to separate them forever. Chris takes a harrowing trip into the dark regions to rescue Ann, a quest paralleling the Orpheus-Eurydice myth. After enduring "hells within hells," Chris finds and establishes contact with Ann, deciding that hell with her is preferable to heaven without.

At the end, Matheson adds a nine-page bibliography on the after-death experience. This rhetorical impulse probably accounts for the novel's weakness as fiction. Our identification with Chris Nielsen is almost entirely cerebral, and the environment in which he operates is neither believable nor interesting. Whatever the validity of Matheson's ideas, his physical conception of the next world is thoroughly mundane. The few animated scenes between Chris and Ann near the end of the novel are too little and too late to save it from its well-meaning dullness.

Since the late 1970's Matheson has devoted less and less of his time to prose in favor of screenwriting and playwriting. His only recent novel, a psychological ghost story entitled *Earthbound* (1982), is a reworking of a twelve-year-old narrative. He claims to have lost interest in the short story altogether, and his only recent ventures in that area have been written in collaboration with his son, Richard Christian Matheson.

However, one of these stories, "Where There's a Will" (*Dark Forces*, 1980), deserves notice; it is perhaps the most graphic of all the man-in-a-trap stories. Charlie awakens to find himself buried in a coffin. Propelled by fear and anger, he slowly and painfully scratches his way out, using only a cigarette lighter and a set of keys. He climbs up through the wet, bug-infested dirt to the surface and stumbles across a highway and into a rest room, where he calls his wife. Her reaction and his subsequent gaze in the mirror reveal that he has been buried for over seven months. Perhaps this latest man-in-a-trap story, with its obvious echoes of Lovecraft's "The Outsider," most vividly underscores the difference that Stephen King has noted between the Old Masters and the new horror writers.

Both stories are about fugitives from the "underground" who seek and make contact with the real world—only to discover to their horror that they are monsters who can have no part of it. But Lovecraft's creature exists in a strange, grotesque netherworld, darkly mysterious and "mythic," and he ascends to the real world up a long staircase, then around a tower, and then finally through a trapdoor and grate. Even when we see "him," we do not know what "he" is. The creature has connotations of the dead come to life, a ghoul or zombie, but it is still an otherworldly monster, an intruder into our world. But Charlie is one of us, and we identify with his struggle to dig his way out. The horror is as much psychological as physical. This difference between the "old" and the "new" can perhaps be most easily seen in that moment in each story when the creature sees "himself" in the mirror:

> I can not even hint what it was like, for it was a compound of all that is unclean, uncanny, unwelcome, abnormal, and detestable. It was the goulish shade of decay, antiquity, and desolation; the putrid, dripping eidolon of unwholesome revelation, the awful baring of that which the merciful earth should always hide. God knows it was not of this world—or no longer of this world— yet to my horror I saw in its eaten-away and bone-revealing outlines a leering, abhorrent travesty on the human shape; and in its moldy, disintegrating apparel an unspeakable quality that chilled me even more.
>
> (Lovecraft)

> Staring back at him was a face that was missing sections of flesh. Its skin was grey, and withered yellow bone showed through.
>
> (Matheson)

Matheson's lesson is simple: the most concrete and familiar can be the most frightening.

Selected Bibliography

WORKS OF RICHARD MATHESON

Born of Man and Woman. Philadelphia: Chamberlain Press, 1954. Abridged version, London: Max Rheinhardt, 1956. As *Third from the Sun*. New York: Bantam, 1955. (Short stories.)

I Am Legend. New York: Fawcett, 1954. London: Corgi, 1956. As *The Omega Man: I Am Legend*. New York: Berkley, 1971. (Novel.)

The Shrinking Man. New York: Fawcett, 1956. London: Muller, 1958. (Novel.)

The Shores of Space. New York: Bantam, 1957. London: Corgi, 1958. (Short stories.)

A Stir of Echoes. Philadelphia: Lippincott, 1958. London: Cassell, 1958. (Novel.)

Shock! New York: Dell, 1961. London: Corgi, 1962. As *Shock I*. New York: Berkley, 1979. (Short stories.)

Shock II. New York: Dell, 1964. London: Corgi, 1965. (Short stories.)

Shock III. New York: Dell, 1966. London: Corgi, 1967. (Short stories.)

Hell House. New York: Viking, 1971. London: Corgi, 1973. (Novel.)

Bid Time Return. New York: Viking, 1975. London: Sphere, 1977. (Novel.)

What Dreams May Come. New York: Putnam, 1978. London: Michael Joseph, 1979. (Novel.)

Earthbound. New York: Playboy Press, 1982. (Novel.)

CRITICAL AND BIOGRAPHICAL STUDIES

Burns, James E. "TZ Interview: Richard Matheson." *Twilight Zone*, nos. 6 and 7 (1981).

Ellison, Harlan. "An Elegant Exaltation of Afterlife." *Los Angeles Times Book Review*, 17 September 1978: 1.

French, Lawrence. "Richard Matheson on *Twilight Zone* and *Jaws 3D*." *Fangoria*, no. 31 (1983).

Goldman, Stephen H. "*I Am Legend*." In *Survey of Science Fiction Literature*, edited by Frank N. Magill. Vol. 2. Englewood Cliffs, N.J.: Salem Press, 1979, 986–990.

King, Stephen. *Danse Macabre*. New York: Everest House, 1981, 317–330.

Martin, Robert. "Matheson in the Movies." *Twilight Zone*, no. 6 (1981).

Nicholls, Peter. "Richard Matheson." In *Science Fiction Writers*, edited by E. F. Bleiler. New York: Scribner, 1982.

Reed, Julia R. "*Hell House*." In *Survey of Modern Fantasy Literature*, edited by Frank N. Magill. Vol. 2. Englewood Cliffs, N.J.: Salem Press, 1983, 725–727.

Sharp, Roberta. "The Short Fiction of Matheson." In *Survey of Modern Fantasy Literature*. Vol. 4, 1983, 1645–1651.
———. "*What Dreams May Come.*" In *Survey of Modern Fantasy Literature*. Vol. 5, 1983, 2112–2114.

Watson, Christine. "*Bid Time Return.*" In *Survey of Modern Fantasy Literature*. Vol. 1, 1983, 90–94.
Zicree, Marc Scott. *The Twilight Zone Companion*. New York: Bantam, 1982.

—KEITH NEILSON

MICHAEL MOORCOCK

1939-

THERE ARE PARADOXES in the career of Michael Moorcock. He has been a hack (and often admitted it), but has won a major literary award. He is devoted to the past, especially to Edwardian England, yet he has become one of the great symbols of modernism in fantastic literature. His work is on the one hand romantic (sentimental), melodramatic, and tearful, and on the other hand antisentimental and ironic. A professed puritan, he introduced into 1960's science fantasy the Cavalier emblems of style (elaborate clothes, cars, houses, makeup) and sex (incest, bondage, troilism, transsexuality, and other imaginative pastimes). A professed anarchist, he is nevertheless preoccupied with property, ownership, and the use of autocratic systems for manipulating other people, not always in an obviously disapproving way.

Something of a legend in his own time and consciously given to ambiguity as an indoor sport, Moorcock himself is largely responsible for the rather silly nature of many of the myths surrounding him. One of his favorite scenarios is the harlequinade. His physical presence (much illustrated in books and magazines) is perhaps another in a series of masks: he is huge, bearded, Falstaffian, and wild-haired, a wearer of opera cloaks in the 1950's, a hippy dude in the 1960's, a retiring gentleman in tweeds and knickerbockers in the 1970's. Yet just as the dandyism of his work is part of a series of Chinese boxes, at the center of which a protagonist frequently will be revealed as ordinary, anxious, and tired, so the flamboyant real-life Moorcock is shy, and since the early 1970's has made very few public appearances.

An author's public persona may not be relevant to his writing, but in Moorcock's case it is surely part and parcel of the interesting and consciously developed metaphor that animates his work. Just as life is seen as aspiring to the condition of art in much of the work of the *New Worlds* writers, so Moorcock's books and his projected self-image seem part of the same performance. We are back to the harlequinade. It is relevant, then, that like Jerry Cornelius in *The Condition of Muzak* (1977), Moorcock was not wholly successful as a rock 'n' roll star. His one album to date (Michael Moorcock and the Deep Fix, *The New Worlds Fair*, 1975) reveals a singer whose voice, far from being raunchy, primal, and swaggering, as some fans expected, is a thin, light, pure tenor that sounds as if it should be singing patriotic Irish ballads or sentimental songs from the turn of the century.

If Moorcock's work is an enigma, then it is clearly a patterned enigma. Indeed, the paradoxes are not merely whimsical or inconsequential; they have been functional from the outset, and more recently have become, in a sense, the subject of his art.

Michael John Moorcock was born on the southern periphery of London, in Mitcham, Surrey, on 18 December 1939. His work has always been that of an intensely urban man, specifically a Londoner, to the extent that he has given the landscapes of Not-ting Hill and Ladbroke Grove, some miles to the decayed west of London's center, as fabulous a role in modern science fiction and fantasy as those of Melniboné or Middle Earth, Mars or the much-mined asteroids.

Unhappy at school, changing schools often, Moorcock left as soon as legally possible at age fifteen. Soon he was able to put his childhood love for Edgar Rice Burroughs to practical use by writing for a boys' magazine-cum-comic, *Tarzan Adventures*, which he edited from 1957 to 1958. From 1958 to 1961 he was an editor for the Sexton Blake Library, which published pulp thrillers. During this period he began submitting stories to the British magazines *Science Fiction Adventures*, *Science Fantasy*, and *New Worlds*.

There was rather more heroic fantasy than science fiction in Moorcock's early magazine stories. The first Elric story appeared in *Science Fantasy* in 1961. Nonetheless, of the first six books published under his own name, four were science fiction. The other two, *The Stealer of Souls* (1963) and *Stormbringer* (1965), told stories of the albino fantasy hero Elric, and of the phallic, blood-drinking sword that in part controls him. (Four pseudonymous works also appeared in this period. The first three, published as by Edward P. Bradbury, are a trilogy, a vigorous Edgar Rice Burroughs pastiche: *Warriors of Mars*, *Blades of Mars*, and *The Barbarians of Mars* [all 1965]. The fourth is an interesting short story collection, *The Deep Fix*, published in 1966 as by James Colvin.)

The four science fiction novels are, at first glance, unremarkable. The style is uneasy and hurried; the action is implausible and melodramatic, producing striking color effects and set pieces rather than any carefully wrought suspension of disbelief. Moorcock's carelessness about and lack of interest in science, and his generally slapdash approach, may have been promising qualities for a potential pulp writer, but a careful reading reveals that even then his thematic concerns were perfectly serious, although they did not really conform to the expectations of most readers at that time.

The Sundered Worlds (1965; reissued as *The Blood Red Game*, 1970) introduces the key idea of the "multiverse," which explicitly or implicitly runs through the whole of Moorcock's work, although in this early form it is something of a science fiction cliché: the idea of a huge (though finite) number of parallel universes coexisting. This was rapidly developed (at first in the fantasy rather than in the science fiction) into the idea of a series of alternative realities in and across which characters play out recurrent roles in a kind of manic, cosmic dance—characters who sometimes, especially in the fantasy, are seen as avatars of heroes and semideities, and sometimes as much closer to the common man.

Characters keep reappearing throughout Moorcock's work, sometimes with the same names, sometimes with very similar names (for example, Jherek Carnelian and Jerry Cornelius), sometimes sharing initials only (Jesus Christ and James Colvin), sometimes linked by style and fate, as are Elric and Jerry Cornelius (both of whom in their respective first appearances—in the story "The Dreaming City" [1961] and the novel *The Final Programme* [1968]—are moved to action by a quasi-incestuous love for a dead sister).

The Sundered Worlds offers a multiverse as a mere notion, which is not much more developed in *The Wrecks of Time* (1967; reissued as *The Rituals of Infinity*, 1971). *The Wrecks of Time* describes, with a feverish though jaunty assurance, the adventures of a Faustus/Falstaff figure (named Faustaff) in his attempts to save a series of doomed, parallel Earths. But by the end of the 1960's, Moorcock had begun to include so many cross-references between books and so many allusions to previous books (which when first published had no obvious connections between them) that the whole body of his work retrospectively has been made to seem a kind of giant, episodic supernovel. (A side effect of all this is that it is not possible adequately to discuss his fantasy in isolation from his science fiction.) If this strategy had been carried out purely on the level of recurrent characters and plot situations, it would have remained rather notional and diagrammatic. The success of the method depends on the substance, not the technique. At the heart of this supernovel lies a massive, passionate, structured concern; the complications and recomplications are a trick of the light, as new facets flash out and the entire crystalline mass revolves slowly before us.

The structured concern to which I refer is present, embryonically, from the beginning of Moorcock's work. We find it in its earliest form as a kaleidoscopic effect, a sometimes dreamlike shifting from one scene to another. Characters and landscapes are protean, metamorphosing, unstable. There is a shifting, disturbing flux. A sense of impending chaos has always been basic to Moorcock's writing, and it becomes an explicit theme early on, notably in the heroic fantasies.

The world of the Elric stories, in all its cryptic, doomed, and bloodstained variety, is structured around the struggle between the Lords of Order and the Lords of Chaos, who battle for Elric's soul throughout. Like Jerry Cornelius in the later and more sophisticated fiction, Elric is searching for a strategy of survival that avoids complete commitment (or surrender) to either of the forces working upon him. He displays an uneasy impartiality, an unstable integrity that is subject to many temporary but spectacular failures, usually in the direction of a Byronic, romantic excess (always doomed, all satisfaction being fleeting). But in the long run he just about manages to stand on his own two feet, despite the seductive lures and potent threats issuing from either end of the metaphysical, ethical, and political spectrum (order and chaos; good and evil; totalitarianism and anarchy).

This is visibly a reflection of Moorcock's own position as writer. The chaos that pervades his books is the stuff of nightmare, but attractive for all that. And although the books show an occasional yearning for serenity, they do not by any means advocate the imposition of law as the right answer. Indeed, the failure of two of the first four science fiction novels—*The Fireclown* (1965; reissued as *The Winds of Limbo*, 1969) and *The Twilight Man* (1966; reissued as *The Shores of Death*, 1970)—is largely due to their being in part political tracts against the imposition of law. They advocate a liberal anarchy, but much of the didactic material is not properly assimilated into the melodramatic adventure stories, so that dogma rather unnervingly alternates with death. Since that time a commitment to political anarchism—left-wing but not doctrinaire—has been a persistent feature of Moorcock's writing and of his editorial policies.

One of the charms of Moorcock's writing is its openness to all kinds of experience, ordered or chaotic. He has always been as sensitively responsive to the zeitgeist as the hairs on a Venus's-flytrap to its prey. A passage in *The Sundered Worlds* anticipates the Moorcock to come:

> The multiverse was packed thick with life and matter. There was not an inch which did not possess something of interest. . . . Here was everything at once, all possibilities, all experience.
>
> (chapter 10)

Openness to experience, of course, became a slogan of the 1960's; and Moorcock, though still very young, was in the right place at the right time with the right talents. In 1963, after its near-collapse, the science fiction magazine *New Worlds* was about to change publishers, and former editor E. J. Carnell recommended the twenty-three-year-old Moorcock as new editor. His first issue was May–June 1964.

Under Moorcock's strong, creative, and sometimes manic editorship, *New Worlds* reflected much of the 1960's ethos (and criticized it too) in a way that no other science fiction magazine managed or even attempted. The conservative members of the science fiction world hated it: sex, violence, pessimism, anarchy, and—worst of all—literary and typographical experimentation had been loosed into their cozy universe. But new readers were found, and the magazine is now recognized as having had a liberating influence on science fiction out of all proportion to its circulation—even in the United States, where it was not published. It was, by and large, literate, flamboyant, iconoclastic, and original, though sometimes paying the necessary price of being pretentious and angst-ridden.

Moorcock made barely enough to live on during this period, and he was forced into the absurdly fast production of novels in order to support the magazine (which had a respectable but not really profit-making circulation). He also had to support his wife and their two daughters born by the end of 1964. (A son was born in 1972.)

During his editorship Moorcock somehow found time to read an enormous amount, focusing on two special areas: the late-nineteenth-century novel (Joseph Conrad, George Meredith, Rudyard Kipling, and others) and more recent experimental fiction (William S. Burroughs, Boris Vian, Italo Calvino, Hermann Hesse, Jorge Luis Borges, and others). The understanding he gained through this reading, and through his editorial work, of the possible structures and nuances of sophisticated fiction resulted in a quite startling increase in the flexibility and assurance of his own writing. (Few science fiction and fantasy writers, sadly, show very noticeable advances in skill throughout their careers, and in all too many cases their early work is their best.)

Nonetheless, much of Moorcock's writing over this period is not very memorable. He was probably writing too fast. The early Elric books remain among his finest work; but while there is much of interest in the subsequent heroic fantasy series, some of the vigor has already been lost with the Hawkmoon stories. The Corum series, another fantasy sequence, was written at the very end of Moorcock's *New Worlds* editorship. Although technically more proficient than some of his earlier work, it seems rather etiolated and sapless. (It also suggests that Moorcock's feelings about Celts are at best ambiguous.) He was responsive to fin-de-siècle writing, and did not always control its studied decadence and dying falls when he used the style in his fantasies.

Moorcock, by the late 1960's, was moving further away from fiction that could be labeled by such generic categories as science fiction and heroic fantasy. In fact, he was to explode completely out of the straitjacket of literary categories in the best of his later works. As suggested above, the heroic fantasies of 1969–1975 seem rather perfunctory in comparison to the earlier ones, and there were only two more novels that could be described as moderately pure science fiction. Both of these are more interesting than the later fantasies, although in neither case is the generic structure capable of sustaining the weight of meaning it is invited to carry. Thus *The Ice Schooner* (1969) and *The Black Corridor* (1969) seem rather portentous, out of sheer top-heaviness.

The Ice Schooner pays homage to Joseph Conrad's *The Rescue* (1920), and to some extent recapitulates the latter's plot, which F. R. Leavis summarized as "the conflict between Love and Honour (a kingdom at stake) against a sumptuously rendered decor of tropical sea, sunset, and jungle" (*The Great Tradition*, 1948). The milieu here, though, is a future Ice Age, and the hero—closer to fantasy than to science fiction stereotypes—is a sailor-adventurer who plies his ship on runners across oceans of ice. It is a very readable story—a moving account of a barbarian hero who is finally faced with the fact that his entropic, frozen world is metamorphosing into a new world of springtime greenery. When asked to adjust to a new life, he refuses.

The Black Corridor was commissioned during a period of total exhaustion for Moorcock. Much of the book was first written to his outline by Hilary Bailey, his wife at that time, and was later revised by him. It is as close to the "psycho-Gothic" domestic chiller as Moorcock ever approached, although the responsibility for the change of mode was probably his wife's.

Moorcock's two most important books of the 1960's open up what has become the main thematic area in which he has worked ever since. They also effectively create a new genre. Tropes and images from both science fiction and fantasy continue to be used, but they are embedded in an ironic structure that cannot be pigeonholed in the traditional generic categories. Two science fiction themes remain very dominant indeed: alternate worlds and time travel. Both, for Moorcock, were means of approaching what was to become the major theme of his work in the 1970's: the ironies of time and history.

Behold the Man is one of Moorcock's most praised works, although I find in it a rather mechanical cynicism that is too contrived to be really painful. In its first form, as a novella (1966), it won a Nebula award. The hero, Karl Glogauer, is a seedy and self-pitying Jew from present-day London who is given to justified feelings of persecution. He goes back in a time machine to fulfill his neurotic obsession: to determine the truth of the Christ story. He accidentally becomes the historical (but insane) Christ himself, and is crucified. The story is cleverly told, especially in the short version (the novelized version of 1969 is a little inflated), but I find it atypically mean-spirited. Moorcock's work is usually more generous, expansive, and even altruistic.

The Final Programme (1968) was written in 1965, at which time three sections of it were published in *New Worlds*, the first Cornelius stories to appear there. It is the first part of a tetralogy, *The Cornelius Chronicles* (1968–1977), which is perhaps more properly considered as Moorcock wishes it considered: as a single novel. But *The Final Programme* may not have been written with so ambitious a plan in mind; and to some extent it seems separate from the other three parts, even though it has been revised three times to incorporate it more seamlessly into the fictional whole.

The plot of *The Final Programme* is (deliberately) similar to that of the first two Elric stories, but now the Elric figure is Jerry Cornelius—a dude, a brilliant scientist, and an international adventurer in the mid-twentieth century. Jerry is a metamorph, a scholar, an assassin, and a spy, with as many lives and as few morals as a tomcat, and an ability to alter reality in the world at large. In *The Final Programme* his character is suffused by a kind of manic gaiety, even when he and his unpleasant alter ego, Miss Brunner, use the final computer program to absorb one another and to emerge as a new, hermaphroditic messiah.

Moorcock's genius for incorporating pieces of his own art into larger, more sophisticated totalities was never more evident than in his use of this self-sufficient *jeu d'esprit* of the 1960's as a springboard for his most ambitious creation. The remaining three novels in the Cornelius saga are *A Cure for Cancer* (1971), *The English Assassin* (1972), and *The Condition of Muzak* (1977). All four books were published in one volume as *The Cornelius Chronicles* (1977), with an introduction by John Clute that is the finest single piece of exegesis I know of in science fiction criticism.

The further into the series the reader proceeds, the more complex is the literary structure. Synopsis is very nearly impossible. The story is multilayered and is spread across the trouble spots and pleasure spots of the globe, sometimes in the twentieth-century world that we know, sometimes in twentieth-century worlds that could have happened if Edwardian dreams of progress within a harmonious Empire had come true, or in worlds that could still happen if our nightmares come true, or in worlds that are somehow metaphorically true to the real world, while factually false. Always the story returns to Jerry's home ground, Ladbroke Grove in London W 11—to "the deep city," as John Clute puts it, the decaying landscape of the randy urban pastoral, just like the places where many of us live.

Moorcock's control of narrative tone by now is utterly assured. The story moves confidently and ever more darkly, as the sound of 1960's merriment begins to fade away and the gray realities of the 1970's begin to assert themselves. It moves through romantic extravaganza, poker-faced reporting of the holocaust (and another holocaust, and a third, spiraling through Apocalypses Now); moves through the wit of the bedroom and of the shambles, through Dickensian wholeheartedness, through abdications and coronations and resuscitations; moves through the whirl of the harlequinade and finally back to the ordinary world where Jerry has acne and his dreadful, indomitable mother lies dead.

Time shifts and turns. History has many routes and lessons thus revealed, or perhaps Moorcock does not know what day of the week it is—or probably and typically both are true. Objects are talismanic: rock 'n' roll records, cars, clothes, the gear and tasty detritus of style and appetite. Helicopters, guns, and drinks are all given their brand names. Time travel has always been used in science fiction, as have alternate worlds, to show us how things could be better, worse, or simply different; but, *The Cornelius Chronicles* ultimately insists, things will remain the same; they were and are the same. Other world lines, other time tracks, other possibilities offer an escape or a salvation that is strictly temporary and emblematic, for none is free from entropy.

Entropy is the other subject of this extraordinary series, but not entropy as a process to be merely succumbed to. Death, rust, decay, holocaust, cold, the lost ball-point pens, and the grease stains on top of the gas stove are real, and Jerry cannot be Harlequin forever. This too is the nature of the catastrophe. But as Pierrot, the sad clown at the sad close, Jerry is still alive. Even entropy, which has no brand name, can be endured.

Jerry is not the whole world. Other mythic figures abound. There is, for example, the threefold goddess (the maiden/the woman/the crone) much beloved of quasi-mystical fantasists with their well-thumbed copies of Robert Graves's *The White Goddess* (1947). She is there, too, in incarnations that are not at all Gravesian or godlike, although Una Persson, the Woman Revolutionary, is often heroic and turns out to be Harlequin after all. Catherine Cornelius is the decadent, dead child; and Mrs. Cornelius, the grotesque and malicious embodiment of the life force, is the most appallingly likable character in fiction since the creations of Charles Dickens.

In 1977, *The Condition of Muzak* became the first science fiction novel to win a "mainstream" literary award, the *Guardian* prize for fiction. Yet with all the talk at that time, no critic seems to have commented on the most remarkable paradox of all: *The Cornelius Chronicles* remains, all of its irony notwithstanding, the last major monument to British patriotism in literary history.

Moorcock's wit, always evident previously, became sharper and more ironic in *The Cornelius Chronicles*, although like most literary irony it is easy to overlook. Many readers seem never to have understood that Jerry is not always an admirable model of the 1960's "swinging" life-style; that element is part of him, but it is undercut by the mockery with which he is regarded. Some of this is a mockery of 1960's excess; some is a kind of mockery of fantasy heroes in general and of the foolishly flamboyant actions they so often feel called upon to undertake. Jerry can be seen as Moorcock's revenge on Elric and Hawkmoon, and on the whole heroic fantasy genre that he came to love like an aging and nagging mistress—better when it was in the next room.

Moorcock was still highly productive at the beginning of the 1970's (nine of his sixty-odd books were published in 1971 and 1972), and he continued to edit *New Worlds*, in its new format as a paperback anthology, until 1973. Then, at least by his own standards, he slowed down.

The second Karl Glogauer book, *Breakfast in the Ruins* (1972), is rather morose and dispirited in its guided tour of representative contemporary crises, both moral and political. A formal and diagrammatic farewell to the fantasy precinct of the multiverse was bid with *The Quest for Tanelorn* (1975), in which the Many heroic analogues are seen to be aspects of the indisputably One hero, who retires. (Elric, though, turned up a little later, looking rather forlorn, at one of Jerry Cornelius' parties.)

But a sprightly wit, less seriously focused than in the Cornelius books, characterizes much of Moorcock's work of this period. Two fantastic novels, loosely related to the Cornelius world, feature Captain Oswald Bastable, a decent Edwardian figure who contrives to deal with life in the alternate worlds by dint of guilelessness, honor, and a certain mental inflexibility, almost as successfully as Jerry Cornelius. (Bastable was borrowed from a series of books written at the turn of the century for children by the fantasy writer E. Nesbit.) The books are *The Warlord of the Air* (1971) and *The Land Leviathan* (1974). (A much later addition to the series, *The Steel Tsar*, 1981, is very disappointing.) But the best witticisms appeared in the Dancers at the End of Time trilogy: *An Alien Heat* (1972), *The Hollow Lands* (1974), and *The End of All Songs* (1976). These stand in the same relation to Moorcock's more substantial work (*The Cornelius Chronicles* and *Gloriana*) as, at a more exalted level, Shakespeare's comedies stand to the history and problem plays. (Moorcock has not yet written a tragedy.)

In much of Moorcock's earlier work, protagonists of a lawful world are tempted by the allure of chaos. In the Dancers trilogy, though, the reverse is the case. At the end of time, during a kind of Indian summer before entropy finally makes the suns wink out, the prevailing post-technological sophistication on a future Earth allows the spontaneous creation of just about anything. But Moorcock's naïve desire in *The Sundered Worlds* for "everything at once, all possibilities," had clearly been tempered by the partial granting of that wish in the hedonistic 1960's. In *An Alien Heat*, Jherek Carnelian, the darling of the last days, meets an unwitting time traveler from the nineteenth century, Mrs. Amelia Underwood, who is very moral indeed. Faced with her stubborn penchant for misery and self-denial, the insouciant Carnelian feels something to be lacking in his own life. Having everything is not enough if it is unstructured, unweighted, and entirely free. It needs to be paid for.

The ensuing farce, punctuated by an excellent series of running gags on the theme of creative anachronism, is a bravura performance carried out with a delicate touch. Some longueurs do occur in the second and third volumes, where the author at several points resorts to funny aliens to keep things moving and where a slight self-plagiarism creeps in as the creative pressure slackens. (It is difficult for a highly productive composer not to relax, occasionally, by playing idle, minor variations on the same riff.) Most of Moorcock's main characters — Persson, Bastable, and others — make guest appearances here. The trilogy is a soufflé, balancing out the richer, heavier dishes in the Moorcock banquet. (*Legends from the End of Time*, published in 1976, collects three fine, ironic, and somewhat fin-de-siècle novellas as a coda to the Dancers trilogy.)

Gloriana (1978) is the other major fantastic work by Moorcock. It is dedicated to the late Mervyn Peake, and pays homage to this writer whom Moorcock greatly admires. He borrows from Peake's great Gormenghast trilogy (*Titus Groan*, 1946; *Gormenghast*, 1950; and *Titus Alone*, 1959) the central metaphor of the great building (here a palace) that stands both as a microcosm of the world and as an analogue for the brain. (The image of an inhabited building as a brain appears several times in Moorcock's earlier work, notably in *The Final Programme*, when Jerry, looking up at his secret ancestral château, reflects "how strongly the house resembled his father's tricky skull.")

Gloriana is the queen of Albion, and at many points she resembles Elizabeth I, the queen of Shakespearean England. Albion is an alternate-world England that splendidly evokes much of the ambience of the Elizabethan court; the novel borrows its structure and imagery from that elaborate, moral-allegorical court poem, Edmund Spenser's *The Faerie Queen*. *Gloriana*, though, is more Jacobean than Elizabethan in flavor. The ghosts of John Webster, Cyril Tourneur, and Ben Jonson seem to hover over the scenario of revenge, malcontents, conspiracy, illusion, and masque. Gloriana's great palace is home and court, museum, laboratory, and map, a

setting for affairs of state, yet (most important) full of secret places unknown even to Gloriana. There is a darker, more dangerous world behind the walls, where the stately beings of the superego cannot easily reach; these beings seem almost unaware of their scurrying, furtive relatives of the id. Gloriana cannot reach all the recesses of her own mind, either. She is a woman trained to maintain order and harmony, working to undo the harm brought about by her mad, malicious father during his reign; but she is nevertheless promiscuous, often unhappy, and unable to achieve orgasm.

This is a book richer in metaphor than anything else in Moorcock's image-laden oeuvre. Traditional ideas from late-sixteenth- and early-seventeenth-century writing (harmony and good governance; hierarchies, correspondences among the body politic, the body physical, and the body spiritual; the flux of the elements, essences of being, conflicts between spiritual and temporal law; and original sin) meld effortlessly with Moorcock's own preoccupations, and are merged into his metaphors as though they were made for one another.

The masque subsumes the harlequinade; formal masques mark the phases of the story, and behind all this is the great masque that *is* the story. The fiction draws attention to itself as a fiction, because a book is a kind of building too, an analogue of the author's brain. (Thus Moorcock, even though he has never eschewed some kind of naturalism, no matter how extravagant the movement and structure of his work, will nevertheless become grist for the academic structuralists' mill by becoming a fabulist also, his fiction consciously a masque, a mask, a made thing, and so declaring itself.)

In *Gloriana*, Moorcock's previously established themes continue — even through the romantic extravagance, the mirth, the masques, the insignia of surfaces — with greater depth than anything before (apart from *The Condition of Muzak*), continually made fresh and new. With masterly control he relates and rediscovers a strategy of survival, suspended between law and chaos. Likewise, he rejects the partial truths of an order and harmony the precarious existence of which depends upon never admitting what is rustling behind the walls, and which for that very reason must crumble, must explode into chaos or into a final orgasm. This final orgasm is the novel's ultimate metaphor, erupting when Gloriana is raped by the black-garbed, amoral Captain Quire—the incarnation of evil, perhaps, or anarchy, possessor of an insatiable intellectual and sensual curiosity that leads him to explore any and all experience. This orgasm is the emblematic paroxysm of joy and pain that might usher in chaos, or that might restore us to the Garden, to Eden, to Tanelorn, to the flourishing of the state—but that, surprisingly and gravely, is followed by a workmanlike, practical sobriety and a serene progress through the winter landscape.

Gloriana belongs to the same multiverse with which the young Moorcock began, within which both science fiction and fantasy, all desires and fears, must necessarily play a role. If Moorcock refuses to fit into the comfortable categories of genre fiction, he does so because the fictional multiverse itself is (as in real life) intractable. Moorcock is barely middle-aged. No doubt the multiverse he surveys holds more surprises yet, although no important fantasy novels have appeared since *Gloriana*. *Byzantium Endures* (1981), his most important work of the recent period, is a serious, well written, ironic, and realistic novel about anti-Semitism, the Russian Revolution, and survival in the city. The theme of the Wandering Jew lies half concealed within it. Mrs. Cornelius, as a young woman, appears as a character, but there is no other link with Moorcock's fantasies.

The War Hound and the World's Pain (1981), on the other hand, is direct fantasy; it could easily, and perhaps unfortunately, be the first in a new series. Ulrich von Bek, a mercenary captain in the Thirty Years War, is offered a pact by the Devil, Lucifer, who after long years is now seeking reconciliation with God. Von Bek is to seek the Grail that cures the world's pain, in return for his lost soul. The novel is a curious blend of insouciant swagger and great bitterness, but it is also rather silly and cannot be ranked as in any way a major work.

All Moorcock's other work in the period 1979 to 1984 is minor (*The Steel Tsar*, 1981; *The Entropy Tango*, 1981) or in no sense fantastic (*The Brothel in Rosenstrasse*, 1982).

Selected Bibliography

HEROIC FANTASY OF MICHAEL MOORCOCK

As the above article indicates, Moorcock's work forms a continuum, and elements of fantasy are present in many of his other stories. A full bibliography of such other books is to be found in the companion volume to this set; see Peter Nicholls, "Michael Moorcock," in *Science Fiction Writers*, edited by E. F. Bleiler. New York: Scribner, 1982.

Elric series in original chronology of publication

The Stealer of Souls and Other Stories. London: Neville Spearman, 1963. New York: Lancer, 1967.

Stormbringer. London: Herbert Jenkins, 1965. New York: DAW, 1977 (differs from previous editions in restoring complete text).

The Singing Citadel. London: Mayflower Books, 1970. New York: Berkley, 1970.

The Sleeping Sorceress. London: New English Library, 1971. As *The Vanishing Tower.* New York: DAW, 1977. As *The Sleeping Sorceress.* New York: Lancer, 1972 (with text revised without author's consent).

Elric of Melniboné. London: Hutchinson, 1972. As *The Dreaming City.* New York: Lancer, 1973 (with text revised without author's consent).

The Jade Man's Eyes. Brighton and Seattle: Unicorn, 1973.

Revised Elric series in order of internal chronology

Elric of Melniboné. (Details above.)

The Sailor on the Seas of Fate. London: Quartet Books, 1976. (Incorporates a revised version of *The Jade Man's Eyes.*)

The Weird of the White Wolf. New York: DAW, 1977. (Incorporates sections of *The Stealer of Souls* and *The Singing Citadel* with some new material.)

The Vanishing Tower. (Details above.)

The Bane of the Black Sword. New York: DAW, 1977. (Incorporates sections of *The Stealer of Souls* and *The Singing Citadel* with some new material.)

Stormbringer. (1977 edition, details above.)

Mars series starring Michael Kane

Warriors of Mars, as by Edward P. Bradbury. London: Compact SF, Roberts and Vintner, 1965. As *The City of the Beast* by Michael Moorcock. New York: Lancer, 1970.

Blades of Mars, as by Edward P. Bradbury. London: Compact SF, Roberts and Vintner, 1965. As *The Lord of the*

Spiders by Michael Moorcock. New York: Lancer, 1970.

The Barbarians of Mars, as by Edward P. Bradbury. London: Compact SF, Roberts and Vintner, 1965. As *The Masters of the Pit* by Michael Moorcock. New York: Lancer, 1970.

The Hawkmoon tetralogy and its sequel, the Count Brass trilogy

The Jewel in the Skull. New York: Lancer, 1967. London: White Lion, 1973. Revised text, New York: DAW, 1977.

Sorcerer's Amulet. New York: Lancer, 1968. As *The Mad God's Amulet*. London: Mayflower Books, 1969. Revised text, under latter title, New York: DAW, 1977.

Sword of the Dawn. New York: Lancer, 1968. London: White Lion, 1973. Revised text, New York: DAW, 1977.

The Secret of the Runestaff. New York: Lancer, 1969. As *The Runestaff*. London: Mayflower Books, 1969.

Count Brass. London: Mayflower Books, 1973. New York: Dell, 1976.

The Champion of Garathorn. London: Mayflower Books, 1973. (Can also be regarded as the third volume of the Eternal Champion series.)

The Quest for Tanelorn. London: Mayflower Books, 1975. New York: Dell, 1976. (Can also be regarded as the fourth volume of the Eternal Champion series.)

The Eternal Champion series

The Eternal Champion. New York: Dell, 1970. London: Mayflower Books, 1970. Revised text, New York: Harper and Row, 1978.

Phoenix in Obsidian. London: Mayflower, 1970. As *The Silver Warriors*. New York: Dell, 1973.

The Corum series

The Knight of the Swords. London: Mayflower Books, 1971. New York: Berkley, 1971.

The Queen of the Swords. New York: Berkley, 1971. London: Mayflower Books, 1971.

The King of the Swords. New York: Berkley, 1971. London: Mayflower Books, 1971.

The Bull and the Spear. London: Allison and Busby, 1973. New York: Berkley, 1974.

The Oak and the Ram. London: Allison and Busby, 1973. New York: Berkley, 1974.

The Sword and the Stallion. London: Allison and Busby, 1974. New York: Berkley, 1974.

A Von Bek novel

The War Hound and the World's Pain. New York: Timescape/Pocket Books, 1981.

— PETER NICHOLLS

ANDRE NORTON

1912–

ANDRE NORTON IS a popular writer of science fiction and fantasy who is not recognized as fully as she should be. Her work always is at least competent and frequently is better. The situations and points of departure in her fiction are intriguing, and her development of these situations is always skillful. In addition, in her works of fantasy she has created and explored a noteworthy and fascinating alternate universe. Although Norton has written for young people, most of her work is aimed toward a much broader audience, and all of her work can be enjoyed and appreciated by people of all ages.

Alice Mary Norton was born in Cleveland, Ohio, on 17 February 1912, the daughter of Adalbert Freely and Bertha Stemm Norton. She attended school in Cleveland, including Case Western Reserve University (1930–1932). Between 1932 and 1950, she was assistant librarian and children's librarian at the Cleveland Public Library, except for a period during World War II. In 1950 she turned to writing full time, also serving as an editor for Gnome Press from 1950 to 1958.

Norton began writing as "Andre Norton" with *The Prince Commands* (1934). Like her other early novels, it is a novel for young people. In the mid-1970's she legally changed her name to Andre Alice Norton. Her first science fiction story, "The People of the Crater," later included in *Garan the Eternal* (1972), was published in 1947 under the name Andrew North. Her first science fiction novel, *Star Man's Son* (1952; paperback title: *Daybreak—2250*

A.D.), began a long list of science fiction and fantasy novels. She has won a number of awards, including the Gandolf and Balrog awards.

Norton is best known for her "Witch World" series, some fourteen books (to date), plus related short stories. These works form two distinct subseries. The Estcarp/Escore novels focus on the powers of the Witches of Estcarp and on the uses and effects of those powers; the High Hallack stories are set across the sea from Estcarp. Although not an accepted way of life among the Dalesmen of High Hallack, magic is prevalent in the places of the Old Ones and in the Wastes that border High Hallack, and the lives of the major characters are touched by the workings of supernormal power. These novels are more varied in the roles and effects of magic than are the Estcarp/Escore novels.

Of the two subseries, the Estcarp/Escore novels are more tightly unified, following a roughly consecutive story line. This subseries includes *Witch World* (1963), *Web of the Witch World* (1964), *Three Against the Witch World* (1965), *Warlock of the Witch World* (1967), *Sorceress of the Witch World* (1968), *Trey of Swords* (collection, 1977), and *'Ware Hawk* (1983).

The High Hallack stories are held together more by setting and general situation than by a common story line; nevertheless, complex connections unite many of these works. The High Hallack stories are found primarily in six novels and two collections: *Year of the Unicorn* (1965), *Spell of the Witch*

World (collection, 1972), *The Crystal Gryphon* (1972), *The Jargoon Pard* (1974), *Zarsthor's Bane* (1978), *Lore of the Witch World* (collection, 1980), *Gryphon in Glory* (1981), and *Moon Called* (1982).

Witch World, the book that introduces this alternate world, is in some ways Norton's richest and most satisfying novel. Thrust into the Witch World without preparation, Simon Tregarth learns the nature of this world and of his situation, and the reader is slowly led into an alien world and culture. Because we identify with Tregarth, who reacts pragmatically but skeptically, our potential incredulity is blunted and a sense of verisimilitude is created.

His entry into the Witch World is interesting. A former colonel in the U.S. Army, Simon Tregarth is hunted by criminals. He is offered escape through the Siege Perilous, known in King Arthur's time to judge a person's worth and deliver him to his fate. Although he is skeptical, Tregarth accepts the challenge. After a brief, wrenching moment, he sprawls on his face on alien turf.

Estcarp is largely a river plain, bounded on the north by the Tor Fens and Tor Moor. Farther to the north lies Alizon, which is at war with Estcarp. On the south, Estcarp is bounded by mountains. Farther to the south is Karsten, which is increasingly drawn into the wars against Estcarp. To the west lies the sea, in the bay of which lies Gorm and on an arm into which lie Sulcarkeep and Yle. Both Yle and Gorm are now holds of the Kolder, people from another world whose goals are antithetical to those of Estcarp. Beyond the sea is the main base of the Kolder. What lies to the east is later revealed to be the land of Escore, the original home of the Old Race.

The people of Estcarp are of the Old Race, heirs to age-old knowledge and powers. Estcarp is a matriarchy of women gifted with the Power. The Power is found only in virgin women. Will, imagination, and faith are thus the weapons of magic in Estcarp, intensified through the jewels that all with the Power wear.

Simon Tregarth introduces new elements into this society. As a professional soldier, he brings new ideas about military strategy. As a person from a technical world, he can understand the Kolder and their methods. Moreover, he discovers he is sensitive to the Power and can use it. Thus, he is important in helping Estcarp temporarily defeat the Kolder and their other enemies. He is, however, an anomaly in this world.

The next five novels in the series develop from the events and implications in *Witch World*. Estcarp's society is rigid and dying. It has had little infusion of fresh life and new ideas for centuries; the ruling witches have set themselves against change. Thus, when Simon and Jaelithe, a witch whom he rescued and with whom he worked, marry, the matriarchate refuses to believe that Jaelithe could retain her powers or that a man could have powers akin to their own.

The matriarchate effectively ensures lack of new direction and growth when it alienates the children of Simon and Jaelithe, two boys and a girl. Each has a different gift, but they are also linked and can act as one, multiplying their abilities. The arrogance of the witches pushes them in a new direction.

In *Web of the Witch World*, although Simon and Jaelithe end the Kolder threat, ferment continues as Karsten and Alizon press the battle against Estcarp. As a result, the witches focus their Power to draw on the power inherent in the land to close completely the mountains to the south, effectively isolating Estcarp and ensuring its decline. While the witches' energies are thus focused, Simon's children—Kyllan, Kemoc, and Kaththea—escape into Escore over the mountains to the east, a blind spot for most in Estcarp.

In Escore the people had explored the Power extensively. Much good resulted, but great evil was also raised. The battles between those forces and their adherents left the land charged with magic, and many had fled. Those who remained avoided arousing the great dangers and created an uneasy peace. In their ignorance, Kyllan, Kemoc, and Kaththea disturb the balance and again bring turmoil into Escore as they try to survive and find their way.

The time has come for Escore to be reopened and for the battles between good and evil to be fought to a definite conclusion, laying ancient evils to rest. Thus, in *Three Against the Witch World*, Kyllan returns to Estcarp to recruit new settlers. He succeeds, and fresh life, untainted by the old, finds its way into Escore. The next three works—*Warlock of the Witch World, Sorceress of the Witch World,* and *Trey of Swords*—chronicle the battles to restore Escore, revealing a great deal about Escore's past as they do so.

'Ware Hawk* is the best of the novels in the Witch World series. Its most significant quality is the power of its telling, in compelling and often lyrical prose, of Tirtha's joining forces with a Falconer and a child of great Power to win a way from Estcarp into Karsten and to her family home, which they had fled during Yvain's harrowing of the Old Race from Karsten. There they find a weapon charged with the magic of the Old Race, but they are captured and brought into Escore, where they bring the weapon to bear on a Dark Great One and defeat him. Thus, we learn of the condition of Estcarp and Karsten after the great upheaval of the mountains, and the cleansing of Escore is continued.

Norton's second Witch World series, that of High Hallack, is introduced by *Year of the Unicorn.* High Hallack is also beset by Alizon and, indirectly, by the Kolder. This land had been peaceful, with life largely centered on the keeps and their large holdings of land, each keep separate from the others. That the Lords and landholders of High Hallack treated with the wandering, shape-changing Were-Riders from the Wastes to the north—a place pervaded by old magic and avoided by most people of High Hallack—suggests the upheaval of the society. The Were-Riders kept their part of the bargain, winning some respite for the Dales, and their price must be met—thirteen noble, healthy maidens as brides for the Were-Riders.

In *Year of the Unicorn,* Gillan and Herrel struggle to gain their true heritages. Gillan feels that she is somehow different from others and is strangely out of place. Thus, she takes the chance to go into the Waste as a bride. Herrel is accounted the least of the Were-Riders out of Arvon, for he has mixed blood and is not able to do the spells and other deeds of the Were-Riders as well as they. He accepts this assessment without bitterness.

Gillan chooses Herrel, who discovers her ability to see the reality underlying the illusions created by the Were-Riders and tries to protect her. She later discovers that she has other abilities as well. Others in the pack conspire against them. Thus, Gillan must learn to use her powers and draw courage and determination from within her. When Herrel joins her, they defeat the rest of the Were-Riders, winning through the illusions and dangers of another world and growing in power and in knowledge of themselves.

The Jargoon Pard focuses on the other side of Herrel's heritage. Lady Heroise (Herrel's half-sister) wants power and plans to raise the heir to Car Do Prawn to do her bidding. Her companion, Ursilla, uses her arts to exchange Heroise's daughter for Kethan, the son born to another couple—later revealed to be Herrel and Gillan. Named Were and harried from the keep, Kethan comes into contact with Herrel, Gillan, and Ailynn.

Living as a pard (that is, leopard)—kept in that form by sorcery—Kethan learns control of himself and of the pard's nature, as well as of the change process. In the final confrontation with the dark forces that Ursilla serves, each of the four—Kethan, Ailynn, Gillan, and Herrel—plays a part in defeating those forces, and new strength to stand against the new assault of the Shadow has been raised and tested.

Written after *Year of the Unicorn,* both *The Crystal Gryphon* and *Gryphon in Glory* occur earlier and show High Hallack before and just after the invasion of the Alizon. *The Crystal Gryphon* and *Gryphon in Glory* are the stories of Kerovan and Joisan; each is the focal character in alternate chapters.

The life of Joisan before the Alizon invade High Hallack is typical of young women of high station. Later, when she and Kerovan face strange adventures, she learns determination and persistence, and she draws deep within her for the abilities that she needs to aid him in his battle against magical forces.

Kerovan, however, must come to grips with who and what he is. Old forces had shaped him before birth, and it is clear that his heritage includes an element that is other than human. Kerovan assumes that his differences make him inferior to others. As a result of learning what forces were involved in his making and drawing on the strengths within him, including those allied to the power of the Old Ones, as well as looking deep within himself, he is at last able to open himself fully to Joisan. He decides to live as a man, forsaking his heritage of Power.

Unlike the other novels in the High Hallack series, *Moon Called* and *Zarsthor's Bane* are linked by similarities of plot and character, rather than by common characters and settings. In both, the central character is a young woman who flees to avoid death at the hands of raiders. Both women have learned to survive in the wilderness with the help of an animal companion. Both help another being who is in trouble and are thus reluctantly drawn into their adventures. Both are driven to their limits, and both of them emerge from the test with a greater understanding of themselves, their resources, and their world.

The three stories in *Spell of the Witch World* are set in High Hallack. "Dragon Scale Silver" tells of the effects of the war and of ancient evil ready to ensnare the unwary. "Dream Smith" shows the dangers and the powers of metal from the Waste and suggests the great powers of the Old Ones. "Amber Out of Quayth" shows the downfall of a man who would use magic for his own selfish ends.

The stories in *Lore of the Witch World* are more varied in setting and situation than those in *Spell of the Witch World*. "Spider Silk" takes a blind girl from High Hallack to an island where weavers produce sought-after material. "Sand Sister" shows life in Tormarsh as Tursla saves Simond, son of Koris, who had been drawn as the victim for a ritual sacrifice. In "Falcon Blood," the defeat of an old evil in the land from which the Falconers came allows a Falconer and a Sulcar woman to survive together. In "Legacy from Sorn Fen," Higbold, a tyrant of the sort who sprang up in High Hallack after the war, is brought to his end by his greed and the magic of Sorn Fen. "Sword of Unbelief" is another story of Elys and Jervon (they also appear in "Dragon Scale Silver" and *Gryphon in Glory*), who battle and defeat an ancient evil in the Waste. "The Toads of Grimmerdale" and "Changeling" are paired stories. Raped, impregnated, and homeless, Hertha calls upon the Toads to carry out her revenge but finds she cannot allow this and helps her victim escape.

Afterward, he convinces her that he is innocent and offers marriage. Her child is born a changeling, and they fight for it, restoring the seal around the Toads and thus removing the curse from the child.

Norton has also written fantasy unrelated to the Witch World. *Garan the Eternal* is a collection of two tales about Garin Featherstone, who becomes Garan in Tav, a land hidden by the mists of the Antarctic. In the first adventure, which is Norton's first science fiction/fantasy story, he must rescue Thrala from the Light from the Black Ones in the Caverns of the Dark. In the second adventure, he relives the life of an earlier Garan during the time when Tav was in upheaval. This volume also contains "Legacy from Sorn Fen" and "One Spell Wizard," a comic tale in which a very minor wizard defeats a wizard of greater power; both stories are set in High Hallack.

Quag Keep (1978) is based on the game dungeons and dragons. Players are drawn into another world by game figures for which they have a special affinity. In that world, they find that they **must** stay together as a group and that they **must** carry out a quest; although they would choose differently if they could, they have no choice in either matter. They are successful, and they also discover how they were drawn to this world; although they remain, they make sure that no others are brought into this world as they were. In the course of the novel, these people learn to work together for the common good, overcoming prejudice and different outlooks.

Norton's fantasies for young people include *Steel Magic* (1965; variant title, *Gray Magic*), *Octagon Magic* (1967), *Fur Magic* (1968), *Dragon Magic* (1972), *Lavender-Green Magic* (1974), and *Red Hart Magic* (1976). *Red Hart Magic* and *Dragon Magic* are representative.

In *Dragon Magic*, the main characters are troubled young people. Sig Dortmund is a slow learner. George ("Ras") Brown is torn between his father's patriotism and his brother's militant support of black power. Artie Jones yearns for recognition from the "in crowd." Kim Stevens, a Chinese boy adopted by Americans, dislikes his new life and the absence of others like him.

Similarly, the main characters in *Red Hart Magic*

are also troubled. Chris Fitton and Nan Mallory feel "displaced" since jobs have kept their parents, who have just married, away for long periods. Chris and Nan must stay with Aunt Elizabeth, a situation that both hate.

In both novels, a "magical" device helps the young people to learn more about themselves and to cope with their problems. Each receives appropriate help that is presented through an adventure appropriate to his or her ethnic background. In *Dragon Magic* the magical device is a four-part puzzle, each part showing a particular kind of dragon. In *Red Hart Magic*, the magical device is a model of an old English inn that Chris finds in a Salvation Army store. Through their adventures, these young people learn what they must in order to grow up.

The sense of wonder and of exploration is strong in Norton's fantasy. Her tales are carefully paced, with the action interesting and exciting. The movement of the plot is rapid; and the details of character, setting, and situation are deftly woven around the action, adding to its interest and depth without impeding its flow. Consequently, the movement through the worlds and societies that Norton has created takes on an importance and interest of its own that can obscure elements that are not immediately obvious.

In creating this sense of wonder and of movement, as well as in the development of all aspects of her stories and novels, the art and skill of Andre Norton lie primarily in her handling of detail. Her plots, like those of most writers, are variations on those that have been common since Homer. However, her skill at using details to vary these plots gives fresh life to them with each work. Similarly, her general themes, though not particularly original, are elaborated through details that give them new life and present them from a different perspective. Indeed, all aspects of Norton's works—characters, settings, cultures, situations, and so on—are enhanced by her ability to handle details aptly and deftly.

For example, *Dragon Magic* and *Red Hart Magic* are very similar in outline but differ greatly in their particulars. Each main character, for all their similarities, is presented as an individual with particular problems caused by his or her situation. Each of their adventures is particularized to match the character's ethnic background and specific problem. Apt details provide a sense of the life and times of legendary Germany, of Babylon, of Arthurian Britain, of Imperial China, and of three different periods in sixteenth- and seventeenth-century England.

Underlying the fascinating surface of action and the exploration of a world very different from our own are a variety of themes and perspectives. Norton examines the relative strengths and weaknesses of various social organizations, including matriarchy; she explores the relationships between human beings and machines, as well as the attitudes involved in working with the machinery; she focuses on the potentials inherent in human beings. The two strongest and most pervasive of her themes are the uses and abuses of power and the ability of individuals to break free of narrow and repressive constraints and to renew themselves from within. In her thematic explorations, Norton affirms such values as the respect for the land, the use of natural powers rather than machines, the recognition that there is a time for action and a time for defense, the awareness that there are proper limits that must be obeyed, and the necessity for intelligent beings to overcome barriers and to work together. Above all, Norton affirms the value and the potential inherent in individuals, as opposed to either machines or societies. Indeed, most of Norton's characters must learn to recognize and use their own abilities in order to cope with problems.

Norton is, more than most writers, a "series writer," one whose individual novels and stories are often related to her other works. This, of course, has significant implications for the ways in which she uses details to tell these stories, to develop her themes, and to build her worlds. In this respect, the Witch World novels and stories are Norton's crowning achievement, for in them she uses detail most effectively to create a living world with a past and a future, as well as a compelling, immediate present. That world is one of immense variety—in its geography, in its life forms, in its societies, and above all, in its human population. The Witch World is wide enough, the possibilities of magic varied enough, and the conflicts sufficiently universal to sustain the reader's interest not merely within one novel but from one novel to the next. This is in part because the recurring characters change and grow from one work to the next as they face different situations. It is also in part because the various themes carry through and develop from work to work (for example, it is only over the course of several novels that the depth and breadth of Norton's understanding of power is most readily apparent). Each novel builds on the base established in the preceding novels and explores another facet of the world, of the characters, and of the themes, not only within each of the subseries but also across the subseries.

Andre Norton is a quiet, competent writer who has contributed significantly to fantasy, even though no single novel can clearly be considered great. Through her fantasy, she has explored societies, cultures, individuals, and relationships, unfettered by the requirements of faithfulness to the world as we know it. Above all she has nourished a sense of wonder at the possibilities still available to us. In the Witch World series, Norton has created a world that is fully as vivid, as varied, and as real as those created by many of the more noted "world builders" in science fiction and fantasy.

Selected Bibliography

WORKS OF ANDRE NORTON

Witch World. New York: Ace, 1963. London: Universal-Tandem, 1970.

Web of the Witch World. New York: Ace, 1964. London: Universal-Tandem, 1970.

Three Against the Witch World. New York: Ace, 1965. London: Universal-Tandem, 1970.

Year of the Unicorn. New York: Ace, 1965. London: Universal-Tandem, 1970.

Warlock of the Witch World. New York: Ace, 1967. London: Universal-Tandem, 1970.

Sorceress of the Witch World. New York: Ace, 1968. London: Universal-Tandem, 1970.

The Crystal Gryphon. New York: Atheneum, 1972. London: Gollancz, 1973.

Dragon Magic. New York: Crowell, 1972.

Garan the Eternal. Alhambra, Calif.: FPCI, 1972. (Collection.)

Spell of the Witch World. New York: DAW, 1972. London: G. Prior, 1977. (Collection.)

The Jargoon Pard. New York: Atheneum, 1974.

Red Hart Magic. New York: Crowell, 1976. London: Hamish Hamilton, 1977.

Trey of Swords. New York: Grosset and Dunlap, 1977. London: Star, 1979. (Collection.)

Quag Keep. New York: Atheneum, 1978.

Zarsthor's Bane. New York: Ace, 1978.

Lore of the Witch World. New York: DAW, 1980. (Collection.)

Gryphon in Glory. New York: Atheneum, 1981.

Moon Called. New York: Pinnacle, 1982.

'Ware Hawk. New York: Atheneum, 1983.

BIBLIOGRAPHY

Schlobin, Roger C. *Andre Norton: A Primary and Secondary Bibliography.* Boston: G. K. Hall, 1980.

—L. DAVID ALLEN

THOMAS BURNETT SWANN

1928-1976

IN THE TIME since his early death, Thomas Burnett Swann has become a remote figure for the reader of fantasy. He seems as deeply embedded in the past as any of his numerous novels and stories, none of which is set later than 1875 and most of which take place in lands bordering the Mediterranean before the triumph of Christianity. To a point, the exigencies of genre publication can explain his obscurity. Of the eighteen books of fiction published under his name, seventeen appeared as paperback originals and have never been granted hardcover publication in English; as a consequence, most are difficult to obtain, and some almost impossible. The eighteenth title, *Queens Walk in the Dusk* (1977), the last of five to be issued posthumously, was released as a limited-edition hardcover by a firm whose output was restricted to this one book; it, too, is not readily available.

Swann was unfortunate in publishing most of his work ephemerally; he was also unfortunate in that the excessive productivity of his last years caused a bunching effect in the release of these titles, with eight novels being published during 1975–1977. As the market for his slender, elegiac fables was never large, the likely effect of a spate of releases was to flood that small market.

There are still further reasons for Swann's sudden disappearance from the marketplace. Of those eight final novels, two are mild, unsuccessful farces utilizing sentimentalized historical figures only dimly familiar to the readership for which he wrote, and three are "prequels" considerably inferior to the texts that they are intended to adumbrate. (*Prequel* is a term that has come into use to describe the very large number of recent science fiction and fantasy stories whose internal chronology precedes that of a previously published story set in the same venue; Swann wrote several prequels.) Only three of Swann's last novels are independent creations that fairly reflect his peculiar talents as a fantasist of nostalgia: *How Are the Mighty Fallen* (1974), *The Minikins of Yam* (1976), and *The Gods Abide* (1976). They were lost in the crowd.

Misfortunes—some of them perhaps self-imposed—dogged Swann's brief publishing career and provide a leitmotiv for any discussion of his work. Although the form in which his novels were published provides some explanation for their swift disappearance, there are further reasons for their neglect. It is clear, for instance, that Swann was more comfortable with the short story and novelette than he was with full-length fiction, yet the latter part of his career was devoted to novels and to ill-considered expansions of earlier stories. It is also clear, as any sustained reading of his fiction should confirm, that the wide variety of settings and characters in his novels is in a sense misleading, because he is a writer whose range is startlingly limited to certain obsessively reiterated themes: the rite of passage from childhood into maturity; the nature of friendship; the loss of innocence, both on the personal level, with the onset of adulthood, and on the cultural level, with the rise of the classic Mediterranean civilizations. All culminate in a constant interlinking of nostalgia and carpe diem tropes.

At the heart of Swann's work lies a remarkably poignant dream of an unattainable ideal childhood. This ideal colors, and in a sense vitiates, the ostensible themes that permeate the eighteen books. This is particularly evident on any examination of Swann's treatment of the rite of passage into sexual maturity, which provides the motive force of so many of his tales.

Again, a glance at the actual presentation of his books to the market may give some hint as to the pervading tone of his treatment of this material. It is always dangerous for a book to be published with illustrations, because any artist's rendering of a world depicted through language is a kind of straitjacket; and many authors, from Gustave Flaubert on, have strenuously objected to the impoverishment of their fictions through the addition of visual material. It seems that Swann had no such qualms. He seems indeed actively to have approved of the rendering of his imaginative universe by the artist most frequently associated with his work, George Barr, whose covers and other illustrations decorate no fewer than seven of his novels; Swann even purchased three examples of Barr's work and hung them in his bedroom.

Barr specializes in cartoonlike drawings that he overlays with a watercolor wash; the effect is that of a lush, somewhat sickly innocence. Although the figures depicted exhibit the exaggerated sexual characteristics typical of popular fantasy art, they have anything but a knowing air in Barr's work, where the effect is rather that of a prepubescent pretense to adulthood and sexual maturity. In this, Barr realizes with remarkable accuracy an abiding aspect of Swann's own vision.

Thomas Burnett Swann was born on 12 October 1928 in Tampa, Florida. His parents were wealthy, and his mother, who survived him, was a significant support for him throughout his life, especially during the difficult final years. After graduating from Duke University in 1950, Swann served in the navy for four years; in 1955 he took a master of arts degree from the University of Tennessee. He had privately

published his first book of poetry, *Driftwood*, in 1952; in all, he was to publish four small volumes of slender, delicate, sentimental poems. Some appear in his fiction. While earning a doctorate (1960) from the University of Florida, in July 1958 he published his first fiction, "Winged Victory," in *Fantastic Universe*, a commercial magazine of fantasy. This story, with six others, remains uncollected.

From 1960 to 1970, Swann taught intermittently at various southern colleges, publishing in the first year his M.A. thesis on Christina Rossetti. He eventually published four further books of criticism or biography, on the poet H.D., of whose classical focus (for example, *Helen in Egypt*, 1961) he strongly approved; Ernest Dowson; Charles Sorley; and A. A. Milne. He also became engaged to a fellow academic, Ann Peyton. Toward the end of the 1960's he became ill, broke the engagement, resigned from his last post at Florida Atlantic University in Boca Raton, and retired to a family house in Knoxville, Tennessee, where he concentrated on the writing of fiction. In 1972 he contracted cancer. He died on 5 May 1976, in Winter Haven, Florida, at the home of his parents.

It was a productive life and, despite his involvement with both teaching and the world of fantasy fandom, a secluded one. Although it would be impertinent to erect a psychological analysis on these bare data, the external facts of his life certainly present him as turning away from the daylight glare of the modern world and remaining as close as possible to his family roots. This unworldliness may explain some of the vagaries of his publishing career — for instance, the oddness of his relationship with the British editor and agent E. J. Carnell, who did much to promote Swann's early career by publishing him in *Science Fantasy* but who subsequently acted as his literary agent with very little success. Whether or not Carnell agented him efficiently, it was, all the same, peculiarly unworldly of Swann, as an American writer, to have his books marketed from England. After leaving Carnell, he submitted material to Donald A. Wollheim, editor of Ace Books and from 1972 of DAW Books, which was ultimately to publish fourteen of his titles as paperback originals; but by remaining faithful to Wollheim, Swann may have forfeited some opportunities to market his fiction in a more permanent form. It is perhaps the case that he did not much care.

He wrote avidly and with scant concern for the fantasy market in general, where high fantasy adventures set in secondary universes were becoming more and more popular and more and more clamorously violent, perhaps in tune with the times. His fiction is invariably set in the past of this world, and his protagonists are generally children or women, sometimes human, sometimes creatures of myth, but all of them oppressed by patriarchy. When, as with Saul and David in *How Are the Mighty Fallen*, Swann does deal with personages on the world stage, he does so in an effort to rewrite their stories in his own terms. For Swann, male adults are redeemable only when they cast off their patriarchal trappings, put down their swords, abandon life-denying heroism, and become capable of making friends with boys, warmly sexual motherly women, and prehuman figures—dryads, paniscs, centaurs, and so forth—whose enforced departure from the world stage Swann clearly sees as analogous to the loss of innocence of children when they grow up to become the wrong kind of men. As children lose their innocence in becoming patriarchs, so the world itself loses its innocence as the gentle creatures of myth are driven underground.

Robert A. Collins' *Thomas Burnett Swann: A Brief Critical Biography* (1979) contains a "Chronology of Swann's World" put together by Bob Roehm. It is a cycle of loss, containing all of the novels and most of the shorter work. Although there are minor inconsistencies throughout from book to book, the oeuvre amounts to one large series, with a prologue, a central grouping of closely linked novels, and a series of epilogues that read as elegiac parodies of the central material.

The Minikins of Yam, set in the dynastic Egypt of 2269 B.C., serves as a prologue to the whole. Pepy, a child pharaoh, gains wisdom, sexual initiation, and true adulthood in his quest up the Nile to discover the true nature of the blight that has afflicted Egypt. His father has, in world-historical terms, rather prematurely attempted to impose a magic-denying patriarchy on the land, and it is not until young Pepy

confronts and accedes to the Isis principle embodied in the ghost of his mother that the warm green fecundity of the female principle can return to rescue Egypt from drought. For a while, the world will remain in balance.

A thousand years later, in Crete, the balance has begun to tip, and from this point any reference to the haven of a golden age will be to something that, like childhood, has passed; no Swann protagonist will fail to be afflicted, at least occasionally, by moments of acute nostalgia. Swann's novels constitute that version of pastoral which deals with the rape of Arcadia. Trapped in their mountain fastness, the nonhumans of Crete who populate *Cry Silver Bells* (1977), *The Forest of Forever* (1971), and *Day of the Minotaur* (1966) are particularly vulnerable to the sexual aggressions and land-hunger of Cretan humanity. Written in reverse order—a movement into the past entirely typical of Swann's character—this Cretan trilogy compresses the theme of the loss of Arcadia into a somewhat confused narrative of the loss of innocence and freedom of the last minotaurs. Some of the confusion undoubtedly arises from the inverse order of composition and from the fact that *Day of the Minotaur*, serialized as "The Blue Monkeys" in *Science Fantasy* (1964–1965), was Swann's first novel, written before he could have more than glimpsed the full scope of the cycle to which he devoted the rest of his life.

Unsurprisingly, then, *Cry Silver Bells* shows Swann at his weakest in the construction of novel-length stories. Into the nonhuman cultures of Crete—interlinked but separate groups of centaurs, minotaurs, dryads, and the like—he introduces two young Egyptian exiles, who are duly frightened and then entranced by the beauty and gentleness of the folk they meet. (This process of introduction Swann had already gone through once, in *Day of the Minotaur*, with greater freshness and with firmer structural point.) The Egyptians are soon exiled from Arcadia by Chiron, the centaur, the vain ruler of the nonhumans; the threat of their deaths in a Cretan bullring provides a somewhat lame pretext for most of the action of this first book.

In *The Forest of Forever* the main themes of the trilogy are developed through the passage into manhood of young Eunostos, the last minotaur; his doomed affair with a dryad; and the incursion of a harsh male human into his idyllic world. Aecus the Cretan steals the dryad from Eunostos and, after she has borne his children, abducts them and returns with them to the world of men. The dryad kills herself. Eunostos lives on, with the hope of the children's return.

Achaeans invade Crete in *Day of the Minotaur*, and the children are forced to flee into the interior, where they were born. They slowly assimilate the values of Eunostos and his compatriots, though it is now too late for any sustained residence in the gentle world of the nonhumans. With the Achaeans come patriarchy triumphant, technology, life-denying religion, and modern man's relentless lust to dominate. The children are betrayed and captured. Eunostos leads a successful counterattack but knows that the war has been lost. With the children—who turn their back on the terrible new world that is being born—he and those who have survived set sail for the Islands of the Blest. We do not witness their arrival.

In his second trilogy—*Queens Walk in the Dusk*, *Green Phoenix* (1972), and *Lady of the Bees* (1976)—the scene is Carthage and Rome, though the first volume, which retells the legend of Dido and Aeneas, cleverly avoids material dealt with in later volumes. *Green Phoenix* injects a cast of dryads, fauns, and other such creatures into the later story of Aeneas. Mellonia, a young dryad, tied as are all dryads into a symbiotic relationship with her tree, has an affair with the doomed expatriate Trojan and, after his death, manages to negotiate some kind of balance between the nonhumans she has come to rule and the men who will eventually be responsible for the Roman Empire. Like the children to whom Eunostos loses his heart in the Cretan trilogy, her child is a halfling, a creature with one foot in the female and one in the male camp. For Swann, the notion of the halfling is deeply congruous with a vision of the saucy but clement innocence of retained childhood.

In *Lady of the Bees*, Mellonia, now almost five hundred years old, takes as her second lover young Remus, doomed to be murdered by his male adult brother, Romulus. Remus, who is constantly lik-

ened to a woodpecker, has the sylvan grace and love of mothering nature of a true halfling. His death and Mellonia's mark the end of any real truce in the hearts of Romans between the warring patriarchal and matriarchal principles; Romulus' guilt-ridden pledge to found a Rome whose rule of law will "resurrect" Remus seems particularly feeble.

The original story on which this novel is based, "Where Is the Bird of Fire?" (*Science Fantasy*, April 1962), is told from the viewpoint of a short-lived faun whose understanding of the world is limited but who all the same conveys a sense of melancholy in his telling that becomes muffled in the flustered mélange of viewpoints through which the expanded version is recounted. Both versions end with the faun's prose poem of longing and relinquishing, but only in the story does his determination to follow the bird of fire (that is, Remus) effectively set a terminal mood: "Where is the bird of fire? Look up, he burns in the sky, with Saturn and the Golden Age. I will go to find him."

Both *Wolfwinter* (1972) and *The Weirwoods* (*Science Fantasy*, November 1965; book form, 1967) are set in an Italy subsequent to the failure of balance represented by the deaths of Mellonia and Remus, and both forsake the world stage for tales of intimate self-realization. *Wolfwinter* is much the finer work, combining the quiet balanced craft of Swann's earlier work with something of the hectic urgency of his last books, though without their incoherences of narrative and tone and their forced, saccharine rhetoric.

The frame of *Wolfwinter* depicts the protagonist, Erinna, grown old; being a sibyl, she confers some advice upon a young man whose young male friend has been murdered. She tells him to remember the Cretans, who "lived in the grace of the Mother and never feared lamplighting time because she had promised them a final, unquenchable morning" (prologue). She then recounts to him her own life, which forms the body of the novel.

Young and virginal, Erinna is seduced by a faun on the island of Lesbos and, as a consequence, is married off to a man from Sybaris, losing her love, it seems, for fauns survive only a few years, and having to leave her older friend, the poet Sappho. In Sybaris, when her husband has the halfling child exposed to wolves, she escapes civilization; rescues her son, Lysis; sleeps with an Etruscan; and is captured by nonhumans in the forest. There she sets up house with the faun Skimmer, with whom she eventually sleeps, after many adventures with humans and nonhumans; reunion with her first faun lover, who dies of age in her arms; a short visit from Sappho; and a descent into hell, from which she returns intact and blessed by Aphrodite. For the reader the heart of *Wolfwinter* lies in the brief autumnal union between Erinna and Skimmer, about which Swann is, as usual, inexplicit:

> He fell to his knees and placed the flowers in my hair, and I thought, "They are little sunbeams, they glow with their own warmth," though of course the warmth came from Skimmer's hands. I felt his breath in my face, sweet with blackberries. I felt the heat of his body, a mantle against the cold. The body of a Faun is a little forest, a place of terror and splendor and tenderness. The body of Skimmer was a forest without wolves.

(chapter 8)

In its slightly lachrymose intensity and seeming ingenuousness, this passage is entirely typical of Swann's writing at its best: it conveys an elegiac sweetness that almost allows one to dismiss from one's response the sense that the creative energies on view have consistently been displaced from their proper locus. *Wolfwinter*, for instance, using the frail, brief lives allotted to fauns and mortals, claims to deal with the need to somehow seize the day, to live so as to merit the blessings of each day as it passes, and to accept the nature of the world, which too soon closes into death or adulthood, without mourning that necessary outcome. It might be thought, therefore, that the natural bearer of a carpe diem consciousness would be the faun, Skimmer, not the human woman, who, however vividly, is rendered by Swann as viewing Skimmer's life in retrospect. The central drama of the book is thus not the locus of Swann's energies.

This turning away from the heart of the reality that he would embrace seems yet another manifes-

tation of the central feature of Swann's life and art — a movement backward and inward that has as its goal the unsullied quietude of the unawakened child. As the child undertakes the rite of passage into sexual adulthood in so many of Swann's tales, one begins to sense a disruptive imbalance, an unresolved discord, because the rite of passage, which is meant to be read as necessary and positive, is almost always counterpointed with a depiction of the loss of balance in the world as patriarchy triumphs. This discord becomes all the more serious when the reader senses that as Swann's protagonists become sexually mature, they escape his creative control; he loses interest in them, and the text drowns in a sentimental bath of deranged pathos — sweet, distressing, perhaps rather attractive to young readers.

Indeed, all of Swann's novels are in fact juveniles. His true protagonists are male children, and the older women who sometimes substitute as protagonists serve as a complex displacement from the prepubertal male child at the heart of almost all the texts. Although the male child may — in terms inexplicit, chaste, and make-believe, though ostensibly saucy — have sexual congress with a mother figure, the undisplaced focus of his attentions seems generally to be a "friend." Bearlike or elfin, simple or preternaturally wise, this friend will be distinguished from "normal" male adults by the sweetness of his scent, the gentle givingness of his nature, and his ultimate vulnerability. Like Remus, he will very frequently be killed, and the true protagonist of the story — like the faun in "Where Is the Bird of Fire?" — will express the only undisplaced forms of mourning that Swann allows in his doomed universe.

Although it is the thematic climax of Swann's long parade of losses, *The Gods Abide* suffers from the hasty foreshortenings and excesses of his late style. At points genuinely difficult to follow, the novel represents an ingathering of oppressed nonhumans into a final haven made ready for them by the mother goddess, Ashtoreth. The book is notable for its expression of a spirited hostility to Christianity, which Swann clearly sees as life-denying, humorless, partriarchal, and disastrously Manichaean.

After *The Gods Abide*, which is set in the fourth century A.D., the world stage has been swept clear of

Swann's folk, and in *The Tournament of Thorns* (1976), *Will-O-The-Wisp* (*Fantastic Stories*, 1974; book form, 1976), *The Not-World* (1975), and *The Goat Without Horns* (*Magazine of Fantasy and Science Fiction*, 1970; book form, 1971), the flow of elegy narrows into defiant self-parody. *The Tournament of Thorns* embodies, and vitiates the plangent clarity of, Swann's finest single tale, "The Manor of Roses" (*Magazine of Fantasy and Science Fiction*, November 1966). Set in Britain at the time of the Crusades, the tale tells of the discovery by a middle-aged widow that she is a mandrake, a creature of the woods who has taken on the semblance of a human being. As the story closes, she returns to her roots. *Will-O-The Wisp* and *The Not-World* rather unamusingly re-create historical figures — Robert Herrick in the first, Robert and Elizabeth Barrett Browning as well as Thomas Chatterton in the second — and put them through their paces as they encounter vestiges of the old Swann universe, cope, succumb, grow wiser, survive.

Oddest of these parodic texts is *The Goat Without Horns*, in which the essential Swann protagonist is divided into two aspects: the boy-man undergoing his rite of passage, in a character based on the minor poet Charles Sorley; and the undifferentiated unsullied genuine boy, impersonated in this case by a dolphin named Gloomer, who narrates the tale. The setting is a Caribbean island. Watching from the waves, Gloomer falls in love with Charlie, a glowing young orphan in early manhood who arrives to tutor Mrs. Menell's daughter. As usual in Swann's work, Charlie becomes enamored of the mother rather than of his coeval and sleeps with her. The girl's father is a were-shark, however, and the plot thickens. Gloomer is instrumental in saving the day, and at the novel's close Charlie returns to him, jumping gayly into the amniotic sea: "A big wave almost inundated him. I dove under him and he clasped my dorsal fin and we swam for the island and the passage and our own green lagoon" (chapter 12). They have become "friends." The world is well lost.

Because of the flood of displaced emotion that distorts most of his work, Swann's novels are far less attractive to read than to remember. What is read is a dissembling artifice; what is remembered can be the pure affect of elegy, the longing for a prelapsarian frolic in the mothering sea, the seizing of the day. Swann is a weak writer who evokes strong memories. His name may survive.

Selected Bibliography

WORKS OF THOMAS BURNETT SWANN

Books
Day of the Minotaur. New York: Ace, 1966. London: Mayflower Books, 1975.
The Weirwoods. New York: Ace, 1967.
The Dolphin and the Deep. New York: Ace, 1968. (Collection containing "The Dolphin and the Deep," "The Murex," and "The Manor of Roses.")
Moondust. New York: Ace, 1968.
Where Is the Bird of Fire? New York: Ace, 1970. (Collection containing "Where Is the Bird of Fire?" "Vashti," and "Bear.")
The Goat Without Horns. New York: Ballantine, 1971.
The Forest of Forever. New York: Ace, 1971. London: Mayflower Books, 1975.
Green Phoenix. New York: DAW, 1972.
Wolfwinter. New York: Ballantine, 1972.
How Are the Mighty Fallen. New York: DAW, 1974.
The Not-World. New York: DAW, 1975.
The Minikins of Yam. New York: DAW, 1976.
Lady of the Bees. New York: Ace, 1976. (Expansion of "Where Is the Bird of Fire?")
The Tournament of Thorns. New York: Ace, 1976. (Incorporating "The Stalking Trees" and "The Manor of Roses.")
The Gods Abide. New York: DAW, 1976. Godalming, Surrey: L.S.P.T., 1979.
Will-O-The-Wisp. London: Corgi, 1976 (really 1977).
Cry Silver Bells. New York: DAW, 1977. Godalming, Surrey: L.S.P., 1979.
Queens Walk in the Dusk. Forest Park, Ga.: Heritage Press, 1977.

Uncollected stories
"Winged Victory," *Fantastic Universe* (July 1958).
"Viewpoint," *Nebula* (May 1959).
"The Dryad Tree," *Science Fantasy* (August 1960).

"The Painter," *Science Fantasy* (December 1960).

"The Sudden Wings," *Science Fantasy* (October 1962).

CRITICAL, BIOGRAPHICAL, AND BIBLIOGRAPHICAL STUDIES

Collins, Robert A. *Thomas Burnett Swann: A Brief Critical Biography and Annotated Bibliography.* Boca Raton, Fla.: The Thomas Burnett Swann Fund, 1979.

————. "Thomas Burnett Swann: A Retrospective." *Fantasy Newsletter*, 6:3 (March 1983).

————. "Swann on Swann: The Uses of Fantasy." *Fantasy Newsletter*, 6:4 (April 1983).

Page, Gerald W. "Remembering Tom Swann." (An afterword to *Queens Walk in the Dusk* by Swann.)

—JOHN CLUTE

JACK VANCE

1916-

JACK VANCE, RIGHTLY admired for his delicious style, is an author of remarkable range, invention, and achievement. Primarily a writer of science fiction, within that field he has turned his hand to space opera, science fiction bildungsroman, award-winning novellas, and virtually every kind of pulp adventure. For a few years he also wrote detective novels—*The Man in the Cage* (1960) received an Edgar—and psychological shockers, such as *Bad Ronald* (1973). At one point Vance cranked out scripts for Hollywood and the *Captain Video* television series, and on three occasions he ghostwrote Ellery Queen mysteries.

Despite this variety, Vance remains best known for two fantasies: *The Dying Earth* (1950) and *The Eyes of the Overworld* (1966). Along with the more recent *Lyonesse* (1983) and *Cugel's Saga* (1983), these novels make up his claim as one of the masters of modern fantasy.

Not that Vance would make such a claim himself. In a world of author tours, science fiction conventions, talk shows, and interviews, Vance refuses to discuss his personal life, interpret his books, or display his photograph on dust jackets. His job, he feels, is simply to write; the forty or so books are what matter, and they, rather than the man, should hold the reader's attention.

John Holbrook Vance was born on 28 August 1916 in San Francisco, California, the son of a rancher and his wife. As a boy he read widely in fantasy—especially Robert W. Chambers, Edgar

Rice Burroughs, the Oz books, and *Weird Tales* magazine. At the University of California at Berkeley, Vance first majored in engineering and later switched to journalism, but left without a degree in 1942. During World War II he served in the merchant marine. In 1946 he married Norma Ingold and thereafter traveled widely—Mexico, Europe—before settling in Oakland, California, where he now lives in a house he built himself.

Sometime in the late 1930's Vance began to write fiction. An editor of that time once claimed to have turned down some of his "pseudo-Cabellian" sketches; these sound like early versions of stories later gathered in *The Dying Earth*. In 1945 Vance's "The World Thinker," a slambang adventure tale, officially inaugurated his career as a professional genre writer, his avowed ambition being to become "a million-words-a-year man."

Normally such an aim would lead to quantity driving out quality. Oddly, with Vance the two could coexist. Just after composing the marvel-filled, ornate stories of the Dying Earth, he was churning out the one-dimensional exploits of Magnus Ridolph—"Cosmic Hotfoot" (1950), for example—to pay the rent. But there were highlights even in the uneven 1950's, especially "Big Planet," in *Startling* (1952), and an ambitious novel about cloning, *To Live Forever* (1956).

In 1961 the Vances found themselves with a newborn son, John Holbrook Vance II. Perhaps this added responsibility, coupled with skills already sharpened, led to Vance's impressive flowering in the 1960's: the brilliant science fiction mystery "The Moon Moth" (1961); the Hugo-award-winning *The Dragon Masters* (1963); and *The Last Castle* (1967), which received both a Hugo and a Nebula. In one year, 1966, Vance brought out six books, including his second major fantasy set on the Dying Earth, *The Eyes of the Overworld*.

In the 1960's and into the 1970's Vance also began several science fiction series—the five Demon Princes books, the four volumes of the Barsoomian *Planet of Adventure*, the Durdane trilogy, and the Alastor novels. Eminently readable and always well written, these books emphasize adventure and at times resemble more sophisticated versions of the pulp short fiction of the 1950's. Vance seemed more distinctive in his oddball singletons, especially in the somber *Emphyrio* (1969) and the lively *Showboat World* (1975). Whatever their success as novels, all these titles offered something that only Vance could deliver: an addictive style, a voice that, once heard, had to be heard again.

To some, Vance's style smacks of old-fashioned pastiche, fin-de-siècle fine writing laced with an ironic Voltairean sprightliness. Hard-boiled realists always chafe at any hint of artificiality, refusing to recognize that all styles are, in some sense, artificial. Vance's sentences tend to be richly ornamented, courtly, measured, and with a sardonic twist. His syntax is never fancy, but the vocabulary possesses a faintly archaic flavor, the result of a flair for odd (but oddly right) names and a historian's desire for precision. The invariably refined diction suggests a civilized observer, a kind of galactic Saint-Simon, who analyzes in detail the social structures of bizarre cultures while also describing the doings and misadventures of various outsiders, misfits, and rebels.

Here is Vance at his richest:

Such was Mazirian's garden—three terraces growing with strange and wonderful vegetations. Certain plants swam with changing iridescences; others held up blooms pulsing like sea-anemones, purple, green, lilac, pink, yellow. Here grew trees like feather parasols, trees with transparent trunks threaded with red and yellow veins, trees with foliage like metal foil, each leaf a different metal—copper, silver, blue tantalum, bronze, green iridium. Here blooms like bubbles tugged gently upward from glazed green leaves, there a shrub bore a thousand pipe-shaped blossoms, each whistling softly to make music of the ancient Earth, of the ruby-red sunlight, water seeping through black soil, the languid winds.

(*The Dying Earth*, chapter 2)

Such sensuous excess can easily cloy or become mere bejeweled cataloging, rather gaudy but insubstantial. Vance skirts this danger, most of the time, by balancing his easy elegance and leisurely descriptive powers against archetypal adventure plots: the revenge saga, the picaresque journey or marvel-filled odyssey, the murder mystery, the novel of education (his most common form), sword and laser epics. In his best work the style supports the action; in his worst, the wry sentences still charm, but the plot may seem trivial.

Vance's other great gift is an ability to imagine convincingly detailed alien cultures, strange yet logical societies, bizarre practices and customs. (He especially enjoys creating and satirizing religion—and making up games.) Sometimes his inventiveness at "world-building" may even overwhelm a story's unfolding. Readers have complained of a tendency for Vance to take an idea—such as the complex evolutionary pattern of "The Narrow Land"—and describe its implications, while neglecting character, theme, and plot. Like Herodotus, Vance would rather display another wonder than try to bring order to his book.

Again like a historian (or cultural anthropologist), Vance tends to convey a feeling of sympathetic observation rather than of close involvement with his characters. He sets down the actions of a protagonist with a cool detachment; seldom does the reader come to identify with him, worry over his fate, or feel his humanity. Vance strives to entertain, and it is his knack for wonders and surprises that keeps us reading. In this sense he resembles a singer of tales more than a modern novelist. We relish the charm, eccentricity, and "humours" of his subsidiary figures, the detailed variety and intricacy of the worlds they live in, and the grandiose, baroque richness of the storytelling.

The Dying Earth, Vance's first book, remains his most famous and admired, a modern fantasy classic. What makes it so distinctive? First, the setting. *The Dying Earth* consists of six, loosely interlocked stories set on an Earth some twenty million years in the future. However, Vance's future hardly recalls the gleaming chrome of the movie *Things to Come* (screenplay by H. G. Wells); instead, it more closely resembles Robert E. Howard's shadowy Cimmeria — a place of ancient mysteries, crafty sorcerers, and hungry demons. But where Howard's world pulses with energy and vigor, Vance's planet reflects the languor, muted resignation, and carpe diem attitudes of the later Romans. This is science fantasy according to Petronius.

"They were gay," writes Vance, "these people of waning Earth, feverishly merry, for infinite night was close at hand, when the red sun should finally flicker and go black." Most of the people in his six stories tend to be magicians, adepts, witches, replicants, picaros, or seekers after enlightenment. Each of them sallies forth on a quest of some sort and along the way encounters various of his world's temptations and terrors.

In the first story, "Turjan of Miir," Turjan has been trying to create artificial human beings in a chemical vat. Unsuccessful, he decides to consult a greater, nearly godlike mage. To guard himself from harm he turns to his books of spells:

> These were volumes compiled by many wizards of the past, untidy folios collected by the Sage, leather-bound librams setting forth the syllables of a hundred powerful spells, so cogent that Turjan's brain could know but four at a time.... What dangers he might meet he could not know, so he selected three spells of general application: the Excellent Prismatic Spray, Phandaal's Mantle of Stealth, and the Spell of the Slow Hour.

Such a passage, though brief, conveys much of *The Dying Earth*'s flavor. The mildly arcane diction—"librams"—and the leisurely narrative pace encourage a readerly submersion in storytelling, rather than a wish to speed the action along. This is proper to a world of punctilio and caution, one where the careless or headstrong come to painful ends. Unwittingly hinting at civilization's decline, Turjan memorizes the spells of others, not his own—and at best can manage only four. Quietly, then, the reader understands that this is a world obsessed with the past, relying on old knowledge rather than new experiment. That Turjan feels obliged to arm himself with spells also reveals that this is a lawless planet, where strength and craft alone will preserve one from malice. Finally, the three spells themselves demonstrate Vance's flair for names. All are evocative and exotic, the first touched wtih a certain elegant refinement, the second alluding to the greatest of all magicians of the past and thus possessing an associated grandeur, and the last touched with a sweet romanticism.

The languid backdrop of Vance's prose heightens the power of his plots of intrigue, violence, lust, and greed. For instance, in the second tale, "Mazirian the Magician," Mazirian at first seems to be an epicurean decadent, cool, gracious, and sophisticated. Then we learn that he has captured Turjan, has reduced him in size, and now passes the time watching the little man run in a maze pursued by a tiny dragon. (Once, he recalls, "he had dwindled a woman small as his thumb and kept her in a little glass bottle with two buzzing flies.") Mazirian, hoping to exhaust his rival into confessing the secret of artificial life, keeps finding himself distracted by a young woman—who turns out to be T'sain, created by Turjan and hoping to rescue him. At last Mazirian hotly pursues the elusive beauty through waste and forest, where he chances suddenly upon a deodand. Does the man-beast attack him outright? Not at all. "'Ah, Mazirian, you roam the woods far from home,' the black thing's soft voice rose through the glade. The Deodand, Mazirian knew, craved his body for meat." Only in Vance would a monster address its intended victim so obliquely, so formally.

In the next story, "T'sais," we first meet Liane the Wayfarer—hard at work torturing a peasant and his wife for information. The man has been beaten and burned but said nothing. "'Attend,' said Liane.

'I enter the second phase of the question. I reason, I think, I theorize. I say, perhaps the husband does not know where he whom I seek has fled, perhaps the wife alone knows.'" And he prepares, with a lilt in his voice and a spring in his heels, to torture the woman. As it happens, he is interrupted by T'sais, the sister of T'sain, forlornly seeking to heal her mind of a skewed vision that perceives nothing but ugliness and pain.

After being attacked by Liane and nearly raped by three brutish louts, T'sain is saved from a deodand by a melancholy hooded young man. Etarr masks his face because a woman he once loved—innocent and beautiful in appearance—turned out to be a monster of depravity: nymphomaniacal, devil-worshiping, sexually obsessed with demons. After enslaving the young man with a magic rune, Javanne made him witness her orgies and gleefully replaced his face with that of the ogre who disgusted him most. Thus T'sais, fair on the outside but filled with hatred within, encounters a man ugly on the outside but fair of heart and spirit. Eventually, the pair are both restored to their just condition—as is, less happily, Javanne.

Besides the quest motif, the first three stories interlock, in the way of a miniaturist Balzac, by taking up a minor character from one tale and making him the protagonist of the next. The fourth story, "Liane the Wayfarer," also completes a pattern among the main characters, who alternate between good and bad, between love and lust.

"Liane the Wayfarer" is the most Dunsany-like of the tales in *The Dying Earth*, reminiscent of such minor classics as "The Hoard of the Gibbelins." Vain, amoral, and lecherous, Liane hopes to secure the delicious favors of the golden witch Lith by performing a trivial mission: the recovery of a tapestry fragment from Chun the Unavoidable. Liane agrees to do this partly because he possesses a kind of dimensional hole into which he can disappear at will. Eventually, he comes to the Land of the Falling Wall, surveys the ominous temple carefully, seizes the tapestry—and discovers Chun hidden behind it. The monster, wearing a robe made of eyeballs, pursues Liane, who jumps nimbly into his quiet, invisible refuge. He is safe there until he hears a voice at his elbow say, "I am Chun the Unavoidable."

In the next story, "Uhlan Dhor," the hero undergoes swashbuckling Conan-like adventures, as he uncovers the secrets of the bizarre, long-lost world of Ampridatvir. The young man's name may seem odd, but it provides a good example of Vance's flair for, and care in, naming. The full name possesses a vaguely exotic Near Eastern flavor: *Dhor* is reminiscent of *d'or*, meaning "of gold," which is appropriate to a nephew of Prince Khandive the Golden; and an uhlan is a soldier used primarily for scouting and skirmishing—which is just what the hero does. Similarly, Cugel the Clever possesses a sobriquet that reveals the source of his name: *Cugel* represents a kind of aural twisting of the German word *klug*, meaning clever.

The last and longest story of *The Dying Earth*, "Guyal of Sfere," completes the overarching patterns of the book: the movement from magicians to human beings, from despair and lethargy toward hope and vigor, from rote learning to personal investigation, from dying to life.

When young Guyal of Sfere asks questions, he is given the traditional answers. Most unsatisfying. The young man decides he must seek out the curator of the Museum of Man, where he will find the knowledge his heart aches after. Following several adventures, including the most haunting of the book—a rendezvous with a beautiful girl who dances to the tunes of death—Guyal encounters the Saponids, who dwell near an ancient wasteland: "Death lingers here, and no creature may venture across the place without succumbing to a most malicious magic which raises virulence and angry sores." Earlier, Vance's people alluded to the near and far past, but only in his final pages does a half-savage mankind remember the radiation poison of the ancients, that potent theme of the classic Stephen Vincent Benét story "By the Waters of Babylon" and of many books since.

Through trickery, Guyal and a village beauty named Shierl find themselves a sacrificial offering, marched into the Museum of Man, where they will presumably be devoured by some evil monster. There is indeed a demon within—a kind of monster of the collective unconscious—which the young couple defeat with the help of the ancient dying curator Kerlin. (The last avatar of Merlin?) To him

Guyal voices his perplexities: "Rather than master and overpower our world, our highest aim is to cheat it through sorcery. . . . I am dissatisfied with the mindless accomplishments of the magicians, who have all their lore by rote." In the end, still eager for knowledge, Guyal stands outside the Museum of Man and, turning away from the dying Earth, looks to the stars. Vance ends with a question: "What shall we do?"

The book's conclusion ambiguously suggests that Guyal and Shierl represent a new hope for the race, a kind of Adam and Eve for the stars. The life that Turjan tried to re-create artificially now has a chance to begin again in earnest, as the spirit of science instead of sorcery broods over the still mind of Guyal of Sfere.

Vance may have derived his vision of a dying earth from a paragraph in H. G. Wells's *The Time Machine* (1895) where the Traveler describes the stillness and melancholy of an empty seashore beneath a red sun. Or he may have meditated on John Campbell's bittersweet "Twilight." Or perhaps there was something in the zeitgeist, for at least two nearly contemporary novels about a dying Mars recall *The Dying Earth*: Leigh Brackett's *Sword of Rhiannon* (1953) and Ray Bradbury's elegiac *The Martian Chronicles* (1950). But, for style, subject matter, and treatment, Clark Ashton Smith must be counted Vance's main influence and precursor.

Indeed, all of *The Dying Earth* might have been generated from a single paragraph of Smith's: "On Zothique, the last continent of Earth, the sun no longer shone with the whiteness of its prime, but was dim and tarnished as if with a vapor of blood. . . . Many were the necromancers and magicians of Zothique, and the infamy and marvel of their doings were legended everywhere in the latter days" ("The Dark Eidolon," 1934). But as Don Herron has pointed out (in an essay comparing the two writers), what Smith does in earnest, Vance does ironically. And that makes all the difference.

Nowhere can Vance's irony be seen to better effect than in *The Eyes of the Overworld* and its sequel, *Cugel's Saga*. Set in the same melancholy time of Vance's first book, these two "novels" — really the loosely connected adventures of Cugel — prefer elegant wit to elegy, delight to despair; their tone is that of lusty fabliaux, suavely retold by Jean de La Fontaine. They are tall tales of the future:

> Cugel was a man of many capabilities, with a disposition at once flexible and pertinacious. He was long of leg, deft of hand, light of finger, soft of tongue. His hair was the blackest of black fur, coving sharply back over his eyebrows. His darting eye, long inquisitive nose and droll mouth gave his somewhat lean and bony face an expression of vivacity, candor and affability. He had known many vicissitudes, gaining therefrom a suppleness, a fine discretion, a mastery of both bravado and stealth.
>
> (*The Eyes of the Overworld*, chapter 1)

Such a sleek con man — part Jim Rockford, part Wiley Coyote — naturally requires suitable adventures to prove his address, and these two novels present them aplenty when our intrepid ne'er-do-well manages to offend Iucounnu the Laughing Magician of Almery. To forestall the Spell of Forlorn Encystment — encapsulation in a constricted pod some forty-five miles beneath the earth — Cugel must steal a certain magic cusp, then journey across his treacherous planet and deliver this ransom to Iucounnu. In *The Eyes of the Overworld* he miraculously succeeds, but at the last moment outwits himself and so is thrust back to where he began his odyssey, alone on Shanglestone Strand on the far side of the Ocean of Sighs. *Cugel's Saga* opens at this point with Cugel once again on the long trek back toward Almery, this time by a different route, but one no less dangerous and dire. Fortunately, he early on acquires a new talisman with remarkable qualities — a scale from an energy creature of another dimension — with which he hopes to tempt and defeat Iucounnu.

Cugel's behavior reveals him to be in the mold of Liane the Wayfarer (though his adventures recall Guyal of Sfere's). Indeed, Cugel may be associated with the amoral antiheroes of the 1960's — J. P. Donleavy's Ginger Man, Michael Moorcock's Jerry Cornelius, Clint Eastwood's Man with No Name. What charms about Cugel is that he is always willing to abandon a beautiful maiden — to death or the fate worse than — to save his own skin. Of course, he will then justify the whole business, with a bit of logic-chopping, as all for the best. This carefree amoralism, enhanced by a velvety diction that John Gielgud might envy, generates immense readerly delight, as does the utterly artificial pattern of Cugel's escapades. At the beginning of each chapter Cugel trudges along, broke, hungry, dirty, and tired. Approaching a village or private manse, he observes there some bizarre custom practiced by the locals. Soon he is invited to join their group and usually does so, hoping to swindle a treasure or purloin a purse. Repeatedly, however, he finds himself tricked into some dangerous or odious enterprise, which he performs with a false gusto until he can initiate countermeasures. These usually prove successful — at first — and he wins the gold or the girl. But invariably at the last moment, due to some trivial oversight, Cugel loses one or the other (or both), thus finding himself again penniless and on the run, albeit a little closer to Almery.

As Cugel makes his way back home, he suffers the hardships of a Ulysses, performs the labors of a Hercules: in *The Eyes of the Overworld* he outwits deodands, discovers a magic bracelet, unleashes the dreaded Magnatz, joins a doomed pilgrimage, accidentally devours the Totality of the Universe, travels back in time, is captured by rat-beings. In *Cugel's Saga* he works a slime pond for treasure, learns the worminger's craft, guards the seventeen virgins (to their general pleasure), encounters a culture where people live on stone columns, flies through the air on a charmed boat, briefly explores another universe, and finally confronts his old enemy Iucounnu. Despite constant reverses in both books, this blustery hero persists in regarding himself as diabolically cunning, able to adapt to any vicissitude:

"The folk are peculiar in many ways," said Erwig. "They preen themselves upon the gentility of their habits, yet they refuse to whitewash their hair, and they are slack in their religious observances. For instance, they make obeisance to Divine Wiulio with the right hand, not on the buttock, but on the abdomen, which we here consider a slipshod practice. What are your own views?"

"The rite should be conducted as you describe," said Cugel. "No other method carries weight."

("The Bagful of Dreams")

As *The Dying Earth* most recalls Clark Ashton Smith, so the two collections of Cugel tales echo James Branch Cabell and the club stories of Lord Dunsany's Mr. Joseph Jorkens. Of the pair *Eyes* is the richer in texture and invention; *Cugel's Saga* is mellower, more loosely written, marred by several weak stories ("The Blue Inn," for example). Still, most people — enchanted by unexpected turns of phrase or event — will hug themselves with pleasure as they read.

After elegy and irony, romance. In *Lyonesse* Vance blends Celtic folktale, Arthurian legend, and children's fairy tale. Like Atlantis, the ancient island realm of Lyonesse once flourished somewhere in the Atlantic off the coast of France (and was the legendary birthplace of Tristan). Although Vance's tale verges on the tragic, it still possesses a springlike buoyancy; this world is young and strong and bursting with life. Principally, the novel recounts the political manipulations of King Casmir of Lyonesse to become the king of all the Elder Isles. To this end he is willing to sacrifice everything — including his daughter, whose childhood and youth are leisurely chronicled in the novel's first half. In its second half, the loosely woven book tightens into a tale of doomed love and thwarted ambition, and includes sorcerers, trolls, a bisexual villain, a lustful priest, a changeling, a magic sword and talking mirror, and two heroes: a son brought up by the fairies and a father who escapes from an oubliette to become a king. Like all good fairy tales, the book proposes many riddles and answers only a few (leaving the remainder for later volumes in what promises to be a series). As King Casmir says, in a closing understatement, "There is mystery here."

What is significant rather than mysterious is that Vance elaborates a much more complex narrative than usual, with complicated, emotionally engaging characters. His more ambitious science fiction — such as *Emphyrio* (1969), with its loving portrait of a father and son — obviously shaped and nurtured this romantic fantasy, which achieves breadth in depicting every class of a society and depth in its portrayal of a half-dozen major figures. Perhaps *Lyonesse* is less original than *The Dying Earth*—many writers, after all, have fallen sway to the romance of the Middle Ages—but it reads as a work of considerable meditation, of leisurely invention. If it can be sustained, the series should prove another triumph for Vance, worthy of a place next to T. H. White's *The Once and Future King*.

A writer as talented as Jack Vance has never lacked for admirers, though he has, regrettably, never achieved mass popularity. Frank Herbert, Poul Anderson, Robert Silverberg, and other authors of science fiction and fantasy have lavishly praised his work. Barry N. Malzberg called him "one of the ten most important writers in the history of the field." Micheal Shea, winner of the 1983 World Fantasy Award for the Cugelian *Nifft the Lean*, began his career with a homage to those same Cugel stories: *A Quest for Simbilis*. And in an essay on the origins of his own somber masterpiece of the far future, *The Book of the New Sun* (1980–1983), Gene Wolfe confessed that at one time *The Dying Earth* was for him the finest book in the world. Many fantasy readers would agree with that enthusiastic statement—except, of course, those who prefer *The Eyes of the Overworld*.

Selected Bibliography

WORKS OF JACK VANCE

The Dying Earth. New York: Hillman, 1950. London: Mayflower, 1972. (The first two stories are reversed in the Hillman edition. The Underwood-Miller [1976] edition is preferable.)

The Eyes of the Overworld. New York: Ace, 1966. London: Mayflower, 1972.

"Morreion." In *Flashing Swords No. 1*, edited by Lin Carter. Garden City, N.Y.: Doubleday, 1973. (Set in the Dying Earth universe, this tale of a dozen rival sorcerers on a bizarre quest begins well, but peters out. Somewhat revised, it forms the last section of *Rhialto the Marvellous*, a further set of Dying Earth stories. See below.)

Green Magic: The Fantasy Realms of Jack Vance. San Francisco and Columbia, Pa.: Underwood-Miller, 1979. (Nine stories, including "Green Magic," "The Miracle Workers," "The Moon Moth," and "The Narrow Land.")

Cugel's Saga. San Francisco and Columbia, Pa.: Underwood-Miller, 1983. Trade edition, New York: Pocket Books, 1983.

Lyonesse. San Francisco and Columbia, Pa.: Underwood-Miller, 1983. Trade edition, New York: Berkley, 1983.

Rhialto the Marvellous. San Francisco and Columbia, Pa.: Underwood-Miller, 1984. (Traces the rivalries and misadventures of a loose fellowship of magicians living in the twenty-first century. It comprises three sections: "The Murthe," "Fader's Waft," and Morreion.")

CRITICAL AND BIOGRAPHICAL STUDIES

Close, Peter. "An Interview with Jack Vance." *Science Fiction Review*, 23 (November 1977).

Dirda, Michael. "A Galactic Night's Entertainment." *Washington Post Book World*, 26 April 1981. (A general appreciation of Vance. Some of this article has been drawn from it and from a review of *Cugel's Saga* in the *Washington Post*, 13 December 1983.)

Edwards, Malcolm. "Jack Vance." In *Science Fiction Writers*, edited by E. F Bleiler. New York: Scribner, 1982.

Levack, Daniel J. H., and Underwood, Tim. *Fantasms: A Bibliography of the Literature of Jack Vance.* San Francisco and Columbia, Pa.: Underwood-Miller, 1978. (Essential. First printings, foreign appearances, later printings, books written under pseudonyms, and—most important—the later definitive cloth editions, on acid-free paper, from Underwood-Miller.)

Platt, Charles. "Jack Vance." In *Dream Makers II*. New York: Berkley, 1983, 159. (A portrait of the artist as a crotchety eccentric.)

Underwood, Tim. "A Talk with Jack Vance." Vancouver, British Columbia: Vancouver Science Fiction Convention Program Book, 1979, 15.

———, and Miller, Chuck, eds. *Jack Vance.* New York: Taplinger, 1980. (An ideal introduction. Eight essays, by various authors, including Robert Silverberg, Don Herron, and Richard Tiedman, with his pioneering "Jack Vance: Science Fiction Stylist.")

—MICHAEL DIRDA

ROGER ZELAZNY

1937–

LOOKING BACK, IT seems wholly appropriate that Roger Zelazny's first professional sales should have been to *Amazing* and *Fantastic*, for from the beginning of his career he has enjoyed mixing genres. As he has admitted, two of his most popular "sf" stories, "A Rose for Ecclesiastes" (1963) and "The Doors of His Face, the Lamps of His Mouth" (1965), were fantasy by the time he wrote them, since he deliberately set them on versions of Mars and Venus that science had invalidated. What the "sf" stands for in these stories is the subgenre "science fantasy," texts of crossover. Yet, as Samuel R. Delany has pointed out, their intensive symbolism is perfectly suited to science fiction; and though they are set on utterly unreal worlds, the stories also can be considered science fiction.

The problem is to define fantasy as opposed to science fiction. Some critics feel they can and do so in a way that denigrates fantasy; Delany's concept of "subjunctivity" is more helpful: fantasy events "could not have happened," while science fiction events "have not happened." In these terms, many of Zelazny's fictions are fantasies that employ science fictional discourse. And sometimes, as in *Jack of Shadows* and the recent Changeling series, he takes great pleasure in forcing a confrontation between science/technology and magic within a single text.

But in fact he turned quite early to writing fictions that were purely fantastic, if sometimes fabular

as well. In all these cases, one feels Zelazny's desire to erase the boundaries that only critics perhaps have erected between categories. The kind of openness to possibility that such boundary-blurring implies is consistent with the thematic tenor of his major works, where his heroes, as Joe Sanders suggests in his Introduction to *Roger Zelazny: A Primary and Secondary Bibliography* (1980), "fight to make the world safe for uncertainty."

Born into a family of Polish origin on 13 May 1937, Zelazny grew up in Euclid, Ohio. He earned a B.A. at Western Reserve University in 1959 and an M.A. in English at Columbia University in 1962. He wrote his M.A. thesis on Jacobean tragedy, and the grandiose gestures of its heroes and villains often turn up in his fiction. He worked for the U.S. Social Security Administration in Cleveland and then in Baltimore, while writing part-time, until 1969, when he quit to become a full-time free-lance writer. In 1975, he and his family moved to New Mexico, where he now lives and writes.

Two of Zelazny's major obsessions fit equally well into fantasy and science fiction: mythology and immortality. From one point of view, most ancient myths are now no more than cultural fantasies. Still, the figures of such myths can focus the resonance effect that Zelazny seeks in his various allusions, both literary and mythic. In science fiction, Zelazny has found ways to grant his protagonists immortality through technology; in fantasy, their immortality can simply be a given. As Delany points out in "Faust and Archimedes" (1969):

> Zelazny's basic premise about immortality is quietly revolutionary. The classical supposition . . . is that given all eternity to live, life becomes gray, meaningless, and one must be crushed by the ennui of experience upon experience, repetition upon repetition. Implicit in Zelazny's treatment is the opposite premise: Given all eternity to live, each experience becomes a jewel in the jewel-clutter of life; each moment becomes fascinating because there is so much more to relate it to; each event will take on new harmonies as it is struck by the overtones of history and like experiences before.
>
> (*The Jewel-Hinged Jaw*)

What counts is not how Zelazny's protagonists become immortal but that they are; and what counts most is what they do with their immortality, for they can use it well or badly; how they do so reveals their true personalities.

If his protagonists are associated with mythic figures, the terms of their immortality contradict the stasis signified by myth. As Sanders suggests, Zelazny uses mythic allusions to give his stories a resonance they would otherwise not have, but he does not cling to myth as a stay against change. Rather, "Zelazny boldly shatters myth and throws away many vital parts; rather than holding to a fixed sense of character and morality, his stories rejoice in the invigorating, mind-straining process of self-discovery and moral growth that myth can stimulate" (Introduction). Since the gods of the various mythologies deployed by Zelazny in his fictions represent unchanging attributes, a character who unthinkingly plays the role of a god also achieves stasis, which is a kind of imaginative death. But Zelazny is a Heraclitean writer: his characters play the roles of gods in order to entertain the possibility that they might eventually grow and change enough to transcend such roles. Zelazny's heroes, especially in his fantasies, tend to be questers, if often unconscious ones. Their quests take them through their roles, not to find out who they are in static perfection, but to discover the possible person they can continue becoming, one who recognizes and accepts change as not only necessary but also welcome.

The function of immortality, or very long life, in Zelazny's fantasies of potential growth, then, is that it provides the time for his characters to mature to the point where they recognize the value of change and growth. Although he works within the parameters of pulp adventure fiction, Zelazny seeks to renew and deepen that vital popular form by applying to it the techniques and stylistic innovations of so-called high literature.

Though full of energy, adventure fiction is often flawed by its adolescent refusal of psychological complexity. Zelazny's protagonists—Corwin of Amber, for example—often begin as typical tough-guy heroes; but through the fictional fact of their immortality, they gain the potential to take the necessary steps beyond the adventure story paradigm. Given "world enough and time," even the most shallow and self-regarding of his heroes will be "struck by the overtones of history," both personal and social, and will make a beginning toward adult individuation. Zelazny's basic subject, says Sanders, is "growth of the character . . . from a particular personality at the beginning of a story into a fuller one at the end, and a recognition that it, too, will evolve into another personality, for it is simply one state in an unending process of growth" (Introduction). Those who fail to change and grow—and Brand of Amber is a tragic and dangerous example—are doomed in terms of both the old adventure story paradigm (where they become simple villains) and Zelazny's extension of it (where they fall into moral and imaginative stasis and are finally left behind, arrested in both text and memory in a typical stance).

Zelazny's first clearly supernatural stories are the four tales of Dilvish, the Damned, published between 1964 and 1967. Later stories did not appear until the late 1970's and early 1980's, and the collection *Dilvish, the Damned* was published in 1982, one year after the Dilvish novel *The Changing Land*. Dilvish is an eccentric example of the ageless hero, for he is of elvish blood; but more important, he has spent two centuries in hell. As the second tale, "Thelinde's Song," informs us, he had won great renown as Dilvish, the Deliverer, in defense of his city. But he dares to interfere with the great black sorcerer Jelerak, who attempts an evil sacrifice of a young virgin. Jelerak turns Dilvish to stone and sends his soul to hell, but somehow Dilvish escapes in the company of Black, a demon who accompanies him in the guise of a metal horse. Dilvish's next acts are once again to defend the cities of his realm. Though all his friends are long dead, he fights for their descendants.

But his basic motivation is established in "Thelinde's Song" when Thelinde's mother, who has been narrating Dilvish's history in the high style, remarks that Jelerak, though very strong, is "not without his problems." In a delightfully sardonic understatement, she tells her daughter why: "Because Dilvish is come alive once more, and I believe he is somewhat angry." Revenge is what he is after, but he can be distracted, and this quality make Dilvish one of Zelazny's more charming heroes. Indeed, though Zelazny does not go into detail about what Dilvish might have learned during his two centuries of suffering in hell, he hints that Dilvish lived a socially responsible life before his act on behalf of another resulted in his being cursed. And in the first four stories Dilvish continues to act for others rather than simply setting out monomaniacally to seek his revenge. Later stories in the Dilvish canon suggest that his time in hell has led him toward the single role of revenger, but he remains capable of setting aside the role to help others and of living on, once the reason for revenge is removed. In this adaptability, he is a true Zelazny hero.

Jack of Shadows (1971) is notable for its cunning juxtaposition of science and magic and for its exploration of its eponymous protagonist's simultaneous longtime refusal to change and his slowly growing recognition that change is necessary, both for his own sake and for his world's. Jack is the cause of change, but he does not seem to change himself, and yet perhaps he does; the novel refuses to offer sure answers on this point. A bare-bones fable in form, it is a good example of what Delany calls reductive, as opposed to intensive, symbolism, yet it does not offer the clear oppositions that fables usually do. Jack is not likeable, but he can be charming, and he is the one active character in the narrative. The world of this book is static at all levels, including that of personality. Characters are stuck in their roles; even Jack must play out his revenge far beyond its successful completion, until an accident forces him to act outside his role. On the nightside, magic works and particular powers wield it within their realms. On the dayside, science works and technicians are in control. Each side views the powers of the other as superstition. Jack, a creature of the twilight whose power is manifested wherever shadows gather, is the only one who can live in both worlds, though he sees himself as a Lord of Power on the darkside and has many lives, as all darksiders do.

Trapped and killed in what later appears to have been a trick of his enemy, the Lord of Bats, Jack escapes from the Dung Pits of Glyve, where all darksiders awake when they are killed. But the Lord of Bats humiliates him further, imprisoning him in a jewel and marrying Evene, the lady Jack intended to marry, who tells Jack she loves her husband as she could never love him. The archetypal loner out for revenge, Jack has but one friend, the fallen angel Morningstar, who awaits the morning that never comes. On his way to the dayside, where he will seek the information he needs to conquer the nightside, Jack passes Morningstar, who tells him he will succeed but may not desire such success when he has it. In a sentence that almost sums up Zelazny's creed, Morningstar says, "Consciousness tends to transform one."

Jack's life as a university lecturer on darkside anthropology is full of comic twists that question the static values of both camps while pointing to the possibility that Jack's consciousness is growing. Eventually he returns to conquer his enemies, having worked out on a computer "The Key That Was Lost." In defeating them, however, Jack ignores consciousness. In order to have Evene, he must put a spell on her, for he cannot steal love. With all his power, he finds he is not satisfied. In another complexly comic move, an old woman brings him his soul in an egg, and though he refuses it he must put up with its complaints. Eventually, when some lesser Lords refuse to maintain the shield that protects the atmosphere of the darkside, Jack seeks out Morningstar and then travels to the center of the earth to destroy the mechanism by which the world is prevented from turning. Although his world and his power are destroyed, he ensures that change will come and will remain in the world. He also grows to accept his soul and to recognize some of the evil he has done. By maintaining a curiously distanced tone throughout, Zelazny simultaneously precludes empathy for Jack and compels intellectual admiration for the cool workings of his narrative. If a bit too thin in texture, *Jack of Shadows* has its own dark, fabular power.

It is not surprising that Zelazny now copyrights his work under The Amber Corporation, for the Amber series is one of his most popular and important works, despite a number of flaws that can be blamed on its eight-year publishing history and on Zelazny's sometimes sloppy habits of composition. Though published in five separate volumes — *Nine Princes in Amber* (1970), *The Guns of Avalon* (1972), *Sign of the Unicorn* (1975), *The Hand of Oberon* (1976), and *The Courts of Chaos* (1978) — it is essentially one extremely complicated story. Even these titles supply many clues to the way the series works, however, as the many witty allusions that they contain point to the formal qualities and intellectual structure of this apparent sword-and-sorcery adventure. To try to outline the many twists and turns of the plot is to essay the impossible; its confusion "is a deliberate mechanism on Zelazny's part," says Sanders, "to show that the characters feel" as confused as the readers. The story begins when the narrator, Corwin of Amber, wakes out of a centuries-long amnesia to realize that he is a Prince of Amber, the world from which all other worlds take their form. Amber is the only true reality, all other worlds being but its Shadows, and the children of Amber can pass among Shadow and control it. But, as the plots and counterplots of his family slowly take Corwin further toward a possible truth, we discover that there is an even more "real" Amber, whose existence is tied up with the Courts of Chaos, where utter disorder rules.

Corwin's siblings at first appear, like him, to be utterly adolescent in their power struggles; they form and reform cabals, they deviously plot against each other; and they have been doing this for eons. Once he knows who he is, Corwin joins in and be-

gins to fight to win the throne apparently vacated by their father, Oberon. But during his centuries of life on our Shadow earth, Corwin has changed; he is no longer as bloodthirsty or precipitous as he used to be. He has, in fact, begun to grow up (and one of the great comic moves of this series is its suggestion that immortals will have an even more drawn-out adolescence than do most people). But, as he slowly discovers, some of his brothers and sisters have begun to grow up too. Because they have changed, their behavior is no longer wholly predictable; the uncertainty principle now reigns in Amber.

A darker uncertainty attaches to the Shadow (connected directly to Chaos) that has invaded Amber. Against such an attack on their world, all the family joins in battle, or so it seems. But seeming and being are difficult to tell apart here; and with each new addition to the series, more wild cards enter the game. This metaphor is, in fact, exact, since a tarotlike pack of cards combines with the Pattern of Amber to give the family members their mental powers over Shadow. As the story proceeds, we learn that Chaos existed before Amber and that Dworkin, Oberon's father, was a rebel Lord of Chaos who created the first Pattern within it. Amber represents Order, then, in constant tension with Chaos; but in Zelazny's grand metaphor both have their place.

The Amber books are a metaphoric construction of the eternal battle and necessary conjunction of Order and Chaos; the structure of the tales is their thematic core. Although they appear to be high-class sword-and-sorcery books, the signs of the subgenre that they display are essentially empty, for the novels are about something else. Despite sword fights and battles, the actual relation of action to talk is definitely weighted toward talk. Talk is the real narrative, the convoluted, devious, interlacing tales that every character tells, either to Corwin or to others, who then often include them in their own stories. Corwin himself tells his tale to a specific listener outside the Courts of Chaos; though it is only in the final volume that we discover this listener is his son, Merlin, who was raised in Chaos by his mother and has never seen Amber. The Amber series is a marvelously complicated palimpsest of narratives.

Order in these books is aligned with language. All

the Amberites are good storytellers with an awareness of the necessary ambiguity of all tales, though some misuse the art. (Brand is the most devious storyteller, yet he turns out to be the most static character, unable to change himself however much he may change his story—the uncertainty principle applies especially to acts of language.) The mazelike Pattern by which they all achieve power and full life is the pattern of story itself, best exemplified for them by the Amber saga, in which they live as only fictions can.

Toward the end of the series, Dara, Corwin's lover from Chaos and mother of his son, refuses to listen to Corwin's side of the story, telling him that she "will settle for the one" side of the story she already has. Her failure to understand how story works contrasts with Corwin's (and with her son's) growing determination to search through the whole exasperating complex of tales until he has made some sense of the many levels of text or memory that he is discovering. In an act of moral understanding, he recognizes that to accept only one version is to refuse the multiple reality that all the stories and their tellers participate in.

Of course, there is much more to the Amber saga than its self-reflexivity. Corwin begins as a tough smart guy out to revenge himself on Eric and some of his other siblings. But his ongoing narration reveals the slow maturation of an ethical being and an adventurous soul who will continue to grow and change after this story ends. Random, the younger brother who sought out Corwin on earth because his power in the family was negligible, undergoes a similar transformation as Corwin watches him throughout. Other characters also have their fascination: though they are types and archetypes, the argument of the series is that they can also be human.

Zelazny's beloved allusions are especially entertaining here; since Amber is the model for all the other worlds, all the myths and fictions to which the names allude are, in terms of this fiction, mere copies of the originals that Zelazny has created. This is a delightfully Borgesian method to further confuse fiction and reality. Zelazny has never been a fantasist of landscape and history, such as J. R. R. Tolkien and his followers. The Amber books allow him to indulge his interest in the evanescence of place. Cor-

win remembers worlds that no longer exist, though other versions, like Oberon's Avalon, may. What is beautiful is what can be (and often is) lost, to be found in memory—that is, in fiction—only. Even the structural flaws and lapses of authorial memory can be argued to reflect Zelazny's feeling that nothing should be or can be perfect, since perfection is stasis is death. All in all, the Amber saga is Zelazny's major achievement in fantasy and a fine, often moving, exploratory fiction.

After completing the Amber series, Zelazny returned to the figure of Dilvish, further deepening his character even as he playfully works out his fate. In both the Dilvish tales and the Changeling books, Zelazny seems content merely to entertain: there is little of the kind of moral exploration that is embedded in the very structure of the Amber narrative. Nevertheless, as I previously remarked, Dilvish remains a charming hero because he can be diverted from his quest for revenge. Although continuing to seek out Jelerak, he always turns aside to help others, making friends in the oddest places as a result. As he says, when Black warns him once again not to heed a probably spurious call for help, "Damned if you do, damned if you don't"; he chooses to be damned for doing.

Zelazny is at his best in stories like "The Places of Aache" (1979) and "Garden of Blood" (1979), where an elegiac tone and a true moral imperative deepen the texture of sheer adventure. The novelette "Tower of Ice" (1981) is the central story in *Dilvish, the Damned*, foreshadowing what will happen in the novel. Dilvish is not even the main focus of the story: the tower is one of Jelerak's holds, but an apprentice now holds it against him. When Dilvish gets there, all he can do is help the apprentice's sister escape while the two powers duel and destroy the tower. In *The Changing Land* Dilvish also finally reaches his goal of confronting Jelerak only to have the wizard snatched away by the punishing gods; he gets justice but not revenge, and he is able to live with that.

The pleasures of the novel lie not so much in following Dilvish as he tracks Jelerak down as in watching the cast of secondary characters play out elaborate and duplicitous games of hide-and-seek in Castle Timeless, which is revealed to be *The House on the Borderland* of William Hope Hodgson, to whom the novel is dedicated and who appears in a minor role. Zelazny obviously enjoys creating a sort of cinematic collage of fantasy motifs and character types—an elf maiden; the resurrected Queen Semirama, who once loved Dilvish's elf ancestor; a college of wizards; various demons, including Black, one of the most interesting characters in the Dilvish cycle; and a lesser god slowly going mad. This comic-opera horror story is great fun—and perhaps something more.

Changeling (1980) and *Madwand* (1981), the first two books of a series, are also good light entertainment. Returning to his early playful juxtapositions of science fiction and fantasy, Zelazny creates a world where magic works and technology is outlawed. Pol Detson is removed to a technological world when his father, a black wizard, is defeated and killed. The child for whom he is exchanged grows up to build things and eventually discovers the ruins of an ancient technology that he revives. In the face of such a threat to the ways of his world, the magician who took Pol away sends him back. Pol discovers his powers and eventually overcomes the technocrat. He also finds out about his father's death and considers revenge, but he grows beyond that. His ability to consider possibilities and learn marks him as a true Zelazny hero. In the second novel, Pol endeavors to learn how to use his powers and becomes involved in some ancient conflicts among wizards. A "madwand," he has great natural ability but little training; still, with a little help from mostly newfound friends, he defeats his enemies, finds an older brother, and begins to lay claim to his rightful place in his world. Later books will undoubtedly take him further in this quest.

Although Zelazny creates some marvelous set pieces, the writing in this series is at times perfunctory. Once again the secondary characters are often more interesting than the protagonist, especially the thief who befriends a wizard, Mouseglove, and the demon who doesn't yet know he is "The Curse of Rondeval," who is also the sometime narrative voice of the second volume. Mouseglove is almost a second protagonist, and he is fascinating because he chooses to deal with people who possess fantastic

powers while he has only intelligence; if Zelazny continues to explore the personalities of those who must interact with power rather than wield it, his future fictions could take some intriguing new directions.

Meanwhile, with his command of a wide range of idioms; his ability to create intense symbolic tableaux; his playful orchestration of allusions from all levels of myth, literature, and popular entertainment; and his continuing exploration of the possibilities that an open universe holds for individuals willing to grow into it, Zelazny continues to provide entertainments of great verve and energy. Moreover, as "The Last Defender of Camelot" (1979), with its wisely comic presentation of Lancelot du Lac in the twentieth century, demonstrates, he can on occasion unite all the aspects of his talent to create a work of elegiac grace. For this reason, Zelazny remains one of our best popular writers.

Selected Bibliography

WORKS OF ROGER ZELAZNY

Nine Princes in Amber. Garden City, N.Y.: Doubleday, 1970. London: Faber and Faber, 1972.

The Doors of His Face, The Lamps of His Mouth, and Other Stories. Garden City, N.Y.: Doubleday, 1971. London: Faber and Faber, 1973.

Jack of Shadows. New York: Walker, 1971. London: Faber and Faber, 1972.

The Guns of Avalon. Garden City, N.Y.: Doubleday, 1972. London: Faber and Faber, 1974.

Sign of the Unicorn. Garden City, N.Y.: Doubleday, 1975. London: Faber and Faber, 1977.

The Hand of Oberon. Garden City, N.Y.: Doubleday, 1976. London: Faber and Faber, 1978.

The Courts of Chaos. Garden City, N.Y.: Doubleday, 1978. London: Faber and Faber, 1980.

Changeling. New York: Ace, 1980.

The Last Defender of Camelot. New York: Pocket Books, 1980. (Short fiction.)

The Changing Land. New York: Ballantine, 1981.

Madwand. New York: Ace, 1981.

Dilvish, the Damned. New York: Ballantine, 1982.

CRITICAL AND BIOGRAPHICAL STUDIES

Delany, Samuel R. "Faust and Archimedes." In *The Jewel-Hinged Jaw: Notes on the Language of Science Fiction*. New York: Berkley, 1978, 173–190.

Nicholls, Peter. "Roger Zelazny." In *Science Fiction Writers*, edited by E. F. Bleiler. New York: Scribner, 1982.

Sanders, Joe. "Zelazny: Unfinished Business." In *Voices for the Future: Essays on Modern Science Fiction Writers*, Vol.2, edited by Thomas D. Clareson. Bowling Green, Ohio: Popular Press, 1979, 180–196.

Yoke, Carl. *A Reader's Guide to Roger Zelazny*. West Linn, Ore.: Starmont House, 1979.

BIBLIOGRAPHY

Sanders, Joe. *Roger Zelazny: A Primary and Secondary Bibliography*. Boston: G. K. Hall, 1980.

—DOUGLAS BARBOUR

LIST OF CONTRIBUTORS

L. David Allen
University of Nebraska, Lincoln
ANDRE NORTON
SAX ROHMER

Brian Attebery
Idaho State University
E. R. EDDISON
ALAN GARNER

W. F. Axton
University of Louisville
CHARLES ROBERT MATURIN

Douglas Barbour
University of Alberta
J. R. R. TOLKIEN
ROGER ZELAZNY

E. F. Bleiler
THE ARABIAN NIGHTS
FRANK BAKER
J. K. BANGS
EDWARD GEORGE BULWER-LYTTON
DION FORTUNE
WILLIAM HOPE HODGSON
ROBERT E. HOWARD
ARTHUR MACHEN
A. MERRITT
TALBOT MUNDY
EDGAR ALLAN POE
G. W. M. REYNOLDS
M. P. SHIEL

Richard Bleiler
STEPHEN KING

Robin Bromley
Columbia University
STEPHEN VINCENT BENÉT

Donald R. Burleson
Rivier College
H. P. LOVECRAFT

James L. Campbell, Sr.
University of California, Santa Barbara
J. S. LE FANU
MRS. J. H. RIDDELL
SIR WALTER SCOTT
MRS. HENRY WOOD

John L. Carr
The Ohio State University
LEIGH BRACKETT

Wells Chamberlin
The University of Chicago
JACQUES CAZOTTE

Thomas D. Clareson
The College of Wooster
FITZ-JAMES O'BRIEN
MARK TWAIN

John Clute
ROBERT AICKMAN
WALTER DE LA MARE

LIST OF CONTRIBUTORS

DAVID GARNETT
RICHARD GARNETT
VERNON LEE
C. S. LEWIS
MRS. OLIPHANT
BARRY PAIN
THOMAS BURNETT SWANN
T. H. WHITE

Alfred L. Cobbs
Wayne State University
WILHELM HAUFF

Richard Dalby
WILLIAM FRYER HARVEY
JOHN METCALFE

Les Daniels
ROBERT BLOCH
FRANK BELKNAP LONG
BRAM STOKER

Michael Dirda
HONORÉ DE BALZAC
GUY DE MAUPASSANT
PROSPER MÉRIMÉE
JACK VANCE

Norman Donaldson
WILKIE COLLINS
W. W. JACOBS
M. R. JAMES
OLIVER ONIONS

Aileen Douglas
JAMES STEPHENS

Charles L. Elkins
Florida International University
HENRY JAMES
ARTHUR QUILLER-COUCH

Mary J. Elkins
Florida International University
OSCAR WILDE

Uwe K. Faulhaber
Wayne State University
WILHELM MEINHOLD
J. K. MUSAEUS

Benjamin Franklin Fisher IV
University of Mississippi
WILLIAM AUSTIN
AMELIA B. EDWARDS
WASHINGTON IRVING

Martin Gardner
G. K. CHESTERTON
LORD DUNSANY
H. G. WELLS

Penrith Goff
Wayne State University
E. T. A. HOFFMANN

Donald P. Haase
Wayne State University
ADELBERT VON CHAMISSO
LUDWIG TIECK

Len Hatfield
Indiana University
MAY SINCLAIR

Robert Hogan
University of Delaware
MERVYN WALL

Marilyn J. Holt
Central Washington University
GERTRUDE ATHERTON
RUDYARD KIPLING

Manfred K. E. Hoppe
The University of Chicago
FRIEDRICH DE LA MOTTE FOUQUÉ

Kenneth Jurkiewicz
Central Michigan University
RAMSEY CAMPBELL
SAKI

John J. Kessel
North Carolina State University
JOHN COLLIER
E. M. FORSTER

Thomas L. Kinney
Bowling Green State University
ARTHURIAN ROMANCES

LIST OF CONTRIBUTORS

Russell Letson
St. Cloud State University
C. L. MOORE

Edgar MacDonald
Randolph-Macon College
JAMES BRANCH CABELL

Willis E. McNelly
California State University, Fullerton
RAY BRADBURY

Julia R. Meyers
North Carolina State University
ROBERT NATHAN

Walter E. Meyers
North Carolina State University
STEPHEN R. DONALDSON
MANLY WADE WELLMAN

Chris Morgan
E. F. BENSON
F. MARION CRAWFORD
R. A. LAFFERTY
FIONA MACLEOD
H. RUSSELL WAKEFIELD

Keith Neilson
California State University, Fullerton
RICHARD MATHESON
THORNE SMITH
DENNIS WHEATLEY

Peter Nicholls
MICHAEL MOORCOCK
SARBAN

John R. Pfeiffer
Central Michigan University
LEWIS CARROLL
WILLIAM MORRIS

David Punter
University of East Anglia
ALGERNON BLACKWOOD

Douglas Robillard
University of New Haven
MARY WILKINS FREEMAN

CLARK ASHTON SMITH
EDITH WHARTON

Erich S. Rupprecht
NATHANIEL HAWTHORNE
JAMES THURBER

David N. Samuelson
California State University, Long Beach
PETER S. BEAGLE
URSULA K. LE GUIN
CHARLES WILLIAMS

Joe Sanders
Lakeland Community College
ELIZABETH BOWEN
AVRAM DAVIDSON

John Scarborough
University of Kentucky
PIERS ANTHONY

Natalie Schroeder
University of Mississippi
WILLIAM HARRISON AINSWORTH

Curtis C. Smith
University of Houston at Clear Lake City
HARLAN ELLISON
CHARLES FINNEY
H. RIDER HAGGARD
ROBERT LOUIS STEVENSON

Frank Edmund Smith
William R. Harper College
A. E. COPPARD

Nelson C. Smith
University of Victoria
JAMES HOGG

Brian M. Stableford
University of Reading
F. ANSTEY
J. M. BARRIE
J. D. BERESFORD
MARIE CORELLI
L. SPRAGUE DE CAMP AND FLETCHER PRATT
CHARLES DICKENS
ANATOLE FRANCE

LIST OF CONTRIBUTORS

THÉOPHILE GAUTIER
ROBERT HICHENS
FRITZ LEIBER
EDEN PHILLPOTTS
JOHN COWPER POWYS AND T. F. POWYS
THEODORE STURGEON

Jack Sullivan
Rider College
L. P. HARTLEY
SHIRLEY JACKSON

Ann B. Tracy
State University of New York, Plattsburgh
M. G. LEWIS

Roald D. Tweet
Augustana College
POUL ANDERSON
AUGUST DERLETH

Devendra P. Varma
Dalhousie University
WILLIAM BECKFORD

ANN RADCLIFFE
HORACE WALPOLE

Diana Waggoner
LLOYD ALEXANDER
TANITH LEE
HOPE MIRRLEES
FRANK R. STOCKTON

Lee Weinstein
ROBERT W. CHAMBERS

John J. Winkler
Stanford University
APULEIUS

Gary K. Wolfe
Roosevelt University
DAVID LINDSAY
GEORGE MACDONALD

Thomas L. Wymer
Bowling Green State University
AMBROSE BIERCE
PATRICIA MCKILLIP

GENERAL BIBLIOGRAPHY

SELECTED BIBLIOGRAPHIES for individual subjects have been prepared by the contributors (with, in some cases, transatlantic editions added by the editor). In addition to general bibliographic sources, the following books have been useful in the overall preparation of this work.

Aldiss, Brian W. *Billion Year Spree: The True History of Science Fiction.* Garden City, N.Y.: Doubleday, 1973.

Attebery, Brian. *The Fantasy Tradition in American Literature from Irving to Le Guin.* Bloomington: Indiana University Press, 1980.

Barron, Neil, ed. *Anatomy of Wonder: A Critical Guide to Science Fiction.* Second edition. New York: Bowker, 1981.

Barzun, Jacques, and Taylor, Wendell H. *A Catalogue of Crime.* Second Impression, corrected. New York: Harper and Row, 1971.

Bleiler, E. F. *The Checklist of Science-Fiction and Supernatural Fiction.* Glen Rock, N.J.: Firebell, 1978.

————. *The Guide to Supernatural Fiction: A Full Description of 1,775 Books from 1750 to 1960, Including Ghost Stories, Weird Fiction, Stories of Supernatural Horror, Fantasy, Gothic Novels, Occult Fiction, and Similar Literature.* Kent, Ohio: Kent State University Press, 1983.

————, ed. *Science Fiction Writers: Critical Studies of the Major Authors from the Early Nineteenth Century to the Present Day.* New York: Scribner, 1982.

Cockcroft, Thomas G. *Index to the Weird Fiction Magazines.* 2 vols. Lower Hutt, New Zealand: T. G. Cockcroft, 1962–1964.

Contento, William. *Index to Science Fiction Anthologies and Collections.* Boston: G. K. Hall, 1978.

————. *Index to Science Fiction Anthologies and Collections 1977–1983.* Boston: G. K. Hall, 1984.

Cowart, David, and Wymer, Thomas L., eds. *Twentieth-Century American Science-Fiction Writers: Dictionary of Literary Biography, Volume Eight.* 2 vols. Detroit: Gale Research, 1981.

Currey, Lloyd W. *Science Fiction and Fantasy Authors: A Bibliography of First Printings of Their Fiction and Selected Nonfiction.* Boston: G. K. Hall, 1979.

Day, Bradford M. *An Index on the Weird and Fantastica in Magazines.* South Ozone Park, N.Y.: Bradford M. Day, 1953.

————. *The Checklist of Fantastic Literature in Paperbound Books.* Hackensack, N.J.: Wehman Bros., 1965.

Day, Donald B. *Index to the Science-Fiction Magazines, 1926–1950.* Portland, Oreg.: Perri Press, 1952.

Goedeke, Karl. *Grundriss zur Geschichte der deutschen Dichtung.* Dresden: Ehlermann, 1884 on.

[Lewis, Anthony]. *Index to the Science Fiction Magazines, 1966–1970.* Cambridge, Mass.: New England Science Fiction Association, 1971.

[Lewis, Anthony, and Whyte, Andrew A.]. *The N.E.S.F.A. Index: Science Fiction Magazines and Original Anthologies.* (Vols. for 1970–1972, 1973, 1974, 1975, 1976.) Cambridge, Mass.: New England Science Fiction Association, 1973–1977.

Lovecraft, H. P. *Supernatural Horror in Literature.* New York: Dover, 1973.

McCutcheon, Ann. *The N.E.S.F.A. Index. Science Fiction Magazines and Original Anthologies.* (Vols. for 1977–1978, 1979–1980, 1981, 1982–1983.) Cambridge, Mass.: NESFA Press, 1982–1983.

Magill, Frank N., ed., [and Keith Neilson, staff director

and associate editor]. *Survey of Modern Fantasy Literature*. 5 vols. Englewood Cliffs, N.J.: Salem Press, 1983.

Nicholls, Peter, ed. *The Science Fiction Encyclopedia*. Garden City, N.Y.: Doubleday, 1979.

Reginald, R. *Science Fiction and Fantasy Literature: A Checklist, 1700-1974*. 2 vols. Detroit: Gale Research, 1979.

Smith, Curtis C., ed. *Twentieth-Century Science-Fiction Writers*. New York: St. Martin, 1981.

Spector, Robert D. *The English Gothic: A Bibliographic Guide to Writers from Horace Walpole to Mary Shelley*. Westport, Conn.: Greenwood Press, 1983.

Strauss, Erwin S. *MITSFS Index to the SF Magazines 1951-1965*. Cambridge, Mass.: MIT SF Society, 1966.

Sullivan, Jack. *Elegant Nightmares: The English Ghost Story from Le Fanu to Blackwood*. Athens: Ohio State University Press, 1978.

Talvart, Hector; Place, Joseph; and Place, Georges. *Bibliographie des auteurs modernes de langue française*. Paris: Éditions de la Chronique des Lettres Françaises, 1928 on.

Tuck, Donald H. *The Encyclopedia of Science Fiction and Fantasy Through 1968*. Chicago: Advent Publishers, 1974 (vol. 1), 1978 (vol. 2), 1983 (vol. 3).

Tymn, Marshall B., ed. *Horror Literature: A Core Collection and Reference Guide*. New York: Bowker, 1981.

Tymn, Marshall B.; Schlobin, Roger C.; and Currey, L. W. *A Research Guide to Science Fiction Studies*. New York: Garland, 1977.

Tymn, Marshall B.; Zahorski, Kenneth J.; and Boyer, Robert H. *Fantasy Literature: A Core Collection and Reference Guide*. New York: Bowker, 1979.

Waggoner, Diana. *The Hills of Faraway: A Guide to Fantasy*. New York: Atheneum, 1978.

INDEX

Arabic numbers printed in boldface type refer to extended treatment of a subject